THE RED CHRONICLES

COMPLETE SERIES

BY

KENDRAI MEEKS

RELUCTANT

RED CHRONICLES
BOOK1

ONE

The amber liquid swishing about in Amy's glass tempted both gravity and my nerves. To separate my blonde friend from the bar: a task much easier put to words than action. Side-eying the clock and the bartender's focus on it, I realized last call was nigh. No need trying to liberate Amy's fourth cup of poison from her grasp and shuffle her to our loft to sleep off her drunk. The regulation of liquor sales in the fine city of Chicago would cut her off soon enough. Besides, after the day she'd had, I couldn't blame her for opting for inebriation, even if it did mean I'd likely end up with her slung over my shoulder on the way home.

"Cock-sucking assholes!" Amy's mouth pulled a double shift, vacillating between drinking and spewing profanities that would make the devil blush. "That's what they are, Geri. Every single man is a cock-sucking, fucking shithead. They can't help it, they're *born* like that."

"Not everyone."

I squeezed my eyes shut, refusing to let memory take me. Cody was gone, and there was nothing I could do about it.

"Oh yeah? Name me one – just *one* – who isn't an ass."

Amy didn't know about Cody. *No one* I'd become friends with since moving to Chicago six months ago knew about Cody, or anything much else about my life back in Paradise. The less I talked, the less opportunity for anyone to figure out that the tiny town near the northern tip of Michigan's Upper Peninsula was populated mostly by werewolves and hoods.

Or that I was one of the latter.

"My dad isn't so bad," I offered. "Even if he's willing to give my mom the benefit of the doubt."

Still, I couldn't shield my roomie from everything. She'd overheard enough of the arguments I'd had with my dad on the phone to get the basic gist. Things in the Kline household weren't exactly Brady-like.

Amy blew a raspberry, leaving a mist of her saliva on the counter. "That's only because your parents' relationship is reversed and fucked up as shit. Your mom is the cock-sucking asshole. Trust me, she'd be welcomed at Asshole Camp with the male part of humanity."

Who was I to argue? What little Amy did know of my home life came from me grumbling about my mother's arrogance, or overhearing me argue with my dad in broken Spanish. One day, I thought she'd caught on to my family secret when she'd declared, "I didn't know there were any of your kind that far north."

My kind? What did she mean "my kind?"

"You know, *Hispanics.*" She said the word like some taboo turn of phrase that could launch riots. "Don't worry, I'm cool with it. Besides, I *love* Enrique Iglesias."

I left the comment to air-dry. First, because even though my dad was from Argentina, the rest of my family tree grew from Central and North European roots. Hood society bucked Western tradition by being matriarchal. Brünhild Kline, my mother-and-matron, embraced her Germanic heritage with the ferocity of a bear, and the identity had been passed down to me despite my *papi's* Latino influences. And second, because Amy wasn't rude, she was only socially isolated. Not so different from me. Only, where I'd grown up destined and trained to police werewolves, Amy had grown up on the Upper West Side where labels were openly accepted, if only worn to figure out someone's proper shelf.

As for men, I couldn't really debate Amy there either. I'd only ever had one boyfriend, and that relationship flatlined when I'd walked in on him in the arms of another woman. Come to think of it, Amy might be on to something. The proxy experience, watching a roommate cycle through a catalog of creeps, suggested that at least as far as the localized stock of the student body was concerned, Amy had discovered the only possible explanation.

"Maybe you just suck at picking guys," I suggested, pushing her hair away from where it stuck to her forehead, held in place by a sheen of sweat. "Six months, Amy. We've only lived together six months and this is man number five you've put up as a token sacrifice. You swear you're giving up men for good, and two weeks later, it starts again."

Amy extended a finger. "But this time I mean it. Sick bastard. I gave Carl my heart and my time, and he turns around and starts sleeping with Tiffany Olson!"

"Maybe you should get revenge."

Amy's brow creased. "Great idea. How?"

"By sleeping with Tiffany Olson, of course."

Our eyes met, and a second later, we both convulsed with laughter.

"I should so do that," Amy said when'd she'd gotten her breath back. "Or better yet, pick up the hottest guy here, make the world's longest, dirtiest sex tape, then post it to Carl's Facebook! That'll show him."

Show him everything he and half the men under the age of 30 this side of Lake Michigan have already seen, I thought.

Just as quickly as the idea crossed my mind, I annexed it to that part of my brain I called "Old Geri's Vault." That I'd been raised with out-of-date, uber-conservative values had never eluded me. Even in high school, the human kids—the Hueys, as we called them—had teased the wolves and me about being goody-two-shoes. My clan and their pack had emigrated from the Old Country and set up far from town, in the backwoods. A fabricated ultraconservative church with a Luddite moral code covered for our isolation and odd ways. The fact that we didn't drink, didn't hang out after dark, and never, ever slept around like the other kids didn't make us fit in with popular culture exactly. The truth of it was, sex wasn't the same for us as it was for Hueys. It had consequences. Irrevocable, life-changing consequences.

I threw back the rest of my drink and finished off the tumbler. Four full servings of ginger ale finally resulted in the expected outcome. I slid off the barstool, maneuvered my tiny purse to rest on my right hip, and leaned in towards Amy who stared at her drink like it was some sort of museum display she just couldn't wrap her head around.

"I have to hit the bathroom. You going to be okay here on your own?"

Her reply came in the form of an alcohol-scented belch. Not exactly as concrete an answer as I'd been hoping for, but there was no way we'd cover the six blocks back to our loft if I was hauling this bladder *and* Amy's comatose body.

As for college bar bathrooms at two in the morning, The Old Kettle's held its own. I noted an absence of paper towels and the presence of a chunky, off-white pool on the floor near a wastebasket. The acidic citrus odor of the soap did a good enough job covering up whatever else may be polluting the atmosphere. If I had had a slide or a Petri dish, I'd collect a sample to examine under my microscope out of utter curiosity. Then again, I thought as I counted to thirty while scrubbing down my palms under the hot water, maybe better not to know what hostile chemical concoction I was bleaching my skin with.

I froze the moment I rounded the corner of the hallway and took in the view of the bar, ice coating my spine, my weapon hand twitching. Wearing a saccharine smile and a costume plucked straight out of a copy of *Hipster Goth Quarterly*, the guy at Amy's side pressed up against my inebriated roommate like he was trying to squeeze 'Amy oil.' Apparently, Revenge Plan B had been implemented. Mr. Too Close was probably the hottest-looking thing within ten city blocks, but unlike Amy, I knew he wasn't cruising for a hookup. Not the kind Amy was after, anyways.

The barman and I exchanged a glance. I doubted he was up on the fact that the man creeping my friend was supernatural, but he was clearly picking up on the vibe that he *was* a schmuck trying to take advantage of someone too drunk to break bread with wisdom. I nodded to the barkeep as if to say, *thanks for your concern, and no, there's no way I'm letting him get two steps out of this bar with her.*

"Geri!"

My leggy blonde roomie pulled her hand from the Friday-night Fabio's cheek. Amy waved me over with the enthusiasm of a child seeing a horse at the county fair for the first time. I crossed, shoving my hands in my pockets, and my sarcasm down my throat. When I got close enough, she gave her impromptu suitor a push in my direction, only to pull him back immediately.

"This is Donovan, and he's taking me to see some art at his place. He said his car is right outside. He'll drive me home later."

Amy winked, just in case I had suddenly become as stupid as she was acting and didn't pick up on the implication.

"But we came here together," I said, giving Mr. Sexy-Paste-Man the stink eye. I couldn't tell if he was on to me the way I was to him. Vampires were city creatures; my kind stuck to the sticks. "Come on, I don't want to walk home alone. Not at this time of night."

Donovan rubbed a thumb over Amy's inner wrist, the vampire equivalent of swirling a glass of wine before scenting it. "Maybe Geri could join us. With your permission, of course."

His hopes were almost as high as his arching eyebrows.

Amy slapped him playfully on the chest. Dropping all pretense of "seeing art," she said, "Geri in a threesome? *Bwahaha!* Doubtful. Geri doesn't... Well, do anything, ever."

"Ever is a long time. Geri, wouldn't you like to try something, sometime? Perhaps even now? Perhaps, with us?"

Was he honestly suggesting I should lose my virginity in a three-way with my drunken roommate and a Mumford & Sons wannabe? This fangie must be young. Young, and not too bright. In a generous mood, I'd give him the benefit of a doubt RE: his IQ. He might be such a newbie that he'd not yet been oriented towards recognizing a hood when he saw one, or know the danger we held, even if vampire control really wasn't part of our M.O.

I reached into Amy's coat pocket and lifted the little slip of wallet that she kept her ID, student card, and a few dollars in. If somehow the vamp did get her away, I didn't want him to have access to any of her personal things. Despite his earlier suggestion, I knew Donovan didn't have a car. His skinny jeans were so tight I didn't even need him to turn his head and cough to sign off on his physical. There was no way he had space for air let alone a car key in those pockets.

I took a step back toward the bar. "Donovan, was it? You mind if I have just a word with you." With my other hand, I stretched my debit card to the barkeep to cover the tab before jerking my head to the left. The vamp drew Amy's hand to his lips, inhaled deeply, and placed a kiss on her knuckles, coiling her tighter in his thrall.

"This will just take a second. Don't go anywhere."

She nodded, almost frightfully, like she was worried she'd be punished if her butt slid one inch off the barstool. "I won't. I wouldn't." As Donovan turned and followed me, she leaned after him, as if pulled by gravity, almost falling off her barstool in the process.

"Can I help you?" he asked with no amount of hidden annoyance when we gained distance.

I pushed my hair from my eyes. "Yeah, you can, actually. Leave my friend alone. She's already met her asshole quota for the day."

His green eyes shimmered, reflecting the neon lights behind the bar. "I just want to show the young lady a good time, and she seems more than willing. Why don't you do like she asked and take her car home? After that, forget you two went out tonight. You won't notice she's not home until the morning."

I felt fuzz in my brain, an odd mental shake as the vamp tried his best to woo me with his power. It was no more than a brush of a stranger's sleeve against my arm. "Oh, please. You really think your mind control mumbo jumbo will work on me?"

"My…mumbo jumbo?" he repeated, going rigid. "Wait, what?"

"How old are you? A year?" I continued unabated as I browsed his features. "I've always been told your type was into Purple Labels, but you look like you hit up the sales rack at Forever 21. Aren't you Chicago clutches famous for being chic and uppity? A student bar doesn't scream out posh night club or executive lounge to me. Which makes me wonder… Is this your fang mitzvah?"

He winced when I whacked him on the shoulder with the back of my hand.

"It is, isn't it? You really planning on taking my drunk best friend as your first thrall? If she had any idea what you really were, she might be flattered."

Donovan's eyebrow quirked as his cool melted away. "You're not a slayer."

Well, at least he'd finally gotten the clue that I wasn't a Huey. "Of course not. The slayers are all dead. No one's seen one since the Andrew Sisters were hot."

"But, how do you know about fang mitzvahs and clutches?"

Boy, this one's wall of secrets held up like a soggy waffle cone. One or two clandestine facts, and he was fine confirming everything I said. Vamp pickings must be slim in the big city.

"I'm a person who knows these things."

He laced his hands behind his neck, leaned in, and attempted awkwardness. Scratch that, achieved it. "Am I really that obvious? I came on too strong, didn't I? Too much cologne?"

"You could dial back a little, not that she'd be capable of picking up on your scent."

"I just thought, you know, couldn't hurt. Plus, the drugstore was running a really good special on Aqua Velvet."

"It *is* hard to let a deal go by. But if you don't mind, can I tell you something else?"

A hood's training in blade techniques started at age four. I could stab a supernatural before I could write my own name. I threw an arm over Donovan's shoulders while slipping Amy's wallet into a small bag I kept hanging from my left hip, clipped to a belt loop. The vamp didn't know about my weapon until he found my silver blade pressed against the soft flesh between two ribs. His eyes went wide, but luckily, his maker had taught him well enough to avoid making a scene.

"Etiquette would suggest you only drink from a willing partner, and Amy isn't sober enough to agree to a handshake."

"But I'd wipe her memory. She wouldn't…"

"You think that makes it okay? You think fang-rape is okay as long as the victim doesn't remember? Even if that were true, Donny, *I* would know, and I don't forget easily," I said, cutting him off and, well, actually cutting him.

Not that a nick into his flesh would do anything serious. Silver blades wouldn't kill vamps. But a knife was a knife, and making a living kebab of his kidney wouldn't exactly feel like foreplay.

"Take my suggestion and cruise somewhere else tonight. And I better not get word some baby vamp got frisky and left a body. I might not be a slayer, but trust me, my kind is just as much a fan of slicing first and asking questions later."

"And you're not going to tell me what that is, huh? Your kind."

"Human biology major. I also minor in Medieval history, but that's just gravy."

"Geri!" Amy whined when the tab got long and the hours grew short. Not the best timing, when I was trying to be all covert and stuff. "Why are you hogging him? He came on to me, not you."

An atypical Amy argument. Usually, she ranted on incessantly about how I needed a social life that extended beyond our small circle of friends and biweekly telephone calls with my dad that ended in yelling. If she hadn't just broken up with another asshole tonight and she saw me this close with a member of the opposite sex, she'd have high-fived me, shoved a condom in my back pocket, and told me to go ride that buck all the way into town. Hell, at this point, if she saw me making moon eyes at a member of the same sex, she'd probably do a back flip.

Donovan looked back over his shoulder, passing Amy a "just a second, darlin'" smile, but kept his voice directed at me. "I've been casing every bar this side of campus for hours. It's closing time, and if I come back to my maker's place empty-handed, I'm staked for sure. I have to have her. I promise, she won't remember."

"As drunk as she is, I guarantee she wouldn't. Not the point. Get out of here, Donovan. We both know your maker isn't going to stake you over one botched prowl."

"Most makers, no, but my maker ain't most makers."

"Grammar and you don't often break bread, do you?" The blade slid a few millimeters deeper, bringing his eyes and his bile back to me. "You seem to be male, so I assume you have balls. Use them. Tell your maker to get off your back and let you do your first thrall right. Now, I'm going to put my blade away, immediately after which you're going to tell Amy some excuse, then scram. Don't make me filet you; neither one of us needs that kind of attention."

He winced when I withdrew my weapon. I caught sight of a small dark red patch soaked into his shirt as he turned, but the wound would begin to heal in seconds. Donovan crossed to the bar, sending Amy into a flurry of the giddies. She stood up, and just as quickly, fell forward into Donovan's arms. He caught her, proving he might have been a vampire, but he wasn't a complete dick.

Amy's breath carried so much alcohol, even I could smell it ten steps away. She plastered herself to Donovan, playing with what could only be hypothetical chest hairs. "Now, where were we?"

Donovan's nervous smile cracked across his face. He pushed her back onto the barstool. "Sorry, babe. I just remembered I have a big exam tomorrow. I have to study."

"An exam?" Amy asked, wide-eyed. "But tomorrow is Saturday."

"Did I say exam? I mean I have a paper to write," Donovan amended. "Listen, it was great meeting you."

"What? No!" Amy practically broke down crying. She clung to Donovan's shirt, oblivious to the fact that it was ripped and blood-stained on one side. "My worst fears have come true. Geri's frigidness is contagious."

"No, really, I think you're sweet, but... Ow."

This time, my blade pierced his back. Again, only deep enough to be a warning, but he got the point. Literally.

"Maybe I'll see you again sometime."

And finally, Donovan turned to leave, all while shooting me a warning fang from behind a curled lip. Once we were alone, Amy tipped me off that she had reached the angry-drunk stage of the night by poking a finger into my chest and mustering the fury of a methed-up tick mouse. "What in the hell did you say to him? He had the look and everything!"

My eyebrow quirked, amused that my sweet, free-love, upbeat roomie thought she could sustain bitterness for more than a blink. "The look?"

"Of course, you don't know the look. No one ever gives you the look. You don't let them get so far as a smile," she prattled as I signed the slip the barman pushed across the counter and stowed my card. "You know, the *look.* The one that says a guy wants nothing more than to take you to the nearest bed, strip off all your clothes, and spend the rest of the night making you scream."

Maneuvering my arm around Amy's back, I spun her toward the door. Even though she was three inches taller than me, I bore her weight without any difficulty. Hoods were stronger than humans. Even without having gone through my formal rites that would awaken all my strengths and abilities, my innate gifts still made hauling a society girl's drunk ass out of a bar after last call a breeze.

"Take away the bed and the stripping all the clothes off part, and I think you've just described the effect I have on every man lately."

"I know, and it's so Sandra Dee. My god, have you ever even kissed a boy?"

I blushed, pushing back bittersweet memories. "Yeah, a few."

She blew a raspberry, covering the side of my face in 40-proof spittle. "I mean like, a full on, I-want-you-right-here-and-right-now type of kiss. Not a peck on the cheek in the church basement." Amy was convinced every person who'd grown up in what she called the "in between places," i.e. not the East Coast and not the West Coast, spent their weekends in Bible school or shooting grizzly bears.

She continued without waiting for an answer. "Don't you ever get tired of studying all the time when you're not in class or working out? Of only ever having a social life when I force you to? Why are you always such a good girl?"

"Sex has consequences, Amy. Especially where I come from."

I felt a hitch in my breath in the shade of the memory. *No,* I lectured myself, moving Amy along faster. *You will not go there. It was doomed from the start, and you knew it. You knew it could never work.* "I'm really not that pristine; we just have different definitions of what bad behavior entails."

"Maybe, but my way is the best way." Amy fell against me as we left the back alley of the bar. The front would be safer, but after last call, it would also be lousy with police looking to make the city a quick buck, fishing out of a barrel as the bars emptied. We got six steps from the door when the world changed its spin.

I looked like a mime trying to rationalize the sudden appearance of a box around me, grabbing at empty air. Amy was gone. Just gone.

TWO

Instinct took over. There was a hunt afoot. Only this time, my prey wasn't a two-hundred-pound werewolf. It was a hipster wannabe who, maybe, soaking wet could make one-twenty. Donovan may have been a baby vamp, but I'd never taken on one of his kind. Would my skills for hunting wolves transfer to hunting a vampirical barfly?

The perpetrator must have been waiting in the shadows; under street lamps I'd pick him out in a blink. The alley, bathed in stripes of fluorescent and gray, took on definition as I honed my vision. The nearby garbage bins provided the assailant with a robust olfactory cover of stale alcohol, cooking oil, and filth. Mixed in the miasma of stench and rot, however, was a very distinct, fresh overlay of cheap cologne and disappointment.

My ears would hear the scratching of mouse feet in the ceiling if there were no other background noises, but this environment wasn't like my family's compound back in Michigan. A few hundred meters away, plastered frat boys and let-it-loose coeds tramped down the street, cackling and wailing. If Amy had been struggling or resisting Donovan's assault, I might stand a chance, but there was nothing. Either she'd blacked out from alcohol, or she'd blacked out from a vampire's knock on her noggin. Either way, I was operating blind, which would make rushing in with fists flailing stupid.

My mother had tried to get me to train for the possibility of facing a vampire someday. I drew the line at knowing ten ways to kill a werewolf. If I ever told her my best friend had died because she'd been right and I'd been wrong, I'd never hear the end of it.

Plus, you know, Amy would be dead. Despite her many, quirky flaws, I really liked my roomie.

Luckily, I had read a little bit about vamps and their abilities. There was a wide river between things a vampire really could do, and what the movies showed. Fly? Not really, but even a baby vamp could set Olympic records in the high jump. Turn into bats? No. The really old and powerful ones could become a cloud of smoke to get out of tight pinches and traffic tickets. One skill they had which Hollywood never picked up on was a form of vocal stealth. Hiding in the shadows wasn't much of a defense against hoods, let alone slayers when they were still around, since our better-than-nifty hearing could effectively echolocate. Either by some magical power grab or evolutionary dumb luck, they had developed the ability to throw their voices, making it impossible to pin down their location just from the sound.

"Come on, Donovan. You know how this ends, right? Hint: it rhymes with 'shmule be read.'"

He refused the bait.

"Amy?" I called into the void, hoping if she was still conscious she'd at least moan. Even with her offline, the sound bounced off nearby objects and filled in some of my blind spots. To the left of me was something large – maybe a dumpster. My eyes adjusted to the dimness, letting me in on a little more. Black bags and boxes that had been piled up until they made a barricade of grease-drenched cardboard lay on my right. "Come on, Amy. It's late and you're drunk. Let's get you home."

Donovan's voice, somewhat mottled by what I was willing to bet was an emergence of fangs since last we spoke, sent a shiver up my spine. His comical and desperate display in the bar made me forget the truth: even a baby vamp could kill.

"Just leave, witch. Your little 'leave my friend be' speech and knife was real admirable, but do you know how much they're going to bust my balls if I show up without a thrall for my own initiation ceremony for the third night in a row? I'm not going to kill her. I just need her to be my first feed."

"One, I'm not a witch. There's no such thing as witches."

At least, as far as I knew.

"And two, you don't have to kill her to screw her up. Or didn't you know thralls can leave residual headaches, nausea, night sweats, and delusional obsessions for up to two months? Amy already gets all that from watching reruns of *Full House*."

"What, you think you're Web MD or something?"

"I'm thinking of applying to medical school."

Donovan croaked a laugh. "Yeah, you obviously got that bedside manner thing down."

Keep him talking, Gerwalta. As long as his mouth was busy spitting back retorts, he wasn't sinking his teeth into Amy. True, he'd want to wait for his ceremony, but if what he said was true and it had been three days since his maker cut him off from secondary feedings of his own thralls, he could be getting bloodlusty and stupid.

Time was running out. I needed to draw him out, kick his ass, find Amy in the shadows, and get her home. Problem was, *he* didn't need to engage *me*. One well-timed leap, and even dragging an unconscious or struggling body, he could outmaneuver me and escape. The only advantage I had was banking on a weakness of many a baby vamp, or hell, most college-aged men: a male ego.

"Take off, bitch. You know you can't take me, and you know enough about us to know we don't kill anymore."

"You're asking to abduct my friend and feed from her on the honor system? Fine, take Amy. Let's see how much they bust your balls when they find out you had to force her to go home with you. All your vampy charm and Jedi mind tricks, and you can't even pick up someone on a college campus infamous for loose women."

That did it. One moment I was alone, and the next, Donovan was a foot from me, huffing in my face. Only, no Amy. No best friend. She couldn't be too far away, but I was still going to have to chase him off or leave him a whimpering pile of vamp goo to search for her.

My training had drilled into me that I should never, not even for a millisecond, look away from a supernatural opponent. A vampire or wolf within striking distance was a creature within killing distance. Then again, I had been pretty avidly ignoring my upbringing and training since I'd run away from home, and apparently, my mind saw no use in kicking in now.

One quick glance over his shoulder in hopes of seeing Amy in the shadows was all it took to find myself a foot off the ground, Donovan's hands around my neck, and me, choking.

The pubescent vamp sneered, his dark intentions bubbling at the corner of his mouth. "My maker said I couldn't kill humans, but that don't save you, does it? Lucky for you, I'm curious. Tell me what you are, tramp, and maybe I'll make your death quick."

My mother's voice screamed inside my head. *Willful, wistful, foolish child! In the heat of battle, the enemy does not care about your bloodline or your wish for diplomacy. The only thing that will save you and anyone you're trying to defend is your ability in combat and your training!*

I wished I was stronger. I wished I'd listened to my mother more and trained harder, instead of going through my "trying to be a normal person" phase. I wished I hadn't run away that night six months ago, when my mother had commanded me to finally take my rites and my rightful place in the clan. Couldn't I have just stuck around one more day, threw myself into the ceremonial fires to burn away my human coil, and gained all my powers? A vamp whose fangs hadn't fallen yet was outdoing me; I couldn't get my fingers winched under his grip on my throat. Was this how I was going to die? With Amy suffering and, even worse, my mother thinking she'd been right about how wrong my actions were?

No, I had to prove her wrong, save Amy, and, most importantly, save myself.

Remember your training. Look for his weaknesses.

Donovan's weaknesses? His ignorance about what I was, and the fact that he could apparently be prodded in the ego with such ease.

I gasped enough air to get out a few words. "Maybe I'm a wolf."

He pulled me right up to his face, and inhaled. "Don't smell like wolf to me."

How would he know? Given the fact that clutches pretty much stayed in the cities and packs in the countryside, I didn't see how.

"So unless you're prepared to tell me what you really are," Donovan continued, "and why I should let you go..."

He never got the words out.

Donovan whipped around, trying to figure out where the empty beer bottle that had smashed into the back of his head came from. It sent a spray of glass shards everywhere, and if he hadn't effectively become an inhuman shield, my face would have been cut to shreds. The glass couldn't penetrate a vampire's skin, of course, but the tall, lumbering idiot at the far end of the alley probably didn't know that.

"Hey, arsehole!" the man called, his voice sounding like an extra from some dry British comedy. "Didn't your mother teach you not to choke women in an alley in the middle of the night?"

Backed by the glow of the street lamps, our interloper looked like a life-sized cutout of a WWE wrestler. The stranger was on the taller side, and either was wearing a full set of protective football gear or had been endowed with the muscles of a Greek god. Broad shoulders pared down to a surprisingly slender waist. A body Amy would have called "a swimmer who'd I like to see up close doing a breast stroke."

But as the wind shifted, carrying his scent on the breeze, I knew that this triangular muscle mass over sturdy long legs also described another type of male. A bristle of recognition went down my back and I squeezed my eyes shut. Why didn't I sense him a long time ago? Or had I? Suddenly, the lurch in my stomach when I'd come out of the bathroom made more sense. I was a hood; the nearness of a vamp shouldn't have any physical effect on me.

The nearness of a werewolf, however...

"Take a walk in the other direction, dude," Donovan said without turning, his clenched jaw and fangs roughening the edges of his words. If he knew how easily the werewolf could snap him like a twig if he wanted, he'd be running. "This doesn't concern you."

What the hell was he doing here, and why was he by himself? Lone wolves were rare, mostly because of how imbalanced they became the longer they stayed away from their pack. Was he one of my mother's informants? He wasn't a member of the Paradise pack; I knew each one of those wolves by sight and smell in either of their forms. I supposed he could just be in town on vacation; most wolves didn't like to travel too far from home but it wasn't entirely unheard of. Would he walk away and leave me to the vamp, once he figured out what I was? The wolves where I came from were respectable members of the community, but this *wasn't* where I came from.

"Actually, I have two rather compelling reasons to be involved," the wolf said, taking a few steps forward. In a dictionary-inspired rendering of the term 'cliché,' he held up both hands and made fists. "I call them Pain and Abel."

Without a second of difficulty in keeping me pinned, Donovan pivoted toward our guest. "Seriously, get along, little doggie."

Great, so the vamp did know. Well, that just made this already complex situation even more so. Looking over Donovan's shoulders, I opened my eyes and tried to pin the wolf with a glare.

"Go," I begged.

The Brit took two more steps, but the interplay of shadow and light still cloaked his identity. "Look, hood, I'm not all keen on helping one of your kind, but an honorable man does what he can. It's not your call."

"A hood?" Donovan appraised me with fresh eyes. Despite that, his expression curdled. "But they're all out in the boondocks."

Exactly one of the reasons I chose this school over all the others. Still, since my cat was out of the bag (side note: what kind of sick bastard kept cats in bags?), I might as well use it to my advantage. Able to find focus and, you know, breathe, I sucked in oxygen, directed all my energy to my legs, and called on my innate abilities for all they were worth. With one triumphant *harumph,* my right foot connected with his balls.

I fell to my feet as Donovan doubled-over.

"*Biiiitch,*" he hissed out, looking up at me from his wounded-manhood stance. "Now I'm going to – *ooooouuuucchh* – kill you!"

With another maneuver that I'd mastered at the age of eight, my knee slammed into his stomach. Donovan hit the ground, and I hit the darkened regions of the alley, looking for Amy.

The wolf drew near, but I didn't think he was stupid enough to get too close to me when I'd just flat-floored a vamp in two moves.

"What are you waiting for? Run."

"That vamp took my friend into the shadows. She's probably passed out. I got to get her out of here before she wakes up and sees a man with fangs."

He pointed absently at Donovan. "Toast him, then, and get the hell out of here."

"Glean the context clues, O Ye of the Moonies. I'm trying to stay under the radar. Toasting a baby vamp on the evening of his fang mitzvah doesn't exactly aid in my incognito-ness."

"Why are hoods all so self-centered?"

My back went rigid. I paused long enough to fix balled fists on my hips and give him my full attention. Mistake. The moment my eyes met his, my knees decided to become conscientious objectors. Such fire, such heat. So much like Cody had been when fired up about something. Still, I managed to pull off a good impression of a righteous bitch.

"Our job is to police wolves. Vamps don't fall under our jurisdiction."

The wolf took two more steps in my direction. Instinctively, my hand went for my weapon, and to the pouch on my belt loop that contained it, only to find it had fallen off in the melee. I knew I should have woven the blade into my hair like usual.

"How can you say that, after what he just did to you? Your kind should be doing something about it. *You* should be doing something about it."

"That kind of decision lays with a matron," I spat back. "In case you haven't noticed, I'm still a nascent."

His brown eyes narrowed on me, rimmed by a glow of green. A vein on his temple pulsed. My mouth went dry. Was he going to wolf out right here? I got lucky that Donovan was a baby vamp; my training — and, fine, the wolf's intervention — was enough to take him down, but I couldn't take on a fully-grown wolf if he wanted to attack. Especially without my silver blade.

He must have picked up on the itch of fear tingling under my skin. A smug half-smile pulled up his lip. "Frightened that I'll eat you, little red?"

My eyes went wide. *Little red.* Was it a coincidence, or did he really know about me? Resolving to reacquaint myself with my spine, I turned back to the task at hand: picking up dripping bags of filth and throwing them behind me. "I don't have time for this. I have to find my friend."

The next pile of garbage I budged moaned. I dived in, finding Amy, conscious but confused, under what looked like an old smoking jacket.

She put her hand to her head as I pulled her to her feet. "What the hell happened?"

It was that moment I was faced with the dilemma: make my already depressed roomie feel even more depressed by telling her she'd been attacked? That the "making her scream" Donovan promised involved forcibly sucking her blood, or...

"You passed out."

...lie to her face.

"I did?" Amy surveyed the nearby shuttering stack of clothing and regret that was Donovan. He keened in his pain, trying to force himself to stand erect.

After how hard I'd kicked him, any kind of erection on his part was going to be hard to come by.

Amy pointed vaguely in his direction. "Is that the guy that was trying to pick me up?"

"Yeap. He tried to bully you to go with him when we came out. You kicked him in the junk so hard it made you pass out."

Amy sobered in 3.2 seconds as she turned toward the street. "And who's the hunk?"

Hunk? I turned, thinking that she might be confusing brawn for beauty, and found myself struck dumb. Now that I had a second to consider the wolf at leisure, I saw what had Amy's radar beeping.

One thing that Hollywood got wrong, was supposing that every supernatural creature was also a supernatural sex bomb. While some were cute, it wasn't inherent to the status. Some were, frankly, ugly as sin. When I looked at this wolf, sin would definitely be part of the description, but more along the "inspiring carnal thoughts" variety.

Standing about six-two, he was just the right combination of muscle and lean sinew. His skin tone and skeletal structure suggested his pack was likely, like my mother's bloodline, descended of the Northern or Eastern European stock. It fit the accent. Like many wolves, his deep brown eyes bordered on black, hiding under bushy eyebrows that, despite the field day they'd present for any beautician, somehow complemented what was probably a persistent five o'clock shadow. In a pair of fitted jeans, a worn denim jacket, and an old pair of work boots, he had country boy charm down to a tee. If not for the fact we were creatures separated by tradition and sanctions, I'd be howling at the moon myself.

As if sensing the question in my eyes, *how do you want to play this, wolf?*, he took the initiative to cover our tracks.

"Passing by and heard a ruckus," he said.

Amy stepped right back into I'm-willing-and-available mode. She was a sucker for accents. And anything cute with a penis.

He continued, "Wanted to be certain you were okay. Plenty of bad blokes in this part of the city. Never know who or *what…*" He winked at me. "…you may come across."

Amy examined him with drunken eyes and sweetheart dreams. "I'd say. Hey, do you want to…"

With a jerk, I pulled Amy along, rushing her past the still seething Donovan. "Thanks for your help," I said, not even turning to the wolf as we hurried by.

"Got to get her home. Like you said, all kind of *bad blokes*, and unfortunately, that's her favorite kind."

Present company, not excluded.

"Thanks for the help. Next time drinks on me, okay?"

"Jello shots off his stomach!"

"Amy!"

THREE

The hungover Huey's bedroom door didn't even crack open until almost 2:30 in the afternoon, though at least she had managed to shower before reintroducing herself to the world of the living. Clutching fistfuls of wet hair, she leaned against the frame of her door and stared at the ground.

"I think I was doing shots of Mack truck last night."

"With Sherman tank chasers," I confirmed.

I'd gone over the usual vamp strike zones the second we were secure in our loft the night before. No puncture wounds. Nothing but a few light scratches. Donovan hadn't in fact penetrated her during those few moments in the shadows. I wasn't really sure what I'd do if Amy had been bitten, but I'd need a better story than 'you passed out' to explain the damage.

Sitting at the kitchen island on a highboy stool, I offered her the cup of coffee I had been refreshing for the last three hours, anticipating her need. "Now that you're sober – well, *soberer* – want to talk about the breakup without the assistance of alcohol?"

She shuffled with the grace of a Teletubby. "I think all I'm capable of at this point is moans. Thanks for the joe."

Amy called coffee joe. I had a feeling it was an East Coast thing, but I couldn't be sure. I'd never been to the East Coast. Outside of a few trips to the Black Forest and occasional ride-alongs with my mother into Southern Ontario or Minnesota, I'd never been anywhere. Even the trips to Germany weren't exactly illuminating. All kids born to the House of Red went straight from the airport to the ancient hunting lodge that served as the ancestral home of our line. A month annually, starting at age seven and until such time as your bloodline matron determined you were ready to receive your rites.

When I'd first met Amy, she was as exotic to me as if she'd been from Brazil or New Zealand. The native New Yorker probably thought I was just as weird.

Me, unassuming Gerwalta Kline, a junior transfer bio major from a tiny little drive-thru town with a population of less than 500. Never mind the fact that of that number, about a quarter were Yooper Werewolves and a few hoods in charge of policing them and the other dozen packs of their kind spread around the region.

Plus, there was the fact that I'd achieved the age of twenty-one and had never slept with a man, which in Amy's world, put me in ranks with Bolivian knife-throwing clowns for rarity.

She assumed the stool next to me and reached across for the package of bagels and the tub of Nutella I'd left out. "The breakfast of champions, hey?"

"Depends, champion what?" I sipped my own coffee, long since cold but what the hell did I care. "You don't want to talk about it? Fine, but I will. How many times are you going to go through this cycle? No man is worth that kind of self-abuse."

"Said like a true virgin," she teased. "There are some men who take a lot more than a drunk night to get over. But don't worry, Geri. This pounding headache and I have learned our lesson. No more dating losers for a while."

I tapped her on the shoulder as I rose to take my empty mug to the sink. "Good to hear you're not giving it up completely."

"Why would I, when the world is rife with mistakes I could still make? Speaking of which…" Amy leaned over the island, grinning. "Did you get his number?"

"Whose number?"

"You know. Tall, dark, and happened-to-be-passing-by last night."

I picked up my plate and pivoted for the sink. "No offense, but I don't think dives-into-an-alley-at-closing-time guy is a romantic prospect."

"Who said anything about romance? Come on, Geri, you can't tell me that even you didn't notice how hot he was. And the way he was looking at you? It was like he wanted to gobble you up."

Gobble me up? It had been a lifetime since a wolf had actually attacked and eaten a hood, but it didn't make the possibility any less real. But that wasn't what shocked me. Truth was, I was dumbfounded by Amy's selective memory. How could she recall such detail about one glare, but when it came to remembering being swooped away by a vampire and thrown in a pile of garbage? No, on that she drew a blank.

"No, I didn't get his number."

The anticipation that had been bubbling in Amy's expression went flat. "His name?"

"Not that either."

She ruminated a moment before shrugging. "Doesn't matter. A man doesn't look at a woman that way unless he's planning on sleeping with her or killing her. You two had a moment. I bet you it's not the last one. Do you really not want a boyfriend, or have you somehow convinced yourself that you're not worthy of one?"

A chill went down my back when I remembered the wolf's intensity. Between sleeping with me or killing me, I had a definite fix on which was more likely. Besides, I'd already dated one wolf, and I'd learned the hard way why that was such a bad idea. Even though I'd been named after the infamous Little Red Riding Hood, didn't mean I'd make her same mistakes.

My nose wrinkled. The snide little reference the wolf made the night before still irked me. Did he really know I was of the House of Red, or had it been complete chance? Did he know that my mother, in a willful attempt to rewrite history, branded me *Die Verräterin*'s namesake?

Amy's quizzical expression reminded me that she was still expecting an answer. No, I did not think the wolf had been tasty, but I did think he signaled trouble.

"What can I say? I'm sexy. I know I am. It doesn't mean I'm going to hop every bus that comes along, just because I think it might be fun to go downtown someday."

"I swear, you're going to force me to hire a himbo just to get you laid."

My eyebrow raised. "A *himbo?*"

"Yeah, you know. A male bimbo? Not her, but a *him*. A *himbo.*"

She stated this all like it was obvious and common. What did I know, it might have been. I hadn't exactly been raised in anything approaching Huey-world culture. Even the humans in Paradise weren't exactly on the forefront of fashion and culture.

"Sorry, but we don't have many *himbos* back in Paradise."

Amy huffed. "I swear, you come from one of the most inappropriately named towns ever." She ticked off its shortcomings, all learned through me of course, on her fingers. "No shopping, no spas, no coffee shops, no life!"

"There's always life, Amy. It has many variations."

"Spoken like a biology major," she deadpanned. "Look, I'm ordering you, if you see Hunky McHunk-Hunk again, bare minimum you are to get his name, his phone number, and his eye, okay?"

"Not okay. Trust me, he's not my type."

My roomie planted two balled fists on her hips and a grimace on her face. "I swear the sacred pinky swear of roommates that I am going to see you actually using that body of yours for something other than gym abuse and as a book-transportation implement before we graduate." Then realizing what she'd just said, her rigidness faded. "Not, like, personally of course. I mean, I'm not actually going to watch you do it. Seriously, though: name, number. You think the universe just throws a man like that into your path at random?"

No, I didn't, and that's what scared me. In general, wolves were rural folk. Part of the reason I had wanted to come to school in the big city was the fact that the nearest pack was seventy miles to the northeast, in a forested region along the Illinois-Wisconsin border. No wolves meant there was also no hood commune nearby. The last thing I wanted to do was have a regional oberst, who no doubt would report straight to my mother, think I was now in her territory and therefore, at her disposal.

Which resurfaced the question: what was a British wolf doing in Chicago anyway, and was he really alone, or did he have a pack nearby?

I didn't know which possibility frightened me more.

I decided I'd been on the pointy end of Amy's knife long enough, and turned the conversation back to her. "You still planning on going to the library, or can you not yet walk straight?"

"Why wouldn't I be able to walk straight? The only guy I spent any time with last night was Jack Daniels."

"You got in a few words with Johnny Walker too."

A sizzling sound permeated the air as Amy sucked in breath through clenched teeth. "Yeah, Johnny... He does things to a girl, you know. Problem is, she usually doesn't remember it afterward." She scooted off the barstool and grabbed an apple from a bowl on the counter. "Library. Supposed to meet my study group at five-thirty. It will be getting dark then. Damn it, I hate walking across campus after dark on the weekends. I always feel like I'm being followed."

FOUR

Amy had been gone for all of ten minutes when I felt it.

Deep in my gut, the curl of recognition. My arms broke out in gooseflesh. Hoods had a certain innate ability to detect when a wolf came near, especially in isolation. Last night I'd probably felt it, but I'd been distracted by the vamp. Now, in my own apartment and preoccupied with nothing more than a blog post on nitrates, I couldn't help but notice when my insides twisted.

Even though the modern, scientific brain didn't want to believe it, there was something mystic in the universe. I'd seen it time and time again. Hell, my family was living proof. After going through the ritual that we called the Gate of

Fire, a fully initiated hood had powers that lay beyond the borders of rational reason. Even a nascent, like me, could hold her own if she played her cards right.

Amy had entertained me when I began putting little silver objects around the flat. A city girl not familiar with the occult, she swallowed the "these are the trinkets of my people" excuse. She accepted it as Bible truth, not even asking which people. The fact that my lineage was from Germany and Argentina suggested I probably wasn't dancing around wigwams as a child. One of the first lessons my mother had taught me was that anything could be a weapon, if you threw it hard enough and had good aim. Even a tea tray, and in particular, a silver one.

It had to be him. There weren't enough wolves in Chicago, especially in my area, for it to be coincidence.

I put my ear to the door. A slow, measured inhale, exhale, inhale, exhale. My grip on the tea tray handle tightened as I mentally charted the consequences of my options. Should I open the door and immediately whack him across the head, or rip off the handle and try to shove it into his chest? Silver always hurt a wolf when they came into contact with it, but the only way for it to be lethal was if it touched the heart or brain. As a nascent, my only hope of coming out of an attack unscathed was to be on the offensive.

Strike last, die first, as my mother would say.

"You know that I know you're on the other side of the door, right?"

As stupid as I felt, I actually shuddered when his baritone brogue erupted. "How?"

"Because I'm a wolf, and you're a hood, and that's how it works." I could practically hear the smirk in his smug voice. "I know you're a nascent, but are you completely ignorant? Or are the wolves where you come from as incompetent as you?"

"Of course not!" Then, realizing how I'd just been cornered into demeaning myself, I guffawed. "I mean… You know what I mean! Were you tracking me last night? Did you send the vamp after my friend to flush me out? Trying to make me scared so I'd go running home?"

"I literally have no idea what you're talking about." Through the peephole, he embodied the art of disinterest. "Believe me, I'm about as happy at our running into each other as you seem to be. Why I didn't just walk away still niggles at my brain. One less hood in the world sounds perfectly good to me."

Jesus Christ, what was his deal? Traditionally, hoods and wolves weren't best buds, but we usually maintained a healthy amount of respect where the other was concerned. At least, where I came from we did. And, if you took "respect" to mean, "We hoods will leave you be as long as you act nice, but step one claw out of place and we will silver your ass."

"Why bother then?"

"Did you want to be murdered by a vamp, or are you just into kinky stuff?" He laughed wryly, running a hand through a head of hair distorted by the peephole to look conical. "I didn't come up the alley to save you. I was worried about the Huey. But while we're on the subject, can I just mention that, usually when a man saves a woman's life, she's grateful? She might even say thank you."

"You're not just a man, and I'm not just a woman. Now tell me why you're here."

"Are you looking through your peephole?"

I pulled back, feeling like a kid caught with her hand in the cookie jar. "No."

"Oh my God, hood. You have to be the most annoying type of your kind. Look, I don't know why you're in the city, and I don't know why you're living with Salty Two-Tits as a roomie. I get the feeling she's not exactly aware that she's living with a wolf-slayer or that she almost got sucked on by a parasite last night. I'm just trying to do the right thing." I heard the rustle of cloth and a shifting of his body from left to right. "Look through the peephole. I mean, again."

A small, rectangular piece of plastic with STATE OF NEW YORK printed at the top replaced his head in my line of vision. Amy's ID stared back at me.

"Both you and your friend dropped your bags in the alley. I figured you wouldn't want the vamp to know where you live."

My mind raced for other explanations. "How do I know you haven't attacked her as she walked up the street just now, and that her ID is all you have?"

"So your theory is I somehow magically knew what building you guys lived in, and was just waiting for the rise of night to empower me, so I could get her ID and find out the exact unit, because *that* level of detail proved too much for me?"

Sarcasm was a tongue in which he was obviously well versed. Still, I didn't believe him. Amy had gone to the library to meet her study group. Without a student ID, she'd be unable to get in.

Just at that moment, I felt my cell phone buzz in my back pocket. Taking it out, I read the message from Amy on the screen.

Got all the way to the library and realized my wallet isn't in my bag. Do you know where I left it last night when we got home?

Such timing was the work of a cruel and bitter god.

"Let me guess, that was her asking if you knew where it was. Am I right?"

"No need to be smug." As I spoke, I sent Amy a message, telling her she'd left it on the kitchen counter. Best not to let her know the truth. She'd be convinced the guy on the other side of the door had tracked me down because he was desperately in love with me after just one glance and that I should take him to bed posthaste. "Leave it outside the door. I'll take it when you're gone."

"Tobias."

Maybe my hearing was failing me. "What?"

"My name is Tobias."

"I don't do quid pro quo with strange werewolves. I'm not telling you my name, and I'm not opening the door while you're here, so just go already."

"You want me to huff and puff, then? Isn't that how this goes?"

"That's the Three Little Pigs, not Red Riding Hood."

"Right. I get the two confused, seeing as they both just show wolves to be evil, when it's really the hoods who are to blame for most of our problems."

Loyalty to my lineage, drilled into me over a lifetime of training, upbringing, and genetics, battled with good judgment. *He's just trying to get you emotional so you'll open the door to confront him without thinking. Then he can attack.*

"No comment on that?" he asked, amusement coloring his words. "Illuminate me, then. What is a nascent hood doing here, all on your lonesome, in an area without wolves? Something tells me this is that famous American teenage rebellion I've heard about. Giving your matron a little scare before you fall into line and become part of the system? Fine, then. Then I'd guess that you're not skirting about Chicago on any sort of official business. In which case, what cause would I have to hunt you down?"

"Yet, here you are," I answered. "And I could ask you the same thing. What's a wolf doing in Chicago, and a British wolf at that? Wolves hate cities."

Rather than answer, Tobias changed the subject. "You got something silver ready to bludgeon me with?"

"Of course I do. I'm not stupid."

"Big words for a girl who, just last night, was nearly strangled in a back alley by a vampire," he said. "I have questions, questions you may be able to answer. I'd prefer to be face to face to ask them. If you're lying to me, I'll see it in your expression. If it takes you silvering me for that to happen, so be it."

My eyebrows rose. "You're volunteering for me to cause you pain? Who's into kinky stuff now?"

"It will heal in a few hours if I don't hold it too long. If it gets me answers, it's a small price to pay."

I had questions too, ones only Tobias could answer. Temptation to take him up on his offer made a nerve in my temple twitch.

"I don't have silver thread. I mean, I do in my bedroom, but…"

"And we're back to the kinky stuff. Okay, as you're not about to wander away from the door for fear of me busting in and chasing you on the way to your chambers, that won't do, will it? What are you holding then?"

I looked with shame and self-ridicule down at my hands. "A tea tray."

He swallowed a laugh. "Because I'm English? Trafficking in stereotypes, I see. Fine, open the door, and we'll trade. I'll give you the two bags, and you hand me the tea tray. It should drain enough of my energy that I won't be at my full strength. You could kick my butt with a feather."

"My fist would do."

"Holding silver, I believe that may just be true."

I closed my eyes, inhaled deeply while calling on my innate abilities, put my hand on the door and…

Under the humming light of my building's hallway, I could see he was definitely the kind of wolf that could devour an unwary hood. Taken individually, his facial features seemed harsh. A strong chin, slightly ridged brow, glass-cutting cheek bones… But when taken as a matched set, they did him well. If one of the Hemsworth Brothers and Gaston from *Beauty and the Beast* had been able to procreate, Tobias could have been their miracle offspring. He stood taller than me, like most mature male wolves, so that he found himself looking down on me. In a literal way, that was. But given the way he was glaring at me, Amy's purse and my tiny bag outstretched at arm's length, the metaphor didn't fall far behind.

I lifted the tea tray in kind. Each of us mirrored the other when our free hands reached for what the other offered. The moment I had the bags in hand, I let go of my silver. Tobias hissed as his fingers closed around the tray's handle, and the burn began to take hold.

I backed back into my loft and reached for a nearby display of collectible spoons on the wall. The silver didn't have to be large or weaponized to be dangerous. Sometimes, a momentary distraction was enough to outsmart a wolf.

Tobias followed me in, looking at me with twinkling eyes. "Is all your silver in the form of kitchen implements? First the tiny little paring knife in your bag, and now this?"

Even though I doubted anyone living in my building would care, I closed the door as he entered. "It's a dagger, not a knife. And FYI, it was forged by my great, great grandmother."

"And so tiny that, in essence, it's just a fancy knife. Nevertheless, I have no interest in attacking you, or making any use of your tea tray, mini spoons, or — I'm guessing the next thing will be candlesticks?"

"This is my house, so I get the first question." Amy's purse and my bag went flying as I tossed them on the floor. "Did you tell anyone about me after last night?"

"Um, no. Did you tell anyone about me?"

"Who would I tell?"

His sarcastic, dry laugh curled my stomach. "You'd report me to the closest matron."

"I don't give a flying pheromone what Chicago's *orbest* knows." His mild rebuke reminded me of my years of training. Years that now seemed wasted, as I had no intention of ever carrying on my family's legacy. "Just curiously, though, does she know you're here?"

"As if you didn't check one of your big brother databases. The people who really need to know I'm here do, so don't worry your pretty little head over it."

I narrowed my gaze on him. "If you're passing through, that wouldn't have been in the records when I last looked. But *why* you're passing through – that's a different question. So tell me, how is it you strolled by last night when I just happened to be nearly attacked by a vamp?"

"One," he enumerated his retort on the fingers of his free hand. His other hand kept a grip on the tea tray. "He didn't nearly *attack* you; he nearly *killed* you. Something, incidentally, you still haven't thanked me for preventing. And two, I believe it's my turn to ask a question. Had you ever seen that vamp before?"

"Not unless you count inside the bar about ten minutes before, when he tried to pick up my friend."

"Right, your friend, Amy. Isn't it weird that I know your friend's name and not yours? If you're going to silver a pup, the least you can do is throw him your moniker. At least then he knows whose name to include in the profanity-laced curses when he's tending to his blisters later."

"Fine. My name is Geri."

He quirked an eyebrow. "Your mother a fan of Mick Jagger's exes?"

"Doubtful." If he wanted a name, I'd give him the name. "It's short for Gerwalta. But *everyone* calls me Geri."

"Your mother doesn't."

I almost sent the spoon flying right into his temple. Had it been my dagger, and had not Amy been due to arrive any moment to get her purse, and that she'd likely notice a mortally injured hulk of a man bleeding profusely on our living room floor, I would have.

Instead, I did the next best thing. I glared. "How do you know that?"

"A hood names her daughter after *Die Verräterin* herself, I'd wager she's got a lot of rep and expectation vested in that name from the get-go." He tilted his head to the side, taking on a canine-like manner. "I hit the nail on the head when I called you Little Red, didn't I? But I thought Chicago was under the control of a House of Yellow."

"The Matron of this region is of the House of Yellow, and not exactly Red's biggest fan. She's - none of your business." Let him take a swig from his coffee pot on that one. "You swear to me you just happened to be passing by? Nobody sent you?"

"You swear you're just here, doing the college thing, and nothing else? You haven't been sent here to chase down leads?" he countered.

"I also take a pottery class on Saturdays, if you must know." This time, it was my turn to be confused. "Wait, leads? There are no reports of supernatural problems in the city since Al Capone's days. And while we're on the subject, how did you know I was a college student?"

"Because I'm not a Luddite." When I just returned a dead stare at him, he rolled his eyes and continued. "Amy talks about you on her Facebook page. I wanted to know if she was hiding something I should be aware of, being that she fraternizes with hoods."

I crossed my arms. "And?"

"And I don't think Amy hides anything. Ever. Just FYI: if you're trying to stay on the down low, you might want to ask her to stop trying to hook you up. What's with that, anyway? Can't you handle your own love life without outsourcing to Manhattan Barbie?"

I made a mental note to talk with my roommate again about my *media mentions* request. Of course, Amy being Amy, she attributed part of my single status to the fact that I wasn't "swimming where the sharks feed." She had no idea the type of sharks I was trying to avoid. The daughter of Brünhild Kline, the Matron of the House of Red, would be a pearl in some dick's collection.

In my silence, Tobias continued. "Three pieces of advice, little red. First, splurge for quality."

Tobias put the tray down on a nearby coffee table. When he pulled away his hand, I noticed only the slightest tinges of red on his inner palm. Holding on to a silver object for so long should have at least given him second-degree burns.

"There's not enough actual silver in this thing to give me watery eyes, let alone neutralize any of my strength. Two, given who your roomie was trying to go home with last night, I wouldn't exactly trust in her judgment when it comes to men. And three, you should know there are vamps in this area, even at your school. Be careful. I'm not saying they're necessarily all bad, but if you're going to be in the practice of performing S&M with them in dark alleyways, I'd at least carry some gold around."

"Gold?" I asked.

"Yes, gold," Tobias repeated, putting extra emphasis on the hardness of the g. "Or don't you know that it has the same effect on them that silver does on us? Bonus advice: get actual gold. Pyrite will leave you feeling slightly foolish."

"Haha, because it's fool's gold. Are all British wolves so funny, or are you a special case?" I deadpanned.

One jab in just the right spot in his ego was all it took. In a moment, we went from standing several feet from each other, to breathing each other's breath. The air whooshed from my lungs as Tobias's hard body pressed against mine. His canines had grown long in the space of a blink, and were mere inches from my nose. His eyes shone like golden orbs, like the eyes of the dog he was when he connected with his animal nature. When he spoke, the sound was distorted, the human words struggling to be formed by a lupine mouth.

"There's very little about this that's funny, hood. Understand? If you get in my way, I will end you."

Adrenaline pushed my pulse into marathon speeds. I struggled to bring the silver spoon still in my grasp up to touch his flesh, but Tobias dominated my every inclination. I couldn't move. My state must have triggered his instinct, and he leaned in, running his tongue over the pulsing jugular on the side of my neck.

Click.

We both turned moments before the door opened. Amy bounced in, as if she had found total sobriety and a Red Bull sometime in the last twenty minutes.

"Hey, Geri, I…. Oh!"

There were unspoken subplots and devious insurgent conclusions in that grin. I knew what it looked like: me with my back to the wall, Tobias's body covering mine, his mouth hovering at my throat. To Amy, this was a finally-making-out-with-a-guy session. To me, it was a barely-getting-away-with-my-windpipe-intact session.

She lingered at the door, beaming at me with the pride of a deviant mother seeing her daughter don a miniskirt for the first time. "Well, well. Lookie here. Hello, stranger. Even through my drunk, I knew you had a thing for Geri. I hope, Geri, you got his name, like we discussed."

Without giving Tobias a chance to speak, and cutting off any prepubescent schemes born of one Amy Popowitz, I pushed the wolf away from me and toward the door. He was too busy pulling back the effects of his partial wolf-out to raise a hint of protest. Also, my spoon might have been pressed into the sensitive skin over his wrist as I forced him by the hand through the room.

"It's Tobias, he was just leaving, and he's never coming here again. He does, and I'll call the cops."

As I shoved him past Amy and out the door, I added, "And you know exactly the type of cops I mean."

FIVE

"Has he called?"

"Being that I didn't give him my phone number, he might find that difficult."

"YOU DIDN'T GIVE HIM YOUR PHONE NUMBER?! Are you *insane?*"

"Not enough to give my phone number to some random guy who first, is hanging out in dark alleys in the middle of the night, and second, is all creepy-stalkery and randomly turns up at my apartment the next day."

"You realize, allowing for slight variation in the details, that you just described about half of the romantic comedies from the 1990s, right?"

I turned on Amy, expecting to see her grinning at her joke. Instead, what I got was a hybrid expression that melded genuine concern with the pity one reserves for idiots.

"You also realize," I said, "allowing for a slight variation in the details, that also describes about half of all unsolved murders in, like, every decade, in the history of the world, ever, right?"

My roomie was not pleased. She shook her head and clicked her tongue like a seventh-grade teacher who'd just caught one of her star students spraying graffiti all over the lockers. For some reason, Amy had decided that I was to be her acolyte, even though I'd told her – though honestly, I didn't give a damn – that I didn't want to complicate my life with guys. Besides, what would happen if I did meet a guy I liked? One of my kind's edicts had been dutifully drilled into me since grade school by my mother. "In our blood is our survival. Outside our blood is our death." Then, as an afterthought, she'd add, "Don't forget what happened to the slayers."

Of course, *that* was impossible. I couldn't not forget what happened to the slayers, because I didn't know what happened to the slayers. No one did, not really. Oh, sure, there were theories on why they'd disappeared. The leading one, the one to which my own mother subscribed, was that their elders had allowed too much marrying and coupling with humans. That was, that slayers bred themselves out of any meaningful existence, producing children whose innate talents weakened with each succeeding generation. At some point, their offspring wouldn't have been strong enough to take rites and become initiates in their community. "City folk," she added with a huff. Too much opportunity for the heart's distraction. Hoods, in her opinion, did well by keeping themselves in communes, limiting involvement with Hueys.

That implied that slayers —and for that matter, hoods —weren't human. Collectively, supernaturals had decided at the advent of genetic testing that such concrete evidence of our existence would be bad. Because of that, I had no proof that we all were, as I suspected, some type of Huey. Then again, if *Die Verräterin* had managed to bear a wolf a child, hoods and weres had to be at least related closely enough for it to be possible.

"This conversation is done."

Gathering my books from the counter, I slipped them all into the backpack along with my keys, wallet, and cell phone. I ducked into the bathroom long enough to slip my dagger, its blade only two inches and its hilt appearing to be no more than a fancy hair clip, into the black braid that roped half way down my back. After what happened in the alley, and after having nearly lost it when I dropped my bag, I wasn't going to be without it for quite a while.

"If you see Tobias, you are to give him your phone number! You hear me, Gerwalta Kline? I have a feeling about this one!" Amy called as I made for the door. "You could see it in his eyes when you pushed him out. That man is on a mission, and you are his objective."

Chicago's weather seemed like a practical joke concocted by a bitter god. I'd expected rain, cold, snow, sleet, sun, and its infamous winds at intervals. After six months, I was still getting used to experiencing all of them during the twenty-minute walk from the loft I shared with Amy to the biology building on the WCU campus. Our saying in Michigan was, Don't like the weather? Wait five minutes and it will change. Chicago weather catered to a clientele that thought that was just too long to wait.

WCU, of course, varied from its infamous and more prestigious city-serving cousins. It wasn't the University of Chicago, and it most certainly wasn't DePaul or Loyola. Most importantly to me, however, it wasn't the dinky community college a half-hour drive from my family's compound, and therefore wasn't a den of mother's spies, who'd report back on any "mischief" I got up to unfitting of the next great hood in her illustrious bloodline.

That I was here still seemed a miracle. My mother had not held back her cackling one iota when, after graduating high school two years before, I'd said I wanted to go away to school. There were no degrees in Hood Studies, and no university in the world offered a course on Lycanthrope Diplomacy and Treaty Negotiations. It was only my father's intervention that allowed me to enroll at community. When it'd come time to transfer or finish my associates, I embraced the old saying, better to ask forgiveness than permission.

The Matron of the House of Red would never have given her permission, and as yet, she sure as hell hadn't mustered up the ability to forgive. At one point, I thought she might never speak to me again. Then I realized I'd never actually be that lucky.

I'd submitted the WCU application in secret and managed to use a small inheritance from my grandmother and savings from a part-time job to cover the first year of tuition and living expenses. Transferring as a junior had plusses and minuses. Plus: I didn't go through all my freshman foul-ups in front of the very same professors who were now mentoring me. Minus: everyone else in the program was already established with a lab partner they'd been with for two years, meaning in an odd-numbered class, I worked on my own without any help.

I double-checked the procedures for the exercise of the day and measured my chemicals with military precision. Wouldn't my mother be proud I'd found some activity that benefitted from the high standard she'd held me to as a child? After twenty minutes or so, I was scribbling notes in my lab book when I felt the presence of someone behind me.

"Casper must really be helping you out today."

I turned and stared at the sweet, aged face of Prof. Hikimoto.

"Sir?"

He took a seat next to me and pointed at my experiment. "You've gotten to step twelve when most of the class is still lingering on step seven. It's hard to believe you've done this on your own. I was thinking, maybe there's a ghost working with you."

"Ghosts can't interact with physical objects. One wouldn't be much help to me."

His face blanked. Finally, he decided I must be joking, smiled politely, and continued. "Your labs are executed with precision and thrift, your test scores are at the top of the class, you have an amazing sense of maturity and self-reliance... Tell me, Miss Kline, you wouldn't be looking for a job, would you? One you might continue on with full-time over the summer?"

I scarcely kept myself from hissing. I may have pulled off my dramatic escape late last fall to sneak off to school, but I hadn't yet considered where that left me when classes got out. I supposed I'd still have my room in Amy's loft; the sublease I'd signed had been for twelve months. But was I going to just hang around Chicago and bide my time? It wasn't like I could go home again.

I shrugged. "Haven't thought about it much. Why?"

Prof. Hikimoto pushed his glasses up his nose and blinked three times rapidly. "A colleague is seeking a few student candidates for a project. It starts as part-time for the rest of this semester and turns into full-time come summer."

"An internship? Like a job? Would I get paid?"

He sheepishly smiled. "You wouldn't be making a lot by any means. But if you were open to doing something that would gain you some industry experience, get you something you can put on your resumé to impress any future employer, I think it would be a great experience."

Future employer? Résumé? It suddenly occurred to me that my glorious rebellion against my mother and the seemingly born-to eventuality of becoming a sanctified hood didn't have to be some sort of late developmental temporary state. I could actually run with this and build a life for myself. I could get a job. An actual job, with a supervisor, paid vacation, dental insurance, sensitivity workshop trainings... and no werewolves.

The inheritance I'd gotten from my grandma and my savings wouldn't last forever, after all. Eventually, I'd either need to retreat home with my tail between my legs, or make my own way in the world. Given the choice, I'd go with the latter.

"I might be interested."

"Oh, wonderful!" Prof. Hikimoto clapped his dry hands. "I'll let Prof. Karmarov know. He's already working with one graduate student on the project, and wanted another. I told him he'd be a fool not to consider you though. He'll get in touch with you about the details. Keep up the good work, Miss Kline. I see good things in your future."

My future? I'd heard the phrase since I was knee-high to a scratching post, but always in my mother's rumbling and demonstrative prognostications. She'd more than expected greatness from me for my own benefit; she demanded it for her own. For our family's. For our *legacy* and *legitimacy*. We were the House of Red, the most prominent hood bloodline in the world, with the most ancient roots, and the one to whom other hoods deferred.

We were also the ones with the biggest humiliation to live down.

"A mother hood names her daughter after Die Verräterin herself, I'd wager she's got a lot of rep and expectation vested in that name from the get-go."

The memory of Tobias's instigation played at the back of my thoughts. Most particularly how he'd chosen to use the word "vested." My mother wanted all the bloodlines to know that she was not only the Matron of the Red Hoods, but that she could rewrite the legacy of our biggest shame by branding a name that had become a curse on her only child.

But I'd turned my back on my mother's attempts to rub clean the cloth of our history, and engrave one of her own using me as the pen. I renounced my birthright, and with that, I'd unmoored myself from the harbor of my destiny. It had all happened so suddenly, I'd never stopped to pause and consider all the opportunities now open to me. An internship at a real company, working for real people, making real money (okay, a small stipend), for real work? It sounded too good to be true.

I walked home on cloud nine, grinning ear to ear and absorbed by the tunes filling my earbuds. Butterflies did a cha-cha in my stomach, anticipation over all the things that could come of this mounting sense of self — a self that wasn't defined and confined by some mystical birthright. Maybe that's why I didn't recognize that in that cloud of butterflies, there were also wasps buzzing. As I dashed across a shortcut back alley on the way between the campus and the apartment I shared with Amy, my pursuer took advantage of my distraction and isolation.

One moment I was shaking my butt to the upbeat song beating in my ears, wrapping a scarf around my neck.

And the next moment, I was kissing my ass goodbye.

SIX

A bitter, familiar taste nipped my tongue. Blood. *My* blood — hot, sticky, and free flowing in a rivulet down my face and across my lips.

Had I bitten off my tongue when I'd been jumped from behind and my body, flattened against the urine-washed blacktop? Taking account of my senses, calling on my innate powers to aid in my awareness, I realized the truth was almost as bad. Crude, long fingers threaded my hair, forcing my right cheek to the ground but giving me a view of my assailant's own head next to mine. A sharp pierce of pain just behind my left ear pulsed, and what blood released at the point of a fang that didn't get immediately sucked up by the vampire flowed down into my own mouth.

"Get off of me, asshole."

My futile demand fell silent over the detritus around us. I recognized him, of course. Donovan, the vamp from the bar. He'd probably been following me since that night, just waiting for a chance at payback. And here I was, a pretty little package of distractedness. How could I be so freaking stupid?

Another deep pull of my blood into his mouth, and I felt the first flirtations with dizziness and pain hit. He was draining me like he couldn't finish the deed fast enough. That's when it hit me. He wasn't just trying to fang-rape me. Donovan was out to kill.

I struggled again, trying to free myself. "I'm warning you, last chance."

His lips, pursed around the wound his teeth had bolted into my neck, curled into a smile I could feel, but he still didn't release the hold.

As I called on all my strength, readying myself to buck him off of me, hoping he didn't take a bite-sized chunk out of my neck when I did so, a rumble permeated the air. Like a sheet of ice, it covered both me and the vamp, and we both went dead stiff.

Looked like someone was about to cut in on my and Donovan's dance again.

The vampire's jaw slacked moments before an arc of fur and teeth knocked him off of me. I scrambled to my feet to find the vamp, who moments before had been grinding my face into asphalt, in much the same position. Only instead of a humanlike creature with its devilish hand forcing his head down, it was the maw of a huge red and black wolf, its teeth on his throat and its massive front paws on his shoulders, pinning him to the asphalt.

I pressed the raw flesh behind my ear and pulled back to find a trickle of blood. The moment the wolf took out my adversary, my body had redirected all my innate strength to healing itself, as if by instinct. I still didn't understand why hoods were gifted in this way. Beyond wielding silver and the few of us that could fly, we didn't have what many Hueys would refer to as "super powers." What we had were human abilities, amplified. Like the Six Million Dollar Man, I was stronger, faster, better than human. Only, as a hood who hadn't completed her initiation rites, I could only be superhuman in a very subpar way.

"How now brown cow? Or should I say, red wolf?"

The wolf didn't loosen his hold of Donovan in the slightest. Instead, the muscles over his eyes shifted, the lycanthrope equivalent of raising an eyebrow.

"You're not going to kill him, Tobias. If you had wanted to do that, he'd be dead."

"Get your damn dog off of me!" Donovan attempted to squirm, but he had about as much luck with that as an elephant squeezing into a tube top.

"*My* dog?" Approaching my would-be murderer, I shifted my weight and sent my foot flying, catching him in the s, sending a sickening, bone-crushing crack echoing off the alley walls. "One, he's not mine. And two, are you really that ignorant that you don't know a werewolf when he's trying to subdue you?"

"Of course I know he's a werewolf!" Donovan bit back. "And I don't care what you are. As soon as this mutt gets off of me, you're dead. Do you know what I got for coming home without prey on the night of my rise? Sixteen effing minutes of sunlight!"

"Sixteen, huh?" I asked, mocking him with fake awe. "Well, that is a very particular number. You must have been very crispy when you went back inside. But judging by your supple, baby-smooth skin, I'm guessing you got your fangs on someone since then. So my question is, did you kill them?"

His tongue peeked out of his mouth, smearing across his bottom lip until a fang stopped its path. "Not yet, but you'll be dead soon enough."

A punch of incredulity hit me in the gut. Even the wolf swayed a little in that.

"My blood?" I said. "My blood healed you that quickly?"

"Who knew?" Donovan asked. "My maker says hood blood is better than Neosporin for us. Told me not to come home until I had drained you dry."

Immediately I knew what I had to do. And I hated it. Hated it with a capital HA.

Pushing up my sleeves, I called on my gifts to embolden my strength, even though the effort halted the healing that had already reduced the pulsing and gushing behind my ear to a dull trickle.

"Let him go, Tobias."

The wolf removed his maw but kept his body planted atop the vamp. His head cocked to the side in a way that almost made me forget he was a wolf. He looked like an adorable puppy hearing a high-pitched noise.

"I'm ready." I nodded, reinforcing my statement. "Let him up on the count of three, okay? One, two, three…"

Several things happened all at once. The wolf leapt, landing soundlessly four feet away – far enough away to give me a window but close enough to spring back into action if I needed him. At the same time, Donovan shot to his feet like a spring daisy. He pivoted with a speed my brain could barely follow, and barreled right toward me.

And then there was the third thing that happened. Me, angling my body and shifting right in time to jump up on Donovan's shoulders, thread my fingers through his hair, and twist.

Body and head flew in opposite directions, each landing with a thud a few feet away. I, however, came down in a perfect crouch, one hand before me to steady myself on the pavement.

Tobias shifted back to his human form, showing me respect by not assuming his nudity would be in any way bizarre. I'd been witness to the naked human forms of wolves of every size, shape, and color since I could remember. There was nothing seeing this one's perfect male form was going to do to me.

Well, at least not with him six inches from me and his finger driving into my collarbone.

"What the hell, hood? You killed him?"

Confusion deformed my expression. "Um, yeah. Wasn't that the plan?"

Tobias's jaw worked. "Did it ever occur to you to rough him up for information first? Maybe query *why* a vamp saw a nascent hood as such a threat? Or, bloody hell, even ask who his maker is, in case he sends another of his mosquitoes after you?"

Now that he mentioned it, it was a little odd. And if I was a fair person, I'd admit that to Tobias. As it turned out, in that respect, I was my mother's child after all.

"One of the primary guidelines I've been taught since I was a child: deal with an immediate threat before worrying about the greater implications."

"So shoot first and ask questions later. Yeah, you're *definitely* a Red."

"What exactly do you think he might have said? Come on, Tobias, it's obvious. He failed his initiation rites. He didn't get a thrall home for his ceremonial induction. His master commanded him to come after me because he wanted him to die, but didn't want to do it himself. I've read stories about vampire justice. You wouldn't believe the consequences."

"I'm guessing the fact that *you* killed him doesn't make those consequences magically go away, does it?"

A lump in my throat threatened to cut off my ability to breathe. Holy shit, no it wouldn't. There were procedures for this kind of thing, protocols. Ones I wasn't familiar with, but that my Matron would be. What I did know was that any maker worth his salt would be seeking recompense for the loss of their child.

Which meant, in a very short span of time, my mother would know I'd slain a vampire. Even if they didn't know I was the Red Matron's daughter, and even if they didn't know my name, word of such things spread through the community like disease. As far as I knew, I was still the only hood in Chicago. That left little room for scapegoating.

My nerves made me go on the defensive. "I was justified. He pledged to kill me. You heard it! If I get called out for this, you *will* witness for me."

"I don't think the testimony of a lone wolf will count for much, do you?"

"You're in Chicago alone?" Were his words ever going to stop punching me in the gut? "How long have you been away from the others?" I held my breath, waiting for his answer.

"Only two weeks."

The rush of air from my lungs carried away some of my anxiety. A lone wolf, without a pack, would eventually go insane. He'd kill without hesitation. My father, a hood of the House of Yellow, had told me tales that still turned my stomach, of tracking lone wolves gone over the edge across the Pampas, and destroying them.

"You've got a few months then. But why is a lone... No, you know what, none of my business. I don't want to be involved."

"Neither do I, and yet, here I am again," Tobias said, running a hand through his hair.

"Speaking of which, how did you end up here this time? You really going to tell me that you just happened to be walking by again?"

"Of course not. I've been tracking his scent since that night outside the pub. He's been following you for two nights, just waiting for when you'd be stupid enough to walk down a dark alley. You know, Gerwalta, I've saved you twice now, when really, letting that vamp toast you would have worked out better for me by a long run."

"Well, then, if you ever chance upon me being attacked by a vampire again, please, don't hesitate to go fuck yourself."

His hands tightened into fists, and for a moment, I thought he was going to hit me. Instead, they just shook at his sides.

"Ungrateful, entitled bitch."

He turned on his heel, lashing his fists into the empty air. When he turned back, I saw the wolf flash in his eyes. Maybe he'd been out on his own longer than he'd claimed. He was already displaying irrational behavior.

"If anyone does come asking you about what went on tonight, you mention one tiny little thing about me, and I will track you down to finish what the vamp started. No one except you knows I'm here. I'd like to keep it that way."

"I'm not exactly going to be shooting off fireworks to let everyone know I nearly got my ass kicked. If you're fine with me taking all the credit, works for me."

"Go ahead. I don't need my ego stroked. And, just so we're clear, this is the last time I'm helping you," he ground out. "So, please, for fuck's sake, don't be an idiot. Lighted roads, no more back alleys. I told you, there's something going on around here with the vamps. They might not fret over hoods in general, but now that one of their babies kissed pavement while out on assignment to tick you off, you'll be on their radar. If they're anything like the vamps where I come from, they're really into that vendetta thing."

Lacing my arms over my chest, I shifted my weight from one side to the other. "Don't suppose you're going to tell me just where that is, will you?"

He answered with a finger pointed in my direction. "I mean it, Gerwalta. Next time, you're on your own."

"Fine by me!"

I barely got the words out before a ripple of fur shot down his chest and over the pulse points around his body. Wolf-Tobias gave me a flash of his sharp canines, the werewolf equivalent of passing me the middle finger, before turning and exiting the way he'd come.

Leaving me alone in a dark alley, with a decapitated vampire corpse.

SEVEN

As a hood, my primary area of study and training had been on how to work with – and when necessary, against – werewolves. That was our purpose. My *abuela*, who lived with us briefly before her death, told me that God had to balance the world when he created supes, all to protect his ultimate creation: man. Wolves ruled the wilds and vamps held dominion in towns and villages. He created hoods and slayers as the buffer between them both, and between the Hueys with whom they shared territory. Slayers were to vamps as we were to lycanthropes: an intermediary between them and civilization and when necessary, if one ever got out of line, a bringer of punishment.

Hoods weren't meant to balance vamps. As I looked down at Donovan's headless torso and torsoless head, I knew why. My stomach threatened to vie for an Olympic gold medal, it was turning so many flips. How could there be so much blood in something that wasn't technically alive?

I looked at my phone. 1 AM. The sun wouldn't be up for hours. Would I have to wait till then for the body to dissolve? Would it dissolve? Or did it explode? I suddenly realized that you could drive a semi truck between the margins of what I knew and what I thought I knew. There were no vamps in the Upper Peninsula. I'd have to go clear to Detroit or over to Green Bay to meet one if I ever got the notion. Realizing I needed advice from someone I could trust, I plopped down, took out my cell, and sent a message to my cousin.

You don't know anything about vampire corpses, do you?

Markus took a painfully long time to answer. *I think I saw them open up for Metal Trap once. They really rock.*

Not a band. Actual dead undead.

Academic interest or practical application? :/

Chest heavy, I sighed and keyed in my answer. *The latter.*

A nanosecond later, my cell rang. In the silence of the alley, the soft trill became Gabriel's horn. Hermes would drip with envy over the speed of my answering.

In my mind's eye, I saw my cousin's herculean frame overtaken by his friend-of-Dorothy mannerisms. "One, where the hell are you? And two, why?"

"Why what?"

"Don't get smart with me, little red." Markus clicked his tongue. "You know perfectly well why."

"I'm in Chicago. I'm going to school here." A fact my mother and father knew, but probably hadn't shared with the family due to shame. "The vamp was trying to kill me, so I sort of just, you know, killed him first."

"*You* killed a vamp?"

I didn't know if I should be proud or offended at the surprise in his voice. "I had a little bit of help."

"But there are no other hoods in Chicago. At least, there's not supposed to be."

"It wasn't a hood that helped me." My voice and my courage shrank. "It was a wolf."

"There aren't any of those either!"

My hand slapped over the receiver, hoping to cover up Markus's shouting. A moment later, I did my best to explain.

"There's at least one. Markus, you can't tell my mom, okay? You can't tell anyone. He's saved me twice, and I really don't want to pay him back by getting word to the *oberst* that he's around. I'm keeping an eye on him. If he gets out of hand, I'll let someone know."

"Are you seeing him? Are you *sleeping* with him?"

"No, and on that note, you should really meet my roommate. You both seem to be overly concerned with my love life. Can we focus on the problem I'm currently having? I need to know about vampire corpses. I know you had some kind of weird obsession with the vampires once. Tell me what you know."

My cheery cousin turned adamant professional. "Method of death?"

"Decapitation."

"Current location?"

I side-eyed the body. "About three feet from me. We're in an alley. I thought they just sort of fizzled when they died. Or melted, or something."

"They're vampires, Geri. Not the Wicked Witch of the West. Are you somewhere that the sun is going to hit when it comes up?"

The alley ran parallel to a street I knew from staring at maps ran east to west. "If there's sun. It's supposed to rain tomorrow morning."

"Doesn't matter," Markus said. "Even if the sunlight is diffused, the body will still turn to ash. It will just take a little longer. Rain would be good, in fact. It's going to wash away all the dust. Of course, you're probably going to want to take all his clothes off."

"WHAT?"

This time, it was my voice that threatened to give me away.

"Think about it, little red. Even without a body, if someone comes upon a set of clothes and shoes laid out like someone deflated inside them, it might draw attention. Make sure to get rid of any identification he had on him too. Now, go on. Strippy, strippy. I'll wait."

"Don't dare ask me to send you a picture of this."

"I'm gay, Geri. Not a necrophile."

Resting the phone on a nearby box, I got to my feet and did as my cousin advised. While true that naked werewolves didn't make me blink twice, something about defrocking a near stranger made me curl my lip in disgust. The smell didn't make the process any more tolerable. Every item removed perfumed the air with Eau d'Vamp, a sickly sweet smell, like tar-covered caramel. When Donovan's body was nude, I picked the phone back up.

"Okay, I did that. Now what?"

"Now, you wait for sunrise. Your fingerprints are all over his stuff. Anyone comes up to him before dawn and calls the cops, you're screwed."

"So you actually just made this harder for me. Thanks, Markus. That's great. Jesus Christ, how did the slayers deal with this crap? Vampires live in cities. They couldn't have just been babysitting undead corpses until sunrise all the time. Someone would have caught them."

"The slayers didn't have to wait," Markus said. "They could conjure sunlight. All they had to do when they killed a vamp was throw a solar flare at it."

"Great for them."

I felt my hackles rise when a noise at the far end of the alley caught my attention. Looking up to where moonlight hit shadows, I caught sight of a slowly trudging silhouette. The way the body shuffled with small steps and rigidity told me it was neither a vamp nor a werewolf. The labored slide-step-slide could mean it was a zombie, even though I was pretty sure those didn't exist.

"Shit, I have to go. Thanks, Markus. I owe you one."

"You mean you owe me one more."

With a click, he was gone.

Donovan's bewildered eyes and mouth, stuck in a last rattling of his favorite cuss word, sat flash frozen in his bulbous head across the way. The person at the far end of the alley stopped, leaned over a trash bin, examined a couple of random objects, then moved on to the next.

I could run for it, but like Markus pointed out — slash that, *ensured* my prints were all over the scene. Nope, I had to stay here and see this through, even if it meant improvising.

When Amy had extolled the joy of giving head, she probably hadn't pictured it quite in this way. I pulled off my loosened, blood-soaked scarf and pawed for Donovan's head. It didn't exactly want to stay in its original position, i.e, at the end of his neck, continually rolling like some partially deflated basketball. Finally, using my scarf, it kept its position, the fabric covering the gap between his *cabeza* and his lower faculties. Taking a breath and ignoring the vomit trying to crawl its way up my throat, I threw a leg over his bare hips and settled myself over his midsection.

As the homeless guy made his way up the alley, nothing more likely to get him to turn and run occurred to me than if he caught us "in the act." Only, after a moment of my theatric gyrations and faux moaning, I realized instead of running away to avoid the gooey awkward of apparently finding two people mid-coitus, he kept his eyes fixed on us.

I froze.

"Don't stop." He shuffled his hands, as if telling me to run with something. "I ain't gonna intrude, just want to watch."

I huffed. "It isn't a public show."

The gruff, grimy man waved a hand through the air. "Not with all your clothes on, it ain't. And your guy doesn't seem to be helping much. Isn't he stiff or something?"

I perused the corpse beneath me. "Oh, he's stiff. And of course, I have my clothes on! It's only forty degrees out here!"

"If you were doing it right, you wouldn't care." Then, turning to Donovan's head, he said, "Never learned to please a woman, have you son?"

And it was at that precise moment that the vampire's noggin rolled out of the scarf.

I moved before realizing I'd made the choice. I was on my feet and had a fist into the man's temple before he had time to do more than raise a hand and bring the question to his lips. If I needed more reasons why I was going to Hell when I died – starting with breaking that whole commandment about honoring thy mother – rendering an innocent albeit voyeuristic homeless guy unconscious was adding to my ledger.

Screw due diligence. I grabbed my things and turned tail for home.

EIGHT

Amy refused to believe that I hadn't actually gone out and "got my v-chip revoked" when I hadn't come home until two in the morning. The night we sat and watched a movie with a no-holds-barred love scene, however, finally changed her mind.

My face morphed into a mask of disgust as the camera zoomed in on the ridiculous facial glitches of the couple as they went into rapid bunny mode. "Is that actually what it sounds like? I don't think I'm going to be able to keep a straight face when the time comes."

"If you come, you won't." She giggled, making a pretzel of my words. "You weren't lying, were you?"

"I generally don't. I *avoid* the truth on occasion."

"Fine, you didn't track down Mr. Hot and seduce him. But if you weren't, you know, with someone, what were you doing?"

I'd regurgitated my rehearsed excuse. "I told you, I got sleepy working late in the lab, put my head down to rest a few minutes, and woke up six hours later."

Technicality number one: I had gotten sleepy in the lab. I just didn't fall asleep there.

"Right, you fell asleep in the lab. Oh, Geri, did I tell you what I got in the mail today?"

I paused in my attempts to down another handful of popcorn.

"My birth certificate!" Amy squealed. "Which is awesome, because I thought it'd take two days at least, you know, given that I was just born yesterday."

"Ha ha."

She rose, taking the bowl of popcorn with her. "Fine, maybe you just were dry humping or fish facing. Or maybe you went all *Breaking Bad* and spent the night cooking up meth in the chem lab."

"We don't do that kind of stuff in organic chem, Amy. It's more like plant cells and stuff. A little genetics, if we get really crazy."

"At this rate, you're going to be a virgin until you're sixty."

I batted my eyes. "Don't you mean, sixty-nine?"

A beige throw pillow became a beige *thrown* pillow as Amy chucked it my direction.

"You're hopeless, Geri. Hopeless!"

We'd only gotten to the awkward morning-after scene in the movie when there was a knock at the door. My hand when to the hilt of my dagger in my hair, even though I didn't sense any wolf nearby. Being attacked by a vamp raised my vigilance. Amy was already to the door, however, her hand on the handle.

"We live in a big, bad, dangerous city, Amy. At least look through the peephole!"

Amy rolled her eyes at me, but still did as asked anyways. "Good call, Geri. Thank god I didn't open my door before making sure it's only a delivery guy."

In the hall stood a nondescript man wearing dark clothes and holding a clipboard.

"I'm looking for *Garwalter,* um, *Girvalter…* Kline, a Mister Kline?"

Amy reached out her hand expectantly. "Gerwalta, and that's her," she said, jerking her head to the side to indicate me on the couch behind her. "You need a signature or anything?"

"Oh, I'm…Sorry, *Miss* Kline. I've never heard that name before. It's very…"

"German." I completed his sentence for him, getting up to take the pen and clipboard. "It's an old family name. Is this it? You just need my signature?"

He nodded, holding out a standard-sized envelope. "Actually, no, I need an answer too."

I looked at the envelope as though I expected it to explain. "An answer to what?"

The delivery guy shrugged. "Not sure. I don't ask the questions, I just follow the orders. I can wait out here. You can close the door if you want. I won't go anywhere."

My mind raced with possibilities. Was my mother trying to get to me through an intermediary since I'd refused to answer her calls? Was Markus following up on my predicament, and doing it in an unusual way to throw off any suspicions of his own mother? Had I won the lottery?

But the last thing I expect was what I actually found. A letter penned elegantly on fine ivory linen paper.

Miss Kline,

I received your information from Prof. Hikimoto, who recommended you as a candidate for the special research project I'll be running this summer, which also includes preliminary lab research this semester. Yamato-san's rave review of your tenacity, intelligence, and performance in his class is encouraging, but it has been my experience that it is always wise to meet and discuss these things in person, in order to review the expectations we both may hold, as well as to discuss compensation. Would you be able to visit me at my office, Browning 359, this Wednesday evening at 8:30 PM? I do apologize for the late hour, but this project is being conducted in what I understand most people refer to as "free time," and our current hours generally run roughly 8 PM to 11:30 PM, twice weekly. (Another consideration before accepting the position.)

Please respond with haste,

Prof. Igor Karmarov

Amy, reading over my shoulder, wrinkled her nose like she'd smelt something foul. "Sounds weird, Ger. What kind of professor asks to meet you at his office at eight-thirty at night, and expects you to work until almost midnight?"

What kind of professor, indeed? My stomach developed a lupine-shaped lump.

"Plus, come on... Igor? Seriously, his name is Igor?" Amy said when I hadn't responded to her original comment. "Does he have a hunchback too?"

"Igor is actually a very common name in certain parts of Eastern Europe." *Like the parts with the biggest of the Old World packs.* "Just because we associate that name with creepy literary characters doesn't mean they do. I heard the name Adolf is even making a comeback."

"It shouldn't. And moms shouldn't name their boys Igor. That's just cruel. Why not Sven? Isn't that Eastern European?" Amy's fingertip drew a line over her lower lip. "Mmmm, Sven."

"That's Scandinavian. But, having grown up with the name Gerwalta, I kinda get what you're saying. It's always sad when people chalk up too much to a name."

I fetched one of my lab notebooks from the kitchen table where I'd been studying earlier and scribbled a reply, before ripping out the sheet and folding it in half.

"Here." I stuck out the sheet to the courier. "Thank you for coming out this late. I really appreciate it."

The courier tipped his head. "Seems to be the only time of day Prof. Karmarov asks us to do anything, ma'am. It was no problem."

NINE

Browning Hall had been built at a time when Gothic architecture was the everything-old-again-is-new-again thing. I felt like I was walking into a military academy, entering under its hatched brick towers and angular windows. A brisk wind chased me through the double doors, laying out a carpet of brown leaves, blanketing the speckled marble floor with the detritus of nature. Even though the building had two perfectly functional elevators, I took the stairs out of habit to the third floor. My training had drilled into my nature a distrust of indefensible blind positions and closed-in spaces.

The room number, 359, eluded me. I strolled down several hallways, passing sequential rooms from 320 to 358, which skipped immediately to 360 a few feet away. A bundle of nerves smoldered in my gut. The meeting was set for tonight, wasn't it? It was Browning Hall, and not Renquist on the other side of campus, right? Had the professor made a typo in his email and not realized it? Maybe it was Browning 259 or even 539. On the edge of nausea, convincing myself I had already lost the job before I'd even gotten it, I made my way back down to the lobby to see if I could find a floor plan for the building when I heard a hiss behind me.

The wall opened.

Not a door. Not even a window, but a *wall.*

What had appeared to be cinderblocks coated in decades of paint cracked, and a corner intersection between the main hall and one of its offshoots proved to be hinged. My left hand went to my head, where the hilt of my silver blade sat camouflaged as a hair clip. A head full of fair hair peeked out, followed by broad shoulders covered in flannel. A moment later, the head swiveled, and I was rendered mute.

Amy would be proud of my reaction. A man with a toothy grin and dimpled cheeks complemented perfectly by deep blue eyes and blonde hair, stared at me. He was college frat boy cocky with just a touch of you-know-you-want-me male model. A perfect specimen of the type of guy my roomie would define as "the type you bed, not the type you wed." The guy oozed sex.

I shook myself from my stupor when I realized he was talking and lowered my hand, leaving the knife in its sheath, woven into my braid. "Sorry, what?"

"You don't look like a Walter, I said, but I'm pretty sure I was sent out here to find a Walter Kline."

"*Gerwalta*, actually," I corrected, holding out my hand. "Everyone calls me Geri."

Except my mother. And my father. And every hood I ever met.

"Geri," he repeated as he took my hand. *Oh, so warm. So soft. So firm. So big.* "Like the Spice Girl?"

"Except for the dancing and singing part." Deadpan, thou art mine name. "Gerwalta's old German. Just kinda hard for people to remember. Are you… Dr. Karmarov?"

Please, oh please no. But knowing my luck over the last six months, I would finally meet a guy I find attractive, and he'd turn out to be forbidden for a different reason than being a vampire.

"Me?" He ran a hand through his hair and laughed at the notion. "I'm Jess Harmond. I'm a student of Prof. Karmarov's. You're Prof. Hikimoto's student, right? The undergrad he was talking about?"

"I am. Now I remember. He mentioned there was already a graduate student on the project. Is that you?"

Grad student? I could do a grad student.

I mean, *date.* I could *date* a grad student.

"Must have been talking about me, yup. So, um, Dr. K sent me out here to get you. He's in his office at the back of the lab. Said you might have gotten lost, because he forgot to mention to you that there's a special entrance for this room. Hope you weren't wandering for too long."

"I actually was, but… No, it's okay."

Was I batting my eyelashes and giggling? Oh, my god, I was.

"But I have to admit," I continued, "even if he had told me that the door was an unmarked piece of wall, I probably wouldn't have found it any faster."

Jess looked behind him with confusion, as though he had no idea what I was talking about. When he saw the stack of pivoted bricks that was the door behind him, his mouth dropped. "How about that? Didn't know what it looked like from this side. This is an emergency exit. We never use it. This building is full of weird secrets. They even say that there was an animal lab back in the WWII days, running experiments on behalf of the government. You know those creepy towers that rise up on the corners of the building on the third and fourth floors? Doc K's lab and office are in one of those. There's an entry from the outside of the building that goes directly up here. The stuff Doc K is working on is kind of… Well, I shouldn't say anything until the two of you talk and you sign the NDA. So," he said, clapping his hands together, "let me take you, huh?"

Yes, please. Suddenly, twenty years of learned self-discipline washed down the drain. My hormones had hijacked my body and were already thinking of ways to casually ask Jess if he had a girlfriend.

Who would have guessed; I actually was female after all.

The room we entered didn't look that much different at first from any other lab in the building. Linoleum floors, off-white walls, several work areas with waist-high tables and black-cushioned stools. At the side of the room stood an emergency wash station, and next to it, a sink over which hung cartoonish signs showing proper emergency technique. No windows, however, and only four ways in or out: the door we had just come through, which looked from the inside far more commonplace and utilitarian than it had from the exterior hall, an elevator well, an arched doorway beyond which I could see a staircase spiral – I was guessing that was Prof. Karmarov's office – and a heavy brown behemoth of a door on the left wall with a large, lever-like handle.

"That's cold storage," Jess said. He must have noticed my eyes trying to figure out the details. "Restricted access, I'm afraid. Only Doc K and his staff researcher. No students allowed."

My hood hunches were piqued. "Why, what's so important about it?"

"Not important, just…" Jess winced. "Sorry, I really can't tell you until you're officially part of the team."

"Yeah, no worries." My eyes drifted up, examining an industrial ceiling dotted at intervals with what looked like an army of pen lights. "Those are some weird-looking light bulbs."

My tour guide nodded. "LEDs, actually. The lab is on an independent power grid, something about making sure that the samples in the refrigeration units stay at the right temperature even if there's a blackout. These lights don't create as much heat and are cheaper to power. Don't tell him I said so, but I think Doc K might be a secret member of Greenpeace. He has that real 'out to save the world' mentality."

"I noticed there are no windows either. I must be going crazy. I could have sworn I saw them on the outside."

"You're not crazy, there are windows," Jess said right on cue, turning an amused smile at me that made the pit of my stomach dance a jig. "Bricked over back in the '80s when this floor was used for storage. The reason Doc K fought for this space when he showed up last fall. I guess some of the samples are photosensitive."

"What, like sensitive to sunlight?"

"Yup."

He guided me towards the turret entrance. Jess opened the door and waved me on.

"Top of the stairs. I'll be here when you're done and I'll show you back down in our exclusive K-Lab elevator. Good luck, Geri."

"Thanks."

I grew dizzy as the turret crawled like a nautilus towards the tower. Memories of old castles along the windy rivers of Bavaria flooded the forefront of my mind. My annual trips to the Black Forest were for training of course, but once, when I was fourteen, my father managed to convince my mother to let me take a week-long side trip with him. We walked through medieval streets, ate chewy pretzels hot from the oven, and even went to an opera. Of course, four days in, our trip reached a dead end. A call went out for need of a hood in a nearby valley. My father was the closest and responded with haste.

I was still convinced my mother had called in a favor to make sure we didn't have *too* much fun.

At the top of the staircase, I found a door that looked more like the entry to a French cottage than a professor's office. The wooden surface, crisscrossed by iron bars with flat-nosed bolts at the intersection, would have been right at home in Lausanne or Burgundy. A wheel and lock were embedded where a plain handle may have been. I wasn't sure the professor would hear my light tapping if I tried to knock, but clueless what to do otherwise, I fisted my hand and raised it in preparation.

I'd barely made contact when the wheel spun and the door opened. The air of the room beyond, colder than that filling the staircase and the lab below, blew past me, making stray strands of my black hair fly out.

A moment later, the hair on my neck went for a similar look, and my hand flew instinctively to the hilt of the blade woven in my braid.

"Peace, Miss Kline. Peace."

The glint off the knife reflected a line of light over the vampire's forehead. I gulped, taking note of my every, numerous disadvantage. He had everything going for him: higher ground, the element of surprise, superior strength. The ability to suddenly sprout one-inch long dental daggers. The only thing I had was a two-inch blade made of a metal that wouldn't even burn him. Oh, sure, if I was lucky, I might be able to sink it in his chest and try to get halfway down the stairs, but that would be as far as I got.

"Who are you, and what did you do with Professor Karmarov?"

A gleam overcame his features, making him look boyish. He wasn't a young vamp. That is to say, when he was turned. If I had to guess, I'd put his mortal age around forty. He was far gaunter than most of his kind; a fact that may be attributable to malnourishment, or simply the roll of the genetic dice. He wasn't unpleasant to look at, but wouldn't stand out in a crowd with his curly black hair dashed in places by gray. An angular nose and a prominent chin suggested eastern European, perhaps even Russian heritage. He held his hands out before him like a cop trying to convince a kidnapper to drop his gun once cornered.

"I *am* Professor Karmarov, and I will not harm you. If you would please sheath your weapon, I can explain."

"There are no vamps at this university!" I retorted, despite the contrary evidence staring me back in the face. "It's part of the reason I came here: no supes."

"Come now, Miss Kline, as integrated as supes are in the mainstream these days, surely you don't believe there wouldn't be *any*. Though, admittedly, most vampires working in academia would think WCU too brow an institution. In my case, it is the fact that others of my kind would tend to overlook this college that led me to locating my lab and my team here."

He may have thought he was calming me, but he only made me more nervous. "Your team? So, you're not alone?"

"There are three vampires working in this lab, but I thought it would be best if you met me first, so I could orientate you to our involvement."

That's when the full implication of what he was saying hit me. "You know I'm a hood."

"Of course, I know." A tinge of smugness crept into his smile. "No need to worry. I see the fear etched into your features. I'm old enough to know the way of your kind. You're pack animals, almost as much as the wolves you counterbalance. You wouldn't be here unless it was meant to be incognito. I assure you, however, how I came to know of your nature and presence here is mere coincidence. I scented you one evening when you were working in the lab."

"Bullshit. If you had gotten close enough to smell me, I sure as hell would have picked up on your presence."

Karmarov clicked his tongue, becoming in stature every bit the professor his human cover suggested. "Firstly, you were likely scent blind at the time, given the particular concoction of sulfur dioxide you were working with. And secondly, I am a very old vampire. The reach of my senses out-performs far beyond anything a hood, no matter how mature, would be capable of. Probably beyond even that of the Red Matron."

I bit my tongue before I blabbed the fact that, as the daughter of the Red Matron, I very much doubted it.

He stepped aside and held out an arm. "Now, if you'd like to come in and discuss the matter as nothing more than a professor and a student engaging in academic exchange, I can tell you more about the project, and why, in particular, you should be interested in pursuing it."

My wordless response was to jerk my dagger a little higher.

Karmarov closed his eyes and sighed. Reaching out with dedicated ease, his hand grabbed the blade. In one clean swipe, he'd robbed me of my weapon and my self-confidence.

"If I wanted you dead, you'd be dead, Miss Kline. If I wanted a snack, between you and me, I'd opt for Jess."

A smile flitted across his face, one I found I couldn't help but share.

"Please, if you decide you don't wish to work on the project after I've had a chance to explain, I'll hold no grudge. But I think you'll find that it is in your best interest to consider otherwise."

TEN

"I know you're a biology student," he started once I'd settled into the chair across from him.

And by settled, I mean sat straight up, eyes forward and trained on him for the slightest implication that he would attack.

"But strictly speaking, this isn't a biology project. It isn't even an organic chem project."

"How about telling me what kind of project it *is,* then, instead of what it *isn't.*"

Karmarov ran a hand through his thinning (or thinned, I supposed, given that he no longer would age) hair. "At the moment, our work is preliminary. We're casting a wide net, not really sure which discipline is going to get us to our goal. I know as a hood, you must be very knowledgeable about wolves, but tell me —how much do you know about vampires and slayers?"

"More about your kind than slayers," I answered matter-of-factly, "seeing as slayers were never really a threat to us."

"Being that they're all extinct, I'd say they're not really much of a threat to anyone," Karmarov observed. "A vampire doesn't speak of his age in polite conversation, but suffice it to say, I'm not young, as you've probably gathered. I've been on this earth for several centuries, and I remember slayers. It was, of course, my natural inclination to dislike them, especially when I was shorter in the tooth. But through the ages, I learned that they served a very necessary and key role. Nature likes balance, and even though a species may benefit short-term from a lack of predators, in the long run, having nothing to stand in the way of its growth and dominance results in more harm than good. Are you originally from this area, Miss Kline?"

Training and a healthy dose of common sense kept my tongue still.

The professor grinned. "Forgive me, of course you have every right not to trust me with such information. Though, if I really wanted to know, as a member of the faculty, I could access your student records with just a few phone calls. I won't, of course, but please take the fact that I didn't as a token of my respect for your privacy and my professionalism in the course of this endeavor."

That fact was too true, and the understanding that he hadn't snooped relaxed my nerves. "I'm from the U.P."

"Ah, the Upper Peninsula of Michigan, yes? Well, then you may be aware of this even more so than most. Do you know what happened to the deer population in the upper Midwest when its natural predators —bears, wolves, badgers, et cetera —were hunted to near extinction during the age of the fur trappers?"

"Of course, I do," I said. Yooper school kids learned about the justification presented by thousands of Michigan deer hunters each fall in class. "The population exploded. There were so many deer that there wasn't enough food for them in winter. Not to mention how having so many of them around stunted forest growth, with them gnawing at everything that shot up out of the ground. It's part of the reason the state pushed deer hunting in the '50s and '60s. They figured it was more humane than letting thousands starve to death."

"Not to mention, venison is also very tasty." Karmarov, sitting on the edge of his desk, leaned in, sending my stomach plummeting. "Not unlike a slayer."

"Unless you're about to suggest to me that the best solution to the overpopulation of deer would have been for them to develop a sudden taste for human flesh, I'm not sure how that's relevant."

"Too true," Karmarov said as he straightened up and crossed his arms over his chest. "What I'm getting at is this. The bear, the wolves, the badgers – yes, they were predators, but they served an essential function, one that, in their absence, evolved into a much more horrific fate. As much as vampires detest slayers, they had a place in our world. In their absence this last half-century, the vampire population has begun to grow unwieldy. We've begun to fight over territory, over resources. No doubt you've heard about the increase in unsolved murders in Chicago. While some of that is merely mortal, some of the less scrupulous of our kind have taken advantage of these events to add to their clutches, including some who are not well adapted for a life of eternal, responsible imbibing of human blood."

An image of Donovan's headless corpse flashed into my mind's eye. *You're not just whistling Dixie, professor.*

He continued. "The honor code which called upon us only to use humans as donors rather than disposable prey seems to be fading into the annals of history. Huey authorities would never think to blame some of these mysterious disappearances and deaths on something as mythic as vampires, so the less morally inclined among us continue to build larger and larger families, unchecked by any limiting force. Though some of my kind may deny it, Miss Kline, we need slayers. If we do not have our balance, we will soon find ourselves stranded in the urban jungles, turning further on ourselves and our values."

"And humanity will be your forest, bitten back in the process." Fine, he had my attention, but I still wasn't clear where I fit into the picture. "So what you're trying to do is...?"

"Easy." He fanned the fingers of one hand through the air. "I'm trying to bring back slayers."

"But... they're all dead."

"I'm not so sure. You must have heard the most popular theory about their disappearance, that breeding with Hueys diminished their bloodlines."

Lectures and rants by my mother flamed the edges of memory. "Once or twice."

"Honestly, I don't know if it's true, but that some slayers did take human mates is undeniable. Though their elders frowned on the practice, it's created a wonderful opportunity for vampires like me who've realized how desperate we are for the counterbalance. You see, the slayers' DNA information has been passed down to later generations, even if dormant or recessive."

"So you're trying to extract slayer DNA?"

He nodded.

"But all the supes agreed that genetic profiling—that intentionally mapping our DNA—would be too risky. Once that information is out in the world, we can't take it back. If any wrong hands got those details, there's no telling what they might do with it."

"I'm aware of the risks. That's why this program is very small, and access to this lab, highly restricted. Besides, for the moment, I'm simply trying to identify and sequence the slayer genome. I have no intentions or plans to do that of hoods, wolves, or vampires."

"But I don't get what good having slayer DNA would be. I know there are some genetic therapies these days, but what you're talking about would be changing the physical composition of a human."

He turned sheepish, something I didn't think a vampire was capable of. "Oh, I'm not talking infection, Miss Kline. Please don't think I intend to con a score of humans into clinical trials that will lead them to become creatures of the night with glowing gold eyes and a ravenous desire for garlic. No, no. On the contrary, all around the globe, there are secret societies, ones who track all supes. Their records are long, ancient. Generation after generation of vampire, wolf, slayer, and hood bloodlines documented. I believe your people use some version of that in order to know the current whereabouts of both hoods and wolves."

"As does your kind track its own," I stated.

Karmarov nodded. "Using these records, it shouldn't be too difficult to track down some slayer descendants, perhaps even ones whose parents or grandparents were fully of that persuasion. The last known slayers only died out a few generations ago. Their mostly human descendants may have strongly related genetic sequences that, with a little tweaking, could *induce* slayerhood, for lack of a better term."

A noble cause, but one still shortsighted. "Just because you make the weapon doesn't mean it will perform well in battle. The body is only a vessel, but what would a slayer be without their traditions, their teachings? Even if you can engineer a slayer, how do you give him the ability to know how to slay?"

The professor stood, placed his hands behind his back, and began to pace. "Thus my interest in your kind."

His interest in…

My head began to shake before I even realized I was smiling. "There's no way the Matrons would agree to such a thing."

Prof. Karmarov looked down his nose at me. "Not the Matrons. I know they're too wrapped up in their power struggles and politics."

"But if not the Matrons, then wh— No, you can't be serious."

"Why couldn't I?" Amusement stretched his mouth into a grin. "Hoods, ones like you who have problems with the way your community is currently conducting itself… Surely a small cadre of such individuals could lend a hand. And in the meantime, your ability to assist in our research would be critical to success."

"How do you know I have issues with hood procedures?"

He grinned. "Would you be here, at University, on your own if not? If you had the ability to change the direction your kind – and mine – are heading, wouldn't you want to?"

I thought back to Donovan, of the gall of a baby vamp openly attacking an innocent Huey, and of his maker sending him back a few days later in a bid to kill me off. If that was the direction the vamps were heading, then Karmarov had a point.

My hesitance was all the answer he needed. "Welcome to the team, Miss Kline. Now, let's talk about your pay."

ELEVEN

Three days later, I had two big problems.

First, there was a slight chance — like, a pencil shaving's slight—that Tobias had been right. What if Donovan's maker actually did want me dead? But if that was the case, wouldn't he have sent someone else to finish what Donovan had proven to be so impotently incapable of? And if he did, wouldn't I totally die in the process? Twice I'd been challenged by a vamp — a *baby* vamp — and twice, I'd come up short and had to be saved by a werewolf.

If my cousins ever found out how pitiful I'd been in the field, I'd never live it down. Not like they would fare much better, though. I'd always been the strongest in my clan, the hood matron apparent who could kick anyone's ass — male or female — that training bouts teamed me with. As a kid, my mom had even arranged for me to spar with the Paradise alpha's son, giving me practice with an actual werewolf.

Later, I fell in love with that werewolf, and I didn't mind so much if he managed to pin me to the ground.

All my life, I'd carried silver on me — be it the two-inch blade with the embellished handle I disguised as a hair accessory woven into my braid, or bangle bracelets that I could use to shove into a wolf's maw if I got attacked. Now, I added gold to my repertoire as well. Finding 14K clip-on earrings proved a challenge, but my shopaholic roomie Amy knew how to source whatever I asked for.

"Why clip-ons?" she asked, baffled by the choice. "Your ears are pierced."

I could hardly tell her because, in the event of a vampire attack, I didn't want to tempt fate further by pulling out a traditional post earring to defend myself, thus drawing said vampire's attention to a wound gushing his favorite cocktail.

"Because of the lab," I deferred. "Some of the microbes we work with down there? Ew. I don't really want to be shoving metal through holes in my body at the end of my shift, having been exposed to who knows what."

The second problem I had wasn't so easily rationalized. I had killed a vampire. Regardless of the reasons that came about, I knew it wouldn't go without notice. Even if the maker had sent Donovan to me with the hopes I'd dispatch him, once they found out who I was, they'd take advantage of it. As my mother had told me, never waste a crisis.

When I saw my father's number flash across the screen of my smartphone, I just about had a heart attack. Truth be told, I'd been sitting on pins and needles since the moment I signed my name to the contract in Karmarov's office. Even though the professor assured me that the project, with its taboo research, was purely an academic endeavor and that no one would have any reason to know of it outside the university, I doubted something so objectionable to wolves and hoods alike would go unnoticed. The Red Matron had connections, with moles and rats from sea to shining sea, and world round.

I hit answer and launched straight into the conversation without any of the usual pleasantries. "How mad is she?"

"How *mad* is *she*?"

I bit down so hard, my tongue stung with the taste of iron. I should have known that if my mother really wanted to find a way to get me on the phone after I'd blocked her number and refused to answer her letters, she'd find a way.

"Hello, Brünhild."

"Insolent, foolish child," the Red Matron ground back with a voice that could have made nails on chalkboards sound like Mozart. "I am both your mother and your matron, and you will address me with the proper respect."

If she was giving me the choice, I'd cop to the one that didn't acknowledge the fact we were genetically linked. "Fine, *mein matrone.*"

If she picked up on the implied *fuck you* with which my tone was imbued, she didn't think it worth sidetracking. Instead, she got straight to the reason she'd finally deigned to speak to me.

"At what level does your shame manifest? How low will you sink, dragging our names along, before you come to your senses? First, you embarrass us by running away when all the family had gathered for your fire. Now, to add insult to injury, you've decided to go rogue and perform duties without edicts or justification? Your father has been worried sick over your safety as a nascent, and now we learn of this."

"Perform duties?" I didn't know exactly what part of Karmarov's research she considered part of a hood's task list. I also noticed that she didn't lump herself in on my father's side for worrying about my wellbeing. "What are you talking about?"

A gurgle on the other end preceded her airy response. "Did you or did you not kill a vampire the other night?"

A line formed between my eyes as my face screwed up. "*That's* what you're calling about? To get on my case about slaying Donovan?"

"Did you suppose I had called to coddle you?" Then, the quality of her voice shifted, becoming smaller, calculating. "Is there something else I should have called about?"

"I'd imagine the list of things I've done since leaving home that you disapprove of could fill volumes." I had long ago learned how to steer clear of the Brünhild

Kline interrogation trap. "Yes, I killed a vampire the other night, but no, it had nothing to do with me acting like some righteous hood. He cornered me in an alley and told me straight up he had been ordered to kill me. I know we generally leave vampires to their own devices, but I kinda thought I was justified, seeing as it was a case of him or me. Why, whose was he? One of the people who pays you off, or someone you owe money to?"

Unfortunately, my mother likewise knew how to ignore my barbs. "Who he belongs to is of little concern to you. Now that he's dead, there's an inquiry. The crèche maker knew a hood was responsible. Figuring out it was you took little thought. How could you be so reckless?"

"*I* was the reckless one?"

"Vampires don't care for our kind," my mother spit back. "If one attacked you, you must have provoked him."

I considered waylaying into my mother about how I was sure a lot more vamps would be *craving* hood blood if they knew the healing power it seemed to have, but screw her. She could unearth that little nugget herself.

Or not. I didn't really give a fuck.

"I didn't *provoke* him. He was trying to claim my drunk roommate for his fang mitzvah, and I told him very diplomatically to get lost. Turned out, he was the kind of guy who didn't like taking no for an answer."

"You were drunk?"

To my mother, that was a worse offense than being a murderer.

"No, my roommate was drunk."

"But you were drinking too," she stated with no lack of confidence. In her book, proximity was probability, and probability, proof. "The Huey girls are a bad influence. What else are you doing? Shooting drugs and sleeping around?"

"Not that it's any of your business, but no."

Silence, then, until at last, she exhaled. "I worry."

My mother sounded like a stranger, a woman for whom genuine concern was actually possible. What game was she getting at?

"Don't be." Then, softening my own voice, I continued. "Look, I'm sorry this made its way back to you. Believe me, the last thing I want is for you to have any reason to get involved in my life. But you're the Red Matron. You're freaking Brünhild Kline. Surely the maker won't come after you for any sort of compensation. I barely defeated him as it was. If he hadn't been so young, or so cocky, he might have gotten me."

No need to mention Tobias's help in saving my skin. The last thing I wanted was for her to start asking questions about how I'd crossed paths with a lone

British wolf. Or, if it was one of her plants, give her a reason to think she was successfully spying on me.

"It would... relieve your father greatly if you returned to us and performed your rites, became a fully initiated hood."

"Tell *dad* that the ability to manipulate silver and see in the dark aren't essential here. The streets are very well lit."

The alleys? Not so much.

She said nothing to that, but I swore for a moment I heard her laugh under her breath.

"I'm fine. I lead a very simple life. I go to class, I train at the gym, and I'll be starting a job soon at school. Once in a while, I go for a drink — not alcohol, in my case, anyways — with my roommate. There's nothing to be scared about."

"Parents are always scared for their children. It cannot be helped." Then, resuming her indifferent tone, she said, "The crèche maker, of course, would take grievance, even knowing his son was in the wrong. Save face, or admit to an unwise induction of a vampire who couldn't even defeat a nascent hood."

"I feel like you're trying to insult me with a great amount of stealth."

She ignored my comment, and continued. "At least there are no wolves there. I was worried some old dogs from that pack down there might come after you to get some payback, but the *oberst* reports they're all accounted for."

"Really?" I asked, an image of Tobias coming into my mind's eye. "Any from another pack, say, on vacation or passing through?"

"No, not a single one. Why?"

"Because that means you haven't sent any spies."

And with that, I ended the call.

TWELVE

Jess and I strolled across the main campus square. Midterms were fast approaching, and most of the student population had sequestered themselves to the study carrels of the library or burrowed down in their dorms. Not being a Huey gave me a slight advantage; as one of my intolerable male cousins used to say, 'We gots smarter than da Hueys.' My memory had always been sharp as well, even for a hood. Sure, I'd study, but I didn't need to become a social recluse.

Especially when the one I was being social with was so enticing.

"So hoods…" Jess started.

"Shhh!!!" I pushed a finger over my mouth before realizing there wasn't anyone nearby to overhear. Even still, I kept my voice down, and my chin curled in his direction to avoid anyone being able to read my lips. "Let's use a different word, even if it seems silly, okay?"

As soon as I'd signed the NDA, Karmarov informed me there wasn't a need to keep secrets from Jess. The Huey had been fully oriented on the particulars of his project team. Having accepted the existence of vampires, something called a hood proved quite mundane.

The adorable boy next to me grinned, but amused me. "Okay, the *Yoopers*…" he said with a wink, using the nickname Midwesterners used to refer to the people of and all things relating to Michigan's Upper Peninsula. "How are all the other kinds of – *you know* – they're all so well known, and the only real reference to your people is a single fairy tale? Everyone knows what a slayer is. Who hasn't heard of Buffy or Van Helsing?"

I quirked an eyebrow. "Who?"

"Come on, you don't know about Buf…"

"OF COURSE I know," I giggled. Yes, giggled. Which, to the untrained eye, may imply I was flirting. "Believe me, if Bram Stoker had written a book about Michel Verdun instead of Vlad the Impaler, Buffy would have worn a cape and hunted down the moon-mad." I shrugged. "I guess part of it too is because we're backwoods people. We're also not quite as, you know, extraordinary as the other… Midwesterners."

"Yeah, those Swedes, man. Fierce."

When Jess managed to bring a smile to my face, he shoulder-bumped me for good measure. Despite the fact that he was five inches taller than me and despite my having trained in hand-to-hand combat since a young age, I let myself be nudged off the path. In the back of my mind, it occurred to me that I might be flirting.

"Care to illuminate a Huey?"

"Well, as y'all are so in the dark, I suppose. What do you want to know?"

Jess motioned towards a nearby bench. We plastered ourselves in place, our bodies turned forward, but our pinkies touching. Pinkie-brushes were a good thing, right?

"First of all, what in the hell is a Huey? I hear Karmarov and his two creepy assistants say it. I mean, I know it refers to people. You know, people not from the U.P."

As a precaution, I took one more survey of our immediate surroundings. With the brick wall of the humanities building at our rear, and the whole of the interior quad nearly desolate except for a few men and one girl too far across the courtyard for me to get a good visual on. They talked amongst themselves, and not concerned with the likes of us.

"A Huey is what we call a human. Sorry, it's not really anything more exciting than that."

He pulled a pack of gum from his pocket and offered me a piece. "You shouldn't make assumptions. I can be pretty damned exciting."

Just why Karmarov had decided to bring a human in on the project was anyone's guess. Jess reported that the other two vamps that served as research assistants barely gave him the time of day, and he was an okay student, but nothing exceptional. Luckily, he'd been a night owl. In fact, Jess crossed paths with Karmarov when he pulled an all-nighter in the lab right before the fall semester finals. At 3:45 AM, the professor discovered a bright-eyed and bushy-tailed Jess in the midst of determining the mass percent composition of an aqueous hydrogen peroxide solution.

Jess leaned in, as though he were about to tell me a secret. The proximity, the smell of him, made my head swirl. The percentage of my own composition that could be described as aqueous shifted.

"So the others get all the glory and Hollywood movies, and all you guys get is a story of a little girl who wanted to go see her grandmother." He let the comment linger, and when I didn't immediately take the bait, he continued. "Any truth to it. You know, the thing about Little Red Riding Hood?"

"*Some* truth." If there was a merciful god, Jess didn't notice the way I hesitated. "The truth is very, very different from the Grimm Brothers, and definitely not something Disney would ever make a movie about."

"Tell me what really happened, then."

I looked at his gleaming white teeth, his strong chin, his total lack of facial hair and fangs, and found myself unable to resist his charms. "My people call her *Die Verräterin,* the Betrayer. She wasn't on her way to her grandmother's house; she was on her way to her clan's compound in the Black Forest. And the wolf didn't want to eat her, he wanted to..."

The words died away, and my thoughts went back in time, to me and a sweet werewolf, doing our best not to cross a line we could never come back from, but wanting to be as close to each other as possible. Cody and I discovered every technical boundary there had been around the term "virginity."

Jess tried to fill in my missing words. "I'm guessing eating her is a metaphor."

"He loved her," I let out in a huff. "And she loved him. They married in secret, in a Huey village where none were the wiser of their natures. They were happy for a short time, our history says. But there're downsides to being a wolf. They're pack animals; their whole psychosis demands that they remain with a pack. The wolf who loved *Die Verräterin* left his pack to be with her. After a little time, he began to bear the burden of his separation. We call it lunacity."

"Hueys know all about lunacy," Jess supplanted. "You've seen how politics works in Chicago, haven't you?"

A smile ghosted across my face. "No, not lunacy, *lunacity*. After three moon cycles, a lone wolf loses his humanity. He becomes the wolf for good. As Little Red's wolf husband veered toward lunacity, the Matron of her bloodline performed her sacred duty. She killed the wolf."

Jess's jaw went slack. "That's one badass mother-in-law."

I nodded.

"So, then what?" he asked, scooting closer to me, the anticipation roiling in his eyes. "No cross-dressing werewolves or huntsman hacking people out of his stomach."

"I've always supposed the wolf dressing in the grandmother's clothing was a metaphor. You know, like a power play, him showing the matron that he could steal her daughter away and control her. I don't know, I'm not really sure where that bit of the fairy tale comes from."

"And the ax?" Jess said.

I swallowed down my nerves. "There was an ax. They used it to cut the baby out of *Die Verräterin*. Then they used it to cut her and the baby into tiny pieces. The Red Matron roasted all three of them like kebabs on silver spits over a sacred fire."

I didn't know why the truth of it should bother me. Still, I found my head hanging low. A moment later, the sorrow flew away, warmed beyond comfort by the feeling of Jess's hand underneath my chin. I looked up, and felt my lungs seize up when the intensity of his concerned gaze met mine.

"I'm sorry."

I licked lips that had gone suddenly dry. "There's nothing for you to be sorry about."

"Of course there is. I asked you to tell the story. If I knew it was so painful for you, I wouldn't have. Tell you what."

As quickly as the heat had started to fill my fingers and dance in the pit of my stomach, Jess was on his feet, leaving me bereft.

He reached for me. "Let's get a cup of coffee and talk about silly things, like the campus football team and how stupid Dean Whitmore is for wearing a toupee in a city famous for its wind."

"Coffee and mockery? It's like bingo night."

THIRTEEN

My body pulsed as I gripped the nearly frozen metal handle to the equally prosaic metal door, the private entrance for Karmarov's lab. As though a piece of ice had been slipped beneath my skin, the frigid sensation shot up the network of nerves, over my wrists, and up to my shoulders. Inside the door, things didn't get much better. As I used the plastic ID I'd been given to call the elevator, the hairs on the back of my neck rose to attention. By the time the door opened, I practically fell into it, and into Jess in the process.

His awkward smile and curious gaze held me in place as I stared at him, wearing the sloppy gooey face of a doe-eyed girl. "Are you okay?"

"What, me?" I finally managed to blink and waved my hand in the air. "Fine, it's just… The full moon sort of throws my senses off."

Throws them into hyperdrive, was more accurate.

To my surprise, when I looked up from the floor and met Jess's eyes, he was beaming.

"What?"

Jess leaned forward, his forehead touching mine as his free hand worked to angle my chin up. "You're all flushed and… Sorry, it's inappropriate."

"No, that's fine. Be inappropriate. What were you going to say?"

No time for the warm wash of liquid goo over me; the door into the lab opened at just that second. Whatever he'd been on the verge of melting me with would have to wait.

I still remembered my first day of work at the state park. I had heard the term "butterflies in your stomach" as a child, but I didn't think it accurately captured the semi-toxic feeling, as though someone had poured acid down my throat so that it could slowly eat away my insides. In that case, I'd known most of the people I'd be working with at the state park. The head ranger, Rick Ryland, had been my boyfriend's uncle, and the only wolf whom my mother had ever admitted to once considering "not a total wretch."

If that day had felt like acid eating my innards, then today, I felt like I'd done a double shot of liquid hot magma with a nuclear fusion chaser. Some things proved similar, however. My boss? Not a werewolf, but a vampire. My mother? Unsupportive. (Or, at least, I knew she would be if she ever found out.) My uniform? Unflattering. I supposed it was only appropriate to wear a lab coat, working in a lab. But as I'd decided that flirting with Jess wouldn't be totally objectionable, I wished it came in a more form-hugging fit and, if possible, in red.

Karmarov grinned at me. "Ready to meet the rest of the team, Miss Kline?"

Before I could follow up, a light tap on my shoulder sent my instincts flaring. Within a heartbeat, I had my petite dagger before me, and Jess pushed protectively behind me.

Amused, and not in the least bit frightened, three vampires wore saccharine grins as they looked at me in my defensive pose, ready to protect a human with nothing but my cunning and a two-inch silver blade. If I'd been a Huey who didn't know any better, I'd have said the two new faces belonged to fellow college students. That is, that they were college aged. The girl I'd place in her early twenties at the time of her turning, and the guy, just a few years younger. How old they really were was anyone's guess. Like most of their kind, they possessed the tempered duality of being completely nondescript and, if you let your eyes fall on them and observe at length, beautiful in a way that defied logic. Despite the fact that both she and he appeared to be Asian, their pallor drew the eye, almost as if they'd covered themselves in some sort of iridescent powder. Her green eyes and his brown ones tracked me as I strove to drive down my instincts and walk step by labored step off the elevator and into the lab proper.

Karmarov assumed his best detached scientist voice to the others. "As I mentioned before, hoods don't experience quite the rabid surrender to animal nature that a wolf does leading up to a full moon, but it's not uncommon for them to have some mild symptoms. It's very fascinating, really. I suspect something at the genetic level, of course. Miss Kline, you can lower your weapon. Neither Kai nor Cynthia are going to harm you. Remember that I discussed this with you, that there were two more vampires working on the project?"

Did he? Looking back in the memories of our conversation, I supposed that he had. Still...

I looked back over my shoulder to Jess, and saw no panic or worry at all. He winked at me, then jerked his chin in the trio's direction.

"They're perfectly harmless."

The female vamp huffed and planted a fisted hand on her hip. "I beg to differ." Then, as if she'd never heard Jess's unintentional insult, she took on the repose of a Walmart greeter, holding out her icy hand. "Hi, I'm Cynthia Wu. I just started my third PhD, this one in bioengineering."

My head slowly dipped. "Your... third?"

"I already have doctorates in PoliSci and Asian History. That second one's a personal passion, of course."

"Of course." I turned to the young male vampire. Like Cynthia, he had the same Far Eastern complexion, but something in his manner seemed much more... western.

"Kai," he said, jerking his head as though he'd just broken the surface of the ocean and was ridding his brow of it.

"Hawaiian?"

His smile went from bubbly to 100-watt. "Oh, you recognize the name. Yeah, totally. Gnarly."

Karmarov, who had been circling in observation, dipped in closer to where we all stood. "You have to forgive Kai's out-of-date expressions. He was turned in the late '80s and I'm afraid he's never let go the vernacular. It's like working with Spicoli."

If Karmarov meant to insult Kai, it fell flat. Instead, the Pacifica vampire beamed. "Totally. The character was *awesome.*"

"No, it's just..." I stumbled verbally, looking in my memories for long ago lessons on the decorum of polite vampire society. "I didn't know there were vampires in Hawaii. Doesn't seem a very welcoming environment. There are certainly no werewolves there."

Karmarov grinned. "Which enhances its appeal for a vampire. Why don't you three get to work while I give Miss Kline a quick orientation?"

Without a word, the others turned to their respective tables and did as instructed. Karmarov flicked his fingers, motioning me towards an unattended table at the far side of the lab.

"Do you remember those secret societies I told you about? The ones that track the goings-on of all supernatural creatures?"

"Of course."

Karmarov continued. "You may be interested to know there is no mention of either slayers nor hoods in their most ancient annals."

"But the hood archives go way back to Biblical times."

He shook off what turned out to be evidence of my ignorance. "Vampires can trace our ancestry as far back as Nineveh, and the wolves, to the building of the Sphinx."

"So there's some truth to the Anubis and Lilith lineage myth?"

This time I had Karmarov at a disadvantage. "Is that something taught in the hood bloodlines?"

I nodded. "We're told the first werewolf and the first vampire were the results of ancient kings breeding with gods. Used that story once or twice to argue myself out of bible school when I was little." *What's with all the one and only god, then,* I'd say, to the point of driving my mother to the end of her wits.

The professor bared his teeth – sans fangs, I noticed – at my quip. "And what origin story do you have for your own existence?"

I searched the cobwebs of memory. "I don't know that we have one."

His finger went up as if to say *eureka!* "Because you were *engineered*. Hoods and slayers both were; that's my theory, anyway. My goal – our goal – is to figure out how, and do it again. In this lab…" His hand ghosted the air at our surroundings. "…we begin that task. Through my contacts around the world, I have amassed genetic samples from all the slayer lines, some as old as the sixteenth century. We will catalog them, work the bloodlines backward, and see if we can't figure out what it was that caused the mutation to begin with."

He reached under the table and pulled out a box of one-inch long glass slides.

"Each table has its own sequencer. What you and Jess will be working on is feeding the slides, one by one, running the analysis, and examining the computer's report for any noted anomalies or uniqueness. It's somewhat tedious, and I'll admit, boring work, but a necessary step for the project to move forward."

Having never worked on anything in a lab dealing with genetics, I found my curiosity piqued. I pulled the tray of glass slides in my direction and picked up the one in the furthest corner, holding it up to the light to examine it. "If slayers went extinct half a century ago, how did you manage to get DNA samples?"

If a vampire was capable of blushing, Karmarov would have. "Unlike vampires, slayer bodies do not burn to ash when exposed to sunlight. In fact, they hold up very nicely."

Realizing the implications, and with my mind's eye suddenly filled with the image of two men in beaten-up clothes tunneling into a slayer grave and heaving out the body, I almost dropped the slide. The look on my face must have tipped off the professor to my conclusion.

"Oh, no, nothing covert, I can assure you. We received permission in most cases from surviving family to excavate. There were only a few gravesites which required less-than-legal-or-ethical attention. Now," he said, looking at his watch, a platinum-plated trinket I was willing to bet cost more than my rent. "I have a teleconference I'm supposed to be joining in a few minutes, and I need time to review my notes. Ask Jess to show you the ropes of working the machine and how to read the results. Oh, and Miss Kline?"

"Yes?"

"If the moon always has such a strong effect on you, you might be wary of taking the elevator up in Mr. Harmond's company when it's near full. I may have brought you in on this project due to your chemistry, but not necessarily the part of it between you and Jess."

"I wasn't… We weren't…"

His finger in the air cut me off. "I know. But let's just say, you both were a little flush."

FOURTEEN

Victor Clements had massive hands. I knew this both from my roommate's reports, and because he emerged from the kitchen of the frat house holding three beer bottles in only one palm.

I clicked my tongue when he offered. "No thanks."

That smile defined sly and sexy. No wonder Amy had fallen for him in the span of a week. He was just the right combination of hot and ill-advised to meet her profile. "Nobody's going to card you here, Geri. You don't have to be such a goody-two-shoes."

"Geri doesn't drink," Amy informed him, taking the bottle her new beau offered and twisting off the top.

Propping himself up next to Amy against the wall, Victor laughed. "What's the point of coming to an Alpha Beta Delta party if you're not planning on getting wasted?"

Before I even had a chance to rise to my own defense, Amy did so for me.

"Amy doesn't drink, Vick. Not can't, or shouldn't. *Doesn't.* Is that going to be a problem, because if this place is only for bingeing, and doesn't know how to show everyone a good time, your frat is kinda lame."

My eyes blinked rapidly as I tried to rationalize this new Amy. Too bad she couldn't be so respective of my lack of love life.

"Thanks, Amy. Victor, like she said, it's just not for me."

Any concern he might have feigned fell away with a shrug. "Whatever. Come on, Amy." He pulled at my roommate's sleeve. "You said you're a physics major. I want you to show me all about getting physical."

And like that, they were gone, the bouncing, mingling crowd swallowing them as they drifted away. I looked around me, hoping that Jess had turned up. I'd texted him as soon as Amy had convinced me to go out tonight. He texted back that he was studying, but he'd try to swing by.

As I wandered into what was probably a dining room under normal circumstances, a flash of pale flesh caught the corner of my eye. The vampire somehow managed to blend into the crowd, and seem to not be a part of it at the same time. He'd been frozen at just the right age to fit the crowd; I'd place him in his early twenties when he'd been turned. Whenever that was had been an era when men wore their hair shoulder-length. His blond locks and flannel reminded me of Kurt Cobain. That he'd been waiting for me to look in his direction couldn't be disputed; the moment our eyes met, he jerked his head to the side, motioning for me to follow.

Normally, you'd tell a child of the night to go screw himself if he tried to get you alone. Me? I'd been almost killed by one of the bastards not too long ago, and I still needed answers as to why. The vamps in my lab were no good. They had all arrived in Chicago too recently to have a grasp on what the local clutches were up to. If I was going to get to the bottom of this, I'd have to do it on my own.

Even outside, despite the fact that the late March air was still pretty nippy, a half-dozen couples sat in armchairs or curled up on blankets on the humble front lawn. The vamp sauntered us past them, not even turning to look at me. When we got far enough away from the frat house for the sounds of the voices within to begin to fade, I stopped.

"If you think you're going to lure me to an alley, know that I'm not going to fall for the same trick twice."

He pivoted with the speed of a sloth. "This will work then. Come closer."

"Nope, I'm good here. If you got something to say to me, say it."

He hesitated a moment, before making his pronouncement in his flat baritone. "Leave Chicago or suffer the consequences."

"Really, that's what you're going to try to pull? Guess what? Every badly written horror movie from the past thirty years called. They want their clichés back."

"If you stay, we will not be held responsible for the consequences. Not the ones for you. Not the ones for your family."

My ire fired within. "My family has nothing to do with my being here."

"That's what you think. Decide what you will. You have been warned." His eyes rolled as he turned and began to stalk up the street. Following him with my gaze, I caught sight of someone I actually wanted to see.

Jess rounded the corner at the end of the block just as Vampire Kurt turned around it. He caught sight of me and waved, picking up the pace to reach me.

"Was that a vamp?'

My hands flew up, and I shot him a warning expression. "Hueys."

"Oh, right." His brow furrowed as he considered alternatives. "Was that a... Swede?"

"Yes, Jess, that was most definitely a Swede. Maybe even a Viking."

Given his appearance, it wasn't impossible.

"What did he want?"

"What do all Swedes want? To be creepy Swedes and act all Swedish. I'm glad you made it, Jess, but I have to tell you, I don't really want to go back in there, if you don't mind."

"Fine by me. I was only coming to spend some time with you anyway. Still, it's a beautiful night. Would be a shame to waste it. What do you want to do?"

The night air filled my lungs as I pulled in a deep breath. The waning moon above still managed to keep the night sky bright. It would be the kind of moon back home that would have lit up the woods when Cody and I would sneak out to meet each other. Not for the first time, I wondered if my ex-boyfriend was even capable of the kind of wistful nostalgia I felt at times like these, or if being mated blocked him from remembering how in love we'd been once upon a time.

Jess snapped inches from my face. "Hello, Geri, you there? You wandered off for a moment."

I smiled my apologies. I might not still have Cody, but Jess was here and waiting.

"You up for a walk?" I asked.

He offered out his arm. "With you? I'd be delighted."

With no real destination, we meandered the edge of campus for an hour, talking about the useless miasma that passed for conversation in the early stages of a relationship. When he laughed at a joke I made, it felt like magic.

Jess motioned to a nearby bench as we passed through one of the college's courtyards. The three-quarters moon rose overhead, lacing my insides with temptation. I never thought I'd miss running through the woods at night. My soul, my body, ached for it. I crossed my arms over my chest, hugging myself, tempering my breath.

"You're doing it again."

One eyebrow angled precipitously as I looked to Jess.

"Acting like you're modeling a straightjacket," he continued. "Am I making you crazy?"

"What? No!" Immediately, my arms and hands lashed out, and I tried to look as non-bundled as possible. "It's just, the moon. It does things to me. It… Oh, jeez, I guess when I say things like that, it does sound crazy, doesn't it?"

Jess slid closer, dripping an arm over the back of the bench behind me. His voice took on a secretive hush, even though there wasn't anyone nearby. "Is it a hood thing?"

"I don't know. I think?" Sitting back, I was thrilled to discover he didn't shy away —or worse, push me— when I leaned my head into his shoulder. "It's kind of like lunar separation anxiety. Ever since I left my clan last fall, I'm uncomfortable in my own skin sometimes. My instincts get stir-crazy."

"That doesn't surprise me," Jess said. "Christmas is just a tradition, but people who are separated from their families can actually become ill from it. You're a strong woman, enduring something like that month after month."

I'm weaker by the day, I wanted to say, but was afraid to admit even to myself that it was true. Every moon that came and went, I felt the urgency to act build inside of me. Running myself ragged and going through forms at the gym took some of the edge off, but even Amy had noticed how my "inner bitch had a regular stopover," joking that she'd never seen a PMS case as severe as mine. Every full moon that passed left residual effects, a hangover that grew longer with each cycle.

Shivers broke me from my inner machinations when the arm Jess had been resting on the back of the bench hooked around, and he ran lazy fingers down my cheek.

"Anything I can do to help?"

I shook my head. "I get through it. But, damn, if it wouldn't cause so much drama, I'd love to dance around the bonfires at *feuernacht* just one more time."

From beyond my view, Jess's other hand circled around. My eyes focused on his balled-up fist, of his fingers wrapped around a lighter. With a flick and a scratch, a petite flame burst from it, dancing, winking at me.

My head rotated, looking up into his grinning face.

"It's not quite a bonfire," he said, "but if it helps, I'll dance around it with you."

And then, I kissed him.

My lips moved over his tenderly at first, disorientating, gauging his acceptance. Within moments, my excitement had turned to panic. Oh my god, what if he thought I was a bad kisser? What if I *was* a bad kisser? Did I have bad breath? What was the last thing I ate? Tuna fish? Had it been tuna fish? How in the hell did I let myself eat tuna fish on the day that I was going to kiss Jess Harmond for the first time? Was it also going to be the last time? Was he going to curl up his nose in disgust and say it had been a mistake? What if I never kissed another boy again? What if, as Amy warned, I died a virgin?

"Geri?"

One eye opened, ready to see him rolling his tongue like he'd just licked a toad. "Yeah?"

He met my gaze with a smolder that shut down all thought and turned on my whole body. "You don't have to think so much about it. Just kiss me."

His wish was my command. I leaned in and pressed my mouth to his again, this time relaxing into his body. Jess's hand moved from my cheek, up the side of my face, over my ear, until he threaded his hand through my hair and angled my head. The position allowed him to deepen the kiss as his tongue entered my mouth. Before I realized what I was doing, my own hands had circled his neck to pull myself toward him.

It all came crashing down when something punched me in the gut.

I gasped and pulled away from Jess, getting to my feet, my hands pushing into my stomach, trying to push down the spasm.

"Geri?" Concerd watered Jess's eyes. "What's wrong?"

"Wolf."

My answer ground out of my throat, an echo of the psychic energy the nearby beast was dishing out. Hoods sensed wolves, of course, but I also had a bit of psychic empathy where they were concerned. Call it animal instinct. Even if a zebra didn't see the lion, instinct told it when it was being stalked. Somewhere nearby, there was a wolf, and he was throwing out serious negative and hostile vibes in my direction.

Jess's head spun, surveying the square. "Where?"

"Close. A few hundred yards, maybe. Jess, go. I need to find…"

But I didn't need to find him. A moment later, when I forced myself erect and went into hunting mode, as if by instinct, my eyes found his.

FIFTEEN

Upper lip curling, teeth bared, Tobias glared at me like a madman threatening death and promising pain. Had he been any closer, I would have heard his growl. Even across the square, I could see those eerily white canines of his grow long and wanton. He wanted to destroy me. He wanted to rip me, limb from limb.

A wave of desire soaked through me. I wanted it more. I wanted *his blood.*

"If you got something to say to me, come say it."

No sooner had I called him out than he turned to run. I was in pursuit without thinking. Jess's voice grew small as my steps grew quicker. Even with the taste of him still on my tongue, I couldn't suppress my predisposition. I had become a huntress, inverting Tobias's nature and intentions, making the prey into the predator.

A werewolf's propensity to run in his animal form would have left me behind in the dust, but as bipeds, a hood held favor. Tobias cut through a crowd of students holding a demonstration in an archway. A woman, knocked aside, screamed obscenities which faded as I too passed her. At the edge of campus, he managed to slip out of view, but he wasn't safe yet. There was no doubt in my mind which way he went. Even from two blocks away, I could hear the rush of water and the clacking branches of leafless trees blown in the night wind inside of LaBagh Woods.

I pushed my body, striving, straining, needing to reach him. If he got more than a few hundred feet into those woods, out of sight from the main paths, he'd shift into his wolf and I'd lose him for sure.

Ground made paste by the barely-above-freezing temperatures and rain of the previous day rendered every footfall a struggle. Luckily, that was true for Tobias as well. I heard his grunt only moments before I saw him. Trying to shake his feet free of the muck, he was already peeling off clothing, revealing a bare chest glazed by a sheen of mist from the damp night air. His hands worked at his belt. Despite the burning in my muscles telling me I was going to pay for this tomorrow, I did what I must. I leapt, tackling him to the ground.

Tobias collapsed, kissing dirt. "Get off me, hood!"

"Not until you tell me why you're spying on me!" I shouted, wrestling his belt from his hips and using it to bind his wrists behind his back.

"I'm not. Ow!" All attempts to bring his arms back around front failed. "Are you one of those Americans raised on a pig farm?"

"Better, I was raised a Yooper."

"A *whaaat*?" His face screwed up as he looked back at me over his shoulder. "What the Dickens is a Yooper?"

"Me." Shifting my hips, I was able to plant a knee between his shoulder blades as my hand filled with his shoulder-length, greasy brown hair. "Why are you following me?"

"For the last bloody time, my being here has nothing to do with you. My God, are all American hoods this paranoid, or are you special?"

"Am I supposed to believe you just happened to show up *again* by chance? And what was that growly thing back there? Are you seriously going all territorial? Oh my god, are you following me around because you have some sort of crush on me? You got jealous when you saw me kissing another boy?"

Tobias let his forehead fall into the mud as I released my grip. "No, you're definitely special. Look, Gerwalta, I swear to you on the haunches of my alpha and father, I don't give a bullfrog's left bullock who you go around kissing. But three times since I came to Chicago I've been on the scent of who I came here to find, and all three times, following that scent led me to you. I'm starting to think you're the one sleeping with the enemy."

"Ha! Shows what you know. I'm not sleeping with anyone."

"Can't imagine why." He shook with silent laughter. "Please get off me. If I have to throw you off, you're going to get hurt."

"Excuse me, but which of us is the badass who just ran down a werewolf and tackled him to the ground?"

"I let you tackle me. Have to admit, your sudden resurgence of BDSM threw me for a loop."

"For the last time, I am *not* into sadomasochism!" I declared and threw my hands up in the air.

Which, it turned out, was a mistake.

The moment I withdrew the pressure of my knee between his shoulder blades, Tobias rolled to the side with such force, I was thrown to the ground beside him. Despite having both his hands behind his back, he moved with lupine grace and speed. His weight atop me rendered my ability to sit up, let alone stand, impossible. Tobias covered my body with his own, his legs straddling me at the hip, making the ability to kick him impossible.

His canines, still extended, skimmed the sensitive skin at the base of my ear, sending shivers through my body.

"One bite, hood," his gravelly voice teased as he spoke into my ear. The feel of his warm breath triggered a gasp, but I wasn't entirely sure it was from fear. Instead, another more feral sensation was boiling my blood. "One bite, and I could end you."

"If you don't want anyone to know you're here, I'd suggest not killing the only daughter of the Red Matron."

He pulled, wide-eyed. "The Red... You're the Red Matron's daughter?"

A smile ghosted my lips, seeing him at a disadvantage. "The *only* daughter. In fact, the only *child.* The only hope for her illustrious line to continue. So while I'm not really into being dead right now, at least I'd go with the knowledge that you'd be joining me after a most painful and dishonorable death."

He changed strategy, whispering against my lips instead as his smoldering eyes looked right into mine. "Maybe instead of kill you, I'll simply take you. We all know what happens to hoods who lay with a wolf, don't we? And you've already been branded with *Die Verräterin*'s name, so all I'd be doing is helping you fulfill your destiny. What would your Red Matron mother think then?"

I tried to deny corrupt impulses firing on full throttle. God, his body on mine felt so good. A pull in the pit of my stomach was sending commands to my limbs, demanding that they get with the program, reach out to touch him. I became uber aware of his domination, how without even his own hands to assist him, he had me at his complete mercy.

And blood of my ancestors help me, I liked it.

But a lifetime of training wouldn't so quickly lapse. An expert in disguising my inner emotions with a war mask, I kept my expression and my movements under command. I gave Tobias nothing he could interpret as weak or manipulated.

"You'd honestly doom yourself to a lifetime of being bonded to me sexually just to piss off my mother?"

"If I am unable to complete the mission I'm here for because of your interference, my life has no other purpose than revenge." He leaned in, sniffing me, running his tongue over the throbbing vein in my neck. "You think I can't scent your arousal, hood? If I tried to take you right here and right now, you wouldn't say no."

I gave him a flash of a toothy grin. "No, I wouldn't." Then, putting all my strength into breaking my right leg free and thrusting it up, I slammed my knee into the big dipper extending down from his full moon. "I'd say *hell* no."

Tobias rolled off me, howling, whimpering, folding himself into a fetal position. I rose to my feet, doing my best to push the muck and leaves off my clothing. He'd be fine in a few minutes, which I hoped was long enough to get the hell away.

SIXTEEN

I'd sensed his proximity for the better part of five minutes when he finally found his backbone and the door to the diner. Tobias plopped down in the booth across the table from me and glared. Glared like a professional Olympic badminton judge, complete with all the, you know, world-class judgey-ness.

"Tobias."

I didn't bother looking up from my *Introduction to Genetics* text. "Stop by so you could threaten to seduce me again, or just happen to be looking for a bite? If the latter, I'd try the lamb. I hear they serve it extra raw here."

He ran a hand through his hair, which, like his clothes and his personality, could do with some serious scrubbing.

"I'msorryaboutsayingthosethingstoyou."

His mumbled frankenword failed to communicate much of anything, but when I looked up at his crestfallen expression, I could tell that it was taking every ounce of remorse for him to get it out.

"What was that?"

"I said, I'm sorry about what I said the other night," he said through gritted teeth. "I shouldn't have implied I could smell your... You know what. It was ungentlemanly, and I apologize."

I closed the book and hitched my chin on a balled fist. "Rare are the occasions when a werewolf is mistaken for a gentleman. However, I'm now positive you're not faking the whole being British thing."

"I'm English, not British. And you're a hood. Most of your kind wouldn't give me the benefit of a doubt when it comes to being human."

"I hear that's often true of the English. Then again, my father is Argentinian, so I may have inherited his biases."

Rather than be offended by my remarks, he dismissed them with a sigh. "I mean, most hoods wouldn't look for my humanity. They'd only see the wolf, the monster, the thing they must beat into submission, dominate, destroy. But you're not like most hoods I've met."

"Two days ago, I chased your ass into the forest, knocked you to the ground, and threatened to gut you," I said. "This is what you consider an improvement?"

"It's better than most of my encounters with hoods back home. But even if you had treated me like that from the beginning, I have to pay up my own fines. Calling you out on what was more than likely a purely subconscious physical response was beneath me." The corners of his mouth twitched. "No pun intended."

I took a long sip of my coffee, fixing him in my gaze, before responding. "You wouldn't be the first wolf who propositioned me."

His face screwed up. "But why would a wolf want to sleep with *you*?"

The way he said *you*, the tone with which he slanted the word, could have been replaced with *the severed head of a camel* or *Charlie Sheen* with the same level of disgust. Glaring, I crossed my arms over my chest and shot a medieval treasure trove of daggers his way.

Tobias, ashen-faced, scrambled to correct himself. "I don't mean *you*, like ew, who would want that? I mean you, who is not only definitely not a wolf, but also a hood?" He leaned in over the table, dropping his voice. "Wolves mate for life, without exception. You'd think someone like you would know that."

It amused me that, of all the things we had said, that was the thing he thought needed to be protected from stray ears. "We were both aware of that. He was willing, I was not. And for your information, we *had* been dating for the better part of two years."

"*You* dated a lycanthrope?" Tobias asked, incredulous. "You, the daughter of the Red Matron?"

"The fact that it pissed off my mom made it all the more enjoyable. In fact she…" I cut myself off. *That,* frankly, was none of his business. I threw up my hands in frustration. "Look, I'm from a tiny town with only five hundred people in it. Pickings were slim. So, yes, if you want to know why I treat werewolves with general acceptance, that's part of it. If you also want to know why I have trust issues with particularly good-looking male werewolves about my own age, I'd see Part A of this statement."

The unintended flirtation was out of my mouth before I realized it. My cheeks burned red, and Tobias took no aims to hide his amusement. Luckily, proving that he was (usually) a gentleman, he continued as if I said nothing.

"Are we good then?"

He extended a hand across the table. A hand that shook even as it waited for mine to join it. Why? Was he stressed? Was he nervous? Was he…

I narrowed my gaze, noticing what at first had escaped my attention. The shine of his eyes had faded. His hair, beyond oily, was now both matted and full of dirt. His clothes hadn't been quite so threaded at the edges last I saw him. Under his eyes, dark, puffy pockets that would have set any doting mother into a tizzy.

I sat up as his hand dropped away slowly. "How long has it been now?"

His eyes darted away, as if he'd been caught in the midst of a lie. He crossed his right arm over his body and rubbed his opposite forearm. I didn't need to specify what I was asking about; it was obvious to both of us what banner the elephant in the room wore.

"Two full moons. I left my pack right after the wane."

Dear god, no wonder he looked such a wreck. "Are you insane? What are you doing lingering around Chicago? Even the strongest wolves can't get through a third full moon without going loony. As young and as far away from your territory as you are, I'm surprised you got through two without doing something horrific to some innocent Huey."

"I was able to lock myself up the last full moon," he said, running a hand over his face. "No one was injured, but it took everything I had just to come back to two legs."

"I don't get it. What is it that's going on in Chicago that has you so determined to stay even though one more month is going to leave you trapped in your wolf form for the rest of your life? Go home!"

Don't put me in a situation where I have to be the one to kill you.

"Do you remember the night we met, Geri?"

The sudden shift in subject gave me whiplash. "What?"

"When you and your drunk friend got cornered by the vamp behind the pub?"

"One, my friend has a name, which you know is Amy. Two, in America, they're called *bars,* not *pubs.* And three, as I told you before, I would have been able to handle it just fine if you hadn't come along."

A silver streak passed through his eyes. "He literally had your passed-out friend stashed in a pile of rubbish and you, dangling off the ground as he tried to choke you to death."

"All part of my plan," I bluffed.

Tobias paused a moment, as though deciding if it was worth it to reopen the debate. "Whatever. My point is: it wasn't coincidence that I was passing by. I had been tracking that vampire all night. He'd had a few other scores lined up that he gave up on when he noticed me tailing him. He probably guessed, and correctly, that I might follow him back to the crèche."

"What possible interest would a wolf have in a baby vamp breeding house located halfway around the world?"

Then, as though I was on a gameshow where a leggy, blonde assistant had just turned over a sign with the obvious answer to the grand prize jackpot question, it all snapped into place.

My throat tightened. "If you're a few weeks away from lunacity, your only hope is to go back to your own pack or find a way to join another. Why don't you?"

"Because I can't. I've been exiled."

SEVENTEEN

My grandmother had told me once when I was a child that magic made werewolves animals, but their sense of community and family gave them their humanity. Without the latter, only the former remained. Eventually, a lone wolf, deprived those connections, would lose his human form. As supernaturally strong predators who didn't fear humans, they'd be a danger to themselves, and everyone around them.

That's when a hood would step in. Asking a packmate to destroy one of his own was an indelible cruelty, almost like asking a mother to slaughter her own child. Hoods had no qualms terminating a wolf gone permanently moon-mad. We killed on sight, and slept like babies. At least, most hoods did.

I was not most hoods. In the space of a few seconds, my mind's eye filled with images of Tobias's wolf form, headless, his blood staining my hands. Fear struck me —not just because I worried for his safety, but because that vision filled me with a carnal pull, a bloodlust I had rarely known.

When I could find the ability to form words again, my voice was high and airy. "You're a rogue?"

"Not by choice," he said. "Don't think I don't know what's coming if I can't amend this soon. I'm running out of time."

"That's kinda my point. I mean, look at yourself. You look like a junkie, like a meth head. Do whatever it takes, Tobias. Beg, barter, get them to take you back."

"They won't," he insisted with a huff. "Not unless I come back with proof, not unless I can show them evidence."

"Evidence of what?"

A grey cloud drifted in over his already gaunt features. His jaw tightened as his teeth ground. Then, with a huff only a broad-chested wolf could make, both his body and his tongue relaxed.

"My pack is based in rural England, up in the north. A few years ago, a vampire clutch moved near our territory, but we didn't care. How would it affect us? They were in town, we lived out in the countryside. Soon, a dead body turned up in the river, then another a week later in a parking lot. Then, a few more. Nothing in numbers unusual for a city the size of Morpeth, and always people who didn't have much in the way of friends or family. It was obvious to me, however, that the deaths bore the common markers of a baby vamp losing control. All happened a few hours before dawn, all without signs of a violent struggle or forced entry, all missing sizable amounts of blood. Still, we didn't think it was our business. Until one of our own became a victim."

I couldn't catch the air before I sucked in a gulp. "But I thought vampires only preyed on humans."

"Me, too. But the Morpeth clutch— it was almost as if they were field scientists, collecting data. They keep logs, write out notes, have a lab where they run experiments."

My eyebrow arched. "How do you know?"

A grim but boastful cock in his smile preceded Tobias's answer. "Because I broke into their compound. During the day, while they slept. The wolf they killed? It wasn't just any wolf, it was my brother."

"What!?" I reached out across the table on instinct, covering Tobias's hand with my own. As expected, the chill I normally got until I'd acclimated to a wolf ran up my spine.

"I'm so... I'm so sorry." Then, *trying* to maintain some proper indifference, I circled back. "But if you knew the vamps were responsible for killing your brother, didn't your alpha see that as justified? Hell, if one of your pack had been murdered, wouldn't that even be his responsibility?"

"It should have been," he agreed, "if it hadn't been the alpha who was murdered."

A double whammy, where pack dynamics and Tobias were concerned. Not only had he lost a sibling, his pack had lost their leader.

"The new alpha refused to listen to me, insisted I was seeing boogiemen in broom closets. Even after I showed him a few of the documents I'd taken. He just took them from me and threw them in the fireplace. Eventually, the clutch ferreted out that I was the one who broke in. They demanded an explanation, compensation. Our alpha rolled over, told them he'd do anything they wanted to keep the peace between our peoples. They wanted me exiled."

"To kill you themselves would have started a blood debt," I said aloud at the realization. "Your offense wasn't enough to ask for your death, but they still wanted you dead. To kill you themselves wasn't going to work, but by having you exiled, they pretty much guaranteed the same result. As a rogue, eventually you'd go mad, and a hood would be forced to end you. But I still don't see how that leads you here?"

Tobias shook his head. "There's another wolf pack just slightly south of us. Two days after my brother died, their beta went missing. I found her name listed on one of their charts, and with a note saying that she would be sent off to Chicago."

"And what makes you think that meant this part of Chicago? It's a huge city."

The dismissiveness evident in my tone made Tobias's words sharp.

"My instincts drew me to this side of town. I caught her scent a few blocks from campus when I first got here. That would have been two days after Kara disappeared. More than three days, and the trail would have faded too much for me to pick up. I've been keeping my eyes open for vampires in this area since then. That vamp who attacked you was the first I'd found in the area since I'd arrived."

"Did you follow him back to his crèche? Poke your nose around there?"

Tobias shook his head. "Bastard might have been hard up drawing in a thrall, but he wasn't completely stupid. The second you and Amy left the alley, he leapt up and took to the roofs. I couldn't keep up with him in my human form."

I bit my bottom lip. "That's why you were so angry when I killed him. Tobias, I'm so sorry. If I had known..."

"If I had wanted you to know, you would have known," he said, stepping in when my words failed me. "I didn't trust you."

"You still don't."

He didn't bother denying it or trying to patronize me. "Why would I? Then again, you haven't reported me to the local matron. I'd know if you had; this area would be crawling with Yellow hoods, trying to figure out who I was and why I was here."

I leaned over the table. "They still might. So, you have any more leads? Crossed any other vamps? Picked up on any other scents?"

"Nothing, but I know she's still here. I get echoes of her every so often. The second I get close to pinpointing her location, though, the feeling disappears. The city... there's too much to hear, too much to smell. My senses are thrown off. As I imagine yours must be."

Truth be told, I could sympathize. I'd passed through large cities before, but never for more than a few hours. My first night in Chicago was a sleepless one. The sounds through the window overwhelmed me. Every hour, a siren, a fight, a cat screeching in the street.

"It took some getting used to, that's for sure. Look, Tobias, I can't make any promises, and I don't know if it will help, but... I know a few vampires on campus."

Fervent eyes across the table glistened. "Where? Who? I have to talk with them."

"Whoa there, Tex."

He'd already gotten halfway out of the booth when I managed to grab his soiled sleeve and drag him back.

"I'm not exactly sure you in your growing lunatic state should be meeting with anyone right now. You go a little too loco and openly attack an innocent vamp, you'll be dead by dawn."

The werewolf across the way chewed on that insult. "But we're stronger than vamps."

"A *pack* is stronger; an individual is going to get his hide sent home in a doggy bag. Just hear me out, okay? You and me, we got a shared interest in this. You're looking for a crèche in the WCU area, and so am I. Whoever sent Donovan after me is still out there. I want questions answered too. Namely, why in the hell do they want me dead?"

"Why haven't you just asked your vampires that question?"

"It's not exactly the kind of thing you bring up right after you start a job. 'Hey, boss, just wondering. I was almost killed twice a few weeks ago by a baby vamp, said his maker ordered him to do it. It's cool, I ripped his head off and stuff, then pretended to be riding his corpse to drive away some homeless guy—'"

Tobias's face screwed up. "You what?"

I waved away the concern. "You had to be there. Anyways, I believe in the saying *don't shit where you live*. But I'm sure I can find an excuse to bring it up on your behalf. Better, even, because then they don't know that *I'm* looking for it too."

White teeth gleamed. Tobias's smile was a thing of beauty. "In a million years, I never thought I'd see the day when a hood helped a wolf. Thank you."

He reached across the table and grabbed both my hands. The moment his flesh touched mine, I felt it again: the bizarre dual sensations of both fire and ice running through my veins. The fire made sense; even I couldn't deny anymore that, at a purely physical level, I found Tobias attractive. If he hadn't been a wolf and I hadn't been a hood, I'd be all over him like sweet on honey. The freezing sensation, however, threw me.

"Where are they? The vampires you know? Can you talk to them tonight?"

I negotiated with the little voice in the back of my head reminding me that the NDA barred me from speaking about the project outside the lab, and that, despite his cheery demeanor, Karmarov could rip my head off like a child decapitating a dandelion if I went about things in an unprofessional manner.

"I'm not working tonight, but I can ask tomorrow."

He scratched the stubble on his chin. "What does that have to do with anything?"

"One of the vamps? He's kind of my boss. I work in Prof. Karmarov's lab, over in the Chem building."

The werewolf, who moments ago had looked at me with a softness usually reserved for Lifetime holiday movies, went cold as Hades. "Really, a lab?"

In a flash, I saw where that instigation was leading. "I'm a hood, Tobias. If there was a werewolf within a block of his lab, I could sense it. I promise you, I haven't picked up the slightest vibration."

"Kara's not part of your local pack. Maybe your senses are off."

"Unlikely, I sense you just fine."

A large hand slicked through his oily black hair. "Maybe if I could sneak in…"

"No. The place has three layers of security, and cameras everywhere. Besides, why would a vampire be holding a werewolf in the Chemistry building? I'm fairly sure the beta is howling at night. Students would hear that."

Tobias huffed, rolling his eyes. "I'm not a freaking bloodsucker, Gerwalta, I don't know why they do the things they do. What is it you work on there?"

"I can't tell you. I signed an NDA."

My words acted as a catalyst, a base being thrown into a vat of highly reactive acid. His grip went from gently coaxing to vicelike. "NDA? What the bloody hell does that mean?"

I explained further. "I started working in Karmarov's lab a week ago. He made me sign a non-disclosure agreement, saying that I wouldn't speak about the project at all."

"Wouldn't… Wouldn't speak about the…"

The crescendo of his tone drew gazes. Hesitant, worried, reluctant men and women who both wanted to intervene, because they thought we were a couple having a fight turned violent, and keep their distance, understanding at some level the predator that Tobias represented.

"This is the closest thing that I've had to a lead since you played pop-goes-the-weasel with Donovan, and you're going to cut me off because you signed a contract?" he huffed. "Look at me. Look at how hard it's getting for me to control myself. She's been away from her pack just as long as I have, and who knows under what kind of conditions. Time is running out for both of us."

"Tobias, you don't even know if the beta is alive."

I'd never seen a man more reverently speak with utter confidence. "She is. I can assure you, she is."

"But if you stay here much longer, you won't be. Look," I whispered as loudly as I dared. "I'll ask the vamps I know, but as a courtesy. I doubt they know anything about a British beta shewolf being kidnapped. And for the love of Van Helsing, *keep your voice down!* People are starting to stare."

Practically throwing my hands back at me, Tobias lounged back in the diner stall, as though reexamining me from a new angle and at a greater distance.

"I was wrong about you," he said at last. "You're not any different at all from the other hoods. In fact, you're worse, because you think you're different. You have all of their weaknesses and none of their strengths."

"If I need to be reminded of my shortcomings, I'll go home and let my mother rip into me. Tobias, honestly, I'm sorry about your brother, and I'm sorry that the other beta is missing. But—"

Leaning in, I called on my nascent power, hoping he could see under the florescent light of the diner the dim blue glow of my eyes. Not that I could muster a real threat if he called me on it, but anything I could do to encourage him to leave wouldn't be in vain.

"You're barking up the wrong tree, if there even is a tree. Come next full moon, if you're still around and can't cross back to your human form, a missing wolf will be the least of your problems. You'll have the Yellow Matron giving her bloodline the order to hunt you down."

"The only hood who knows I'm here is you." With all the coolness of a poker player, he matched my position. Hovering over the table, his eye shone yellow. "I don't think you're eager to be tied up in hood business, which means you'd have to come after me yourself. Make no mistake, if you try to get between me and my mission, I'll huff, and I'll puff, and I'll kill you dead."

Something in his eyes struck fear in me in a way his proximity did not. There was something much more than anger or bravado. There was… sadness. Longing. Desperation. Every moment of his day must be measured in the ticking of the clock. He knew he could save himself. And for some reason, he knew he'd never forgive himself if he left the lost beta behind.

Despite my training and my instincts telling me to match his glare tit for tat, I found myself softening. It must have been evident in my own expression; a moment later, he pulled back and looked at me with a cocked head and a raised eyebrow.

I reached again across the table. "Tobias, she's not in the lab."

My confidence and the table shook when he slammed his palm down on it, cracking the Formica top. "Just mind your own!"

And with that, he rose and chuffed his way out onto the street.

EIGHTEEN

The weight of each sunrise and sunset pulled at my soul. Three days after the encounter in the diner, and I still couldn't shake the memory of Tobias's glare. His words had made a direct demarcation in my life. His eyes haunted me, eyes that begged for something, anything, to give him solace. No matter what I thought, I knew it wasn't in fact a cry for help. Nevertheless, I found myself questioning my place, wondering if it wasn't my duty to aid him, even if he didn't want it.

What would my mother do in this situation? She'd have listened to Tobias fully, then she'd take every clue he could offer, find the missing beta, and destroy them both for good measure. Thank goodness Chicago wasn't my mother's territory. The Head of the House of Yellow, Matron Consuela Renanta, ruled her sanjak with a silver fist and a jaded eye. Nevertheless, she had always been more tempered in her approach to policing the wolves under her jurisdiction than any red hood I knew.

Maybe I should go to her and relay what Tobias had said? If there were two wolves stuck in Chicago against their will and on the edge of moon madness, wouldn't she be the most likely to expediently solve the situation?

No, it wouldn't work, *couldn't* work. As certain as Tobias seemed that Prof. Karmarov was somehow involved or must know something, there was no way he'd agree not to bring up the suspicions if Consuela became involved. There would be no good outcomes if hoods became aware of the genetic profiling and engineering Karmarov was undertaking, even if it had nothing to do with us. Not to mention, it would cost me my job.

What to do? I needed advice, advice from someone who I could trust to keep my worries to himself, who would ask the right questions but not too many questions.

I didn't remember making the decision to dial the phone number when I already found myself listening to the ringing on the other end of the line. When the call connected and I heard my father's voice, however, all my words left me.

"Geri?"

It had been weeks since we'd spoken, and like most conversations since I'd left home, it had been more a brawl than a friendly chat. The sharpness of his absence in my life intensified in the simple fact that he said my name with love every time I called. Each conversation with my dad was a fresh canvas, and he left it up to me what colors and shapes to paint.

"Hi, Papi. I, *um…* I need your help."

"Are you in trouble?"

"No, I'm fine." Taking a deep breath, I gathered myself from the edge of tears. "I need some advice is all."

A smile blossomed in his voice. "Is it about a boy?"

"Kinda." Better he think I had some sort of college crush than learn that I might have to kill a rogue wolf who'd gone over to lunacity. Or worse, help one I barely even knew. "But you have to promise, this stays between us, okay? I don't want Mom knowing anything about it. Especially given what she did."

"You know she was only trying to…"

"I don't care why she did it," I snapped, feeling the bile rise within me. "It was wrong."

"I am not defending your mother's actions." My father's voice softened. His Argentinean accent, usually a thick smoke that blanketed every English word he spoke, weakened. "For what it's worth, Cody is happy. Very happy."

As if that should salve the pain I still felt over losing him. Over being lost to him. Instead of lingering in the heartache, however, I pressed on.

"So, the guy," I said, in as light a tone as I could manage. "He's putting himself out on a limb to help someone, even though it's going to hurt him more to do so than to just walk away."

"A martyr complex," my father declared. "Not unlike your mother."

"My mother?" I asked in disbelief. "Mom is the most selfish woman in the world. You're married to her, you should know."

My father clicked his tongue. "Your mother is many things, but selfish has never been one. Unless you want to talk about taking on the burdens of others, and then she is a glutton."

"I think we'll just need to agree to disagree on that."

Silence came from the other end of the line, until at last he sighed. "In regards to your... *friend.* Sometimes we convince ourselves we alone can make something right. Then, it becomes more than a desire. It becomes a calling, a mission. We think suffering is part of the solution. Sometimes it is, but usually, it's better to share your burdens. We are made stronger by calling on our friendships, never weaker by denying them. The only way to help a martyr is to recognize his struggle, and to help ease it if you can. Just make sure you're not a victim in the process. Now, if you don't mind me asking, as a concerned father of course, is this friend a *boy*friend?"

"No, nothing like that. He's a ..."

Werewolf, my mind shouted to complete. I refrained. No need to give my father the impression that history was repeating itself, and certainly no reason to betray Tobias's privacy. My father might be the more compassionate and approachable of my parents, but he was still a hood. Not to mention, he was of the Yellow bloodline. Consuela might be a distant relative, but they still had a connection.

Tobias didn't have to help me out that night in the alley. He didn't have to help me again when Donovan cornered me with orders to kill. He didn't need to let me go the night he'd gotten the better of me in LaBagh Woods. He hadn't had to do a single kind, frankly life-saving, thing that he'd done for me. If for no other reason, I owed him for that.

"I think I know what I need to do then. Thanks, Papi."

"You're welcome, *bonita*. And since you called, I will take advantage of the chance to speak with you and beg you again, come home."

"I can't. Not yet. Maybe not ever."

Something my dad said, however, made me realize I'd be stupid to pass up an opportunity to ask the Red Matron's second a question.

"Hey, Papi, before I came here, I checked the records to see if there was any wolf activity in the city of Chicago itself. There wasn't back then, but it's been a while. By any chance have you..."

"Twice a day," he said before I could get my full question out. "I know you are a big girl, but I am still your father. Of course I look."

The heretofore unnoticed tightness in my chest melted away. "And?"

"No wolves," he said plainly. "Not that I am too concerned. Wolves don't like big, noisy, dirty cities, and Chicago is certainly one of those." Then, pausing, almost as if my silence on the subject suggested something, he added, "Why do you ask?"

"It's nothing," I said, even though it clearly was. Tobias hadn't been lying; no one knew he was here. He either truly was a rogue, or someone had gone through a hell of a lot of work to keep him off the radar. "Just thought I might have sensed… something the other day. But maybe I'm just getting a cold. You know how sometimes I confused the sniffles with the other thing."

My father went to no trouble to cover the suspicion in his tone. "You know, Gerwalta, if you were to come home, go through your rites, your senses would increase and you wouldn't…"

"No," I interjected. "I can't support… Dad, you know what she's doing is wrong."

"My Hilly has her reasons."

Not wanting to insult my father, and all too ready to blast my mother, I decided that was enough. "I have to go, Dad. I have to get to work. Thanks for the advice."

"Of course, *bonita*. Call me back later and tell me if you listened. *Te quiero*."

NINETEEN

"Cynthia?"

The vamp in question only deigned to speak to me when necessary. I'd decided against asking Karmarov about Chicago clutches after his reaction to my initial inquiry regarding crèches. The senior vampire told me the location of his kind's "nurseries" was privileged information, and that as a vamp without a local clutch affiliation, he wasn't in a need-to-know position. Cynthia, however, had reportedly lived in Chicago on and off for the last few decades. She wouldn't give me addresses and local bar reviews, but she might offer up some general information.

"What, hood?"

"I was wondering — just curious, you know, because we don't have such a thing where I come from — are there any crèches around here?"

The olive-skinned researcher held up a slide at eye level, as though not trusting the readout her screen gave her. "There's usually a few in a city big as this. Why? Want to bat for the other team?"

My nose crinkled. "I don't think hoods can be changed."

"Want to feel what it's like to be bitten then? I hear some Hueys find it very pleasurable."

The phantom pain of Donovan's fangs buried in my neck and the pull of his mouth on my blood echoed through my body. My hand went to my neck, rubbing the spot. "Not really. But I wouldn't mind seeing one. You know, just for research. We don't get exposed to much vamp culture way out in the woods."

She turned to me, clearly doubting my thin veil of an excuse. "You know they wouldn't exactly welcome you there, right? A crèche is very tightly protected by its maker. The second they discover what you are, you might not walk away from it – whether or not you mean any harm."

"Would there be a way for you to know what I am unless I told you?" I asked. "Can a vampire sense I'm a hood the way a wolf does?"

"Why would we need to sense hoods?" she said. "You're no threat to us."

Spoken like a person who had never met my mother.

I bit down the impulse to defend my kind. As my father often reminded me in lessons on negotiation, sometimes it was better to be underestimated. Instead, I shrugged and acted as though her insult was water and I was the backside of a duck.

Jess, overhearing the conversation from where he typed research notes on a lab computer, raised an eyebrow. "What about me?" he asked. "Can you sense me?"

What an odd question, I thought. Didn't he know that to Cynthia, he was food? It was like asking a stoner if he could tell when someone was smoking pot nearby.

The vampire's little button nose twitched as she folded her arms and stepped closer to where Jess and I shared a station. Far too bunnylike for a vampire, I thought. Vague memories of reading *Bunnicula* as a child while hiding in the linen closet filled my mind's eye.

After a moment, she crossed her arms over her chest, and surveyed him from the ground up with a scowl. "Yes, but all I get from you when I focus is that you have no fashion sense, and that you probably taste like chicken."

His head tilted down as he tried to pin down what was so off. I agreed with Jess's apparent confusion; in his white Ralph Lauren sweater that let the casual observer pick up on the outline of his chest and a pair of green slacks, I thought he pulled off preppy collegiate pretty damned nice.

And he tasted so much better than chicken.

"Wolves hunt using smell." The vampire grinned, leaning in and running a finger down Jess's chest. "But vampires? We're visual creatures. You'd be better if you left a button or two open on your shirt. Better yet, white tees and tight jeans. No collars."

In a flash, her fangs dropped. Cynthia let out a hiss as she showed off her ready weapons, sending all the blood in Jess's body south and all mine to my head. Was she actually taking him under her thrall right before my eyes? Clearly, this was not a case where being underestimated was going to help me keep what was mine.

I had my blade out of my hair and pressed to the base of her neck before I could manage to blink.

"Try to enthrall my boyfriend, and you and I are going to have a problem, Cindy-Loo Wu."

Clearly an empty threat. I was no match for a vampire in a one-on-one and we both knew it. Fangs aside, if she wanted to go one-on-one in a bitch-off, I was pretty certain I could hold my own.

"Your boyfriend?" Cynthia looked as though she was struggling to swallow laughter, which just made me all the more pissed. With a hiss, her fangs snapped back up into her jaw and she took her hand back. Jess, confused but still lingering in the endorphins enthralling triggered, shook off his confusion. "Well, isn't that sweet?"

The moment Cynthia wandered off, I felt a different type of burning in my cheeks, this time from embarrassment. That turned to anticipation, however, the moment I felt Jess pull me back against him and whisper into my ear.

"So I'm your boyfriend, am I?"

I reached behind me and ran a finger over his cheek. "I was rounding up."

"Do it more. It's very sexy."

Heat blazed through my body. Despite the fact that three vampires were within earshot, I found my back arching as my breath hitched. I turned my head back over my shoulder, licking my lips and all but begging aloud for Jess to kiss me. The pressure of his hands on my hips ticked up as his pupils dilated.

Only a very loud, very insistent, very professorial clearing of a throat across the lab kept me from turning and throwing myself into his arms.

"Miss Kline." Prof. Karmarov didn't look up from the rack of test tubes he was squirting liquids into. "That's not the kind of chemistry we study here."

Both my and Jess's faces crackled into smiles born of frustration and temptation, sealing us together.

"Sorry, professor," I called as we both repositioned ourselves at our station, grabbing two slides each to feed into the machine for scanning.

His eyes focused on his work, Jess whispered, "Later, maybe."

I knew he was keeping his voice down because he assumed the vamps wouldn't be able to hear it. I, however, knew better. "They can hear everything we're saying."

I looked over to the table where Kai and Cynthia worked at inhuman speeds, marking up slides on their display. Cynthia remained as mushmouthed as ever, but the corner of Kai's mouth ticked up, providing evidence for my presumption.

"I don't care," Jess said. "It's none of their business."

A whole tropical rain forest full of butterflies fluttered in my stomach. "I know, but it's a bad call to try and get to third base with your boyfriend at work, even if you can blame it partially on the fault of it being that time of month."

Jess's face screwed up, and I rewound the record in my head to figure out why.

"I mean the moon phases," I quickly amended. "The hormones go completely out of whack, and the closer to a full moon, the wilder I get."

I blushed over when I saw the mix of wonder and, if I wasn't mistaken, strategizing in his eyes.

"Don't think you're going to take advantage of that, Jess Harmond," I warned, though the smile in my voice matched the one on my face. "I still can't believe I'm telling you stuff like this."

"Some sort of family secret?" he asked.

I swallowed a laugh. "Hardly. We're not exactly chatty about stuff in my family. The only time I brought it up with my mom she completely shut down. It was like I was asking her which sexual position was the best one."

Jess grinned. "I'd be happy to discuss that one with you too."

TWENTY

Dear Miss Kline,

Reports are that your work on the Helsing Helix program has been exemplary, and it is therefore with great honor that I confirm your internship with White-Whitman Labs this summer. Your appointment will commence one week following the end of the spring academic term, and will conclude one week prior to the beginning of the fall term. In addition, you will have up to five days of your choosing as personal enrichment and/or vacation

"Inga Rosethorn?"

I read the name out loud, enunciating like a student in a language lab training his mouth on new vocabulary. It wasn't that I didn't know the name. It was that I knew it too well.

"Not *the* Inga Rosethorn?"

Across the desk from me, Prof. Karmarov twirled in his old-school, wooden office chair, a risqué piece of furniture given that the material was one of the few that could penetrate vampire flesh and kill them.

"I suppose my answer to that depends on your clarification."

Was he being deliberately difficult, or just setting me up to give away what I knew?

"The most powerful vampire in Central Europe?"

The corner of his mouth ticked in annoyance. "Well, then, the answer to that is no. She doesn't live in Central Europe anymore. She relocated to Chicago two years ago."

"Holy shit, Vlad's firstborn?"

My voice bounced off of brick walls. Slapping my hands over my mouth, Karmarov shooed away my immediate concern.

"Cynthia and Kai are on an errand. I doubt very much that Jess heard you." He leaned over his desk nonetheless, as if there was still a reason to be discreet despite what he'd just said. "I'm not sure how *you* know that, but most vampires don't. It would be wise to keep that knowledge to yourself."

"I'm sorry, I didn't know. I..." I took a pickaxe to my memory, trying to dig out the context. "I think I was at her house once, as a child when I was visiting Germany with my mother."

One of Karmarov's eyebrows arched. "*You* met Inga Rosethorn?"

Funny, he'd only said *you* yet I heard so much more than that.

"Being the Red Matron's daughter has privileges. And I don't know if I actually met her. I just remember having to get very dressed up and thinking the food at her house sucked." But he was missing my obvious question. "What in the world is someone like Inga Rosethorn doing working as the internship coordinator at a Chicago biomed lab?"

"You probably think someone of her stature would have a very high-profile title, don't you?" Karmarov asked. "CEO or Director, perhaps?"

"I've always been led to believe that vamps are really into prestige." Insofar as my education had covered topics to do with the undead, a primary theme had been the importance they placed on deference and the perception of —if not actual— dominance.

"Amongst our own, perhaps. But in a position requiring interaction with the Huey world, it's sometimes best for our more prominent luminaries to hide in plain sight. Meanwhile, behind the scenes, they're the ones running the show."

In the back of my mind I thought about a brilliant genetics researcher who could have easily gotten tenure at any Ivy League institute instead of settling into the unassuming role of an assistant professor at a fairly insignificant regional university.

Was Prof. Karmarov hiding in plain sight? If so, hiding from what?

Whatever. As far as I could tell, Karmarov spent all his waking hours not teaching his one course in the evenings, in the lab. Did he ever actually leave this building? The work he was heading to tap out slayer DNA was already a hidden motive; I couldn't possibly imagine he had time to have a triple life going on.

"Cool. Hoods mostly just take jobs where they interact with the packs in day-to-day settings. You know, like bankers or teachers or veterinarians."

"Veter…" The word died and his lips curled into a smile when he realized the joke. "Ha! Because they're…. Right, well, yes. I suppose that makes sense. Wolves and hoods tend to settle in rural areas or small towns; vamps and slayers in large cities. Well, slayers did until…" He sighed. "But that doesn't matter now. I'm close, Miss Kline. I can feel it. Soon, we'll have enough complete sequences that we can move to phase two."

"Phase two?" I scooted to the front of my chair. "What's phase two?"

"Developing gene therapies, of course. Ones that could perhaps trigger the slayer abilities in adults with an existing genetic predisposition."

"I'm sorry, professor, a *predisposition*?"

He shied. "I imagine despite all your kind's attempts to keep procreation within your community, there's been a hood or two who's gone looking beyond the edge of the firelight and ended up with something to show for it."

"One famous one in particular."

Any humor in his eyes died. "My apologies, I didn't mean to imply something like *Die Verräterin*. What I mean is, there are humans with a slayer somewhere in their family tree. Our goal would be to identify those individuals and recruit them, if appropriate, into a genetic therapy trial. We're also looking at the possibility of a genetically engineered infant. We could literally birth a new generation of slayers. Genetics is amazing. So many possibilities, so many ways to correct our wrongs."

"You know, Test Tube Slayers wouldn't be a bad band name."

This time, the smile failed to break across his face. I took that as my cue to leave.

"Anyway," I sighed, holding up the letter. "I suppose I should get downstairs and get back to work if I want to hit the ground running this summer. Thanks, Professor. Please tell White-Whitman that I'm delighted to accept their offer."

An hour later, as I stood side by side with Jess in the lab, I could still feel the effervescence tingling my inside. The letter stuffed in my nearby backpack filled the room with helium and any second, I would break out into an epic giggling fit. A job. *I* had an actual job in Chicago. Until now, I'd been afraid that I was going to have to take up Rick Ryland's offer to work at the state park for the summer, as I had previously. That would mean going back to Paradise, a town much too small to hide from two people I vehemently did *not* want to see: my mother, and my ex-boyfriend, Cody.

"What has you so giddy?" Jess asked without looking away from the slide he was pulling from the scanning machine.

A hammer shattered my bubble. What if Jess hadn't also been offered work for the summer? What if there had only been one position, and I had gotten it? What if he hated me when he found out? It was funny: even though Jess and I had only known each other for less than two months, and even though we'd only gotten to the point of calling each other a couple in the last few days, he'd already fashioned himself a little comfortable nook in my isolated life. Suddenly, the idea that he'd not be there had me panicked. My chest felt tight as I attempted to iron out any abrupt signs of emotion from my voice.

"Jess, what are you doing this summer?"

He shrugged. "Haven't thought much about it. Dr. K was talking to me the other day about maybe staying on with the project over the summer. Why?"

The ache under my ribs melted in a warm gush. "Thank god."

Something in my voice must have tipped him off. The slide pinched in his fingers tinkled as he dropped it back into the tray. He turned and reached for me, as if by instinct, knowing I needed comfort.

"Come on, now." With a gentle pull, he wrapped me in his arms. "What's all this for?"

"Nothing, just…"

His finger pressed to my lips. "You were scared I was going to take off for the summer and find myself someone else? Someone better than a badass hood, like maybe a yeti or something?"

My anxiety immediately turned to frustration. I play-slapped his chest. "There's no such thing as yetis!"

"You're not supposed to exist either, but you feel real to me."

The proximity of him, the yearning that burned inside me that I hadn't felt in ages, that I swore I could never feel again, roared to life. Not content to let his kiss be a mere touch of lips, I laced my hand through his hair and kept his mouth working against mine, massaging his kiss and coaxing the flames of desire within him. Within *us*.

I only stopped when my more sensitive ears picked up on what I was sure was a very intentional book drop in the office upstairs.

"It's impossible to get away with anything naughty when vampires are nearby," I said, smiling against him.

"I know," Jess replied.

"Good thing there's only another hour to our shift. Maybe we can go somewhere where *no one* will hear us."

"Just so you know—" Karmarov's voice found its way down the winding staircase. "I'm going to close this door for a while so I can concentrate. Please try to control yourselves. I understand you're both college students, but seriously…"

Looking at each other, we both struggled not to laugh from the awkwardness. Jess unwove his arms and turned back to the table, closing the lid of the box he'd been working on while I was meeting upstairs with Prof. Karmarov.

"Or we might be done now. We finished scanning and cataloging all the slides on this tray. We need another, but Kai and Cynthia are gone. No way to get into the refrigeration room."

"Karmarov can probably let us in." Glancing over at the vampires' workstation, however, I caught a glint of light that reflected off a set of keys.

I crossed the lab to the vamps' workstation and grabbed Cynthia's set of keys. "She left these behind. Are these only lab keys? I thought they had her house key on them too."

Jess didn't seem as concerned as me. He shrugged. "Maybe she left them on purpose so we could get another tray. She's constantly on our backs for being so slow, but even she had to realize we'd get through the first one by ourselves with time to spare – even without superhuman speed."

"Speak for yourself, slowpoke. I *am* superhuman." Barely. Not as much as I'd be if I finally ceded to my parents' wishes – my mother's *demands* – and completed the hooding rites.

With one balled fist planted on a hip and the others jingling the keys, I contemplated the options. One, head back upstairs and beg Karmarov for permission. Doable, but wouldn't we come off as little kids who felt like they needed to ask permission to turn on the TV? After basically just being told to mind our raging hormones and not touch each other in inappropriate places, not really a dynamic I wanted to reinforce. Or, I could just grab out another of the trays from the shelf and Jess and I could actually get our work done. And maybe, just maybe, Jess wouldn't refuse if I suggested he walk me home, or laugh at me if I invited him to come upstairs for a few minutes.

After all, Amy would be gone tonight. She'd moved on – and, more or less over the last few weeks, moved in – with her latest featured boyfriend flavor. Not that I expected that to last. Still, Jess and I could take advantage of the situation to Netflix and Chill.

Hell, we'd been getting so hot lately, chilling was the only thing we had left to do.

I caught a mischievous grin on Jess's face and knew he was thinking the same thing. With one toss and catch of the keys, I crossed the room to a metal door with a head-sized viewing window and covered over in a new layer of brown paint with every change in the White House since Eisenhower. I'd never been in here – both Cynthia and Kai had insisted on refreshing our supplies whenever we ran low. As expected, wire shelving units held several dozen encyclopedia-sized trays. I entered and went right when suddenly, my insides rebelled. I felt like a fist had grabbed onto my belly button and twisted.

"Whoa!"

My hand caught the shelf next to me just in time to keep me from falling. My other hand laced over my stomach, as though trying to keep the contents in place.

What the hell was this? Did the vampires booby trap the fridge somehow? I knew Prof. Karmarov's work required a certain level of security, but if it was really this important, they wouldn't possibly have left the keys to the assets just sitting around like that, would they?

My lingering inside the fridge must have worried Jess. The next moment, as I struggled to stay on my feet, I heard him call out.

"Everything okay, Geri?"

What was I going to say? *No, I think there's some kind of chemical defense in here; hurry up so it can get you too?*

As a hood, I wasn't immortal in the way vamps were, and I didn't have the physical resilience of a wolf, especially as a nascent, but my biological fortitude was more robust than any Huey's. If whatever in this fridge was having this effect on me, it'd probably knock Jess right on his ass.

I focused on the box of slides nearest the entry despite its composition where the others were plastic, gave myself a 1.8-second internal pep talk, grabbed it, and bolted.

And plowed smack dab into Jess's chest.

His hands braced my shoulder, keeping both me and the box containing the tray from crashing to the ground.

"What happened? You look as white as a ghost."

A corner of my mouth twitched. "Oh, the charm..."

A moment later, the weight lifted from my hands as Jess took the box under one arm, and looped the other around my waist, guiding me out. He groaned as he tried to close the door behind him with a foot.

"Jesus Christ, that thing is heavy. What's it made of, lead?"

The box with the tray tinkled as he set it on the table, making me fill with dread. Had the slides inside come out of their slots? Had they broken? Remembering how Karmarov said they had been collected — mostly postmortem — at great expense from around the world, I felt the roil in my stomach intensify.

"Jess, the slides..."

"Can wait," he interjected, now turning his attention to me. His strong hands braced my shoulders as he pushed me down on a lab stool. Three iterations of his face swam in my vision as I tried to focus on the middle one. "What happened?"

My voice sounded raspy, winded, as though I'd just finished running ten miles. "There's some sort of booby trap, a chemical barrier or something, in that room. The vamps wouldn't be affected by it. I should've... I should've guessed they'd do something like that."

Jess's back straightened. He looked to the fridge's entry across the room, narrowing his eyes. "Why would they need to booby trap the fridge? You sure you just didn't knock something over?"

"No, I would have heard if I did, even if it was small. Oh, my god. Jess, you came to the door, you breathed the air. Are you okay?"

His face scrunched up, as though he'd just realized that fact the same moment I did. He looked himself over, like signs would be smeared across his shirt. "I feel fine. I was only at the door; you were all the way inside."

True. Still, my resistance to such things should have been five times his.

"Jess, can you open that tray of slides?"

His hands dropped to his sides. "What? Why?"

Gaining my feet on shaky legs, circling behind the stool and using it to prop myself up, I struggled with my equilibrium. Only one thing ever had this kind of effect on me – being close to a werewolf, one that was emotionally distraught.

"Please, Jess, Just open the box."

He took two steps back to the worktable. Keeping his eyes fixed on me, as though expecting my head to explode or something, Jess reached out and slowly, slowly tipped the box open.

A wave crashed over me, a blind force pushing me down. Their pain, their torment, their fear, their hate. It fed into my soul, the gut-wrenching torment of a century of wolves, brought to a bitter end.

I didn't know how I knew, only *that* I knew. These slides were from werewolves who had all lost their mates.

I fled, crossing the room and heading straight to the elevator, pushing the button over and over.

Jess, horror-stricken, slammed the box shut and ran to me. "Holy shit, what the hell? I've never seen anyone move so fast."

"Werewolves!" I said, my voice tight.

He pivoted, doing a full three-sixty. "Where?"

My hand stretched out, one finger targeting the source of my disruption across the room. "Those blood samples. They're not slayers. They're all werewolves. I have to… I need to go home."

Jess became a rock at my side. I leaned in, clutching at the fabric of his shirt. His eyes were full of concern and laced with panic when I looked up at him. "I'm taking you home."

Without another word, my feet swept out beneath me as Jess's arms caught me. I cradled next to his body as he walked us into the elevator.

"Miss Kline, Mr. Harmond – what's going on? I thought I heard a scream. I…"

Prof. Karmarov's puzzled expression, seeing us staring back at him from the elevator as he stood frozen on the stairs, was like looking at a still life. I wondered if, from his perspective, it looked like Jess and I had been caught in another of our borderline amorous moments. Something in the way I was clinging to Jess, like he was rescuing me, must have tipped him off. His gaze pivoted, landing next at the workstation where the slides full of werewolf DNA still sat.

His wide eyes swung an arc from the table back to me.

"Gerwalta, I—"

Instinct must have pushed the scream from my throat. I had been trained since a babe in diapers to anticipate a werewolf attack, to mentally steel myself for a lycanthropic onslaught. Vampires, however, were another thing altogether. I had no sufficient defense. If he came for me, I would die.

Jess's arms tightened around me. We swung, Jess pivoting on the spot so that his body protected me. Never mind that I was the stronger of the two of us, that I would be the one who could at least stand up to a vampire, even if I knew I wouldn't be able to persevere in such a battle. Jess, however? He'd be nothing more than flesh food.

And yet, he protected me. He placed himself between me and danger.

I'd never felt more afraid and more overwhelmed by appreciation in my life than at the moment I realized I was falling for Jess, and that Prof. Karmarov's fangs were bare as he leapt in our direction, an arm outstretched to grab me the second he got close enough.

The elevator doors closed just as a tremendous thud slammed into the outer metal doors.

TWENTY-ONE

The ceramic mug warmed my hands, casting out chills that racked my body after the initial adrenaline had burned away.

Jess laid his hand on my knee as we sat on the couch. "You couldn't have known."

"I could have." I buried my chin in my chest. I didn't want him looking in my eyes. He'd see my shame, and as fragile as I felt at the moment, I didn't know that I'd be able to keep from telling him the truth. I did know. Tobias told me. Only, I refused to listen.

With two fingers crooked under my chin, Jess lifted my gaze to meet his. "I promise, whatever it is, I won't tell anyone." Then, choking out a laugh, he added, "You think I go around telling people I've spent the last two months working nights in a secret lab in the Browning Building with three vampires and a hood?"

Of course, he didn't.

"What is it about that tray that upset you so much? And don't just say it's because they were werewolf samples. That doesn't come close to telling me what's actually going on."

The lump in my throat doubled in size. With dull eyes, I studied Jess's features, noting both his compassion and concern. A furrowed brow deepened as the clench of his jaw tightened. His hand, still on my knee, massaged gently, kneading a patch of flesh warmed by his efforts. He wanted to help me, to understand. He was being there for me, as cliché as that sounded. And I realized, only by showing him my weakness, could he truly understand my strength.

He was worthy. He had put himself between me and an attacking vampire. He didn't ask why I needed to leave or try to argue me out of it; he just helped me do what I needed to do.

Closing my eyes, I sucked in a deep breath through my nose before pushing it, and the truth, out in a fine stream. "I'm not like other hoods."

A glimmer of a smile twitched on his lips. "Since you're the only one I've ever met, I'm going to need you to expand on that."

"All hoods have certain skills," I continued. "Innate strengths. But after our rites, after the Gate of Fire, they're off the charts on the human scale."

"Sounds more exciting than catechism," he joked.

"A few of us can even…" I swallowed down my nerves, hoping this wasn't the stone that was going to crumble any credulity he allowed me. "…fly."

"Fly?" Jess's eyes went from thin slits to white orbs floating in a red cloud. "What, like Superman, or something?"

"Why do you think superheroes have capes?" I teased. "It's taken from us. Or, at least, we think it is. You see, we're called hoods because we actually do wear hooded capes. The weird thing is though, they're kind of… um, magic."

How much more of this could I tell him without him running, screaming through the door, never to talk to me again?

"You've heard how werewolves can be killed with silver, right?"

"Isn't that the popular story? A silver bullet to the heart?"

I nodded. "But did you ever wonder how that was done before guns were invented?"

Jess shrugged. "I assumed with spears, or really, really good slingshots."

"I *am* thoroughly trained in archery. In fact, the wrist bow is my favorite weapon. Hard to wear it around Chicago without getting looks, though. But a hood doesn't need anything but the silver. We can wield silver."

Jess's forehead wrinkled. "What does that mean, *wield* silver? Like you hold it out in front of you or something? Hate to break it to you, but Hueys are pretty good at that too."

"I'm sure you're very good at holding silver, dear, but what I mean is, we can manipulate it, command it. After we go through the Gate of Fire, silver obeys us. We can shape it into anything we want. We don't need a gun to shoot a wolf in the heart. We just need a bit of silver and proximity. FYI, either the brain or the heart is fatal. The brain is usually easier to reach."

He held up his hands, enumerating the facts so far on his fingers. "So hoods can kick ass; wield silver; hear, smell, and move faster than humans – excuse me, *Hueys;* a few can fly, and... anything else?"

"That's pretty much it. Except..." I sighed, running my hands through my hair. "Like I said, I'm special. I have a particular skill my mother wanted to utilize. I can sense wolves."

Whatever anticipation had been building in his eyes deflated like a balloon zipping across the room. "Sense wolves? Is that all?"

Was he serious? "Think how useful that would be to a woman whose job includes hunting down troubled wolves to kill. All hoods can sense when one is within a dozen feet or so, but that's not much better than using your eyes, is it? But me? Sometimes a half-mile away. Not as much here in the city, though. I don't know if it's all the buildings or because there are so many people, but I only get a few blocks here. My mother believes, if I went through rites, I could have a sense of proximity unlike any hood that's ever come before."

Proving that Jess loved playing Devil's advocate, he kept drilling for the importance of this seemingly insignificant ability. "Does she have a constant need to track down and kill wolves? From what you said before, the role of a hood is more of a deterrent."

"It *should* be."

It used to be.

Setting the half-empty cup of cooling tea on the side table, I tucked my feet up underneath me and turned toward Jess.

"But the supe world has gone high tech. My mother and her cabal believe the best deterrent is total control. Shortly after I was born, they started a registry. They pitched it to the packs as a way to expand their communities without all the risks and costs involved in travel. A way to find new mates and keep their traditions alive. They registered in droves. But what it's turned into is a way for self-righteous hoods to control pack movements. It's as good as 'Show me your papers' in the dark days of Europe."

Understanding dawned in Jess's features. He may have been a chem student, but he had a basic understanding of social science. "And let me guess, the packs have retaliated by hiding from the registry, by not reporting themselves. And your ability to perceive them…"

"Makes it harder for them to hide," I said, completing his thought. "But it gets worse. My mother is the Matron of the Red Hoods. Matrons have unrestricted and *unmonitored* access to our history and archives. She says there's a precedent for someone with my talent. When they took rites, not only did their range and degree of perception increase, but they could throw the sensory direction in reverse. Basically, they could make themselves into a beacon that the wolves could sense."

"To trap them," Jess said. "Like setting out a leg of lamb tainted with poison."

"Exactly. So, I've put off taking rites. I don't want to be that. I don't want to be her tool to clamp down on innocent families. I don't want to be part of their system of control."

My soul sighed when, after a few moments of mental digestion, Jess opened his arms and invited me in. In all the years since my mother had shared her vision for my future — *our* future, she'd put it — I had only opened up to one other person. In that case, only after years of building trust, of knowing he wouldn't use the information against either me or my family, did I accept him as part of my life. When I found out the potential I held, his curious reaction had been to comfort me as well. As I fell into Jess's hold, as his arms circled around me and he gently rocked me from side to side, the recollection of that moment when I finally had a confidant doubled back on me, up to, and including, the moment that it had all been taken away.

Cody. With a she-wolf. Mated.

At my mother's insistence.

Sweet turned sour in my mouth, and my body went rigid.

Jess stopped on a dime, but he didn't pull away. "Did I do something wrong?"

"No!" How could I let this ghost rise up between us? Jess was trying to support me, and all I could do was push my damage between us. "It's not you. It's…"

But my words died, along with any hope that I'd ever get over what my mother had done to me. I didn't remember tearing up, but as I pulled myself out of Jess's arms and wiped a sleeve over my cheek, I pulled it away to find the splotch of dark gray where my tears had wet the fabric.

Jess swept a warm palm over my cheek, cupping my face and drawing my eyes to his. "Whoever it is you're remembering and whatever it was they did to you, I'm not them."

The corners of my mouth twitched. "You're psychic now?"

"I don't need supernatural abilities to see that you're hurting." He pulled my face forward just enough to ghost a kiss over my lips. "What your mother did to you what she expected you to do– is horrible. But I'm sure she only did it because deep down, she thought it was the best way to protect you. With a power like that, and if your kind really has become so restrictive of the wolves, I don't doubt that would make you a target." Another light kiss, and he swept the hair that had fallen in my face away as he beamed at me. "It's a good thing the wolves don't know."

I sucked on my bottom lip before whimpering, "One does."

Compassion turned to a critical need to protect. Jess's jaw went rigid as his hand dropped away. "Who?"

"My ex-boyfriend, Cody."

I didn't know if it was because he could see the lingering emotions in my eyes or if that my ex was a werewolf that made Jess prickle. His muscles tightened under his skin, as he labored to keep his expression neutral.

"We broke up last year," I clarified. "I'm sure if he wanted to use what he knows about me for any nefarious purpose, he would have done so by now."

Confusion still marred his features. "From everything you told me before, I don't understand how that even happens. How does a hood end up in a relationship with a werewolf? Aren't you guys like the Hatfields and McCoys?"

"We don't exactly have family picnics together." I shrugged. "Small town dynamics. Paradise has less than a thousand people in it. Between hoods and werewolves blending into the Huey population, choices are few. Plus, I suppose Cody was sort of my teenage rebellion. We started dating our senior year of high school. I guess at first I was using him to piss off my mom, and he didn't mind – another chance for a werewolf to tick off a hood. But we actually hit it off. We were together almost two years."

"And why did you…" In a guttural click, he cleared his throat. "Why did you two break up?"

I arched an eyebrow. "Is that relevant?"

Defiance defined his stance as he laced his arms over his chest. "Just want to know if there's some asshole out there with an axe to grind, or who might hold some sort of petty jealousy if… when he finds out we're together."

"You don't need to worry," I assured him, putting a hand on his knee. "He's married now."

"That may be true, but…"

My hand went up, stopping his words. "No, you don't get it. Wolves mate for life – that goes for both the purebred animal and for the supernatural hybrid. Once a wolf consummates with a mate, adultery is a biological impossibility. Their DNA won't allow for it."

"Yeah, but you and he…" Jess coughed out, framing what he thought was an obvious end result of a long-term romance. When he caught the hurt look in my eyes, his smile fell. "Really, not even once?"

"The consequences… I always thought it would be so selfish of me. The moment we – *you know* – he would be bound to me for life, but I could change my mind at any time, leaving him trapped. Or if I was killed doing my duties… You've never been around a werewolf who's lost his mate, Jess. You can't understand the pain they go through. Think if I left him on purpose, what that would do to him? Most lone wolves we encounter separate from their packs on purpose. Death by hood is something I've heard of a few times. With me and Cody—I loved him too much to ever put him in that kind of situation. And then, he mated Lisa, and any romantic feelings he had for me… They're all irrelevant now. *I'm* irrelevant now."

"Actually, you're pretty much the only thing I care about right now." In a bold, quick move for a Huey, Jess pulled my hand from his mouth before stroking my cheek. "So, you're a… I mean, are a … What I mean is…"

"Yes, Jess, I'm a virgin."

He went wide-eyed at my bluntness.

"Don't act like it's a big deal, because it isn't." No matter what Amy thought. "I'm not ashamed or proud of it, and it's not something I'm holding on to out of any sort of sentimentality or moral code. The situation has just never happened."

He looked like he was trying to swallow a fishbowl. "I… Gerwalta, I want to…" Finally, he swallowed down his nerves, sat up straight, and turned towards me. "I'm not saying right now or today or even anytime soon, but when you're ready to…"

I didn't even let him finish the sentence. All it took was me remembering how this defenseless Huey, oblivious to how easily a vampire like Karmarov could have eviscerated him, put himself between us without hesitation. I remembered how he'd come into our crazy world, where there were such things as vampires and hoods and werewolves, and hadn't even blinked. The man who could dive into the deep end of the pool and break to the surface of the water without even gasping, who put my safety over his sanity, was a man I wouldn't soon let go.

I crushed my lips to his with a ferocity even I hadn't known was possible. After blinking away his confusion at the sudden move, Jess kissed me back, his hand raising to lace through my hair, angle my head, and deepen our connection. Without breaking away, I drew myself up and threw a leg over his lap. As I straddled him, places I'd let go dormant within me sparked to life, and I felt my senses – all of them – awaken.

"Geri?" He pulled back, looking up at me with awe. "Your eyes are glowing blue."

I nodded. "That happens whenever my primal instincts are aroused."

"Primal instincts?" A seductive grin parted as he ran the tip of his tongue over his top lip. "I like the sound of that."

His hands made their way under my shirt. With lithe fingers, he traced lines over my ribs, circled around my back, and unhooked my bra – all while kissing me with a languid patience that made the ache growing in my belly more pressing. Would he take off my shirt, or did he expect me to do it? He'd have to give up my mouth first, and Jess seemed to have no intention of doing anything like that.

The next moment, however, when his hands came back around and he used the pads of his thumbs to entice my desire, I threw back my head and gasped. Too long. It had been too damn long since I'd felt like this. God, I'd missed it.

With one corner of his mouth arched, he leaned in to kiss my neck. "If my fingers do that to you, imagine what my mouth is going to feel like."

Oh, Valhalla. In my mind's eye, I pictured him carrying out the task. Heat shot down my spine. Suddenly, my moaning altered, becoming a gruff grunt.

Not because I had had any sort of negative reaction, and not because I wasn't close to going over the edge from just a little bit of foreplay, but because I'd suddenly picked up on the presence of a werewolf.

One who, based on how strong I could sense his proximity, was more than likely just on the other side of my front door.

My hands became fists as I shifted my weight and climbed down from Jess's lap, leaving him in a comical pose, kissing air. I'd unsheathed the silver blade hidden in my hair by the time he'd shaken off the confusion and stood.

"What? What is it?"

With a slash across my mouth, I signaled Jess to stay quiet. Not that it would matter. Even if Tobias hadn't heard him, he more than certainly could smell Jess.

Pointing at the door, I mouthed the word "werewolf" and signaled for Jess to stay where he was. Then, I turned around, the knife held out in a striking position.

"What do you want, Tobias?"

For a moment, all I could hear was his breathing in response. Quick, shallow, racing – as though he'd just run a marathon.

"Tobias?" The blade dropped a little lower as concern replaced my annoyance. "Why are you even still here? I thought you left Chicago. Didn't you and I discuss the consequences if you go lunar?"

"I found her."

I didn't need to ask who; that much was obvious.

"Okay, but what do you..."

"I need your help," he said, his breaths evening out. "I can't get to her. I… tried… and I… It's dark, and I think she's…"

Suddenly all my heistance disappeared, replaced by a nagging concern that even I didn't understand. He was losing his humanity already. I'd never seen a wolf go through the process of going moon mad; I'd only seen the final result when, stripped of the ability to hold a primate form, one struggled to connect with his humanity, and even then, only from a distance, safely behind my mother's warrior pose.

"Tobias, you need to go home. Please, don't do this to yourself."

Don't do this to me.

His voice cracking, he sounded as though he were on the edge of tears. "I know where she's being held. I need to save her. I need to save her and… I don't know. She's been away from her pack for too long, but she's a beta. Maybe she's stronger. Maybe she can come out of the wolf for one more cycle. But me… If I don't, there won't be enough of my human mind left to save her. I have to free her. You have to help me."

Was he really rambling on like this, knowing I had a Huey in the room with me? How crushing was his desperation, to chance exposure like that? Knowing it was a bad idea, and knowing I'd regret it in the long run, I reached out, took the door knob in hand, and slowly leveraged it open.

And that was when the world went black.

TWENTY-TWO

"Is she going to be okay?"

"Why do you care?"

"I don't. Just seems like a waste, you know, given what she said about what she can do."

Voices reverberated off walls I could not see, before crashing into a void. One man, one woman, both speaking at ease just beyond where my body had been strewn out over a cold, stone floor. Either they didn't know I was awake, or it didn't matter.

The woman's voice, laced with contempt, continued. "She's too valuable to damage too much. For now, anyway."

The voices grew faint, moving away as my mind labored to focus on their timbre and tones. Both were so familiar, but placing them proved just out of reach;   either because the way it reverberated cloaked it from my recollection, or because my brain had been scrambled when someone hit me over the head.

Speaking of which... *fucking ow.*

With a shaky hand, my fingers inspected the crown of my head. Dried blood caked my hair, but the wound had already begun to heal. I must have been hit. Or maybe I fell down and hit my head? Yeah, how likely was that? What happened? One minute I was mauling Jess, thinking I'd finally make Amy proud, and the next...

Jess! Oh, my god, what about Jess? Panic took me to my feet, and across the room. Fist a-flailing, I pounded the thick glass wall, beating out a fervent rhythm and screaming at the top of my lungs.

"What did you do with Jess? He's just a Huey, you bastards!" More fist thumping, more useless braying. "I swear, if you've hurt one single hair on his head."

The two who had been conversing grew suspiciously quiet. Above me, electronic gears clicked. The sound was one with which I was overly familiar. A remote-controlled security camera repositioned to take me in. Behind me, the recognizable old brickwork that made up the exterior of the Browning Building, but filtered through another wall set before it, one that seemed to be both thick and clear, like some sort of glass. It was mirrored in front of me as well. Both walls to the left and right appeared to be made of concrete, and none of them in any direction had a visible door that I could see, leaving me to wonder how I'd come to be deposited here.

"What is this, some kind of racquetball court?"

Instinct told me I wasn't here by chance, and no way was this something Hueys were behind. Supes were involved, no two ways about it. I reached up to my braid, loose but still woven on the back of my head, and felt for the hilt of my constant weapon.

No sheath, no knife. Nothing. Whoever had taken us knew the decorative clip in my hair wasn't merely for fashion's sake; it hid one of my only defenses.

As I turned my head, my braid scraped across my shoulders, teasing the skin just under my cotton shirt. It reminded me of Jess's touch, which in turn reminded me of his voice. And in that moment, I knew who was talking just out of sight.

"Jess?"

He slipped into my field of vision and stood in front of the glass wall. My eyes cataloged him, looking for any signs he'd been injured. My boyfriend was pristine, not a scratch on him. But the way he looked at me, detached from any warmth or familiarity, told me something was off-kilter. Suddenly, the truth hit me.

My hand massaged my wound. "It was you."

"In fairness, I was aiming for the wolf," he acknowledged. "But when you heard my tranq gun fire, you dove in front of him, pushed him out of the way. You hit your head when you fell."

"You were trying to get Tobias?" My words rang in my head.

"I've been after him the whole time. He was my mission. You were bait."

Looking around at my surroundings, other truths fell into place. I was a prisoner, and after a moment, I even realized where. Jess had told me it himself that day we first met, hadn't he? How there were supposedly secret labs under Browning where animals had been experimented on in the war era. I was in a holding pen. Sending out my senses, however, I didn't pick up on any wolf in the area.

Tobias had gotten away.

My gaze held his as I sent all the animosity I'd kept from my voice out through my glare. "I don't believe you. You're not that smart."

He sizzled under my attention, shifting his weight and staring at the floor. A moment later, he was no longer alone. Cynthia appeared with preternatural speed, crossing her arms and cocking a hip.

"No, Little Red, but I am." Cynthia sneered, clicking her tongue. "He was told to distract you from what any decently trained hood would have picked up on in the lab. If he had had half a brain and gone into the fridge himself to get another tray of slides instead of letting you do it, you never would have stumbled onto the werewolf samples. Lucky for him it led to you two being in the right place, at just the right time."

The werewolf genetic samples, I'd almost forgotten about them. My mind indexed everything that had happened leading up to the moment where the sorrow of dozens of wolves pressed on the edges of my consciousness. The box had been so heavy because it had been made of silver.

But how had they come to have werewolf samples? The hoods and the wolves had agreed together, that unlike vampires who could mind trick their way out of explaining their unique physical traits, we would have no such luck. We went to extreme lengths to make sure our genetic information never went outside our communities. Something still didn't add up, and I had a feeling the missing numbers to balance this equation lay in the unknown quantities of Cynthia's cryptic statement.

"Right time and right place for what?" I asked.

She grinned, the way one does at a child who'd figured out how to get on the counter and break into the cookie jar: with equal parts appreciation and malice.

"You were never supposed to be part of this project, Geri," Cynthia said. "I only let you come on board because Karmarov insisted you'd be of value to him. *I* don't care about restoring the slayer lines. I don't care, because…" She reached behind her, stroking a hand under Jess's cheek like she was teasing a dog's muzzle. "Not *all* of them are gone."

No. No way. It couldn't be. I appraised Jess with newfound understanding. "You're a slayer?"

For the first time since revealing himself as an accomplice, he smiled. "My father was one of the last."

So he was half-slayer. I leaned forward. "That puts me in a bit of a quandary, doesn't it? I'm pretty sure it would be a bad thing for me to kill an endangered animal, and yet, I so want you dead."

His cocky grin mocked me. "An hour ago, you were ready to sleep with me."

"Yeah, well, an hour ago I didn't know you were scum, so…"

Cynthia's hand flew up, shooing Jess away. "Run along now, dear. I have some things to ask Little Red here."

I'd find a way for Jess to get his comeuppance eventually. For the moment, I enjoyed how he huffed in frustration when his sugar mama sent him to play in the corner. Left alone, Cynthia set about inspecting me with more leisure, as though admiring a dress in a shop window.

"Exactly how did you do it?"

I quirked an eyebrow. "Do what?"

She rolled her eyes. "Get the werewolf to become so obsessed with you? I thought wolves mate for life, and I don't see anything about you that would lead a bonded male to turn his back on his mate."

"Well, Cindy Loo-Who, that could be because your assumptions are wrong. Tobias isn't mated yet." I found myself giving up information without a second thought, the hurt and bitter truth of it still serving as a poison to loosen my care. "Besides, he doesn't care a lick about me. He's just a wolf at the end of his rope. He only reached out to me because he's pulling at strings."

"And that's why he twice defended you against one of my children?"

A ringing abounded in my ears. "Your children?"

"Oh, come on, Geri. Haven't you figured it out? When you asked which crèches are in the area, I convinced you not to bother. Didn't it occur to you I did that because I had something to hide?"

"Wait, so you're telling me that…" My mouth went dry, my mind raced to piece together the clues. "*You* sent Donovan."

Cynthia nodded. "Yes, and thank you so much for taking care of him for me. He was *such* a disappointment. I told Kai that, but I'm afraid my Hawaiian son is a bad judge of character. I've sent him on a mission to find a replacement now. Luckily, he's decided to scout at Northwestern instead of WCU. In the meantime, I got to see if the werewolf intervening in your fight was just a fluke, or if there was really something going on. And lucky me, the moment you were in mortal danger, Mr. Furry showed up. Want to tell me again there's nothing between you two?"

"There's nothing," I assured her. "I can't stand Tobias. I've been trying to get him to leave for months."

"Too bad he didn't listen. Since he stayed, however, I'll make use of him. Just as I'll do with you."

"Me?" I asked. "What possible use could you have for me?"

"I don't mind getting blood on my hands, when the time comes for the wolves to die. But why should I, when I have a wolf-slayer at my disposal?"

I barely contained my laughter. A glow grew in Cynthia's cheek, as though she still had the power to blush.

"What's so funny, hood?"

"Just that, you think it's possible for me to kill a werewolf," I said. "I haven't taken my rites yet. I couldn't kill a wolf any more than Jess could. Besides, what could you and Karmarov want to learn from the wolves that isn't already known?"

Cynthia jerked her head back and cackled. "Karmarov? My dear, he's a hopeless, idealistic academic. Igor's gone soft in the tooth. I'm just making use of this fabulous facility he has access to. I'm afraid what I'm after has very pragmatic intentions."

"Yeah, like what?"

A maniacal grin stretched across her face. "I'm going to decimate the wild wolves, just like we did the slayers. And when they're all gone, there'll be no one who can stop us. Say you can't take on a wolf? Fine, I'm sure I can derive other projects where having a hood at my disposal will prove useful. Settle in, Gerwalta Kline. You could be here a while.

TWENTY-THREE

Hours must have passed, but how many, I couldn't know for sure. Even denied a way to see outside, I sensed dawn inherently, followed by the pull of the sun across the horizon and the late afternoon rise of the moon, and again, sunset. Had Amy noticed I never came home? How long would it take before my non-presence alerted her there was something wrong? And when she started to ask questions, would Cynthia send out a vamp with a little more tact and success to derail her curiosity? Somehow, I had to get out of here before that happened. But more importantly, with the full moon approaching, I had to get out of here before Tobias and his fiancée lost any hope of avoiding moon madness. How I was going to achieve: one, breaking myself out; two, breaking out two wolves being held prisoner by up to three vampires and a partial slayer with unknown abilities; three, getting them back to their packs half a world away before the full moon; and four, keeping my roommate both safe and ignorant of all the above, I hadn't the foggiest.

Halfway through the day, I awoke from a dreamless sleep to find a cloth sack on the floor next to me. In it, a water bottle, some fruit, cheese, and bread. I took a few sips of the water, and set the rest aside. I wasn't about to eat anything Cynthia and Jess gave me. Besides, I had gone through several training exercises that forced me to endure without resources for up to a week. Going twenty-four hours without grub wasn't about to do much to me. Other needs, however, didn't respond to willpower as well.

"Unless you expect me to designate a corner for you to hose down once a day, I could really use a potty break," I called out to the void.

At first, I thought my words may have gone unheard. A few minutes later, however, the good old professor himself came into view.

"I'm really very sorry about this, Miss Kline," Karmarov said, his words soft, his gaze tender. "I never intended for you to become one of Cynthia's subjects."

I kept my eyes trained on him, emotionless, giving him not the slightest satisfaction to see how betrayed I felt at having trusted him. "You know, something you said to me once makes a lot more sense now, about how some of your kind with a lot of power hide in plain sight? Which leads me to wonder, who exactly is Cynthia?"

"A vampire whose confidence I'm not interested in losing," was all he said. "If you need to use the facilities, I'd be happy to accompany you."

"I haven't needed to be accompanied to the bathroom since I was three."

Apples blossomed in his cheeks. "Of course, I wasn't suggesting that I would be in the restroom with you. I only meant that I would take you."

"I guess if you're my only choice, we just have to go with that, don't we? Now, how do I get out of here? I don't see any door."

No sooner had I asked the question than Karmarov squatted, taking on a frog pose one moment, and rocketing into the air the next. Getting over the twelve-foot wall presented as much of a challenge to him as stepping over a rain puddle. He landed just a foot from me without much of a sound, not even to my sensitive ears. I took a step back, reflexively feeling myself outmatched in his presence.

The professor held up his arms. "I'm not going to hurt you. I'm sorry to say this, but the only way for me to take you out of here is to carry you. The iguanas who were kept in this enclosure years ago didn't have much need of doors, and I'm afraid the ladders that used to allow the researchers access from the gangplank above have long since disappeared. So have many of the gangplanks."

I assumed zombie pose. "Fine, carry me then."

Karmarov blinked twice in quick succession. "Just like that, you trust me to be that close?"

"I don't trust you at all, but I know what my abilities are, and I know roughly what yours are. I'm a nascent hood. You're a centuries-old vampire. If you want to hurt me, I can't really stop you. Besides, my bladder is about to explode."

He took me in a you-Jane-me-Tarzan hold, all while wrinkling his nose. "I admit, one thing I do not miss about being mortal is the need for such indelicate functions. Hold on, the g-forces involved in the leap are a little hard for a mortal to endure."

The hall that ran between the four different enclosures didn't give me much clue about how I could get out of here, or where Kara might be. Whitewashed cinderblocks gleamed under humming fluorescent lights. The scent of bleach stained the air. At the end of the corridor lay a windowless metal door.

"How does the university not know about all this?"

Karmarov's eyes roamed the edges of the room. "I've been able to make the records say the experiments carried on here during the war era have left the room unsafe for use. Hueys take every quarantine sign at face value."

When we reached the door, he swiveled in front of me, waiting, staring at me like he was studying my reaction to see if I appreciated the ugly brown paint that covered it.

"Nothing?"

Nothing what? What was he getting at? "Full bladder."

He tipped his head to the side. "Interesting. And if I open the door?"

The world shifted. A roil of my stomach only momentarily preceded a swirl in my head. My mind raced from annoyed curiosity to shocked understanding. There was no doubt, none whatsoever, that there was a wolf nearby. I'd known from Jess's loose lips that they hadn't gotten Tobias. What was Karmarov doing, pointing out to me that the English wolf was nearby? The sensation that tugged just below my belly button matched perfectly the effect he'd had on me the other times we'd been close. It had to be him.

Bracing me from behind, Karmarov pulled me over the threshold and into a vestibule with three doors: one to my left through which I could see a somewhat rust-dusted enamel sink and toilet, the one behind me we had just passed through, and another to my right, an unremarkable wooden door like any in the Browning Building above.

"I'll give you two minutes," the professor said, pushing me through the door on my left. "Use it wisely."

Even though my mind raced with the overload of thoughts, I still needed to attend to biological needs. That effort addressed, however, I knew exactly what Karmarov wanted me to do. The only question was why. He obviously wasn't about to rebel and act out against Cynthia and Jess on my behalf. What, then, was his end game?

But I couldn't think about that now. I only had forty-five seconds, tops, to do what needed to be done. I pulled in a breath, slow and steady, through my nose, and exhaled a deep sigh through my mouth. In the cracked mirror over the sink, my eyes brightened, a tinge of silver lining my brown irises, as I called on my innate abilities. I pushed my senses out, taking in the size and shape of everything around me. Inside my chest, a warmness formed.

Please, Tobias, I don't know if this will work, but if you sense my proximity, move toward it. I'm here. I'm here, and I think Kara is too.

Pounding on the door made my heart race. Looking down, I realized my hands had been under the ice- cold running water as my mind drifted. I reached up and turned off the faucet.

"Sorry, just washing up."

Karmarov gave me an expectant look as he opened the door and ushered me out. "Did you take care of what you needed to do?"

"Yeah, I think so."

"Good," he said, motioning back towards the heavy metal door. The painted *silver-plated* door, through which I'd never be able to sense a wolf. "I want you to know, Miss Kline, that no matter what Cynthia says, I didn't lie to you. I really am trying to find a way to restore the slayers. Unfortunately, Cynthia's research is the one that is getting all the attention in our little community right now. Genetics is all the rage, even among vampires."

"Trying to make sure all vamps have blue eyes and blonde hair, or whatever characteristics it is you consider preferable?"

"As you are a red hood descended from Germanic bloodlines, I can't help but take some amusement at your statement." Karmarov again took me up in his arms, preparing to jump. "What is the number one problem werewolves face?"

"Besides my mother?" I deadpanned.

"Diversity, Miss Kline," he said, ignoring my quip and taking another effortless stride through the air. It was easy to imagine why peasants of old thought vampires could fly. The way they defied gravity would certainly leave one with that impression.

"It's ironic that while our population is exploding beyond the capacity of city centers to support it undetected, werewolves are becoming more and more isolated. Destruction of habitat affects them the same way it effects any species."

Reflex pushed me to counter, to tell him about the matrons' database for tracking the packs, before thinking better of it. Karmarov might be playing things down the middle, or he might just be acting the friend to see if he could find out what I'd already stupidly told to Jess. Instead, I thought about Tobias, about how he'd mentioned the clutch that moved into his region when a nearby city had grown large enough to sustain it, leaving the packs that lived on the town's edge antsy.

Karmarov set me down gently, giving me enough space to feel somewhat, if foolishly, at ease as he continued.

"And yet, in this information age, where our *virtual* boundaries have all but disappeared, we're even more in danger. Supes have become overly cautious about reaching out to other communities, not sure who to trust. One cannot blame them, I suppose, but it does have effects. Their gene pool is narrowing. Packs that have exchanged mates for centuries now are pushed further from each other, and we all know how werewolves disdain long-distance travel."

"But I've never heard anyone mention anything about the packs being in danger due to lack of genetic diversity. If that was an issue, don't you think I'd have heard?"

Karmarov grinned, as though letting me in on a secret. "So you're suggesting someone is keeping that information contained? If one were to entertain the idea that such a thing might be happening, then one would have to ask himself – or *herself* – who would have such power, and more importantly, the motivation to keep such knowledge private."

I didn't have to ponder that beyond two quick blinks to know the who. The Matrons were the only ones with unfettered access to the database our kind had spent the last few decades developing, who communicated openly and frequently through clandestine means about their local issues. They claimed it was to help wolves find mates across packs: an excuse I'd never bought. But was this it? Was my mother and her ilk actually trying to solve a problem among the wolves no one had yet admitted aloud? If so, then why keep it secret? The answer to that kept itself hidden in the details.

"Are you familiar with animal husbandry, Miss Kline?"

I shook my head. "I'm not from the part of Michigan with farms and feed lots. We're copper and timber in the U.P."

"But surely you must understand how some farmers... even dog breeders, will go to great lengths to control mating and produce the ideal stock." Karmarov turned, eyeballing the top of the holding cell. "Of course, wolves have natures which won't allow for trading out partners once a mating occurs. You are aware of the bond that werewolf couples experience, are you not?"

I swallowed. Hard. "Firsthand."

If he recognized the pain in my throat and the crack in my voice, he made no acknowledgment. Instead, he leapt, landing just on the outside of my pen. Karmarov turned back to me, pushing his hand to the glass.

"Control is about more than doing, Gerwalta. It's also about undoing. Think about that." Then his hand dropped away. "If you need to use the facilities again, just call. I can come down from my office at any point tonight. Cynthia and Jess are otherwise occupied."

TWENTY-FOUR

Towards dawn, Karmarov brought me more food.

"I need to use the bathroom again."

I couldn't be sure of the meaning of the smile that blipped across his face before disappearing. "Of course."

Once in the small lavatory again, I was hit with the same awareness as before. Somewhere very nearby there was a werewolf. This time when I emerged, instead of striking up a conversation with me, Karmarov took me through the third door, to a small room, on the wall of which were several lever-handled silver doors.

I was standing inside a morgue. Or at least, what had been a morgue. The outdated décor suggested the room hadn't been refurbished for some time. Yet, the level of cleanliness, right down to the subtle scents of bleach and formaldehyde, suggested it had undergone some recent upkeep.

Cynthia stood at the back, clicking her fingernails on one of the refrigerator doors.

"What do you feel right now, hood?"

If she thought I was going to cooperate, she had another thing coming. I bit my tongue, crossed my arms, and smirked.

"Fine, be that way."

Her nail-polished fingers wrapped around the lever of the unit and pulled up. When the door opened, a sheen of condensation wafted out, dissipating just inches from the rim and replaced by a gentle flow of mist. Ball bearings whirred as Cynthia reached in and pulled out the slab, on which the man's body lay. Without any clothing and covered up to his chest by a white sheet, I couldn't gather too much about him, other than the obvious that he had been stout and built when he'd been alive.

"Anything now?" Cynthia raised an eyebrow.

"Don't know what you're expecting," I said. "I guess I'm vaguely curious why you have an autopsied body in the basement?"

Cynthia blinked. "His name was Nick Somfield, and he was an alpha."

And with that, I suddenly felt too many things. Sadness, disappointment, regret, anger, confusion. She wanted a reaction, she got a reaction. My fist convulsing, I practically growled my answer. "Tobias's brother. You murdered him."

A corner of Cynthia's mouth rose. "Nonsense, Geri. I harvested him for study, the way one does with any animal. I'm going to assume, then, that you had no idea what this man was until you learned *who* he was. How delightful to hear! Igor, bring her along."

In a few swift moves, the body of Tobias's brother disappeared into the cooler as Karmarov nudged me out of the room and up the hallway. When we stopped abruptly, it was before a holding cell not so different from the one in which I'd been, with one big exception: it had a door, one on which the lock was molded in silver. Only one kind of prisoner would need such a pricey precious metal.

She must have been a true sight to behold before her captivity. Echoes of beauty still traced the edges of her face. Dressed in ragged clothes more ripped than whole, I wondered how many times she had put herself through the rigors of a transformation. That she had tried to get out in her wolf form was evident; the cinderblock wall at the back of the cell bore a number of claw marks. I had no doubt about who the woman with dull mocha skin and a frizz of matted, unkempt hair was. Only, it didn't make sense. She was a mere dozen feet from me, but I couldn't pick up any sense of her at all, not the way I did with the other wolves. I was blind to her lycanthropic nature.

But that wasn't what really concerned me. What did concern me was how a supernatural being could look so haggard. How little had they fed her for her body to waste away like this? How little did they care for her?

I lashed my head to the side, fury erupting in my voice. "What kind of monster are you?"

"The kind that always gets her way." Cynthia's smile beamed. "But for what it's worth, I can say that we are not entirely to blame for her state. No, not entirely. Kara's been offered a diet from hamburgers to raw lamb. I even had some human flesh given to her, just in case she was a wolf who enjoyed that kind of thing. She barely eats or drinks. She spends her days sleeping, and her nights when we aren't running tests on her howling. She used to take on her wolf every night. Now, I think she's lost interest in it."

I ground my teeth. "She hasn't lost interest. She's losing control. She's on the edge of lunacity. She's probably scared to take her wolf at this point. She may not be able to find her way back."

Cynthia laid a finger on her chin and tilted her head. "I've always wondered why the werewolves were so resistant to being their stronger selves."

"You really don't get it, do you?" I pointed at the poor woman beyond the glass, who so far hadn't even been able to move her head to look at me. "This *is* her stronger self. She's on edge of losing her control, but she's holding it in. You have no idea how hard that is for her."

"Such humanistic sentimentality. But then, I wouldn't expect a *nascent* hood, to understand what true power is. You've never felt it."

"I have, the moment I turned my back on my mother and refused to become the weapon she wanted me to be."

"A hood?"

The whisper came from within. Both Cynthia and I turned, taking in Kara's desperation with surprise.

Cynthia stepped back, pointing at me. "Not just any hood. She's the Red Matron's only daughter. Are you quaking in your boots, Kara?"

The she-wolf's head fell, her eyes growing distant and her voice small. "I fear nothing now, except the moon."

Cynthia turned back to me, rolling her eyes and waving her hand. "She's been saying that for days. I don't know what she means."

Did vamps really not get moon madness? If Cynthia didn't know, I wasn't about to tell her. Luckily for me, Cynthia didn't even inquire. Instead, she asked me the question I had been dreading.

"Now, what I want to know from you is, can you sense her?"

I swallowed down my nerves, kept my pulse steady. "No, I can't."

The vampire actually clapped and jumped, looking so much closer to her physical age than her actual one. Even Karmarov, standing just beyond us, seemed taken aback by Cynthia's sudden childishness.

"You've made me very happy, Geri. That's exactly what I wanted to hear." Her head jerked to the side. "Okay, Igor, put her in now."

"What? Wait, no!"

Normally, going into a room with a werewolf would be no problem. But this wasn't normal. The she-wolf had obviously been put through hell, and was on the edge of losing herself. On top of that, if her pack had the same adversarial relationship with hoods, leaving her as spiteful and vindictive as Tobias, she wasn't exactly going to suggest I pull up a chair and have a cup of tea.

Karmarov's touch could have been rougher. As manhandling went, his was civil. Nevertheless, as he undid the silver locks and corralled me through the door, I couldn't ignore the fact that he was shoving me into a room with a nearly feral fucking werewolf. Moments before I passed through, however, he pulled me close, putting his mouth to my ear.

"You're going to need every bit of your abilities to get out of this one, Geri."

Great, so he was going to both imprison me with my eternal foe and taunt my total lack of uber magical skills. Perhaps he'd also like to give me a papercut and pour lemon juice all over it.

Not knowing what else I could threaten him with, I hit him in the only way I could think. "You're never going to get tenure like this!"

Next thing I knew, I lay prostrated on a cold, misty floor. I looked back over my shoulder just in time to see Karmarov turn the lock again, before he and Cynthia slinked away. No need to stand around to see how this went down; a camera was mounted on a tripod in the identical cell across the hall, its lens turned directly on us.

The most important thing: not to panic. Panic was born of assumptions. I couldn't assume that Kara was about to leap up and shred me limb from limb, even though the over-under on that was a thin line requiring a microscope to see.

Backing myself to against a wall, I sat, noting how her head hadn't moved at all. Was she trying to ignore me, or honestly indifferent to my presence? It didn't matter. The only way I could see to gain a foothold in this situation was to engage her in conversation, and hope I could pull out the strength of her humanity by making it her focus.

"I'm Geri… *Gerwalta* Kline."

"The daughter of Red Matron." Kara's lips barely moved. "About time the hoods became involved. Red Matron might be the only one strong enough to defeat a vampire."

"Actually, she doesn't know. Only I do."

"Then I am doomed."

Forgetting all caution, ignoring all instinct, I rushed to Kara's side, laying a hand on her shoulder. "No, you're not."

"And just who is going to save me, hood. You?" Finally, she looked at me, and I immediately wished she hadn't. Her bloodshot eyes barely reflected light, and the bags under her eyes and purple patches on her cheeks told me she'd been physically roughed up as well as mentally imprisoned. That, or she'd injured herself thrashing around, trying to force her body from one form to the other.

I wanted to ask how long she'd been here, but I already knew the answer to that. The variable wouldn't be measured in the number of days, weeks, or months, but in the simple fact that however long it was, had been too long.

"I'm only a nascent," I admitted. My own words sounded like a rationalization, like an excuse. Like an apology.

"Of course you are. Why wouldn't you be?"

"Do you, um, mind if I ask you something?" Purely a rhetorical lead. "Do you know why you're here? What are they trying to accomplish with you? Why are the vamps after the wolves?"

"Isn't it obvious? Because we have the ability to fight them. Assuming they don't gang up on us when we're driving along a country road one night." Her head shook, as though freeing herself from the belief. "Five of them ganged up on me. I was on my way to see my boyfriend. They ran me off the road, then bound me with silver chains. Two days later, I was here."

"And you've been here ever since?"

Her face soured. "You think they let me traipse about the city on weekends do you?"

"No, I just..." It was going to sound crazy to her, I knew it would. "I can't sense you. You're different somehow."

"Am I? It wouldn't surprise me." Her chest shook with silent sighs. "So many things they've done to me. I don't know them all. When life had mercy, I was not awake. And when it didn't..."

"I'm so sorry, Kara." As tears pricked the edges of her eyes, I knew I needed to keep her focused. As loose a grip as she had on controlling her form, becoming overly emotional could trigger a change. I had no silver, and no ability to access a full hood's strength. If she changed, I was dead. If I died, so would she. "You said you were on your way to meet your boyfriend? Is that all he is, really? Because the way Tobias tells it, you and he are practically mated already."

With that single name, her face brightened. "Tobias? How, how is that possible?"

"He's in Chicago looking for you." I pulled away, if only to give her a moment to adjust to that fact without any distraction. "He's been trying to convince me that you were in Browning this whole time, but I didn't believe him. I'm in this building most days of the week, and I never got a blip from you."

The brow of Kara's forehead creased. "What a barmy! If he's been here the whole time, he's just as close to going over the edge as I am. Stupid, dumb dog."

"Actually, Kara, I think he might be our way out of here."

She lifted an eyebrow. "There is no way out of here."

"I think there might be. Only, we have to wait for daybreak when the vamps are asleep."

TWENTY-FIVE

I didn't know if it was desperation, an inability to concentrate on anything but her sanity, or just a total lack of credulity led Kara not to argue. A few hours after I'd been placed in her cage, Cynthia and Karmarov sauntered by, on their way to their day rest, with Jess close on their heels like the little sissy sycophant thrall he was.

Cynthia glared at us, disappointed. "She's still alive."

I didn't bother to ask which of our continued existences pissed her off most. Kara, as when I first entered, stayed seated on her folding chair, motionless except for the slow rise and fall of her shoulders as she breathed. I remained in the corner of the cell, searching for a comfortable sleeping position.

"We'll use it to our advantage then." Cynthia turned over her shoulder to Jess. "I want to see what happens when the full moon rises and Kara takes on her wolf. For that to happen, they both need to survive the day."

I raised my voice, flustering them to be reminded I could speak. "Just put me back where I was before. It would be hard for even the most determined werewolf to get to me through a silver-plated wall."

Amused, Cynthia nodded at me approvingly. "You've figured out our little design secret, have you?"

"Yeah, but I'm not really sure what you hoped to achieve. Whatever you did to the stiff you got in the morgue and this wolf, I can't sense them. You've... masked them somehow."

"And just what makes you think that those are the only wolves we've had down here since you've been on campus?" She leaned over, putting her hands on her knees. "Where do you think all those little samples in the silver box upstairs came from?"

Then, turning back to Jess, she said, "Careful with the hood. They're trained to use anything and everything as a weapon."

Jess bobbed his head. "What do I do if they go after each other?"

"Then make sure you are recording. We should still learn enough from the brawl to know if Igor's chasing ghosts."

The professor's back went rigid, his fists balling. His serene voice belied obvious frustration. "I've been studying blood and tissue samples since the invention of the microscope. DNA samples since the technology came along to make it possible. I know what I saw, Cynthia. I'm not wrong about her."

"And yet, the wolf lives." Evil manifested as a grin on Cynthia's face. "At least for now. When the full moon comes up tonight, we'll see if your theory holds any water."

"It will hold the ocean," Karmarov assured her. "But I stress again, there are other ways to go about this. Ones that don't risk Gerwalta losing a limb, or worse, her life."

"A deal is a deal, Igor. I promised that if she survives, she's your guinea pig. I didn't promise you'd get all her associated limbs in the process."

For the first time since I'd met him, I saw anger take hold of Igor Karmarov. His fangs lowered in a second. That single alteration, combined with the narrowed eyes, bowed head, and creased forehead, let one see that, while subservient, the old vampire was not some domesticated beast that Cynthia could dismiss at will.

"What good is she to me if she's rendered incapable of fighting?"

"What does that matter to me?" Cynthia twirled a hand through the air. "Besides, I thought you only wanted to study her genetic makeup. Wouldn't that be more efficient if you only had to cart her arm or leg around from place to place, and not have to worry about feeding it, washing it, taking it to go potty?"

"Understanding why she is the way she is at a genetic level is only part of my query. I also have to see how that genetic uniqueness…"

"Blah, blah, blah." Cutting him off, Cynthia raised her hand to her mouth, slowly working her jaw through a languid yawn. "I've heard it before. Don't worry. I'm sure we'll wake up tonight and find your precious hood still intact. Jess, remember: any changes, wake us. We might be a little slower than usual during the day, but we can still take care of a weakened werewolf and a nascent hood."

The two vampires continued past our cell, heading up the hall, beyond my vision. Jess, however, lingered, taunting me with his glare. He pointed to the camera mounted outside and pointed at our cell.

"If you decide to try to kill each other, at least try to make it look sexy."

Even distant Kara growled at that one. Jess squared her in his gaze, then licked his lips, before slithering out of sight.

The werewolf turned her weary head my way. "Now what?"

I settled myself back in the corner, using it to support myself in a sitting position and leaning my head to the side.

"Now, we sleep a little. We'll need strength tonight."

"I'm afraid that, if I sleep, I will never wake again to see the world through human eyes."

"You will, Kara. I promise. Try to get some rest. I can't do this alone."

TWENTY-SIX

When I awoke a few hours later, lying on the floor, I found myself surrounded by fur. Confused, I rubbed the sleep from my eyes and pulled myself up to sit. Beside me, a white belly of fur served as my pillow. My eyes went to the chair where Kara had been sitting when I'd fallen asleep. Nothing there, except a few scraps of cloth that no doubt had been the threadbare clothes she'd been wearing before.

Kara raised her snow-white snout. The fur over and leading up to her eyes abruptly turned gray with specks of red. Silver and black fur rimmed her neck like a scarf. Despite the thickness of her coat – typical for wolves from northern environs, though I suspected some of her lineage came from North Africa due to her human form – it didn't hide the fact that her skin hung loose about her, as though someone had deflated a wolf-balloon, leaving just enough helium for it to skirt the floor.

It wasn't night yet, so she must have taken her wolf deliberately.

"Can you change back?"

A thin, hollow whine answered me. She looked toward the camera trained on us both, then back to me.

"Ah, you don't think you should. Got it."

Her head tilted to the side, the wolf version of "what are you doing?"

"You ready?"

A weak yelp.

"Good. I'm going to get Jess to take me to use the bathroom. When he brings me back, be ready to act."

My whole body shook as I took to my feet and bounced in the direct line of the camera. If jumping around like a stranded person on a desert island at a passing boat didn't get Jess's attention, I wasn't sure what I would do.

"See someone you know, Geri?" he ground out when he came into view.

I avoided his jibe and stuck with the plan. "I need to use the bathroom."

Jess lifted a finger and pointed to the corner behind me. "Go ahead."

"Seriously? You can't expect me to just sit around in my own pee. Besides..." Jerking my head back toward the she-wolf, I drew his attention to the obvious. "...probably not a good idea if I go about 'marking territory' in a cell with a werewolf on the edge of going moon mad."

With a slanted eyebrow, he weighed my claim against his limited knowledge of werewolf behavior. "Is that true?"

"You've seen a dog lift its leg on every third tree, haven't you? Don't give werewolves too much credit just because they can take on a human form. In their heads, they're more mutts than men. Come on, Jess. I've really got to go."

The stoniness of his face began to show cracks. "Can't you just hold it? It's almost dark. The vamps will be back soon."

"You know the saying, when you got to go... Come on, my bladder is about to burst."

A tiny twitch, then a sigh, and finally Jess slipped his hand into his pocket, pulling out a key. He slipped it into the lock, but paused to point at Kara before turning the silver deadbolt.

"You show a single canine, you'll regret it. I got silver oxide spray, and I'm not afraid to use it." He dropped his hand to pull a small container out of his pocket, holding it next to the deadbolt like he was positioning a gun to dissuade a prisoner from charging.

If he thought a diluted mist of Ag_2O was about to stop a full-sized, mature she-wolf just hours away from full moon, he was a few trees short of a forest. Still, I wasn't about to clear him of his delusions.

"Listen to him, Kara. No reason for you to get hurt just because of my human biology. Okay?"

The wolf picked up on the cue, and yelped her acknowledgment.

Jess wasted no time in scooting me up the hall once I was out of the cell. He probably didn't suspect I was taking notes of every little move he made. The smallest part of winning a battle relied on muscle; both my parents had taught me early that my brain counted as my greatest weapon.

In the back of my mind, I began to index his behaviors and assets. Silver oxide spray: right pants pocket. Key to Kara's cell: left pants pocket. Being that he was right-handed, that made sense. It was a mistake, however, as silver oxide wouldn't deter me in the slightest. I was a hood; silver was my friend. I might not be able to command it yet, but he'd have better luck trying to douse me with seltzer water.

His left side, his weaker side, became my target. He'd try to either kick or hit me with a left, bringing it — and the key — closer.

"Because we never got a chance to talk after I knocked you out, let me make one thing clear," Jess said as he pushed me toward the bathroom. "Every minute I spent with you was torture. I belong to Cynthia."

"Yeah, I know how that whole thrall thing works. Sounds like she's in your head, nice and deep. Funny thing about that is, you don't realize what it means."

Let it fester. Let him try to figure it out.

Jess huffed. "What's that supposed to mean?"

At the bathroom, I turned back around. "Nothing, it's just... Vampires weren't the subject of my training, so I could just be wrong. But, as far as balances go, seems like, to have an equal playing ground, a slayer wouldn't be able to be put under thrall. If you are part-slayer, the genes must be recessive in you. I highly doubt anything Cynthia and Karmarov come up with in their research will ever work to awaken those properties in you."

I paused, turning around and leaning against the frame of the door coquettishly.

The seeds of doubt began to germinate. "What do you mean, if I'm part-slayer? Of course I'm part-slayer."

"I'm not saying you aren't. I'm just saying you're probably not slayer *enough* to be useful to them. You're just convenient. And if there's one thing I know about vampires, the second you stop being useful to them, then bam! They wipe your memory clean and send you off." I pressed a finger to my chin, feigning deep thought. "I wonder what cover story they'll come up with? Car accident that left you with amnesia? Experimental drug that fried your brain? Rare genetic condition that led to big gaps in your memory? Yes, that's it. That would fit in with the fact that you've been receiving payment for working in the lab of a geneticist."

"You have a creative imagination, Geri, I'll give you that."

"It's too bad we didn't get a little more time before Tobias showed up. I could have shown you just how creative I can be."

"You?" The word came out as an airy chuckle. "A virgin?"

Sticking out my chest to offer up what my cousin Markus mockingly called my "hood goods," I lowered my gaze, putting on the schmaltz. "Only technically. Remember, I dated a werewolf for two years. Just because we successfully kept ourselves from going all the way doesn't mean we didn't find ways to have a hell of a time. I have a catalog of skills that don't require a full immersion."

"And am I supposed to believe that you want to share these skills with me, even though it turns out I'm one of the bad guys?"

A shrug, one with my left shoulder a little higher than the other, reached Jess on a purely subconscious level. Animal instinct drove the predator to square an attack on the weaker side. The side where the muscles didn't show as much strength. With a devious smirk on his face, Jess raised his left arm, using it to ballast himself against the wall as he leaned toward me. When his mouth began to angle toward mine and his eyes closed, I wondered what lottery I had won to have him fall into my trap so easily. Just as I was about to wrap my hands around his waist and distract him with a kiss, however, he paused.

Jess's eyes flew open. "You think this is working?"

With a vigorous yank on my right side, I fell down into the bathroom. Cold tiles under flat palms, I pivoted from the heap I'd landed in on the floor and looked up at the dominating figure before me. Jess, both hands balled on his hips, sneered at me.

"Like I said, I'm Cynthia's." He pointed to the porcelain pot at the edge of the tiny loo. "Do your business, and get on with it."

The moment the door was closed, I leapt to my feet and stuffed the key into my bra. I had to be quick. Making a show of using the bathroom, I turned on the faucet labeled "C," closed my eyes, and centered my mind, pulling on all the nascent power in my body, and hoping Tobias hadn't given up, that he was still close enough.

How stupid of them to somehow put a silver coating around the holding pens, but not the bathroom. It was like giving me a periscope to see into the world above the surface. At first, I wasn't sure if the niggle poking at the edge of my nervous system meant he was close, or if the consequences of limited food and water had begun to have an effect. After one more deep breath, the sensation sharpened and normalized, then, heightened. Tobias – at least, I'd assume it was him, since I didn't know of another werewolf in Chicago – drew near. My senses flooded with awareness of his proximity. I felt the corners of my mouth dance, even as I remembered my mother's words.

You're only a nascent, and the wolves find themselves drawn to you. When you complete your rites and walk through the Gates of Fire, they will not be able to resist. You'll be able to lure them away from anyone, to anywhere. You'll never have to chase a wolf the way the rest of us do. When you want, the wolves will come to you.

A pounding rhythm on the door brought me back to the here and now.

"Time's up!" Jess bellowed, then rapped the door again.

My eyes flew open, broken from my reverie, to find myself staring at the mirror. My eyes glowed, the typical rim of light blue outlining my irises. If I could will it away, I would. There would be no hiding it from Jess once the door opened, and backed into a small room without a weapon, he'd have the advantage in any sort of attack.

Something must be usable as a weapon. With a single sweep from left to right, I cataloged the bathroom. Its Spartan design didn't offer much possibility, not even a plunger next to the toilet I could use as an impromptu bat or bar of soap on the sink to throw as a distraction. The only available item: a thinned roll of toilet paper on the back of the toilet.

Wait a minute – the toilet!

In a blinding moment of inspiration, I had my plan. I dropped to my knees, hugged the toilet, and did the best impression of vomiting I could manage.

"Jesus Christ!"

Three steps took Jess across the length of the bathroom. The moment I sensed him leaning down to inspect me, I acted.

Gripping the edges of the toilet seat, I yanked with all my strength. The porcelain lid separated with a crack, flying through the air and catching Jess under the chin, sending him reeling back and flattening against the wall. Had I been stronger, he may have gone out with one blow. No such luck.

He stumbled to his feet, dazed but dangerous. "You're going to pay for that one, Geri."

Teeth gnashing, I said, "Bill me."

He charged again, but it was opening night in the Gerwalta-will-not-go-down-easily Season, and I was ready. Faking a blow coming down on his right, Jess's arms went up to block me. I pulled back, but the distraction was just long enough for me to swing a kick right to his groin.

Doubled over, the so-called semi-slayer was all too easy to pick off. A hard conk with the rim of the toilet seat to the back of his head, and he was out. Jess's body slumped, his head landing under the sink and his face flat against the floor.

I didn't know if he was actually part-slayer, or if that had been a lie Cynthia told to manipulate him. If he was, he might, like hoods, heal more quickly than humans. The last thing I wanted was for Kara to be stolen of her already-limited strength by the silver oxide spray he carried. I reached into Jess's pocket, pulling out the miniature bottle, before emptying it into the toilet and flushing. As I shoved it back into his pocket (nothing like a false sense of security to distract a foe), the now-empty bottle pinged when it hit something.

Reaching in, something palm-sized, plastic, thin, and rectangular filled my hands. Jess's student ID? Of all the things to carry around in his pocket in Cynthia's dungeon, why that? Was there a secret student café I hadn't yet discovered in Browning's basement as well?

I stepped over his body and ran out in the hall, down to Kara's cell. She found life when I shoved the key in the lock and opened the door.

"Come on, I don't know how long he'll be out for, and the sun is already setting."

Kara yelped, rushing through the door as soon as the crack allowed for it. I dove back in only long enough to grab the dress that still sat on the chair. It may be torn and dirty, but it would have to do for the moment. Together, we hightailed it up the hall, in the direction we had seen the vampires running. After a few more similarly designed cells on either side, we came to an elevator lobby. Instead of call buttons, only a small, plastic opaque inset appeared next to the doors.

We looked at each other with equal confusion: me, gawking; Kara, tilting her wolf head.

Could it be so simple?

I reached into my pants pocket, pulled out Jess's card, and held it up to the black plastic inset on the wall. A beep preceded an electric hum, the sound of gears working and cables... cabling, as the elevator shaft shook gently.

Keeping my eyes glued to the doors, waiting for them to open and ready to attack anything and anyone that might be inside if needed, I said to Kara, "I know it's really close to sunset, and that even in your best condition, that would make it hard to change back to human, but can you?"

I'd seen wolf mannerisms all my life. I'd grown to be able to read their body language like a spoken tongue. Kara all but vocalized her question: Why?

I pointed at the elevator. "Tobias is near. I sensed his proximity. I... I actually was able to make him feel mine somehow, to like, call him here. I don't know how. Anyway, wherever this elevator opens, it's still going to be somewhere in Browning Hall. As soon as we find Tobias, I'll get both of you to my place before the sun sets; it's not too far away. But between here and there, you need to be human. We'll never be able to get away with two werewolves walking across campus. You may look a lot like huskies, but the fact that you're as big as miniature ponies won't go unnoticed."

Confusion, anticipation, trepidation... all passed in Kara's expression, until finally, she settled on determination. Gaining her paws, the wolf arched her back. Gray fur became consumed by a plane of mocha flesh. Elbows and knees took shape. A maw shrank back, morphing into a mouth and button nose. Soon, where there had been a canine stood the emaciated frame of the she-wolf in her human form.

Kara took to her feet and held out a hand for her dress. Like me, she had long ago let go any awkwardness at being nude.

"But what will happen when we get to your apartment and the moon rises?" she asked, slipping her clothes over her head. "And how will we get back to our packs before the moon sets? England is six hours ahead of Chicago. There's no way for us to travel that far in that amount of time."

"Maybe it won't be necessary? After all, you slipped into being human easily enough just now. Which was… really impressive, by the way, given how weak you are."

"I am beaten, but I'm still a beta." With a mournful huff, Kara shook her head. "*I* might be able to come back to flesh tomorrow morning, for one more night. But Tobias won't. If he left England the same time I was taken, he's on the edge of going mad."

"One thing at a time, Kara. First, we need to get out of here. I have a tranquilizer at my apartment. If you show signs you're out of control, I'll dose you. Don't worry about Tobias. I have a plan to help you both."

Her eyes went suddenly wet around the edges. "Why are you doing this? What kind of hood goes to such lengths to help wolves, ones that aren't from her territory at that?"

I didn't have time to answer her before the elevator stopped, and the doors opened up to an eerily familiar sight. Wire shelves and long gray boxes filled with slides. The air of the refrigerated room mixed with that of the elevator, forming a mist as chilled met warm. I led Kara, taking tentative steps, wondering how I had been in this room before and not noticed an elevator shaft.

As the doors closed behind us and I turned to see, I realized just how. Somehow the elevator bay had been disguised to look like a regular patch of wall.

Kara took a place beside me, gauging the scene with equal curiosity. "Why have an elevator hidden inside a deep freezer?"

"Because," I said, pointing at the door, "if it wasn't someone could look in here and see it. Karmarov's lab may have restricted entry, but it's still university property and must be accessible by some people on campus. Probably custodians and security, at least. But they didn't want anyone to know this was here. Karmarov himself said he fudged university records to make it look like nothing useful was still down here."

I shook out the confusion and refocused on both the plan, and the tingling in my fingers and chest that told me Tobias was near. So tingly, in fact, that I didn't doubt he was on the same floor with us. We just had to get out to find him. Hopefully Jess's student ID opened the main elevator down from the lab too, since as far as I knew, my ID was still in my bag back at the apartment.

Kara reached out to touch the door. Wisps of smoke wafted from her fingers the second her hand clasped the handle. She groaned, pulling back her scorched palm and holding it before her eyes, looking at her own hand as though it had betrayed her.

"Silver," I concluded. Now I realized why there were so many obvious layers of messy paint over the door. The whole thing must be made of it. Or at the very least, plated in it. "In case any of you escaped, a last measure to try to keep you in."

"Or one to try to keep others out," Kara said, dropping her head. She turned to me. "Do you still sense him being close?"

"Very close." I raised an eyebrow. "You can't?"

She shook her head, her gaze falling to the ground. "Whatever they've done to me, it had some effect. I couldn't sense what you were either when they brought you to me. Whatever the vamps are up to, they're putting us in serious danger. We need to know when an enemy approaches."

Catching my awkward pose, Kara shrugged.

"Sorry, no offense, but hoods where we come from aren't like you. They'd as soon chain us to a tree as look at us."

"The ones where I come from aren't much better."

I reached out, wrapping my hand around the handle of the door. Unlike Kara, I felt warmth, a sense of familiarity. The silver wanted to speak to me, but I still did not know its language.

"Ready?"

The werewolf's chest rose and fell through a cycle of deep breaths. Finally, after a moment, she gave a jerky nod.

Neither of us could move the moment after we got through the door. What we were seeing was impossible.

Tobias, in the lab.

Bound in a silver cord, and standing between Prof. Karmarov and a very smug Cynthia, my silver blade at Tobias's throat.

TWENTY-SEVEN

"Kara, run!"

"Silence, dog!"

Cynthia yanked the silver cord, dragging Tobias closer.

Beside me, Kara whimpered. "You shouldn't have come. There's nothing you can do for me."

"Sounds like at least one of you understands the situation. Now…"

The Asian vampire pressed the blade to the werewolf's throat, drawing a pebble of blood. Air siphoned between Tobias's lower lip and teeth as he bit away his pain. The attempt to hide his suffering fell short; I had no doubt Kara understood her beloved's pain. Tears welled in the corner of his eyes.

"I will always come for you," he ground out. "I am thine, and thou art mine."

Cynthia ignored them, continuing to bark out ultimatums. "Let me make this really simple for you. Here's what's going to happen. The professor here is going to hit the lycanthropes with a heavy sedative. Geri, since it seems you've been able to outwit my thrall, you will go with Karmarov. He needs to do a few tests on you. Then, we're all going to take a little drive."

"Are you crazy?" I barked out. "They'll be moon mad by morning. They've been away from their packs for too long. They won't be able to change back to their human form."

"I don't really care." Cynthia shrugged. "Besides, this bitch isn't going to be useful to me for too much longer. I'm as likely to eat her as keep her come morning."

My nose wrinkled. "You're eating wolves?"

"Well, eating might be an overstatement. More like, drinking unto death."

Prof. Karmarov brought himself even with the other two. "If I can suggest, Miss Xin, sunset is minutes away. Handling the two werewolves will become exceedingly difficult after that. It may be wise for us to take action now, and deal in dialogue later."

"Not yet."

Cynthia handed off Tobias to Karmarov before sidling up to the she-wolf. Kara, chin stiff and teeth bared, let out a warning growl.

Cynthia's hands flew up in surrender. "Easy there, wolf, I only want to follow up on the line of questioning we've been going over the last few months." Pressing the blade to Kara's throat, she leaned in, whispering in her ear. "Now, who is the pretty boy who's crossed an ocean and stalked this side of Chicago for three months, looking for you?"

"Tobias Somfield."

"I knew that much from his immigration files, sweetie. Try again, and this time—" A bead of blood pearled where the tip of the blade punctured Kara's collarbone. "—tell me what I want to hear."

"He's my…" Kara bit back tears, bit back anger. "He's my mate."

I felt my world shift at the revelation. The next moment, I was struck dumb. Why would Tobias hide the fact that he was mated?

"How sad. That explains how he could follow us so easily. You are bonded – even though you've not officially been given permission by your alphas. You naughty, naughty wolf. But it's obvious he loves you. Look at him, traipsing about the city, looking for any clue to find you. He even buddied up to a hood, he was so determined. He wanted her to hunt you when he had failed. Do you love your mate, Kara?"

"Yeah," Kara sighed, her voice cracking. "I love him. Tobias, I love you."

The wolf finally showed signs of life, pulling at his restraints, trying to get closer. "You bloody vampire, stop! You've hurt her enough. Let her go!"

Cynthia stuck out her bottom lip. "Not nearly as much as you have, lover boy. Tell me, can you sense her? Just a few feet away from her, can you feel the pull all wolves feel when they are near their mates?"

This time, it was Tobias who lost all resolve from his features. Lowering his head, he shook it mournfully. "No."

"And yet, you made a pretty straight line for this lab when you came huffing and puffing in. If it wasn't the draw of your promised mate, then what exactly led you here?"

I went cold when, with anger in his eyes, Tobias snarled at me. "Somehow that hood keeps luring me to her whenever she's in danger. Evil cow, are you happy now? Now that you sprang this little trap and both Kara and I will die?"

"Okay, I seriously have no clue how you think I'm in on this," I replied. "FYI: I've been a prisoner here for the last two days."

I turned to Karmarov. "Why? What possible value is a nascent hood to you?"

Any compassion or collusion I may have thought I'd picked up on in the dungeon faded. The professor's monotonous tone showed no emotion.

"I have theories, but only theories. Is it just you, or all Reds who have your traits? I need further study. More test subjects."

"Further study? Why, you old…"

The room echoed back Kara and Tobias's groans. Inside myself, I felt the echo of the same force that pulled on them, forcing them into submission, robbing them of their humanity. I didn't need a mirror to see that my eyes glowed with the faint light of my power. Behind me Kara fell to all fours, her bones breaking, her skin prickling as hair follicles multiplied and bubbled. When changing at will, a wolf could mitigate the pain of a body remaking itself. When forced by the moon, the process was the worst kind of torture. At least, Cody had described it that way. I had no doubt now as I witnessed the moon-induced transformation with virgin eyes.

For the first time since Kara and I had emerged into the lab, the vampires showed their nerves. Karmarov dropped the silver thread that bound Tobias.

The metallic twine pinged as it hit the floor, searing a path over the paws of the massive red and white-furred wolf. Cynthia stumbled backward, my silver blade falling from her grasp, as Kara's maw, still half-formed, chomped at her.

The vampires' only concern became the wolves. It should have been mine as well. A wolf under the pull of a full moon made for a foe even the bravest and strongest of hood matrons gave proper due. Having two, both more than likely doomed to be trapped in their lupine forms from moon madness, in a confined space? It wasn't a question of if I would get killed, it was a question of if my parents would be able to recognize my mangled corpse.

As metamorphized forms found balance on four legs, I dove for the silver blade. I didn't know what I could do, but I was useless without a weapon. The moment I had the blade in hand, my feet went out from under me. Before I could come to grips with the blurring scenery around me, I found myself upstairs in Karmarov's office, Karmarov standing next to me. I knew vampires were fast. I didn't know how fast.

I brandished the blade before me, a comic impression of a person who thought she stood a chance to calm the storm with a whisper. "Why?"

Shame filtered his eyes as he dipped his chin. "You are unique."

"How? Because I wanted nothing to do with this world?"

His hands threaded through my hair as snarls and groans, crashes and destruction, crawled up the winding staircase from the lab below.

"You can choose the type of person you want to be, Gerwalta Kline. Don't be the kind that runs away. You have to be in the game to change its outcome."

"So, what? You're helping me again? I'm dizzy at all your side-changing."

The professor became streaks before my eyes, moving with such velocity that I couldn't track him. In two blinks, he had crossed his office, opened a desk door, and sent his antique wooden office chair crashing against the wall, breaking it into several pieces in the process.

Karmarov rounded his desk to shove a handgun into my grasp. "Have you been trained in firearms?"

"I'm the daughter of the Red Matron. I've been trained in everything but compassion." I took note of the furry red-feathered dart in the loaded weapon. "Only one dart? But there are two wolves out there."

Karmarov turned. "I'm not giving it to you as a tactical weapon. It's for defense. The blast is strong enough to pierce a werewolf's hide, but it may take a few moments for the sedative to have an effect. Use whatever defensive maneuvers you've got hidden up your sleeve. You still have Jess's ID?"

I nodded, despite my confusion.

"Good," Karmarov said. "Make for the elevator. Sounds like both wolves are busy trying to take down Cynthia, but if your running triggers one of their instincts and it tries to attack, shoot it. You get out, no matter what, okay?"

"What? No way. I am not leaving Kara and Tobias behind so you two can throw them in a cell and use them as test monkeys."

Karmarov's patience began to fade. "Didn't you hear what Tobias said? He can't sense Kara. The experiment is over. We found a way to uncouple a werewolf bond."

Was I hearing what I really thought I was hearing? The vampires had discovered a way to undo the bond between mating wolves? Impossible. That bond glued packs together. Mates were so true to each other, adultery in the werewolf world had never been witnessed. Packs were family, an interconnected web of devoted pairs who'd fight to the death for each other and their progeny.

"But that would entirely alter the nature of the species."

"Correct," Karmarov confirmed. "Now you see why we have to stop this. If Cynthia survives this battle and she figures out that I let you get away on purpose, all my work will have been for nothing. Get out. I'll become smoke, go to the basement, and make sure Mr. Harmond's memories also conveniently disappear. If anyone asks you about me, you must never tell them I aided you, understand?"

Every new truth revealed twisted my old understandings into tighter knots. "Just whose side are you really on?"

"I'm on the side of life, Miss Kline." He winked at me. "Good luck, and until we see each other again."

My gaze shifted, from the open door on the far side of the room, to the empty office, and then to the weapon in my hand. My eyes fell on the splintered fragments of the wooden office chair, wondering how a creature who could cause such destruction without even intending it, could also show such tenderness for a few werewolves and a nascent hood.

And I wondered if he thought I was really going to do as he asked.

No matter what Karmarov said, I wasn't going to abandon the wolves. Even if it cost me my life, I wasn't about to be the kind of hood — I wasn't going to be the kind of *person* who cared more about saving her own skin than those in peril. Still, I was only a nascent, and two wolves on the edge of madness and under the pull of the full moon were just as likely to kill me as accept my aid.

Looking at the gun, I realized what I needed to do. Below, I'd only have one shot. I needed to make it count.

Before me was chaos made fur, fang, and flesh. The four workstations where a few days ago I had scanned slide after slide, oblivious to the dungeon and prisoner three floors below me, had been laid to waste. The tabletop machines lay in broken pieces on the floor. The assorted vials of solution and cleaners, pools of broken glass.

Amidst the chaos, Cynthia stood in the center of the room, acting like some sort of centrifuge that spun the wolves out every time they got within reach. Kara and Tobias took turns throwing their bodies full force, only to have them lashed in the corner. I lifted the tranq gun, fixed the vampire in my sight, and waited for the coast to be clear. Pressure built on the tip of my finger as I started to squeeze, but I stopped dead in my tracks when Cynthia caught me on the stairs. The momentary distraction was all Tobias needed to settle his teeth around Cynthia's wrist.

A terrifying screech emanated from the vampire's mouth as she flung her arm, taking the red wolf for a ride through the air. Drywall shattered as his body crashed. Kara, instead of repeating the pattern of fronting an attack against the vampire who had held her hostage for three months, sped to the side of her beloved.

In the act of turning her back on that same woman.

In a blur, Cynthia found her way to one of the workbenches left in disarray. The silver box that started my last few days of horror lay among the debris. Its hinges proved no obstacle; Cynthia merely grasped ahold of the box's lid by the edges and yanked, and it came off. With no more challenge than it would take me to fold a paper plate, so she too managed to contort the lid, rolling it, altering it, making it into a conic tube.

Cynthia raised the newly molded weapon over her head; I raised the gun.

The vampire brought her newly forged weapon down with a yowl.

Silent, the reluctant hood within me pulled the trigger and shot.

TWENTY-EIGHT

The doors of the elevator connected to the dungeon opened just as the she-wolf and female vampire became lifeless forms on the lab floor. Karmarov held a still unconscious Jess in his arms, as easily balanced as if he were carrying a stack of blankets. Confusion overtook him, his eyes narrowing.

"How?"

I held up the tranq gun as evidence. "I'm sorry, professor, I had to repurpose your chair. I replaced the dart with a piece of wood."

"You were supposed to use it against the wolves. Your job was to get away."

"No, my job was to protect the wolves. I'm a hood. That's what I'm supposed to do."

But his unspoken implication remained true. I hadn't protected the wolves. Kara's body lay in a red pool, which grew larger by the moment. I held my breath as Tobias's paws touched down in his mate's blood, sniffing at her neck. The she-wolf made no movement. I looked to Karmarov.

His expression drooped, confirming with a somber shake of his head what I feared true. "She's dead."

My legs felt leaden, the gravity of each step heavy, as though I was walking down into a dark destiny that would pull me under. "Tobias. Tobias, I'm so sorry. I– "

"Geri, stay back!"

But Karmarov should have saved his words for himself. The moment Tobias accepted that his mate was dead, his ire turned on the sole person left who had contributed to her imprisonment. Ice and fire shot up my spine, instinct telling me to defend. But who did I defend? The vampire who had lied to me, only to save me? The werewolf who had repeatedly saved me, but detested me?

Trepidation made Karmarov's movements deliberate. With exceeding care, he rotated, setting Jess on the floor. He put his hands up, backing away. The wolf held himself in parallel, a rumbling growl on the air. Teeth bared, Tobias assumed an attack posture, looking for just the right moment to spring.

"I understand your anger, Mr. Somfield, but please know, I'm on your side. I'm so sorry about Kara."

As though his daring to speak Kara's name was the only thing standing between Karmarov and her mate's rage, the werewolf pounced. Tobias pinned the vampire to the floor, becoming a torrent of teeth, fur, and revenge.

Across the room, rapid-fire quandary pelted my determination with conflict. Karmarov had helped me, but did that make him my friend? Tobias had saved me from death twice, but did that mean he'd hold back from killing me if I put myself between him and the vampire? No matter what the professor did for me tonight, the fact remained that he'd knowingly held a kidnapped woman in a dungeon for months while Cynthia performed who-knew-what diabolic experiments and rendered countless tortures on her. Who was I to deny Tobias the right to avenge the death of his mate? It was just, an act even my mother would likely give leave to.

All this didn't change, however, the two central truths that led to me reaching into my pocket to slide out the tranq dart I had very carefully put there. One, Tobias had been right; the vampires were up to something. Whatever that something was, it spread far beyond Cynthia and Karmarov. Any chance we might have to discover what the tapestry this very loose thread came from looked like might die with Karmarov. And two, if Tobias did succeed in killing the vampire, there was no guarantee that I wouldn't be next.

A streak of red sailed through the lab, pinning Tobias's hindquarter, drawing a yelp from the wolf. His maw rose, dropping Karmarov's arm, an appendage that now was a shredded, mangled collection of rent flesh and purple sinew, looked down his back, and then to me. With the gun still held out in front of me, there was no denying from where the shot had come. I saw confusion fill his eyes, betrayal. The emotions evident in his character hit me in the stomach as good as a fist. Leaving the vampire behind, the wolf rounded, a fearsom growl in my direction as he pulled limbs refusing to comply beneath him.

Karmarov stumbled to his feet, trying to push the torn bits of his arms still attached to the bone into some sort of submission. "Quick, Geri, leave! I'll take care of this."

Take care of this. Those four words confirmed in no uncertain terms that this project, whatever it was, didn't begin and end with this lab. Someone was going to hold Karmarov accountable. Someone was going to want to know what happened.

"What will you tell them about Cynthia?"

He pointed to Kara's body. "The prisoner was able to escape when her moon madness finally set in, and overpowered Cynthia."

I looked to the pile of fur and paws, the slow rise and fall of Tobias's chest. "And him?"

Prof. Karmarov shook his head. "I don't know. They knew we were trying to capture the mate who had followed Cynthia from England when she brought over Kara. I can just say that we were unsuccessful in apprehending him. It doesn't really matter, does it? I saw it in his eyes when he had me pinned. He's on the edge of losing his humanity. Come sunrise, he'll stay trapped in his wolf form. Sooner or later, one of your kind will come for him. If there is a god and mercy still in this world, it will be sooner."

"So what, we just let him go, more animal than man, in a city full of people? You don't know wolves like I do, professor. His instinct will drive him to seek out a remote place. Between here and where that ends up being, however, will be thousands of people. Anyone he perceives to be the slightest threat, he'll kill."

The professor squared his jaw. "The only other alternative is that either you or I kill him first. There's no need for you to have more blood on your hands. I'll do it."

Desperation made my actions bold and movements swift. "Don't!" I bellowed, surprising myself as much as Karmarov with my strength as I jerked him back. "There's another solution."

"I don't encourage keeping a lupified werewolf in the dungeon."

"Not that either. There's a chance that I can still save him from going permanently moon mad. Professor, you saved my life tonight. I still don't understand why. If I leave for twenty minutes, can I trust that no harm will come to this werewolf?"

"Why, what are you going to do with him?"

I shook my head. "I'm still not sure if I can trust you. But if I come back and Tobias is unharmed, then I know I can start trying."

The vampire's eyebrow arched. "And what if you come back to find him dead?"

"Then it will be no worse fate for him."

Karmarov's cold corpse fingers sent a chill through me when they landed on my shoulder, squeezing gently. "I will do him no harm. You have my word. Now go, do whatever you need to do. As for Kara, I will put her in the morgue below. If you're able to save her mate, he can bury her properly when he's ready."

"Thank you, Professor."

"It's the least I can do, Miss Kline."

Amy glared at me, totally unimpressed by my sudden presence.

"So you finally stopped smooching up Jess long enough to come home and change your clothes, huh?"

"What?"

My blonde roommate stretched across the kitchen counter, taking her phone out of her purse. After a few flicks of her screen, she read aloud, "'Amy – OMG, finally happened with Jess. I'll be staying at his place for a while. Text me if you need anything. P.S. He was really, really good.'"

A wave of disgust filled me, and I slammed the door.

Amy's spine straightened. "So I take it that it didn't end well."

"I didn't sleep with Jess," I declared as I peeled off my shirt and headed for my closet. "He stole my phone."

And knocked me out. And took me prisoner on behalf of his vampire master.

"We broke up." It was as close to the truth as I was willing to take her.

Amy's voice was lined with suspicion. "So, then, where have you been for the last three days?"

What was I going to say? It wasn't like I could tell her the truth. With Cynthia dead, I didn't think that Amy would be in any immediate danger. Sure, Karmarov might still turn out to be playing me, but even if that was true, that meant that, for the moment, he wasn't about to strike out against my roommate and risk losing my trust. If Tobias was still alive when I got back to the lab, then I had zero doubt Amy would be safe while I was gone.

It felt like a layer of my skin came off with my bra. God, I wish I had time for a shower. Amy didn't bat an eyelash at seeing me half-naked. She'd learned very early on that I didn't consider nudity that big of a deal.

"I was with, um…"

Suddenly, her face exploded into a grin. "Oh, my god. You were with him, weren't you? The guy from the alley?"

Sure, why not. "Yup, you caught me."

"So you did lose your v-card?"

I slithered into a white t-shirt and some cargo pants. "I still don't know why that concerns you so much, but no."

Braiding my hair, I managed to dive into the bathroom and out of her sight long enough to weave my grandmother's silver blade into a newly tied braid.

"Then, what were you doing for the last three days with him?"

"Comforting him. His wife died."

"His wife? Whoa, you mean he's married?"

"Not anymore." I grabbed a rucksack out of my closet. The weapons within clanked and pinged as metal and wire jingled. "Amy, I'm going to be gone a few days. If anyone comes here looking for me, just say I'm away at a concert or something, okay? The last few days were really stressful. I need to go offline and relax."

"You sure nothing's wrong, Geri? You're acting really strange."

"I'm sure. Once I get where I'm going, I'll see if I can cancel out my old phone and get a new number. Once I do, I'll let you know what it is."

When the doors opened into the lab, a tightness that I'd refused to acknowledge melted. Tobias's wolf, sitting in the middle of the floor, breathed easy. If not for the destruction still evident around him, no one would be the wiser than anything was out of place.

Well, other than a werewolf sleeping in the middle of a science lab.

Karmarov's eyes found me across the room. He sat on the floor, back to the wall, with his legs out in front of him. His black hair with gray outbursts remained disheveled, and a certain weariness in his eyes made me wonder how much the events of this evening had taken out of him.

Stepping into the lab, I let the bag at my side fall to the floor. "Jess?"

"I woke him up long enough to place him under my thrall. Towards morning, I'll have him move out to one of the benches in the college courtyard and change his memories. He'll think he went to a frat party and drank too much. The last few months, just mundane memories of scanning slides. The fact that they were samples of slayers would be an inconvenient truth for him to recall."

I swallowed. "And what will he remember about me?"

Karmarov's eyes narrowed. "It wasn't entirely fake, you know. Yes, he may have been acting on Cynthia's orders to cozy up to you, but the man I saw with you isn't too different from the man he'd actually be without her control. In fact, I could make him believe he's in love with you. You'd practically have yourself a devoted slave."

A bittersweet sting hit the back of my throat. Would the fact that Jess's feelings were nothing more than subterfuge change the feelings I had grown to have for him? After all I had been through the last few days, wouldn't it be worth it to have Karmarov do the very thing he offered to do, just so I could have the satisfaction of engineering a very embarrassing, public break-up?

But when I looked to Tobias and remembered what he'd gone through to try and save his mate, I knew my answer. I wouldn't make a mockery of real love that way.

"It's better that he forgets everything about me. I've betrayed my family secrets too much as it is." I turned to Tobias. "Can you help? I pulled my truck up to the receiving dock downstairs. I don't think I'm strong enough to carry him all on my own."

A smile bloomed on Karmarov's face. "Of course." Without the slightest bit of struggle, the vampire stood, crossed to the slumbering werewolf, and scooped him up. "If I can ask, Miss Kline, if your plan fails, will you kill him yourself?"

I shook my head. "I'm not allowed to kill a wolf without the leave of the matron in whose region it is. Plus, I don't think I'm capable. I'm still a nascent."

"No, Miss Kline. You are so much more than that. More than you understand. Perhaps, more than I understand."

As the elevator doors closed us in, my voice became so much smaller than my confidence. "When I come back to Chicago in a few days, will you tell me what you mean by that?"

"No, all I have are theories, and misinforming you could have tragic consequences. But I promise you, if the evidence ever makes itself clear, I will not hesitate."

TWENTY-NINE

Night, black and beautiful and a salve to my nerves, enveloped us all the way along the Lake Michigan coast. I recalled with envy who I'd been when I'd been a southbound traveler along this same route just eight months ago. That Geri bubbled with anticipation, fizzed with pride at having finally escaped her destiny and her calling. The person I was now bore the shame of that nearsighted optimism. I kept thinking back to the confusion evident on Tobias's face, confusion that reflected my own at the inability to sense the presence of his mate. Had I listened to my mother and taken my rites, would my abilities have been heightened so much that I might have picked up on the fact Kara was imprisoned a few floors below Karmarov's lab? Brünhild had been right about my ability to lure wolves – at least, given how it now seemed clear that I had done just that with Tobias, drawing him to the very heart of the Browning building when Kara and I needed him most, what could I have done with the full scope of my abilities unleashed?

Otherwise deserted roads were dotted at intervals with truckers and the occasional minivan. Outside of Gaylord, I stopped to gas up. After grabbing an anemic-looking ham sandwich from the cooler, I pulled off into the shadows of the parking lot. In the bed of my truck, covered by a tarp, Tobias looked more like a bear I'd bagged and loaded up instead of the massive red wolf he was. Karmarov said the tranq should keep him down the entire trip, but he didn't know werewolves like I did. Open brown eyes met mine. If he could do more than eye me, he made no attempt. Not that I expected it. The body may have survived, but Tobias's soul was DOA. He'd probably hate me for what I was about to attempt, but I couldn't not try. I pulled the syringe from the glove compartment and gave Tobias just enough of a dose for him to sleep off the last few hours.

Not too much. When we got where we were going, I'd need him awake.

But more than that, I'd need to hope that Cody's father would hear me out.

Once we passed the forty-fifth parallel, speed limits became mere suggestions. The blue glow of the clock dash affirmed what I could already feel instinctively; we were running out of time. Inside, I could feel the pull of the moon towards the horizon, despite the fact that a frigid mist and clouded sky greeted us as we crossed Big Mac and touched down in the Upper Peninsula. By the time the highway devolved from the eight-lane monster at the bridge, to the two-lane country road dotted at intervals with potholes and roadkill, I had officially entered panic mode. What was I going to do if I didn't make it? What would I do with a moon mad, permanently lupified werewolf once we got to Paradise?

I didn't have to wonder. The moment my mother found out that Tobias was on her turf – and she would find out – he was a dead wolf walking.

A faint glow of pink already tickled the horizon when I pulled into the Paradise Pack commune, and with it, another realization. Holy shit, what was I doing going into pack territory on a full moon? Just because an alpha maintained the ability to shift back to his human form during a night such as this didn't change the fact that the other wolves couldn't. A nascent hood wandering into a pack of inebriated animals? Stupid. Doing that while dragging a strange wolf into very claimed and established territory? Potentially suicidal.

But as I slammed the car door, leaving the headlights on to provide illumination to the landscape before me, I could hear a few dozen wolves just beyond the forest's edge, gathered close to see what idiot had come into their territory on a full moon. It didn't take long for the first of them to emerge from the forest. No doubt they had heard a car approach, but whether or not they recognized it as mine, I couldn't say. Once, my rust-kissed truck had been a common sight in this area. I stopped by on my way home from work three or four times a week. The Paradise Pack had every right to hate me; I was the daughter of the hood matron who controlled their region with fire and ice. But to them, I'd always just been little Geri Kline, Cody's girlfriend.

A grey-and-black-pelted wolf with deep black eyes made no sound as he trotted toward me. About ten feet away, he stopped, cocked his head, and let out one gentle yip.

"Rick!" I dropped to my knees, forgetting all trepidation. Any tension I still felt eased when the pack's beta nestled up to me and placed his maw on my shoulder, the werewolf-to-human version of a hug. I pulled back and held his head in my hands. "Rick, where's Mr. Ryland? I need to talk to him. Like, man-to-man talk, and it can't wait for sunrise."

Rick turned his head to the edge of the forest, where the silhouette of another pack member shifted from animal to human. At first, the muscular frame and youthful features threw me for a loop. Werewolves did tend to age well, but Cody's dad was in his mid-sixties. Even for a supernatural creature, the alpha's appearance challenged my memory. As the figure stepped into the direct beams of my truck's headlights, however, the understanding of who stood before me sent me scuttling back.

"Cody?"

I had often pictured what it would be like to see my ex-boyfriend again after the way things had ended between us, with him telling me he wanted me to be happy, and me knowing that, having lost him to a she-wolf with whom he'd been his father to bond, I probably never would be. In those visions, I'd never pictured myself shrinking back, scared of his hostility, of his anger. The Cody who fixed me in his acidic glare now didn't want happiness for me; he wanted me dead.

As though picking up on the vibe flowing between us, Rick rounded on all fours, a droning, warning growl rumbling in his chest. At least I still had the beta's affections, even if my ex apparently wanted to kill me.

A scowling Cody turned to his uncle. "I'm not going to hurt her, Rick! Back yourself down."

I did a double take as I watched the beta whimper, his ears falling back over his head. Suddenly, the truth of why Cody was able to shift back to his human form became painfully clear.

"Your dad?"

His brow flinched. "Ask your mother."

"I try to avoid her at all costs." I didn't know what I expected by admitting it. Would he think I was disavowing my family, my clan, my kind? How would that change the way Cody saw me? Did it matter? "I'm so sorry, Cody. I didn't know."

"Yeah, well when you left, you made sure to do it completely, didn't you?"

Such disdain, such bitterness.

"What do you want, Geri?" he asked, getting to the point. "And why do you have an unconscious wolf in the bed of your truck?"

Right, stay focused. Given how much contained anger rolled off of Cody, taking my chances he wouldn't order me chased off the land or even worse, hunted down, might be stupid. I rounded to the back of the truck and untied the ropes holding down the tarp.

"This is Tobias Somfield. He's a lone wolf, turned away from his pack in northern England. His mate was kidnapped three months ago. He's been in Chicago since then, looking for her."

"Three months?" Cody asked, his muscles uncoiling themselves as his arms fell to the side. "Is he…"

"He was showing signs of lunacity before the moon pushed him into his wolf last night," I confirmed. "I came here because you're his last hope. If he's still without a pack when the sun rises, he's likely trapped forever, and we both know what that means."

Cody turned to the lightening sky. "But that's just minutes away."

"Which doesn't give you long to make this decision," I said, pulling off the tarp. "If you don't accept him, and given that I've brought him into my mother's territory, it's likely she'll order his execution as soon as she discovers he's here.

I want you to know, however, that I will assume full blame. If she orders his death, I will give it to him mercifully."

The Paradise Pack alpha took turns examining the wolf in question, and me for signs of insanity. "You said he came looking for his mate. Did he find her?"

I nodded. "Yes. Unfortunately, it was too late. She died last night."

I could fill out the details later.

Behind us, Rick leapt lithely into the bed of my truck and nosed Tobias. A moment later, the wolf bared his teeth, huffing. Though I was adept at reading the general context of wolf communication, I couldn't grasp a word-to-word conversation the way a real pack member could. Whatever Rick said to Cody, the latter's temper flared again.

"Why does he smell like vampires?"

No. I was absolutely not going to open up that conversation when Tobias literally had minutes between him and lunacity. "Accept him in this pack, and I'll tell you everything. Cody, the sun's going to rise any minute. Whatever your feelings for me, whatever my mother has done to you, you know me. Last night, Tobias lost the single most important person in the world to him. I know what that feels like. Please, don't make him lose whatever humanity he can hope to have after enduring that too."

My words hit him between the eyebrows. Cody's forehead wrinkled. He wasn't to blame for what had happened between us, just as I wasn't to blame for what did. Still, some small sliver of guilt must have remained. I only prayed now it was a big enough piece to wedge its way into his sense of compassion.

"Fine," he huffed after a few moments. "But you know how this works. I can't just decide he's mine and that's that. He has to accept me. He has to acknowledge me as his alpha, and given that he's passed out—"

I dashed to the glove compartment before Cody could even get through the rest of the sentence. The second shot that Karmarov had provided me lay within, a drug he promised me I should administer only if I wanted Tobias "to go from unconscious to ready to run a marathon in ten seconds flat." He also advised me that I should probably stand clear of the werewolf the second the drug was administered, for my own safety. As I plunged the needle into Tobias's shoulder, however, ten seconds became two.

The English wolf leapt to all fours without time for me to even jump down, throwing me from the back of the truck. Rick took guard over me as Tobias, confused and lackadaisical, fixed me in his sight, his maw wet with saliva, his hackles raised.

I couldn't comprehend the eruption of fur before me. In the time it took me to blink twice, Cody had shifted back to his wolf, throwing the red wolf off balance, knocking him to the ground. Fear and fangs vied for power, but Tobias was no match for the alpha. They'd barely begun when Tobias yelped, letting himself be pinned to the ground just as the first rays of dawn cut through the unfurling canopy of spring above.

I gasped when rough hands and strong arms surrounded me, caging me from behind. My nerves frayed, my patience shot, my instincts cried out to fight. But when the familiar scent reached me, and I understood who held me from behind, all vigor evaporated.

Rick Ryland's voice was a calming salve. "I hope this isn't too awkward, given that I'm naked and everything, but damn it, kid, I was worried about you."

I couldn't help but let out a small laugh. "I'm trying to ignore that fact."

Seeing wolves naked was one thing. Feeling one brush up against me from behind, even if he was practically like family, was a whole different basket of fish.

Rick backed away, tapping me on the shoulders. "Come on, then. Cody's going to need a little time with this pup to get him properly obedient."

THIRTY

My soul felt as warm as the cocoa in the mug Rick gave me as I sat at his kitchen table. "So Tobias accepted Cody as his alpha?"

"After a few four-lettered words, yes." He took a seat across from me, sipping from his own mug of something that smelled suspiciously of whiskey. Since he'd done me the courtesy of putting on some sweatpants and a flannel, I decided not to call him on it. "Colorful language your new wolf has."

"He's not my wolf. He's not my anything."

"And yet, you drove him hundreds of miles in the dead of night to make sure he didn't go moon mad." The beta side-eyed me. "You know most hoods would have just waited for the sunrise then killed him at dawn, don't you? Your mother would be so ashamed if she found out you actually gave a damn about one of us."

"Rick Ryland, you do say the sweetest things."

The door to the garage opened behind me, and I knew who it was just from the look on Rick's face. A beta demurred to no one except his alpha. The way Cody's uncle popped up to his feet and offered his chair like the Queen had just walked in meant it could be no one else. The alpha swiveled the chair, straddling it as he lumbered down. Gone was the anger, filled in around the edges by equal parts resolve and sadness.

"He's taken to the pack," Cody declared. "A few moments more and he would have been gone. I'm still worried. Parts of his humanity may have slipped away, or it could just be that he's in mourning and that's why his mind is so distant. The sadness he feels over losing Kara, it's so palpable, Geri. I don't know if I've done him a favor or not, taking him in."

That Cody knew Kara's name should have surprised me, but it didn't. No doubt Tobias cried it out in his struggles. "You have, Cody, and I can't tell you how much I appreciate it." Without realizing my own actions, I reached across the table. The old familiar thrill ran through me when my hand landed on his, the feeling of possession and pride that I'd reveled in for years when Cody had been mine. Now, however, that feeling carried with it a sense of bitter poison, as though I'd gotten to the front of a long line but only by taking cuts. I pulled back, burying my hands in my lap beneath the table. "I couldn't bring myself to let him go. Not when I knew your dad... you might take him in."

"My dad would have accepted him, too, Geri. He would have done it because you'd be the one to ask him. He loved you. Despite the fact that you're a hood, you were like his own daughter."

A cacophony of unspoken words filled the air between us. The hows, whys, and why nots filled pages of dialogue. Finally, I swallowed hard, and pulled the one written in the boldest font out of the air.

"What happened? Did my mom really do it?"

"Yes! No... I'm not... We're not sure." He ran a hand through his spiky brown hair. "I shouldn't have said that. It's just... Shit, Geri, I'm pissed at you is why. You just upped and left like a fart in the wind. Even if we broke up, you're still my friend. Or at least, I thought we were."

No one had ever labeled Cody as an elegant speaker, but I'd forgotten how he could cut right to the chase in a blink. Probably helped make him a good alpha, frankly.

"I'm sorry, but in my defense, the last time I saw you it was the morning after you mated Lisa, which was also the morning after you asked me to marry you, so..."

"Did you think I was lying when I told you that you were still my best friend?" The pain in his heart became water in his eyes. "You know I had no control over the decision to mate with Lisa. And then when my dad died... You loved my dad almost like you really were his daughter. I expected more of you."

Unanswered phone calls from my father weighed heavy on my mind. Papi had never been a fan of texting, and my voice mail had long ago filled up with his attempts to talk me into returning home.

"I didn't know. If I had… But that's no excuse, Cody. You're right. I should have at least talked to Rick, or even my cousin Markus. I'm sorry. I'm so incredibly sorry, and soon I want to take the proper time to sing his song at the moon."

The corner of Cody's mouth quirked when I'd offered to perform a werewolf mourning rite. "You're not a wolf, Geri."

I kicked him under the table, reviving a tiny bit of our old camaraderie. "Hey, aren't you the one who said I was like his daughter? I might not hit all the right notes. Hell, I might even accidentally yelp some four-lettered words in Lupinese, but I'll remember him in the way he would have wanted. Now—" I leaned forward, folding my hands and placing them on the table. "My mom. Do you really think she might have had something to do with what happened?"

"Your mom keeps such a tight leash on everything, it's hard to imagine something happening that Brünhild Kline doesn't know about. Dad disappeared right before Easter. Your mom said as long as he wasn't posing a danger to himself or others, it wasn't any of her concern. That was six weeks ago. Three weeks ago we… We know when an alpha or our mates die, Geri. I can't explain it, it's instinct somehow. We knew he was gone, and I took his place as alpha."

"I should have been here." I already loathed the fact that Kara's blood was on my hands. Now did I have to accept Mr. Ryland's too?

"What would you have been able to do?" Cody asked. "I can't even say something went wrong. Maybe he had a heart attack out in the woods somewhere. Maybe he got caught by a poacher. Maybe he went out fishing alone on Superior and got caught in a storm."

"And maybe what happened to him is the same thing that happened to Tobias's mate," I interjected.

That stopped Cody dead. "So what happened? He won't talk about it. Can't blame him. It's still too fresh."

"Some vamps are running genetic experiments. I don't know exactly why, but they're altering wolf DNA."

"Vamps?" Cody leaned back in his seat, crossing his meaty arms over his chest. "Not good. But we haven't picked up on any scent around here that would suggest vampires have been traipsing about the woods."

A long screech and the knock of wood on wood drew both our attentions. I looked over Cody's shoulder to see Tobias, looking the most ragged I had ever seen him, come through the door. He wiped a dirty hand over an oily face and stopped short when he saw Cody at the table.

"Alpha," he said, growing smaller where he stood. "Apologies, I was looking for the hood. Beta told me she was in here."

My ex-boyfriend stood, vacating the chair and motioning for the newest member of his pack to take a seat. "I don't know how things operated in your old pack, Tobias, but in this one, we're family. You call me Cody, and my uncle's name is Rick. You go around giving him a superiority complex, I'm worried you'll have to settle up with Aunt Kathy."

Tobias became the very model of obeisance, a coat that, as the beta of his old pack, I was sure he didn't feel fit him. "Yes, Alpha. I mean… Cody." His eyes flashed to me, then back to the floor. "Can I speak with the hood?"

Cody looked to me for acknowledgment, asking my permission with his eyes. I gave him a silent nod.

"Her name is Geri. And while she's a hood, and not pack…" Warmth filled his expression, pouring out of him and into me. "… she's as close as you can get. Don't go giving her any titles, either. She's already carrying around one that bogs her down enough as it is. Geri—" Cody leaned over, putting a hand on my shoulder. "—I'm going to be right outside the door listening. You feel in any danger at any point, you just say our old catch phrase, okay?"

Tobias eased once Cody left the room, but the old determination that had once made every movement of his bold and purposeful had left him. His body surrendered to the seat, dropping like a bag of flour. He steepled his hands and leaned into a prayer pose. I gave him room, both physically and emotionally, sitting back in my chair and waiting for him to talk first.

Finally, it came out. "Why didn't you just kill me?"

I labored to keep my tone even. "Because that's not who I am."

"That's exactly who you are. You're a hood. Hell, if you'd let me make it to sunrise, I couldn't have even held it against you. I was on the edge, I felt it. But you've pulled me back to live like this." His hands reached out in either direction, motioning broadly to the modest kitchen with mustard yellow counters and pea green synthetic floors. "In a foreign land, with a pack I don't know, without the mate whom I love. You don't know what it feels like, Kline, to lose the one whose life gave yours purpose."

Beyond the screen door, Cody half-turned his head, looking over his shoulder.

"I know a little bit about how that feels." I swallowed down my memories. "Listen, Tobias, I can't pretend to understand fully what you've gone through, but if nothing else comes out of it, know this: you were right. There is a group of vampires, and they are up to something. What it is exactly, I don't know yet. But with your help, I'd like to find out."

"My help?" The bitterness in his voice poisoned the sarcastic laugh he let out. "Why should I help, when I repeatedly came to you, only to be turned away? I saved your life twice, and the most I got from you in return was 'sorry,

I know I'm technically a hood, but I don't actually want to be a hood, so you're on your own.'"

His sharp words hit their mark, making my insides squirm as my sense of righteousness attempted to claw its way out of a slew of guilt. "You're right. I have no right to ask for your help, and even less to expect it. But in that case, let me help you, Tobias. Kara was murdered. Let me help you avenge her."

"I don't believe in all that life-for-a-life bollocks."

"No, then what about two lives?" When he just stared blankly at me, I grew a pair of my own bollocks and told him the truth. "When I was in the dungeon of Browning Hall, Cynthia showed me the body of another wolf. She said it was the alpha of a pack from England. That, combined with the fact that you're his spitting image, would suggest to me she's the one who killed your brother."

His face cycled through a slew of emotions: surprise, frustration, confusion, anger, and then confusion again. "But Cynthia is already dead. You killed her, I remember that. Other than Karmarov, there is no one else to hold accountable for what happened to my brother and Kara."

"I think Karmarov is on our side," I said. "He saved my life. He could have killed you easy, and he didn't. And while I'm not exactly forgetting that he helped throw both your mate and me in a dungeon, we need his help. There's something bigger going on here. Something that goes beyond my college campus and a few vampires in Chicago. What we need to do is find out who they are and exactly what they're up to. And then, once we know that, we can hold every one of them to the fire. Until we do that, every wolf is a possible target for their experimentation."

"You're talking like a hood. Like a real hood, one who actually wants to protect us rather than kill us. I thought you had no interest in your birthright?"

"I don't. But I got blood on my hands now. Kara's blood. If I had listened to you, I might have been able to save her. If I don't listen to the voice in my head telling me now that this is nowhere near over, who knows how many more will die? But I'm still a nascent. I don't have the strength or the skills to go this alone. I need your help."

Tobias leaned back in his chair, contemplation in his gaze. "I'd need permission of my alpha."

"Done!" Cody shouted out from outside with such ferocity, we both flinched.

Tobias lowered his voice. Why, I'm sure he couldn't say. He'd have to know that Cody would still be able to hear us. "He accepted me in his pack, but I have to wonder why. He seems eager to get rid of me."

"It has nothing to do with you," Cody said, forgoing all illusions of privacy and coming back in through the screen door. "Until Geri takes her rites, she hasn't a chance against a wolf that really wants to do her harm. I doubt she'd do much better against a vamp. Once upon a time, before hoods and slayers, there was just us and them. We were the vamps' balance. Maybe it's time we try that out again."

An invisible ball of awkwardness bounced on the table between us. Lucky for me, Tobias wasn't about to correct his new alpha in front of company, and I wasn't about to give the FYI to my ex-boyfriend that validated his – well, alpha male attitude.

"I swear to you, Cody, I will protect her with my life." Then, under his breath, he added, "Again."

Cody let the jibe go and turned to me. "Geri, once he gets rested up, he's all yours. But he's been through a lot and he's in mourning. He needs a little time. Can you wait to go back?"

I shook my head. "I'm still worried for my roommate. She's a Huey, but this whole mess first started when a vamp tried to pick her up in a bar. It could have been coincidence, but I'm not sure. I need to make sure she's okay. Plus, I have final exams in a few weeks, and I haven't studied at all yet."

"Still bound and determined to do the college thing, then." The alpha grinned. "Good. If you just upped and gave up because you had lone wolves and vampires after you, you just wouldn't be my Geri."

I bit my tongue, reminding him that, as a wolf mated to another wolf, I wasn't his anything anymore.

"You can't go back alone, though. Take Kimmy."

My eyes went wide. "WHAT?"

This time, it was the alpha who flinched. "Come on, Kim's great. She's been wanting to get away for a while. If you think your roommate wouldn't care if you had a houseguest, that is."

"But she's so..." Loud. Awkward. Rambunctious. Muscular. Cody's cousin on his mother's side remained the only girl in the history of our high school football team to get the MVP trophy. "Kim."

Cody considered that a moment before making a counteroffer. "If you prefer, I can send Lisa. But I warn you, you're not exactly her favorite person."

"No, Kim will be fine." Much better than your mate. "I'm sure Amy won't mind a bit. And if I tell her that Kim and I are dating, she might even insist she move in."

RELINQUISHED

RED CHRONICLES
BOOK 2

THE SEVEN RAVENS

Though his heart ached for a daughter, Fortune blessed the king with seven sons. Until, at long last, the family welcomed a girl. But the infant's constitution was weak, so much so that the king feared his daughter should pass from this world before provisions were made for her soul. He therefore hastened to have her baptized.

The king sent his seven sons to fetch the water necessary. Each wanted to be the hero in their father's eyes, and so they fought over who should lower the bucket into the well. In the melee, the bucket fell in. The brothers then fretted over the king's reaction should they return without that for which they had been dispatched.

After several hours, the king grew impatient, and called out in his anger, "Such godless sons as have I! They have forgotten their task and taken to revels, feckless and unworried for their sister's fate. Fie upon them all! Would that Fortune would make them ravens, that they may caw about the land as the heathen progeny that they have grown to be!"

Fortune shared his anger, for she perceived as did the king. Hardly had the curse fallen from his mouth than she breathed life into his words. The brothers' flesh rippled with feathers, and seven birds flew from the well.

The king regretted his hasty curse, but knew Fortune had done only as asked. He was to blame for his sons' fates. When the king admitted his guilt to Fortune, however, she too regretted her hastiness. To relieve their common suffering, she ensured that the little princess grew strong in both beauty and kindness.

The princess knew not her father's mistake, nor the fate of her brothers, until one day, while walking near the very well where the folly had occurred, she chanced upon an old woman who pointed her long, bony finger. "Woe, maiden, for though thou art tall and lovely, your beauty and breath came at such a price! Seven ravens have you for brothers, and they flew from the hearth of your father, discarded and forlorn."

The princess had known that once she had these siblings, but the king grew sad whenever she had asked of their fate, and so she had stopped asking. Now, guilt sprouted in her heart, and she decided that she must find her brothers, break their curse, and unite her family once more.

She left by night, hidden by the mists, taking only that needed for her journey: her gray cloak, her satchel, and a tiny dagger, given to her by her father, to prepare what food she may find along the way. She walked east, until she came to the very precipice of the sunrise. The sun, careless and distant, burned her flesh. She knew her brothers could not be where neither she could go.

Next, she journeyed west, until she came upon the great moon in its sky. The children of the moon crawled and uncurled from a forest basked in light. "We smell flesh," they said, licking maws. "Flesh, which smells to us like prey."

Frightened of the moon children, she ran away, to the land which sat in darkness, between the moon and the sun, where only the stars could see her. Here, she found a cave blocked by a glass door, and a key made of bone. But when she tried to use the key, it vanished into air. The keyhole looked familiar, and thinking what a waste it would be to come so far and be stopped by nothing more than a lock, she took a dagger from her belt to slice off her own little finger.

The door swung open. The child she found inside asked after her quest.

"I come seeking the ravens," she said.

"Fortune has led you here," the boy said, "for this is where they dwell. They have taken to their hunt at present, milady, cloaked by the darkness so none may see their shame. Come into the hall, sit at the table, while I am about my business."

The child set out seven silver plates filled with meat, and beside each plate, a golden goblet filled with red wine. For many hours, the daughter sat waiting, her eyes growing hungry with the meal displayed before her. At last, her hunger overcame her. She put the dagger down on the table, before taking one bite from each plate, and a single sip from the vessel beside it.

No sooner had she partaken of the seventh goblet than a great wind swirled in the cave, and seven shadows came through the door. Frightened, the daughter hid behind a rock, even as each of the birds took a place at the table.

"*Caw!* Who has – *caw!* – been eating at our – *caw!* – table?" one asked.

Another said, "This bite is that of a – *caw!* – human."

The biggest of the ravens cried out, "Look, it is Father's dagger, but was it not Father who cursed us? Surely he is not here. How, then, came it to be here? Would that it was our sister, so that we know we suffer our fates that she had lived."

The princess, knowing that her brothers held still love in their hearts, revealed herself. "It is I, come to free you from your curse, and unite our family once more, if Fortune grants it."

The little boy smiled, and in a sigh, took on his true form, Fortune. "Use your father's dagger," she said, "and into each cup and on to each plate, place a drop of your blood. If your brothers then partake of your offering, and if they have repented, I will again make them flesh, and I will make it known to your father that his legacy has been restored."

It was done, and so as Fortune promised, soon the seven brothers stood by their precious sister once more. They made their way back through the land of the darkness, where upon they came to the King's castle.

The brothers charged the gate, and within found their father. The King shed tears upon seeing his sons return, made men once more. He opened his arms to welcome them, whereupon they each in turn fell upon him, growing beaks which they used to rend the flesh from his body. Into the night, they chewed long upon the marrow of his bones, tasting the bitterness of their vengeance, until at last, their eyes fell upon the princess. They forced her to consume their father's heart, whereupon she threw her head back and screamed. But her screams faded, as did her flesh, and soon, where the princess had stood, remained only a single raven.

ONE

In the past month, I'd thoroughly kicked the asses of a pseudo-slayer and a bitch of a vampire. But today, *my* ass had been kicked.

By an Organic Chemistry final.

"I swear to God, I'm never going to need to know so much about carbonyl compounds, like, ever." I let gravity pull me back into the cushy confines of the overstuffed armchair.

Bubbly and blonde, Amy Popowitz, my fearless roommate and only close friend in Chicago, rounded the kitchen island, poking a spoon into a bowl of bulbous black orbs. "Told you Org Chem was Satan's Bitch."

Amy was the type of girl you'd swear was all about sales at Saks and rating the best mani-pedis along Michigan Avenue, while secretly being the smartest person in the room. At least, book smart. When it came to relationships, she flunked every subject, dating a parade of losers that made the Chicago City Council look like angels. She'd just broken up with her latest flavor, Victor, the week before finals, when he'd dared study for his architecture exam instead of her own flying buttresses.

I hitched my head up. "Is that why they say the Devil smells like sulfur?"

"Do they say that?" A stream of whatever gluten free, organic, no soy chia seed sludge she'd learned from Gwyneth Paltrow this week dribbled from her mouth. "I thought it was brimstone."

"It *is* brimstone. Brimstone is sulfur. You seriously didn't know that?"

Her face drooped. "What, I'm supposed to be smart about religion now, too?"

A *clomp, clomp, clomp* preceded Kim into the room, bringing a scowl to Amy's face and a smile to mine. I had to admit, Cody's cousin had grown on me. Once you got over the fact that her combat boots only came off when she laid down to bed each morning, Kim drew you in with her unabashed refusal to be anyone other than herself.

In Amy's eyes, this was also Kim's worst flaw.

"Geri, I thought I heard you come in."

An obviously fake and overly accentuated wink pumped up the level of awkward in the room. Kim was a werewolf, and I was a hood. She sensed me as soon as I got out of the elevator, just as I had picked up on her vibe from down the block. Amy knew that Kim and I were keeping something secret from her. Given that the shewolf only appeared to my roomie as a very butch woman who slept in my room all day and could drink her under the table every night, however, Amy had newborn suspicions on why I wasn't as interested in men as she thought I should be.

"How did the last final go?" Kim asked.

"It went, and for the moment, that's all I care about."

"She aced it. That's what Geri does with all her exams." Amy's confident comment could have been sincere, or, as I suspected was actually the case, was an attempt to win me back from Kim. For a huey, my roomie threw out more territorial markers than a new alpha.

Luckily, diplomacy was a skill wolves cultivated from childhood. Otherwise, they'd be in constant honor battles to the death.

Kim's grin stretched wide, pride beaming. "Geri's always been great in school. She was our valedictorian, you know? And Cody was the salutatorian. It was so cute when they got up to give their speeches and they kissed instead of shook hands."

A PDA that almost set my mother on the prowl, if I hadn't convinced her the Paradise Pack's son had done it deliberately to piss her off.

Amy's eyes went wide as the bowl clanked unceremoniously to the tiled counter. "She kissed a *boy* in front of a whole crowd of people?"

The shewolf grinned at her superior knowledge of my past. "They *had* just started dating at the time. And 'crowd' might be an exaggeration. If I remember right, they were the only graduating students that year. Our entire school had less than fifty students all together."

"Boyfriend?" My roommate examined me with the eyes of a stranger. "There was a boyfriend? How could you not mention a boyfriend?"

I squirmed, wishing one of the powers in the hood catalogue was the ability to turn back time and keep werewolves from blabbing. "We broke up right before I moved to Chicago. I wasn't trying to hide it from you. It's just…"

Understanding filled Amy's eyes. Her expression softened. "Oh, Geri. I'm sorry. I didn't mean to dredge up something painful. But, now that I know, it totally makes sense why my tactics haven't been working. Here I thought you were all innocent and shy, but you just had a broken heart. I bet he's a bastard. I bet he's sorry every day that he lost you, and he can suck on it, for all I care. He doesn't deserve you."

Thank goodness the low rumble coming from Kim across the room was drowned out by the passing of the El-Train a block away. I shot to my feet and pushed five fingers into the shewolf's chest, hoping to make her realize she was taking a defensive posture in front of a clueless, and over all well-intentioned, huey.

"It was nothing like that, Amy," I interjected, reining in Kim's hackles. "Our relationship just ran its course is all. He's actually a really good guy who is still a friend. And FYI, he's also Kim's cousin."

Amy's nose wrinkled. "It really is a small town up there, isn't it?"

I'd barely gotten out "When you sneeze, it makes the front page of the paper," when there was a knock at the door.

Kim shifted from emotionally defensive to cautiously territorial. Someone who had to knock on your door in Paradise was usually trying to sell you something, or serve you. Rarely, a bewildered fudgesucker might chance upon the packlands way out in the remotest part of our U.P. town, but it was rare and upset the pack for days afterward. Yet another reminder why werewolves were not well suited to city life.

I glared at Kim, gently pushed her tense form away from the door, and attempted to answer without a scene. A reed of a man wearing khakis, a navy jacket, and a brown ball cap stood on the other side. He blinked in rapid succession through coke-bottle glasses tinted pink, alternating his gaze between me and the monarch envelope in his hands.

"I'm looking for a Grrr… Grrr… *Walter* Kline?"

"Gerwalta," I corrected, offering out a hand. "That's me."

A clipboard I hadn't noticed tucked under the wing of his jacket swung in my direction, as did a pen pulled from his pocket. "Sign please?"

"Of course. Have you been asked to wait for a reply?"

No need to wonder who had sent a private courier. A quick read-through, and I folded the message and stuck it in my pocket. Just to be on the safe-bordering-on-conspiratorial side, I'd burn the letter later.

"Tell him I accept."

The courier nodded, tipping the bill of his cap. "Thank you, miss. I'll make sure he gets the message. Then, I guess…"

Thank god Amy could always be counted on to instruct us backwoods folks on the manners of mainstream civilization. She rounded me, holding out a bill of modest denomination. "You have to forgive her. She's not from around here."

"Thank you, miss." He accepted the tip and turned to leave, but not without giving me a reproving side eye.

I closed the door and racked up another debt I owed the New Yorker, and not just in terms of money. Amy served as my Obi Wan to the ways of living in the city.

"So pizza guys, waiters in sit-down restaurants, taxi cab drivers but not Uber drivers, and now delivery men?" I asked, checking my list of he-who-shall-be-tipped.

"Ones who bring hand-written correspondence? Yes. The Fedex guy? No. Unless he's cute, and then you use it to start a conversation that eventually leads to sex."

Kim chuffed. "Surprise, another pick-up-guys tip from Amy."

"What can I say? I like to receive big packages on my door step. Just because they're not one of your recreational activities…" Amy trailed off. "What did the note say, Geri? Anything wrong."

"Nothing wrong. Just a follow up on that research project I was working on earlier this term. The faculty who was running it wants to know if I can swing by tomorrow night and discuss my final report with him."

As good a cover as any, and not technically a lie. Not that I hadn't told Amy a few white lies since we'd met the previous fall. I wasn't about to explain to her, however, that the project I was working on had been a shill operation posing as research into identifying the slayer genome, but was actually some sort of prison where werewolves were being used as lab mice for reasons I had yet to understand. Moreover, I was so not going to tell Kim that either. Cody knew what had happened, and Kim had only been given vague instructions to "protect me from obvious threats" in Chicago without explanation. Pack didn't need reasons. If the alpha gave an order, they obeyed.

The shewolf bolted the front door. "I'm going to be going back home for a few days. If you don't feel like going there alone, you'll need to wait for me to come back."

Throwing the back of her hand against her forehead, Amy feigned care. "Oh, no! You have to leave? But we're having such a great time with you here!"

The werewolf didn't pick up on sarcasm easily. Kim, while a bit rough around the edges, was too kindly a soul to assume vindictiveness from tone. "Big family event I can't miss. I'll be back on Wednesday."

Karmarov's note suddenly seemed too well-timed. Since I'd come back from Michigan, he'd avoided me like the plague. I suspected it was for my own good, but I had to admit I was getting antsy. The job I took under him was supposed to transition into a summer internship with the sponsoring Chicago-based company. Now that I'd killed one of my coworkers and bashed another over the head with a toilet seat, I assumed the offer had been rescinded. Sending me this note right as the full moon grew nigh and my werewolf-slash-bodyguard would be heading out of town to run with her pack? Had Karmarov worried about being in my presence while I had a predator gifted with superhuman senses staying in my house? If Kim picked up on the scent of vampire on me, even operating only under Cody's vague orders, who knew how ugly and confused things might become?

The shewolf's hand on my shoulder roused me from my reverie.

"Come home, Geri. Have a little break now that your finals are done. Rick would be happy to put you up for a few days if you don't want to be at your folks' place."

Rick would put me up for any reason, or for none. Despite the fact that I was a hood and he the beta of the Paradise Pack, Cody's uncle was almost as close to me as my own father. Temptation to agree to Kim's proposal danced on the tip of my tongue, but I couldn't pass up a chance to talk with Karmarov. Since my internship wasn't to be, I'd have to head home soon enough, anyhow.

"I still have a few school things to wrap up first, but tell Rick that if my old job at the park is still open for the summer, I'd like to take him up on his offer. I'll need to save up some money to get me through the fall term."

Two

With a thud, my overburdened backpack found ground. No luck at the bookstore; turned out both my biochemistry and my genetics textbooks would have new editions next year, making my copies worthless. Well, not worthless, per se. Lots of knowledge in both those behemoths. What they lacked was market value, and if there was anything I needed right now, it was market value. The balance of my bank account resembled the floor indicator of an elevator plummeting toward the lobby level.

"As much as I appreciated the old-fashioned feel of a hand-delivered letter, I'll remind you that you do know my email address."

Karmarov kept his eye anchored to the end of a microscope. "Until your generation figures out how to hack ink and paper, I'll use it whenever possible."

"There are so many holes in that thinking, swiss cheese would be jealous."

My sarcastic quip was rewarded by a half smile from the vampire. "I don't like email. In my day, if something was important enough to write down, it was done with delicate penmanship, a sharp quill, fine linen paper, and sealing wax. Nowadays, hueys cut out half the letters from each word, constantly fire messages back and forth, and yet don't seem to communicate much at all. Sad. Did F. Scott Fitzgerald perfect the play of syntax and lexicon only for modern men to slice it as thin as stir fry ginger?"

"Fitzgerald? You seem more a *Beowulf* guy to me."

Karmarov huffed. "I'm not *that* old, Geri."

Pulling back from the microscope, he jerked his head at it, inviting me to look. I pressed my eye to the viewer and took in a cosmic starry sky balanced on the surface of a glass slide. It was a genetic sample, a small slice of bio material not unlike those I had been scanning into a machine earlier in the semester for the professor. The goal? Build a slayer genetic catalog, the first step in an attempt to resurrect the species.

"What am I looking at?"

He hesitated, then reached down to the base of the microscope, nudging the device with expert precision. Under the scope, the sample went from being inert, to dancing a salsa, almost as if the blood and tissue still was attempting to carry out its biological impetus.

I couldn't stop the gasp. "Whose is this?"

"Mine," he answered in a stoic tone. "But whose it is is not nearly as important as when it was taken. Ask me that question."

"Okay, when was it taken?"

"1968."

My back went rigid as I jerked myself up. "A sample taken from you fifty years ago is still alive?"

"Alive as I am. It shouldn't still be alive. It really shouldn't. I admit, it has me thrown for a loop." A coy smile brightened Karmarov's face. "Me calling myself alive is a bit of a misnomer, isn't it?"

"I suppose that's why we have the term 'undead.' You're clearly not alive in the traditional sense. You don't get sick. You don't age."

He crossed his arms and leaned back against one of the nearby lab tables, where a few months ago, Jess Harmond and I had worked side by side. "Life is a fatal disease, Geri, no matter how it's manipulated. It kills all of us in the end. Immortality is relative. As best as I've been able to deduce, what vampirism does is arrest the aging process in the soft tissues. Organs, flesh, hair. But in the bones, in the marrow, it—"

He trailed off when he caught me gawking.

"It's not relevant to our current predicament," Karmarov concluded, waving a hand vaguely through the air.

"Is it relative to what Cynthia was doing?" I asked.

Despite Igor betraying his own kind in helping me to kill Cynthia, he still hadn't been forthcoming about why he'd played along with her act for two days, all while I was held prisoner. Nor had he volunteered any further details of what she had actually been doing in his lab.

"Not in the least," he said. "And just so you know in no uncertain terms, the community in which Cynthia was operating isn't the same as the one I move in."

"So you know *who* she was working with?"

My hopes fell to the floor together with his downcast eyes. "I do and I don't. I accused her of certain associations, but I cannot be sure that she was actually acting directly with them, or only because of them. Until we're able to confirm that, I think it best, for your own safety, that I withhold that bit of information. Vampires are not fond of notoriety."

"Except Dracula," I chuffed.

Igor complemented with a laugh of his own as well. "Even he would tell you he'd have been much happier if Bram Stoker had never written the book, even it if is *mostly* wrong. As for this slide—" he tapped the microscope with his finger, "—I was curious is all. Think of it more like giving myself a health screening. Tell me, how is Mr. Somfield doing?"

"Last I heard from Paradise, not too good," I said, relaying the facts as best I could without letting my emotions bleed into my tone. "He's still in mourning, of course. It's a permanent state for a wolf that loses a mate. The bitterness and hopelessness fade, but they never shake the sorrow. It's with them constantly in the empty spaces between breathing in and breathing out. Add to that that he was forced to submit to a new alpha half a world from home, and that he's basically dependent on strangers for everything from food to a place to sleep to toilet paper, and he's in rough shape."

"When he has reached a place where he feels he can see to his dead, they are here waiting for him. I will make certain that any cost associated with a proper burial is mitigated."

"That could be a while. Professor——"

"Geri, call me Igor. Unnecessary huey honorifics annoy me."

"Okay, then, *Igor*. How is it that Tobias's brother ended up in Chicago?"

"When Cynthia showed up demanding lab space, she had his body with her in tow. I wanted nothing to do with her research, but I had to oblige. Politics, I'm afraid. To bar her from the facilities would have resulted in too many consequences."

I tilted my head, inspecting his features. "You told me once that she was someone you didn't want to get on the wrong side of. Care to expound on that?"

"No, and for your sake, you're better off not knowing." He smoothed out his lab coat. "What you do need to know is that my contacts at WWL launched an investigation, but they accepted my rendition of events as truth. I told them that the wolf in custody crossed into lunacity. Cynthia unwisely attempted to subdue the wolf, but it overpowered her and killed her. I tried to fight, but was only able to slay it after it had destroyed her."

"Did you ever notice how you refer to Cynthia as *she* and Kara as *it*."

The professor's eyes searched the ground. "I am an old vampire, and some of my oldest habits are difficult to break. In any case, as much as I hate to say it, you should get used to me using some rather dismissive language, both about wolves and you, when we begin our work at WWL next week."

My eyes became saucers. "What?"

"Your internship starts Monday." Concern crept into the wrinkles at the corners of his eyes. "Don't tell me they didn't give you the orientation letter?"

"Would it have come through a courier like your messages do? I..." Wait, what was I going on about? "I still have the internship?"

"They bought my story about how Cynthia died. There's no reason for them to retract the offer. Unless you no longer feel you'd be safe?"

"I'm the daughter of a red matron, I'm never safe."

A bitter reality, but a true one. In the hood hierarchy, my mother wasn't the only matron of the Red Hood bloodline. There were two others, one still in Germany, and one in Australia. Like the hueys we posed as being, so too had supes been forced to migrate away from ancestral homes through history. My mother, however, was infamous, the most powerful of her status. Because of that, Brünhild Kline had been branded by wolves as a sort of boogie man with whom they scared their cubs. More than once I'd heard even the Paradise mothers warn unruly children that "Red Matron comes for cubs who don't behave." As much as I drew shame from it, my mother's reputation as a hardnosed, vindictive executioner afforded me some protections. I'd been away from my clan for almost a year and hadn't been hunted down by one of her enemies or, worse, an ally.

My reality fractured, dual impulses of dread and excitement swirling together to form a directionless miasma of purpose. If I still had the internship, I wouldn't have to leave Chicago, retreating to Paradise like an ashamed puppy with her tail between her legs, relying on the charity of friends to keep her clothed and fed. If I did take the internship, I'd likely be in the midst of vampires who knew, at least tangentially, I was connected with the deaths of, not one but, two vampires in the last few months. Surely if my mother knew I'd killed Donovan, others did as well?

"After everything that happened, do you think going into a den of vampires – corporate vampires – is safe?"

"All corporations are vampiric in their own way. It's their nature." He examined me at length, trying to diagnose my wrinkled nose and bitten bottom lip. "I'm not going to pretend that this endeavor is devoid of danger. Some are still uncomfortable with the way your killing one of Cynthia's children was handled. The only form of death a vampire respects is at the hands of a slayer. Your mother had to offer some serious money to the crèche to make the problem go away."

"My mother *what*?" I interjected.

The professor reached to the mat of thin brown hair atop his head and scratched. "You didn't know," he concluded. "Cynthia demanded compensation from your bloodline, even though she sent Donovan after you with the hopes you'd kill him. We're contrary creatures in so many ways. Being a vampire maker means having your cake and eating it too. Your mother paid. In silver, of course."

"She does have a preference for metal over paper."

A half-smile lifted the right side of Igor's face. "She's a hood, that goes without saying. But *we* prefer tradable currency. Still better than lead, I suppose."

I wondered if the debt had come from our family's silver stores, or if my mother had lifted the trinkets off tourists passing through Paradise over spring break. One of the tactics she'd taught me at a young age was that a hood is never without a weapon, if hueys adorned in silver are near.

Not in my case, of course. I wouldn't have the talent to steal the finery of passing crowds by commandeering their silver until I took my rites.

If I took my rites.

"In any case," Igor resumed, "I'll be moving my work over to their facilities this weekend. You're expected at orientation on Monday morning, eight-thirty. Most of WWL's operations are legitimate huey-world activities; all interns – even those working for me – have to make the lawyers happy. Of course, in your case, you're also going to have to convince a few supes that you're trustworthy."

"Is there a reason I shouldn't be?"

He looked at me like a child who didn't understand the adult world. "Yes, you're a hood. We're not traditional adversaries, but trust won't come easy, and you and I both know, you're not entirely deserving of it."

I put on my best poker face. "What do you mean?"

His eyes narrowed. "You'll be watched closely until they come to trust you. They might also suspect you're a mole working for your mother. Rumor is that the Red Matron has been poking her nose around down here, trying to find out what you're up to. You must convince WWL that you have turned your back on your family, that you are not your mother's shill."

It was like asking me to prove it was night by pointing out the stars, all while yelling at me for the sun being gone from the sky. "That won't be difficult at all. It's true."

THREE

A third ring taunted me with the promise of conflict diversion. Voicemail would be a blessing. I wondered momentarily why I should be nervous. Wasn't working at WWL going to help with the whole "spy on the vampires and figure out what the hell they're doing kidnapping and killing wolves" thing? They didn't seem to be using them for food. Kara hadn't had any fang marks on her that I'd noticed. Although I'd only had a passing look at the body of Tobias's brother, Nick, nothing gruesome suggesting a violent vampire-induced death sparked in my memory. I knew whatever they did to Kara messed up the mating bond she shared with Tobias; she couldn't even sense her own mate standing in the same room. It still didn't mean I knew why, though. What reason would there be for a vampire to unmate wolves?

During a pause between ring two and three, moments away from safety, I realized my nerves had nothing to do with vampires, and everything to do with the werewolf whose number I'd just dialed, one who I wished to high heaven I could stop loving as easily as he'd stopped loving me.

"Geri?"

"Hi, Cody. You got a few minutes to talk?"

"For you? Always!"

How could he do it? How could he so happily receive a call from me, and talk to me like I was a fifth grader trying to sell him Girl Scout cookies? Bouncy and cheery, like he wasn't the man who had been able to make my head spin without ever technically having slept with me?

"What's up?"

Deep breath in, deep breath out. Stay focused. "Did Kim get home all right?"

His voice took on a hesitant vibration of awkwardness. "Of course. She got a flat outside of Green Bay, but she changed it easy enough. You know Kim. She'd carry that old Chevy of hers home if she had to."

The image of Cody's burly shewolf cousin hoisting a pickup over her head filled my mind's eye. I wasn't sure she was *that* strong, but I bet she came damned close.

"Good to hear. Did she, um, tell you and Rick that I was coming back home to work for the summer?"

"Sure did. Glad to hear it, too. It's hard to keep Tobias from hitchhiking to Chicago as it is. He thinks you're knee-deep in vampires down there, having all the revenge fun without him. Now that you're coming back for a little while, maybe he'll kick back and actually work on getting to know the pack. For a communal animal, he does have a terrible introverted personality."

My bottom lip called out for mercy as I bit away my nerves. "What do you think he'd do if I *didn't* come home for the summer?"

The alpha on the other end of the line measured out some silence before asking, "Why would that happen?"

I pushed a thumbnail into a bar of soap on the edge of the bathroom sink. "Because I still kinda, sorta have an internship with WWL."

"That vampire corporation? You can't be serious. Not after what happened. No, Geri, I won't allow it."

The nerves that had danced on the edge of my tongue moments before stood to attention and declared war. "You won't *allow* it?"

"No, I won't. Jesus Christ, it's bad enough as it is that you're still in Chicago. Kimmy said you were coming home in a few days, or I'd never have let you stay there alone as it is."

Suddenly, my blood boiled for an entirely different reason. "I'm not a member of your pack, Cody Ryland. You can't command me to do anything."

"You may not be pack, but you're family. I protect you just like I protect them."

The wounds of my broken heart still festered, and the sharpness of the pain made me lash out. How could he tug me around like this? Sure, I could stomach being Cody's friend, but assuming he was responsible for my safety, like he had when we were together? Had he no mercy?

Poison laced my words. "Exactly which part of your family am I? I'm certainly not your girlfriend any more, unless your wife is an exceptionally open-minded shewolf."

"Don't get that way, Geri. Don't act like a… Like a…"

"Like a hood?" I interjected. "Is that the word you're looking for? Because, whether you like it or not -- whether I like it or not, that's what I am."

"Which is all the more reason why you can't go waltzing into some big city company run by vampires!" He huffed. He puffed. He, I was willing to bet, ran a hand through his hair. "I'm sending Kimmy back tomorrow to get you and bring you home."

"You do, and I'll silver her the second she walks through the door."

"You, silver *Kim?*" A low chuckle filtered over the line. "Yeah, that's really going to happen."

Heat shot up my spine, arched across my neck, and landed on my tongue. "You seem to be confused. I didn't call to get your permission to stay here, oh Great Alpha Wolf of the Paradise Pack. You have no alpha's prerogative with me. I'm telling you what I'm planning on doing. Three wolves are dead that we know about. One of them, your dad. Now, I may not be a righteous hood. I know I'd have no hope of defending myself if I ever got in a real fight with a supe. You don't have to remind me of my weaknesses. My mother spent years making me well aware. But it appears I do need to remind you of my strengths."

"Geri, I didn't mean that—"

"Nascent or not, I'm still going to get to the bottom of what the hell is going on. I've been trained in defense, espionage, and negotiation. I may not know as much about vampires as I do about wolves, but I know a hell of a lot more than you do. Remember, the slayers are all dead; they can't protect you. The hoods are all prejudice; they *won't* protect you. So either you can get with the program that *I* am going to protect you, or you can go fuck yourself."

"Geri, come on, I'm only thinking about your safety. I'm not saying you couldn't—."

I heard the flat door open and close behind me. That alone was reason enough to hang up, but I didn't need any further motivation.

"I've said all I need to say. Good-bye."

Amy did a double take as I pressed my screen to end the call and threw my phone into the couch cushions with the power of a major league pitcher.

"If I didn't know better, I'd call that a break-up call. But you don't have a boyfriend, so what's up?"

Fuming, balled fists on my hips, I paced. "It was my ex."

"The one you told me yesterday was god's gift to women?" Amy asked, amplifying my comments with an extra-large speaker. I nodded. "Reassessing that assessment, are you?"

"You could say that." Deep breaths and calming thoughts helped me get under control. When I opened my eyes again, I was glad to see that Amy had moved into the kitchen, totally ignoring my temporary rage. She moseyed from sink to fridge, getting out the elements of a turkey sandwich.

"Where did you get your contacts?"

Her question threw me for a loop. "What?"

"Contacts," she repeated, her gaze drilling into mine so deeply, I felt like she was trying to give me a visual lobotomy. "They, like, glow when you get really emotional. They must be triggered by your pulse or something. I had a friend in New York who was really into cosplay. Don't ask — I have no idea exactly *what* she was supposed to be dressed as. Schoolgirl slut with the ability to conjure lightening, I'm guessing. But she had this little stick-on lightning bolt thing she'd put on her forehead that could actually sense when her pulse spiked, and then it would flash. Are your contacts like that?"

"I don't know what you're talking about. I don't wear..."

It was then I caught sight of my glowing eyes reflected in the silver tea tray kept on an eye-level shelf. The blue was faint, but they must have been like flashlights when Amy had first walked in. Arguing with a wolf, even over the phone, could apparently spike my nascent instincts.

I quickly bought in to her assumptions. "Oh, my god. I must have forgotten to take them out. They're so thin I forget they're in. Yeah, they, um, they react to my pulse."

I turned, making a show of taking imaginary plastic slips out, all while trying to quell my fighting instincts that had fired up my eyes in the first place. But then, of course, what would I do with these imaginary contacts? It wasn't like I could just slip them in my pockets. Ew, contacts with pocket lint? I made my way to the bathroom while Amy, a sandwich pressed between her two dainty hands, followed.

She spoke, even though I closed the door. "That's how I knew you liked him, you know."

"Liked who?"

"That one guy, Tobias. That time he was here, you looked like you had a power plant going on in your head."

I almost choked on my laugh. "Did not."

"Did too. You were all flush and angry and about to jump him. I have a sense for these things. A nearly inhuman, supernatural sense."

If only...

"I *was* angry, but not because I wanted to — what's the term you used, jump him?" I asked, all while wondering just how long I had to stay in this bathroom to pull off the ruse. "Besides, as I'll remind you, he was married."

"Could have been unhappily. Might have been looking for a little side action."

"Not the case on either count." I opened the bathroom door, hoping the time I'd spent inside was sufficient. My eyes, in any case, had returned back to their dull hazel default. "Even if that's what he was after, what about me would make you think I'd ever do something like that?"

"You can't possibly be that frigid. You're an attractive, intelligent, dare I say, sexy woman. You're in the big city, away from all that backwoods, ultraconservative 'no one shall touch me lest we be bound in holy matrimony' culture. Even if you're not into hookups, you can't tell me that you don't at least want to play the field a little. Come on, don't you ever get lonely?"

I pulled a bottle of water from the fridge. "Why should I? I have you here."

"We both know I'm a poor excuse for a first date." Crestfallen at her own comment, Amy wrapped an arm over her stomach to palm the opposite elbow. "And trust me, experience says I'm not really that good of a second or third date."

The sadness in her eyes hung heavy on my heart. Amy, a serial hookup artist, specialized in relationships that fizzled quickly and left her sobbing. For a brief time, anyway. At first, I thought it silly. Maybe, though, what made her so upset was that it caused her to devalue herself.

I reached out and stroked her arm. "You're so much better than all of them, Amy. You know that, right? I keep wondering why you waste yourself on such scumbags."

Her puppy dog eyes caught me. "And I keep wondering why you don't share yourself with someone worthy. Have you ever thought how unfair that is, that you have so much to offer, and you never even think about offering it?"

I'd never thought of Amy as particularly strong. The blow she'd just delivered on my psyche, however, left a bruise.

Sober words followed sobering thoughts. "That never occurred to me."

"Yeah, well..." Her words trailed off, the thoughts capped by a shrug. Then, as though someone had flipped a switch inside her, Amy was her usual bright and bushy self again. A smile pulled wide across her face. "Maybe that can be your summer project while I'm gone."

"While you're gone? Where are you going?"

"Back home, of course. You don't seriously think I'd hang around in Chicago when I could spend summer in New York, do you?" Her next words came across in song. "Darling, I love you, but give me Park Avenue!"

"You're leaving, for the whole summer?" I raked my gaze over the apartment. Why, I couldn't say. Did I expect an explanation to be sitting on the couch?

"Oh, don't worry. I'm not expecting you to carry the rent or something. I'll still be throwing in my part, even if just to keep the lease. If you can't do that, you can get someone to sublet your room over the summer. Someone not totally scuzzy, if possible."

"I… um. I'm actually going to be staying here. You remember that internship I thought I lost? Well, turns out I didn't. I start Monday."

Before I could come to grips with reality, Amy wrapped me up in a hug. Maybe she was supernatural, some sort of preternatural hugging monster heretofore unclassified in the hood annals.

"That's wonderful," she said, totally ignoring my stoic non-response. "I was so worried about you going back home. I know you and your folks don't get along, and I couldn't imagine you having to stay with them the whole time. You'll be much better here, even by yourself."

Awkwardness pulled the corners of my mouth into a grimace. "I suspect Kim will be coming back."

My roomie pulled herself off me and held me at arm's length. "You two… You aren't a… couple, are you?"

"Well, I have seen her naked at least a dozen times, so…" I had to swallow the laughter or else risk cackling. "No, we're not a couple. She's not my type."

"Oh, good, because… You know. I mean, nothing wrong with it if you were. Just…" Amy let me go and walked back to the kitchen. "Never mind. I don't know why I said anything at all. I think Kim is… swell."

"Swell?" I repeated. "First, the 1950s called and they want their vocabulary back. Second, I thought you hated her. You two are always bickering."

"I don't *hate* her," Amy protested. "I'm just not very compatible with her is all. Plus, I don't know if this makes sense, but she's a little… intimidating. When we went out all together, every time she caught some guy checking you out, I could have sworn she growled at them. You may not think she's your type, but I'm not sure that street goes both ways. She treats you like a bone she has to bury just to protect from others."

"Kim's nothing like that. In fact, she told me she wants to get mated… *married* pretty soon. Anyway, the last thing I want right now is to get involved with anyone."

And the last thing I wanted ever was to be involved with any kind of supe.

Four

Old Bessie, my darling truck, groaned and jiggled whenever we hit a speedbump, but she got out to O'Hare and back. After Amy left, however, our loft felt like a bag of bones, a structure with a purpose but lacking in anything that made it move and hum. It surprised me how accustomed I'd grown to the huey's presence, even cared for it – despite the fact that Amy Popowitz had appointed herself the leader of her own personal "Gerwalta Kline must be deflowered" campaign.

I liked, and hated, the realization that I missed my roomie. But, life went on, and the next day, I had to be at WWL by eight-thirty. Thus, I found myself bright and early staring in the mirror at my pathetic attempt to look semi-professional.

My closet was a fine assortment of denim bottoms and cotton t-shirts, mixed in with a few sweaters and hoodies. Back in Paradise, I had a few pieces that could be defined as formal, but of the Old Germanic style and meant as ceremonial garb for hood holidays or *feuernacht*. At 7:31, I grabbed my worn-down backpack, slid my ever-present silver dagger into my braid, and made to leave, wanting to scratch every square inch of my legs trapped inside the second-hand business casual slacks I'd picked up the day before. Three steps from the door, my muscles cried rebellion and halted me in place.

No, it can't be. Not now!

The feeling I got when an unknown wolf approached me was like the one you got as a rollercoaster ticked and clicked its way up the first big hill. A wolf I did know, however? It was the ride down, the pulse-spiking, wind-whipping rush of adrenaline that prompted your fight or flight instincts.

I'd just gone down Space Mountain, a plunge in my gut so rapid and pulverizing it could only be one particular wolf who stood on the other side of my door.

"Huff, puff, Geri."

My backpack thudded to the floor. The last time I saw Tobias had been when I'd left him behind with the pack in Paradise, just a few days after I'd barely gotten him there in time to save his life. An echo of the guilt I felt then formed in my gut, like a mother leaving her disabled child in the care of a nurse. I knew it was the right place for him, but I still felt the burden of his care. In the intervening time, the worst of his pain had ebbed, but even now, standing before him, his conflicted feelings mixed with my own. Part of him wanted to cry at the sight of me; I was the only one besides Igor who had been present when his mate died. We would forever be bound by that tragedy. Yet, reality didn't bow to grief. I was still a hood; he was still a wolf. Our instincts drove us to hate each other.

I didn't want to hate Tobias, but I couldn't be seen as weak and sympathetic either. For a hood to appear weak to a wolf was to open herself to danger. She lived thereafter at his leisure.

Tobias's face crumpled when I threw open the door, seething. "It wasn't an order, you know."

I cocked my head to the side. "What are you talking about?"

"The huffing and the puffing," he answered.

I took a moment to draw back my rage at his sudden appearance. How dare he just show up out of nowhere, when he had no right to be so soon a widower and away from the comfort and support of his pack. How dare he bring this baggage back to my door so soon.

"Why in the hell are you here?"

He pushed past me, and for once in my life, I wished the rule about not being able to enter a home without an invitation applied to werewolves instead of vampires.

"Well, right this second, I'm here because I have to piss. Where's your loo?"

My hand lashed out, indicating the door. Without so much as a thank you or a word of explanation, Tobias dove for the "loo," closed the door, and proceeded to moan as he relieved himself.

"Did Cody send you?" I yelled through the wooden slab covered in layers and layers of paint.

"God, this feels so good. I drove here straight from Paradise, didn't stop." With another grunt, the grotesque virtuoso urination stopped, the toilet flushed, and the faucet came on. "By the way, whose idea was it to name that bloody little puissant tourist trap Paradise? I'm thinking it was the same dullards who came up with Greenland. The waterfalls are nice, though."

"I repeat, why are you here?"

The door opened to reveal the werewolf using Amy's frilly pink hand towels to dab the moisture from his hands.

"You're kidding, right?" he asked, a bit of gruff in his timbre. "Remember about a month ago when a certain vampire held you prisoner and killed my mate? And then, how you asked me to help you figure out what was going on, so it doesn't happen to others?"

"Of course, I remember. But you're in mourning. I can feel the sadness on you. It's … sticky, heavy. Vampires are immortal, they're not going anywhere. The problem will still be there once you've taken the proper time to…"

"To what? Get over Kara?" he demanded. "That's never going to happen. I might as well be here, trying to keep it from happening to others."

All at once, every muscle in my body went tense. "Has it happened to anyone else?"

"Not in Paradise," Tobias said. "Once Cody relayed what had happened to me and you down here, your mum suddenly snapped to attention. She's been running perimeter checks around the packlands twenty-four, seven. And speaking of your mum..."

I'd never stopped to think about it, but as soon as Brünhild Kline was aware a foreign wolf had suddenly joined the pack, she'd probably dragged him in for questioning. I'd never told Tobias, or Cody for that matter, that what had happened was any kind of secret. It also explained why she was snooping around Chicago, like Igor had said. Me mixed up in vampire business and coming across a lone wolf? She probably cursed my name every hour, on the hour.

"Did she hurt you?"

"No. But I had to bite my own paw to keep from hurting *her*. I've never heard a mother talk about her own daughter the way she talks about you. What exactly did you do to piss her off so much?"

"It seems to have started with my birth, and went downhill from there," I answered. "Don't forget, she named me after the most heinous traitor in our bloodline, in *any* bloodline. Just in case you were wondering if Gerwalta is a common name among hoods... yeah, no. Look, Tobias, I get that you think you're ready for this. I understand what you're going through."

"You *understand*?" The werewolf's nostril flared. "Did you feel your soul collapse? Did you have to come to terms with the fact that the only person you will ever love is gone, and that you now have to live another fifty or hundred years without them?"

I wondered.

My silence fueled Tobias's righteousness. "That's what I thought. Cody and I agreed I'd return to Chicago with you at the end of the summer, but *someone* just had to go and get herself an internship at Vampire Inc., didn't she? So your choices were me, or spending June, July, and August with Kim."

"Oh, god, no." The wall clock triggered my adrenaline. "Look, I now have forty-one minutes until I have to check in for orientation. WWL is in one of those really big buildings downtown. If you think you're going to be tagging along with me to work, think again."

"It's daytime, I'm sure you're okay." Tobias plopped down on the couch, his brow fretting. "But your shift under Karmarov in their labs will be at night, right? We'll have to figure out some way for you to stay in touch with me when you're at work."

I pulled my phone from my pocket and held it up. "Like texting, maybe?"

He shook his head. "I don't use those things. They track everywhere you go."

"I'm sorry, *who* tracks you?"

"Who do you think? The bloody ho—" Clearing his throat and folding one leg over the other, the wolf turned sheepish. "Well, the ones back in England do."

"I can assure you that my clan does not track wolves through their cell phones. My mom grumbles whenever she just has to use a computer to check the database. I've even heard that the Yellow Matron down south doesn't have electricity."

"Say what you will, but I know what I know." Tobias rested his chin on the crook of his fisted hand. "Smoke signals probably won't work in the city. Morse code? You could get a flash light and spell out words from a window."

"We can talk about it later," I said while shoving my boot-loving feet into feet-hating heels. "If I don't make orientation, I won't have anything to tell you. And I only have – shit, I'm going to be late. Where are you staying?"

The wolf scratched himself behind his ears. "I suppose I could stay in the car. Rick gave me his old truck."

The Paradise Pack's beta and Cody's uncle, Rick Ryland, would give you the shirt off his back if you needed it, just as long as it wasn't one of his favorites. He'd also give you a punch in the gut if that's what you had coming. Charitable, yes. All sugar and spice and to-every-wolf nice? Hell no.

"Where did you stay when you were in Chicago before?" How had that never occurred to me? Surely Tobias hadn't been roaming the streets for three months.

"There was an old guy not far from the university. Lived in an old run-down house. He thought I was some kind of stray."

I slapped my hands over my eyes to keep them from bugging out. "You were walking around the city as a wolf?"

"He never suspected anything. I think his eyesight wasn't so good. Best part was he fed me too. Meals on Wheels? Turns out, not too bad."

"Well, you got lucky. And you're not doing that anymore." I blew an exasperated breath out. "I can't believe I'm actually going to say this, but since Amy's gone home for the summer, I think you should stay here."

"And have your smell constantly in my nose? No thanks."

"I mean temporarily, until we figure out something else."

He chewed the air before his shoulders slumped. "Fine. I take it Sally Two Tits—."

"AMY."

"*Amy* won't care if I take her bed, will she?"

"Her only complaint will be that she wasn't here to share it with you." I heaved my backpack off the floor and threw it over my shoulder. "I *need* to go. Seriously, like ten minutes ago. I'll be back after work. If you want to take a shower, there's some towels under the bathroom sink. Should be enough soap and shampoo in there for you to use."

"I hope it's not that frou-frou smelling stuff."

"You're in a house where two college-aged women live. Of course, it's frou-frou stuff." At the door, I turned back, making a show of pulling in a deep inhale through my nose, then letting my face sour. "Think of it as a charitable act."

FIVE

I entered the lobby of WWL at 8:29:37 AM. Before I could congratulate myself at having arrived twenty-three seconds early, the security line leading up to two metal detectors cross-checked me. Backwoods naiveté still dealt me the occasional blow, even a year into living in the city. Of course, there was security. WWL occupied the first twelve floors of a thirty-two-story building in Chicago's financial district, the rest of the space rented out to financial institutions, law firms, and various other professional outfits. It needed to be secured. Also, you know, vampires.

"Miss, please keep moving forward."

A female guard waved insistently in my direction, her eyes narrowing on me as a man pushed past me to join the line. Suddenly, I realized that I'd managed to do one of the most suspicious things possible: freeze the second I saw security.

I shook off my nerves and stepped forward. "Sorry, guess I'm a little in shock."

She took my backpack and laid it down on the belt of the scanning machine. "Never seen a security check point before?"

"No. I mean, yes, of course. Just..."

Plastering on faux awe, I surveyed the three-story interior lobby with the look of Dorothy taking in the Emerald City. Come to think of it, there was something a little odd about the quality of the light bouncing around. Did it actually have a greenish hue?

I continued, "I didn't know buildings like this existed. Back where I come from – the Upper Peninsula, ever heard of it? – the biggest building in town is where we keep the snow plows parked in summer. This sure beats a pole barn."

The guard gawked at me, scrutinizing my sanity, before grimacing and pointing at the body scanner. After a minute or two – because unlike me, the other people waiting in line knew the routine – I advanced. A red light and buzzer went off the second I stepped through the body scanner. The guard flexed her finger, directing me to step back.

"Ma'am, if you can step over here, I'll need to do a secondary search."

The second her fingers traced over the hilt of my dagger, making my insides squelch and knowing her discovery of my weapon was just moments away, and, of course, having no idea what that would result in but assuming it was nothing good… a familiar voice called out.

"Charlotte!"

Igor Karmarov veritably sauntered from the elevator, across the lobby. I'd never seen the professor be anything less than an adamant professional, even in the midst of a vampire-werewolf battle with lives on the line. The confidence with hints of mischievousness he imbued with each step threw me for a loop. Only when Charlotte went crimson and her pupils dilated did I understand what was going on. *Impossible.* Was I really seeing this? Was it really happening? It wasn't the enthralling taking place right before my eyes that had me questioning my sanity, but the standing in a glass-walled lobby on a bright, sunny day in Chicago and *not* bursting into flames.

"Morning, Iggy," Charlotte sing-songed.

"Good morning, Charlotte." Igor winked. Actually winked. For an old man, he still had moves. "I see you've found Miss Kline in the nick of time. I just called up to the Internship Coordinator to see if she made orientation. I should take her up right away."

His hand took me by the elbow and attempted to drag me away, but Charlotte extended a finger and an objection.

"Just a second, Iggy. I thought I felt something in that braid of hers. Probably nothing, but—"

The polarity of the air shifted as Igor bore down into her mind with his power. "It *is* nothing, Charlotte. Nothing to worry about at all. In fact, you don't even remember the slightest thing being suspicious."

"No, nothing at all," a dazed Charlotte agreed as she swept my bag off the other end of the conveyor and handed it to me. "You better get up to that orientation, now. Mr. Speck hates people who are late."

Igor dipped his head. "Thank you, Charlotte."

"Enthrall security on a regular basis, do you?" I asked Igor as he led us towards the elevators. "*Charlotte* seemed to know you quite well, *Iggy*."

The professor modeled the term nonchalant. "I've taken of her vein before."

With that chilling matter-of-fact delivery, I was reminded I wasn't in the packlands and this wasn't a hood compound. WWL was run by vampires, and how many, I had no idea. At their head sat the firstborn daughter of Dracula himself. The second I got cocky here could be the second I got myself into serious trouble.

"The security in the work zone proper isn't so easily counteracted," Igor continued. "Bringing a weapon into this building again would be unwise. Only dumb luck saved you this time."

"Acknowledged. Do you mind if I ask how you're able to be here at all given current atmospheric conditions?"

Igor smirked. "You mean because we're in a lobby bursting with sunlight, and I'm not bursting *from* sunlight?" He pointed to the transparent walls that framed the expansive foyer. "The glass has a filter that keeps us from going poof. I have the same thing in my car. That, and some underground garages, allows me to be here for a few hours after sunrise, should I desire."

"And you desired?" I asked as the elevator opened, allowing three or four people to come out as we queued to get in.

"I wanted to be certain you got to the orientation on time. And if you didn't. Well... Luckily, we don't have to address that hypothetical. Take care to be on time, please. I will not always be here to save the day."

"You have too little faith in my ability to get myself out of trouble."

He stifled a laugh as the elevator dashed towards floor six. "Perhaps."

The hallways of WWL didn't scream out "This place is run by vampires." Not that I had a huge catalog of experience to compare, but if forced to describe the motif, I would say "a dull assortment of neutral-toned paintings on off-white walls and benignly-patterned carpet. Textbook corporate facilities." I wondered where the labs were, and if that floor looked like something out of a hospital.

Igor put a hand on my shoulder and turned me up a hall. I bristled at his touch. Even though I'd come to accept that the vampire indeed was on my side, it didn't quell instincts born of generations of breeding. At the door, a stout, red-haired snap of huey stood, a clipboard in hand and a scowl on her face.

"Igor," she said, in the same way someone might say "locusts."

"Good morning, Thelma. Miss Gerwalta Kline here to check in for orientation."

Thelma pushed black-rimmed, coke bottle glasses tinted pink over the bump of her bulbous nose. "Mr. Speck's instructions were clear. *No tardiness.* Those who are late, are cut."

Again, the air shifted, dull electricity humming through my body as Igor leaned in, pushing his power out to the strict woman.

"Surely an exception can be made for interns hand-selected by senior staff, such as myself."

Unlike Charlotte, who acquiesced like water to gravity, Thelma only stared back, deadpan. "No use in trying to enthrall me, Igor," she said, flicking the lens of her glasses. "My prescription got upgraded. Now, unless you got another trick up your sleeve, I'll trust you to show Miss Kline out."

The professor blew out a huff through pursed lips, looking at the wall as if it had some kind of solution written in graffiti. I, however, wasn't about to let some paper-pushing hard ass screw things up. If this Thelma knew about enthralling, and thus vampires, I was willing to bet she knew about other supes as well.

"Have you ever heard of the Red Matron?" I asked.

The administrative bouncer blinked twice. "That old battle axe? Of course, I have."

"Then you know how crazy she can be."

Thelma's slow nod matched up with a sly smirk. "Oh, yeah, I've heard she's some kind of modern day Xena. A real shoot first, there's no need to ask any questions type of loon."

We shared a laugh. Until, that was, I leaned in close and whispered, "She's my mother."

Thelma's eyebrow arched. "Are you honestly trying to pull a do-you-know-who-I-am maneuver?"

"Well, that depends." Calling on my nascent power, I shot energy through my body, making my eyes glow pale blue. It didn't have too much of an effect, until I pulled my silver dagger from my hair and held it to her throat. "Tell me, Thelma, do you know who I am?"

Nerves made her giggle. Her arm whipped back, indicating the door to the meeting room. "You're our newest intern at WWL. Go right on in."

"Despite your best efforts, I fear you may be your mother's child." Igor walked me past the petrified woman and opened the door for me. "Try to get through orientation without pulling a knife on anyone else. I'll see you in the lab tonight."

Six

To think, all my life I'd fretted over dying at the hands of a werewolf, when really, these high-heeled shoes would be the death of me.

The second I got home and walked through the door, the black pumps came off my feet and landed on the top of the garbage bin.

"These were clearly invented by a man!" I yelled, stuffing them down. "Probably the Marquis de Sade."

Tobias peeked out of the kitchen, a dishtowel strewn over his shoulders. "Bad day at work, hood?"

"No, bad day *to and from* work, wolf," I growled back. "But work wasn't all that great either."

He patted his hands dry as he came around the corner. "You smell like vampire."

"And you smell like lilacs. I guess you used Amy's body wash then."

"Yours was something called English Garden. It was too close to home for comfort."

I surrendered to the couch, thanking sweet mercy as its cushions embraced me. I took a survey of the living room and kitchen island. "Have you been cleaning?"

Tobias sat in the armchair to my right. "Slept a couple hours. Took a shower. Then, I had nothing to do. I, um, I have to have *something* to do. If I don't, I think about..."

Sadness pulled his features towards the ground. He didn't need to finish the sentence.

I sat up, softening my voice. "About this morning. It was rude of me to..."

"Rude is when you tell someone their cooking bites. You were being a bitch," he said, cutting me off. Just before I could get my ire raised again, he added, "but I should have warned you I was coming, and why."

"I stick by what I said back in Paradise. We'll get our answers, but we're dealing with vampires here. I know wolves; you guys are all in, or all out. And when you decide to do something about a situation, you want it taken care of right away. But we're going to have to be, well, a bit more 'hoodish' on this."

"Hoodish?" he repeated, one eyebrow arched. "You're not going to ask me to put on a cloak and kill stray dogs, are you?"

Don't be drawn in. "I mean methodic. We're hunters, trackers. We're used to looking at the big picture, taking in the whole environment, and trailing leads until we're sure we can come out of a confrontation victorious. Right now, we only know that the vamps involved with Cynthia are up to something that's killing wolves or, at the very least, seriously altering lupine behavior. We don't know what exactly, we don't know how, and most importantly, we don't know why."

"That bitch vamp who killed Kara said why. Because they want us out of the way."

I shook my head. "I don't think she meant all wolves when she said that. I think she meant us specifically. Think about it: there's really no reason why a wolf would pose a threat to a vampire. You guys generally don't overlap territory, you're not competing for food. There's no reason for you to be in conflict. There's something bigger behind that goal, and we have to figure out what it is."

"Which is why you're working at WWL. So, then, orientation. What was that all about?"

Now that we were getting to the meat of my day, I shrank back from the reality of its paltry quality. "There's about twenty interns for the summer, but I seem to be the only non-huey."

I didn't mention that among that lot was the brain-bleached huey I'd almost had sex with on this very couch and who turned out to be a conspirator of the vampire I'd killed, Jess Harmon. My handsome but heinous ex held no memory of what I was or what had happened between us; Igor had scrambled his brains to a fluffy goo. Jess only recalled my name was Geri, and no, not like the Spice Girl. Outside of that, I was practically a stranger to him.

Tobias's face screwed up. "And vamps?"

"Igor, briefly, when I first arrived. Then, none. Like you said, daytime."

"You're sure that Igor is on our side?"

"If he's not, he's doing a really good impression of it. Trust me, the second I suspect it's otherwise, things will change."

"This still doesn't feel right. How can you continue to work for someone who held you prisoner for three days?"

My face soured. "I'm not."

The wolf cocked his head. "I don't understand."

"I was supposed to be working with Igor, but at the end of orientation, when we were given our badges, mine said mailroom."

Tobias drew himself up to the edge of the cushion. "Mailroom?"

"As in, sorting the mail in a room designated for that purpose. Much to my chagrin, it was not a metaphor. P.S., My supervisor is a man named Doug who hated me on sight. Anyways, I was so shocked, I didn't say anything. How in the hell am I supposed to figure out what WWL is up to if I have to spend the next eight weeks licking stamps? And to top it all off, it's the day shift! I don't know. I have to talk to Igor, figure out if it's a mistake or something."

The bubbly expression on Tobias's face was either adorable, or insulting. "Day shift in the mailroom? But that's perfect!"

"Why, because now you won't have to get all uber-overprotective when there aren't so many vampires around?"

"Let me introduce a little wolf rational into your oh-so-holy hood logic." The chair nearly flew back when Tobias sprang to his feet. "Yes, fewer vampires during the day shift – if any – means it's easier for me to obey my alpha and protect your life. But a good wolf knows that stealth nets more kills than charging. No one's going to bat an eyelash if a new intern who doesn't know her way around *accidentally* goes some place she's not supposed to be. Don't you see? This is a good thing."

Committed to my sulk, I chewed on his words but tasted only reluctance. "Did I mention the mailroom also runs the shared printers for the whole company? Can't wait until I'm running all around, dropping off everyone's printouts of cat memes and cookie recipes."

Tobias reached out and grabbed my hand, dragging me up. "Are you daft? You said you were the only supe in the orientation, yes?"

"Yeah, so?"

"How likely is it, then, that most of the hueys who work at WWL have no idea what you are? It's the perfect disguise. You're going to be a nobody, and no one pays attention to a nobody." He stuck a finger up between us. "Someone else's hubris is their weakness and your strength. A rabbit on a hill can see far, but he can also be seen from afar even better."

He must have read the confusion in my face.

"It's one of the tenets we're raised on," Tobias continued. "The Six Silver Rules, we call them, handed down from generation to generation. Sort of like our Ten Commandments, only for how to avoid hoods and be good wolves."

"Tobias, I've studied werewolf culture and history all my life. I've never heard of something called the Silver Rules."

"And that just proves my point. You don't know what you don't know." Putting his hand on the small of my back, the wolf guided me toward my room, shoving me in and closing the door. "Change into something you can get dirty and sweaty. City life is making you weak. We're going for a run. If we're lucky, we'll find somewhere we can spar a little too."

Seven

"I'm just as surprised as you are," Igor said when I called him later that night to catch him up on the last few days – despite the fact that Tobias had made me run so hard and so long, I could barely move. "But for me to voice my objection would likely do more damage than solve any problem."

"Do you have any idea why my assignment changed?" I asked, reaching for a water bottle on my side table.

"The vampire who runs WWL – actually runs it, not the huey figurehead who works the dayshift – she knows you're a hood. I had to, of course, disclose this fact before recommending that you be offered a position. If I had not, it would have made it look like I was trying to hide something. Perhaps she decided that having the Red Matron's daughter involved in research might not be prudent."

My instinct to defend myself warred with the reality that there was indeed reason not to trust me. My intentions were not purely academic or professional.

"By she, do you mean Inga?"

The fact that my initial offer letter had come from the firstborn daughter of Dracula hadn't faded from my memory.

"Yes, Inga," Igor confirmed. "Generally, she will grant any request I make. Then again, I don't really make that many. But, at the beginning of the day, it is at her discretion to place you as she sees fit. For what it's worth, I agree with Tobias. There is a certain level of flexibility that comes with being in the mailroom that you would not otherwise have."

I grumbled my agreement, though the ache in my shins and hips tried to convince me the only compliment I should offer where Tobias was concerned was how good he'd look wearing a silver choker.

Igor continued, "I think it goes without saying then, Geri, that it will be necessary for us to keep up appearances should we ever see each other at the office. A quick greeting will not be out of line; WWL knows you were my student worker last term. But if we are seen discussing anything together, it will be noted and reported upon. We shouldn't be seen lingering about, talking."

"That shouldn't be hard, seeing as I'm going to be working 10 AM to 6:30 PM each day, and the sun isn't even setting until 7 or 8 this time of the year."

"True, true. But like your wolf says, keep your eyes open. It's the best way to see things."

And so, I went forth in my summer position as a corporate gopher and busboy.

A week into my position, what I'd learned so far sounded more like a book report than any sort of espionage communiqué.

I'd already known that WWL occupied the bottom third of the building. I'd come to find out, however, that there were an additional three floors underground, one of those only an executive parking garage. The company trafficked in a number of industrial and consumer goods and had researchers in material science, engineering, chemistry, biological endeavors and of course, genetics. The glass in the lobby, for example, wasn't only for vampire benefit; it had actually been developed for use in regions of the world where solar rays were so strong, air conditioning threatened energy supplies. Big buck customers reigned from places like Singapore and Dubai. Hospitals treating patients whose therapies or conditions made them sensitive to the sunlight also purchased large lots.

The two subterranean floors beneath the parking garage required the highest clearance to enter. I knew this from experience, as security guards had cornered me both times I tried to go beyond their elevator lobbies, guns drawn. As Tobias had predicted, saying my presence was beginner's mistake and claiming ignorance got me out of any trouble.

From a glance in daylight hours, the vampire-run corporation didn't vary from what I imagined huey-led corporations were like. Workers typed, mid-level managers held meeting after meeting, and every floor had a breakroom and a stout but kindly receptionist ready to guide visitors and employees alike.

A few things, however, differed. Firstly, Inga Rosethorn's office, as well as those of the "v-staff", wasn't located on the executive floor. Those, I assumed, were to be found in the subterranean levels and behind heavy layers of security. Secondly, as demonstrated by the woman outside the orientation room who had called Igor on his attempts to enthrall her, not all hueys were completely ignorant of the supernatural leadership. Those entrusted with the knowledge bore two telltale signs. First, the most obvious to my eyes, two aligned circular scars on their necks suggested they'd been fed upon. Second, like Thelma, they wore eye glasses in which the lenses had been tinted pink. How odd, I thought, that they were simultaneously being used as food, and being shielded from enthrallment.

Doug Marsen didn't wear the pink glasses and try as I might, I saw no way his collar could ever be loose enough to serve as a meal. Doug was my supervisor. Not my boss, but my *super*visor, he informed me when I reported to the mailroom. As in, he had a superior overview of how things in the mailroom worked. Doug had come to WWL six years before from an Assistant Manager position at a shipping and office supply store.

"Personally, I have no idea why you were assigned to me," Doug said. "I certainly don't need the help. I have three fulltime employees, and we handle everything just fine."

"I'm not sure either, sir," I answered, even though in hindsight I realized he hadn't asked a question. "But I'm happy to do whatever you need me to do."

Doug planted fisted hands on his hips. "Oh, you'll do whatever I need you to, but you won't be happy about it. A mailroom is an essential part of the modern company. Your generation thinks everything can be electronic. Mail, meetings, books. Some things, however, must be wrought in the physical world. We are the anchor that keeps all they do up there—" he pointed at the ceiling "—grounded in reality."

True to Doug's prognostication, I *didn't* find that my work made me happy. I spent the first half of my day sorting bins of mail on to different carts. I spent the second half of my day pushing those carts around the various floors and offices of WWL and dropping off their deliveries. Even though my duties gave me an overview of the movers and shakers in the company as Tobias had predicted, I worked the day shift. I only ever saw hueys, and very few wore the pink-paned glasses.

By the end of the week, I was pretty sure my internship at WWL was a waste of my time. Then, one package changed my fate.

Eight

"Floor twenty-seven?"

I looked at the box in my hand, branded with the logo of the online retailer from which it came, and thought for sure there was a mistake – despite the fact the shipping label clearly said WWL on the company line. First, we didn't have any offices on the twenty-seventh floor. And second, there was no customer name for me to make the delivery to anyway.

I held up the box for Doug's examination, shaking it a little. "Should I drop it with the mailroom of one of the other companies?"

"Nope, that's the correct address. It's a mixed use building you know."

"So you said. I don't know what that means, though."

"It means that parts of the building are business use, and parts are residential," Doug lectured as though he were talking to a child. "All of WWL's corporate offices are on floors B4 to 12, but some bigwigs live in the upper stories. Seeing as there's no name on the label, it's probably a sex toy."

The package in my hand suddenly felt dirty. I dropped it on my cart, deciding that I'd work my way up the building, finishing my shift with the twenty-seventh floor deviant.

"Don't you mean B3?"

Consumed with the tablet in his hands, Doug said, "What?"

"B4," I said. "You said our corporate offices run from B4 to 12. But the cargo elevator only goes down to B3."

Doug outstretched a hand and shooed me away. "Don't waste my time with details, okay? I have far more important things to do."

"I didn't mean any disrespect. I'm just curious, is all. Is there a B4?"

My modicum of reticence earned me invisibility, which I supposed was better than rebuke. Doug said nothing more as I turned heel, and pushed my overburdened cart toward the cargo elevator.

Officially, my shift ended at six-thirty, but on the eighth floor, I had the opportunity to meet Ms. Theodate Lamare, though her reputation had long preceded the formal introduction. As one of the regular mailroom staffers had told me, *Theo,* as she was called for short, was the company gossip. "Talk a rooster out of his feathers," were the exact words. She pinned me with her grin and set about interrogating me in the kindest of ways for my life story. When all I gave was my place of birth, and the fact that I was a student on a summer internship, she instead rambled on for a half-hour about her *own* life. By the time I'd managed to escape her cubicle, the clock read seven and I still had two more floors to go. Even though I knew the workers would most likely be gone, I also knew that Doug's head would explode if I left undelivered packages in the mailroom over the weekend.

The moment I stepped off the elevator, I felt like I had emerged into some alternate universe, where the WWL building wasn't labs and offices but a five-star hotel. Gone were the off-white vinyl floors, replaced by a shiny black stone surface. Dark purple walls covered in silver scroll work reflected the soft light of the interior fixtures, confusing the visual landscape. At intervals, stained wood doors alternated with the sort of minimalist framed art that could only have been created by a kindergartener or a master.

Dark. Everything was so dark. This place definitely housed vampires. Wolves and hoods both preferred greens, reds, and yellow environments – things that reminded us of forests and fields. Vampires and slayers, however, lived lives clinging to shadows, shunning not only the sun, but also the moon. Consequently, their crèches and their clutch compounds were said to be pale, colorless, gothic abodes washed in blacks, browns, and blues. The twenty-seventh floor was like walking into a room meant to be outfitted with black lights.

Without a name, I didn't know who to ask for when the door opened. *If* the door opened. The vamp resident at this hour, in this time of the year, would be on the edge of waking for the night. Even though the interior hall didn't have any windows, instinct told me that the sun outside had begun to sink into the horizon.

The low-level hum of an air conditioner beyond the thick, wooden door muffled the soundscape. As I counted to ten, then knocked again, I had begun to accept that the vamp wasn't up yet. No sooner had I taken out my clipboard to mark the delivery as incomplete than the door opened.

All I saw was taut olive flesh, and white, fluffy cotton, riding low and hugging hipbones sculpted by either Satan or the gods.

"Can I help you?"

His words should have had me raising my face to meet his. Unfortunately, my eyes had grown a mind of their own, and independently decided that his washboard stomach had spoken.

Rudolph Valentino's doppelganger stared back when the gravity of his grin drew my eyes up at last. A little younger, maybe. At most, I'd put him at twenty-five. God had blessed him with a face that proved His existence, while the devil had given him the kind of body that would make you question your own. The only thing darker than his eyes was his spiky black hair. The fact that he was more or less naked, with an asterisk being the towel wrapped around his waist, didn't seem to bother him in the least. That I was gawking bothered him even less. He might have expected it. Women had probably fallen down at his feet all his life. He might have wondered how I still remained standing.

That made two of us.

The pulsing vein on his neck and healthy skin tone ruled out him being a vamp. Huey executive, then. A freshly showered one at that.

I pushed the box forward. "You have a package for me."

My cheeks burned when I'd realized what I'd said.

He reached out, wrapping his hands around the box. "I think you mean that the other way around." He held up the label for inspection. "Oh, my new frosting tool. I've been waiting for this."

"Frosting tool?" I asked. "That's not really what's in there, is it?"

It was probably inappropriate of me to ask. It was *definitely* inappropriate for me to imagine the things I wanted to be in the box.

"Think just because I'm all buff and have no body fat, that I don't enjoy the delicate art of making buttercream rosettes?"

"No, I don't think someone like you eats much sugar."

"I assure you, I've been known to enjoy the occasional sweet." He maneuvered the box inside and set it down. "The key is to make sure you work off the calories right afterward, but tell you a secret? Working off the calories is twice as fun as eating them."

The air in my lungs went AWOL. "I'm sure. Well, goodnight."

He stepped into the hall, towel and all, as I began to push my cart back toward the elevator. "Don't you need me to sign for this?"

"Internal mail delivery, no need."

"But how else am I supposed to ask what your name is?"

Turning to look over my shoulder, my brow furrowed. "What are you talking about?"

He crossed his corded arms and leaned against the wall, as though he wasn't nearly naked. "The second I saw you checking me out, I said to myself, 'Self, she's into you. Find out who she is.' I tried sneaking a peak at the ID badge hanging from your belt, but I can't pull off staring below the neckline as well as you can. So instead, I was going to wait until you asked me to sign, and then say it was unfair that you were finding out my name, when I didn't know yours. Now, it's not a great plan, but it's the best I could come up with in the fifteen seconds that have passed since I opened my door and now."

"Do you make plans often?"

"Deliberate ones." His eyes quickly skimmed down my frame. "My success rate is practically Roman."

"Even the Romans lost some battles." I turned to leave.

"Caleb."

"What?"

"My name," he repeated. "It's Caleb. Now we're uneven. Settle up, or ruin your reputation as a profiteer, mailgirl."

Were all city guys this slick? "It's Geri. Geri Kline."

"Well, then, Geri Kline, the next time I have a package, I'll expect to see it in your hands."

NINE

By the time I'd crossed town and hopped off the El, the blue sky above had softened to shades of pink. I pictured Tobias, huffing and puffing and brooding by the door. I dashed into the small Asian grocer near home to pick up something for dinner. The ethnic fare was so foreign to my backwoods understanding, but one thing I could say for certain was this: Thai food wasn't half bad. More than that, it was cheap, and surprisingly well-liked by a werewolf who thought that blood pudding was the height of haute cuisine.

Suddenly, there was a buzz against my hip bone. I pulled the phone from my pocket, prepping myself for a sales pitch from the unfamiliar number. "Hello?"

His voice arched in confusion. "Hello? Geri?"

"Tobias?" I looked around, like I expected him to be hiding behind the mango display. "How are you calling me?"

The wolf refused to engage in chitchat. "You were supposed to be home an hour ago."

"I got hung up at work."

Best not to mention the terry-clothed hottie. Not only was it none of Tobias's business, but I didn't have to rub it in his face that while his love life was tragically over at the age of twenty-four, mine was still wrought with possibility.

"What number is this?" I continued. "Where are you calling me from?"

"I got a mobile." The tone he employed sounded like he was admitting to getting picked up by the cops for public indecency.

"Because you finally realized it made sense and it was the best way to stay in touch with me when I'm not home?"

"No, because Cody ordered me to," he huffed. "Also, I got myself a job."

I double blinked, standing with a plum in my hand. "Why?"

"Because it's not right of me to take advantage of you," Tobias said. "If I'm going to stay here, I have to help. It's only right. Plus, it helps keep me from thinking too much."

"It's going to get better eventually, Tobias. I promise." I knew I should offer a kinder ear, but I wasn't in the ideal place to have a conversation with a werewolf about his lost mate, even if one-sided. "What's the job?" I asked instead, hoping to distract him.

"Dog walker." The wolf coughed a laugh. "Another reason for the phone. I needed something that would pay cash. I'm still not legal here, am I?"

"I guess not. Dog walking, huh? I think that's a great idea. Domestic dogs fall into line for someone like you, don't they? That's what my mother said when I asked why we didn't use them as tactical tools."

The smile came back into his voice. "The dogs I walk will toe the line if they know what's good for them."

"They sure will. Listen, I'm sorry I'm late, but I'll be home soon. No need to worry."

"Oh, I'm not worried," he rushed to assure me. "If there was a problem, I'd *sense* you needing me."

I moved towards the front of the store, toward the cash register. "And therefore, I'm okay?"

"It at least means you're not being choked to death by a vampire in an alley. I'm not sure you're ever really okay."

Good, a short line. Just one old woman at the counter, and one shifty looking guy in front of me.

"Did you pick up on anything when I got that horrible papercut around two this afternoon?"

"Don't joke. If something happens to you, Cody will kill me. Like, literally. Where are you anyway?"

"Just a few blocks away at the Thai market."

Like a dog spotting a ball, excitement peppered Tobias's words. "Are you getting dumplings? Please be getting dumplings."

"Don't worry, I'm getting dumplings." I shook the package as though he could see it, stepping forward as the old woman collected her things and left the shop. "I'll be home soon. Put a pot of water on to boil."

"Okay, but I'm not doing it for you, hood. I'm doing it for the dumplings."

"Tobias Somfield, I never imagined anything but. Bye."

I slid the phone into my pocket and let my backpack fall from my shoulder onto my forearm. With wallet in hand I looked up, surprised to see the elderly Asian man behind the counter taking out a wad of cash to hand back to the man in front of me. Guy must have given him a hundred for the avocado in his hand.

Only, I suddenly realized, he wasn't holding an avocado.

He was holding a gun.

No sooner had my blood pressure shot up than the man pivoted. I must have gasped, maybe even cursed, though I couldn't remember making a sound. Something brought his attention to me, and the second it was there, his bloodshot eyes settled on the wallet in my hands, open and dotted with green bills.

"You know what they say. Every little bit."

He reached out to snag my cash, grinning, until I turned to stone. A hood's strength taunted my resolve as I held back what was mine. My attention fractured, taking in every aspect of the scene, analyzing what worked for me, what worked against me, and what could go either way.

A gun, pointed at me. Could I survive a shot? Not this close. Not a chance.

The door, behind the man with the gun. Even running my fastest, I'd never make it.

The old man, gathering the money and putting it into a paper bag, like a well-rehearsed act. Even if I did run, there was no way he could. I *could* throw my wallet toward him, creating a distraction and shifting the gunman's attention long enough to sneak by, but where would that leave the shopkeeper? What kind of person would that make me?

A survivor, my mother would say. *A hood triumphs.*

The power welled up inside me, longing to be unleashed. Even a nascent could take on this foe. Yes, if I managed to unarm the thief, there was no doubt I'd win in a hand-to-hand battle. Only, that camera over the counter would capture every moment of it. I'd save myself, and doom my ability to keep my secrets at the same time. Even if I was willing to expose myself, it would be unfair to subject Tobias to the consequences. He was my secret now too.

I had strength this huey could only dream of, but my greatest power in this moment was letting go.

The wallet slipped from my grip.

"Good decision, little girl." His grimy fingers pinched on to my twenty-six dollars and pulled them out. The rest of the wallet he had no use for. The thief tossed it to the floor, leaving me with my student card and my Michigan Driver's license, but somehow poking holes in my identity. He turned then, back to the old man who had finished bagging the money and was holding it out like a sacrifice.

And then he was gone.

I hadn't realized how tense I'd become until, just me and the old man, my body relaxed.

"Are you okay?"

The old man nodded, shaking off his fright. His broken English shook. "I okay. I okay. You okay?"

I nodded, then bent down to pick up my wallet. I'd barely gotten to my feet when the door of the shop opened again, the bells mounted on its frame jingling.

This time I wouldn't be caught unaware. My hand reached up to my braid, grasping for my weapon, only to find empty space.

That's right. You didn't take it to the office. You are powerless. You will always be powerless until you take on your hood.

Desperate to prove myself, fighting the mocking voice inside me, I swung my fist, another of my mother's rebukes echoing inside my head. *Strike last, die first.* My knuckles popped as they hit a solid mass of muscle.

"Gerwalta!"

The werewolf's voice brought me back to myself and to the moment. His strong hands took me by the elbows, shaking me. How was he here? Why?

"Snap out of it, it's me."

Without thought, I surrendered and let myself be caged by him.

"I guess I was in mortal peril, huh?"

Tobias managed a laugh while holding me at an awkward angle. "Even more than usual."

TEN

"It was really nice of Mr. Aromdee to give us the dumplings. You know, considering the circumstances."

Tobias fixed me with a questioning glare, as though I just declared it was kind of the hangman to have given the rope as a souvenir.

I shrugged. "I mean, we still got dinner. Just cost a little more than I was expecting."

"*Just cost a little more than you were expecting?*" he echoed as he set my backpack down on the kitchen island. "Gerwalta, what kind of hood lets herself be taken advantage of by a huey? You could have kicked that guy's ass. Why didn't you fight back?"

If I had hackles, they'd be raised. "He had a gun drawn just inches from my stomach. Unless he happened to be shooting silver bullets, I wouldn't have stood much of a chance."

"Don't tell me you haven't had any anti-weapon training. Surely Red Matron wouldn't make you rely only on silverwielding."

A memory of my mother staring down the barrel of a shotgun at a Canadian wolf who'd forced himself as mate to one of Cody's distant cousins flashed in my mind. I shook my head, forcing the images away.

"Think about it. Crime happens every day, but if a seemingly weak college student went all ninja on a huey, you think no one would notice? Local media loves a David and Goliath story. They'd swarm. Do you think the vampires would let me stay at WWL then? Plus, Chicago falls under the yellow bloodline's control. Do you think the yellow matron wouldn't chase me down and kick my ass for getting so much attention?"

"A Yellow Matron? Is she something I should worry about, being here away from my pack?"

I shook my head. "As long as we keep our heads down, we'll be okay. Consuela is traditional. She loathes cities. She'd only come up here if you were... unaccompanied."

Tobias shifted. "You mean she trusts you to babysit me."

It would be insulting to deny it, but I didn't have to add insult to injury by confirming it directly. "Consuela likes me. Like, a lot. The last few times she visited Paradise, she made it a point to remind my mother that I'm as much a yellow hood as I am a red."

The wolf didn't know what to say to that.

"My dad is from a yellow bloodline that migrated from Spain to Argentina about a century ago. It's almost unheard of for a hood born of a mixed bloodline to take rites in her father's rather than her mother's command, but it's not unprecedented."

A steady drip of reason began to seep into his understanding. Tobias's tension ebbed, his jaw softened. "I guess I can't blame you for protecting yourself."

"*Us*," I corrected, grabbing the package of dumplings and crossing to the stove. A pot that Tobias had put on to boil before my weird wolf-calling ability had made him run out the door had nearly gone dry. I turned off the burner and took the pot back to the sink to refill. "I was protecting *us*. Right now, the vamps have no clue I have a werewolf staying at my place. I get any sort of notoriety, they're going to start looking at me a little closer. You know where that leads: to us being no closer to figuring out what's going on at WWL, assuming there is something going on."

"Are we any closer to figuring out what's going on there?" He settled himself at the table. "You've been there a week."

"I've told you what I know. Some hueys are in the know, and I'm pretty sure the WWL vamps fear their being discovered. Why else give them those weird, pink-tinted glasses that block enthralling?"

"I still don't see how that would do any good," Tobias mumbled. "Would any vampire be so easily out maneuvered by corrective lenses?"

That had been bothering me as well, and I suspected there was more to it than I saw on the surface. "Oh, there is one more thing I found out today. There're some executive apartments on the upper floors. I had to make a delivery to one."

"Executive apartments? A clutch living on site, maybe?"

I hadn't thought of that. "I thought clutches were more like highly-fortified compounds than luxury lofts."

"They're on a high floor in an office building, with a dozen layers of secure zones beneath them. Sounds pretty luxurious and fortified to me. In the olden times, vamps tended to go for castles surrounded by villages or mansions in the middle of a city. The clutch in Morpeth had a block of rowhouses, even though they used one in the middle most. But in a modern city, especially the kind you Americans have that grew big in the last century or two? Living in a collection of flats would makes sense for a vampire, even if it does put them literally high in the sky."

"The design of the floor was definitely vamp-friendly. No external windows, no mirrors. But there's one problem with that theory: the unit I made a delivery to had a huey living in it."

A very delectable huey who smelled like rosemary soap and who probably looked as great in a tux as he did in a towel.

"Was he wearing those weird glasses?"

"No." He wasn't wearing much of anything. "Maybe that's something they only do at the office."

Tobias settled his chin on his balled-up hand. "A meal maybe?"

"A bleeder?" I asked, supplementing the term I'd always heard used to describe someone who willingly allowed vampires to feed off them. "Maybe, though I didn't see any fresh feeding sores on him."

"Vamps are smart. Maybe he's fed off of somewhere you couldn't see," Tobias suggested.

In my mind's eye, I recounted the ample canvas of Caleb's flesh, barely stopping myself from hitching a breath at the recollection. If a vamp could hide the evidence in what remained unexposed, they must have a terribly small mouth. "Doubtful."

The werewolf sitting at the table grimaced. "A huey living among vampires, or even under the protection of WWL... There's something worth looking at there. You should find out more."

Was the werewolf actually telling me that spying on Caleb would be beneficial to our pursuits? Well, how about that? Business and pleasure, all in one.

"In the meantime, we need to keep you on top of your game."

My eyes closed, as did the prospects of getting to bed before midnight. This wasn't exactly the kind of big city Friday night I'd been picturing when I'd left home last year. "You want to make me run again? Fine, but I need to eat first."

"Not just running. We need to do more than that. You're... going native."

I wasn't sure if he meant it as an insult, given the obvious. "I am a native. You're the foreigner."

"It's only ten forty-five, and yet, you look like you're about ready to collapse."

"I've been living as a huey since last September. Excuse me if I'm not as nocturnal as I used to be."

"That's not what I mean. When is the last time you trained?"

Oh, now he had to be joking. "We've been running ten miles every night since you came from Paradise."

"That's not enough. I remember how fast Karmarov and Cynthia moved when Kara..." His voice choked up, before he pushed on. "Vampires are faster than wolves. Even if you had taken rites, you couldn't outrun them. If it comes down to you facing off with a vamp, your only hope is to stand your ground and fight. Right now, you'd be a biscuit for them."

"You missed your true calling as an inspirational speaker, Tobias."

My quip backfired as the werewolf's face screwed up, flushing sallow cheeks behind the dark scruff of a barely-there beard. "I'm not trying to inspire you, hood! I'm trying to make sure you don't die. I'm trying to make sure you're still alive to work with me and avenge the wolves taken from us. It's bad enough you're a nascent, but you're arrogantly letting what little ability you have atrophy and go to waste."

"So you got a chance to visit my mom when you were in Paradise and get a list of all her pet names for me. May I remind you that a few months ago, even as a 'weak and arrogant nascent,' I was still able to run you down and tackle you."

The wolf in him grabbed control. Anger burned in his eyes, and I could tell he was on the edge of shifting from the override of emotion as he leapt up from the table. In three steps, Tobias had my arms over my head and my back to the wall. His canine teeth grew, elongating into twin needles that could remove my larynx in moments. Instinct roared to life within me, a primitive drive to fight back: *strike him, mark him, dominate him.*

Kiss him.

"You only caught up with me because I was starting to sink into moon madness," he growled, bashing my wrists into the wall to emphasize his power. "I was weak. Even then, I could have easily killed you if I wanted. Luckily for you, I decided that if I couldn't appeal to whatever small sense of honor, or – dare I say it, duty? – lay within you, I was going to manipulate you through your body, to get you to help me."

"Through my body? What are you talking about?"

He leaned in, sniffing at my neck. The proximity threw my pulse into overdrive, and not merely born of fear. I let my head fall to the side, exposing my throat to him.

"That," Tobias said, pulling back. "Do you even realize that you keep submitting to me?"

Imagining the scene that had just played out from his perspective, I understood what he was talking about.

"I just offered you my neck," I said in time with my understanding. The practice was used in two ways in the packs. First and most obvious, as a sign between two wolves of any gender that one recognized the superiority of the other. The second, in the mating ritual for the female to show that she accepted the male as her mate, and was submitting to him. Cody made no secret of how crazy it drove him when I acted like a wolf. I didn't realize until now how enticing it was for me, too.

"Do you even realize how dangerous that is, Geri? You're attracted to me. Beyond being fucked up, think of all the ways I could have taken advantage of that."

"But you were mated; you couldn't possibly…"

"I *am* still mated." He cut off my words with a growl. "Even if she's dead. A wolf would do anything… *anything* to save his mate. I'd even degrade myself by sleeping with a hood."

He let go my wrists, but held me captive with his stare. My soul withered. Raised to believe myself superior to the status of any wolf, I realized suddenly that Tobias had been raised the same way. I was a lesser being in his eyes, a pest that infringed on his pack's freedom. He hadn't sought me out because of his faith in my abilities; he had sought me because he lacked faith in his own. I was a last resort, and one that had cost him far more than just the love his life. It had cost him his pride.

"I'm sorry." The words tumbled from my mouth before I could stop it. Pride told me I had nothing to be sorry about. My own guilt told me better. "WWL is wrapped up in this somehow. Or at least, some vamps who work there are. I'll figure it out. I'll find a way to stop them. And you're right; I have been letting my skills go dull. But you're wrong about one thing."

The wolf raised an eyebrow. "And what is that?"

"Neither of us have much experience taking on vampires. We need to know how to fight one."

"Remembering your experiences in alleyways, I'm forced to agree with you. But how do you suggest going about that? If you think that appearing on a local news show after fighting off a robber would be bad, I assure you that stalking down street vamps and picking fights with them would be worse."

I crossed to the stove and put the dumplings into a steaming tray.

"When the student is ready, the teacher appears."

ELEVEN

A slip of cloud illuminated by the waning moon shifted the colors cast on the ground below. Silver hues with blue overtones danced across green leaves and an earthen base baked and cracked under the unyielding summer sun. I wondered if the vampire we waited for had ever looked as that ground did now. Memories whisked my thoughts away to my last confrontation with Cynthia's progeny, Donovan, shortly before I killed him.

My maker says hood blood is better than Neosporin for us. Told me not to come home until I had drained you dry.

Tobias's voice broke me from my reverie. "You sure he's coming?"

"He said he would."

"Yeah, but is he *actually* coming?"

Unlike the werewolf seated on the passenger side of my old Chevy, my worry wasn't about if the undead professor would show up, it was about whether the cops would. The state park campsite an hour's drive from the city was closed for remodeling, but I'd been a teenager in a rural region once. I'd been caught by the cops a time or two in places I shouldn't have been in the middle of the night, though those were cases of patrolling as a hood. Luckily, in a small town like Paradise, where everyone knew each other, at least by name, all I'd gotten was a ride home in the back of the cruiser to give me "a good scare," and a warning.

I didn't know the name of the town we'd come to, but that also meant that they didn't know my name either.

Just as I was about to pull out my phone, we caught sight of a pair of headlights driving up the access road, toward the riverside campsite. Igor Karmarov must be a savvy investor, or have been putting drachma away since he was in baby fangs. The silky, black luxury ride he drove easily had a six-figure price tag. Any hopes for inconspicuousness flew out the window. His sweet Daddy Warbucks wheels next to my rusted-up Chevy? It shouted out something funky going on.

Tobias got out of the truck, crossed his arms, and proved that, despite being a werewolf, he was first and foremost, male. He gawked over the car, his mouth watering as well enough as if a tray of venison steak had just pulled up beside us.

Igor closed his door and hit his key fob. Two high-pitched, double beeps flattened in the humid air.

"Mr. Somfield." The professor stepped forward, offering out a hand. "I wish to offer my condolences and my regrets. Geri tells me you have accepted my apologies by proxy, but let me assure you that I'm dedicated to doing whatever it takes to end this madness. Unfortunately, for the moment, that means pretending I'm a team player, not waging an open war on my own kind."

Tobias's mouth worked, jaw grinding over jaw, as he fought the part of himself that wanted justice, and the part that desired vengeance. "Thank you," he coughed out, barely biting back any tears and feeling emotions so poignant, I felt wary in the wake of his proximity. Then, the wolf rounded on his grief, his tone leveling and his demeanor, businesslike. "We need your help, professor."

"So Geri's message said, even though I'm not sure meeting this far out of the city is completely safe. We don't know who – or what – may be lurking out here. By the way…" His gaze refocused on me, amusement teasing the corners of his mouth. "The number you contacted me from was not your own."

Was he accusing me of something? "It's actually an online phone number my cousin and I used to use to send messages without our mothers finding out. It's registered under the name Dora Knockers."

Even Tobias grinned at that.

I shrugged. "We were thirteen at the time. I agree with you, Doc, but Tobias and I realized a problem we had, and you're the only one who can help us."

With a furrowed brow, Igor stuck his hand into the pockets of a trench coat, which he wore despite the muggy conditions of a midwestern summer. "And what is that?"

I swallowed my nerves. "We need practice fighting a vampire."

Igor blinked twice, let out a laugh, and turned back toward his car. "Out of the question."

Before I could take two steps in pursuit, Tobias beat me to it. "You can't expect Geri to go into that office building full of vamps day after day unprepared. She's spent her life learning how to fight werewolves. Surely you could spend an hour giving her pointers on fighting vamps. If anyone finds out why she's really there, she needs enough know-how to get away."

"It's not that what you're saying is wrong," Igor said as he wedged himself behind the steering wheel. "It's that it can't be me. I made a vow that I was never going to put myself in that situation again."

I picked up the conversation. "You also promised me you were going to do whatever it took to help me get to the bottom of WWL's involvement with wolves. Don't tell me you're going to help build a house then expect me to bring all the tools on my own."

"Your analogies are lacking. You might want to– "

Both Igor and I fell silent as the front windshield of his car fissured into a hundred pieces.

Red fur and heaving chest, the massiveshoo wolf lorded over the car, denting the hood. Closer to the size of a black bear than the purebred animal, the sight of him both thrilled and terrified me. With gleaming teeth bared and the rumble in his chest droning, I knew that what Tobias had said earlier in the evening had been right; if he had wanted to kill me, the task would be all too easy.

The vampire was less impressed with my associate's display.

"Are you insane?" The door nearly fell off its hinges, Igor threw it open so hard. "Do you have any idea how expensive this car is!"

Tobias turned to me, yelping out a few canine phrases. I couldn't understand wolf word for word, but Igor didn't know that.

"He says if you don't agree to help us, he's going to rip off the rearview mirrors," I said, making up a translation on the spot that captured a threat rendered in mannerisms and yaps.

Igor, however, called my bluff. "You have no idea that's what he said, and even if he was saying that, it won't change my mind. I'm already doing everything I can. Don't ask any more of me."

"I appreciate all that you're doing. But since I'm stuck in the mailroom, I'm going to have to stick my nose into places an intern shouldn't be. Me coming up against a v-staffer isn't an if, it's a when. I'm not saying make me be able to fight like a slayer. I'm just saying that a few pointers would be nice."

"You want a pointer?"

The hard ground rose up to meet me as I lost my footing. At first, I thought that Igor had pushed me. Only a moment later did I realize I'd been thrown off balance by mere air, a veritable sound wave that took me down as he sped past. When I looked up, it was to find the normally mild professor, teeth long and gruesome, eyes black as coal, holding Tobias by the scruff off the roof of his car. The wolf whined, not being injured, but understanding that he was at the vampire's mercy.

"Take your rites," Igor said. "That's the best thing you could do to help everyone. You have the potential to be among the strongest of the hoods, and you abstain out of pride. Use every weapon you have, starting with yourself — that's my *pointer*."

"Release the wolf."

My hand arched over my shoulder, tightening on the handle of the silver blade woven into my hair. Whipping it back in front of me, the metallic blade went flying, embedding in Igor's thigh. Silver wouldn't kill him, but that didn't mean a dagger into his ancient muscles hurt any less.

Tobias's body flattened against the earth, a sickening crack of bones that turned my stomach. The vampire cursed in a language I didn't recognize as thin, white hands wrapped around the blade of my grandmother's dagger, unplugging a wound oozing thick, black blood.

I threw myself in front of Tobias, shielding his body with my own. "Set a finger on this wolf again, and next time I'll nest my blade in your brain."

My threat failed to have much of an effect as he studied my weapon.

"So fast," he mumbled. He looked down on my defensive position, all anger erased from his face. "Are you certain you haven't undergone your rites? I've never seen a nascent who can move with such speed."

An ache formed in the pit of my stomach. "My mother wouldn't be constantly riding my cape if I had."

"No, I suppose she wouldn't." The vampire tossed my blade on the ground about a foot in front of me. When I looked from it to him again, he'd moved to the ground so swiftly, I wondered how he was unable to dodge my volley a moment ago.

"Fine, we train," he declared. "But not tonight. I have to ride back into the city and drop my car for repairs, now that you've ruined the glass. It's a good thing you're not working under me at WWL, Geri, or I'd dock what it will take to make this right from your pay."

Behind me, Tobias shifted back to human form, and though naked werewolves had no effect on me, it clearly disturbed Igor. His eyes became bobbers, floating on a plane of reality that didn't dip below Tobias's chin.

"Something tells me you can handle the cost just fine." Tobias braced me from behind, his palms sliding under my elbows and guiding me to my feet. "But first I want to know what you meant when you said you made a vow to never confront a hood again."

Igor's shoulders slumped. "I have the blood of too many on my hands."

"Hoods?" Tobias's hold on my elbows tightened.

Igor shook his head. "Hoods, slayers, wolves. Even my own kind. You'd think after so many years, I'd learn to outlive the shame. Some regrets refuse to dull. They are a blade that sharpens, cutting less frequently, but deeper each time it swings."

"Fine, I'll bite. What made you so guilty then?" I asked.

The vampire turned his eyes to the skies. "Once, I longed for power, control. I wanted to be a king among my kind, a prince of darkness. I built a family that supported that vision. I chose children foolishly. My legacy is the destruction they have wrought. So many dead. Whole slayer lines abolished, hoods and wolves pushed from their lands. One day, I had an epiphany, and realized what the true legacy of my actions were. I made a vow that I would never again intentionally harm another supernatural creature."

The wheels of my mind began to whirl. "When did you make this vow?"

A darkness crept into Igor's eyes, a panic of a man whose secret had become known. "Fifty-three years ago."

I swallowed my nerves. "After they were all dead."

He didn't try to deny it. "I thought, if I could just destroy their food source, *maybe* I could defeat them. I swear, Gerwalta, I'm not that man anymore."

"What man?" Tobias asked confusedly.

I pulled my keys from my pocket, took my dagger from the ground, and without taking eyes from Igor, backed to the truck.

"He's the reason the slayers are gone," I said. "He killed them."

Twelve

The only upside of discovering that the one vampire I'd grown certain I could trust had let me down was that Tobias gave me a day to mope. Or as he put it, "regroup and reevaluate our options." Hope waned. My chances against a vamp were paltry at best. Without proper training? Smaller than a fly bite on a moose's butt. I needed guidance. I needed strength. But how could I possibly trust a man who had admitted to killing off the last of the slayers, even if the purpose of his work now was to resurrect them?

"Maybe you shouldn't go to work today."

I sighed as I pulled a bagged lunch from the fridge. "We need the money."

He flinched, and it only took me a moment to figure out why. Over the last two days, and more so, in just the three weeks since Tobias had shown up on my doorstep, the frequency of "us" and "we" trickled in to our discussions. Somehow, we'd become a team, one made of traditional foes whose instincts still pushed them to hate each other.

"I can walk more dogs," he insisted as I turned for the door. "It's not a lot of money, but every little bit helps, right?"

"Fine, get more clients. But until you do, rent is due next week. I have to go, I'm going to be late."

"Are you sure you're going to be safe?"

I paused at the door, the wolf at my back. "Tobias, I know Cody sent you here to protect me, but we both know there's only so much you can do. Everyone – huey, wolf, or hood – takes a chance with each step. I'm at least going to make sure my steps count for something."

At the office, I drifted through my duties efficiently, but detached. At lunch, I sat with the huey interns, all of them assigned to office positions on the floors above ground, and wondered if I was wasting my time keeping my head down and my eyes open. Had I been assigned to Igor's lab as expected, I'd have access to records, experimental spaces, research notes. Now all I had access to was the supply closet. Nothing suspicious in there except three dozen cases of correction fluid and a hobgoblin's boatload of rubber bands. I checked email on my phone, surprised to find one from an address I didn't recognize.

It's not what you think.

For some reason, I felt the same for Igor that I'd felt two months before with Jess when I found out he'd been using me to get to Tobias. Only this time, there was a tinge of regret. Feeling anything but repulsion for Igor, knowing what he'd done, didn't make sense in my head. But something niggled at me, a low-level hum that I owed him a chance to explain.

On Wednesday afternoon, after loading my cart with deliveries, sorting from lowest floor to highest, I was surprised to find another package destined for the twenty-seventh floor. This one, however, required a signature, meaning I'd have to see Mr. Perfect-in-just-a-towel again. Even if I was trapped working at WWL, at least it came with benefits.

This time when he answered the door, he qualified as clothed, even if "clothed" meant only an undershirt and boxers. Did this man not own any street clothing? Moreover, did he not go into the offices below at all? The time on my phone made it perfectly clear that it was still huey working hours.

Rubbing sleep from his eyes, his mouth curled into a sly grin when he saw me at his door. "If it isn't Geri. Geri Kline."

Despite the doldrums in which I'd anchored myself, I couldn't help the blush in my cheeks as I extended my clipboard. "I have another package for you, Caleb."

"I know. I mailed it to myself."

"You... Why would you do that?"

"Why do you think?" He winked, sending the butterflies in my stomach into a coordinated flight routine. "Even paid extra for certified delivery so you'd have to see me for a signature."

"There are easier ways to talk to me. You must know I work in the mailroom. I'm there all morning. Come by any time."

"Thanks for the invitation." He took the clipboard from me to fill out the receiving slip. "Not much of a morning person though."

"A night owl, are you?" I asked as he handed me back the clipboard. "Me too until... Wait, is this... Is this your actual name?"

"You knew my name, Geri. It's Caleb."

I turned around the clipboard and shoved it into his chest. "Is this some sort of cruel joke?"

"I used to ask my mother the same question. As a kid, all the other boys at school called me Kale-Club."

"No, not your first name." Huffing, I pointed at his scrawl. "You signed Caleb V. Helsing."

His hand rose tentatively to brush the back of his ear. "Yeah, so?"

There were three possibilities. One: Helsing was a more common name than I had realized, and it was mere coincidence. Two: it wasn't coincidence, but the name had come down through the subsequent generations, even if the legacy had not. Or three, the man standing in front of me was actually a born and bred member of the most infamous slayer line ever.

I decided to take a chance. Leaning in, I whispered, "Helsings tend to be night people, from what I hear."

Caleb gawked at me. "Sorry?"

In an awkward gesture, I threw the clipboard on the cart behind me. "If you're going to slay vampires, you'd have to be."

A moment of confusion, and then, before I could rationalize the movement, Caleb pulled me into his apartment and slammed the door behind us.

"Who sent you?"

The air in my lungs came whooshing out as he threw me against the wall. Gone was the coquettish, irrepressible flirt, replaced with narrow eyes and a hunter's glare. In a moment, I'd gone from butterflies, to scorpions. My instincts reared outside of my control, calling on what strength I had. I knew my eyes were glowing blue, because suddenly, Caleb's hand dropped as he stepped back.

"You're a... You're a hood."

Not a question, a statement.

"House of Red," I confirmed, peeling myself off the wall and trying not to gasp too loudly. "And you claim to be a Helsing. Big words, but do you have any proof?"

Caleb lifted his right arm, bringing his hand to shoulder level. With a twitch of his fingers, a small orb appeared, a baseball-sized globe that threatened to blind me.

"Proof enough for you?"

I couldn't really be seeing this. It had to be a trick. I needed proof. My fingers danced through the air, reaching for the fireball dancing over his palm. Just before I touched it, Caleb slapped my attempt down with his free hand and closed the other, forcing the sphere out of existence.

"Are you crazy? That's solar energy! You want third degree burns?"

"Yes, if it will prove this isn't a dream."

Caleb ran a hand through his hair, huffing. "It isn't a dream. But no one's supposed to know. Shit, I... I need coffee. You want some coffee? I'm going to make some coffee."

My father once told me that mysteries were like a rash. Sating the itch of one dangerous question only caused more to arise.

"You're a *slayer?* You guys are supposed to be extinct. Are there others? And why are you *here,* of all places, holed up at WWL?"

He muffled a laugh as I followed him into the kitchen. "Coffee first. Questions after."

Now that I was no longer pressed against a wall and wondering if I was about to be locked in a fight to the death, I took time to examine my surroundings. Caleb's apartment looked like a high-end hotel room crossed with an interior decorating magazine. Following him into the kitchen, I found a landscape of shiny black appliances with chrome highlights and ebony marble counters. He worked the controls of a coffee machine that looked like it had been lifted from a Roman coffee bar. He prepped twin cups of espresso with a single pushed button, then put one in front of me. The kitchen didn't have a proper dining table. Instead, two tall stools sat on opposite sides of a cocktail table.

"Questions one at a time, please, allowing for one swig of joe between."

I brokered a smile. "Not an evening owl?"

"What can I say, Geri? I like spending as much time in bed as possible."

I ignored the innuendo and pressed on. "I've been told my whole life that the slayers went extinct. Obviously, that's not the case."

"There's no question in that statement."

"Fine then," I said. "How are you alive?"

"Because my parents loved each other very much, and it led them to do things that resulted in my being born."

"Seriously, Caleb! Do you have a clan?"

A slow sip of coffee, slurped with relish. "Slayers don't live in clans. Or clutches or packs, if that's your next question. We're more of the traditional nuclear family model, with a shorter coming-of-age period. I left my home and New York City ten years ago, when I was fifteen."

"Fifteen?" I was certainly capable of surviving in the wild by that age, but not on being a functioning adult in the huey sense of the word, legally or practically. "Why so young?"

"Since my parents were murdered, it seemed the right thing to do at the time."

My humanity fought my hood nature. My mother would tell me, "Don't get emotionally involved. Keep a clear head so you can stay an impartial party and mediate with logic, not feelings." My hand froze midair over the table, unable to cross to give the simple comfort of a touch. Caleb observed my spontaneous attempt at miming with no shortage of amusement.

"And here I was told all hoods were stoic, detached wolf-killing-bots."

My hand dropped to the table. "We don't just go around killing wolves." There was a bit more annoyance in my voice than I would openly admit to. "We're supposed to help keep the peace. We're more like security guards."

"Who have some kind of magic ability to form silver into any weapon you want and can fly," Caleb countered. His eyes grew wide with excitement. "I've always wanted to see what that looks like. If I got out some silver, could you change it into a bell or a statue of Angelina Jolie or something?"

"No, I'm only a... Wait, we're not talking about me. We're talking about you, and how a slayer is living in a building owned and operated by vampires."

My memories of Igor's admission rebounded on me. Security in the building was tight, and even though I could crawl all about it delivering packages all day long, I knew even then that I was constantly subject to surveillance. An open door didn't mean unfettered ability to move about.

My mouth went dry. "Are you being held prisoner here?"

"Prisoner?" He laughed, his tanned cheeks taking on a beautiful reddish glow. "Is that what you think? No, Geri, I can come and go as I wish."

"Then you... work for WWL?" It seemed the only other logical conclusion.

"No, not really." His features relaxed and Caleb grew somber. "I guess if you had to put a label on it, you'd say I'm a refugee."

Thirteen

Refugee. A small part of me wanted to scoff at the term. I equated it with heartbreaking images of scrawny children dressed in rags, running through mazes of tents or old women carrying sacks on their backs as they trooped through mountain passes to avoid border crossings. The image of a handsome young man who could summon sunlight in his hand and lived with a killer view of the Lake Michigan shoreline didn't square. Then again, I so far had no evidence that his clothing expanded beyond towels and cotton blend undergarments.

"Refugee? What are you refuging from?"

"From vampires."

Awkwardness made a fist and aimed for my gut. "I'm sorry if you were unaware of this, Caleb, but WWL *is run* by vampires."

The man across the table from me exhaled and pinched the bridge of his nose. "You honestly think I don't know that?"

"You didn't know I was a hood."

"How would I even begin to imagine that?" he threw back. "You're supposed to be out in the countryside, roaming through leafy forests and collecting apples on your way to grandmother's house, not pushing a mail cart around a Chicago skyscraper."

"Oh, man, you have really bought into the Grimm brothers PR job, haven't you?"

"Always envied the wolf in that." He winked. "I always wondered what a hood would taste like if I ever got a chance to eat one."

Dizzy with the implication, I moved on. "Stop that, be serious. You're going to have to help me understand this. If you're running from vampires, why are you knowingly hiding behind vampires? Is it, like, some sort of hiding in plain sight thing?"

"No, it's like a good vampire/bad vampire thing," he said. Caleb laced his hands and set them before his now empty coffee cup on the table. "You sure you want to know this? Why I'm really here? I don't know if you ever heard the expression, but a little bit of knowledge…"

"…is a dangerous thing," we said together.

I continued on alone. "One of my mother's favorite idioms, and one of her justifications for making me study combat or arcane pieces of history so fiercely. But yes, I want to know."

"Okay, then. The truth is, I'm probably one of the best slayers in the world."

He paused, giving me an opportunity to laud him, I assumed, but all that came out was, "Well, you're probably one of the only slayers, so…"

"Touché." He stood, taking his empty cup and my untouched one to the sink. "Even if there were others, though, I'd still say that. I've been hunted since my parents died. Six times, I've come face to face with a vamp, and five times I slayed it."

"And the sixth time?"

"I barely managed to get away," he admitted, staring off into space. "The five I killed were pretty young, half a century at most. But that sixth one? He was one of the Ravens. I'm a gifted slayer, but even I couldn't take on a daemon."

A chill crept down my spine, radiating out to my extremities. "Demons? Are those real?"

"Not *demon, daemon.* It refers specifically to one of the vampires in the Dracule line. It's the word the ancient Greeks used for a creature somewhere between a god and a man. To a huey, a vampire's abilities would seem divine. You know how they twist our truths. Hoods become one single, innocent young girl attacked by a wolf while going to grandmother's house. Slayers become either an elderly Danish quack or Sarah Michelle Geller. And the Seven Sons of Dracula become…"

"Ravens," I said, cutting him off.

"The Seven Ravens." The slayer grinned at my insight. "Dracula's daemon progeny: one daughter and seven sons. The Grimms got that right. The rest of the details, not so much."

"My cousin told me a version of it." I repeated the story as I remembered Markus relaying it over a *feuernacht*, years ago. "He said that Dracula's sons were supposed to protect and defend their clutch against a rival group moving in from the east. Especially his daughter. But the brothers ended up hating Daddy Vamp. Dracula couldn't bring himself to kill his own progeny, so instead, he sealed them inside a mountain."

My face screwed up. "That part of the story never made sense to me. How would Dracula, or any vamp for that matter, seal anyone inside a mountain? Do they have some secret rock-altering ability no one has told me about?"

"No, and honestly, I don't get that part of the story either. If slayers knew the truth of it once, it's been lost now. But somehow, Dracula managed to contain them for centuries. Until about fifty years ago, that is."

I felt like a child at story time, sliding to the edge of my seat. "What happened fifty years ago?"

"Dracula died."

"He did? But I thought he was the one vamp a slayer never bested."

Caleb crossed his arms over his chest and leaned back in his chair. "A slayer didn't best him. Time did."

My curious expression pressed him to continue.

"I bet you hoods are the same as the hueys on that. You think vampires are immortal."

"They're not?"

He grinned, amused by my naiveté. "Not in the way it really matters. When a huey is folded into a crèche and undergoes his change, yes, the baby vamp stops aging, doesn't get sick anymore, and basically becomes indestructible short of a massive sun burn, decapitation, or wood to the heart or brain, but immortal? There's this great old saying from where my people come from: five hundred to the day, then pass away." He shrugged. "I mean, it's not exactly that clean and easy, but yeah, a vampire will last about five hundred years, give or take a decade or two, and then it turns to stone."

His yarn had hit a snag. "Wait a minute. If that was true, there would be all kinds of awesomely accurate statues of vamps all over the world."

"They turn to dust when struck directly by sunlight," he said, as though it were the most obvious thing in the world. "And for the ones that go stony somewhere where the sun would never find them..."

He held out his hand, sparking another luminous orb on his palm. I winced, my retinas burning.

The memory of babysitting the baby vamp I'd killed in the alley, just waiting for the sun to rise and destroy the evidence of my slaying him, I ground my teeth. "Isn't that convenient?"

Closing his hand, Caleb again squashed the sphere from existence. "So, anyways, like I was saying, fifty years ago, the Count finally kicks it, and the Ravens are set loose on the world. My people were already dwindling in numbers then. Guess we fell prey to affluence just like anyone else. More wealth, less children, younger generations not wanting to uphold the traditions of the elders. You now, that kind of thing. Then, too many slayers started taking hueys for mates. A huey-slayer kid might have the gift to fight vamps, but beyond that first generation, it's a crapshoot."

Wouldn't my mother be pleased to learn she'd been right on that theory.

Caleb continued. "When the Ravens returned and started picking us off, we were pretty much doomed. And that's why I'm here: because they're still out there, and they won't stop until each and every slayer is either dead, or their prisoner. The vamps at WWL, though, protect me."

"But why?" I asked, trying to digest the massive history lesson I'd just been given. "I get why a vamp might like to see a slayer dead, especially if it came down to a life-to-life face off. But why are Dracula's sons so determined that slayers go extinct? Which, by the way, everyone assumes they are."

His tightening jaw suggested either frustration or bluff. Caleb knew the reason, he just wasn't sure if he should – or *could* – tell me. After a few moments of his silence, and myself knowing the importance of keeping secrets, I moved on.

"Okay then, if you can't tell me that, then what's in it for WWL? Why grant you asylum?"

Out of nowhere, Caleb clapped and got to his feet. "Well, it's after dark and I'm willing to bet you should have clocked out by now. Unless you want to hop in the shower with me, which is normally what I do after coffee in the evening."

"Another time, maybe." I slid off the chair, inwardly groaning as I anticipated the ten-mile run that awaited me when I got home. Thunder rumbled in my head as lightning struck my brain. "Hey, Caleb?"

"Geri?"

I took a step closer, relaxing my features, putting on an air of vulnerability. "You're trained to defend against vampires, right?"

He deadpanned, pointing both index fingers at himself. "Slayer."

"Right." Another small step, the lowering of my gaze. "Can you teach me?"

The vein on the side of his neck ticked. "*You*, a hood, want to learn how to fight vampires?"

"Don't think of me as a hood. Think of me as a girl from the country, alone in the big, bad city for the first time, all on my lonesome, who just happens to end up working at a company run by vampires. It's been happening more lately, hoods having to fill in for slayers and take on vamps who've gone a little batty. All the bloodlines are reporting it, but we're still not trained for it. All I'm asking is if you could teach me how to defend *myself*, if it ever came down to it?"

He was either calling me on my bluff, or falling into my trap. Either way, when he took a step toward me, his eyes looking at my lips, I had to wonder if I bought my own con. His proximity sent my head spinning.

"If you were just some huey girl, and you found yourself squaring off with a vamp," he said, his voice husky, "you wouldn't stand a chance. But you're not a human girl, are you, Geri?"

"No, I'm not."

"Then you might. You know what? Sure, why not? If for no other reason than when the Ravens do find me, and if I am the last, our skills will live on. But I have to warn you—"

He moved again, his step bringing us chest to chest. He leaned in, his lips just inches from mine.

"—I fight dirty."

He's going to kiss me. No sooner had the thought occurred to me, and my eyes fluttered closed, than a breeze whisked through my hair. By the time I opened my eyes, Caleb was already at the door of the kitchen into the hall.

Apparently, vamps weren't the only ones who could move with superhuman speeds.

"I really have to book it," he said, disappearing down the hall. "Meet me tomorrow night at seven at the executive gym. I'll trust you can show yourself out."

FOURTEEN

I ran home from the El, dizzy from the day's events. Not only were the slayers alive, but one was going to give me lessons on how to defend against vamps. And he was hot. And a flirt. And god damn it, even if I had no intentions of flirting back for any other reason than manipulating him to fit my own needs, it felt good to be flirted with. Coming off of two relationships that had ended both in their own uniquely tragic ways, I had started to doubt that I'd been meant to have any sort of appeal as female. Yes, Caleb might be playing up my attraction to him for his own ends, but it was hard to think what those ends might be.

Other than the one possibility that was the aim of males of any species. To my own surprise, that didn't sound too bad. For the moment, however, I had to deal with another male, one whose only intention for me was to serve as a vehicle of his revenge and to buy dumplings.

"You're late." Tobias glared at me the moment I walked in the door. "Again."

"Sorry."

I dropped my backpack on the couch and shimmied out of my street shoes. After I found out I'd been demoted to the mailroom, I didn't bother with anything that gave an air of professionalism. The high-heel shoes I'd worn to orientation ended up in a dumpster somewhere. As I walked to my room, peeling off work clothes so I could change into my yoga pants and sports bra, the wolf trailed me, sniffing deeply.

"What's that?"

For the briefest of moments, I stilled, before forcing myself to keep moving. Hopefully, he thought my quickening pulse was merely because he was standing in my room as I changed. Wolves knew better than to expect a blushing damsel around their own nudity, but hoods weren't as loose on the practice of bearing all.

"What's what?"

He inhaled again, closing his eyes, concentrating on the profile. "You smell different. It's... some animal I never smelled before."

I wasn't a liar, but I knew when to conjure a truth for my own sake or somebody else. I could have, of course, told Tobias about Caleb without mentioning the part about him being a slayer, but I was pretty sure I couldn't do it without grinning like a school girl, suggesting I had a crush that would distract me from my work. The last thing the grieving wolf needed was to see me being giddy over a guy.

"Had to make a delivery to one of the labs today. Must have been whatever chemical concoction they were working on. Why, what does it smell like?"

"It smells like…" He fell back to sit on my bed. "Sunshine? I don't know if that makes sense, but that's what it reminds me of. Are the vampires trying to manufacturer sunshine?"

"Science has already invented sunlamps, so I doubt there would be much money in that."

"Probably not. God, it's clinging to you. I should throw you on Amy's bed and roll you around for a while."

I stopped mid-shoe. "What?"

"Amy's bed," he repeated through a half-smile. "The traces of at least six men are in that mattress. I'd much rather smell sunshine than that."

"Right." *Change the subject, change the subject.* "So, coach, what's on the itinerary for tonight? Ten-mile run, five-mile swim in the river, then burpees?"

"Remember the woods you chased me down in that one time?"

La Bagh Woods. Both he and I scoffed at the name when it came up before. I'd been raised in the tree-choked innards of Michigan's Upper Peninsula. Tobias's packlands nested on the edge of the largest national park in England. Chicago's paltry attempt at a woodland made both of us snicker.

"Yeah, so?"

The wolf stood, marching through the door. "We're going there. Now that you're getting a sense of your agility and endurance again, we need to rekindle your hunting skills. I'll expect you there in a half hour."

"You'll what?" I slid my phone into my bra. Not a fan of pockets, it was the only place I'd found to keep it. "What do you mean you'll expect me there?"

"I'm going ahead to hide from you. Wait ten minutes, then run."

So I wouldn't be getting out of running after all.

He continued, deaf to my groaning. "I'm your target, and this time, when you find me, I'm going to attack. Be ready; I won't be going easy on you."

"Come on, Tobias. Like you said, I wouldn't stand a chance against you if we were actually to go at it. I'm still only a nascent."

"That's no excuse." Grabbing his house key, he headed out the door, squeezing in just before it closed. "And it's certainly not one that the vampires are going to accept."

The night when I'd first chased the werewolf through these woods had been before I understood why he was in Chicago. Before he'd shared with me that he'd been drawn there by the abduction of his mate, and that he'd been searching for her for two months, a dangerous amount of time for a wolf to be away from his pack. Then, he'd hit me with the hardest truth of all: he was a rogue. Exiled from his pack and disowned by the alpha, Tobias's fate had been all but sealed. He'd go moon mad, and as soon as the Yellow Matron who controlled this area discovered that, he'd be dead.

A waxing moon peaked out from a break in the clouds, reminding creatures of the night that the cycle was nearing its zenith. Two hours past sunset, the park was officially closed, but I could still hear a handful of hueys scattered through its dales and canopies; whether they were homeless, lovers stealing a few moments together, or others up to illicit activities, I couldn't be sure. Chicago's famous winds battered the leaves of the trees above. Rain clouds seeded the air with their scent, and a distant rumble suggested we had a half-hour until they arrived and deluged all caught out of doors. Verdant rolls twisted, turning yellow in the momentary silver glow.

The wind made tracking difficult. I could sense Tobias on the air, but the gusts dispersed and folded his aroma, making a mockery of my sense of direction.

Before I left home, I'd grabbed my wristbow. Wearing the weapon in the city might bring unwelcomed attention, but who could blame a single girl for having some sort of protection on her? Besides, it still wasn't the weapon I wanted. My hands longed to wrap around my crossbow, a gift from my father on my fourteenth birthday. For Tobias's sake, I'd switched out my normal silver arrow tips for rubber ones. The design inflicted blunt trauma, but didn't pierce the skin. Any werewolf worth his canines wouldn't get more than a bruise from them.

Finally frustrated by the lack of cooperation the elements offered, I closed my eyes and used my senses. The low-level buzz of his proximity hadn't diminished since I'd come into the park. Without concentration, however, it was just a directionless sensation. Suddenly, his location revealed itself, not with my eyes or my ears, but with my mind. Tobias waited twenty yards away, hidden in some shrubbery. My eyes opened just in time to see his lycanthrope form pounce over the hedges. White, gleaming teeth bared, he attacked. I lifted my arm, took a blink to aim my training arrow, and fired.

The wolf yelped when the dull projectile knocked him right between the eyes. Tobias's charge ceased, and his confusion began. Sitting back on his haunches, he pulled off the closest thing a two-hundred-pound wolf could to annoyance.

"Oh, just change back!" I huffed out. "You know there's something you want to criticize and I'll be more pissed off about it if it's in human."

He did as I suggested, and then, immediately after, he did as I had predicted. "You have to stop doing that!"

I blinked twice. "Being an expert mark?"

"No!" he shouted, flailing his hands in the sky. "Using this weird hood mumbo jumbo thing you do that makes me track you down. It's like you're shouting out, 'come eat me, wolf, for I am near and tasty.'"

"I'm sorry, but did or did I not also just shoot you between the eyes?" The cool grass blanketed hard earth still warmed from the sunny day as I plopped down. "If that had been one of my silver arrowheads instead of the rubber ones, you would be dead right now."

"And if I had been a vampire," he shot back, "I'd have moved even faster, and you'd still be dead. Why do you close your eyes anyway?"

"Helps me concentrate."

"Helps you lose, is more like it."

Tobias circled around a tree to grab his discarded clothing before crossing to where I sat and bringing himself into compliance with public decency laws. "What does it matter, anyway? You're already half way through your internship, and we're still not any closer to knowing anything."

I shared his frustration on that, but I didn't really know what to do. Every attempt I'd made to snoop around was blocked by security, and the others with whom I worked were either too far embedded to be trusted, or too ignorant to be useful.

Maybe Caleb could become a resource? After all, he'd shared a boatload of sensitive information with me, without me having to work all that hard to get it. All it would take would be a few subtle threats implying he wouldn't want those secrets to get out to get him telling me what I needed to know.

I shook my head, and threw away the notion. No, I wouldn't rely on my mother's tactics, even if, currently, it might be my best option for actually learning anything. I sighed, lying back on the ground, observing the play of cloud and moon above. We'd need to go soon, or risk being caught in a tizzy of a thunderstorm.

I threw my hands up to the sky, fanning my fingers like the air was fur I could pet. "Don't you love when there's a storm coming? Even in the city, you feel a little like being in Paradise. Oh, if only..."

"You really like it there, don't you?"

"Of course I do, it's home. Or at least, it used to be." I turned to look at him. "It's funny, that while I've always wanted to get away from my mom, I never actually wanted to leave home. I love where I grew up. I always pictured myself living there."

Tobias grinned. Maybe he and Kara had had plans too. "What would you do there, though, if you weren't a hood?"

"You'll laugh."

"Will not." He crossed a finger in an x-pattern over his heart.

"I wanted to be a school teacher," I admitted. "I always pictured myself grading papers at night and making scones on weekends. And I'd have a dog. Not a wolf. Not even a German Sheppard. I'd get a pug or a corgi that wouldn't even be able to walk full speed because I'd fatten it up so much. Yes, Tobias, that's what I wanted. Maybe it's what I still want. What about you? You planning to go back for *feuernacht*?"

"That's what you guys call it. To us, it's just full moon." He finished buttoning up his shirt. "I survived three months here just fine. I don't need to run back to Paradise every lunar cycle."

"Just fine? You were on the edge of lunacity."

"The edge of it?" He looked over his shoulder at me. "I'm living with the daughter of Red Matron in one of the biggest cities in North America, helping her infiltrate a corporation run by chemical-happy vampires. If this isn't mad, I don't know what is."

I chewed on that for a moment, surprised at how little offense I felt. "If you stay, we'll need to find a place for you to spend the full moon. What were you doing before?"

He raised a hand in the air dismissively. "I'd tip off animal control about an out-of-control stray, then make sure I stayed on mark until they came to pick me up. In the morning, I'd fall back to human and just let myself out before any of the workers came in."

"I love how you say that like it's obvious."

"Isn't it? Why, you have any better ideas about where I should pass the moon?"

For a moment, I thought about the dungeon under Igor's lab back on the UWC campus. Despite the bad memories, it would serve the purpose. Except, that would require me to make amends with Igor. No way in hell.

"I don't suppose I could just lock you in the bathroom?"

"Not unless you have great faith in that flimsy, hollow door and its ability to keep me from busting through to hunt you." Tobias's face screwed up. "Geri?"

"Tobias?"

"Can I ask you a question?"

"Seems that way."

His eyebrows became arches. "What?"

"Never mind. Yes, go ahead. Ask away."

He pitched himself up on an elbow and turned to me. "When you took me to Paradise, it was full moon. Our instincts those nights are crazy, more animal than man. How were you so sure you could go into the heart of the packlands and not get yourself killed?"

It was a question I had been asking myself since it happened. "I didn't."

"And yet, you did. Why?"

I shrugged, as well as I could while lying on the ground anyway. "It was the only way I could think to save you. I knew that if I couldn't convince Cody's dad to take you into his pack, I was basically signing your death warrant."

"And then you showed up, and instead of Bob Ryland…"

"It was Cody who was alpha," I said, cutting him off, my voice cracking. "No good deed, et cetera…"

Silence clouded the air around us as he sank back to eyeball the sky. A few moments later, his voice turned unusually gentle.

"It's hard for him too, you know."

Confused, I turned my head toward the non-sequitur.

"For Cody," Tobias clarified. "He loves Lisa. How could he not? They're mated, but… I don't know. A wolf can't commit adultery; it's biologically impossible. But I guess what I mean is, where you're concerned, there's a lot of regret and… guilt?"

"You two must have got close in just a month if you're having those kind of heart-to-hearts. What an inspired bromance."

"We don't talk about it." The werewolf's flat tone admonished my presumptions. "I recognize it in his eyes when he looked at you, that day in his kitchen. If anyone else had asked him to let some foreign, strange wolf into the pack, he would have said hell no. But he felt like he owed you. He was making amends."

Nerve endings that had grown dull with time twitched in response to the stimuli. Despite that I was coming to think of Tobias as a friend, I feared I'd still be willing to cleave his heart from his chest with my silver dagger if someone assured me it could bring me back Cody's affections. But what was done, was done. I had to just get over the fact that that ship had sailed. It had been a stupid fantasy anyway, thinking a hood and a wolf could ever truly be together.

"He didn't owe me anything. And neither do you. Want to go another round? We might have time before the storm hits."

Tobias shook his head. "There's no point."

This time, it was me propping myself up to glare down at him. "What do you mean?"

The werewolf lifted himself off the ground, then turned to offer me a hand. A useless, although not totally unappreciated gesture.

"I can't sneak up on you, and you have no problem chasing me down. Your peculiar special skill makes chases pointless."

"We could try a little hood-to-paws," I suggested, boxing the empty air. "Maybe just a frontal assault. I used to do that with Cody, but I think he went soft on me whenever things got too heated."

He lifted an eyebrow.

"Get your head out of the gutter, Somfield. I mean we trained together. It's actually how we first discovered we were attracted to each other."

The werewolf clicked his tongue. "No point in that either. You're no match for me. As long as you're a nascent, you're hopeless."

"Oh, come on, Tobias! Give me something to work with here?"

He squared me. "Work with this: Until you take your rites, you're no match for me. Do it, and you actually stand a chance. Maybe."

An ache registered in the back of my mouth as I ground my teeth. Was he secretly in collusion with my mother? "I'm afraid that might cause more problems than it would actually solve right now. Anything else?"

"Full moon is in two nights," Tobias resumed. "Maybe you can call in the tip to Animal Services instead? Otherwise it might look like the same irresponsible owner keeps losing the same dangerous dog."

"You're giving me permission to call the authorities on you? Sounds fun."

Fifteen

"You really don't have to stay. I've done this before."

Tobias shimmied out of his worn jeans and folded them neatly before handing them to me. It was still a few hours until sunset, but it was better that Animal Services seize him before he fell completely under the moon's influence, when he'd have little ability to clamp down on his instincts. Wolves were not irrational killers, but werewolves did hold a primal instinct to detest hoods. All the more reason he didn't want me near when the sun finally set.

"Would it be bad if I admitted I'm here for the entertainment?" I stuffed his clothes into my backpack and slung it over my shoulder. "If I wasn't so conditioned not to take pictures of anything relating to supes, I'd be snapping this like Jimmy Olson."

My eyes lingered on the sinewy muscles moving under his fair skin. Tobias's thighs could crack coconuts. He looked like a body of water, his navel the place someone had tossed in a stone and his muscles the corded ripples that radiated outward. He was... a fine example of the human form of a werewolf. I was a hood, yes, but I was still female. Only a few hours until full moon, my emotions were raw and near the surface, including those typical of a college-aged girl without any sexual outlet.

"You know what you need?" the werewolf asked.

I licked my lips, thinking of all the naughty ways I could answer. "What?"

"*Feuernacht,*" he said, snapping me back to reality. "How long has it been since you danced around a fire? It does for you what running with a pack on full moon does for us, resets our humanity. You don't vent that energy soon, it will take you bad places."

My argument caught in my throat, and somehow the truth slipped past. "If I go home, even just for *feuernacht,* my mother will force me through my rites. I couldn't come back to Chicago."

He raised an eyebrow. "Why not?"

"It's not too different from alpha's prerogative," I said, referencing the compulsion a pack member fell under when his alpha gave him a command. It wasn't that it was impossible to disobey, but only the strongest wolves could try. Even then, it often got them disowned. "If my mother opens my Gate of Fire rites, and I pass through, I'm hers to command. Then, all this..." I motioned to me, then him, then the city at large, "is over."

"I get why you wouldn't want that." He planted his balled fists on his hips, concentrating. "Then you need to toss yourself off."

The heat within me shriveled as a bucket of cold water washed over it. "What?"

"I don't like saying it either. But this power you have, this connection we share—" He looked up at me from downcast eyes. I didn't know if the heat in them was anger, or lust. "I feel it, what you feel."

My mouth took on guppy status as I struggled for words. What was I supposed to say? It wasn't untrue, but if he thought a few merry-go-rounds at the edge of a sacred fire or me getting my jollies were the problem, he didn't know that much about hoods.

I cleared all confusion from my expression, making my face rigid, my voice, detached. "I'd feel this way about any naked man in front of me. It's not about you. It's about the moon."

Tobias took steps, bringing him inches from me, and sending my instincts into overdrive.

Kill him.

Take him.

He leaned in, bringing his lips inches from mine. "Tell me you'd resist if I tried to kiss you right now."

My hand twitched, though I didn't know if it was from the impulse to pull the silver dagger from its usual hiding space, tucked into my braid, or if I wanted to reach out and run my thumb over Tobias's bottom lip. I was a hunter, but what was I hunting? If I kissed him, the distraction could be used against either of us.

"Don't forget what I am, wolf. I'm still as likely to slay you as avenge your losses."

Our standoff ended as a truck at the end of the alley pulled to a stop and two doors closed, followed a moment later by a male voice. The air shifted around me, and I didn't have to look to know that Tobias had taken on his wolf.

Two people came around the corner of the alley. One, a stout mocha-skinned woman, and the other, a tall, scrawny white man. They both wore black slacks and khaki-colored uniform shirts. The man held a long poll with a retractable noose on the end. The woman held out a cell phone, her eyes alternating between the screen and the alley. Even from this distance, I could read the names on their embroidered tags.

"Miss, we got a call about a stray," Simon said.

I looked around. Tobias was still near, but had somehow hidden himself from open view. Made sense. How weird would it look for a "feral stray" to be calmly sitting, awaiting capture?

"Yeah, that was me," I said, exaggerating the act of looking around. "He was here just a minute ago. Not sure where he got to."

Right on cue, the massive red wolf emerged out from behind a garbage bin, teeth bared and a growl rumbling in his chest.

It hit too hard, too fast, and in a whirling moment of clarity I knew that I should have listened to Tobias and just left. Here, there was a wolf, and behind me, there were hueys. A full moon rose overhead, dragging away my ability to be rational, propelling my instincts.

Protect them. Defend them. Destroy the wolf.

I bit my tongue, fighting the urge to pull my dagger out and attack. Tobias must have sensed my urges; a moment later, he was sitting primly on his back haunches, then fell to the ground, and rolled over, offering his belly. It was a display for me, not the hueys. He was reminding me he was no threat, that I didn't need to take him on. That we were not enemies.

"That him, Doris?"

"Yeah, that's him, alright."

The gun fired before I had a chance to think. Panic filled me, all blood draining from my face. They shot him? They *shot* him? My instincts threw themselves into reverse, and my pull to destroy became a need to protect. Without thinking, I dove, throwing myself over Tobias's body, my silver dagger wielded in my hand.

The two officers, the woman still holding the gun out, took a step back. The man leaned in to the woman.

"I hate calls from PETA nuts."

Doris, however, ignored him. "Whoa, there, young lady. Put the knife down, and step away. You don't want to be anywhere near that dog. It could take up to a minute for the sedative to set in."

"Sedative?" I dropped my knife and turned, examining Tobias. On his neck, a red-feathered dart peeked out from his thick coat. His eyes were glassy, but there was still a hint of fight in them.

No, not fight. What I saw, I soon realized, was a reflection of my impulses. He wanted to protect me, but the drugs flooding his system prevented him.

"Yes, a sedative," Doris said, closing in, attempting to pull me back from the limp canine body on the pavement. I didn't resist, taking to my feet. "We've dealt with this stray before. Third or fourth time we're picking him up. We need to make sure it's the last time."

"The *last* time?" I repeated, as though that was a foreign term, the meaning of which I couldn't grasp. "What do you mean, the last time?"

Simon approached with his stick, putting the loop at the end around Tobias's throat. It barely fit. A werewolf was twice the size of their animal world kind, and even the mightiest Mastiff would pale in comparison to his bulk.

"He keeps escaping," the man said, tightening the restraint. "Might have tried adopting him out, but that growling thing he's doing? Aggressive behavior. Too risky. We're going to have to put him down. Damned shame. Every time we've picked him up, he's been a sweetheart. Such a beautiful dog, too. Probably some sort of wolf-mastiff hybrid."

"God save us from the wolf hybrids," Doris muttered, maneuvering me behind her back. "Never lose their wild streaks."

Not knowing what else to do, my mind took fantastic leaps. "I'll adopt him!" I blurted out. "Give me a few minutes to go grab my truck, and I can take him home right now."

Doris's sappy expression suggested she'd pegged my type perfectly. "We understand where your heart is at, sweetie, but after a dog of this size shows this kind of aggression and habitual escapes, we can't risk it. Besides, he's not safe enough to leave roaming the streets."

Safe? You're *going to be the one who should worry about being safe if you hurt my wolf.*

With desperate eyes, I turned to Tobias, hoping he could somehow tell me what to do. He labored just to keep his eyes open. The sedative was dragging him under. I had to fix this without his help. Unfortunately, I could only think of one way to do that.

Crow wasn't my favorite dish, but I'd eat it if it meant saving Tobias.

SIXTEEN

On the horizon, the pink blush of dawn grew warmer by the minute. Chicago was to have one of its bright and beautiful summer days, full of sun, dangerous conditions for a vampire to be out and about. With that in mind, I rushed to close the door. Even then, he winced in pain. The orientation of the street put the rising sun at my back, flushing a curtain of ambient rays over the professor when the door had opened.

It was hard to say who was the more rigid as the car moseyed away from the curb outside my building, me, or the undead vampire behind the wheel. On the phone, I had been straight-forward about what I needed, and totally upfront about how awkward I felt asking him to help me after our last encounter. He in turn had admitted that he wasn't sure I'd have spoken to him again.

"So, how did he get taken by the dog catcher exactly?" Igor asked.

I explained the fact of the matter, then went silent once more.

The summer sun peeked up around 5:30 AM this time of year. The shelter wouldn't open until 8, but it maintained a twenty-four hour emergency pet drop with someone always on duty.

"I'll use that as our in," Igor explained. "Once I take the attendant under thrall, I'll get him to lead me back to where the strays are kept. If they really think Tobias is a public safety hazard, they'll have him separated somewhere."

"Won't you look strange coming in without any animal, though? I checked their website. It says the night attendee has to buzz you in."

Igor notched his head toward the backseat. "Already thought of that."

I turned, and gasped the moment I saw the little ball of fluffy joy. I'd always been told by schoolmates that cats hated riding in cars, but the silky white Persian in Igor's backseat looked as concerned with our mobility as a tree with the rain.

"A cat?"

"Her name is Buttercup."

"As in..."

"Twoo luub," Igor invoked. A more oddly timed quote of *The Princess Bride* I had never heard. "I love that movie."

Despite holding the same opinion, despite the stressful conditions that had brought us back together, and despite myself, my chest shook with laughter.

"What?"

"What?" I asked. "You quote one of the most cultish chick flicks of all time, oh big bad vampire, and you don't think I'd find that funny?"

"It's a good movie. One of the best. I didn't cease to have human emotions and interests when I became a vampire, Geri. I just became capable of inhuman acts. Vampires are huey at heart. You have to stop thinking all we do is brood over young virgins and stalk unsuspecting maidens in the dark. What's the point of having eternal life if you're never going to live it?"

"But you don't, do you?"

His brow furrowed, pristine fair flesh unmarred by the defused sunlight coming through the WWL-made windows. "Don't what?"

"Live forever," I said. "Vampires aren't immortal. Not in the way that it counts the most."

"No, we're not." I respected that he wasn't going to try to deny it. "Who told you?"

Should I tell Igor, especially after he'd admitted playing a role in the reason the slayers were supposedly extinct? I wasn't exactly sure the nature of his relationship with WWL, but I did know the company funded his lab at the university. If he didn't know of Caleb's existence, I was sure there was a good reason. On top of that, I owed Caleb's secrets respect.

I shook my head and fashioned my lie. "My mother told me something about it once."

"And how would your mother... Oh, that's right. She knows Inga. I suppose that's not all she knows, then, is it?" His grasp on the wheel tightened. "No, Geri, we're not technically immortal. It's not exactly a secret to those who go looking for the knowledge, but it's not something we share openly."

Along with their ages, I recalled from an earlier conversation. Could a reason for that be because a vampire near the end of his days grew weaker, not unlike a huey? Would knowing an opponent was turning 499 this year put him at a disadvantage?

The car slowed to a stop as a sign for the West Chicago Animal Shelter came into view. Igor moved the gear shifter to park and turned to grab a pair of sunglasses and a panama hat that really didn't mesh with his college-prof-on-the-weekends attire.

"Geri, you're going to do something for me."

I watched him pull his docile cat from the back seat and wondered how a man who could be so gentle with such a tepid creature could turn on a screw to be so cold toward me.

"And what exactly is that?"

The cat hissed at me as soon as it got a good view, as if it hadn't even known I was in the car before.

"You made a friend recently, Geri. One with a very nice view of the city."

Ice shot down my back and drained the color from my cheeks. "I don't..."

"Don't try to deny it. I have friends inside of WWL too."

"Fine." Trying to push back some confidence into my manner, I straightened on the edge of my seat. "What about him?"

"I need a genetic sample."

It sounded too stupid to be real. "What, you want me to just walk up to him and ask to swab his cheek?"

"You're a hood of the red line. I'm sure your mother has trained you in a number of tactics needed to get information. You pick the one you think best suited to the situation."

"And what are you going to do with it if I do?" I asked, sounding like a petulant kid threatened with grounding if she didn't get her grades up.

"Do you want me to save your wolf or not?"

He slammed the door and stooped over, his hunter's eyes sharpening on me. The hat and angle mostly shielded him from the sun, but a sliver landed across his throat. The spot began to redden, as well as if someone had tagged him with a can of crimson spray paint.

"I'm not a complete humanitarian. I'd like to think we're becoming friends, but there are things going on here bigger than just you and me. If you have some information I need, I will get it from you, either through your kindness, or at the cost of it."

He knew what my answer would be, and ten minutes later when Tobias emerged wearing a lifted Animal Services uniform and slid into the backseat, I knew I had no choice but to do exactly what Igor Karmarov wanted.

"Are you okay, Tobias?"

He looked like he'd been licked up and down by the cat that Igor just threw on the seat beside him.

He answered in a voice as flat as his expression. "I don't like being tranquilized. I don't like it at all."

Without saying a word, I reached my hand back over the seat, putting it on his. He gave no indication that it made the slightest difference.

"Worst part of it was, though," he continued, "I saw them bring in one of the dogs I walk on my normal route. Dead. Hit by a car."

"Oh, Tobias, that's awful. I'm sorry. Was it an accident?"

"Accident?" He seemed confused by the term. "No, that's why it's so sad. It was suicide. He told me he was going to do it the other day. I didn't believe him, or maybe I did. But how could I tell her owner that her dog was planning to off itself, and you know because it laid out the detailed plan for you while you walked it on the Navy Pier?"

SEVENTEEN

I hovered my employee identification over the reader again, only to get the same result. Total denial. Not entirely surprising. I couldn't recall anything from orientation or reality suggesting that interns would have access to the executive gym. Even my ID, programmed to let me into most of the offices during the workday, was set up to be invalid from 8 PM to 6 AM. When I'd asked my mailroom supervisor about that, Doug's matter-of-fact reply had been "to make sure the interns don't treat the offices as their own personal hook-up lounge."

That may have been true at any other company, but at WWL, I suspected that huey interns were barred overnight for other reasons.

Finally, on my third useless try, there was a beep. Not because my card had worked, but because the one Caleb extended past me did. He stood behind me, close enough that if I looked over my shoulder, we'd be cheek-to-cheek. As it was, the heat of his proximity made the hairs on the back of my neck stand to attention.

Smooth. The guy was smooth. Flirt level: expert. A fact I would need to turn to my advantage to hold up on my end of the bargain with Igor.

"I believe it's customary that when a man takes a woman out, he should open the door for her."

He rounded me to take the handle of the now-unlocked door, but I got to it first, pulling it open and motioning him inside.

"Hoods are matriarchal," I informed him. "You don't need to worry about huey expectations. They're more likely to upset me than flatter me."

Unfazed, the slayer stepped into the gym, his eyes never leaving mine. "In that case, I can't wait to see how you try to flatter me. FYI: I'm a sucker for flowers and chocolates."

"I don't do either one."

"Well, then, stretch out and let's see what you do do."

Any qualms I had about us possibly being walked in on by any of the huey executives passed quickly when Caleb informed me that only residents had access to this gym.

"Though the other residents don't really need it, if you catch my drift."

"So you're the only non-vamp living in the residential section?" I asked.

"I guess if you define 'living' as being an animate, thinking being even if also an undead, blood-dependent bug, then yes."

Caleb issued me protective gear: gloves, a chest cover, and a head wrap. I had to shake my head when he didn't provide himself the same. Did he really think he had that much of an advantage over me?

"Doesn't sound like you have that high of an opinion of them."

"I look at a vampire the same way I look at a politician: down, until given a reason to do otherwise. Box as a warm up?"

The gloves strapped on my hands made dull thuds as I hit them together. "You sure you don't want to strap something on? I probably hit harder than most girls you've fought."

"Being as I've never fought any girl, I'll take your word on that." Caleb walked to the center of the large square mat on which I stood and raised his hands, starting to bounce around. "What about your people? You get along with the wolves?"

"If by get along you mean do hoods take the role of authoritarian overlords, boxing packs into their lands, and constantly surveilling their movements," I threw a left jab, which he easily ducked, "then yes. Most wolves are pretty good people. I suppose like any society, it's got its peaches and its bad apples. My clan keeps the bad ones on a tight leash."

He jabbed at me, but I ducked, letting his fist meet air. "You said you're a red, right?"

I nodded, landing a fist on his bicep. The blow might have found purchase, but the slayer didn't so much as flinch.

"Daughter of the Matron, in fact. They'd be my clan someday, if I hadn't renounced them."

"Can I ask you a question?" I lost a step when a hit landed on my left shoulder, and the gear distributed the force across my upper body. "Is what they say about

Little Red Riding Hood true? That her own mother tore her limb from limb with silver blades, and roasted them over a fire?"

"More or less. Silver something, anyway. The form the matron chose to wield it to eviscerate her, the wolf, and their baby? We don't know for sure. I've heard variations."

"Man, you hoods are sadists."

I didn't need the reminder. In fact, hearing it from someone else's mouth only made me recall how much I hated the legacy with which my namesake had saddled me. Even leaving my clan and my birthright behind as I had, I'd never outlive her reputation among those who knew of our kind.

"My mother is the queen of the sadists." A left, a right, another left, and I'd regained my lost ground.

"Is something she did the reason you need to learn to defend against vampires?"

His question made me go still. I dropped my arms and stood, petrified. "What?"

"Come on, Geri. You didn't ask me to show you defensive moves as part of some damsel-in-distress seduction scheme. And it's not like the WWL vamps are going to come after you, seeing as there's now a paper trail that would cause them problems if they did. So I have to wonder, why are you really here?"

My mouth went dry as I tried to force false words over my tongue. But I couldn't. I couldn't ask Caleb to share slayercraft with me under false pretenses.

"I killed a few vampires not too long ago," I admitted. "A baby, and its maker. The maker didn't really care for its baby, but unless I've strongly misunderstood your world, makers are valuable. My tracks are pretty well covered, but if anyone ever finds out I was involved...."

My voice trailed off, and I realized it was because of the total lack of drama in what I'd said. Maybe saying it aloud was the first time I'd allowed myself to acknowledge just how big a danger I'd be in if word ever got back to whoever Cynthia's friends had been, or any of the other progeny of her crèche. Jesus Criminy, for the first time, I realized I didn't even know how many vampires that would include. Were vampire makers of the only child, or the Brady Bunch variety?

Caleb's mouth hung half way to the floor. "*You* killed a vampire, all by your lonesome?"

"*Two* vampires." Technically, Tobias had had a hand in killing Donovan, but I didn't think that kind of detail mattered much. "It was a lucky set of circumstances. Circumstances that would be difficult to reproduce on demand."

A pleased smile scraped over his face. "You must realize if the maker's kin ever track you down, there's going to be hell to pay. I might as well make the exchange rate work in your favor. Gird your loins, Geri. Let me show you what a slayer can really do. Ready?"

"Ready for wh—"

My eyes couldn't even follow Caleb, he moved so fast. One moment he was before me, and the next, I was on my back and he was looking down at me.

"Lesson one…"

With a hard yank and a blur, I was back on my feet, gasping and dizzy. His voice reached from across the room, a distance of thirty feet he had crossed in the time it took me to look around.

"Slayers are vampires' balance, and the only way we'd outrun one of them is to be just as fast. And since you're not one of us, that means that we – and they – can outrun you too."

"If that's true, then how the hell am I supposed to have a chance?"

"By using what you can where you *are* on equal footing," Caleb said. "That basically leaves two options: your body, or your brain. Also, use their weaknesses against them."

I folded my arms over my chest. "Which are?"

In two blinks, Caleb again stood before me. Like, right before me. If he leaned in, we'd be kissing.

"Blood," he said, raising a hand to my neck and tracing a fingertip down the path of my jugular vein. The act left me struggling not to lick my lips. "As fast as they are, as strong as they are, the change they go through when they enter a crèche alters their brain. Like sharks, once they smell blood, it's almost impossible for them to resist the urge to at least investigate. It will bring them in close. And when they're as close as I am to you now—" He ran the pad of his thumb over my bottom lip "—and distracted, they are at their weakest."

"I can sympathize."

Caleb grinned and dropped his hand. "Unfortunately, I'm not a vampire, so your blood – and your proximity – has no effect on me. But, now that I've taught you how to bring a vamp into a zone where you might actually stand a chance, let's practice the short game, huh?"

Throwing off the act of being able to move so fast it would make the Flash weep, we took turns initiating mock attacks. Caleb still held the advantage; he was older and stronger. Nevertheless, with a lifetime of training, bolstered by my work with Tobias over the last month, I held my own. Caleb only landed two hits, apologizing profusely on each occasion. When he learned I only took his pauses to double my attacks, however, all apologies went out the window.

After two hours, we decided we'd had enough for the night.

"Well, I'll say this: you certainly don't need much in the way of basic training on my side," he said. "Now, are we going to get dinner, or do you just want to have drinks?"

Confused, I stood with the boxing gloves in hand. "What?"

"Didn't you understand this was a date?"

"Why would I think it was? You didn't ask me out."

"*You* asked *me* out when you asked me to show you how to fight vampires."

"That wasn't me asking you out. That was me asking you how to defend myself against imminent death."

"Romances have started in worse ways," he quipped. Caleb extended an arm and pointed to a set of doors on the far side of the room. "Shower suites. You should find most everything you need inside."

"Thanks." I grabbed the bag of clothes I'd brought and headed toward the door on the right. "But I feel the need to clarify: we're not starting a romance."

"Oh, silly hood, we already have. You just haven't realized it yet."

Among my various superpowers I counted one not unique to hoods, and while convenient, not one worth bragging about: I could get in and out of a shower like a storm blowing through town. It didn't surprise me, therefore, when I emerged four minutes later to find that Caleb still hadn't finished. When an opportunity walked up to you and gave you a business card, you took it.

"Any sample will work," Igor had told me when handing me the glass specimen tube. "Blood is best, but that might be hard to come by. Saliva could prove a challenge too. But if you get me a few hairs, I can probably do fine with that."

"Hair?" I had asked, my face twisted with disgust. "Yuck."

"You can try to get a semen sample. It would definitely give me a robust genetic profile, but its collection might be a little demanding on your part."

"Hair, it is!"

Only, how was I going to get his hair? If I crawled around the gym, looking for hair on the mats, I'd have no way of knowing if it was actually Caleb's. Plus, ew... I could just kiss the guy, using it has a cover for running my hands over his head and yank a few strands in the process. That idea seemed feasible, only kissing Caleb might introduce complexity.

I crossed my hands, bit my lip, and pondered. The idea struck me with a dull thud. The risk of getting caught? High. The consequences if not discovered: nil. The ease with which I could do it? All the ease.

The other shower suite proved to be a mirror reflection of the one I had used a few minutes before. An anteroom just beyond the door included a table laid out with individual toiletries —single-use soaps, shampoo, mouthwash— even disposable, pre-pasted toothbrushes. To the left was a second, smaller room, one with just a toilet. Ahead, a frosted glass door fogged over in mist led to a shower area.

And in the shower, under the spray, Caleb was singing.

Perhaps I'd become too used to the manners of wolves – both Cody and Tobias were the "pile on the floor" variety of men —and that was why seeing Caleb's workout clothes neatly arranged on the table in a perfectly folded pile surprised me. I shook out his shirt, and found a few hairs quickly enough. They fell into the specimen bottle, and without any pockets in the pants I'd brought to wear, it went the only place I could think of: inside my bra. Replacing a perfectly rectangular fold to the top of the stack, I was ready to make my escape. My hand was on the handle when the song behind me stopped.

"Something I can help you with, Geri?"

Every muscle in my body pulled taut. Should I own up to the fact that I was in the room, or slip out and hope he chalked it up to his imagination.

Caleb continued. "As far as supersensitive ears go, I'm willing to bet hoods got it slightly better, but I can still hear you."

The water shut off, and my panic turned on.

"I'm… I was just… I'm sorry."

The shower door behind me creaked as it opened. The moisture poured into the much cooler changing room, as little, hazy droplets appeared suddenly before my eyes.

"Don't be," Caleb said. "I like it when a woman is aggressive."

My eyes shut and my pulse booming in my ears, I only knew he was so close to me when he lifted my still-wet braid and shifted it to the right side of my neck. A moment later, his mouth, wet and soft and sweet, lowered to the junction of my neck and my collarbone.

I couldn't move. I wanted to, desperately, in so many ways not right for a Sunday. But as invested as I was with the sensations his mouth and his tongue brought on, I couldn't shut off the little voice screaming in my head, which then turned into speech.

"You're not wearing a towel, are you?"

I felt his lips move into a smile against my skin. "Aren't hoods used to nudity?"

"Hoods are used to being around naked *werewolves*. You're not a werewolf."

His mouth moved to the sensitive skin behind my ear. "And what about hoods? Are they known for their naked ways?"

"A hood's hood is kinda what makes her a, you know, hood."

"A shame, that."

His hands circled my waist, pulling my hips back until my backside was against him. My eyes rolled, and I couldn't stop the moan that escaped.

"Caleb, I need…"

One roll of his hips, and I felt my control slipping. Caleb's hands maneuvered to the front, making for the bottom of my shirt. If I didn't stop this now, he was going to find more than he was bargaining for on my chest.

"Stop."

His hands, his movements, his hopes —they all fell still. He heaved a heavy sigh. "You sure?"

"Yeah, I'm…" Why not block him with the truth? "I've never… done *it* before, and as exciting as I'm sure this would be, I don't want to have my first time be in the shower of an executive gym at WWL."

"No, it should be something better than that," he agreed, backing away. "Challenge accepted. In time, of course. Be warned, Geri, and please forgive the pun, but I always *rise* to the occasion."

"I won't forgive it. It's not a good enough pun."

He laughed at that. "Okay then, Kline, you and your innocence get out and give me a chance to get dressed. At least I can take you for the best pizza this side of Chicago."

Eighteen

The next day, as I clawed into the office, I thought about calling in sick to work for the first time in my life. It wasn't that hoods never got sick – I remembered being stuck for a week in bed with the chicken pox when I was six. It was that I in particular seemed to have a very robust constitution. Until it met deep dish, sausage and pepperoni, that was, and robust became defunct. That, combined with the fact that I was burning the candle at both ends, working at WWL in the day, training with Tobias, then Caleb, late in the night, and fitting pockets of sleep in the crevices where those things overlapped, and I'd come to look like a strung-out addict by the time July rolled in.

I was half way to the women's bathroom at lunch time, hoping to grab a 15-minute nap in one of the stalls, when my supervisor's voice reached up the hall.

"Kline, hold back a minute."

I knew better than to roll my eyes. Unfortunately, the part of my brain in charge of "you know better than to" had already gone on break. "What?"

Doug's jaw worked, but he seemed to overlook my rebellious teenager impersonation. "The boss wants a word with you."

"I thought *you* were my boss. Or are you talking about yourself in third person? If that's the case, you should know *this* intern knows her rights, which include a thirty-minute break after four hours worked."

Some people got angry when they were tired. Some cried. Me? Apparently, I verbally attacked supervisors.

Doug was not amused. Standing in place, he cocked a hip and gave me an "oh, really?" glare. "Do you know how many deliveries you made today?"

What was this, a pop quiz? "Twelve or so? My clipboard is on the shelf in the annex if you want to check."

"The correct answer is six," he said, ignoring my lip.

I quickly slogged through my mental catalog, counting out the stops on my fingers. "There were at least ten."

"No, Geri. There were only six that you *delivered.* The rest of them, you merely took to places they didn't belong. *That* is called *misdelivering.* So far, today, you have delivered six packages, and misdelivered four. Do you know what batting six hundred gets you?"

I glared at him. "I don't even know what that means."

"Didn't you ever play baseball as a kid?" Doug continued. "You spend half your time wandering in places where you have no deliveries to make, and the other half dragging your feet. My god, Kline, we work in one of the easiest jobs in this whole company: take this thing from Point A to Point B. Ants have been doing it for millions of years, yet after a month you're actually getting worse it at."

A bit of the guilt my mother had honed in me over the last twenty years peeked its head. "I'm sorry. I was out late last night, and I…"

His hand shot up, cutting me off. "The extent of my concern for you only lasts between 10 AM and whenever you clock out for the day, and concern might be too strong a word. You're an intern, and that means by default your position is supervised by the director of HR. Go tell her about your crazy night out on the town and see how she reacts."

"The HR director?" I saw her name in Palatino ten-point type in my memory, affixed to the bottom of my original offer letter for the summer internship. "You mean Inga Rosethorn?"

The agitated, middle-aged man in front of me blanched and threw his hand over his mouth. "*Never* call her by her first name. You will address her as Miss Rosethorn or sir, yes sir."

"Does she have a preference?"

Doug smacked his hands together. "She sent a message just now that you'll no longer be working under me. You know what that means, right? Just a suggestion, Kline. In your next job, don't treat the company like the jungle for your own version of Dora the Explorer."

I walked off the elevator, and into a cliché. If you had asked a Hollywood set designer to fashion something for a scene in which the supernatural villain was to be played by Meryl Streep a la *The Devil Wears Prada*, Inga Rosethorn's office would have been the unholy creation of that vision. Whatever carpenter had been in charge of its construction, they must have hit Home Depot on the day black marble was on sale. The floor, the tilework cut into a diamond grid that went half way up the wall, the shelves built into the walls… they were all made of it. Furniture was sparse. Two modern-styled ebony armchairs sat perpendicular to a black lacquered, bean-shaped desk carved with ivy and fleurs-de-lis.

Thug 1 and Thug 2 had met me by the elevator the moment I'd exited. They didn't tell me who they were, and I didn't have to ask. T-1 closed the door behind him while T-2 jabbed a meaty finger at one of the armchairs. My field of vision longed to be filled, but the office held little in the way of curiosities after they'd left. I tried to imagine what my mother might do, armed with the knowledge she was about to sit face to face with the firstborn daughter of Dracula. First, catalog every route of ingress and egress, keeping eye on both from where an attacker could come, and to where she might escape. In this space, the only way in or out was the door through which I'd come. I turned, eyeballing the distance from my spot, thinking how long it would take me to cross it and what I might be able to use as a weapon to get past the guards.

When I turned back, all plans and thoughts came to a screeching halt. Behind the desk, a file in hand and her hair pulled back in a spartan bun, sat a woman who had materialized from nowhere.

"The vents," she said.

I cocked my head to the side, chiding myself inwardly for having adopted one of Tobias's werewolf mannerisms. "Sorry?"

"You were wondering how I got in here when the door behind you is the only way in or out." She extended one delicate lily-white finger toward the ceiling, where an air vent had been built over her desk. "A very useful means of travel for our kind during daylight hours in a structure such as this. Your next question, I imagine, would be how the clothes travel with us when we become smoke, to which I would counter: how does a creature made of bone, flesh, and organs manifest itself as a particulate and reincarnate in its original form to begin with? Not knowing the answer to that, the clothes question has never captured my interest."

If I had seen her as a child, seeing her again sparked no memory. What was perhaps most surprising was how unremarkable Inga was. She had the kind of face you'd see in a crowd and forget the next moment. Dark brown hair pulled into a severe bun, topping off a slim face from which a hook nose erupted. Her bottom lip didn't measure the width of the top one, making it look like she constantly pursed her lips. A thin woman, she might stand five foot four in heels. A strong wind could topple her frame.

"I guess we're not beating around the bush, are we?" I asked.

"Bushes hate being beaten. I should know; I contributed large sums of money to several of their less successful campaigns," she said distantly, more absorbed by the file in her hands. "You're the daughter of Red Matron, and I'm the daughter of Dracula. What do you remember of me?"

"Just going to your house."

"Not surprising. You were very young then. And now you're… my, seems you'll be twenty-one next week." She opened her mouth, displaying two long, piercing teeth – the only weapon a vampire ever needed, and one they were never without. "We should celebrate with a drink."

My right hand twitched, wanting for my blade.

"But luckily for you, I'm well fed here." Her face lowered back to the papers before her. "You're a student at Western Chicago University, I see. Never heard of a hood who came to the big city for college."

Suddenly, I doubted this meeting had come about just because I'd misdelivered a few packages. Wouldn't Doug be disappointed.

"You were originally invited into the internship program to work with Igor, mapping the slayer genome." She dropped the folder to the desk and steepled her hands. Illusions of her plainness blew away with a single look. Her eyes… Not quite blue, not quite silver, but somewhere in between. Like Lake Superior when it froze, Inga had eyes the color of nature's indifference to man. "Were you disappointed when you showed up on your first day to discover that you were assigned to the mailroom?"

I made a mental note to ask Caleb if what I heard about vampires was true, and that they were sensitive to dishonesty the same way lie detector machines were. Not knowing that at the moment, however, I decided that honesty was my best – maybe my only – policy.

"Quite a bit, actually."

"And why do you suppose I put you there, under the supervision of that horrid little man?"

I sensed a trap, and didn't know which way I should step to avoid it. At least I could take comfort in the fact that she didn't seem to like Doug any more than I did. "Igor thinks it's because you assume I'm a plant, spying for my mother."

She bit the end of her pen. "You've been caught several times snooping around areas you had no place being."

"I'm not spying for my mother." A truth that, nevertheless, didn't shift all of the suspicions she might hold about me aside. "But I'm still a hood, and from the forests. It's in my nature to map out my surroundings. Instinct, really, telling me to know my turf."

Inga's face fell. "Is that what it was? How disappointing."

I cleared my throat and shifted in my chair. "At the same time, it's let me stay in the city instead of going back home to the job I worked last summer, so there's that."

"Ah, yes." Her index finger pinned down a page where I assumed my work history appeared. "At the... state park? I'm sure you're much happier here than being immersed in the swish and sway of the forest and roar of the waterfalls, in a place where hoods and wolves run free."

Not knowing how to respond to that, I didn't.

Inga looked up again as she leaned back in her chair. "Would you care for a glass of water, Miss Kline?"

No sooner had she asked the question than the door behind us opened. I didn't turn to see who came in; I assumed it would be one of the same strong arms, just waiting for the obvious cue to enter. The new arrival came to stand beside me, leaning over to offer me the drink. I didn't look until I had to, and then looked away as quickly as I must, unless my shock be too evident. I couldn't stop my pulse from racing, though, and as Jess Harmond passed the glass to me, I saw a smile crawl across Inga's face for the first time in my peripheral view.

"Thank you, Jess. I wonder if I might ask for one more thing before you go?"

If Jess had been a dog, his tail wagging could have powered Chicago. "Of course, Miss Rosethorn. Anything."

Inga jerked her head in my direction. "Do you know this woman?"

I swore that my blood froze. Igor had said he'd altered Jess's memories, but would another vampire, one older and from a regal bloodline, be able to untwist his knots and release the truth?

I looked to Jess, playing along, forcing a lip-deep smile onto my face. He examined my features with the scrutiny of a young sculptor studying *The David*.

"We met at orientation. Other than that, maybe I've seen you around campus?" he asked. Then, realization dawned in his features, and my stomach fell to the floor. "Oh, I think we met at the library once. You do go to WCU, right?"

"Thank you, Jess, that will be all."

With his mistress's dismissal, the POS I'd almost slept with slunk out of the room, no care to the fact that he'd been sent off so unceremoniously. Enthralled, then. Definitely enthralled.

"Tell me, Miss Kline, how is it that Jess Harmond has no clue who you are, when according to Igor's own work reports, you two worked together at his WCU lab last summer?"

Again, I decided that honesty would be best, though I'd pour it sparingly and into a glass I knew the shape of.

"Prof. Karmarov told me he tinkered with Jess's memory after Cynthia Wu's death. I didn't ask for details. A vampire's prerogative, I guess."

The vampire's head angled, and I could see contemplation working behind her eyes. Either she bought what I'd offered at face value, or she was saving up her doubt to spend it at a later date.

"A shame what happened in Igor's lab," Inga said. "Xin was one of the most respected makers in the Americas. Many clutches vied to acquire her offspring."

With a gentle manner, I held up my hand and shook my head. "Please, I don't want to know any more than I already do."

With that act, I tipped the scales in my favor.

"Wonderful." Inga clapped her hands and rose to her feet, inviting me toward the door. "You are a credit to your mother, Miss Kline. When Red Matron and I met several years ago, we reaffirmed that there was no place in the vampire world for you."

Remembering what curiosity did to the cat, I didn't ask. Her cold, lithe arm settled over my shoulder, so feather light I wondered if she were touching me at all.

She continued, "When Igor put you forward as a candidate to assist him here this summer, I was reluctant. I wondered if she had not taken my sage advice and was sending you as some kind of interloper. But now I see, you're only here to serve your own purposes. That, I can respect."

How could she both praise and demean my mother in the same breath, and which side of that statement did I rally against? Did I care either way?

"I'm here because I agreed to continue my work with Prof. Karmarov. I find his passion for restoring slayers a worthy endeavor."

Cold, mauve-colored lips drew close to my ear. "But we both know that the slayers aren't extinct, don't we?"

I stopped in place, pulling back to look into her smug expression.

"Last night shortly after sunset, security informed me that you had tried to access the executive residence gym. Unsuccessfully, until Caleb Helsing showed up, that was."

"I take it you've been tracking me." I couldn't blame her. My mother had had our own training facility laced with a surveillance system not two summers before. If the hoods were doing it out in the sticks, surely a vampire-owned skyscraper in the big city had enough cameras in it to qualify as a reality show.

"No, but of course, we do monitor the hallways and some of the shared private areas to see who goes in and out." Her eyes rolled to look toward the ceiling. "As well as a few select air vents. I wasn't surprised to learn that Caleb engineered a second meeting with you. He's what I believe hueys your age call 'a player,' and you aren't displeasing to the eye. I thought, perhaps, you were to be just another of his conquests. Then, when I saw him moving the way only a slayer can move in front of you, I knew he'd let you in on his little secret."

"I won't tell anyone."

Why did I care if Inga Rosethorn thought I'd tell no one or not? But of course, I knew. My whole reason for being at WWL had been to figure out what Cynthia and her ilk were up to where the wolves were concerned. After more than a month, and with only four weeks left in my internship, I hadn't found out anything, and every effort to do so had ended in failure.

As quick as lightning, I realized what I had to do. Courage filled me as I pushed away my fear. I turned on heel and locked gazes with the daughter of Dracula.

"*If* we can come to an understanding."

She lifted a hand to my cheek and patted it. "It's so cute that you think you have any ground to negotiate. Consider it a privilege that I'm only firing you, Miss Kline."

Pulling away, I turned, crossing my arms over my chest. "Oh, I don't think you want to fire me."

"I'm quite sure I do."

"You're keeping Caleb a secret from Igor. Imagine if he found out, the trauma that could cause."

Any trace of amusement evacuated Inga's face. "You know how easily I can kill you, right?"

"I know you're capable of *killing me.* But I've been an employee here for five weeks. I go missing, this is going to be one of the first places authorities are going to look. And by authorities, I don't mean the Chicago Police."

That heated up the vampire's cool demeanor. Dealing with one hood was child's play. A whole clan, however? Difficult, even if Inga called in her more long-toothed employees to help.

"I imagine you're a fan of the saying keep your friends close and your enemies closer. Hard to get much closer than working in a lab right inside the heart of your operation on your dime."

I had her hooked; I could tell by the way she squinted at me.

"And precisely what is your offer, if you stay on?"

I grinned. "Igor likes me. He thinks we're friends. I could use that to find out just how much you should or should not trust him. Put me on his project. Give me access to his files, his communications. I'm an expert in investigating misdeeds. It's what I was born and bred to do."

Inga chewed on that a moment before finally, relenting.

"But if at any point you're not upholding your end, you'll be subject to termination." Her grip enveloped my hand, making my bones crack. "You have so much of your mother in you. I find that... surprising. Report to Lab 3 tonight at 9 PM. I will ask my assistant to inform Igor that you will be joining his team,

and I'll let you know when I expect you to report."

Nineteen

Two packages of premium dumplings landed on the table with a thud. Tobias, canine deep in a bowl of discount curry, moved only his eyes and not his head to look up at me with his quizzical expression.

"I have the best news ever."

Mid-suck on a mouthful of vindaloo, he gave no response.

"Come on, ask me," I whined. "Or is courteous curiosity after someone comes in the door and throws down top grade pork dumplings not a thing the English do?"

He lowered the bowl. "We're in the general nature of telling everyone too bubbly over their basket to sod off. But, if you Americans need that sort of thing..." He cleared his throat and held his hand aloft, taking on the form of an overly dramatic Shakespearean actor. "Verily, maiden, what delights thee so that thou wouldst return to our domicile bearing the pasta-pocketed pigs of orient east?"

I plopped down in the seat across from him. "My emotions are wasted on you."

"Ah, something we can agree on. So, then?"

"Inga Rosethorn called me into her office and threatened to fire me, but I blackmailed her into transferring my internship to Igor's lab."

The wolf's face curdled. "Let me get this right. Your source of cosmic joy is that you made an enemy of Dracula's daughter and because of that, will from now on be working under the vampire who admitted he was the reason slayers went extinct and was also part of a conspiracy that murdered my mate and held you in a secret dungeon for three days?"

I nodded. "Isn't that awesome?"

Tobias let his fork clank against the bowl as he rose from the table. "I don't know if it's because you're American, or because you're a hood, but there's something seriously wrong with what tickles your fancy."

"Come on, Tobias. Don't you see? This was the original plan. I work with Igor, while using the access to WWL's files to see who Cynthia's conspirators were and what they were up to."

"Conspirators? That's a great word. Perfect, in fact. Because think about what that means: there were other vampires working with Cynthia, and we don't know who or why. In fact, it could have been WWL and Inga Rosethorn for all you know."

"If it is, I'll be able to dig that out by accessing the research logs!" I said. "Igor says Cynthia wasn't funded by WWL, but she was using his lab's facilities. That information all backed up daily on WWL's servers. If there's anything I'm going to be able to find there, that's how I'm going to get to it."

Tobias shoved away from the table and crossed to the sink. "You mentioned blackmail as well. What information could you possibly have that Inga wouldn't want to get out?"

The moment of truth never sets up an appointment to let you know when it's coming. It just shows up at the door with a suitcase and a machete.

My voice grew tiny and my righteousness shriveled. "There's a slayer living on the twenty-seventh floor."

A werewolf's sense of hearing outstripped huey's several times over. When Tobias asked me to repeat myself, his hand cupped around his ear, I knew it wasn't because he hadn't heard me. He simply hadn't believed me. I never knew a wolf could blanch. Their pulse beat so strong, they were often flush with color.

Tobias. Blanched.

"Impossible."

I shook my head. "I thought so too. But he *is* a slayer. He was able to pin me to a wall and conjure a ball of sunlight on command. Not to mention he runs faster than my eyes could follow."

"Not that there's a slayer," Tobias mumbled. "That you would discover something like that, and keep it from me."

Guilt twisted my insides, smashing my pancreas into prune paste. "His being there is kinda a secret."

"And your loyalty to him is more than your loyalty to—Oh. Wait a minute. I get it."

Letting go of his rigid stance, Tobias grinned. The anger, pushed down within him, became a concentrated undercurrent between us.

"You fancy this guy."

"I... I..."

What was I, some pimply teenager being caught sexting? Why did I feel like I should be guilty for being attracted to someone? Tobias wasn't my father. He wasn't even clan. I shot some courage into my spine and reminded myself that not only did I have my big girl underwear on, but that was the only kind I owned.

"Yes, I do." Then, so he didn't think I was some kind of lovesick puppy, because I did still value his opinion for reasons I couldn't even begin to fathom, I added, "But that's irrelevant. Tobias, why are the vampires funding Igor's research if the slayers aren't extinct?"

The skin over his mouth suckered. "Isn't it obvious? Because they only have a male."

That simple statement, that obvious truth, caused a flurry of understanding to come crashing down on me. One thing I had learned in my life was that two seemingly contradicting truths could exist in parallel. Wolves hated hoods, but they were still good people. Physics explained in simple terms how the world worked, but in ways that taken together were very hard to understand.

Caleb was a refugee, and WWL was using him.

Logic lined up the next question. "Why does WWL want to control the re-creation of slayers? What's in it for them that they're covering all their bases?"

"And why are they folding you into whatever goal that is?" Tobias added.

My head snapped in his direction. "What are you saying? That I'm being played?"

"If keeping this slayer they have secret was so critical, they never would have let you near him. Inga Rosethorn *wanted* you to learn about him. WWL *wants* you working with Igor."

"WWL wants me *spying* on Igor." I felt the color drain from my face as I came to grips with how gullible I'd really been. "*Dios mío*, she even got me to suggest it, like it was my idea."

Tobias leaned back on his haunches, balancing his forehead on the points of his fingers. "Just because they can't enthrall creatures like you and me doesn't mean they can't manipulate the shit out of us the old-fashioned way."

"I *am* being played." I picked up my shattered self-confidence and pieced it back together. "I'm going to quit tomorrow. We'll go back to Paradise. We'll figure something else out."

"Like hell we will."

When I turned from the sink, Tobias was inches from me. Our living together had worn away the intensity of my instincts around him. I'd been feeling it for a while, and now, I had a demonstration of my numbness to detect him as danger. The wolf could have lifted his hands and snapped my neck in that moment. Instead of resort to such violence, however, Tobias wielded an emotional weapon.

"You owe me," he growled. "I've been sitting here, twiddling my thumbs, for weeks, trusting you to act. Werewolf blood is still on your hands, and the only way you're ever going to wash it off is to find out why Kara was killed. Until you do that, your debt is unpaid."

I couldn't deny the weight of it, and the possibility that Cody's dad might have suffered a similar fate still niggled at me. But strange experiments on werewolves having anything to do with resurrecting slayers? Where to draw the dotted line that might connect them?

I was barely twenty-one, and already, my lapses of judgment, my inability to act when actions could count, created burdens that were now forcing my knees to buckle. Just because I bore a name of an infamous hood didn't mean I had to become one myself. The world was fresh with opportunities for me to earn my own shame, and it seemed I was prepared to pursue those opportunities without regard to my own life.

"You're right. I have to see this through. Even if Inga's playing me, I have to let her."

"And try not to get killed along the way," Tobias added.

"Would you care?"

"Of course, I care." His hand planted on the table as he leaned over, putting his face right into mine. "I'm not innocent in this either. I should have found her sooner. I shouldn't have lived when she died, but I did. Now, my life is an obligation to her memory. Plus, if anything happens to you, Cody's going to kill me."

Lifting my eyes, I locked gazes with him. "If not for Cody, would you care though?"

The wolf before me gnashed his teeth. "Because of your indifference, I have lost my mate. Before that, I lost my brother. After, I lost my country, my pack, and my will. What the bloody hell do you think?"

"I think part of you would be happy to see another dead hood."

He shot up, and I didn't miss the way he worked his fists. "Beyond genetics, by what qualification are you a hood? You don't dance around fires in the full moon. You barely even trained in Chicago until I got here. Hate hoods as I did back in England, at least they respected clan like we do pack. But you? You have both of your parents, just a short drive away, and you refuse to even talk to them. Even though doing so would mean you could take your rites and be ready for the battles that are no doubt coming. But you, *Gerwalta* Kline? You're not a hood. Not in the ways that really count."

Something about what he said, something about the disdain with which he said it, lit the embers of anger within me. I'd barely realized I had moved when I was on my feet, reaching for silver – any silver – my fingers could find. The only thing nearby was a modest collection of decorative teaspoons I had mounted to the wall by the refrigerator. I moved like a scythe, cutting across the room, picking one of the spoons from its braces, and sending it spinning toward Tobias.

The wolf grinned when he caught it effortlessly from the air. It never would have pierced his hide, of course. It was only a teaspoon. But, it was silver, ninety-seven percent if I recalled.

The smile on Tobias's face melted as the metal leeched away from the utensil, and into his skin. Within moments, the werewolf, face contorting, groaned as he gathered enough strength to let the spoon drop to the floor. The pain was sharp enough to take him to a knee.

I lorded over him, making all my five-feet, seven-inches feel like a mile. "Tell me again I'm not a hood."

Accusing eyes full of rage and hurt lifted from the floor, tears welling. The skin across his palm cracked and sizzled. "Silvering me doesn't change my opinion."

Any sense of righteousness fizzled. I reached out to help him, falling into a cascade of regrets. My efforts were met with a snarl. Tobias huffed, pushing away my hands, holding his injured hand up to examine. When he looked back to me, there was no doubt of what I was in his eyes now.

Worse than a hood, I was a traitor.

"You and me? We're through. Make sure to watch your back every way you go, Geri, because I won't be there anymore."

Twenty

I stared at my phone, propped on the table next to my bed to display the time, as first the numbers grew, then reset, then started their upward climb again. At 4:30 AM, a rosy glow beat the intrinsic sense inside me that dawn approached.

The sleepless night brought clarity, a lack of rest my penance. What Tobias said had been right. If I had listened to him when he first came to me for help, none of this might have happened. Kara might still be alive. But that wouldn't have saved his brother, and it more than likely wouldn't have saved Mr. Ryland. Atonement came when the blood on my hands had been washed away. To survive whatever trap Inga Rosethorn was weaving for me, however, I'd need to be at the top of my game. What I wanted didn't matter anymore. My life was no longer, would no longer be, my own.

Should I just swallow my pride and take my rites? After, maybe I could convince my mother to let me do what needed to be done. Would she, though? Brünhild Kline wore a hood woven of indifference to wolves and a love of control. She'd lived all her life in tandem with the Paradise Pack and, despite that, her relationship with the Rylands was that of a brute authority, issuing ultimatums. If I went through rites, walked through the fire, and became one of her vassals, she'd use me and my ability to lure in the wolves for all the wrong reasons. Why couldn't Tobias understand that I might be stronger if I became a righteous hood, but I was a better ally to our cause as a nascent?

I needed him to listen, but the only way Tobias was going to hear me out after what I'd done was if he was forced to. Which meant, I was going to have to call *him*.

Sleep clung to the edges of Cody's voice. "So you do still have my number. Your timing still sucks, though."

Any joy I took from his voice fell away as the woman in the background spoke. "Who is it, baby?"

The sound of smacking lips conjured a vision in my mind's eye: Cody rolling over to kiss his mate before crawling out of bed. "It's just Geri, pup. You go back to sleep. I'll talk out in the living room."

Just Geri.

"What's wrong, Geri?"

"Why do you automatically assume something's wrong? Can't I just call to chat?"

"The fact that you haven't called in two months would suggest not. Plus, I got a text from Tobias who said, and I quote, 'your hood is a conceited slag who can protect her own sorry, secretive ass.' Not sure what a slag is, but I'm guessing it's not a compliment."

I bit my bottom lip. "I didn't know that he checks in with you."

"Of course, he checks in with me. I'm his alpha. And as his alpha, I should feel obligated to take his side. Only, the 'slag' he's talking about is you. You got an open mike. Tell me why I should reprimand the newest member of my pack."

"Because he's just so… moody. And stubborn. And all he does is sit around the house and brood all day long while I go to work. I mean, he *did* get a job, but still, it's only a couple hours a day. I get that he's frustrated by the lack of progress on finding anything out about why the wolves are being targeted, but he doesn't seem to understand that I'm just a nascent, and that WWL is run by vampires that could snap my neck in moments if they got the notion."

"Nah, it'd take them at least a minute. You'd put up a hell of a fight."

I laughed despite myself.

"Don't forget that Tobias lost his mate just a few months ago. He's still grieving. He may be grieving forever."

"I know. I KNOW. But you know what the weird thing is? He doesn't seem to be mourning her. At least, what I feel from him isn't like what I feel around other wolves that have lost their mates."

Cody ruminated on that in silence for a moment before saying, "Maybe it's different in cases of unnatural death. All the wolves you've been around here in Paradise lost their mates from old age. Most knew it was coming months in advance. God, I still think about the way Reina had to watch Harold being eaten alive by cancer."

Harold Klimt knew he was dying for two years before finally succumbing to the disease. I was eleven, and just starting the part of my training that saw me accompanying my mother into the packlands on routine meetings with the alpha and beta. My unique gift, the ability to sense wolves, didn't end at their proximity. Like the wolves themselves, heightened emotional or physical sensations transmitted to me, like a radio signal coming in over an AM channel in the middle of the night. A week before the end, Brünhild put me in the van and drove me to their home. She saw Harold's pain and Reina's suffering and shrugged.

I felt it viscerally, and spent the next week crying, both from what they felt, and from my inability to understand what was happening to me.

I choked back my tears even now, recalling that time. "Me too."

"With Tobias," Cody continued, "who knows? Plus, we don't know exactly what them vamps did to Kara before she died, and if the effect of that spilled over to him at all. Didn't you say that whatever they did to her, she couldn't sense his proximity anymore? Just at a psychological level, think what that had to have been like."

My brow furrowed. "Are you saying that whatever they did to her, it might have had a physical effect on him, even though he wasn't even directly subject to the same condition?"

"Mating bonds are funny things." The alpha laughed under his breath. "Lately whenever Lisa gets a craving for pickles, I look down and see I've eaten a whole jar without even realizing it."

"You don't like pickles."

"Don't I know it?" Cody said. "The second I see what I've done, I feel like throwing up."

I thought about what else Tobias had thrown at me during our fight, and brought up the one thing he said that I couldn't help but argue. "Cody, do you think I'm being selfish by not taking my rites?"

"You still think Brünhild's theory might be right? That you taking your rites would weaponize that weird empath thing you do with us?"

I hesitated to tell him that that "weird empath thing" was actually getting stronger on its own. Knowing that the fire melded a hood's power and proofed it, how could it not make that ability in me stronger?

"I have no doubt. But you and I also know that's not the only thing that comes from the fire. If I take rites, my mother is my commander. No way she's going to let me come back to school, especially in Yellow's sanjak."

"Not to mention, it would make her happier than a pup with a plaything," Cody added. "I don't know much, but I know anything that makes your mom happy is dangerous ground in my eyes."

The smile that crept across my face felt so bittersweet, tugging at the heartstrings of memory. Cody and I, hidden in the forests, trading barbs about the dominion that constituted my mother.

"Still," he went on, "can't deny it would make me breathe a little easier, knowing you could take care of yourself if things ever came down to it."

"You think I can't take care of myself?"

The ice that had crept into my voice forced him to rush to correct himself. "You're a tough chick, Geri. You know you are. You've kicked my ass multiple times when I was shorter in the canines. It's just that..."

"You're stronger than me now," I deadpanned. Even I knew better. When we grabbled as thirteen-year olds, my superiority came from advanced training and the fact that, typical of teenagers, I had matured earlier than Cody did. Now, years later, there would be no hope if I were to take on Cody in a fair match. He'd have my throat before I could scream. "Don't worry about hurting my feelings, Cody. You know I prefer honesty to kindness."

He sighed. "If only there were a way to take rites and not be under your mother's thumb on the flip side."

"Yeah, and if rivers could run backwards..."

A distance crept into his voice. "Maybe they can."

"They can't," I assured him. "I had world geography my first year at community. Even there, they knew that rivers do not, in fact, flow backward."

"No need to lord your superior education over me, Kline. I gots brains too. I was just thinking, remember the time I teased you about being ketchup and mustard, since you're the child of a red and a yellow?"

"You mean the time you threatened to put me all over your hot dog?" I asked. "What does that have to do with... Oh. Oh, I see what you mean. But that seems a little extreme, don't you think?"

"This is an extreme situation. Just don't forget it's an option." He returned to the serious situation at hand. "About Tobias. Try to be a little more compassionate, okay? I know you're all silver nails and barbed wire, but even a werewolf needs a gentle pat on the head every so often. I'll order him to go back to your place, but that's all I can do. I'm an alpha, not a miracle worker. I can deliver him to your door, but I can't force him to forgive you. Making things good with him? That's all on you."

"I'll do my best, Cody. Thanks."

TWENTY-ONE

The werewolf occupied the couch, his arms resting on the back, spanning the width. How acute was his sense of smell? Could he still detect hints of Jess? I hadn't been able to for at least a month, luckily just the time Tobias showed up to stay with me. Then again, my sense of smell wasn't as good as his. Neither, it seemed, was my stubbornness.

Coming back to the apartment had been an imperative. When an alpha gave a direct order, the wolf at the receiving end only had two choices: obey or break his covenant with the pack. After Tobias had experienced firsthand the dangers of being without pack, of being literally moments away from permanent moon madness and stuck in his animal form forever, he must not be too eager to relive the experience.

But that didn't mean he had to be happy about what the alpha required him to do. Tobias clearly was not happy.

I shifted awkwardly on the armchair perpendicular to the couch. "Can we just try to talk?"

He hadn't said a word. Not when I opened the door. Not when I closed it. Not for the five minutes since I'd said the last thing, when I asked him if he wanted something to drink or needed to get some sleep before talking. I'd even gone off to take a shower and get ready for work, hoping he'd settle in and unwind a bit. No luck.

He glared at me, then turned his head back to the spot on the wall that had previously consumed him. "It's unnatural."

Okay, cryptic talk was still talk. "What is?"

"That I'm here."

"I know. Living in the city took some getting used to for me too. It's so… busy. Noisy. Impersonal."

"I don't mean here, Chicago. I mean here, in this apartment." Now when his eyes settled on me, it was with a murderous glare. Not that Tobias would hurt me. He couldn't. He'd sworn to Cody to protect me with his life, and hate it as he might, he couldn't go back on that. "Who in the hell are you? What kind of nascent hood can command an alpha like that? What kind of alpha listens? What kind of pussyfooted pack have you forced me in to?"

I bit my lip, knowing that from Tobias's perspective, and seeping into the scars of his experience with the green hoods of the British Isles, infamous for their pigheadedness and military style, I must have looked as though I were my mother — a heartless matron who bullied respect from the packs in her sanjak. After all, I'd taken him, a foreign wolf with no connection to the Paradise wolves and on the edge of lunacity, to them on a full moon and gotten the alpha to accept him on the spot without an argument. Such adoptions were rare and generally only the result of an arranged mating to diversify a pack's gene pool. Even then, the negotiations and courting could take months.

"You think I forced Cody to accept you."

"Are you going to tell me you didn't? Why else would an alpha accept someone like me? I have nothing to offer a new pack. I cannot be mated again, and I am too damaged to mentor any young pups. I have no kindreds in Paradise. You, hood, have put me in Hell."

"Actually, Hell is in the lower peninsula."

The joke flew over his head, and didn't exactly pair well to the serious moment.

I slid my hands over my jeans. "I didn't force Cody. He took you because it was the right thing to do. And because he's my friend."

He examined me, disgust curling his lips. "He… *feels* for you, almost like you are pack."

"I almost was."

His disbelieving glare forced me to continue. I got to my feet, pacing.

"About a year ago, a few days before I left for Chicago, Cody asked me to marry him. My mother got to Cody's father, made him invoke alpha's prerogative and forced him to mate Lisa. I showed up at Cody's house the next day to tell him I'd decided to accept his proposal, to find him in post-mating bliss."

A tenderness played behind his eyes, but Tobias was still unconvinced. "The pack never told me anything like that."

"I suspect Lisa has something to do with that. She knows Cody could never really cheat on her, but he still considers me a friend. A best friend, maybe, and I would guess she doesn't like it. I can't blame her. It's not her fault what happened. She was just another pawn my mother played."

"And you… you still *love* him."

"Like that matters." When had I started to cry? "I know it's not the same, Tobias. I know what you're feeling is ten times, a hundred times, infinitely worse. But I do understand some of what it's like to lose your mate, because in all the ways that really matter, I lost mine. For a while, all I wanted was revenge. If someone had come to me then and said they'd take out my mother for what she'd done, I'm not sure I would have said no. But I do know that if I had said yes, and then they let me down, I'd be pissed, like you are now."

"I'm not…" His face tightened, before he laughed once. "No, I am pissed. But it's not all you. I feel… emasculated. For the past two months, everything I need has been forced on me by you, directly or indirectly. Who my alpha is, where I live, even the food I eat. I'm not that much of a bleeding bastard. I know your intentions are good, but when you decided to take control over what I was allowed to know or not, that was too much."

"I should have told you about Caleb," I blurted out. "Finding a slayer was a huge thing, and it was wrong of me to keep it from you."

His eyes returned to the floor. As he shook his head, his shoulder-length hair swished over his shoulders. "That's not what I'm talking about."

"What then?"

"I'm charged by my alpha to do everything within my power to keep you safe." His eyes lifted to meet mine, begging. "Everything in my power includes forcing you to do what it takes to protect yourself. Take your rites, Geri."

"It's not that simple. As soon as I do, I'm under my mother's command. It's not as binding as alpha's prerogative, but…"

Memories echoed in my head. My sweet cousin, Markus, had been a gentle spirit before his fire. A fiercely trained warrior, but one who believed the power of the dialog was stronger than silver. On the other side of his rites, however, he fell right into line with the red ways of discipline. He'd never been brutal with a wolf – not that I knew of, anyways – but he had garnered the reputation of being the go-to hood to deal swiftly with any of the moon mad in the western stretches of my mother's sanjak.

I lowered my gaze, trying to hide the second appearance of tears. "I'm not sure who I'll be on the other side. Plus, since it's me, I could be more of a danger to you than I am now. I couldn't go on, knowing I'd hurt you, that I'd hurt anyone in the pack."

Tobias leaned over the space between us, putting his hand on my shoulder. "But right now, you're hurting yourself. You're losing control, Geri. Hoods are our balance, because in many ways, you have the same abilities and weaknesses."

I shook my head, both because I was confused, and because his tenderness and proximity made me itchy. "What are you getting at?"

"You threw silver at me. Thank god it wasn't anything sharp, but…" Tobias's hand moved from my shoulder to splay in front of my eyes. Across the inside of his palm, from below his pinky down to the heel, a blistered stripe of skin bore the evidence of what I had done to him the night before. "If it had been, you might have damaged me more. Lunacity, Geri. You're going moon mad."

"Me, a lunatic?" My face screwed up. "That's ridiculous. Hoods don't get mood madness."

"From what the Paradise Pack says, your mother keeps your clan on a very tight leash. All hoods put through their fires before they can legally vote. How old are you now, twenty?"

"Twenty-one last week."

Could what he was saying be true? Truth be told, the first few full moons away from my clan had been tortuous. Then, the pain faded, replaced by crazy emotions, wild mood swings, passion both sensual and senile. Sure, all hoods got a little loco come full moon, but did they get as crazy as I got?

This time, his hands raised to my face, cupping both cheeks. "I know the consequences of taking your fire, and I can hardly believe I'm actually trying to power up one of your kind, but you have to take your rites. If you don't, you're going to end up like I almost did." A smile broke across his face. "Only, I don't have some ex-girlfriend in a clan somewhere to take you in, not that that would work for your kind."

I echoed his chuckle just for a moment, until the sliver of truth in his joke stuck in my brain. "Actually, it might."

"What might?"

"Seeking out alternatives," I said, turning to look for my phone. I had to talk to Markus, and if he agreed with the crazy idea running through my head, there'd be more phone calls after. "Good news, Tobias. I think there's a way of taking my rites that doesn't involve my mother."

"Well, that should go over well with that old battle ax. How soon can this be done?"

That was the catch, wasn't it? "Nascent hoods can only take their fires on full moons."

"But that's not for another three weeks," he chuffed. "What are we supposed to do between now and then?"

"Isn't it obvious? Continue playing into Inga's hands. I work in Igor's lab at WWL, glean what I can off of Caleb about defending slayers, and keep my eyes open for when the status quo changes. My internship doesn't end for a while yet. We'll still have two weeks after I take rites to get out."

"You do realize though, that if we find ourselves on a sticky wicket, you won't be able to come back to Chicago. It would be too dangerous, even with your full abilities. Cody would never..." Tobias smacked the roof of his mouth with his tongue and rolled his eyes, forcing the admission through deceptive mannerisms. "*I* would never let you."

He pretended to wince when I kid-boxed his shoulder. "Tobias Somfield, I do believe you're becoming my friend."

"Great, because you have such a wonderful history with having wolves as friends."

Twenty-Two

With each driving swing, my aim grew more precise.

Caleb dropped the boxing pads, shaking out the impact of my last hit. "You keep this up, I'm going to have to declare you an honorary slayer."

"I don't think it works like that," I said as I readied my next attack.

The actual slayer in the room raised the whole-body shield from the ground just in time to keep my foot from landing in his chest. For two weeks, I'd been pushing the limits of my endurance. Living a nocturnal life again helped. Now that I was working in Igor's lab, and consequently my schedule had shifted from six hours starting late morning to five hours starting at 11 PM, I could use the earlier part of the night for training, and fall asleep with the sunrise. Tobias got Tuesday and Thursday, running me up and down the shores of Lake Michigan, and Caleb met me on Mondays and Wednesdays in the WWL executive gym. Fridays involved me sitting in a chair across from Inga Rosethorn for an hour, giving a selective report on Igor's undertakings. The old vampire wasn't stupid. He'd known I'd been sent as a mole the moment I walked into his lab. Luckily, he also made sure to keep up appearances of a professional-only relationship in front of the other workers, three hueys all wearing the pink-hued glasses. Likewise, the professor coached me on explaining the work we were doing to Inga without raising any red flags.

Though I wasn't sure there were any red flags I could raise, even without the coaching. I took up my work right where I had left off at WCU, by scanning slides into the database. Meanwhile, Igor's activities involved the "pinkies," as he called the hueys sporting pink glasses.

"They're part of an experiment in neurocybernetic research," Igor had explained when I asked. "We're trying to see if we can hack the part of the brain that vampires effect when we enthrall someone. The goal is to make hueys who are immune to our mental powers. It would be highly useful in daytime security provisions."

At the tail end of my shift, under the auspices of uploading my daily lab notes into the research logging system, I sifted through the thousands of similar reports filed by WWL workers around the world. The v-corp took global conglomerate to a new level, and I recognized subsidiaries in at least a dozen countries and in as many industries, from automotive manufacturing to food products. I knew any research with supernatural overtones would be coded or somehow obfuscated. With two weeks of digging, nothing on Cynthia's work, or anything that appeared related to werewolves in any way emerged.

I was running out of time, and worse, I was running out of faith.

Training with Caleb had proven one thing so far: I'd never be as fast as a slayer, or have one's ability to throw a ball of concentrated sunlight. Thanks to Caleb, however, I did know now that vampires' strength peaked with the new moon, not the full moon like wolves. Also, the best way of engaging one in battle was to first engage him in conversation.

"They're very arrogant if they feel intellectually challenged. Whether or not you can match wits with them doesn't matter." Caleb shrugged. "I don't know. Maybe it's something that happens to them in their rebirth. Something in their brain that overrides their fight-or-flight instinct. If you can strike up a conversation with a vampire, you don't need to chase them. You can walk right up and fight face to face. You get them engaged, and they're too distracted to smoke. Hey, I've been meaning to ask you something."

"Shoot."

"That jumping-into-the-fire thing you mentioned," Caleb said. "Does it hurt?"

"Doesn't seem too. I'd call bullshit on it if I hadn't seen it a dozen times. It's not that we're impervious to burning, just fire doesn't seem to have an effect on us. Got a hell of a scar on my ankle, though, that proves red-hot pokers work just fine."

Caleb threw me a cold bottle from a minifridge at the side of the gym. Apparently getting distracted by talk wasn't reserved for vamps. "What's the whole ceremony like?"

I cleared my throat. "Um, well... There's some sort of speech, usually by the mother of the hood taking rites. The nascent makes a pledge to serve the matron, to protect wolves from the harm of hueys and hueys from the harm of wolves, though that part of it is a bunch of hooey if you ask me, because we threaten them so much more. Then the matron of the bloodline presents the nascent with a silver medallion, the group chants some ancient bunch of hoopla no one really knows the meaning of, and the matron pushes the nascent into the fire."

"Really? Military honors?"

"It's not a medal," I contested. "It's a big silver disk. You're supposed to make it into some shape when you emerge from the fire, as proof that you're now, you know," I used finger quotes, "'a real hood.'"

"So your family gathers around, and your mother throws you into a bonfire. I used to think our coming-of-age ceremony was brutal."

I seated myself at the edge of the room, back against the wall. "What do slayers do?"

Caleb plopped down beside me. "It's just your mom and dad, or some stand in if they're no longer kicking. They put you into water – in my case, a swimming pool -- and both throw a solarium at you."

My eyebrows made way for my hairline. "A solarium?"

"Yeah, you know..." Caleb presented his hand, a Ping-Pong sized ball of light radiating over his upturned palm. "One of these guys. They're called solaria. Oh, and also, there's pizza. At least, there was at my ceremony. I don't know if that's standard practice, though."

"And after being hit with a ball of sunlight?"

His fist closed, the little ball of light sinking into his skin. "Phenomenal cosmic powers."

"That's from *Aladdin*."

"Still true." After a few laughs, he continued. "After that, you get your final training. Kind of like an internship. You tag along with your parents when they go out to patrol. I think it's a lot like you guys with the werewolves. Ninety-nine percent of vampires just want to live their lives in peace, occasionally getting together for a dinner party or a rave. We only deal with problem children."

"Not so much raving or dinner parties in packlands. They do have really awesome barbeques, though."

"I'd expect nothing less from meat eaters. Well…" He bounced to his feet with a vigor Tigger would envy. "Ready to try kicking my ass again? You almost got me to lose my balance this time."

I pushed myself off the ground. "If I wanted you on your back, Helsing, you'd be on your back."

"If you want me on my back, Kline, all you have to do is ask. I like when the woman's on… *Oohff.* Wow, that was a good one. Give it to me again."

I hadn't waited for him to take up any protective gear when I'd punched him directly in the chest. Inga Rosethorn had been right about one thing; Caleb was definitely a player, one of those guys whose flirt button was always flipped on. Once I accepted it, I kind of enjoyed it.

I was about to land another fist, this time to Caleb's left shoulder, when my phone rang. With a raised finger, I asked for a break. Caleb took to boxing the air, keeping himself limber.

"Cody?"

"Hey there, red."

The smile in his voice suggested good news. "My dad was willing to talk to you?"

"Shit, Geri. Your dad has never been a problem. Hell of a good guy, I think the world of him. How he ended up with the Red Dominatrix is the question."

"Aaannddd?" My voice stretched out like taffy.

"And he got a hold of her. And she's said yes."

My squeal froze Caleb in place. He paused, mid-jab, and examined me for signs of injury or insanity. Waving a hand, I tried to tell him not to worry, but he came to stand by me anyways.

"That's great news! Where?"

"Where do you think?" Cody asked. "Right here in Paradise."

The man had gone from the bearer of good news to stupid in two seconds flat. "Are you insane? Whose stupid idea was that?"

"Your dad's, and he wasn't negotiable on it. He made it a condition of helping."

The joy I felt moments ago curdled. "My mom's going to find out. She's going to find out, and she'll make sure it doesn't happen"

Cody reassured me. "Your clan will be too busy with *fueurnacht*. Your mother won't have a clue; we've worked it out. Just make sure you're here well before sunset so I can move the pack far enough away to avoid problems. You got lucky when you came here with Tobias during full moon. You have no idea how many commands I had to keep growling to keep the others from attacking you."

I'd never considered that. The day I'd brought Tobias to Paradise, all I had been thinking of was him. I trusted in the alpha, who I assumed was still Cody's dad, knowing me well enough to keep the others at bay. If it had been Bob Ryland and not his son, would the results have been different?

"Thank you, Cody. I really appreciate this."

"No problem, red. You and Tobias just try not killing each other until you get here."

"So once we get there, it's okay?"

"Once a smart ass, always a smart ass."

Caleb did his best not to look wild with curiosity when I got off the phone, but the excitement bubbling just below the surface drew him out.

"Must have been some good news."

I nodded. "I'm taking my rites. I won't be a nascent anymore."

Twenty-Three

"I would be remiss if I didn't mention that the needle seems unnecessary for someone like you."

Igor may be old, and he may be an academic, but he still had a sense of humor. A goofy grin spread over his face. "I find analyzing samples is difficult if I eat them first. Besides, I don't like causing people pain."

"You drink from hueys, don't you? I'm sure that doesn't tickle."

"Hueys can be enthralled. They don't feel a thing. You would feel something. You would feel something quite terrible."

My free hand went to my neck, rubbing the spot where Donovan the Baby Vamp had attacked me several months before. "I know."

He pressed a cotton ball to the red dot left as the needle pulled out of my vein, before laying a bandage atop to hold it in place. The vampire whisked away the vial holding my blood. Whether securing it from others, or taking it out of sight before I reconsidered, I couldn't say. When he returned to the room, it was with a green lollipop the size of a quarter pinched in his fingers.

"A reward, for being such a good patient."

I should turn down the treat; I didn't want to come off seeming childish. But candy was candy.

"Thank you, I try." I slid myself off the counter and the wrapper off the candy. "What is it you're thinking to find, Igor?"

His eyes brightened. "I have no idea, and I can't remember the last time I was this excited. The work I was able to do on your blood when you were…"

"A prisoner locked in your basement," I completed when he could not.

He coughed away the awkward moment. "The machines I have at the university aren't as good as the ones here at WWL. I've never been able to compare a hood profile before and after rites. I'm eager to see how, if at all they differ."

"What about slayers?" I asked. "They have their own kind of rites, too."

"Yes, well, I wasn't interested in genetics at the time there were enough of them around to ask for the privilege."

I let that rest in the air a moment before saying, "What about that sample I brought you from the guy upstairs. Have you gotten any results from him yet?'

Igor stared blankly at the wall. "What sample?"

Was he kidding? Did I have to endure one of the best kisses of my whole life for nothing? "*The* sample. The *only* sample I've collected from an executive locker room this month."

"I don't know what you're talking about."

"Don't know what I'm talking about? Igor, seriously, if you-"

My pointed, wagging finger stuck in the air as Igor grabbed my wrist. The weight of his years, the gravitas of his power bore down on me through his glare. "There was no sample, Geri. Do you understand what I'm saying? You never gave me anything."

I understood the message, but I couldn't comprehend the messenger. "If you say so, Igor. If you say so."

TWENTY-FOUR

Old Bessie choked and coughed that last few miles, but she delivered Tobias and I safe enough, even if a little dizzy from the fumes. Half of me wondered if she'd be able to make the trip back to Chicago.

The other half of me was hoping I'd be in any kind of shape to make it. I'd spent my whole life anxious over taking the actual rites, I'd never paused to think with any detail what life would be like on the other side. Maybe because I didn't want to envision my mother's grip coming down on me any harder. Maybe because I didn't want to imagine that I'd resist her.

Tobias tapped my shoulder, bringing me back to the moment. "You in there, Gerwalta?"

I pulled the key from the ignition I'd switched off a minute or so before. "Yeah, just nervous I guess."

The werewolf's jaw worked, grinding teeth.

"Okay, now what's wrong with you?"

He chuffed. "I don't feel comfortable leaving you alone to go through something like this."

"Unless you're prepared to challenge Cody for alpha and assume control of the pack so you can be human during a full moon, I don't see that happening," I said. "I won't be alone. Consuela will be there, making sure the ceremony goes through without any problems. When you come back in the morning, all this will be over, and I'll be a righteous hood."

"A *righteous* hood?" he asked, grinning. "Well, you'd be the first."

"Not like *righteous* as in virtuous. It's what we call a hood who's gone through their rites. First you're a nascent, then you're righteous. Don't the green hoods in England use that term?"

"If they ever spoke to us longer than to insult our mothers and bully our fathers, I'd let you know."

Could my kind really be so cruel where he came from? Or was this just years of guided hate talking?

"Come on," I said, getting out of the car. "We have enough time to eat something before Cody leads the pack into the Hiawatha. I could smell those ribs on the grill miles ago."

"You eat all you want. I prefer wild game on full moons."

"Great, more for me then."

Cody threw open the front door and his arms. I stepped into his embrace, feeling like a fire wrapped inside a soggy blanket. The press of his chest against my cheek still sent desire spinning in me, but to push him away would cause more problems than it'd solve.

"This is it," he said, rocking me gently. "Excited?"

I could have responded in so many ways, none of which were appropriate with a married man. Instead, I just sighed and thanked him for helping to set everything up.

"No problem." Cody let me go before reaching a hand out to shake with Tobias. "Good job putting up with her. I know it's not easy."

"She placates me with dumplings," Tobias declared flatly as he bypassed the alpha to drop my bag inside the door. "I'd like to head to my room and get a nap in before sunset. I'm stifled by the city. I need to run as much as I can tonight."

"Room?" I asked, looking behind me. "What room? Where do you have a room?"

Cody picked up my duffel bag and heaved it over his shoulder. "You don't need my permission to take a nap, Tobias. But you sure you don't want to hang out, have a beer? Lisa's kept a few of the burgers on the raw side for you, just flamed them enough to get a little dark on the outside."

My mouth watered. Cody and his uncle had got me hooked on what they called "Wolf Sliders" a while ago.

Tobias tapped his belly. "I'm keeping room for rabbit. I give your Yooper woods this: the coneys are delicious."

"Cody, honey?" Lisa slid open the glass door connecting to the backyard open. "I thought I sensed a hood, but hard to tell with... Oh, Geri. Hello."

My head simultaneously threatened to explode and implode, and it wasn't because of the cute way that Lisa wore her hair. Nor was it because she had just called the man I loved "honey." It wasn't even because a small part of me still blamed her for my losing him, even though I suspected she had as much choice in the matter as Cody had had.

It was because the tray of burgers she carried rested on a visible swell of her stomach, given to her by a man who a year ago had pledged to love me and only me forever.

The solid mass of muscle behind me became the only thing keeping me from falling. Tobias managed the impossible, he held me up, while not touching me at all. It took me a moment to realize that what bolstered me was his compassion. I sensed it so acutely, it had a physical effect. Looking over my shoulder, the smallest of nods confirmed I wasn't imagining things.

"On second thought," Tobias said, circling around me and heading for the back yard, "who am I to turn down a seat at my alpha's table?"

I tamped down my emotions — all of them like a classroom of toddlers screaming to be taken to the bathroom by the hand — and turned my eyes to the floor. I would not make this awkward for them. It wasn't their fault. Neither one of these people had ever intentionally hurt me in any way.

"Just as long as you realize it's only a picnic table," Cody called after the wolf.

"Lisa." My tongue wanted to employ a derogatory term that, nevertheless, was technically accurate for a female werewolf. "Thank you for agreeing to let me stay here."

A smile fluttered across her face. "Of course, Geri. No bother at all."

A silence that threatened to bloom uncontrollably between us broke when Lisa pivoted to the kitchen, setting down the tray of barely-cooked meat.

"You must be exhausted after that long drive. Maybe you'd like to rest up a bit? Or if you want to grab a burger and go sit out back with the others, I can bring you something cold to drink."

"Others?" I turned to Cody, all thoughts of the little wolf the alpha's mate carried set aside. "What others?"

Cody ducked around a corner and dropped my bag in the room that used to be his. Now that his father was gone, had he taken the master suite? Where was his mother staying?

"Your cousin Consuela got here earlier this morning," he said. Almost as if reading my mind, he continued. "Don't worry, we brought her up Farm Tuck Road. We didn't drive her near the hood compound or through town at all. Your mom wouldn't have sensed her."

"Hoods don't sense each other." Why would we need to? We weren't supposed to be a threat to others of our clan. "Who else is here? We agreed this should be done on a need-to-know basis."

"And I've kept that in mind," Cody assured me. "In the pack, it's just me, Lisa, and Uncle Rick. Tobias, of course. And from your side of it, there's Consuela, and..."

"Hola, mi bonita."

My father hadn't changed much in the year since I'd last set eyes on him. Hoods, as a rule, aged well, keeping limber and agile well into their sixties. My dad could pass for a man twenty years younger. Except in his eyes, where sadness had sacked away his youth. I wanted to believe it was because of my mother's frequent indifference towards him. Divorce in hood families wasn't common, but it wasn't unheard of. How someone as sweet and compassionate as my father ended up with my mother to begin with had always thrown me for a loop. Why he stayed with her threw me for an Alpine mountain pass.

"Papa." My voice cracked even as I chided myself. *He sided with* her. *He tried to keep you from Cody. He would have disowned you the moment you two were wed.* I put the cauldron of silver boiling in the pit of my stomach into my throat. "You're here, so I assume Brünhild is only shortly behind."

My father's smile faded under my glare. "She thinks I've gone to visit Consuela. Please, *cazadora...*"

As my father stepped forward, and I fell back, Tobias put himself between us. Whether it was because he'd sensed my conflict through the connection we seemed to share, or through old-fashioned body language, I couldn't say.

My dad's voice took on an authoritarian tone. "Step aside. You have no right to keep me from my daughter."

"The name's Tobias, and I have pledged to protect this hood with my life," he said in his rough English accent. "So not only do I have the right, I have the duty."

Looking over the werewolf's shoulder, I caught my father eyeing Cody questioningly.

The alpha shrugged. "Come on, Pietro. I wasn't going to let Geri go to the big city without anyone there to have her back."

"You told me Kim was with her. Not some wolf I do not know, who isn't even of this pack. If I had known..."

"If you had known, what, papa?" I cut in, pulling Tobias back to stand beside me. "Would you have followed your wife's example? Intruded in pack politics and bullied them into submission? Invalidate all my choices, hoping I'll give in and fall into the role of the obedient daughter who always does what father and her Matron say, even when it's wrong?"

A second person came through the sliding door, suggesting there might be a whole village of people milling around in Cody's back yard. The woman with auburn hair woven in a braided spindle atop her head and olive skin stepped into the living room wearing fatigues. A clash of commando style and the beauty of Latin goddess in her late thirties, Consuela Carlito de Reina presented a striking figure – especially in a room dominated by Yoopers and a token Englishman. The ice in her glare reminded me so much of my mother's.

"Such disrespect, Gerwalta?" Consuela spotted Lisa, still holding the tray of burgers and waiting to the side of the room. She crossed, took the tray, and set it on the counter, before turning back to me. "Not a good start for us. Respect of elders is a high priority among the *Amarillo*. Do you not realize how much your father has risked to get me here today, for you? If your mother finds out he was involved, she could expel him from her clan."

Tobias, still at my side, ran a hand through his hair. "The *Amarillo*? You mean, the yellow hoods? But Geri's a red. Why is a yellow matron here?"

Consuela jumped in. "Perhaps if we sit, I can explain. Gerwalta and I must come to terms anyhow. Pietro?"

Consuela stepped to the side, inviting us into the backyard.

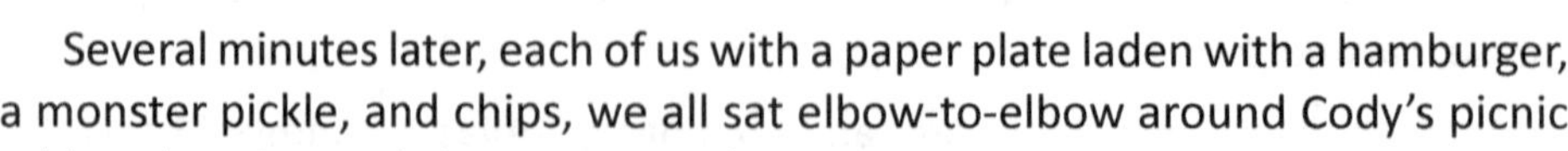

Several minutes later, each of us with a paper plate laden with a hamburger, a monster pickle, and chips, we all sat elbow-to-elbow around Cody's picnic table, when Consuela began to speak.

"Most bloodlines marry amongst their own," she began. "Distant cousins, of course. We do not favor incest. Occasionally, as in the case of Pietro and Brünhild, a union from two different lines may occur. Geri's lineage, therefore, is not solely as a red. She is also Pietro's progeny. Almost always, the children of such unions cross their fires under the color of their mother's line. It is possible, however, for a daughter such as Geri to be taken in by the Matron of her paternal line."

"So instead of being a red hood, I'm going to be a yellow," I said to Tobias, who seemed confused by the whole pitch. "But I'd still be righteous. I'd just be subject to Consuela's orders instead of my mother's."

Tobias's brow furrowed. "Like she'd be your alpha?"

"I would be her Matron, yes. And as her Matron, I'd expect her to live in my sanjak, and pledge loyalty to my line," Consuela said. "When time comes for her to wed, she will take a Yellow as her spouse."

Pietro cleared his throat and steepled his hands. "Consuela has agreed to defer her claim on Geri until she finishes college. My cousin controls a very large swath of land. Chicago is its northernmost tip, but she has hoods as far south as the Louisiana Bayou, and from Oklahoma to Alabama. Within that space, Geri may live where she likes."

"As long as you come when summoned, and go where commanded, you may make your home wherever you decide," Consuela added. "I am not like your mother. I do not demand that my hoods live breathing down a pack's neck."

Cody and Lisa exchanged glances. Natives to Paradise, they knew firsthand the truth of that insult.

"But Geri wants to live in the Upper Peninsula when she finishes school," Tobias said. "She wants to be a school teacher, have a pet dog and make scones on weekends."

My cheeks burned as I tried to melt into a pool while the others all shared confused expressions, having witnessed a werewolf prattle off my vision of domestic bliss.

Except for Consuela, who continued undeterred. "I don't care if she bakes banana bread and has a parrot, but she will live in my sanjak. If Geri is determined to stay in her mother's region, then she should have the Red Matron to conduct her rites."

"It's a reasonable request, Matron." My back cracked as I put some steel in it, sitting up straighter. "I regret, however, that I have to ask one more thing."

She crossed her arms as her left eyebrow took on the shape of a boomerang. "And that is?"

"Tobias and I are working together to investigate some vampire activity in the city. It's possible that that will take me longer than the year of school I have left."

"Investigation?" She said the word like she didn't understand the meaning. "Just what are you investigating?"

My eyes went to Cody, then Tobias. For some reason, I felt like the decision of whether or not to share the details fell under their purview, not mine.

Surprisingly, it was Lisa who answered. "Two of Tobias's native pack and my father-in-law have been killed off in the last year. Both Tobias's mate and his brother's bodies ended up in vampire hands."

Consuela's head whipped to the alpha seated at her left. "What happened to your dad?"

Put on the spot, my ex shifted in his seat. "We don't know for sure. He disappeared one day when he went out fishing. Never came back."

"And the Red Matron, she did not investigate this?" Consuela asked.

My father leaned in. "Brünhild felt that there was no evidence to suggest any foul play. 'A huey-styled death,' she called it."

More like she thought one fewer wolf in the world wasn't a bad thing, I thought. To have said it out loud would have mocked Cody's feelings however, and put my father in the role of defending my mother — a role in which he could give an Oscar-worthy performance and which wouldn't advance the conversation at all. Instead, I said what was defensible.

"It's best that my mother isn't involved. If the evidence ends up leading back to Chicago, as the Red Matron, she'd have reason to subjugate your sanjak, Consuela. Her turning a blind eye to this keeps your region safe from her meddling."

"Subjugate a sanjak?" Tobias asked. "One, what in the hell is a sanjak? And two, why would Geri's mother be able to take over yours?"

For a moment, I thought how much of a distance there must be between the pack Tobias was born into and its hood clan. Then, I recalled how the Paradise clan had been ignorant of most of the hood ways of governance before I had become Cody's girl and a fountain of information.

Maybe Bobby Ryland had other reasons for tolerating my non-traditional relationship with his son. Then again, it was possible the green hoods in England simply called their territory something else. Hoods didn't lack diversity in our own way; certainly, the hoods of the Steppe and those in Africa didn't use words like *feuernacht* and *mein kind.* I was still thrown by the fact that my Central European ancestors adopted an Ottoman term like sanjak into our lexicon as it was.

"A sanjak," Consuela said, "is the geographic territory a Matron controls. The hoods in the Balkans adopted it about five hundred years ago when the Ottomans took control of their lands. As a yellow matron, only three things can take control of my sanjak away. Death, the eldest matron of my bloodline – but she lives in Spain and they say is fruitier than banana – or the eldest matron of the Red Blood Line. Brünhild Kline could become a dictator in our world if she wanted to. Rumors are, she's considering it."

Both Consuela and I looked to my father, but on this subject, he remained mute, staring straight ahead, mouth tight, jaw clenched. I, however, had suspicions. It wasn't my mother's desire or ability to seize control I debated. The problem lay in how to get the wolves in the annexed regions to accept it. A dictator was only as strong as her strongmen.

A hood who could sense wolves up to a mile away and act as a beacon, drawing them helplessly as moths to flame? My mother had been waiting on me. She had been waiting for me to take rites so she could have my power. A wolf's greatest strength wasn't his ability to fight, it was his ability to *choose* to fight. What I could do would undermine that. I'd draw them to the battlefield, lead them to slaughter.

"I'm prepared to accept your terms, Consuela, if you can accept mine."

The corner of the yellow matron's mouth ticked up. "You have a deal, Miss Kline. Now eat. You will need your energy."

Twenty-Five

In a closet just a few miles away, hung a tunic of leather, lace, and red ribbon, custom-tailored to my body, with matching leather gauntlets and quiver. It had been a present from my mother on my sixteenth birthday, the hope being that I would wear it a week later in a sacrificial fire. She hadn't known then that I was three months into dating the son of the Paradise Pack alpha, or that coming to know the wolves through informal visits to the packlands had me questioning everything I'd ever been told about their character and worth. I'd used the excuse of needing more training before taking on duties, so that I wouldn't let her down. Then I used the excuse of attending the local community college, with my father's aid in convincing her it was worthwhile.

Today, I had no more excuses. I would walk the fire under the full moon wearing a pair of worn jeans and a purple t-shirt. On the other side, I'd conjure my hood for the first time. Only, instead of red, I'd wear yellow. It shouldn't make a difference.

So why was I feeling like a traitor?

"Out with it, then." Tobias found me at the edge of the woods, staring blankly into the forest beyond.

"Out with what?"

He grimaced in frustration. "I don't know why it is that we have this connection, but it's made me into a damned Geri-gauge. I feel whatever's in here—" He reached out, tapping two fingers on my sternum, then to my bottom lip. "—no matter what this claims. Out with it. I have to go in a few minutes."

Fine. He wanted to know, I'd tell the wolf who lost his mate to vampires my petty problems.

"I guess I had more wrapped up in being a red than I realized. Now tell me how stupid that is, especially since I had decided not to take my rites at all."

"It's not stupid."

Wide-eyed, I turned on him. "It's not?"

He shook his head. "Your bloodline is more than what color your hood will be. It's your clan. It's your family. And sometimes…" He pivoted to a squeal in the distance where Cody and Lisa kissed, near where my father and Consuela had built the pyre to be set ablaze after sunset. "…you don't realize how much that means to you until it's taken away."

Memories of the conversation we'd had in the diner resurfaced. It seemed like forever ago, when Tobias explained to me the events that led to him coming to Chicago. Along the way, he'd not only lost his mate, he'd lost his pack. The alpha turned him out, exiling him. Misty recollections blew away when Rick Ryland, naked as the day he was born, called from across the clearing.

"Pack, get your asses over here. Time to take off."

In another twenty minutes or so, the sun would set. Taking the wolf wouldn't be an option for them at that point; the full moon's dominance of the sky would force them through it. Leaving early would allow them to drive deep enough into the forest to give us a sufficient buffer. A werewolf under the light of a full moon could be more animal than human, and a hood in the heart of their packlands could trigger their defensive instincts.

Tobias put a hand on my shoulder, locking our gazes. "You're still going to be you on the other side of that fire, and you will still be my friend. You got that?"

"So we're friends now?"

The wind whooshed from my chest as he pulled me into his arms, wrapping me in a blanket of warmth both physical and emotional. "You're my only friend anymore, Geri."

He let me go, giving me a little, playful push as he turned away. "You tell anyone in the pack I said that, and we're going full fairytale reenactment, though."

"Meaning what? You'll huff and puff and blow my house down?"

I felt a blush in my cheeks as he simultaneously walked away and began to strip off his clothes. "That, or I'll lure you towards my bed until you get close enough to eat."

The pyre wasn't necessary. I was about to burn to ash on the spot.

Logs crackled, falling in on themselves as the embers beneath pulled them down into the heart of the flame. The yips, yowls, and howls of the pack reached out across the distance, dancing on the breeze coming off the lake, weaving moist fingers up the hills. To my left, my father sat on a sawed-off log, doing everything in his power not to look at me.

I sighed as I adjusted the second-hand gauntlets Consuela had given me. "Just say it. You know it's eating you up."

Credit to the man for dropping the front as soon as I called him on it. "Are you seeing him?"

"No."

"But you're living together. I heard Cody say so."

Sometimes in the eyes of a parent, one plus one equaled thirty. "For convenience, and only temporarily. My roommate went home for the summer. Tobias stays in her room, I stay in mine. We're friends, nothing more."

"You used to say that about Cody."

"And now, I can say it again." I dropped my hands and turned towards my father. "There's nothing romantic going on between Tobias and me, and there never will be. His mate is dead, and I'm part of the reason why."

Thrice, he blinked his confusion. "Were you hunting her?"

"No, and I should have been. If I'd hunted her, I'd have saved her. I didn't want to be a hood. I refused to get involved."

He mulled that over as he held his chin. "So you feel like you owe him something."

"You could say that."

"I hope, *mi bonita*, that you do not feel you owe him your life."

"We are ready to begin!"

Consuela's proclamation brought my father and me to attention. The fire burned steadily, rebellious licks of orange and blue flame leaping from the pyre. It seemed small in my eyes, the top barely coming up to my navel. My mother's fires on *feuernacht* put out smoke trails that could be seen three miles off shore.

"Your mother always keeps one hood turned toward the packlands on a full moon," my father explained when I asked. "If we build the flame too high, the smoke could alert the lookout."

"The size of the fire is not important," Consuela cut in as she took a small, black satchel from a duffel bag she'd dragged out to the fire. "What matters is the size of the heart of hood for whom it burns. Gerwalta, how is your Spanish?"

"Barely passable," I coughed out. "Why?"

She stood and turned toward me. "Because I am not a red. Reds conduct their rites in Old Germanic. The *Amarillos* use either Spanish or Arabic. I thought of the two, you might know Spanish better."

"She knows Spanish," my father intervened, hitting the ground with his ever-present walking stick for emphasis. "I made certain to raise her knowing enough. She cannot speak with fluency, but she will be able to understand what you say."

Had he foreseen that one day it might be necessary for me to take this path? That I'd abandon the House of Red? If so, why hadn't he ever told me?

Consuela gave a slow nod as she pulled out a silver disc from a black sack tied to her belt. I presented my hand eagerly, my palm itchy, wanting the silver. The metal had always called to me, but I never could speak to it as the righteous could. A thrill shot through me when I realized that soon, that would no longer be the case.

When she resumed in Spanish, my brain became consumed with rendering the words back to English. My father's foresight turned out to be useful.

"You have seen this before with the red ceremony, and our way is similar. The most important thing is accepting the fire. You must not hesitate. If you do, it will recognize the nature that rebels within you. Do you understand?"

I'd never heard that was possible. Then again, reds weren't known to hesitate when claiming their birthright.

"I do." The cold metal in my hand warmed and vibrated, as though it too had agreed to the accord. "Don't we need more people here to do this?"

Consuela shook her head. "Only the matron and the *nasciente* are necessary. The clan's presence is only for social reasons. It's a family event, no?"

I side-eyed my father, who puffed his chest out. With an inhale, and a slow exhale, Pietro Kline awakened his powers. A roll of smoke from the fire wafted his way, smoldering over his shoulders and down his back, until it stilled and solidified, brightening into the mustard yellow cloak of his native clan. His silver bracelets shone like liquid mercury around his wrist, the metal ready to obey his command.

"I represent the family."

So he did, if by no other virtue than he was the only one here. If I had more time, and if I could trust no one else would have found out, Markus's presence would have been welcomed. My heart ached thinking about my cousin, and how I'd no longer be part of his clan. Hell, after my mother found out I'd become a yellow, she'd probably disown me. I'd be lucky if my dad was still able to take phone calls from me on the other side of this.

Turning back, I saw that Consuela too had summoned her hood. Like the Red Matron, her power covered her face in a half mask, as the silver running in her veins turned her eyes into shining disks in the night.

"Steady yourself, child. This is the worst part."

The bottom of my stomach leaked into my ankles. "What do you mean the worst —"

Complete silence. The fire burning before me did not crack. The wind around us made no whistle. My father, stationed on the south pole of the fire, moved his lips, invoking the chant that would trigger whatever supernatural power fed the magic. Phrase after phrase he uttered, but my ears perceived nothing. Even my own voice in my head went mute.

Then, the medallion in my grasp began to hum.

No, not the medallion. It was the fire. Discordant voices whispered, competing for my attention. *Go away. At last, you are here! You are not worthy. We've waited for you for so long. Come inside the flames.*

I focused on the last one, trying to pull it out from the web of sound weaving itself into my brain. Flames contorted in my vision, becoming fiery fingers coaxing me. It wanted me. The fire *wanted* me. But not nearly as much as I wanted it.

Consuela's hand folded over my shoulder. I nodded with vigor, signaling her that I was ready. I'd burn, and gladly. I'd be her clan; I'd serve my matron. I yearned for the pyre. With a push, I fell forward, the flames licking my skin, my vision turning blood red. Bleeding skies and howling winds consumed my senses. Swaddled in flame, I threw back my head and bellowed. Every part of my anatomy tingled, as though I'd been muted all my life before now, and suddenly, the volume had been pushed to the max.

Then, pain. Coldness. Separation. Despair.

With a hard jerk, my body folded backward, sending the silver in my hand flying. Panic raised its flag beside me, looking wildly left and right, seeking out the reason that where I expected heat, I found only ice. When the air exploded from my lungs, the reason for my discombobulation became clear. It stood five-foot-seven, had glowing silver eyes, and whisked through the air like a giant crimson raven.

"Put me down!" I belted, hitting my mother in the chest.

Brünhild cradled me as though I was no more than the babe she'd born twenty-one years ago. "You don't really want that, do you, daughter mine? We are at least twenty feet off the ground."

Consuela let loose a torrent of Spanish curses that could shame a bordello. "Brünhild, how dare you!"

My pleas brought only my mother's jest, Consuela's curses triggered her ire. As quickly as we'd taken to flight, we floated down, landing between the yellow matron and the fire.

"How dare I? How dare *I*?" Brünhild dropped her arms, letting me regain my feet, though one cold, callused hand still wrapped vice-like around my wrist. "How dare *you*? You come into *my* sanjak, working against me with *my* husband, attempt to awaken *my* daughter on *feuernacht* and claim her for *your* clan, and how dare *me*? I could have your hood for this."

Though at least six inches shorter, Consuela's diminutive size did little to curb her attitude. "I am well within my rights to claim her! She's as much an *Amarillo* as she is a red. And, *she* came to *me*. Pietro knows why you really want your daughter's rites so badly, and he felt he had no choice but to help."

"And both he and I know why Gerwalta must *never* be an Amarillo, as do you!"

Those words, that declaration... it chilled the air around us. Something thick and wet and mucked in bitterness lay within them, though what, I couldn't see.

My father stepped back from the other side of the fire. "*Mi amor*, don't. Gerwalta can wait no more. It is becoming dangerous. She *must* take her fire."

Brünhild turned to her spouse, sneering. "Et tu, Pietro?"

In a blink, I was free. With a flick of her wrist, my mother's silver formed into her favorite weapon, the short sword. Most hoods preferred the crossbow or even throwing knives; distance helped keep one safe. My mother, however, liked to feel the blood flow over her fingers when she killed.

"I have never denied Gerwalta her fire, *you* have. By masking her relationship with that wolf, by indulging her foolish desire to go to college, by giving in to her every flight of fancy! I would have welcomed her to the fire years ago, if not for your coddling."

Even if a fierce and righteous hood, Pietro Kline was a gentle man not given easily to anger. My father *raged*, his fists clenching, the veins on the side of his neck pulsing.

"I have done nothing more than protect her from *your* devices until she was old enough to decide on her own."

I grew tired of being discussed in the third person while perfectly present. "Great mother of all, I am old enough to decide anything on my own that I damned well please."

"Silence, nascent!" With a swish of her wrist, her sword pointed at my chest, its tip hovering a few inches from my heart. "You are my progeny. You will take your fire under me, and none other. I am the only one who can protect you from the Ravens when they come for you. And they *will* come for you."

My heart leapt into my ears. "You know about the Ravens?"

Of course she knew. What she didn't know was that I did too. Red rage gave way to the clouded features of the terrified.

When she spoke, her voice trembled through purple lips. "They've come for you already."

My mother had killed werewolves. My mother had faced vampires. My mother looked at the time teasing the corners of her face and the blood running from her veins and shrugged it off. She feared no creature, supernatural or otherwise, that I had ever seen.

At this moment, my mother dreaded all.

Her face shifted, from wide eyes to a steely-glared determination. "It's not too late. The moon is still overhead. We will build you a fire, and I will perform rites so that you may claim it."

She grabbed my wrist and yanked, trying to take me back into her arms. I knew the moment she did, we'd be airborne. Flight among hoods counted as the rarest of gifts, but one which ran in my red bloodline and which my mother had discovered after her fire.

Pulling, tugging, her grip remained. "I refuse. I will never be one of your hoods."

"If you are anything else, they will kill you," she continued, trying to bring me under control. "That was the agreement."

"What are you talking about?"

No answer this time. At least, none from my mother. But as she stilled, I knew she sensed with intensity what had been a low-level buzz for me since I'd arrived in the packlands earlier that day. Wolves grew near. More precisely, one particular wolf, who in our confusion had come close to the fire.

Both the hoods across the fire called their silver into battle form. My father's walking stick was no simple accessory. It was the canvas on which he formed his weapons. Now, it became a bow, though other times it could be an ax or a sword. His choice of weapon suggested restraint. He didn't want to hurt the wolf, only encourage him to keep a distance while still able to defend us. Consuela, I was surprised to see, preferred her silver in the form of a chain. I wondered if that meant she planned to take the wolf captive, or if she planned to strangle it.

Both would be sorely surprised, for neither would I allow to harm the brooding red wolf approaching us.

Tobias took one look at each of his opponents and stopped his advance. The light of the fire behind us crackled in his eyes, giving him a demonic air.

My mother hissed. "This doesn't concern you, wolf. Leave now, and I won't hurt you."

Inside my head, something between a voice and growl spoke words without form. Tobias was... asking me? Asking me if he should attack? Yes, that was it. Somehow, Tobias was asking me something, inside my head.

"No, don't!" I said aloud to him. "She'll gut you if you do."

My mother wrenched harder, doubling her efforts to move me. "It is worse than I feared. Pietro, for Geri's sake, we must force this to happen."

One more pull, and she won. The ground melted away, leaving my feet scrambling in air for purchase. Before I could focus and find out which way we were traveling, however, we halted. The growl was far too close. I looked down, and saw Tobias's maw filled with my mother's boot, before a moment later, he in turn was knocked away by a blond wolf with a slightly swollen belly.

I needed to protect them; my mother wouldn't tolerate such lupine revolt, and the fact that Lisa was pregnant wouldn't make a lick of difference to her. Brünhild couldn't counterattack and fly me away at the same time, however. I fell, she flew – straight for Lisa. I moved faster, hurting myself, becoming the shield between them.

I couldn't say for sure what happened next. A silver blade pierced my side, the burn of injury becoming flame in my veins. Then, the fire took me down, burning me to ash.

Twenty-Six

Voices swam around the deep end of my mind, where trapped in a fog I tried to find the surface of the water.

"Is it normal to be out this long? Seems to me that's a really long time."

"Every patient is different, but she should be coming out of it soon."

"Will she be in pain? Is she in pain? Oh, god, she's in pain, isn't she?"

"Calm down, Cody, or I'll have to kick you out. You shouldn't even be here; you're not an immediate relative. Speaking of which, why *are* you here? Didn't you and Geri break up? I thought I heard that you married Lisa Jenkins."

"I did. But, Geri's like my… She's like my family. She *feels* like family."

"We'll tell that to the nurse if she comes by. I'm sure it's totally allowable under our 'only family and feels-like-family' policy. If I didn't know you…"

"Yeah, man. I know. I appreciate it. Really, I do."

"Wait. Yup, looks like she's waking up. Remember, calm."

Light had never been so harsh. It streamed in from a nearby window, falling over my eyes, as though God had gotten new batteries in his flashlight and decided to try them out on my retinas. Slowly, the room came into focus. Instruments beeping, tubes on my arms, a weary-face werewolf at the end of my bed, fretting. The other voice belonged to a huey I thought I might recognize. Maybe someone I knew from Paradise? What was he doing here? Come to think of it, what was I doing here, and where exactly was here?

"Don't try to move, Gerwalta," the blond-haired man dressed in army green scrubs said. He jotted something on his clipboard, looked up again at a monitor next to my bed, and jotted a few things down. "My name's Kevin Turner. You were a sophomore the year I graduated."

"Kevin." My voice was less than a whisper. I couldn't remember a time when my mouth had been drier. "Of course. Am I in the hospital?"

Cody took over then, weaving a cover story no doubt. "You got into a little trouble out in the woods last night. You fell, and got jabbed in the stomach by some sort of old broken pipe. I found you and rushed you here."

Standing behind Kevin, the nurse didn't see when he winked at me, a gesture I found frankly insulting. Did he think I was new to the whole living-in-a-secret-society thing?

I tried to stretch a hand out, feigning grace, but the pain that shot through me bit away my will. I sucked in a breath through clenched teeth as Cody reached out to ease my burden.

"Easy there, little red. You're going to rip out your stitches."

Kevin slid his pen into a holder on the side of his clipboard. "I'll ask the doctor to swing by, Geri. He'll review your injuries and tell you how to care for them after your discharge. Try not to move too much. Luckily that pipe didn't hit any major organs, but you're still going to have a hell of a scar. "

As Kevin left, I tried to sit up. I'd barely lifted my head when the room went into a tail spin, forcing me back to my bed.

"What really happened?"

Cody smiled, placing his hand on mine. "We can talk about it later."

"Or we can talk about it now," I insisted. "Last thing I remember is falling toward the ground when Tobias showed up. Oh, my god. My mom tried to slay Lisa. Is she… Is…"

"She's fine. You kept her from getting hurt." The joy in his eyes was the most beautiful thing I ever saw. "She's the alpha's mate. I guess the whole pack seems like her responsibility too. The second Tobias took off, tearing up the forest to get to you, she followed. I didn't even know she could move that fast."

"And Tobias?"

As a wolf that had shown open hostility to a hood, my mother would have had jurisdiction to silver him. If he resisted that, she could even kill him under our codes.

"Tobias escaped without a scratch. A little pissed at you, though. Says now you've saved him twice, and he owes you too much already."

"Bull shit. It just makes us even." I managed to prop myself up higher on the pillow at the cost of any dignity. "Who injured me? Was it my mom or my dad? And why am I here? Hoods heal quickly from minor injuries inflicted with silver, and that's the only thing either one of them had last night."

A fact I knew from years of training and many run-ins with something pointy and metal.

"Anyone else get hurt?"

Comfort left his features as he shifted his weight. "Hurt? No, not really."

I knew this werewolf. I knew him in a semi-biblical fashion. I could tell he was hiding some tall truths behind those short words.

"Cooooddddy?"

His chest fell, and with it, the barrier he'd kept around the truth. "I wasn't there. Two bloodline matrons on our territory? I had to keep the pack safe. I only know what Tobias told me."

"Well, that's a start, so start."

The werewolf ran a hand over his spiky hair. "You probably figured out the big part of it. Tobias sensed you were in danger. He bolted, even though I told him he should just leave it alone. I guess when he saw your mother trying to whisk you off, he went a little crazy. Brünhild laid into him and Lisa, but you threw yourself between them. She ran a sword right through you."

Should it have surprised me that my own mother stabbed me? But what she'd really cut when she ran me through wasn't my body, it was the last vestiges of tenderness I held for her.

"And my father?"

Cody's eyes watered. "He left with Consuela. Banished."

"Banished?" Now the ire that I'd tempered down raged within me. "After all the shit she's done and he stayed standing beside her? After everything he's sacrificed to solidify her matronship?"

"It was part of the compromise."

"Compromise?" I asked. "Are you telling me that even as I lay there, bleeding, they opened some kind of negotiation? I don't even understand what there would be to negotiate."

The lines of his face hardened, his voice grew husky. "She still wanted Tobias slain. Your father intervened. He agreed to be banished in exchange for Tobias's life."

"But that makes no sense. My mother wouldn't spare a wolf *and* lose my father. There's no gain in that for her. Cody, something doesn't add up about this. Are you sure Tobias told you everything?"

All of a sudden, the alpha couldn't meet my eyes. I reached out, trying to sense his emotions. My injury must be dampening my strength. Or maybe whatever medicine crawled through my veins from the bag dripping steadily to my right dulled my abilities, but I got an empty read on the werewolf.

Tears pricked the corner of my eyes. "There's more."

"There's more," he repeated. The wolf turned to me, an apology written into his eyes. "I don't understand how, Geri, and I sure as hell don't understand why. But the way Tobias explained it, your mother used the fire to do some sort of ceremony. At the end of it, he… *lost* you."

"Lost me? What in the hell does that mean, lost me?"

"Hey, I hear she's up. Can I come in?"

My head swiveled as the werewolf I'd nearly sacrificed myself for came in through the door, looking like he'd been dragged through sewage and left on the side of the road. How long had Tobias been lurking in the hall? More importantly, why hadn't I known that?

The machine turning my pulse into an audio feed picked up tempo, driving harder by the moment. With each increase in pace, Cody's eyes grew wider.

"Geri, stay calm. You're going to rip your stitches if you move too much."

Had I moved? Yes, I had. I'd sat up. I'd swung my legs over the side of the bed. I'd started to plot my mother's murder, all without knowing it.

Nurses rushed in, first Kevin, and then a small Asian woman with the strength of a musk ox. They wrestled me onto the bed, pulling straps as if from thin air, tying me down to the mattress. Any other day, I'd had been able to throw hueys like them off me with ease. But today wasn't any other day. Today was the day after my mother had revoked even my nascent abilities, and left me mortal.

Twenty-Seven

Igor pulled back from the viewer of the lab instrument he was using to examine a genetic sample I'd given him a few days before. He'd done his best to comfort me when I returned to Chicago, but the moment he learned what had happened to me, I could see it in his eyes: I was an outsider now. Powerless, pointless, and without clan. I was a lark set free in a world of crows and told to learn to sing a new song, all while having my voice silenced. I wasn't a hood, but I wasn't a huey. I belonged nowhere and with no one.

"Well?"

He mustered his professional decorum and used his professorial, detached voice. "Genetically, you're no different. You are still you. But at a deeper level, there's... damage."

"Damage is what happens to a car bumper when it hits a tree," I said. "You can say what it is I really am: relinquished. She's stripped me of my powers. She's rendered me inert."

At least he respected me enough not to try and correct me. "The type of damage I'm seeing in your cells? It's almost like you've been irradiated."

"So, can we fix it?"

The vampire dampened a nervous laugh. "This isn't my area of research. I..."

"Bull shit," I said, stopping him on the spot. "You've been studying slayer DNA for years. I know Cynthia had her own little silver box of wolf specimens. Don't you dare pretend that there isn't a cache of hood genetic information out there you have squirreled away."

"Hoods don't give us samples," he said. "You know firsthand that it's against your codes."

"And I also know that you took a sample of mine when Jess dragged me into your dungeon. If it wasn't to study us, then what was it for?"

"It wasn't to study *all* hoods. It was just to study you. You're..."

"Yeah, unique," I said, sealing the fate of his argument. "I remember you using that word, and huey or hood, I got enough brain cells to patch together that that was a comparative statement."

The sands of his features shifted, until finally settling on resolve. "Fine. I have a few — just a very few — hood samples. But the subjects had died long before I came into possession of their bodies, and the structures were far too decomposed to be robust. But even if I had hundreds, thousands of hood DNA lines at my beck and call, I couldn't answer your question. What happened to you is beyond science. At some point, the super supersedes the natural. Why can I turn to smoke and still retain consciousness? How does a slayer create solar energy and still not burn? How do hoods make silver liquefy and reform into perfectly forged weapons with only the power of their minds? How does a matron inflict radiation poisoning on her only daughter?"

He motioned to his bank of instruments.

"If there's a way for one of these to be able to tell me that, I assure you, I haven't found it." He lowered his voice. "You mentioned you can no longer sense wolves. Any other effects?"

"You mean other than I'm as weak as a wet noodle and I can't keep my eyes open past 11 PM without six cups of coffee? No, other than that, I'm just my usual, peachy self."

The professor paused in his ministering. "How many cups of coffee have you had tonight?"

"You don't even want to know, Igor." I sucked in a breath and repeated with a bit of gruff, "You *don't* want to know."

A knock at the door cut off our conversation as the ex-of-a-worm known as Jess Harmon slithered into the room.

"Jess, good to see you."

Igor extended a hand, falling perfectly into his roll of clueless coworker. He wouldn't call out Cynthia's ex-mind slave as having now found a bigger shark to stick his lamprey mouth on to. Though, given that there were vampires involved, perhaps that analogy ran the other way.

"How is your internship with HR going? Inga can be quite a piledriver."

His face blossomed into glee. "Oh, Ms. Rosethorn is wonderful. I've learned so much from her this summer. I hope you're still not upset that she snatched me away from you."

"Not at all. You clearly had the skill set she needed."

Jess's skill set: young, semi-athletic, easily enthralled, happy to be a blood buffet.

Jess turned toward me, reaching to take my hand as well. "Gary Kline, right? I think we met in Ms. Rosethorn's office a few weeks ago."

"Geri, actually. Sorry, but I just handled a sample of a live flu virus. You might not want to touch me right now."

His arm fell to his side and that fake smile schlepped off his face. "Um, okay, thanks. Sorry to interrupt your work, but Ms. Rosethorn would like to meet with Ms. Kline. Do you mind if I steal her away for a few minutes?"

"No, of course not." Igor cleared his throat, an unnecessary act for any vampire. "Geri, we'll pick up this discussion later, okay? In the meantime, I'll look through my files and see if I can find anything."

"Have a seat, Ms. Kline. Jess, can you please call Mr. Helsing and reconfirm my appointment with him?"

Smooth as cream in a cup of coffee, her eyes flashed up just long enough to see if the name caused any changes in my expression. Any other day, it might have. I'd found even alone that a mere mention of Caleb could up my pulse and blush my cheeks. A purely physical reaction, of course. Base animal instinct. Today, she got nothing from me. I was too red from crying, and my pulse already accelerated by caffeine, for any noticeable change. I hadn't even spoken to Caleb since I got back, other than a text to tell him I wouldn't be making it to our normal training session, no explanation given.

"You wanted to see me?" I asked after several moments when she said nothing more.

Inga pulled a sticky note off her desk and held it to eye level. "I had a very interesting chat earlier this evening with the Red Matron."

I went rigid, my mind exploding into all the possible paths that could lead out from that comment. "Oh?"

"It seems..." she lowered the note. "That you have been relinquished."

Any bitterness in my voice could poison the WWL well. I may be a de facto huey, but I was still determined to unearth anything there was to inform me of what Cynthia and her ilk had been up to.

"My mother disapproves of my choices," I said flatly. Then, taking in the full breadth of what had just been said, I added, "She called you to talk about me? How did she even know I was working here?"

A tease of a smile on Inga's lips annoyed me. "Your mother is a very powerful woman, Gerwalta Kline, and like all women in power, she knows the value of a good informant. She has several in the city that have been keeping an eye on you since you moved here last year."

"Are you one of them?"

"I am no one's watchdog. But your mother and I... Well, let's just say that our interests have occasionally overlapped." Her eyes returned down. Good god, for a creature with supernatural speed, she could certainly stall with the tenacity of a sloth. "She asked me to fire you."

"She wants me to come crawling home with my tail between my legs, begging for forgiveness," I said.

"And will you?"

"Never."

"Then, you can stay." She waved a hand through the air, dismissing me. "But I'd suggest being careful around the v-staff. Under my orders, none of them have tried to sample you, despite great interest. I'm not sure you'll hold much appeal in your current state, but the reasons for the ban disappeared with your powers. But there, I'm being presumptive, aren't I? Perhaps you'd like to be tasted. In which case…"

She looked up, flashing her fangs.

"Not interested," I said, rising from the chair. "And between you and me, we both know why I was banned."

For the first time in our interaction, something I said made Inga flinch. "And why is that, Ms. Kline?"

"For the same reason, my mother relinquished me. Because there's something about me that's different. Or at least, there was."

"But you don't know what, do you?" The arrogance was back in her voice, and with it, my ire.

"Does it matter anymore?"

Inga grinned. "No, it doesn't."

Twenty-Eight

The rest of my night ran on auto-play. Under the auspices of being an intern in Igor's lab, I marked up graphs of data and fed them back into a computer.

In the past, routine work held no appeal for me. I detested treading water; I wanted to swim all the time, and usually against the stream. Now, my depression took comfort in the banality of rote processes. Open a tray, take a slide, scan it, mark it, repeat. Brainless work that didn't demand reflection. The last thing I wanted to do was think about anything I did having an impact in any way on anything. If I was to be a being without purpose, I'd revel in my ineptitude.

Halfway through my shift, I rose to use the bathroom, distracted. The second I turned around, I ran into someone who had managed to sneak up on me without my noticing.

"Sorry, I didn't... Oh, hi. What are you... Can I help you with something?"

I couldn't even pretend to be sorry I was no longer working with Doug Marsten, my supervisor while I'd been in the mailroom. He'd been a boss, nothing more, and a snippy one at that. He had always looked at me as an unnecessary addition to his well-running machine of a division. I'd thought he'd be happy to be rid of me, frankly. The way he glared at me, however, made me think I'd still managed to piss him off with my very existence.

"Gerwalta Kline." His mouth pulled tight into a toothless smile. "So I guess now you're too good for the mailroom?"

I wasn't sure what he had been told about my transfer, but given WWL's general on-a-need-to-know-basis attitude, I suspected little.

"Turned out to be a clerical error," I said, creating alibis on the fly. "I was supposed to be here in the lab from the beginning. Someone in HR messed up the paperwork. I'm a biology student at school, you know, so this is kind of a good fit for me here."

"I never wanted you in my division," he muttered, his fist unusually tight. "But they put you there, so I changed around our procedures to make work for you. Work which now is going undone, since you unceremoniously left."

"If I had known there was a going-away ceremony, I'd have been there with bells on."

My humor died on the altar of sarcasm.

I wasn't sure why Doug would be hell bent on me staying under his supervision, given how much trouble I caused him, what with using my deliveries as excuses for wandering to areas where I had no business being. If I didn't know better, I'd say the man was about to explode. The vein on the side of his neck pulsed, and though Doug might not be aware, the vampire who was now my supervisor had taken notice of his normally overlooked presence. No doubt the driving pulse beating in the middle age man's chest sounded like a fast food jingle to Igor. He crossed the lab to our position, careful to move at a human pace to keep up appearances.

Doug didn't wear pink glasses; he wasn't in the know about the true nature of his employer.

"It's Mr. Marsten, isn't it?" The vampire extended a hand. "Doug Marsten?"

I may have imagined Igor's handshake being a little more firm than was likely needed. It could be a threat, or it could simply be that the vampire was out of practice with scaling actions for huey consumption.

"Yes, and you're Igor Karmarov," Doug said, dropping his hand as quickly as he could. "You've stolen my employee away."

Igor crossed his hands over his chest. "Technically, Geri is an intern, not a staffer. I'm sorry for the confusion the clerical error caused. She's a wonderful young woman; I can understand why you miss having her in your division."

Doug took two measured steps back, glaring at Igor the whole time. "Oh, I won't miss her. You can be sure, I won't miss her."

And with that, he turned and left the lab.

I cocked my head to the side. "What the hell was that about?"

"Not sure." Igor shrugged. "He's always seemed an annoying ass to me, but perfectly suited for his job. A strong proponent of doing things methodically and strictly according to protocol. I guess you made a bigger impression on him than you thought."

"I guess so."

As Igor went back to his workspace, something niggled at me. The vampire's read on Doug matched my own; my ex-supervisor did like procedure. He liked rules and regularity. I still remember how I'd gotten in trouble because of my desire for a regularly-scheduled rest break. He was the type of boss that wanted you clocked in and out with military precision.

Which made me wonder why the man who clocked himself in precisely at 7 AM had visited me in Igor's lab four hours before his shift began.

At 4 AM, when the two other technicians, two women in their twenties with the rose-tinted glasses, took off at the end of the shift, Igor caught me in the lobby.

"I can give you a ride home, if you don't want to take the train."

"You mean you can give me a ride home, if I don't feel *safe*," I returned, calling him out on his kindness.

Igor buried his hands in his pant pockets. "You think just because you're a huey now I see you as weak? You stood up to the red matron. Any woman who can do that can take care of herself just fine, and I don't think superhuman strength or a predilection towards silversmithing played any part on that. You're going to be okay. You'll find your way in life, it just won't be in the same way you thought."

My whole body sighed, weary and warped with woe. "Thanks, Igor, but I'm good. Actually, I think I might just hang out here for a while."

His eyebrow arched. "In the lobby?"

I shrugged. "Morning shift will start coming in soon. I should watch them, so I can observe them in their natural habitat and adopt their odd, huey ways."

I felt like a bird snatched from flight when the professor pulled me into his embrace and wrapped his arms around me. "There's a chance, though I'm not sure completely about it," he said into my ear, "that you might be able to cross into my world now. I would sire you if you wanted to, Geri. I'd be proud to call you daughter."

Someone on the outside of the supernatural world might find the offer an insult. I knew, however, that a vampire only offered to sire a huey of great potential, though what my potential in his eyes might be, I didn't know.

"Thank you, but right now, I don't see that happening." Despite my sorrow, I found myself returning his hug.

He pulled back, holding me at arm's length. "Offer's on the table, if you ever change your mind."

With Igor's exit, it was just me, the night security guard, and a sole custodian, vacuuming in the corner, in the lobby. I should go home. Tobias was already thinking I was going to jump off the Sears Tower or something after how much I sulked around my hospital room. For the first time since he'd met me, he hated not being able to sense me, saying it was a comfort he'd didn't realize he'd had. I was glad of it, though. I didn't want him feeling the emotions that consumed me now. They would only drag him back down into the mire of his own loss. I wasn't sad just because my birthright, which I swore for so long I didn't want, had been forcefully ripped from me. It was guilt that ripped at my soul. I'd saved Tobias, kept him from going moon mad, more or less forced him to take to a new pack, so that I could alleviate myself of the burden I'd taken on when Kara died. Now, as a huey, what hope was there for me to make good on that debt? How would I ever be able to navigate this world of wolves and vampires as an outsider? Now that I'd been turned away from my clan, what protections did I have? My mother had disowned me. A relinquished hood was scarcely better in this world than a lone wolf.

I had failed him. I had failed myself. I had failed Kara, and Cody's dad, and Tobias's brother. I had failed every wolf that would fall prey to whatever it was that Cynthia's ilk was up to.

"Geri?"

Caleb's smooth tenor broke my reverie. I looked up to find him dressed in, of all things, a tux, with sleek lines and no tails. He'd loosened the collar and unbuttoned his shirt, his bowtie lopped around his neck like a dead butterfly. Behind him, a man I recognized as Thug 2 who stood outside Inga's office during our first meeting waited, both intently focused on us, and disinterested.

"Always sit in the lobby after your shift?"

My eyes narrowed on him. "How do you know it's after my shift?"

His eyes tracked down, pulling my attention along for the ride, to find I was still wearing my cleanroom suit.

"Oh, yeah. I was just really tired when my shift ended. Guess I forgot to change."

"Well, I have to say, of all the women I've seen wearing hazmat suits, you pull it off the best." He held out a hand. "Come up with me. Have a drink before you take off."

"You are a terrible flirt, you know that."

"On the contrary, I'm rather good at it."

Thug 2 barked goodbye to us at the elevator, heading down as we headed up. For the first time, we weren't alone in the hall when we stepped off on the secure floor. Caleb waved to a vampire with mocha skin I recognized from Accounting wearing an Armani suit as he keyed into his own unit. Inside he invited me to have a seat in the living room, a space the size of my whole apartment with modernist, black leather furniture that would make Amy flip and a view of the Chicago skyline that would make Amy throw off her clothes and beg to be savaged.

Then again, a brick wall might have the same effect on her.

He took off his jacket and threw it over an armchair before sitting down to wrestle off his leather shoes. "Hope you don't mind me loosening the penguin suit a little. I hate dressing up."

"But you look so good like this."

The slayer actually blushed. "Are you coming on to me, hood?"

The little twinge of playfulness I felt died. "I'm not."

Caleb coughed a chuckle. "No need to be so disgusted by the prospect. Shock you as it might, you wouldn't be the first. Not even the first tonight."

"No, I didn't mean that." And before I could realize what I was doing, it came gushing out. "I mean, I'm not a hood. Not anymore. My mother relinquished my powers. I'm… I'm only human now."

Confusion mired his features. "What does that mean, she took away your powers? Is that even possible? I thought you were going home so you could go through your fire ceremony thing. You're saying the opposite of that happened?"

It felt like I had a ten-pound weight dangling from each ear as I nodded. When I looked up to catch the pity I knew Caleb *must* be wearing, I found myself instead looking at a man who had just found out his cancer was in remission.

"Oh my god, Geri! That's excellent news!"

Credulity took the express elevator down and fled the building, putting as big a distance between me and it as possible. "What?"

Caleb moved from the armchair and sat beside me on the couch, taking my hands in his. "Do you know what I'd give if I could stop being a slayer? Think about it: you can be anything, be anyone, you want to be. You're not tied down to a legacy. Geri, you're free."

"But I…"

He stopped my word with two fingers pressed to my lips, freezing me in babbling fish mode. "This gives you a clean slate. You can write whatever story you want for yourself. Sometimes the only way to find our true path is to be driven from the wrong one."

I eyed him with the sharpened glare of a mad woman on the edge. "You got that from a fortune cookie, didn't you?"

"That doesn't mean it's not true." He let go of one hand and moved it to my forearm, squeezing. "Do you know how jealous I am?"

In the last ten seconds, the focus had somehow shifted from me to him, kicking me in the ass and reminding me that the whole world didn't revolve around me getting the very fate I had spent years wishing for, and now suddenly, didn't want.

"How can you say you don't want to be a slayer? You're the last of your kind! The survival of your whole species depends on you!"

It was like I'd shown him a mirror, and he didn't find the image pleasing. Caleb pulled back, his face contorted.

"I don't mean I'm ashamed of it or anything. But in this world, in this place, it's the worst possible thing to be."

I scooted to the edge of the couch, trying to get his eyes back on me. "Why? I thought you were safe here?"

"I am, but at what cost?" He looked up at me. "Those who would exchange their freedom for security deserve neither."

He wasn't going to get out of this can of worms he'd opened in a baggy sealed with a Benjamin Franklin quote. "What haven't you told me?"

He hesitated only a moment. Then, as he started his shoulders drooped. "I tell myself I'm a refugee. In some ways, that's true. But would they let me leave if I wanted to? No, because Inga needs me. I'm the key to her whole scheme."

"What does she want you to do?" I asked. "Kill the Ravens? Could you even do that?"

"Do you remember when I told you there was one vampire I faced and I barely escaped with my life?"

I nodded. "You said it was one of the Ravens."

"An ex-Raven, actually. Inga left them after Dracula died."

If he thought I'd be surprised by the reveal, he was let down. I'd already known that Inga was the firstborn daughter of the infamous vampire. Adding that to what he'd told me before about the Ravens lined up perfectly.

"Go on."

Caleb licked his lips. "I went a little crazy after my parents died. I didn't see the difference between good vampires and bad ones. They were all bad ones in my eyes. Then I crossed Inga's path. She let me dig into her for a while, before easily handing my ass to me on a plate. She told me she wasn't going to kill me. Sometimes I wish she did. She had bigger plans. She brought me here, taught me how to fight, gave me money, clothes. Even women. I thought she was taking pity on an orphan kid, and I began to see vampires differently. Then a couple years ago, she told me we were ready to move to the next phase. Said she had some genetics wizard working on a DNA therapy that would make, and I quote, 'a viable female.'"

"As in, a female slayer?" I asked, my stomach already broiling from the direction this was going, remembering how Tobias had foreseen this very thing.

He nodded. "Turns out Inga wasn't only keeping me here to keep me safe. I'm an investment to her. Slayer blood is... *Ach,* how do I say it? You remember when I told you that vampires aren't actually immortal?"

"Yeah, you said they die after about five hundred years."

"Unless they don't," he said. "Slayer blood is like a fountain of youth for a vamp. It can heal them, even if they're on the edge of death. But more than that, it can keep them alive far beyond their natural – or, um, *supernatural* lifespan. How long, I don't know. Maybe forever. But I do know as time goes on, as they get further and further from five hundred, they need greater supplies of blood to sustain themselves. You see, Geri. That's what really happened to the slayers. We didn't just go extinct. The Ravens killed most of us, but kept some of us alive to breed, to keep as cattle. And now, to fight fire with fire, that's what Inga's going to do. As soon as she has a viable female slayer, rendered by genetic therapy, then I'm her stud. Literally. She's going to use me to create her own herd."

"But why? I don't understand what her motivation would be."

"To undermine the Ravens racket," Caleb said. "Dracula left his entire fortune to Inga. It's how she pays for all this." He held out his hands, indicating the posh spread around us. "The Ravens draw enough blood from the slayers they have to sell at a high price to vamps running out of time. It's funny, right? You'd think 500 years would be long enough for anyone. Just goes to show you, some people are never satisfied. Geri? What's wrong? You've gone as white as a sheet."

Why had my mother feared the Ravens would find me? Why had Inga Rosethorn been open to me coming into her world? Why did Igor Karmarov say I was different in a way he understood, but refused to tell me? Because knowledge was a dangerous thing. What I didn't know couldn't hurt me. But what they knew could kill me.

"Caleb, I think I'm a slayer."

A blank stare turned into a gleeful smile as he laughed. "Good one."

"No, I mean it. I was attacked by a vampire after he'd been scorched not too long ago. As soon as he drank my blood, he popped up like a freaking daisy on the first day of spring, completely healed."

As soon as he understood I wasn't joking, the Devil hired him as an advocate. "But you're a hood. You sense wolves and dance around fires on full moons, right?"

With that question, the pain was back. "Not anymore, I'm not."

Caleb looked like he had just reminded me that my puppy had died. "Shit, I'm sorry. I didn't mean it. It's just… It's impossible, right? There's no way you could be a slayer."

"No, I suppose not." My shoulders drooped. "But I am still a biology student, and for some stupid reason, I thought if I was, then maybe this trying-to-engineer-a-female-slayer problem would be solved. Maybe I could…"

…have a purpose again.

…be special again.

…not be alone, like you are.

The words died in my throat, but Caleb, the consummate playboy, picked up the threads.

"Geri Kline, are you saying you're into me?"

"I swear to god, Caleb, if I say yes, and your next answer is 'but not as much as I'd like to get into you,' *wink, wink,* I will kill you — even if that's tantamount to slaying a bald eagle."

But the slayer wasn't laughing. Instead, he was looking at me — looking at *me* — with an intensity I hadn't sensed for the better part of a year. Jess and I fooled around a bit, but it had never gotten to an emotional level. He looked at me like Cody used to, like he wanted to eat me.

Caleb leaned in, his lips hovering over mine. "I've wanted to do this since the first time I saw you."

I swallowed my words, hoping my nerves would copy. "I… I haven't… I don't…"

The moment his lips touched mine, I knew anything I said on the contrary would be a lie. All too soon, it was over, and the cool air fell over my face. I opened my eyes to see him on his feet, holding out his hand.

"Let me distract you for a while."

Twenty-Nine

I was going to kill that alarm clock. I just had to find it first.

"Caleb!"

The slayer gave up a dull grunt when I poked him in the side. How could this man move so fast on his feet, and yet, be completely unresponsive in his sleep? Any vampire able to keep his eyes open during the daylight hours could sneak up on him while leading a marching band.

"Caleb! Where in the hell is your alarm clock?"

His attempt at speech came out as a single, yawned frankenword. "Idonthaveanalarmclaa...."

The trill tones repeated, and I realized that the sound wasn't a clock at all. It was my cell phone, which if I remembered right, was in my pants pocket on the floor.

The slayer rolled over as I pushed his arm off of me and tumbled out of bed. I grabbed my clothes and waddled out of the room. Tobias's number lit the screen, and I noticed that a series of missed calls and unread text messages preceded it.

I shut the door of Caleb's bedroom behind me and began to redress myself while balancing the cell on my shoulder like a boss. "Hello?"

The wolf huffed out. "Oh my god, you're alive."

"Alive? Of course I'm alive."

"You didn't come home from work, and then I called Igor and he said you'd left the same time he did, and... Where are you? Are you hurt? Are you trapped? Whatever it is, I'll come get you."

"I'm..." Blind emotions twisted my insides. It wasn't that I wanted to keep my relationship with Caleb secret. It's just that I didn't think it was any of his business. "I'm still at WWL, actually."

"Since this morning?" The relief in his tone gave way to wariness. "Doing what?"

I balanced my forehead on the fingers of my free hand. "Things."

"Like, the sort of things that would help us figure out why my mate was kidnapped and my brother, murdered?"

The man really knew how to ratchet up the guilt. "Not so much."

"Oh, see, because I *thought* that might be it, being as that was supposedly the whole reason you were there."

"Tobias, I..."

"Don't." He cut me off with growled words. "Unless your next words are 'I actually did find something out' or 'I'm about to go look around for clues' then I don't want to hear it."

My hackles went up, my nails digging so hard into the heel of my hand, I wouldn't be surprised if I looked down and saw blood.

"Look, I'm the one who's been coming here for the last two months, sticking my neck out, putting my own life on the line, to snoop around. I even tried to take my rites for you. And you know how that ended: my mother relinquished my birthright. Now I have no hood, no clue, and no more interest in your monopolizing my guilt. I have my own uses for it, okay? So you can just back off."

"Back off? I've been here since June, WALKING DOGS JUST TO GET THROUGH THE DAY. I'm a pack animal, isolated, but have I gone out trying to socialize? Have I tried adjusting to the city? Do I have ANY OTHER PURPOSE than to protect you and hope you just do what you god damned promised me you were going to do? How much further back do you want me? What, should I take my wolf twenty-four hours a day so you can keep me on a leash and check me into to doggy daycare while you're at work?"

"I'm not trying to emasculate you, but we both need to come to terms with the fact that I failed. I don't even have my innate power anymore. I'm sorry, Tobias, but if there is an answer here, or even a clue about what they were doing to your mate and your brother, I don't have a way of finding it."

His growl ripped across the phone. "Fine, I'll do it myself."

The hairs on the back of my neck rose. "What do you mean?"

"Just what it sounds like." In the background, a door slammed shut. "If you think you failed, what choice does that leave me? Let's see if having a werewolf show up in their lobby at WWL shakes some fruit from the tree. Your boyfriend had been trying to find me, after all. The ones who killed Kara and Nick must want me for something."

"No, Tobias, you can't. They'll— Oh, my god!"

As the call ended, every nerve in my body came alive as Caleb laid a hand on my shoulder from behind. Before I could rationalize my actions, I had leapt to my feet and had him on the floor, his hands pinned over his head, my legs straddling his waist. He let me, of course. As fast as he could move, and as slow as the human version of myself was, there was no way it was otherwise.

His eyes took on a sultry sizzle. "Huey Geri is aggressive. I like it."

My body fought my heart on a course of action. The body wanted the slayer beneath me, but for all the wrong reasons. He would distract me from the pain brewing in my heart, remembering that a werewolf with nothing to lose was on his way to this building, intending to do something that would surely get him killed.

"I guess you're still a night person." Caleb loosened his hands from my grip and moved them to my hips.

"I didn't say no this morning because of the time of day."

"You didn't say no. As I recall, your response was 'not yet.' That not yet gave me a lot of hope."

My sense of determination felt like a marble statue on a pillar of sand. "Caleb, stop…"

"Are you sure?" He reached up and landed a hand on the back of my neck, pulling my mouth towards his.

I let a ghost of a kiss pass before taking back control. "Something's come up."

"I know you've never done this before, but that's what it's supposed to do."

"No, Caleb, I don't mean your… Look, I have to go."

Caleb closed his eyes, exhaling his frustration as I crawled off of him. His libido came into check as he wove his fingers behind his head, looking like a cool-as-ice kid from an anime. "Anything I can help with?"

"Not unless you want to talk a crazy werewolf out of rampaging his way into the WWL building."

His cool lost some chill. "A werewolf in Chicago? And he's coming here? Why?"

I offered him a hand off the floor. "Because he's convinced that the vamps here know something about the reason his mate died. And, because I'm relinquished, I'm powerless to stop him."

"Relinquished? You mean, that 'de-hooding' thing? So, you can't do anything special? I thought you were just being dramatic this morning."

He didn't mean that to hurt. Ignore the pain. "This hasn't happened to anyone else in my lifetime; I'm not sure the full effect. I don't know what to do, but I have to do something, even if I am a nobody now."

He cocked his head to the side. "You think you're a nobody just because you're not a hood anymore?"

"What I mean is, I'm on my own. I'm going to stop this, but the consequences? They'll be entirely on me. I can't ask you to get involved. You're too valuable."

My phone in pocket, I walked to the door and slid my shoes on where I'd thrown them the morning before. Suddenly, I jerked back, tugged by the belt loops on my jeans. The slayer threw me back against the hall of his entryway, forcing air whooshing from my lungs. The intensity in his eyes sent my heart racing. Either he was going to kiss me hard, or kill me – possibly with the same act. My mouth had no sooner opened to ask what the hell he was doing then his hand came down over it, silencing me. His eyes rolled to the left as his head jerked. The heat within me cooled when I heard the knock, and froze when I heard the voice that came over the security call-in speaker.

"I know you've got one of your love bunnies in there, Caleb. Don't worry, I'll enthrall her. She won't remember anything."

The next thing I knew, I was inside a bathroom, staring at myself in the mirror, as Caleb reached inside the shower stall to wench on the water.

"Don't talk. Vampires can't smell for shit, but they can hear a mouse sigh across a football field," he said without any explanation. "I'll get rid of her as soon as I can. *Do not* come out of this bathroom until I come and get you, okay?"

Ignoring his directions, I whispered as quietly as possible. If vampires could really hear that well, I was pretty sure a slayer would have the same gift to some degree. "She would have heard me talking already if that's true."

Caleb made short work of drying his hands on a towel by the sink. "All these executive units are more or less soundproofed, or the vampires they're meant for would never get any rest. She must have opened up the call button and heard your heart beat. Luckily, she didn't hear your voice, or she'd have busted the door down."

"Inga already knows we met. I'm pretty sure she thinks we already slept together."

What I thought would be a bombshell didn't make the impression of a raindrop in Lake Michigan. "She specifically told me *not* to sleep with you. Why she thinks she can make those kinds of decisions for me is crazy. I'll explain more later. Just, please, stay here and don't say a word."

"But, Tobias—"

He leaned in and pecked a kiss on my lips. "Stay."

And then with his crazy ability to move like lightning, Caleb was gone.

I put my ear to the door, straining to hear. If it had been a week ago, no problem. Without even my innate abilities, I only got every third or fourth word, mottled by the door and the steady drum of the shower hitting an empty stall. If vamps could hear so well, would Inga think it weird that the water obviously hit only the shower stall floor and not anything else? I grabbed a set of towels rolled up in a basket and threw them under the spray, altering the acoustic profile.

Every moment that ticked by added weight to my shoulders. With each breath, Tobias came closer and closer to doing something stupid. Like others of her kind, Inga probably rose for the night about a half hour before sunset. That meant I had less than that to find a way out of this bathroom and sidetrack the werewolf. Yes, he could change at will anytime he wanted, but a werewolf could only grasp the height of his power after sunset. As irrational an action as Tobias was about to take, I prayed he'd stall long enough for that advantage alone.

With a shaky hand, I reached for the handle. If I snuck out of Caleb's apartment unseen, would there be any reason for Inga to think I was anything more than one of Caleb's random hookups?

No oracle or imagination in the world could have prepared me. From a half inch sliver, the shocking view came into focus: at the end of the entryway, Caleb stood, his back against a wall, and Inga Rosethorn, pinning his arms over his head as she sucked eagerly at his neck.

Instinct overrode rational thought. The door almost came off its hinges, I threw it back so hard. In the time that passed from my discovery until I was attempting to pull the vampire off my – Friend? Boyfriend? Lover? – Caleb had one moment to fix me with wide, pleading eyes, fearing that my life was about to end.

For a moment, I thought it did. As my vision blurred and my body slammed to the floor, I couldn't feel my arms, my legs, my back. Inga had me at her mercy as the hallway light behind her formed a halo around her head. Her long, elegant fingers curled around my windpipe, cutting off my airway.

"You!" the vampire gurgled through the blood still sliding down her throat. From the right corner of her mouth, one crimson dot drew a line down, tempting gravity on the curl of her chin. "Bad timing, Miss Kline. Your mother has disowned you. I could take your life this moment if I wanted, no repercussions."

Desperation corralled thoughts running through my mind into shoddy pens in danger of being trampled. Was this it? Was I going to die? Would my mother regret disowning me when she found out? Would Amy mourn me? Would Cody's pack rally to avenge me? Would Tobias ever find out the truth? Would he wise up and call off his kamikaze mission, or would my death be the first of others tonight?

Inga snarled. With all the strength it took to flinch she could crush my windpipe. That, or slam my head backwards, crushing my skull. So why didn't she? Her teeth clamped, she hissed, winced, fighting pain. But pain from what?

Then, I saw it.

The lines at the corners of her eyes softening. The skin of her neck becoming supple. The creases around her mouth filling in. Inga never looked old to my eyes; if forced to venture a guess, I'd have said she was in her late thirties when turned. But that all changed in a heartbeat, as before my very confused eyes, the years slicked from her face, leaving her looking no more along in life that I was.

"Inga!"

The hallway blazed bright. When Inga dropped me and moved aside, turning toward Caleb, I saw why. On the balls of his hands danced two solaria, poised and ready to burn her to ash. The look on his face threatened to redefine the term "cocky." He bounced the orb in his right hand like it was a baseball.

"Your call, sweetheart. It would be a shame for you to come out of here all crispy when I probably just gave you enough life to keep you going for a few more months."

What?

"You!" My back felt like it'd been whacked with a crowbar, but I managed to sit up. Inga glared at me like a bug that had crawled out from under the refrigerator. "He's keeping you alive. You're... You're keeping him prisoner so he can keep you alive."

The math added up. I'd never been a history nut, but I did remember enough about Dracula to know that Vlad the Impaler had lived about five hundred years ago. If he'd died fifty years ago, like Caleb had said, it stood to reason that any of his children might be reaching the end of their unnatural lives as well.

"This is the arrangement you were talking about?" My mouth went dry as I turned eyes on Caleb. "She keeps you safe from the Ravens, and you keep feeding her life?"

Soft eyes held me, and I wondered if it was because he pitied my lack of understanding, or wanted sympathy for his. "There's hardly any of us left, and anyone the Ravens find will either be killed or taken prisoner. Inga used to be one of them, and because of that, she's one of the only vamps who they fear. She knows their weaknesses."

"You think you have it all figured out, don't you, Kline? So much like your arrogant mother." The vampire crossed her arms and leaned against a wall. "I'm more this slayer's prisoner than he is mine. His blood keeps me alive. Without him, I'd be dead within a few months."

"And what about after he's gone?" I asked. If there were any holes I could poke in her justification, I'd do it. "Slayers aren't immortal. Caleb will die eventually."

"A fact I'm well aware of. My father gave me no illusions when he brought me into his crèche that I would live forever. I accept that I will eventually depart this mortal coil. But until I can commit to stone knowing my brothers preceded me, I'll do whatever it takes to stick around. And now that you just had to know..."

Inga clapped thrice, immediately after which the front door opened. If Caleb's loft was as soundproof as he thought, I wondered how anyone outside had heard. However they picked up on the signal, the three guards dressed in black surrounded me without a direct order. The ease with which they handcuffed me disgusted me. I should be able to fight my way out of this, but now I would pay for trying to have my hood and wear it too.

"Inga, please." Caleb tried to round one of the guards, but deferred to their deterrence. "Is this really necessary?"

The vampire had stopped listening to the slayer. Instead, her vile glare fell upon me. "Your mother begged for your life, you know? When she brought you to see me all those years ago, I suggested that you be killed. Your mother, however, convinced me that I didn't have to worry about you interfering. I guess she was wrong."

"My mom's been wrong about a lot of things when it comes to me. Pegged you right, though. Said you were a bloodsucking parasite only interested in making money and bullying people beneath you, like all the Dracule."

Come to think of it, if the Ravens were Dracule, and she thought they'd be after me, that explained much of her hate and fear where they were concerned. Of course, that would be assuming she cared about me enough for it to make a difference.

"Oh, so it's because I'm a *Dracule,* is it?" Her powder-white chin balanced on a balled-up fist, the corners of her mouth tugging into a sinister grin. "Well, Miss Kline, I think you're in for a very big surprise."

Thirty

Once, as a teenager, while out on a training exercise in Pictured Rocks Park, I slipped on a loose patch of ground and tumbled off a cliff and into the lake. I survived the fall fine, but after hours of treading water and yelling, a gathering storm tiptoed my direction as the icy fingers of Superior curled into my veins. Trapped on an impregnable rock face and knowing I'd drown when my energy finally failed to keep me afloat, reduced me to panic. Luckily, an early morning kayaker heard my last attempt to scream. Somehow, I lived to tell the tale.

The helplessness I felt at this moment, seated beside Caleb in Inga Rosethorn's office, knowing that Tobias was walking into a vampire-assisted suicide, took me back to those last moments in the water before I'd been found. This time, however, even if I called out with a megaphone, there'd be no rescue.

My arms had been cuffed to the chair, though what threat Inga thought I might pose anymore, who knew? When finally, the door opened after several silent minutes, Inga beamed, looking at the man who had entered behind me.

"Good evening, Igor."

As he came even with the chairs, assuming a place between Caleb and myself, I couldn't lift my eyes to look at him. Igor, however, fixed on me just long enough to deduce my situation and formulate a response.

"I assume you have a good reason for handcuffing my intern, but I can't wait to hear it."

"Oh, I do. But first, may I introduce Mr. Caleb Helsing?"

If there was any sort of standard etiquette for the meeting of a slayer and a vampire, it didn't differ much from huey interactions. Caleb stood, presenting a hand, wrapping it firmly around Igor's when he returned the gesture in kind.

"Mr. Helsing," Igor said, as though he were greeting the chair of the Chemistry Department. "Prof. Igor Karmarov. An honor. I have known and barely escaped persecution by many of your ancestors."

One of Caleb's eyebrows rose. "Can't say I'm familiar with a Karmarov bloodline."

"Taking our bloodlines as a surname hasn't caught on in the vampire community the way it did with slayers," Igor answered matter-of-factly, offering no further clarification than that. Instead, he turned to Inga as Caleb sank down into his seat. "If you wanted to shock me by revealing there's a slayer in the building, you've failed, Inga. I've known about him for a while, though I only was able to confirm his status with a genetic workup a few weeks ago. The question I have, however, is why you've been *attempting* to hide him, while simultaneously providing support for my research?"

"Your research?" Caleb asked.

I reiterated what I knew, both to remind them all that I was still here, and that I wasn't some malleable huey they could expect to melt away. "Igor is the one cataloging slayer DNA."

"And therein, we have the explanation of why I have been aiding your research," Inga resumed. "One slayer is little good to anyone, if he cannot renew the species. We *will* be able to renew the species, won't we, Igor?"

"The trials are producing promising results. In the meantime, you may want to capture his sperm so it can be used when the time comes. In case, for some reason, he doesn't survive that long, and assuming that you haven't already... *captured* it. Now," Igor pointed back over his shoulder at me. "If we can return to the fact that you have my intern handcuffed to a chair?"

"Ah, yes. Well, you see, the funniest topic came up just a few minutes ago when Geri, Caleb, and I were having a talk up in his flat. Oh, by the way, something I'm able to get away with because all those slayer samples you keep in your lab create just enough buzz for my v-staffers in residence to not suspect a living, breathing slayer is actually living here. Thank you for that."

Igor remained silent at the sarcastic jab. Finally, after several moments waiting for her mark to find its target, and realizing it hadn't, Inga continued.

"The Seven Ravens," she said. "I'd like Geri to hear it from *you* why they're such a threat."

Grimacing, Igor turned toward the door. "I would prefer not to be a part of this."

No sooner had he taken a step than Caleb was on his feet, a solarium burning at the end of his outstretched hand, little flares kissing the tip of Igor's chin.

"Please, Professor. My parents were killed by the Ravens. If you know something I don't, I'd consider it a personal favor if you'd share it with me."

Igor's eyes stayed fixed on the solarium, neither frightened nor indifferent. "Are you sure? Sometimes, knowledge is its own price."

"I'll take my chances."

With a flick of his wrist, Caleb encouraged Igor to move back from the door. Only when Igor pulled up a third chair, moving one from a conference table at the side of the room to the space between Caleb and myself, did the slayer draw the power back into himself.

"So be it," Igor grumbled, before composing himself and adopting a straight-forward academic monotone. "You probably think that the Ravens were the sons of Dracula, but as I said, vampires have not taken to the human habit of branding each child with their father's surname. Any vampire of the Dracule crèche is a Dracula, including Inga. Including the Ravens. In fact, the human often referred to as Dracula, Vlad the Impaler, Prince of Wallachia, is one of the Ravens, not the patron of the bloodline. He became a menace to his maker. An embarrassment. A mistake. But a maker cannot kill his child."

"Wait," I interjected. "Do you mean it's impossible, or it's just not socially acceptable among your kind?"

"It's fatal," Caleb explained. "Anyone else can kill them, and it's just fine. But for whatever reason, if a vampire destroys another made in his bloodline, whether a predecessor or successor, they share the death. It also means makers tend to be very careful about who they bring into their crèche. It takes a vampire with wisdom and gravitas to be able to command baby vamps."

"Both of which Vlad's maker thought he had. He was…" Igor's head dropped, "…sorely mistaken. Not all vampires can be makers, but for some reason, that's not true in the Dracule line. Every Dracula is cursed with the gift, including Vlad. In a short time, he had managed to turn ten of his most trusted soldiers. They raged over the land, drinking Ottomans and Transylvanians dry."

"But there are only seven ravens," Caleb said.

Inga rounded her desk. "Vlad was so bloodthirsty and arrogant, he didn't think a slayer was a threat. Until a few of his own children were picked off, that was, and then, he swore to destroy them all. One by one, his Ravens hunted them down, burning them alive or impaling them on poles. At last, my father vowed to end the Ravens' reign of terror. Killing them, however, wasn't an option. Luckily, the wolves were equally upset by a vampire who'd already proven he had no respect for the lives of other supes. The House of Dracule and the wolves of Wallachia managed to drive the Ravens back into my father's fortress, where the trap was sprung."

Igor pointed at the dominating woman lording over all of us. "It was Inga's plan. The Ravens were hosted to a brilliant feast, and trusting their father, they took to their daybeds thinking they were safe. The wolves worked from sunrise to sunset, sealing them in the room where they slumbered brick by brick until finally, they were trapped."

"So fine was the mortar made by lupine hands that even as smoke, they could not escape," Inga continued. "So they stayed. For a little while anyways."

Igor's face took on shades as his brow furrowed. "As I recall, *someone* aided them with an escape from their father's castle. Someone who, I should very much hope, has learned her lesson. Luckily, they did not remain free the second time for long."

I sat up, grasping at the truths hidden in the old fairytale. "But how did they get out, and how did they even know that slayer blood could push them beyond their unnatural life spans?"

Inga straightened her back, eyeing Igor. "*Someone* found out where they were imprisoned and took it upon himself to destroy them for good. When the slayer opened the wall, the creatures inside, driven mad with bloodlust, likely took his life in moments. Slayer blood is the closest thing vampires have to a drug. It feels different in our veins, fuels us like no other creature."

Igor shifted in the chair, becoming suddenly focused on a Klimt painting hanging on the opposite wall. "The Ravens are ravenous and power hungry, but they are not stupid. They must have put together quickly the power slayer blood held. In less than a century, they've managed to decimate the population."

"Caleb is the first slayer I've seen this millennium," Inga said. "It was a miracle when we crossed paths four years ago. Since, I have made it my duty to protect him."

Something about that still didn't add up, however. "If everything you said is true, you have to be older than the five hundred years Caleb told me you guys last. If you didn't have access to his blood before four years ago, how are you still alive?"

Inga and Igor exchanged a look laden with secrets. When Igor gave a slight bow, their unspoken truth began to reveal itself. *She* was asking *him* for permission to answer the question. Inga deferred to Igor. I'd seen the pattern in wolf families for years. Only two relationships demanded such obeisance, that of any member of the pack to the alpha, and likewise, any younger wolf to an elder one. In a vampire clan, that relationship could be instilled in the same individual.

I looked to the man beside me, my heart racing. Igor's head snapped my way, no doubt picking up in the spike in my pulse.

With a dry mouth, the words cracked as I said them. "How is it possible, Igor?"

A smile spread across his face. "You figured it out."

Caleb, however, had not. "What? Figured out what?"

Before any of us could say anything more, the door behind us busted open. Within a heartbeat the two vampires had moved with speed my eyes couldn't follow. Inga shielded Caleb, her arms spread wide and her teeth bared. I found myself suddenly free of my manacles, but caged by Igor, who held me under his wing like a mother bird.

Inga eased when she saw the intruders were her own WWL security detail.

"I said that we were not to be disturbed."

Four guards dressed in the black gear typical of their kind stood with guns at the ready, wearing goggles tinted the suspicious pink color of the vampire-aware human staffers.

The one closest the door rotated his weapon, taking his aim to the ceiling. "Apologies, Miss Rosethorn, but there's a 1335 situation on the ground floor. You need to evacuate immediately."

The vampiress scowled. "A breach of the lobby? By who?"

I didn't have to wonder. I knew.

Tobias.

Thirty-One

In the back of my mind, I'd still been expecting to sense him when he was close. Perhaps at some level, I'd even hoped he'd be able to sense *me* as he had so many times before when I was in danger. But in my new normal, neither of those things were possible.

The senior guard did a visual sweep of the room. "V-staff have been alerted and have smoked away. We suggest you and Dr. Karmarov do the same immediately."

Inga shook her head. "Caleb is only safe with me."

The guard didn't try to argue. Inga was the boss, after all. "Then you need to come with us ASAP so we can get you to the roof. What about the woman?"

"Lock her in the room as soon as Caleb and I are clear. Igor will stay here and see to her defense if it becomes necessary."

"What? No!"

The attempt I made to rush forward fell flat when Igor pulled me back. I could no more fight against his power than I could run full speed into a hurricane.

"Stay," he said as he pulled me back. "This is the safest place in the building there is, and I won't let anything happen to you."

Inga rounded her desk, pulling Caleb along with her. "Hurry."

"Are you kidding?" Caleb bellowed, yanking back on the insistent pull of the vampire who had him by the wrist. "No way I'm leaving Geri behind, especially not after what she's been through."

My rising panic over what lay behind the melee distracted me from going all weak-kneed over his concern. "Inga, please. I know what's going on. This security breach is all because of a single werewolf, one I can probably talk down if you give me half a chance."

"There's no such thing as a *single* werewolf. Not unless he's a lone wolf, in which case he's as likely to be moon mad as not," Inga said. "You picked a great time to be relinquished of all your power, hood."

"He doesn't have lunacity," I assured, trying to put myself in front of her. She continued to plow forward despite my pleas, with Igor shuffling along behind us. "But he's not in his right mind either. He lost his mate a few months ago and he's convinced WWL had something to do with it."

She threw back her head and cackled. "Why would my company have anything to do with that?"

Throwing on speed, Igor placed himself in his progeny's path.

"Because we did, Inga."

The move brought the whole party to a stop. Inga blinked in confusion. Perhaps she'd grown accustomed to her maker's passive manner and forgotten that by age and by lineage, Daddy Dracula was the superlative creature.

She squinted at him, as though trying to crush him with her eyelids. "*We,* or *you*?"

Igor rolled his head to the side. "His mate was being held prisoner in my facilities at the university by Xin."

The female vampire bared her teeth, including a set of characteristic fangs that had snapped into place out of nowhere. "How could you? You know she sides with *them.*"

"She was no less my daughter than you are."

"What the–?" Caleb lifted his free hand to pull his dark locks. "Inga, this guy is your... *This* scrawny little pen-pusher is Dracula?"

The vampires, however, were stuck in their own family drama, no interlopers allowed.

"Cynthia was vile," Inga said. "If she hadn't had such a large crèche under her full of loonies she barely controlled, I'd have found a way to get rid of her years ago. Why didn't you just tell me that's what she was doing? I would have intervened."

"I didn't know if you could be trusted. You *were* a Raven at one point, after all. I still hadn't ascertained which side you were on. But now–" His eyes flashed to Caleb before again falling on his daughter. "I see you are on the side of right. Continue to be. Let Geri do as she asks. This wolf is acting out of vengeance, not malice."

Mentally pacing with her eyes fidgeting in their sockets, the hard resolve of Inga's features began to melt. "She's not a hood anymore. I'd be sending her against an enraged wolf to be slaughtered."

Igor placed a hand on his daughter's arm. "No, you'd be sending her to save a friend."

Inga chewed on the notion for a moment, her face screwing up before she relaxed into her decision. She nodded once, then turned to one of the junior officers. "Give her your side piece."

"Why?" Anxiety coiled in my gut. "I'm not going to shoot him."

"You may feel differently when a two-hundred-pound, enraged dog is charging at you at full speed." Inga wrapped her hands around the handle of the revolver before transferring it to me, shoving it into my grip. "I'm not saying to kill him, Kline. Shoot him in the foot, get him to back off."

The gun couldn't absorb any of my body heat before I shoved it back into the guard's grip. "Everything I need to resolve this is in your office, except your word that you'll give me the time and the chance to talk to him."

"Five minutes," she declared, looking at a gold watch on her wrist. "Starting now."

If I did manage to get Tobias to take on his human form again, I needed to thank him for forcing me through so many late night and early morning runs. In the span of a minute forty, I'd managed to dash back into Inga's office, up three flights of stairs, and into the lobby, hardly breaking a sweat.

Hunched down on all fours, a rumble emanating from his chest and bordering on a bark, the red-and-brown werewolf veritably vibrated with hostility. Six men bearing a smaller version of the gun Inga's personal security used surrounded him. Some twenty feet away lay a pile of torn clothing and the shattered remnants of a destroyed metal detector. Tobias must have taken his wolf either right before or right after the security check point. The lobby guards may have been in the loop of WWL's supernatural executive body, but their lack of pink-hued eye protection suggested otherwise. Given that, I had to wonder what they'd thought when a six-foot tall English bloke became a crazed wild animal right before their eyes.

One of the lobby guards on the opposite side of my approach spotted me running and held up a hand without taking his other one off the trigger. "Ma'am, stay back. This is a … It's a rabid… It's…"

My feet drove a frantic rhythm against the tick-tock of an imaginary clock inside my head. "He's not rabid. He's a werewolf. Step back, I know how to handle him."

My voice shifted Tobias's focus. The moment he saw me, it was too late. He crouched, and before he could pounce, one of the security guards shot.

"No!"

He never stood a chance. The rent-a-cop hadn't spent years training to take on supernatural foes as had I. His femur cracked under the strength of my kick, making him fall to the ground, beating his weapon by a heartbeat, wailing. It took only moments for the other five guards to turn. They'd only been taught to take on an opponent as an individual, that much was apparent. Falling in on me from all directions, they were too close to each other to risk shooting. They might take down a colleague in friendly fire. I became a tornado of jabs, juts, and kicks, all while conscious of the fact that the werewolf who started this fracas was not in the mix.

With the guards down, I turned and found myself eye level with Tobias's maw. His front paws rested on the body of one of the guards I knocked out, giving him the ability to stand face-to-face with me while still in his wolf.

I held out both arms, showing him my empty hands. "I'm not here to fight you, but you have to think about what you're doing. Raging through here is only going to get you killed. Is that how you want to die, throwing a temper tantrum? How in the hell is that supposed to avenge anyone?"

Another growl and two paws forward toward my stance suggested I'd screwed something up.

"I know you're frustrated," I continued. "I know you're pissed off at me because you think I'm becoming part of the problem, that it seems like I'm wallowing in self-pity because I lost something I never really wanted anyway. Or…" My heart turned traitor, pushing truth to my tongue. "At least, I didn't think I wanted it. Not until it was ripped from me, and I understood how much it actually meant. But I can't change it now. All I can do is *try* to make sure I don't lose something I know I can't go on without. Tobias, you're my friend. Please, you don't want to do this, especially after what I just learned."

Cats may be curious, but canines were rabid to chase down a bone once shown. The wolf before me shrank back, his jowls yipping as he looked to the ceiling. Contemplation, werewolf style. I knew the look well.

Finally, after a few precious moments, Tobias sat back on his haunches and exhaled. The edges of his being shifted in form, the fur sinking back into skin, the hindquarters growing awkwardly long and limber as his chest disproportionately squared and filled in. In a few tense breaths, the man consumed the wolf. Tobias, however, hadn't lost his temper. He shot to his feet, shoving a finger in my chest.

"Explain."

A scuffling behind me suggested the others had arrived. The human guards may no longer be a threat to Tobias, but Inga and her personal security detail were not a half dozen minimum wage lobby cops. She was a genetically-perfected killer, and I'd seen enough even in my brief observation to suspect the team surrounding her were ex-military. In the back of my mind, I wondered if my time was up, if they'd rushed up here to see if I was even still alive or just plain shoot the werewolf who caused all the commotion.

Tobias, for his part, took no notice. He glared, drilling me with the expectations of the righteous.

I swallowed down my fear. "Stand down and I will."

He snarled. It wouldn't take but a blink for him to lose control and shift back. Two blinks, and at this distance, he could have my throat between his teeth.

"I thought I could trust you." His raw tone was still more animal than human. "And you go and spend the night with that… that slayer? Is that the way of it? Why am I even here, Geri? So I'll protect you when you get in a scuffle, and look the other way so you can buddy around with the enemy and sleep with traitors the rest of the time? I'm through being patient. You're using me. For protection. For companionship. For your own devices. In return, I'm no closer to my vengeance. *You promised me vengeance!*"

Could I deny I didn't have some self-interest in his presence? The wolf had begrudgingly saved my ass on more than one occasion. "You're right; I have been using you. But please, if you don't back down, Inga's men are going to kill you."

Even as I said it, three red dots appeared on Tobias: one on his heart, one on his neck, and one between his eyes.

The werewolf's chest puffed up. "I can survive gunfire."

I took a step forward, plunging my hand into my back pocket. I pressed my chest to his ribs. "But I can't."

Before he could be any the wiser, I'd managed to swing out my hidden arm, throw it around his back, and clamp the other manacle on my wrist.

Thrashing, the werewolf tried to shift. One lick of the silver on his skin, however, brought the process to a stop. Luckily for me, Inga sprang for the good stuff. Although the weight of pure silver made keeping the metal aloft and not touching him difficult, its concentration meant that it burned Tobias like a son of a bitch whenever it came in contact.

"Fucking. Hood!" The words made their way past a jaw clenched in pain. "As soon as I get out of this, I'm killing you. To hell with what my alpha says."

Another brief bump sent us both reeling, as Tobias tried to pivot away from the metal, and I became a rag doll being tossed about by a spiteful master.

"You can't. Cody made you swear to protect me. You break that vow, you break your connection to the pack. As you Brits say," I put on my best fake accent, *"fancy being a rogue again?"*

"For the last time, I'm English!"

Inga appeared beside us from nowhere, having moved so quickly even the werewolf I'd chained myself to winced in surprise. Warmness wasn't a natural display for the daughter of Dracula. I'd have guessed being saddled with that title resulted in an existence requiring vigilance. With a wave of her hand, the surrounding guards took two steps back, lowering their guns slightly. Except for one, who kept his sights set on Tobias. Damn it that I wasn't taller. Despite my little ploy, the fact that in his human form the werewolf towered over me by more than a head left a vulnerable target exposed. A werewolf could survive a shot to the brain, as long as the bullet wasn't silver.

Something told me Inga's security detail had bullets of several varieties.

"My name is Inga Rosethorn, Mr. Somfield, and I'm—"

"I know who you are," Tobias growled. "The fangy gobbler that runs this place. Geri tells me everything. Or, at least, she used to. Why did you kill my brother? Why did you kidnap my mate?"

Inga didn't bristle the slightest. "I didn't. My sister did; I had no part of it. But I can tell you *why* she did it."

Another blink, and Igor appeared on the fray, and trailing shortly behind him, Caleb. Igor stood next to his daughter, one of his hands settling on the chain that bound Tobias and I together. I read the strategy in that move; he'd rip it apart if things went south. It wouldn't help. If Tobias shifted and I was this close, I'd become his prey before even a vampire could intervene.

"Tobias, listen," Igor said. "Inga's figured it out. If I hadn't been so wary of where her allegiances lay, I would have learned it before now and let you and Geri know."

The father and daughter reunion must have taken place in the few minutes since I'd left them downstairs. I only hoped what Inga had shared and what Igor had learned justified me strapping myself to a lupine time bomb if he didn't like what they had to offer.

Tobias's eyes moved as would have his body, if he were not naked and forcibly embraced by an ex-hood bearing silver. "Make it quick, or I'm coming at you — even if it means through her."

"Your brother was an alpha, and your mate, a beta. Is that correct?" Inga asked.

Tobias let out a gruff grunt and nodded.

"Your kind's blood is a powerful restorative for *our* kind," she continued. "Supernatural blood is always better to us, but not all supernatural blood is equal. Slayer or hood blood keeps us going a few months. Werewolf a few years. But for some reason, nothing bests unmated alpha or beta blood. A few feedings from one of them can keep a vampire on the edge of death alive for years."

The wolf grimaced. "My brother may have been a bachelor, but Kara *was* my mate, even if she didn't survive to be formally brought into my pack."

Here, Igor took over. "We all are declining in numbers. *All of us.* There are fewer packs than there once were, and few vampires know of the power of wolf blood, let alone that of an alpha or beta. Cynthia was trying to find a way to reverse the bonding process. With your mate, I fear she almost succeeded."

I spoke aloud the realization as it hit me. "That's why Kara couldn't sense you, even when you were standing right before her." Then, a sicker thought. "Cody's dad?" I asked Igor.

He shook his head. "Cynthia's crèche was already reeling from relocating to Chicago from England. It would have been difficult for her to travel that far out of town without her children in tow. I doubt so many vampires could come into packlands overseen by a Red Matron without notice."

Inga's head tilted. "But if she were working with the Ravens, might one of them have wandered through the area to rendezvous with her? You know Vlad's children have a tendency to stalk forests."

"It's possible," Igor agreed. "Geri took this internship for the sole purpose of uncovering this information. Even though it took some serendipity to get to this point, we are here. We know why your brother and mate were killed, and we know by who. Inga and I are partially to blame for the Ravens existing, and we're prepared to make amends. We could really use help from both of you."

Tobias's eyes softened, anger ebbing in the revelation. "Can I trust their word?"

Apparently, he still trusted mine if he credited me with making that declaration. "Yes."

"More importantly—" His throat bobbed as he swallowed. "—can *you* still trust me?"

I turned my neck, offering him my jugular. "I've never stopped."

Every hair in my body stood on edge when he leaned down and pressed a closed kiss to the pulse point just below my ear. "Never doubt yourself again. Everything you just did, you did *without* your hood strengths. Dammit, Geri, don't make me do something this extreme again to prove to you how powerful you really are."

"You mean this was all a set up?" I asked, pulling back to gawk at him. "You nearly got yourself killed just to give me a confidence booster?"

"Well, not just for that." He looked at the vamps behind me. "We now know who our friends really are, and cleared WWL of any involvement."

"Aren't you a smart puppy?"

His forehead pressed to mine. "I just tried being a little more *hoodish*, is all. You might actually have something with this strategy and planning thing."

I was just about to turn around to Inga to ask her to unlock the manacles with the key I hoped she still had, when a flash of something at the edge of the room caught my eye. The pain hit me before the sound, a great burning anguish, rending flesh, flaming heat below the skin. I threw back my head, bellowing, trying to pull myself away. The act pressed the silver again to Tobias's back, forcing him to mirror my pain.

"Caleb, no!"

Inga's cries couldn't move fast enough. Nor could Igor's feet. My head turned, following Caleb's solarium as it flashed across the room. Doug Marsten stood on the second-floor landing that overlooked the lobby, a revolver still stretched at arm's length. He had a split second of realization to know that his life was over. The solarium hit him like his own personal nuke, burning a hole clear through his gut and setting his clothes ablaze. The body-with-a-peephole fell to its knees, the remnants of a scream on his face, before Caleb's second volley removed his head.

Tobias shimmied himself out of my arms, hissing each time the manacles connected with his skin. When free once more, he leaned over me.

"Someone help! She's been shot."

By my former supervisor from the mailroom? But why would Doug shoot me? Doug had never worn the pink glasses. He was day shift, so it shouldn't matter. Only, it did matter, didn't it? Those without pink glasses weren't protected by WWL's anti-enthralling tech, making him the perfect proxy for a vampire who wanted a mole on the inside.

Like the Ravens, for example.

Caleb appeared at my side, trying to push Igor away. "Back off, vamp! You shouldn't be anywhere near this much blood."

Modesty be damned, Igor had already started ripping off the bottom of my shirt. The bullet pierced my left side, just below the rib cage. Now that the initial pain had passed, the sensation centralized where the injury had actually occurred. Only, as I took a few deep gasps, the pain itself began to ebb. Warning flags went off in my analytic brain.

"I'm going into shock!" I called out. "You have to get me to a hospital."

Caleb, Igor, and Tobias stayed unmoving, hovering over me.

"Did you hear what I said?" I repeated. "Hello? GSW with possible internal injuries. Call an ambulance."

Tobias fell back on his ass, running his hands through his unkempt hair. "How is that possible?"

Frustrated, I sat up before the thought of how stupid it was to attempt such a thing while bleeding from the gut was. "Jesus Criminy, what now?"

I ran a hand over the spot as the vampire and slayer observed, slack jawed. The place where there should have been a wound was only a damp bump. Under the skin, something moved, rising to the surface. A dull burn subsided as my body rejected the bullet Doug had introduced in to it. Fresh skin webbed itself over the entry point as I pulled my hand around to see the pebble of silver on my palm.

"But, I'm not a hood anymore," I muttered. "The silver shouldn't heed my command."

Igor grinned. "I suspect it always has."

Thirty-Two

"The point is that *Tobias* is fine."

"God damn it, Geri, will you stop changing the subject."

I had never lied to Cody, but over our years together, I had become very adept at framing things in a way that centralized what I thought was important versus the critical point of telling him anything that would make him go all alpha male. Now that he *was* actually an alpha male, that method seemed to have lost its charm.

"You were shot, but you're not hurt at all? How is that possible?"

"The bullet was silver," I said. "I can't really explain it. Neither can Igor. Relinquished hoods are supposed to be de facto hueys, but seems like my body didn't get the message. Somehow, it just kinda said to the silver, 'demon, be gone,' and it was."

"If the bullet was silver, it wasn't meant for you."

I exhaled my nerves as I bent and snuck a look into the lab through the glass door. Igor hovered over Tobias, the werewolf in human form laying belly down on an examination table, while the vampire tended to some pretty nasty silver burns.

"The guy who took the shot was the mailroom supervisor. As far as we've been able to find out, he's never had any firearms training. We found his cell phone in his pants pocket. He called someone just a few minutes beforehand. The order to take a shot at Tobias must have been a crime of opportunity, not something planned in advance."

Cody hummed his agreement across the line. "You said this was the guy you worked under at the start of the summer?"

"Yeah, so?"

"You don't think it's coincidence that *that's* the guy who these Raven characters decided to enthrall? Someone who could keep an eye on you and report back to them?"

I told him I didn't think it was coincidence at all, before adding, "but that doesn't explain why the Ravens would want Tobias dead."

"Why would any one up to something evil want to kill someone? Because they know something they shouldn't know."

The alpha had a point there, but I wasn't sure what to do with it. "I'll ask him, but I don't know what that would be. The whole reason I came to WWL was to find out answers. Why would I do that if Tobias already knew?"

"He might not even know what he knows. Maybe you're not asking the right questions," Cody suggested. "Bring him home, Geri. We need to dive deeper into what happened before he showed up in Chicago."

"Just have a few things to wrap up, then we'll get on the road. Keep in mind that the semester starts in two weeks, so I can't stay at home too long."

"I like that."

My face screwed up as I slid off the counter I'd been sitting on in the lab's storage room. "You mean, *'I'd like that.'* Grammar and you still not breaking bread, huh?"

"I know what I said, Gerwalta," he replied, my full name serving as rebuke. "I mean, I like that you're calling here home. It is, you know? Even if you're not a hood. Even if your damned mother thinks that chanting some mumbo jumbo that keeps you from being able to bend metal with your mind and get spidey sense for wolves was the right thing to do, our packlands... our *pack* will always be your home."

I bit my tongue, marking only the second time I'd withheld the truth from Cody.

You'll always be my home. "Thanks, Cody."

"No problem, Little Red. You tell my wolf to call me when he's off the operating table. I need to make sure he's okay, and you know I mean more than just his body."

I gave Cody my word and ended the call.

Later, the five of us sat around a table in Inga's personal flat, a posh suite of rooms on the floor below Caleb's. Tension still hung thick in the air, a sense of humidity forecasting the storm that would soon blow into our lives.

"I guess my first question," I said, eyes looking up from the mug of tea to Igor, "is why Dracula is hiding the fact that he's still alive?"

"Alive as one of your kind can be, anyway," Caleb added. "And while you're at it, mind telling us, if Vlad the Impaler isn't the infamous Dracula most people think of, why he's called that?"

Igor's eyes went to the table. "My clan was powerful, as am I, but we had no renown outside of our own world until I took in Vlad. Within a few years of his leaving my crèche, the whole of the Balkans knew our name. He became Dracula, as far as the hueys were concerned, even though I am the current patriarch of the Dracule bloodline."

"And you couldn't kill him because it would destroy you?" Tobias asked, having gotten the basics from me throughout the night. "If only you had been a little more self-sacrificing."

Igor took the jibe in stride. "I didn't think in those days that he *was* too strong for my control. History buries our triumphs in the shadows of failures. Besides, I still had Inga to protect."

"Inga?" I asked. "Why would Vlad care about Inga?"

"Because I am Vlad's daughter," she said, flat as if she were reading the time off a clock. "Biologically, that is. As a vampire, I am also his sister. No matter, when I helped Igor to contain the Ravens, he swore revenge on me as well."

"I turned her at Vlad's behest," Igor continued. "He made me believe that his rage and anger were because his beloved daughter would die a mortal death. But what he really wanted was much worse."

For the first time, I saw vulnerability crawl across the vampire's unblemished, snowy complexion. "He wanted me to destroy Igor. He kept it secret from me that I would die in the process."

"Vlad valued his soldiers more than his own flesh and blood," Igor said. "Inga he saw as expendable. What he didn't see her as was capable of making her own decisions. Once I understood his intentions, I swore to protect Inga over all. She is my daughter as much as if she were of my own human line. I knew, that as long as there was a chance he may return, I had to stay alive. To protect her, and to protect all my line."

I shifted in my seat, gnawing on the realization that in killing Donovan, I'd killed a descendant of the Dracule. My ease only lifted a moment later when he added, "Those who deserve my protection, anyway."

Tobias folded his hands and leaned forward. "So, Cynthia?"

"My youngest daughter," Igor said, "corrupted by Vlad's ideals. She, too, sought unmated beta and alpha wolf blood. Only, it is so rare to come upon now. Oddly, it is that fact that keeps the Ravens from spreading the secret of their longevity to others. Supernaturals or not, the laws of demand and supply remain true. Until they can figure out how to *manufacture* ideal supply lines, the Ravens will keep our family's knowledge contained. Cynthia was attempting to develop a treatment which would undo the genetic-level effects of werewolf mating. I fear that she had come quite close to achieving that goal when Geri killed her."

Caleb turned to me, eyes wide and smile beaming. "I knew you offed a vamp, but you actually slayed a Dracule?"

I confirmed it in the tiniest of voices, keen of the uneasy glances of the two vampires across the table from us. When Caleb picked up on the tension, he managed to wipe the smirk from his face and clear his throat.

"I mean," he said, "terrible tragedy. Sometimes these things need to be done."

Tobias, as with the last few hours since he'd met the slayer, ignored him to the best of his ability. "The last time I saw Kara, we couldn't read each other. There was no pull between us, like there had been. Is that because of what Cynthia did to her?"

"I fear it is," Igor confirmed. "And I'm not fool enough to believe that Cynthia wasn't reporting back her research results to other parties. Geri and I scoured

WWL and my own lab records. Wherever she was keeping her notes, it bypassed both systems. One of the Ravens, Timur, is a gifted scientist. Likely, she found a way to deliver her research findings to him to carry on."

I folded my hands and mirrored Tobias's stance. "What about you, Igor? Vlad is from the fourteenth century, meaning you're at least that old. What's keeping you alive?"

"There is a family in Spain. We have an arrangement. I supplement with the occasional human, of course, but no more than a well-behaved vampire should, and always within the Faust protocols."

Tobias and I exchanged blank expressions. Caleb, as well, was stumped.

"They are not as widely taught now as they once were. Perhaps when I have less pressing matters on my mind, I will share them." Igor fanned his fingers through the air. "In any case, very few vampires know the secret of slayers blood, and rarely do they come into contact with wolves or hoods to have opportunity to learn anything of them. Still, my sons have cost this world too much. I thought, perhaps, if I were able to resurrect the slayers, it would in some way make up for the damage my bloodline has perpetrated. If they returned, they could fight the Ravens. The events of today show we must move from a defensive mindset, to an offensive one. Even though we were able to erase the memories of the huey guards in the lobby, Doug was able to become enthralled despite our preventative efforts."

A muffled chuckle struck the air. Mine, I realized. "If you don't mind me saying so, your 'preventative efforts' are shit. Pink-colored glasses? All a vamp would need to be able to do is to take some huey's glasses off and, boom, there's a mind slave."

Igor and Inga exchanged a knowing look.

"*That* was not the preventative measure," Inga said. "The elevators are misted with a scentless, almost invisible aerosol that coats the eye and prevents hueys from being susceptible to enthralling. It naturally flushes out after a few hours. Ironically, it's the fact that you were relieving Doug of some of his duties that made him a better pawn. He wasn't using the elevators as much. Our method keeps new enthrallment from occurring, but it doesn't undo that already in place."

"And the glasses?" Igor asked. Nice to see I wasn't the only one not in the know.

"They're only issued to our trusted staff as a sort of club badge, a device that fools them into thinking they've been given some layer of protection the others don't have," Inga said. "It also lets our v-staff know without too much trouble who's open to being fed upon."

Igor folded his arms over his chest. "The autopsy may reveal something about Doug. Deep, sustained mind control leaves brain damage. If I find any, it may reveal how long he's been under the Ravens' control."

"Actually, I think you two missed the biggest reveal of all here," Caleb said. "The bullets he fired weren't huey, and they weren't slayer. Ours are made of wood. They were silver. Whatever it was that happened, that guy was prepared for a random werewolf to come charging in, and without much advance notice by the looks of it. You may think you run a pretty tight ship here, Inga, but seems it's sprung a leak somewhere."

The vampire on the pointy end of that accusation took the snip in stride. "That leak will be found, and it will be plugged. Full of lead, if necessary. In the meantime, Igor is right. We can no longer hope for the best. We must go about doing our worst. The Ravens must be destroyed."

"Now we're getting somewhere," Tobias said. "I'm ready."

Caleb took to his feet. "I'm in, too."

The female vampire set sail a verbal assault. "Absolutely not. Far too dangerous, and you're far too young and inexperienced. Besides, you're a—"

"Slayer," Caleb completed for her. "I'm a slayer, Inga. Tracking down and killing evil vampires is my reason for existing. Don't think for a second you're going to drop me in the kennel and be on your merry way."

A low rumble vibrated in Tobias's chest. I laid my hand on his. "He doesn't mean anything by it." Then, standing, I added, "I'm in too."

"Why?" Caleb asked. "What skin do you have in this game?"

I laced my fingers with the werewolf's. "We're pack. I won't let him go into this alone. It might help, too, that I'm still the daughter of the Red Matron. Even if I am relinquished, I doubt many know that. My name is still exploitable. Plus, my body just mended from a silver bullet. I don't think my mother swept away quite as much of my power as she thought she did. So, the Ravens? What do we know about where they are?"

Inga looked to her father, who, after a moment of contemplation, gave the go-ahead dip of his chin.

"We know exactly where they are, actually," she said. "Their arrogance leads to notoriety. They keep a residence along the Golden Horn."

"Right, the Golden Horn," I said, clapping my hands together. "And where exactly is that?"

"Istanbul," Caleb said. "Where I was born."

RAVENING

RED CHRONICLES
BOOK 3

PROLOGUE

With growing scorn, she observed the revelers in the street below. Brünhild Kline detested revels. She abhorred festivity. She disparaged all those who celebrated Mardi Gras without a care for this world or the next.

And yet, she so wanted to be one of them. It could never be, of course. Duty. Duty to herself, to her kind, and to her birthright had kept her grounded and alienated since she was a little girl. The only time she'd forgone the burden laid upon her as a red matron, indulging her heart instead of obeying her head, had laid the foundation for the battle taking shape just over the horizon. The cynical voice deep within her said this was one war her stoicism and command could not win. Brünhild persisted. She would win, *must* win. It was her *duty*.

A string of plastic beads landed by her feet where she perched on the balcony just as this thought crossed her mind, just as her *indulgence* opened the door to the suite in the background.

A metallic clack echoed off the thin, pasteboard walls covered in faded yellow wallpaper. Brünhild kept her eyes on the street below; she did not require the benefit of vision to sense his movements. His presence had always registered on a visceral level; the first time they'd met, it had been what drew her to him. Over the years they'd spent together, she'd become numb to the sensation. But now, after eight months of separation, it pricked at her, like a tantalizing form of foreplay.

Her knuckles became pearls on the railing of the balcony.

"I wasn't sure you would come."

Pietro's hands ran over her hips, his grip firm as he pulled her back into his frame and lowered his mouth to the junction of her neck and shoulder. Heat crawled under her skin, electrifying her senses.

"Could I deny you?" he mumbled against her skin.

No, he couldn't. The fact both thrilled and saddened her.

Brünhild closed her eyes against traitorous thoughts. "After what I did to you, I'm not sure how you can even bring yourself to speak to me."

He nipped his way up to her earlobe. "I understand why you banished me."

"I didn't banish *you*."

She yielded to Pietro's attempts to pull her away from the line of sight of the drunken masses below. An amorous couple on a balcony in the midst of this celebration wouldn't get a second look, but if their eyes glowed silver in the haze of night, avoiding attention might prove difficult. She only wanted *his* attention.

Her breath caught as his hands worked at the belt buckle. "The red matron banished a member of her clan who had openly defied her."

"I know."

"And yet, you still desire me."

It couldn't be a question. There was no doubt of it. Brünhild merely stated an intellectual observation.

"Blame it on my Latin blood if you must. You knew that when I chose you, you would be the only for me. It is an eternal fact." Hot breath over her eyes whispered the words that had always made her knees go weak.

And Brünhild Kline did *not* have weak knees.

"*I am your sacrifice.*"

For the first time since Pietro had entered, a pang of guilt licked at Brünhild's resolve. She loved her husband; she had always loved her husband. But when they had decided to be together, the red matron made it clear that her first priority would always be to her clan. Pietro was already so gone on her by then, he'd have agreed to anything to be with her. Little had she known the depth to which his self-sacrifice would be forced to plunge.

"It must be torturous to you, to be..." Brünhild bit her bottom lip as her husband managed to pull her shirt off over her head. "...separated."

Bare from the waist up, she turned in his arms, ran her hands over his shoulders, and laced her fingers behind his neck. She'd never known of eyes so black, and when the silver hue overcast them, Brünhild felt no full moon could ever be more beautiful than her husband's hungry gaze.

"Each breath is death." The kiss was light, foreshadowing the rapture to come. "Reanimate me, *mi amor. Sálvame.*"

Later, as they lay in the bed, spent and euphoric, the hum and squeal of the streets unfettered by the late hour, Brünhild sensed that Pietro wouldn't remain mute on the elephant in the room much longer. At last, he invited it into the open.

"It would have been fine, if she'd been a yellow."

"Perhaps."

Pietro hitched himself up on one elbow, running the finger of his free hand over her flushed cheek. "Then why did you stop it? Do you doubt Consuela's valor?"

"Not in the least. Your cousin is a righteous hood, and she honors the yellow bloodline with her leadership. But our daughter... I cannot risk putting her under anyone else's command. Gerwalta's power will be too great, and her blood, too much of a temptation."

"Then why leave her defenseless?" Pietro queried, the smile chased from his face. "Why relinquish her powers? Is she in any less danger because she's a huey?"

Brünhild shook her head. "I *didn't* relinquish her."

From elbow to palms, Pietro jolted up, his unkempt, gray-streaked black locks flipping. "But I saw you do it. I *heard* you speak the words."

She rolled over, her gaze falling softly over memory. "There is no such thing as being relinquished. It's an old hood's tale, one we mothers tell our children to scare them into submission. I did nothing more than hit her with silver flame. It would have shocked her, temporarily damaged her, but no matron can take her power away. She believed it, and the silver flame added to the perception. The mind is a powerful thing, Pietro. Gerwalta's, more powerful than most."

No need to look at Pietro to sense his confusion. She could feel a vague sense of it tingling in the air around her. "You used silver flame on our daughter, when we both know that—"

"We know nothing," Brünhild interrupted as she slipped from the bed and grabbed her clothes from the floor. "We can't. Gerwalta isn't you, and she isn't me. There hasn't been a child like her born for centuries. Neither you nor I have any idea what the effect will be."

"There was an effect," Pietro countered. "Cody says she is relinquished. The wolves can't sense her anymore, nor she them."

Brünhild frowned; whether it was because her banished husband had just admitted to staying in contact with her custodial pack, or because he knew more about the state of their daughter than she did, she couldn't say. "The longer it takes her mind and her body to realize she's not, the better. Perhaps the Ravens will not be so eager to get their fangs on her if they believe her a huey."

"We should have told her about them long ago. Ignorance is never an excuse, but we've made it her only choice." The matron's groom shook his head. "It's already been months. How much longer can we hope for the effects of the silver flame to last?"

Through a squinted gaze, she scrutinized his expression. "Not too much longer. Besides, it could be a benefit to her for the time being, being perceived as weak. A dull blade inspires less terror, though its *potential* to kill is no less."

"Then we must hope her edges sharpen soon."

The red matron spun, her dulled pupils growing silver. "Why?"

Pietro stood, ambivalent to his nudity. Unlike her, he felt just as strong in his own skin as when he donned his hood. "They are planning on going after the Ravens."

"When?"

"After graduation. And that *boludo* wolf is going with them."

Brünhild wondered if her husband's dislike of Tobias Somfield was simply because the latter was a werewolf, or because Tobias was English. Argentines could hold a grudge.

"Good."

Any heat remaining between them dissipated with the spike in Pietro's anger. "Good? How can you possibly think our daughter spending time with that mutt is good?"

She crossed to him and planted a kiss on his pursed lips. "Because then they must come back within three months, mustn't they? Otherwise, the wolf will go moon mad. And in the meantime, Markus will shadow them."

"Markus?" Pietro repeated, as though it were a word in a foreign tongue whose pronunciation was uncertain. "You want to send Markus to Istanbul?"

One perfectly drawn eyebrow arched. "Is there something wrong with that? You know he's had some fascination with the Dracule since he was a child. He is young, but he is a fine and righteous hood."

"Yes, but he is..." Pietro smirked as his hands pantomimed whatever words could or would not come from his mouth.

"I am aware of my nephew's proclivities. It is irrelevant. He is the right man for this situation. Besides, he is more vested in her safety than any other under my command."

Her husband flinched at the implication. Banished, Pietro could offer no official duty as a member of the House of Red, even if only by marriage. Taken in by his cousin, a yellow matron, he also could not elect to make the journey himself. After the standoff with Brünhild, Consuela's readiness to upset the indomitable red matron so soon was small.

"You still hold hope that Markus and Geri will someday be joined." He side-eyed his wife. "I fear that's a stock which holds no cattle. It's against both their natures."

"What do their natures matter?" Brünhild pulled on her second boot, making the leather creak. "It was against my nature to marry you, but I did."

"And you regret every day of it," Pietro said flatly.

This was one thing of which she wanted Pietro to be certain. "I have never regretted who we are, Pietro. I've only regretted who life forced me to be, and what it cost us all."

ONE

"GODDAMN IT, GERI! DO WE LIVE WITH A YETI?"

A hot iron pressed to my feet would not have woken me faster. I found my silver blade in hand and held ready for attack. Luckily, reality caught up just in time.

Any other person might flinch at having their roommate brandish a knife. At the very least, they might give said roommate TEN FREAKING MORE MINUTES TO SLEEP IN ON THE ONLY DAY OF THE WEEK THEY COULD. Amy, however, had danced this dance before.

"Put your butter knife away. Like I said, I'm a New Yorker. It ain't a gun, I ain't gonna run."

The silver blade found its way back into the sheath hidden under the pillow. "And this is why werewolves make better roommates."

"What the hell does that mean?"

"Nothing." The pillow's warmth had already started to leach away. "It's Sunday, Amy. Why, in the name of Godric's Hollow, are you waking me up before nine?"

"Because our bathroom sink looks like the floor of a dog-grooming parlor, and your boyfriend—"

"For the five thousandth time, Tobias is *not* my boyfriend."

"Since he's your shack-up honey, then, I'm laying the ability of our bathroom to be braided at your feet."

Chances of getting back to sleep: zero.

Chances of me being required to decontaminate the bath: higher than James Franco at a Snoop Dog concert.

I rolled out of bed, pushing sleep from my eyes and eking resolve into my determination. "And for the *six thousandth* time, I'm not sleeping with Tobias."

"Methinks the lady doth protest too much."

"Fine, we are *technically* sleeping together, as in we slumber in the same room. Rarely, when we're both home and sleeping at the same time. And FYI: *He* makes his bed on the floor."

In a discount dog bed I'd brought home as a practical joke and which he actually decided he liked.

The blonde cocked a hip and twirled a braid around her finger. "Send him to my room, then. I mean, really... Minus the fact that his personal hygiene practices are seriously deficient, and that he has some sort of obsession with dumplings that I'll just never understand, why can't the two of you get together? I know his wife died, but that was, like, a year ago. Even Puritans would roll their eyes at you."

Cast the girl in one university production of *The Crucible*, and suddenly she thought she had a PhD in American history.

How could you explain to your huey roommate that the man who had been sleeping in your room since the beginning of the school year was a widower werewolf who would never love again, and that she stood as much chance of a hook-up with him as grapefruit taking on a semitruck? You didn't. You just rolled your eyes, sighed, and repeated your boilerplate response.

"Tobias and I are only friends. It's never going to happen between us, and most importantly, it's never going to happen between the two of you either. So just let it go."

Just as I turned to the coat closet to grab the bucket full of cleaning supplies, the front door opened and the werewolf with burning ears came in.

He was suspiciously unshaven.

"Ladies." Tobias pushed a cardboard tray holding two cups of coffee toward us. I had never thought that werewolves were psychic, but could there be any doubt he'd foreseen Amy's anger? "Mocha for Geri, soy milk latte with two pumps of mango syrup for Amy."

Even a werewolf would flinch when a huffy, blonde New Yorker growled.

Amy snatched the coffee away in a fit. She pointed a finger in Tobias's chest with her free hand. "This doesn't excuse anything."

And with that, she went in her room and slammed the door.

Tobias's confusion drew lines in his forehead. "What was that about?"

A methodical sip of mocha with my eyes open and staring over the rim of the cup at the werewolf proceeded my answer. "Did you shave last night before you left for work?"

"Yes, but I…" Memory called up guilt and invited it to the party. "Shite, I didn't clean out the sink."

Shoving the basket of cleaning supplies into his arms, causing him to drop the empty tray, I nodded. "*Yet*, Tobias. You mean you haven't cleaned out the sink *yet*."

A werewolf could pull off an amazing amount of reticence once you got to know them. Without further prompting, Tobias snatched the fallen coffee caddy from the floor, went to the bathroom, and began to excavate.

"Quickly, please!" I called at the door. "I just got up a minute ago, and nature is calling on speed dial."

He paused to look at me back over his shoulder. "Do you think sometimes that there's reasons hoods and wolves aren't supposed to be bosom buddies? I don't want to know about your toilet habits. We'll never be that close."

"This from the man who yesterday told me and Amy not to open Netflix until he got out of the pisser."

"That's different."

"How?"

He shrugged as the last bit of hair-flecked soap scum transferred onto the sponge. "Because I'm a guy."

"And THIS is one of the reasons why hoods are matriarchal, because we clearly are the better sex."

When I slipped back out of the bathroom a few minutes later, he took up the conversation right where it had left off.

"Speaking of sex..." Tobias grinned. "Guess who's coming back on a midnight flight?"

Any ire within me faded in the wake of such a delicious tease. "He's coming tonight?"

"That part will be up to you, won't it?" Looking all smug and superior, Tobias nodded as he deposited the bucket back in the coat closet. "Got the word from Inga's assistant last night. No idea if they found out anything, though. I don't think Clark is that in the loop on his boss's personal life."

The reminder that Inga Rosethorn was the center of WWL gossip as having a boy-toy lover, i.e., my boyfriend, Caleb Helsing, and that she regularly whisked him away to exotic, foreign locales, burned in my gut. Even though I knew the rumors were nothing, and that Caleb himself admitted that, for once, he didn't enjoy his sex-god reputation, the fact that that woman put her fangs on him regularly to drink his blood and keep herself alive still smarted.

"It's about freaking time. They were only supposed to be gone for ten days. I want to know what the hell they were doing for a whole month."

"I can draw you a chart of the mechanics, if your mother never gave you the talk."

My fingers pinged his rock-hard chest. "They are not sleeping together."

"Why shouldn't they be? After all, you and Caleb aren't."

"Oh, I see. 'Toilet habits' you want nothing to do with, but my sex life is open grounds for analysis."

"You don't have a sex life, Geri. You have to actually have sex to have a sex life."

I crossed my arms in the perfect act of childish petulance. I could tell the werewolf that Caleb and I had actually decided we'd make the beast with two backs when he came back to town, and that that, in part, was why his being gone so much longer than anticipated was so annoying, but why should I? "And just what makes you think we're *not* sleeping together?"

"Because you don't smell any different."

"I'm not going to believe for a second that makes any sense. Got any other theories?"

I almost dropped my coffee when Tobias put his arms around me and pulled me to him. Within moments, my body went into high alert. My breath hitched when Tobias lowered his mouth to mine, just inches away from kissing me. He might be an ass sometimes, but he was, in fact, a very sexy ass (with a very sexy ass) who loved to tease me with his looks. With his shoulder-length brown hair tied behind his head, his biker-inspired stubble, and a body that set off the tingles, the werewolf's human form could make a nun give up her vows.

A knowing smirk pulled taut the corners of his mouth. "Once you've been with him, I won't be able to do this to you."

I tried to keep myself in control, even as little demon voices called out inside me. *Kiss him. Take him. Be with him.*

"I'm not a wolf, Tobias. I won't bond with him that way. I won't have what you and Kara had."

The reminder of his slain mate's name loosened a bit of his hold on me. Still, his hands stayed on my waist as he tried to shake off the sadness. "If he doesn't at least make you feel like you should, then you shouldn't be with him to begin with."

Just at that moment, Amy's door opened as she emerged with a backpack slung over her shoulder. As soon as she caught sight of us, instead of going all squeaky with delight at our proximity, she just rolled her eyes and huffed.

"Oh, my god, will you guys just fuck already and get it over with? This will-they-won't-they thing is getting really tedious." Without giving me a chance to respond, Amy pushed a plain white envelope into my face. "Here."

I broke away from the werewolf to take it. "What is this?"

"Your tickets."

"Tickets?" Tobias said, moving to the fridge to grab a pint of milk to chug. We'd given up on coaxing him into using a glass months ago. "Tickets for what?"

"For my play," Amy said. "Remember? My senior performance for my drama minor? You two said you'd come cheer me on."

Nervous chuckles filled the room as Tobias and I exchanged manufactured smiles. "Oh! That's tonight? I must have forgot to put it on my calendar. But, yeah, looking forward to it."

"I'm not, but I'll be there." Tobias winced when I elbowed him in the side. He quickly got the hint and corrected his rudeness. "I mean, I don't like being in tight, packed crowds. Of course, I'll be there, Amy. It's the least I can do to thank you for letting me move in."

Amy admonished him with a glare. "The very least. Especially since I didn't *let* you move in. In fact, I remember the promise being 'it's only for a few weeks until he finds a new place.' Curtain time is seven-thirty. I have to go. We're sneaking in one more dress rehearsal before show time. See you tonight."

The second the apartment door closed, Tobias spun on me.

"Okay, two things. One, please tell Amy about Caleb so she stops trying to make you and me happen. And two: please, please, don't make me go to this."

"I can't tell Amy about Caleb. Officially, Caleb doesn't exist, remember? He's contraband. And two, I'm not making you go. I'm going to support my friend."

His knuckles blanched as his hands became fists at his side. "And de facto, that means you're making me go."

"It wasn't my decision for your alpha to order you to ensure I never went outside without a supernatural escort at night. Believe me, having you walk me to Caleb's apartment, then waiting for me outside isn't my idea of convenient."

"Well, at least we can come together on that," he huffed. Tobias leaned against the wall, disguising a yawn with the back of his hand.

"Go to sleep. *Comfortably.*"

He raised an eyebrow. "I thought you told me no more sleeping in my wolf since that time Amy almost walked in on me?"

I waved a dismissive hand. "She'll be at the theater the rest of the day. I'm just going to take a run and spend the day studying. Only have one more final exam and then I'm free."

"You're an ex-hood who's likely on the kill list of a fifteenth-century Transylvanian vampire prince. Free is the last thing I'd call it."

"Dr. Taylor's threat to my long-term well being seems more imminent at the moment. I'll grab my things from the bedroom so I don't have to come in and disturb you later."

"Actually, then, that sounds like a right good thing." Tobias's hands went to the row of buttons running down his shirt, starting at the top, opening a pathway my eyes longed to tread. Suddenly, he paused, meeting my stare. "I thought 'all the better to eat you with' was my line."

I shook my head and stuttered through embarrassment. "Sorry. I just…"

A catch of sorrow crept into his voice. "Yeah, I know. You miss your boyfriend. But maybe hold that heavy-lidded-eyes-and-parted-lips thing for Caleb. He'll appreciate it more. Now, weren't you going to take a run?"

I clapped my hands and rushed into my bedroom to ferret out two sets of clothes. "Yes! I definitely need to take a run."

And then, maybe, a cold shower.

TWO

                              Where are you?

    Walking.

                    "Walking" is a verb. The
                    question I asked can only be
                              answered by a NOUN.

    Bloody Chicago.

                    Did you have to use that word?
                    You do know I have a legendary
                    clutch of vampires who want to
                              kill me, right?

    Keep it up, and there'll be a
    werewolf too.

                    Just get here already. Or
                    should I wander the streets
                    unprotected and look for you?

"Don't you fecking dare, Geri."

Mesmerized. I was freaking mesmerized. The werewolf who had just walked into the theater lobby had two fashion modes: security uniform for when he was at work at WWL, or blue jeans and tees when he wasn't. Three, if you included fur as a mode. What Tobias did not do, or at least had not done in the time I knew him, was formal.

Where he got the three-piece suit from, I couldn't begin to imagine. The things I actually *could* begin to imagine, however, were not appropriate for a woman with a boyfriend. The man defined the term "rugged hot." His ever-present stubble combined with the dark navy of his slacks and jacket to present a rock-star-at-the-Grammys feel.

The illusion of him as a confident, easygoing playboy melted away, however, as Tobias observed the packed theater lobby. Werewolves were creatures who favored wide open spaces or forests. Crowds distressed them. Suddenly, I realized how much I was asking Tobias by being here. His heavy breathing wasn't from rushing over; it was born of anxiety.

I wrapped my hand around his and flinched when his grip tightened. "Just a bunch of hueys. No threats. Focus on me."

"I'd focus on you better if you had dressed up like I did."

"Tobias, no one is dressed up like you." I pulled him towards the entry, digging the tickets out of my pocket.

"I've never been to an actual theatrical performance before. This is how everyone dresses for the annual Royal Variety Performance they have on the telly back home each year."

"Well, on the northside of Chicago at the WCU Arts Complex, jeans are just fine. Not that any woman here between the age of eighteen and eighty is going to complain, mind. But where did you get the getup?"

"I called Igor to ask where I could get a suit on short notice. Twenty minutes later, there was a tailor at our door. Seems like being rich lets you do things like make all manner of manservants magically appear. We should definitely try being rich sometime."

The usher guided us to our seats in the third row, stage left, right on the aisle. Hopefully having access to an escape route would ease Tobias's nerves somewhat.

"If I were still a hood, I could wield silver, and make us very, very rich. Not as rich as Igor, I'm willing to bet, but comfortably cozy."

With a newfound revelation, his head swiveled in my direction as he settled into his seat. "Bullocks, I've never thought of that. Why aren't all hoods rich, then?"

"Discipline. Values," I answered. "We can't *make* silver, so what we do have, we hoard. Besides, you can't exactly toss a few ducats up on the counter to pay for things, can you?"

Other theatergoers milled around. As expected, women eye-screwed Tobias as they walked by. It was nothing new. Women were drawn to the wolf, and I frequently got acidic glares from those who thought I was touting hot property out of my price range. Normally, I'd just ignore the fact, but today, when he was already nerve-wracked from being enclosed on all sides by hueys who liked Arthur Miller, chancing anything setting off Tobias's protective instincts seemed like a bad idea.

I unlaced our fingers and drew back my hand, only to have him snatch it back and wrap the back of my hand in both his paws.

"Please." He stroked my knuckles like he was petting a cat's ears. "If it's okay?"

"It's okay." I leaned into him, easing the strain on my arm on the armrest. "Only you're going to have to put up with my head on your shoulder or my hand's going to go numb."

"You say that like it's a bad thing."

"A numb hand is a terrible thing."

He coughed a laugh as the house lights started to lower. "Always ready with a quip, aren't we?" Before I knew what was happening, and done before I believed it, Tobias turned and kissed my forehead.

The next hour and a half was the longest of my life. He never let go of my hand, and I never picked up my head. That was, at least, until the end of the third act.

I couldn't recall if Amy had shared with me many details of the play in which she was starring. For example, I didn't remember hearing her say she was, in fact, *the* star. Her ability to pull off the part of the deceptive, selfish, manipulative Abigail Williams astounded me. The character Amy played was the antithesis of her own. I wondered if her ability to render the role so believable was just her doing the opposite of what she herself would do. Except for the part where she wanted to sleep with John Proctor so bad. *That* was full-on Amy Popowitz.

Tobias leaned down to me, his voice barely a whisper. "I've seen the film version of this at least ten times. I don't remember fog."

I shrugged. We'd read it in high school in our stilted teenage awkwardness, but I couldn't stand Winona Ryder in anything. "Everything's more dramatic with a fog machine."

As the billowy clouds filled the stage, however, the growing worry on the faces of the acting company suggested the fog was assuming an unwritten walk-on role. All about the stage, college kids dressed up as Puritans looked on with utter bafflement as the low-pressure system entering stage left stole the scene.

Amy shook away her confusion, trying to recover her character and get the cast to do the same. "Oh, Mary, this is a black art to change your shape. No, I cannot, I cannot stop my mouth; it's God's work I do…"

My roomie's hands went to her throat as another of the cast members shouted out her complicated line, "Abby, I'm here!", followed by a guy I knew to be a freshman wearing a gray wig adding, "They're pretending, Mr. Danforth!"

Amy fanned herself, the fog thickest around her. "Oh, please, Mary— Don't… Don't…"

When Tobias yanked back his hand and stood, my first impulse was to bemoan the loss of my headrest. A moment later, the actors themselves began to scurry around the stage. The fog cleared for just a moment, and what the fuss was punched me in the stomach. There, nearly doubled over, stood Amy, her hands on her throat, her face red, the other members of the cast attempting to pull away the white collar of her costume as she gasped and coughed.

"Tobias?"

He didn't look at me. He didn't hesitate. One moment he was beside me, and the next, he had bounded up on the stage and had Amy in his arms, rescuing her from hitting the ground in the nick of time.

"Call an ambulance!" he bellowed, and even as he moved, the fog moved with him.

The fog moved *with him*.

"Oh, my god. Amy!"

The werewolf leapt off the stage just as the director ran on, his eyes tracking Abby Williams.

"My star! My ingénue!"

The crowd gathered in, making my stomach tighten. Tobias had been nervous in a group of this size in tight quarters; what was he going to do when he thought they might be intending to harm her? Was he going to wolf out right here and blow our cover? Would the yellow matron who controlled this territory send one of her righteous, or would Consuela come in person to terminate my friend? More importantly, what in the hell was wrong with Amy?

A man on a cell nearby put a hand on my shoulder. "The paramedics are on their way. You know her?"

I nodded. "She's my roommate."

The man acknowledged me with a jerk of his head and pressed the cell back to his ear. "Okay, I'll ask her. The dispatcher wants to know if she has any allergies."

"She's allergic to cats."

"And what medical conditions. Does she have any of those?"

"It's not a medical condition!" I dropped to my knees and tried to do the impossible. My hands strained the smoke, but I couldn't find anything tangible. The vampire who was doing this had no interest in being caught. "Leave her alone, asshole!"

Just as Amy's face went from red to purple, Tobias sucked down air so deeply, he had to arch his back to contain it. As he exhaled with all his might, the fog blew away, but not before an airy voice whispered in my ear.

You have been warned. Stay away.

And then, the vampire was gone.

THREE

"This is all my fault."

Tobias played with a strand of my hair that had come loose from my braid and fallen across my eyes. My head moved in time with the cycles of his breath. "No, it's not."

I sat up and glared at him. "So it's pure coincidence that my best friend was just attacked by a vampire in front of a large crowd?"

"Of course, it isn't coincidence, but that doesn't mean it's your fault. Don't own their shame, Geri."

I'd been arguing the point with him in the hospital waiting room for the better part of two hours. He wasn't going to budge, and neither was I. A quick sweep of the waiting room confirmed that, other than a shabby, bearded man wrapped in three layers of flannel snoozing on a pleather-wrapped loveseat, we were alone in the sterile, copacetic space. Other than the faces on some thirty-odd magazines spread out over every flat surface, no one was around to hear us.

"They know about us," I concluded, changing lanes. "The Ravens know we're coming for them. Now that graduation is near and we're about to leave for Istanbul, they're sending off warning shots."

"Seems that way."

The flat tone of Tobias's response made my head swivel. "Doesn't that bother you?"

"No, I think it's a good sign." My dumbfounded expression forced him to continue. "Of course, I'm pissed they came after Amy, but they wouldn't send a warning to us if they didn't see us as some sort of threat. Yes, Geri, they know we're coming. And now, we know they're scared."

"You know, this kind of shit is originally why I left home to come to Chicago. All I wanted was to be normal, *not* to have anything like threatening vampires or crazy wolves—no offense—hounding me. But instead of getting out of the supe world, I've only succeeded in sucking Amy into it." The memory of seeing my roomie fainting, turning unnatural colors as the life leaked from her, reverberated in my mind, sharpening my anger. "I'm going to kill Vlad myself."

Tobias grinned and pulled me back to his chest, kissing my forehead and encircling me with his arms. "That's my girl."

A rush of warmth flowed through me, and for a moment, it was almost like I'd recaptured my hood senses. My eyes tilted up to Tobias's; his beard didn't hide his smile. Was he feeling it too? The glow of it overpowered my senses. I opened my mouth to speak when a bell rang, followed a moment later by the elevator doors at the far end of the lobby opening.

I was out of my seat the moment he appeared. Igor, grinning in amusement, sidestepped Caleb and I as we devolved into hormonal creatures, more octopi than humanoid. Even if it was a hospital, truth was truth: I hadn't seen the guy in a month.

"Thank god you're okay." The slayer covered my face in kisses as I wrapped my arms about him. "You are okay, aren't you?" Another kiss on the cheek, another on the nose, all as I bobbed my head to answer his question. "I was so worried when you called. Igor picked us up and brought me straight here. Damn it, I missed you, Ger-Bear."

The woes of the world took a respite when his mouth finally lowered to mine. Caleb's kiss was like the man who gave it: full of sunlight and warmth, and as likely to set me afire. I allowed myself three seconds of dismissing everything that existed besides him and me. When Igor started to get the rundown from Tobias, however, the time and place slapped me back into the moment.

"It was one I hadn't smelled before," the werewolf was saying to the patron of the Dracule line. "Musky, spicy, like a shop that sells incense."

"And the accent?" Igor asked, his eyes unfixed as he sorted through his memories.

Tobias shook his head. "I didn't hear it. Only Geri did."

That was news to me. Caleb and I uncoiled as I walked toward the vampire and the wolf. "What do you mean, you didn't hear it?" I asked. "Your hearing is, like, ten times better than mine, and it was so loud."

Igor repeated my previous scan of the room. He must have considered the other occupant as little a threat as I did. "A smoked vampire can finger into your ear. It can seem like he's talking right into your brain. Even a werewolf would have difficulty overhearing. Did the voice appear to be male or female?"

"Male," I grumbled. "I didn't recognize the accent. Then again, the only ones I'm fully aware of are Yooper, Argentinian, and British."

"English." Even under present circumstances, the wolf would still correct me on that. "Igor, any ideas?"

The vampire bit his bottom lip. "It's not enough to go on. I might be able to get more clues when I talk to Amy."

If I had hackles, they'd be raised. "Why do you need to talk to Amy?"

His deadpan expression was tinged with pity. "To learn what she experienced, and then to erase her memory, of course."

Instinct drove me to step up and block Igor's path—even though he made no movement toward the patient area. "I don't *want* her memory erased."

Igor chuckled. "Geri, please. We can't have an innocent huey running around with the recollection of being fogged by a vampire. At best, other humans think she's crazy. At worst, she develops PTSD from her near murder. Think how traumatic this must be for Amy. Don't you want her to never have to deal with that again?"

The truth lingered in those words. I knew it, and I couldn't deny it. Having lived my life as a huey for the better part of a year, however, gave me a little more sympathy for their powerlessness when faced with a supernatural threat.

"This wasn't a random attack. The Ravens did this, and unless we're willing to capitulate, I don't see why they'd consider Amy any less of a target if we go forward with our plan to track them down. Once we leave for Istanbul, Amy's going to be on her own. The only thing that will possibly protect her from another attack is her instinct to be afraid. You're not going to do anything that dampens that at all. Her life may depend on it."

"But—"

I cut off the vampire's argument with the tip of my silver blade pushed to his throat. Just because I was a huey didn't mean I'd stopped being prepared. The only thing sharper than it I could wield was my glare, which I did.

"It's not negotiable."

"Understood." Nonplussed, Igor stepped back. My blade couldn't inflict any mortal wound on him, but it wouldn't exactly tickle. "In that case, it's on you to tell her something that lets her process this. What, prithee, do you think you can say to her?"

Tobias, who'd slunk back to the least comfortable chairs ever, spoke up. "You could tell her the truth."

The ballsiness of the statement made all three of us turn to see if he'd grown a second head.

The werewolf shrugged. "Igor's right; her memory should be wiped. But if you're not going to do that, then…"

"*Et tu*, Brute?"

Tobias grimaced. "I don't speak Greek, hood."

"It's Latin," Caleb corrected with no little amount of smugness. He did so enjoy any opportunity to outshine Tobias. Which, given his slick sophistication, was frequent. "I agree with Geri. Fear and braveness are powerful defenses when paired. The question is *what* to tell Amy, not what to make her forget. It should be something powerful, but not traumatizing."

"She just was traumatized. Or what would you call a huey being—"

Tobias cut himself off as his eyes scanned the room and focused on the corridor which led to the exam room. A moment later, Igor assumed the same stance, then Caleb. What they could hear I now relied on huey-powered eyes to confirm. A russet-skinned doctor, equipped with a stethoscope and a clipboard, studied each of us in turn.

"I'm Miss Popowitz's doctor. Are any of you a family member?"

Igor stepped forward, and even without being able to see his face, I'd grown to recognize the shift in the air that occurred whenever he took someone under thrall.

"We're all family members," the vampire said, pointing at first himself, then each of us in turn. "I'm her father, that's her sister and brother, and her sister's boyfriend."

The doctor twitched, his mind fighting Igor's influence. Finally, after several tense moments in which I was beginning to mock up a case of the whinnies to get past administrative red tape, he coughed. "Yes, of course. Well, we just wanted to let you know, she's fine. We're still not certain what happened. Our leading guess right now is there was a malfunctioning fog machine that hadn't been cleaned out in a while. If untended, those things can become little breeding grounds for molds and bacteria. We're still waiting for a few more routine tests to come back, but she should be ready to go home shortly. As a precaution, she shouldn't be home alone tonight, just in case there's something we missed. Will any of you be staying with her?"

I stepped forward. "Yes, of course, I will."

Caleb's shoulders fell. He didn't hide the frustration he felt. No doubt he, like me, had anticipated tonight being a milestone in our relationship. What was to be done, though?

Meeting his eyes, I mouthed to him "tomorrow night."

The doctor acknowledged me with a nod. "Good. Just be sure she gets a good night's rest, and don't hesitate to give us a call or come back in if she has any problems tonight."

FOUR

Back home a few hours later, Amy hit the *end* button just after three AM. I'd never met her parents; George and Katrina Popowitz didn't care for Chicago, and despite repeated efforts, I'd never succumbed to Amy's attempts to drag me to New York City. Nevertheless, it spoke to their credit that they took a call from their daughter in the middle of the night and that they had to be convinced three times in the ten-minute conversation not to hop a plane and come force her into passive convalescence.

"I guess I'll head to bed, then." Amy smiled and reached for me. Or at least, I thought she was reaching for me. When her hand settled on Tobias, however, I wasn't the only one who felt the awkwardness about us sharpen. "Thank you, but next time I'm about to pass out on stage and you sweep in to save the day, I insist... Don't hesitate to perform CPR. Mouth-to-mouth saves lives every day."

Tobias grinned, a gleaming set of teeth setting my own irrationally on edge. "Glad to see you're okay."

As Amy's cheeks blushed, and she turned way too coquettish to be talking with a grieving werewolf, my concern for her health took a nosedive. Amy let out a little yelp when I pushed her toward her room. "Your doctor said you needed rest. Go rest."

"But you guys seem wide awake, maybe we can just stay up and hang out?"

I clicked my tongue. "When you're the one with the PhD in medicine that says that, we'll do it. Good night, Amy."

Tobias admonished me when I'd shut her door.

"What?"

Annoyance colored his words. "Let the poppet have a little comfort."

"Oh, my god. You have never sounded more British than you do right now."

"I'm not..."

"British." I dismissed him with a wave of my hand as we both made our way into my bedroom. "Yeah, I know. All I'm saying is, I know Amy's I'm-coming-on-to-you script. You're too sweet to shoot her down, so I did it for you."

"Just because I can never love again doesn't mean I don't like to be flirted with." Tobias closed the door and locked it—a precautionary normalcy since the time Amy had nearly walked in on him wearing his wolf. "This wouldn't be an issue if she understood *why* I could never be with her."

I paused at the closet, a hanger in hand as I took off my sweater. "I thought we discussed that back at the hospital."

"I said one thing, you said something different. That's not a discussion, it's an opening statement." His finger went to work trying to loosen his tie, but all the effort resulted in was a tighter knot. "Bollocks! Do you see now why I hate wearing monkey suits?"

He huffed and puffed and ripped the tie into shreds.

No doubt about it. If Tobias's suit was going to survive to see another night—and it should, because every woman benefited from the vision—I'd have to be the one to rescue it from his wolfie ways.

I waved him to me. "Oh my god, just come here."

As the puppy obeyed my command, I continued, "Don't get me wrong, I love Amy. I never thought I could be real friends with a huey. Even before I was one, Amy proved me wrong, though. But to bring her into our world... I'm not sure Miss I-got-it-at-Saks-and-not-on-sale can handle that. There's a reason we keep hueys in the dark. Believe me, I know all those ones at WWL who are privy are going to regret it someday."

"And what I'm saying is that, as of tonight, Amy *already is in* our world." He stilled my hands as I undid the last button of his dress shirt and pushed it aside, taking my eyes off the bottom of his undershirt and back to his eyes. "Geri, she was attacked by a vampire and we didn't hesitate to rush in to protect her. If we had ignored her, so would they from now on. Our compassion for her has condemned her; they'll come for her again if they think it's likely to rattle us. She needs to be prepared. She has to know, for her own sake."

The truth of his words struck guilt deep within. I pulled away. "It's like being pregnant—she can't just know a little. She's in all the way or out."

"At least on the inside, we can protect her. Help her protect herself." Tobias shimmied off the shirt and pulled the undershirt over his head. "I'm sure Inga could assign her security until we deal with the Ravens. If we're lucky, her guard will be some sexy, buff vamp who's really into smart and loyal blondes."

"Tobias Somfield, we are *not* fixing Amy up with a vampire!" Realizing the volume I'd reached, I threw a hand over my mouth.

Tobias turned his head, angling his ear. "I think she's asleep. Speaking of which..." He went to work on his belt, and I suddenly found I needed to be very busily reorganizing my drawers. "You seem spirited tonight. Reclaiming some of your nocturnal habits?"

"Adrenaline, I guess. Plus, I drank a lot of coffee before I left for the theater."

"Why, did you want to be—" His words dropped off as a rustle of cloth suggested his pants had done the same. "Oh, that's right. Caleb."

I didn't know why I was admitting it to him. I shouldn't be. What business of Tobias's was my love life? "We had a big night planned."

"And I would have, what, stood guard while you guys finally got busy? Knitted and read magazines?"

"I hear there's a new issue of *Fangs & Fur Monthly*." My attempt at humor died on his grimace. "I don't know. I guess I assumed you'd just hang out in the lobby or the employee gym, like you always do. But let me point out again, not my fault. Blame the fact that you're my after-hours security detail on Cody."

Tobias coughed a laugh. "Oh, believe me, I blame a lot of things on Cody," he mumbled. "I got a sheet wrapped around myself, Geri, so you can stop pretending to be looking for the perfect pair of socks. God, you've become so proper. As if you haven't seen naked wolves all your life."

I had. Of course, I had. But Tobias wasn't just another wolf. He was Tobias, the werewolf who slept on my floor, curled up in a ball of fur, and occasionally, when I was about during the day, in my bed, naked as the day was long.

And long seemed the operative word in that analogy.

"Since when is modesty something to be ashamed of?"

"Since it's not your nature. I don't care if you're technically a huey now; you're still culturally a hood. And as a hood in the way that counts, you should understand that what I'm saying is right. Amy needs to know. Unless you want to—and I use this phrase only as a metaphor—throw her to the wolves. And by wolves, I mean Ravens. And by Ravens, I mean the evil pack of vampires who've already killed at least two of the people I love and, likely, one of yours."

Damn him and his ability to manipulate my emotions. "Fine, you're right." But if he thought I was the only one in for a penny, Tobias was about to get smacked in the head by the whole pound. "And if she's going to be in the know, she should probably come to Istanbul with us."

A shell-shocked werewolf in his huey form clutching a bed sheet proved to be an amusing sight. "What?"

I crawled into bed, despite the fact that I was still wearing most of my street clothes, minus my jacket, shoes, and socks. "What good is it to tell her and then just leave her behind? We should offer to let her come. Let the Ravens see I protect my own, and at the same time, we can get her trained up a bit while we're there. After all, you and the others will be sleeping all day long. It'd be nice to have someone spend the daylight hours with."

"Daylight hours? Trained up a bit?" Tobias repeated as he turned his back and dropped the sheet to the floor.

I didn't look.

For too long.

He continued as he nudged around the pile of blankets atop the dog bed into an agreeable form. "What exactly are we going to train Manhattan Barbie to do?"

"To fight. Or at the very least, to defend herself. I can teach her how to handle a blade, you can teach her some wrestling, and I'm sure Caleb can teach her some martial arts. He's actually quite good at Krav Maga."

"I don't see how learning to play video games is going to protect Amy," Tobias said through a yawn. "Unless the Ravens are going to take the battle into *World of Warcraft*, probably not much good for Amy to master either."

"It's *not* a video game. It's a type of hybrid boxing-judo-other-stuff thing. And don't pass her off so easily. The woman didn't flinch this morning when I pulled a knife on her."

"Did she try to wake you up early again?"

"She's got spirit," I said, ignoring his quip. "With a bit of patience and motivation, she could hold her own."

"Not if she can pay someone to hold it for her."

"Look, it was your idea to tell her anything. I'm just saying, that's going to have consequences. *These* are the consequences. Are you going to help, or should we reconsider having Igor toss her memory around?"

I reached over to the wall and flicked off the light, but his voice still reached through the darkness.

"Seeing as I can't stomach the alternative, yes. But if you think she's convinced you and I should be a thing now, just wait until she knows I'm a wolf and you're a hood. *Were* a hood. You know what I mean."

"Why would that make a difference?"

"Because it's Amy. Doomed relationships are her superpower."

FIVE

I'd grown up in the supernatural world. Never had there been a time when I'd been in the dark, and never had there been a time that I thought it was my place to bring people into the light. It wasn't that no hueys knew of the supe world, as the several dozen vampire-aware hueys at WWL attested. It was that hoods (and wolves, frankly) by nature didn't trust outsiders. In my twenty-two years, I could think of only one I knew who was intimately integrated into our society, and she to the point of immersion: the gatekeeper of Schloss Wolfsretter, the reds' ancestral estate, deep in the Black Forest.

Hueys were so not my area of strength.

"So, Amy…"

She looked up expectantly from the couch, balancing a ballpoint pen on the palm of her hand.

Okay, so now what? "What was it you said you were doing after graduation?"

Her head cocked to the side. I'd gone from zero to what-the-hell in one-point-two seconds.

"What? Oh, going home, I guess. I'll probably go to grad school in a year or two, but I just want to take some time and live a little, you know?"

"Oh, I know. I'd like to live too. Ideally, of course."

"What?"

Heat pricked in my cheeks as I tried to overcome the oddness. "I mean, I'd like to have an adventure. I'm not in a rush to go home. I'd like to wait for all that stuff with my parents to blow over."

Amy set the pen and notebook down, her eyes softening. "Still on the outs, are they?"

"In a way. They're not talking to each other, and neither of them is talking to me." I took a seat on the armchair next to the couch. "Anyway, I was thinking, would you be interested in going on a trip with me? I mean, it's not just with me."

Her eagle eyes narrowed in my direction. "Is Tobias going on this trip too?"

"Yup. Also Inga Rosethorn and Prof. Karmarov."

Any amusement she wore melted away. "The creepy boss lady from your internship and the creepier biochem prof who has his weird lab at school?"

"They are not creepy!"

"They are the definition of creepy," Amy insisted. "I looked up that Inga woman after she offered the job to Tobias. There's nothing on her anywhere online. How does an executive from a big corporation like that stay off the web? More importantly, why? Why? Because she's up to freaky shit, is why."

"Or just likes her privacy."

She continued, undeterred. "And I took one of Karmarov's classes my sophomore year. There's just something about that guy that gives me the heebie-jeebies. You and Tobias are going on a trip with them? Is that what's really going on between you? There's some kind of weird cult thing or something, one that makes two people who are obviously attracted to each other sleep in the same room but resist temptation?"

"As I keep telling you, there's nothing going on between Tobias and me, and there never will be." Oh, shit. This was my break, wasn't it? I scooted to the edge of the cushion. "Actually, there's another person coming on the trip too. His name is Caleb."

Now I had her hooked again. "Caleb? That's a sexy name. Is he cute? Is he *available*?"

"Yes, he's cute. But no, he's not available. He's actually… my boyfriend."

The pen flew as Amy sat bolt upright. "No. Fucking. Way."

"Yes, way." I quelled my tongue which wanted to add, *though not so much fucking. At least, not yet.*

"I can't believe it! Yes!" The woman actually squealed and clapped. "I have so many questions, I don't know where to start. Is he cute? Is he a good kisser? Does he dance? Hell, do *you* dance? Does he ever wonder why he's never been to your house? Has he been here? Have you been sneaking him in for quickies when I've been gone? What about the whole Tobias situation? How does that all work? Have you guys talked at all about a three-way?"

"Amy!"

Her eyes went wide. "What?"

"No, no three-way—and we will never discuss that possibility again." Now that the cat was out of the bag, I guess I had to outline the whole thing from the beginning. "Caleb and I met last summer during my internship. He lives in the same building WWL is located in."

"Oh, penthouse view. He must be rich then."

I scanned my memory. "To tell you the truth, I'm not sure if he has any money. He's… *friends* with Inga Rosethorn. I don't think he's exactly getting charged market rent rates."

Amy chewed on that a moment. "Influence is almost as good as money. So, how is he in bed?"

I gulped. "Um…"

A switch went off in Amy's brain. Her beaming pride became withering scorn with a scrunched-up forehead and a tilt of her chin. "How long have you two been together?"

I counted out on my fingers. "Officially? I guess about eight months, although he travels a lot. And, of course, Tobias and I head back to Michigan all the time, as you know."

"Eight months, and you haven't slept with him yet?" Amy cleared her throat, laced her fingers, and set her hands on her lap. "So he's as much of a prude as you are."

"Caleb is the polar opposite of a prude!" I exclaimed. Wait, was I *bragging* about my boyfriend's licentious leanings? "The situation just hasn't… if you'll forgive the pun, *arisen*."

She put a hand to her forehead and sighed. "Of course, it hasn't arisen. You won't let it. Ever since I got back from New York last fall, you don't leave the house unless Tobias is with you. And also, you've kept this Caleb guy secret from me for, what I'm sure, are good reasons, but that makes sneaking him in on a night Tobias works impossible."

I held up my two index fingers. "Actually, can we pause there and drill down a bit? That's what I wanted to talk to you about: why I kept him a secret. You see, Caleb comes from an old family with a lot of enemies."

But Amy was not hearing it. "Yeah, we'll get back to that later, but I would be remiss as your best friend if I didn't stage an intervention, and to do that, I need you focused on the problem: Tobias."

"So Tobias is a *problem* now?" If I had hackles, they'd be raised. Again. "You've been suggesting that the solution to everything wrong in my life—and possibly a way to bring about world peace—is to sleep with him."

"That's before I knew you were dating a member of the Mafia."

"What in the hell makes you think Caleb is in the Mafia?"

"You just said it yourself: old family, lots of enemies. Wait." Amy bit her finger. "Is Tobias some sort of bodyguard that Caleb arranged? That would actually make sense."

"No, Tobias is not a bodyguard. Well, actually he is, but *Caleb* isn't the one who sent him."

"Feds?" Amy asked. "Or what are they called in England? MI6? Is Tobias some sort of British agent, using you to get to Caleb's family?"

I pressed my fingers to my temple. "This is not going how I pictured it."

Again, my roomie steamrolled forward. "'Cause if that's not what's going on, then you really need to get him out of your life. Oh, sweetie, don't get me wrong. I'm not saying anything bad about Tobias. I like him a lot, even if his living here has exploded our Drano budget. It's not your fault, you're too close to the situation to see it clearly. But him living here is clearly cockblocking your love life—both emotionally and physically."

When had trying to tell Amy about the supernatural world become a discussion about my love life? "This isn't what I wanted to talk about."

"But it's what you need to hear. Listen, Geri—" She reached out and rubbed my arm. "Ever since you came to me two years ago, brokenhearted and ignorant because of your small-town upbringing, it has been my mission to ensure that you fully seize the opportunities your life holds. I got excited for a while when you were seeing the Jess guy, but he turned out to be a flake."

"Actually, he turned out to be using me to get to Tobias."

"Ah, so that's what happened." Understanding brightened her eyes. "Point is, this is what I wanted for you all along. You've been with this guy for months. Obviously, you have feelings for him. And if he's not a prude like you, and he's still hanging around this whole time, it's got to be because he feels something pretty damned compelling for you too. Don't blow this. Tobias has lived here for almost a year now. I know he still misses his wife, but like I said: a year. He should be able to fend for himself now. You can still be friends, I'm not saying you shouldn't be. But please, be a big girl and do what's right: move Tobias out of your bedroom, so you can get Caleb into it. Even if Tobias is only a friend, trust me, it's like with dogs. They mark their territory. Tobias is marking you, and that's why things with Caleb are so dull."

"Amy, please. I really need to talk to you, and it's not about Caleb or Tobias. Well, okay, that's not true. It's all about Caleb and Tobias. And me. And other people too."

"If you're about to tell me you're in some kind of cult, then I have to admit, I already had a suspicion."

My train of thought plunged off a bridge. "Why would you think we're in a cult?"

"I don't know... Your tendency for being nocturnal? The way you usually disappear on full moons, and even if you are around, you act like you're all hyped up on something, the way you put silver trinkets all over the house when you first moved in, your weird obsession with Thai dumplings..."

"Lots of people like Thai dumplings. It doesn't mean they're in a cult!" My hair fanned out from my face as I blew out my frustration. "I was trying to tiptoe you into this, but looks like I just have to lay it all out. Tobias is a werewolf, my boyfriend is a vampire slayer, and even though it's confusing, Inga Rosethorn and Igor are both vampires. Not only that, but I used to be what in German is called a *wolfsretter*, but most people just call us hoods now. I'm actually an indirect descendant of Little Red Riding Hood, and no, not the Disney version of Little Red. In fact, I'm even named after her, which isn't all it's cracked up to be, since in my world, she's about the evilest hood who ever existed. Which is ridiculous, because actually *my mother* is the evilest. And, oh yes, my mom... Last summer, she performed a rite of denial which ripped all my powers away, so that now I'm basically just as huey as you are, but with a lot of combat training. Oh, and FYI: that's what you are to us, a huey. We call humans *huey*."

By the time I finished my screed, I'd worked up both my heartbeat and my lungs. Perched on the edge of the armchair, I watched a wide-eyed Amy glare at me. Finally, after a few silent moments, she blinked, stood, and patted me on the shoulder.

"I'm only going to say this once, Geri, but it's said with love. You're too good a person to ruin your life with drugs."

And with that, she slipped into her room.

SIX

"She thought you were high?"

Across the table, seated far from the other patrons of the Italian restaurant near WWL, I couldn't tell if Caleb was horrified or about to break out laughing.

I shook my head, quelling the temptation to cackle. "Ridiculous, isn't it?"

"Depends." Caleb drew a bread stick to his mouth. "Are you?"

"On drugs?"

"Yeah."

I squirmed in my seat, doing my damnedest not to slither out of the black tube sock substituting as a dress in the process. The moment Amy found out I was going out on a date with the boyfriend of whom she'd only recently become aware and with whom, after eight months, I had not yet slept, she had blocked the door and refused to let me leave in anything less. Or, more aptly put, anything more.

"I took some aspirin a week ago when Tobias threw me down too hard in the gym."

The ire of Caleb's inner caveman swelled. "He what?"

"It was nothing." I took a quick sip of the sparkling grape juice. "The fact that I'm not still a hood doesn't mean a thing to the Ravens. I train. Tobias helps. He doesn't go easy on me just because I'm not supernatural anymore... at my request. Sometimes, I get a little bruised."

"Well, that stops now. If anyone's going to slam you on your back too hard, it's going to be me."

"Speaking of which..." The flute balanced on the edge of my lip, a dramatic pause for a dramatic effect. "How's Inga?"

The slayer worked his jaw. "Inga and I do not have a thing going on. Yes, she likes drinking my blood—perhaps a little too much—but my neck is where anything physical between us begins and ends."

I did like to tease. "And the trip? Was it successful?"

I waited through his slow, steady chew of the steak he'd shoved in his mouth. "Only confirmed what we already suspected. The Ravens are in Istanbul; the question is where. It's a big city, you know. Almost fifteen million people, two thousand square kilometers of land covered in buildings folding in over themselves. Finding them will be no easy task, nor a quick one. You sure you want Tobias going along? Unless I misunderstood, a werewolf has to be with his pack on a full moon at least every three months to keep from going insane. Finding the Ravens' clutch could take years, and that's assuming we don't tip them off and they go scurrying."

Amy's comments replayed in my inner ear. It wasn't the first time Caleb had said something that suggested putting some distance between the werewolf and myself, but this wasn't the time.

"Tobias actually has a bigger dog in this fight than I do, if you'll forgive the pun," I said. "I kind of just stumbled into this whole Ravens-werewolf thing. No one is sure if Cody's dad's death had anything to do with it or if it was just coincidence. But we know for sure that Tobias's mate and brother died because of the Ravens' quest for eternal life."

He cocked his head to the side. "And what about what your mother said last summer?"

"About the Ravens finding me?" I shrugged. "My mom has enemies all over the world, of every species. Besides, you heard what Inga said. She only *suggested* my mom kill me when I visited her as a kid because she was scared my wolf-luring ability would be too useful to them. As usual, I think my mom's real fear was having a situation where she wasn't the one totally in control of me."

"Speaking of control…" He leaned over the table, his voice drifting into a husky register. "I'm having a difficult time with mine."

The corners of my mouth twitched. "Good thing we're so close to your place then."

In retrospect, the fact that we shared the elevator with Caleb's WWL-assigned bodyguard was probably the only reason I didn't lose my virginity on the ride up. The moment the slayer closed the door to his apartment, however, the game was afoot.

His hands hovered over the curves of my body, as though it were a glass figure he'd break. "Damn, whose idea was this dress and where do I send the thank you card?"

I stepped back toward the couch, kicking off my heels. Pink-tinted walls, more glass than frame, ringed my silhouette in city light. "Amy insisted."

"Makes me wish you told her about us a long time ago." Caleb's grin spoke a silent promise as he, too, shook off his shoes and let his suit jacket fall to the floor.

"You saying you don't like the way I dress?"

My feigned offense had him stupefied. "What? No. Damn it, no. I didn't mean—"

His words died on my tongue as Caleb came close enough for me to grab by the tie. I worked my mouth against his, hoping he understood tonight wouldn't end the way the others had. Tonight, this was going down.

When he pulled away, breathless and flush, I giggled. "I was just teasing."

His hands anchored on mine, pulling me to him at the hip. "I hope not."

Amy's dress didn't last long, but neither did Caleb's suit. After a few minutes spent becoming more naked and less clothed on the living room couch, Caleb cupped my backside as he pulled me up. I threw my legs around his hips, locking my ankles behind, never letting his lips leave mine. In the bedroom, silk sheets, chilled from the night air flowing into the room through a vent, made me shudder as he laid me on the bed.

Caleb stood at the edge of his bed, his heroic briefs putting up the only other remaining barrier between him and my innocence. "What's the shiver for? You afraid?"

"No, the sheets are cold."

He grinned as he leaned forward and hooked a finger on the waistband of my underwear. "We'll have to make sure we heat them up pronto, then, won't we?"

This was it. This was finally going to happen. I dug my heels into the edge of the mattress as I lifted my backside, helping Caleb's effort. The garment dropped off the end of his finger and out of sight, after which he sent his own briefs to keep them company. When I settled back, Caleb followed my arc, crawling over me as I scooted up the mattress. His lips met mine. His hips shifted. Heat raged.

And yielded as ice took my body.

Caleb froze over me, one hand beside my head, the other hooked under one knee in an attempt to pull it over his shoulder. "Geri?"

It wasn't the sheets that were cold; everything was. The air, my body, my desire. In a snap, all the warmth of the world fled. Even the feel of Caleb's touch blistered beneath my skin.

He let my leg fall. "It happened again, didn't it?"

"Can't." It was the only word that I could utter, though five thousand more were battling in the back of my throat, wanting to charge across my tongue.

He stared at me, awestruck. "Can't what?"

"This." I scooched back, working my back up the headboard and covering myself with the sheet. "Oh my god, Caleb, I'm sorry. I don't know why it happens."

Caleb pushed himself off the mattress, cursing under his breath. "We were so close."

"I know. Damn it, I hate this. I want to be able to do this."

When he came back into view, he wore a silk robe that complemented the gray slate shade of his bedding. "You say that, but you never do anything to change it."

Defensiveness shot through me. "And what, exactly, do you think I can do? Go to a doctor? What would I say? That I'm unable to get too hot and heavy with anyone since my mother stripped me of my powers?"

"Of course not, I just…" Groaning, his hands mussed his ebony hair, setting bits of it pointing in a hundred directions. "What about Igor? He might be able to figure something out."

"I can't go to Dracula to discuss sexual dysfunction. It's just too weird."

Caleb fell back on the bed, and by the rise in his robe at a suggestive place, I could see he was still open to engaging in bedroom politics. "We've got to do something, Geri, or we're never going to have sex." He chewed on his thoughts for a few moments before adding, "You don't suppose it's something psychological, do you?"

"You're saying I can't have sex with you because I'm crazy?"

He tried to bring levity to the situation…

"I've always thought a girl would have to be crazy not to want to screw me. You're just providing empirical proof."

…and failed.

"I'm not crazy," I assured him. "I want this. I want *you*. It's just… I don't know, maybe you're right. Ever since I was a little girl, I've been lectured on the importance of having the right kind of mate. *Hoods beget hoods* was one of my mother's slogans. Maybe it sunk in deeper than I thought. Maybe all the years spent blocking myself with Cody trained my body to cut itself off at a certain point. Maybe it's something else altogether. Some sort of nascent hood, biological cockblock."

He ran a hand over his face, laughing into his palm. "Only you're not a hood. Not anymore."

Feeling like shit wouldn't help this situation at all, but it seemed to be the only thing I was capable of at the moment. I shimmied under the sheet, settling down on my side, facing away from Caleb.

"I'm not much of anything, am I?"

A moment later, the silky robe became the only barrier between Caleb's body and mine as he threw an arm over me and nuzzled his nose under my ear.

"You're so much of so many things," he said, kissing my cheek. "We'll get there, I promise. And when we do, it'll be worth the wait."

"Yeah, well, it's a long time coming."

"Touché." His fingertips brushed down my arm, over my hip, and past my navel. "But at least we already know that, even if we can't seal the deal, I can still fill the inkwell."

I rolled back over, flattening my back on the mattress as his head disappeared beneath the sheet. "Your metaphors suck."

"Luckily, so do I."

SEVEN

My body was a lost connection of tissues and bone, held together more by theory than fact. Why was Caleb so focused on us having actual sex? We were doing a damned good job making each other happy without it, so much so I was convinced actual intercourse was going to be a letdown.

All I wanted to do was sleep. This was my last week of Chicago living and, while I didn't feel any particular affection for the city itself, the freedom and sense of self-determination I'd found in it seemed anchored to the top of the Sears Tower. Later in the day, I'd start packing: some things into boxes to go to a storage locker Inga had arranged for, some things into suitcases bound for Istanbul. In two days, Tobias and I would head back to Paradise one more time so he could run with the pack for the full moon. It would set off a three-month timer, near the end of which we still knew, sadly from experience, that Tobias would start to deteriorate mentally. A few days before the third full moon, he'd need to come back to Paradise, or suffer eternal lunacity.

Though, judging by what I found him doing on the couch when I crawled in just after sunrise, he might have done so already. Tell the guy he could go home and I'd wait until daylight to return safely alone, and he did weird things with his newfound time.

"This is how you took advantage of your night off? Watching foreign *Sesame Street*?"

The wolf turned away from his phone perched on his knees, whereon a purple puppet that looked like the result of crossbreeding Cookie Monster with a cow prattled on about god-only-knew-what in some weird language.

"You look like a mummy in that dress." His tongue stilled as he closed his eyes and inhaled. "And it didn't even work. Struck out again, huh?"

My spine went rigid. "My sex life is none of your business."

"True. Also, I don't give a damn." Tobias chuckled as he hoisted a bowl of cereal he was holding up to his mouth and took down a spoonful, after which he pointed vaguely to the screen. "I've been trying to pick up some Turkish for the last few weeks. Kid shows are easiest for learning; they tend to repeat phrases over and over and keep the vocabulary simple."

I plopped down on the couch, scooting close to him so I could see the screen. "Inga, Igor, and Caleb all speak it already, and it's a very international city. I don't think we're going to have much use for it."

"Well, call me a wolf, but I don't like to be dependent on anyone except my pack."

"And me."

"You wish."

We both laughed under our breath, watching the puppet on the screen go through the motions of preparing breakfast. If the program was to be believed, in Istanbul, I'd start the day with cheese, olives, honey, and bread.

"I hope there's more meat than what that's suggesting."

"Don't worry. Another of the shows I've been watching is a restaurant review program. There's no shortage of meat. *Et*, they call it. Or, if you prefer, *kuzu*."

"What's *kuzu*?"

He turned to me, a grin on his face. "Lamb. Succulent, moist, tender lamb."

"Oh, I do like lamb."

"Yes, you do. Fluffy, furry, little well-roasted lambs. Juicy as rain."

I tried to ignore the way his eyes lingered on my lips, then internally scolded myself for seeing things that weren't there. *Caleb failed to win your castle, and now you're looking for weaknesses from lesser fortresses.* Tobias couldn't be attracted to me; it was physically impossible. But me? Yeah, he'd pegged my primal draw to him the first time I'd chased him down, knocked him to the ground, and straddled him. Plus, given my history with Cody, that I could feel such attraction to a wolf despite my genetics wasn't theory, it was proven fact.

"What about pork? Have you learned to say that?"

My question broke the tension as Tobias threw back his head and laughed.

"What?"

"It's a Muslim country, Geri."

"Yeah, so?"

"Yeah, so…" He reached out and mussed my hair and, in that simple move, restored our sibling dynamic. "Sorry, love. No pork."

"Not even sausage?"

"Not a single link."

"Okay, I'm rethinking this whole going-after-the-Ravens thing. I didn't realize I'd have to sacrifice bacon as part of the process."

He stretched to the table to set down his phone and his empty cereal bowl. "I'm sure we'll find acceptable substitutes." With that, he stood and pulled me to my feet. "You look like you're about to fall over dead. Let's get you into bed."

"Maybe the second time will be the charm."

Once, when I was still a hood, I felt on a visceral level the moment a wolf came within a certain perimeter. Amy, though a huey, had a similar talent, only her body alerted whenever a sexy man between the ages of twenty and forty said anything that included the words "you" and "bed." Her bedroom door almost cracked down the middle from the force of her throw. Despite the early hour, my roommate looked at me, to Tobias's hand in mine, and then back at me.

She took on her best chiding mother hen tone. "Didn't we talk about this yesterday?"

Tobias leaned back, stretching, yawning so wide he yelped a little. "What is she talking about?"

"I'm talking about your presence and the not-coincidental lack of advancement in Geri's love life, mister."

My chest rose and fell. "If it's any consolation, we got to oral tonight."

The wolf let go my hand and put his hands over his ears. "Blimey, Geri, no. It's none of *my* business, but you just wallop Amy with that kind of disclosure without so much as a prod?"

"I have best friend rights," Amy retorted. "And good. But remember what I said when I sent you to him wearing that?" She pointed at what little bit of a dress I was wearing. "It was supposed to be *the* night. Why am I finding you curled up on the couch with Lord Grows-a-beard-a-day when you're supposed to be waking up in Caleb's bed?"

"Amy, I love you. I really do, but I don't understand why you've appointed yourself as my personal intimacy manager."

The blonde curled her fists and shook. "Because I want you to be happy!"

The moment Amy stepped over the line from cute-but-awkward concern to whiny-bordering-on-rude insistence, Tobias put himself between us.

A move which Amy appreciated none too well. "You!" Her right hand pelted Tobias's chest, a drop of rain in the river of his physique. "Don't you see that she's too hung up on you to give this Caleb guy a chance? I get that you lost your wife, and believe me, I'm very sorry for you. Really, I am. But you can't keep interrupting her chance at happiness like this. It's not fair to Geri."

"You think I'm here because I want to be?" Tobias crossed his arms and belly-laughed. "If only you knew what's really going on here."

"What, you mean your werewolf-little red thing?"

Wide-eyed, Tobias's head swiveled in my direction. "You told her?"

"Isn't that what we agreed to do?"

"Yeah, but I didn't know you actually told her." Tobias turned back to Amy, his hands squeezing her upper arms. "You have no idea how much of a relief that is. Bet it came as quite a shock, huh?"

My roomie blinked thrice in rapid succession. "You don't think I actually believe that, do you? Come on, just be honest. You're in love with Geri, but you're too guilty about falling for someone else so soon after your wife died to admit it, and too scared about being alone to deny it. How is she ever going to have a relationship with Caleb when she's got all that waiting for her at home? Either make a play for her, or get yourself out of the game!"

But Tobias proved uninterested in Amy's early-morning therapy sessions. Instead, he went about pulling his undershirt off his head. "Guess this means I don't have to worry about not doing this in front of you anymore, then."

In the three seconds that it took Amy's eyes to catalog Tobias's bare chest, him to undo the fly of his jeans, and his form to shift from two legs to four, Amy's skin went from cardinal to cadaver. It was one thing to be told your third roommate was a werewolf. It was another thing entirely to watch him prove it.

I swooped his jeans and T-shirt off the floor as I followed Tobias towards the bedroom. "We didn't get to this yesterday, Amy, but it should go without saying: this is a secret. Now I trust you'll have questions, and we'll be happy to answer them after I get some sleep, but I'm beat. Good night. Or well, you know, good morning."

EIGHT

"Silver bullets?"

"True. *Kinda.* Any silver, actually, but it's only deadly if it hits the heart or the brain. Otherwise, it just burns like a son of a bitch. It can scar if left on the skin for a long time, though."

"Do vampires really change into bats?"

"Nope. They can alter into some kind of gaseous state, though. Just don't ask me to explain how it's possible. No one really knows, not even the vampires."

"Are they really immortal?"

Tobias and I exchanged a look across the front seat, understanding passing between us. The werewolf balanced his left arm on the window ledge and a lie upon his lips. "That part's mostly true, but anything that can live, can die."

We'd made a pact before leaving for Paradise this morning: now that Amy was in on our secret, we'd answer any question she had, *unless* the answer was one a supe wouldn't normally know. Hoods and wolves, who more or less lived as long as hueys, were blind to the truth about a vampire's post-conversion life span being only five hundred years or so. From what Caleb had said, they preferred that knowledge to remain guarded.

After the first half of the trip to Paradise being filled with the inane questions we'd have expected, my roomie dug up left field to toss some inquiries at us.

Does a vampire have to drink human blood, or is animal blood okay?

Would it get drunk if it sucked from someone who was already drunk?

Where does a hood's hood come from? Is it magic? Magic really exists?

If a hood and a slayer had a baby, what abilities would it have?

That last one made me squirm, and my discomfort made Tobias grin.

Amy picked up on it. Always observant. "What? What'd I say?"

When I didn't answer, Tobias did. "Geri's boyfriend is a slayer. My guess is you tapped into a nerve a little too close to her heart on that one."

"Oh, my god." A gasping Amy wore a grin that could power an incandescent bulb. "You have a superhero boyfriend? And you're not hitting that every night? I mean, all that power, and you're just—"

"Like I said, we're getting there," I said, cutting her off. "Besides, other than being superfast, being able to throw little balls of sunlight, and being ever-so-slightly stronger, slayers' *other* skills aren't inherently greater than a huey's. One thing I can tell you right now, Amy: you have to overcome all the brainwashing Hollywood has done on you. Supes aren't de facto attractive, porn-worthy sex gods. That's just not how it works."

"Speak for yourself, Geri," Tobias piped up, taking the exit off the main road that led to the packlands. "I am amazingly talented in the sexual arts."

As Amy cackled in the backseat, slapping her hands, heat crawled over my skin, though whether from embarrassment, anger, or some other emotion, I didn't want to know.

"Kara must have really appreciated that," I mumbled, and then hightailed our conversation out of any topic that could make me imagine Tobias in the act of anything. "Supes aren't superheroes, Amy. Remember that. In fact, some are the opposite of heroic."

The Paradise Pack numbered a few dozen adult wolves, spread out over sixteen different primary bloodlines between whom family trees interweaved. To describe the packlands as a compound wasn't quite accurate; without any fences—which would have been an abomination in any wolf's eyes—the twenty-three homes built at odd intervals around a central clearing weren't technically more than a neighborhood. Other than being completely surrounded by and punctuated with pine trees, the style was distinctly European village in formation. Only, instead of a chapel at its center lay a multipurpose meeting house hewn of local timber, big enough to fit a crowd twice the pack's size. When they'd settled in Paradise a century ago, the alpha at the time said it was too small. How times and culture had changed.

Amy wore tension like a second shirt. Moving with the grace of a stick bug, she crawled out of the backseat of Tobias's hand-me-down extended cab pickup, the vehicle kept to her back like a rampart. In some ways, I had to admire the tactical prowess with which my big city roomie maneuvered. *Safe ground behind, a means of escape in sight, moving forward with awareness of what lies beyond.* My mother would be proud. But, as we were in friendly territory, and as every werewolf within a fifty-yard line of sight of our car had stopped to survey the interloper, the signals of *I'll-kill-you-or-die-trying* she was giving off didn't bode well.

I slipped to her side, weaving her hand in mine. "Wolves can smell fear, Amy."

She shook her head. "I made sure to put on lots of perfume."

Even Tobias grinned at that.

Ahead, the crowd turned when a tall, solidly-built woman dressed in white broke through the crowd. Amy's grip threatened to push all the blood from my hands.

"Is that who I think it is?"

No need to answer. Within moments of a visual confirmation, Kim, wearing a wedding gown worthy of a princess but barefoot, peeled away from the pack and was bolting in our direction, arms held wide.

"Hi, Kim!"

A dull thud made me turn my head. Amy's back pressed against the Chevy, her hand searching behind her for the door.

"Amy, what are you doing?"

"She's a wolf!" Her hand found the handle and lifted just as Tobias palmed the door, keeping it from opening.

"Have you gone bloody mad?" the wolf demanded. "Why does that matter?"

"It doesn't. It's just... She's so..."

As did a wolf recognize the weakest animal, so Kim went for Amy first, pulling her up into her arms, yanking her off the ground, and spinning her around.

Crimson strains stretched across Amy's face. "STRONG."

After Kim had finished immobilizing my roommate, she took me and Tobias in turn.

"I'm so glad you were able to make it." Kim's grin could light up the Sears Tower.

"We're happy to be here, and very, very happy Cody agreed to let Amy come along." I pulled my bag out of the front seat of the truck. "Congratulations on your mating. I hear he's quite your equal, but I doubt that's possible."

Kim blew out a raspberry. "I still beat him at arm wrestling two out of three, and even that third time, I'm usually throwing it. Amy, I hear you're in the know now?"

"Seems that way." Amy swatted away the question and the mosquitoes buzzing around her head. "To tell the truth, finding out Tobias was a werewolf was shocking. Finding out you are kinda makes sense."

My insides squirmed as the jab meant for Kim washed over me. Tobias took a step closer. Whether he was doing it because he thought he might have to defend Kim or defend Amy, I couldn't say.

But Kim just threw her head back and howled. "Knew you were an observant one from the start, Popowitz. Kinda had me wondering how you didn't figure it out earlier, frankly. No harm done. Come, meet my mate, and I know Cody and Lisa are eager to see you too."

Lisa spotted us first, even as she bounced the baby on her knee. She stood, and automatically, the awkwardness bloomed between us.

"Geri, Tobias, so good to see you." She shifted her weight to examine my cowering roommate behind me. "You must be Amy. I'm so glad you could make it for Kim's wedding. She's told us so much about you."

"I didn't mean to be such a bitch to her. If I had known she was a werewolf…" Amy's words died on her tongue. "Oh, god, is that still an insult here, *bitch*? Because wolves are a type of canine and a female canine is a bitch, and I didn't mean—"

"Kim," Lisa interjected, cutting off the babbling blonde, "has a strong personality. A strong *everything*, really. I can only imagine that stuffed in a city apartment, she was in a concentrated form. But she's only ever said kind things about you, Amy, so I don't think you have anything to worry about."

Cody's mate had become quite the diplomat, as further evidenced when she turned to me.

"Cody says you're graduating next week. Congratulations, I know he's very proud."

Don't be a bitch. "Thank you, Lisa. Wow, Jenny's grown like a weed since we were here just two months ago." I reached out to twirl a tiny curl of the baby's hair on the end of my finger, admonishing the jealousy on a low boil in my soul whenever I had to talk with the she-alpha. "Before you know it, she'll be tearing all around these woods each full moon, giving my mother fits."

The air stifled despite the pleasant lake breeze that snuck from the shore into the woods.

Tobias cleared his throat and put an arm around Amy. "Come on, Barbie. Let me introduce you to the infamous Cody Ryland."

As he began to pull her away, Amy leaned into him, still unaccustomed to a wolf's enhanced hearing. "*That's* who he left Geri for? Not hard to believe. She's a knockout."

Lisa closed her eyes and grinned. When she opened them again, the mask of indifference was gone. "I know this is awkward, but is it ever going to be not that way? You're still a big part of Cody's life, Geri, but so am I. We have to get past this."

"There's nothing to get past. Neither of us did anything wrong. It's just…"

"You still love him," she interceded. I didn't insult her by denying it. "But you know he's bonded to me now. Why do you keep torturing yourself like this?"

I looked around. Luckily, the music of a four-piece band in the corner helped to lay down enough background noise that none of the other wolves had heard. At a table about twenty feet away, however, Tobias and Cody sat side by side,

Amy opposite of them with her back to me. The two wolves watched me and the alpha's mate through suspicious gazes.

I reached out again and tickled Jenny, making the pup squeal with laughter, playing off our conversation as standard pleasantries. What could I tell her? That ever since my mother rejected me from my clan, the pack was the only family I had? That even though I'd been dating Caleb for the better part of a year, I still hadn't felt one-tenth the emotional bond with him that I had with Cody? That I was afraid Cody only let me continue to visit the pack because of the guilt he felt from what had happened between us, and that I was scared he'd turn me away as soon as he knew I'd fallen for someone else? I couldn't even admit half of this to myself, let alone to her.

"I'm trying, Lisa. I swear, I am. But hearts don't listen to reason, not even for a hood."

"The day a hood listens to reason, I'll throw a parade." She played off the comment with a smile that exploded onto her face, and as quickly faded away. "I understand what you're going through, Geri. I know you think I don't, but you don't know me that well. I'm just begging you, please, today, try to squash it more than usual." She looked to her mate, love beaming in her eyes. "Don't make him do something he's going to regret."

"What does that mean?"

Lisa shook her head. "Nothing. Something stupid. Forget I said it. You better go. Get business out of the way so we can all stuff ourselves with cake before sunset."

<hr>

"One of the Ravens, Timur, has been spotted in the city in the past few weeks. Igor and Inga say they move in pairs, and rarely ever all in the same location. Wherever you find one, though, there's guaranteed to be another nearby. More than likely, it's Vlad."

Cody stared blankly, letting the intel sink in. When we'd first told him of our plan to chase down the vampire that may have had a hand in killing his father, he'd been gung-ho for the idea. Since, the more he learned about the rumors surrounding Igor's wayward offspring, the more his fervor cooled. Where we'd been certain last fall that he'd have no problem giving Tobias leave to make the trip, now doubt lingered.

He fidgeted with a tattered tablecloth stretched over a decades-old folding table. "What's to stop them from killing you the second you arrive?"

I scooted to the edge of my seat. "Igor says Vlad modeled his clutch after the Ottoman court of his era. He thinks of himself as some sort of vampiric sultan, I guess. He'll kill when he has to, but he prefers politics first."

344

"Inga and Igor can't kill him," Tobias took up. "To do that would be to kill themselves. Igor thinks he won't consider a single werewolf and a relinquished hood a threat."

Cody's face soured. "That's because you're not."

Tobias's hand took mine under the table, squeezing, silencing my automated retort, before letting it go. "Don't forget, we'll have Caleb too, an actual slayer. Once we ferret out the Ravens' location and their behaviors, it's just a matter of divide and conquer."

"One young slayer against at least two vampires born of the most infamous lineage ever, with a member of my pack and one of my best friends forming shallow ranks. Still don't like those odds, Tobias."

"That's because you haven't seen what Caleb can do," I said. "He isn't just any slayer; he's a Van Helsing. One infamous line against that of another, and vengeance for Tobias's mate? Vlad won't stand a chance."

"Yeah, well, you're dating the guy, so your assessment ain't exactly without bias, is it?" Cody turned on Tobias. "What do you think? Is this slayer going to be able to stand up to the Ravens?"

Tobias steepled his hands, leaning into their support. "I don't worry about Caleb taking on Vlad. I'll be more surprised if he ever learns to stand up to Geri."

I reached out, running my fingers over Cody's, drawing his attention from the frayed checkerboard pattern to my face. A nostalgic tingle ran up my arm, an electric buzz I had once thought was because I was a hood and he was a wolf, but now I suspected was more because he was a boy and I was a girl who loved him. "Cody, please. Tobias has a right to avenge his lost ones. Give him permission to come."

The alpha grinned, turning my hand over and cupping it with his. "If I said he couldn't go with you, would it stop you?"

Tobias chuffed. "If you think saying *no* works with Geri, you clearly don't know her as well as I do."

Cody's eyes pivoted to his packmate. After a moment, without letting my hand go, he rose and pulled me up to my feet. "Let's dance, Little Red."

"Wha— What are you... Cody, this is no time for... Hey!"

He spun me in a circle as the speakers blasted the band covering an old U2 ballad. Cody's cheek pressed against mine, sending dueling impulses firing through my body. Half of me wanted to stomp his foot, and the other half wanted to knee his groin.

"What are you doing? You're a mated wolf with a child, and you're dancing with the daughter of the red matron at your packling's wedding!"

"*Shh!!!*"

He pulled back only long enough to admonish me with his glare, before immediately resuming the white man shuffle. Even with the proximity, hearing his words was difficult. The realization that this was sort of the point set me at ease, and I fell into a left-right-left sway.

"Your heart doesn't speed up when you say his name."

"Who's name?"

The alpha huffed. "Your slayer."

"I'm not sure I'm following what—"

"When you touched me, your pulse spiked. Maybe you couldn't hear it, but I did, and I'm pretty sure Tobias did. I can read my pack's emotions in their mannerisms. You're *saying* one thing about your faith in this slayer, but Tobias is telling me you're not as sold on him as you seem to think."

"I'll remind you: I'm not in your pack. Hell, I'm not even in my mother's clan anymore. Besides, I have complete faith in Caleb's ability as a slayer, whether or not my heart speeds up."

"Good to hear, but I'm still having a hard time understanding his motivations. Your Caleb was on this path before he met you, and if he's as great a slayer as you say, why does he need you? More weight makes a heavy tow."

"You think he'd just, what, up and leave me behind?"

"He might. And if you break his heart on this epic quest halfway across the world, what happens to Tobias? What happens to you? Jesus, Geri, just love the guy, will you? Get over me, and let someone else into your heart. Your life might depend on it."

I didn't know when the music stopped. I didn't know when we'd become the center of attention. I did know, however, that every single wolf glaring at me throughout the hall reared to defense when I smacked their alpha.

I caught Lisa in the crowd over Cody's shoulder, shaking her head.

A dumbfounded Cody raised his hand to his face and rubbed the imprint of my palm on his cheek. "Once a hood, always a hood, huh?"

Proving I had no talent for knowing when to quit, I stood my ground. "How dare you or *anyone* tell me what to feel about you? In the last two years, have I once asked you to betray your wife? Have I ever used any of my abilities to cause a single member of this pack any harm? Even though it has cost me my family, my birthright, and may cost me my life, I've *never* asked for you to care a lick for me since the moment we were through. Since, one day after you asking me to marry you, I walked in on you in the arms of another woman. *Mated.* So don't you dare stand there now and try to order me to get over you, like it's just a decision I have to make and, poof, it will be done. No matter how much you think it, I'm not a member of your pack; alpha's prerogative doesn't work on me. You can't order me to stop loving you, and you sure as hell can't order me to love someone else. My heart is the one thing I won't sacrifice for you, or for anyone!"

It took to the end of my screed to realize at least six of the pack had formed a ring around their alpha, teeth bared, on the edge of taking on their wolves. Nothing lay between me and their anger but the order of their alpha. I looked into Cody's eyes, and for the first time, I knew the depth of heartbreak.

He sneered at me, at the ex-friend who represented regret and youthful indiscretions. At the outsider who he had welcomed into his pack, who now had betrayed that trust by showing him up in front of everyone. By calling him out and laying blame at his feet tailored by another, of forcing him to act.

My hands shook. Not with rage, but with nerves. The wall of words I'd just built stood between me and grace, and I'd dug the moats too deep to cross it.

"Oh, my god. Cody... I'm so... I don't know..."

"Rick!"

The beta of the Paradise Pack emerged from the crowd, gently pushing the awestruck bride aside.

"Yeah, Cody?"

"Accompany Miss Kline and her huey guest to their hotel. Advise them not to venture into the woods tonight. I can no longer guarantee their safety from the pack, especially on a full moon."

"You got it, Cody. Geri, you need to grab a purse or anything?"

Before I could answer, Amy was at my side, her fingers lacing mine and squeezing some strength into my resolve.

"I got her stuff, and I got her." Ignorant or ignoble? Either way, she stood with me against them. "We can find our way to the hotel just fine, thank you very much. I'll get us an Uber."

Rick cleared his throat. "There are no Ubers in Paradise, Miss."

Unperturbed, Amy hooked my elbow and forced me erect. "Fine then, we'll walk."

Tobias pushed his way forward. "I'll take them."

Cody shook his head. "I asked Rick to..."

"I said, *I will take them.*"

This time, Cody ceded, even as my heart sank deeper. What in the hell was he doing? It was one thing for me to tell off the alpha, but as a member of the pack, Tobias could get disowned for the same act. I couldn't let that happen to him again. I *wouldn't* let him become a rogue again because of me.

"Tobias, you don't have to. I'm not worth it."

The werewolf turned, leading the way through a crowd that parted before him, a blast of anger through narrowed eyes his only response.

When I'd left Paradise for Chicago two summers ago, fresh from my boyfriend being mated to another, I thought the seven-hour drive was the longest of my life. It didn't compare to the twelve minutes of eternity spent in the pickup truck, seated between Amy and a very rigid, silently seething Tobias.

NINE

"Are we getting more drunk, or less sober?"

"I'm more drunk, you're less sober. It's your first time drinking. Getting *more* drunk would require a basis of comparison."

I sighed as I swirled the little bit of liquid left in my glass. "My love life has finally driven me to drink. I held out twenty-two years almost. That's pretty good, right?"

"It's excellent! Only, now I guess I know why none of my prodding ever worked." Amy's hand rubbed my shoulder, as I, slumped over the bar, huffed. "Two years, and he could still hurt you that bad? You must have really been crazy over him."

A ping in the air kept me from having to comment right away. The message on the screen from Kim got straight to the point.

Don't worry about it. Made the wedding memorable.

Amy read the message over my shoulder and nodded. "I sold Kim short, I think."

"Yeah, but she's still pack. If Cody had said to rip me to shreds, Kim would have. They all would have."

"Not Tobias," Amy said. "Or that Rick guy. You might have been too distracted to realize it, but they were both sizing up the situation, looking for a way to intervene."

"Rick is a beta; one of his jobs is to keep Cody in check. A beta can counter an alpha without jeopardizing his place in the pack."

"What about Tobias then? What's his excuse?"

As I lifted my head off the bar, I realized that Amy was right; Tobias had stood up for me. Or had he? Werewolves weren't mindless drones; even though obeying the alpha was written into their DNA, at the end of the day, their opinions and their actions were their own. I played back the memory, analyzing the scene that had passed a few hours ago.

"Tobias didn't disobey," I finally admitted, both to myself and to Amy. "Cody's order was for Rick. If Cody had said point blank to fall back and let Rick bring us here, Tobias would have obeyed."

One could argue that Cody would have given that order, if Tobias hadn't cut him off.

"Still, given that everyone else in that room looked like they wanted to kill you, pretty brave of him."

"*Stupid,*" I amended. "The word you're looking for is *stupid.*"

"In what way?"

"Tobias is still pack. We still need Cody's permission for him to go to Istanbul with me."

"With *us.*"

Confusion turned my head. When I'd brought up the idea with Amy last night, she'd laughed at it. "You changed your mind?"

Amy took another sip of her second whiskey sour before smacking her palate. "I'm going to Istanbul with you. You said that these bad vampires..."

"SHHH!"

The bartender was busy talking to another customer at the opposite end of the bar, but still, I wasn't unaware that our voices had been growing louder in the two hours we'd been sitting at the bar, getting more and more drunk.

"Those bad *people*, then," Amy amended, whispering. "That they were the ones who attacked me, and that they'd try it again if they thought it would do any good. Well, I just helped you stand up to a pack of dogs, so I'm guessing any shot I had at claiming the title 'innocent bystander' is gone. So, yes. I'm coming with you, and you're going to teach me how to fight, okay? That's the deal. And in exchange, I'm going to teach you how to fall in love."

I attempted not to choke on my drink. "*You're* going to teach me how to fall in love?"

Amy blinked at me in rapid succession. "What, you think I don't know how? Geri, I almost fall in love five times a year. You don't think it's on accident, do you? It's a carefully controlled and deliberate process!"

"Granted, but what I need help with isn't falling in love. I did that just fine. What I need help with, apparently, is falling *out* of love."

"Silly Yooper, it's the same thing. There's no better way to get over the old guy than to get hung up on the next one."

"So you're telling me that you can teach me to fall in love with Caleb?"

Suddenly, the confident gambler decided to hedge her bets. "Caleb specifically? We can try. I mean, you just can't fall in love with *any* guy. He's got to have the right package. And no, I'm not just talking about genitals. Though, don't get me wrong, those are important too."

"I'm going to need another drink for this." I leaned over the bar, trying to ignore the way the room went along for the ride. Prior to tonight, I'd consumed alcohol on three occasions, each more ceremonial than celebratory. In the past ninety minutes, I'd set a lifetime personal best. Or worst. "Randy? Another?"

As the orientation of the room took time to catch up with me as I sat back up, I decided worst, definitely worst.

"Oh, my god. You really do know everybody here, don't you?" Amy asked. "I thought you were just joking, but you've been able to call everyone by their name since we got to the hotel."

"I don't know the tourists." With a wide swing of my arms, indicating the roomful of Johnny Detroits and Jenny Chicagos, I disavowed any suggestion of omnipotence. "But Randy here, he was my PE teacher in high school."

"And her driver's ed teacher," the balding, gray-haired man in his sixties said as he topped off my glass. "Speaking of which, I hope you're not planning on getting behind the wheel to head home after this tonight, Gerwalta."

"Nope! I'm staying here, pretending to be a tourist. Didn't you hear that my parents disowned me?"

Randy tried to hide his laugh. "Sounds like your mom hasn't changed. But your dad, too? He's always seemed to me like an okay guy, not the kind to turn out his daughter. Anything I can help with?"

"Not unless you can convince the old battle-ax to let me have my hood without being her minion, not really."

As Randy's face screwed up in confusion, Amy put both her hands on my shoulders. "Don't pay any attention to her. She's been babbling stuff like that for an hour. I should probably take her up to the room now."

She threw a stack of bills onto the counter, which Randy's fat hand pawed and swished away. Amy tried to tug me to my feet, but both my mind and my body refused to budge.

"But he just got my drink!" I protested, two hands, both seemingly connected to my right arm, swinging out to grab the glass. "I mean, *I* just got *my* drink. When I get upstairs, I'm going to pass out. If you're going to tell me how I'm supposed to fall in love, I need to know that now."

Amy leaned in, whispering in my ear. "If I tell you, will you promise to go after? You're getting kind of belligerent. People are starting to look at us."

"Tourists always gawk at the locals. We're like a zoo exhibit for them: 'Come see the amazing Yooper, who lives seven months a year in the snow, survives on a steady diet of pasties, and knows sixteen ways to use lake ice as a natural resource.'" I pounded the bar with my fist, making my refilled glass spill over the edge. "Now teach me, oh wise one. How do I fall in love?"

Amy huffed, but relented. "You need to assess four things. First, do they think the same thing about food as you? I don't care what so-called experts say: if you get to Thanksgiving, and one of you wants a turkey stuffed with pork sausage while the other wants a tofurkey, it's never going to work. Second, do you both want to live in the same kind of place? I can't tell you how many guys I've met whose bones I would have jumped posthaste, but it turned out they were country folks. I know it seems superficial, but so much about what we want out of life is wrapped up in where we want to live. Our pace, our shopping, our vacations, our expectations about family: all is geographically-oriented. If you've assessed those two factors, and the guy meets those conditions, you can move on to assessing quality three."

Her convoluted logic had me drawn in, and I was an acolyte sitting at the feet of the priest.

"What's number three? Job prospects?"

"No, silly, sex appeal." Amy said it like it was the most natural thing in the world. "If looking at him doesn't make you want to rip his clothes off three times an hour, then the relationship has no hope. Physical things only slow down with time. If you don't have that spark right at the beginning, you're never going to have it."

I ran the mesh of Amy's filters over the view of my current relationship. Food that we both liked? I guess we had that down. I mean, our dates often included going out to eat, and so far, we never ended up anywhere where there wasn't something each of us could eat. Sex appeal we definitely had down, excepting for some weird thing on my side that had so far prevented any actual sex. But as for wanting to live in the same place? The discussion had never come up.

"Wait," I said, realizing Amy's lesson wasn't done. "What about the fourth thing? You said there were four parts of the rubric."

"No one says rubric, Geri," she chided. "But yes, the fourth thing. This is crucial. You have to identify one thing about the guy you hate. And I'm talking really, really loathe here, like, makes you contemplate murder."

"And that's it? Three things you have in common, one thing you hate, and then boom: love?"

"Well, no, it's not that simple. But it's not much more than that. See, falling in love is the process of meeting someone, overlaying them into your life, and then, letting them sink into all your nooks and crannies. Don't give me that face, Gerwalta Kline, and get your mind out of the gutter! I'm talking about emotional nooks and crannies. The first few times you're meeting someone, you focus on just getting to know what those four factors are. Then, once you think you got them down, and he fits in on the first three factors, you sit down and talk to yourself. You say, 'Self, here is a man with the same appetites and the same goals as me, and who I want and seems to want me. And here is the one worst thing about him that I can say. Given that worst thing, am I willing to accept him for all those other reasons?' If the answer is yes, you let yourself fall in love. If the answer is no, dump him."

It was brilliant. And stupid. And genius. And ridiculous.

"And this is how you find yourself in love with a different guy every other month?"

Amy threw a hand over her heart. "Have I ever said I've been in love?"

"No. I just assumed that—"

Her upheld hand cut me off. "I *almost* fall in love frequently, but I've never bottomed out there. That last part, the worst reason ever? That's what gets me. So far, I haven't found anyone to make it over that hurdle."

"I did," I mumbled, remembering what had driven me to be where I was right now. "But you forgot rule five: if he's a werewolf mated to another, all bets are off."

"And with that, I think we're ready for bed, don't you? Thanks, Randy! Couple of bills for you here on the counter."

At three in the morning, the moon summoned me.

Green numbers on the clock next to the bed flashed four-forty-five. Four hours since I'd plopped down, with Amy's help, into my bed. It had been the only way to keep the room from spinning. I may have never been drunk before, but I'd heard enough stories to know recovery didn't come this quickly. As I sat up, what greeted me wasn't nausea; what greeted me was clarity. Crystal clear, clearer than I'd been in almost a year. Every sense reverberated: scent, taste, hearing, sight—even the ability to sense the wolves. I could feel them, out there, beyond the highway and the forest's edge. Under a cooperative nighttime sky, the pack darted around trees and bushes, chasing squirrels, rabbits, even a few deer. In their wolves, they were at one with nature. Stripped of their humanity, they reached the zenith of their inherent natures.

It was a dream. A glorious, enrapturing, surreal dream.

Silver daggers in the form of moonlight sprayed down from the sky, pierced the land, fell over my bare arms like raindrops, wetting my skin with power. Shoes were needless in this nocturnal walk. The pavement of the road between the hotel and the trees gave way to gravel beneath my feet, then the soft, downy grass of late spring. The forest and the human world dueled in a gentle fault line.

I didn't know how long I strolled in the woods, but at some measure, the sounds of the shore and Lake Superior's surf dissipated. The nearness to the pack pushed down on me, but so did the alpha's order to ignore me, not to approach me. Agreement, consensus, concurrence.

Dissension.

He hadn't listened to the alpha. He refused to turn his maw on me.

Tobias's wolf held a kind of grace even Cody had never had in my eyes. Was it because of the foreign climate in which he'd been raised that made his coat smoother, led his tuft to be slimmer? Other than perhaps Rick, he was certainly larger than the other members of the Paradise Pack, even in huey form. Tobias was just so... built. Broad shoulders, a firm chest, abs I could bounce a dime off. With his mix of red and brown fur, rings of white around his paws and his maw, he was the most beautiful wolf I'd ever seen.

And he was staring at me. Under the influence of a full moon. And me, here, in nothing more than a pair of boy shorts and a cami. Even in a dream, this seemed stupid. They were more beast than man under a full moon, and I'd never been more mortal.

But I'd been raised a hood, hadn't I? Even if I'd never succeeded in taking my fire, there was nothing wrong with my brain.

Other than the fact it was floating in booze.

Dogs could smell fear; a werewolf could taste it. Deep breaths, and focus. *I am a hood. Silver flows in my veins. No pest shall pester me. No beast or man shall conquer me. I am a red. I am the blood that flows through the veins of the earth. I am the warrior which keeps the wolf at bay. I am power. I am strength.*

I was no longer a hood. Mosquitoes, trying to tap my veins, found the deed insurmountable as the old teachings instilled in me all my life rang and became a mantra, though reality niggled at my confidence. Even if the bugs swarming around me thought otherwise, I was nothing more than a huey.

I held up my hands and flinched. "I'm not armed."

Tobias's head tilted to the side. If he'd been a man, he'd have been smirking at the idea a weapon would make any difference. That, or the animal within him was deciding how to best dispatch me.

Dream or not, I didn't want the memory of being ripped to shreds by a werewolf under a full moon. "What I mean to say is, I'm not going to try to hurt you. I'm just... dreaming. Even still, you shouldn't *try* to hurt me either. It might affect our friendship when I wake up."

Two more steps toward me, and I knew I should be running already. Both our eyes turned to the forest canopy as a crow made its presence known, cawing has he leapt from the branches of a fir to the leafy extension of a budding oak. A symbol, I was sure of it. I'd have to remember to google it later. When my eyes dragged back down to the earth, however, no interpretation was needed. A man stood before me: one with broad shoulders, a firm chest, and abs I could bounce a quarter off of. (My memory suggesting a mere dime before had proven faulty.)

"What are you doing here, Geri?"

Despite taking on his human, Tobias spoke with a growl. It had taken the man to reveal the anger of the animal within.

"Dreaming, of course. You?"

"You think you're dreaming?" He shook with silent laughter. "Maybe you're right. Maybe I am." A mud-caked hand dragged through sweat-drenched hair. "This can't be real."

"That's because it's not. I'm a huey now, and there's a full moon overhead. It should have no effect on me, and a more animalistic effect on you. Ipso facto: we're dreaming."

Three more steps, and he reached up to stroke my cheek. "If it's a dream, right now doesn't matter. It doesn't have to make sense."

"Nope. I suggest we try something crazy, then. I've always wanted to be a—"

But I was never able to admit to Tobias that I'd always wanted to feel what it was like to take on a wolf. Because the next moment, I couldn't say anything at all.

Tobias was kissing me.

Lips sweet with nectar, a brow wet with dew. His hands cupped my face, turning my head, letting me feel the intoxicating pull and suckle of his mouth. I moaned, reaching for his shoulders, wrapping my hands around his neck. His arms encircled me, pulling me hard against his body, firing the hood's soul within me. Old voices, long thought dead, spoke inside me.

Kiss him. Take him. Mate him.

As his mouth slid over my neck, all the feeling within me started to ebb. I closed my eyes, gasping, whimpering his name. My world turned upside down as Tobias swept my feet from under me. His chest felt so warm beneath my cheek. I leaned into his chest, letting his body heat reflect my own. The gentle left-right sway as he carried me through the forest lulled me. Soon, I couldn't keep my eyes open.

<h1 style="text-align:center">TEN</h1>

Amy called it a hangover. I called it proof of why cultures that shunned alcohol had things right.

Tobias arrived to pick us up the next morning, though I drove all the way back to Chicago while he and Amy napped in the back of the crew cab. Too many times, I caught myself snatching peeks in the rearview mirror, wondering if the lips which looked chapped in the light of day could be soft in the night.

And then I reminded myself that I already had a boyfriend, and that one dream didn't magically make Tobias any less of a widower wolf who would be forever bonded to his mate.

Back in Chicago, a message from Inga's office informed us that she and Caleb had left already, traveling to Istanbul via Tel Aviv.

"Israel?" Amy asked, reading the note over my shoulder. "Why?"

"Old vampires don't like email or phone calls or even fax machines. Inga's been corresponding with old friends, trying to find one the Ravens have approached to offer their life serum thing to. She's hoping one of them will lead us to their exact location. Right now, we don't know for sure."

"Okay, then why is Caleb with her?"

I shrugged, not wanting to admit aloud that that same thought passed through my head five times a day. "She's very protective of him."

"Yeah, well he's *your* boyfriend, so she better not try anything sketchy or I'm going to let her have it."

"You haven't even met him yet. What if you think he's scum or a player or something?"

"You, pick someone bad?" Amy's face screwed up. "I don't see that happening."

"Remind me later to tell you why Jess and I broke up."

A box on my bed with a note from Caleb passed along regrets for missing my graduation, but the present inside almost made up for it.

Just because you can no longer wield it, doesn't mean you can't make it shine. Very proud of you. Love you.

Amy snatched the card from my hand and held it at arm's length, whereupon she examined the page with the intensity of a homicide detective. "Geri, if you're serious about this guy, then get serious about this guy. You're going to lose him if you don't."

"What?" I grabbed the note back. "How in the hell do you know something like that from twenty words?"

"Because I'm looking at the only ones that matter. *'Love you.'*" Her finger pointed out the key text. "There's no 'I' there. He's—what's the phrase?—tipping his heart. He wants to show you what he feels, but he's scared of rejection. Scared, because he has a lot more invested in the relationship than you do."

Tobias cursed as he finally emerged out of the bedroom a few hours after sunset, the first words he'd said other than "I'll pump" since leaving Paradise.

"What the bloody hell is she talking about?" he said to me, vaguely motioning to Amy.

"She's pretending to be the love guru again," I said, opening the box and holding up the contents for the werewolf's inspection. A silver crossbow charm the size of a dime pivoted from a thick chain of the same material. "Inga and Caleb left early. This is Caleb's graduation present to me."

Tobias grimaced. "Perfect. Now if I try to strangle you, I'll get third-degree burns in the process."

"So your alpha *has* ordered my execution."

"On the contrary, he's officially instructed me to accompany you to Istanbul because, and I quote, 'Geri's too irrational right now, and if something happens to her you could have prevented, her bitch of a mother will take it out on the whole pack.'" The werewolf coughed a laugh into the orange juice container as he stood in front of the open fridge. "Might be willing to test that theory after what happened."

I white-knuckled the handle of the fridge door as I pushed him back to close it. "Damned alpha."

"Can we get back to what's really important here?" Amy interjected. "If this Caleb guy is really as hot and sexy and sweet as you say, why are you not treating him better?" Her suspicious glare turned on Tobias. "Or do you have something to do with that?"

"Me?" Tobias stuck a thumb into his own chest. "Don't lay this at my paws. I've been telling her for months to sleep with the guy."

I threw up my hands at both of them. "As much as I appreciate you both trying to engineer the cashing in of my v-card, let me reassure you, I'm making that move only when I'm ready."

"Well, of course, sweetie!" Amy's mannerism shifted from grilling best friend to sympathetic sister. "No, I'm not saying put out before he gets out. No! I'm just saying, if you got a great guy, why are you being so resistant to building a *real* relationship with him?"

Tobias took a bite of bagel and shrugged. "I don't care, I'm just sick of having to wait around at WWL for you. If you started staying whole nights with him, I'd get half my life back."

Amy snapped her fingers. "Another great reason. Look, I have to go change over my laundry downstairs. When I come back, you and I are going to sit down, talk this out, and make a plan."

Finally, with Amy out of the room and Tobias talking again, I could bring up the were-elephant in the room.

"So Cody isn't that mad with me?"

The werewolf looked at me like I'd just suggested dumplings were disgusting. "Actually, I'd say he's right pissed. You called him out in front of the pack and, by the way, made a fool of yourself in the process. If you were pack, he probably would have renounced you to save maw."

A fool of myself? How dare he? "Like your alpha did with you?"

My verbal arrow hit its mark, and Tobias flinched. "It's not the same."

"Okay, I'll grant you it's not *exactly* the same. You were trying to prove to your alpha that vampires were involved in your brother's murder and your mate's disappearance, but you acted out of love."

"You telling your ex-boyfriend—your married-and-mated-with-a-child ex-boyfriend—that you were still in love with him wasn't heroic, Geri. You weren't trying to right a wrong or alert others to danger; you were just shopping for sympathy."

"Sympathy?" I spit the term back in his face. "May I remind you that *Cody* was the one who brought up my feelings to begin with?"

"Because every time you look at him, all dreamy-eyed and lovestruck, you weaken his position as alpha. He—" Tobias stumbled over his own realization as his flashing eyes went from me to the ceiling. "He set you up. He knew exactly how you would react, and he did it on purpose to create a scene so he could save face."

The notion turned over in my head only for a moment before my mind filled in the other part of that conclusion. "He did it because that was the only way he could let you go with me to Istanbul for the summer. He had to solidify his authority *and* make me look pitiful, so the others wouldn't question why he was letting you go chasing after a hood. Not even a real hood anymore, a former hood."

Tobias ran a hand through hair badly in need of a cut. "Cody might be better at pack politics than I thought him capable of." The werewolf extended a hand. "Peace?"

I wrapped my hand in Tobias's. "Until the next time we have a reason to fight."

ELEVEN

"What about your parents, Geri?" Mrs. Popowitz asked as Amy and I posed for pictures in caps and gowns. "Did they make it into town for graduation? Amy says you're from Minnesota. That's not too far away, is it?"

"Michigan, actually," I corrected. "Unfortunately, my parents are very occupied running the family business. They couldn't make it."

Truth be told, I'd been a little upset by the fact that neither my dad nor my mom had talked to me since last summer. But, as Amy's parents reminded me, I didn't have an exclusive on dysfunctional family drama. She had a feather of a mother and a stone of a father.

"Yes, I understand how hard it could be to get away," Mr. Popowitz grumbled. "Yet, somehow, I managed to do it, and I run a Manhattan law firm."

"Never you mind him, dear." Mrs. Popowitz practically cooed as she ran a gloved hand over my cheek. I didn't know if it was good genetics, or a great plastic surgeon, but she didn't look to be more than a few years older than her daughter. "But is there no one here at all for you? How tragic."

I bit my lip. It didn't feel tragic until she had said something. But then, wading through the crowd, wearing the darkest pair of sunglasses I had ever seen, strode my unwitting bodyguard.

"Actually, there's one person."

I squealed as his embrace picked me up off the floor and set my legs pinwheeling through the air.

"Damned proud of you, Little Red. Even though I don't understand what the hell it is you're going to do with that degree."

"It's just official documentation that I'm smarter than you."

"Could have told you that without you wasting all that money on tuition."

My feet tingled by the time Tobias set me down. He played nice, shaking hands with Amy's parents, then asking what they thought about their daughter's plan to join us in Istanbul for the summer.

Mr. Popowitz's face screwed up, as though he'd just smelled something foul. "Istanbul?" He turned to his daughter. "I thought you said you were going to Europe for the summer."

"Istanbul *is* in Europe," Amy sighed. "Or at least, half of it is."

You could have polished a blade on his sharpened eyes. "Amy Helene Popowitz, how can you even think to go to such a backward country for the whole summer?"

I snatched the werewolf's hand before he could try to slither away. If he had opened this can of worms, the least he could do was stick around to watch them crawl out.

Amy, however, must have anticipated her father's objection, and came out fighting with silver-studded facts. "Actually, *Daddy*, Turkey has a higher GDP than both Switzerland and Austria, is one of the world's leading producers of textiles, hazelnuts, and tobacco, and has the highest levels of education of any Muslim country in the region. *They've* even had a woman prime minister—something America still hasn't managed."

Mr. Popowitz looked off in the distance at nothing in particular. "If there was a woman worthy who'd run, we would have."

"But... Turkey," Mrs. Popowitz persisted. "It's rather dangerous, isn't it?"

"How is New York City different? Or the United States?"

Her father pushed his black-rimmed glasses up his nose. "And when do you leave for this escapade?"

"Tomorrow night. We have a direct flight out of O'Hare."

Mrs. Popowitz took me and her daughter by the hand and walked us toward the door. "Oh, that's soon! Let's make sure you both are well fed before then. I hear they don't have any pork in that country. Can you imagine? A whole summer without bacon."

Tobias winced as I elbowed his ribs.

<hr>

"I can't believe a place like this really exists."

Ignorance was a fertile field in which surprises grow.

I'd been to large cities before: Detroit, Frankfurt, Munich. And of course, two years living in Chicago. Metropolises on their own, I'd thought, were interchangeable, after you got past a few distinguishing landmarks or sports stadiums.

Istanbul was a city defined by landmarks, one which a modern city had managed to grow into the cracks of and cocoon over the outside. Even Schloss Wolfsretter, the majestic, ancestral home of the House of Red and current de facto United Nations building for my entire species, would fade into the background among such colossal edifices. As I looked out over the European side's skyline from the cabin of the massive SUV Igor had waiting for us at the airport, snaking its way up the Asian coastline, a crick in my neck began to throb from all my head turning.

Igor grinned, although he too kept his eyes fixed on the living museum landscape. "Five hundred years since I first saw her, and she still has the power to make my heart beat."

"Wait, you mean your heart's not beating?"

Amy's question proved to be a bucket of cold water that awoke all of us to reality. Istanbul released its mystical hold on our attention, and our conversation turned inward.

Igor smiled. "Beating might be an exaggeration, but it functions, just in a much different way, from what I've been able to gather." Once he'd learned that Amy was definitely and enthusiastically in the know about the supernatural world, he'd decided that knowledge trumped ignorance, even if he wasn't sure of this particular huey's trustworthiness as yet. "It's been difficult to know much about how vampirism changes the internal organs and biochemistry of the subject. As we heal from minor injury so quickly, and given that when we do die, our corpses turn to ash as soon as they're struck by sunlight, it's been impossible to learn much through postmortem examination."

"But you're obviously still able to function humanly," Amy countered. "How, without a pulse? How do your muscles get oxygenated? Wouldn't you have continual strokes without it going to your brain? And what about digestion? You drink blood, which doesn't have that many nutrients or other essential things like fiber? How in the hell do you survive?"

"I still exercise regularly."

The attempt at humor fell flat. Igor cleared his throat and continued.

"All good questions, and ones I myself long to learn the answers to, Miss Popowitz. Despite centuries of study, both in books and on my own person, the best I've been able to deduce is that *that* is the primary reason we drink blood. Whatever infests or infects us when we become vampire—call it a virus or call it magic—keeps our bodies in a perpetual state of rejuvenation. It cannot, however, deliver oxygenation. In effect, we drink blood to breathe."

Amy's expression soured. "But you'd need to drink it, like, all the time."

Igor allowed an acknowledging nod, then added, "Then again, with practice, one can hold one's breath for a very long time."

Amy could accept that Igor was a vampire, but she couldn't accept that he had as quick of an intellect as she did. She settled back in her seat and turned her eyes back to the city. "You can't hold your breath forever."

According to Igor, I shouldn't be deluded into thinking that traffic would always be so accommodating, as the drive from one side of the Golden Horn to the other usually took several hours. Our advantage? At two AM, streets were merely crowded instead of congested.

Tobias looked down at the waves below the bridge when we passed over, each rise kissed by light from both sides of the strait. "There's more history in the square mile around us than England and America hold together. Really makes you ponder things, don't it? How insignificant our existence is in the bigger frame of things?" His bottom lip pulled in, and a glisten on his cheek gave away what he struggled to hide in his voice. "Kara would have loved this."

Like the city reflecting in the waters below, I turned my thoughts back to the mangled histories that had brought each of us to this moment. If I hadn't hesitated to say *yes* when Cody had asked me to mate him, I would be his wife now. Perhaps I'd even be sitting by his side this very moment, bouncing our baby on my knee. If Tobias had convinced me sooner to help him, Kara might still be alive. But then, who would be here to fight the Ravens?

I leaned into him, resting my head on his shoulder. "She would have."

As Igor paid the driver (and selectively poked at his memory to delete too much detail about us), the rest of us unloaded our bags from the back of the car.

"It smells like fish and piss," Tobias grumbled.

Amy paused, taking a moment to thoroughly scent the air herself. "I'm only getting the piss. Your nose must be better than mine." When Tobias gave her a *I'm a werewolf, remember?* glare, she followed up with, "Oh, right, yeah. Well, I'd rather be able to smell the fish, frankly."

"And I'd rather smell anything." I sucked down another lungful of air. Supernatural abilities denied, the profile proved limited. "Seriously, all I'm getting is..."

"Bread." Igor cut me off as the car pulled away. "There's a bakery across the street. You're smelling the yeast proofing the bread. In an hour or so, when the ovens fire up, you'll swear you were back in your mother's kitchen."

We all turned deadpanned expressions on him.

"Seriously, none of your mothers baked bread?" Igor shifted his weight. "We'll get a loaf in the evening when I rise, if they're still open. It's the next best thing. Empires universally result in two things: slavery and fine cuisine. The latter remains after the former has arisen."

The sidewalk leading toward the house before us seemed to be more worn down than welcoming. The structure, three stories high but only the width of two cars, still held an echo of beauty. At its zenith, it must have drawn the eye and inspired envy. Its wooden boards had long ago let go any hold of paint. The door, a dark-stained thing laced over with iron girders, looked like something salvaged from a pirate ship.

"Suddenly, I'm thinking coming to Istanbul wasn't my best idea." Amy examined the home with a displeased eye. She turned to Igor. "You're, like, an ancient vampire. Aren't you supposed to have luxurious mansions all over the world?"

Igor shrunk back, throwing his coat over his arm. "I suppose you also think I should only wear black capes with high red collars and seduce young virgins with my radiant sex appeal."

"One: ew, you're old. And two…" She pointed to exhibit A: a three-story structure held together by nostalgia and a few remaining nails. "If there was a building in Manhattan that looked like this, it would be surrounded by a security fence and plastered over with signs saying *condemned*."

Igor found a key underneath a pot of pink flowers resting on a stoop before the front door, a metal relic longer than his hand that may have been as old as he was.

"That is by design. We're here to find the Ravens, hopefully while not being found ourselves. We want to lie low. I do have a house here—a beautiful home out on one of the Prince Islands. I'm certain Vlad would have someone watching it. Too risky to stay there."

"If this isn't *your* home, whose is it then?"

Tobias's question echoed my thoughts. Immediately following which was, why here? For the past three minutes, I'd been scanning the run-down building's edifice for security concerns. Other than the bars overlapping the windows of the first floor and the front door, little inspired hope in me that this house would stand up to a rainstorm, let alone a Raven.

Igor turned the key. "I rented it online. Please remember, if any of the neighbors asks, we're a group from the university, here doing research about street cats. Also, let me tell you one thing about this country: it teaches you not to focus on outward appearance. There is often something surprising hidden behind the veil."

I stepped around Amy, pressed forward by hope. "Are Inga and Caleb here? I got a text from him yesterday saying they were on their way to Istanbul."

The vampire, his hand flattened against the door, paused. "None of you are supposed to be using any devices."

Amy looked up from a tiny lit screen. "I thought that meant just for the flight."

Before my friend could blink, our honorary *in loco parentis* had her device in his hand.

"George Orwell failed to foresee that you all would be the ones holding the cameras on yourselves." With one simple gesture, Igor closed his hand, reducing the phone to e-waste. "No smartphones, no computers, no telephone calls. Inga will be bringing devices we can use that are guaranteed to be secure."

While Amy mumbled her grievances, I was still stuck on the one thing with which I couldn't reckon. "Caleb?"

Igor motioned me into the house. "Soon, Geri. I promise."

He'd been right about one thing: the exterior concealed what the interior revealed. Not to say that I felt like we'd just stepped into something swanky like Caleb's WWL flat or posh like a suite at the Ritz, but the home held its own in terms of quality. Hardwood floors were covered in aged yet intricately-patterned rugs. Clean, white-washed walls hosted a gallery's worth of paintings and prints, many of which framed the very skyline we'd observed driving in.

Igor set down his bag inside the door. "That over there," he pointed to the right, "is the sitting room, though they call it a salon here. The kitchen is at the back of the house, along with a bathroom if any of you want to freshen up. There's only two bedrooms upstairs, but they're both pretty big. The third floor is one large room, empty of furniture at my request. I thought you all could use it for sparring and as a space to train Amy, like you were talking about."

"Only two bedrooms?" Amy asked. "So, who gets what?"

Igor seemed confused by the question. "I thought it would be obvious: the women get one. The men, the other."

Embarrassment warmed my cheeks. "I thought Caleb and I would get our own room?"

"So I'd get Tobias?" The blonde licked her lips. "Sounds good to me."

"No." Tobias put his paw down. "Don't take this the wrong way, Amy, but no. There's no way I'm sharing a room with you."

"Amy and I will share a room," I said, stepping in to play diplomat. Caleb would just have to join me at the negotiating table when he arrived. But something still didn't add up. "What about you and Inga, Igor? Where will you stay?"

"Ah, yes! Where is—Ah! Here it is." In the middle of the house, between the entryway and what I assumed was the kitchen, the vampire opened an old wooden door that echoed the front door's style. Beyond, a staircase descended into a dark pit. Must and dew scented the air. "*This* is why this house," he said. "A cistern. Empty, of course. In the old part of the city, there's hundreds of them. Every grand home or even apartment block in Byzantine or Ottoman times had one, and a number of them still survive in one form or another today. A favorite of vampires for day rest, of course."

Amy's nose turned up. "Ew, you sleep in water?"

"Not so much these days, but once upon a time, it was quite usual for a vampire to prefer a water bed, if you'll forgive the pun. You see, nature likes balances. Ours is a slayer, of course. But even they, in turn, have a weakness, don't they?"

"I was thinking the weakness was that whole not-being-undead thing," I deadpanned.

The professor continued very professorially. "Water, Geri. A slayer can conjure a solarium and burn a vampire to ash, but they cannot do so while standing in water. Yes, back in the day, a cistern was the very height of vampiric sleeping arrangements."

I bent down over my suitcase and foisted out a smaller bag from within. "Whatever floats your boat. Or, your body."

Tobias side-eyed me. "Please tell me that isn't what I think it is."

"Of course, it is."

"But they won't even do you any good anymore."

"They make me *feel* safer." The silver tchotchkes clanked as I palmed two of them and pulled them out. "They're small, and I'll make sure they're nowhere that you're going to just casually rub up against one of them."

Amy crossed her arms. "So, you're going to stuff them into your bra then?"

TWELVE

"I've never understood the term *food coma*, but I think I'm going into some kind of torpor."

Amy folded her arms over her stomach and fell back, groaning. By the time we'd awoken late in the afternoon the following day, most of the bakery's stock had been depleted and was already turning hard. Still, food was food. Crumbs were all that remained of the second loaf of bread we'd polished off.

Her eyes swung around the room as another smile crept onto her face. "Can you believe places like this exist? Igor wasn't kidding when he said 'behind the veil,' was he?"

I dipped my chin. "It certainly wasn't what I expected when we first pulled up outside, that's for sure."

Yes, the interior of the house was just as aged as the exterior, but it wore its years clinging to remnants of a former glory. Instead of individual pieces of repositionable furniture, a permanent row of low, wide couches ringed the edge of the room, festooned with lace coverlets. At the center of this U-shaped configuration, a table which looked more like a giant copper plate sat atop a collapsible base of wooden peg legs, its circumference edged with poufy floor cushions. This, I came to understand, was also the dining table.

"We'll have to make sure to get some lira soon," I said as I lay down on one of the couches. "We were lucky that guy at the counter was willing to take pity on a few American tourists who only had dollars."

Amy lay on the floor parallel to me, her blonde hair a contrast to the red-tinted rugs covering the floor throughout the house. "I told you, I could have used my card. They accepted them; it said so on the door."

"No, we're here on the down-low, remember? We want to avoid electronic breadcrumbs as much as possible. No credit cards."

"There's no way they'd know to follow my records, though. I mean, I only decided to come with you a week ago, and I shouldn't be any interest to them. I'm just a looney."

"*Huey*, Amy. The term is *huey*. Like, a human-y creature: *huey*. Not sure who came up with it, but—"

The front door had opened, and both our resident vampire and werewolf were still asleep. I'd rolled off the couch and drawn the blade from my hair before Amy could even blink.

"Geri, w—"

"*Shh!*"

Putting a finger to my mouth, I ordered her silence. Amy was a quick learner; she sat up but didn't make another peep. A drawn-out, deliberate creek of a floorboard near the entrance suggested an intruder moving with deliberate haste, but in our direction. Jumping on the couches let me move toward the door without the same giveaway, but the element of surprise would only last until we could look each other in the eye.

Years of training took over, as I began to categorize assets and liabilities. *Huey behind me, so I can't run away. Silver blade would be ineffective if it's a vampire, but given that it's still daylight, it probably isn't. They might have a weapon. A gun or a knife. A knife I can handle. If it's a gun, only try to take him down if the physical match is pretty close, and get control of the gun ASAP. Scream for Tobias as soon as silence is no longer a benefit. Get Amy to run away if you can't control the situation. Hostages, not homicides. Anyone here isn't here by accident. Hold and interrogate. Find out who sent them, and what they were sent here to do.*

"Igor?"

The voice struck at the chords of my memory, but the tune seemed out of place. My hand planted on the floor; it would be my ballast point so I could round out a kick low and sweep out the intruder's feet.

"Hello? Anyone here? Geri? *Oofff…*"

With the coordination of a tiger's pounce, I dropped my blade and had him on the ground, my legs thrown over his hips and my hands on either side of his head. Only my goal wasn't to incapacitate any longer; it was to hold and to kiss.

Caleb laced his fingers behind his head as he slipped into his mask of smugness, a golden grin greeting me. "Looks like somebody missed me."

"Maybe a little."

I giggled as he rolled up, exchanging our positions. A solid weight against my thigh told me he'd finally taken my advice on always having a weapon. As Caleb leaned down and renewed our kiss, a halo of blonde hair emerged from the background.

"Please tell me this is the boyfriend."

I almost burst out laughing when Caleb pulled away and found a stranger brandishing a vase of dry flowers as an improvised weapon. Realizing we were no longer preparing for a real-life action movie fight scene, Amy let the vase lower as her eyes glassed over.

"On second thought, please tell me he's *not* the boyfriend. Wow."

Caleb turned back to me. "Is she a werewolf? And mind, I only ask because she's drooling."

"No, she's a huey, and she's only drooling because my boyfriend is hot and there's nothing Amy likes more than hot men. Now, stand up and let me introduce you to her properly. After that, you're going to tell me what the hell you and Inga have been up to."

"If you insist. But after that, you're going to tell me why in the hell there's a huey in our house, wielding flower vases."

Our house. That phrase shouldn't have sent my mind abuzz, but... *buzz.*

"Fair enough."

THIRTEEN

"Technically, I haven't aged in centuries, but for some reason, I feel suddenly very old. Did I just walk onto the set of some new CW series where an ex-hood, a slayer, a werewolf, and a token huey have to fight evil monsters on the streets of the city?"

Igor sized up the four twentysomethings lounging in the living room. Tobias had just joined us a few minutes ago. The vampire's head swung to take in the scope of the room.

"Where is Inga?"

"A 'hello' to you, too, professor." Caleb stood and cleared his throat, shaking Igor's hand, before they both took seats on the couches. "Inga's still in Üsküdar, over on the Asian side. At least, she was when I left the hotel this morning. We got in last night, but that's as far as we could make it from the new airport before dawn. I'm going to guess when she woke up a few minutes ago and found me gone, she smoked out of there pretty quickly."

"You crossed the city alone?" Igor Karmarov had never fit the "disapproving father figure" role better. "Caleb, you of all people know how dangerous this city is for someone like you. For anyone, frankly."

"It was daytime. I wasn't going to be tagged by any fangs," my boyfriend returned. "I've barely seen Geri for the last three months. Knowing she was just a ferry ride and steady walk away, I couldn't wait anymore. It was fine. Besides, you forget two key facts: one, I was born here. I know the city. And, two…" A ball the size of a tangerine burst into existence on his open palm. "I could have handled a vampire if one wanted to tango."

Amy's mouth dropped to the floor. "He's Harry freaking Potter."

Tobias yawned and stretched both his physical muscles and his sarcastic ones. "And how, exactly, did you get into our ultra-secure facility?"

The slayer pointed his free hand over his shoulder, back toward the door. "Found a key under a pot of flowers out there. Maybe not the best place to leave that?"

Igor failed to be impressed, despite blinking as the solarium stung his irises. "This isn't Chicago. These aren't little offshoot clutches spun out from the Old World. We're in the Belt of Blood, and the Ravens circle it daily."

"Belt of Blood?" Looking to Tobias, I saw he was just as perplexed. "What is that?"

The vampire grimaced. "The traditional territory of the Dracule clutches. It spreads from Vienna, down through Asia Minor, then up into the caucuses. There's a reason this region is known for its vampire lore. It came of age with the Byzantines, fled west and east with Christians into the Hapsburg and the Czars' courts, then folded back in once the Ottomans seated themselves."

"That last part thanks to Vlad Tepeş," Caleb added.

Thank goodness that I had Amy, whose innocence couldn't be condemned, to ask the questions that would have revealed my ignorance. "Wasn't Vlad the Prince of Transylvania? Why is he so obsessed with Istanbul?"

"It's a bit Freirean, I'm afraid."

Our blank faces drove Igor to frustration.

"Seriously? Two of you just graduated from university in the last forty-eight hours, and nothing?"

"If it was a biochem thing, I'd know it," I offered. "Obviously, it's not some kind of molecule."

More annoyed scowling. It was almost like being back at home with my mom.

"It's the concept that an affronted or oppressed population will assume the characteristics of their oppressors when they gain power," Igor explained. "As a human, Vlad and his people—That would be Wallachia, Amy. Transylvania refers to the region at large.—were at the mercy of the Ottomans. His entire royal line ruled at the leisure of the sultan. As children, Vlad and his brother Radu were even political prisoners at the sultan's court."

Caleb nodded, presumably heading off our confused expressions. "It was a very common practice in the ancient world, and not just for the Ottomans. A good way to ensure that a conquered people didn't rise up against you was to give incentive for toeing the line. Even Augustus took Cleopatra and Marc Antony's children into his own home after they died."

"Even though the children were technically prisoners, they were treated as royal guests, given an education and furnished with a lifestyle nearly on par to the sultan's own children," Igor resumed. "But Vlad never forgot who reigned over his people, though his brother sided with the Turks, even helping them conquer Constantinople in 1453. It left an imprint. When he escaped the confinement we'd placed him in, he came here, vowing to live out the luxurious life his people's blood and tears paid for, by literally living off the blood of his enemy's descendant."

Amy's eyes couldn't get any wider. "If Shakespeare had known about this, he might have written a vampire play."

Igor waved off the comment. "Politics is a constant, perpetual motion. The only difference is the players."

The growl rumbling through Tobias's chest preceded his shift, and within moments, all hell had broken loose. The werewolf tensed his haunches, balancing on all fours amid a pile of ravaged clothing, as I in turn drew my blade and covered Amy. It seemed to happen all at once: the front door flying open, the bank of smoke that rushed into the room, the smoke taking form, slamming Caleb against the wall, and Igor rolling his eyes at it all.

"You bastard!" Inga Rosethorn practiced control like a Zen master. A foot off the floor and pinned in a vampire's grip, Caleb looked nonplussed. "How dare you pull a stunt like that? I thought you were dead! I thought they'd gotten you. I thought after everything, I'd failed."

"But I left you a note on the dresser."

"I KNOW YOU LEFT ME A NOTE ON THE DRESSER!" Her nails nicked his neck, and I had to fight the urge to leap in and pull Inga's hands off my man. "Which was even more stupid. What if the Ravens had come for you? They'd know exactly where to find you. Do you ever think about *any* of the consequences of your actions? How pussy-whipped are you?"

"I object to that." My words turned a spotlight onto my presence, and a vampire seething anger lashed out in my direction. "Most hood women would consider such dominance over their beau a compliment."

Caleb took his protector/attacker's wrists in his hands. "I'm fine, and look around: no ravens. Not even sparrows."

"Inga, enough," Igor said. "I've already lectured him. Let it go, and by that, I mean him. He's a man in love. They do irrational things."

"If he doesn't learn to master his emotions, the irrationality is going to get him killed," Inga grumbled as Caleb resumed his feet. Now free to observe the room at large, her eyes fell upon a somewhat flushed huey. "Who are you?"

The blonde stood and threw out a hand to the seething vampire. "Amy Popowitz, and I'm apparently the token honey."

"Huey!"

"Huey," Amy corrected. "I'm assuming you're the beautiful Inga Rosethorn I heard so much about."

Inga took a moment to look at Amy's hand as though inspecting it for defects. Finally, her tensions eased, and she gently slid her own out to meet the greeting in kind, if without kindness.

"Miss Popowitz, a pleasure." The words were flat, emotionless, scripted. "But you should not have come. This is no mission for a huey. I doubt even Gerwalta's readiness."

"Oh, I know. From what she's told me, she's pretty much useless now."

"Hey!" My hackles raised in the wake of my best friend's betrayal.

Amy continued as though I'd said nothing. "But since I was attacked by a vampire in front of a theater full of people, I thought if I came along, I'd stand a better chance of surviving with you, Igor, and Caleb around."

Inga raised a suspicious eyebrow. "And Tobias?"

Amy swatted the air. "What's a werewolf going to do to a vampire? Bark at it?"

Tobias took on his human, complete with outrage. "Bark at it? Don't forget who—"

I lashed my arm out over Tobias's chest, keeping him from pouncing. Maybe he didn't yet see what was going on, but I'd certainly caught on. Genius. Amy was a diplomatic genius. In a few brief moments, she'd managed to turn a centuries-old vampire to her favor.

The corners of Inga's mouth ticked up. "Indeed. Well, I still think it foolish that you are here, but at least you will prove to be most entertaining."

"Inga?"

The female vampire's head snapped to her vampiric father.

"You said something about what you found out in Tel Aviv?" he continued. "I think we should all hear that. Let me make some tea, and then I want you to tell *all of us* what you've learned."

We sat dispersed on the couches, drinking from the tulip-shaped cups that had perplexed me when I saw them in the kitchen earlier. Igor handed each of us a spoon about half the size of a normal one.

"Tea is the lubricant of the tongue in Turkey, as well as the wallet. Even if you don't like it now, you need to acquire a taste for it. It will be given to you everywhere you go, and I mean everywhere. Learn to drink vast quantities of it in a way that doesn't stress your pulse or your bladder."

The brew, a mildly bitter tonic with hints of bergamot, didn't quite satisfy the palate like coffee, but it did warm the insides. Despite the fact that it was now early June, something about the house made the drafty interior a bit chilly.

"As we suspected, the Ravens still make their clutch in Istanbul. As in the ancient world, it is still one of the most convenient bases from which to operate."

"Operate?" I asked. "That's an interesting word choice."

"It is an intentional one," Inga confirmed. "We knew that Vlad's discovery of the power of werewolf blueblood to sustain vampire life after the natural death was due had been used for political advantage. Seems he's also using it for financial gain as well."

"He's still selective about who he allows into his inner circle," Caleb added, even as his fingers traced lines over my palm. "Not just anyone is chosen for the treatments. A run-of-the-mill clutch holds no interest for him. He grows friends in gardens of influence, and seeds it very carefully. Our contact assured us that one does not seek out the Ravens; the Ravens seek out you."

Tobias set his untouched tea down on the copper table. "But how would the Ravens even know who to approach? How are they getting their information about potential clients?"

Inga and Caleb exchanged a weighted look, one that then turned on me.

"No." It was impossible. How would that even happen? "Not the hood's tracking software? But that's only used to keep a tab on werewolf populations, to help create matches between different packs and flag potential lone wolves."

Tobias mumbled into his shoulder. "Big brother, watch thyself."

"It is the same software the hoods use, but the hoods are not the ones who created it. *That* dubious achievement came from the Line of Dracule. Your mother—or some other matron—received it from us."

Tobias leaned back on the sofa, looking oddly Roman as he held up his half-empty cup and swirled it, setting the tea leaves collected at the bottom spinning. "So vampire tech was implemented by hood overlords to control werewolf populations. If they weren't all dead, I'd say the slayers are the only clean ones in this."

"I'm not dead." Caleb's fingers laced through mine. "But I'll admit that I'm not that clean. I can, in fact, be very dirty."

"Yeah, well good luck with that," Amy muttered. "You're sharing a room with Tobias."

Inga pushed on as though no one had interrupted. No doubt she was accustomed to Caleb's twisted tongue. "A tool isn't inherently good or evil. It's the intent the user brings to it that determines its utility. In any event, it seems that Vlad and the Ravens are very good at what they do. Several I contacted in Amman and Tel Aviv have been approached. None have any idea how to find the Ravens on purpose or where they're located."

"That's a shitty attempt at building a client relationship," Amy said. "There's something missing there. They'd have to know that some would stew over a decision like that, and want to change their minds. How were these vampires told to get in touch if that happens?"

Inga grinned. My little huey roomie proved impressive when pitching in the big leagues. "They were told if they changed their minds, they were to come to Istanbul. No further instructions than that, not even if they should come to the Asian or the European side."

I chewed over the revelations. "There's something fishy about that. Something missing. Can vampires sense each other's proximity the ways hoods and wolves can?"

"Wait, you know when each other are near?" Caleb passed narrowed eyes over Tobias and me.

"Not me anymore. But yeah, before my mother did her little disowning ceremony."

"The only good thing to come of that whole event," Tobias added. "I'm no longer a living Geri-emotion-meter. Thank god that happened before this trip."

I turned over my shoulder to examine the werewolf lounging on the couch behind me, managing to stay serious despite the comic vision of him, naked, with a pink throw pillow covering up his unmentionables. "What's that supposed to mean?"

"Nothing. Just… I'm in a crowded city, stuck indoors, and I'm jet-lagged. In short, Red, I'm in a foul mood."

"So our first objective should be finding out where the clutch rests during the day."

Inga's statement made my eyes twitch. "Why?"

Beside me, Caleb released my hand and rolled to the front of the cushion. "Because that's the best time to kill them, when they're asleep."

"Kill them?" I nearly choked on the words. "Without even talking to them?"

My boyfriend looked like a deer caught in headlights, not really sure if there was more danger in staying where he was or dashing off in another direction. "Baby, that's the whole reason we're here."

"It's not entirely why we're here." Tobias sat up finally, putting an emptied cup of tea on the table. "They're going to die, trust that. But sounds like Vlad Inc. isn't just an old boy's cricket club. If they're distributing, they have a network—whether that's a handful of others or hundreds. We off them without understanding what kind of network they've built up, we'll just be clearing the corner for someone else to set up shop."

Igor, who had remained silent, finally stirred. "I agree with Tobias, though I do think we need to be cautious. The moment he feels you're a threat, he'll destroy you."

"What, and you're safe?" Amy asked.

"We are of his blood," Inga said to the unaware. "A vampire cannot kill another of his bloodline. It destroys him in the process."

Amy snapped her fingers. "Well, isn't that a meatball?"

Caleb poured himself another cup of tea. "With all due respect, Igor, I think we're better off destroying the Ravens and letting the chips fall where they may. Once it gets around that there's one slayer still out there and he killed off the most infamous vampire of all time, anyone else will think twice about following in old Vlad's footsteps."

"I am in agreement with Caleb," Inga said. "We tried to be rational before, Igor. We thought we could handle this problem ourselves by sealing the Ravens away until their time to expire had passed. Somehow they survived, and now, we must deal with the consequences in a way that leaves no opportunity for survival. Every moment they're left to live, we risk the lives of all supes. We're not trying to defeat our enemy, we're trying to destroy him."

"So where do we look?" I posed. "I mean, this is a HUGE city. Something like ten million?"

"Plus five million more," Tobias said. "You really did *no* research before coming here, did you?"

"Not the kind that would go into a third-grade geography report, no. But I now have a very thorough and appreciative knowledge of the weapons used by the Ottoman military over its very long history."

Tobias rolled his eyes as if to say "Hoods!" Igor, however, stayed focused.

"The city keeps adding new neighborhoods on its edges, but I'm pretty sure Vlad will have selected a location in the old parts of town, more than likely on the European side. Remember: he's dangerous, and in part because he's learned to be tactical. Wherever it is, he'll have chosen a place that is easily defensible and has access to sufficient humans for feeding."

"In one of the biggest tourist destinations in the world?" I asked. "That doesn't narrow it down at all."

FOURTEEN

Each of us came from a different lineage: slayer, hood, werewolf, and huey, but we had one thing in common. Jet lag had turned our world on end. Even Caleb, who had come from Tel Aviv, a single hour of difference, reeled from the shift.

"Don't expect this to be common, Amy," Tobias warned. "As soon as we adjust to the time difference, we'll be sleeping through the day. I'm so knackered right now."

"I'm not exactly bouncing off walls here," Amy returned. "But if I'm not allowed to go outside at all by myself at night, and only in the daytime with a 'special' chaperone, then you'll be up and dragging my ass around the city whenever *I* like."

"If you let me train you, I'm sure we can get that changed."

She rolled her eyes at my platitudes. "Like me knowing how to throw a knife is going to do me any good."

"It's not just knowing how to fight, you know." Caleb turned the corner, leading us into a crowded corridor lined on both sides with what looked like a flea market. "Most people like you know how to tell when a situation is suspicious, and most people like us only want easy targets. You figure out how to recognize when you should just leave some place because something doesn't add up, you'll be ten steps ahead of where you are now. The best defense is a good offense, as they say."

"Actually, I think it's the other way around. And lest you forget, when I was attacked, it was on a crowded stage in front of... well, a crowd." Amy coughed as we passed through a flume of smoke rising up from a brazier on the side of the road. "Where in the hell are you taking us? This looks like something out of *Aladdin*."

Caleb stopped and swung around. "You know *Aladdin*?"

"Of course, I do. It's only one of the best animated movies ever made. Answer my question."

Caleb grinned, took Amy by the hand, and walked her backward under an archway bearing the seal of the Ottoman Sultan.

"Manhattan Barbie, welcome to Shangri-La."

If not for the fact that I knew this wasn't a Christian culture, I would have sworn we'd discovered Santa's workshop. We were mice in a maze, and cheese lay in every direction, making it impossible to know which way to run first. Ahead: leather, spices, exotic and massive glassworks designed in intricate patterns. To the left, polished metal, most of it jewel-encrusted, sparkled. Even without my supernatural abilities, the sight of so much silver made my insides hum. To our right, bags, books, buttons... Anything a heart could desire outside of illegal activities had its place.

Amy roused herself from her reverie with a clap of her hands. "I'm going to buy one of everything."

Tobias raised one eyebrow. "You don't even know all of what's in there."

"Doesn't matter." She could barely move forward with anything but her eyes. "I'll figure out what it all is later."

<hr>

Two hours later, I'd learned two new things about Amy. One, she had a penchant for painted tea sets, and two, she could haggle with a tenacity that left Caleb wondrous.

"I used to think no one could negotiate a price like the Turks," he said, shifting a bag filled with silk scarves from one arm to the other. "But Amy? She could talk a potato out of its own skin."

I nodded. "And she's limited by the fact that I'm only letting her use cash. Think of the damage she could do if I told her she could use her credit cards."

The slayer sucked in air through pursed lips. "That might actually cause an earthquake when we went back to the rental. So much weight might shift tectonic plates."

"Fifty-five!" An olive-skinned man standing three inches shorter than the New Yorker pushed five sausage fingers and a bunch of attitude into Amy's face.

"Fifty!" Amy held her ground. Her own fingers she left at her side. "And that's still more than it's worth."

A series of Turkish curses followed, after which Amy shoved her purse back into a bag at her side and walked away.

"That's it?" I asked. "Fifteen minutes of back-and-forth, and you're going to walk over five lira?"

"Oh, Geri…" She grinned a smile that failed to conceal mischief, deliberately moving slowly to where we waited. "Watch and learn."

Just as we all turned to walk away, the man from the booth called out, "Miss! Miss! Come back. Fifty, but only because you are beautiful."

Caleb leaned into me as the victorious blonde turned to close her deal. "With that sort of cachet, you could probably get some things for free while we're here."

"Caleb Helsing, did you just call me beautiful?"

"Implied it, actually. Why don't you try for one of those skimpy belly dancer costumes over there?" He lifted his free hand and pointed to a diaphanous concoction of muslin, bedazzled by belts of silver coins. "I know it looks pretty flimsy, but remember: you won't be wearing it for long."

"Is our relationship at the 'will you wear this lingerie for me' stage?"

"We'll never know unless we give it an honest try."

"Oh, please." Tobias, two stalls away and looking at some woolen socks, of course could hear us just fine. "At least warn me if you guys are going to talk about your sex life so I can—"

When a dog caught on to a suspicious noise, what followed was a typical series of mannerisms. He'd stop all action, go still as the dead, and tilt his head in the direction from which the noise had emanated. Werewolves were no different.

"Caleb, get Amy." I wasted no time in explanations, and Caleb thankfully didn't ask for any. He went about the errand as I made my way to the wolf. "What is it?"

Tobias sniffed, tasted the air, then sniffed again. Even I was picking up on the subtle hints of lupine essence swirling in the air. My sense of smell might be average now, but it had been finely attuned to that particular profile.

"How many?"

He didn't look at me but, instead, began to turn a slow circle. "One, but mixed with recent scents from at least a dozen others. She's alone, but she's not a loner."

"She?" I didn't know why I expected the werewolf to be male, but a little nudge in my gut told me the eyes of a man were upon me. Then again, in this crowded venue, that could be coming from any corner, from any kind of creature.

Tobias lifted a hand, pointing at a booth a few stalls up, to a little shop selling leather goods and postcards for tourists. "There."

Amy and Caleb rejoined us, the former with no reserve of cool about being pulled away from her hard-won victory. "This had better be good."

"Geri, look." Above the entry to the door, a silver plate embossed with looping, decorative script hung. "Caleb, can you read it?"

My boyfriend clicked his tongue. "I can read Turkish but only in Latin script. If it is in Turkish, it's from the era when they still used the Arab alphabet. That means at least a hundred years ago."

"Sounds right. We haven't used these in about that long." I took another step toward the shop, sending a chill of anticipation up my spine. "It's a Writ of Authority."

Tobias huffed. "Jesus Christ, even the crazy greens in England did away with those in Victorian times. That can't seriously be current, can it? I mean, this whole building is hundreds of years old. It has to just be a relic, right?"

"It might be, except there's definitely a wolf in that store, standing under an ancient hood marker declaring them in compliance with its enforcement. Something tells me no proud wolf would leave that up for just decoration."

"Wolf?" Amy's complexion went ashen. "As in, werewolf? Here, in the middle of the Grand Bazaar?"

Caleb's fingers crackled with power until I pulled at his fingers, forcing the solar rays to dampen. "She's scared. You're going to send her into a panic."

He proved incredulous. "And you know this... how?"

"Basic common sense." Though that wasn't the whole of it. I was basically a huey now; insights into wolf emotions were meant to have been a thing of the past. Nevertheless, something in my gut told me I was right. Chalk it up to experience. "Let me talk to her, tell her we don't mean any harm. Tobias will come with me."

The wolf stepped in front of me. "Let me lead. Let's not make her think I'm your bodyguard or anything."

I gave him my best fawning southern belle eye flutter. "But you *are* my bodyguard."

"Reason number five we need to get this wrapped up quickly. You're ruining my rep."

The shewolf froze from head to toe, except for her eyes. Those darted around, cataloging what weapons I might be carrying—two deep green marbles rolling in a game of chance. At her wrists, flesh twitched, as though she fought the instinct that told her to shift into a form better suited for fighting, before the *Homo sapiens* part of her brain kicked in and reminded her that she was in a crowded marketplace filled with thousands of huey tourists.

Standing behind Tobias, I raised my hands and showed naked palms. "I mean you no harm."

She flinched, but otherwise remained still.

"Shit, I should have asked Caleb to come with me. I assumed you'd speak English. All the other shopkeepers do."

When Tobias stepped forward, his shadow falling back over mine, backlit by a skylight at the top of the booth, she eased, even if just to allow him to approach without argument. Tobias ate up the space between them in cautious, tiny bites, until he stood just inches from her. For a moment, neither moved, locked into each other's gazes, until at last, her eyes shied to the floor. My werewolf leaned into this new one, scenting her neck as they both began to turn a slow circle. After a moment, he stood still and let her round him alone, all the time drawing scents off her person. It was... one of the most bizarre things I had ever seen, and yet seemed entirely appropriate.

After what seemed minutes but must have been only seconds, she lifted one hand to Tobias's brow. Instinct drove my hand to the base of my braid, where it gripped the handle of my grandmother's silver blade.

"Geri, wait!"

Tobias threw a hand out in my direction. The shewolf paused, waiting to see if I'd obey. When I did, her hand continued its northward trek, until delicate fingers touched Tobias between the eyes.

The werewolf sucked in a heavy breath. "Thank you."

What was he thanking her for? Regardless, a moment later, she turned to me with questioning eyes, and I realized she was asking him for guidance where I was concerned. Tobias's head turned toward the juncture of roof and ceiling, and the shewolf turned away from him and toward me, taking three light steps and no more.

"*Başliksiniz.*"

I looked to Tobias for guidance. He offered none.

Instead, it was the shewolf who clarified. "You are..." Her hand swept back over her thick black hair, then raked down her chin. "*Başlik.*"

"Oh, you mean a hood."

I knew the term for my kind in a few languages; Turkish was not one. One might think I should have learned, knowing I'd be spending at least my summer in Istanbul, but how could I have anticipated that here, in the midst of one of the largest metropolises in the world, I'd cross paths with a creature who loathed both cities and crowds?

"I am. I mean, I *was*. I..." I stuck my hand out, hoping this western tradition held. "My name is Gerwalta. *Geri.* Everyone calls me Geri."

"*Ben* Tobias. *Ben de kurt.*" Tobias's try at a foreign tongue was admirable, but muddled. Even having no idea what he was saying, I could tell. So could the shewolf, it seemed. "What's your name? Do you speak any English?"

"Little." The shewolf nodded and finally shook my hand. "I am Ayşe."

"Good, because beyond *I am a wolf*, my Turkish only includes the names of foods and a few of the colors."

Speak slowly, I wanted to say as I watched the wheels of Ayşe's mind spin, trying to suss out what the brawny foreigner had said.

"Are you alone? Are there others here?"

After a moment's contemplation, the shewolf sucked in her bottom lip. "This store? My pack store. This month, I run. Another month, somebody else run. Why hood?"

Her question was for him, though she gawked at me the whole time.

"She's my friend." A simplistic answer, but not an untrue one. "Your pack is near?"

She nodded. "We live near."

That took me by surprise. "Your pack lives here, *in* Istanbul? A whole pack, in a huge city like this?"

"Istanbul is not one city. It is many cities." Then, eyes back to Tobias. "You come eat us?"

He guffawed. "Cannibalism isn't my thing."

"I think she's asking you to dinner." Someone had to save the male from his own lack of social insight. For whose benefit I lowered my voice, I couldn't say. It wouldn't impact her ability to hear, that was for sure. "Say *yes*. There're supes in the city. They might know something about the Ravens."

"I know, but there's no way an unfamiliar pack is going to feel comfortable having a hood in their midst."

"But I'm not a hood, remember? Is there anything we could do to convince her I'm not a threat?"

He chuckled beneath his breath. "Yeah, but you won't like it."

"Something painful?"

He hedged his answer, looking off to the side. "Depends on how you define pain."

Even though I was a huey, I knew my tolerance was high, and passing up an opportunity like this would be foolish. Not to mention, our rushed words in low tones had Ayşe growing suspicious. We must have looked like a bickering couple, like I was some domineering wife refusing to let my husband go out for his bowling night.

"Do it."

His eyebrow arched. "You sure? Your boyfriend's not going to like it."

My back became a board, my shoulders squared. "If it helps lead us to the Ravens, he'll understand."

"Okay, I hope you're convincing."

The second Tobias's mouth lowered to my ear, instinct I'd thought dead sprang to life. *Kill him. Subdue him. Kiss him.* His hot breath on my neck heated not just the skin beneath my ear, but all along my chest. I longed to turn around, and put those lips on another part of my body. When his teeth grazed my skin, I had to suck on my upper lip to keep my breath from rushing out.

The words were forced, but his tone was clear. At least to a stranger who didn't understand the type of relationship we had.

"I *am* going to accept this invitation, Geri," he growled out. "You have no say in this decision."

"I wh—"

His hands threaded through my hair and pulled my head to the side, his elbow resting on my shoulder, and before I spoiled the ruse, I finally got with it. Eyes to the floor, I let my head fall to the side and my tongue go silent.

Tobias yanked back, examining me. Had I the will, I would have loved to see his face. I didn't doubt he was eating this up with a silver spoon.

Well, a tin spoon, anyhow.

The shewolf took two steps toward us, her hand up cautiously before her. On one of the shop's business cards, she jotted down an address. "Tonight, at eleven."

FIFTEEN

"Igor, will you talk some sense into Geri's head?"

The invoked vampire lowered a pink-tinted newspaper and looked at the slayer across the room. "I'm not sure I could stuff more in there. It's already pretty full."

Caleb threw up both his hands. "Oh, come on!" Pivoting, he began to join decades of former residents in wearing down the carpet beneath his feet. "We can't let a relinquished hood go traipsing about alone with a foreign pack of werewolves. Have you ever read a single fairy tale? These things don't end well."

Seeing that silence was not to be found through simplicity, Igor folded his paper and set it on the kitchen table. "Actually, if I recall *Little Red Riding Hood*, she survives just fine."

"And she's not going in alone." Tobias emerged from the stout refrigerator, an empty glass bottle in one hand and a milk mustache over his lip. "I can guarantee you, no way in hell I'm letting her be eaten."

Oddly enough, my boyfriend's nerves failed to be soothed. "Well, great. Now that I know that, go on ahead."

"They think I'm Tobias's looney." Dots of tangy pepper paste clung to my fingertips, a mess caused by haste. I sucked each off in turn. "And, can I remind you, I'm still a highly trained warrior. If things turn ugly, I know how to do ugly."

Igor blinked thrice. "They think you're insane?"

"No, not a looney. A *looney*, a werewolf groupie." I stood to take my plate to the sink. "Some packs and hood clans are loose on the no-humans-knowing thing. I'm not sure if it's a reference to the moon or to being crazy, but that's the term. Anyway, Tobias is smart. He put on a little dominance display that convinced the shewolf in the Grand Bazaar I was one."

Accusation burned in the crimson hue of Caleb's cheek as he turned to Tobias. "You *dominated* Geri?"

The werewolf shrugged. "Figured at least one of us should."

The solarium, the mere size of a pebble, whizzed by Tobias's head and singed a spot on the wall. Tobias might have pounced back, and Caleb dove forward, if I hadn't created a barrier between them the moment the words were out.

"Okay, boys, enough. Can we focus on our luck? There's a werewolf pack in Istanbul! Think about that: supes in the city who aren't vamps. It would be stupid of us not to try to see if they know anything more than what Ayşe already told us."

"Did she really tell you anything, though? You said her English wasn't that good. Baby..." Caleb cuffed my arms as he drew me in. "I know you can kick lupine ass, but a whole pack versus you and one other wolf? You have to see what a bad idea this is."

Rolling up on my tiptoes, I pressed a kiss to his lips. "We'll be home by dawn."

Amy had often boasted New York was the city that never slept. Istanbul was the city that never blinked.

"It's crowded and lacking wide open spaces, but I can see how this works for the nocturnal." Tobias surveyed the crowds milling through the long street, a stack of cafes, shops, and bars, past street performers forced to occasionally pull their acts aside and allow passage of a restored streetcar. "This is like Chicago in the middle of the day. Everything's open. Have you ever seen so many hueys running around on a Tuesday night?"

"It certainly is beaming with life. I don't like it. Too many people. It's making me nauseous."

The wolf side-eyed me. "Sure it's the crowd?"

"What else would it be?"

"Seems you and Caleb can't stop having rows."

"Relationships don't come prepackaged. They take work, and working out."

"They also take compatibility. And at some point, *intimacy*."

The pig squeal of a laugh leapt out of my throat. "One, that's none of your business. And two, we *are* intimate, even if that hasn't reached its..." I searched the air for the right word.

"Climax?" Tobias suggested, wearing a smirk. "I agree, it's not any of my business. And, god knows, I'll kill you if you give me details, but I can't help but recall a very unfortunate, very public spat you had with my alpha not too long ago. Can't help but thinking he might have had a point. Maybe you are hung up on past loves."

"What would you say if I said that to you? That you need to just get over Kara, that you're too young to spend the rest of your life pining over her?"

"I'd probably rip off your arms."

"How much do you like your arms, Tobias?" A rickety *chug-chug-chug* pushed the crowds to the side of the street, all of us compressing as the tram passed. "Speaking of which, how is this going to go over? I'm supposed to be a looney, but I'm guessing they know you're a widower."

"You heard Ayşe offer her condolences in the Bazaar, didn't you?" He didn't wait for my answer. "I've been asking myself since earlier today what my motivation for keeping a looney around would be. I'm guessing it comes down to sex."

"I'm not sleeping with you just to strike up a conversation with a few werewolves. I don't care if it lets us find out where Vlad buys toothpaste. Besides, I thought it was impossible for a mated wolf to be adulterous."

He grimaced. "Emotionally, it is. Physically, I hear it can be done. I've been told by a few wolves who've lost their mates that it's possible, just to scratch the physical itch. Takes years, though. I could suggest that because Kara and I only had a few months, and we were never officially mated under a full moon, our bond wasn't as strong."

"Sounds good, if you're comfortable with that." I sidestepped a man handing out flyers. "I don't get that. What would be the appeal of sex without the emotions?"

"Only a virgin would ask that."

"I hate you sometimes."

"Only sometimes? I must be doing something wrong."

Ayşe hooked us with gray eyes staring out from behind a black veil. In the market, she'd been dressed in slacks and a loose cotton shirt. Now she looked like someone freshy arrived from Tehran. Fear rimmed her irises, wide and glossy. It was enough to make us pick up our pace once we'd spotted her at the back of a crowd gathered around a man performing a puppet act.

"Is something wrong?" Tobias put a hand on her arm with a tenderness that made me question how *itchy* he was becoming.

"No wrong. Just…" Her eyes went to where buildings met sky, a luminous patch of stars dimly nodding in the background. "Tonight there is…"

"A hood." Tobias's eyes flashed to the sky. "She's nearby. I can sense her now, too."

I couldn't help my own impulses. I turned, surveying the visible, looking for the impossible. A black hood? I'd never actually met one, but I'd heard tell of their particular preferences in silverwielding. Scimitars, it was said, and daggers the size of a man's fist. But that wasn't what really thrilled me. The black hoods were famous among our kind for another reason.

They hunted with falcons.

"Is there something the pack has done to get their attention?"

Ayşe shook her head. "Only, I should not be on the street."

With my eyes still fixed against a barren blue-black sky, confusion closed in on me when Tobias wheeled me around, saying "You're fine. I'll protect you."

Protect me? Protect me from what? Only then did the moment return to me. I was supposed to be a looney. Ayşe recognized me as a hood in the Bazaar, though how, I still didn't understand. But as a hood-turned-looney, I was the worst form of apostate.

Never had my Betrayer namesake clung so tightly to my skin.

I feigned confusion and relief, nodding vigorously as Tobias's hands cuffed both my arms. "Thank you."

"Hurry." Ayşe pivoted and waved us along. "We must go before she is angry."

"Angry?" Tobias said. "About you being out on the street? That doesn't make any sense."

"My pack is not like other packs. Soon, you will understand."

SIXTEEN

Alleyways branched out from the main street, narrower by the turn, until at last, in a place without light and where my eyes struggled to distinguish motes from minarets, Ayşe stopped. The metallic clacking of keys was followed by the tenor groan of rebellious hinges yielding.

"You see, Geri?"

The same moment she asked the question, Tobias's hand pawed mine, lacing our fingers together. "I will be her eyes."

My pulse raced, *from surprise*, I told myself, and I wondered if he'd done it on purpose to help sell our ruse.

Three steps into the passageway, Tobias pulled me to a stop. "There's stairs, and the corridor is too narrow to go down side by side. You want to be behind me or in front of me?"

"Front, please."

With his hands on my hips, holding me out at arm's length, we descended.

"You can put hands on my shoulders," Ayşe offered in front of me. "The stairs are old. Not safe."

Pride warred with practicality. I looked over my shoulder to Tobias behind me, despite the fact that I couldn't actually see anything.

"Have I mentioned lately how much I hate being a huey?"

"Not in the last hour."

Twenty-six steps, then a downward-sloped passage with an irregular floor, and another flight of stairs, making a total of sixty steps.

"Ayşe, do the basements go down this far?"

She shook her head. "Basement? I do not know this word."

"Where are we going?" Tobias clarified.

"Home."

"Home?" I found the idea ridiculous. "You mean you live underground?"

Suddenly, light exploded around us, swallowing darkness. Pain pierced my retinas. A thousand lanterns burned on the periphery of my vision, birthed by one celestial orb in the middle. Even Tobias threw an arm over his eyes from the shock of it, though as a damned supe, he adjusted quickly.

There could be no doubt the man before us was a wolf. Tall and wide and replete with muscle, his frame radiated power and poise. Golden eyes took stock of us from a face fortressed by facial hair—black, with outshoots of gray whiskers. He held an electric lantern aloft and, wrapped in a tattered, floor-length black trench coat, presented a dominating appearance. Tobias slumped his shoulders, bowed his head, and lingered. All signs that could point to a single truth: this man was an alpha.

He must have been advised that we spoke no Turkish, as accented English tumbled from his mouth. "I am Serhan of Pack Pera. Who are you, and do you represent your pack?"

"No, alpha." I'd never heard Tobias so soft-spoken before, not even when addressing Cody. "My name is Tobias Somfield, of the Paradise Pack. Alpha's prerogative brought me here."

Serhan's eyebrow arched. "How is that?"

Without raising his eyes, Tobias jerked his head in my direction. "I protect this woman on his orders."

"She is not your consort then?" Suspicion filled his gaze. Ayşe had apparently told a different story.

Consort: I much preferred that word to *looney*.

"No, but she was an unmated consort to my alpha. She is a friend of wolves. Ayşe invited me at the Bazaar to dine with you tonight. It would be rude for me to refuse a share of your hunt, and because of the duty I hold to my alpha, I could not leave her behind. The shewolf likely told you of my display earlier today. I was not attempting to deceive, only to expedite. I ask welcome for me and my ward at your haunches, and bring no rival."

Who was this formal wolf and where had my Tobias, who earlier in the day had yelled at me to "get out of the pisser," gone?

Serhan's mouth cycled, as though chewing on Tobias's explanation. "She is a hood."

"Relinquished."

The alpha sneered. "What difference does that make? Istanbul is home to a hundred spiders weaving ten thousand webs. My pack wishes to be caught in none of them."

I grew tired of being spoken of in the third person. I knelt, holding out my arms for display and rolling my head to the side. "My name is Gerwalta Kline, daughter of Brünhild Kline, Red Matron of the Americas. I seek only peace and conversation at your fire."

The alpha blinked his surprise. "You have a talent for lupine etiquette."

"I was the consort of an alpha," I said, weaving the loose ends of my truth with the slack weave of Tobias's lie. "I know many things."

Tension built palaces in the space of a few moments. In the midst of our conversation, the shadows had grown shapes, sulking out of the darkness, a dozen eyes burning me in effigy.

At last, the alpha abated. He raised his left hand, turning it once as though screwing in a light bulb. In that motion, his pack eased. Where animosity had festered, hospitality emerged. Tobias took my hand again, pulling me along as wolves, young and old, female and male, fell in behind us, urging us along. When the ceiling above us rose and the walls tapered out, both Tobias and I were struck dumb.

Neither cave nor chamber, the space in which we found ourselves merited confusion. As high as a cathedral, and yet, with earthen walls like one of the old day shelters of the Black Forest, the wolves dwelled in an archaeological wonder. In the midst of it, a fire burned. Not too large; so deep beneath the ground, I suspected that the temperature remained largely unchanged through the years. No, the fire was merely for light and, perhaps, comfort. The smoke rose, filtering through a ceiling from which pipes dropped and plants grew down.

"A place for dead." Ayşe had managed to sidle up to me without my realizing. She'd rid herself of the traditional cover in the interim, adding to my suspicions of why she felt the need to wear it on the huey streets above. "How do you say… a tom?"

"A tomb," I corrected, then looked instinctively for crevices where coffins rested. None could I find, but perhaps the pack had removed them? "Ayşe, is this where you live?"

She nodded. "Some of the time."

"But why? Why are you here in the middle of the city, and not out in the mountains or the woods?"

"Because here are jobs," she said. "Our place in the Bazaar? It feeds us all."

"The leather shop," Tobias said. "The labors of your hunt?"

Serhan laughed, inviting us to sit by the fire. Several younger wolves, no more than nine or ten years old, vacated the space. "Have you seen a single cow or sheep in this city since you arrived?"

A woman appeared, wearing a brown skirt from under which her bare, besmirched feet shuffled, her hair tied back in a white scarf like an extra from *Fiddler on the Roof*. She deposited bowls of a thick stew into our hands, then dropped a quarter loaf of the same type of crusty bread Amy and I had gorged ourselves on a few days ago atop it. Given that there was no utensil, I suspected the bread was meant to serve as both side dish and spoon.

"Only this, and on the plates of the cafes in the street above." Tobias played the conversation like a string section called on to answer a bellow of horns. As one trained all my life for diplomatic pursuit—though, my mother had sneered, diplomacy was art beyond the grasp of most wolves—I had to admire the ease with which he took to the calling. "Another pack provides the product then?"

Serhan acknowledged it. "All with permission of the onyx hoods. Permission purchased by a steep percentage of the proceeds."

The anger that shot through me wasn't because I took any offense on behalf of the hoods, but because I couldn't believe the unfairness of it.

Serhan seated himself across from me, examining me. "Something troubles you, Miss Kline?"

"I recognized a silver decree posted above your shop today, even if it was in another language." *Pause to swallow the lamb stew.* "A Writ of Authority, official permission to operate your shop? The reds outlawed that sort of practice a century ago. And you, living here, stories below the city in a crypt, forced to stay out of sight? What kind of old-world practices are these?"

Serhan leaned forward. "Where is it you suppose you are at? This is not the Americas, or England. Nor are we in the gleaming shadow of Schloss Wolfsretter. This is Istanbul. This is Constantinople. This is Byzantium. We are not some privileged, pampered pack. Your modern world is all boxes. A cradle when you are a baby. A house when you are an adult. A coffin when you die. We are the *gökkurt*, descended from Asena himself. No one will confine us in a box, not even the onyx."

I leaned forward, searching for recognition in Tobias's expression, but he seemed just as clueless as I was, confirmed a moment later when, his mouth full of potatoes and lamb, he leaned forward.

"Asena?"

"Yes, Asena. The father of us all. Come, now, Tobias, you must know?"

A dribble of broth raced down his chin. "I'm sorry, no."

A grin crossed Serhan's face. He rose to his feet, encouraged at intervals by the claps, the cheers, the shouts of his pack. From out of nowhere, a violin rang out, scratching against the surface in an echo of the daily calls to prayer the city above rang out with five times a day.

"*Aramızda kim Asena'yı tanımıyor?*" His arms akimbo, Serhan spun. His wolves shouted a response as he pointed to several in turn. Then, back to us, he brought his long, dirt-encrusted finger. "What wolf does not know Asena? A wolf who does not know Asena does not know how he is a wolf."

"I am a wolf because my father and mother were wolves."

The alpha shooed away Tobias's retort with a wave of his hand. "But why was your father? And his father before him? And his before him? Because of Asena. We are *all* his children. It was he whom the shewolf chose to father our people, and she by him who gave birth to the ten packs. So werewolves came into the world, but we... we are sons of the eldest pup born of Asena, Ashina. We are the truest wolves."

I elbowed Tobias in the side. "So maybe you're not English after all. You're descended from Turks."

My guardian ignored me. Rightfully.

"And have you been in Istanbul all this time?" Tobias asked. "Living here, beneath the city?"

"We have always been Turks, and so our packlands have moved with the fate of our ancestors, as have the Turkish hueys. From the Steppe, to the Caucasus, to Anatolia, and into the Balkans. Our pack was among those who took the city from the Romans."

But that brought up a question in my head that the others didn't seem concerned with. "And what about hoods? Um... *başlık*?" I asked. The mere utterance of the word sent a hush of the gaiety of the pack. "Where did they come from?"

Serhan's smile flatlined. "Do not you know? Your kind who flies? Your kind who speaks to birds?"

"Birds?" I almost tugged Tobias's shirt sleeve clear off. "Tobias..."

His hand lay over mine, stilling it and my words. "Protecting this relinquished hood is not the only reason I... *we* are in Istanbul, Serhan Bey. We're here trying to find someone. Several someones, actually."

Serhan fanned the air. "In a city like this, finding one is difficult. Finding many, easy. Who is it you seek?"

"He has had many names," I said. "A vampire. A *very* old vampire. Most know him as Vlad."

The name. So simple: four letters, one syllable. For all that, *v-l-a-d* might have spelled *stop* or *silence*. Even the wolves who stayed some distance from the fires on the edges of the crypt stilled. In the chamber, a chill descended upon me, upon *us*. I felt at once old worries rise. A moment ago, I'd been surrounded by a clan of people who had welcomed me into their home, such as it was. Now, I felt the weight of lupine curses.

And only one wolf who would defend me.

I focused in on Serhan as I shot to my feet, my hand clutching the silver dagger's hilt. The alpha needed but give an order, and the pack would take their wolves and rip me limb from limb. Instead, Serhan turned to Ayşe, barking out gruff foreign words before, without any further explanation, he whirled, trouncing off into the darkness, diving into shadow.

Ayşe's disappointment was palpable as she began to lead us back the way we'd come in. Neither Tobias nor I needed ask what had transpired, though I was certain that he, like me, desperately wished to learn the *why*. As we reached the street, Ayşe covered herself and led us back toward the main street.

"We can find our way from here, Ayşe," Tobias offered. "That hood is still nearby. I can sense her. Both Geri and I apologize for any offense we committed. We never meant to upset you."

"It is not... the word you use, *offense*?" The shewolf rounded a corner, practically clinging to the walls. "It is *haram*. You say, I think, forbidden? Yes, *forbidden*, for us to talk about the Ravens."

I fisted Tobias's shirt. "You do know about them!" Despite the daggers Tobias shot me, I couldn't let this go. "Please, Ayşe, tell us what you know. We promise, we won't tell anyone."

Tobias sighed. "Geri, she's under alpha orders. She can't say a thing. Come, the hood that's patrolling is very close. Let's not get anyone into trouble, or get noticed ourselves. Good night, Ayşe. Thank you for letting us sit at your fire."

The girl nodded once, turned to go back into their subterranean landscape, then halted. Inner conflict pulled tight the expression on her face. "Advice?"

Was she asking for it, or offering to give it? Tobias nodded some sort of acceptance.

"Birds that hunt need to soar high," Ayşe said. "But please, do not look for them. You will die. That is all I can say."

SEVENTEEN

"Baby, you have to let this go."

I was trying. Damn it, I was trying. "But they were opening up to us! And then I had to make a mountain out of a molehill. One tiny mention of birds, and I blurted out Vlad's name, and then we were personae non gratae. I swear I have that 'awkward non-sequitur' award of the year cinched this year."

I could only hope that Tobias had some luck in getting them to accept our apology. When he told me earlier in the morning he was going to find Ayşe at the Bazaar and offer our regrets, I had begged to come along. He'd insisted that it would go over better without me there. When even Caleb agreed it was probably better to let the wolves work it out among themselves, I deferred.

Amy, however, had not. The second she found out Tobias was on his way back to that magnificent place, she was out of bed and on the prowl in record time.

Caleb continued massaging my shoulders, relieving the tension that had me wound up his primary objective. "One, let's try to limit Latin phrases to one per statement. And two, I don't think there's any casual way to bring up the Prince of Darkness in polite conversation. You saw an open window, you jumped for it. I would have done the same thing."

"No, you would have gotten one of the female wolves alone, then turned on your awesome sex-god powers and charmed the information out of her. In Turkish too."

His mouth came down the juncture of my neck and my collarbone. "Sex-god powers? How would you know about those?"

With the shifting mood, I softened my voice. "I've never left your place unsatisfied."

"*Mmm*, true, but you've never left my place entirely... fulfilled."

"If the brochure is that great, I can only imagine the actual view is mind-blowing."

"Oh, it's *blowing*." His hot breath funneled through pursed lips as he blew on my ear, sending a wave of anticipation up my spine. "We're home alone. We should take advantage of that."

My head tilted to the side, giving Caleb de facto permission to ply willing flesh with his demanding mouth. "Technically, Inga and Igor are home, even if they're in torpor in the cistern."

"They won't hear us if we go upstairs, which leaves only one question: your room or mine?"

I could see it in my mind, how simple this would be. I'd stand, turn to Caleb, offer him my hand. He'd take it, stand as well, and kiss me. We'd fumble our way upstairs, taking only brief glances beyond each other to navigate the climb and then, the door, and then the bed. We'd take turns robbing each other of clothing, piece by piece surrendered to the floor, until ultimately, we'd stand before each other wearing only the balance of our confidences.

I'd call out his name when he entered me, and think of another…

That broke the vision, and suddenly, what my body had wanted, my heart denied.

I needed more time. I needed more distance. I needed to just convince myself that I had to move on.

I needed an excuse.

"Caleb?"

His voice vibrated against my skin. "Mmm?"

"I've been thinking." I swallowed hard, trying to block out the sensations he sent spiraling around my body as his hands encircled me from behind, one of them sneaking its way under my shirt. "This is going to sound…" *Crazy? Puritan? Prudish?* "…old-fashioned, but I think I want to wait."

Clearly, his blood had already vacated his brain for other parts of his body, as he asked in a dreamy tone, "Wait for what?"

"Wait for this," I said, pulling away, turning to face him. "I never thought I'd be so traditional, but where I come from, this—" I motioned between us. "This doesn't happen until marriage. I thought I could do this, but you've seen what happens when I try. I think it's because, deep in my heart, I know that I want to wait."

Undeterred, the slayer leaned forward, balancing on his hands as he ghosted a kiss over my lips. "I bet parts of you deeper down think otherwise. And I'm willing to go searching for those parts. Way—" *Kiss.* "Deep—" *Kiss.* "Down."

He fell facedown onto the couch as I took to my feet. He'd only sat himself up when I turned to face him from the hall.

"I'm sorry, but I'm not negotiable on this."

EIGHTEEN

They dragged themselves in before the morning light, each wearier than the last. Igor and Tobias had scouted most of the districts on the Asian side, each night ringing out further into districts springing to life on the edges of the eternally-growing city. Three weeks of effort, and nothing more to show for it than the discovery of a few good all-night kebab houses. Inga and Caleb, in the meantime, had cut lines through the European neighborhoods, testing even the endurance of an immortal.

"Cities should not be allowed to grow so vast," the vampire lamented as she fell back on the couch, brown hair falling like a halo around her. "Damn Istanbul. It's like a cancer, a giant, pulsing tumor spreading across continents. Give it another hundred years, and this city will cover the world and strangle the whole planet."

Amy managed to wander in just as the vampires made it home. "I think it's going to bump into Beijing and, well, frankly, all of China before that can happen. Morning, Geri. We still on for the boat ride today?"

Tobias looked up from his breakfast of fried sausage and egg. "Boat ride?"

"We're taking a Bosporus cruise."

Caleb ran a hand over his face. "Great. We'll spend our nights looking for villainous vampires, but you guys pretend to be tourists and take in all the sights. What's the point in having that training space upstairs if you're only going to use it for yoga?"

"First, Geri has actually been teaching me a few attack forms, so there." Amy peeked over the fridge, a carafe of orange juice in hand. "And two, we thought it might be a good idea to see the city from a different perspective—especially since you won't let the poor hueys go out at night all defenseless and alone. Seriously, you guys have been at this for three weeks, and have nothing to show for it but a cryptic message from a werewolf who now refuses to talk to you. The worst thing that happens is that we get nothing out of it."

Caleb sat up. "And the best thing that happens is that you get *someone* out of it." He turned to me with begging eyes. "Geri, come on, you know she only agreed to this to scope out guys, right?"

"Caleb Helsing, are you calling Amy a flirt?"

"I'm calling Amy the female version of me." He blushed under my scornful gaze. "The old me. Before I was with you, I mean."

I slipped my cell phone and bottle of water into a backpack and threw it over my shoulder. "I'll make sure she behaves. And uses protection, if it comes to it. In the meantime, you guys get rest. Only two nights until full moon. We'll have to spend tonight finding someplace to stash our own werewolf during it."

"I still volunteer my room."

The slayer's hand lashed out in response to Amy's quip. "See? That's what I'm talking about."

<hr>

The only revelation that emerged from our two-hour cruise was that there were dolphins in the Bosporus Strait, something which made total sense in hindsight but which I hadn't anticipated.

Amy folded her hands and leaned against the railing. "It really is a beautiful city. Isn't it?"

"Indeed."

"And you still want to go back to Paradise?"

I shrugged. "Not Paradise, maybe. But someplace like it, not too far away. Sault Ste. Marie, maybe."

Sunlight bounded off the water, forcing Amy to shield her eyes. "And then?"

"And then... what?"

With a sway of her arm, she indicated the city, as though it were evidence in some court proceedings. "The world is so big. You got your degree, you can go so many places with it. What are you going to do in the backwoods of Michigan? What is Caleb going to do? I picked up on his type the moment I met him: likes fashion, fancy restaurants, clubbing. One-hundred-percent city boy. You think he's going to go along with the Suey Ain't Mary plan?"

"Sault Ste. Marie," I corrected. "Why is it that he'd have to go along with it?"

"Hello? Because he's your boyfriend, and he's going to either want to be in the same place as you, or stop being *with* you. Seriously, Geri, what was your goal when you came to Chicago to begin with? Let me interrupt you, because you probably don't know, and I do: You were trying to escape Paradise. Even if you're not willing to admit that to yourself, that's what you were after. You either have to accept that Caleb is part of that escape, or let him go."

The words struck me harder than if I'd fallen in the waters below. "You're blowing things way out of proportion here. I'm only twenty-two. *Barely* twenty-two. I don't have to make those kind of long-term decisions yet."

"Sorry, but you do," she countered. "Didn't you tell me just a few days ago that, before the two of you hit it off, he was a bit of a lady's man?"

"By his own admission. And Inga's reports. So?"

She rolled her eyes. Something I was saying really watered the stupid tree. "If a guy like that goes cold turkey it means he's found—and believe me, even I can't believe I'm using this term—'the one.' Caleb is planning a life with you, and if you're not doing the same, you got to let him know. Trust me on this."

In the eddies swirling off the boat in the waters below, murky visions of a life with Caleb emerged. Running from city to city, always in hiding, unless under the protection of a vampire who already admitted she was living on borrowed time. Tall buildings, landscapes of concrete, crowds of people everywhere. Everywhere. So many people. And kids. He'd want kids. Lots of them. He was the last of his kind, after all. At the very least, it was his duty to procreate. And what would I be then, but a breeding sow, raising slayers who I couldn't even get to understand the kind of person I'd been before my mother had relinquished me?

Amy's hand settled on my back. "You see it, right?"

"I do." The words cracked when forced over a dry palate. "But he loves me."

A softness overcame her. "All the more reason to end it."

Only a blind man could stare at the sun and deny its light. "Damn it, you're right."

"I know I am. Now, let's talk about Tobias…"

My hands went up. "Whoa, remember that big talk about werewolves and hoods you and I had a few weeks ago? Tobias was mated, and wolves mate for life. No exceptions."

"I know," she said. "But there's something between the two of you, something… dare I say, primal? You two just click. Like, platonically, even if the physical stuff is never a part of it. Which I can't believe I, of all people, am saying, but that's not so bad, is it?"

"Oh, yeah, we'd be great together. Long walks through the woods, baking cookies, sighing mournfully in unison each morning. Twice on Sundays. No, Amy. A life with Tobias means living with the Paradise Pack. It's me watching Cody and Lisa and their perfect little cubs running around for the rest of my life under the shadow of my mother's domain. It's about the worst thing I could think of."

"Yeah, I suppose so." Her eyes settled on one of the boat's crew handing out glasses of tea on the aft deck. Igor had been right; tea really was everywhere. "Too bad Tobias didn't get hit with that serum stuff that vamps have. It could solve all of this."

"That serum was designed to work on alphas and betas," I said. "Tobias is neither."

"How do you know?"

"Because he's not. It's that simple. Cody's his alpha, Rick's his beta."

"And back in England…?"

"His dad, then his brother, then… I'm not sure. Someone else who kicked him out."

"And Kara was a beta in her pack. Isn't that what he said?"

I nodded. "What are you getting at?"

"Nothing, just based on everything I've learned about werewolves and hoods and slayers so far, there's a lot of heriditary stuff involved in the way you guys determine leadership. Now, I might think it outdated and undemocratic, but if that's the way y'all roll, fine. *But* in that case, wouldn't political marriages be a thing? Wouldn't it be weird for Tobias, son and brother of an alpha, to be mated to another pack's beta?"

"Amy, I don't know where you hide all these smarts, but they're amazing."

"Mostly I keep them in my bra. If guys are going to stare at the girls anyway, they might as well get an education in the process."

"I think several of your recent boyfriends should be given honorary doctorates, then." Master's degrees at least. "But even if it's true, that he has the genetic inclination for being a pack leader, that doesn't make him an alpha."

Amy now turned all her attention on me, forgetting about the tea guy. "What would?"

"You mean, how does a wolf become an alpha?"

"Yeah, I guess."

"Well, that's simple," I said. "The previous alpha dies, and he rises to take his place—whether that's through the agreement of the pack, or through a formal challenge for leadership. Or he starts his own pack, but that's something that hardly ever happens. It takes a wolf of extreme strength, both physical and mental, to do something like that—not to mention the fact that he risks lunacity in the process."

Amy's head tilted to the side. "Lunacity?"

Even if the last few weeks had seen Amy take a crash course in all things supernatural, there were still some gaps in her knowledge.

"Lunacity," I repeated. "Or what we usually call moon madness. Wolves are so orientated towards pack that their psychology hinges on it during full moons. They can only go a few lunar cycles away or they become their wolf forever. It drives them crazy, makes them very dangerous. It's an obligation of the hoods to eliminate a wolf who gets to that point. I've seen three in my life." My chest tightened at the recollection, of being at my mother's side as she dispatched a creature trapped in fur but with remnants of a human soul I could still sense. "I hope I never have to see it again."

"But what does that have to do with becoming a new alpha?"

"A wolf who decides to try and be his own alpha has to have three things: an ability to make it through three lunar cycles away from his pack without going insane, the release of his previous alpha, and a beta wolf who's willing to risk the break as well. That's the part that stops most defections. One can rebel, but getting a beta to buy in at the risk of going insane and permanently wolf is almost impossible. It's generally only done in times of war and famine, to give the pack the best hope of surviving by immigrating into new regions."

"I see." Amy laced her fingers together. "Maybe you can live in Suey Ain't Marie and he can commute to the pack? Is that a thing?"

"Afraid not."

"Damn it. Well, then, I might have to resume my get-Geri-hooked-up campaign."

"I could jump into this water right now, Amy."

"Go ahead. I double dog dare you. More than that, I double *wolf* dare you."

NINETEEN

Tobias stood at the door, staring at his upturned palm.

Stalling.

I put down the book I'd been reading, a droll history of the Ottoman system of government. "You seem to be treading water there, chief. You sure you're comfortable with this?"

A wispy grimace preceded his words. "What choice do I have? Unless you want to tie a saddle to me and ride me through the streets."

I snapped my fingers. "Damn, I didn't pack my saddle, and I never learned to ride bareback…"

"Based on your tepid love life, seems you haven't learned to ride *barefront* either."

Switching the subject ASAP was the only way to keep from blanching. "Scared you can't trust the Pera Pack?"

He barely bobbed his head. "Ayşe's sticking to orders; she still hasn't uttered a single word to me when I've approached her in the Bazaar. Luckily, she still *listens*. I told her I needed shelter for the full moon, and that I'd wait down the street for an answer. A half-hour later, another wolf came to tell me I could pass the night with them, as a lupine courtesy."

"The last thing the alpha of a pack trying to avoid attention wants is some foreign wolf to run about on full moon, causing trouble with hueys," I concurred. "If I had my hood, I'd build a silver cage for you in your bedroom upstairs."

"So your suggestion for an alternative to passing the moon with a local pack would be to imprison me. You still want to claim you're not into BDSM?"

"Try chaining me up sometime and see."

His eyes jolted away as a spark of crimson warmed his neck. Were Tobias's jabs about rough play a cover for his own proclivities? How interesting.

"I still can't believe Caleb convinced Inga to go with Igor to Spain for the weekend." The werewolf shoved his overseer-approved phone into his back pocket. "I guess you were right about his charm, huh? Even convinced the daughter of Dracula herself to give in to him. How did he manage to do that?"

"By promising we wouldn't step a foot out of the house after dark until they got back. I think he even pinky-promised."

"So you, Amy, and Caleb are planning a quiet night at home?"

"Oh, hell no. Amy would open a pop-up Kama Sutra studio. Caleb and I are going out to dinner, then he said something about going to see Hagia Sophia."

"He lied to Inga?"

"He prefers to think of it as a technicality. We aren't stepping *a* foot out. We're using both feet."

Tobias laughed. "Remind me never to get into a negotiation with a slayer. Slippery eel, that boyfriend of yours. Hagia Sophia… That's that big church-turned-mosque thing, right? Is it even open at night?"

"I think we're just going to walk by it. He said there's a beauty to it you can only see at night."

He grinned and tapped me on the shoulder. "So he thinks taking you to a huge church is going to finally get you into bed? Told you telling him you were 'waiting for marriage' would make him think you're a religious nut."

"My sex life is not a venue for your comedic efforts."

"No, it's the venue for your own."

The sepia orb crawled its way out from behind the city skyline, pulling me in a way I hadn't felt in months: anticipation, dread, longing, desire. A familiar swirl of extremes that, in my huey existence, left me anxious. Or, maybe it was because I'd planned to talk to my boyfriend about how I didn't see our relationship as having legs—despite the fact that it brought us all the way to Istanbul to track down an infamous vampire and, eventually, kill him.

"The moon sure is pretty tonight."

Caleb turned a smile to me that made the cosmos in the sky above dim in comparison. "It's not the only thing."

"Caleb..."

Any effort to peel away was met with an equal effort on his part to pull me closer, which ultimately resulted in his tugging my arms behind my back and holding them there.

"You need to just accept the fact that you're beautiful, Geri. Every time I bring it up, it's 'oh, Caleb, stop.' It's like you don't want me to compliment you."

"Oh, god no. Compliment away. It's just..."

Not yet. Not out of nowhere.

"Predictable."

He brushed a kiss over my lips, and I tried not to notice how good it felt, how my bottom lip tingled, how my body instinctively leaned into his, chasing the kiss.

"It's possible," he admitted as he pulled away and we resumed our leisurely stroll along the avenue. "You're the first woman I've been with long enough for my wit to become seasoned. I'll try harder in the future."

Worms crawled through my belly. *Change the subject.* Beside us, an ancient wall stood, each of its stones meticulously shaped and placed, like a puzzle. "I thought you were taking me to see Hagia Sophia. Isn't this the old hippodrome?"

Just then, a doorway emerged in the wall, an old (though probably hundreds of years newer than the stonework surrounding it), heavy metal thing that looked like it had been recommissioned from a submarine.

Caleb flicked the padlock that held it closed. "That's new."

"That's new?" I repeated. "You've been wherever this leads before?"

"Not in about a decade or so, but yeah."

"What is it?"

The slayer shifted his body, blocking the view of his hands from a group of nearby Asian tourists. If they saw the glow that radiated from his palm, turning the obstacle into a molten sludge, they probably just thought it was a cell phone screen lighting up. Liquid metal dripped to the ground as hinges groaned, pulled on for the first time in who knew how long.

"It's like Hagia Sophia's slayers-and-guests-only entrance."

Doubts refused to be dismissed. "You sure you know where this goes?"

"Unless a two-thousand-year-old passageway has been rerouted in the last decade. Don't be nervous. It's full moon, the weakest time of the month for vampires, and I was running through these tunnels before I could read."

I feigned surprise. "I didn't know you could read."

"There's a lot of things I can do that you still haven't found out about."

Caleb's solarium became a lantern, giving definition to a passage sloping downward. I was getting jealous of how many diverse applications there were for the slayer talents.

"First, werewolves living in an old Byzantine crypt, and now, slayer passages underneath one of the most historical parts of the city?" I stepped over an old drainage pipe laid over our path. "It's like this city is built over a foundation of supernatural haunts."

"This city is built over a foundation of everything," Caleb said. "This part was a passage of the Roman hippodrome. The Byzantines ignored it, but then the Ottomans built stuff on top of that. Istanbul is like cultural moussaka. Slayers have been in this city since it first took shape, but Hagia Sophia and these passages are some of the only remnants of that history."

I pulled my hand back out of his. "Slayers had something to do with building Hagia Sophia?"

"Not building it, just *how* it was built. Whoa, just a second."

I tried to blink definition into being as Caleb's solarium faltered, plunging us into darkness. The slayer slowed our pace, and a moment later, I realized why. Since we'd entered the tunnel, there'd been the sound of dripping, of water pooling at the bottom of walls. As I stepped forward into a cool stream deep enough to cover my ankle, I hoped to high heaven the source was underground and not runoff from the streets or, worse, bubbling up from the sewer.

"It would be really great if you could turn the lights back on. I'd like to see what I'm stepping in so I know if I'm going to need a tetanus shot."

His sloshing feet at least gave me a direction to follow.

"Should be just a few more steps. And yeah, we're through."

My feet cleared the stream just as the cavern around us illuminated anew.

Caleb bounced the relit solarium on his hand. "One defect with these little things: they can't be conjured when I'm standing in water."

A memory resurfaced, of Igor saying much the same thing when we'd first arrived at the rental house. "That was only, like, three inches of water. That tiny bit is enough to flatline you? Maybe those solaria aren't all they're cracked up to be."

"Oh, they're cracked. Just wait until you see why." He took my hand back and hurried me along the path as it twisted and pivoted underneath the streets above. "It will be easier to show you when we're inside. Come on, it's not too much farther."

I could search through a thousand libraries, each with ten thousand books, for a hundred thousand years, and never find words sufficient enough to describe it.

Caleb let go of my hand, allowing me to drift on the breezes of beauty and history, interwoven with stone and light. Hagia Sophia struck me dumb and left me incredulous. It rose above, around, tunneled underneath. It captured the limits of my imagination then mocked it. It was like man had tried to cage heaven. Mineral veins and dozens of stone panels lay over walls and beneath my feet, drawing my attention to a ceiling circumscribed in Arabic letters around a mighty dome above us, punctuated with uncovered mosaics in the apses.

"I have never felt more huey… More *mortal*, than I do at this moment."

Caleb nodded. "My mom used to say that peasants and sultans were equals when they entered here, that it was the only building on the face of the earth so vast in scope it rendered the arrogance of small differences mute. It's… I mean, look at it! It's maybe mankind's greatest achievement, am I right? But it's more than just a church, or even a mosque. Remember what I said about slayers influencing how it was built?"

"Yeah, but how?"

Shyness grabbed a man who'd rarely known its company. "Geri, for all we know, I'm the last slayer."

I cocked my head. "What does that have to do with Hagia Sophia?"

"Because this building, Geri… This big, boisterous, beautiful building is part of my legacy. Inga and Igor have, um… you know, *donations* from me. If I die, they may be able to rescue my kind back from extinction. But being a slayer isn't just genetics, it's training and culture. Igor says he talked to you about hoods training slayers if it ever came to that, but someone needs to carry on our *legacy* too."

"Caleb, I still have no idea what you're talking about."

"Here, let me show you."

He extended his right hand and conjured a solarium. The lemon-sized balls of light were powerful little things, powerful enough to kill a vampire, to turn him to ash. But as it rose at a measured pace upward, controlled, I assumed, by Caleb's will, the most magnificent thing began to happen. Not only did its light cast a warm glow over the interior of the structure, but the beams began to fracture, to turn in on themselves and bounce off mosaic-covered walls. Reds, greens, golds, yellows: a spectrum of brilliance turned into the center, collecting below.

I had to hold up a hand to protect my eyes, stung from the magnificent display. "What is this?"

"This is why this building was made the way it was," Caleb said. "Before the Ottomans converted it to a mosque, every inch of that dome and most of the walls were covered in glass mosaics, all designed specifically for this. This building is both a place of worship, and one of defense. In the Byzantine times, slayers protected this city from vampires. Vlad changed that. Vlad made this his sanctuary. Someday, Geri, a slayer might be able to stand here as I do now, and if the Ravens are here, it will be enough to destroy them all. I hope."

Already boggled by the structure for its own sake, I could hardly grasp the revelation. "This is why we're here, isn't it?"

He didn't deny it. "If we spook one Raven, all we'll do is send him flying. We have to get them all here—or somewhere like it. And when Vlad and the others stand here, they'll die. Inga knows this, Igor knows it, and now you know it."

"But what do you expect me to do with this? Why did you tell me?"

He dropped his hand, and despite the act, the solarium continued to shine above. "Because one day, it may be one of our children who has to undertake this."

"One of our... Caleb, I—"

The heat of his kiss made the ball of solar rays above seem cold by comparison. I'd tasted desire, and longing, and lust, and love. Caleb's mouth on mine spoke of it all and more. It spoke of negotiations, offerings, outcomes. It promised family, a place, meaning. It proffered all this to me with a bonus of pleasure.

This man would do his damnedest to make me happy. He'd make me his.

"Caleb, stop."

In the most technical sense, he did. His lips lingered just beyond mine as our breath mingled. When had I begun breathing so hard? When had I come to be completely wrapped in his embrace? With open eyes, I could see just how brilliantly his light shown, as though the fire of desire uncurling within him, within us, fueled the solarium in the dome above.

"If this is because I told you I wanted to wait until marriage—"

"It's not." He licked lips which then curled into a smile. "I mean, that's a bonus, but that's not why I'm asking. I don't want to go through any more of this life without you. I can wield the sun, but you are my light." He reached up, laced his fingers through my hair.

A touch, a kiss, a brush of his lips on my neck. His sunlight shone above, and the moonlight fell on the building from outside. Both born of the same fire, separated by the lattice of history and purpose. It stirred my veins, lit my desire. I wanted him. God help me, no matter how selfish it was, I wanted him. Let his light outshine mine; I'd be warm in his.

His lips went to my ear. "I love you, Geri. Please say *yes*."

"Caleb, I…" My heart fell back into shadow, and my body shook. "…can't."

The brilliance turned blistering. His solarium doubled, tripled in size.

"What?"

I pulled back from him as flares licked up his arms, singing the sleeves of his shirt.

"I want to. God, Caleb, you have no idea how much I want to believe that you and I could work, that we could make a future together. But we have completely different expectations about what we want, about where we see ourselves."

"How can you know that?" With both hands on either side of my face, he pressed a hard kiss to my lips. "All I want is you. We'll find a way to make it work."

I shook my head, even as he held it. "But I know what I want, and as much as I *like* you, Caleb, and no matter how much I tell myself to just let a good thing happen for once, I don't love you. I won't do that to you. I won't make promises that someday it could change, when I know it won't."

In a snap, hope turned bitter.

"How can you know?" Caleb dropped his hands and backed away. The brilliant sphere above began to descend, moving in parallel with him. "You don't even know who or what you are. You're too wrapped up in who you *used* to be to think about who you could become."

"I know you're angry, but you don't need to—"

"Or maybe Cody was right. Maybe you are too in love with him to ever give anyone else a chance."

Now the heat radiating in the place was my own. "How do you know about that?"

"Just because you won't talk to me doesn't mean the others won't."

My fist clenched so tightly my nails cut flesh. "Amy."

"Tobias, actually. And here's the kicker on that one." His arms flailed through one revolution. "He did it because he actually thought Cody was right. He told me—*begged* me to step up if I had any intentions of being with you, and get you to forget about him. But you can't, can you?"

"*Tobias* told you?" But that didn't make any sense. Yes, he was *my* friend, but Tobias hated Caleb. Why would he encourage the very man he told me wasn't good enough for me to woo me? "It's not about Cody. That was all over two years ago."

"Ha! That's who you think *him* is?" He threw his head back and barked a laugh, and as I faced the slayer, I saw my shadow stretch before me. "You think you can never love me? If that were true, Geri, you'd see the relationship you're choosing over ours. That you've already chosen. Fine, good luck with that. Just remember, when you wake up from that fantasy, that you and I can actually work. Better hurry, though, because I can't wait forever."

I began to run even before he'd finished turning, making to exit from one of the main doors instead of back through the underground passage we'd used to sneak onto the grounds, even as the aurora of Caleb's solarium chased along.

"Please, Caleb! Don't—"

My words died in a blaze of red and orange. Fire blinded me, bound me. It seeped into my veins, trying to consume me.

I wouldn't let it. I breathed it in, and made myself its master.

Little made sense when I walked in the door: how I got back, where I had been, how much time had passed. All I knew was that I was tired. So crushingly, utterly tired. Every bone and every muscle ached. If this house had a bathtub, I'd draw one up and probably drown falling asleep in the soothing waters. My skin felt two sizes too small for my body, and scorched.

The full moon dipped low in the sky, taking my determination with it. My body surrendered to gravity as I fell back into the low couches in the parlor. Tea. I wanted tea. I didn't have the strength to make it. Habit took my hand down to my pants pocket. Maybe someone had texted. The device proved useless, however, its plastic frame bubbled from the heat of the solarium. The cracked screen wouldn't even light.

The night outside waned, and I wanted to chase it as it blinked out. I closed my eyes, and ran into its oblivion.

TWENTY

The tide pulled in, the tide pulled out. Each wave rolled me, a gentle cycle of taking and giving. The water became flesh and wrapped itself around me.

My head rolled into his shoulder as he scooped me off the couch. "Why are you sleeping down here? I thought Caleb said you guys were staying down at some fancy hotel in Beşiktaş."

How did he know about that? No matter, I shook my head as he navigated the narrow staircase. "Never made it."

"Please tell me you guys didn't do it like dogs in some back alley." A chuckle rumbled in his chest. "As a dog, even I look down on that."

"We didn't do anything. We broke up."

He stopped, and my legs gave out beneath me as he set me on my feet. "What do you mean, you broke up?"

I could barely get my eyes open. God, why was I so tired? Depression? Stress? "He asked me to… I don't know, he wanted me to teach our children something? I think he might have asked me to marry him."

The werewolf sniffed the air. "I'm guessing, by the fact that Caleb's not here, you said *no*."

He could know the truth, but he didn't need to know the whole truth. "In so many words."

"And how did he take that?"

"He hit me with a solarium."

"He what?" With a jerk on my shoulder, Tobias spun me around, examining me for damage. "I'm going to kill him. What happened? Where are you hurt?"

"I'm fine?" A hint of surprise took my voice up a few notes. "No damage, other than a ruined cell phone. I must have just caught the edge of it."

"Thank god." The werewolf ran a hand through his hair. Fretting. My reliable, tough werewolf was fretting. "You smell different, though. Did he at least apologize?"

I tried to think back to the aftermath, but all I could draw was a huge blank. "I'm not sure. It's no big deal. I'm obviously okay. I'm not even sad about the break-up, except we still need him. Has he called you at all? Texted?"

"Only once saying I shouldn't worry about walking in on you two because of the fancy hotel thing. He's probably there, licking his wounds. Come on, let's get you into bed."

"Can I… Can I come sleep in your room?"

Tobias gasped out a laugh. "Geri, that's hardly…"

"What?" I asked. "Appropriate? A good idea? We slept in the same room in Chicago for almost a year while I was dating Caleb. How is it a worse idea now that I've broken up with him?"

"Because you're…" He held up his hands, fingers splayed, as though he could gather the explanation from the air and press it into a ball. "…grieving."

"I am *not* grieving." I could cock a hip with the best of them. "Fine. I'll go to sleep in my…"

I had barely turned to storm away when, seizing me by the arm, Tobias tugged me back the opposite way.

"You're so frustrating, you know that? You think this is about you. Seriously, how can you be the singularly most informed hood I've ever known when it comes to werewolf behavior and still be so utterly clueless?"

He pulled me into the bedroom he and Caleb shared. The footprint was identical to the one Amy and I had on the other side of the house, the exception being a blanket hung over an east-facing window to block out morning light. It made sense for two nocturnal beings, but I was surprised at the relief I felt in the dark. The door shut with a little too much force. I didn't need my old hood skills to see I'd ticked off the wolf somehow.

"I can go back to the couch if I'm that much of a nuisance."

"Makes no difference. My Geri-meter has never turned off."

I blinked as his form took shape in the darkness, features inking themselves on my irises. Maybe the room wasn't as dark as I thought.

"What does that mean?"

"The others can't sense you anymore," he said as he peeled off his shirt and pelted it against the floor. "And you can't sense them. But you... The intensity changes, but I can still sense *you*. It hit me like a brick wall about a block away: your sadness, your confusion, your guilt. I'm awash in it. *Grief*, Geri. Don't think for a moment I'm not familiar with its markers. I've been stewing in it since the day my brother died, since my mate was kidnapped."

"I might be a little down, but it would be insulting to you to say breaking up with Caleb affected me even one-tenth the way losing Kara did you."

"Yes, it would."

His hands went to his belt, undoing the buckle. Suddenly, my emotions could be described as anything but grief.

"A small cut still bleeds," Tobias said. "If another of my pack suffered, I'd comfort them. My instincts say to... *comfort* you? I suppose that's as good a word as any."

A tiny drop of conflict rose in my stomach, even as Tobias's pants dropped to the floor. Yes, he was a wolf—which included, on full moon nights as last night had been, going commando.

"Meaning?"

He pointed to the bed. *His* bed, not Caleb's. "Lie down."

I swallowed. "And you?"

"Well, I bloddy well can't sleep in his bed, if that's what you're asking," he said. "That slayer wears too much damned cologne. It's hard enough being in the same room with him."

The laughter came despite its improbability.

"I'll take the floor, just like back in Chicago."

"In your wolf?"

He turned the other cheek. Literally. "Yeah, so?"

"Right after a full moon? Aren't you tired as hell?"

"On so many levels. What's the difference?"

"Then share the bed with me." I couldn't believe what I was saying. "Besides, I... I need you to be..."

"Comforted." He turned, and I managed to keep my eyes locked on his. "But we both understand that comfort has definitive limits. Right?"

I nodded. "Right."

TWENTY-ONE

Instinct told me we'd slept through the day, even if the blanket over the window kept the changing angles of sunlight from confirming it. Oxygen flooded my muscles as I stretched long, then let my body go limp. I couldn't remember the last time I'd felt so rested.

Tobias's arm fell over me, pulling my body back into his. Air flooded my lungs as I drew in a breath. He held me. Tobias held me. I was a relinquished hood in bed... with a wolf. And I *wanted* him to hold me.

"I'm so hungry, I could eat a whole lamb."

"Me, too. I'm famished."

"Famished?" Tobias lifted his head enough to glance at me through one open eye as I looked back over my shoulder. "I think my English is rubbing off on you."

"We say *famished* where I come from."

"Do not."

"Do too."

"I have never heard an American use the word *famished*, ever."

"Can we get back to the discussion about the lamb?"

"Indeed." His head collapsed into the pillow. "Lamb dumplings, with that tomato sauce they put on it. We should get dressed and have breakfast at that place down the street again."

"Dumplings. God, I want a whole plate of them."

He squeezed me, which I convinced myself was the same thing as a hug, even if his side of the hug came without any clothing.

"Ask Amy if she wants to go. I need to get some clothes on."

"It's still daylight. She might not even be here."

"She's right outside the door."

I shot bolt upright. "How do you know?"

Tobias grinned as he rolled off the bed. Naked.

Still naked.

"I'm a wolf, remember? I can hear her."

No sooner had he made the declaration than the pounding started at the door. "Gerwalta Kline, I know you're in there. Tell Caleb he's had you long enough. I need details!"

Tobias turned to me, his brow furrowed.

"She thinks I've been in here with Caleb since last night."

"Reasonable conclusion. I don't think she knew about the fancy hotel either. What are you going to tell her?"

I headed for the door. "What do you mean? I'm going to tell her the truth."

"Geri, wait. Let me at least—"

But it was too late. The second I opened the door, Amy's eyes filled with the scene: me, in the clothes I had worn last night; Tobias, wearing nothing but the blanket he'd just ripped off the bed to cover his wolfie bits.

No Caleb.

"Oh. My. God."

My hands flailed about in a mad attempt at distraction. "This isn't what it looks like."

The blonde stuck out one accusatory finger. "So you didn't spend the whole day curled up in bed with Tobias?"

"We only slept together."

I shot daggers at the wolf, even as he scrambled to pull up boxers under the protection of our bedspread. "That kind of statement is not helping."

Turning back to Amy, I continued. "Yes, we slept together. *Literally*, and only *literally*."

Confusion pulled her quirked expression out into broader definition. "So you *metaphorically* slept with Caleb, then came home and crawled in bed with Tobias for some *literal* sleep? Is this some sort of ritualistic, supernatural mate-swap thing?"

"Oh, my god." Tobias growled as he pulled a shirt over his head. "I don't know if it's a girl thing, or an American thing, but do you really just up and ask about each other's sex lives without a thought?"

Big words from a wolf who was constantly on me about mine.

Amy enumerated her virtues on her fingers. "One, it's more of an Amy thing than anything else. And two, you said there was no sex. Did you want to revise that statement?"

The wolf brushed past us. "It remains none of your business."

And with a *thwack!*, the bathroom door was closed and the shower came on.

Alone, she assaulted me and dragged me down the stairs. "Start at the beginning, tell me everything. I thought you said you were going to break up with Caleb last night?"

"I did break up with him. But unfortunately, not until after he'd asked me to marry him. Mate him. Be his baby mama? I'm not sure which one he was going for, but he didn't take it well."

I then explained the fact that he'd whacked me with a solarium, which turned the blonde into a banshee bent on revenge.

"That bastard!"

"I don't think he meant to hit me. I think he was just pulling the energy back into himself, and I got in between. It didn't hurt me. I mean, I don't think it did. I don't remember being in any pain. In fact, now that I think of it, I can't really remember anything that happened after that."

Amy's brow furrowed. "How did you get home?"

I scraped at reluctant memories. "I'm not sure. I just remember walking in the door an hour or so before sunrise and collapsing on the couch."

"And Caleb?"

A big blank spot there too. "Probably just needs some time. Actually, can you text him and make sure he's okay? My phone kinda melted."

She grimaced, even as she pulled out her device. "You still haven't explained how it was that you came to be sleeping next to a naked werewolf all day long."

Heat prickled across my chest. "I just didn't want to be alone, is all. I swear, we didn't do anything. Remember, he can't."

Amy held one hand up. "Look, Geri, I'm not your mother. God knows I'm not, given how much time I spent the last two years trying to get you hooked up with someone. Which... was my fault. You're not the hook-up type. You're the automatic long-term commitment type; I see that now. Anyways, the point is, I'm not going to stand here and pretend like I have any business telling you what to do with your love life, but I will say this: allow for more than twenty four hours between breaking up with your slayer boyfriend before curling up next to your I-swear-he's-just-a-friend werewolf buddy. Even if it's platonic, and even if it's platonic because of some weird mates-for-life condition. You guys are still here on a mission, and if you have to continue to work together, you need to… well, continue to work together."

A knock at the door below drew my attention away, and I spoke to Amy over my shoulder as we went down the stairs. "It was a moment of weakness. And when Caleb comes home, I'll make sure he knows how much of a friend I still consider him. Has he texted back yet?"

"In the last sixty seconds? No."

"He could be asleep. The sun just set, after all."

The man standing outside the door was no doubt a local: A button-down shirt, black hair, olive skin, and a mustache that looked like he'd chopped off a squirrel's tail and glued it to his upper lip. He said a few words in his native tongue, none of which either Amy or I understood.

"He says he has a package for the woman of the house."

Amy and I both looked at Tobias like he'd grown a second head as he joined us in the entryway.

"How in the hell do you know that?" I asked.

"Unlike the two of you, I've actually been studying Turkish while we've been here." The werewolf said a few words back, highly shaped by an English inflection, and dug a few coins out of his pocket. The man nodded his thanks, placing a linen envelope in Tobias's hand in exchange for the tip. "*Teşekkür ederim.*"

I closed the door and engaged both its locks. "Must be a message from Igor. He *loves* being a pen pal and it reeks of vampire."

"Faintly. Like it's been near one but not touched by one." Tobias put the missive to his nose, inhaling. "*You* can smell that?"

"Of course, I can smell it." Then, what Tobias had actually said hit me. "Not touched by one? Is Igor using scribes now?"

Two questions which needed to be answered immediately. When Amy put her hand on my shoulder, I wondered why. Only when her fingers massaged my tension did I realize how clenched up I'd become.

Fine linen paper turned to scraps as Tobias ripped open the envelope.

"Well," I said after a few tense seconds of his eyes playing a tennis match across the page. "What does it say?"

He shook his head. "I don't know. It's not English. It's not even in English letters."

"You mean roman script," Amy corrected as she grabbed the paper from the werewolf's hands. "This is Cyrillic."

"And you read Cyrillic?" I asked hopefully.

The blonde grimaced. "Cyrillic isn't a language. It's an alphabet."

"So what languages use it then?"

"Lots. Russian, Ukrainian… It's used for most of the Balkan languages."

Even as I asked it, even as Amy's eyes went unfocused as she looked into her memory, the pieces had started to fall into place. "Romanian?"

She pondered that a moment, her mouth pursed, lips pulled left. "No, though maybe once upon a time. I mean, Turkish used to be written with Arabic script, didn't it? Why?"

Tobias and I exchanged a look.

"Because," the werewolf said, "Vlad was Romanian." Tobias pulled out his phone, plucking out digits. "We need to get Igor or Inga on the phone now."

"And Caleb!" Amy added, pulling out her own phone.

I pushed her device back down. "There's no point trying again. The Ravens have him."

TWENTY-TWO

"If I had only told him what he wanted to hear…"

"Then you would have been lying."

Amy's rebuke nipped my latest downward spiral of guilt in the bud, even if only temporarily. An hour had passed since the delivery of the letter, and though we still had no idea what it said, couldn't even state with certainty that Caleb was in fact a hostage, we all felt it. Only, where the others were merely perplexed and worried, I was manufacturing self-blame like I was planning to sell it wholesale.

"The last slayer is dead, or will be," I muttered, staring off into space. "And it's all because of me."

"Seriously, you have to stop. We don't know anything. You're jumping to conclusions. Plus, can I remind you that the only one to blame for any crime is the criminal?"

A scratch at the front door made both of us jump. An hour ago, when I'd opened the door to the messenger, I'd done it without a second thought. The last tendrils of sunlight had still streaked across the sky, and that fact had filled me with a false sense of security. Now, with night having descended over Istanbul, every person in the street had become a monster in my mind. A city of fifteen million heinous creatures, all wanting to destroy us. I'd even convinced myself that my ability to sense wolves had returned. The Pera Pack would mount an attack posthaste, as contact with us would eventually lead to retribution on their account.

Amy, however, had found a way to keep a level head, even as my nerves wrapped me in a ball. She looked at the peephole then, bearing some frustration, opened the door just enough to look out.

Tobias's snout pushed into the opening, the precursor to his giant wolf's frame making its way inside. He shook off the mist that clung to the night, spraying the air. The moment the door was closed behind him, he shifted back to his upright form.

I stood, handing him the pile of clothes he'd discarded before heading out. "Anything?"

The werewolf shook his head. "As soon as I got out to the main street, there were too many scents for me to pick out that messenger's. I would have tried going a few blocks in other directions, but I was already getting a lot of worried looks from the locals." He pulled up his jeans and buckled them. For once, Amy seemed not to take any delight in having a naked man in her presence. "There may be plenty of street dogs in Istanbul, but a wolf the size of a pony still sets everyone's teeth on edge. Anything from Igor or Inga?"

Amy pulled out her phone and looked at the screen. "No, but Spain is two hours behind here; it still won't be sunset there for another hour."

"And you sent them a picture of the letter?"

"Of course, but I don't think we have to wait."

She held up her phone and turned the screen our way. On it, a photo of the letter we'd received and, overlaying the lines of text, boxes outlined in red, on top of which English words were superimposed.

She turned the screen back in her direction. "These online translation engines aren't exact, but it's more than we know now. It'd be better if it was printed instead of handwritten."

"Enough, woman!" Tobias exclaimed. "What does it say?"

"Remember, this may not be completely accurate, but…" Amy focused on her phone. "*Think you victor my field? I keep your crusader, want monarch. Throw yourself. I am finding where raptors sit in a high place.*"

She shrugged as the two of us gawked at her.

"I told you, it's not perfect. Look, just try to think *around* the literal translation. The first sentence, 'think you victor my field,' sounds like some arrogant ass boasting about something. Heard enough lines like that through many a break-up."

Tobias balanced his chin on a cupped fist. "One thing we know about Vlad, about all the Ravens, is that they're very full of themselves, so that fits. The crusader is probably Caleb, but sounds like they wanted someone else instead."

Already I was pulling on my boots. "I don't care who they wanted. Who they're getting is me."

"Like hell, they are." Tobias seized me by the forearm, pulling me to my feet. "What do you think you're going to do, Geri? Even with your hood abilities, what *could* you do? Silver doesn't harm them."

"Not on its own, but I still haven't met something that can survive without a head."

"So, what? You're going to magically find a highly-dangerous clutch of vampires we've been searching fruitlessly for for over a month and chop off all their heads, just like that? And without a weapon? I thought you were the one who said we needed to interrogate them first."

"That was before they kidnapped my boyfriend."

"Ex-boyfriend." Amy slid her phone back into her pants pocket. "You two broke up, or don't you remember that part?"

Of course, I remembered! But what had happened afterward? The recollection stunned me for a moment, and I saw myself last night in my mind's eye, running after Caleb as he slayer-walked out of the museum. He'd been moving so fast, what possibly could have caught him? I couldn't. Not that I was as fast as a slayer, not even when I'd been a nascent hood. The only thing as fast as a slayer was a...

"They were there." Realization slapped me in the face. "The dome of Hagia Sophia has windows. Anyone could have seen the light of that solarium."

Amy passed Tobias a look of confusion. The werewolf only grimaced and shook his head. The historical pictures that covered the walls of the rental house had been telling us the answer the whole time. Hell, even Ayşe had told us. We'd wasted so much time when the answer had been in front of us since we'd arrived.

"Remember what Ayşe told us last time she was talking to us? I thought it was a metaphor, telling us not to mess with the Ravens, because they were too dangerous. It wasn't a metaphor at all."

I crossed to the living room, where, over one of the low-slung couches, a painting of Istanbul at its height under the Ottomans hung. The modern city lay anchored on so many of its great monuments. Many of these buildings had been raised under the early sultans, but some of them stretched back to Byzantine times.

"Think. What did Inga and Igor tell us about the Ravens? About Vlad?"

Tobias pulled alongside me. Was he starting to see it too?

"They'd be somewhere that was easily defended," he said.

"Somewhere that wasn't built by the Ottomans. Somewhere that had large crowds nearby," Amy added, making us a trio before the painting. "A place where there were lots of tourists without places to be, people to be accountable to. Easily fed from. Easily used without anyone noticing."

"Vampires can't smell worth a shit, but they can see the faintest light," I said. "Caleb thought we were inside, on a full moon night nonetheless. He didn't think there would be any danger in showing me. But they saw it. They can see almost the whole city from there. It was like a... Like a..."

"A giant bug zapper."

The werewolf and I both gawked at the huey.

"What?" Amy asked. "You've never seen one of those? It's like a cone and the light attracts bugs and then it zaps them—"

"We know what a bug zapper is!" Tobias growled back. He refocused on the scene before us. "The whole time, and we've been running around in its shadow." The werewolf cupped his hand over his chin, pulling on a beard that became more permanent by the day. "It's the perfect place. They're protected by a thousand eyes, and by the fact that they're in a fucking tower. It will be hard, but I think I can do it."

I rounded on him with speed a cheetah would envy. "You're not going anywhere near the Ravens. It's my fault they got Caleb, and I'll be the one to get him back."

"Unless we're going to wait for Inga and Igor to come back, which I'm guessing would be tomorrow night at the soonest, assuming that the professor can't leave Spain until he gets a belly full of his special diet blood, then it has to be me. I'm not going to let two hueys get themselves killed by Count Dracula."

A squeak erupted out of our token huey. "Oh, I have no intention of going anywhere near them. Got my fill of intimate time with a bad vampire when one turned into the smoke monster and tried to kill me in front of a live studio audience. But Geri's right, Tobias. It can't be you."

"Amy, no matter how much you've learned about our kind since you came into the fold, you don't know what you're talking about."

"Actually, she does." Shame took my eyes to the ground. "Your brother and your father were both alphas. Even if you weren't an alpha, you still have the blood markers to be one. Remember what Igor said? Alpha-beta blood is one of the most powerful elixirs for a vampire to extend his life."

Tobias's teeth ground. "I can't let you go in there defenseless, even if that's true."

"I'm not defenseless. I have a lifetime of hood training in both combat and negotiating. Just because I can't move as fast as I used to or that I'm not as strong doesn't change that. Besides, being a huey in this circumstance might be an advantage. I'm still the daughter of a red matron, and I doubt a vampire as arrogant and self-involved as Vlad or the other Ravens would know that I've been relinquished. Knowing I'm a matron's daughter will make him think twice about killing me. Worst-case scenario: he decides to feed from me."

The werewolf let me speak my piece, then shook his head. "You really think that's the worst-case scenario?"

"It's the worst one I'll let myself think about."

TWENTY-THREE

All my life, I'd known the weight of eyes. My mother's admonishing glare, my father's sympathetic gaze, the pensive stares from werewolves as I accompanied different members of my clan on rounds to regional packs. The scowls of other hoods during summer training trips in Germany when I would best them in competition after competition. Eyes had mass, gravity. I felt it now, the anchor of a dozen eyes upon me as I stood at the base of Galata Tower, weighing me down with expectation, confusion, surprise.

Intrigue.

Despite the crowds of tourists milling about, some chatting, some seated at nearby cafes, taking in an early dinner, others snapping pictures of the tower above the square, I felt utterly singular. Was this really so different from the forests and rivers and stones I knew as home? Only there, my goal was to sneak up on the prey without it knowing. This time, I had to attract the hunter, being just another beast.

The hunter needed bait, however. I lifted a hand to my head and wrapped my fingers around the hilt of my dagger. The familial weapon sighed from the sheath buried in my braid. Balancing the blade on the tip of my finger garnered little in the way of attention from the crowd. When I started to toss it into the air in a series of complex routines, however, a small crowd gathered. When I added fighting forms to the presentation, they fanned the edges.

I felt like my old self in this moment: driven to the middle of an expanse, waiting for the challenge that would soon make itself known. Even though I'd made Tobias promise not to come anywhere near here, I felt his stare too. The liar. Familiar, comforting, almost like a warm blanket on a cold night. I swept the crowd, wondering if I could catch sight of him, but when I came about three-quarters of the way through my turn, a man stood before me who had not been there a moment ago.

Black hair, feathered, haphazardly tossed and styled. A shirt as blue as the tiles that decorated so many of the Ottoman architectural wonders, opened down to the third button to show the sculptured, fuzzy chest beneath. Gray slacks and a suit jacket. A thick mustache that seemed the fashion among the natives. Native: he looked like one, but an air of otherness about him suggested anything but to trained eyes. He snatched my hand, his black eyes fixed on the drop of blood that pearled where my blade had nicked a finger.

"Merhaba, canım. Dün gece nereye köştünüz?"

I shook my head. "Don't speak Turkish."

He grinned. Such white teeth. No fangs. They must be retracted. "English, then?"

"Or some really basic South American Spanish."

"Alas, my Spanish hasn't advanced beyond the sixteenth century. Your owning of a pulse suggests yours was born after that." He looked at me with a more intense inspection, as though determining what dress would best suit me. "Most hueys would consider escaping from us a blessing. How intriguing that you returned to be captured willingly."

Escape? I escaped the Ravens?

Despite the mixture of pride and confusion warring inside me, I had to maintain outward indifference, annoyance. Disdain. *If you make their concerns seem petty, you make their players feel powerless,* my mother would say. *Set them ill at ease by letting them think their goals have no value for you. Then they must appease you in some other way to get what they want. Then,* you *can make demands.*

"What makes you think my being here has anything to do with you?"

He lifted my finger up to the level of his eyes, examining the trickle of blood that had begun to crust over. "Either you're not as skilled with a blade as you assumed, or you yourself set a beautiful trap to get our attention. I understand you Americans have a concept called 'finger food.' I must admit, I did not think it so literal."

I managed to snap my hand back seconds before his lips closed over the injury, leaving him holding air.

"Where I come from, people like you have to ask permission to feed. I haven't given it."

He dropped his hand and stepped to me, bringing our chests into contact. He'd seemed taller a moment ago, but I realized, as our gazes locked, that he was, indeed, the same height as I. His slender fingers petted down my hair, tracing an eventual line over my chin.

"A Raven is not given permission to do as he wishes. He takes what he desires."

An adversary must be equal at the very least. I mirrored the vampire's action, raising my own hand to cup the dominant jawline. Anyone else seeing us in the crowd would think us lovers.

"So I've learned. Give him back to me, or I'll be forced to take him back. I promise, if it comes to that, the consequences will be drastic."

The glint in his eye sharpened. Possibly from amusement. Possibly from the longing sparked by my racing pulse. Or both.

"Vlad will find you most interesting."

"I imagine the feeling will be likewise." I dropped my hand. Now that he'd confirmed he was one of Dracula's clutch, and not the man himself, I wouldn't touch him. It would suggest equity. "Summon him."

The vampire took the hint that the locus of this cat-and-mouse game had shifted. I'd played myself beyond the first maze.

"He's not here."

"How convenient."

"Do you suppose we reside *here*?" The vampire motioned to the tower overhead. "It's merely our... official place of business. He suspected you'd come tonight. He made sure we had someone waiting for you when you arrived."

"Sorry, who?"

The vampire shook with silent laughter. "In time, you will call him *master.*"

TWENTY-FOUR

Boot heels pounded on cobblestones. Tourists and locals swirled in a miasma. Ten steps from the tower, a sharp right, fifteen steps along the adjacent street, two steps off the curb into the black SUV that had arrived right on cue. A slamming door, and the weight of his stare lifted. Tobias had lost sight of me behind tinted glass. There was no doubt the werewolf was in the crowd, or that he was now panicking about what to do. On two legs, he'd never keep up with a vehicle, even in Istanbul traffic. On four legs, the feat was possible, but impractical. A two-hundred-plus-pound wolf in a highly-packed tourist area running as though he were hunting prey, though? The huey authorities would shoot to kill without a second thought.

The Ravens had chosen their perch well.

Two men sat in the front seat, textbook goons: slicked-back hair, three-piece suits, holstered guns peeking out. Vampires or enthralled hueys, I didn't know. The man who'd harvested me slid into the backseat from the other side and leaned over, a slip of cloth in his hands.

"May I?"

I very much doubted that. "Why not just enthrall me? Erase my memory when I leave?"

He didn't wait for permission to secure the blindfold over my eyes. "*If* you leave. And if you leave, it must be for certain you will not return."

"Am I being taken prisoner?"

The goons in the front seat chuckled. They understood English. Was that important?

The vampire beside me wore his smile in his voice. "You are an honored guest, until such time you give us a reason to dishonor you. No matter what my sister claimed, we are not bloodthirsty monsters."

"So, I'm not a prisoner, but my boyfriend is?"

No answer to that. This vamp either was unaware of Caleb's capture, held an opinion on his detainment contrary to his master's, or had been instructed not to discuss the matter with me. No point in further attempts at information; he wouldn't provide it.

"Do I at least get to know your name?"

"I thought my sister would have told you that already."

"I know the names of all the Ravens, but I don't know which you are."

After a few moments, his answer came out clipped. "Timur."

"Timur," I repeated, inking the feel of it on my lips.

"And you?"

"I am eager to meet Vlad."

Power wasn't about who knew the most; it was about who was able to share the least and still get what they wanted.

Perhaps an hour had passed when the SUV parked. Timur and I kept our silence, though the driver and other passenger kept up a conversation I could make neither heads nor tails of. When the car came to its final stop, Timur circled to my side to open the door, guided me out by the hand, and gave the car time to drive away before the blindfold was removed.

The structure before me looked more like something from Prague or Vienna than Istanbul. Six stories high and covered in vines, the mansion was definitely fit for a prince. Though its size blocked my view of the exterior and periphery, the taste of the air and the profile of the soundscape convinced me it was either right on the water, or within a block or two of it.

"Does my master's abode meet your expectations, *yenge*?"

That word I knew. Literally, it meant *aunt*, but it was also used casually the way Americans used *ma'am*.

"I don't frequent with fifteenth-century Wallachian princes-turned-vampiric-sultans, so my expectation had no basis. It's a very nice home, if that's what you're asking. Does my opinion matter?"

"A question I myself am asking."

Timur opened the front door and led me into a hall donned with appointments that reflected the exterior's luxury. The floor: marble. The walls: fine linen wallpaper. I would bet a ten-spot that the frame of the mirror we passed was gold-leaf.

"We rarely entertain outside our own community, so the level of luminosity was somewhat debated. Do let us know if it needs correcting."

Meaning, normally the house was kept dark. Vampires only needed the dimmest light for efficient vision, far less than a hood or even a werewolf. Though, as I realized in reflection, it could also be that any huey victim gathered for feasting might not be able to detect their attackers.

"It's sufficient. Thank you for the consideration."

"Of course."

When we entered the main salon, I would have bet that I'd been magically transported to Buckingham Palace or Versailles. Not that I'd visited either, but I'd seen pictures. Every furnishing evidenced extravagance, every material and means of decorating, precise and expertly arranged. A marble fireplace captured my attention. In the midsummer, no flames danced within. Instead, its craftsmanship blazed, as did the red-haired, fair-skinned woman sitting before it in an ivory wingback chair, a mound of yarn on her lap.

She flashed big blue eyes at me, knitting needles frozen in place. Having expected the legendary Nosferatu himself, I wasn't sure what to make of her.

She, likewise, gawked at me, unmoving. Was she shocked? Scared? Disturbed at my presence? Her plaintive expression suggested all and nothing.

"Alexandra." Timur assumed a place at my side in utter silence. "Would you please allow the room? *He* would like to have a private audience with…"

"Alexandra may stay."

Mist became man, and myth became material. How I could have wondered if Timur might be Vlad back at the tower dumbfounded me now. Vlad's artists had painted him well, and the only thing time had touched were his fashions. The coffee-colored hair no longer dropped in gentle waves about his shoulders. It was trimmed, feathered but short, and his face no longer naked, but bearded. His billowy, black pants reminded me of something from a Middle Eastern fairy tale. He didn't wear a shirt. I traced back to memories of my year of study in preparation for this moment, and couldn't bring to mind one authentic rendering of him bare-chested, but I doubted any artist could have accurately captured it.

Maybe the stonecutter who'd perfected the fireplace, since it seemed to be of the same material.

"Timur, see that our guest has tea?"

As the lesser Raven pushed a tulip-shaped glass to a heated samovar on a nearby table, Alexandra stood, holding her work tight into her stomach. A tiny slipper peeked out from the bundle of yarn. "I'd prefer to leave, my lord. Her kind scares me."

Vlad grinned. "My dear, what harm do you suppose a relinquished hood could deliver from which I could not save you?"

Timur handed me my tea, even as tension dug into my gut. Somehow, the truth of my condition had found its way to Istanbul.

A faltering smile flickered on the woman's face. "None, my love. You would save me from any danger. But I'm weary at the moment. I would, with your leave, rest."

Vlad took the woman's hand and planted a kiss. "Of course. Go, I will come to you later tonight."

My veins iced over from her frosty glare as she passed me on her way out. Only, between her ire and her stately manner, the purpose and source of her disdain sat in a mire I couldn't digest. When she was gone, Vlad turned his attention to me, replacing tenderness with annoyance.

"My message was meant for Inga."

"Inga is in receipt of your message." I assumed by now she'd be awake in Spain. I wondered what Amy had told her?

"If that were true, you wouldn't be here, Gerwalta Kline."

It didn't faze me that he knew my name. Or, at least, that was what I told myself.

"You took Caleb. I want him back."

"No, and not merely because Mr. Helsing's residence with us has been most efficacious," he said, motioning to another seating area away from the fireplace, in a corner of the room before two massive, arched windows through which the lights of the opposite shore and of the few boats bobbing on the waves shimmered on the water. "Is that why you've come, in some vain attempt to recover Inga's pet slayer?"

My mother's lessons echoed in my brain. Sitting tall I hoped made me look more formidable, though what effect, if any, that would have on a legendary vampire, who knew? As I caught sight again of the silver-plated samovar, I longed for the abilities of a righteous hood. If I could draw it to me and shape it into a disk, I'd just slice this bastard's head off.

"I'd also like you to tell me who else knows about the power of unmated alpha blood, what the serum is that Cynthia derived to undo the mating bond, and where you store that serum so that I can destroy every last drop of it. But for the moment, let's start with you returning my mate."

"Your *mate*?" Vlad's eyebrow rose. "I thought only werewolves took mates. There are no werewolves here, not unless your token beast managed to track you across twenty kilometers of traffic. What did Caleb say his name was again? Oh, that's right." A grin emerged, one tailored to show off prominently extended fangs. "Tobias."

I hoped he saw the embers burning in my cheeks. "I'm talking about Caleb. We're a couple, or didn't he tell you that part?"

He may have tried to hide it, or perhaps Vlad assumed that a relinquished hood, a de facto huey, had eyesight too poor to see how he winced. In this moment, I knew that part of our lives, Caleb had managed to keep hidden. Why, though? Was it because remembering my response to his proposal hurt too much, or because his feelings, despite the rejection, were strong enough he'd done it in an effort to protect me? If the latter, then Vlad wanted something from him. Something that he was refusing to offer up, and he feared that having me would create leverage the Ravens could use to force his hand. Either way, I'd have to play this out very close to the chest.

The vampire changed directions. "You don't seem to be frightened, Miss Kline. You do know that it would take me only a few bats of the eye to sink my teeth into your neck and rip out your throat, don't you?"

"If you're simply playing with your food before eating it, then I'm dead already and there's no point in fretting. Even if I am relinquished, I was raised a hood. Women of my kind do not fear men."

Vlad splayed his hands out. "Perhaps this is why the slayer is so resistant to our encouragements. Perhaps you have trained him to fear you more than he fears any vampire."

Yes, they were negotiating with him, but for what? "You'd be wise to learn from his lesson."

The vampire threw back his head and laughed. Unlike the suggestions in any number of horror films I'd scoffed at through the years, Vlad's laughter was full-bellied, whimsical. Lightening.

Attractive.

"So, Caleb is yours." Taking to his feet, he grabbed me by the hand. My untouched tea crashed to the floor, sending a shatter of glass and spray of drink over the tile.

Vlad watched with some amusement as the liquid became a rivulet heading toward the fireplace. His eyes tracked its path, as did mine in turn. The stream ran over the hearth and into the fireplace proper. Only, instead of pooling, it fell into oblivion. That fact alone was curious, but I found myself focusing on the cleanest grate I'd ever seen. Silver? With gold leaf on all of the nearby knickknacks, should it surprise me that Dracula burned his winter fires on a grate made of precious metal?

"A simple accident. Don't worry, it will be dealt with." After a moment, Vlad pulled me up. "Would you like to see your mate, Miss Kline?"

"I wouldn't *like* to see him." Despite the fact that it gave away my excitement, there was no way to slow my racing pulse. "I *demand* to see him."

Vlad turned another amused smile on me as he guided me towards a staircase at the edge of the room. "Oh, I find that, despite myself, I do *like* you, Miss Kline. Very much, indeed."

Whereas the bottom floor had high ceilings and an open concept, the vampire's head barely gained clearance upstairs. We emerged in a hallway dimly lit, wide and long but with few doors. Not a single window in sight, not even at the end of the hall where it reached a dead end. The walls on this floor had been painted a dark blue, crisscrossed by a repeating geometric pattern not unlike those I'd seen decorating lamps and plates in the Bazaar.

"For a Romanian prince, so many of your tastes seem local."

Vlad gave my comment a nod of acknowledgment. "For many years after my father turned me, I was a raving nationalist, I must admit. Do you know my story, Miss Kline? I do not wish to bore you by repeating things you already know."

"I know a story about you. Whether or not it aligns with the one you know of yourself, I can't say."

"Bravery and wisdom," Vlad said. "I see why so many are so drawn to you. I, too, have tried to use my many years to gain wisdom. I like to think that, in this house, I have cultivated an artifact to that growth."

"Oh?"

"Indeed. Over the centuries, I've even learned to embrace certain aspects of the Ottoman's legacy. For example,..." His hand fanned out, indicating the wall. "...the motifs. And another system I had not the scope to recognize until I had learned to let go of my human attachments to concepts like nationality and tribe."

In this course, we reached a door. Surveying left and right, I realized it was the only door on this side of the hall. Vlad's hand curled around the knob, just as a devilish smile curled the corners of his mouth.

"And though it took me many years to understand how to properly implement it, they also had the best way to assure the survival of their bloodlines."

When the door opened, I wasn't quite sure what it was I was seeing. An open space, a room two stories high with a loft above, open to below. In the loft, a dozen or so beds sat at intervals, and below lay a lounging space populated with cushions, couches, and low tables. And women. Lots of women, as many as there were beds above. Finely dressed, all sitting about on luxurious couches. Some did needlework, some drank tea, some even played instruments in a corner. Alexandra sat among them, her eyes still in her knitting.

The edges of my face pulled tight as I turned to the vampire. "You keep a harem?"

"With one important difference."

"Geri?"

I took two steps into the room, pivoted. It couldn't be. "Caleb?"

There, in a puffed-up imitation of an armchair, wearing three beautiful women as clothing, sat Caleb. Swollen lips and purple blooms over his neck suggested just how warm they had kept him too.

From behind, Vlad leaned down to whisper in my ear. "As you see, he's simply pined over you since he's been here."

The slayer stood, his lampreys falling off with a pop. In the space of a few blinks, he'd crossed the room and stood before me. "Why are you here?"

"To rescue you, of course. Here I was thinking you were being tortured and drained for some kind of Ravens' blood-bender, and instead, you've spent the last twenty-four hours making out with half the harem?"

A low rumble bounced off the walls as the vampire laughed, echoed in moments by any number of the blood slaves sitting at intervals throughout the room.

"Oh, my dear," Vlad said. "Is that what Inga led you to believe? That the moment I got my hands on your dear *mate*, I would hang him by his heels and let his precious blood flow into a trough?"

Caleb stepped to the side to look around me at Vlad. "Mate?"

"Did you not know that you were mated to her, Helsing?" Vlad asked. "She seemed quite insistent that you were."

The mate in question righted himself, his hands balled into oppressive fists. "My recollection about what she wanted from me in a relationship is quite different."

"Seriously?" I pointed around the lavish suite, at its in-floor fountain, at its pitchers of fruit water. Seriously, fucking fruit water? "This is okay with you?"

"It is, Geri. It's more than okay. In fact, you can say I've had a sort of awakening."

Just then, a third hand grew out of Caleb's side. Or so I thought, until it was soon joined by an arm attached to a body. A body that most girls would kill for. A body that "old Caleb" would have loved to spend some time with.

"Come back to us, Caleb. We're getting lonely without you."

Caleb smiled back over his shoulder. "In a moment, Konstantina. I have to deal with something first."

The black-haired beauty rolled up on her feet and pressed her lips to the slayer's ear, sucking on his earlobe as she slowly extracted her hand from him. When she pulled away and retreated, I didn't miss the "awakening" going on in his pants.

Taking three steps toward me, Caleb stared me down, his face only inches from mine. "You shouldn't have come here, Geri. Inga lied. The Ravens haven't killed the slayers at all. They've preserved them. They've freed them from oppression."

"They've freed…" The words died at the back of my throat. Who was this man, and what had he done with my Caleb? "How can you say that? They killed your parents. They killed all the slayers."

Caleb shook his head and stepped back, even as each of the dozen women in the room rose to their feet. The familiar orb glowed atop Caleb's hand as he held out his arm and opened his palm to the sky. My eyes went wide as each of the women mirrored the act, conjuring tiny balls of sunlight like his. Only Alexandra remained sitting, her knitting now in her lap.

Slayers. They were all slayers.

"*These* are my people," Caleb said. "These are the slayers. And it's with them, not you, that I'll find happiness. Good-bye, Geri. Good-bye forever."

I couldn't find it in me to resist when Vlad's arm draped over my shoulders. "Come now, Miss Kline. Your *mate* has had his say. Unless, you'd care to join him here?"

Caleb paused in his retreat, turning his head back over his shoulder. Even as shivers chased up my body, I saw it: the momentary flinch in his expression.

"Like I said, *Sultanim*, she's nothing more than a huey now. The women here would eat her alive. If you didn't, that is."

Vlad balanced my fate in his grin. "Either might be entertaining."

"If you want my continued cooperation, you'll strongly consider how much her presence disturbs me."

Wait, he didn't want my help? He knew that I was still highly capable of kicking ass. We had been sparring together for a year. We knew each other's rhythms, and joining the harem would be a ticket to set me up under the nose of the enemy. There was only one thing I could think of to explain his words: he *was* playing a part. He didn't want *me* to be here, either. There was a plan afoot, one he needed Inga to trigger. I was only getting in the way. I was only going to get myself killed.

That, or it wasn't a plan at all. He really meant it.

Impossible, but without the ability to get him alone, what could I do but play along?

I had to be the hood. I had to be in control.

"You've enchanted my mate somehow, Vlad." I swallowed my nerves. "Which leaves me to wonder, are you making me an offer, or an ultimatum?"

"I do not kill in such haste, no matter what Inga suggested." Again, the prince paid attention to my neck, this time with his mouth, not his tongue. "I have tasted hoods before, but never relinquished hood. The bouquet of your skin is earthen, metallic. Does silver still run in your blood?"

"Not likely." I was, as he so duly noted, relinquished. "Are you planning on drinking me?"

He pulled back, holding me at arms' length. "I would love to do so much more than that. Miss Kline, you've managed to pique my interest in a way few can. What kind of relinquished hood seeks out vampires and claims, even if in a poor attempt at some ill-conceived rescue, that a slayer is her mate? Most hoods I've met would curl in disgust at the prospect of having to partner outside their own bloodline, let alone across the divide. Yes, I would have you, if you would consent, but alas, to what end? Vampires cannot chase scents as do wolves, but did you know we can *smell* emotions?"

A prickle chased up my spine, sending all my hairs standing on end.

Vlad fingered the ends of my braid, pulling it to his nose, inhaling my secrets. "Heartache, longing. There is a scent about you, a remnant of another who holds your heart, but threw it away."

Cody. How strong must his hold be that even, two years later, the vampire could sense it?

"It is in this way I know you cannot be had in the way I take women."

The collection of female slayers dispersed, still balancing balls of sunlight on their hands, giggled like some sadistic Greek chorus.

Vlad finally peeled himself away from me and circled the room. "They laugh with joy. I love each of my beauties. But in turn, they love only me. Isn't that right?"

"Yes, *Sultanimiz*," they cooed in unison.

He ran a hand tenderly over the ebony cheek of a particularly statuesque slayer. "I demand complete obeisance. I would be the only man you'd owe fealty. So, unless you're willing to surrender your love for whomever this man is who wound up your emotions so tightly..."

"Good luck with that," Caleb mumbled under his breath. At last, he closed his hand, and with it, the female slayers did too.

The vampire feigned disappointment. "Then, to the dungeon with you."

"What the hell?" My inner Geri erupted out of my mouth before I could stop her. "You said it wasn't an ultimatum!"

"Not where your life is concerned. But you didn't just expect that I'd let you walk out of here of your own free will, did you?" Vlad clicked his tongue. "Come now, Miss Kline. And here I had attributed to you such intelligence. Did you or did you not come in response to summons I sent my sister? Did you not surrender yourself to me in her stead?"

"I..." Did I? "I don't recall mentioning the word 'surrender' at all."

He flicked away the inconvenience of small differences. "All the same."

I didn't remember making the decision to turn and run; I just did, exploding into the extensive corridor through which I'd first come. Almost at once, the soft lights dimmed, leaving all sides inked black. Though, perhaps, not as dark as I thought. After a blink or two, with my pulse pounding in my ears, my eyes adjusted somewhat. Details remained concealed, but structure took on definition. How I managed to get to the stairs without any of them catching up with me, I'd never know.

The last several stairs were managed in a single leap, as I pivoted and turned back towards the front of the house. The grounds were enclosed, I knew that much. How I intended to break out of a secured clutch, I couldn't fathom. One step at a time: first, to get outside.

"Not so fast."

Icy fingers lashed around my neck, and the lower half of my body, subject to physics, swung forward, making a pendulum of my legs. Timur held me with such little effort, it surprised me that he didn't just break my neck in two.

"We offer you hospitality, and you respond with—"

Silver streaked the air. Blade rent flesh. This song I knew like a lullaby.

The world rose to smack me as the vampire released his grip. Hungry lungs, flattened by the impact, gasped for air. Somehow, I managed my feet, ignoring the gurgling of the creature behind me, and propelled myself forward.

Just beyond a gate, presiding over the corpse of one of the men who earlier had driven me across the city, was a dominating, broad-shouldered man cloaked in red. His face was obscured, but I knew him on sight. It didn't mean I understood how he'd come to be here.

Suddenly, Markus called out in warning. "Geri, behind you!"

I turned just in time to see fangs and death. Only, seconds before the other man who'd been in the car sunk his fangs into me, he burned into dust in a terrific orange glow. Through a curtain of his ashes, a familiar face: Alexandra.

She'd thrown the solarium? But, why?

"Hurry, or they'll be upon us. Flee!"

I shook my head. "Caleb—"

"Is safe as long as he continues his ruse," Alexandra said, cutting me off. "Run, fool. Return only when your victory is assured."

With that, Markus took my hand, and we fled into the night.

TWENTY-FIVE

Amber fingers, luminescent strains of gold and red, beamed from behind patchy storm clouds, smacking my retinas as Markus drove us over the bridge between Eminönü and Karaköy, absent of cars at this early hour.

"You know you won't be safe in that house you've been staying in anymore, right?" He kept his wincing eyes pointed ahead. "Come nightfall, they're going to descend on that place like harpies."

The first words he'd spoken since helping me flee the Ravens' compound formed a lecture. My mother would be proud. He'd allowed me silence after he'd told me to get into the car parked just outside the gates of the mansion, though that might have also been self-preservation. We were two hoods wrapped up in a vampire family drama; neither of us should be here. Both had reasons to call the other out.

"How long have you been following me?"

"I arrived in Istanbul before you did, by an hour or so, anyways," Markus reported matter-of-factly. "As soon as I got word that you'd boarded the plane in Chicago, I hopped on the next departing flight out of Frankfurt."

"Frankfurt?" It didn't take me but a moment to put together the pieces. "My mother's at Schloss Wolfsretter?"

"No, your mom is still in Paradise, but she's had me there on standby since the beginning of June."

"Why would she send you to spy on *me*? She's already disowned me. Relinquished me. She's never cared about vampires killing other vampires."

"I'm not here to spy on you." His stoic face crumbled under the weight of his own lie. "Okay, yes, that's one of the reasons she sent me. But believe it or not, my primary mission here is to protect you. You have to stop thinking your mother is some kind of monolith who only casts one long shadow. She might have banished you from the clan, but that doesn't mean she loves you any less. Come on, you're still her daughter."

"If you think, for a single moment, I'm going to buy that on any level, you're crazy." Then, grabbing at any scrap of humility I could muster, I added, "But I probably would have been locked in yet another vampire dungeon if you hadn't helped me, so thanks. Speaking of which, what the hell is it with vampires and dungeons?"

He pulled up outside the house I'd been sharing with the others. No sooner had I gained my feet getting out of the car than the front door opened and a massive lupine form bounded out, leapt clear over my head, and landed atop the sedan Markus had stolen off the streets.

My cousin, still decked out in his hood, silver still brocaded over his chest in wait for his command, held out his hands. "Easy, wolf. I'm not here to hurt you, but if needs be..."

"Tobias!"

The brindle wolf swung his head in my direction.

"He's from my clan," I explained, pointing. "And one of my best—"

"Freeze!"

That the werewolf would pounce towards an unfamiliar hood after what had happened last night didn't surprise me. What did surprise me was Amy in the doorway, pointing a small handgun (pink, no less) into the street.

The silver plate over Markus's chest shimmered. He'd weaponize it quicker than any huey pulling a trigger if he really thought there was a threat.

I threw my hands into the air. "Oh, my god. We're separated for a couple hours, and suddenly both of you are crazy." I turned and pointed at the blonde. "Amy, put that away, and Tobias…" My accusing gesture swung to the wolf. "…come inside and change back. We have to talk and we don't have a lot of time."

Amy kept the weapon squared. "Who's the hood?"

"His name is Markus. He's my cousin."

"Your cousin?" As the barrel of the gun sank toward the ground, Amy's eyes rose toward Markus. "Is he single?"

Markus scoffed. "Hardly."

That was news. "You have someone now?"

He nodded, his glee practically misting the air. "Yan. He's quite a looker. Oh, and I look. *Often.*"

Amy's face fell. "Why do the hottest ones already have boyfriends?"

Tobias skittered through the door and past Amy. The moment he was safely out of view of the street, the familiar groan of a body reforming itself spilled beyond the doorway.

The wolf merged into the conversation without even slowing down. "What is one of your mother's minions doing in Istanbul?"

"Me?" Markus pointed mockingly at his own chest. "Oh, nothing. Taking in the sights. Saving my cousin from Dracula's compound. You know, the usual tourist things."

That knocked the wolf on his ass. "What?"

The shock of Markus's statement created an opening for us to get in off the street. As soon as the door was shut, I set about explaining what had happened after I disappeared from under the tower. By the time I'd finished, Amy had put away her gun, and Tobias, his apprehension.

"When he drove away with you, I did everything I could to keep up," the wolf said. Luckily, he'd managed to shimmy into a pair of sweatpants while I spoke. "I lost you after a few blocks. Speaking of which…" He pivoted to Markus. "…how were you able to follow them?"

"By understanding my enemy, and by accepting my own limitations." My cousin laughed and pulled out his phone, waving it about as Exhibit A. "Only a slayer can run down a vampire, and I don't know this city well enough to outdrive them. Thank goodness for technology."

"A tracker?" Tobias asked. "How?"

"Embedded in silver and moving with the target." Markus tapped his chest, sending a ripple over the liquid metal clinging to it like armor. "Hoods can make silver do whatever we want. Not really that hard."

The wolf took my hands and pulled them to his lap. "I'm so fecking sorry, Geri. I shouldn't have given up so easily. I ringed the district until I started to get worried about Amy here alone. I was hoping you'd shake them and make your way back."

I put my hand on his shoulder. "It's not important. What we have to focus on now is that the Ravens know where we are, and at nightfall, you can bet they're coming for us. We have to find somewhere else to go, somewhere they don't know about or wouldn't dare come."

Tobias crossed his arms. "Agreed, but where?"

The pivotal question. None of us really knew the city very well, definitely not as well as the Ravens. If only Inga and Igor were back.

"Have we heard from our vampires yet?"

Amy jerked her head. "They said they'll fly back first thing after sunset tomorrow, but that still won't get them here until about midnight local time. They also agreed with me that you were stupid to go after Caleb on your own. Inga says she can handle things."

"I know just how Inga would *handle* things," I said. "She'd have gone in there and killed Caleb instead of let Vlad have him alive. Text her back, Amy. Tell them I'm okay."

The blonde pulled out her phone and began keying in the message. "Should I ask them where we should go hide?"

"Not unless you want them to give you directions to your own grave," Markus piped up. "This isn't some fifteenth-century blood gang. I saw the security system they had in place at that compound. Motion sensors, laser lines, infrared. I have no doubt they have your phones tapped at this point. Anything you send back and forth with them is going to give you away."

Amy dropped her device, her face ashen.

"Don't worry, Amy. I doubt you've told the Ravens anything they don't already know."

I picked up the device. A glare was all it took to get Tobias to present his phone as well. He pulled it out from some of the cushions on the couch and handed it over. I took both devices to the door of the cistern, and walked away satisfied when I heard the plop below.

"We're in the same situation if we leave anything written here," I continued. "We have to worry about ourselves right now. Reconnecting with Inga and Igor comes later. Markus?"

My cousin stood to attention. "Yes, matron?"

I didn't know if he meant it as a dig, or if he was just so well trained to respond to a commanding hood female. "One, don't call me that. I'm not even a hood anymore, let alone a matron. And two, you've been stalking around this city for over a month. Any suggestions?"

"I've been following *you* around. I only know the places you went. So unless you're going to spend the rest of your time in Hagia Sophia…"

I perked up. "Hagia Sophia? Why do you say that?"

"Just that the vampires who attacked you there seemed unwilling to go in for some reason."

My hands went to my temples, squeezing as if this would somehow press the memories up and out. "We were attacked by vamps?"

Markus's eyebrows lowered; he examined me for signs of sanity. "Don't you remember?"

My hands dropped as I shook my head. "I can't remember anything between being hit by Caleb's solarium and coming home the next morning. You were following me?" This time, the tone was optimistic. "What happened? What did you see?"

But all my hopes fell to the floor with his expression. "You disappeared."

"Disappeared?" I asked. "What the hell does that mean?"

"I don't mean into thin air," Markus clarified. "As soon as that Caleb guy came out, he saw the vamps and he did this, like, swishy thing with his arm?" The hood demonstrated a move that looked like someone bowling without a ball. "Then the solarium—side note: how awesome is that? Just like I read about!—followed him out of the museum. I saw you for a second when it hit you instead. Looked like it knocked you out, though why it didn't burn you to a crisp, I'm not sure. Your boyfriend couldn't conjure up another one before the vamps took him. As soon as the goons cleared out, I scrambled down from my hiding spot and came to help you, but I couldn't find you anywhere. I'd assumed you'd run back from wherever it was you got in to start with."

I replayed the events leading up to Hagia Sophia in my head. "But Caleb and I came in through old slayer tunnels underground. You didn't follow us down there. Even if I am relinquished, one of us would have heard you. How did you know we ended up at Hagia Sophia?"

"That tracking device I mentioned? It *is* embedded in silver." The hood at the end of my glare flinched. "In the handle of your dagger, specifically."

"What?" My hands went to the weapon's usual hiding place, buried in the wrapping of my braid. I pulled out the silver dagger that had been my constant companion since I was thirteen, a gift bequeathed by my paternal grandmother upon her death. "How in the hell?"

Then the pieces all fell into place. How easily my mother had known when I was in the packlands, how she descended on my attempt to be awakened by my distant cousin, the yellow hood Consuela, how she never seemed to worry about me while I was in Chicago.

I dropped the dagger to the floor. "All this time… And it's been…"

Markus groaned. "We're wasting time. We can catch up on what I know as soon as we get somewhere safe. Come on, we need to think! Where can we lie low?"

Amy spoke with peculiar softness. "Lie low?"

"Yeah, somewhere that's not friendly to vamps," Tobias repeated.

The blonde rolled through a slow nod. "Vampires don't like werewolves, do they?"

The only member of the species in attendance quirked an eyebrow. "Not traditionally. Why, you want to all line up behind me and hide?"

Amy grinned, a daring light in her eyes. "As much as I'd like to have any excuse to stand behind you and do anything, that's not what I'm getting at. I was just thinking, though, you said that the pack of the girl from the Bazaar, that they keep hidden from all the other supes in town. Do you think they'd give us a place to hide?"

Tobias and I exchanged a weighted look, before the werewolf said, "Serhan specifically told us he didn't want to get mixed up with anything."

"I know, and I want to respect that," I said. "But Amy's right. And it's the only thing we have on such short notice."

TWENTY-SIX

"It's weird. I didn't expect the daylight to reach down this far underground. Sure is a lot easier to see my way around this time."

Tobias paused the briefest moment to look back at me over his shoulder before resuming our downward trek into the abyss that was the Pera Pack's crypt.

"It's not any lighter," he said. "Not that I can tell. Markus, what do you think?"

That made me halt. Like in some cliché TV sitcom, Amy slammed into me. Luckily, unlike some cliché TV sitcom, it didn't knock me over or send me facedown into some awkward-yet-sexy position with Tobias.

I helped my friend gain her footing on the step next to me and turned to my cousin at the tail end of our procession. "When were you down here?"

But it was Tobias who responded. "Don't you remember when we were here the first time?" he said. "The wolves all sensed a hood. They assumed it was one of the black hoods, but there are no black hoods in Istanbul. Are there, Markus?"

My cousin only held out an attempt at innocence for a moment. Markus had many qualities as a person and as a hood, good and bad. An ability to lie was not one of them.

"The Pera Pack isn't in the Wolfsretter registry," he confirmed, referring to the database the matrons had for tracking packs. "If there ever was a hood patrolling this area, she did so without any guidance from the black matron based near Bayburt."

"So this is an illegal pack?" I asked. The term tasted like ash on my tongue; even hating the overlord tendency of my mother and other matrons like her, I still jumped right back into their lexicon on the spur of the moment, didn't I? I rounded on Tobias, eager to offer up an apology, but the disappointment in his expression convinced me not to try. Instead, I turned back to Markus. "So you followed us down here before? And I suppose you immediately reported it back to my mother?"

"I'm a righteous hood, Geri, but I'm not an asshole. I don't report anything back to your mother that she didn't *very specifically* tell me to report. At no point did Brünhild say to me, 'Markus, if you find any evidence of an unrecorded pack living in a decrepit tomb under the city, let me know.' Besides, *you* would know what would happen if I did, and I repeat, I'm not an asshole."

Amy, who uncharacteristically had kept pretty mum since we'd entered the tunnels under Istiklal Street, finally piped up. "What would happen?"

The shame I'd felt moments ago tripled in mass. "The matron of the region has the right to order the execution of its alpha and relocate the remaining pack members in any way she sees fit. It's been decades since something like that was done, though. I can't imagine any matron today doing something so heinous."

"The Wolfsretter database wasn't even around until the 1980s," Tobias said. "That means this pack has been in hiding at least since then, but I'm not convinced it was the hoods they were trying to avoid."

Weariness leaked into the cracks of my suspicions. "Who, then?"

Tobias shook his head. "Later. Geri, help Amy. We need to get a move on; if Serhan refuses to shelter us, we only have a few more hours of sunlight to find somewhere else."

When Tobias and I visited the Pera Pack before, I remembered that it seemed to take forever to descend, the whole time thinking I was about to trip over the edge of an abyss in the dark and fall to my death. This trip felt longer. Maybe the fact I could see this time tricked my brain into perceiving time through a strainer.

"Shouldn't we be there by—"

"*Shhh!*" Tobias whipped around, a finger pressed over his lips. Why he thought keeping quiet would help, I wasn't sure. A werewolf's sense of hearing put a huey's to shame, and even I had been able to hear the footfalls ahead of us. If I could hear them, they had no doubt heard us for much longer. The pack knew that someone was approaching; the only question was why they hadn't confronted us already.

And then I realized why: because a hood walked among us.

No sooner had the truth dawned on me than fur and fury flew before my eyes.

Serhan's wolf cleared Tobias easily, the alpha's ability impressive even more so due to the fact that he made the leap both over a really tall man and up stairs. Within moments, the rest of the pack were upon us. Snarls, yips, growls. *Posturing,* I hoped. Years of training overrode logic, and before I could ridicule my own response, I had the handle of my blade pressed into my palm.

To my surprise, the alpha let Markus be. I, however, was on my back before I could mount a counterattack. A maw dripping with saliva opened, sending hot breath smelling of carrion wafting over my face. Somehow, I'd managed to take the blow unharmed, though a wolf of Serhan's size could break every bone in a huey. His back paws anchored on the ground, while his front paws pinned my shoulders. My blade could still give a werewolf a wound that would take weeks to heal. The task wasn't beyond me, not even in this diminished, relinquished body. But as Serhan's pack looked on from the edges of the fracas, I knew that offing their alpha would be pushing down one domino in a line I'd need to topple to survive.

"Please." Gritted teeth deformed the word. "I don't want to hurt you, but I'll protect my own."

The alpha barked, a mocking sound approaching laughter. His maw jerked to the right, alerting me to the state of the faceoff: Markus lay under a pure white wolf, while Amy, looking as scared as I'd ever seen her, had her back against the wall and a small brown wolf inches from her upheld hands. My cousin retained his dagger, but the member of the pack holding him had his wrist clamped in his jaw, blood trickling down. The pain must have been immense, but Markus's discipline kept him contained. A pack would swarm wounded prey.

Tobias remained in his mortal form, the lone member of our party unmolested. Part of me wished he'd take on his wolf and kick Serhan's ass; the other half of me swelled with pride when, instead of lash out, he attempted to negotiate.

"Alpha, hear us out." Tobias sunk to his knees as his chin tucked into his chest. "I beg you."

The wolf lording over me turned; the dagger in my hand lowered slightly. A series of yips and low growls built a wall of language I barely understood but in which Tobias was fluent.

"I give my word, they mean you no harm," Tobias responded, chancing to bring his head up just enough for his eyes to catch mine. "Geri, please?"

Metal on stone sent a dull ping echoing through the air. Moments later, Markus's blade joined mine on the floor, though I couldn't say if he'd dropped it on purpose or lost the ability to hold it against the pain.

Either because wolfspeak wasn't as universal as I thought, or because he wanted me to taste the bile in his words, Serhan took on his mortal form, paws becoming hands, long fingers hooking over my collarbones.

"I told you never to bring this hood here!" the alpha belted out. A moment of confusion passed before I realized that, in fact, I hadn't been in this exact part of the underground before. The reason it seemed to be taking longer than last time wasn't my imagination; at some point, Tobias had redirected us. "And now, you bring not only one, but two, and a huey too? I could have your scruff for this."

Even knowing I lived at his pleasure, I couldn't tamp the ire that rose in my gut. "Hurt a single hair of his hide, and I will divest yours of every strand, one at a time, with excruciating and deliberate slowness."

The alpha spared me one disgusted glance before lashing out at Tobias. "You said she wasn't your consort. You said her feelings were for your alpha. And now, *this*? Explain."

Did he care so little for his pack that he wouldn't rip apart anyone who tried to harm one of them? Would he expect me to do any less? Of course, I'd defend and avenge Tobias, just like he'd do for me. Just like he was doing for Kara. Because that's what you did for someone you loved; you protected them no matter what.

For someone you loved...

Truth fell upon me like light through a door opening to a dark room, illuminating a path to escape my own haze of confusion. No sooner had I admitted it to myself than Tobias spoke it aloud.

"She's in love with me."

Markus squealed out a laugh, but Amy grinned, like the rest of the world had finally woken up to what had been obvious to her all along.

Serhan pushed himself off of me. Clearly, a woman in love wasn't a threat. He rounded on Tobias. "And you? Do you love this wolf killer? Have you betrayed your own kind?"

"No. My moon eclipsed with the passing of my Kara. I will forever be her true mate."

Even though I knew Tobias's words weren't meant to cause pain, his response cut through my soul. No time to adjust, however. Revealed and reviled from one moment to the next, he sped to clarify.

"But she is a warrior, and a friend, and my alpha considers her pack. Geri isn't like other hoods; she cares for wolves. She's lost her clan, her birthright, and almost her life, all to help me avenge my kin and my mate."

A roar leapt from Serhan's throat, bouncing off the walls of the subterranean cavern. "A hood, a member of the pack? Ridiculous!"

"It's true," Tobias insisted, and even from my position on the ground, I could see his fists roll and tighten. He didn't jibe with being called a liar. "I swear on the mercy of your maw and my throat in kind."

Both Markus and I gasped, though in my peripheral vision Amy's head quirked to the side. Inside a pack, a wolf's life was always at the mercy of his alpha, though rare were the occasions where something so heinous caused one to lose it. It was a far worse fate to be disowned, to be sent into the world a loner, destined to go mad. Outside a pack, however, a wolf had few options to represent his loyalty. In offering his throat to the Pera Pack's alpha's maw, Tobias had presented his life in place of his honor should Serhan call for it, and Cody wouldn't have a leg to stand on for recompense. Tobias had potentially laid his life down... for me.

Not for you, stupid hood, a voice inside me mocked. *He just finished saying he doesn't love you, that he could* never *love you. He needs you to get to the Ravens. He needs you and Markus to lead him. Without you, he will never have his revenge.*

At last, the alpha's demeanor shifted. Serhan cocked a hip, amusement pulling up the corner of his mouth. "Never did I expect to see the day a wolf would offer up his throat to protect a hood."

Tobias nodded. "You and me both."

The alpha let out a single laugh as he moseyed over to where Markus remained pinned. The heel of Serhan's foot balanced on Markus's injured forearm, making my cousin wince. "And what of you, boy? Do you have any wolf who would risk his neck for you?"

Markus's red hood shimmered before dissolving into mist. Perhaps he thought he'd be less of a threat without his cloak on display. "My orders are only to protect Geri. If you're not a threat to her, then I'm not a threat to you."

With a jerk of the alpha's head, the wolf atop Markus took his leave and let my cousin sit up and tend to his wound.

"I'm not going to hurt anyone either." My former roomie blew a stray hair from her eyes. "And I don't think I'm ever going to get used to wolves transforming into naked men on a whim. Just FYI."

Serhan looked to Tobias for clarity, but the English wolf just shook his head, as if to say, *hueys are just like that.*

"Very well then, Tobias," the alpha resumed. "What is it you want?"

"Shelter." His throat bobbed as he swallowed down his nerves. "Only for a few nights, until we can plan our next move. Weapons, if you have any."

Serhan rubbed his chin as two of his pack in their mortal forms arrived to offer him a pair of pants. "Weapons? Depends on what you seek." A pointed look at Markus also spoke to me. There'd be no silver among any pack-provided weapons, that was for sure. "As for shelter, you must tell me from what, or is it, from who?"

"The Ravens," Tobias replied. "They're after us. All of us."

"Not me really," Amy piped up.

Tobias's eyes shifted for just a moment before focusing back on the alpha. "Except for her."

The alpha eyed a place on the floor, nudging it with his bare feet. "You are a very curious wolf, Tobias Somfield. Loved by a hood whom you do not spurn, but defend. Traveling the world, away from your pack, in one of the largest cities of the world. Hiding from vampires. What is it that drives you? What is it that causes you to act out against your wolf?"

"The Ravens killed my mate." His lips quivered, even as he struggled to hold back a tear. "They killed my Kara, as well as my brother and my father. They denied me my pack. They denied me my legacy."

"Denied you your pack?" I couldn't stop the question from forming on my lips.

Tobias could have ignored me, but he didn't. He fixed on me, his conflicted gaze almost an apology. "I wasn't disowned from my pack because I challenged the alpha. I was forced from my pack because I was the alpha, and another challenged me. I lost."

Amy beamed, blind to the fact that, in our world, what Tobias had just admitted could get him killed. Not by a hood, though that would have certainly happened if he had gone moon mad. By any other wolf. *Weeding out of the weak and the wretched,* I remembered Cody explaining to me once when I asked him of the old-world practice. *An alpha can mess up, he can screw up pretty damned bad. But if he gets to the point where his pack rejects him, there is no place for him in this world.*

I held Tobias's gaze only a moment longer before turning on Serhan, awaiting his reaction. To my surprise, the Pera Pack's alpha grinned and put a hand on my wolf's shoulder.

"You are like us now," he said. "*Hayalet kurtları*, ghost wolves."

Tobias's eyes widened. "You are..."

"The castoffs of a long-forgotten alpha," Serhan interrupted. "This is why we hide from other supernaturals. If another pack or a hood learned of us, as the descendant of a ghost wolf, that knowledge could be deadly."

Markus's hand massaged his wounds. As he worked his hand around it, the glint of metal caught the dim light in the chamber. Silver: he dressed his wounds with his own weapon. It would heal him faster, as it would with any hood, but it would also make his blood temporarily toxic to any wolf. I had to wonder which he had intended.

"The black hoods control this region," my cousin said, stepping forward. He might have been the most reasonable member of my mother's clan, but he was still a righteous hood, a fact reinforced by his next words. "They know nothing of you. If you shelter us and help us get what we need, I swear that will stay the same."

Serhan allowed an amused grin to plaster over his face. "And the world as I know it remains unchanged."

TWENTY-SEVEN

"I'm guessing there were parts of that I didn't understand. Ouch, shit."

I grabbed Amy just in time to keep her from falling. Or, really, from falling again.

"Jesus, watch where you're stepping."

"Sorry, it's just so goddamned dark down here. How are you not falling down like I am?"

With three blinks, I tested out the landscape. If anything, the environment had brightened, almost as if we had reached the edge of a sphere of light. A few more steps confirmed it, as the mouth of the path in front of us, sloping upward, appeared like a halo.

"Your eyes just suck." I ignored the laugh she made under her breath. "Honestly, I think there's some of that I don't understand either."

Like why the pack's stall in the Grand Bazaar displayed a Writ of Authority, like they expected a hood to show up at any moment for inspection. Or why Tobias kept the fact that he was a toppled alpha from me.

Or how he knew I was in love with him even before I did, and why fate kept giving my heart away to wolves I would never be with.

Tobias walked at the head of the procession like an honored diplomat. Markus, Amy, and I trailed several yards back, surrounded by werewolves of both forms, like the spoils of war to be paraded for Caesar. When we finally arrived at the end of the tunnel after an hour's slow walk, I could have sworn we'd covered miles. We could have been anywhere under the city now, even on the other side of the Bosporus. The door ahead looked modern, a precursor to the shocking sight beyond it.

"You seem surprised, hood."

Serhan leaned casually against a refrigerator, nursing a bottle of yellow soda. I looked back over my shoulder and discovered the door connecting to the tunnels had been disguised as a pantry in an otherwise mundane kitchen. Other wolves passed further into the house without regard to my wide-eyed amazement. Windows on either side of the room let me know that the sun outside had begun to set.

"It's a house," I said, sounding as simple as I did dumb.

"You didn't think we *lived* in the underground, did you?" The alpha sneered. "Surely you didn't think we'd bring strangers into our packlands on a first visit."

It was a clever subterfuge, and even though the sting of their lack of trust shouldn't have surprised or offended me, I found it still did. "I'm not exactly up on the habits of urban wolves, so forgive the gap in my judgment."

Before Serhan could snap back at me, I felt heat at my back.

"We need to talk."

Tobias's hand wrapped around my arm, just above the elbow, as he led me out of the kitchen, through a hall, and into a bathroom. The space was hardly large enough for him, let alone the both of us. Werewolves had a superb sense of hearing in their animal forms, but it wasn't much hindered in their huey form. When Tobias reached behind me to open the water faucet to its full capacity, what could follow but something he wouldn't want anyone else to hear?

"What's our next move?"

Planning? He brought me in here to talk about… planning? Fine. I could do the emotionless soldier thing. Hell, I excelled at it.

"We send Markus out to do recon," I said. "The Ravens only know there's another red hood in town, but they don't know which one or what he looks like. He can sniff around without attracting attention. Once we know what the fallout from last night is…"

"I'm not talking about that." With a touch far more delicate than I realized was possible, the werewolf fingered a lock of my hair that had fallen from the braid in the tussle with the pack, sweeping it aside. "I'm sorry I had to say that you loved me. I needed Serhan and his pack to think there was some deep-seated reason you were helping me. No wolf would believe a hood would help a wolf avenge a mate simply because she thought it was the right thing to do."

Disappointment burned in my cheeks. Tobias had lied. Or, at least, he'd thought he'd been lying. "You were on the spot. It was the first thing you came up with. I can play along with it. Don't worry. I'll try not to make it too awkward. But what about what you said?" I asked, thinking back to his words in the underground. "Was is it a lie, you being an alpha?"

His bottom jaw worked before he answered. "It shouldn't be a surprise; you already figured out it was in my bloodline."

"Why didn't you just rekindle?"

"What, you mean start a new pack?" The werewolf's eyes sparkled with amusement. "A wolf creates a new pack from a place of strength, not by the consequence of his weakness. Besides, it takes a strong wolf to survive that process. My brother and father had disappeared, and I already knew my father was dead. I wasn't in the place to handle that kind of emotional challenge at the time. The only thing I was doing was trying to free Kara before I went moon mad."

My chin dipped. "I know how you felt. I didn't want to be a hood at all after Cody…"

The memories tugged in my veins, and the familiar ache resurfaced. For the first time in two years, however, the pain was just an echo. For the first time, the reverberation of it didn't box me in. And knowing that, I could finally let it out.

"Between my mother's demand that I be what she wanted, and Cody's expectation that I be the opposite, I realized I didn't want to be either of those things. Now, I'm not, and I can't believe how much that loss means to me. Not to mention it set off this whole trail of events that's led to us being on the run, separated from Inga and Igor, and Caleb getting caught by the Ravens. If I'd just said *yes* when Cody asked me, or been the obedient daughter my mother wanted, we'd never be here."

"But then you never would have come to Chicago. I'd be dead along with Kara. Plus, you just wouldn't be my Geri." Chills dashed up my spine as his fingers laced through my hair. "We're going to get him out, I promise. Him, and all the slayers who want to escape."

"All the slayers who *want* to escape?" My weight shifted as Tobias dropped his hand. "You think there are some that don't?"

"You still think they're all pretending to like their situation," he said. "But is it really such a stretch of the imagination to suppose some of them do? You fell in love with a wolf. Why would a slayer deciding to be part of a vampire's harem be so different?"

Confusion clouded my thoughts. "But we're still going to kill them, right? The Ravens?"

"Of course."

"Then why would we leave behind slayers to make them stronger?" I asked. "If we cut off their supply to supernatural blood, even if we didn't find a way to kill them in battle, they'd eventually die from that alone."

His eyes shifted, as though he could see through the closed door to the wolf pack beyond. "They'll just find a new supply. For all we know, the Pera Pack might be like some emergency rations or special reserve for them."

Anxiety punched me in the gut. "Then our mission just became a lot more complex. We rescue the redhead who helped me escape, and any other she wants to bring. And Caleb, of course."

"If *he* wants to come."

Fire shot up my spine. "You don't honestly think Caleb wants to stay, do you? Come on, Vlad killed his family."

Tobias's head swiveled back. "What he said to you when you saw him... Maybe he was telling you that he felt he could protect the slayers in the harem better from the inside. Or maybe... I don't want to hurt you, Geri, but maybe he was telling you the truth."

What could I have said to that? That part of me wished it had been true? That if Caleb's heart could be so easily converted, I'd probably dodged a bullet? Hell, for all I knew, slayers were polyamorous to begin with. A harem might be Caleb's ideal situation. But something in my gut told me that wasn't the case. *The redhead was pregnant. That room had no other males, and a vampire couldn't be the father.*

"Where are the men?"

Tobias blinked thrice. "What?"

"Somebody fathered Alexandra's baby. It couldn't be Vlad or any of the other Ravens." The wheels of my mind spun. "There have to be male slayers somewhere in the compound."

The werewolf balanced his scruffy chin on a balled-up fist. "That doesn't change the pressing issue. If we are able to free them, then what? We've never made plans for something like this. 'Kill the Ravens' was pretty straightforward and didn't require any back-end tasks."

"We really need Inga and Igor on this part, don't we?"

"Wouldn't hurt." His massive chest compressed as he pushed out a breath. "I bloody hate being dependent on other people for things. Okay, fine, how do we reconnect with the good vampires?"

"I'm not sure. For the moment, I think we just have to make a plan without them."

A knock at the door made us both jump, followed by a string of Turkish I was certain had a few choice phrases.

Tobias reached behind me, his body pressing mine into the sink. His lips pressed against my ear. "Thank you, by the way."

I tried to ignore the way his nearness pureed my insides. "For what?"

"For being here," he said. "Until I had to think on the spot about why you came along, it never occurred to me that you're doing it entirely for other people."

I shook my head. "They almost destroyed the slayers. They're after wolves. It's only a matter of time before they come for the hoods. I'm doing this for all of us. Mostly, though, I'm doing it for Kara."

The name echoed across his face. "For Kara?"

"If I had listened to you when you first came to me, we might have been able to free her. She might still be alive. I know that, Tobias. I know that her blood is as much on my hands as it is the Ravens'."

His hand dropped from the faucet, cutting off the sound of the water.

"She'd have liked you."

"She did like me, I think. At least, for the short time we had together."

A moment later, both his hands laced behind me. Tobias and I were already touching, but somehow, he found a way to pull me closer. I blinked my confusion as he lowered his lips to mine.

Seconds before they touched, another fierce round of knocking jolted us.

Tobias was out the door before my eyes could open.

TWENTY-EIGHT

Wolves and hoods were never meant to break bread, let alone bake it side by side.

Perhaps because I was relinquished, or because the Pera Pack had come to see me as Tobias's pet, the wolves in the expansive home tried their best just to ignore me. Except for Ayşe, who had overcome her initial distrust to use me as an anthropological data set. Her fascination with hoods made me feel like I was being interviewed for what would turn out to be a tell-all book.

Markus, however, had a completely different experience.

"They all look at me like, at any moment, I'm going to wield my silver into a machete and take their heads. I swear that one with the two little kids wants to rip me up and feed me to her pups."

I sighed as I put away the last of the freshly-washed tea cups on a shelf over the sink. Guilt had driven me to become obsessed with relieving the burden of their household chores. "Think of it from their perspective. You're the monster from every one of the bedtime stories they've heard. Not to mention, you're a behemoth. *And* a foreigner. Basically, the only thing you've got going for you is that Serhan is curious about you."

"Honestly, I'd prefer he was a little less curious about me."

I dropped the damp towel over a rack to dry. "What is that supposed to mean?"

"I feel like he's cataloging me, like he's studying me for posterity. I think you and I are the first hoods this pack has ever seen. And since your abilities are offline, he's using me to figure out the best defensive strategy."

I hadn't sensed quite that vibe coming off the alpha. Not that I could say with any certainty anymore. "If I were an alpha, or even if I was a matron, I would do the same thing. I wouldn't hold it against him. In fact, I admire him for it."

"You would." Markus snatched a cup—and my ire—from the shelf and poured himself another portion from the constantly-brewed pot on the stove. "You want to hear my report or not?"

I motioned to the nearby table. In the week since we'd fled our rental house near the Bazaar, we'd had the same routine. The pack went about their normal business. Most of the adults, and even a few of the older teenagers, had jobs. The mothers of young wolves used the night to take their pups out. Anywhere else, little kids running around on city streets would have drawn judgment, but not in Istanbul. Anytime of the day, the population trafficked all the avenues, alleys, and byways, almost as if each citizen had a shift to report to for that distinct purpose. If a pack had to live in an urban center to stay off hood radar, Istanbul may have been one of the best places for them to blend into abnormal huey traffic patterns.

Markus alternated between spying on the Raven compound and looking for life at our old rental. He hadn't seen either Inga or Igor, though I told him that wasn't unexpected. I was certain they'd been trying to call us, and since the only one of us with a phone was Markus (who refused to call them, since it would tip off my mother about his having been discovered), they must have suspected the Eminönü house had been compromised. I suspected by now they'd also ditched their burner phones and phone numbers for new ones.

After getting myself a matching cup of tea, I took a seat at the table. "Give it to me."

"That's what he said."

"Markus, I know you're my cousin. Don't take this the wrong way, but I hate you."

"There's something going on at their compound," he said, getting serious. "Lots of things being taken away. The fact that they're coming in after dark tells me it's something they're concerned about overseeing personally."

"And the slayers?" I stared into my tea, its waters a whirlpool.

Markus shook his head. "Other than the one you said was named Alexandra, no sign of them. *She's* outside frequently, either alone or with that other one who took you from Galata."

"They must trust her then," I concluded. "Odd, since she was the one who blasted Timur with a solarium that let me get away."

"Yeah, about that..." My cousin rubbed the back of his neck. "Are you sure it was a solarium, and not, like, a flare gun or something? I'm not as much of an expert as Igor and Inga are. I mean, obviously, right? But I've never found any stories of a vampire who was able to survive one of those things."

I hadn't thought about it before, but now that he'd mentioned it, it did seem odd. "Maybe they can change the intensity somehow?"

"What, like on *Star Trek*?" Markus mocked holding up a communicator to his mouth. "Slayers, set solaria on stun. I repeat: stun only."

"Fine then, ass. What's your idea?"

"That the vampire wasn't really hit. They can move fast, Geri. Wicked fast. Your huey eyes might have thought you saw that guy take the brunt of the solarium, but he might have ducked out of its path long enough for it to miss him. But, getting back to Alexandra... She has a pattern."

My eyes widened.

"Every night, about an hour after sunset, she's driven a few blocks from the house and takes a walk at a park on the water. There's a dock there. She walks out to the end of it and spends ten or fifteen minutes just sitting, meditating or something. Then, she gets up, walks back to the car, and goes back into the compound."

"Any escorts?"

Markus leaned back. "Just one. Not that guy, Timur, and not Vlad, based on your description of him. It must be one of the lackeys."

My hands gripped the tea cup as resolve filled me. "I have to talk to her."

"Are you insane?" Markus belted out a laugh. "Out in public, where anyone can see you? And here your mother always said you were the best hood when it came to sneaking around that she'd ever trained."

The reminder of my mother sent a shiver through me, one that left a fleck of doubt at the back of my brain about my ability to pull off this plan. "Camouflage is all about not being noticed, not *not* being seen. Conservative women here wear full veils. Even Ayşe does when she's on the street at night. I'm sure she'd let me borrow it. I'll be just one of many hueys on that dock. The vamps won't even know I'm there."

"If that's what you want to do, let's do it. Or do you need another day to plan out the details?"

"I'm already operating on borrowed time here." My eyes drifted to a calendar hung on the wall over the tiny kitchen table. Even though the labels of days, weeks, and months were in a foreign tongue, members of the pack had circled full moon nights. Half of the time Tobias could be away from the pack without consequences had already fled to the historical record. Moon madness could begin to peek around the edges of his behavior at any point. So far, there'd been no sign of it. Perhaps staying with wolves slowed the descent, but our luck wouldn't hold out forever. Neither, for that fact, would Caleb.

"We go tonight. Which means... I better get some sleep."

"I can't believe you're sleeping in the same room as Tobias."

I couldn't ignore the hint of jealousy in my cousin's voice. He'd made no secret of the fact that, as far as wolves went, my best lupine friend would be a pretty sight to wake up to every morning.

Heat flared in my cheeks, but I turned to hide it. "We slept in the same room together in Chicago for almost a year. It's no big deal."

"That was before he outed how you feel about him to an entire foreign pack."

I lowered my voice. Just because I didn't think any of the pack were near us in the house didn't mean they still couldn't hear us if we didn't take care. "It was a lie, a story to explain why I would act unlike other hoods."

"A lie?" I didn't think I'd ever seen Markus wear a wider grin. "You keep telling yourself that. You look at him now the same way you used to look at Cody Ryland."

Any semblance of amusement melted from my face as I turned to the sink to rinse out my cup. "And look how that turned out."

My cousin's words replayed in my mind like the cries of an annoying crow, building a border to sleep. I lay next to Tobias on the bed, staring at the back of his head as cycles of breath moved his body in a gracious arc: rise, fall, rise, fall. We'd been permitted a room usually reserved for newly mated couples—a fact that only made our presence in it all that much odder. Amy had been given the option of setting up a pallet on the floor, but decided instead for a spot in the pup room.

I questioned her motives.

Markus slept under a makeshift canopy on the roof; both he and the wolves thought it best.

Late in the morning, sleep used me as its plaything. The pack's commune had no air conditioning; wolves had methods of coping with excessive heat ingrained in their bodies. No such luck for ex-hood hueys. Early afternoon licked at my chest, at my neck. The only options for cooling off were either to go jump in the shower, or to lose the few articles of clothing I had on.

It's no big deal, my hood brain said. *Wolves don't think about nudity the way non-wolves do. You know this. Remember that time Rick caught you and Cody out in the woods and you had nothing on your top half but your bra? The two of them thought it was no big deal. If your boyfriend didn't get all crazy about it when the two of you actually* had *been fooling around, Tobias won't even notice now.*

But you will, the female part of my brain countered. *Now that you know you love him, you want to make things* more *awkward? He's a widower, for goodness' sake! Keep your shirt on and just sweat it out.*

Ten minutes more, with the perspiration pooling in the hollow of my neck as I lay on my back, staring at the ceiling, and I could take no more. I sat up and began to peel the drenched cami from my body, only to pause, the bottom half of the shirt covering my face, when the weight of his eyes settled on me.

"It's hot," I muttered. "If it makes you uncomfortable, I can keep it…"

When Tobias rolled over and his hand pulled down my shirt, a tiny part of me shriveled, chastised for the audacity. When he draped his hand over my waist, hooked my hips, and pulled my body flush to his, spooning me, that same tiny part of me stuck its tongue out and blew raspberries.

His lips hovered over my ear. "The key to overcoming heat…" His mouth trailed down my neck like a vampire sizing up a juicy vein. "…is *not* to fight it. It only makes you that much more flustered."

"Flustered?" The word came out as a laugh. "What a British thing to say."

"It wasn't a lie, was it?"

I didn't have to ask him to clarify. Despite the sudden shift in the air between us, I knew what he was asking. "No, it wasn't."

"I knew. I can feel you, Geri. It never stopped, just softened a bit. These last few days, though, it's back, full force." He laughed against the back of my neck. "You really are one fucked-up hood, aren't you?"

In the miasma of his psyche, flecks of every emotion I felt swirled, but the dark ones pulled at him heavier. So wrapped up in the wash of what came over me, it took me a moment to reflect on what he said and truly hear it. Only then did I realize the truth.

"I can feel you." I turned over on my back so I could look him in the eyes. "Like I used to. Like I could before my mother stripped me of my powers."

"About time you figured that out." Tobias ran a hand through hair moist with perspiration. "Anything else occur to you?"

"Yes, actually." I leaned over him, putting a hand to his cheek. "I'm in love with you."

My lips had barely come down on his when the door crashed open, and something that seemed truly impossible walked in the door.

One of the slayers I recognized from Vlad's harem, Konstantina, holding Amy by the hair.

The man beside me disappeared, a wave of fur and tooth and fury taking form, all while I wrapped my hands around the handle of a blade I knew I would never wield against a slayer.

Amy dropped to the ground, calling out as Konstantina's foot prodded her further into the room.

"Did you really think we couldn't track you down?" the dark-haired vixen asked, stepping over the crumpled mass of my friend weeping on the ground. "Did you really think you could hide from us?"

Tobias lunged forward, but a wolf wasn't as strong in the day. With a lash of the slayer's arm through the air, the wolf went flying. His body surrendered to the ground, motionless.

"You bitch!"

My foe grinned at my outlandishness. "Caleb will find it so *interesting* that I caught you in the arms of a wolf. Almost makes me want to drag you back, just so you can see the reaction of the man who cried from guilt after we made love last night, all because he felt like he had betrayed *you*."

Realization unfurled in my stomach. If she wasn't here for me, who was she here for?

"The werewolf, Kline," the slayer said, as though she could work out the question burning through my mind. "Though on second thought, he'll be much more compliant if we have you to dangle over him."

At a snap of her fingers, two thugs ran in. That the Ravens had hueys on call during the day was something I'd foolishly never considered. Before I could believe what was happening, a hog-tied Tobias whimpered and yelped, and their eyes turned toward me.

Ravens were one thing, but I refused to take out hueys, and harming a slayer would be like cutting up a bald eagle. Trapped in a corner, there was no solution for escape that wouldn't leave the carpet soaked with blood.

The blade crashed to the floor, the sound echoing against a backdrop of pandemonium in the rest of the house. This was no random smash and grab; this was a coordinated campaign, one to instill terror and seed confusion.

The slayer beamed at me with approval as her two thugs stilled. "Surrender, then?"

"I never surrender. I just know when to cause a distraction."

All three perpetrators' eyes bulged moments before they swung around, just in time to catch Markus's silver whizzing through the air. The lemon-sized pellets knocked the two huey's skulls, rendering them unconscious. The slayer, however, could move as fast as a vampire, and did so. Markus fell back into the hall from the force of her impact as she rushed past him.

Taking Tobias along with her.

TWENTY-NINE

Markus blew a rebellious lock of hair out of his face even as he shifted his weight, trying to gain comfort against the pull of his restraints. "Wolves always blame hoods whenever something goes bad."

"In this case, I'm not sure we're entirely innocent."

His hefting sigh took his eyes to the ground and his chin to his chest. "Geri, I have to warn you, I think you're going native."

"Meaning?"

"Meaning," Markus growled, "you're siding with wolves. Wolves, Geri! The very creatures we're born to defend against? To keep in line and buffer from humanity?"

Superiority was hard to cultivate while tied to a kitchen chair, but I did my best. "The only side I'm taking is the truth's. This pack has somehow managed to stay off our radar for at least forty years, and who knows how long before that. Then, within a few weeks of allowing hoods into their midst, their home is invaded by some Stockholm syndrome-suffering slayer. If I didn't know better, I'd swear they'd enthralled her."

"Slayers can't be enthralled. It's impossible." Markus looked up with eyes brightened by realization. "I read an entry in an old manuscript once, though, that said they're actually stronger in the daytime. Seeing as one threw a massive wolf over her shoulder and ran at warp speed with it, I think we can consider that confirmed. They got in through the tunnels too. Did you know that? Tunnels, I'm quite sure they didn't know about, seeing as they would have stumbled onto the Pera Pack before now, if they had. Bet that was another thing your boyfriend blabbed."

"Tobias?" *Raspberry.* "Don't be stupid."

"I was talking about Caleb." My cousin's eyes became vicious slits. "Wait, did you just call a werewolf your boyfriend? Oh my god, you *have* gone native. You're in love with a werewolf. *Again.* Your mother was right; there's something wrong with you on a very deep level. Your wiring is all kooky."

"Well, you know my mother. She's always right." Pulling at my restraints did nothing but frustrate me. Why try, then? If a righteous hood like Markus couldn't find a way, I didn't know how a relinquished hood like me stood a chance. "Did you say *wiring*?"

"Yeah, wiring," Markus repeated. "W-I-R-*ing*. Why, does that surprise you?"

"Nothing my mother says disparaging about me surprises me. Only, I think I know why neither one of us can get through these restraints now."

"Yeah, why is that?"

I cringed as I pulled again, recognizing at last why the hairs on my arms were all standing straight up. "Because it's insulated, electrified wire."

Markus chewed on that a moment. "Well, shit. Isolated wolves, but they still know our weakness. Sons of bitches."

"Not exactly an insult for a wolf. More a statement of fact, actually."

"You're not funny, Geri."

When the door opened, we both closed our mouths and faced forward, eyes blank. Hood training always assumed the superiority of our kind, but it allowed that certain circumstances might favor temporary capture. *Arrogance lubricates the tongue and rusts the blade. Your opponent will never allow you inside his head, but if he feels you are defeated, you're no longer a threat. Sometimes, letting them believe you've been bested leaves them at their worst.*

After the raid, when the pack was in chaos, it had become all too easy for them to turn their ire from the Ravens (like we *told* them) to the "true outsiders" in their midst. As hoods, blame fell upon us like snow on a field. Markus had wanted to fight; he easily could have extracted us from the home. But how many dead wolves would that leave? Even one was too many. Plus, if I had any hope of rescuing both Caleb and Tobias, I was going to need help, even more than Markus could give. At my urging, he had stood down. The pack had wasted no time in securing us.

Ayşe's grim features painted a new mask on her otherwise cheery face. The shewolf entered from the tunnel just beyond the kitchen door, flanked by two other female wolves whose faces I'd come to know from afar, but whose names I had not yet learned.

"Serhan was taken."

Weird, I thought. Wolves were a patriarchal society. Was it because this pack was also of a Muslim persuasion that women were being sent to interrogate another?

"Amy?"

Ayşe's face flickered. Perhaps she hadn't expected my concerns to lie with anyone but myself. "Safe."

"Where?"

"Another house. Other side of Istanbul."

"Thank you."

The shewolf's eyes widened. "You thank me for this?"

"You're protecting my friend. Of course, I'm thanking you."

She needed to keep the upper hand, which meant not acknowledging my gratitude. "Why did the Ravens take Serhan?"

"Because he's an alpha," I explained. "A vampire only lives for about five hundred years after he's changed, but the Ravens have discovered that the blood of other supernaturals lets them keep going past that. The blood of an unmated alpha or beta has that power. That's why."

The wolf didn't miss the conflict between my statement and who had been taken. "But Tobias is mated. Why take him?"

"Yeah, Geri," Markus piped up. "Tobias is mated. Illuminate us on how you expected that all to work out."

I let the emotion drain from my eyes. "I don't know. Maybe they didn't know either. Maybe they took him when they had a chance, to worry about the details later."

Through pinched features, she eyeballed me. "Lie."

I should have listened to Tobias and studied some Turkish. I wasn't sure if, in her broken English, she was calling me out, or giving me a demand. "Ayşe, please… If I tell you why they really have him, it would put you in more danger than you are already in."

Her shoulders eased. "Do you really love Tobias?"

"Yes."

"Ah, that." The shewolf's finger wagged, and with it, I felt the room lighten. When Ayşe spoke again, it wasn't with the heavily accented drawl I'd grown accustomed to, but with words flowing like honey. "That is the truth. Do you know why I ask you, Gerwalta Kline? Do you know how I trust now that you are telling the truth, and that you are not like other hoods?"

"Geri?" Markus stared at me, but with his head turned towards the wolves. "What's going on?"

"What's going on, Markus, is that I now understand why this pack was in hiding," I said. "They're an anathema."

Ayşe's face curdled. "I do not care for that term."

"And I don't like to be called relinquished," I said. "But that's what I am. I know what it is to be rejected by your own kind, the way a pack whose alpha line is female would be. *Serhan* was never the alpha, was he?"

Ayşe shook her head. "My beta. An uppity one at that."

Both Ayşe and I winced as Markus's chair screeched across the floor. Even if it only moved him an inch or two, he was going to give it his darnedest. "So *you're* the alpha? And somehow, you speak excellent English to boot."

"Of course, I speak excellent English!" Ayşe snapped. "I attended one of the best English-speaking universities in the country. *We* are not typical werewolves, Mr. Kline. Once the others of our kind rejected us, we were no longer bound by their traditions. Nor did we fall under your jurisdictions."

"No, I get that," I said. "I just finished my BS in biochemistry."

"Really?" Ayşe's face brightened. "I just got my master's in organic chem."

She delved in the evil arts.

"If I can interrupt your girl bonding…" Markus interjected. "Your beta is gone, and our… Tobias is gone. Along with our slayer, so we really need to get out of here and rescue them while we still know where they are."

"Slayer?" Ayşe rose from her chair and turned a lazy circle. "There are no slayers. They're all dead."

"That's what we used to think too. But last year, I met one."

"Who she dated," Markus added.

"And who she just broke up with." I shot him daggers before turning back to Ayşe. "I'm sorry this happened. I'm sorry they found you. Believe me, I am. But now that they know about you, now that you're living right under their noses, they're not going to leave you alone. We have to deal with them, and if we're going to have any chance of that happening, we need to get the slayers out as well."

Ayşe's lips pursed. "We know the Ravens only by reputation. We have no idea where they are."

Now that Markus had begun to see the path to our liberation, his mouth became a lot more productive. "We do. In fact, I've been casing their place for the last week. But what my cousin seems to be forgetting is that the Ravens' compound is like Fort Knox."

Ayşe laced her arms over her chest. "Fort Knox?"

"It's a saying we have in America," Markus clarified. "Meaning, it's highly secured. Armed guards, multiple gates, and all manner of video, infrared surveillance, motion detectors... Not to mention it's full of vampires, and slayers who may or may not be loyal to them."

"And this slayer who you 'dated...'" The alpha used finger quotes. "He is a mole? Someone who will help us from the inside?"

Awkwardness skewed my features. "Not exactly. In fact, he might have bought into their cult. I'm not sure. But what I do know for sure is that the Ravens are now holding two people who are very dear to me, and there aren't many people in this world I care about. One way or another, I'm going to find a way to get Tobias and Caleb back and free the slayers, or die trying."

She digested this with steady, thoughtful repose. "Was Tobias assisting you in this quest?"

"The Ravens killed his mate, his father, and his brother. I was assisting *him*."

"He was right. You are unlike other hoods." The she-alpha stopped before me and reached out to pet my braid. "It makes me wonder..."

In quick words of her foreign tongue, the alpha sent her two backup dancers away, though I was certain not so far that they couldn't bound right into the room if they were needed. When it was just the three of us, she crouched in front of me.

"Let's say I did release you," she said, tapping my knee. "Can you guarantee that you will return my beta to me safely?"

It felt like I was shaking my head in a vat of molasses, so heavy was the weight of the deed. "I can only promise I'll do my best to free him."

Suspicion spooled out into a string of diminishing width. "The problem remains, how do we get into such a fortified compound?"

We.

"I'm not worried about getting in. I already know how to do that part. I'm worried about getting out. I did it once, but it was only because a slayer helped me."

"And your cousin, you ungrateful, little urchin!" Markus rebuked.

I ignored his whining. "I was hoping to talk to that slayer tonight. Markus discovered that she takes a trip each evening to one of the parks near the Ravens' place."

"That must be Bebek Park."

Markus nodded. "Yeah, that's the one. It's—Hey, you said you didn't know where they were."

"I don't," Ayşe affirmed, a mischievous smile on her face. "But as I said, rumors. Speculation. My pack has lived concealed in this city for over five hundred years. We know every corner, even if we choose not to visit them. We also know its weaknesses. Istanbul's weakness is the same as Constantinople's, as was the same of Byzantium: it is surrounded by water."

"And the Ravens' compound is right on the strait," I said, as anticipation began to tingle all around me.

Ayşe stood, a grin spreading across her face. "They'll expect us to come to the gates. They'll never be looking for an attack from the sea. Slayers fear water, and they don't think anyone but a slayer could ever be a threat to them. Once you're on the inside, we must work quickly."

"And the escape?" I asked.

"The same way we came. There is a huey who brings the products we sell at the Bazaar from Izmir. His boat will be far enough off the coast so as not to be suspicious. When we have everyone ready, a single flare will have him at the vampires' seawall within sixty seconds. Now, Little Red, tell me how it is you're planning to get in?"

"That's simple enough," I said. "Escorted by Vlad through the front door."

THIRTY

Not a single shopkeeper denied Ayşe's request, and few even questioned it. Traditional wardrobe in my size? Done. Silver bracelets—just to loan out for the night of course? Granted. A bit of these wires and those electrical components, and some of this perfume and a little of that makeup? They would send her a bill when they got around to it, *if* they ever got around to it.

Markus held up one of the silver bangles, turning it in his hand and capturing a video on his newly-acquired cell phone.

Ayşe tightened one of the stitches just below my hip bone and paused. "What are you doing?"

"If you want me to change this back to what it looks like now after we're done with it, I'm going to need to remember what it looks like. I'm a hood, not a jeweler. It's going to be tough enough as it is."

The alpha shook her head. "I still think it will give her away."

"It won't," I assured her. "A hood always has silver on her somewhere. Vlad must know something about hoods, as old as he is. He won't think twice about it."

"But she's relinquished," the alpha argued.

"She'd still wear it for...senti*metal* reasons."

Even possibly sending me to my death, he finds ways to joke.

"She got away with having her dagger with her last time, but I'm not risking that again. If something goes south, I want to be able to find her. You hear that, Geri? Something bad happens, I want you to rip off this silver coin—" He held up the fake in his hands. "—and swallow it. If I don't get you out of this alive, your mom is going to order my execution."

Markus set down the phone and placed the bangle in his flat palm. In moments, the circle melted inward, becoming a pool of liquid metal. Into the molten goo, he dropped one of the little doodads the electrician had been able to scrounge up for him, before commanding the silver into the shape of a token styled like one of the reproduction Ottoman coins that decorated harem costumes sold in the Bazaar. A costume, for reasons I still couldn't comprehend, I was wearing.

"I feel like a reject from the touring company of *Aladdin*. Ouch!"

"Hold still!" Ayşe, crouched at my side, clicked her tongue. "If I don't get this side sewed properly, you're as likely to lose your pants as well as your head tonight."

"Believe me, Geri, of all the ways to lose your pants, in the process of outrunning vampires is not one." Markus held up the completed belt, a string of coins and bells that he snapped around my hips before standing back to admire. "You know, if Cody had ever seen you in this outfit, you might have never lost him to that slut."

"Her name is Lisa, and she's not a slut." The belt rotated on the tips of my fingers as I hid the odd silver coin with the embedded tracking chip in the back. "And, seriously, you want to bring up Cody right now?"

"Cody?" Ayşe tied off the stitch and took to her feet. "Tobias's alpha?"

"The same," I confirmed.

"So you were—or possibly *are*—involved romantically with *two* werewolves." The alpha turned to Markus. "Is this normal for hoods where you come from? In this part of the world, they'd rather kiss a goat than shake hands with a wolf."

"I don't think it was his *hand* she was shaking."

"Markus!"

"What?"

"Cody and I are *not* involved. In fact, based on our last encounter, he may hate my goats. I mean, *guts*." My arms akimbo, I turned once, giving my two companions the full scope. "So, how do I look?"

Markus balanced his chin on a balled-up fist. "Like an extra from the touring company of *Aladdin*."

When Timur's gaze fell on me under Galata Tower, he couldn't hide the grin.

"If you're trying to blend into the native population, you should know that, even in Ottoman times, costumes of this style were worn only by whores." The vampire sidled up to me, his eyes kept on a crowd that seemed to expect me to break out into some kind of performance at any moment. "Not to say it doesn't suit you."

An elderly couple approached, speaking a language I didn't understand. They seemed to be asking to take a picture with me. I happily obliged. "You're not surprised to see me."

"We have both your boyfriend and a wolf with whom you were curiously found in the throes of passion. Of course, I am not surprised."

"We were *not* in the throes of passion!" No sooner had I snapped than I mended. "When I visited before, Vlad made me an offer. After further consideration, I'd like to discuss that possibility with him."

"Is this then a demonstration of that American phrase, *dress for the job you want*?" He shooed away the two tourists with the camera, who were busily trying to shove a folded bill into my hand. "That offer was made before you escaped and killed two of our staff."

Don't back down. Don't allow his rejection. "Which should prove all the more why I'd be a treasured addition. Plus, there is the fact that I was a hood. The daughter of a red matron, even."

The vampire's curiosity piqued. "Why would that be useful to us, precisely?"

"See this mark?" I rolled my neck to the side, showing off my scars. "That was done to me two years ago by one of Cynthia Wu's children after he'd been punished with sunlight. My blood completely healed him in a few minutes."

Timur stood firm, his feet planted at shoulders' width and his arms crossed. "Impossible. News of something that miraculous would have reached us."

"News never got out. Right after that, I ripped his head off his body. Now, do you think you might have a use for me?"

Gone was the space between us, despite how foolish it must have been to move so quickly with so many tourists watching us. As though Timur himself realized his folly, his eyes scanned the perimeter.

"If what you say is true—" With his back to the crowd, my back to the tower, long, hungry fangs descended and deformed his words. "—do you know how much danger that would put your people in? Why would you make something like that known?"

"Because your boss has outmaneuvered me twice and taken away my people. I'm not easily overcome, Timur. I figure the only choice I have against someone like that is to either go down fighting against them, or rise up fighting *for* them."

Those fangs could be the death of me, but that grin would be the end of him. Timur raised a hand to eye level and flexed his fingers, as though inviting someone over. Temptation to look filled me, but I knew better than to break eye contact. Instead, I relied on my ears, telling me that again a car had just come to a stop at a nearby curb, ready to whisk me away.

THIRTY-ONE

Each day, the city became more mysterious, even as the streets became more familiar. Within a few minutes, I understood we weren't heading the same direction as we had the first time. Had the Ravens moved after my escape? Were there multiple fortresses around the city? Did I just fall into a trap, and Timur was doing nothing more than taking me to a more convenient place to drink me and dump my body?

"He wants to show you something first."

I blinked my confusion. "What?"

No chaperones or chauffeurs this time. Instead of a massive tank of an SUV, the vampire had bundled me into a pavement-hugging sports car with only two seats. At a red light, Timur pointed ahead. Even from this low-to-the-ground vantage, I could see the ancient walls rise just a few blocks ahead.

"Vlad wishes for you to accompany him on a private tour of the palace. He said it would be *illuminating*."

"Is that some kind of solarium joke?"

Timur shrugged. "Vlad is not in the nature of making jokes. No Raven is. I understand you've spent time with our sister."

Nerves alighted and wormed their way into my gut. "Inga."

The light turned green; the car pulled into the intersection. "Then you understand."

"A harem costume?" Vlad's lips pressed against the back of my hand, testing my resolve. "How fortuitous. I believe you can see the future, Miss Kline."

If I could wield silver, the coins on my belt would purchase your head being cleaved from your body, bastard. But what good would that do? The other Ravens would still have Caleb, Tobias, and the others.

"We see only the present," I said. "It is only within our power to determine how far into the future our adversaries are permitted to see."

Vampires had no pulse, so I couldn't be sure how a flush could overcome Vlad. Had I not known better, I'd have said it was lust coloring his cheeks. After a few unintelligible words to Timur, an exchange was made. The soldier left, and the prince led me by the hand, strolling beside me.

"Have you visited Topkapı yet, Miss Kline?"

"I'm willing to bet you've been spying on me long enough to know the answer." Before us appeared a set of magnificent doors, with grandeur on a scale that made the castles I'd seen in Germany come off as fixer-uppers. "This barbican looks medieval."

His eyes brightened. "You know about architecture?"

"I know about castles and fortresses." I pointed to the turrets on either side rising above the stone archway gate. "This was either built as a nostalgic throwback in the nineteenth century, or during the Middle Ages, at a time when whoever lived here suspected they might actually be invaded."

Vlad gave a slight nod as the doors, which had swung open by powers unseen, closed behind us. "They were wise, the Ottomans. It took me years to understand. Years to appreciate, to *accept*. Then, even longer to learn their ways. Eventually, my wisdom exceeded their own."

"You do have the benefit of a much longer life span," I noted. "One that is getting longer all the time, I hear, thanks to all the wolves you've killed."

"All in the name of progress."

I bit down so hard, the taste of blood teased my tongue. Hopefully, he couldn't sense it. *Play along.* "Where are we going?"

"The slayers whom I guard have grown up in my care. They know this world. You, however, are what my girls would call *yabanci*. A foreigner. An outsider. If you are to decide to join my harem, I wish you to know its origins."

"I know the basics," I insisted. "Many women, one all-powerful man who gets to have them all to himself whenever he wants. Sex slaves."

"*That* is the ignorant orientalist view of what the Ottomans—of what *I* have established. Call one of my *haseki* a sex slave and she'd laugh. Or kill you. They are quite lethal, as beautiful as they are. I believe you received a small demonstration this afternoon from Konstantina. No, the true purpose of a harem isn't sexual indulgence, Miss Kline. It's legacy."

"To create heirs, right? But a slayer can't be turned into a vampire, and you can't impregnate them, so how does that work?"

"I suppose this is one of the areas where my harem varies from the one that once thrived—" He pointed to a group of buildings, two stories high and as wide across as half a football field. "—in these very buildings. The slayers nurture not my biological progeny, but those reborn of the Dracule. *That* is their purpose: to sustain my life, so that my own purpose may endure as Sultan."

At this, Vlad paused, looking into the sky and spreading his lips wide. Gleams of a waning gibbous moon illuminated fangs that seemed to grow longer from the effect. "Did you know that werewolves once protected this very part of the palace? History says it was eunuchs who guarded the sultan's family. I am sure there were *some*. But who showed the greatest loyalty, and who the sultan entrusted with his inner sanctum, were the mated werewolves who were incapable of being with any woman other than their mates. That, too, is my revenge. I deny them that luxury."

I struggled to push out sound through a mouth gone dry. "*That's* why you're undoing mating bonds? As some sort of revenge against a sultan who died five hundred years ago?"

"Rarely are my reasons so simplistic. Your Caleb told me what you thought, that unmated royal wolves provide the best sustenance for my clutch to endure. There is some truth to that, though it was not the impetus for my serum to be developed. What I wished to do—what I *am* doing—is to destroy the werewolves from within. True, I could send my clutch to pick them off one by one. But there are thousands of them around the world. So much time and expense and coordination, when none of that is necessary. You see, Miss Kline, what we discovered is that destroying the mating bonds of the alphas leads to the deterioration of the pack as a whole. Alpha's prerogative becomes impossible. The fealty which keeps them true devolves. I have the luxury of forever, thanks to my slayers. I can wait for the process to play out over several generations."

"But without werewolves, what is the purpose of a hood?"

One of his eyebrows raised precariously. "An interesting query, isn't it? In your case specifically, perhaps one which I may help answer. You have so much to offer: an interest in genetics, familiarity with all forms of supernaturals, and an instinct for hunting down werewolves. In turn, I can offer you every comfort, every luxury you would ever desire." As he slow-walked us back to the main courtyard, he reached out his hand to me. "Join my harem, Gerwalta Kline."

"Your world would never offer me one thing."

"And what is that?"

My hand traced down the curve of my hip, taking his eyes for the ride. "What of my own legacy? What of wanting my own family?"

"I didn't take you for the motherly sort." Vlad licked his lips. "I have the resources required for that, of course. If I didn't, my crop of slayers never would have endured beyond the first generation."

"You know my proclivities. I am the namesake of The Betrayer." I leaned into him, twirling one of his dark curls around my finger. "Promise me my choice of wolf instead."

"If that's what you desire." His hands finally detached from his side to wind around my hips, pulling me close. "Do we have an accord?"

"Not yet." I pulled back. "Caleb told me this palace is a museum, and that there's quite a few Ottoman treasures here."

"Does my *haseki* desire diamonds? Art? Golden teapots?"

"A hood has no use for any of those." I leaned in, ghosting my lips over his. "Show me the weapons."

Desire curled in his eyes. "As you wish."

We walked in silence back across a stone path. A guard stationed at the door held an impressive weapon of the modern era, but gave no heed when he spotted us.

"Do you have every person in this place under your thrall?"

"There are less taxing ways of ensuring their acquiescence," Vlad said. "They are on my payroll."

"And they aren't worried they'll get into trouble?"

"What part of 'I am the sultan' did you not understand, Miss Kline?"

The room we entered, longer than wide and filled with display cases, came to life with a flick of a switch. My mother would have cried. I was on edge myself. The pieces of the collection were not only impressive, they were works of art: khanjars with jade hilts, kards embedded in granite, scimitars as long as my body... Arrows arranged in a quiver of tanned leather, gilded at the edges with copper... Iron helmets engraved with scrollwork so complex and elegant, its place on the battlefield could only be to make the enemy understand the vast wealth of the foe they faced.

And in one display case, though not the fanciest or most ornate, was a smaller sword, slightly curved, embedded in a wooden hilt that called to me. A typed slip of paper held in place by two pushpins was in several languages, the English of which read, *Kilij, 17th c., Balkans. Older,* a voice in my head said. *Much older.*

My hands flattened against the glass. "Beautiful."

Vlad couldn't hide his surprise. "Of all the treasures in this room, *this* is the one that you're drawn to?"

It was, even though far more exceptional pieces surrounded it. "It…" I cut myself off just in the nick of time, just before saying *it calls to me*. Because it couldn't. I was relinquished, more huey than hood, and not in any way, shape, or form on speaking terms with silver. It was impossible.

But I'd sensed Tobias, hadn't I?

What was happening to me?

Vlad leaned in closer, as though he could get between me and the glass. "Does it please?"

"Yes." I raised my weapon hand, wishing I could make this glass dissolve and take that sword by the handle. I hungered to feel the hilt pressed to my flesh.

When the vampire snapped his fingers beside me, I managed to draw my attention away just in time to see the guard who had previously been standing just outside the room scurry in. Vlad said a few words; the guard blushed and made excuses. A few more words from the vampire, this time spoken around fangs, and the guard dropped his argument and rushed away. Moments later, he returned, a set of keys in his hand. I watched, mouth agape, as the very sword I'd been drooling over moments ago was removed and rushed from the room.

"Done. It is being loaded into my car as we speak. The weapons curator will also be happy to entertain any questions you have regarding the sword and its history whenever you care to make an appointment with him."

"Loaded into your…" Evil dead or not, that was absurd. "You can't just remove a four-hundred-year-old sword from a museum!"

"I already have." Two blinks, and the vampire was no longer feet away; he was standing before me, his hands in my hair. "I will compensate the museum for the financial burden. That, or offer a similar piece from my private collection. I hope this gift sufficiently demonstrates the dedication I have for my *haseki*— my *favorites*—Gerwalta. If you give yourself to me, I give myself, and so much more, back to you."

I didn't know why I felt the need to argue a present I was never actually going to receive with a man whose moral compass pointed towards a different pole than mine. "That sword must be worth thousands, maybe even tens of thousands of dollars."

"Your worth is far greater, and ten times more rare." His head tilted, as though he were mapping my side profile. "You have named your terms, and I have accepted. Are we in agreement, then?"

"I don't remember you presenting your terms."

"Mine is singular: loyalty. Not only to me, but to the whole clutch. If you are discovered to betray us, you will die. If we ask of your body, you must give it."

"Didn't you just chastise me for saying the women of your harem are sex slaves?"

He laughed at my ignorance. "We require only your blood. Anything more is at your own discretion, just as long as your lovers are friendly to the Ravens. My ladies mingle with the males of their kind at their leisure."

Which meant there were male slayers still alive. The question was where? If the females had ready access, somewhere in the compound or very nearby, I'd imagine.

For the third time, he offered his hand in the style of a suitor asking a belle for a dance. "Agreed?"

Do it, the voice inside me said. *You're going to kill him anyways, and you'll buy the others more time to infiltrate the house if you keep playing along.*

Putting my hand in his, I gave one quick nod. Then, my world flew out of control.

My mouth fractured, a silent scream cut from my throat, as his fangs pierced my neck. The pain flashed through my body, every nerve reacting to the attack. Then, numbness, almost as if, instead of the vampire's bite, I'd been injected with morphine. The ache ebbed away, replaced with a subtle chill and sense of euphoria.

Intoxication took me hostage as the prince drew back, his eyes wide and his lips crimson with my blood.

"Im...possible."

Equilibrium was such a challenge, I dared not try anything as complex as speech. Instead, I just looked at him, goofy and aloof.

"Someone lied to you." Vlad ran a hand over my hair, brushing back the stray hairs free of my ever-present braid. "They lied to you—lied to all of us. And now I know why."

"What did you... Why am I..."

The high-pitched trill coming from inside Vlad's coat pocket overlaid my incoherent mumbles. Amused, Vlad grinned as he pushed a finger to my lips while holding the phone to his ear with his other hand.

"Perfect timing, Timur. I believe I have just succeeded in getting Miss Kline to—Oh, really? Oh, very interesting. Yes, of course, bring around the car."

He slipped the phone back into his pocket. The way his expression shifted in the intervening moments sobered me. Curiosity curdled, leaving behind only resentment.

"The funny thing about this, in hindsight, is what I've just managed to do, I did without you having to canoodle me. Perhaps you're more like your mother than I supposed."

"Sorry?" Fingertips pushed into my temple finally steadied the room. "I don't have any noodles. I like dumplings, though. Why… Why am I so dizzy?"

"The disorientation is temporary, and will ease with rest," Vlad said as he took me by the hand. "Rest, I fear, you won't be getting for a while."

And with that, I stopped trying to keep a hold of both gravity and reality. I slipped into my own daydream, unaware of the nightmare that awaited me.

THIRTY-TWO

Pain shot through me as Vlad slammed my face into the wall beside the fireplace in his massive home, rocketing me awake. My eyes shot open. Hungry, desperate lungs ate up air. With a twist of his wrist, I collapsed to the floor, panting, kissing carpet.

"An hour ago, I was prepared to offer you use of the mating suite for you and your lover. Now, I have to ask myself, how tight should I make your chains?" A kick in the side brought blood to my mouth. "And should they be silver?"

Because a werewolf would try to free me if they weren't? If he succeeded in killing Tobias, I doubted any would even let out a sigh at my death. Certainly not the Pera Pack, who must be blaming Markus and me for their discovery. Certainly not the Paradise Pack, whose alpha had sent me packing.

With a twist of my arm behind my back, Vlad pulled out my curdled cry and straddled my waist. The agony shot through me, from my wrist to my shoulder blades, and the strain bit into my resolve. I turned, catching sight of the sword he'd gifted to me sitting on a nearby table, the belt of coins discarded beside it. If only I could get to it…

"Just because I can't kill you without killing myself doesn't mean I can't cause you inexorable levels of pain. Act out against me, and this will be the baseline of your suffering."

"Wait, what? Why can't you kill…" Did I really want to finish that question?

The prince's hands flattened against the floor on either side of my head. He lowered his upper body, pressing his cheek to mine. "The bite I took: you said it felt different. Didn't you realize why?"

"Because I'm relinquished?" It was the only thing that came to mind when I compared Vlad's attack with that of Xin's child.

"Oh, you're something all right, but relinquished isn't what I'd call it. It's because what you felt was a maker's bite. My blood now flows through your veins, Gerwalta. You are of me."

The dim hall blurred in my vision, but I didn't need my eyes to see the truth. "That's how you keep the slayers from revolting. You've taken them hostage. You've made them Dracule."

"True that we cannot turn a slayer, but Igor discovered long ago a maker's bite will immunize a vampire from his victim's solarium. Sadly, though, it only works with the females." I could feel his smile stretch out next to my face. "As I said, I learned from the Ottomans well. Mehmed tried to infect me, to drive his ideology and his politics into my veins, to *internalize* my slavery, and make me my own captor. And that is what makes my *hasekis* so compliant: my blood is in their veins."

"You've given all the slayers in your harem the maker's bite. If they killed you, they'd die too."

"You really are quite the smart one, aren't you?" Vlad stood, finally ending the onslaught of pain. I struggled to push myself up on all fours. "Though sadly, their solarium can still knock us out for a few hours. Also, that still doesn't keep them from escaping. That doesn't assure their loyalty. Have you figured out that part of it, hood? Have you?"

No, I hadn't. I searched my memory, recalling the salon where I'd seen all the female slayers lounging, Caleb the only male in their midst.

The only male.

"By threatening the men." Agony ebbed as I rolled to my knees, struggling to my feet. "But how? How could you keep them from killing you?"

"Every supernatural creature has its weakness, doesn't it? Vampires: sunlight. Werewolves: silver. Hoods: electricity. And slayers?"

Vlad's arms wrapped around me just seconds before the scenery became a blur. Moving so fast played havoc with my lungs, leaving me a coughing mess when we came to a stop in his back garden, lights dancing like pixies over the Bosporus.

"Water." The vampire grinned as he beheld the vast resources surrounding his home. "A slayer forced to stand in water is powerless to conjure their damned solaria. Oh, yes, I learned. The way to keep power in check isn't with chains around the wrists, but with chains around the heart."

Igor's explanation of why he'd rented the run-down house in Eminönü bubbled up in my memory. *In the old part of the city, there's hundreds of them. Every grand home or even apartment block in Byzantine or Ottoman times had one, and a number of them still survive in one form or another today.*

"There's a cistern under the house."

"And I flood it just enough to keep their power—and their hopes—dampened. The moment one of the women acts out against me or tries to flee, the males pay the price. Alexandra could tell you from personal experience. I killed her husband only a month ago when *she* tried to escape."

My eyes flew shut, but the vision still danced on the back of my eyelids. "Caleb?"

"Your Caleb resisted the charms of my beauties far longer than I supposed he could, given how long you denied *him*. Let me guess: every time you got close to consummating, your body rejected the experience?"

I refused to dignify the question with an answer, or acknowledge even to myself that the reminder Caleb had slept with one of the slayers hurt. Instead, I huffed, glaring at him like my eyes could rip off his head.

The vampire planted his hands on his knees and bent over, laughing at my quivering frame. "That was pretty much the way of it, wasn't it? And the way you're staring at me, like you're shocked that I knew that, tells me that you *don't* know what's so special about you."

Fury fueled my strength, rage drove out the pain. The shaking stopped, and though I moved slow, I rose to my feet.

"I know what's so special about me."

Straight back, flashing eyes, firm voice...

"I am Gerwalta, namesake of The Betrayer, and I will be the one to ensure *you* never hurt another living soul, even if it does kill me in the process."

The vampire nodded, amusement brightening his features. "A nice sentiment, but all bluster, I'm afraid. You see, you don't have any power. You're nothing but a relinquished hood."

The cloaked figure in the tree at the edge of the yard crouched, the silver in his hand dancing.

"I have the best power of all: allies."

Blood sprayed across my face as Markus's weapon found its mark. Crimson rivulets drained down the vampire's mouth as he keeled over. Markus pounced, another ball of liquid silver at the ready, even as his eyes scanned me for injuries.

"No broken bones," I reported, even though I suspected at least a few ribs were cracked. "I'll heal. Ayşe?"

"She's sweeping the perimeter, taking out any guards who would see us escaping from the seawall." Markus turned to the house. "Tell me where we're going."

I pointed to the second story, even as we ran towards the doors. A silver spear through the neck could only sideline Vlad for as long as it took him to pull it from his throat and heal. Given the power of my blood on a vampire from my last encounter, I didn't suspect that would take too long.

"The women are there. The men are in the basement. I suspect that's where the wolves are too. There's at least one other Raven on the property, probably along with a handful of other vamps of later generations."

"So you go up and I go down?"

"No, we both go up. This house is expansive, and we need someone who knows it."

<hr>

Markus eyeballed the two headless corpses outside the entrance to the harem. "If I had known beheading them was so easy, I'd have done that with Vlad. Nice sword by the way." He balanced my new weapon in one hand, examining it before handing it back to me. All his silver had gone into piercing Vlad. Literally. "Where'd you get it?"

Not a story I wanted to go into right now. "Just saw it downstairs and thought to grab it as we came through." I searched through the pockets of one of the victims of Markus's attack. "These vamps were young. I don't think a Raven would have been as easy."

Light spilling from a newly-opened door blinded us. I threw my free arm up, creating a band of shadow over my eyes. The measure against so many cocked and loaded solaria proved useless, as did the sword I grasped.

"We're here to save you, but we need Alexandra's help."

With a wall of ebbing luminosity behind her, the redhead stepped forward.

"Is this why I saved you?" she barked. "Just so you could get us all killed? What kind of fool are—"

"A hood!" I shouted. "A hood who knows that, as long as the Ravens survive, we're all in danger."

Another of the slayers, a dark-haired one with brilliant blue eyes, cackled. After a few blinks, my eyeballs toasting like marshmallows, I realized I knew her. This was the slayer who had taken Tobias. "Idiot! Even time could not defeat them. What makes you think a *wolfsretter* stands any chance?"

"Because I'm not a *wolfsretter*. I'm something much more dangerous: a woman in love with someone they've taken. I will not be stopped. Not by reason, and not by regret."

Alexandra let her solarium extinguish, along with the fury in her features. "After Caleb did what he'd been put here to do, the Ravens took him below with the others."

I shook my head and let my sword fall to the side. "He's not the one I love."

At that, most of the others dropped their defenses as well.

"If not him—" Alexandra inched forward, confusion marring her features. "—then who?"

"His name is Tobias Somfield. He's a wolf."

The room repolarized, as all eyes went from me and Markus, to Alexandra herself. The redhead's eyes dropped to the ground as her hand rounded the child within her, cradling it in her grasp.

Her brilliant blue eyes sparkled with tears when she looked up. "You know of our limitation?"

I nodded, even though Markus managed a muffled "no" in the background.

"We'll figure out how to kill them all later," I said. "Today, our goal is freedom. There's a boat, just a few hundred meters off the seawall behind the house, waiting for us."

Alexandra gave a curt nod before turning to a woman with mocha skin and coal-black eyes. "You must be swift, Rashidi."

The slayer drew back, like she'd been singled out for ridicule. "There are too many guards at the gates."

"I'm not suggesting to lead them through the gates."

Rashidi went ashen. "Surely you're not suggesting we attempt to escape by diving into the strait. We'd be powerless in the water, you know that."

"The only power you will lack in the water is the power to destroy a vampire. If you are brave, and if you are steadfast, you will not lose the power to save yourselves."

Markus stepped between the two women. "Swim far away from the landing, straight out, staying as close together as you can."

My cousin drew one of the two flare guns we'd brought from inside his hood. "After fifteen minutes, if we're still not there, you fire this. They'll come pick you up. Don't wait for us. If we see the flare, we'll know you've gone. We'll find another way."

Rashidi glared confusedly at the hood before her. "Why are you helping us?"

"Because it is the right thing to do." Markus closed her hand with his own around the flare gun. "Which, frankly, isn't enough for me. But I know Geri. She's not going to get out of here unless all of you are safe, and I can't get out of here unless the same's true for her."

THIRTY-THREE

Every creak of the stairs signaled our defeat.

Alexandra noted my nerves. "The home is old, and it was shaken harshly by the last great earthquake. Don't worry, I will know if one of the staff approaches. We can sense vampires the way you sense wolves."

Probably not the way I sense wolves, I thought.

A keypad outside a white door beeped as the slayer punched in the code, a feat that Markus found suspect.

"Does everyone have access to the dungeon?" he asked as he swished a ball of liquid silver around in his hand. At least that obnoxious harem costume belt had come to some practical use. Otherwise, my cousin might have insisted on requisitioning my new favorite weapon. "Doesn't seem very secure."

"It's a cistern, not a dungeon," Alexandra replied. She held up a hand at shoulder level, sparking a solarium to light the stairway below. Three feet under a modern lattice, the walls morphed suddenly from smooth concrete to rough plaster. "Each man is secured with chains. We do not have the keys to those. The access is necessary for... visits."

The presence of a baby bump on the slayer told me what kind of visits.

"And the wolves?" I asked, fretful of the visions my imagination was conjuring. "Are they down this way too?"

Alexandra shook her head and took another step. "Not anymore." She swallowed, and I didn't miss the crack in her voice. "I suppose they decided that the wolves needed to be kept somewhere the slayers couldn't access."

The moment we splashed into knee-deep water, her solarium coughed out. Luckily, the buzzing, dull lights stringed up the hall were powerful enough to see.

"Are there any more Ravens in Istanbul other than Timur and Vlad?"

"Not right now. They travel in pairs, and rarely are the others here," Alexandra answered. "When they are, it's only for a few hours, just long enough to receive a treatment."

Remembering how Inga had been "treated" by Caleb's blood, I didn't need to question that part. "So we only have to worry about where Timur is, then. Maybe we'll be lucky enough to avoid him."

"Timur is already down here, lying in wait."

Sloshing water created ripples as Markus stepped around me to catch up to Alexandra. "Why didn't you say so sooner?"

The redhead paused to blink at him in confusion. "Were you expecting this to go smoothly?"

Markus's cheeks went crimson. "Why should anything be easy at this point?"

Suddenly, a low-level buzz tickled my hairline, and a lurch of my insides pulled in the direction to the right, to a space that seemed to be just more of the ancient foundation. Only, the direction in which I was drawn wasn't the one Alexandra was leading us to.

I pushed my hand flat against the wall. "It's him."

Markus came alongside me, weaving the strands of silver around his arm like a chain and pressing his palm flat against the plaster. "How can you feel that? You're relinquished."

I ignored his question, and posed one of my own. "How do we get in?" I eyeballed my sword, wondering, if I sliced into the wall and managed to break through, would its weakening bring down the whole house atop us?

"Get in where?" Alexandra asked. "The slayers are in a room up ahead."

As far as I could see up and down the corridor, there were no breaks in the wall, which arched overhead like an excavated cave. "There's a chamber on the other side of this wall. The wolves are in there. I can feel them. I can feel..." His name—his presence—almost broke me. "Tobias."

Markus joined me. "There's no way you could possibly sense the wolves."

"Tell me I'm wrong, then."

"You're not, but it's impossible—"

We both yelped when Alexandra's fingers laced through our hair and yanked us along.

"You swore to save the slayers!" she whispered. "They come first. After that, your wolves."

Tobias. My heart reached for him, latched on to him, and yearned for physics to break its own laws and let him pass through the wall to me. With every ounce of my being, I focused on getting my message to him. *I am here. I will save you. Just be strong.*

But Alexandra was right, and if she were to be believed, there was a Raven in wait ahead. I twisted from her hold as Markus did the same.

"The slayers first," I agreed. "But how do we kill Timur? We don't have any wood."

"Markus will take off his head." Alexandra turned, guiding us forward. "Without wood, it's the only way to kill a vampire."

Markus trudged on. "Or if we can get you out of the water, you can burn his ass with a solarium."

"Out of water, he can simply smoke and escape. Water weakens both vampire and slayer. They can't evaporate, but we cannot summon solaria. Besides, Geri and I can't kill him."

I gulped, hoping my cousin would chalk up Alexandra's declaration to the fact that I was relinquished and, therefore, unequal to the task.

No such luck.

"And why would that be?"

"Because Vlad has infected her," Alexandra said. "As he has done with all the female slayers. If we kill a Dracule, we kill ourselves."

"Whoa, wait." Markus's hands went out to the side. He came to a halt and turned on us. "Are you saying that a vampire's bite makes them immune from harm from their victim?"

Alexandra shook her head. "Only a maker's bite, only from the Dracule, and only in a female slayer. Or, it seems, a hood."

Realization dawned on me. "That's how you were able to hit Timur with a solarium and he didn't die?"

Alexandra's brow furrowed. "This is a topic I will gladly expound upon, at a later time when we are not all dead or imprisoned."

"I have got to write that down, and Geri, we're going to have some major tests to run. Okay, if I'm going to kill him, you should probably let me get in the front and I should—"

But Markus never got to say what he was going to do. One moment he had pulled out ahead of us, the silver under his command warping into a hanger sword, and the next, he was on his back in the water, his head submerged, and a vampire atop his frame. His weapon flew backward, splashing my face as it plunged beneath the muddied surface.

Even if they couldn't smoke, water had no apparent effect on a vampire's strength.

Alexandra tried to advance, but I pulled her back.

"You go," I said. "Save your people. I'll take care of him."

"But how will I cut the chains?"

The weapon in my hand vibrated, as though reminding me she was still here.

She. Swords didn't have genders, but something about this one felt particularly… feminine.

I pushed the hilt into Alexandra's hand. "She'll cut through them."

The slayer examined me, then the sword. "But this sword is so…"

"*She* will cut through *them.*"

This time, Alexandra didn't argue. One more glance at Markus struggling to break free of the Raven's hold, and the slayer nodded and turned on her heel, calling over her shoulder as she did, "Remember, you are Dracule. Kill him, kill yourself."

I reached down into the water, tracking in my mind the arc I'd watched the hanger sword fly. Its handle practically leapt into my hand, and I shot up, getting a quick feel for the weight of the short sword in my grasp. A relinquished hood didn't have the power of a righteous one, but if I didn't do something, my cousin was going to die. Alone or not, I had to act.

Ayşe, we could really use you down here.

"You'll let my cousin up now."

His muscles, his strength, his abilities: nothing helped Markus to free himself. The vampire was too strong.

"This hood is an intruder," Timur purred, not threatened or even concerned in the slightest. "I couldn't possibly let him live. And since you can't kill me, I—"

As the blade bit into his flesh, the cloth of his shirt severed and blood rolled down his elbow. Timur shrank backward, his hand clasping over rent flesh. I put myself between him and Markus, fretting at the sound of my cousin trying to clear his lungs.

"I can come pretty close to killing you without actually doing the deed."

"Pretty little *wolfsretter.*" Even as the blood flowed down Timur's arm and dripped into the water, the wound began to knit itself together. "A shame that you're born of a supernatural line already. You would have made such a glorious Raven. You have an innate taste for blood."

"You're really going to love this then."

The water slowed me, but my arms remembered motions ingrained from years of training. I lunged, forward and to the right, using the momentum to drive a strike into the vampire's shoulder. Instead of taking the blow, Timur utilized his speed, unhindered by the deluge, to clear him from my path. That was fine; it was further away from Markus.

"Your blow was a fluke." Timur shifted again, advancing several feet up the corridor, toward the direction Alexandra had run. "Unfortunately, playtime is over. I have work to do. Just because we're going to kill the slayers doesn't mean we can't salvage their blood first."

Kill the slayers? Caleb! "I'll die before I let you hurt them."

"That's not completely off the table," Timur returned.

The hairs on the back of my neck tingled, and all at once, I knew we weren't alone.

"Hey, Markus? You good back there?"

"Yup. What do you need?"

I held his weapon up. "Something good for shooting down a Raven."

"I can do that."

The vampire turned, but I'd already hurled the hanger sword with all my might in his direction. Under my cousin's influence, the metal liquified, bending and twisting in midair. Within seconds, what had been a sword grew long, cylindrical. The arrow caught Timur in the back, right under his left shoulder blade.

When he pivoted to us again, a drop of blood dripped from the arrow tip that stuck out of his chest. "Did you really think your Tinkertoy was going to stop me?"

"Not at all." Markus grinned. "But it distracted you long enough for *her* to get here."

When a werewolf's growl rumbled through the air, the exhilaration had me on cloud nine. The Pera Pack alpha leapt, clearing over me and Markus as we crouched down.

For one terrifying moment, I saw it: fear. It sunk into the cracks of Timur's arrogance, seeping into his veins. Long, ebony fangs took the vampire at the throat, cutting off his screams. Soon, his body disappeared beneath the water, only his hands and flailing feet breaking the surface. Red waves washed from the tumult, painting a crimson sheen over the water. When his severed head floated to the surface, the tension left my body.

Ayşe shifted back to her huey form. "How did you do that?"

"I'm not sure. I didn't think I'd be able to throw hard enough for the arrow to go all the way through his body."

The shewolf shook her head. "No, not that. I mean, how did you call to me?"

I blinked away the confusion, even as we reached the end of the hall where Alexandra was cutting the chains off the last of the male slayers. "Yeah, well, all kinds of crazy shit going on tonight, I guess."

Inside the room, a dozen men in varying states of health and wearing only T-shirts and Bermuda shorts stared at me, the red-cloaked hood beside me, and the green-eyed woman with wild black hair who was more than a little nude. Those shorts alone had me wanting to kill Timur all over again. Unkempt facial hair hid their expressions, but two things became clear right away: they were young, and they were overall healthy. I looked around, expecting to find a dungeon straight out of a Hollywood movie, but it looked more like a partially flooded Ikea showroom. Clinical, spa-like even.

The slayer must have read the confusion in my face. "The water level can be controlled. It's only raised when the doors open and someone comes down here."

"Then why don't they just use their solaria to melt the chains?" Markus asked.

"Because they were never awakened."

I peered around the group of men, looking for the owner of the voice I knew so well. A moment later, he emerged. With bags under his eyes and his shirt stained with blood, there was still no doubt, this was my slayer. I crossed to him and threw my arms around him.

"Caleb." His name drew guilt to my tongue. "I'm so sorry. I don't know what happened. I… Are you okay?"

"I am now." His hands threaded my hair, pulling my head to his shoulder. "I was so scared I'd killed you. God, I wanted to tell you when you showed up in the harem, but I knew if I showed them how much I really loved you, they'd know I'd been playing them."

"Killed me?" I looked up into his eyes. "What do you mean, killed me?"

"When we were leaving Hagia Sophia, the night the Ravens took me. The second I cleared the exit, I saw them. I pulled my solarium from the church, but I didn't know you were running after me. It hit you. I saw you disappear. I saw you burn into dust."

"Burn into dust? I didn't burn into…"

No. No way, it was impossible.

"I didn't give myself to the flame," I said. "I didn't let the fire take me. *I* took *it*."

His face scrunched up in confusion. "Give yourself to the flame? What does that mean?"

"We'll have to talk about it later." Wrapping my hand around his, I pulled him from the room. "I have to save Tobias. He's still here somewhere."

"I'll help."

A red cape dashed into my peripheral vision. "Geri! Come on!"

Caleb pushed me behind him. "Who in the hell are you?"

Markus guffawed. "Calm down, Helsing, I'm one of the good guys."

"There are more vampires approaching." At the top of the stairs, Alexandra pushed the last of her clan through the door. "And Vlad is still nearby, but I don't know where. He must be smoke. They're always harder to sense when they're smoke. We have to get to the boat. He can't chase us over water, but my people have never had to face vampires in battle. We've lost the skill."

Caleb took Alexandra by the hand. "Just follow my instructions. Geri, if you're going to get the wolves out, you don't have much time."

I nodded. "Then we better get going."

THIRTY-FOUR

I ignored the thrill that ran through me. It sparked too many questions, and confusion would only slow me down. Later, I'd concern myself with how I could feel the tug of dawn kindling in my veins, though even without too much effort, I'd begun to understand what had happened to me that night at Hagia Sophia. I just didn't know *how* it had happened.

Alexandra sparked a ball of sunlight on her outstretched hand, at the ready in case one of the vampires infesting the front of the house reached the back before the slayers were clear. "The sun rises in a few minutes. We'll be safe outside, but in the house, we're still at Vlad's mercy."

"But Vlad is outside, injured," Markus said.

Ayşe shook her head. "Trust me, he's not. He's in the house."

Looking for us, no doubt. "Thank you, Alexandra. Caleb?"

"Yes?" He took my hand in his. I pushed down the need to rebuff his feelings; apparently, he'd thought our argument at Hagia Sophia had been no more than a passing lover's quarrel.

"The others have been imprisoned for who knows how long," I said. "They may be weak. Help them. A boat is coming as soon as we fire the flare. Please, don't let anyone drown."

"But I won't leave—"

My cousin cut him off. "I'll make sure she gets out, lover boy. Just do what she says, there isn't time for debating."

The slayer hesitated only a second, until the features of his face shifted into resolve. Caleb leaned in, kissing me hard, as though for the first time. Or perhaps the last.

"Hurry," he said. "We need to talk."

"I will."

The first time I was in the house, I'd dismissed the silver and gold that interplayed in Vlad's décor as emblems of vanity, trophies of a vampire who considered himself a sultan. But hadn't he himself said his actions were rarely for a single purpose? A silver grate may be just vanity, but it could also hold back a wolf trying to escape.

I pointed at the fireplace, to the shining grate. "Markus, can you reclaim the silver?"

"Gladly."

My cousin extended his arms, beckoning the metal. It obeyed readily, liquifying, flowing through the air to wrap itself around his chest, his belt. As soon as he'd finished the task, I turned to Ayşe.

"I can go first."

The alpha shook her head. "No, Serhan might attack you, not knowing we are working together. And if your wolf attacks *him*, we'll have too much chaos on our hands. Let me go first."

As Markus had said to Caleb only moments before, there wasn't time for debate. I nodded and stepped aside. The shewolf shifted, flesh giving way to fur and tooth to fang. The lithe creature disappeared down a hole easily big enough to pass a small sofa through.

Markus waved me on. "Someone needs to stay up here to pull you all up. There's no way your huey arms could handle the load."

My back straightened. "I'm not a huey."

"Relinquished isn't much better."

I put my finger on one of the gleaming sheets melded to his forearm. "I'm not relinquished either." The metal under Markus's influence refused to obey my command, but it still vibrated in response to my call. "Though apparently I need to figure out the whole commanding silver thing."

Markus gazed at me, wide-eyed. "How is that—"

"Possible?" I said, cutting him off. I put my sword on the ground in front of the grate as I turned to shimmy the bottom half of my body down. "We'll have to worry about that later. Take those cords from the curtain, use them for rope. Throw me my sword as soon as I'm in and clear."

"Will do."

With only the light that came from the portal above, my eyes took a few moments to adjust to the dim space. As the dark took on definition, I caught sight of Ayşe licking Serhan's ear. In his wolf, the Pera packling's frame heaved, his breaths congested. Around one of his ankles, a silver clasp had burned his flesh completely away, exposing bone. My sword made quick work of the chain. Markus would have to coax the metal from his wound once we cleared the room.

And there, on the far side of the room… was Tobias.

I ran over to where he sat, on the ground, inspecting him for the worst. Like Serhan, a silver manacle cuffed the werewolf, connecting to a chain that kept him from moving too far. Bubbled skin seemed to be the worst of his damage, and as I ran a finger under the metal band, I figured out why. Tobias's hair, oily and grimy, at first concealed the self-injury. Several handfuls of hair had been ripped from his head, which he must have used to create as good a barrier as he could manage between his skin and the silver.

The naked man crossed his arms and leaned back against the brick wall of the chamber. "Took you long enough."

Was he serious? Now? He was going to give me lip *now*? After I made sure he was safe, he was going to be in so much trouble.

I yelled up to Markus. "Pass down the curtain cord, Serhan's in really bad shape." Then, crouching down to Tobias, I ran my hands over the manacle and tried to get the silver to heed my command. It obeyed, thank god, losing definition and melting away. "I'm *so* sorry that I had to put together a coalition to invade the Ravens' stronghold, and that you were inconvenienced. I hope you didn't—"

But before I could say just what I hoped he didn't, Tobias drew me into his lap, threw his arms around me, and pressed his lips to mine.

His lips… so tender, so firm, so demanding. He waxed and waned the pressure, pulling me closer. If I hadn't broken the moment by mumbling into his mouth, he might not have ever let me go.

"You can't even let me kiss you without being contrary, can you?"

Serhan yipped from above as he cleared the tunnel, probably from the shock of having the metal leached from his blood. Ayşe turned, tilting her lupine head in confusion at discovering our intimate position.

She wasn't the only one confused, though. "How?"

The wolf turned sheepish, averting his eyes, looking everywhere except at me. "It doesn't matter."

The Pera Pack alpha barked before taking her turn to escape. Tobias held up a finger, the international sign for "one second, please."

"It does *too* matter." My hand flew to my mouth. "Oh, my god. They gave it to you, didn't they?"

"It's not just because of the serum." He didn't try to quell my fears. "There's been something between us for a while. We both knew it. We both felt it. We've been connected for… God, maybe since we met."

"But you're mated!" I said again. "It's impossible. You can't…"

"I can. I *do*." He finally looked at me again, but instead of remorse, daring filled his gaze. "Believe me, I've tried not to. But since we kissed the first time, I can't deny what I feel."

"Since twenty seconds ago?"

His hand ran through his patchwork hair. "Shite, you don't remember the night in Paradise, do you? You never talked about it, so I assumed you were too embarrassed. And believe me, I've had nights of guilt, thinking I'm somehow being unfaithful to Kara by loving you. I've tried to stop. But I can't. I love you, Geri. Whether or not it should be possible, it's true. And I didn't need the serum to realize it. I only needed the fear that I'd lost you."

"The night in Paradise?" Memories cast themselves on the back of my eyelids. *The full moon. He took on his human, even then. He kissed me.* "You were human on a full moon. You… Cody exiled you."

"No, he didn't. I asked to be released. I wanted the chance to be an alpha again. I wanted to free myself, free *you*, from Paradise."

"But who is your beta?"

But it wasn't Tobias who answered. It was Vlad. "Now *that* is the most interesting part of this all."

We turned to find him standing at the exit, his body solidifying from a cloud of smoke.

"Markus, run!" I shouted, even as Tobias shifted me behind him.

"Try to lay a hand on her, vampire, and I will rip you to shreds."

Vlad chuckled. "I have no intention of harming a single hair on her pretty little head. Offer me a thousand unmated alpha wolves, each holding a bar of solid gold, and they still wouldn't be as valuable to me as she is."

Tobias stood straighter. "That makes two of us."

The vampire ignored the statement, and set about pacing through the room. "Earlier tonight, when I tasted your blood, your secret revealed itself, Miss Kline. How you and your whole cursed race kept something like this hidden for so long is beyond me, but now I realize: you weren't hiding it at all. You don't know. If you had, you never would have let me bite you. You would have killed yourself first."

"I'm still wondering if that wasn't the right thing to do in hindsight." I eyeballed my sword where I'd dropped it when Tobias embraced me, halfway between us and the only means of exit.

"I have become a legend among men, but creatures like you? You are the legend I longed to find," Vlad continued as though I'd said nothing. "I honestly didn't think one could ever come to be, given how strict your hood matrons are on the mating and breeding of their bloodlines. *Hood begets hood,* isn't that a favorite idiom of theirs?"

"And cryptic vampire begets cryptic vampire," Tobias mumbled. "You've already killed too many people I love, demon. You got something you need to tell Geri, do it now. I'll be ripping out your throat in about twenty seconds."

Vlad halted, leaning forward as he spoke, like he was trying to provoke a dog tied on a leash. "They never killed the baby."

The sharp turn threw me for a loop. "What in the hell are you talking about?"

"*Die Verräterin,*" Vlad said. "The Betrayer: so called because she broke the most sacred of hood laws and mated a wolf, bearing his child. Oh, I don't doubt that Gerwalta Faust and her wolf *did* fry on silver spits, but it seems even the heartless harpy matrons could still be melted by the coquettish curls of a tiny, helpless little cub mongrel. It lived, and *you,* Gerwalta Kline, are not only The Betrayer's namesake, you are her direct descendant." He paused, his eyes kept locked into mine. "Isn't that true, Father?"

THIRTY-FIVE

Igor seemed more shadow than solid, or maybe it was the aspect of light that was changing. Above, dawn tickled the horizon. If only Tobias and I could get by and out of the house, the sun would assure our escape.

"Geri, Tobias, are you unharmed?"

"Oh, Father, they are my guests! They have been well treated, I promise. Now, do not change the subject!" Vlad rebuked. "You were always one who believed confession was good for the soul. Confess now. Confess the truth about this hood that you've helped keep hidden."

"This has to stop, Vlad." Igor labored to keep his expression even. "Hunting down other creatures, extending your mortality on the blood and bones of the innocent."

"You're one to talk." Vlad pointed back over his shoulder. "How long before you drain her for your own gain?"

I shuddered. "Igor, what is he talking about?"

"Didn't you hear me, hood?" Vlad bemoaned. "You are a direct descendant of The Betrayer. Hood, yes, but also descended from wolves. It has come down to you over a dozen generations. And my father…" He paused, shooting daggers at the man. "…kept it hidden for his own benefit. How else could a vampire live five hundred years beyond his vampire mortality?"

Tobias gasped. "But that would make you a thousand years old."

"A feat only possible with the rarest of supernatural blood," Vlad confirmed. "Slayer blood is rich, but burns away quickly. Even the blood of an unmated alpha or beta might give us another hundred or so years. But the blood of an *asenaic*? The legends say it can let a vampire live forever."

The knuckles of Igor's hand popped as he made fists. "*Nothing* lives forever, and I've only extended my life until I found a way to end yours."

"And Inga's?" Vlad asked.

Some degree of certainty ebbed from the elder vampire's expression. "I could not bear the weight of my many years alone."

"You wouldn't have had to, if you had shared your knowledge with me instead," Vlad hissed. "So, Gerwalta Kline, you see now why I could not let you go. You are the way I will live forever."

But my mind was still stuck at a point in the conversation from sixty seconds ago. "There's no way my mother is descended from wolves."

Igor's head dipped. "You're right; she's not."

"But if she's not, then—" Impossible. *Im-poss-i-ble.* "My dad?"

"I suspect that's why he was turned away from his own clan," Igor said. "And why he loves your mother when nobody else would, having done what she's done to her own daughter. He's mated to her. *Bonded*, like a wolf."

"And that's also why—" Vlad interrupted, "—I'll be going after him next."

No, not another life.

I lunged, the sword flying into my grip as I angled it for Vlad's chest. The vampire smoked, and I flew forward, landing in the belly of the hole.

"Quick," Igor said, pushing me up through the hearth above. "Into the sunlight."

"But Tobias!"

"You're more important! And I can't—"

A cacophony of snarls, growls, and cries filled the chamber below, rebounding on the stone of the hearth overhead. I pulled myself out and dropped the sword on the floor before lying down on my stomach and reaching back into the hole.

"Tobias!"

His wolf appeared below. He leapt, claws digging into the earthen sides of the tunnel. For one brilliant moment, the amber pools of his eyes met mine, and then, the tunnel gave way.

I barely moved in time to save myself as the stone edifice of the fireplace surrendered to gravity, collapsing in.

"Tobias!"

Markus appeared from nowhere, dragging me back, his words a jumble.

"...now!... Boat... flare... no time!"

THIRTY-SIX

Inga threw the blanket over my shoulders. "They might have survived."

I slurped a sip of my tea, slow and deliberate and as loudly as possible. "I'm sure Igor and Vlad survived just fine. A vampire doesn't need air to live. Wolves do."

Markus, his hood subsumed back into nothingness, shimmied below deck. "There's no word from Ayşe or Serhan. Either they swam off in another direction, or they tried to go out through the street and were overcome." He took a seat beside me and turned to Inga. "How did you finally find us?"

Inga looked away. "Brünhild."

That finally snapped me out of my haze. "Are you telling me she knew where the Ravens' house was all this time?"

The vampire shook her head. "We looked everywhere for some clue of you. *Everywhere.* Finally, last night, when we still couldn't find you after a week, we called your mother. Igor felt... *I* felt that she deserved to know you were missing. *She* knew where we could find you. She told us where to go."

"Your mother has access to the data I pulled off the dagger," Markus said, running a hand through his hair. "She must have looked at the history of where you'd been and figured it out."

But the reminder of Inga and my mother's history triggered a memory of something the vampire had once said. "Was the fact that I'm part-wolf why you suggested to her that I should be killed?"

Inga blanched. "Geri, you were a child. I didn't know—"

"WAS IT?"

Neither shame nor my glare would let her deny any longer. "I knew the danger of your pedigree being discovered by the Ravens was too great. I worried that Vlad would find you, that he'd seize you and succeed in his quest for immortality. It wasn't *you* I suggested she kill, but the chance that the propensity of your kind to breed with wolves would allow you to become some kind of vampire superfood."

Inga grabbed a newspaper from a seat nearby and blocked the sunlight that streamed in as Caleb opened the door. As soon as he closed it, she lowered it, awaiting his report.

"Only one unaccounted for," the slayer said. "A slayer named Haim."

His name means life, I thought, tasting the bitter irony. *And now he's dead.*

Caleb continued, "All in all, a successful rescue. The captain also says he just got a message from Ayşe over the radio. They had sent a member of the pack along with Amy to protect her, just in case. She gave us that wolf's phone number. He'll escort her safely to wherever we want to meet her, though she also strongly suggested we get out of Istanbul before nightfall."

"It is essential that we do, for both our safety, and those of the slayers." Inga's dalliance with emotions ended as she turned to Markus, all business. "I can arrange a private plane for this afternoon. You said you knew a place we could take refuge. Where?"

My cousin shifted in place. "Schloss Wolfsretter, in Germany. It's far from any vampire clutches, deep in the Black Forest."

"Seriously?" I evil-eyed the hood across from me. "You think the matrons would agree to let the home of our archives, our high council, and our training facility be overrun by slayers?"

Markus coughed a laugh. "I'm not planning on asking for permission. We'll worry about their reaction once they have it. Until then, it's the right thing to do. Besides, it will be us soon, won't it? Neither one of us is stupid, Geri. Vlad was already running a de facto slayer-breeding program. Now that he knows the power of a wolf-hood hybrid, a—what was the word he used?"

"*Asenaic,*" Inga supplied.

"Right, an *asenaic,*" Markus resumed. "It's just the logical thing for him to do. He's going to take hoods, and he's going to make them breed with wolves, and then he's going to use the babies as Capri Suns."

I shook my head. "You're wrong."

"What?" Markus's face distorted, his brow furrowed. "Come on, seriously? It's like a recipe, he's just going to follow it."

"No, he's not." I stood, making my way to the door. "He won't have to. You don't seriously think I'm the only one, do you? After a dozen generations coming down from Gerwalta Faust and—" A curt smile bit across my face. "He doesn't even have a name in our history, does he? Gerwalta's mate? We just call him 'the wolf,' as though that's all he was. I guess immortalizing him as an animal lets us forget his humanity."

I would end that somehow. I'd reach back across time, and restore my ancestor's name and his dignity.

I shook my head. "I can't have been the only one. We're going to Schloss Wolfsretter? Fine, then we'll make good use of our time there. We'll turn the archives inside out. We'll dig through them until we discover the truth. And then, we'll work our way forward. We'll find them. We'll find them before he does."

My cousin had the good sense not to oppose me. "Absolutely."

The captain didn't know what we were or why we'd been fleeing from a mansion on the Bosporus at five in the morning. He just wanted to know that he'd be paid for his trouble. Inga made sure the lira flowed like the waters around us.

The summer sun warmed my skin as we passed under the bridge, and Alexandra, raising a hand to block the sunlight, stepped up beside me on the deck.

"You mustn't lose hope. We survived for decades after the world thought we were dead. He can survive a short time until we find a way to free him."

"I saw a fireplace come down on his head, Alex," I spat back. "Tobias was a wolf, but he was still mortal."

"I have seen the brave survive fates worse than death." The slayer wove an arm around me. "Forget your eyes, what does your heart tell you?"

"That I should stop falling in love with wolves." I thought of Cody, thousands of miles away, of his pretty wife, and their chubby little baby. "I'm sorry, I don't mean to be bitter. It's probably best not to talk to me right now."

She nodded, pulling back her hold. "When it is the right time, I will be here. And for what it's worth, so will Caleb."

Caleb. In all my grief, I'd never paused to think of his. "He might not be when he finds out I'm in love with another man."

"You put so little faith in others. It does not surprise me, when you've had so much practice not putting it in yourself."

I gripped the rail, shifting my weight as the boat bounced over the wake of a passing freighter. "I've never lacked faith in myself."

"Not in your ability as a hood, but in your ability to love and to act in the way love demands of you, I think that's not true." Her hand tapped my shoulder as she turned to go. "Stop trying to be what other people have told you you are. Start being who you *really are*."

Who I really was. But who was I?

I was a woman who had loved and lost twice. I was a hood who had been relinquished by her own mother, and somehow—though I still didn't know how—had found her way back to her birthright on her own. I was the namesake and scion of The Betrayer, who, in turn, had been betrayed and lied to by her own blood.

I was Gerwalta Kline: *asenaic*, mate to Tobias Somfield in my heart if not by deed, and I would win back my wolf and have my vengeance.

The red orb of the east burgeoned in its fullness, chasing away the last remnants of the night, and I accepted the road it lit before me.

And then, I threw back my head, and I howled.

REBELLIOUS

RED CHRONICLES BOOK 4

PROLOGUE

BRÜNHILD

"But it's all in German!"

With that, I knew my daughter and nephew were up to no good. I could practically picture her behind the closed study door, my seven-year-old's ebony curls flopping around as her head tilted to the side the way it did whenever she was puzzled. *Like a confused pup.* I shuddered and banished the thought with haste. The last thing I wanted was to credit any lupine tendencies to my own child. Pietro didn't have any such quirks, nor had his mother, who was also an asenaic. What made my daughter so different?

I knew the answer to that question, however. *I* did.

Inside my study, the children continued their banter.

"Of course, it is!" Markus said. "We're in Germany. Did you think it would be in Farsi?"

"What's Farsi?"

"It's another language," my nephew said.

Only two years older than my Gerwalta, my cousin's first born thought he knew everything. For certain, he knew far more than he should. Markus had started reading at four and had yet to stop. The child was insatiable and his parents had quickly discovered that great care must be taken when leaving digestible materials around the house.

Gerwalta huffed. "Well, I've never heard of it."

"Doesn't mean it doesn't exist."

"Where do they speak Parsley?"

"*Farsi,* not *parsley.* And I don't know. In Farsistan?"

A pause, followed by a clunk as the pair took another book down from shelves I myself hadn't perused since being elected. The study had been my mother's when she, too, was Grand Matron, but books and administration had never been my wheelhouse. Execution was. I leaned in, just as curious as the children about what they may find.

"Look!" Markus said. "This one has illustrations."

"What are *iller stations?*" Gerwalta asked.

483

"No, not iller stations, *illustrations.* Pictures that go along with the writing. Smells weird though. Old. And… whoa! Geri, look! Your name is in this book!"

The door flew open without another moment's hesitation.

Filling the door, I invoked all the outrage I knew a mother should feel at catching children in the act of doing something forbidden. Planting balled fists on my hips, I glared them into guilt, and in its shadow, saw the two children diverge. Markus bristled, as if the only misdeed was being caught in the act. Gerwalta withered, her eyes cast to the floor as she shrunk back into herself.

Like a shamed dog.

The boy started to construct his rationalization, sitting in plain view with the ancient leather-bound book open on his lap. "We were just looking, Aunt Brunnie. You said yourself that we should read more about hood stuff."

"That is true, but that does not mean you should be in my study without permission." I turned to where my daughter cowered in the corner. "Come out, sweetheart. It's okay; I should have told you to ask first. This isn't like at home. Now that I'm Grand Matron, you'll just have to get used to me having things you cannot see. It's not because I'm trying to keep anything from you." *Liar.* "It's just because I owe it to the hoods and wolves under my command to respect their privacy. Now," I turned back to Markus, "what is it you've found?"

His pokey little finger landed on a bit of highly-embellished script. "Isn't that Geri's name?"

I bent over and took up the tome, surprised by its lightness, and began to page through the text. "Indeed, it is."

"Why does one of Grandma Sabine's old books have Geri's name?"

My eyes fell instinctively on my daughter, whose eyes shone bright with intrigue, even if she refused to ask the question herself.

The next page's illustration was of a lupine, his dual nature shown by having the head of a wolf and the body of a man, and a red hood beside him with a baby in her arms. "It's a testimonial of our ancestor, Helga the Restorer, about *Die Verräterin*. You both know this story."

All hood children were told a simplified version of the infamous Little Red Riding Hood. The real story, *not* the fairy tale. A werewolf and a hood had fallen in love and wed, despite her mother, the Grand Matron, forbidding their union. They had a child, which angered the Matron so much, she ordered all three executed. The wolf ate his bride's mother in defense. Helga the Restorer carried out the subscribed punishment in lieu of her mother, running them through with a silver spit and roasting them over a fire just outside the outer bailey walls.

"*Die Verräterin?*" Gerwalta stepped forward at last. "The one I'm named after?"

"You're not named after her," I insisted, stroking my daughter's cheek as I balanced the book on the other arm. "You just have the same name."

"But everyone says I am," the girl pouted.

"You're not. When they tell you that, just say what I told Grandmother Sabine: that your name in Old German means 'woman with spear.' It's a proud warrior's name, one which was common in our bloodline for centuries. It is time that it is so again."

It was a partial truth, but the child was too young to know the rest.

I pulled my hand back, flipping pages, finding ones less yellowed by age. They'd been added later, obviously, but why? After the details of the Betrayer's misdeeds and punishment, what more was there to chronicle? A great deal, it seemed, and it should have been no surprise. After all, my own mother had known the truth, that the babe born to Gerwalta Faust and her alpha mate Andreas Baron had not, in fact, been executed. That truth, concealed at the time with the aid of the powerful Dracule paterfamilias Igor Kharmarov, had been reintroduced to my mother shortly after she became Grand Matron. These pages bearing her penmanship documented the recovery of the lost bloodline, tracing the heritage back through the centuries.

The final entry tore at my insides.

On my orders, Brünhild visited Igor K.'s blooded-born, Inga R. She sampled young Gerwalta, confirming my worst fear. The vampire advises the child be terminated before discovery, a heinous act neither Brünhild nor myself are willing to entertain. It cannot be known for certain what powers my granddaughter's blood will hold after she takes her fire, or even if she will survive such an ordeal. Her choice of mate is also highly likely to influence her nature, for such is the way of wolves. Brünhild has been advised that Gerwalta should be arranged to wed one within her own house, preferably someone unable to give her children, if one can be identified, so as to contain further iterations of her condition. To deny the child an opportunity for a full life weighs on me heavily, but the alternative is far too dangerous for us all. In the end, I blame myself for not acting sooner, and for my own contributions to the whole matter. The missteps of the House of Red, past and present, have resulted in a child that could empower our enemies and weaken our alliances. I will counsel Brünhild to do what's required so that our truths are never discovered. I pray this tainted blood dies away. There can be no defeat of the Ravens if ever they become aware of the child who never should have been.

The plan fell into place without thought. "Children, go find the castellan and tell her I wish to have an inventory of everyone who had access to this room during Grandmother Sabine's tenure."

The young hoods looked at each other, quixotic.

"What's tenor?" the girl asked.

For once, her know-it-all cousin had no answer.

I placed the offending text on my desk and pushed the children toward the door. "It means during the time she occupied the office of the Grand Matron."

"Oh." Markus turned back over his shoulder. "But she was Grand Matron FOREVER. Like, before you were even born."

I nodded. "I know, and it will take Rebecca a while to put that list together, but I must have it. You're not to come back until it's ready, okay? In the meantime, practice your swordplay."

Markus let out a rambunctious laugh. "Swordplay."

Gerwalta paused, turning sharply. "Did we do something wrong, mommy?"

"*Mutter,* not mom." The ache in my heart brought a tear to my eye. "No, my dear, of course not. I just have work, is all. Now, go. I'll see you later for supper."

They scampered down the stairs then, the echo of their descent and laughter from their play growing softer with each step. I waited until even my sensitive ears could hear no more. Turning back to the study, I closed the door, locked it, checked the lock again. The book felt heavier when I picked it up the second time, weighed down by secrets. A few unspent logs still rested in the fireplace rack, perhaps where my mother had placed them before her death two months ago. Good, that meant they'd light fast and burn hot. As soon as I had the stack arranged, I placed the leather-bound text atop, held out my right hand, and brought forth a silver orb.

I burned our past under the light of a harvest moon, hoping that the embers did not carry forward in time to set us all ablaze.

ONE

MARKUS

Triberg had never been a prominent town in history, but that didn't stop the tourists. I know, because one of the summers of our training spent in residence focused on local history, both ours and the hueys'. The kitsch-seekers started descending in droves in the '50s, right around the time the haze of second great huey war was settling down. Some came here because, frankly, it's freaking gorgeous. The mountains peaking up on the edge of town, the fall colors, the hot Berliners and Viennese college students flooding into the region to do some "male bonding..."

The Black Forest may have once been known for its isolation and, well, *blackness,* given it used to be so damned dense you couldn't see five feet into it, but nowadays, it was all about cuckoo clocks, alcohol-soaked cherries on chocolate cakes, and thermal pools. Is it any wonder that I loved trips to Triberg when I was a young man looking for other young men? Tourists are so easy to pick up, especially in a roman bath after a long hike through the countryside.

But what brings people to Triberg *specifically* are those waterfalls. I mean, I get waterfalls. Niagara is, like, one of the most impressive things God did with the earth. Even the Tahquamenon Falls by Aunt Brunnie's compound are crazy awesome. Triberg's are the biggest in Germany, and just a short hike from the parking lots at the base. You can hear them from every part of town, just like you can see the top of the cliff that rises above the valley from there, too. Believe me, if the House of Red had known when they built their homestead centuries ago that their beloved castle would be one of the most Instagrammed buildings in the whole of Badem-Württemberg, they would have avoided those falls like the plague.

Interestingly enough, avoiding the plague *was* one the selling points for building here, so far from any sizable population center. See, history lessons *do* come in handy.

Luckily, Schloss Wolfsretter (note: a fancy German frankenword meaning "wolf watcher," like we're some kind of damned lupine peeping tom) developed a bit of a reputation. The tourist guides even tell unsuspecting saps to be smart. "Former residence of a family made wealthy through ownership of the local silver mines, it is now a corporate retreat for a private religious order, and protects its borders aggressively. Take pictures from afar, but do not attempt to visit. You can find licensed postcards at the village gift shops."

But, you know, tourists... Some of them are dumb. A few still crawl up that mountain each year, either boldly driving up the paved road in their airport-issued Beemers, or attempting to hike it in through the woods. Every year, they're escorted back down at the end of a sword or axe. Not that they remember that particular fact afterward. My grandmother, Grand Matron Sabine Kline, wised up and hired a resident vampire. He does the hoopy-loopy thing and clears up huey memories. As a race, we may be old-fashioned, but we're not completely stupid.

I was six the first time my parents forced me to attend "Camp Wannawhackawolf." Geri was only four, but as the direct descendant of the leadership, her school breaks were sacrificed on the altar of hood bureaucracy since she was a baby.

I can't really remember much about that summer except that it was the first time I'd seen a vampire, and they were cool as hell. Back then, the undead-in-residence was an old Welsh rabbit named Regina Flanders. She showed me how she could turn to smoke and made the one huey who lived in Schloss Wolfsretter think her underwear was a dinner napkin. Aunt Brunnie was *not* impressed, but I was. Though she wasn't officially supposed to encourage my curiosity about her kind, Regina sent me emails a few times a year with links to a few places to pick up insight. Which was, like, uber cool of her. Then, when I was thirteen, I showed up for summer training to be informed that Regina had "moved on to another opportunity."

Lucky her, I thought, because by that time, the "summer camp from hell," as we'd described it to our huey friends back home, had ceased to be anything Geri and I looked forward to. I mean, how many summer camps required its attendees to drill martial arts forms from four continents, to learn how to land an arrow in the heart of a squirrel from two hundred meters out, or to study semi-magical chants in half a dozen antique languages?

And did we ever weave a lanyard?

Not. One. FREAKING. Time.

Anyways, Triberg…

One big advantage of Hood HQ being a short drive from a big tourist trap was that you could drive around in cars worthy of a mafia flick and locals would just think you were an uptight banker from Frankfurt. The reason security freaks loved big, black SUVs so much wasn't hard to understand. They were sleek, powerful, roomy, but mostly, their shaded windows and boxy confines leant a certain amount of secrecy to the riders. Or so the theory went. As I pulled the Mercedes SUV to a halt outside the only vehicular entry gate to the compound, the last thing I was, was covert. Hard to stay secret when the only road traversable by a car wound two thousand feet up a mountain in plain view of the village in the valley below, the headlights a moving marker of my position in the night.

I rolled down the window. "Two fries, six cheeseburgers, and a kiddie meal please – extra ketchup."

A click preceded the tinny voice speaking perfect German that came from the box. "Name, clan, and sanjak, please."

Whoever was on duty either had no sense of humor or didn't speak English. Or both. I sighed, piecemealing together the broken language I'd been taught in my youth. "Markus Kline, House of Red, American Midwest under Brünhild Kline."

"Thank you, please hold." The speaker clicked as the castellan's office searched their schedules. Schedules I wouldn't be on, because screw them, I shouldn't need an official invite to enter my clan's ancestral home.

Another click. "Mr. Kline, we don't see authorization for your visit."

"Jesus fricking Christ."

"He's not on the schedule, either."

Inga rolled her eyes and crawled over my lap to get closer to the speaker. Her extended finger wagged at the box like it was a disobedient puppy. "I don't know who you are, but *this* is Inga Rosethorn, and if you don't open this gate and let us in right now, I will personally drain you with my own two teeth."

In German, she sounded even more threatening. And hot.

What? I'm gay, not dead.

The nerves in the voice of the on-duty guard were unmistakable. "Hold please." *Click.*

I fixed Inga with my best side-eye.

The vampire turned a blank expression to me, five inches from my face. "What?"

"Well, first..." I gently pushed her back to her seat. She gave in. Of course, she did. There was no way a hood, even one with my brawn, could force a vampire to do anything. Not without a sharp sword or wooden stake, anyway.

"And, second," I continued once she was back in the passenger side. "Remember on the drive up when I said, 'don't say anything. Just let me handle it because you're going to go vamp psycho and piss them off?' That's the kind of vamp psycho I was talking about."

Inga crossed her arms. "What do I care about pissing off hoods?"

"Seeing as we're coming here begging for their help, I think the answer to that should be, 'a hella lot.' Unless, of course, you're thinking of killing them all."

"A hostile takeover of the compound?" She balanced her chin on a beautifully manicured finger. "How many do you think are inside?"

I wasn't sure if I should tell her because, one, duh, who gave up that kind of information to an outsider? And two, I was scared the number wouldn't dissuade her, and if that was true, yikes.

The speaker clicked again. "Matron Chin has authorized your visit. The gates will open momentarily."

I closed my eyes and grumbled a curse under my breath. I hadn't known Inga long, but it only took a few minutes in the company of the infamous 'Daughter of Dracula' to discover her arrogance. The simple victory would only fuel that fire of conceit.

"Psycho vampire, you were saying?"

"Shut it, Fangs."

The moon above was no more than a sliver in the sky. Tomorrow, it would be nothing. The castle had undergone some modernization efforts through the years, but unfortunately, that didn't include any sort of exterior lighting past the entry gate. The last thing the Matron Council wanted was any way for the hueys in the valley below to get a better view of what happened on the mountaintop.

Inga's eyesight, however, beat mine to Hell. "So, this is the infamous Schloss Wolfsretter?" She twisted in the passenger seat as the car pivoted up the switchback road. "Funny, I thought it'd be bigger."

"You've never been here before?"

Inga looked at me like I'd just said the most ridiculous thing in the world. "Is there a reason I should have?"

"Just, you know… You're one of the oldest vampires kicking it, and this is the center of the hood universe, so I just figured, you know, you big wigs getting together and such…"

"Vampires don't have big wigs," she said indifferently. "Except for Vlad, and then, only because he is a power-and-fame-hungry asshole who made himself renowned through infamy. I think Igor was here once, many centuries ago."

"Really?" I pulled the car into a spot alongside a half-dozen other well-intentioned stealth mobiles. "Why?"

Inga shrugged. "The list of things my father has done of which I know little is long and varied. He's always told me the knowledge of his acts would only be a burden, one he did not want to pass along to me. As time passed and I cultivated secrets of my own, I came to share that sentiment."

"I'm a little jealous of that. My mom tells me everything. And I mean, EVERYTHING. What she ate, who she played poker with, when her bowels are giving her trouble."

Inga's face curdled.

"Just saying, if your dad could give my mom a little lecture on holding back, that would be just peaches and cream with me."

For the first time in our acquaintance, Inga's resolve broke. Her eyes went to her lap and her voice softened. "If he survives, I'll be sure to pass along the request."

A vampire playing the guilt card? That was new. "Look, Inga, I didn't mean to…"

Her hand shot up, halting my words. "No need for platitudes, Mr. Kline. Every child expects their parent to proceed them in death. Just because mine is immortal does not change that."

I leaned across the seat, placing a hand on Inga's arm. "I'm so sorry for your loss."

"My loss?" The vampire turned indignant. "Igor is still alive."

Awkward. I pulled my hand back. "But he was buried underneath half a mansion with a blood-thirsty, egotistical maniac who thinks he's the sultan of the vampire world."

"Tobias was also buried, yet Gerwalta knows he survived."

I didn't hold out much hope of that, either. "I'm not sure Geri even knows what day it is. She's barely come out of her room in the month we've been here. I'm all up for bitch-slapping her with reality if she doesn't get out of the denial phase soon."

"Gerwalta is not mourning Tobias."

"What do you call barely talking or eating while sitting alone in your room, staring at the ceiling?"

"I call it, 'coming to terms with a massive shift in your understanding of the world and your place in it,'" Inga said so plainly, I suddenly felt foolish. "She's spent her whole life being trained to hate the very thing she's found out she is. Even if she was rebellious and claimed to eschew many of those beliefs for herself, it does not mean others have. Not all hoods are as accepting as you are about her newly-revealed nature."

I looked to the castle, wondering if Yan was inside. "I do know something about having your nature judged by society."

"Then accept that Gerwalta knows what she's talking about." Inga opened the car door. "Tobias survives, as does Igor."

***

Rebecca Krantz was part security guard, part old maid, and three parts den mother. One thing she was not, however, was spry. Not that I held that against her. It wasn't like the olden days when the castellan had to actually be daytime caretaker and watchman for the castle, defending it with both sword and honor. Now, each sanjak was responsible for providing two hoods for a year of duty, young folk who staffed all the compound's needs, from security detail to custodial service. Even the cooks were hoods. Rebecca just sort of... kept everyone in line.

She was also the only permanent huey resident of Schloss Wolfsretter, and had been since she'd arrived as a teenager in 1945. By tradition, the Castellan had always been a human woman. A woman, because the hoods were a matriarchal society that held the so-called "fairer sex" as the dominant one. And a human, because no bloodline affiliation meant no bias towards or against any of the twelve houses.

She did have a soft spot for me, though.

"Bibi!" I threw my arms out wide on sight of the old woman looming in the doorway.

She feigned indifference, looking down her nose at me. "Come to tease me again? Butter me up with flattery and try to woo me into bed?"

I let my face screw up. "But, Bibi… *You're* the one who hits on *me*."

"Damn right, and I'm tired of getting the cold shoulder. Now get over here and lay one on me!"

Rebecca's hands took a little tour south as she hugged me, letting my backside have a wee squeeze. Whatever. The old gal had survived a world war, the age of disco, and the holier-than-thou attitude of three Grand Matrons during her tenure. I wouldn't berate her for a little harmless pinch.

As soon as I was free, Bibi turned her attention to the slender brunette behind me. "And what about this one? Someone Yan's going to have to fight off?"

Inga examined her fingernails. "Not if he wants to retain his eyes."

Rebecca ignored the comment. "He's been asking about you, you know. Almost like he was expecting you, which I said was silly, since you were not officially recalled from Istanbul."

"Not my fault. I've been writing to Aunt Brunnie for almost a month, asking her to give me clearance so I could haul tail up here. Or at the very least, give him permission to hike down to RotHaus so I could just plain get tail. I finally got tired of waiting. By the way, Bibi, this is Inga Rosethorn of the House of…"

"Inga will be fine," Inga said, cutting in and holding out a hand in the modern custom. "You're just a human."

Rebecca's face soured, sensing a backhanded compliment.

"Never mind her," I said, putting my phone away again after shooting off a text to my boyfriend. "She's not great with her people skills. Listen, Bibi," I pulled the old woman aside, "why's Chin on duty? I thought Reyhan was in charge?"

"The Matron of the House of Black left a few weeks ago," Rebecca said matter-of-factly. "Apparently, there's been some unrest in the Bosporus."

I rubbed the back of my neck. "Yeah, we might have had something to do with that. Whatever. If Chin is the one here, then I need to see her and ASAP."

"Who's Asap?" Rebecca asked.

Inga cast her rolling eyes to the sky. "And I'm the one who's out of touch?"

Rebecca's spine stiffened. "Now, listen here, youngin'. I've been the castellan of this schloss since before you were in diapers."

Two gleaming fang daggers jutted out of Inga's mouth. "No, you listen here, youngin'," she spit back. "When I was in diapers, your great, great, great, great, great, great…"

My spidey senses told me to move the hungry vampire away from the blood-filled human. "And... we're walking. Bibi, page Chin, won't you? Inga's getting a little cranky. I'll need to get her home soon and put her down for a nap."

"But, Markus dear, the council is in session. Matron Chin won't come out, not unless it's an emergency."

"Oh, it's an emergency. Please, sweetie?"

The sugar sealed the deal. Rebecca grinned. "Okay, dearie. If you think it merits it, but they will want to know exactly what kind of emergency." She leaned forward, into the gossip, as it were.

I sucked on my lip for a moment as I paced out an explanation. "The slayers aren't extinct, but they will be without help. Currently, the twenty or so left are holed-up in Aunt Brunnie's house down in the village."

"Slayers? Well, I haven't seen one of them... Must be about fifty years, since that one stayed here that one time for a while." Rebecca nodded. "I'll announce you at once."

"Thanks, babe. Please also let them know that Ms. Rosethorn will be accompanying me in."

Rebecca clicked her heels like the soldiers of yore before shuffling off.

Inga swiveled. "I have no intention of appearing before the Matron Council."

She was kidding, right? "Then why in the hell did you insist... and I mean *insist,* that you come along?"

"To protect you in case the Ravens were lying in wait. They were not, and you made it into the compound safely. I am a vampire, it is not my place to assert myself in the midst of hood governance, as long as you'll get the council to issue them aid and defense."

"Hood governance?" I echoed. "Inga, this isn't the UN. You're not Belgium and I'm not Barbados, appealing for aid. This is a cross-section of the supernatural world coming together to prevent the exploitation of an oppressed and endangered... Oh, actually, it is kinda like the UN, huh?"

Inga ignored my screed. "As I said, not my place. I've lost too much time already. Now that I know the slayers will be protected, I must go."

"Go?"

She looked at me like I had two heads, neither of them particularly attractive. "To rescue Igor, of course."

"To rescue Igor?"

Inga spat what I assumed was an ancient Wallachian curse. "I swear, you are worse than a parrot."

"How in the hell are you going to rescue Igor? You can't kill a Raven without killing yourself. Plus, it's not like they're going to just be hanging out in Istanbul. They've moved on, and you have no idea where. It took you weeks just to find out which house they were in when you were in the same city, and that was only because I tracked them when they tried to kidnap Geri."

"Actually, I have some idea."

"Great then. Share with the class, Rosethorn."

"I am not your teacher, Mr. Kline, and I'm certainly not your friend."

"Which leads me to wonder, what *are* you exactly?" I crossed my arms, fixing her with a withering glare. "Don't think I haven't noticed the way your hungry eyes keep sizing up Geri. She might be too down in the pits of despair to notice, but I'm not. You could drink any huey in town. Hell, you keep drinking Caleb. I know, I saw the fang marks, even though he's trying to hide them."

The vampire raised an eyebrow. "Spend much time starrng at men's necks, do you?"

"Caleb is a hottie. I stare at his everything!" I retorted. "Stay on topic. What's your stake in this, Inga?"

The crack was fleeting. So fleeting I'd bet that she didn't think I saw it. But I did; that tiny flash in her eyes, a look of pain, a look that begged for mercy.

But a moment later, the stonehearted vamp swept away the cameo of humanity. She turned on her heel. "I will call if I discover anything about the wolf's whereabouts. Tell Geri that I promise that much."

Before I could get another word in edgewise, the daughter of Dracula became a pillar of smoke and dissipated before my eyes.

At which juncture, Rebecca returned. "They're ready for you, Markus. Have to say, the news about the slayers caused quite a stir." She scanned the bailey. "Where's that woman?"

Shaking my head, I made for the inner gates. "Stepped out for a smoke."

TWO

GERI

The sky cried openly, even if I could not.

More fall leaves rusted away by the day. I sat and stared out my third-floor window, as the eroding canvas of trees laid a carpet over the span of the village to the west, to a point where the earth swelled up from the valley floor. Beyond that, a mountain, one which seemed out of place with its stark cliff towering over the land below. Schloss Wolfsretter looked like building blocks arranged by a child at this distance: a rectangle, a cone, a few squares. In my mind's eye, however, I could see its marble entry way, the stone-floored council chambers with its antique throne and tapestries reveling of the glories of the House of Red past. I could envision myself running across the chess board of its inner bailey. Tasting hazelnut soup on my tongue and hearing the wind twist its lithe fingers up the cliff when I fell asleep at night, cloistered in the Grand Matron's residence at the top of the tower.

A few years ago, teenaged me had despised that place, saw it as a center for indoctrination that bred hate for the man I loved. Now, my heart ached for it, knowing that I might never walk its halls again. A werewolf hadn't set foot inside in half a century, as far as I knew. What sane wolf would? The ghosts of their ancestors may still haunt the corridors and passageways. If they were unlucky, they may join them.

The street beyond the walls of my mother's private villa away from the compound, RotHaus, glistened under the street lamp, a spotlight that stood achingly empty. Wishing to see Tobias's form fill in the shadow and stride toward my door was foolish on so many levels, not the least of which was that he had no idea this house existed. Even if he'd managed to escape the Ravens, how would he find me?

But he hadn't escaped. How did I know? I didn't. But in the quiet moments between waking and dreams, I felt his presence in a way that couldn't be explained by logic, sensed his desperation and loneliness. He was alive, but I didn't know why or for how much longer.

Amy walked up from behind, putting a hand on my shoulder. "They're going to say yes. They have to."

She'd confused my wistful street-staring for worry over the fate of the slayers. I couldn't blame her for it; it was where my thought *should* be. A month ago, we'd rescued the last members of a supernatural species thought to be extinct, from imprisonment by the very creatures they were meant to balance. If not for the Istanbul wolf pack, we'd never have made it out with our lives. Here, we were hardly safer than if we stood in the middle of the street, protected only so much as the Ravens feared venturing so closely to the center of the hood world. Our only hope was to get the Council of Matrons to accept the slayers as refugees.

Which should have been as easy as asking, but anything involving a single matron never was, let alone a dozen of them. Markus was the only righteous hood among us, the only one who could appeal to the council. But to do that, he needed an official invite. One we expected to come soon after he relayed a message to my mother that he'd returned from Turkey. One that never came.

"No, they don't." I wasn't being pessimistic; I was making a projection based on years of keen observation. "Hoods are very insular. Outside of dealing with wolves as much as they need to, they keep to themselves. It's like a cult."

Amy cocked a hip. "Then why send Markus to ask? Why don't we just keep running? All we're doing by sitting here is giving those vampire creeps a chance to catch up to us at as leisurely a pace as they want."

When I'd told my cousin I thought we were wasting time approaching the council, it wasn't simply because I felt defeated (which I did) or tired (which I was) or indifferent about what the hell they would decide to do (which I was earnestly trying to convince myself was true.) In the absence of slayers, there had been occasional appeals for help when a vampire got too big in his fangs for comfort, but only when another of his kind didn't solve the problem first. Now that the slayers were back, not extinct, and in need of consolation and protection? Great, but they wouldn't consider it their problem.

"We're here because this is our best hope of finding the slayers shelter," I said. "They need sanctuary, aid, resources. The women know how to use their power, but the men don't. Half of them can't even walk up the stairs without getting winded. They need rehabilitation, rest, and the money we were able to pool together is running out."

Amy, however, thrived on positivity. How could she not? She found a new boyfriend with the changing of the month, each time hopeful *he* was "the one" until the *homme du jour* proved a disappointment. That never ended the cycle though, one powered and buoyed by the fact that Amy always had faith in one time being *the* time.

The blonde crossed her arms over her chest. "Well, even if they do say no, so what? If the hoods won't help, we'll just find someone who will."

"Like who?" I pulled my brown hair, a rambled mess without definition, out of my face as I looked up. "The vampires certainly aren't going to do anything. Even if most of them are decent, none of them are going to take on the Ravens."

"The wolves then."

I scoffed. "Yeah, right, the wolves. Like that's going to happen, them going against the Matron Council and their Machiavellian edicts."

Amy sat down beside me. "We help ourselves, then."

"*We*?" I fixed my friend with a withering stare. "Amy, you're not a part of this. You're not a hood, not a wolf, and you certainly aren't a slayer. Your best bet would be getting the hell away from us and setting yourself up off the grid for a while. Unless you want to discuss the process for becoming a vampire, I'd watch how we use the term 'we.' This is a supe crisis, and you're just a tourist."

The blonde's blood boiled, reddening her cheeks and sending her shooting from the room. A stray impulse told me to jump up and chase her, apologize for being rude. The wiser part of me knew what I said had been the truth.

Caleb slipped into the door, because apparently no one trusted me to be on my own for too long. Great, yet another person with whom I had a complicated relationship coming to comfort/lecture me. I turned back to the window, but this time, not because I was looking desperately for any sign of Markus, but because I couldn't bring myself to look at the slayer who had confessed his love for me, asked me to marry him, then got cozy in the harem before my 'no' grew cold.

"You shouldn't be so rough on her, you know." He slipped his hands in his pockets, looking back over his shoulder in Amy's wake. "She's loyal, brave, compassionate, all things I'd take over mystical silver-wielding or sunlight-throwing powers any day of the week. Even if she does have the worldly concerns of a 1990s Teen Flick Drama Queen."

"She shouldn't be wasting time…" I cut myself off before I said something I couldn't take back.. "If Amy stays with me, I'm going to get her killed."

"What makes you think that?"

"The Ravens already tried to kill her once, and that was before I knocked one of them off and stole all their gourmet meals."

I didn't have to be a bitch though. I'd apologize later. Again.

"Right. Okay. So, anyways, I've been sent in here to kick your ass."

I raised an eyebrow. "Meaning?"

"Meaning… It's time to stop moping. It's been a month since Istanbul, and sitting around being sad isn't helping."

I spun in my seat, making no secret of my anger. "We're not sitting around being sad. Our best shot at defeating the Ravens is with the backing of the Matron Council. Even if I think it's a waste of time to ask, Markus is right that we have to try. Your people are undertrained, underfed, and under some delusion that I can give them what they need. I'm just a twenty-two-year-old woman from a tiny village in Michigan, Caleb. I'm not capable of being a healer, a therapist, a trainer, or a general."

"And… what? You think as soon as the Matron Council bestows its magnanimity on the slayers, you're just going to pass us along and wipe your hands clean?"

My fists clenched so hard, I'd not be surprised to find I'd drawn blood. "I don't owe the slayers anything. In fact, it's just the opposite. I should have spent the last month hunting down the Ravens and rescuing Tobias. Instead, I'm stuck in the Black Forest, playing house frau."

"Bullshit. You might spend your nights here, away from everyone, but you're barely sleeping during the day. Amy says you spend hours when everyone else is asleep training yourself ragged in the basement."

"Of course, I am. I'm going up against a six-hundred-year-old vampire with a god complex and his four closest buddies. You don't overcome someone like that by knitting socks. Or should I just rush into where my mate is being held prisoner and wing it?"

"What makes you think Tobias is still alive?"

"What makes you think he's dead?" Anger crackled in my bones, an impulse to find something silver and push it into a weapon threatening to consume me. "You and Amy are just the same. You don't get that this is what *I* have to do, but I can't get to it until the Matron Council gets its *head out of its collective ass* and agrees to take care of you all."

The door leading from the underground garage opened, taking me to my feet and all the blood from my face.

"He's back."

 Caleb, on edge of boiling over, threw the door open. "Good, let's go hear whether or not your terrible burden is over."

I was just about to dredge up another retort when Markus's booming voice called out across the house. "Oh, my god, seriously! Geri! Geri, your slayers are threatening to kill someone."

Caleb and I, drawn from the mire of our own conflict, exchanged a look of concern before rushing down the stairs. Markus, donning his red cloak like something had spooked him and using his body as a human shield, stood before a tall, slender man with dusty rose skin and hazelnut eyes. The scene did not explain itself, which forced me to demand to know what the hell was going on.

Markus kept his arms akimbo. "Hell if I know. All we did was walk in the door."

Alexandra, in all her gravidity, still held herself out as unofficial overseer of the group, and appeared willing to kick anyone's ass to prove it, pregnant belly or no. She stood a few feet away from Markus, balancing a solarium in the palm of her hand.

"That man is a vampire!" the slayer said. "We did not come all this way just to be taken again."

"Yan is NOT one of the Ravens," Markus insisted. "After everything I did in Istanbul to bust your asses out of Count Creepy's mansion, do you think I'd use you to open up an all-night buffet?"

Something needed to be done before things got out of hand. Only thing was, I couldn't figure out which side of the conflict I least wanted pissed at me.

Amy didn't have a side, or as had always proven to be the case, a filter. The blonde huey pounded down the stairs. "Oh my god, are you seriously telling me that despite all your radical superpowers, you all are still just as bigoted and ignorant as the rest of us?" The shockwave snatched the attention from the standoff, and centered it on her. "Markus, who is this and why is he here?"

But it was the vampire who answered the question, speaking in so gentle a voice, I'd have not heard him without superhuman abilities. "My name is Yan, the resident vampire at Schloss Wolfsretter. I'm Markus's boyfriend."

Amy's face screwed up as she eyeballed my cousin for the briefest second. Was she more surprised that he was gay, or that he was with a vampire? "Okay, *Yan*, my name is Amy, and I have to say, as the only non-supe in this house, I get where the slayers are coming from. See, they were being held hostage by Dracula and all, so we'd just kind of like to know… Are you going to hurt them at all? Because there's, like, twenty slayers here, and I'm sure if a few hit you with their weird sunlight things, you're going to go boom, along with all the rest of us."

Alexandra tutted. "Solaira do not harm slayers."

"Might blast all our clothes off, though," Caleb piped up from the top of the stairs. "Not that that would be a bad thing."

The vampire, perhaps sensing the de-escalation, and picking up on how the odds would be stacked against him, demurred. "I have no reason to hurt anyone. I am an honorable vampire; I do not drink from someone without their permission."

"Or without my permission," Markus added. When Yan gave him a *Really, that's what you want to say right now?* look, he clarified. "What, we're a couple now. I'm just saying, if you're going to suck on anyone's anything," Markus's hand shot up in to the air, "the line starts here."

Amy, blushing like a peach, turned to Alexandra. "If he were to try anything, can you end him immediately?"

The pregnant slayer bounced her solarium like a child's plaything. "In seconds."

"Good enough." The blonde dropped her arms to her sides. "Now, kids, we're all going to play nice until someone gives anyone a GOOD REASON not to. Okay? I'm talking injury, not insult, so everybody, chill."

The slayers grumbled, even as they began to break up and move toward parts of the house other than the large living room that had become a de facto gathering spot. Yan drifted behind Markus like a shadow as the latter made his way toward me.

"A word in private?"

I tried to keep the bitterness from my tone, but I'd never been very good at faking. "Why? We all know the Council said no."

As Markus reached the top of the stairs, he seized me by the arm and turned me toward my room, despite my still-body routine. "I said, 'a word in PRIVATE, Geri?'"

"Okay, fine. Don't be so dramatic."

Once the door was closed, Markus set about his briefing. "Okay, so the part you know: the request to offer the slayers sanctum was denied."

"You don't say?" I deadpanned. "I told you they weren't going to accept them."

Markus grinned. "But they *are* willing to accept them."

I shook my head. "What are you talking about? You just said the request was denied."

"The Council of Matrons has offered the slayers housing, provisions, and assistance with reacclimating to the outside world, in exchange for something."

I wracked my brain for the logic behind that lunacy. "For?"

Markus fixed a furrowed brow and glared. "For killing the Ravens."

I didn't have time to stop the cackle that erupted. "Ha! Is that all? What is this, the *Wizard of Oz*? They want to send a helpless, displaced people to take on the wicked witch?"

"We're not helpless." Caleb reappeared in the doorway, leaning against the frame with his arms crossed. "Overpowering vampires is what we were made to do. Each and every slayer in this house has the potential, they just need time and training."

"If you'll excuse an outsider's observation," Yan interjected as he came in as well, because apparently there was a party in my bedroom and everyone was invited, "at least one of them seemed more than capable—and willing—to kill me just a few minutes ago. Actually, at least one of the women was."

Caleb closed the door behind them. "That was Alexandra, who, by the way, says none of the males went through awakening ceremonies. They're wet noodles, like a nascent hood. Something I'll need to remedy soon."

Markus snickered, but Caleb just rolled his eyes.

"Get your mind out of the gutter, Kline."

I tried to subdue the crawling sensation that swept over my skin, remembering that I'd suffered the same at my own insistence until recently. How that had changed, I was still uncertain. But I'd made that choice for myself, and I raged at the idea of keeping another from their birthright by force. But this wasn't about me.

"The fact remains, they are... well, *nascent*. Even the women, who know how to use their power, haven't been trained in combat. How could we take that kind of offer to them?"

"Okay, first of all," Markus said, "*we* are not offering them anything; the Matron Council is. And second, Caleb is right. This isn't an oppressed people, they were hostages. They're like us, Geri. They're supes. And supes don't get mad, they get even."

I balanced my forehead on the tips of my fingers. "What does Inga think?"

"Inga? Oh, she…" Markus's cheeks reddened as his eyes sought butterflies. "She, um… took off. To do recon, I think. She said she'll call if she finds out anything."

Damn her. What gave her the right to go look for her father, and leave me here to deal with the mess her brothers had wrought?

But since things were left to me, as everyone had somehow decided I was the leader of this little party, I was prepared to lay things out as they were, without any heroic upsell. "I don't feel right about this. Markus and I have been trained as warriors all our life, and we barely managed to escape. And that was only with two Ravens on the scene. You can bet your ass that next time, they're bringing all their forces. Without the hoods standing beside them, the Ravens will shred them."

Caleb shrugged. "So we train them." He turned to Markus. "You said the council was willing to forward us some provisions?"

"Yeah. As far as shelter, they deigned to allow us to remain here at the RotHaus, though what any of them could do to make us leave, I'd like to know. It doesn't belong to the Matron Council; it's Aunt Brunnie's personal property. But the food and weapons they talked about would help. We do make some gnarly silverware, you know."

"Then we'll accept the offer," Caleb said. "And between the three of us, we can train them pretty quickly."

Yan leaned forward. "I can assist with pointers on the best attack methods that work on vampires. *If…* the slayers are comfortable with my presence, of course. And if they promise not to actually kill me."

Caleb clapped his hands. "Great, so it's all settled then. We'll draw up plans, break them out into groups, and get going right away."

Had they all gone insane? "Look, it's not that I don't care about the slayers, but I have to stay focused. The Ravens have Tobias, and I have to save him."

Markus dared my ire. "I don't see how those two goals are mutually exclusive."

Yan raised a finger. "I'm sorry, but who is Tobias?"

"It's complicated," Markus said at the same time I said, "He's my mate."

Markus tried to reconcile the two statements. "Tobias is the werewolf Geri found in Chicago two years ago when his mate was kidnapped and then killed by the Ravens. Indirectly, anyway. He was with us in Istanbul, but Vlad Tepeş took him prisoner."

Yan turned back to me. "Then how is he *your* mate, if *his* mate was killed? Werewolves mate for life."

Markus and I exchanged a look, one in which he asked permission to share my secret. I shook my head. The fact that he was asking, however, let me know I could trust my cousin. As much of a gossip as he was, if he hadn't told his boyfriend, he wouldn't unless I said it was okay.

"They do," I said while chastising myself internally to be more careful with my words in the future.

Yan's voice ticked up a note. "Did you mean 'mate' the way Australians use it, like friends? I can never keep all the variant forms of English in check."

"No, I mean I love him. And he loves me, I think, only…"

Of all the people I had no right to expect to come to my rescue, Caleb did. "The treatment the vamps were using on the wolves plays around with their hardwiring," he said. "We're not really sure what the consequences are yet, but when I was their prisoner, I overheard talk about undoing lupine societies from the inside out. Seems Vlad still has a bit of a chip on his shoulder about the way things went down in the Balkans back in his day. He blames the wolves and he wants revenge."

That seemed to put an end to the vampire's confusion, as he nodded once. I made a mental note to thank Caleb later. Hell, it wasn't really a lie, what he'd said. Vlad had told me as much, and I didn't have any reason to think Drac was lying. Still, something niggled at me. My attraction to Tobias was easy enough to understand, even before I knew I was part-wolf. Not only was he buff and hot in a rough-sexy type of way, he'd saved my ass too many times to count. But his attraction to me? Had I been imagining it in the early days? Purely physical, of course; I didn't dismiss for a moment his feelings for Kara. But still, could a bonded wolf be drawn to someone not their mate? Was there something in the archives that could explain the aberrant behavior?

The curiosity had my mind wheeling, and was about to take control of my feet.

"Markus, which matron is on duty at the Schloss?"

"Chin Zhu, why?"

Good. I didn't know Chin personally, but that made it more likely that she wasn't one of my mother's allies.

"Let the slayers know what the council has offered," I said. "I think it's a fool's deal, but ultimately, it's their decision to make. I need to run an errand."

"Run an errand?" Markus asked. "You mean you're actually leaving your room? Where are you going?"

"I want to see if I can appeal to Chin's better nature."

THREE

Inga had told me that if Tobias and I were truly mates, one of us would know if the other died.

"But we never actually… you know," I'd said to the vampire.

Inga had merely smiled ruefully, the way only those grown wise with age could. "But you're some sort of wolf-hood chimera. I wouldn't expect the way mating works with you to be the same. In any case, you love him. I think there's a power to that that goes beyond whatever magic or supernatural talents we have. It's anchored in our humanity, and if that anchor slackens, you'd feel it. Just like I would, if something happens to Igor."

I'd stumbled for words. "You're not… You and Igor, I mean, you…"

Vampires couldn't blush, but she'd given it her best attempt. "No, Igor and I do not now nor have we ever had a sexual relationship. The love of family we feel has bonded us for centuries, even in the times when I was too pigheaded to accept it gracefully. That's why I feel safe telling you that if you feel Tobias is still alive, then he is."

He was. I could feel him somehow, like the warm feeling you had long after finishing a good meal. His existence fed me. But at the same time, I couldn't ignore the implications. If Vlad hadn't killed him immediately when we'd left, he had bigger plans for him. But what?

In the meantime, since leaving Triberg was on hold, I had another wolf to rescue. This one, from the pages of time and the shadow of infamy. Somewhere in my family tree was a branch upon which a noble lupine sat, maligned and overwritten by the so-called shame of *seducing* Gerwalta Faust. I intended to trim back those overgrown twigs and reclaim his dignity.

"Name, clan, and sanjak, please."

The voice piping through the speaker when I pulled up to the security gate of Schloss Wolfsretter wasn't one I recognized, but that meant little. Hoods from around the world and from every clan rotated through the House of Red's ancestral home.

"Gerwalta Kline, House of Red, American Midwest under Brünhild Kline."

"Gerwalta… Kline?" The tremor in the woman's voice was impossible to ignore.

"Oh, you've heard of me." I turned down the music playing on the car stereo. "I'd like to request a word with Matron Chin. I understand she's in charge at the moment."

Which begged the question, why wasn't my mother here?

"Matron Chin is in session, and…"

The gate attendee either neglected or didn't bother to turn off her microphone as her tongue turned to German, the Schloss's official language even if most everyone actually conversed in English these days. Despite the attempt at secrecy, I still picked up on a mention of "Die Verräterin." The notoriety of my 'betrayal' preceded me.

Good, knowing who they were dealing with would save so much time.

Finally, the voice came back full and steady. "Miss Kline, according to our records, you have been relinquished by your matron. Therefore, you have no official sponsorship or standing."

"Mom remembered to fill out all the paperwork, huh?"

She either ignored what I'd said, or chalked it up to rhetoric. "Relinquished hoods may not enter the compound."

"Right. Remind me, what's your name?"

The uncertain voice drew the answer out like taffy. "Beatrice Jones, House of Green."

That explained the vaguely British tone of her voice. "Beatrice, what does *relinquished* mean to you? Other than the fact that my own mother has disowned me, I mean."

"A relinquished hood is one who has had her powers revoked by her matron, and is rendered, as close as is possible, a huey," she said as though reading the answer from a book.

I beckoned a silver bangle on my wrist into action, holding my hand in the direct view of the camera just over the speaker. My influence liquified the metal, boiling it into a pool of cool liquid that swirled on my palm before it obeyed my command and took the form I envisioned in my mind's eye. The tiny, shiny Buddha didn't vary too much from the kind you'd find an any Eastern goods gift shop, with the exception of its prominent middle finger erect on its right hand.

"As you can see," I said, "I'm not relinquished in the way that really matters."

"That does not mean you're a righteous hood."

This chick really wanted to piss me off, didn't she? I plastered on my best fake smile and dipped my voice in honey. "Call Matron Chin, please, or I'm going to crash my car through the gate."

A new voice spoke. "Do that, and you'll be dead before you can hit reverse."

Bingo.

Chin Zhu, a white hood from the lush valleys of China, had a history of disagreeing with my mother on matters of policy and practice. That she was talking to me took me by surprise, but I tried not to jump to the conclusion that it meant she disagreed with my banishment. It might, though, and if it did, she might be willing to agree to what I was about to ask. One could wedge open opportunities if only they knew where the cracks were.

Her German was pushed through a Mandarin sieve. "We are just about to retire for the day, Miss Kline, so if you would be so kind as to state your business succinctly, I would appreciate it."

"Thank you, Matron Chin, for your consideration. First off, I wanted to ask why the council refused to offer the slayers sanctuary."

"Perhaps Markus miscommunicated our answer on that. We *are* offering them sanctuary, if they agree to…"

"If they agree to anything to receive aid, it is not sanctuary," I interrupted. "If you have conditions, then what you're offering is payment. How is that fair? We thought the slayers were extinct for fifty years. Now we're dictating the terms of their rebirth?"

"*We* are doing nothing, Miss Kline. You are no longer a member of this community." A long sigh crackled through the speaker, and when Chin spoke again, her tone was more annoyed than authoritarian. "I'm not Grand Matron; I can't unilaterally decide to harbor the enemies of such a powerful vampire as Vlad Tepeş without your mother's approval."

"His enemies?" My voice shot up an octave. "They were his prisoners."

"I'm afraid that in this case, it's a matter of semantics."

"Slavery is never a case of semantics."

"Geri, please!" Chin huffed. "I want to help. Trust me, I do. But this isn't a dictatorship, and there are members of the council who aren't eager to set us up on a collision course with the Ravens, especially given the involvement of someone like you in the situation."

Had my mother spilled the beans about my true nature to the council? Had the Grand Matron of the legendary House of Red admitted her own daughter was part wolf and that our story of *Die Verräterin* wasn't entirely true? As much as I tried, I couldn't picture the proper Brünhild Kline giving up that kind of info without a fight. No, whatever Chin was talking about, it had nothing to do with Gerwalta Faust or my connection to her. What did she mean, then, someone like me?

Chin continued before I could figure out how to ask without giving anything away.

"Now, if the whole of your business was to come seeking resolution to a situation already resolved, then—"

Panic pushed my pulse into the red. "Wait, Matron Chin, I... I want to examine something in the archives."

"You know you can't..."

"Just for a few minutes," I interjected, even as I tried to keep the desperation in my voice contained. "Then, I promise, I'll go away and stop bothering you. Markus can be the liaison between the council and the slayers, but I really need to examine the logs of the condemned. You can be there with me if you want."

"Logs of the condemned? Why would you want to study the darkest parts of our history?" For someone not related to me, Chin managed to perfect the tone of a scalding mother. "Miss Kline, this must end. You have no right to ask us for anything. I can't make you leave Triberg, but I can have a tremendous amount of influence in the council's discussion about the slayers. If you want us to help them, keep your head down and stay away from Schloss Wolfsretter."

"Five minutes in the archives. Please, Chin, I..."

The floodlights mounted above the gate flickered on, rendering me blind. My arm went up to block the assault, but as my eyes recovered from shock and the figures standing just beyond the gate began to take shape, I knew the discussion was done.

Hoods dealt with other hoods in the weaponry that made sense to us: swords, daggers, slings and arrows.

With humans, we used guns.

Which, oddly, would work on a hood too, especially if you managed to shoot her in the heart or the brain. But one didn't serve water in wine bottles just because it also quenched thirst.

I ground my teeth and the tires as I navigated the SUV through a three-point turn and headed back down the road.

FOUR

I managed to get back to the safehouse without hitting anything more than the proverbial wall. And the steering wheel, several times. By the time I parked the car, keyed in past the security door, and made it inside the yard, rationality had abandoned me. I paced in the backyard, the grass still crisp with frozen dew, as the sky began to yawn in the east. I couldn't let the slayers see me like this; they were already on edge.

What I wouldn't give to run. In my youth, the mountain had been a playground for me, the only condition was never be seen doing inhuman things by all-too-human eyes. Now I felt like an animal caught in a trap, held in place by the slayers, and able to see an escape I could not obtain without chewing off my own foot.

In the corner of the yard sat a stack of hay bales, propped atop each other to create a target for archery practice. If I had my grandmother's dagger still, I'd hurl it over and over just to work out my frustration. Without it, I used a bit of silver I repurposed as a bangle to create a tiny penknife. The meek impact of so small a weapon didn't satisfy, but it still felt good to chuck it at something I could pretend was Vlad's face. When that failed to vent my ire, I turned to my fists, imagining the vampire was standing before me.

"So."

Shoulder punch.

"Many."

Chest jab.

"Damn."

Groin kick.

"Obstacles!"

One final blow to the side of the stack sent hay flying directly into Yan's arms.

I startled as the vampire dropped his catch and ran a hand over his brow to clear the debris. "Did you know I was here, or was it just coincidence?"

Met with the fact that I was no longer alone, my posture eased. Incrementally. "How would I know you were here?"

His bleached hair bounced when he jerked his shoulders. "From what Markus says, you are not like the other hoods. Perhaps you have some special ability to sense us, like the slayers."

"None that I've noticed." I didn't want to be rude, but I also wasn't in the mood to be hospitable. "Did you need something, Yan?"

The vampire restacked the bales with the ease of a waiter picking up a dropped spoon and setting it back on the counter. "Not me, *them.*" He pointed back over his shoulder to the house. "Markus says the slayers have come to see you as some sort of Jesus figure."

Even though I wasn't particularly religious, I still curled in disgust at the comparison. "I wouldn't say that."

Yan twirled his right hand in the air. "You know Markus. He's given to hyperbole. But at the very least, they hold you in great respect and have put their fate, at least for the moment, into your hands. You have great sway with them, and with their opinions of things."

"And this is leading…. Where?"

"I mean them no harm, Miss Kline," he continued from behind a twisty smile. "Like most vampires, I was under the impression their kind was extinct. I admit, their resurrection has me… curious. Perhaps in my questioning of their circumstances, I came off as aggressive. They have misinterpreted my interest for something sinister, when really, I am in awe of their survival. I was wondering if you'd be willing to say a word on my behalf, to set them at ease?"

I stepped forward to draw the silver penknife from the recesses of the hay, curling it back into a bangle on my wrist with a thought. "No."

"No?" He repeated the word as though unclear of its meaning. "Perhaps I have also offended you in some way? Or is it because I am a vampire, and one of my kind currently holds your lover hostage?"

"It has something to do with the vampire part, but it's not about me."

And then, for reasons I couldn't quite fathom, I began to lecture in the backyard of my mother's estate to a vampire who was basically a stranger and sleeping with my cousin.

"Hoods are raised to believe werewolves tiptoe along the edge of humanity, that lupines are only a hair's breadth from being consumed by their animal natures and going apeshit on hueys. Since the time I was little, I felt in my bones that wasn't right. I opened myself up to that possibility, so much so that I fell in love with one of them. My world hinged on his kiss, on our ability to overcome our natures and be together, despite traditions, biology, rules, my mother… And then—"

A silent laugh fell into my shoulder as I buried my head.

"And then, reality bitch-slapped me. All it took was one night for that illusion to break under its own weight. And that left me afraid. So very afraid, probably more than I even admitted to myself at the time. Not of lupines really, but of the idea that I might trust one of them—any one—with my heart, and suffer that loss all over again. Loving Tobias is the bravest thing I've ever done, and now… Now, I may have lost him, too. So, I'm learning that the fear is a good thing, Yan. It protects you. It keeps you from putting yourself in the path of danger. These slayers… Some of them spent their whole life under the Ravens' control, and for them, *every* vampire right now is a Raven. So, no, I won't 'say a word' on your behalf, because I know the danger of that. They *shouldn't* trust you."

I sighed, turning away from his sagging shoulders and pitiful frown. Great, I had to be an asshole, didn't I? Guilt condemned me to say something nice. Close to nice? Not so mean, anyway.

"Look, Yan, for what it's worth, they probably shouldn't trust me, either. I have no idea what I can do to help them."

"No, I... understand." As much as a vampire could, Yan folded in on himself. "Thank you for your honesty. It makes me wonder, however, if I should keep my distance, stay away from the house. At least until such time as I can offer more than my passing curiosity."

"What if that never happens?"

I didn't know if I was asking for his benefit, or for mine.

Yan only shrugged. "In my many years, I've learned that 'never', never happens." The vampire straightened out, before fixing me with narrow eyes and an amused smile. "If only more hoods were more like you, Miss Kline."

"Like me?" I guffawed. "Falling in love with their historic adversaries and given to violent outbursts?"

"Perhaps. Your crowd is far too straight-laced for my taste." He grinned. "Markus is an exception, of course. But no, what I mean is, I wish they all were so passionate about doing right, that they're willing to be ostracized to do so. You are an inspiration."

"Now that's a high compliment. And... one... I'm not completely at ease with."

"Well, then, Geri Kline, I hope you grow into the impression you've made on me through the years, because it is mighty, as are you."

My mouth dropped open. "What do you mean, through the years?"

But just at that moment, Markus emerged from the door on the backside of the garage. "Yan? Are you back here... Are you... Oh, Geri?" He held up when he caught sight of me. "I didn't know you were back. And with my boyfriend. Talking."

Yan, beaming at my cousin, crossed the yard, pulled the solidly-built hood into his chest and brushed a kiss against his lips. "Amor, I think I will run into town for a bite. Can I bring you back anything?"

"Greek sailor, if you find one."

The vampire grinned. "I would keep him for myself if I did. I think I will sleep up at the castle today. Your house is quite full with guests and I would not wish to cause you to accommodate another."

"I told you that it doesn't matter," Markus said. "We can sleep in that attic for all I care. Just don't..."

But the vampire didn't hang around to argue. One more quick peck on Markus's cheek, and Yan dissolved into a smoky patch that rushed over the grounds and out of the yard.

My cousin passed me the stink-eye. "Okay, what the hell? Why are you cockblocking me? Did you tell him he couldn't stay here?"

"No." I mean, I didn't say 'thou shall not commit adultery with my kin in the house of my mother' or anything. "What does he mean he's going to stay up at the compound?"

My cousin looked at me like I was stupid. "He's the resident vampire. You know, the one the Matron Council employs to wipe the minds of any hueys that see something they shouldn't? How did you think I met him?"

"Maybe using one of my methods? Work in his university research lab. Or be really old-fashioned: storm his house to free his prisoners," I deadpanned before realizing my attempt at sarcasm was probably the most honest thing I'd said all day. Which, of course, reminded me that the slayers—and Tobias—were in greater peril with every passing hour. And me? I could do nothing about it.

The weight of incompetence pressed down on my shoulders, pushing my back against the hay bales and my butt to the ground. "Why am I here, Markus? Why am I just... *hovering* here?"

Markus softened, leaning down next to me and putting a hand on my shoulders. "I'm taking it Chin wouldn't give you the time of day."

"I never even left the car. Shame for them, really. It would have made shooting me easier."

Markus's mouth dropped open.

"They *didn't* shoot me, obviously," I amended. "But they did draw against me, so... You know, three-quarters intent, or something like that."

My cousin mused a moment before saying, "Actually, it's a good thing they refused to let you in."

"Good? How in the hell is that good?"

Markus slid down on the ground next to me. "Because I'm willing to bet they don't know you're an asinine."

"*Asenaic.*"

His hand cut the air. "Whatever. The point is, your mother did everything she could to keep that secret, and no matter what you think of her right now, I don't think she did it for any other reason than to protect you. Outside of this house, hardly anyone is hip to that nugget, and maybe we shouldn't just go throwing it around willy-nilly."

"Duh, do you really think I was born yesterday?"

Markus buried his chin in his shoulder, his voice growing soft. "Well, I mean, you wouldn't have to *tell* them."

"Hoods have many great powers." I, for one, was totally digging silver wielding, now that I could do it. "But I'm pretty sure being psychic isn't one. How else would they know? Can matrons read minds and no one remembered to tell me?"

Actually, thinking back on a few times when my mother had caught me trying to sneak off and see Cody back in high school…

Markus gawked at me like I had just said the most idiotic thing ever. And he was a fan of Monty Python. "They'd know the way any hood knows when a wolf is near. They'd sense you."

Ice shot down my spine. "Markus Kline, are you telling me you can *sense* the wolf in me?"

He nodded. "I mean, not *all* the time." He ran a hand through his brown, wavy hair before cleaning it on his sweater. "It's weird, though, the energy… I mean, it's definitely wolf, but not consistent or very strong. I only get whiff of it when I'm as close to you as I am now. It cycles with the moon. Except when you're near Tobias, and then it gets crazy strong. Or at least it did that last week in Istanbul."

I looked into the distance, into nothing and everything in particular, seeing the light that lit the room, though the room had seemed empty before. "Because we're pack."

He laughed. "That's ridiculous. I mean, even if you *are* descended from D.V.'s kid, that was, like, more than three centuries ago. There's no way the tiny bit of lupine DNA you got is going to line you up for beta duties."

He had a point. Possible to have a few traits? Yes, very. Likely that it was strong enough to bond as pack? Unlikely. But the moment I said the words, I felt the weight of truth fall into my hands.

Markus continued, "I mean, what's next? You going moonmad if you two are separated for too long?"

I glared at my cousin. "You think I'm holding it together *now*?"

"I'm serious. If you're wolf enough to be in pack, that probably means you're wolf enough to be struck with lunacity." Suddenly, Markus's eyes brightened. "Have you tried taking your fur yet?"

I rolled my eyes. "Pretty sure if that were possible, it would have happened by now."

"Yeah, but you're different somehow, right?" He pulled closer, putting an arm around me. "I mean, even on a hood level. You can wield silver now, but you never took your fire. Maybe whatever happened to you that made that possible, also ramped up your wolfishness."

He could have a point. "It's possible. We'd never know for sure without proper studies. Test and control cases. Lots of lab work."

Suddenly, Igor's absence became tangible. What a field day he'd have with me in his lab now.

My cousin's face screwed up. "You're thinking too much like a scientist, not like a hood."

"What in the hell does that mean?"

"We're at least a dozen generations down the line from when Gerwalta Faust got Black Forest fever. You really think you're the *only* descendant?" Markus paused as his eyes filled with thought. "The line is actually on your dad's side, you said, right? From the yellow hoods? Don't you have any cousins from his clan? I'm sure if we got in touch with Pietro's family in Argentina we'd discover other aesthetics."

"*Asenaics*." I shook my head. "Remember how we agreed I should keep this on the DL? I don't think reaching out to my extended family is down or low. Besides, my dad doesn't have any family left except my mom and me. My *abuela* was the only closely-related person on his side of the family, and she died ten years ago."

The hood beside me balanced his chin on a balled fist. "If we could look at the archives, we'd be able to trace back, then see if there were any special mentions of anyone in the annals who howled at the moon and hunted tasty villagers."

Humor finds no anchor on a soul worn down by sorrow. "That's what I went to the Schloss to request, but Chin wouldn't listen. Now that she knows what I was after, they're not going to let you anywhere near them either. I'm surprised they haven't ordered you to disown me too yet."

"Chin can't touch me. I'm still under the Grand Matron's orders to watch and protect you. Even if those orders came down because she's your mother and she's using the rights of the throne to benefit her own family, none of the Matron Council would dare to override Aunt Brunnie without good reason."

I wouldn't be so sure. The disgust in Chin's voice when she spoke about not acting on behalf of my mother still echoed in my memories.

"I wish there were some other source we could go to, but all the archives have been centralized at Schloss Wolfsretter since it was turned over to the community."

"You don't think ancestry.com would be able to trace back our family that far, do you?" Markus asked. I mean, we still paid taxes and bought plow horses and stuff."

"Doubtful." My shoulders slumped. "Right now, I'd settle for just knowing his name. Why, Markus? Why is Gerwalta Faust's name a firebrand of traitor to us, but her mate is considered so shameful we know nothing about him?"

"Probably because back in those days, no one cared about the wolves but the wolves." A tiny, sarcastic laugh escaped him. "Not that we've come very far since then."

We sat, letting our ambitions war with our adversity in the battlefield of our minds, until a cannon exploded behind my brain, taking me to my feet. "Oh my god, Markus, you're a genius."

"That's what I keep telling everyone."

I ignored his cheekiness. "Somewhere in my family tree, there was a baby born to Gerwalta Faust and a wolf whose name we don't know. We can't get to our records to see if it's there, but we can get to the wolf's."

"Great idea," Markus mocked, "except lupines aren't known for their archival skills. Before the Matron Council had the database, all that kind of tracking stuff just happened... ad hoc."

I grimaced, knowing Markus was right. The hoods had had to keep records. They had wealth, land, contracts, correspondences with kings and sultans. The wolves in most of Europe had been farmers or laborers, often making a living at the pleasure of their overseeing matron. The hoods, or *wolfsretters* as they'd been known back then, didn't treat the packs under their protection as anything much more than cattle.

Old fairy tales weren't told to inspire hope or recall legendary love. They were tools to sow seeds of fear and hate. *Little Red Riding Hood* was used to tuck my kind's children into bed and implant in our minds how lupine leanings would corrupt us and lead to our ruin. If Gerwalta Faust's "crime" had led to an alpha's execution, the wolves would not have soon forgotten, either. Their histories might not record numbers and contracts like ours; likely they weren't written down at all. They were howled at the moon, barked in the trees, spun around warm hearths on cold winter nights...

They were oral.

"The wolves may have passed down the story, like we did," I said. "Only, the other side of it. A warning to their pups of the danger of letting your guard down around a hood. That's our next move, Markus. If we can't turn a light on the wolf, we're going to look for his shadow."

FIVE

Pastels were an odd color choice for maps. The gentle yellows, tranquil blues, and pastoral greens used to color the different countries of Europe belied a history wrought with conflict, death, and hatred. True, the continent had been more or less peaceful during my lifetime, but then again, huey political boundaries didn't correlate much with ours. The supe map would be colored in radical reds, angry purples, and confusing grays, a swirling confusion of push, pull, and parry. Borders were fluid, set down in the cardinal directions based on the dominance of whatever pack claimed—and kept—territory.

Cities belonged solely to the vampires, as they had been since ancient times, their conflicts played out on urban turfs. Although in recent years, they'd spilled out from beyond those traditional hunting grounds. Thus, the whole reason Tobias came to Chicago from sleepy little Morpeth, Northumberland. If the slayers had still been around, would I ever have met the man I'd come to love? Did I owe my happiness to the imprisonment of a dying race? That I could only have him because his mate had been experimented on to the point of death by Vlad's supporters?

All things I needed *not* to think about right now. *Focus, Geri. This isn't just about you and Tobias. Other hoods could be in danger, and they may not even know it.*

Markus, Amy, and Caleb waited until sunrise before converging in the kitchen. On the floors above, the nineteen other slayers had divided the available rooms in ways that suited them, though the pregnant Alexandra had been granted a solo suite.

Markus briefed the other two on what both he and I had already discussed.

"After '48, when Schloss Wolfsretter was converted from the residence of the House of Red to the administrative headquarters of the whole hood world, the pack that had been rooted in the Triberg area," he pushed his index finger over the very town on the map we currently occupied, "fractured into two packs and relocated. Most of them went here." His finger skirted to a region some 200km to the southeast. "The Oberstdorf Forest. But a few went in the opposite direction." His hand traversed down a minty green border region to a Pepto-Bismal shaded country. "To the highlands just below the Austrian border."

Caleb crossed his arms and leaned back in his chair. "Start with the bigger pack. More mouths, more opportunities for oral traditions to be handed down."

Amy nodded. "As a life-long gossip, I agree. If we drive crazy fast, we can be down there by nightfall."

"You know, Geri, this actually is one time when being relinquished is going to help you." Markus turned his eyes up to meet mine. "You're not a recognized member of the community, so you don't have to go through the formality of telling the alpha you're coming to the packland or letting the local matron know you're there. You can just wander in at your own risk."

I grimaced. "Yeah, but it also means you can't come with me. Most wolves are kind, but having a rogue hood show up on their land uninvited might leave me wishing I had backup."

Amy quirked her head to the side. "*Local* matron? You mean there's more than just Geri's mother?"

"More than one?" Caleb coughed a laugh. "The hoods are like a paramilitary organization. Very organized, very tidy, dividing the world into controllable zones of dominance."

"Actually, our current set up is something based off the Ottomans," Markus countered. "One grand poohbah at its head, from the royal family, if you will, though all bloodlines *technically* have a claim. Then there's a council of advisors, and locally, each region has its own governor. The Ottomans are the reason we call them sanjaks, which unlike almost everything else, is so not a German word."

Amy's hand circled vaguely over the map. "So, you mean, like, the whole world is parceled out, and you guys... The House of Red?... are the hood royal family?"

"There's no one in Antarctica," I said flatly, vaguely motioning at the map. "Or most of Oceania. Australia has a few packs and a matron, but that's because of immigration. Lupines aren't native there."

"I like how you ignored the part about being royal," Amy said. "Does that mean your mom is..."

"The Sultan, the emperor, the master of the universe... Whatever way you want to think about it," Markus confirmed. "As long as she has the backing of the Council of Matrons, Aunt Brunnie's word is law to all the hood clans."

"Which, as you pointed out," I interrupted, "no longer includes me." I watched the light go out from Amy's eyes, knowing my friend had already been constructing some sort of Disney-inspired saga in her head. "Right, so that's my plan. I need a few hours of sleep, but then I'm going to set out for Austria."

The three people across the table blinked in rapid succession.

Caleb shook his head. "You can't honestly think we're letting you go alone."

"Of course, you're going to," I said. "The bigger need for security is here. If the Ravens show up while I'm gone, Caleb can lead the assault and Markus knows all the hideouts and escape routes from Triberg. And Amy can't come because, well..."

"Because Amy is a weak huey who will snap like a twig," she said.

A sheepish smile crossed my face. "I wouldn't have put it like that, exactly."

The blonde folded her arms over her chest. "Doesn't make it untrue, though, does it? No worries. After being attacked by a vampire, I'm not eager to be mauled by a werewolf, bested by pixies, or in anyway assaulted by whatever other creatures are out there."

Caleb turned back to his original point. "I'm pretty sure we don't have to worry about pixies, but there's still five Ravens left alive and they're going to be gunning for you. They might be thinking hard about heading into Triberg with the Hood HQ sitting right up the hill, but once you leave the Black Forest, who knows? Unless you're planning on not sleeping for two days straight or stopping to use the bathroom at some roadside gas station, you need someone to cover your six. You're *not* going alone."

I leaned back from the table. "I agree, that's why I want to take Yan."

"Oh! I'd love to go!"

All four spun the moment his voice called out, Caleb even balancing a conjured solarium on his open palm. Markus meanwhile pulled his hidden silver into a blade. Not to be outdone, Amy brandished a banana swiped from a bowl on the nearby counter.

Though, in her defense, it was a very *large* banana.

Yan wore a crooked grin. "You can put down the produce, Miss Popowitz. Potassium's effect on the undead is overhyped."

Markus, realizing his lover had entered without a sound, reclaimed his silver and circled the others, arms open.

"Sweetheart, what have I told you about sneaking up on me like that?"

"Don't, or you may inadvertently chop my head off?"

The male hood pushed the vampire's cheeks between his massive hands. "I mean, not *off*, probably, but still..." He graced a kiss over the vampire's lips. "I thought you went home. Have you been hanging out here the whole time?"

Yan's eyes landed on me, like a child constructing a cover story after breaking his mother's favorite vase. "I... um, changed my mind. I smoked in through the garage just before the sun came up. I've been hanging around in the heating vents."

"Heating vents?" Caleb's query wasn't directed at anyone in particular. "I never thought about it, but makes sense. Inga used to use the heating system at WWL to get all over the building. How are we going to defend against that, if the Ravens try to break in?"

"We can't," I said. There was no point in false optimism. It would get people killed. "This house wasn't designed for that kind of defense. Keep working with the slayers on sharpening their skills. For the ones who are in good health or haven't been through their awakening, start them working on some defensive forms." I jerked my head in my best friend's direction. "Amy, too. Just because she's not as strong as the others doesn't mean she should be left defenseless, in the event of pixies or whatever."

But Caleb wasn't distracted by my request in the least.

"You knew Yan was still here." The slayer's narrowed eyes focused in on me. "How?"

I huffed. "How else? Because he's a second pair of eyes ordered to watch me."

The vampire dared feign confusion. "Miss Kline, I'm afraid I don't know what you're—"

"My only question," I interrupted, "is *who* gave the order? My mother or Chin?"

At that, the game came to an end. Yan grimaced. "Matron Chin."

"Wait, what?" Markus took a step back from his boyfriend. "Why? I thought that was my job."

Yan's hand rose to stroke down my cousin's cheek. "Because I volunteered. If it wasn't me, it'd be someone less amenable to presenting you all in a good light. I was strategizing." The formalities of lovers' reunion aside, the vampire turned to me. "As long as you can provide me a safe place to shelter during sunlit hours, I would be happy to accompany you to visit the Austrian packlands."

"She's not going to Austria, and she's definitely not going in the company of a vampire." Caleb planted his finger on the Oberstdorf Forest. "Geri, your chances are better with the bigger pack. If they turn out not to know anything, it's not that long of a drive to the other settlement."

"I don't care how short the drive is," I snapped. "I know it's irrational, but I'm going with my gut on this. Besides, the pack that's stayed further away from civilization is the one less likely to have given into modern distractions. The oral traditions would hold up better through the years."

"Actually, there's something to that," Amy said. "You know, I read this one article I came across about this remote valley in the east part of Turkey where the people speak a whistle language. Like, complete with verbs and nouns and stuff, only in whistles. I guess the sound carries, like, a mile over the valley. But now they're afraid the younger generation isn't going to learn it, since it's not the most efficient way to communicate anymore, given that everybody has a cell phone."

By the time the blonde huey finished, the rest of us sat with jaws unhinged.

Amy looked at her fingernails. "Why are you guys always so surprised when I know stuff? I'm not the Daphne of this Scooby gang, you know. Supes don't have exclusive rights on useful information."

I shook off my surprise before continuing. "Yan, I still would like to have you with me. A vampire can move with speeds I can't, maybe get us out of a critical situation. But this isn't hood business; any information I get isn't for her consumption."

"I'm already *not* going to tell her you're an asenaic," the vampire said with a wink. When my face morphed into a mask of shock, he pointed back over his shoulder. "I was back there, listening, remember? No, I'm just supposed to report if you try to make any contact with other *hoods.* I was very careful about what I was agreeing to."

Amy threw her arms out at that one, though. "Come on, Geri, you barely know this parasite—" Her eyes dashed to said *parasite.* "No offense." Then landed back on me. "—and you're just going to get in a car with him and drive off? What if he's just waiting for the perfect chance to kill you?"

Yan's hand splayed over his chest. "I would sooner destroy a Picasso."

I didn't think I was worthy of that level of reverence, but Amy was only being a concerned friend. "If his goal was to kill me, he would have done it when we were alone in the yard. Anyway, if Markus trusts him, I trust him. Only, I'm not sure how I'm supposed to keep a vampire out of the sunlight in a car?"

"I thought the answer would be obvious," Yan said. "You are a hood. Encase me in silver."

I felt like I'd been asked to join a BDSM gang, when I had already said I didn't whip that way. "Can't we just use a Tupperware bowl or something?"

As if we had anything that Donna Reed in this house.

Yan shook his head. "I don't mind being trapped in something, but I must be sure it's sunlight-proof. There may be alternatives, but I'd prefer it this way. I know most vamps can withstand a few hours, but my skin is a little more... sensitive."

"And you're trusting me to do that? To entomb you in silver?"

"Of course." Yan looked surprised that I'd even ask. "Markus trusts you, therefore, I trust you."

"Thank you, Yan." I turned to my cousin. "While we're gone, put in some appearances at the compound. I don't want the council to forget that they still owe the slayers if the slayers agree to take that damned contract."

Markus nodded. "I'll do what I can. In return, make sure my boyfriend doesn't die."

"You mean die again?"

"Seriously, Geri." Markus's face drained of any jest as his hand wrapped around my forearm and squeezed. "He's my Tobias. Don't damage him."

I looked back over my shoulder, at the vampire who was now quietly watching with a cocky grin on his face. "I'll get him back to you unblemished. I promise."

SIX

For centuries, supe intellectuals and philosophers had debated whether or not those once known as "dark ones" were still, or ever indeed had been, human. Opinions varied, bolstered by evidence and counter-evidence, varying degrees of facts, and even a few so-called divine revelations. Even the supernatural races were not immune from crackpots and self-appointed prophets. At the end of the day, since hoods, slayers, and werewolves could still *breed* with hueys, the collective summation was that, technically, we were only a different type of human.

Vampires, however, who could only infect hueys with their condition to create progeny, were classified as humans, but diseased. To me, the answer was simpler. A vampire could love and be loved, and was at liberty to make decisions based on will, not instinct, if they so chose.

Unconditionally, they were human.

Maybe that's what drove Igor to study supernatural genetics, I thought as I maneuvered the car through another gentle mountain curve. He was of an age when all maladies came with some level of social damage. What would it be like to live as a supernatural leper? Did he see himself as having some communicable disease, and see the slayers as a cure?

Retracting from completion of grand theories and biological classifications, even I admitted this was perhaps the oddest road trip I had ever taken. Under the light of the blazing sun, the others and I had agreed I'd be safe to drive on the main highway that led south out of the Black Forest region and over the Austrian border without my watchdog awake. As the sun dipped toward the horizon, however, and the purple shadows of the mountains stretched long over the highway, I turned to the urn-like container belted into the passenger seat beside me. To the untrained eye, it would look like nothing more than a full-sized coffee thermos, though without any seams. How would anyone suspect it held a vampire inside?

I reached across the divide, tapped a finger on the vessel and pulled the silver back up my arm, past my shoulders, and commanded it to plate the planes of my abdomen. I didn't want any of it in sight when I met the pack. The smoke held the container's shape only a moment, so concentrated that it looked like I'd only changed the color of the thermos rather than the materials it was made from. A blink, however, and the cloud swirled, taking on mass where moments ago there had been only miasma.

Yan stretched out long in the seat the moment he was reconstituted. "Thank you. It was getting rather itchy in there."

He put on his seatbelt, though I doubted a car accident would do anything to him. Unless it managed to take his head off, that was.

I turned down the retro German pop station I'd been listening to for the last two hours, more to annoy me and keep me conscious than to entertain. My annual Herbert Grönemeyer quota was full in one sitting. "We've got two more hours until we reach Zeihern. It's not completely dark yet, but the direct sunlight is gone. I have to stop for gas, and I'd feel better if I wasn't alone when I did so. You're not going to burst into flames or anything, are you?"

"A vampire doesn't burst into flames, we dry out, then scorch, then dissolve into dust," Yan said flatly. "The light is defusing quickly. I will be fine with this limited exposure."

"Groovy. So... Want to take turns changing the radio station or have awkward conversations about our lives?"

Yan shut off the radio. "Have you consummated your relationship with your wolf lover yet?"

"Awkward conversation, then." I flicked on the right blinker as I merged toward the exit. "No offense, Yan, but that's none of your business."

He continued as if I hadn't spoken. "In the old days, these things were so much simpler to deduce. If we observed two creatures going into a room together for the day then coming out in certain unkempt ways, we could assume intercourse had occurred. Nowadays, though, your generation has no set rules for social engagement. You and Mr. Somfield, in fact, have been cohabitating for sometime without any intercourse occurring as best we can figure, but..."

The brakes cried to the high heavens as I slammed them down. As soon as I was assured there was no one coming up behind us and I wasn't blocking the exit, I spun in my seat.

"Who in the hell do you think you are, asking me that kind of stuff?"

Yan shrank back in his seat, finally rediscovering his shame. "Apologies. Time and isolation have made me unpracticed in the art of social convention."

"Ya think? My sex life is none of your business. How would you like it if I asked what you and Markus do behind closed doors?"

"Markus prefers keeping the doors open..."

My hand shot up. "Oh, my god, that mental picture is going to haunt me forever..." I tried to clear my mind. "How does that happen, anyway? And before you get into details I don't want to know or will ever want to know, I only mean how did the two of you end up together?"

"You *know* how curious he is about vampires, and since I came in to the employ of the hoods a decade ago, he's always been at me for details. I suppose in the last year or so we just sort of… clicked. It has not been without some negotiation. My position necessitates certain… *acts* which come into conflict with our relationship."

"No offense—I love my cousin—but he isn't the 'lie to my face and I'm okay with that' type."

"Oh, I don't *lie* to him," Yan rushed to clarify. "I've grown too old to put stock in the benefits of artifice, but both of us understand that our harmony depends on a bit of unscripted discord in the distance. I have no doubt he has his secrets as well."

Remembering that Markus hadn't told Yan I was an asenaic, I knew that to be true.

"Not that I'm going to answer, but why would you ask me about sleeping with Tobias?"

Yan's eyes brightened. "Ah, so you have—"

"STILL none of your business."

He drew inward. "One of the things that brought Markus and I together is our interest in the other's peoples. Just as Markus is curious about vampires, I have always been curious about wolfsretters. *Hoods,* as you say currently. I've endeavored to learn as much about your history as I can."

The full implication of what Yan said took shape in my brain. "What do you know about what really happened to Gerwalta Faust?"

"The only record I've ever encountered about those events was one penned by her sister, Matron Helga Faust. But there are… rumors."

My ears perked up. "Yeah?"

Yan nodded. "That the Betrayer wasn't Gerwalta Faust at all, but her mother."

That didn't make any sense, even if I didn't buy the commonly-held version of the story as true. "How so?"

"As the saying goes, 'history is penned by the victors, the truth buried with the victims.' Have you not ever wondered why Helga is called 'the Restorer'?"

I chewed on my lips as I moved the car back into drive. "No, but I guess I should have. Anything you can add to that?"

His hands flattened on his legs, rubbing his knees. "One story I heard was that Gerwalta Faust's mother, Gunda, had a last-minute change of heart about her daughter and saved the baby from harm, staging its death and secreting it out of Schloss Wolfsretter."

Hope fluttered in the pit of my stomach, making me dizzy. "Do you think that's true?"

"Oh, yes, Miss Kline, I do. It came from a very reliable source not given to spreading gossip."

"Yeah, who?"

"Igor Kharmarov."

Holy shit. Igor? Had he known the whole time that my ancestor survived? How? The answer to that question would have to wait until the next time I saw the professor again. If I *ever* saw Igor again.

Yan leaned forward, examining me across the divide. "Are you okay, Miss Kline? You've gone pale."

"I'm fine." I wasn't. "Call me Geri, though. And do you mind if I give you one word of advice before we get to the packlands?"

"Of course not."

"Don't ask any of the lupines about their sex lives."

SEVEN

We left the car parked on the side of a dirt road and moved with lithe steps across grass crisped with frozen dew. Ahead lay six cottages clustered in the midst of a clearing, braced by several utilitarian structures. A little further up the hill stood the remnants of an ancient barn, moist and moss-covered, looking like one of the postcards the summer tourists gobbled up. The style was similar to ones still seen at intervals in the Black Forest, though fewer of the structures remained with each passing decade.

A half moon peered over the mountains, lighting the settlement.

"Which house do we try?" Yan asked. "Or do you suppose the pack is out running?"

I closed my eyes and inhaled, testing the air for hints, sending my senses coursing over the landscape. Then, I felt it. That little tug, a quiver which grew into a wobble in my gut. They were there, up the hill and concealed by the forest, roughly a kilometer away. They'd been moving in the opposite direction, but the moment I reached out to them, I may have inadvertently changed that. Suddenly the pack was on the move, closing in fast. But not all of them. Several of them were closer. Much closer. I didn't need any supernatural powers to know that part. The frosted, lit windowpanes of one of the residences gave it away to the naked eye.

"Markus ran this pack through the database. Four males, six females, four cubs ranging in age from two to thirteen. Two females are with the two younger cubs inside the biggest house." I lifted a finger, pointed to the two-storied structure that lay furthest from where the road ended.

Yan's jaw dropped. "Remarkable. Your senses are so well-tuned as all that?"

"Actually, I'm just using deduction." My finger flicked up. "That's the only house with its lights on and smoke coming out the chimney. You should know, though, that the rest of the pack is charging toward us from that ridge up there."

"I can hear them," Yan concurred. "I am surprised you can, though. I know hood hearing beats a human's, but it is nothing compared to a vampire."

No sooner were the words out of his mouth than the first lupine broke through the tree line, only eight hundred meters to our right. She was tailed by the rest in quick succession, the pack moving in a way I'd rarely observed myself except in nature documentaries. Their circular formation complimented with yips could only be interpreted in one way: they intended to kill.

"We have a plan, right?"

The nerves in the vampire's voice were undeniable. Wolves and vamps didn't often cross paths due to their different habitats, but the archives of our peoples included a few times a pack took on a lone vampire and ripped it to shreds. A single vamp may be stronger, but a lupine was just as fast and, in a group, could pull down anything.

"Kinda." I pushed Yan behind me. "Not sure this is going to work, so be ready to smoke unless you want your throat ripped out."

"I can't smoke when I'm scared."

Brave of him to admit as much.

"Besides," Yan continued, "Markus loves kissing my throat."

I readied myself to move. "So didn't need to know that."

A wall of barks and growls fell over us, an onslaught that pushed every button my hood instincts had. *Strike them. Slay them. Damage them.* I lectured my wolfsretter brain, in German even. *No! This will work.*

Or so I hoped.

It was funny. All my life I had listened to the drive of my nature pushing me to act in ways prescribed by breeding and genetics, and never considered that wolves did the same thing. And since new revelations had me seeing everything from a new perspective, I figured the right thing to do might be the *opposite* of what instinct demanded.

"Yan, do exactly as I do when I do it."

My eyes would be glowing silver now, but there was nothing I could do about it. The wolves ripped up ground. Twenty meters. Fifteen meters.

Behind me, Yan's voice shook. "Geri?"

Ten meters.

Five.

"Geri!"

"Now!"

In the blink of an eye, I folded in on myself, dropping to the ground, burying my head down between my arms, assuming a fetal position on the ground. One of a vampire's greatest strengths was the ability to move with superhuman acuity. Gravity didn't pull on Yan any harder than it did me, but I still heard the thud he made even before I'd assumed my position.

The pack surrounded us, and for a moment, when a few pushed their snouts into my hair and clothing, one even nipping my ears, worry gripped me. Would they attack, would they bite? Would they *kill?* One raked a paw across my head, hopefully just to get a better view of my face. No further comment from Yan, so either he had a remarkably high pain threshold, or the wolves hadn't touched him.

"Explain yourself."

The man's scorched voice, drenched with the thick accent of the Austrian mountains, told me that at least one of the wolves had shifted back into his human form. I fought down the impulse to look up and continued to kiss dirt.

"My name is Geri Kline, relinquished hood of the House of Red, disavowed daughter of Matron Brünhild Kline," I said. Or at least, I hoped I'd said. I'd been raised to speak basic German, but fear was getting the better of me and I wasn't sure I'd said it right.

A lupine's hot breath huffed against my ear as I awaited response. Without my eyes, my ears became my only view of the scene. Quiet whispers wove together in a tangle, the unfamiliar threads of voices difficult to discern. The gruff man—he must be the alpha—spoke with a female. It was the woman, not the man, who addressed me next.

"Why do you travel in the company of a vampire?"

To my relief, Yan answered for himself in German perfected as though god damned Goethe himself were drafting a new work on the vampire's tongue.

"It is my honor and privilege to accompany Miss Gerwalta Kline into your beautiful packlands. I yield to the grace of your Konigswolf, offering my respect and vow that I am here without issue, seeking no claim but a hope for friendship."

I cried out as a firm hand twisted my hair in its grip and pulled me to my feet. I couldn't help but whimper, even as I told myself to do so was to broadcast weakness.

But you are *weak, Geri,* a little voice inside me mocked. *A strong hood would not have thrown herself like pearls before swine.*

The naked, middle-aged woman who held me at arm's length didn't seem interested in roughing me up though, or of actually causing pain. In fact, she looked at me... confusedly, with deep earthen-colored eyes and skin nearly as fair as the snow that topped the nearby mountains. Her appearance struck the eye, gave me pause for a reason I couldn't quite put words to. It wasn't beauty, per se. No, it was some sort of power I sensed from her. She was gentle, but formidable. Dominant. Powerful.

"Your name is Gerwalta?"

"Yes, ma'am." *Ma'am?* "Like the Betrayer."

The woman's face curled. "Who?"

Not all wolves knew of the hood legacy, it seemed. In fact, not all hoods knew more than the name, like a title of a book they'd been read as children rather than a real person, an archetype of evil without the need for context.

"Gerwalta Faust," I clarified, "the Betrayer."

As we spoke, other wolves shifted back into their huey forms, one of whom, a young woman who couldn't be but a year or two younger than me, leaned into the wolf who held me captive.

"It could not be coincidence," the first said.

The other woman clicked her tongue. "Coincidence is never coincidence." She turned back to me. "What business does a relinquished hood and a vampire have in these packlands?"

They were never going to believe me. "I came to learn your stories."

She laughed, turning to the gravel-voiced man and finally releasing her hold on me. "Did you hear that, Lukas? She says she wants to hear our stories. Lies! A hood wants to hear nothing from a wolf but 'Yes, ma'am' and 'no, sir.'"

I tried to wet a mouth that had suddenly gone dry. "Please, I've driven all the way from Triberg just for this. All I want is to talk to you, ask you a few questions."

The young woman smiled and stroked my cheek. "And we will do our best to answer."

Lukas took half a step forward. "Ann-Marie, you cannot possibly—"

Ann-Marie snapped her fingers and gave Lukas a vicious scowl, silencing him, making him sink back. How curious a behavior for an alpha.

"The road from Schloss Wolfsretter is long," Ann-Marie continued. "Come. I think dinner is just about ready. Go to the alpha's home. We will dress and join you shortly."

By this time, all the wolves but two had scratched back into human flesh. As though Ann-Marie were a grand marshal leading a parade, they all fell into line behind her, six naked bodies walking through the crisp Alpine landscape as though strolling across a Brazilian beach in the height of summer. The two in fur pulled up the rear.

Or *rears,* as the case may be.

Yan drew himself beside me, his eyes fixed on a rather svelte male who looked to be in his early thirties. "Are they always like this? So liberated? So nude?"

I nodded.

"But you don't seem fazed by it at all."

"It gets old after a while."

It didn't.

"Really?" The vampire grinned. "So when you see Mr. Somfield…"

In an instant, my face flushed. I had, of course, seen Tobias shift from fur to flesh before, but that had been in a time when we'd either been battling for our lives, or before we'd admitted our feelings. Thinking on it now, I didn't picture myself being so blasé the next time.

Yan clapped me on the shoulder. "Save your breath, Geri. Your pulse says it all."

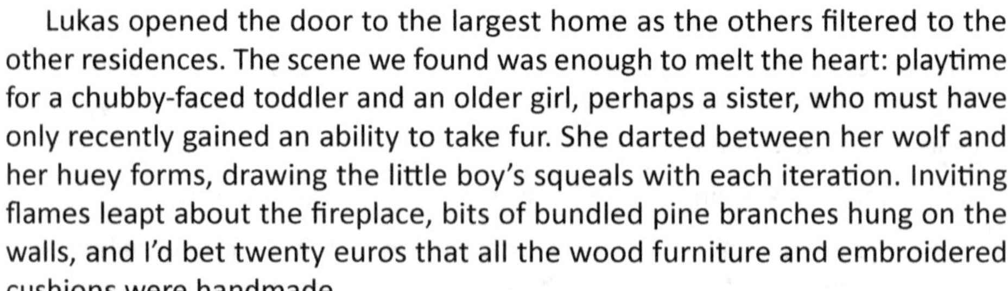

Lukas opened the door to the largest home as the others filtered to the other residences. The scene we found was enough to melt the heart: playtime for a chubby-faced toddler and an older girl, perhaps a sister, who must have only recently gained an ability to take fur. She darted between her wolf and her huey forms, drawing the little boy's squeals with each iteration. Inviting flames leapt about the fireplace, bits of bundled pine branches hung on the walls, and I'd bet twenty euros that all the wood furniture and embroidered cushions were handmade.

"At ease," Lukas said to the two attending shewolves as they leapt to their feet, instinctively seizing the children and shepherding them behind them. "They are guests. The hood is Gerwalta Kline, the vampire is her chaperone."

Both women's faces blossomed into silent smiles, and one with luxuriously long and thick black hair said, "Look at her eyes! How curious."

I blinked my surprise, suddenly self-conscious and uncertain how to respond.

Luckily the other, her hair bobbed short and blond, spoke instead. "Like the hoods." She fixed me with a diagnosing study. "But I don't sense—"

"No, wait." Something shifted in the air around us, and the shewolves grinned. "How odd."

Yan needled around my side. "I don't suppose you ladies would be willing to speak on what you're experiencing?"

The blonde wolf's smile soured. "I'm sorry… You are?"

The vampire stuck his hand out. "Janus Sousa, born of the Varanasi Creche and of the Rajani bloodline, currently resident vampire employed at Schloss Wolfsretter."

None of these facts seemed to meet with lupine approval, as they both eyeballed the proffered hand for a few moments before turning their attention back on me.

"Is your name really Gerwalta?" the blonde asked. "Like, honestly? It's not just a pet name you picked up?"

"A pet name?" My face curdled. "Not unless someone really hated me. *Which* my mother does, so…"

The blanket of awkward I'd just thrown out settled, dampening the conversation. Luckily, it was at this point that Ann-Marie returned, wearing a black knit poncho and blue jeans. "Ladies, I wonder if we might borrow the room for a few minutes?"

Both the women ceased staring at me and turned to the children, still engrossed in the pleasures of the young girl's quick-change routine.

Ann-Marie settled on the couch, inviting me, and I'd presume, Yan, to take up the nearby chairs. "Before anything else, I have to ask what brought you to *us*?"

How to answer it in a way that wouldn't put the wolves on the defensive? "Are you familiar with the hood stories about the Betrayer?"

Ann-Marie grinned. "You mean Little Red Riding Hood?"

I grimaced. "Kinda, but not exactly the Grimm Brothers version."

The shewolf exhaled and fell back into the couch. "Why don't you tell us the hood version of the story, then?"

"Well, it's not a version. It's the actual story. Back in the 1600s, a hood of the House of Red became the mate of a werewolf from the Triberg pack. *This* pack's ancestors. It's the biggest crime a hood can commit."

"No huntsman and his axe, then?" Ann-Marie's eyebrow arched.

I curled in on myself. "The story *we're* told as children is that they were hunted down by the Red Matron, chopped into pieces, and roasted on silver spits over a fire on *Feuernacht* as punishment, but I don't think that's true." I knew it wasn't, but I wasn't about to cast out all my secrets. "I'm hoping your version of the story gives an alternative picture."

And his name. Please, I just want to know his name.

"Let me see if I understand." Ann-Marie smoothed out the bottom of her black poncho over the tops of her legs. "She both chopped her own daughter into pieces *and* roasted her over a fire, you say? If you'll pardon the pun, it seems a bit of overkill, doesn't it? But the hoods are given to violence. I should have guessed their version would end with blood and torment."

Yan perked up. "Blood?"

Ann-Marie ignored him. "My ancestors would be appalled to know how the hoods have corrupted their story."

My head sped again, though I tried to pull back the anticipation. "Are you saying that this story *has* been passed down in your pack?"

"Do tell." Yan inched forward in his seat. "And please, emphasize any parts that include blood."

Ann-Marie took to her feet, and I was suddenly aware of how the gaze of the only wolf who remained behind, Lukas, rose with her.

"Geri," the young woman held out her hand, as though she and I were schoolgirl friends. "Might I interest you in a walk, just the two of us? I don't believe you've ever visited these packlands before. They really are quite beautiful, and I'd be honored to show you."

My instincts screamed at me to say no. *An unfamiliar, young wolf with an unusual sway over the pack wants to get you alone. It cannot be for any good reason.* My head jerked in Yan's direction, though if I expected to find any counsel in his eyes, he left me wanting. He watched with an invisible tub of popcorn. Hoping that being alone with Ann-Marie would let me be more open about the reasons I'd come, I swallowed my fears, reached up, and accepted the shewolf's hand.

EIGHT

Winter came earlier at higher elevations. Despite the fact that it was only mid-October, we'd not had to climb far up the mountain to find snow beneath our feet. Wolves preferred forested regions (insofar as the packs that lived where it ever snowed at all) in part because the tree tops offered refuge against the accumulation of the white stuff. What did float between branches and firs to the ground was protected from the sunlight, reducing the chance the surface would melt in the day, only to refreeze after sunset. A space up ahead where the timberline met the cleared land came into view, but it seemed so odd that the wolves would build their residences so in the open, a fact I remarked upon as we walked.

Ann-Marie smiled. "A bold move on our part, perhaps? Who would ever think a pack living so in the open would have so much to hide? But that's not the story you came to hear, is it?"

"Does it have anything to do with why you all fractured off from the wolves who settled in the Oberstdorf Forest?"

"Indeed. The schism resulted from a difference of opinion. Curiously, Geri, do you know why your clan fractured and went to America?"

Honestly, I'd never given the thought a moment's consideration. "Probably the same reason a lot of Europeans were moving around that time: the hope of a better life. There were already wolves and hoods in America, of course. The Orange Clan, the first lupines…They're still around, but not as many. Mostly in the plains states and southwest."

"I've read about this, native peoples pushed out of their lands. Why should supes be immune from such cultural shifts?"

She mused in silence for a moment, though I didn't know if it was because she needed to digest the thought or she was hoping I'd say something. But the question was rhetorical, wasn't it?

Finally, Ann-Marie continued. "I know why you're here, Gerwalta Kline, daughter of the Red Matron. There's a reason you came to us for stories and not the Oberstdorf Forest."

I drew to a stop to fix her in my gaze, but without pausing, Ann-Marie pulled me onward.

"Let's keep pace. I should try to get back home sooner rather than later. I know it makes Lukas nervous when I'm out here alone."

Because she was young? A woman? Alone with a hood?

As if she'd heard my internal question, her face broke out into a drunken smile. "He wants me to be his mate, made a formal offer a week ago. I think he's afraid if he isn't with me every second, he'll miss me giving my answer."

"And do you know your answer?" I asked.

Her head bobbed. "But if I told him right away, what fun would that be? Ah, yes, we're almost there."

I trudged on. Up the mountain slope, tall pines dusted with snow created a verdant crystalline view that disguised a measure of both breadth and width. As far as I could see, there was nothing ahead to arrive to, other than more trees. "I wasn't aware we had a destination."

Ann-Marie grinned, her eyes scanning the treetops. "Anytime one moves forward, it is always with a destination, whether or not they are aware of it."

"You're very philosophical for a wolf."

The statement crossed my lips before I'd had a chance to bite my tongue. Instead, I bit my lip, waiting for a rebuke that I was totally owed. Instead, Ann-Marie let out a single laugh.

"I'm sorry," I scrambled. "I didn't mean to—"

Her hand rose, cutting me off. "No need. You were raised a hood, I was raised a wolf. We both have been forced to believe that the other should fit a certain mold, and it confuses us when we meet with experiences that make us question who the other is, for it also makes us question who *we* are. Besides," she turned a warm grin my direction, "I could also say that I've never met so kind a hood."

Even the indirect insinuation left a mark, one I couldn't slight the shewolf for. Through stories I'd heard from Tobias, and after the Matron Council's rejection of the slayer refugees, I had begun to see my own people with an outsider's eye.

Feeling a shiver that had nothing to do with the cold, I pulled my jacket tighter about me. "You didn't think I was too kind when Yan and I arrived earlier. Your pack looked like it was out for blood."

"That was not about you being a hood." Ann-Marie drew to a stop, as did, it seemed, the falling snow, the wind through the trees, and the rotation of the earth. "That was about an unknown wolf venturing into our packlands."

When I'd used my ability to detect the wolves, I hadn't realized the feeling went both ways. But it wasn't like I was about to come out and admit that. Ann-Marie was going above and beyond to be hospitable, but who knew what she'd do if she knew I could summon her kind. "What unknown wolf?"

"You don't need to hide your secret from me. In fact, you can't. I perceived you the moment you drove up our access road. The others did not, of course, but that's to be expected."

"But I am not of your pack."

Asenaic or no, I was still certain the other laws of lupine nature applied. Wolves had a tremendous sense of smell. Their vision was pretty keen as well, though it paled in comparison to a vampire's. Where the "super" of "supernatural" really came into play, however, was in their ability to communicate while in their animal forms. *Not quite psychic,* Cody had once explained when I'd asked about it. *But we have a sense of each other, both in terms of what we're trying to say and where we are. If another member of the pack is inside my house, I know it before I walk in the front door.*

But the skill wasn't omnipresent. Like a closed-circuit system, that power only extended to members of a pack. Or so I thought…

"True, you are not," Ann-Marie admitted. "Nor are you of my pack, and how could you be? But I think a hood mother would not name her child Gerwalta casually. It would have made you a pariah among your people. The Grand Matron is exceptionally brave, I think, to do this. But it doesn't matter. Even if your name were Philomena or Tsa-Tsa, I would suspect you were of my bloodline. Let's keep walking. We're just about there."

Walk? How could she walk with that kind of bomb thrown at my feet?

"Your bloodline?" My head shook without consideration that it may seem insulting. "That can't be. I'm a hood."

"Who also has a wolf ancestor."

My mouth felt like someone had stuck an overly starched, dry washcloth in it. "Are you descended from Gerwalta Faust?"

The young woman blushed, took me by the hand and coaxed me onward in body, but away in mind. "Oh, dear, no. But my ancestor was the brother to the Guardian's mate. Just a few more steps, now, Geri. Come now, it's just over in that glade there. You'd never know it, but until a century ago, there was a hunting lodge here, one with a splendid summer garden. It's all gone now, of course. But the marker remains. My pack thinks the forest itself protected them, growing around it."

"Ann-Marie, please." I seized back my hand. "I don't want to be rude, and I sure don't want to come off sounding like a hood, but I demand you to tell me what you're talking about. Who is the Guardian? Where are we walking? How did you know we have a common ancestor? Have the wolves known this whole time that Gerwalta Faust's baby lived?"

In short, why was I lied to all my life, while others knew?

The shewolf looked as though she had a secret threatening to bust through at any moment. She pointed to a place behind me, over my right shoulder.

"Read it."

I spun.

At first, I'd thought I'd been put on. What lay before me was just another tree, even if deformed, like some superhuman force had bent it to his will, compelling the trunk to bulge and bubble about four feet off the ground. But as I let my eyes relax, *words* began to take shape. The plaque may have once gleamed, but now its silver was exposed, tarnished. My fingers danced over it as my powers reached out, calling to the silver that lay in the pine's embrace, asking it to shake off its age and weathering. Where a moment before the letters could barely be perceived, they now shone out, reflected in the ambient light of the forest.

The Old German script proved so embellished and elaborate, it was a barrier to understanding. Perhaps Ann-Marie sensed the trouble I was having; a moment later the shewolf was at my side, her finger bouncing along with each elucidation while still keeping sufficient distance so as not to be burned by the element which was a poison to her kind.

"Here lieth the body of A. Baron, born 16 April 1662, aged twenty-five years, died 12 November 1687, and wife, born 3 December 1666, died 12 November 1687, aged twenty-two years. May they be together in death as they were so briefly in life."

Impossible. "*This* is Gerwalta Faust's grave?"

"Pah! Gerwalta *Faust!*" Ann-Marie chuffed. "This is the grave of Gerwalta *Baron*. She and your ancestor didn't have some casual *fling*. They were desperately in love, enough to rebel against both their traditions to be together. And when the hoods attempted to punish the entire pack for that perceived sin, it was Gerwalta who negotiated the peace, and kept them from being destroyed. This is why we call her the Guardian."

"But my people, we call her the Betrayer. We…"

The words caught in my throat. That word, *Betrayer*. I'd heard it, spoken it, thought about it all my life, and never really understood. Every hood knew Gerwalta Faust's story, that she'd committed the biggest crime for one of our kind by becoming the mate of a wolf, but that hadn't been her betrayal, had it? *That* was not the act for which she was forever branded in our histories as Die Verräterin.

"She started a civil war."

"She started a *revolution*," Ann-Marie clarified. "She encouraged wolves to stop accepting their suppression and demanded hoods cease their tyranny. The Matron did not seek her death because she'd mated a wolf. Gerwalta died because in her heart, she became one of them. Even now, my indirect connection with the Guardian earns me prestige in our pack. No doubt you picked up on how they defer to me, or how in awe they were when they learned who you are."

The tears didn't make sense, but what did anymore? The woman who I'd been raised to revile, with whose namesake I'd been cursed and branded… was someone completely different than I thought. And knowing that, I didn't know who I was, either.

Embarrassment flushed my cheeks, heated my temple. I leaned into the warped pine, one arm rising to give my forehead a place to settle as my free hand traced the letters of the plaque.

"A. Baron," I read in time with my ghosting hand. "Ann-Marie, is there any chance you know what his n—"

"Andreas." Ann-Marie anticipated the question. "Andreas Baron, brother to Stephen, from whose line I am descended. That, by the way, is a secret I am trusting you to keep."

"A secret?" Confusion warped my features as I turned to the shewolf. "Why would you need to keep *that* a secret?"

For the first time in our discussion, the kindness in Ann-Marie's face fled, as did the color. "Because, according to *hood* history, neither Stephen nor Andreas had surviving descendants. Andreas and Gerwalta's child roasted on a silver spit over a full moon fire, and Stephen was killed when Gerwalta slayed him on the steps of King Ferdinand's castle. But you and I are proof that never happened. I am protected here, away from the other packs, with the grandsons and granddaughters of a few wolves who believed my grandmother's life and lineage was worth protecting. Someone did the same for you. Do not work to undo that too quickly. The day may come for wolf and wolfsretter alike to know the truth, but that time is not now."

"But I—"

I didn't know, and as words became escape artists, my thoughts hid away, making my mouth agape without purpose.

But Ann-Marie was not done. She took my hands in hers. "Wait for it. Don't try to talk. Just let your mind quiet, and the thing you must know will in turn, make itself known. Deep breaths, Geri. That's it. Now—" She gave my arms a little shake. "Ask it: the same question that has burned within me since I was a little girl and my father told me the truth."

I searched my heart, searched my mind, both reeling and racing and driving my thoughts in a million directions. Across the web of confusion, one thread pulled taut, and I grasped it.

I looked to the shewolf, the tremble in my voice flattening. "Why did the matrons lie?"

"I've told you my truth." Ann-Marie leaned forward, squeezing my arm. "Now go find yours."

NINE

"So anyway, I guess Ann-Marie's grandmother came from Ireland when she heard the pack would be moving away from Triberg. She said by then, the wolves had lost Andreas Baron's side of the story, and her grandmother thought it was a good time to be reminded, since they were going to be out of the shadow of Schloss Wolfsretter and all. That's what caused the pack to divide. The ones who believed her came down here, the rest ended up in the Oberstdorf Forest. By the way, did you know there used to be more wolves in Ireland than people?"

"Actually, I did." Yan put on the blinker before changing lanes. "I have to wonder how Ann-Marie knew about the graves, though. Or how they ended up here when the Betrayer was executed in Triberg."

My head quirked to the side. "I didn't think about that. She thinks—like you heard—that Gerwalta's mother must have taken the baby and fled. If Andreas and Gerwalta's bodies *were* burned, there would be nothing left but charred bones after. Moving bones is much easier than moving corpses."

"They are."

He spoke with an air of confidence that sent a shiver down my spine. I shouldn't ever forget that while Yan seemed to be a pretty passive and go-along-to-get-along type of guy, he had lethal capabilities that could cut me down at the drop of a hat if I wasn't vigilant.

He must have sensed the mood shift, as he took one glance at me, plastered on a huge smile, and moved the conversation to lighter fare. "Sounds like the two of you bonded right away, then."

"We did." I looked out to the horizon, where a thin line of pink sliced the blanket of night. "Sun will be coming up soon. I should... um, put you in silver, I guess."

"Probably best if I pull over first." Yan laughed silently at his own joke. "I saw a sign a few kilometers back that said there's a service station coming up. I'm okay with a little bit of sun until then. Besides, Markus likes a man with a nice, golden tan."

Good. Not about the tan; I couldn't care less what my cousin's proclivities for his paramours were. But even though I didn't want to admit it out loud, I liked having someone to talk to. Someone who didn't have a dog in the whole hood-versus-lupine show was especially welcomed. No pun intended.

"What did you do, by the way, while Ann-Marie and I were out?"

"Mostly, I entertained the pups."

"Meaning?"

"The kids returned when you left, and I don't know...." He shrugged. "They'd never seen a vampire before. They wanted to see my fangs, know if I really drank blood, if I hated garlic... The usual. But I was happy to answer. And bless the parents, they encouraged the curiosity rather than shame or dissuade it. For such an isolated pack, they are amazingly progressive."

"That's not surprising, seeing as they also call Gerwalta Faust the Guardian instead of the Betrayer."

"One man's terrorist is another one's freedom fighter, as the saying goes." He was silent for moment, before slipping in, "Still..."

"Still?"

The corners of the vampire's mouth notched downward. "Please don't misunderstand. I'm glad to hear you've gotten a fresh perspective on your ancestor. I believe that will help you deal with the trials you have coming. But something about what you've learned... It creates more questions in my mind."

"Such as?"

"Ann-Marie said Faust led a revolution against the hoods."

"Yeah, so? Every culture in the world has had uprisings. Why should supernatural ones be any different?"

The vampire turned, even as he guided the car off the exit ramp. Just in time, too. The first crimson ray of sunrise peaked over the mountains, stinging both our eyes. Only in Yan's case, his actually turned red.

"Why doesn't your history record anything more than this one betrayer, and not a movement? Who was doing the revolting and why?" he asked. "What would victory have looked like, and did they achieve it? And most importantly, who was her enemy, and who, her ally? That is probably the question that gnaws at me the most. One rebelling hood does not an insurgency make, after all. There must be a greater context to the events of that era. One, it seems, that may still be having ramifications now."

"Maybe." Any sense of satisfaction I'd gathered during my visit dissipated. "Were you a journalist in your human life? You got a thing for framing questions."

"No, I was a steward under the Portuguese flag."

"Like, on an airplane?" He didn't seem that young. That was, he didn't *look* much older than his mid-20s, but way of dress and manner of speaking didn't suggest he'd been too long a vampire. Based on his formality, I was actually guessing later Victorian era.

"No, not an airplane." He pulled into the station and up to an empty pump. "You said Vlad was surprised when he bit you to discover you were an asaenic."

"Yeah, he said he didn't think any of us truly existed."

"And the most famous asaenic, you've recently learned, was born right around the time the Ravens were entombed," he said. "You don't honestly think that's a coincidence, do you? I mean, Gerwalta Faust's story is infamous enough in supernatural circles that the Ravens would have undoubtably been aware of at least the possibility. Even if they hadn't known contemporarily, they must have heard since resurfacing in 1945."

I bit my bottom lip, remembering what one of the female packlings had said. *Coincidence is never coincidence.*

"I suppose so. But maybe he just meant he knew it was possible, just not likely. Hyperbole isn't the sole art of the hueys."

Yan clicked his tongue. "Or he wasn't talking about what you thought he was talking about. Think about it, did he actually say he thought *asenaics* were impossible?"

My brain tried to pull out the details from a detritus of emotional trauma. "I... can't remember. But if he wasn't talking about asenaics, what was he talking about?"

"A wonderful question."

I rolled myself through a stretch before getting out of the car. "Maybe it's time to pay the matrons another visit, shake them for the truth. Or at least, as much of the truth as they know."

He grinned. "Shall we storm the castle? I've been employed at Schloss Wolfsretter for over a decade now. It's been a good run, and I would enjoy the distraction."

"I was thinking more like sending Markus to appeal to their better natures. You know, with threats of violence and the such."

Yan rolled his eyes. "What makes you think my Markus would rise up against his own? Other than having an unnaturally strong interest in vampires and their history, there isn't a rebellious bone in him."

I kept talking as we got out of the car, doing the pass-and-gas routine. "What do you call him taking on the Ravens with me in Istanbul?" I settled in behind the wheel. "A peaceful protest?"

"I call it following orders." Yan closed the door behind him, trapping in the interior of the vehicle a subtle odor of singed hair. "Your *mother's* orders, as you'll recall, to aid you in whatever mad quest you were undertaking insofar as to keep you from harm."

"Maybe, but I don't think my mother ever anticipated I'd take on Dracula himself. If she had, she'd have probably told Markus just to call when I was killed."

"Of course, she anticipated you facing down Vlad. Or, at least, planned for the contingency."

"You almost make it sound like she was trying to help me. Trust me, she wasn't. I'm quite sure Markus also had orders to kill me if the escape from Vlad's took a turn for the worse. It's part of the unofficial hood handbook; the scorched earth policy. Now—" Making sure no one was watching, I pulled down the silver grafted to my arms under my sleeves. It pooled in my hand, then took on the form of a jar. "Ready to play Aladdin again?"

The vampire crossed his arms and frowned. "You give your mother too little credit."

"On the contrary, I credit her with a great deal, just very little of it to do with my welfare or happiness. Now," I tapped the container, "smokie-smokie."

He closed his eyes. "Okay, but only because I do not savor a hellish sunburn. We shouldn't let this go. I have a feeling what happened back then has a lot more to do with what's happening now than you might think."

"I do too. But all those answers are at the end of this drive."

TEN

AMY

"Oh, god, I— Ahh!"

Caleb was beside Alexandra in a flash, but for all the good it did, he might as well have taken his time. She was pregnant, not under attack. Unless slayers had some sort of "do not break water here in this totally badass training gym hidden behind a secret wall in the basement" power, I didn't see what his Flash impersonation achieved.

Show off.

Caleb braced her. "Alex, are you okay?"

The gravid (isn't that an awesome word? I picked it up reading Bronte. It only means pregnant but it sounds so much more... intellectual) woman squatted against the wall, holding her bulbous stomach like a bowling ball. Or at least, like the way *I* held a bowling ball.

"I'm fine." *She didn't look fine.* "The baby kicked. Very hard. And possibly, ruptured my spleen."

Caleb drew Alex to her feet with a great deal of tenderness as he spoke from the side of his mouth to the dozen or so slayers working in the space. "Okay, everybody, let's call it a night. Hit the showers and grab some dinner before you turn in for the day." Then, once they had filtered out, he said to Alexandra, "I told you, you shouldn't be down here. You should be upstairs, relaxing. I know you're a badass chick, but you're also carrying the future of our race in there, and she gets preferential treatment. Hey, Barbie?"

He was talking to me. Of course, he was talking to me.

I raised an eyebrow. "Yes, Buffy?"

Caleb grimaced. "Can you help Alex back upstairs? I'm going to practice a few more forms before bed."

I mockingly inspected his backside. "Your *forms* look fine to me."

Caleb pointed toward the door, even as he turned away. "Help. Alex."

Alex put a hand on my shoulder. "No, Amy. I'm fine. The pain has passed, and I don't want to become a burden for anyone. I'll be fine."

And with that, the toughest pregnant chick I'd ever met waddled out the door.

I tried to draw from my limited prenatal knowledge, which claimed extensive breadth on the first 15 to 30 minutes of the process and was a little vaguer on the latter parts. "Alex is huge. Shouldn't we, you know, start making plans for the delivery? Is there some kind of special slayer OB-GYN or something? It's like a regular birth, right? Or do you guys have tentacles or something that fall off when you get older?"

"Yeah, like fifty of them. I still have one." Caleb worked his body through a series of blocks and jabs. "Markus has asked the hoods if they have a midwife on retainer, one familiar with supe birth. Turns out, their staff physician serves that role. She'll make herself available when the time comes, if we're still here."

I wasn't a werewolf; I didn't have hackles. Still, I felt mine rise. "What do you mean, if we're still here? I thought the slayers accepted the contract, that we were staying."

"They did, but you see what they're like," Caleb said, turning to me, his bare chest so very *glisten-y*. "The men can't even conjure solaria, and the women don't know how to use them properly. *None* of them has any weapons or combat training. They're not ready to take on a clutch of vamps with centuries of strength and experience behind them."

"You guys literally make liquid sun. How hard can it be to hurl it at something?"

"Oh, ye of little…" His eyes went to my chest. "Well, not those."

"Ha ha, a tits joke. I never heard one of those before. Now answer my question."

Caleb picked up a towel and dotted it against his forehead. "Fine. It's like this: a solarium only has a ground life of three to five seconds, and vampires are quick enough to dodge out of the way if the assault isn't made close enough. They'll have to know how to strike hard and run fast before we encounter them. And if the Ravens come here first…" Caleb swallowed. "Then they'll be hardly more able to defend themselves than you are."

Heat flooded my face. "No thanks to you."

"No thanks to me?" Caleb threw the towel against the wall. "I'm sorry, Barbie, but did I miss the part of orientation where you were my responsibility?"

"You told Geri you'd help me learn how to fight." I crossed my arms over my chest. Not to push up my cleavage, but *que sera sera*.

"*Geri* isn't my boss. And since she broke up with me, she's not really my anything. I'm being nice because the welfare of my people needs me to be and because we're both after the destruction of the Ravens, but you can bet I'm skipping town the second that's no longer true. Besides, Geri already taught you basic self-defense, and that's about all you're going to master as a huey that will stand any chance."

I took two steps forward; Caleb eyeballed my advance with some sort of malicious glee. "So you're saying if I kick you in the balls, it will hurt just as bad as it would a human male?"

"Of course, the anatomy is the same. We just—"

Thwack!

"What the fa— Owwww..."

There are times in life when you wish you could just roll back your memories and frame a picture. Seeing smug, self-important, cocky Caleb double over would have gone up on my fireplace mantle, if I lived to have my own place again.

"Why did—" A terrible wheezing noise. "—did you—" A delicious cough. "—do that?"

I bent at the waist, bringing myself eye-to-eye with him. "I was trying to see if you were right. Guess you were. All I have to do is kick a vamp in the nutsack and I can run away screaming. Oh, unless he's smoke!" I shot to my feet. "Then what the hell do I do?"

Caleb shook his head, braced his knees for support. "I wasn't..." *Hack*. "Damn that was hard."

"That's what she said."

What? I couldn't help it. He left that window too wide open not to crawl through. Even though I very much wanted Caleb to choke on his own tongue for treating me like some defective teacup that couldn't hold a cuppa, part of me lightened when he grinned at the joke.

Gasping, he righted himself. His recovery time was miraculous. Next time, I might want to kick him twice. "I suggest you do the same thing you do with men: date them. That sure seems to get rid of them fast enough."

"Oh, and here comes the sequel."

But before my hand could connect with his cheek, he'd fetched the assault from the air, holding my arm in place.

"Amy..." So he *did* know my name. "Can I tell you a little secret?"

"A supe with secrets? How novel."

A momentary flicker of his customary annoyance, but it faded in a blink. "I wish I could teach you, but some things vamps do a huey could never counter. Smoke, for example. A slayer can push it away with solarium blast, but since you can't summon those—"

My confidence dripped to the floor, taking my righteous posture and the tension in my arm along with it. I dropped the attack and turned to leave. "No, I guess not. Sorry I kicked you in the balls."

"Amy, wait—"

No sooner had I turned to leave than he was before me.

"Not that I enjoyed having my testicles against the back of my teeth, but I guess I deserved it a little. I haven't been very nice to you lately, or like, ever."

"No, you haven't, and I don't get why." I spun on my heel. "Even when I thought Geri was crazy for not hooking up with Tobias—before I understood why, I mean—and she was dating you, I was telling her to put her big girl panties on so you could take them off. It wasn't like I was trying to undermine you or anything."

He buried a laugh into his chest. "Geri's right. You don't have a filter."

"And… you're right back to insulting me in the blink of an eye. So, bye."

"Shit, no, I wasn't insulting you."

This time, instead of rounding me, the bastard tugged me back by the arm. I was two seconds from a second attempt at a ball-drop chaser when his words alone stopped me.

"You've already mastered your weapon."

My hand paused at my side. "What weapon?"

"This." He motioned vaguely to my body. My *whole* body, from top to toe. "This façade you've got where people believe this is all you are: a materialistic, man-eating, dumb blonde. But really, it's like your shield. It keeps back the danger until you gauge your enemy, find all his weaknesses, and exploit them. And that honesty you have? That's your sword. No, it isn't going to overpower a pair of fangs, but a warrior learns to choose his battlefield. Yours is interaction, relationships, and I'm willing to bet you're undefeated there, aren't you?"

Only when my lungs cried out for air did I realize I'd stopped breathing. What the fuck? What the actual fuck?

"If you mean, did anyone ever break up with me instead of the other way around, then the answer to that is a brilliantly red hell no."

He crossed his arms, examining me like I was a piece of art in which he'd just found a heretofore unnoticed brush stroke, framing the muscles of his chest. Caleb had, like, one percent body fat, but damn, it didn't make him look bad.

"It's because all you've done so far is sparring," he said. "Practice runs with opponents you knew you'd best. But be advised, Amy Popowitz, you're working up to something, I know it. You're going to find a worthy adversary someday, one who's going to hit you blow for blow, one who's going to pin you to the mat and get a few blows in before you even realize what happened. And you know what?"

His arms fell to his sides and my jaw went to the floor as Caleb stepped in closer. The no-man's land between us suddenly became a one-man land. One man who was crazy hot. And half-naked.

And touching me.

The slayer's heated breath parted my lips, the angle of his head tilt demanded me to reciprocate.

I managed to lick my bottom lip. "What?"

An inch, a half an inch, a quarter of an inch. My eyes closed…

And reopened to him, six feet away and laughing.

"Oh, come on, Barbie!" Caleb struggled not to double over. "Did you really think I was going to kiss you? I'm still nursing my broken heart here."

Oh, he so didn't want to try to out-burn me. "Actually, when I passed your room yesterday, I heard you nursing something else. Pretty sure it wasn't your heart."

I hadn't, but by the way that smile fled his face told me I'd stumbled on to the fact by dumb luck. Might as well play it for all it was worth. "Which is odd, because aren't you sharing a room with Mikael and Ezekiel? Or were they watching?"

"They were asleep, and I haven't… You shouldn't have…" Red as the dawn, his wide cheeks burned. "If you tell *anyone*…"

I put up my hand to end his suffering. "Chillax, Buffy. My lips are sealed."

His frame relaxed.

"If…"

And again, he was a wall of nerves and steaming eyes. Oh, it did my heart good.

Caleb asked, "If what?"

"If you stop putting a huey down and help me learn how to fight."

"Stand around and observe all you want, but I kinda got the weight of my race on my shoulders here. I don't have any extra time to…"

I cupped my hand, made a rude gesture, and winked.

"Okay, fine. Fine. But don't expect me to go easy on you just because you're—" He motioned finger quotes. "—fragile. And top heavy! Get a damned sports bra or some duct tape or something. But mark my words, Barbie, you'll regret this. I'm going to be on your ass more than any of your fly-by-night boytoys ever were." In a flash, he reclaimed the towel he'd thrown against the wall and tossed it my direction. "You've got a little bit of drool there on your chin, by the way."

"Hey, if I wanted you to kiss me, then you'd be—"

And then, he was.

And damn, he was good.

Or so I was beginning to suspect. By the time I'd actually become conscious of his lips on mine, it was over, and he was glaring at me.

Because that's what you do after you kiss a woman hard and fast, you *glare* at her.

And just as I was about to lay into him for daring to be so bold, and yell even more at him for making it so brief, the door to the training studio opened.

I pushed the asshat in his asschest to get him the assaway from me.

"Oh, good, you two are going at it." Geri walked in, Markus trailing right behind.

"What? No, we weren't. We're—"

Panic told me to get distance, but then I realized there was distance, a great deal of it. I was standing alone in the middle of the room, and Caleb was in the corner, mocking forms.

Geri's eyebrow rose. "So, you're not training? Because this looks like training, and I should know."

"Nope, this is training," Caleb said, punching the air. "Amy's great. Really progressing, keeping me on my toes."

"Really?" Markus asked. "Because to my eyes, all you two have done in the two days Geri was gone was bicker and bitch at each other."

"Like he said, I'm keeping him on his toes, and you don't do that with casual pleasantries," I said. And then I changed the subject, because I so did not want anyone spinning any sentence that would diagram Caleb and I in the same compound subject. "So, did they know anything?"

"You could say that."

Geri ran a hand through her hair, shaking out her ebony locks. God, why did she get supernatural powers *and* supermodel hair? It wasn't fair. She and Yan then launched into a summation of their discoveries, and with every sentence, Caleb and I took turns dropping our jaws.

"And so..." She folded her hands together. "After Yan and I talked about it in the car, we think it might be worth trying to find the other asenaics by looking for anomalies in *huey* history."

Caleb's face screwed up. "Why? I don't understand why that's what this all led to."

The vampire and the hood exchanged a look, but it was the first one who talked. "Because while we do not have access to the hood archives, we do have access to the internet. And knowing what we do now, that the lupine version of the Betrayer's story mentions at least one prominent huey, we might find threads that will at least point us in the right direction."

"But you live up at the Schloss, don't you have access to the archives? You know, somehow?"

Why were supes always so cloak-and-dagger? I pushed Caleb back, trying to ignore the jealousy of my other body parts toward my fingers. "I think what Nancy Drew here is trying to say is, can't you just go all smoke monster and look in these archive thingies, even if you're not supposed to? Assuming you're not supposed to. Are you supposed to?"

The man tried to diagnose me with a cocked head until a moment later, he shook off whatever thoughts had been going through his head. "No, I'm not supposed to, and yes, of course I have. But the archives are not what one might call complete, especially the further back you go. Until recently, the different bloodlines operated more or less independently, and without a universal method of cataloguing or the same priorities of what should be written down, there's big blank spots in the histories. For example, I can tell you that now, knowing the name of Geri's wolf ancestor, there is no mention of his execution in the list of the condemned. To clarify, huey history is no different, but much more of it has been digitized."

"We might find nothing," Gerwalta added. "But we're going to look just in case. Every day, those asenaics are more in danger. I'm not sure how long the Ravens can go without feeding, but it's been six weeks now. Unless there are other slayer harems they have in other places, they'll need to feed soon."

Caleb grabbed a towel from a stack on a shelf and went about dabbing off his glisten. It was a crime worthy of jail time. "Let me take a shower, and we'll get to it then."

ELEVEN

GERI

"I think I found something."

As though moving through well-rehearsed choreography, everyone stood and circled around Amy's computer.

I squinted, trying my best to comprehend what I was seeing. "Okay, explain."

The blonde huey expanded the view of the scanned document on the screen, pulling out the details of highly embellished text. Letters took on definition, but definition brought no clarity.

"Seriously?" Amy blinked rapidly. "None of you read French?"

Caleb, Markus, and I exchanged expectant looks that fell away when the truth became clear.

"I'm only good for English, German, and some basic Spanish," I said.

"Me, just the first two," Markus added.

Caleb took on a cocky grin. "English, Turkish, Hebrew, Spanish, and Romanian."

Amy held up a finger. "You forgot Pomposity, which as I understand is a common dialect of Bastard."

Any hope of Caleb explaining the sudden hostility that had grown between him and Amy in the last few days was met with the latter only shaking his head in a "don't ask" type of way.

Rather than dig any deeper to unearth that mine, I stayed focused. "Amy, can you read it for us?"

My huey friend beamed. "Of course, Geri, I'd be delighted." Then, turning to her screen, motioning to bits and pieces of the image as she spoke, Amy began. "So just a little north of here is a region that's gone back and forth between France and Germany through the centuries. I figured since all of you probably had the Germanic sources covered, I'd skim through French archives and see if there were any unusual events or mentions of things in the 1680s. And here—" Her right index finger zeroed in on the swoopy text "—I found a letter from the Bishop of Alsace to the Cardinal Montblanc written in the year 1685 which reports a rash of livestock deaths throughout Southern Germany by, quote, 'a pack of abnormally vicious wolves.'"

Markus and I exchanged knowing glances.

Caleb stood erect. "This isn't news to you two."

I shook my head. "We all know that one; we think it's where the Little Red Riding Hood fairy tale came from. There was an anathema alpha—"

"Like Ayşe in Istanbul?" Amy interjected.

"Exactly, like her," Markus confirmed. "Female alphas used to be considered some sort of defect that made the wolf dangerous. I don't think that's true, of course, but this one actually was. She was able to lure away betas from a dozen packs to make her own family. The House of Red tracked her down and killed her before she managed it. Unfortunately, not before they ate their way through the countryside."

Caleb turned to me. "And what about the betas she lured away? What happened to them?"

I shrugged. "They went back to their packs, I guess. I don't remember hearing anything different. If they had been killed as well, our stories would have boasted about it. Through history, hoods have been pretty decent at sticking to our own laws about when we could use lethal means to curb wolf behavior, but our ancestors prided themselves on putting down the slightest infractions with brutality."

Amy spun around her chair while also spinning her eyes. "Oh my god, you guys really *can't* see the forest for the trees, can you?" She stood, passing to the sink and drawing herself a glass of water. "Geri, didn't you say this shewolf you met in Austria, that her ancestor was Andreas's brother, who supposedly died?"

"Yeah, so?"

"So?" The glass lingered at her lips. "If Andreas was an alpha, isn't it possible his brother may have been a beta? And if the House of Red was involved in tracking them down, then isn't it possible Gerwalta Faust could have been the one to let him get away?"

As she finally tipped back the glass to drink, her long neck stretched and her throat bobbing with each swallow, I tried to stitch together her logic.

And then, I did.

"But that would mean she let him go on purpose." Every revolution starts with a single act of rebellion. "But why would a hood do that? If she'd had been caught at that time, she would have been exiled. Or worse."

Caleb rubbed his chin. "But she *was* caught and killed. You guys tell the Betrayer story like it took place over a couple of days, but the chick had to have time to fall in love, get knocked up, and pop the kid before the ax fell. Why is it so ridiculous to think the love story started earlier than you think, too? Or is it told in your books that one day, Gerwalta Faust came down with the must-mate-a-wolf flu and went searching about for the cure?"

Amy pointed at the slayer. "Only you could take a beautiful fairy tale and reduce it to getting knocked up."

"Well, that's what happened, wasn't it?" Caleb said, defending himself. "Ergo, we are here."

It didn't seem possible that could be coincidence. But then, something triggered in my brain. I went back to my own computer and went about searching the web, even as the others looked on with concern. When I found what I was after, I flipped the screen around.

"The wolf of Ansbach?" Markus read the title of the article aloud. "Oh, come on. We've disavowed that one for centuries. That was just village idiots getting their superstition on."

Amy swooped in, eyeballing the text through squinted eyes. "In 1685, the same year of the letter I found? Except if that graphic's to be believed, that guy... um, werewolf?... actually ended up dead."

I turned the computer back, looking closer at the accompanying picture of a human-bodied wolf dangling from a scaffold. "Obviously it's not Andreas or his brother, but if there really is a connection between Gerwalta Faust and the wolf epidemic, this might have been part of it. We can never really *know*, but it feels right to me."

Coincidence is never coincidence.

"If only we could get into the archive, then..."

The computer dropped to the table as my chair flew out behind me. Startled, Amy coughed, choking on the water mid-swallow. Markus and Caleb were beside me in a moment as I turned my face to the front door, gaging the distance of the uninvited guests I sensed outside.

In my peripheral vision, Caleb turned to my cousin. "Markus?"

"No idea," Markus answered, even as he leeched the silver hidden beneath his clothing to form a two-pronged knife. "Geri, who is it? Do you know?"

Did I? One was coming closer but moving at too steady a pace to be covert, and too leisurely to mount an attack. Not that whoever it was would stand any chance if he were. There was only one of him, and three of us ready to kick ass.

Three and a half, if you included Amy.

"Amy." I spoke without turning. "Tell the slayers to shelter down. Quickly."

Without asking a question, the huey obeyed, scurrying to the stairs.

Caleb rounded my right side. "Shelter from what?"

Not vampires; that he'd be able to perceive.

Before I could answer, though, the approaching party finally came close enough for Markus to pick up.

"A wolf," he said.

I shook my head as proximity delivered clarity. "Two wolves."

Markus squinted. "No, I'm only getting one. He's not dodging around or anything. He's making a straight line for the front door. Could it be... Geri, you don't think—"

"It's *not* Tobias," I said, cutting him off. "But I know these two. I've felt their presences before." Definitely the one, and I thought the other, though I just couldn't place either. "I... God damn it, really?"

Light brightened the grand room as Caleb conjured a solarium. "Tell me who it is, or I'm going to blast them back across the Rhineland."

No time for a witty retort. No sooner had I turned to the slayer than the doorbell rang.

Which marked the first time in fifteen years of staying in the house that I had ever heard it.

Caleb did a double take. "Well that's unexpectedly civilized." Then, raising his voice, he called out, "Who's there?"

Silence for a moment, and then an unsure timbre reached through the wood. "Hello? I'm, um... I'm looking for Geri—Gerwalta, I mean. Shit, you think she's really here? I'm looking for Gerwalta Kline. Is she... Dude, are you sure this is the right house?"

Markus honed his weapon and made his way to the door. "What is *he* doing here?"

"He who?" Caleb asked. His solarium stayed at the ready, just in case.

I was on Markus's tail. "My ex-boyfriend. Who will be leaving as soon as I see what idiot wolf is with him and how they both knew this house even existed. Markus, wait. Let me answer."

"I can hear you, you know," Cody said from the stoop. "And you shouldn't call this guy an idiot. It's very disrespectful."

My movements arrested, drawn up in the fantasy. Could it be Tobias? The energy I felt was wolf, but weak, barely perceptible. But that didn't make sense. How would Cody have found Tobias? And why would he tease me with it if he did? Why would he be that cruel?

Oh, yeah, that's right. Because Cody was an asshole who kicked me out of his packlands for having the audacity to refuse to kowtow to his edicts like I was some god damned wolf.

Forget that I kinda was.

A head full of steam, I reached for the door, prepared to waylay into whatever bastard wingwolf my ex had in tow.

"Cody Ryland!" I bellowed. "How fucking... dare... y..."

But the insult died on my tongue when the beaming, warm, welcomed man standing outside stepped forward.

"Hola, *cariño*," my dad said. "We need to have a talk."

TWELVE

Caleb stared at Cody like the werewolf was some piece of abstract art, the meaning of which he just couldn't grab.

"You're her ex?"

Cody nursed his beer. "Yup."

Caleb shook his head. "It's just that you're so muscular and rustic and brawny and... and nothing like me."

My father, sipping apple tea, turned pleading eyes on me. "Who is this man, and why does he smell like an Abercrombie & Fitch?"

"This *man* is Caleb Helsing," Caleb answered on his own behalf. "And FYI: it's Kenneth Cole."

"You're the slayer she was talking about last summer?" Cody took one look and hacked a laugh. "Wow, you are *so* not her type. But tough break. I was pulling for you."

"Me, too. Even asked her to marry me," Caleb boasted. "I understand you did that once too, right before you slept with one of your packlings."

"Caleb!" Shit, I so didn't want to deal with an arrogant slayer and a back-woods alpha butting heads right now. "Caleb, you should probably track down Alexandra. Make sure the red alert didn't stress her out too much. Markus, give Amy and everyone else the all-clear. I need to speak to these two alone."

Minor grumbles followed, mixed with Markus recounting the details of the dramatic history of my first hood-werewolf romance, the last sentence of which I perceived being, "so they found other ways of expressing their feelings..."

Cody eyeballed the pair until they were all the way up the stairs and out of sight. "You were really engaged to that guy?"

"No!" Even I was shocked by the insistent tone. "I mean, he proposed, but I was already planning on breaking up with him before then. But let's talk about you." I spun a chair around and sat cowgirl style. "First of all, Papa. Let's start with... I don't know, maybe with my whole life being a lie and work up from there."

"You've learned about our... unique heritage, I take it." My father folded his hands atop the table. "I think you are hyperbolizing, niña. Very little of your life was a lie. Your mother and I only kept one tiny truth from you, and it was only for your own good."

"Really, Dad? The Betrayer's baby survived, a secret that I could maybe overlook if I wasn't her namesake and, it turns out, her descendent. We have wolf blood in our veins. How is that a tiny truth?"

His gaze cast off into the distance. "I was supposed to be the last, so that the line would die with me. But then I met your mother, and..." He made a vague gesture with his hands, something that seemed to say 'one thing led to another...'

Which was fine. I so didn't need to know the details of my own conception.

I crossed my arms. "She wouldn't have married you if she knew. You know she wouldn't have."

"Oh, no, cariño, she *did* know," he said. "It was how we met. She was sent to Argentina to deliver the edict that I would be forbidden to have children. Your grandmother relented, saying she'd permit just one more asenaic, hoping her strong bloodline would wash away any lupine leanings. We did not expect the wolf nature to manifest in you to such a degree. It has varied throughout the centuries, sometime reinforced when different asenaic branches partnered. We kept you in the dark, hoping to marry you off to a hood who..."

"Hood begets hood," I said. "Yeah, I remember that line coming up often when I was dating the bastard who broke my heart." My eyes flashed to Cody. "No offense."

The instigated werewolf threw up his hands. "Your mom's words, not mine."

My father, crestfallen, continued. "You have always wondered how I could stand by while your mother grew stricter by the years. It is because *she* is my mate, niña. I am bonded to her, and I love her no matter what she did to me, or what she did to you." His hand sought mine across the table. "I saw the pain it caused you, every time, and I suffered with you."

The little girl inside me who longed for her father's comfort melted, if only for a moment. Until, that was, the woman I'd become seized back control. I leaned back in my chair, crossing my arms over my chest and turning my attention to the alpha seated to my father's left.

"And you?" I said to Cody, jerking my chin. "Why are you here? Last time I saw you, you were kicking me out of your packlands."

My father turned on the alpha. "What?"

Cody guffawed. "I mean, she didn't give me a choice. She questioned my authority in front of the whole pack."

"She is a hood!" my father said, his Latino-hands-of-reinforcement bobbing through the air. "That is her nature."

"And I'm an alpha," Cody shot back. "Geri was causing some of my wolves' fealty to falter. The pack knows her, loves her like one of their own, and believe it or not, some of them actually think I'm a bastard for mating Lisa, just like Geri, even though I only did it because of alpha's prerogative. I was going to have wolves going rogue if I didn't do something." Then, the focus of his rationalization swung my way. "But I've never stopped caring about you. And then when Pietro came to ask me to come along, letting me in on your secret... I realized how much it all made sense. Your instincts on lupine nature, your ability to understand some of our wolfish, how we were so attracted to each other..."

"Well, guess what? You finally got your wish!" I said. "I don't love you anymore. I only love—"

Even the pain of saying his name cut deep across my tongue.

"Tobias." Cody grinned. "And that's great, Geri. I'm glad to hear that. Only, Little Red, you know that's a dead-end street. Tobias already had his mate; his heart is always going to belong to Kara. It's obvious to anyone you two are good friends. Great, even. But it will never be more than that. I'd hate to see you throw away any chance of a full life."

"Oh, my god." I turned to my dad, and away from the unspoken words I knew Cody wanted to say, *by falling in love with another werewolf you can never have*. "Mom banished you."

Pietro's eyes grew wide. "How did you know?"

"Because if you were still getting communiques from a matron—*any* matron— you'd know what Markus reported to the council a few days ago." I crawled to the edge of my chair. "Vlad Tepeş has some personal, historic beef with werewolves. He's exacting his revenge by unraveling their mating bonds using some sort of genetic therapy. He wants to destroy them from the inside out, and he doesn't care how long it takes. Tobias's mate was one of his victims. He undid her mating bond."

"Does it affect both mates, or only the one subjected to this..." Pietro's hand turned circles in the air. "...therapy?"

"We're unsure. When Kara died, Tobias still went through the same pain I've felt in other wolves who've lost mates. But was he unaffected?"

I remembered both the kisses we shared: one under the full moon in Paradise, the other moments before I'd lost him in Istanbul. I remembered that he loved me, had loved me for who knew how long before either of us had said anything.

It's not just because of the serum...

"He must have been," I surmised.

Cody barked a laugh. "Be that as it may, genetically altering all the wolves in the world would take decades, centuries maybe. If old Drac really wanted revenge, he'd just kill them. He seems more than capable."

I held up a finger. "You're thinking like a mortal, but Vlad doesn't. In his opinion, the wolves undid his country, his family, and his legacy, so he's going to do the same to them. A vampire has the luxury of time, as long as he has the right kind of blood for fuel."

My father narrowed his eyes. "What do you mean, the right kind of blood?"

I didn't know how many hoods were in on the vampire secret that they were not, in fact, immortal, that after five centuries or so, death would still claim them as it did any creature. Unless, of course, they fed off other supes. Even in such circumstances, I wouldn't betray the whole species for the sins of the few.

"The Ravens have a… condition," I said. "And the only treatment is supe blood. Werewolf blood works, slayer blood is better. But the best blood is asenaic." I met my father's eyes, seeing the understanding form within. "Like the kind that comes from the descendants of Gerwalta Faust and Andreas Baron."

My father's olive skin blanched. "This is why your mother was so worried about them finding you. All this time, she led me to believe it was because they wanted revenge."

"Revenge?" For the first time in this conversation, I was the one left in the dark. "For what?"

"For their capture," my dad said. "The Ravens were trapped for many centuries, encased in silver urns crafted by the House of Red, and kept in the vaults of Schloss Wolfsretter."

Though I knew the sky outside to be as clear as a bell, I had no doubt that lightning had just struck my brain and stopped my heart. The world came to a halt, then just as soon, sped up again, all too fast.

When I could find the words to speak at last, my hoarse voice surprised all of us. "What do you mean, we trapped them in silver and kept them at the Schloss?" A dry palate made talking difficult. "Igor told me Inga trapped them with the help of some Wallachian lupines and entombed them in some air-tight wall."

My father blinked his confusion. "The first time, yes. I understand that is what happened."

"The first time?" I balanced my temples on my fingers. "The *first* time?" I repeated, louder, even rudely.

"Yes, the first time. The slayers found out about it, and blamed the wolves for interfering in their affairs. They discovered where the crypt was and opened it, intending to obliterate the Ravens, but they were bested. After that, the House of Red took a contract to trap them in silver urns. The silver was even blood-claimed, so that none might open it."

Cody verbalized my unspoken thoughts. "What is blood-claimed silver?"

My father's eyes went to the table as he shook his head. "A barbaric practice, one long banned. A hood can become the sole master of a piece of silver by threading the metal through her veins and passing it through her heart.

Once upon a time, it was a rite of passage when a hood took her fire and was presented her silver medallion. As a demonstration of becoming righteous, they blood-claimed it. I have read that the pain was excruciating. There are even stories that some died from it. But as all hoods can command silver and form a plethora of deadly weapons, it is a way for us to gain an advantage over other members of our race."

My thoughts turned back to the sword I'd been gifted by Vlad in Istanbul. It had felt different from any other silver I'd ever handled, almost like it had its own memories. Could that have been it?

"Looks like you got yourself mixed up in some deep shit, Little Red." Cody grinned. "Makes me glad you got Tobias here protecting you." He scanned the room. "Where is he, by the way?"

"Wherever Vlad Tepeş wants him to be," I retorted. "He was taken prisoner when we freed the slayers."

My father's eyes nearly bugged out of his head. "What?"

"I guess that hasn't gotten to you either, then." I folded my arms over my chest. "So, tell me, Papa, if you didn't come here because of my mate's disappearance and not because Mom told you to, then why did you come? More importantly," I turned on Cody, "Why are *you* here? I hope it's not for an apology for what I said at Kim's wedding, because you're not going to get it."

The werewolf clearly wasn't ready to mend fences, either. His acidic gaze fixed me long and hard as he drew another pull off his bottle of Schwarzbier before saying, "I'm here because of Amy."

"Amy?" Okay, that I hadn't been expecting. Why would my ex-boyfriend care anything about my huey friend? "What does Amy have to do with anything?"

"She took off to Istanbul with you back in June, and she hasn't contacted her parents since," my father filled in. "By the time late July rolled around, her mother got worried enough to hire a private investigator, who found out your friend emptied all her bank accounts the day before you left, hasn't used any of her credit cards since the first day or two you were gone, and other than going through passport control when you landed in Turkey, hasn't triggered any official records in three months."

Cody took over from there. "When the PI showed up in Paradise and started sniffing around for clues last week, that raised the packs' hackles."

"Oh my god." My head turned to the stairs, as though I expected to see my bubbly, blond friend there. "I had no idea. I never even asked her... I mean, how would that come up, anyways?"

Cody grunted. "Maybe by you being a little less self-involved and remembering that the people around you have their own lives, that this isn't some sort of dramatic play where all the characters enter and exit the stage just to move your plot along."

My father growled. Actually growled.

But the alpha wolf wasn't impressed. "What? We agreed we were going to give it to her straight, didn't we?"

"Straight does not mean cruel," my dad snapped. "*Niña*, what Cody means to say is, especially where hueys are concerned, you have to be far more appreciative of the fact that they do not come from our world. They have attachments that will follow them if you bring them in."

But it sounded like Amy had been trying to break those attachments. Meeting her parents, I understood she and her father didn't have the greatest relationship, but she seemed to get along with her mom okay. Why would she cut them both off?

"I'll talk to her, ask her to reach out to the folks with just enough information to pacify them. I'm sorry that hueys infiltrated the packlands. But that still doesn't explain why you came all the way to Germany. I mean, you could have called. My phone number is different but Markus's is still the same, and I'm sure mom told you he was with me."

For the first time since they'd arrived, my father's face curdled. It was up to Cody, the fount of cruel truth, to explain.

"I'm here to make sure Amy does what needs to be done. And in the event that she doesn't, *assure* she's convinced otherwise. And if it turned out that she hadn't phoned home because of some terrible fate, I came to make sure any evidence went away."

I blew a raspberry. "What were you planning to do, eat her?"

His dead stare made a chill run the length of me. "If needs be."

My spine electrified. "Well, needs *don't* be. Amy's fine. Like I said, I'll talk to her. So, now that's out of the way, I'll trust you two to find your way out."

"When you're up against both the Matron Council and Vlad Tepeş?" my father asked. "Absolutely not."

"I'm sticking around, too. Tobias may not be my packling anymore, but that's only an official thing. He's my friend, and I'm going to make sure he's rescued." The alpha let out a gravelly laugh. "Oh, Geri, you just have to have some lupine in your life or you get into trouble, don't you?"

I was too tired to deal with sexist, wolfish crap. "You sure that Lisa's going to be okay with that?"

"She'll understand. She cares for Tobias, too." The empty bottle thudded on the table. "So, where do we start looking?"

I turned the chair around. "We don't. He's not my focus right now."

The alpha went wide-eyed. "Maybe you don't love him as much as you think you do, then. If it were my mate—"

"But it's not," I said, cutting Cody off. "Despite what you think about how self-absorbed I am, the truth is that I have others depending on me right now. For one," I jerked my chin, "the houseful of slayers upstairs. Maybe the last of their kind, and considered by Vlad to be stolen property. The Matron Council in their *magnanimity* refused sanctuary. Instead, they offered them a contract. Full social and financial support, but only if they agree to kill the Ravens."

My father's jaw dropped. "*Dios mio*. Surely this edict was not issued with your mother's knowledge."

"Who knows?" I said. "Markus says Mom hasn't been in residence since right after we left for Istanbul, and she hasn't been checking in, either. I don't suppose either of you know where she is?"

The men exchanged puzzled looks.

Cody stretched out in his chair. "She was in Paradise over the summer, but since the middle of August, your aunt has been overseeing the roost."

A fact I was sure his pack was thankful for. Markus's mom was slightly less regimented than her older cousin, *my* mother. Still, even a kind warden is still a warden.

I continued. "Matron Chin is sitting in the big chair right now, and she's not too interested in anything Markus has to say. I tried getting in, but no-go as I'm officially relinquished."

"And the slayers?" Cody asked. "Did they take the contract?"

"Of course, they took the contract. They have nowhere else to go. Or at least, their best bet for the moment is near the hoods. The council might be refusing to grant them humanitarian support out of the kindness of their hearts, but we all know that if the Ravens stride into Triberg and try to get away with anything, the hoods will have their heads."

My father nodded. "Yes, which is why you should not feel guilty about leaving here to go find Tobias. The slayers will still be shielded by the proximity to the Schloss."

"I *am* leaving, but you see, there's another group of people counting on me for protection. And they're in even more danger, because they don't even know it yet."

Cody and my dad exchanged a questioning glance, but neither knew what I was talking about.

"The other asenaics, the ones in Spain," I said. "Since Vlad discovered I exist, and since I'm currently out of his reach, he's going to have to find the next best thing if he wants to continue his… his therapy. You might have been the last asenaic in the Americas, Papa, but there's still others of our line in the Old Country, aren't there?"

At least he had the guts not to deny it. "But I do not know where. My line comes from the north part of the country, and this is all I know."

I pursed my lips. "We need to ask Inga Rosethorn."

My father narrowed his eyes. "What do asenaics have to do with her?"

"The same condition that Vlad has, she and Igor do, too." It wasn't the whole truth but it would suffice for now. "And the two of them have been treating it for years with trips to Spain. Igor was also taken prisoner by Vlad. I'm not sure if vampires are susceptible to torture, but if so, it won't take long for the Ravens to find out. That's why I'm going to Spain. It's not the most likely place for me to find Vlad."

And since I doubted he'd leave his prizes behind after I'd robbed him of his harem, I could assume Tobias and Igor would be going along for the ride.

My father stood. "I will go with you."

"Dad, no. I'm going to be traveling light. You'll only slow me down."

"Fi! *Me* slow *you* down? Don't be ridiculous. Besides, your Spanish is not so good."

"What are you talking about, my Spanish is fine."

"You think that because you only speak it with me. I know what all your mistakes mean. When do we leave?"

I grinned. "Just as soon as I can pack up the car and get supplies together, which should only take me until morning. Oh, and talk to Amy, of course. I'll just go…"

Without warning, a scream rent the air: a terrifying, shrill cry that took me flying through the house and up the stairs.

Footsteps pounded behind me, even as a voice in the back of my head warned about the slayers finding yet more strangers in the house. None of them would have noticed, however, because they were all too focused on the huffing woman in the midst of them when I got to the third-floor hallway, being braced on one side by Caleb and on the other by Amy.

Alexandra's face broke into a smile as she caught sight of me, even as her teeth clenched. "Geri, I think it's time."

THIRTEEN

At some point, coffee would cease to substitute for sleep. I couldn't have drunk more of the stuff unless Starbucks introduced an IV Latte. Hour eighteen came and went, with no more babies in the house than there had been when Alex's labor had started. The screaming had started in the thirteenth hour (my father and Cody agreed as the self-declared senior experts in childbirth, that the first part of the labor didn't really hurt that much). The slayer women took shifts, two or three at the time in the impromptu birthing suite that heretofore had been Alex's bedroom, to fetch ice chips, refresh the water basin, or give Alex a new hand to squeeze the blood from as she suffered through the pain.

Dawn, however, arrived in eerie silence.

No one spoke. I suspected because none of us wanted to acknowledge the obvious. But as I finished my sixth mug and set it on the coffee table in the great room, truth took on a mass that refused to be contained.

"Something's wrong."

My father on the sofa beside me pulled me into the wing of his embrace. "We do not know that, *niña*. Have faith, all will be right."

A door opened on the floors above, bringing with it a fresh swirl of scented air. Antiseptic, I'd been told, as well as some aromatherapy oils because, apparently, hood medical care had caught up to the 1970s. Petunia Creed (whom Caleb had already nicknamed Patchouli Reed) pawed down the stairs on lithe feet. Doctor though the slender woman in her early sixties was, she was also a hood of the House of Green. Like all supes, her physical appearance belied her years, as did her endurance since she'd arrived at the house.

We shot to our feet as though a head of state had just entered the room. When she chose to address me as the point person for all that was going on, I had to wonder why. Still relinquished, I had no right under our customs to expect more than a curt nod. Even my father, merely exiled, had status over me.

"She sleeps between contractions," Petunia began without precursor. "But she's growing weak."

Caleb stepped forward. "And the baby?"

The green hood side-eyed the slayer. "Are you the father?"

"Me?" Caleb stuck his thumb into his chest as his face burned crimson. "No. No, definitely not."

"Shame, that," said Petunia. "The genes would be strong. The baby, as far as I can tell with the limited instruments at my disposal, endures, but that could change quickly. I rarely recommend sending one of my patients to a huey hospital, but at this point, I believe it's the prudent choice. I, of course, am not familiar with slayer delivery norms, and none of the females above have attended the birth of one of their own, but most hoods deliver in an eight- to ten-hour window and I can't imagine it's much different. I suggest she be taken to the hospital in Lahr as soon as possible."

Amy pivoted, making for the stairs. "I'll put together an away bag."

Markus headed to the garage. "I'll warm the car and pull it out in front. Should I put the back seats flat so she can lay down?"

Petunia nodded to his disappearing form. "Yes. A few blankets and pillows will also help keep the bumps of the road from causing her too much pain."

My father took the acquisition of sufficient linens and throw pillows as his duty, speeding off to a closet where we kept such things.

That left Caleb, Cody and I, looking to Petunia for marching orders.

"Does Alex know about this recommendation?" I asked.

The physician bobbed her head. "I advised her of the risks, both to go or not to go. She agreed with me that it was better safe than sorry. A slayer birth is a rare event. She said there had not been one in the fifteen years she was held as one of Vlad Tepeş's harem. We need do all we can. We should have made arrangements for this at a private clinic in advance."

"We weren't expecting her to give birth for a few more weeks," Caleb said. "According to Alex, she's only eight months along, and barely."

Petunia chortled. "Eight months, my eye. If anything, she's overdue. I'll want to move her between contractions in as easy a way as possible, and I'll need the help of that cousin of yours, Miss Kline, to carry her down just as soon as he's back."

Cody stepped forward. "I can do it."

The midwife looked at the alpha like she wanted to deliver a knock to the side of his head.

"What do you think I'm going to do, run away with her, eat her?" Cody huffed. "I just want to help."

Caleb stepped in closer. "Take him at his word, Nurse Ratchet. If Geri trusts him, then he deserves it."

Petunia's eyes rolled to the ceiling as she turned back toward the stairs. "A slayer and alpha, vouched for by a relinquished. What is this world coming to? Fine, come along. Miss Kline, I'll trust you to make sure this whole kit and caboodle goes off as planned. I will phone ahead to the hospital and let them know to expect us shortly."

We looked like a circus train driving into Lahr. Two cars, each full of fretful twentysomethings, supplemented by one senior physician smelling of the Grateful Dead and one middle-aged Latino looking like Antonio Banderas's slender brother.

The silky black SUV took the lead, deference given to the transport of the woman actually in labor. As instructed, the back seats had been laid flat, and my dad proved he had missed his calling as an interior designer by making use of sheets, pillows, and blankets in a short space of time to make it as comfortable of a bed as could be had. The shaded windows made my seeing Alex impossible during the twenty-minute trip, but I hoped that Petunia and Amy, both of whom were beside her, had found a way to comfort her. Yan had also rushed down to the house just before the sun had arisen, advised that his telepath services may be needed.

"Who's the vampire?" Cody asked from the backseat.

"His name is Janus Sousa, but he goes by Yan." In the passenger seat beside me, Caleb assumed responsibility for answering. "He's employed by the Matron Council at Schloss Wolfsretter. He swirls the memories of any hueys who manage to get into the property or who spread rumors they shouldn't."

Anya, a willowy reed of a slayer woman who'd been Alex's friend in the Istanbul harem, perked up at that. "So that's true? Vampires can change memories?"

The werewolf turned on the slayer. "How can *you* not know that?"

Affronted, Anya choked out her answer. "We were only taught what the Ravens wanted us to know, and had little contact with the outside world. All of us were born in the harem, or arrived there as children before our parents could train us. In fact, until Caleb arrived, we believed that only female slayers could conjure solaria."

I caught Cody's eye in the rearview mirror. "They were prisoners."

The werewolf became very sheepish. "Oh, um… Damn, I didn't know. I'm sorry. I'm just surprised, you know? I mean, like, you never saw them using that power?"

"It doesn't work on us any more than it works on slayers or werewolves," I said to a crestfallen Anya. "Don't feel ashamed that you didn't know. I mean, Markus and I had an extensive library of information on the natures of all supes, and neither of us had any idea slayer pregnancies only last eight months."

The polarity of the atmosphere changed with Anya's giggle. "That I *do* know. There haven't been any successful pregnancies while I was in the harem, but there were several stillbirths. Nine months, more or less, just like hueys.

I remember because that ninth month, the pregnant *haseki* would always be put into a private suite. Never did any good, though. The baby always died."

Reading the anxiety that hatched over Caleb's face, I leaned across the front seat to place a hand on his knee. "It will be fine. Alex is going to deliver a strong, healthy baby. She hasn't endured so long just to lose it."

His eyes tracked the car in front of us. "I hope so."

I'd spent more time in hospitals in the last few years than all the years previous collectively. What struck me was how similar the experience was, whether it was Marquette, Michigan or Lahr, Germany or even Chicago. Maybe the sterile atmosphere could only result ultimately in the same bland-but-functional environment?

A pond of taupe-colored fabric chairs was docked around a pine-paneled table holding an odd collection of fashion magazines, newspapers, and well-worn children's books, the chairs numbered just enough to seat us all. Markus and Yan, noodled together, thumbed through a copy of the German edition of *Cosmo*, I eyeballed a local newspaper published in Munich, and Cody tried to make sense of a picture book in which two kids bounced on a dragon's tummy.

A cell phone rang.

Caleb pressed the device to his ear. "Halo? ... Ah, Inga, how kind of you to remember that any of us exist. Thanks for saying bye, by the way. ... Hmmm? No, nothing too much, just sitting at the hospital, waiting for Alex to give birth, you know, just shooting the breeze and all. What?" His eyes surveyed the room. "No, it's just us here, no one else. ... You sure about that? Fine, just a second." He lowered the phone to his palm and pushed a button on the screen. "Go ahead, you're on speaker."

"Have you all lost your minds?" the eerily-sedate voice of the vampire demanded without pretense. "You've taken a slayer to a huey hospital? Are you insane?"

"It was her choice, and advised by the hood physician," Caleb said, holding the phone up. "She's been in labor for a whole day at this point."

"Let it be for thirty days!" Inga shouted. "But let it be in Triberg! Do you have any idea what you've done, exposing her to outsiders and having her registered in one of their computer systems?"

"Do you think we're a bunch of first-time supes?" I asked. "She's here under an alias, one created by the Matron Council. They've given new IDs to all the slayers."

A pause suggested Inga hadn't counted on that. But the vampire proved she had more than one arrow in her quiver. "What of the doctors, though? If they do any basic blood work on her, they're going to figure out she's not human. Hell, they'll suspect something's wrong when her pulse and blood pressure are so irregular, and that's going to results in tests, notes, data in medical systems..."

Yan leaned in toward the phone. "I am here to make sure the hueys take no notice of Miss Alexandra's abnormalities, nor that they have any memory of her when we leave."

"Who..." A pause more pregnant than the slayer we'd arrived with. "...is that?"

Yan shrank back, suddenly silent. But Markus wouldn't stand for any slight of his boyfriend.

"*That* is Yan, and he's going to make sure everything is kept secure. Don't worry, we got things covered."

Inga's voice became alarmingly pinched. "Yan, who?"

The black-haired vampire buried his chin into his balled-up fists. "I am blooded of the Varanasi Clutch."

"I see," said Inga, followed by a space during which I could practically visualize the woman examining her fingernails with disdain. "I will arrive back in Germany tonight, and come directly to the hospital. If there is a single doctor left in that facility who even remembers what Alex's hair color is, there will be trouble. Do you understand, Watcher?"

Yan licked his lips. "Yes, Dracule, I do."

"Good," the vampire cooed. "I thought you might. Now, get that baby born, and as soon as I arrive, we leave, whether the doctors think she's ready or not."

And without a further word, the connection dropped.

FOURTEEN

My gaze shifted between cutting and curious when I turned eyes on Yan. Even surmising that the Varanasi and Dracule had some kind of tension didn't do me much good. After all, the Ravens were Dracule, and I had a whole Texan cattle industry worth of beef with them, despite Inga and Igor also being born of that clutch.

Any chance of follow-up would have to wait. Petunia arrived right in time to catch our shell shock but to keep additional bombs at bay.

"The doctors agree that we've waited on the natural thing to happen long enough," the green hood said. "Alex is being prepped for the operating room.

She'll be going in in the next ten to fifteen minutes, just as soon as the epidural kicks in."

Caleb stepped closer. "And the baby?"

Petunia's face blossomed. "She's a strong little lass. But she is showing some signs of stress, so it's good we got here when we did." Then, the glow of her cheeks faded. "Only…"

"Only what?"

Who asked? Who didn't?

She frowned. "The OB-GYN asked Alex permission to perform an ultrasound. Poor child hadn't had one, she said. The image was…" As Petunia's voice drifted off, Yan rounded the lobby. "I'll start containing the abnormality."

My pulse pounded. My breath hitched. Something was wrong, and it was my fault. "Abnormality? What kind of…"

Instead of illuminating our understanding or alleviate our worry in the least, Petunia turned her staunch expression square on me. "Alex would like to talk with you before it's too late."

The weight of collective stares threatened to collapse me.

"Me?" I asked, just as surprised as any of them. Anya had gone in with her the moment she'd been wheeled off, after all, so it wasn't like she was alone. "Why me? Caleb should be there; he's a slayer. Or Amy; she's been helping Alex pick out baby furniture and names. I'm… I'm…"

What? A hood? A no one? Relinquished?

But I knew what I was. I was a broken woman who was beginning to fear her mate was dead. I was bad luck. I was a malcontent. I was the last person Alex should want at her side as she welcomed her first-born child into the world.

I felt my head shaking before I'd even realized I'd said no.

Petunia planted balled-up fists on her hips. "Miss Kline, perhaps you've never been present at a birth before, but here's a helpful tip. Whatever the mother wants that's not a danger to her baby or herself, she gets." The elder hood pulled the surgical mask back up over her mouth. "I'll come to retrieve you in a few minutes when we're going into the OR."

As the midwife made her exit, I suddenly felt like I was the one in need of medical attention. My heart was going to thud right out of my chest.

Markus put an arm around me. "No worries, cuz. It's easy. You just tell them to breathe and push."

Caleb slapped Markus upside the head. "Alex is having a c-section, Einstein. The doctors are going to remove the baby surgically."

"You mean, they have to cut into her whoo-haa?" Markus's face curdled. "Oh my god, I'm so glad Yan can never do that to me."

As the boys bickered and Amy rattled something off about the shortcomings of the female body, I gathered my courage. I'd taken on ruthless vampires and stood up to my alpha ex, but facing a mother giving birth was twisting me into knots. One thing Alex did not need was to be the one reassuring *me* everything was going to be okay. Time to step up and get my act together.

"Caleb?"

"...I mean the biology alone would be impossible, so..."

"Caleb!"

The slayer snapped to attention, wide-eyed. "Geri?"

"I don't suppose you're aware of any slayer birth traditions or anything?"

He guffawed. "We don't give birth to aliens or anything. Plus, how the hell would I know?"

"There's the naming ceremony," Markus offered.

Leave it to my cousin to have some forgotten piece of historic slayer lore in his head but be completely clueless on what a caesarian section was.

"How does that go?"

"Yeah, Markus." Caleb crossed his arms over his chest and cocked a hip expectantly. "How does that go?"

"During the first sunrise after the birth, you're supposed to hold up the baby to the first light of dawn to introduce it to its birthright, while proclaiming its name. Usually it's something done by the dad." He frowned. "Hey, do we even know who the dad is? Seems like that should have come up by now, but I haven't seen Alex being particularly Jane Brady with any of those slayer guys."

"When I asked her once, the only thing she said was that it didn't matter," Amy chimed in. "He's dead."

Another bitter inheritance this child would be born into.

Caleb got a sly look on his face. "I don't think it was a slayer, though. Probably some huey staff the Ravens had. Anya and the others say that Alex never got together with anyone in the dungeon as far as they knew, and there wouldn't have been much opportunity, you know."

I shouldn't be spending one brain cell on trying to puzzle out something that wasn't any of my business, but it did draw my curiosity. Given that the slayers were so important to Vlad, surely he would have been eager to, for lack of a better word, breed them. Would he have tolerated a hybrid? Was he so desperate for any of them to reproduce he'd accept any pairing that resulted in a child? Or was it possible that Alex had found a way to have a little happiness, confined as she was? Although, frankly, her restrictions hadn't seemed as bad as the other slayers'. Vlad exulted Alex over them all, doting on her, treating her with her own personal care and tenderness.

The same man who held my mate bound in silver and wanted to kill his own father. How very ... odd.

"Well, at least we know that Vlad didn't knock her up."

Amy slapped Cody's chest quicker than I was able to. The blond huey didn't fear the big, bad wolf one single bit.

Returning to the room, holding a mass of pink scrubs, Petunia cleared her throat. "It's time, Miss Kline. Take these. You'll put them on over your clothes after you scrub up."

If any of these people hurt Alex or her baby, I'll flay them with their own scalpels.

I put my hand against the wall to steady myself, flooded with a sense of protection that perplexed me.

"Miss Kline?" Petunia's callused hands had a remarkably light touch. "Is something wrong?"

"No." *Yes.* "Just had a weird moment there, a little overcome." *Like I needed to protect something with my life.*

Petunia patted my shoulders. "Stress, perhaps. And I bet you haven't gotten anything past those lips but coffee since this whole episode started yesterday, have you?" She helped me regain my balance. "You're lucky you're relinquished. That wolf of yours from America... He's got a peculiar type of energy. Took me a while to get used to it, too. Makes me wonder if all American lupines are like that. The ones back home in Wales aren't."

What the hell was she talking about, *peculiar energy*? But then I remembered what Markus had said, how he could sense me now at times, the way any hood could sense any wolf when they got close enough. I hadn't thought about that when we called the hood's physician down from the castle. Cody's arrival, it seemed, had come at just the right time to serve as camouflage for my true nature.

Petunia gave me a gentle nudge toward a set of swinging doors at the end of the corridor. "Come along, now. This young one has waited long enough."

I yielded. "Petunia, thank you for this. For being here for Alex, even though she's not a hood."

"Pash! A baby is a baby," the old woman said. "I can't blame it for its parentage."

In the back of my mind, I wondered if she would have said the same thing back in 1687, if she'd been asked to assist in the birthing of my nameless ancestor.

In the OR, the medical staff moved with deliberate speed around Alex, stopping only a moment to acknowledge Petunia and me. The slayer's head stuck out from a surgical poncho, a tent that was tied down at the level of her shoulders and fanned out toward her feet, opening her most private areas to the inspection of the doctor and two nurses busily preparing a slew of instruments on several trays.

To be exposed in such a way to strangers. What more would this creature have to endure?

"Geri." She managed a smile, even as her voice cracked. "Thank you for coming." Then, moving her gaze and tilting her chin the slightest, Alex spoke to Anya and Petunia. "Can we have a moment?"

Anya let go of Alex's hand. "Of course." Petunia pushed a palm to Alex's cheek, telling her she was a brave woman, a mother of the future light. Despite this passing in English, I suspected at least one of the nurses wondered what the two were getting on about, as she stopped in the laying out of instruments for a fraction of a second.

As a hood and as a woman, I knew that's where the truth often revealed itself: in the slivers of time between understanding and obfuscation.

I assumed the tall stool at Alex's side, still warm from its previous occupant, and took her hand. "It's almost done now. Pretty soon, you're going to be holding your baby."

She grinned. "I have been holding her for eight long months."

"Yeah, but now you'll be able to put her down, too."

"Miss Denver." The doctor leaned in over the top of the tenting, looking the slayer in the face. His English proved good, even if heavily accented. "We will make the first incision in just a moment. If you want your guest to stay, it is okay, but if you want either Miss Anya or Petunia back, we should ask them in now."

"I'd like Anya," Alex returned, "but if you would, just a moment?"

The doctor nodded, then went back to his position down the bed. "But quickly. We do not want to cause you or the baby anymore stress than is necessary."

And I'd add myself to that list. "I don't want to rush you," I said, "but it seems you have something to say to me. Best just to say it then."

The jerk of her chin was so minute, I'd have missed it if I didn't look for it. "I want you to know that I didn't hide the truth because I was ashamed. I hid it because I didn't know who I could trust. Now I know, I can trust you."

Where was she going with this? "Of course, you can."

"My baby, Geri..." Her eyes drifted down to the regions of her body now embargoed. "The life she would have known if you had not helped us—"

Thank god she was cognizant to mind her words with an audience. "When you liberated us from Dracula's harem" might have changed the temperature of the room.

"The opportunity she will have now, possibilities that would have been impossible before… What I'm trying to say is, will you do us both the honor of being Mina's godmother?"

The skin on my nose crinkled. "Who's Mina?"

"Why… The baby, of course."

"Oh? Oh! Oh, goodness." So much for that naming ceremony then. Either Alex wasn't aware of the tradition, or the absence of a father had encouraged her to make do without.

I didn't really understand where this was coming from. I mean, yeah, the gratitude made sense, even if it landed on me with a wallop as a reminder that, in exchange for the slayers' freedom, Tobias had lost his. But did she mean would I be some sort of protector? A godmother? An executor of a vast slayer estate Alex had heretofore failed to mention should something happen to the mother and until little Mina turned twenty-one?

Part of me hesitated, and I recognized that part, at last, for it was: the selfish me who Cody had so accurately pointed a finger at (not that I'd ever admit that to him). Remembering what Petunia had said, that a pregnant mother gets whatever she wants as long as there's no harm in it, however…

My hands wrapped around Alex's. "Of course, Alex. I'd be honored."

The slayer didn't need to conjure a solarium to shine. "Thank you. You have no idea how much that means to me. Now, I hate to push you along, but I have to see to this one little thing."

I couldn't help but laugh. "If you insist. I'll send Anya back in on my way out."

Which should have been the joyous end of a long and arduous day, but my true nightmare was only just about to begin.

The hall was empty as I hit the linoleum floor, smelling vaguely of antiseptic and lemon. I'd managed to break my fall, but couldn't move. All four limbs worked to keep me right, even as my frame shook from tip to toe. As the first cries of a new soul who claimed the air as birthright and her life as her own filled my ears, the ground beneath my palms tilted. *She's mine.* The voice in my head chanted it, declared it, repeated it like a mantra as old as earth itself.

She's mine.

I am yours.

She is ours.

Three voices, all of them singing in perfect harmony.

The first voice, mine.

The second, and how I did not know but knew it was utterly true, was Mina's.

And the third...

The third was Tobias's.

My eyes shot up, as though he might be standing there, with his worn-out jeans, scratching the five o'clock shadow that showed up at 9 AM each morning, while offering me a bowl of dumplings. The hall remained empty, but my head remained full.

"Tobias?" I asked.

Aloud? Or was it just in my mind? I didn't know.

"She's ours, Geri," he answered. Or did he? Could he? "The pup is pack."

He had to be talking about Mina, but that was impossible. Mina was a slayer. How could she be—

Alex never talked about the father.

Vlad had treated her like a goddess.

The pregnancy had only lasted eight months.

A werewolf, free of his mating bond, could love again...

Finally, the realization took me to my feet. "Tobias?"

I blinked, and suddenly, what I was seeing wasn't the hospital my logical brain knew I was in, but a small, square room built of ancient rose-colored brick, smocked over at intervals by beige stucco. I was on the floor, my hands bound behind me, while Vlad and another male vampire sat on cushioned, baroque-styled chairs.

"Once I have its lover, then the plan will all be in place, Massimo. It will give us the tools we need to be both masters of life and death."

Massimo, the archetype of a Byronic beauty with his prominent jaw, ebony locks, and olive skin, clutched the top of a silver-crested cane anchored before him. "You assume, Vlad, that we all want such things."

Vlad blinked. "Are you saying you want to die?"

"I am saying that I have very little left for which to live." The man shook his head, then passed me—Tobias?—us?—a sympathetic gaze before turning back. "Why live forever without purpose, when you can die happy with pride and with love?"

The man rose, and Vlad followed.

"You and yours may take shelter in my clutch, as requested, but I suggest you depart for Spain as soon as you've made arrangements. In the meantime, you *will* observe to my edicts while in Venice. We adhere to modernity, Vlad.

No drinking to excess, and erase the memories of those from whom you do imbibe. Tourists work well, especially those who themselves have had a little too much to drink."

The fingers on Vlad's hand flexed. "You presume to lecture me on remaining discreet?"

Massimo's eyes shifted to where we were huddled on the ground once more. "You travel with both your sire bound by oak and an asenaic in bondage, Dracule. Such acts in our world draw attention. I bid you good evening."

And with a tip of his fingers off his forehead, Massimo (and his walking stick) became smoke and flew away.

Vlad, chest heaving, anger in his eyes, turned on us. "You'll pay for your words, wolf. You were told to *remain silent.*"

When I spoke, it wasn't with my voice, but Tobias's. "Even if I were rendered mute, my heart will cry out for her so loudly, the deaf would hear."

"Is it torture or love that's made a poet of you?" Vlad stomped the four paces it took to cross the room. "And I do detest both the love and poetry of amateurs."

Without warning, the vampire's fangs latched onto our neck, the pain rippling through my body. Our screams rang out, walled in by brick and bitterness. The vampire pulled what he desired from us, then retracted, then… was just gone.

Our breath heaved. Our wounds bled. Our hopes withered. The brick sent a chill through our body.

"I will find you. I will save you."

Did I say that to Tobias? Did he say it to me? I didn't know. A moment later, bitter, toxic fumes filled my nose. I blinked, and suddenly, the brick wall was gone. The pain was gone. I was still here.

In the hospital, with a very concerned doctor muttering something in German to me that didn't register.

"I'm fine," I said in English before remedying with, *"Mir geht's gut."*

She seemed doubtful as she explained that she'd just come up the hall to find me on the ground. "Not unconscious," she said. "Just staring blankly. Miss, do you need medical attention?"

I shook my head as she helped me to sit up. "I just need food. I haven't eaten anything in… two days?" I said.

We both turned as the doors of the OR behind us opened and a beaming Anya, draped in the requisite cleanroom attire, peaked out. "Tell everyone, Geri! It's a girl! A healthy, beautiful, baby girl!"

FIFTEEN

The redhead's delicate eyelashes fluttered open.

Alex's movements were slow, but the doctors had warned they would be. She'd gone through nearly twenty-seven hours of labor from start to finish, then endured a c-section. The staff said she'd be healed enough for release in three to five days. The staff didn't know supes healed in half the time of a huey.

Ignoring the vampire hovering over her bed, Alex's gaze searched the room and found me sitting in a nearby chair, rocking a sleeping Mina.

"Is she okay?"

She was better than okay. Holding Mina felt like I was holding home in my arms, and she wasn't even mine. I gave the slayer a smile. "She's perfect. Absolutely perfect."

Inga pushed an index finger into Alex's chin, directing her attention back. "You have some explaining to do, sparky. Who else knew the father was lupine?"

Alex tried to sit up, but one painful shift of her frame told her why that wasn't a good idea, and she surrendered back to the bed. "Vlad knew. Timur, too. Other than that, I don't know."

"And what about the wolf?" Inga asked. "Do you know who he was? What pack he was from?"

"What pack he was from? The wolves that the Ravens held…. Ahhh… Ahh!"

Yan flew to the bed, putting a hand on Inga's when the latter's fingernail drew blood. "Perhaps you can remember, Miss Rosethorn, that Alex is not our enemy. She has committed us no wrong, and she is recovering from major surgery."

Violet eyes flashed anger. Then, with glacial coolness, Inga's features eased. Her hand dropped back to her side as she feigned clearing her throat, waiting for Alex's answer.

The slayer shook her head. "I speak English, Ukrainian, Turkish, and the Raven's form of Romanian. The wolf spoke none of those."

Something about that answer set Inga at ease, and I itched to know what. Regardless, now wasn't the time.

The recovery room door opened, and a short man with a pot belly and brown-rimmed glasses bustled in, carrying a clipboard. "Miss Inga, madame?"

"Yes, Doctor Altz?"

Earlier in the morning, Inga had marched into the hospital like Patton arriving to the front, despite the sun lingering overhead. A quick arrival was worth the sunburn she'd endured, it seemed. Within five minutes, all the doctors and nurses that Yan had already corralled and began to process were under *her* sway, taking each of their breaths from her sighs.

Yan had looked simultaneously impressed and ill.

Dr. Altz flipped open that charts. "As you predicted, the patient's blood pressure and pulse are slightly elevated, but steady. The baby, however, seems to have the opposite result. We're concerned that her temperature is low."

"I wouldn't worry about it," I said. "A wolf's temperature runs slightly cooler than a huey's."

Speaking up only brought Inga's attention back to me, the last place I wanted it to be. The vampire had been shooting me daggers since she'd shown up.

"What happened, Geri? Igor raved all about your amazing ability to sense wolves at a distance none of your kind ever had. How did you not sense the baby?"

I'd been pondering that myself. "The only thing I can think of is that Alex's body—a slayer's body—created some kind of barrier that interferes with whatever it is that lets me do that. As soon as Mina was out, I could sense her."

"Any of you had any other insights?" she drove on. "No inklings? No nudging suspicions? Any visions?"

At the word *vision* I almost spilled about what had happened to me in the minutes after Mina had been born, but instinct told me to hold back. Besides, it probably had been a hallucination. Wolves weren't telepaths in the traditional sense; neither were hoods. There were no precedents for any supe saying they'd actually inhabited the mind of another and seen with their eyes.

"None," I said instead. "I assumed – we *all* assumed – that the baby was wholly slayer."

Before the vampire could follow up her line of questioning, I launched into one of my own. "Alex, it sounds like you met the wolf, but if you couldn't speak, how did you two... you know, come to an understanding about what was to be done?"

The woman in the bed blushed. "The act of procreation does not require words, as you know."

Embarrassment became a flame in my cheeks, but luckily Alex wasn't in a position to see.

"Vlad had offered me the option of having—what is it called?" Alex's eyes drifted through the air, searing words. "An injection?"

Artificial insemination seemed too course a term to say while holding an infant. "I understand. But you didn't choose that. Why?"

The slayer's fatigue pulled at the corner of her eyes. "I did not survive in the House of Tepeş by being ignorant. I learned when to listen, when to be deaf, and when to ask questions. I've spent years making Vlad feel he was my living god. He trusted me. Once, when he thought I was asleep in his bed, I overheard a phone call he took."

I tried to ignore the implication, even as my mind raced to judgement. But how was that fair? Alex had been worse than a prisoner, she'd been a slave. Whatever advantage she made of her limited choices wasn't for me to berate; I knew from experience that knowledge was power. She'd have done it not only for herself, but also to keep the other slayers as safe as she was able. Martyrdom didn't always mean the death of the body. Sometimes it means the death of the soul.

I placed Mina in the clear plastic bassinet the hospital had provided and made sure she was tucked in tight. "Do you know who he was talking to?"

Alex shook her head as I took a chair at her bedside. "A vampire, for certain. Vlad said something about how he wished he could destroy his father, but he'd need a miracle to do it and survive. You know that about them, right? That vampires who kills a member of their own bloodline kill themselves in the process?"

I nodded. "Yes, Igor told me."

A faint smile ghosted her face, then flitted away. "Right. Then, whomever he was talking to told him something that made him happy, exceedingly happy. To delight Vlad when he is in such a mood is to sift diamonds from mud. I pretended that I just woke up and asked what the good news was. When he explained he'd learned a way to kill Igor and explained how, I asked for the honor of being the vessel. Vlad agreed, saying if any of the slayers could seduce a wolf to lie with them, it was me."

"That sounds like my brethren," Inga hissed. "I'm sorry that happened to you, Alex, but I don't understand what you're getting at."

"Of course, you don't," Alex said. "Like all vampires, you don't want context, you only want what you feel is critical. But you never understand that humanity is where the context lies."

Inga choked on the retort, taking none too kindly to being lambasted.

Perhaps because she was so tired or just tired of acquiescing to vampires, Alex continued unabated. "My people have clung to our stories. Maybe you would call them legends, and maybe that's all they are. They've been handed down for so many generations, it's impossible to know what's true and what's made up. One talks about a lupine who took two wives: one slayer and one hood. Both bore him children. One night, a vampire descended on them, eating first the lupine, and then his wives, and then he came to the children. First, he consumed the blood of the babe born to the hood, and it gave the vampire incredible strength, fueling him with power. Then, the vampire ate the child of the slayer, whose blood made him weak, and eventually, killed him."

Inga mused a space before saying, "If this is true, it would change things radically."

Alex's head angled as she took me into view. "At first, I carried the child, hoping that the story was true. I would sacrifice a child born to such circumstances to save my people. Then I was rescued, given a chance at a life, a real life, with my child. Now, the last thing I want is to lose her to them. Please, Geri, swear you will protect her."

I moved to the edge of the slayer's bed, pulling her hands to mine. "Of course, Alex."

Behind us, Inga paced. "If that story *is* true, it means Mina would be… Would be a way to kill the Ravens. The child must be harvested at once."

I shot up from the bed and spun on the vampiress. "What?"

Inga blazed with hope. "Just think about it, Geri: the Ravens arranged for this baby's conception with the intent of drinking it. All we have to do is let them."

I was in front of the bassinet before I realized I'd even moved. "No one touches the baby."

The temperature of the room had shifted, and suddenly, we were no longer three women with fates bound by a common enemy. I was pack, a status extended by virtue of blood to Alex, and Inga… Inga was a jaguar, stalking the young I protected.

"Come on, Geri," she said, creeping forward half-step by half-step. "Don't you want your *mate* back at your side so you can finally be together? You and I both know killing Vlad is part of that process. The other Ravens are tough but not undefeatable; we've already proven that. With Vlad, the rest will fall in short order, but we must kill him. Let me take the baby. I can still leave tonight if I move quickly."

"We're not doing anything that is going to bring a lick of harm to this child." My arms went wide, but not in a mere display. As the vampire dripped toward me, I called out the silver hidden under my clothing, fashioning it into a chakram. I'd never fought with the Indian weapon before, but the circular throwing ring had an edge as sharp as a sword, and could be used up close as well – both advantages when fighting a vampire.

Inga blinked thrice. "My, my. Been doing some research, or did someone watch *Xena?*"

No idea what that meant, I answered instead by positioning my weapon. "We are not using this baby as a weapon."

"Why not? She's not that precious. Alex got knocked up by a wolf; it shouldn't be hard to get another slayer to do the same."

Revulsion roiled my insides. "Their race is dying and you want them to be some kind of anti-vampire breeding factory? Not to mention what that does to a wolf."

"We'll use unmated wolves, then. Since they automatically love whomever they first bed, what's the big deal? Besides—" Inga held up a hand. "We don't even know if it will work. Worst case scenario: I use Mina as a peace offering, Vlad takes me into his fold again, and then I can work from the inside to destroy them."

Across the room, Alex labored to sit up. She did better this time, propping herself on her elbows. The sedatives they'd given her during the c-section were wearing off, but that didn't mean she was in any state to anchor a battle. "Give me one shot and I'll end this discussion."

"Don't move, Alex, or you'll rip your stitches. Don't worry, I'm not letting her touch Mina."

The vampire flexed her fingers, cracking each knuckle like a string of fireworks. "I tried the nice way, hood. Now we do this my way."

And before I knew what had happened, I was flying through the air.

SIXTEEN

AMY

Someone had brought their pug to the hospital, and when I'd nodded off, it had crawled up into my lap and made itself at home.

No, wait. Check that. It was Caleb. *Caleb* had crawled up into my lap and made himself at home. Or at least, his head had.

"Get off me." I pushed him practically onto the floor.

He startled awake like all supernaturals... uh, *supes* did: leaping into full battle position. What was it with this crowd, did none of them have to rub the sleep from their eyes and spend five slow and confusing minutes trying to figure out which frat boy's bachelor pad they'd passed out in drunk the night before? Every time they were shocked awake, they expected Lord Voldemort to be attacking.

Luckily, he hadn't conjured a solarium, because that probably would have really freaked out the thin, middle-aged woman dressed like an LL Bean commercial in the chair across from us. I mean, I knew that since Inga had arrived, she had all the doctors and nurses involved with Alex's case sequestered and Criss Angel-ed, but down here in the main waiting room, it was still clueless hueys.

Which, for once, didn't include me.

I rolled up my copy of *Der Spiegel* and hit the slayer on the thigh. "Who gave your head permission to be on my lap?"

"What? I fell asleep." His stance eased. "And if you want to give me permission to put my head somewhere else, by all means."

Luckily, German middle-aged auntie didn't seem to speak English. I, however, did. What the hell was it with this guy? How could you so openly flirt after you'd just had your heart broken? Besides, totally inappropriate innuendo was *my* thing. Caleb Helsing was beating me at my own game, and he didn't even like me.

By the way, what was there about me *not* to like?

The slayer sauntered to the automatic coffee machine. "How long was I out?"

I turned my wrists out to him. "Do you see a stopwatch?" My eyes went to the clock over the world's most pristine goldfish tank. "It's five-thirty. Morning or evening, though? We've been at this hospital so long, I've lost track."

He shoved a coin in the slot, and automatically a disposable cup popped into existence underneath the dispenser as it spouted out liquid humanity. "Morning. The sun is about to rise. Probably why I fell asleep. That, or you bored me to death."

"Believe me, Buffy, if I could kill you by talking, I'd never shut up. Now, stop being a self-centered bastard and get me a cup of coffee, too."

"Your wish is my command, Barbie."

Despite the lip, he did as asked, shoving a scalding plastic cup into my grip a few moments later. Inspired by joe, I finally untwisted myself from the awkward position forced by trying to sleep in a waiting room chair, bending at the hip, elongating my frame, puffing my chest out to stretch my lower back. I did *not* miss how Caleb's eyes clung to me during the whole procedure.

"Didn't Inga get here, like, three hours ago?" I asked. "I thought she'd just go through and mind zap all the particulars and we'd be out of here." I took a survey of the waiting room. "Where are the others?"

"Cody and Pietro are sleeping out in the car," Caleb said between sips. "Markus and Yan are upstairs, helping to run doctor and nurse interference."

"Why? Is there something wrong? Is the baby okay?"

The slayer shook his head and then, annoyingly, crossed his arms and beamed at me. "You're very cute when you're concerned with someone beside yourself."

I stood and shoved a finger into his chest. His very solid, very defined chest. "I'd say the same of you, but I don't know what that looks like."

Those soft lips curled into a mischievous grin, one I wanted to smack off his face.

With my lips.

Hot coffee scalded my hand as Caleb threw me against the wall, knocking all the wind from my lungs. I'd had aggressive lovers in the past, but this was borderline Christian Grey-level shit and I was not having it.

Especially not in these clothes.

But no sooner had I drafted a witty way of saying "fuck you" that simultaneously said "fuck me" then I figured out Caleb wasn't attempting to ravage me. Not unless a slayer's idea of getting to first base was to paste you to the nearest flat surface with their backs pressed into your chest.

Which begged the question: were slayers' danglies on their frontside like ours, or to sleep with Caleb would I have to reinterpret the term "reverse cowgirl"?

"What the f—?"

Boom. Crash.

I'd never heard anything about earthquakes in Germany, but it would have been hard to miss the way the whole building shook.

The slayer peeled himself off me and shoved me toward the exit just in time to see LL Bean high-tailing it likewise. "Get out of the building, now!"

Caleb almost managed to get away before I grabbed him by the collar and dragged him back. "What's going on?"

"Fighting. Not sure who. Go to the car in the parking lot. Send Pietro and Cody in. Might need their help. Hurry!"

In a blur, my hand was empty and Caleb was gone, leaving me unprotected, and worse, unravaged.

Sigh… Maybe I should try to sneak out of the house and hit up the local bar scene when we got home. Apparently, I *needed* someone again. Always did, eventually, and it had been… what, six months since that graduation party at Delta Mu Xi?

Did Triberg have a bar scene?

Ignoring the throbbing of my scorched fingers, I instead focused on the destruction of my last pair of blue jeans as I headed toward the exit, all while things were crashing somewhere behind me. All around, frightened chatter turned into panic as patients and hospital staff alike fled the building.

I turned to look up to the three-story structure, knowing Geri and Alex were on the second floor. Right where a bright light flashed moments before the windows blew out from one side of the building.

"Holy—"

Women screamed. A child cried. I looked up, only then realizing I'd fallen to the ground, a moment later to be pulled to my feet.

Cody shoved keys into my hand as Pietro whisked by. "Get the car ready. We might need to make a quick getaway."

"They're still up there." My head jerked to the place where a patch of wall had simply ceased to be.

But Cody didn't wait for a reply. He flew as fast as two feet allowed, running the opposite direction of the crowd.

This was bad. This was super, mega bad. Some serious shit was going on upstairs, and they wanted me to go start the car? I looked over my shoulder and found it parked just twenty feet away, past cement barriers that would keep me from bringing it much closer. The key fob had a remote starter. As long as I didn't lose the keys, it was fine.

Slipping them inside my pocket, I circled back.

The good news was, Lahr was in the middle of nowhere. Nowhere being the Black Forest region. Well, technically, it was sort of on the upper northeast side, but there weren't many people there. Caleb said Inga had created a safe zone around the area where Alex was recovering. Other than Geri, Markus, and Yan, there shouldn't have been anyone there when whatever exploded went boom.

Oh, except a poor, helpless baby.

I wasn't exactly what one would call "interested in kids," but just because I didn't go gaga over mini-humans didn't mean I'd let one get hurt if I could do anything about it.

As I reentered the building, I came to the sudden realization that I really had no idea where to go, other than up. Luckily, the steady stream of people heading in the opposite direction gave me some clue. Near the stairwell, a man wearing a security uniform, his chest pumping and his face uber white, talked over a red phone. He held out a hand as I passed, saying something very German.

"Sorry, I no *sprechen*."

"Explosion!" he warned in an accent so heavy, I'd have to pay extra fees to take it on a plane. "You no can go in the—"

I hit the stairs and didn't hang around to hear the rest. At the top, I could turn right, down a sterile hallway, or left, down a sterile hallway with a window at the end. The glass in the window was still intact. I thought that was as good a reason as any to hang a right. A few doors down, I heard growling. A few more steps, a thundering voice wove into the mix.

"... can't let you do this."

Caleb? My feet picked up the pace, as did my heart.

I rounded the corner and passed a door. Like, one on a wall, only not hung by hinges. The smoldering rectangle bore a perfect shape to fit into a frame that now stood empty.

On the side of the room without windows, or really, much of a wall anymore, was Geri, holding a bundle of pink blankets clutched to her chest, winged by Markus and Pietro. Yan and Caleb stood in front of the trio, the slayer balancing a solarium on his hand. Also, there was a wolf. Like a massive, hulking, would-make-my-mother's-chihuahua-shit-itself wolf. Alex was still in the hospital bed, and from what I could see, unconscious.

Inga's back was to me, but I'd learned enough about supes in my limited time to know they all probably knew I was there. Hearing me or smelling me or their earlobes tingling or something... The supernatural really got the royal flush of hands when it came to the five senses.

And... that made me wonder what Caleb's mouth could taste like.

"Silly slayer!" Inga hissed. "Don't you see? This is the solution! That babe has the power to kill the Ravens. All I need to do is present it to Vlad, and finally, your kind will be saved."

"We are *not* sacrificing a baby!" Caleb snapped. "Back down or else."

Inga crossed her arms. "Are you going to kill me, Caleb? You couldn't do it when I found you, and you're even more compromised now. Now, hand over the baby. I don't want to hurt anyone."

"Hurt anyone?" I'd never heard Geri's voice so worn, so broken, not even when we left Istanbul. "You killed Alex!"

My racing pulse went still as I sucked up all the air in the room.

And surprisingly, *that's* what drew the vampire's attention.

Inga spun. "Why, hello, Amy."

Caleb looked past the vampire. "I told you to wait in the car."

"Alex is dead?" No, that couldn't be possible. She'd just given birth. She'd just gotten free, god damn it, all to die here, in the middle of the Black-Fucking-Forest? "How? When?"

I closed my eyes against the sting of tears, but in doing so, also closed them against the signs of danger. I flew forward. When I opened my eyes, I was five feet farther into the room then I'd been before, and Inga had me trapped, one of her blood-red fingernails at my throat.

And that's when it hit me, I was going to die.

"Caleb!"

Caleb? Why the hell, among all the people in this room, was I singling him out.

"It's okay, Amy." He inched forward, but Inga dug her nails deeper into my skin, and then under it. A hot line of blood trickled down my neck, soaking into my shirt after rolling over my collar bone.

"Careful, Caleb," Inga warned. "Little Amy is just a huey. I could kill her before you had a chance to blink."

The slayer cocked back his weapon. "You do, and I'll kill you here and now."

"Like I said, how? Share a secret, Amy?" The vampire's lips hovered next to my ear. "I've had a theory that this is part of the reason that Caleb is such a manwhore. His solarium has performance issues, so he bangs everything with a pulse to feel like a man."

Anger fringed my fear, burning away its fumes. "Probably why you're so jealous," I said. "Having no pulse, he never gave you the time of day."

The vampire's chest shook with laugher. "Oh, I do like you. I'd hate to kill you. Geri? Give me the baby, and that doesn't have to happen."

I locked gazes with my best friend, shaking my head. "Don't you dare, Kline."

Geri nodded. "I won't, Amy. I won't."

The wolf—Was *that* what Cody Ryland looked like with fur?—chuffed.

I turned my eyes back to Caleb. "Throw it."

His eyes went blank. "But it will kill you."

"If you don't give Inga the baby, she's going to kill me anyway," I said. Even if what the vampire said was true and Caleb's supernatural power had performance issues, it had to hurt like a son of a bitch, right? "Besides, I got nothing to live for. No job, no home, no boyfriend. My father hates me, and my mother thinks I'm the reason he hates *her*. Saving a baby from a wacko vamp would at least give my death some purpose, even if my life has added up to zero net gain."

Said vamp tugged me a step backward. "The girl makes sense, Caleb. Now, *hand it over* or I'll take you too, Geri. Your blood could keep me going until Doomsday."

Geri got the fire of the gods in her as she put a hand forward and morphed silver into some kind of ball. Because the best kept secret in history is that you can kill a vampire by bowling at it.

My friend sneered. "To the death, then, Inga."

Amy's death. I mean, that's what they meant, right, being that I was the hostage du jour? I closed my eyes, trying to buy my sales pitch. I could see my mother weeping her crocodile tears in my mind's eye, but I could also see Geri, actually crying.

Fine, I'd die. At least I'd be the hottest corpse ever.

The grip around me loosened and the floor smacked my ass suddenly. A moment later, I found myself sitting in a puddle of something dark and crimson. A thud next to me drew my attention. Turning my head, I found a body without its own.

Pietro Kline stepped away from the non-human shields that had gathered around the baby. *"Gracias, Dio."*

Was he smiling? Grimacing? Having gas? Any of those was possible based solely on the half-grinning, half-kidney-stone-passing expression he wore.

I followed Pietro's gaze, swiveling, my arm losing its grip from the slick sheen of blood pooling out over the floor. What I saw didn't makes sense. A red hood, brown hair pulled into sober braids that twisted like a crown around her head, and a silver sword dripping red.

An actual, fucking sword. In the post-op recovery room.

At the end of the woman's arm, the head of Inga Rosethorn, frozen mid-bitch. She (the sword-wielding badass, not the decapitated vampire) looked down on me, both literally and, I felt in my huey, huey soul, figuratively, and asked, "And who in the hell are you?"

SEVENTEEN

GERI

I stepped past my father and fixed my mother with the most acidic glare I could manage. "Her name is Amy Popowitz, and she's my friend."

My mother ground her teeth. "Markus, explain."

Markus cleared his throat, even as he pulled his silver away from the twin daggers he'd fashioned in the heat of battle. "Her name is Amy and she's—"

"Amy Popowitz!" I intervened. "As I just said." If Brünhild thought she was going to pretend I didn't exist after what she'd just done, she had another thing coming. "And she doesn't have to explain herself here, *you* do."

But one didn't get to be Grand Matron by being easily emotionally manipulated. Ignore me she had decided to do, and ignore me she would. "Markus, please help Miss Popowitz to her feet and take her to the bathroom to wash off. Quickly. Sunrise is eleven minutes out, and you need to be on the road in six."

Friend though he may be, my cousin was still a righteous hood, and fell right back into being the perfect little soldier when the Red Matron snapped her fingers. He hoisted Amy to her feet, even as her left and right legs attempted to swap sockets. "Whatever you do, don't get any of it in your mouth. Inga was a Dracule. Very potent maker bloodline. Even a few drops could start the process."

"The process?" Amy asked, clutching his arms for support. "What process?"

"Becoming a vampire, of course." He said it like he was telling her water was wet. "Unless that's what you're after."

Amy shook her head. "I can't even eat a pink steak, I don't think I'd have much luck with sucking down human blood."

They rushed off to the bathroom, Markus closing the door behind them.

"You there." Mother pointed at Caleb. "Have you gone through rites?"

The slayer's eyes hadn't left Inga's dripping head since it had left its owner's body. "I have."

"Good." Brünhild tossed the head atop the corpse on the floor. "My sympathies for the loss of one of your own, but now is not the time to grieve. There mustn't be any evidence of her existence when the authorities get here. Is it true that your dead dissolve in water?"

"What?" Caleb seemed shocked by the sentiment. "Um, yeah. Yeah, it is."

Brünhild jerked her head toward the bathroom. "As soon as they're out, take that one's body and wash it away with haste."

Cody shifted back to his human. "Oh, come on, Brünhild. You can't possibly think you're going to be able to cover all this up in less than ten minutes, do you?"

The Grand Matron quirked an eyebrow. "How long have you known me, Cody Ryland?"

The werewolf fidgeted, which paired with the fact that he was naked, upped the awkward level. "Um, all my life, ma'am."

"And you doubt my ability to do this?"

Cody cocked a hip and shied his eyes. He may be an alpha, but he had also lived years under my mother's direct authority and worse, on numerous school field trips on which she'd chaperoned. "Um, no ma'am, sorry."

Brünhild picked up some gauze sitting on a tray at Alex's bedside and proceeded to wipe off the blood from her short sword. "I won't ask what's brought you all the way from Paradise, but we will talk on this, Alpha. Janus?"

The diminutive vampire promptly appeared at my mother's side. "Yes, Matron?"

"Markus will evacuate this lot as soon as he emerges with the huey. You and I will stay behind and handle the fall out. We need everyone to believe this was a gas explosion, a terrible accident that claimed the life of mother and child. Can you handle that?"

Yan tipped his head. "Of course, Matron. And I should advise you also that I can hear the sirens of the emergency vehicles and authorities approaching. You should probably reclaim and hide your silver."

Without arguing, my mother held up her weapon. A solid object one moment, its edges shimmered and turned in on themselves, flooding down her sleeve and under her cloak. A moment later, the flowing garment itself faded from existence, revealing an odd choice for slaying wear: a smart pantsuit. So, she was going to act the role of a huey while Yan mind-wobbled the actual humans to believe every lying word that came from her mouth, huh?

Part of me actually admired the forethought.

Markus emerged from the bathroom with Amy, her blond hair still dripping. She wore nothing but a pale pink hospital gown that clung to her curves at unnatural angles.

Her words barely managed to sneak past her chattering teeth. "I feel violated. Seriously Markus, you have no idea how to touch a woman."

"Gee, let's wonder about that, shall we?" Markus pushed Amy forward into my arms, then heeded Caleb's request to help pick up Alex's body.

Propping Amy up, I pushed the two of us forward. "Strike first, die last, is that it, Mother? Thanks to you, my one lead on where to hunt for the other asenaics in Spain is gone."

Keeping up her "Zero Geri" policy, she continued to ignore me. "Markus, are there enough cars here to transport everyone back to Triberg?"

"Yes, Matron. We have two SUVs parked outside."

"Good. Cody?"

The werewolf turned. "Yeah?"

Brünhild's eyes drifted down. "Clothe yourself." Then nodding to Markus, she said, "Take the others and go now. Only Janus and the slayer are to stay. I'll need their assistance to contain this damage."

Markus hesitated. "Matron?"

"Yes, Markus?"

Just at that second, Mina's little grunt rose through the silence, as though asking in my cousin's stead, "What about me?"

For the briefest second, my mother didn't have an immediate response. The hesitation was over in two blinks as she steeled herself. "Yes, take the baby too."

"Got it." The brawny hood clapped twice. "Let's go, crew. We got to move."

Cody, who had found a pair of green scrubs in one of the supply doors, pulled a simpering Anya to her feet. The poor dear had become the victim of her own fight-or-flight instincts in which she'd gone the unspoken third route: don't make a move, shut down completely, and hope it's all just a bad dream.

"Come, sweetheart. She's gone, and that's terrible, but we need to get out of here."

My father assumed Amy as his burden. Perhaps to help me. Perhaps out of concern for her. Perhaps just because it brought him within a few feet of his wife for even the tiniest of moments. Brünhild tracked him, but never once did her resolve crack. As the others started toward the door, following my mother's orders without question, I lingered. The anger dwelling within me had finally reached critical mass. The barrier would no longer hold.

"Wait a god damn minute!"

Stopped in their tracks, everyone swung their head in my direction. Except my mother, of course, who only let her expression fall into one of general annoyance.

But I was here, and I would be seen *and* heard. "The last time I saw you, you attacked me, banished me. You made it perfectly clear that I was nothing to you, that I was *relinquished*, disowned, an outsider to the world in which I'd been reared and raised. And now you're just going to show up out of nowhere and start commanding around my friends and commandeering my choices?"

"*This* is largely the result of your choices." *For* the first time since she entered the room, Brünhild squared her gaze on me. "Besides, isn't this what you wanted? *Not* to be a hood?"

"Yes, it was." My tone leather, my jaw steel, I chewed my words. "Only, I never *was* a hood, was I? And you knew it. But you still tried to force me into the role, tried to force me to be your little protégé, all the time knowing I was an asenaic."

She smirked in annoyance. "Your point being?"

I held my arms out wide. "How could you do that to me? How could you do it to Papa? How could you torture the people you supposedly loved when their only fault was being who they are? How could you be that much of a... a bitch?"

That one word, one I'd thought thousands of times, but never had the guts to say, finally cut a lash across her resolve. My mother towered over me, easily five inches my better, and lowered her voice in a way that somehow made it feel louder.

"How dare you? Everything I have done was to protect my family." She pointed at the corpse laying prone on the floor. "That woman, the vampire you thought was your friend? She wanted to kill you when you were four years old, but I stopped her. And have you ever asked at what price? No. She knew the Ravens would take you, use you, bleed you. You want to know why I forced you to train harder, to know more, to be tougher than even my own mother, one of the most infamous and cruel matrons ever to wear the red cloak, ever did of me? It's because making you this tough was the only way to make sure you'd survive."

I bit back tears, even though whether they were born of pain or of anger, I didn't know any more. "But what kind of mother pushes away her own child?"

"One who knew the cost if she didn't. Do you think it didn't hurt me, having to constantly hurt *you*? I ached with every cruel word and bitter pronouncement, but it had to be done. You had to be self-sufficient, self-reliant. You had to be able to run, as far and alone as necessary, to keep yourself safe. Any attachments I fostered in you would be to your detriment. If you're expecting an apology from me, you're going to be waiting a long time, because it's not coming. I'm not your friend, Gerwalta. I'm your mother. My job is to provide for your needs, not your desires, and what you need to do right now is haul ass. Now *move*."

Cody's arms around me reminded me that I still had a body. "Come on, kiddo. We're keeping the others."

Shaking out my confusion, I surveyed the room and found it was only him, my mother, and myself. And just like that, we were moving. At some point, we must have gotten into one of the SUVs. It wasn't until I was laying in the back on the impromptu cot that had been set up for Alex, the baby placed in my arms and Cody laying across the way from me, that I even became cognizant of the fact that we'd left the parking lot.

"Like old times, huh?" The werewolf reached out, rubbing my arm. "You and me, laid out in the back of a vehicle after one of your mom's screeds?"

The joke brought no joy. My soul was bleeding, and beside me lay an infant who was suddenly… mine. Mina flinched, her arms flailed, her limbs out of control.

"She's so…" *Helpless? Useful? Doomed?* "Orphaned."

His comforting smile faltered. "She is."

"Inga and Alex are dead."

In my mind's eye, the events of the last twenty minutes replayed in a loop of terror. Inga charging Alex's bed, the slayer's attempt to send a solarium at her attacker. The magic somehow robbing her of her energy, turning back on her, and her body falling limp to the cot. Caleb screaming as he dove, getting to the new mother too late. The havoc of all of us trying both to protect Anya, and not hurt Inga, who was, after all, our friend. Or so we'd thought.

The moment the vampire's body had fallen away from her head as my mother's sword cleaved her in two, because she was the only one who understood who Inga really was.

"She saved us, Cody. She flew us out of Istanbul, she… She supported Caleb, gave Tobias a job, got him fake papers to make it possible for him to stay in the US… She was our friend, and my mother just cut off her head. She's dead because I'm a… Because…"

"Because she was trying to kill you." The voice was my father's. Based on the way it projected through the car, he was at the wheel. "For the second time in your life, she threatened to destroy you. Your mother took her word once, and Brünhild does not give second chances."

Of all the faults I could assign to my mother, this might turn out to be the biggest yet. Brünhild should have let Inga kill me when I was four. I never would have lived my life, my very existence a burden to my family. Cody's father might still be alive. Tobias never would have been captured by the Ravens. And Alex… She might still be a prisoner in Vlad's harem, but she wouldn't be a corpse that my ex-boyfriend had been ordered to dissolve in a hospital shower.

This child would still have hope.

"I have no idea how to care for a baby, especially not one like her."

Cody's eyes narrowed. "Why would you need to care for her, Geri? What is she to you?"

A source of guilt? A debt I owed?

The truth brought a smidgeon of warmth to my shaken spirit. "She's pack."

The alpha's mouth quirked. "What do you mean, she's pack?"

The last few words I'd exchanged with the slayer before the doctors made the incision replayed in the back of my mind. "Alex asked me to be the baby's godmother. I said yes. And then… Cody, am I going moonmad? Is this how it starts, with delusions?"

His voice remained soft, but a lilt suggested suspicion. "Why, did you see something?"

"I'm not sure. I passed out, and maybe it was a figment of my imagination, or… It's impossible. I thought I heard Tobias's voice inside my head, like he was whispering right in my ear."

He grinned his relief. "No, Geri, you're not going moonmad. *That* was a quickening."

"A quickening?" I repeated the term like it came from a foreign lexicon, even though I'd heard the term all my life. "The weird thing that happens when an alpha accepts a new member into their pack? But Tobias is my alpha, and he's hundreds of miles away."

I tried to quell the odd thrill that ran through me when thinking of the roguish and rough Englishman in that way. Genetics and hormones made odd bedfellows.

Cody placed a finger in Mina's hand, the tiny creature gripping for dear life. "Might have been a proxy acceptance. I've heard of it, but it's uncommon. The distance doesn't matter, though. You've probably just never heard that because, well, you know, werewolves aren't exactly globetrotters in general. The quickening happens to the whole pack, not just the alpha."

"You're saying I'm acting as some kind of proxy alpha?" I asked. Cody bobbed his head. "But that can't be. One, I'm a woman. And two, I'm barely even a wolf."

"Being an alpha isn't all about the bloodline. It's about attitude. It's about who's willing to step up and do what needs to be done to keep the pack safe in a time of crisis. If that doesn't describe you, Geri, I don't know what does. Men make kings. Wars make rulers."

Even with all the crush of truth and tyranny and trouble, the thought warmed me. "Then I *did* hear Tobias, because I had a quickening. Because I'm wolf enough."

"Tell you a secret, Little Red? The day you stood up to me at the wedding, when I told you to back off of your moping, I felt a…. I don't know, some kind of snap."

"I told you, I'm not going to apologize for that."

"No, Red, that ain't what I'm driving at." He pulled his hand back from the infant's grasp and wiped it down his face. "I mean, I felt you *leave* me. Not physically, but like, metaphysically. I'd always joked you were pack, and then you up and proved it by becoming a rogue. And then damned Tobias went right after you, didn't he?"

My memories traced back through that night, to the first kiss Tobias and I had shared, a sweet recollection that I didn't understand until much later had been real and not a dream.

"I suppose he did." But any sweet delight I took in the thought of being bound to Tobias that way ceded in the larger bitter implications. "But that means I'm running out of time. I was barely able to save Tobias from lunacity once, and that was when he was with me. I have to find him, and soon. But where?"

"You said something about Spain."

"I was going to try and find the other asenaics," I said. "Igor said he'd been getting his blood from a special source there. Igor will lead the Ravens to them eventually, sooner rather than later. They've already moved as far west as Venice."

The werewolf's forehead wrinkled, but I summed up my explanation by saying only "long story."

"The hood archives wouldn't have that kind of information?" Cody asked.

I shook my head. "Our history says that Gerwalta and Andreas's baby died with them."

"But you got this inheritance from your father," Cody said. "Just trace back his bloodline, then wheel it forward."

"My dad's family immigrated to Argentina from Spain three centuries ago. I can go back and find the origins, but moving forward through the generations... The Casa de Amarillo is a few hundred hoods spread out across the western Mediterranean basin."

My finger traced down Mina's cheek. The child, strengthened perhaps by her semi-lupine body, turned her face into my touch.

"I don't have time to covertly work my way through that big of a list, and that's assuming the Yellow Matrons gave any candidates permission to talk to me. I'll need to figure something else out and quick. I can't let Tobias go moonmad, and I can't let Vlad hurt him any longer."

"Don't worry, Little Red, we're going to find him. And after that... well, I'm not sure what kind of relationship is possible for you two, but at the very least, you'll have your friend back."

I grinned at him as my eyes fell closed. "You mean *another* friend back."

EIGHTEEN

Bitter wind bit my skin, jolting me awake. A weapon! I needed a weapon! Instinct beckoned my silver skin to yield to my command, but found it lacking. Didn't matter. I could kill with my fists. Break bone with my kick. Claw out eyes.

"Geri!" Cody yelled. "Stop! You're going to hurt Mina."

Mina? Who's Mina?

A tiny cough rose from a bundle of warmth beside me, opening the gates of memory that sleep had closed with mercy. Sunlight stung my eyes, pouring in from the open back hatch of the SUV, a sea of bright in which Cody's face swam. Clarity came in both mind and body as the backdrop of circumstance returned. The last time I had seen the edifice behind the werewolf had been from this same car. Then, however, a dozen hoods bearing guns pointed my direction had stood between it and the outer bailey walls. Now, there was just Cody, Amy, Anya, and my dad, all staring at me with a mix of concern and fear.

"I'm fine."

No one had asked it aloud, but they were all screaming it with their eyes. I sat up, turning to check on the child beside me. In body, Mina was fine. Except that she was hungry. And wet. How did I know? The former by some odd instinct. The latter, because the smell was undeniable.

"We're going to need diapers," I said, even as I worked to undo the bundle of soiled blankets. Would that I could wash her, but that formalities of Schloss Wolfsretter demanded ceremony, procedure. *Time.* Babies were not unprecedented or even uncommon in the keep. How could they be, when our matriarchal society put women in most the leadership roles, and demanded them to reproduce? It was also true, however, that self-reliance remained a core value. When you came to the compound, other than food and basic toiletries, you were expected to bring what you and yours needed.

"Come on." Cody tugged gently on my ankle. "Let's take her inside and then we can worry about that."

I shook my head. "She'll catch her death in cold. I have to wrap her in something dry. Doesn't someone have a coat or something?"

They wore blank expressions. We'd fled the hospital with such haste, none of us had had time to grab anything. I hoped Caleb, Yan, and my mom remembered to clean up the various things we'd left behind.

My father stepped forward, closing his eyes and drawing on his power. As he did, the threads of his ancestral garb formed about him, draping him in the yellow cloak of his bloodline. He undid the tie at his throat, spinning it around. "Here. Wrap your *niña* in this."

The offer, both of the garment and of the indication that Mina was somehow mine pinched at my heart. The act, however, made clear what needed to be done for this to be true.

"Thank you, Papa, but..." I shook my head as I turned back to the cub beside me. Since claiming my fire—though still uncertain how that had come to be—I'd not tested myself in this capacity. Now, the moment had come, and it was critical that the bloodline cede to my request. I closed my eyes, calling on the ancestors of my clan, saying internally the summoning charm I'd been taught since childhood.

Ancestors, cloak me in your wisdom and let my bloodline be my shield.

Its weight on my shoulders warmed, while simultaneously reminding me of the burden of my legacy. Having not even been sure I could summon my red cloak, I'd put off the attempt, afraid of what it would mean if I proved incapable. Now that I found I could, I worried what that meant for an asenaic.

My father beamed at Mina and me as we crawled from the back of the vehicle, pride of such depth one might think he was looking at his own grandchild in my arms. He shepherded us under his wing as we turned toward the open east gate of the castle.

"Are you ready? The Council will have questions, make demands."

My jaw tightened. "I have a few questions and demands of my own."

Rebecca Krantz stood at the door, a solid archive of huey pride and fortitude. Gray hair and deep wrinkles around her eyes didn't detract from the fierceness of her heart.

"Welcome home, Miss Kline." Uniformed in her custom black slacks and beaten up brown bomber jacket, I could tell she wanted to say so much more, *do* so much more. Hug me, kiss my cheek, tease me about some secret romance... She'd never had children, and so the young hoods of the Schloss had become the family she'd never bear herself.

Beside her, Chin stood, resolute and severe in every way a woman of her stature could be. The wind picked up, blowing out the trail of her bloodline's white cloak, even as her eyes settled on the bundled baby in my arms with disdain. She'd read the child as a wolf; hoods couldn't sense slayers.

"At ease, castellan."

She wouldn't even address Becky by name? What an ass. Or was she just ticked off at having to oversee a formal affair in the middle of the day when she'd much rather be upstairs in bed?

Chin continued. "Miss Kline, the Grand Matron phoned about an hour ago. She wanted us to relay to you that she, a slayer, and Janus Sousa have contained the scene, and let you know that she ordered us to relocate the other slayers from your family's private residence in town to the compound."

"Where are they?" Anya stepped forward. "Where are my people?"

Chin tilted her head in Rebecca's direction. "Miss Krantz volunteered her personal residence within the castle walls for their use. The space is not as ample as RotHaus where you've been staying, but they are making do and getting settled until we are able to figure out what comes next."

My eyes flashed to the old woman beside the matron, who stood a little straighter than before. "Thank you, Becky."

Rebecca gave a quick nod. "I'm as good in the keep dormitory, ma'am, and they needed the space. I remember what it's like to come away from prison and feel the need to have a safe place."

I motioned to those standing behind me. "Perhaps Amy and Anya could be shown to the castellan's cottage as well?"

"No, your mother's orders are that everyone in your party be kept contained until her arrival." Chin gave me one disgusted glare before pulling at the corded silver belt wrapped around her waist. With the slightest effort, it melded into a stream of silver, then quivered into its next iteration: a pair of double manacles, a set that bind both feet and hands. "I suppose we can forgo this for the pup, but for this lupine..." Chin held up her creation.

Cody coughed a laugh. "You've got to be kidding me. What is this, the middle ages?"

Chin bristled. "*This* is the House of the Wolf-Watcher, and these are the terms. No wolf may enter here unless he be bound by silver. For you to be invited alone is exceptional. If you want to escort this relinquished ingrate…"

As Chin took a step forward, so did I, placing myself between the Matron and the alpha. "The *ingrate* objects."

Chin sneered. "May I remind you, Gerwalta, that you have no official standing here? I could order you off the property right now."

"But you let me past the gate this time," I said. "Pretty sure that wasn't your decision, which means you're not the one deciding anything right now, are you?"

She lifted the chains again. "Regardless, this is our way. Now, step aside or…"

Moments before I called on the silver rattling in her hands, Cody gently pushed me aside.

"Easy, Geri," he said. "I'm a big, bad wolf. I can take a little burn. Go ahead, Matron, then let's get little Mina here seen to, huh?"

The bravado, a display. The moment the metal arced across Cody's wrists and ankles, the smell of seared flesh tickled my nose, turning my stomach. Cody tried to conceal the pain, almost managed it. The corners of his mouth flinched, giving away his pain. I felt out the silver in my mind, willing it away from his flesh, but as we began to follow Chin from the outer bailey to the inner one, he jostled, making the task exceedingly difficult.

Amy pulled up alongside me. She'd grabbed one of the sheets from the collection in the car and fashioned herself a toga over the hospital gown. *Of course,* Amy knew how to make a toga from bed sheets. Rumor was, Amy was amazing in the sheets. My father, realizing the inappropriateness of Frat Party attire in the sacred homestead of my bloodline, threw his yellow cloak over the blond huey's shoulders.

"This is it, isn't it? The castle where they burned Red Riding Hood alive?"

My teeth ground. "Not the greatest thing to bring up right now, but yes."

"Sorry, I just like, you know…" She blew out a long breath. "You don't think they're going to do that to you, do you? Because New York doesn't go out like that. I'll kick whoever's ass you need me to."

"Thank you, Amy, but no." I looked back over my shoulder, sizing up Markus, my father, and Anya. The men, eyes straight forward, were pillars of calm and determination, but the slayer…

I decided to harbor the bundled baby in Amy's arms. "Can you hold Mina for a minute?"

"What?" She pulled back a step before rushing to recover our gate through the inner bailey. "I don't know how to... What are you... Oh, okay. I guess."

I caught the look as I turned, the one that told me this was Amy's first time holding a baby, but it wouldn't be the last. She was positively smitten, even if a little out of her element.

"Anya?"

My voice snapped her out of her reverie, and she turned to me as though surprised to discover she wasn't alone. "Sorry?"

I pulled up alongside her. "I know you're in pain. Alex's loss was sudden and unnecessary, and there will be time to mourn her. But I need your help right now."

"My help?"

I took my voice as low as I could make it, slowing our steps even more. Ahead, Cody hissed, my ability to pull the burning metal from his flesh broken by distance.

Just to be safe, I pulled the slayer into my arms, hugging her, using the proximity to whisper in her ear. "You must say that Mina is mine."

"But she's Alex's..."

I squeezed her tighter. "I know, but when Alex asked to talk to me before the c-section, it was to ask if I'd be Mina's godmother. Hoods will recognize that as old law if others corroborate it. I'll need everything in my power to keep her under *my* protection. If they learn Mina's blood can kill the Ravens, they won't see a baby, they'll see a strategy."

"Surely they wouldn't..." She shook in my arms. "But she's just a baby."

"Exactly, help me protect her." Finally, I pulled away just as my father and Markus passed us. As long as my testimony came first, neither would conflict me. I hoped. Markus, while my cousin and good friend, still walked two paths that might eventually diverge. Anya, however, had no reason to cover for my lies.

I stroked her cheek, brushing away a tear. "Please, Anya, for Mina. For Alex."

She bit her lip, resolve firming her features. "For Alex."

NINETEEN

No one knew the exact year Schloss Wolfsretter had been erected, but the best guesses placed it in the thirteenth or fourteenth century. When it had only been the home of the House of Red and not a de facto administrative center for the whole race, the current council chamber had been the red matron's throne room. The rectangular space could easily host fifty people or more, but its current furnishings were only arranged for thirteen. The massive oaken table sat at the far end of the space, one chair for each member of the matron council, each in turn representing a bloodline. The House of Red had two seats, of course, for the role of the Grand Matron demanded her to act without regard to heritage. Or so the official line went. By consequence, the reds usually dominated.

I'd spent many an hour in this morbid place, hidden away in a corner, observing at my mother's demand. No one had ever said it aloud, because the thing was obvious and understood, it would have felt unnecessary to say. I was the heir apparent, and as such, I needed to understand the power and limitation of the office I would someday assume. Seeing how my mother could dictate her form of justice, handing down edicts and judgments that lacked humanity, had soured me on the prospect at a young age. I found no reverence, therefore, in the stone walls moored in the dark ages of Europe's past, or in the tapestries hung on them that recalled the valor of my more famous ancestors. To the right, Hlin the Conqueror's sword pierced the heart of Kroon the Konigswolf under the mighty tree that once dominated this cliff. Its stump, worn smooth and uneven after centuries of use, still sat on the far end of the room. Once, it was said, it had been carved with magnificent reliefs, antlers twisted into it to enhance its terror. The tapestry to the right held its subject in the middle, her blond hair and silver bo staff front and center. Behind her, the castle, looking then much as it did now, ruled the mountain peak, and beside it, a mighty bonfire. As a child, I'd thought it as no more than a representation of *feuernacht*, a sacred fire burned under a full moon into which a hood would plunge to assume her powers and her place in the community. Only when I'd gotten older did I notice that the fire wasn't burning from logs, but from the bones of three figures caught in its grasp, each with a spit through their bodies.

Amy's eyes took in the reds and blues of another of the tapestries, and Chin didn't let the opportunity go to waste.

"Helga the Restorer," the white matron said. "Sister of the Betrayer and avenger of her mother's death."

Amy leaned in "That's supposed to be Gerwalta Faust's sister? Boy, she needed work on her eyebrows."

Chin's own unnurtured eyebrows arched.

Amy drove on, proving that filters and she did not break bread. "How come the sister is the one who gets the credit? I thought it was the Betrayer's mother who sentenced them to die?"

"Because the wolf ate Gerwalta's mother, leaving Helga the honor of executing the sentence and bringing the offenders final justice."

Amy's nose crinkled. "So when the Brothers Grimm wrote about the grandmother being in the wolf's stomach..." Amy's voice tapered off. "Not a story."

The Matron's eyes bulged. "A broken clock is still right twice a day, even those two cuckoos."

"Kinda makes you wonder..." The huey gave the tapestry a second appraisal. "...are there other fairy tales that are true, too?"

Any chance for reflection or refuting was lost when Rebecca Krantz cleared her throat and proceeded to make an official announcement in German.

Amy leaned into me. "What did she say?"

Any need to answer was cut off by the doors to the chamber being thrown open.

My mother's command rattled the rafters. "English!"

My mother's boots quaked the floor, or perhaps it was the beating of my own heart that shook me. She marched into the council chamber, a heavy sack pulled down at her side, her red cape billowing out behind her. Behind her, Yan and Caleb, both of them looking as spent as two supernaturals could be. Caleb's anxiety eased when he caught sight of us, making his way in our direction. Anya went to him, pulling him close. They'd lost one of their own today, and perhaps that death meant more than one less slayer. A little hope must have died with Alex as well.

Yan tracked my mother, taking the sack from her and continuing his way out the other side of the room.

"From this point forward," my mother said, spinning into her chair, "everyone is to speak English! I want this matter addressed posthaste, and some of those involved do not understand German. Chin!"

The disagreeable white hood, heretofore prideful as a peacock, suddenly bowed beneath the weight of my mother's presence. "Yes, Grand Matron?"

"The slayers? Did you bring them into the castle grounds as I ordered?"

"Yes, Grand Matron. Except for this one—" Chin acknowledged Anya. "—they are in the castellan's house. We have activated all security features on your home in town as requested. If anyone further enters, it will be known within moments."

"Excellent." Sweeping her way across the room, Brünhild took the dominant seat at the head of the table.

"Security features?" I asked. "What security features?"

"The place has more bugs than a Sunday school picnic," Markus said. "Sorry, Geri, the information was embargoed."

I turned to my mother. "You were spying on us the whole time we've been there?"

No wonder she'd known to look for us at the Lahr hospital.

Brünhild ignored me, continuing her orders. "Open the council at once."

Chin's olive skin blanched. "But, Matron, it is midday, and everyone is asleep. Certainly, we should wait for…"

"Did I stutter, Mae?" I may have imagined the tiny frown I thought I saw flit across her face. "Now! There is no time to waste."

Without further ado, the White Matron swept from the room.

Brünhild's arm struck out, her finger pointed in Amy's direction. "You!"

Amy held the baby with one arm while the thumb of her left hand buried in her own chest.

"Yes, you, girl. The one with little common sense and even less intelligence."

"Okay, it's going to be like that then." Amy took three steps forward. "Excuse me, but I don't recall asking your opinion."

"I don't have opinions," my mother said. "I have convictions. This evening, you will be driven to Munich. We will provide you the necessary papers and airfare to anywhere in the world you'd prefer to go, but it will be a one-way ticket. Henceforth, you will remove yourself from the supernatural realm. You will be kept under observation to assure this, and if there's any hint of you attempting to reconnect with anyone present or exposing our secrets, you will be dealt with swiftly. There will be no warnings."

My friend's face could light London. "Who in the hell do you think you are? You don't get to tell me who I will or will not associate with."

Part of me cheered the outburst. And part of me wanted to push Amy to the ground before the metaphorical daggers my mother was shooting became literal.

Caleb cleared his throat and took a knee. "If I may speak, Grand Matron?"

The formality won over my mother just enough to get her to agree.

"Miss Popowitz should not be forced out," the sly slayer continued. "She's a known associate of your daughter's and has already come under vampire attack once. Moreover, she's been of great assistance to my people as they've tried to adjust to the outside world. If you would defer her fate to us, and if she herself would not object, I'd like to ask that she take up residence with us. We need someone with her skills."

Even I had to quirk an eyebrow on that one. *Skills? What skills?* Luckily, I was able to keep the thought to myself.

"Very well." Brünhild's face melted around the edges. "Does the huey agree to consign herself to the community of slayers?"

All eyes fell to Amy, who had commenced flapping her jaw noiselessly and pulling the bundled child a little tighter to her chest. Finally, she managed to squeak out, "What does that mean exactly, 'consign'?"

My mother rolled her eyes. "It means that you will be honor-bound to their service until such time as both parties agree to dissolve the arrangement, if any. In short, you will be their Rebecca Krantz."

The huey followed my mother's gesture in the elderly castellan's direction, took one look at Becky's aged frame and plain clothes, and swung back, panic-stricken.

"I can still wear designer brands, though, right?"

Brünhild hissed through clenched teeth as she uttered a string of German curses.

"Okay, yes!" Amy blurted out. "I agree to consign. Or be consigned, or whatever, to the slayers. Just, please, don't send me away."

My mother raised an eyebrow. "The pact is thus made and recognized. But tell me, huey, why are you so desperate to remain among us? Surely you understand the danger this will put you in."

Amy's backbone grew three sizes. "Because they're my friends. Real friends who don't like me just because of the size of my bank account or my cup size. Well," she jerked her head in Caleb's direction, "except for that one, maybe."

Brünhild fixed Caleb in his gaze. "From what I hear, that one accepts all comers."

Before the slayer could react, Amy pushed him back with her shoulder.

Which gave me an opening to step forward. "Mother, the…"

Her hand flew up. "As has always been, in these walls, I am Matron first. Now more than ever."

I swallowed my anger, promising myself to feed from its reserves later. "Fine, *Matron*. Before the council arrives, I want you to know that this baby is now under my protection." I took Mina back from Amy's hold. "Before you and the council go off making plans for her, just remember that nothing is happening to Mina unless I agree to it."

Bitterness laced into my mother's tone. "Who died and made you its mother?"

"*Her* mother did. Before Mina's birth, before you barged in, silver blazing, and sliced off Inga Rosethorn's head, Alex asked me to be the baby's godmother. I accepted."

"Were there witnesses?"

Anya's voice was tiny. "I did, I witnessed it."

Brünhild was unimpressed. Perhaps she sensed the lie. "Let me rephrase that. Did any of the *righteous* witness this?"

I clutched at my throat. "That's never been a requirement before. A pact was made between two supes grounded in honor and witnessed by a third. Our laws should allow for that claim to stand on its own."

Brünhild's hands became fisted hammers. "When both parties acknowledge such pacts, and are recognized members of their community. This slayer's word may serve on behalf of her fallen kin, but yours must be likewise validated."

I took a step forward, my teeth gnashing. "Then rescue Tobias Somfield from the Ravens, and let him give testimony."

Check. Mate.

Brünhild's brow furrowed, her chest heaved as she fumed the anger in her heart. "Why would *he* know anything of this child?"

Cody's voice, evidence of his weakened resolve, cracked. "Geri had a quickening, Ms. Kline. They're bonded now, and anything you do to that baby is only going to hurt your daughter even more."

"Bonded? How would a child of a slayer bond with a werewolf?" My mother's face went ashen as she leapt to her feet. "Are you saying that child is an illustrian?"

"And by legal rights, your granddaughter!" My father, silent until now, used his words with great economy, dropping the mother of bombshells on the bombshell of all mothers.

I, however, was still caught up in what she'd said before. "What's an illustrian?"

"An illustrian is a..." Brünhild fell back into her chair, her eyes glossy. "It's impossible. How would such a thing come to be? The slayers were living in Vlad's harem, and surely this did not come about by accident. A vampire of his age and status would surely know that bringing an illustrian into the confines of his clutch would be like pouring poison into the well."

It took my mother stating what should have been the obvious question for me to see the obvious answer.

"He created it to kill Igor." The words echoed in my ear before I realized I'd been the one to say them. I looked to the others, daring any one of them to correct me.

No one said a word, until my mother spoke, clutching her stomach. "Very well. Until such time as the alpha wolf Tobias Somfield can present testimony, I recognize temporary guardianship of the babe born to Alexandra, a slayer, and an unknown wolf, to Gerwalta Kline. But, daughter," her eyes pleaded as she looked up at me. "I must point out the obvious: The child is a slayer, a race endangered and in desperate need of every one of its members. Are you sure it's in the child's best interest to be raised by a..."

"A hood?" I supplied when Brünhild proved unwilling or unable to give me even that recognition. "Was it in *my* best interest to be raised by one?"

The blow landed right where it was aimed, my mother's pride. Brünhild winced. "Are you of the opinion that I did you some disservice by refusing to let Inga Rosethorn kill you all those years ago?"

"No, of course not." I tried to swallow my fear and almost choked on it. "You did me a disservice by knowing I was different, and refusing to accept me as I was."

"I was protecting you from a knowledge that would make you a target."

"The only thing you protected me from was the lies of our ancestors." I ran a hand over Mina's soft head as the babe lay peacefully in my arms. Her eyes cracked open, searching. "I will never treat my daughter that way. She will know all that she is, because there's no shame in any of it."

"There is no shame, but there is great danger." My mother looked up. "The child could be weaponized."

Instinctively, I moved closer to Anya and held Mina tighter. "I'll kill any who try."

"I have no doubt." As Brünhild rose, circling the table, part of me wondered if this was the moment I'd have to fight my mother. Instead, only her gaze touched the babe I held, examining from a few feet away, before turning on my father. "This child is *not* my grandchild." Then, softening ever so slightly and bringing her eyes to me, she added, "But it is still an innocent. The council will not be made aware of what she is, but they will sense her wolf nature. How will we explain?"

Was she actually asking me for advice? "Tell them she's mine and Tobias's, that the request to have Petunia's help for one of the slayers was just a cover because *I* was the one who was pregnant."

I'd never gotten out of the car the day I tried to convince Chin to let me in, so she wouldn't have known from seeing me that I wasn't pregnant.

My mother fanned her fingers through the air. "Petunia attended Alexandra, though."

"She would say that was a cover, if the Grand Matron ordered her to."

"You are suggesting we lie, the very sin you just laid at my feet not three minutes ago."

My mother never spoke just for the sake of talking, and even though she could be cruel, she was seldom spiteful. I sensed that, perhaps, highlighting the conflict was an effort to ask me not to be so hasty of her judgements.

"I realize that," I admitted. "Maybe if I had more time to think, I'd have a more honorable solution. But as you like to say, honor is a currency bought over years and spent in minutes."

It was as good as I was going to get: owning up my hypocrisy while not absolving hers.

She bowed her head. "I will speak with Petunia once the council adjourns, then."

"Whoa, whoa, whoa!" Cody stepped forward, keeping his arms as still as possible to avoid the silver slipping onto unmarked flesh. "Geri, think about this for a second. The last time I checked, it would still be a capital offense for Tobias to sleep with a hood. You say Mina is the result of him and you getting together, there's no point in rescuing him from the Ravens. As soon as he's free, the council will command his execution."

We all spun as my mother let out a Disney villain-worthy laugh.

Which, for some reason, pissed me off. "Something funny, mother?"

She buried her smile into her fist. "How could the council convict Tobias of anything? Geri's been relinquished for over a year."

Cody persisted. "Yeah, but she's a still a hood, so—"

"Not in the way that matters to them." My words cut off Cody and everything else I had been thinking. "When Tobias and I finally manage to be together, it won't be a crime." I spun on my mother. "Did you do this on purpose?"

"What? Disown my only daughter and my sole heir just to keep her from harm?" Though she tried to keep her face flat, I saw the miniscule flicker at the corner of her mouth. "That decision was made for many reasons, but none of them was to appease your heart."

"I know it wasn't." I closed the distance between us in three steps. "It was to appease your own."

And for the first time in many years, I threw myself into my mother's arms.

TWENTY

AMY

My mother read *Alice in Wonderland* to me when I was nine. She was drunk at the time, probably doesn't remember it, and I'm sure embellished it with her interpretation of what the mouse-in-the-teakettle and falling down the rabbit hole were meant to symbolize, but the metaphors didn't elude me the way sobriety often did Mrs. Popowitz.

Seeing Geri forgive her mother after two-plus years of non-ending under-her-breath instigations about what a sucky mother Brünhild had been ranked up on my "miracles can happen" list with painless dentistry and the legalization of pot. Yeah, none of those things had fully happened either, but they were goals people worked towards that might actually come to be totally true. I just hoped that as Geri fell down the rabbit hole, she didn't forget what had led her there to begin with.

No sooner had Geri and Brünhild had their Hallmark moment (and yes, I did hear Pietro's sniffle) and separated than the worst fashion catwalk featuring the least beguiling hooded-cloak models of all time marched in. As we collectively fell back, I heard Versace turn over in his grave all the way from Triberg. Each matron wore a different color. I'd known from discussions I'd had with Geri that the other bloodlines existed, I guess I just didn't realize how many there were: twelve in all, one of them dressed in red like Geri's mom and another dressed in yellow like her dad would have been if I wasn't using his cloak as a poncho. I tried not to think about how that meant Geri had grown up in a ketchup and mustard house, but once the thought popped into my head, I laughed out loud.

Chin slithered into her chair at the council table. "Silence, huey interloper!"

"Matron Chin!" Brünhild's voice lacked any of the softness it had had just moments before. How could she so easily flip from secretly-protective mother to badass *mutha* in a blink? I wanted to be this woman's acolyte.

The Grand Matron's acidic stare corroded the white hood seated to her right. "Surely you did not mean to insult the slayer's castellan and our guest."

"The slayer's...." Chin's throat bobbed as she swallowed down her shock. "I did not realize the slayers *had* a castellan. My apologies, Miss...?"

"Popowitz," I said. And though I had no freaking clue what a castellan was (seriously, did she tell me off?) or what my role was supposed to be as one, I wasn't about to let a shame door go unused. "Matron Chin, as the *kaz-ellen*, speaking for the slayers, and given what went down yesterday, I wonder if we can review the terms of the contract you have in place with my peeps right now."

Brünhild blinked. "Your *peeps*?"

"Yeah, you know..." I pointed vaguely behind me. "My peeps. My tribe. My *slay-yahs*."

The Grand Matron cleared her throat. "Mr. Helsing, does Miss Popowitz have the permission of the community to speak on its behalf?"

Which, of course, everyone knew was a resounding, 'no the hell I did not.' I'd just been annexed into their community not ten minutes ago – when would they have had time to do a welcome-and-please-take-a-seat-as-our-representative-on-the-student-council mixer?

Even Geri was giving me the wide-eyed treatment, but what were this bunch of silver-sycophants going to do, kill me? Come on, I had an American passport *and* an American Express Black card. Both had been left behind in Istanbul, but still... Since Geri had made me call my parents and tell them where I was at during the long wait at the hospital, I at least had contacts on the outside who knew where I was and how to raise a diplomatic crisis.

I didn't wait for Caleb to answer. "I'm new at supernatural negotiations, so I have to ask what might be obvious to other people. Is it customary to offer refugees aid only on a quid-pro-quo basis in this neck of the woods? Because where I'm from, that's called exploitation."

Chin sneered. "You'll find our customs do not often align with what the huey world..."

But Brünhild put her big ol' bitch shoes down on that squawk. "Matron Chin, is this true?"

The Asian matron guffawed. "Grand Matron, you yourself have discussed with the council many times the danger posed to the wolves by the clutch of vampires that calls itself the Ravens. Is it not our duty, therefore, to seize an opportunity to eliminate them when it presents itself? They are *slayers*, after all. That is their reason for existing, to destroy those vampires who would throw the supernatural world out of balance."

Geri stepped forward at that. "The supernatural world *is* out of balance! And don't try to act like you're suddenly so concerned with the wolves' wellbeing, either. Matron Smyth: I've heard some very *interesting* stories from one of your former lupines about the way the House of Green treats its subjects in England, which makes me think that the biggest threat to them isn't vampires, but hoods."

Chin found Markus and focused on him. "Mr. Kline, did you not report Vlad Tepeş's own claim that his intent was to dismantle the foundation of lupine society by undermining their ability to bond? How is that not a threat, then? One we must bar against by any means possible. The slayers came to us looking for help, and we've offered it, though it is not our place to do so. Did they not receive food? Shelter? Weapons? Even a physician for the delivery of that…" Chin motioned at Mina "…thing."

When Brünhild got herself a fist full of white cloak and pulled Chin's face to her own, even I could tell the shit was about the hit the fan.

"It is a *baby*, not a *thing*," she hissed. "A very special baby, as the case may be. Do you even know who the mother of this child is, Matron Chin?"

Obvs quaking in her leather boots, Chin shook her head. "No, Grand Matron."

Brünhild's eyes dashed to Geri. "My own daughter."

"Impossible." The Green Matron clicked her tongue. "The child is wolf. We all can sense it. Unless… Unless your daughter has lived up to the name." With that, Matron Smyth rose to her feet. "I call for a vote of confidence in the leadership of Grand Matron Brünhild Kline. How can she lead us with such obvious conflicts of interest?"

Geri's mom… was *piiisssseed*. But, like, in a quiet way that made her more terrifying than before. It was like Hannibal Lecter had become a fairy tale character. *I'll eat your liver with some magic beans and a nice chianti.*

Yan coughed a laugh. "What conflict? Their interest is highly compatible. It is merely your ingrained biases and animal natures which sets you at such odds. Your common humanity should bring you together, not enable you to destroy each other."

Meanwhile, a woman with drop dead brown eyes and sandalwood skin, wearing a black cloak, spoke up. "*We* are not the animals, Mr. Sousa, they are. Quite literally."

"Are you not?" The vampire motioned to Cody. "Look how the blood weeps from his wrists where the silver burns. And for what? Has he committed some crime? Demonstrated some behavior which marks him as dangerous in your eyes? No, you bind him in poison merely because he dares to be in your presence."

A guttural sound ripped from Chin's throat. "It is not your place to speak on hood-wolf relations. Hold your tongue, leech."

"Leech?" The normally sedate vampire who'd even managed to make me think he was a pushover spoke in a hissy voice. Oh, fur was about to fly. Or fang. Or… whatever. Metaphors are too cerebrally challenging around supes.

"You spiteful, power-hungry wench. I am four hundred and fifty years your senior. How dare you address *me* that way?"

Brünhild drew to her feet, pulling silver out of her ass for all I could tell. All I knew was that her hand went up empty, and by the time she slammed it down on the table, she had a freaking mallet formed on the end of her fist. The ricochet of its ramming brought all tongues to a sudden standstill.

Except for Mina, who chose this moment to work a gentle whimper into a full-blown howl.

"Enough!" the Grand Matron bellowed. "This bickering achieves nothing. Let me confirm that any contract made with the slayers was done without my knowledge or consent. Miss Popowitz, tell your people that I absolve them of any expectations and that our assistance comes without strings."

I felt everyone's eyes on me. And, honestly, if I could turn my eyes clear around in my head, I'd be looking at me, too. "Um, will do?"

Brünhild bobbed her head. "Now, Matron Chin, a motion has been made for a vote of confidence. As the vice-matron, it is up to you to recognize the motion or not. What say you?"

Chin made an attempt at a backbone, straightening in her chair and turning hungry eyes on the gaggle of matrons. One by one, they turned their eyes. With each tick of her head, the ego so big she must have built up some hefty calves touting it around deflated a bit. I saw the moment she realized it was a no-go; all the features in her face melted like that horrific scene from *Raiders of the Lost Ark,* only less *liquid-y.* "I do not recognize the motion."

"Good, now that that is out of the way…" Brünhild resumed her seat. "Inga Rosethorn is dead."

Exclamations went up around the table, before a hood wearing a brown robe asked, "How?"

The Grand Matron exchanged one look with us watching in the peanut gallery and said, "Beheading."

"Good," Smyth said. "The slayers have only been back a month now, and they are already bringing balance."

"No, I am the one who killed her," Brünhild corrected.

Even the easy-going Black Matron recoiled at that. "But she has been our ally for decades!"

"No more," Brünhild said. "I have spent the last few weeks ferreting out her activities. I believe she was attempting to find a way to reconcile herself to her brothers, and rejoin their cause. She would have betrayed the slayers under our protection given the slightest chance, as she was attempting to steal the baby when I killed her."

I was so not up on the Dracule family drama, but even I knew that was bad. Looking to Geri and Caleb, I found two people who defined the expression "shell-shocked."

A matron wrapped in pink, but dressed in something that looked more like a floor-length head dress then the other's riding cloaks, leaned forward. "Markus has briefed us on his findings in Istanbul, that the Ravens seek to undo lupine social structures in some sort of ill-conceived form of revenge," she said, sounding like that Bollywood movie that one boyfriend made me watch. "But I am confused. How is it that this involves us? Other than our protection of the slayers, and that conflict could be remedied by negotiation, why are they our concern?"

"Why are they our concern?" Geri stepped out of the shadows, her jaw hanging. "You just said it, Matron Ramathan: because they're threatening to undo lupine social structure."

The Pink Matron blinked away her surprise. "Our purpose does not include assuring that werewolves remain bonded couples and happy families. Our role is to serve as a barrier between them and humanity, and to destroy any who threaten life."

Geri threw her head to the side. "Oh, please. I am so sick of hearing that hoods are some golden, virtuous race that protects hueys from animalistic heathens. Wolves *are* human, and our oldest stories say our *purpose* was to protect *them* from humanity, not the other way around. If anything, *we're* the subhuman creatures, not them."

A hush descended over the matrons as they took the brunt of Geri's vocal bitch slap. Finally, Chin, so flustered she could barely speak, leapt to her feet, turning on Brünhild.

"Will you not punish such insolence, Grand Matron? How do you stand by and allow your own flesh and blood to desecrate our sacred calling that way?"

"By remembering that we do not have a *sacred* calling," Brünhild said, as cool as spring rain. "Nor is our history without fault. We have committed great atrocities, some even in this very building. I will not fault Gerwalta for speaking truth, no matter how bluntly."

"Atrocities?" Chin fell back in her chair. "What atrocities?"

Brünhild crossed her arms over her chest. "As if I need mention the obvious."

"You *cannot* mean the affair of Gerwalta Faust."

"But I do, Chin. I mean that very thing. It is a blemish on our race, more because of our celebration of it than the deed itself. But at least, there is a path for us to remedy some of those injustices." Brünhild paused, catching her daughter's eye. "After all, as Gerwalta so appropriately stated, our true calling is to protect lupines. We can do that by protecting those most at risk: the asenaics, the descendants of Gerwalta Faust."

That knocked them righteous bitches off their rockers. Some gasped, some gawked, and at least one of them looked like she was going to town on someone. It wasn't sexy.

Pinkie was the first to recover. "Are you saying that the offspring of the Betrayer survived?"

"Survived, thrived, and multiplied," Brünhild confirmed. "Though for numerous reasons few of that limb of the family tree endure. In truth, there are only five. And as the Grand Matron, I tell you this now: our current priority is protecting them *and ourselves* by destroying the Ravens. There is to be no confusion on this. Once this mission has been completed, then I will pass word to those five that if they wish to disclose their identities, my office will accept them openly. I am currently determining their location. I will consider who should be included on the team and notify those called for duty as soon as I reach my decision."

I wanted to look at Pietro and Geri to see what their reaction was to that, but at the same time feared doing that would be like flashing a big, huge neon sign in their direction.

Jolly Green lifted a hand. What did she think this was, elementary school?

"Yes, Matron Smyth?"

Smyth cleared her throat. "I took a vow to serve this council and execute its agendas, and I won't pull back from that. However, the question remains unanswered. Why are Ravens so intent on finding these asenaics? Is it part of their scheme against the wolves?"

"In a way, yes, and for the moment, you need know no more."

Apparently, that statement brought the gavel down on the meeting, because when Geri's mom stood up, everyone else did too, and began filing out of the room.

"Rebecca!" Brünhild called. "Please show everyone to your cottage. I know it will be crowded, but better uncomfortable with us than at risk in the valley below."

Rebecca raised an eyebrow. "Everyone, sir?"

"Yes, everyone." Then, Brünhild paused, raising a finger. "Except for Pietro. He and I have business to discuss. Show him to my quarters. I will be there shortly."

Pietro grinned, as did his wife in return. Wow, great to see even Geri's dysfunctional parents still got their groove thing on. Maybe my parents would find a way to pull it together eventually.

Hey, vampires were real and slayers were a thing, so the totally absurd could happen, right?

"Matron?" Cody said, holding up his oozing wrists.

But it was Geri who stepped in. "Oh, my god, I'm sorry, Cody. In the heat of the moment I forgot all about that. Here, let me."

And zip-a-dee-doo-dah, she magicked his restraints right off.

Before I could look back from the scene, the Grand Matron was gone.

TWENTY-ONE

BRÜNHILD

I wound my way up the tower, each step a measure of my increasing anxiety as I wondered who I would find waiting above.

As an asenaic, it was not surprising that Pietro often had dueling instincts, the hood and the wolf in him in constant struggle. His ability to balance and reconcile what would drive other men insane had drawn me to him from the first time I'd met him. That did not mean, however, that he could always maintain stability. There were times, fleeting but frequent, when his lupine half placed us at odds. Luckily, that nature had also claimed me as mate, and no matter how I wronged him – and how much I may deserve his disdain – the fury that would flare up refused to endure.

I didn't deserve him.

He deserved so much more than me.

He stood by the fireplace when I entered the study, his eyes fixed on the sack Yan had left on my desk on my orders.

"Is that what I think it is?"

"Yes."

"So it is true. She is dead." His throat bobbed. "At last."

My inner grand matron pushed me to make some grandiose statement, something along the lines of "*Yes, at last the vampire who killed both your grandfather and my father, and threatened to kill our daughter, is dead. May she forever more burn in the hottest fires in hell.*" But though I felt a burden ease in knowing Inga Rosethorn could no longer threaten my family, I couldn't be the grand matron right now. Not when my heart-made-flesh looked back at me with his soft, loving gaze, resolve and relief shining through. All I wanted at this moment was to be Pietro's mate, to fall into his arms and tell him that justice had finally been done. The world knew my strength, the hoods obeyed my commands. But only my husband saw my cracks, gathered together my broken pieces, and held me together.

We met half way between the door and the fireplace, my head pressing into his shoulder as his arms locked around me.

Pietro kissed my forehead. "When Markus told me you were tracking her, I was so afraid. If she had discovered you…"

"She couldn't."

"If I lost you, Brünhild…"

"You never will." I pressed my lips to his. "Like you said our first night together, we stepped off the cliff together. I'm in for the fall, no matter how far. *Siempre.*"

"*Siempre.*" My mate's hand stroked my cheek. "*Mi familia es mi plata.* My family is my silver."

As his hold loosened, I felt the air shift around us.

"*Mi Corazon,* Gerwalta is…" His words tapered away.

"Coming into her own," I said, completing his sentiment. "She has learned to harness both her lupine and hood strengths. I worried the day may never come, and now, her power is even more than I could have imagined."

A line formed between Pietro's eyes as he crossed his arms over his chest. "How, though? You stopped her from being claimed by the Casa de Amarillo. How is she able to wield her silver, having never taken her fire?"

My eyes went to the floor. "Markus says when they were in Istanbul, there was an… incident. Caleb Helsing hit her with his solarium. *Accidentally,*" I quickly amended as my husband's wolf threatened violence. "He was trying to defend her, but she was caught in the crosshairs. I don't know what to think, Pietro. Perhaps it was providence. It managed to wake up every part of her, give her the defenses she needed just in the nick of time."

Pride beamed from his eyes. "Alexandra's death was a tragedy, but it is a blessing that the illustrian baby has come here; who better to mother such a child than one whose own nature is likewise drawn from so many roots?"

There was truth in what he said, but I also knew that until we defeated the Ravens, young Mina's existence was under the very same threat Gerwalta had been for years. Vlad Tepeş saw the enhancements crossing supernatural species gave the blood of those born to multiple natures as no more than a weapon he could wield.

"She needs every ally, every strength we can give her." I paused, knowing my husband would be reluctant to believe what I was about to say. "Including having her mate at her side."

Pietro's eyebrows arched. "So you've finally accepted that Markus and Gerwalta will never wed?"

"Each other?" I asked, my voice flat. "When wolves fly."

My soul renewed with his laugh. Soon, however, Pietro continued in earnest. "We will rescue him then. Perhaps Vlad's *serum* is a blessing in disguise. It will allow this wolf to love our daughter."

My insides curdled. "It seems at first blush, but I was able to finally track down the one who developed it, a Dracule by the name of Xin. I forced the truth from her before she died."

My husband's face screwed up, but he didn't ask. He knew my methods to procure information, even if he didn't agree with them. "And?"

"And, the results are valid. A therapy of the serum, administered regularly, will weaken the lupine bond. It does not destroy it, however, it only masks it. After the therapy is discontinued, its effects dissipate. Within a few weeks, the bonding rebounds. From Vlad's perspective, it wouldn't matter. A few weeks of unmade bonds is long enough to corrupt the foundation of lupine society."

"So even if we rescue Tobias Somfield—"

I shrugged. "He is also an asenaic, though his only hood ancestor appears to have been the Betrayer. Like the Muñezes, the residual enhancements are very weak. Still, we do not know. Perhaps having a genetic baseline, the serum's ability to hold in his system will prove stronger than with the other subject the Dracule tested."

Pietro mused a space before his head dipped in a single nod. "There is a chance then, and if a chance is all we can give to our daughter for happiness, then it shall be done. But for me, *mi Corazon...*"

He crossed back to the table, his hand disappearing inside the bag. Little blood remained in Inga Rosethorn's severed head; she must not have fed for several days before cornering my daughter in the hospital. Pietro's hands threaded her hair, pulling it high into the air. He locked me in his sight.

"*Por mi padre, por favor.*"

Silver flame, fed by a bit of the metal I kept always wound around my arm, lit the air, licking across the space, and found its target with a preternatural instinct.

As the vampire's head turned to dust, a smile spread across my mate's face.

I hoped somewhere in the afterlife, his lupine grandfather found peace as well.

TWENTY-TWO

GERI

You'd think it was the first baby they'd ever seen. Maybe it was. Alex had mentioned there hadn't been any pregnancies for some time. Which... made me begin to wonder how I was supposed to just randomly bring up the topic that that should probably change soon.

Hey, since you guys might be the last of your kind and you're not getting any younger, perhaps consider having sex like crazy so you don't actually die out, okay? Start now if you like, I can go in the other room.

I mean, unless they wanted to actually cease to be a species, they'd better get to the baby making. At least they had Caleb with them. As soon as the sole surviving Helsing was able to get over our break-up, I had great faith in his ability to... well, hold the opening ceremonies.

"Isn't she the sweetest thing ever?"

Teiko was the only female slayer of Asian heritage, but like all the women, she'd been raised in the harem speaking English, Turkish, and Vlad's own dialect of Romanian. She was also one of the most beautiful women I'd ever met. Petite, but with ebony locks that would have fallen past her waist if she didn't twist the mass of it around her head like a crown. Her amber eyes twinkled, reflecting the fire burning in the hearth.

Teiko finished wrapping up Mina's diaper the way Petunia had demonstrated when she'd stopped by earlier in the evening to also inform me she was *good with the plan.* "I can't believe Alex named her Mina. It's so cliché."

I tapped on the tablet sitting in my lap to close the map of Spain it displayed. "What's cliché about it?"

Amy sauntered in from the kitchen, handing Sergei, a ruddy-faced blond stick of a man, a cup of juice. "Come on, Geri. Even I know that one. Mina, you know? From *Dracula*?"

I shook my head. "I'm sorry, still not getting it."

The blond huey rolled her eyes. "Didn't you have to take that lit class your freshmen year? Oh, I forgot, you were a transfer. Mina is the name of the English prude old Drac tries to bone in that book by Bram Stoker."

I let out a scoffing laugh. "Everyone in the supe world knows those huey knockoffs are hogwash."

Amy fixed me with her best 'oh-really' stare as she settled on the floor at Teiko's feet. "Just like the Grimm Brothers?"

"Yes, just like the Grimm Brothers," I said without thinking. "Like the hoggiest of washes."

"I don't know about that." Amy began counting out a point on each finger. "They did sort of nail that it was a *red* riding hood, when it could have come from any of the clans. And Grandmother's house?" She motioned vaguely in the direction of the castle. "Matron's house. Eating the grandmother, the huntsman coming after the wolf and killing him? Hunts *woman* maybe, but that even sticks."

"Not to mention," Teiko added, "Bram Stoker had an affair with a slayer."

Amy's eyes went wide. "No way!"

"Totally." Teiko grinned, pleased at having an audience. I foresaw the beginning of a beautiful friendship between these two. "You mean Caleb didn't tell you?"

Amy and I exchanged a look.

Just at that moment, the indicted himself came into the room, carrying an armload of baby supplies some of the hoods residing in the castle had gathered. "Tell them what?"

Teiko rose, taking Mina along with her. "That you got an Irish writer in your family tree."

Caleb blushed. "He wasn't part of my family tree."

Even I found my curiosity piqued. "It's true, then?"

The slayer collapsed into a chair at the table next to me. "Kinda? Albert Helsing and Bram Stoker had a passionate, lustful, and *brief* relationship. They still managed to be on good terms long enough for Albert to give Bram the four-one-one on Vlad. Stoker, of course, changed the details and added a "van" to our family name, but he got lots of things right, too."

Amy's mouth dropped open. "How is that not the first thing you tell people when you meet them?"

Caleb smirked. "Tell me, Barbie, did Geri lead with 'I'm named after the famous Little Red Riding Hood and FYI she actually is considered a traitor by my people' the first time you met her?"

"No, I think she told me she'd just moved away from a place called Paradise, and I made some smart-ass comment about why would you leave Paradise for Chicago."

But the wheels in my mind were spinning. Grimm Brothers, fairy tales, the truth in our world…

"My mother in her study with the leather book…"

Everyone turned on me, Caleb saying, "Pretty sure it was Mrs. Peacock in the foyer with the pipe wrench."

I stood, putting a hand on Caleb's shoulder. "I was too young to read back then. Markus and I snuck into my mother's private office and there was an old copy of *Little Red Riding Hood*. No, that doesn't sound right. Why would *we* have a copy of a Grimm fairy tale? But it was? I think it was. I… I can't remember." I stood and started for the door. "Teiko, can you watch Mina for a while?"

"Geri?" Caleb was just a step behind me. "Where are you going? We all agreed we needed to just lay low and rest for a day or two."

"I'm not leaving the compound. I just have to go see something in my mother's study."

"Right, and where is that?"

I pointed up. "Top of the tower."

He looked incredulous. "They wouldn't even let you beyond the council chambers yesterday. You and mommy might have bridged a gap a bit, but you're still relinquished."

"I am so not relinquished, and I'll slice anyone who insists I am."

My body ricocheted off his arm as he strapped it across the door. "Exactly, you have enemies there. You can't just go gallivanting about."

I gently moved his arm to the side. "Relax, Helsing. I know how to stay hidden. I was walking these hallways before I could even crawl."

His face screwed up. "How did that work exactly?"

"Don't mark up my metaphors to full price. What I mean is, I know this castle, inside and out. I can get in from the cliffs."

Caleb blinked his surprise. "That doesn't sound very secure."

"It is, though," I insisted, even as I summoned my red cloak into being, its gentle weight falling like a hug upon my shoulders. I could get up to the tower covertly, but I still had to get across a courtyard full of young hoods in the midst of training. Looking like one of them, conveniently with my face hidden, was a golden ticket. "No one else but the Grand Matron knows about it."

"And everyone in this room who heard you say it exists."

I stifled a laugh and pulled silver I'd left in a ball on a side table over my skin, hiding it from view. "You can't open it. It requires a special key that only hoods can use."

"Hello!" Caleb clapped. "This isn't medieval times anymore. Those kind of things can be made with 3D printers. I know your kind sticks to the sticks, but you got to keep up to date with modernity."

At the door that led into the courtyard, I paused. "Excuse me? Which one of us just earned a BS in Biochemistry and which one of us thinks Penthouse Forum is high literature?"

"It was just one copy, Geri. I told you, I don't normally read those things."

But I was done arguing.

TWENTY-THREE

A carpet of homes, shops, streets, and just… brown… spooled across the valley. The irony of Schloss Wolfsretter's secret entrance was that it was in open view. At least from the village below. Probably not so much a consideration at the time it was built, given the lack of telescopes, binoculars and zoomable cameras held by medieval laity. Night cloaked my presence, however, the maturing moon masked in clouds. The stairway that led to the true base of the tower was nothing more than a series of stones that extended out about the width of two hands from where the earth dropped away. A thin margin for error, but the twenty steps I'd need to take with nothing below me but a fall didn't concern me. That fact that the gathering storm parading across the valley sparked lightning in the distance, did.

Basic rule of metallurgy: silver is the best electrical conductor.

Hoods were mortal. We were born, we aged, if somewhat more gracefully than hueys, and we died. We were amazingly resistant to disease, counted superhuman senses and strengths as assets, and could make silver our bitch, as

Amy might say. It was in that last gift, however, that we also found our greatest weakness. I'd never had to fear it before; as a nascent, the lightning would not seek me. Now, having claimed my fire, that would no longer be the case. Wolves had always known the best way to outmaneuver a hood was in a storm. We didn't dare expose ourselves to them, because when lightning struck near enough, it would reach out a finger to us and strike us dead.

Even though the storm was far away, if I took too long at my task, it would be too late to escape the same way. I'd either need to find another way out, or a place to hide inside until the danger had passed.

The silver wrapped around my arm obeyed my command, pooling into a thin stream that siphoned into a crevice beneath a stone bearing the crest of the House of Red. Liquid metal snaked its way deep into the structure, finding the lever at last when it had gone so far as to be nearly out of my command. With a shift in my mind's eye, the silver solidified, forming a chain. With a hearty tug, the lock released, and the faux brickwork concealing the chamber tilted in.

Into a tunnel of darkness even my sensitive eyes could barely distinguish. *Great.* I'd been so quick to leap at the chance, I'd forgotten basics like the need for freaking lights when ascending a foot-wide staircase entombed between two massive stone walls.

"Here, let me help."

"Holy shit!"

The brilliant light struck my eyes and nearly made me lose my footing. Caleb grabbed me just in time with his solarium-free hand and threw me into the tunnel.

"Sorry, Geri, didn't mean to scare you. Just thought you could use some help."

"Some help?" He winced as I pelted his chest, ignoring the fact that he'd plunge to his death if I did so too hard. "What in the hell are you doing here? I'm trying to be all covert and stuff. Did anyone see you? Did anyone *follow* you?"

"All the nascents were heading indoors when I passed through. I guess even if they aren't allergic to lightning, still sucks to be in the rain. I ran through fast; they probably didn't see me."

I'd forgotten that a slayer could run almost as quickly as a vamp. "Good, but you shouldn't have come. If I get caught inside, it's bad enough. Bringing an outsider into the Grand Matron's private study? It looks like my mother's matronship isn't as secure as it used to be, and that will be major capital for her enemies."

"Relax, Geri. You forget, I'm the master of sly. Besides..." He took a few steps up, calling up a solarium as he did. "...you forgot a flashlight. Pretty cool hidden door trick there, too. How did you open that before you could wield silver?"

"I didn't." The way illuminated as we began the four hundred and eight spiral steps it would take to reach the top. "Not from the outside, anyway. I've only been down here once, about a decade ago. My mother showed it to me in case I ever needed to make a quick escape."

"Does that happen a lot here? Emergency escapes?"

I shrugged, despite the fact that being in front of me, Caleb couldn't see. "I don't think so. I think she just thought that I was finally old enough that I'd keep it secret. Guess she was wrong."

"If it helps, I promise I won't tell anyone."

"Especially not Amy."

He paused, looking at me back over his shoulder. "Why would I tell Amy of all people?"

"I don't know, you two seem to have a way of getting in to one-uppings." I gave him a little push, urging him on. "Why did you do it, by the way? Offer to make her castellan of the slayers? You guys don't even have a castle."

"Maybe not, but I have a corporation. Or at least, a big part of it."

"What are you talking about?"

"You don't think I was giving Inga my blood out of the kindness of my heart, do you?" He laughed as he turned forward. "Everything was very quid pro quo. Inga got biweekly feedings. I got a big slice of WWL ownership."

"Wait, so basically you're…"

"God-maddening rich, yes." Caleb shrugged. "Amy will be well-compensated, don't worry about that. Should finally get her away from those self-involved parents of hers, too."

"Why do you care about that? I thought you hated her."

"I don't hate Amy. I just hate being around her. And you didn't hear her side of the conversation when she called home. After the 'thank god you're alive' part, I kinda questioned if they really were. Thankful, I mean. I don't know exactly what they said, but after a few minutes, she just went all quietlike, letting them get their licks in. Can you imagine what you have to say to Amy Popowitz to make her mopey? Oh my god, how long is this staircase?"

"Just keep going. You do realize you just guaranteed being around Amy for, like, well, until you figure out how to get rid of her, right?"

"She'll be free to leave at any point. Tell you the truth, though? I don't think she's going to. Amy's a drama junkie, and being in our world has given her a steady supply. Notice she hasn't man-shopped once since we left Chicago?"

"During which time we've been hunting vampires or running from them."

"Exactly," Caleb said. "No guys. Girl just needs a new thrill every couple of weeks."

Finally, the stairs ended. The Grand Matron's study wasn't as private as the official residence on the several floors above the tower were. It wasn't uncommon for her to host meetings with other matrons or even passing hoods here, though only by invitation. While on my side of the entry, the door looked like something taken from a barn, from inside my mother's study, it was hidden behind a very large painting of the Schloss made in the eighteenth century. I pushed it gently, checking that the coast was clear.

And came face to face with my mother.

Reclining against her desk, her arms folded over her chest and wearing street clothes, I had to wonder just how long she'd lain in wait.

"Well?" she asked, a slow, impatient draw in her voice. "Coming in or not?"

Not knowing what else to do, I pulled myself erect and crawled in. "Caleb is with me, too."

"I assumed it'd be him, since I sensed no wolf. Well, hurry along, then. I do have other matters to attend."

I looked back in the portal at Caleb, jerking my head. Hesitation lingered until I gave him a death glare. "I didn't ask you to come along. Now suffer the consequences."

"You know, Geri, if you wanted to come off as the nagging wife, you really should have said yes when I proposed." The slayer stepped in, and as soon as we were in the room proper, proceeded to act like we'd just arrived for a scheduled appointment. Extinguishing his solarium, he offered his hand. "Mrs. Kline, Grand Matron, you're looking lovely this evening."

Brünhild rolled her eyes. Then, pushing herself off her desk, leaving Caleb's hand hanging, she circled toward the fireplace. "You're still officially relinquished. If my adversaries find out I've let you into the tower, they'd have my head and yours."

"I know. And I'm sorry. I know it's exceptional that I'm even being allowed to stay in the compound. But..." Why was I twisting my hands? "I think Vlad is heading to Spain, and I think he'll have Tobias with him."

"Interesting, but it doesn't explain to me why you're in my study. So, tell me, why exactly did you break in here?" She folded her arms over her chest and stared into the fire.

Caleb launched into in a seeming non-sequitur before I had a chance to come up with a convincing lie. "Grand Matron, let me explain. To start with, vampires are not, in fact, immortal. They get about five hundred years after they're reborn in the creche before becoming ash. But they can extend their lives by drinking supernatural blood. I mean, wolf doesn't do anything special for them, but a meal of slayer or hood blood every couple of weeks keeps them going."

"Which was why Vlad kept his harem," I jumped in. "They hunted down most of the race but kept a select few to breed and live off of."

"And asenaic blood not only keeps them alive, it makes them even more powerful." My mother's eyes met mine. "I know all this."

Of course, she did. She probably knew a lot more than I did about tons of supernatural lore. If only she'd ever shared with me the stuff that truly mattered.

"Papa told me he was meant to be the last of his line in the Americas. He said those words very exactly, which tells me there may be others of our kind in Spain, where Papa's family immigrated from. I know Igor was visiting them, drinking from them. I need to find out who those people are and warn them about Vlad, and I need to be there if the Ravens show up. *When* they show up, because they're already on their way."

"Really?" She arched an eyebrow. "And what makes you so sure?"

I gulped down my nerves. "Because during the quickening, I heard Vlad say as much. That was a few days ago now. They're either already there, or about to be."

If this surprised my mother, she showed no signs of it. Instead, she looked bored. "You still have not answered my question. Why are you *here*?"

I sucked in a breath and all the courage I could summon. "Because I think there's a book here that lists the history of the asenaics. I'm pretty sure it's the one I was looking at once when you caught Markus and me snooping around. I need to see it, so I know where to go."

Brünhild walked forward, bracing her hands on the back of a guest chair on the opposite side of her desk. "Last chance, Gerwalta. Why. Are. You. Here."

Confusion drew my eyebrows down as I tried to figure out what I was missing. Then, suddenly it dawned on me. She didn't mean just in this office. No, her question was so much broader than that.

"Because I love Tobias," I said. "Because I want him as my husband, and I want to be his mate."

"He already had a mate," my mother said. "Her name was Kara."

I nodded. "But Vlad's got some kind of gene therapy that's unraveling the wolf instincts. Undoing bonds. Tobias had already been exposed to it in Istanbul. I know because he... He kissed me."

Though that didn't explain it all. He'd told me he loved me before the Ravens had taken him, kissed me before he'd been lost to me, but I didn't want my mother aware of his idiosyncrasies any more than was necessary. It might give her fodder later to condemn the man I loved.

To my surprise, my mother smiled. "Finally. And if you don't remember that from here on out, you're not going to succeed at anything."

Expecting fire and getting only kindness, I found myself aghast. "You're … not … mad? All my life, you've drilled into me that hood begets hood. You even tried to convince me to marry Markus, for Christ's sake."

Caleb blew a raspberry. "As in your cousin?" he asked. "Ew."

"Such pairings are not uncommon in our society, Mr. Helsing. And given the extraordinarily small gene pool your kind will be swimming in for the immediate future, I think you'll find they'll be somewhat common in yours." Then, focusing back on me, she added. "I was trying to find you a protector, because I've always known this day was coming. Markus loves you, though sadly, not in the way I would have liked. I appreciate Cody Ryland, but I never thought of him as the kind who could be a leader. Happily, he's proven me wrong on that account. Now, Tobias Somfield… He's good for you."

I swallowed my disbelief. "What?"

"Do you not think I above all people could be sympathetic? I love your father, even knowing that I'm supposed to hate him, even want to destroy him. You need to be sure you feel that for your wolf, because even if I, the Grand Matron, accept you, that does not mean everyone will."

I was dead. Or in a coma. Whatever was happening, it couldn't be real. "Accept me?"

But in my mother's characteristic fashion, she considered the matter closed as soon as the words were out of her mouth. Pushing herself off the desk, she spun in the direction of her bookshelves. "I destroyed the book you're talking about. I cannot show it to you."

And… there was reality, crashing back down around me. All the hope I'd felt? Like pure oxygen, it caught a spark and leapt into flame. "What? Why? You… *Son of a bitch,* how dare you destroy something that—"

Caleb pulled me back, putting a hand over my mouth. "You really need to work on your communication skills. Don't you get it? She didn't destroy it to piss you off. She did it to protect you and your dad. Which, based on my limited knowledge, sounds like what she's been doing all her life."

My mother softened. "Perhaps this one is more than a shameless flirt and pretty face. Here I thought his only abilities were flattery and insolence."

"No, Matron, I can be as insolent as fuck. You could have asked Inga herself, if you hadn't killed her. Forget about the book, Geri. Remember in the council meeting when your mother said she was closing in on the Ravens' location? Your mother knows what you're after."

I turned on her, tapping a foot. "Well, do you?"

Emotions cycled across Brünhild's face. Annoyance, disappointment, finally... acceptance. "At the council, I mentioned there are five. Two, of course, you know: you and your father. Three more survive in Navarre, on the edge of the Pyrenes. Pedro, Elenara, and Indigo Muñez."

"Indigo?" Caleb's voice filled with glee. "'Ello, my name is Indigo Mon..."

His words turned into groans as I elbowed his stomach. "Not the time, Helsing."

"What is he...?" My mother looked at my ex like he was a mental patient.

"Something about vampires and slayers," I said. "They have a thing for *The Princess Bride*. Pedro, Elenara, and Indigo Muñez in Navarre. Got it. I'll leave just as soon as I have my supplies gathered."

"Just like that, you're going to flee?"

Was she kidding? "What would keep me here, our warm and sentimental relationship? You think one hug in a moment of weakness overwrites the years of disdain and cruelty? Look, I *am* thankful that you've given the slayers refuge, that you recognized my claim on Mina, for saving us from Inga. But you lost me the moment you kept me from *my* birthright. You attacked me with silver flame, mother. *Me,* your own flesh and blood. How did you know it wouldn't kill me?"

The barely visible lines on her face grew taut. "It was never my intention to hurt you. I had hoped it would... It doesn't matter anymore."

Struggling to keep my voice even, the heels of my hands bore the grunt of my frustration. "Thank you for telling me the names of the other asenaics. I'll do what I can to let them know the danger they're in."

Just as I turned, she said perhaps the only thing that could get me to stay. "There's a reason, you know, why Tobias Somfield can love you."

I tried to burn her with my glare. "Because it can't be my charming personality?"

Her jaw worked. "The book you saw? It contained more than just the details of the yellow bloodline from which your father descended. Stuck in the pages was a letter written to my grandmother in 1944 by Igor Kharmarov."

I tried to downplay that fact. "What does that have to do with Tobias?"

"Gerwalta Faust gave birth to a healthy asenaic baby. And *that* child, when she matured, had twins. The father, by the way, was also lupine."

I didn't know why that knowledge caused a pang in the pit of my stomach. I had *two* wolf ancestors erased by time? How many more secrets were hidden in my blood? "How would Igor know that?"

"Because he's the one who raised Bianca Baron."

"Gerwalta's daughter?" I scoffed. "Are you serious? Igor would have told me."

"Besides," Caleb chimed in, "a vampire would never raise another supe's baby. Especially not a Dracule. It's just not in their nature."

"I suspect he would not have done it, if he had not felt some guilt. You see, Gerwalta Faust was not, in fact, called the betrayer because of her affair with Andreas Baron. It was because she learned of a plot by the Ravens to destroy werewolves; likely the same plot they're playing out now, only enhanced by modern science and technology. She was ordered to stay out of it, but she refused to not fight for the wolves. It is Gerwalta who entombed the Ravens in jars of silver."

Someone had just shot my brain with a confusion cannon. "Wait a minute, you're saying Igor... The sweet little professor with a pet cat, raised the Betrayer's kid?"

"And her twins, until he became aware of the hyper-restorative power of their blood. He knew then that this new asaenic bloodline could restore the Ravens to power if ever they escaped. He even separated the twins, untwisting their fate. One whose nature proved more hood than wolf was adopted into the Casa de Amarillo in Navarre. The other, whose nature tended towards lupine, was sent faraway to England, where he was raised wolf."

"Wait a FREAKING minute!" I fell back into the chair behind me. "Are you telling me that Tobias and I are... That we're... I'm in love with my cousin?"

"A very distant cousin, yes," my mother said flatly, like she was only confirming it had rained that morning.

Caleb coughed a laugh. "Five minutes ago, you didn't raise a huff at the idea of marrying Markus, but someone you shared a grandma with three hundred years ago? Oh, be still my scandalized heart."

My head whipped back and forth so hard, my brain pingponged. "You're saying Tobias is also..."

But when I took two seconds to think on it, it fit. Tobias had been attracted to me even before Kara died, something that should have been impossible. He'd been able to sense me from almost as far away as I could him, more so than any other wolf I'd ever met. Most convincingly, he'd fallen in love with me before Vlad had ever done anything to him.

"An asenaic, yes." My mother put into words what I couldn't find the strength to do. "As is my husband and my daughter. You seem convinced that I am against you, Gerwalta. Maybe that's part of your wolf nature, too, or maybe we're just a typical clashing mother and daughter. But I assure you, everything I have done, every secret I have kept, has been to protect my family."

"If that's true, help me now."

For the first time since Caleb and I had emerged, Brünhild wore surprise. "To do what?"

"Include me on the team going into Spain."

"Geri, you are my daughter, and I love you. But I am also the Grand Matron, and you are not recognized as a member of this community. I couldn't possibly include you on the team. Besides, Vlad will want you above all others. I'd be handing him a gift-wrapped package by sending you."

"I know. And I know that's against our… *your* traditions. I'm asking you to do this not for my sake, but for the sake of those asenaics. I am one of them, they're more likely to trust me than the leader of the community who has shunned and ignored them for three centuries. Then I can also be there to save Tobias. Besides, no one you have here is a better fighter than me. You know that."

Her eyes went to the fireplace. "I'd need to get the council's blessing before agreeing to that."

"But I thought you were the Grand Poohbah," Caleb said.

My mother swung an acidic glare his way. "It isn't a dictatorship, Mr. Helsing. I am a queen who serves only with the support of the nobles. They have so far let go my insistence to use our resources to track Gerwalta—they are all mothers, after all, and understand my concern—but as you saw, support for my office is waning."

Daring her objections or worse, her indifference, I stepped forward, taking one of my mother's hands in mine. "Please, after I save Tobias and warn the others, I swear, I won't ask you for anything again. I will go about my life alone."

It took a moment, but at last, Brünhild's fingers hooked around mine. "I have to consider the ramifications. There are *some* matrons," her eyes shifted accusingly to the side, "who do not believe the slayers are worth protecting at all. I will not exchange your heart for a whole race's welfare. I'm sorry, but I cannot include you on this mission."

I dropped her hand and my expectations. "I see. Caleb and I can go out the way we came in." I took a few steps back towards the hidden door.

"However—"

My mother's words arrested me. I spun, my heart racing, my thoughts filling in all the ways she could finish that sentence. "Yes?"

"As I am no longer *your* matron, I cannot forbid you from being any particular place at any particular time, and if Markus, while visiting you in Rebecca's cottage, were to accidently mumble the plans in his sleep today before we depart at sunset, how could I hold it against him?"

"Are you saying—" Why was my mouth going dry when there were such salivating developments? "I can be part of the mission?"

"No, I'm saying I can't stop you from undertaking your own mission. Understand, Gerwalta, if dangers arise which force me to choose between aiding my own team or you, I am obligated to them first. However, as your mother, I cannot advise you to abandon your heart. You must do what you must do."

This tender moment died on the sword of Caleb's ill timing.

"Great, so now I have to choose between *two* different teams to be on?" He ran his hand through his perfect 'do. "Don't suppose we can flip a coin?"

"You're not going." "You're not coming."

Brünhild and I locked gazes right after our synchronized words.

Caleb took a moment to wipe away his shock before clearing his throat. "Why?"

"The slayers need you," I said. "You're too valuable to risk against the Ravens."

"Not to mention," my mother continued, "you're the only surviving male of your kind we know of who's gone through his rites. Just as with our kind, only a female matron can awaken the gifts of her clan, so too must the other male slayers rely on you to do the same when the opportunity arises. If you die, then your race ends with its current generation."

I turned to my mom. "I didn't know that."

"Why would you? You've never needed to."

"You got to be kidding me!" Caleb moaned. "Geri, look at me. I told you not long after we met that the Ravens killed my parents. If anyone has the right to go after them, it's me."

I couldn't deny his rationale, but as much as I'd be loath to admit it, my mother was right. "We can't risk it. You have to stay here and keep working with the slayers. Didn't you say you wanted to try and perform rites with some of the guys this coming new moon? You need to get them ready for that."

"As the saying goes, I don't have to do anything but pay taxes and die, and I'm really good at tax evasion." The slayer crossed his arms over his chest. "Neither of you wants me on your team? Fine. I'll make my own team. You aren't the boss of me."

Brünhild grinned. "Mr. Helsing, I admire your drive, but if you do not comply with my order to stay settled here, I will..."

"I'll tell Amy that you have a crush on her," I inserted.

My mother spun on me, brow furrowed, lips pursed. Caleb, in the meantime, threw his hands up in surrender.

"Okay, I yield. You play dirty, Kline. So dirty."

As we grumbled our way back down the hidden staircase, Caleb in the front to light the way, he said, "Mind if I ask you about something you said back there?"

"Why not? You seem to know all my secrets now anyways."

I imagined his smile. I'd give that to Caleb, he smiled more than anyone else I'd ever met.

"When you said your mom hit you with silver flame, what did that mean?"

"I told you about that," I said, my hand tracing the wall with each step. "My dad tried to arrange for me to take my fire with his bloodline, the yellows. My mom found out, freaked out, and relinquished me to keep me from claiming my birthright."

"Yeah, you told me about that, but you didn't mention anything about silver flame. I've never heard of it."

"Of course not, it's a hood thing."

"A common hood thing?" He paused, looking back over his shoulder.

"I mean, not common. Really rare, in fact. So is flying, but she can do that, too. Hardly any hoods can anymore. It's a trait we seem to be losing through the generations."

He turned back and trudged on. "If you say so. All I'm saying is, I've never heard of silver flame until now."

And as I followed him, I had to wonder if, outside of my mother's ability, I had ever heard of it either.

TWENTY-FOUR

I'd made many mistakes in my life, but so far, none so big as writing off Amy Popowitz as a man-gobbling, college coed more interested in getting drunk and screwing guys than being bothered with actual relationships. I'd also underestimated her grip, and if she didn't let me go soon, she might choke me to death.

"You're acting like I'll never see you again."

"What? No, I'm not. Of course, I'm going to—"

I wrestled myself out of her hold and held her at arm's length. "We don't say anything. No goodbye, no good luck. We just go do and get back."

She wrinkled her nose. "Well, you guys suck then."

I pulled back and made a final check of the weapons in my sack. Silver, of course, several bricks of it, but there was also a titanium curved blade I was itching to try out. Wooden bullets and a gun with just enough force to project them without splintering rounding out the kit. "I'm sorry you can't come along, but…"

"But I'm just a huey," she said for me. "I know. I get it. I'm getting better at the hand-to-hand stuff, but I'm not an idiot. I'm not ready to do things at your level yet. Hell, those twelve-year-olds playing Mulan in the courtyard could kick my ass. But, now that I'm a Casper…"

"Castellan."

"Whatever," she said. "I should spend my time figuring out what that means. I'm sure it involves regulating Caleb's conquests. The slayers didn't get out of a vampire's harem just to be dragged into his."

"I'm sure you'll keep everyone in line."

I turned to Anya, who held Mina in her arms. Lupines led the growth curve, but even I was shocked by what one week had done.

The baby's eyes followed me, predatory senses already developing.

"She's tracking you," Anya said. "She knows you're her m—"

"I'm not," I cut off the slayer. "Please, Anya, don't put me in that role. I'm her guardian, and that's all."

I was so not ready to be anyone's parent, let alone a mythical creature whose blood was the opposite of mine, with the power to steal the life from a vampire instead of extend it.

"Remember that Petunia will be stopping by to check in on her every day."

"Of course, we'll expect her."

"Hey, Little Red!" Cody escorted my dad up the walk, Pietro's own weapons kit hanging heavy at his side. I got a nod as my dad passed by and Cody hung back. "I really feel like I should be going along on this wild ride."

I shook my head. "Lisa's going to deliver any day. You need to be there when she does. Family first, pack second. And, frankly, neither Tobias or I are either of those things to you."

His hand cupped the back of my head. "You're always going to be family to me, Geri Kline. You're like my weird sister who I used to make out with."

"You always know how to spoil a tender moment, don't you?"

He pulled me to him then, kissing me on the forehead. "I'm going to turn on my phone the second I land in Marquette. You let me know when you're out and you got him."

"And you let me know when Lisa delivers," I said. "I want to kiss that baby when all this is over. And tell Lisa I hope she's well."

And for the first time since Cody and I had broken up, I really meant it.

From the outside, the van we were allowed to borrow to "do some sight-seeing" didn't look that different from any other vehicle. On the inside, though, it was perfect for supes. The driver and front passenger compartment had been outfitted with the same kind of glass Igor had had in his car back in Chicago, allowing Yan to sit comfortably in the middle of a sunny day without scorching. I hadn't even considered asking the vampire-in-residence to come with us, but in his improvised "sleep talking," the offer had been made via Markus. How could I turn that down? To my surprise, my mother hadn't ordered him to stay behind when asked.

"So what happens after all this?"

My father's question from the driver's seat broke me from my reverie. "What do you mean?"

"You get your wolf back, your mother kills the Ravens, and what after that?"

"I haven't really had a chance to think about it." More like I hadn't wanted to get wrapped up making plans for a future that may never come to be. "Happily ever after, I guess?"

"*Niña*, you know it's not that easy." His gentle voice wore down the edges of the harsh reality. "Even if your status means there's no official crime, the biases of lupines and hoods will make you outsiders almost anywhere you go."

"I know. But I can't plan for a world of infinite possibilities. I just want to hope for one that has a chance for Tobias and I to be together."

As mates, a couple. I longed to say both of these things, but feared putting so much debt into a prospect that may not pay off. Then, thinking about what that might mean, and realizing that, no matter how odd it was, my dad was one of the few people on earth who I could ask, I said, "Papa, did you *bond* with mom? Like, you know, the first time you two…"

"We made love?" He grinned and shook with silent laughter. "There is no shame in saying it. We *have* been married a very long time. Why do you ask? Are you hoping for that, or scared of it?"

No. Yes. "Tobias already had a mate, and when Kara died, he suffered like any lupine would. Maybe he'll love me because of what he is and what's happened to him, but what happens if he's the only man I can ever love and it doesn't work out?"

"That is not a question you need to ask. The only question you need to ask is, is he worth the risk? For me, that answer was yes. We've had our moments."

"Like when she exiled you from the clan?"

Dad shrugged. "For standing against her edict to aid my daughter, which I did willingly and knowing the possible ramifications. Should I have *not* done that?"

"Of course, you should have!" Despite the fact that it had also led to my relinquishing. "I just don't understand how you can forgive her."

"Ach, *niña*. Your mother did not exile me. The Grand Matron did."

"Don't start that. She tried to pull the same thing on me, too. You can't just divorce the two like that. She's only one person. What was it Abuela used to say? Don't try to be everyone to everybody, because we all only get one grave."

"Sage words spoken by another asenaic, who knew what it was like to live two lives," my father said. "You and your mother are more alike than you realize. You struggle to find common ground, because you don't realize you're standing in the same exact spot. Same view, different eyes."

In the middle row, Yan's cell phone beeped. He fished it out and read the screen. "Markus says the Muñez siblings have been moved to a secure location. The Yellow Matron in charge of the region says they've also confirmed the Raven hideout. You were right, Geri. They're there."

I'd never doubted my instincts for a second, but having them validated with so little effort wasn't completely reassuring. I tried to ignore the implications and stay focused on the matter at hand. "Where?"

"They're holed-up in an old residence of Igor Kharmarov's. It's dilapidated now, probably hasn't been lived in for years, but all vampires of a certain age who've passed this way know of it."

I nodded. "Once we're close enough, I should be able to sense Tobias's whereabouts."

Yan looked up from his phone. "How close is close?"

I shrugged. "If the location is relatively open and sparsely populated, a mile or so. With Tobias, it varies. Why? I don't know. Moon phases, moods, distraction? Maybe everything."

Did the fact that we were both asenaics have anything to do with it, like we were operating on a closer frequency? I had to wonder. Then again, my father was also of the same bloodline, and he had never spoken about any greater ability in proximal sensitivity. Come to think of it...

"There is a chance, though, that whatever the Ravens did has changed that," I admitted out loud *and* to myself. "I won't know until I know, I guess."

My father smiled. "He is your mate. You will know, always."

TWENTY-FIVE

We pulled off to the side of a mountain road just before sunset, into a field covered in dry grass amid a grove of tall, thin trees topped with plasticine leaves. The car used by the official hood team sat unguarded, empty of any occupants.

My dad turned to me. "Anything?"

With eyes closed, I focused on the hum of energy that presented itself whenever Tobias came into my proximity. Concentrate as I may, there was no sign.

Dad laid his hand on my shoulder. "Don't force it. We're still two kilometers from the house. It means nothing."

I got out and surveyed the view, leaving Yan in the car. He'd await the final moments of twilight to avoid losing any of his strength to the sun. In the distance, gray mountains highlighted with white patches picked up the amber shafts of light coming from the west. As soon as night rose in its fullness, this landscape would glow under the shine of a full moon. The snow wasn't deep — one would have to round up to say it was an inch — but it did serve as an archive of those who'd gone before. I squatted down, examining the contours of the footprints heading south.

"Mother, Markus… Matron Smyth, I think. These two, I don't recognize."

Pietro knelt down beside me. "I suggested to your mother that she recruit two of the local clan to accompany the mission, to avoid political questioning. More than likely, that is them."

My dad pointed to the southwest. "Igor's home is just over that ridge. We agreed that this distance would allow us to have a sufficient staging ground."

I pressed my hand to the hood of the late model vehicle Markus had parked. "Still warm, but barely. Given the temperature out here, I'd say that means this car was turned off about fifteen or twenty minutes ago."

"According to plan," my dad added, rising to his feet. "Your mother will engage the Ravens, attempting to draw them away from the home. While they are distracted, we will locate Tobias and if we can, Igor Kharmarov, and free them."

"I'm not sure what kind of state Tobias is in." I fished out one of the silver bricks, a chunk of metal the size of a chalkboard eraser, and pooled it over my skin. "He might not be able to keep his huey form if he's too weak."

"We could always call off the mission, try again tomorrow night."

I shook my head. "You know Mom won't back down now that she's in the field. Besides, tonight is the second full moon since we've been separated. He's got to be starting to lose his grip on reality. I hate to say it, but I want his animal brain to be the one in charge of his body tonight. Instinct should get him to run when the chance comes."

Even if that means leaving me behind. It was something I was prepared for. Vlad wanted my blood too much. If he captured me, he might torture me, even take advantage of me as he did with Alex, but he wasn't going to kill me. To free Tobias, I'd endure that.

"Just let me get the silver and weapons I brought out of the trunk. As soon as it's dark, we can—"

The opening car door drew our attention. Dad and I turned to see Yan, his hands shoved in his coat pockets like the cold actually did anything to him, strolling across the way.

"I thought you were going to stay in the car until the sun was completely down, to keep yourself from losing even the smallest bit of strength?"

He nodded. "There are but a few minutes until then, and your father needs assistance."

Suddenly panicked, I turned to my dad still standing by the car. "Assistance with what? You look fine."

I felt the air shift around me, felt the change of direction in my soul, even before my father's head finished its fall.

With a blink, my world flipped. Yan's arms caged me. Silver threads raced through the air, a network of spider webs that laced over my arms and legs, drawing me into a hold. My mind raced even as my limbs flailed and my mind tried to comprehend the impossible. It was silver, just silver, but why wasn't it obeying me? Why did it refuse to yield to my command?

My father couldn't bring himself to look at me. "The silver is blood-claimed. It obeys only me."

I'd been named after the Betrayer, but I was the one being betrayed. Blood-claimed silver? But didn't he say the act was banned, that it caused horrific pain for the one who claimed it? Why would my biggest champion my whole life put himself through that, just to trap me? "Papa?"

The intensity of his gaze knocked the breath from my lungs. "When you were born, your mother and I vowed to do whatever it took to protect you from harm. That holds even if it means protecting you from yourself."

Every movement drew the taut threads tighter across my skin, even as my sadness turned to fire. "You have no right! He's *my* mate. He's *my* responsibility."

"And you are mine." Crossing to me, the metal about me moving at his command and allowing my legs freedom just long enough to collapse beneath me, leaving me in a sitting pose, my father's hand cupped my cheek. "I promise, *mi corazon*, I will save him. Now, no more discussion. We're losing precious time."

I closed my eyes, resigned to the fact that to struggle would only hurt more. "You're losing something far more precious than that."

My father paused, looking back over his shoulder. "Time can heal an injury, but it cannot restore the dead."

I shook my head. "Tell yourself that if you want, but the full moon is still rising."

A threat full of hope and lacking all capital. My father said no more as he and Yan made for the nearby trees. I flexed every muscle, trying to break the hold of the cords around me, but to no avail. No magic could force it either. At this point, I only had one choice.

If the silver would not yield, it would have to burn.

And I along with it.

TWENTY-SIX

AMY

"So this is the archive, huh?"

I examined the rows and rows of leather-bound books and piles of scrolls with all the interest of a fruit fly to Styrofoam, i.e., zero. But for some reason, the last place on Becky Krantz's itinerary for my personal tour of Schloss Wolfsretter was the one she seemed proudest of. She looked on it now like her own grown child striding across the stage at graduation to make his valedictorian speech.

"It's, um… very nice?"

It wasn't. True, it was nicely *organized*. And I'd add that it was surprising to find in the subterranean floors of a medieval castle. What was a climate-controlled high security library room straight out of a Nicolas Cage film doing in the dull patina of Schloss Wolfsretter? And what did the hoods have that was so coveted it demanded this level of Mall Cop Mecca-hood anyway?

"It is my pride *unt* joy," Becky said. "When everything arrived here in the 1940s from all over the world, it was a mess. Just boxes and boxes of records, every family using its own classification system. And preservation? The only things the hoods know how to preserve is a grudge. But now, you see. Years of labor, all for this, and it is marvelous."

What could I say? I didn't want to be a dick and not appreciate something she obviously bled and sweated for. "So I guess you know a lot about wolves and hoods then."

"Of course. I am, perhaps, the world's foremost expert in lupine and wolfsretter genealogy."

"Wolfsretter?"

"*Ja, wolfsretter.*" She nodded. "It is German for 'wolf-watcher.' Until recently, this is what the hoods were called."

"Watchers, huh? Sounds voyeuristic." Then, finding a place where maybe the old castellan and I could share some common ground, I adapted my conspiratorial tone. "Bet you came across some dirt in all these documents, huh?"

Her face curdled. "Of course, but I managed to clean all the documents without damage. I am a phenomenal archivist."

"No, I don't mean like *dirt* dirt. I mean like, dirt. Scandals. The dark underbelly of wolves and wolf-writers."

"Wolfs*retter.*"

"That's what I said." I put an arm around her, pulling her close. "Tell me, Becky, what's the juiciest thing you ever read in all these books?"

"Juicy?" She shrugged. "The hoods are not *juicy*, as a rule."

I could have guessed that, having lived with Geri for two years.

"Surely there's something." I gave her shoulders a little squeeze. "Come on, just between us castrati."

"Castellans."

"Right."

"Well... I suppose it would be the story of Hamunshet."

"Becky Shantz! You kiss your mother with that mouth?"

Becky's smile fell away. "My mother died in Auschwitz."

Awkwardness put on its gloves and punched me in the gut. Jesus, I couldn't just *not* make a joke for once. "Oh! I'm sorry... I didn't mean to..."

Luckily, the airlock around the door decompressed, and in walked tall, dark, and stuck-up, presenting me with a merciful deflection.

"Caleb!" I exclaimed like he'd just brought me to the edge of release. "Just in time. Becky was about to tell me about the story of He-Man Shits."

The castellan clicked her tongue. "There is something quite wrong with your ears, girl."

Caleb must have sensed my utter tumble into graduate-level social guffaws and allotted me a moment of mercy. "Go easy on her, Becky. You have to remember, Barbie here was raised in a place where the most exotic thing she encountered in everyday life was the halal food cart outside her hot yoga studio."

I balled my fists. "It was a kosher hot dog stand, moron."

He laughed away my retort. "Did she mean to say Hamunshet?"

"Yes, you know the story of the first hood?" Becky grinned.

Finally, someone who didn't try her patience. Caleb just charmed everyone, didn't he?

Asshole.

"If you mean the ancient Egyptian priestess who got knocked up by Aten the sun disk god and had twins? Yeah, I know that story," Caleb said. "My mom used to tell me it at bedtime when I was little."

"Well, that explains something." I cocked a hip. "No wonder you're so sex-obsessed. You were programmed to fall asleep thinking about divine boot-knocking."

The slayer squinted at me. "She put it in kid-friendly terms, of course. Only, Becky, Hamunshet gave birth to the first *slayer*, not the first hood. It's the reason we have the power of the sun, being that we're descended from the *sun disk god*."

I looked to Caleb, who looked at me, and I looked at Becky, who looked at Caleb.

"You don't honestly think that's true, do you?" I asked. "I mean, there's no such thing as Egyptian gods. Mythology is the invention of man."

"So is money, but I'm a devout worshipper."

Becky shuffled to a shelf on the far end of the room and pulled out a box about the size of a loaf of bread. "Here, I will show you."

She moved it to a table and opened it, pulling out a scroll. As she unrolled it, the fragments pasted over a clean linen cloth came into focus, looking like something out of an old monster movie. In the center, a woman wrapped in a beautiful white dress sat on a throne, the sun blazing over head and its rays shining down on her. On each knee, a baby, one who shone so brightly its features were difficult to distinguish, almost as if it *were* light. The other, robed in a blue cloak, but with silver eyes.

"There's the whole of it," Becky said. "The oldest version of the story I've been able to find. Came here from the House of Black about fifty years ago, but I've found mention of this through much of the hood literature."

I traced my fingers over the edges of the papyrus scroll. "Caleb, I'm no expert in this. I mean, a priestess impregnated by a god? Way above my pay grade. I'd laugh it off, but a year ago, if you had tried to convince me vampires and werewolves were real, I'd have said you were even drunker than me. If there's any truth to this, it means—"

"It means that slayers and hoods come from the same origin. That we're in some way… the same race."

TWENTY-SEVEN

GERI

A howl pierced the air, falling on us from the edge of the woods, just as the moon came up.

Local wolves, of course. If there were hoods in this region, there would also have to be lupines. During full moons, packs roamed their lands, consumed by their animal natures, more beast than man. Obligated to walk on four legs, only alphas and the occasional beta could keep their huey form under its power. I used to fear meeting one on a *feuernacht,* suspecting such a meeting could turn into a kill-or-be-killed situation.

My mother had always speculated that once I took my fire, the wolves would heed my summons. Under the light of the silver moon, I drove awareness into my soul, beckoning them, appealing to them.

Help me. My mate is a prisoner, and I am trapped by those who've betrayed me.

The words turned and twisted in my head, radiating out, a beacon for any help. After a few minutes, sweat beaded my forehead, even as the night descended and the temperature dipped.

The howls faded.

And then, padded paws crunched the snow.

Golden fur rimmed a brown face. Smaller than the packlings I'd been raised with, the alpha still commanded grace, his tenuous steps as lithe as they were determined. He must not have been expecting to find what he did when he'd descended from the hills, for when he suddenly shifted into his huey form, he wore a screwed-up expression.

"You're a hood," he said in a form of Spanish that sounded more lyrical than my father's.

I shook my head. "*Soy una* asenaic. Um… *Soy una muceta pero soy también una loba.*"

"Both a hood and a wolf? Is that possible?" he continued, scratching his unkempt black hair. "What did you do to me? How did you make me feel like I *had* to listen to you?"

"Please, I don't have time to explain. My name is Gerwalta Kline, and I…"

"Gerwalta?" he said, cutting me off. "The Betrayer?"

I gulped down my anxiety. "Her descendant. Her… Her heir. Please, my mate is being held prisoner a few kilometers from here. I need to get out of these silver cords and save him. Can you help me?"

His eyes swept over me, taking survey of my situation. "What is this, some trick to get me to touch the silver? Playing a joke on us, are you? There are other hoods near here tonight; we have sensed them. They must be near now, hiding. You have a bet or something, don't you? See if you can trick a wolf into getting burned."

"No tricks. I swear, I'm not lying. Please, the cord is woven too tight for me to unravel. If you'd just loosen it a bit, I could do the rest. You're an alpha at full moon, I'm sure you're strong enough to bend it. You can rip off one of my sleeves or get something out of one of those cars so you don't have to touch it."

"You are a hood, no? You should be able to will the cords away yourself."

"Normally, yeah. But these are…" I struggled for a word in Spanish I knew that would work. "Defective."

"Defective?" The alpha's face curdled. "If you are a hood who cannot wield silver *and* a wolf is not burned by it, it is *you* who are defective. I don't believe any of this." He turned. "I'm not falling for your tricks, hood. A word of advice: next time you play this game with another wolf, do not claim your name is the one all hoods loathe."

He turned tail, reclaimed his fur, and ran.

"No. No, please!"

But it was no use. I was alone, I was bound, and I was trapped. Or was I? Part of my training had been learning to get out of tight situations. Surely I could do that now? First step: to stand. Leaning forward, I folded my legs underneath me, getting ready to jump. The moment I did, however, I discovered that my father wasn't an idiot. The cords were looser at my ankles, but still restrictive, and threw off my balance. I called out as my body paralleled to the ground, the earth rising to meet me.

The moon laughed above as I rolled on to my back like an overturned armadillo. "Give it up, Geri Kline," it seemed to say. "I've seen this story before. Now just sit there like a good little red riding hood and wait for mommy and daddy to return. You're not going anywhere."

Which I might have done, if not for the fact that I knew, if the decision came down to freeing Tobias or killing Vlad, there was no way my werewolf was getting away. Through the forest and over the river in the valley, my mother and father, my cousin and his boyfriend, and even a few hoods took on the Ravens. I had to get out of here. I had to be the one there to make the right choice.

And I was going to do that... how?

I was a hood and wolf, why couldn't my strength be enough? I pulled and pushed, trying to stretch the metal. Nothing. It was too strong. I was not strong enough.

Frustration caught spark, sending anger raging through my limbs. Twisting, turning, crying out to the night until my throat was raw, I screamed. No, I refused to be sidelined. I refused to be relinquished. I *would* find a way out of this.

The cry started in my heart, clawed its way up my throat, and ripped from my body with the power of my ancestors. Soon, the fire was not only emotional, it was physical. I opened my eyes and looked down at my body, watching silver flames dance over my fingers. The melting started slow, the bands on my wrists and arms dropping to the ground. Too amazed to be curious, I pushed my palms in turn to each of the cord's stress points. My ankles, my shoulders, my arms. In a moment, I was free. The second none of the cords remained, the fire snuffed itself out.

And I ran. Across the field, through the forest, through the splashing ice cold water of the barely-a-river, until it came into view.

Moonlight clung to ancient alabaster walls of a structure more tall than wide, its sharp dimensions punctuated with arched windows and doors alluding to a Moorish past. Perhaps not authentic to the period, but the influence was there. Five or six stories high and with only one apparent way in or out, the path was clear as my feet ate up ground between the forest and the house.

When the lurch in my stomach grabbed me, stopping me dead in my tracks, my control almost abandoned me.

He was near. *He was near.*

But he wasn't moving. Not away, not toward me, not at all. The sensation remained constant, growing in strength only as I forced my feet to work. Part of my instincts told me to call out, to tell him I was coming. The wiser portion of my brain remembered that wounded animals fell first to predators stalking the night. Igor's old home lay no more than four hundred meters ahead, but the same distance to the east, my heart stood still.

I saw it then, the low rise of a masonry wall more ruin than foundation. Light footsteps carried me across the open earth. A well. Or what remained of one. Even as I leaned in to peer down, I knew what I would find, but that did not stop the pulse of anticipation and woe as I did so.

"Tobias!"

Either he hadn't heard me, or he couldn't. Even from thirty feet overhead and with the moon above at such an angle that he was left in shadow, there wasn't much of him I could see. His lupine form lay motionless, drawing my worry.

He's not dead, I lectured myself. *You'd know it if he were dead.*

"Tobias, answer me or I'm coming down there."

Nothing, not even a flinch of an ear or a cycle of breath. I looked around, hoping to find a rope or some kind of ladder even. Nothing but empty, cold ground. Then I remembered the silver I'd grafted under my clothes before we'd arrived. If my father could make a cord to bind me, surely I could make a rope to climb down into a hole. I reached for it with my mind, demanded it do as I willed.

Only, nothing happened. No rope, not even a tiny little string.

I pulled off my coat and looked for the metal, my eyes demanding to confirm what my senses already felt was true. It was gone. All of it. Whatever magic it was that had let me melt my father's bindings must have also claimed the silver plated against my skin.

There was nothing to do then but jump. I threw my legs over the walls of the well, took a deep breath, and let gravity pull me down. My feet planted on either side of his head.

"Tobias? Wake up!"

A rising and falling frame proved he was, in fact, still alive. My hands pulled up his maw. He was thinner than the last time I'd seen him, but his body seemed in good condition. Why was he here, and how was I going to get him out? The effort would strain my abilities, but I could probably lift him. But to do that while attempting to climb the well-worn, icy walls of a dry well? No way. I'd just have to hope I could find a way to wake him up.

I closed my eyes and tried to sense the pack that had roamed the hills, hoping if I got them to where I was, they might have greater sympathy for one of their own than their alpha had had for me. On the edge of abilities, I found their energy and gave it a slight tug, asking them to circle back to me. The alpha's direction shifted, but just as soon as the string between us pulled, it again went slack.

Suddenly, footfalls on the ground above took my attention skyward. A head blocked the moonlight from my view above. "Gerwalta?"

"Mother?" I leapt to my feet. "Mother, I found him! He's here. Tobias is here. He's okay, but unconscious and… Mom, you can fly! You can get us out of here."

The next sound I heard made my blood boil and freeze at the same time. "Oh, I don't think that will be happening, Geri."

With a shard of moonlight cast over his features, his eyes looked even more intense, his surreal beauty threatening. Vlad wore his usual cock-sided grin as he turned to my mother, who I realized had her hands tied behind her back, likely bound in electrical wire. "You see, Matron? I told you she'd fall for my trap. Never doubt the pull between mates. The magic that binds them also makes them blind to danger."

I'd done many things in my life to invite my mother's disappointment. My days and nights seemed meted for her disapproval. Never before had she looked at me with such disappointment.

And for once, I felt I deserved it.

TWENTY-EIGHT

Wind flew from my lungs, leaving me gasping, powerless. Electrical wires, charged by a small battery pack taped on my back, encircled my wrists, leaving my hood abilities inert and my hands bound. A moment later, the vampire threw Tobias down beside me. He was still fast asleep, knocked out by whatever drug Vlad had given him. I struggled to survey the area around me, searching desperately for the others, but all I found was Vlad and my mother seated at a table, both with cups of tea.

"Miss Kline." The vampire raised his cup my direction, saluting me. "I wonder if you now regret refusing a place in my harem?"

I rolled onto my back and managed from there to sit up, despite the ache in my ribs. "My only regret is not slicing off your head when I had all those swords around me."

"Ah, yes, that would have led us down a different path for sure." He took a sip, smacked his lips, put the cup down. "Your mother and I were just talking terms, but ones concerning you were just wishful thinking until you arrived. Thank you for your haste."

"Terms?" The question was directed at my mother, who had the gall to be stoic. "What terms?"

But it was Vlad who answered. "The offer on the table is this: you will stay with me, provide me and my clutch with your blood, and I will allow you and your wolf to live a rather comfortable and accommodating life under my protection and let all the other fools we've captured tonight go free. Refuse me, and everyone else dies...while you? You will only be able to wish that you were."

I mused silently for a moment. "Sounds awful, like the one the sultan gave you. Life in a gilded cage, comfort but no control. You think I don't see the insult?"

"What do I care if you do?" Vlad snipped. "It will not render your choices altered."

"Why am I so important to you?" I spit back. "You have my mom at the table. Offer to trade me and Tobias for your whole harem back. You can set up your little breeding compound where you like and feed indefinitely."

My head swung back to my mother, but her expression revealed nothing. Defiant and uncompromising, she'd admit to no fault, whether or not there was one to be had. Was she a prisoner too, or had she gone in with the intention of meeting Vlad as her equal? Where were the others? Markus, my dad, Yan? The two yellow hoods? I searched her expression for some tenderness or clue, but found none.

Vlad's eyebrow perched curiously. "Your mother tells me Inga is dead, that she turned on you. Tell me, Geri, how well did you know my dear, departed daughter-turned-sister?"

"Well enough to know she hated you." I spit out the blood pooling in the side of my mouth. "Makes two of us."

"Ah, and you're witty. I shall enjoy your humor in the years to come." Vlad stood, bringing his teacup along with him as he paced in my direction. "Truth is, Inga never should have been turned. She didn't have the constitution for an immortal life. I blame myself, really. You see, when she was no more than my *human child,* I neglected her. Abused her, even. She grew up with what I believe your generation calls daddy issues. She's spent her eternal life running between two father figures. Me and Igor, Igor and me. The last turnover was about twenty years ago. I didn't realize that when she was giving regular checkups to my young slayers, she was also slipping a little something extra into their vitamin shots. Left all the male slayers infertile. Oh, Inga was kind-hearted. As much as a vampire can be, anyway. She didn't want to *kill* the slayers to keep me from feeding. She just wanted to make sure I wouldn't get my hands on any more. Then, the cycle flipped, and she was off with Igor again. She was on her way back to me soon enough. Inga always came home again."

A swirling of emotions made it impossible to react. What Inga had done was horrendous, but was it the best possible solution to an untenable situation? How many more slayers would have been bred in captivity if she'd not sterilized the males? How we'd remedy that in the future was a problem for another day.

"So you see, Geri," Vlad continued, "while I adored my slayers, would have been happy to keep them forever, I've known for some time that source of sustaining blood had an expiration date. I was so delighted when Caleb wandered onto the scene. One vibrant, fertile stud for all my lassies. Inga thought it would make up for her previous transgressions. I was starting to worry, thinking I might finally die... in sixty or seventy years, when my slayers died out. But then, my sister surprised me with one final offering."

In a blink, he dropped the tea cup, crouching down beside me and pulling me up by the hair. "Hamunshet's gift. Oh, dear one… I *would* take your father. I would keep the Muñezes. I would even barter back my slayers for the right offer. But all of them put together aren't worth a single blade of your hair. All I need is you. Oh, and the children you and this asenaic—" His head jerked in Tobias's direction. "—will produce. And your children's children. And *their* children's children… Perhaps with the occasional outsider thrown in to keep the gene pool healthy."

Confusion swirled in my soul. "What makes *me* so special, Vlad? What makes *you* so deserving?"

My mother cleared her throat, pivoting in her seat. "I think that what my daughter means is, while it's true her veins carry wolf blood, we're three centuries down the line. Whatever elixir asenaic blood seems to be for you, surely the effect would be increased by a fresher coupling."

Vlad, amused, pulled back. "Are you offering me an alternative, Grand Matron? Unless the offer is the illustrian I was breeding—"

"I told you," my mother interjected, "I killed it. Her and her mother."

What was she talking about? Mina was alive, and Brünhild hadn't killed Alex. Alex's death had been a tragic consequence of forcing so much power into an attack when she was already so compromised.

"And Inga all in the same swoop," Vlad acknowledged. "Yes, I recall. You have a remarkable sense of bloodlust. And all this leads me back to Geri."

"The pick of any under the command of my office, every twenty years!" The mirror cracked, and my mother's inner demons took control. The words flew from her lips with a passion I'd rarely witnessed in her. The air of desperation clung to each syllable. "And the forced acquiesce of an acceptable wolf mate, in perpetua. I can make that happen."

Venom laced my tongue. "Mom, you can't!"

Her eyes drilled into me. "Silence! You are not a righteous hood. You have no say in my decisions."

Vlad stood, taking two steps to my mother. One of his long fingers traced a line down her cheek. "The time for feigning ignorance is over, Brünhild. You know as well as I do why I want Geri. I've tasted her blood; I know what she is." He leaned in, his tongue darting out. A slick line of saliva marked the path Vlad licked up my mother's jawline. "And I know what *you* are."

I saw everything and understood nothing. For the first time in my life, Brünhild Kline was… scared.

Her words trembled over lips gone white. "She doesn't know. No one does."

"Know what?" I inched closer to the table as well as I could in my position. "What is he talking about?"

"Funny thing, supernatural blood," Vlad mused, backing away. "It's a genetic chemistry lab, all the ingredients stable on their own, but mixed together in different proportions, and BOOM!" His clap made both of us shake. "Explosive results. Huey blood keeps a vampire alive until for some reason, after half a millennium, the magic just dries up. I can drink slayer blood and that's, well... yummy, really. Hood and werewolf blood, a little more gamey, and not quite as powerful. But cross a werewolf with a hood or a slayer, you get liquid life and death. And I thought *that* was the ultimate cocktail. But then... Then I tasted the blood of one who had all three creatures running in her veins."

My mother's eyes fell closed.

"All three?" For some reason, I took the question to Vlad, who seemed to be the only one willing to give answers. "That's impossible."

"Hood begets hood." Brünhild's loathsome words melted through a sighing resolve. Her eyes shone as she lifted them to meet mine. "Words I tried to drill into you. Words my own mother drilled into me. She never wanted me to repeat her mistake."

My world turned red. "No. No, that's impossible, Grandpa Germain was a hood."

"Yes, Jacques Germain *was* a hood," my mother said. "But he was not my father."

The words echoed in my head, but repetition didn't bring clarity. Three bloods ran in my veins... The hoods of my mothers, the wolves of my fathers, and the slayers... My grandfather was a slayer? My *mother* was *half-slayer*?

Suddenly, Caleb's words while descending from the tower came back to me.

All I'm saying is, I've never heard of silver flame until now.

When I pressed my brain, I realized that I hadn't heard of another hood with the talent either.

Except for... me.

Vlad held his hands to the sky. "And truth, like a blanket, grows heavy and smothers out our misconceptions." The vampire refocused on my mother. "Geri and the wolf are mine, payment in kind for my slayers."

The monster returned to my side and reached down, his cold, bony fingers threading through my hair, pulling me to my feet by the scalp. I refused to offer him the pleasure of my cry, and filtered the pain through clenched fists and ground teeth.

"What say you, Miss Kline? You, your wolf, and eternal comfort, or just you and all the others be damned?"

My acidic glare met his. "How about neither and you go take a long walk on a sunny day?"

"Do you need further incentive?" His chin lowered into his chest. "Very well."

At the far side of the room, where there may have once been shutters or a pane of glass, only a window frame remained. Vlad pulled me to it, forcing me to look down below, to a clearing where a man stood tied to a tree. For a moment, I assumed it must be one of the local hoods. The cloak distinguished the captured as a member of Casa de los Amarillos, but I couldn't find familiarity in the swollen, broken skin or the blackened, bloodshot eyes. Only when I noticed the patch of solitary gray hair just above his right temple did I realize the truth.

"Dad! Let my father go, you fuc— *Ah!*"

Vlad yanked me back, his cold cheek pressed against mine, sending a pain shooting down my neck. "Do you know what happens to a vampire when he does not feed, Geri?" he asked, his voice distorted by fangs. "I think it's much like what wolves experience: a form of madness. The onset is quicker, though. It's been seven weeks since Istanbul, when you were kind enough to leave my father behind, who I've made certain hasn't had a drop of blood in all that time."

I shook my head. "Igor's strong. He can endure it."

"In his prime, perhaps, but at his age?" Vlad laughed. "If not for his kinship with your distant cousins here in Navarre and their blood, he would have disintegrated long ago."

Below, guided by two other vampires I assumed to be members of Vlad's clutch, Igor emerged from out of my line of sight. Ragged, pale, skin on bones, he was a fading echo of the vampire I'd come to know and trust over the last two years. His brown eyes found me, and a momentary sadness made the depth of his suffering reverberate.

As he turned his head, Igor saw my dad. Like an unrepentant criminal being led to the gallows, he bucked, struggling against the hold of his captors, crying out words in a language I didn't understand.

"What are you doing?"

Vlad grinned. "Have you ever been to a zoo, Miss Kline? I haven't, but I understand animal feeding times are quite a draw."

"Feeding time?"

It didn't make any sense. Vampires didn't need so much blood as to kill their prey. Such deaths were usually the result of intent, or the consequence of inexperience.

"Is this a threat? This will only make Igor strong again."

"Oh, make no mistake, as hungry as *my* father is, *your* father will not last long. Even when he is restored, Nicolae and Petru, my Ravens, will easily overpower him."

Fear kicked in at last, my heart pounding like a wild thing in my chest. The decision was in my hands, but its implications burned. Say yes to Vlad, and my father lived. Say no, and watch as he methodically killed every person he'd captured tonight and force me through who knew what kind of tortures until, at last, battered and used up, he disposed of me, too.

"Niña!" My father's eyes caught mine from below, blazing courage. *"Te amo. Siempre te amo.* Tell your mother, I forgive her."

"Pietro!" My mother's voice broke in its fierceness. "Vlad, no. I'll do whatever you want. I'll—"

Vlad waved his hand, and the two vampires below let loose their charge.

I closed my eyes, for even what my ears heard overwhelmed. My dad's cries gargled through blood, and my mother's through terror. But despite refusing to see it, I suddenly *felt* it: his anguish, his despair, his life ebbing away... The wolf within my father reared its head, let out one last sorrowful howl, and fell into darkness.

My knees gave out on the spot just as the vampire released his hold, letting me collapse. "I forfeit."

He curled a hand around his ear. "What was that, Miss Kline? Do speak up."

"I said, I forfeit!" I threw my head back to fix him with a stinging glare. "Tobias and I will stay with you. We'll... We'll *breed*. But let the others go, and swear you'll leave them be forever."

"Not so fast." Vlad crossed to where my mother sat, her face covered in tears but her expression molded by hate. "Your word as well, Brünhild. Your daughter and her mate remain my guests for life, and you will forget she even exists, understand? If I ever catch a whisper that you or any hood under your command is so much as looking for me, I'll destroy you all."

My mother's words came through restrained tears. "None under my command shall pursue you. I swear this as the Grand Matron of the Wolfsretter."

A drunken grin spread across Vlad's face. "Ah, the old names. I do like them. Ladies, we have an accord. Hurry up now, Matron. Time for you to grab your little commandos and be on your way. Oh, but before you go..."

The vampire crossed the room to where a shopping bag had been left on the floor. I'd thought it garbage, some bit of refuse left behind in the rundown abode by a squatter. I should have known better. Vlad crossed to my mother as his hand went inside the bag. What he pulled out seemed impossible. A blade. A *silver* blade, one only a few inches long with tiny jewels encrusted in its hilt.

As a weapon, it was useful, though not big enough to do any serious damage to a vampire. As silver, it was useless. For the first time in my life, I understood why such an object had been bequeathed to me instead of merely being recycled into another form: it was my grandmother's dagger, and the silver must have been blood-claimed by her.

Vlad used the dagger to slice away the electrical cord binding my mother before turning the hilt and shoving it into her weapon hand. "A token of good faith. Your daughter left this behind in Istanbul. Take it with my good wishes."

The self-proclaimed sultan snapped, and with that, a fourth and fifth vampire walked into the room. Reality hit, punching me the stomach. All five Ravens were here. If I just had a way to attack, we could take them all down now.

And leave Tobias unconscious and open to attack, trusting in the honor system that they wouldn't go after him? Smart move, Kline.

The only way we'd take them out like this was if we set off a bomb. As a rule, supes didn't deal in explosives. We were of the old world, and fought with its rules. Only, as I thought about all I'd learned tonight, I realized, we *did* have a bomb. Two in fact, and now that Vlad had unwittingly given my mother a fuse to light them, the plan forming in my head just might work.

"Mircea," Vlad said to the vampire on the right, who couldn't have been any older than me when he was turned. "Escort our guests to town. Do not release their bonds until daybreak. Mihnea?"

The other vamp, a man who could have been Inga's brother based on his looks, dipped his head. "The sedative we gave Mr. Somfield should be wearing off soon. Once he's awake, please see him and Miss Kline to a containment chamber before daybreak. They will have much to speak on once they are able to talk."

Mihnea bowed. "Yes, Sultan."

I struggled to my feet and then, with all the mock obeisance I could muster, bowed my head. "Your Grace?"

Vlad, on the edge of leaving the room, turned, his face aglow. "Ah, see. She is learning. Well done, Miss Kline."

"Thank you, Sultan," I continued, my eyes kept low. "You won, I'm yours. But please, let me say goodbye to my mother. It's the last time I'm ever going to see her."

He weighed the request, his eyes tipping from side to side, before ceding. "Very well, but quickly."

Playing up an inability to move, the restraints on my arms and hands stretched with my efforts. "Can I hug her?"

"My, my, aren't we suddenly sentimental?" With a jerk of Vlad's chin, Mihnea followed unspoken orders.

Brünhild Kline felt light in my arms. A spirit, a shell, a hollowed heart that beat despite its owner wishing to die, all hidden behind a brick wall. I wouldn't question it; I was barely holding on myself. But grief was a luxury I could not afford.

I wrapped my arms around her, pulling her drifting form into my hold. "Please, mom. Please."

No response, not even a sigh. My chin on her shoulder, I looked to the silver in her hands. The dagger my grandmother had left to me, *my* dagger. Would it be enough?

"Mom," I sighed. "I'm going to be okay. *We're* going to be okay. You have to relinquish your love for me, just like you did before. Do you understand?" I squeezed her even tighter. "Relinquish it *the same exact way.*"

God willing, Vlad thought nothing of the tiny gasp my mother made, nor understood its significance. No wonder there were no other hoods who could command silver flame. It wasn't a *hood power.* It was a unique skill commanded by a rare individual. My mother's silver flame must be some kind of solarium, and *that* was the craft of slayers.

"I know it seems impossible with what's happened, but is it something you think you can bring yourself to do?" I pulled back to find her red eyes as wide as saucers.

She nodded, looking as astounded and shell-shocked as any widow should. Was it subterfuge, or sincere? Could it be both? "I know you'll persevere," she said. "You are strong. Stronger than I ever dreamed. But your... mate?"

I nodded, my confidence drawn merely from earnest hopes and solemn prayers. "He's strong..." I leaned in the tiniest amount. "...like me, remember? And tonight I realized, in the ways that really matter, *I'm just like you.*"

Her eyes went to the comatose wolf on the floor, then back to me. She opened her arms, inviting me, even as Vlad huffed in the background.

"My daughter, my child."

A raw energy crawled over my skin, leaving gooseflesh in its wake. Then, suddenly, heat. Warm, hot, burning, *blistering...* My mother's power electrified the air, making the hair on my arms stand on end. The last time she'd hit me, the shot had robbed me of my abilities for months. Then, I'd only been a nascent. Now, I was so much more. Hood, wolf, mate. Mother.

If I lived.

She kissed my cheek and—

"I relinquish you."

—silver flame lit the room.

TWENTY-NINE

Flames licked my limbs, then bore deeper. Down, down, down into the very marrow.

"Gerwalta!"

My mother's voice was so close, and yet, distant, mottled.

"Gerwalta, run!"

A hard smack brought my attention to the pain, reared my instincts to defend. Focus summoned me back to the present, to a place where I was under attack. Run? From what? Oh, yes. From Vlad.

From Vlad.

With a gasp, I plunged back into reality, falling to the floor where Tobias lay, awake but confused. As was I; he was no longer in his wolf.

"Geri?" Sluggish, he pulled himself onto his elbow. "Geri, what are you doing here?"

I pulled him to his feet. "No time. Run."

All around us were howls of pain, cries of anguish. One particular wail stole my attention, and when I looked, I couldn't explain what I saw. It was a vampire, one of the Ravens. Only, where there had been flesh and bone, all that remained was sinew and blood. The image of charts hung in my Human Biology lab back in college resurfaced in my body, and I knew what I was seeing: the human form, ripped from all flesh.

The vampire surveyed himself in disbelief, trying to come to terms with what had happened. He was a walking anatomy model, a cross-sected corpse that nonetheless was still living. Another monstrous body stumbled into view, its front side scorched as well as peeled, and they took to confirming their worst beliefs.

My mother tugged on my clothes. Clothes? How did I still have clothes when we'd just managed to peel the flesh off of four of the world's most powerful vampires in a single blast?

Explanations would come later, when we weren't dead or prisoners.

I scanned the room as my mother helped me get the werewolf to his feet. "There's only four."

"Vlad smoked away a moment before the blast." She shook her head, pulling Tobias's arm over her shoulders. "I don't know if it hit him or he got away. Hurry!"

"Silver flame, mother… It's—"

"Later!" she yelled as we raced down the stone stairs, emerging at a terrible scene.

Igor and my father, both tied to a tree. The vampire, staked through both shoulders and at the hip, blood still smocked across his chin. My father, his head lulling to the side, half of his throat missing.

"You!"

Tobias stumbled as my mother dashed away, crossing to the vampire with terrible, ferocious speed. She drew the stake from Igor's stomach. The vampire cursed, calling out for a long dead saint.

"Please, do it!" he wept. "Kill me. I deserve death. I deserve *much worse.*"

"Mother! Mother, we don't have time." Even as I said it, I was shuffling as best I could with Tobias in tow. "We have to run."

Shrieks erupted in the house behind us, hideous bemoaning wails that soon took on depth and breadth.

"The vampires," my mom said, snapping her gaze. When she looked back at Igor, and at the stake in her hand, poised over his heart, it was as though she were discovering both fresh. "Redeem yourself!"

Igor swallowed his cries as best he could. "How?"

"You're going to die tonight, Igor Kharmarov. Either by me stabbing you now, or by you attacking your brood. Which will it be?"

He whimpered his response. "I can… only kill… one. Then… I die."

Without asking him to say more, Brünhild dropped the stake in her hand, took the other two stuck through Igor's shoulders by the heel of her hand, and yanked them out of him. Igor fell to the ground.

"One life then for the one you took from me. Survive, Igor, and I will hunt you to the ends of the earth and destroy you slowly."

No words from the broken man I'd once respected as a mentor, just a silent nod of acknowledgment. Her eyes fell then on my father. Brünhild lifted his head with the palm of her hand, pushing a kiss against his white lips. "*Siempre, mi amor. Siempre.*"

"Mr. Somfield!" And like that, she was all business again, all emotion gone from her face. "You'd best take your fur."

"Do you think I'd be in skin if I could bloody take my fur?" he snapped. "Something happened. I can't pull myself through."

Another bellow in a tongue my ear did not know, this one closer to the front door. They were coming. The walking corpses were on their way.

"Mother, the Ravens!"

Brünhild pointed to the trees in the distance. "Take him and go. Do not wait for me."

"What?" Was she serious? "But the Ravens will…"

"There is another pit around the back of the house where they threw Markus and the yellows assigned to help us out. Yan went there to rescue them. I will rendezvous and we will make for the cars together."

"What? How do you know that?"

She held up her hand pulling down her sleeve to show me some kind of electronic device strapped on her wrist. "The Ravens didn't even think to look. He was listening the whole time. Until we used the silver flame anyway. We had codes for different contingencies worked out in advance."

More rambunctious curses from voices dipped in pain, and their forms appeared in the doorway. "The bitch matron dies last and slowest. Kill the rest. Kill them all!"

My mother's eyes went wide as she pushed us in the right direction. "Go!"

They started for her before she even turned, their advance slowed by their condition. They didn't notice Igor's presence until he was on them, the snarling, yipping fight happening at a speed my eyes couldn't comprehend.

Tobias assumed his own feet and wrapped his hand in mine. Moments later, we were running as fast as we could. Weighed down with sorrow and the effects of silver flame, we drove forward, pushing beyond our limits, until Tobias doubled over, his hands on his knees.

"What's happening to me?" he said through gapping pants. "Why can't I take my fur?"

"Silver flame."

His wide eyes looked up. "The stuff your mum hit you with when she relinquished you?"

I nodded.

"I don't understand what that means."

"I don't either."

In the distance, wolves howled out. Under the light of the full moon, a pack was only as tame as the alpha demanded. An alpha could be reasoned with, as I'd experienced earlier, but if any other wolf encountered us, they'd be just as likely to attack us as not.

Taking to Tobias's side, I tried to pull him along faster. "We have to keep moving."

He jerked up when a second howl came. "We should ask them for help."

His feet trudged. One step. Two steps. Three...

"They won't help. I tried."

The moon above became playful, skipping its way across the night sky in and out of patchy clouds, making the forest a patchwork of blues and grays, blues and black, over and over again. Perhaps that is why I didn't see the cloud of smoke rushing toward us.

"Tobias!"

It came upon us like a swarm of wasps, encircling us, blinding us to direction. We swatted the air, trying to push away the assault, but every movement only made the blanket around us tighter.

"Geri!" Tobias shouted out. "Take my hand."

I reached but found only air. A moment later, the man I love called out for me, his voice trailing on the breeze, growing distant.

"Tobias!"

No answer came, even as I grew dizzy, turning in all directions, arms out, desperate. The taste of ash on my tongue, I coughed, until finally, everything rushed to a stop. I opened my eyes. My hands were empty, but on the ground a few feet away, hideous charred lips drew back in a sinister grin.

"Now, you are ours."

The monstrosity of bone and sinew bared his fangs. Nicolai? Mihnea? The others? I didn't know which Raven it was that seized me, and it didn't matter. They were all equally deadly.

"You did this to us!" he hissed. "Give me your blood, and undo it!"

"No, wait, I—"

Cries broke the air as fangs sunk deep into my neck. *My* cries, I realized, though the beating of my pulse in my ears dampened the sound. My hands planted on the monster's chest, trying to push him away, but I could feel my strength draining away, pouring into him, healing his temporary wounds. The thrum of my heart drowned out all other sounds, and soon, echoed in the vampire's chest.

He was killing me. Or at least, he'd bring me as close to death as he could. I knew the vampire wouldn't really let me die, he'd only make me wish I could.

Only when he'd had his fill did he pull back, grinning. Even as my eyesight blurred, I could see it: the transformation. Fresh flesh spun in webs over him, stitching together a plane of perfection silver flame had singed. His hair, mussed and scorched, became fine and flaxen. Those smiling lips rejuvenated, taking on a rosen glow even a vampire couldn't hope to achieve.

Almost like he wasn't a vampire at all.

If not for his hold on me, I may have fallen to the ground. The very next moment, I did. Not because the monster had let me go, but because he pushed me down.

One fang curled over his bottom lip as he paced my direction, even as I made a feeble attempt to back away, my elbow pushing me up.

His hand went to the button of his slacks. "You need to be taught your place, girl. You are ours now, and we will have you in any way and every way we desire."

"No." *Jesus, no.*

Any normative calm was gone. The vampire growled his words. *"Anything and everything,* you insolent, mortal cur."

No fucking way. I refused. I REFUSED. But what could I do? Even as my mind raced, routing a dozen solutions, finding ways to escape, nothing would work without a weapon or at the very least, my strength.

In a moment, he was on me, pulling at my clothing, robbing me of my security. The world began to fade. Trees, sky, ground... all narrowed into a pinprick of light. This was it. I'd failed. Not just Tobias, but everyone. Mina, Amy, Caleb and the slayers... even my mother.

Cold wind and icy snow pushed into my naked flesh as his renewing body covered mine, pushing my shoulders into the ground and pinning me at the hip with his weight. I closed my eyes, helpless, telling myself that I'd do no one any good as a martyr. This was not death. I would survive this, and in time, the vampire would pay. They all would.

I bit my lip and tried to think of anything else but this place and this moment. If I had stayed present, I may have heard it: the rustle of leaves, the approaching of a foe. My eyes shot open when the vampire's weight flew off me, and the sound of conflict filled the air.

A few feet away, my attacker, mounted by Igor Kharmarov, stared up at the wooden stake poised for his heart. Igor closed his eyes, his weapon arcing through the air, and plunged it into the vampire's chest.

The Raven didn't last another breath, his limbs going numb within a moment. Igor, chest pumping, looked down at the body in amazement before turning to me.

"Did he... Did he..."

I shook my head. No, he hadn't. I'd escaped. Barely. I was, however, injured. Broken ribs, dislocated shoulder, a neck still dripping blood. But it could have been worse. Far worse.

Igor staggered to his feet, and it was then that I saw it: his true age coming over him. He'd held the youthful face of a man in his late 30s for hundreds of years. Whatever magic that bound him to the survival of his progeny, however, began to take back what fate had given him. Igor himself realized it too, holding up his hand, watching the wrinkles appear before his eyes.

"I'm dying," he said. "As I should. My debt has gone unpaid for too long, and I killed your father."

He had, and I should have hated him for that. I should've killed him myself. I couldn't, though. I wouldn't.

"You couldn't help it," I gasped. "They starved you."

"I gave in to the monster." His black hair lost its shine, then its color. Sixty had come and gone, and his body drove onward, the vitality of his face fading, bags forming beneath his eyes. "Geri, you must kill them, all of them, or they will hunt you to the ends of the earth. They will hunt Tobias. They will… They w…"

A curdling noise cut off his words as the brown of his eyes turned black. Igor's feet gave out from under him. His ripped and tattered clothing coughed the dust he became as he hit the ground.

I didn't know how long I lay there, bleeding, naked, scared, alone. When movement caught in the corner of my eyes, all I knew was that it was him.

My wolf.

I knew he spoke, because I could see his lips move, but only a dull palate of sound pressed against my ear. Tobias's arms pushed under my frame, lifting me into his hold, carrying me through the forest.

"Igor…"

He stopped, looked down at me, mouthed "what?"

"Igor saved me. He's dead."

A swish of red, and suddenly I began to warm. A cloak. A hood's cloak. I turned my head, only vaguely aware of the pain in my neck, and saw Markus. I could feel Tobias's voice vibrate his chest. No, not his voice. He was growling. Growling because Markus was trying to pull me away.

"No!" I shook my head. "I stay with him. I'll *always* stay with him."

Markus mumbled something I couldn't make out. A cloth pressed into my neck. From where? I didn't know. It staunched the flow of blood, but even I could feel my lightheadedness. Perhaps the loss was already too much. Could I be dying? Could my world be fading from my sight? It didn't matter. I'd saved Tobias, and that's what I'd come to do.

"Geri?"

His hands pinched my chin, turning my face to his as my eyes fluttered closed.

"My hearing must be coming back." I smiled. "I heard you say my name. Say It again."

"Geri…"

Geri…

Geri…

THIRTY

AMY

Three quick taps on the door before Caleb's head peeked in.

"What's the point of knocking if you're not going to wait for me to say if you can come in or not? We might want to add etiquette lessons to the slayer training program."

Tall, dark, and presumptive smirked. "If I were here to see you, I'd have waited, but I'm here to see her." He pointed to the bundled baby in my arms.

As if Mina understood she had a gentleman caller, her tiny little blue eyes opened, scanning the room, finding the arrival. I swear, that child was already smitten with her Uncle Caleb. He was going to spoil her rotten.

"You seem to have taken to being an auntie pretty well." He settled down on the bed beside me, reaching up to stroke the billowy puff of red hair on the baby's head. "I thought you said you wanted nothing to do with babies."

"I don't. But Mina isn't a baby. She's… like a little kitten."

"She's half-werewolf."

"Fine, puppy then. My point is, she doesn't scream and shout and act like the world is ending because of a wet nappy or anything. She's special. And I like her just fine."

Who was I kidding? I loved the little thing. We all did. Hell, even the hoods who saw her in the courtyard when we'd taken a walk earlier went gaga over her, and according to Markus, most of them were so high-and-mightiest, they questioned the reverence of saints.

"At least tell me you're here because you have news. Did they finally say Geri and Tobias could have guests?"

The sparkle in his eyes dulled as his hand and eyes dropped away. "No, they're both still isolated from the others at the top of the tower. No one's allowed up there except Brünhild and Petunia. Even Markus says he's embargoed."

Damn it. It had been two days since they'd come back from Spain, since the horrific word that the mission to kill the Ravens failed. Well, wasn't totally successful, anyway. Three had been whacked, I'd heard from Yan. The Grand Matron managed to take out two during the escape, and Igor Kharmarov had given his life to destroy another. That left three, one of them being the Big Bad Daddy Vamp, Vlad Tepeş. As sad as that was, worse news came later: Geri's dad had been killed during the mission. Officially, Pietro had been exiled at the time of his death, so he wouldn't be allotted any memorial. Which, IMHO, was sucky on the hoods' part. I mean, damn. But unofficially, his death painted a gray cloth over everything and everyone, most of all Brünhild, who'd left the compound soon after getting back to Triberg, and hadn't been seen by anyone since.

Mina grunted, her little lips puckering and drawing me from my reverie. "Looks like someone is hungry again. I swear, at the rate this child eats, she should be the size of a sewer rat by next week. I better make up some more formula."

But before I could get three steps to the door, Caleb swooped her out of my arms. "I got her. You get some rest. It's late."

"It's only 1 AM."

"And you're still a huey," he said. "All good little girl and boy humans should be tucked up in their beds by now."

"I'm not good. Or little. And if there's any word from Geri, I want to know."

"I promise, if anything comes before morning, I'll let you know. Get some shut-eye. The others and I will be on Mina duty through the night." He shifted the baby from the cradle of his arms to his shoulder, giving her a little bounce. "We'll count on you to handle the day shift again."

"In that case, I think I'll grab a few hours then. You guys might sleep during the day, but this little one doesn't seem to give a damn that she's supposed to be nocturnal." I extended my arms over my head, inverting my steepled fingers and feeling a beautiful stretch down the sides of my midframe. "Thanks, Buffy. Sometimes you don't totally suck."

"That might be the sweetest thing you've ever said to me, Barbie."

Little Mina's eyes caught mine as the slayer turned away. I'd blame being tired for why the shut off key in my brain didn't turn in time.

"You'd be such a good daddy."

Caleb froze. Turned his head halfway back toward me. Turned it back toward the door.

And left.

THIRTY-ONE

GERI

His scent filled my senses. My hand reached for his, which was stroking my cheek. "Tobias..."

Slowly, the world came back into focus.

I opened my eyes to see beauty. My love, my wolf, my mate, smiling down at me. He'd grown a full beard, which, combined with his usual mess of shoulder-length hair, made him look like a lumberjack who'd escaped a Pacific rainforest, but I didn't care. I'd take him bald or wild, just as long as I had *him.*

I reached up, tracing my finger over the significant beardage. "Hi there."

His eyes closed as he huffed out his relief, his forehead falling to mine. "Bloody hell. I thought I lost you. I thought you'd never wake up."

"I rescued you," I said, like that was the perfect counterargument to being comatose. "I came for you."

He grinned as he pulled back. "Yes, you did. You total badass, you did."

But with consciousness came memory, and the realization of the cost for his delivery.

"My father..."

His smile dissolved. "I'm sorry, Geri."

Panic struck my heart. "Markus? My mother?"

"They're okay. Mourning, but alive."

"And the Ravens?"

He shied away his eyes. "Your mother killed two. Igor a third. Three, they presume, fled."

I pushed myself up by the elbows, ready to jump to my feet, but stopped when I realized I was in a bed.

With Tobias.

I sat up, observing the space. No doubts about where we were. The carved wooden bed frame, the dark velvet bed curtains, the large oval window that opened out to the view of the valley below.

"This is the Grand Matron's suite. This is my mother's bedroom." I turned to Tobias. "And you're here."

The lupine blushed, pushing himself off the bed. He adjusted the bathrobe tied around him as he took to his feet. "I swear, nothing happened. I've been in my wolf most of the time, just as soon as I was able to do it again. I only took on my skin when I noticed you were waking up."

"No, it's fine. I—"

I threw off the blanket and discovered I was dressed in a white nightgown that ran down to my feet and its sleeves to my wrists. A bandage covered a patch of skin where I suspected an IV line had dripped a steady bead into my veins.

"How long was I out?"

"Three days under. But that was only because Petunia induced it. She wanted to make sure the worst of your injuries healed before you could argue with her. I guess everyone thought you'd fight your way back to Spain if they'd woken you any sooner. Good thing hoods heal with superhuman speed. It's still red and swollen, but the skin has closed over."

"Three days? I've been out for three days. And you've just sat there the whole time? How did you get up here? Wolves aren't allowed in Schloss Wolfsretter without being bound in silver. To have a wolf in the tower, though? I'm surprised the council didn't riot."

He smirked. "I'm sure they weren't happy, but no one's going to attack the decisions of a grieving widow."

His words trickled off just as my sadness rose anew. My dad. If he hadn't bound me in blood-claimed silver, I would have been with him when he'd been captured. Maybe I could have fought off the Ravens with him. Maybe things would have been different. Maybe... so many things. Nothing could be done when a page was turned. The story stopped for no one. His was just another name of the fallen now, joining Igor, Inga, Kara, and Alex.

Alex!

I leaped up. "Oh my god, Mina!"

Tobias's mighty arms caught me as I tried to fly by. "Hold up now, explain yourself."

"Mina, the baby," I said, pulling back. "She's... It's complicated. But she's mine. *Ours.* I mean, she's pack. Our pack. She's our..."

"Daughter?" The wolf grinned, pulling me into his embrace. "Is that the word you're looking for, Geri? Our *daughter?*"

I swallowed, even though his scent was making me dizzy. "I'm her godmother, and, well, her mother died, so I just assumed... We can talk about our kids... I mean, if you ever wanted to have kids, but with Mina, given the situation..."

Tobias brought his hand between us, pushing a finger against my lips. "*Shhhh.*" A moment later, his mouth replaced the hold as the werewolf brushed a kiss across my lips. "I felt the quickening, too. I knew she was ours. And if that is as a daughter, then we have a daughter."

The girly parts of me wanted to swoon, but the hood parts of me were doggedly practical and wanton of formality. "We're not even mates yet. Not in any real way. Seems like things are out of order: first kids, then becoming a couple? Assuming, that is, that you meant what you said in Istanbul. And that whatever happened to you these last weeks hasn't changed...."

"You and I will have a proper munch later and discuss what happened. But let's get this set right from the get-go." Another brush of his lips, this one softer, and yet, more intense, chased by another. "I love you, and I have every intention of mating you just as soon as we can make the arrangements."

"I love you, too..." Another visit of his mouth on mine, and I was positively melting in his arms. "...but is that even possible?" I threaded my fingers through his mangy hair, pulling him closer, deepening the connection. "Can we be together, that way?"

He bit my lip before pulling back to examine me. "There's only one way to find out."

His hands gathered the nightgown as he inched higher, building a delicious anxiety with every bit of territory he claimed.

I licked my lips. "There's no rush, Tobias. After what you've been through... If you need time to..."

"I don't need a moment more to know how I feel about you." He paused midway, kissed the rise of my hip bone, dotted the planes of my stomach with his lips, the white folds of cloth filling his hands. "And if there's one thing I've learned, it's not to waste time doing what's proper, when you could spend your time doing what's *possible.* I love you. I am *in love* with you, and I don't want to lose you again. I want you as my mate, my friend, my lover, my companion. I want you as the mother of my pups."

Logical and rational Geri tried one more hostile takeover of my brain. "They'll never understand. Not the hoods, not the wolves, no one. Our lives will be..."

He paused, looking up from where his two fingers had hooked around the top of... when had someone put underwear on me?

"Hard as hades?" he said, pulling down the cotton band with aching deliberateness. "Yeah, I know. But at least at the end of the night, I'll be with you."

No panic, no pain, no sudden anxiety. Nothing but peace. His eyes stayed locked on mine as he pulled himself over me, and as his mouth closed in on mine, so did his heart.

He was my wolf.

And I was his.

EPILOGUE

I bit my lip, sensing in every fiber of my being what even the patch of sky I could see through the windows above had yet to acknowledge. Dawn was coming.

She was not.

Tobias pulled me under his wing, squeezing my shoulder. "It's not about you or Mina. She's grieving the loss of her mate. She needs time and space to do it however she needs to."

The old familiar streak of guilt ran the length of me. *Kara.* Tobias's words weren't derived from assumption, but from experience. But he was a wolf; my mother was not. My mother was the Grand Matron, head of the House of Red, and one of the toughest women ever to walk the earth.

"I just wish she'd let us know she's okay," I said. "I mean, I know she's not *okay,* but that she's safe. We don't even know where she is. And if something happens to her…"

"*Shhhh…*" The lupine pressed a kiss against my forehead. The shift of my body made Mina flinch in her sleep. Tobias kept his voice low, trying not to wake her. "Nothing will happen to Brünhild Kline. And now that I'm back, nothing's going to happen to her daughter either." He ghosted a finger down Mina's cheek. "Or *our* daughter."

A rush of warmth filled me. *Our daughter.* Tobias and I had had one of the quickest progressions to establishing a family in history. Here we were, parents, despite the fact that we'd only slept together for the first time two nights ago.

And the second time the same night.

The fifth through eighth times, in the past twenty-four hours.

His lips claimed mine for a kiss that was all too brief. Barely had we touched when the doors leading to the courtyard of the inner bailey opened and Rebecca shuffled in.

The grin on her face brought a blush to my cheeks. "Are you ready, or do you want me to watch the baby and tell everyone to wait so you can sneak a quickie in the armory?"

Tobias cleared his throat and pulled back his focus to the ground. How curious that a wolf was so prudish when it came to a little raucous humor.

Then again, he *was* English.

"No, Becky," I said. "The sunrise waits for no one. Thank you, we're coming now."

The castellan winked and left us alone, leaving the door open in her wake.

Formal affairs required formal attire. My cloak materialized into existence with my beckoning, falling over my shoulders and covering me down to my calves. I shifted Mina so I could cradle her with one arm and offered my free one to Tobias. "Bailey or call Becky back and head to the armory?"

"Stuck in a room surrounded by silver weapons?" Dousing the residue of his blush, he hooked his arm with mine. "Even with you, I'd pass. I'm still chuffed they let me stay without chains. But… maybe you could wear *that*—" His free hand motioned vaguely at my cloak. "to bed? Like, *just* that?"

"Tobias Somfield, are you telling me you have a hood fantasy?"

"No, Geri Kline, I'm telling you I have a little red riding hood fantasy. And I promise, I *will* try to eat you."

Shivers went down my spine. If not for the pink beginning to tickle the horizon, I'd hand Mina off that very second.

Though we wouldn't get as far as the armory.

⁂

Markus planted balled-up fists on his hips, personifying the concerns of the slayers, hoods, two asenaics and two hueys paying witnesses. "Anytime *please,* or we're going to miss the sunrise."

"Okay, okay!"

Despite the nip of the early winter air, all the research Yan and Markus had done in the few remaining slayer texts suggested the ceremony required the child to be naked. Amy took up the blankets as Caleb unwrapped our illustrian burrito, holding them at the ready to swaddle Mina the second the ceremony concluded.

"We gather today to welcome a new beam of light."

An uncertain Caleb Helsing was an amusing sight. The slayer clutched the index card in his hand as though it was his lifeline as he managed a newly-awoken-and-more-than-a-little-confused-about-being-naked baby in the crook of his other arm. Caleb's shiver didn't go unnoticed, and it wasn't because of the cold. Even Amy had noted the very thing I was coming to suspect: as the only awoken male slayer and the only one with substantial defensive training and world experience, he had defaulted to being the leader of his kind, and that prospect scared him to hell.

"As the sun falls upon her now," he continued, the formality sounding like a foreign tongue on his lips, "may it fill her with life, lighting a path of righteousness and honor, and into a world where she is known as…"

Cue: my line.

"Mina Alexandria Petra Kline," I said. "May the sun blaze her name into the hearts of her people, and light the path of righteousness—"

"Yeah, righteousness and honor," Caleb mumbled over my words, cutting me off. "I already said that part."

He pivoted, just as the sun peeked over the eastern ridge of the sky. Its amber light seemed to be drawn to her, the beam setting my daughter aglow, the baby golden in Caleb's arms.

"Mina Alexandria Petra Kline, you have been accepted by the sun. All here bear witness, a slayer is born."

"A slayer is born!" said every single slayer in the compound, standing in witness.

As the clapping and cheering arose, Amy's patience snapped. She swooped in, coating Mina in folds of wool.

Tobias waited until the clamor had died away before clearing his throat, calling the crowd's attention. "And as alpha of the..." He turned to me. "What pack are we?"

A good question. Packs were generally identified by the region or town in which they lived. But where did Tobias and I live? We didn't have a home anymore, and who knew when we would again.

But we did have *something* in common that bonded us together, something which very few others could claim.

"I believe that's the asenaic pack, dear."

He grinned. "Bloody right we are." A swooping kiss sealed the deal. He turned back to the crowd. "As alpha of the asenaic pack, I claim Mina Alexandria Petra Kline as one of my pups, under my protection and the protection of all my packlings."

"So just you and Geri then?" Caleb couldn't help a little sarcasm.

I turned my face up to Tobias. "For now."

I mean, we were having lots and lots of sex, so things could happen...

The subtext of my comment didn't fly over Amy's head. "Finally! Okay, now that you've gotten over that hurdle, I need to educate you on advanced practices."

A growl rumbled through the chest of the alpha beside me.

The blonde huey threw her hands up in surrender. "Fine. But if a copy of the *Kama Sutra* should show up in Geri's library someday, you'd thank me for it."

Before I could frame up a witty response, my words died in the air. The rays of the sun took on shape, an object that seemed distant in one blink solidified the next into meaning. My mother landed in the midst of the bailey without pretext.

"Mom, I—"

Tobias pulled me back, shaking his head. Had he sensed something I hadn't, or did he just want me to give her space?

Brünhild took in the scene through a confused expression. "What is this?"

"A slayer naming ceremony," I said. "We're doing it as best we can figure out from research. Mina has just been recognized as a member of the slayer community."

"And as a member of my pack," Tobias said. "She's slayer and wolf, and we'll all protect her."

"An illustrian will need such protection," my mother concurred. She looked at the baby in Amy's arms. "And who will protect the protectors?"

Tobias and I exchanged a look. "We'll watch out for each other. Wherever the slayers go, Tobias and I will follow. We'll… We'll make our pack where they settle their pride."

"A *pride* of slayers?" Caleb asked. "Is that what we're calling it now?"

Teiko called out, "You're sure as hell not calling us a harem anymore!"

"I like pride," the normally silent Sergei nodded. "Like lions. We are fierce."

My mother, I could tell, did not agree, but with the slayers at least she understood where her opinions should cease. "Very well. But your *pride* and your pack will not be alone. This child is the daughter of my daughter, by cause if not blood. By this, she is also hood."

"But, mother," I pulled away from Tobias. "I'm relinquished. How could Mina be—"

"I decree it so," she said, cutting me off. "You are restored. From this day forward, all asenaics are recognized members of their houses." Her eyes went to Tobias. "Do you understand my words? *All* of them."

I turned back to my alpha. "Tobias, I think she means you."

The werewolf blanched. "Me? I ain't no bloody hood, and don't you dare go…"

"*All* asenaics, Mr. Somfield," Brünhild cut in. "Remember, our laws still dictate that a wolf and a hood may not join in union. I can acknowledge those with documented bloodlines, even if they're not wholly hood, but my power to change the laws are more limited, especially in current circumstances." My mother grinned as she walked past him, patting his shoulder. "Welcome to the House of Red, *son*."

"Reclaim my father!"

My sudden outburst arrested Brünhild in her tracks. She turned her head back over her shoulder part way. "That I could, Gerwalta, but Pietro's crime was not his heritage. As I said, my ability to change laws is…"

"But does anyone know why you exiled him?" I cut in. As matron, she didn't have to explain her actions unless she chose to, and knowing how much my mom loved my dad, she never would have spoken a word against him like that.

The corners of her mouth lifted. "Disobedience is the only notation I made on the decree."

"Then say it was a lie," I said. "Say you did it because you discovered he was an asenaic. Grandfather him into your decree. Don't let him die in shame."

"It will not bring him back in any way. It does not change what happened."

"If it is written down, then it does." I crossed to my mother, laying a hand on her arm. "Gerwalta Faust *wasn't* Gerwalta Faust when she died. She was Gerwalta Baron. She was a wife, a mother, an alpha's mate: things I never understood until I saw her grave marker. The writing made her truth real. Don't doom my father to dying a criminal when the only thing he did wrong was try to help his daughter."

I didn't know if I asked too much. My mother's leadership had been so strained already, but if I didn't try to move her on this, the cost would be so much more than her matronship. She stood to lose the honor she felt in being my father's wife.

Slowly, the Grand Matron nodded. "Very well, I hereby pardon Pietro Kline of his crimes and restore him as one of the righteous."

"Thank you, mother." Later, I'd talk to Rebecca about arranging a formal remembrance, but one step at a time. "You know he's worthy of it."

"I know he is," she agreed, "but am I worthy of being a martyr's wife? I... I do not think so."

As she turned, crestfallen, and made her way into the castle, I prayed that was a question neither Tobias or I would ever have to ask ourselves.

RIGHTEOUS

RED CHRONICLES BOOK 5

SCHLOSS WOLFSRETTER

1687

They were almost there. A few more steps and they'd be safe.

Andreas held Gerwalta up on the stairs as another labor pain struck. Or it could have been that he held on for his own support. Wolves didn't favor heights, and Gerwalta fought with all her strength to keep the silver stairs near the top of the tower solid beneath their feet.

"Walta?"

"I... will... not... let... us..." The contraction gripped her, her womb constricting, driving fire into her core, crushing her determination. Gerwalta doubled, pushing her hands out in front of her, catching the edge of the steps.

Andreas breathed a sigh of relief as the stone landing held them up. He stopped on the stair above, turned, blanched. He was so gaunt, so unnaturally wane and weary in a way she'd never seen any other lupine. Gerwalta never knew a werewolf had the capacity to become beleaguered, but that had been before she and Andreas had been forced to flee, running the length of God's green earth just to keep their own lives. He pulled Gerwalta to her feet. Or tried, for the pain still held her captive, and even her strong will proved incapable of resistance.

"Walta, please," he begged, gently coaxing her. "Just a little more, my love. We're almost safe."

Her words were more cries now than voice. "I'm coming."

The wolf found a shade of white lighter still and assumed it, even as he whisked them into the first room he came to: the Matron's bedchamber.

"I am sorry, Walta. This will hurt."

Without warning, her mate heaved her up, pulling her into his arms, and carried her to her mother's bed, even as the bolt of anguish gripped her once more.

"Andreas!" She squeezed shut her eyes against the suffering, seeing red without the benefit of sight.

"A moment more, love. And... we are here."

Gerwalta took what relief she could from the cool sheets beneath her thin, torn frock. Andreas knelt at her side, pushing pillows under her back. "I don't know what comfort I can offer but ask it of me and I'll do it."

"Just promise me that you'll do whatever it takes to make sure our child survives."

The lupine wrapped her frail hand in his, drawing Gerwalta's white-knuckled fingers to his lips. "I swear to it."

The tender moment passed as the ache of labor lit her body on fire. Gerwalta dropped Andreas's hand, planted her palms flat against the bed, threw her head back, and screamed.

"The baby is coming."

These words were not from either of them, but from a third who had just entered the room.

Andreas teetered on the edge of shifting. "If you try to hurt her now, Matron…"

"Cease your fight, cursed wolf!" Gunda Faust snapped, even as she closed the door behind her and worked to move what heavy items the room offered in front of it. "Do you think I fought beside you below just to kill you up here? Now, step aside, unless you know how to birth a baby. Guard the door. The others will make their way here soon enough."

The emotions cycled through the lupine's face. Anger, spite, frustration, and finally, acceptance. "If another member of your clan enters this room, I'll tear

them limb from limb, but please, save my pup."

ONE

"But you must see that the best way forward is together. If we don't ally as one nation against the Dracule, then…

Mother's words cut off as hysterical curses poured over the phone line. She passed a look around the Council Table in the Schloss's former throne room. Instead of other matrons, however, only Markus and I were seated there to lend silent sympathy.

With a huff, Brünhild continued, "I would remind you, Yanyu, that regardless of half of the Council's retreat from Germany, I am still Grand Matron. Think of that twice before threatening me again."

Once upon a time, I would have believed in fairies before the idea that someone would try to out-bitch Brünhild Kline. Now, our allies in the Hood Houses had fallen away like flies. The first to bolt: no surprise. My mother had barely finished decreeing that all asenaics were now recognized members of the community when the House of White's matron showed Schloss Wolfsretter her backside. The Greens followed in her wake fast enough to share a cab to the airport, taking away the Atlantic seaboard on both sides of the ocean as safe zones. God willing, Vlad didn't decide to head to NYC because the Big Apple was now a Brünhild-Kline-can-suck-it designated zone.

Pressing her forehead against a balled-up fist, Mother waited for the other voice to a give her an opening, and then...

"Of course, I understand that what I've done has gone against centuries of tradition by treating werewolves as our equals, but we both knew the day was coming. When the most powerful and vicious vampire in the history of creation declares war, you find your allies where allies are to be had. What better time to move us forward? And if you'd just listen to reason, then..."

The other side went dead.

Markus's words wrapped around the lollipop he sucked. "Guess the House of Orange is a no?"

Brünhild closed her eyes. "Indeed." She cycled a breath, then turned to me. "Where does that leave us?"

I examined my notes. "So... pretty much all of Asia and the UK have told us to go to hell. Casa de Amarillo is still with us, though that's probably more because they're the ones who helped hide the asenaic line all these years. And... the blues are confirmed, so if the vampires invade either the Fjords or Minnesota, we're golden."

My attempt at comedy was a drop of water on a hot stove. Pushing off my sarcasm, I set aside my notebook. "It's a fifty-fifty split, but *Mädchen*, that's more than enough. There are only three ravens left, and Vlad's just one vampire against, what, a few hundred of us?"

"He's not just one vampire, Gerwalta. He is the vampire. And with Igor Karmarov dead, he's now the paterfamilias of his bloodline. It's a position many still revere." Brünhild let out a long exhale as she planted her hands on an old, ornately carved chair and leaned into a stretch. "And I fear he may be targeting the other asenaics now."

Behind us, sitting on the side of the room, Tobias coughed a laugh.

The Matron spun. "Something amusing you, Mr. Kline?"

"Mr. Kline? My name is..." Tobias's face screwed up. "No. No dice. You are not going to stick me with my mate's family name just because you decided it's convenient if I'm one of you now."

I crossed my arms. "And what's wrong with taking the wife's name? Or did you assume that because you're a man, I'd take yours automatically?"

"Why wouldn't you want to be a Somfield? It's a great name. Geri Somfield. Gerwalta Somfield. Mrs. Somfield. Rolls off the tongue like sugar now, don't it?"

He stood, walking… no, stalking toward me. Tobias raised his hand to trace a finger down the bridge of my nose and over my lips. "Don't you want to be my missus, Mrs. Somfield?"

Behind me, my mother chocked on her annoyance. "You two must learn quickly there is more to marriage than constant sex."

"I'm a slow learner, Matron." The corner of Tobias's mouth pulled up. Given only a few days, he'd learned all the best ways to piss my mother off. "But I do hear it also comes with tax benefits in your country. Maybe even a green card."

The chair legs groaned as Brünhild pushed them into the table. "I hope that at least you're using protection. This is hardly the time to knock up my daughter."

And she, it turned out, had learned how to push all of Tobias's buttons.

"You're very crass for an old autocrat, you know that? What I was laughing at," he said, like that part of the conversation had been on pause and all he had to do was hit play again, "what made me so giddy, is that I guess it should come as no surprise that there are other asenaics you know about and we don't. You were covering up quite a few things, it seems."

"Yes, I was." Brünhild crossed her arms. "If I didn't, old school traditionalists like Zhu and Smyth of the House of Green would have hunted them down and killed them long ago. So, you're welcome, Tobias, for my efforts which kept you and your family alive all these years."

I sucked in a breath through my teeth as I turned to watch the crater of that verbal shell form.

Tobias's hands balled into fists. "Last I looked, I'm the only one left standing. Dracule killed my brother and my da. And, oh, my mate, too, so… tell me again why I should thank you?"

My mother's eyes tracked to the floor, a gesture anyone who didn't know Brünhild Kline the way I did would take for shame. Only, my mother didn't do shame. There was only ever one reason for the matron to not look you in the eye.

"Mother, you're hiding something."

She didn't deny it. Why would she? It was her privilege as the unquestioned—well, until recently unquestioned—leader of our people to keep whatever secrets she wanted.

I stepped forward. "Fess up."

"What do you think she can tell you, Geri?" Tobias said. "That my father and brother aren't dead? I buried them myself. That Kara isn't dead? You were there for that funeral with me."

An image of Tobias's first mate's grave in the Paradise cemetery flashed in my mind.

"No, Tobias, I would not tell you they're alive, nor deny that I was aware of the possible target they represented for the Dracule as soon as the Ravens were set free and began to regain influence and power. But there is at least one other member of your bloodline who carries the asenaic traits, and more than the fear that Vlad may come for her, I fear that she may welcome it."

My mate was the picture of a man who stood on the edge of a precipice with the balance about to be knocked from his feet. "I don't have sisters, aunts… Both my grandmothers are dead. Who possibly could there still be?"

Brünhild lifted heavy eyes. "Your mother."

TWO

Between us Mina fussed, refusing to go down easy for the day.

"I just can't believe it," Tobias mumbled for perhaps the fifth time since we'd settled into bed. "My mom died when I was eight. I *felt* it happen. You can lie about some things, but you can't fake a preternatural sensation like that."

"You believe what my mother said then?" I continued to tap Mina gently on the bum as she lay on her stomach, a trick we'd learned to coax her to sleep.

"Your mother might hide more secrets than Houdini, but I've never heard anyone accuse her of openly lying."

"Unless you include lying by omission." Just because my mother and I were on speaking terms again didn't mean we were going to suddenly become the Brady Bunch. Deciding not to kill my mate started us down a path towards reconciliation, but the pain of years couldn't be sewn up in just a few weeks.

"Not going to pretend that it's good, love. She should have told you about your true heritage. Spun my head around to find out I was part hood. Finding out your 'true blood' mother is half slayer over your asenaic father's corpse? Must have burned like a bitch." Tobias grimaced. "No pun intended."

"Whatever. We can't change the past. We just have to move forward with knowing what we do now." I pulled back my hand as Mina finally nodded off. "So, when do we go?"

"Go?" His brow furrowed.

"To England," I said as I stood, gently scooping up the baby to put in her bassinet.

Tobias, god bless him, rolled on to his feet and headed for the windows. "Why would we go to England? I'm not homesick, if that's what you're thinking."

I blinked away my surprise. "You don't want to see your mom?"

"Why would I? The green hood who told Brunhild about her said she appears to be living there of her own free will. If that's true, it means she left her family willingly. Or at the very least, she chose not to come back to us. Good riddance, I say."

"You don't honestly believe that's true, do you?" I said as I pulled off my sweater. Schloss Wolfsretter made for a good postcard, but at the end of the day (or the beginning of one, as the case might be), it was still a medieval castle and drafty as hell. "Why would a mother leave her kids and husband? And don't tell me it's for the city life. London ain't all Mary Poppins and Paddington Bear. Plus, it doesn't explain why you felt her die. We have to go. You need to know the truth."

Tobias unbuckled his belt. "I don't need anything but my mate and my pack. Dumplings wouldn't hurt, though. God, Geri, when's the last time we had dumplings? Is there a Thai restaurant in Freiberg?"

"Your mom is alive, Vlad the Impaler wants us dead, and you're thinking about dumplings?"

"What? I'd share." He moseyed my direction as his pants fell to the floor.

Things I knew about werewolves: they feared heights, hated perfume, could tell a fake diamond from a real one without a microscope...

And they never wore underwear.

My jaw dropped at the sight of the luscious figure before me. The time with Vlad had taxed his body, but muscle had begun to rebuild over hardcore sexy sinew. The cuts and bruises had mostly healed, leaving behind virgin flesh in a body that was anything but.

He pulled closer. "See in the sunrise with a root, pet?"

I guffawed. "We just got Mina to sleep." My head jerked in the bassinet's direction in the adjoining alcove.

He twirled a lock of my black hair around a long finger. "We've learned to be quiet enough." I felt his smile as he pushed a kiss beneath my ear. "Usually."

"Fine." I let my shirt drop to the floor and wrapped my arms around his neck. "Root me, Mr. Kline."

The whole "who takes whose name" question? Yeah, it hadn't been settled.

The warning in his eyes promised delicious payback. "Why, Mrs. Somfield, you devil, you. I ought to take you over my knee and..."

I pressed my lips to his before he could finish his sentence.

The next night, I was trying to score in a completely different way. In a sparring match, with a slayer, in Schloss Wolfsretter's underground training gym.

"Damn it, stop moving so fast."

Caleb ducked as my swing went wide, sending me spinning. "Think Vlad's going to slow down for you? Vampires are lightning-fast, and a slayer's only chance is to be just as quick, if not quicker."

"I'm not a slayer!" Another punch flew over his shoulder as he lunged to the left. "Let… me… hit… you…" I said, each word punctuated by another attempt to land a blow.

"We're not dating anymore." Caleb's flattened hand drove hard into my shoulder, sending me staggering back. "I'm not going to pull my punches. Vlad won't."

Barely grabbing my balance back in time, I froze. "Wait, you mean the entire time we were together and training, you let me hit you?"

"I mean, I was trying to get in your pants and I…"

A drop of silver grafted beneath my shirt heeded my unspoken command, racing up my shoulder, down my arm, and into my hand. Caleb flew as the metal powered my silver solarium—or "lunarium" as we'd been calling it—and blasted him to the floor.

"Da fuh…." Chest working, hands bracing for the impact, Caleb turned up wide eyes on me. "What the hell, Geri?"

"What?" I played innocent, letting my hands drop out of attack position. "You said solaria don't hurt slayers, and a lunarium is a really weak solarium."

"I said they don't burn, not don't hurt. And that was, like, point-blank range. Seriously uncool." He peeled off his singed shirt to examine the damage. Reddened skin looked more like a probable bruise in the early stages than a burn. "You know what? If Vlad comes for you, I'd lead with one of those babies as big as you can make it, then slice off his head while he's trying to catch his breath. That might actually work."

I offered out a hand to help him up. "Are you sure that I just shouldn't let him try to get in my pants? Seems like that could work, too."

Caleb grunted as he regained his footing. "Geri, I didn't mean anything. I was trying to make you mad enough to hurt me."

"Big check mark on that one." I examined the training tape I'd wrapped my hands in when we started, watching it fall to the ground, blackened and ashy. "Word to the classically untrained: anger is dangerous in battle. When you fight angry, you're not focused on what defeats the enemy. You're focused on what makes you feel you're getting your way, and that's a guaranteed way to lose."

His hand swung as he pointed at the floor. "Did you or did you not just land me on my ass because you were angry?"

I shook my head. "Like you said, it was point-blank range, and you were giving me an open window to strike. In actual battle…"

"Save it. I've heard all your hood-wolf blah blah blah…"

He turned, grabbing his bottle of water from a table on the side of the room. I tried to ignore the slim but solid definition of his torso as he lifted it and tipped it, pulling the muscles of his arms to attention. Memories of my mouth exploring that plane of flesh resurfaced. If I hadn't already been flush from sparring, I'd light up red on the spot. Oh, I had no intention of doing anything, but there was a little bit of jealousy on the edges of my consciousness for the woman that would eventually land that in her bed each morning.

"Slayers and vampires don't think like hoods and wolves," he continued after he'd had his fill. "We're all about the passion, the heat of the moment. You fight fire with fire if you don't want to get burned. Or, in our case, a deadly allergy to sunlight with balls of magical solar energy."

"I guess that's why you all sleep around so much? All that passion and being in the heat of the moment?"

Caleb feigned confusion.

He was a terrible actor.

"Come on, Amy tells me what goes on in that cottage. She said it's practically a reality show."

He crossed his arms over his chest and clicked his tongue. "Excuse them for celebrating their liberation by engaging in a little adult recreation."

I couldn't tell from his tone if I'd actually insulted him or if his flirtatious nature was just acting up. "Maybe I confused habit for nature where you're concerned. Just because hoods have such a stick up our asses—or, I mean, don't—about sex doesn't mean I'm dissing slayers for being the complete opposite. I'm just… you know, kinda curious."

"No, it's not that, it's just…" Goofy smile and all, Caleb leaned back into a wall. "I mean, this isn't awkward for you? Talking about those kinds of things with me?"

"I'm not asking for intimate details, just a view from forty thousand feet. Besides, I'm mated now. Anything we discuss about the physical is just academic." It so wasn't about the fact that since discovering that I was one-quarter slayer, I wondered if that was why I'd been such a… rebellious teenager, going against tradition to date not one, but two werewolves. "Come on, Caleb, I'm not stupid.

I got the player vibe off you the first time we met. I know you got around before we were together."

"Yeah, well… I did, but I'm not going to do that anymore."

I leaned in, putting a hand on his arm. "Performance problems?"

"What?" A gurgle erupted from his throat as he gagged on the suggestion. "No. No! It's just…" Caleb pushed off the wall, running a hand through his glistening ebony hair. "It was different when I thought I was the last slayer, you know? Because I could sleep around and it didn't really matter. Not like I was trying to knock anyone up. Just the opposite, in fact, because I figured if I was the last and under so much pressure, any kid I had would get it just as hard. Then I met you and you weren't one of my kind—at least, I didn't know you were part slayer then—and my perspective changed. For the first time, I thought there might be a chance. And now…"

I read the writing of his unspoken words. "Now that you know there are others, you feel like you have some kind of holy mission."

"I mean, I wouldn't call it 'holy.' I'm not exactly saintly over here. But, yeah, I feel like it's time to grow up, settle down, raise a family. Be a man and all. Be the leader my people need."

My hand moved up to his shoulder, squeezing. "You're going to be awesome, and I get what you're saying. But I don't think that means you need to give up on love. You deserve that."

He shrugged. "Who knows, maybe I'll find it." Caleb's eyes glistened when they met mine. "Why couldn't it have been with you?"

Awkward personified walked into the room with a marching band in tow. The slayer's hand lifted, cupping my cheek. The pull between us… it was a delicious nostalgia, like an old favorite song that had suddenly come on the radio and made you want to relive the first time you'd heard it. He started to lean in, his eyes drawing closed, and I….

Tobias bounded through the door, chest heaving, eyes wide.

Although nothing had happened (other than my heart going full rabbit mode), Caleb put distance between us, whisking across the room in a flash, leaving me alone to face my flustered mate. A curl of anxiety blossomed in my belly. Had he seen us? I'd been a moment from putting my hand up, pushing Caleb away. *Turning the radio off.* Surely after all we'd been through, Tobias wouldn't think I'd betray him?

Remember who you were named after, my inner voice heckled.

I do, I told it. *But I also remember who I* am.

The werewolf walked over to me, eyes downcast. "Okay, we're going."

I put my hands over Tobias's chest when he stepped into me, giving my heart space to slow its roll. "Going where?"

"England, of course. We're going to London."

My anxiety began to ebb. "We'll make arrangements and leave tomorrow."

On the far side of the training room, Caleb motioned himself through fighting forms, as though he'd been doing that the whole time, completely uninterested in my presence and existence. Maybe he was a better actor than I thought. "Does that mean I can sing the song now?"

We both turned on the slayer with blank expressions. "Song?" I asked.

Caleb put up his index fingers and stuck them to the sides of his head. "Aaaa-oooo, Werewolves of London. Aaaa-oooooo!"

Beneath my fingertips, I felt the muscles in Tobias's chest ripple. "That song is a bloody insult to lupines."

"Dude, chill, I didn't know. It's not like I was trying to…" Caleb cleared his throat and clapped his hands. "Great, London. Why are you going to London?"

"To rescue my mother before any vampires find her."

Caleb stumbled back. "I thought your parents were dead."

"So did we," I said over my shoulder before turning back to my mate. "What changed your mind? I thought you decided she'd left you and you were going to do the same to her?"

Tobias shook his head. "Even if she is scum for leaving, that doesn't mean she deserves to be a blood bag for some youth-worshipping vampire to suck."

The slayer's ears perked up. "Vampires?"

Annoyance curled my features. "I'm sorry, when did you become a part of this conversation?"

"I think it was the moment you mentioned vampires," Caleb said. "If you're up against the undead, I'm going with you."

Tobias dropped away to flash his teeth. "Stay out of this, lightning boy. It's a family issue."

Caleb shook his head and crossed his arms over his chest. "Not if it involves vampires, it's not. Look, I don't like the fact that I've become the de facto Don Corleone of the slayer world either, but if you've got an opportunity for me to make someone an offer they can't refuse, I'm not going to let that slip by."

"Oh, well, since you want to come along for the right reasons…" Tobias held his hand up and flashed me a look that was so New Jersey it was hard to believe he wasn't American. It practically screamed, 'What is it with this guy? The size of the pair on him!'

Time to use my one-fourth slayer, some-complex-math-formula-portioned-sized wolf, and the bred-in practicality of a Red Hood to be the peacemaker.

"Tobias, honey, I think it actually makes sense if Caleb came with us."

My mate spun on me. "Why? The two of us can handle anything that happens just fine."

"But if we run into an unfriendly vampire, it *would* be an opportunity for him to gain a reputation."

I could feel the pulses of anger under Tobias's skin. "But it's my mother."

"But our daughter is half-slayer, and you and I can't help that part of her. Mina needs them to be strong enough when the time comes to help her understand her own power. Caleb being their superhero action star is a big part of that, and this is a way for him to gain clout."

He turned his eyes on me. "Is that what I just saw when I came in? Caleb helping you understand your slayer... parts?"

Damn, Tobias *had* seen us. A thousand curses screamed in my mind, but my heart overpowered them all. I knew where my heart lay. Leaning in, I planted a kiss against his lips, curled my hands around his back, and focused all my energy on making Tobias feel the strength of my emotions. When I pulled away, the big bad wolf was howling at the moon from the waist down.

I flicked his nose. "I don't need anybody but you to help me understand my... parts."

Coughing, Caleb threw a towel over his shoulder as he walked by us. "I'll let you guys have the room, then. Just remember to wipe everything down when you're done. And don't be too long. We're sending the others away at dawn."

Tobias waited until we were alone to reach up and stroke my cheek. "You wanted me to come and tell you when Mina woke up."

I sucked in my bottom lip as the heat between us plunged into ice-cold water. "Do we really—"

He pushed an index finger to my lips. "We've been over this. The closer Mina is to us, the more danger she's in. At least until we off the Ravens."

"But who can protect her better than us? And how will I be able to keep focused not knowing she's okay? And what if Amy can't get her to sleep or she comes down with a cold or..."

Tobias pushed a finger against my lips, stopping me. "You and I have to agree on this now, love: Mina will *never* be safe. The most we can do is kill anyone who tries to harm her. That's why we're sending her with the slayers to Chicago. They'll protect her while we do away with the enemies she already has. And if the slayers don't take care of her..." He gave me a one-shouldered shrug. "... then they really *will* be extinct."

THREE

Six cars sent exhaust swirling through the early winter air. Most of the slayers had already found a seat, but one passenger had a special place in the second car from the front of the queue. One with a five-point harness and facing the rear.

I kissed Mina's head for the three dozenth time. Every time I puckered my lips and exaggerated the sound, she smiled… and my heart broke a little more.

"Okay, Geri, let me have a turn." Tobias swooped in and took the baby from Amy's arms, lifting her in the air. "Come, little pup. Give me enough honey to tide me over."

Amy pulled up alongside me as Tobias twirled away. "You'd think he got a custom-made suit the way he's slipped into being a dad so easily."

My heart leaped because, apparently, I was a totally sappy wife. "It's just because he's a wolf," I said. "They're really family-oriented. Even if Mina was someone else's pup and just a packling, he'd—"

"Geri, stop it."

I turned to my friend. "Stop what?"

"This." Amy vaguely motioned to the air between Tobias and me. "You're in love. You're married. Or… well, whatever, close enough. You got a good man who cannon balled into becoming a father overnight, and more importantly, he finally made my little red into a woman. It wasn't just dumb luck or instinct or whatever else you want to write it off as. It's because you deserve to be happy."

"I know, but all this coming together like it did…" Sandcastles fell with the smallest push of water. "What if this is the best it gets and it's all downhill from here?"

Amy threw an arm over my shoulders. "I'll take downhill from this any day over uphill from my love life."

The slayers sitting in the courtyard turned and rushed to their rock star as Caleb walked into their midst. Amy's feet stayed planted, but her imagination put on its sneakers.

My head jerked in Caleb's direction. "*That* looks like your kind of hill. Why don't you climb it and lay out a picnic? Maybe if you put out a good spread and…"

"You're killing my metaphor and turning it ugly, Kline," Amy said, cutting me off.

But she wasn't getting off that easy. I nudged the huey with my shoulder. "There's chemistry between you two. I picked up on it."

"Doesn't matter, I'm not taking your sloppy seconds. Besides, Caleb is effectively my boss now, both like, supernaturally and corporately."

Okay, fine. I wouldn't try to play matchmaker. But was it so bad I wanted an excuse for my best friend to stay in the supe world as long as possible? "Your parents must have been thrilled to hear you got a good job at WWL."

I didn't know what Caleb's motivation had been in drafting Amy as his human interloper, if he'd done it to give her an excuse to stay in our world, or as a roundabout way for him to stay in mine. I didn't even know if slayers needed day people the way hoods once had, a huey face to interact with the diurnal world while the supes were all tucked into their wee little beds. Regardless, it was decided that the slayers, having only recently been liberated from captivity and with varying levels of experience with the world outside the Ravens compound, could benefit from having a "mortal liaison." Officially, she'd be Caleb's executive assistant when he returned to Chicago to take over WWL. Unofficially, she'd be an ambassador from the huey world to the supernatural one, helping a rediscovered species find its place once more.

Amy shrugged. "Mom was more perplexed than anything. Wanted to know why I was going to stay in Chicago when I could come back home and work at her store selling overpriced dresses to underdressed women. And Dad… has yet to share any comment."

Tobias swooped back then, redelivering Mina into Amy's arms. "Now remember, she likes you to tap her backside when she's trying to fall asleep. Nappies are fine but only cloth; none of that paper-plastic thing you Americans fancy. The pack outside Chicago is already building up a breast milk supply; they'll drive it down to you as soon as you arrive and every few days after that. Mina's going to want more than milk soon, though. Huey baby food is fine but try mixing in a bit of ground lamb or goat when you get a chance. Raw, *always* raw. That top tooth is about to break through, and she'll be wanting fresh meat."

Amy's jaw dropped. "*Fresh* meat? Tobias, she's only six weeks old."

"Lupine babies mature faster than your lots'," he said. "A wolf knows how to wolf it down, we say."

Amy's smile was short-lived. "You guys are going to be safe, right? I thought that was the whole point of staying here in Triberg. 'The one place Vlad wouldn't dare attack,' you said. Now you three think you can go all James Bond and stuff and just pull some kind of high-level extraction without anyone chasing you?"

"It's not an extraction," Tobias rebuffed. "My mum is an asenaic, but she might not even know that. We're just going to give her a head's up and offer her protection with us if she wants it. Honestly, I'm hoping she doesn't."

Amy nodded. "You know, Tobias, if I had known that you had so many mommy issues, you and I could have bonded much sooner."

"I don't have mommy issues." The werewolf huffed himself into calm.

"No, he's not me." I opened my arms, pulling in my friend. "Come on, Popowitz, one for the road. Take care of all them slayers until Caleb gets back."

Cradling Mina in one arm, Amy put her head on my shoulder. "Keep him with you as long as you like. Or just dump him in the Thames and let him get nice and soaked so his powers don't work. Seriously, he's letting this *solari* thing go to his head. Thinks he's the slayer messiah."

"More like Moses, except instead of Egypt, he delivered his people out of Turkey." I backed away enough to trace a finger down my Mina's cheek. "Seriously, though, watch out for her teeth. She could take off your pinky if you're not careful once that tooth drops."

Amy laughed, but her gaiety flatlined when my face remained stoic. "Seriously, there were like, at least five other subleases when you showed up in Chicago. You had to rent mine?"

"What can I say, Amy?" I reached out and squeezed her shoulder. "You needed me."

What became abundantly clear in a period of about two hours was that, of the three of us, I was the only one not prone to seasickness.

Caleb's head hit the door post, his eyes cast wide across the water to the land undulating beyond. "I've been watching the same spot on the shore for about ten minutes now, Geri. It's not working. I still feel like I'm going to hurl. Any other tricks?"

"Not unless this boat has some secret stash of ginger candies. I can't believe you guys. This is the Thames, not class three rapids. It's one of the gentlest rivers there is." I stroked Tobias's hair as his head lay across my lap. "What's your excuse? Don't tell me wolves don't like water. Every male in Cody's pack is an avid fisherman to the point of domestic unrest."

"No, not a wolf thing, just a Tobias thing." He clutched his stomach. "You sure we can't just ring the doorbell? You know, the one by the door on the front of the house, by the door, on land?"

"We're on too many hit lists these days to wander into supe territory blind. And besides, just because I sense a wolf, it doesn't mean it's your mom." Not to mention, the wolf I did sense had an energy that was hard to hold on to. Like she was blinking in and out of existence. I wanted to size up the subject with my eyes before plunging forward with my hopes.

I set down the binoculars, freeing my non-nursing hand as my naked eyes swept for movement. Shuttered windows had refused to yield clarification. Tobias and I discussed using my ability to lure wolves to me, but that could cause more problems than it'd solve if the person inside was, in fact, *not* Margaret Somfield.

I shivered as I examined the petite, wood-sided houses standing in a tightly packed row, each with just enough yard between for a grown man to pass. Sneeze, and your neighbor could toss you a box of tissues without leaving their house. It certainly wasn't a place I'd have suspected of hiding forest folk like a lupine. It was so crowded, so restricted.

"Something about this feels off," I said, shaking my head. "It's much too urban for a werewolf to be comfortable for too long."

And it must be able to sense me by now. Why wasn't it investigating my presence? Was it hiding? Or as Markus had suggested, was it possible I was "reading wolf," and indetectable in the way our kinds usually were to each other?

"Okay, that's enough of this." Without warning, Caleb assumed the captain's chair—as much as there was one on the wee fishing boat we'd rented for the night—and turned on the motor. "We're going in and getting this over with."

"Caleb!" Immediately, the craft skipped over choppy waters. Both my hands shot out, grabbing the sides of the boat like that could stop our advance. "What are you doing?"

"Life is short, Geri, and I have to pee, so we're going to go knock on the door. There's no point to this charade. I don't sense any vampires; you only sense one wolf. Everything checks out."

The dock built along the shore had been intended for a boat with a little more height than ours, but that didn't stop Caleb from making the leap like it was a stepping stool. He might be a total flirt and a male, but he wasn't exactly without impressive badass bona fides. Tobias and I followed in his wake as soon as the boat got a little closer. Three steps on, I put my hand up, forcing a halt.

Tobias circled in front of me, ever the protective mate. "What is it?"

I shook my head, unsure. "Do you smell... muscle cream?"

The werewolf took in a thorough sample of the air. "Yeah, and... butterscotch."

"It's a toffee, actually."

All three of us assumed attack forms as a figure emerged from an open door on the backside of the house. He must have been waiting there, watching us for who knew how long. Close up, I could see that the windows weren't impenetrable because of curtains like I'd assumed; they were severely tinted. No, not just tinted... they were outfitted with Athenian glass, the same thing WWL used on their lobby back in Chicago.

Why would a werewolf be staying in a house made day safe for vampires?

A question for another time. For the moment, that wasn't my biggest concern. The man with a long-barreled pistol in his hand was. *Idiot,* my mother screamed inside my head. *You were so hung up on if there'd be supes, you never stopped to consider the possibility that there may be hueys.*

He appeared to be in his late fifties or early sixties, a stack of wrinkles across his forehead and his high hairline the start of some serious salt and pepper. His raised eyebrows suggested surprise, but quickly those eyes beneath them narrowed. Diagnosing, examining. He wasn't scared of us, that was for sure, but he wasn't exactly happy to find us there, either.

I'd put a twenty on a hopeful wager that he had silver bullets in that weapon.

Caleb cleared his throat and assumed a relaxed posture. "Good evening, sir. I was wondering if I might use your loo? That *is* what you call it here, right? The loo?"

The tan corduroys and college prof sweater combo didn't match the gruff, barking voice. "Do you mean the pisser?"

Caleb clapped his hands. "Yes, the pisser. Aptly named. Do you mind if I...?"

With a grimace, the huey hooked a thumb in the direction of the house. "Second door on the right through there."

"Great, thanks!"

Within seconds, I was yelling at air as the slayer disappeared inside the house. Typical, thinking with his dick. (Even if it wasn't sex but a full bladder channeling its will through his manhood.)

The huey flicked up the barrel of the gun. "Now, care to illuminate me on what you lot were doing on the Thames at 1 AM, piddling just off our dock?"

Tobias stood before me, a wall of muscle growling lowly, bearing his teeth and sparing few words. "Step out of the way, old man."

"Men." I rolled my eyes. Seemed I would have to be the diplomat. "Sorry for the weird entry, sir, but I promise, we aren't here to cause trouble. We're looking for a woman named Margaret Somfield. Someone told us she might be here."

The old man chewed on that. "Might," he said in a tone that made it hard for me to know if he was giving an answer or asking a question.

Whatever. I'd take the chance. "Would it be okay if we spoke with her? This is her..." I pointed vaguely in my mate's direction. "A relative of hers."

Doubt clouded his expression in the form of squinting eyes and a lifted chin. "Relatives who arrive on a fishing trawler in the middle of the night?" He lifted the gun, aiming for my chest. "What kind of fool you take me for, stupid girl?"

That was the straw that broke the werewolf's back.

Tobias lunged forward, grabbing Mr. Huey by the collar. "I'd take you for a dead fool if you don't step out of the way." His voice, like his will, could barely hold back the animal within. "Insult my mate again and I'll..."

The gun fell to the ground, and when it did, my world exploded.

"Tobias!"

Pain blossomed under my ribs like a meat hook had run me through, tied to a cord that was being yanked forward. Sucking in a breath through clenched teeth, I doubled over. I pushed a hand into my stomach, against the pain, expecting the warmth of my own blood.

Only, when I pulled my hand back, there was nothing but clean flesh.

"Geri?"

Tobias was at my side in a moment, bracing me. Mr. Huey lay in a heap; no doubt he'd been dropped or thrown when I'd cried out. The pile o' mundane twitched, telling me he hadn't been killed in the act.

"What's going on?"

I stood up straight, slowly, cautiously, looking around like the answer to that was over by a stubby little garden gnome. Tobias's fingers wrapped around mine as he pressed the back of my hand into his palm. "I thought he shot me, but..."

Another wave crashed. My world went red as my eyelids slammed shut, my jaw seizing and my breath flying from my lungs. This time, I gave in to the pull, finding that the pain ebbed with movement. Another step, and I felt the wringing of my kidney slacken. A third, and air refilled my lungs.

"Love, words." Tobias framed me, his arms on my hips, ready to catch me if I faltered.

I took another step, then another, each one bringing more and more comfort. "Something is... compelling me... forward."

His furrowed brow lifted as understanding came into his eyes. "It's like when you do your thing, pushing and pulling wolves, only with hoods."

It made sense, somehow. "You never said she could do that."

"How would I know?" Tobias let me go, lifting his gaze and his voice toward the house. "Stop or I swear by God, I will rend you limb from limb, mother or no."

"Mother?" The huey pushed himself up on the palms of his hand. "You mean you're one of those little brats she left years ago?"

Tobias ignored him, thank god, turning to me instead. "Do it back to her, Geri. Make her come out here and face me."

"But, Tobias..."

Spit flew from his mouth, his voice a cawing bark. "Do it."

I'd never seen Tobias so mad. Not when Kara had died. Not when Vlad Tepeş had captured him. Not even when I'd silvered him in the WWL lobby what seemed like a lifetime ago.

With a single nod, I dug in my feet and focused on the shewolf's energy, digging in my mental daggers and pulling on the tether that connected us. The sensations morphed from anguish into curiosity, then panic, each shade darkening as my pain lightened. She fought me, she begged me, but my hood nature fed on the wolf's weaknesses. The more she resisted, the stronger I became.

And then… she was just *there.*

Gray hair, wild and long, fanned out, its tendrils curling down over her shoulders and past her hips. She wore her years in her curves and her suffering in the bags beneath her eyes. The skin over her neck was a patchwork of pink and gray. They'd fed on her. Not recently, but consistently. Jesus, how many times would a vampire need to fang a lupine to inflict so much permanent damage?

Her tired, bloodshot eyes rose slowly as I released the pressure, sending me stumbling back. I reached for Tobias, but he paid me no mind. His universe was the haggard form standing in the garden.

"Mum?"

She gave a slow nod, looking out through memory and regret. "Yes, Tobias, it's me. And you never should have come here."

FOUR

CALEB

As I closed the bathroom door behind me, I was sure Tobias and Geri were as confused as a chicken in an igloo. But what was I supposed to do? Obviously, there was no vampire threat. The huey threw us for a loop, but one old human wasn't anything either of them couldn't handle. Which meant, the only thing to really confront in this situation was an awkward mother-son reunion. Family politics was nothing unique to supes or hueys, however, and I wasn't about to be a witness to that kind of drama.

Besides, I really, really had to go.

Zipper. Toilet.

Ahhh…

Was that pine tree scent? Good choice.

And then, I heard Geri cry out. Shit, couldn't the two of them go one damn place without getting into trouble? I zipped up like my life depended on it and bolted.

At the back door, I found myself looking at the backside of a woman, her hair gray and straggly, her figure… not bad for an old chick, frankly. But when she turned her head, giving me a view of her neck, my whole body shuddered. Underneath a dimpled chin: fang scars. A minefield of them. Mrs. Robinson had not only been fed on, she'd been milked routinely.

My eyes were the sole part of my body in motion as I dragged my gaze over her. "Margaret Anabel Somfield?"

She spun. "Maggie. Just Maggie. And who the bloody hell are you?"

Well, I could see where Tobias got his elegant conversation skills. "My name is Caleb. I'm a friend of your son's. Well, I mean, not *friend* really. More like, a colleague? I mean, he kinda stole my girlfriend, but we're keeping things professional, and…"

With every roll further into rambleland, her eyebrow arched higher to the sky.

I cleared my throat. "Point being, I'm here to help Tobias and Geri. Bad people are looking for … *people* like you. He's come to offer to take you somewhere safe."

"She *is* safe here," the old huey said, taking a step forward and drawing his hands from his pockets. "And if she's not now, that will because of you lot showing up, won't it?"

In an instant, my solarium sparked, its light pushing long shadows behind the huey, making a giant shadow puppet on the cottage wall behind him. I didn't even think about if he'd understand what was going on or if he was aware of the supe world. Who cared? He squared his stance and tightened his jaw. Huey Union Jack here had his hackles up, and I wasn't about to be taken by surprise.

"Now, son, put that away before someone gets hurt."

"Don't think so." If I fucked up my first mission as the Solari, there was no way I was ever going to last as head of my people.

Only, as usual, Geri refused to just let anyone else have a moment. "Come on, Caleb. He's just a guy. Besides, I'm not sensing any fear from Maggie. I don't think she's in any danger."

"Then why does her neck look like it's been used as a motorcross track?" I said. "Do you know how much feeding it would take for scars like that to stay on a supe?"

A storm blew across Maggie's expression. She dropped all her nerves and summoned her inner bitch, marching between me and the dude. "Yes, I do. And

Horace here saved me from the ones who were doing it, so pop off, muffin, and click down your Zippo before I eat your throat slowly. I'm not going anywhere."

"Jesus, Mary, and Joseph, Helsing, put that thing away before you blow up the house and everyone in it." Tobias ate up the in-between, drawing equal with his mother without dropping the scowl. He drew her attention, forcing her to turn. "You don't want a safe escort out of England, *Mum*? Fine, I don't give a fang. But I'll be damned if I'm going to leave here without an explanation of just how you faked your death and why you never came back."

Maggie scowled, talking through her teeth. "You want to know what happened? Fine, I'll tell you, but after you'll leave and never come back again."

Horace turned toward the house. "Guess I'll put on the kettle." His eyes narrowed on me as he moved inside. "My hob works fine, slayer, so you can put out your fire."

I'd give it to Somfield, he had the patience of a saint. No one spoke more than utilitarian words as the others settled around a table. Well, "settled" was perhaps an overstatement. Resigned, maybe? On one end of Horace's eight-seater was Maggie. On the other, the much-confused son. Geri flanked him while the huey attended to servicing drinks. I stayed on my feet, my solarium a hidden marble in my hand. Something about this wasn't adding up. According to the werewolf, his mom had died when he was a kid. She'd have to be scum to have kept her continued existence hidden out of some vengeance. I didn't like Tobias, but that was personal. He wasn't a bad guy. So why was his own mother treating him like some unwanted pest? It's like she *wanted* him to leave, but why?

That, combined with the fact that Horace the Huey and Maggie knew I was a slayer and weren't shocked to see one of my kind alive, concerned me. Outside of the hoods at Schloss Wolfsretter, who knew we were alive and kicking?

Only the Dracule.

The gravity of the room pivoted from Tobias to Geri as Maggie diverted her attention to the woman sitting beside her son.

"You're the hood I sensed."

Geri's face screwed up in the cutest way. "I'm Gerwalta Kline. *Geri*."

"Kline?" Maggie repeated, tasting the name on her palate. "Isn't that the same as the Grand Matron?"

"She's my mother. But I'm also, well..."

Tobias's hand skimmed over Geri's as he laced their fingers together. "Mum, Geri is my mate."

The shewolf went bug-eyed. "You mated the…" Maggie choked on her words. "You're with a…"

Tobias pulled forward in his chair, his arms stretching across the table. "Geri's not just a hood. She's an asenaic. Like… Like us."

"So you know." Maggie's mouth snapped closed, her jaw working, before she finally said, "And so is she. Well… I've heard the rumors that the Reds were keeping a secret."

"Speaking of secrets…" Tobias tapped the table. "Where in the hell have you been all my life?"

Maggie's arms crisscrossed her chest. "I suppose you want me to tell you some glorious story about how I really wanted to come back to you but couldn't, don't you? Well, you and your hinny can pick right on up and tow along now if that's what you're after, because you won't get it."

Tobias chewed on the words, his clenched teeth absorbing the brunt of his anger. "So you wanted to leave your family behind, did you?"

"Dinna say that now, did I?" She lashed her head to the side to stare at the wall. "No mother wolf with love in her heart would *ever* want to leave her *bairn*."

"So just me da, then?" Like the fog rolling over the river outside, Tobias's Geordie accent seemed to thicken. "Did he know that when you mated? That you were capable of deserting your family without consequences?"

Maggie gestured to her throat. "Does *this* look like there wasn't consequences?"

Horace tried to lay hands over Maggie's shoulders, but she managed to shoot to her feet just in time to avoid him. My eyebrows knitted. There was something here I wasn't seeing, and the curl of anxiety tinkling in my gut told me things weren't going to move the direction we needed them to if we just left the wolves to their pissing match.

I leaned forward. "Tobias, let her say her piece. We can't stay here all night for you two to Dr. Freud it up in here."

Maggie took that as an invitation, or just continued like I'd never spoke. It was difficult to say.

"No, your da didn't know what I was when we mated. But when I became pregnant with your brother, I felt he should know. He still loved me, he said, but how could he not? He'd mated me. *Bonded* to me. I could tell him I was the Grand Matron herself and his heart would have remained true. But as time went on, his *behavior* changed. He could love the part of me that was a wolf, and hate the part that was a hood, all at the same time. It was hard to know which I'd get each day: loving alpha or big bad wolf. Then one night, I had to go into Newcastle to fetch some things. That's where the vampires found me."

Even at the mention, the solarium in my hand pulsed.

"I thought nothing of it, of course," Maggie continued. "I'd seen vampires before, and we just mutually ignored each other. Not that day. Those ones seemed to know I was different and that made them curious. They managed to feed off me, but I got away somehow. And when I came back home, the Big Bad Wolf was waiting. Your da refused to believe me, insisted I'd wanted to be with them, that they wouldn't have been able to feed off a true werewolf unless she wanted it. He… He exiled me from the pack."

Lie detection wasn't in the slayer play deck, but I'd been to enough bars in the world to recognize the tells. Maggie might have the others fooled, but she was either straight up lying, or dancing around the truth. Only curiosity about what she hoped to achieve kept my tongue tied.

The incredulity etched into Tobias's face began to soften, however. Maybe that was the point. "But what that would have done to him… To the pack…"

"You and your brother were so young, you probably couldn't tell between the sensation of an exile and a death. Your father told me if I ever tried to return to corrupt his boys, he'd make me pay."

Geri, her hand in Tobias's, spoke with unusual softness. "But how did you survive without a pack?"

Maggie huffed a smirk. "Those Newcastle vamps? They started collecting wolves to keep me from going moonmad. Tracked me down a few days later when I was too distraught to resist. Then for years, others would join. But those poor wolves who they captured…" Maggie shook her head, her eyes falling to the table. "I can't explain why, but one by one, they'd go moonmad, and I wouldn't. Because I'm an asenaic? Possibly, but who can say? I didn't know what that truly meant, only that it was shameful, that the enemy's blood ran through my veins. The vamps fed off me for years, only letting me off my chains during a full moon. Over time, I lost the ability to heal. The scars," she ran a hand over her marred skin, "are the result. I thought I was in a Hell I'd never escape, but it couldn't be worse. And then one day, *she* showed up."

Tobias asked the obvious question, even as Horace slipped from the room. The others were too distracted to notice or care, but I listened as a drawer in the kitchen opened, then to Horace rummaging around in it, and the sound of the drawer closing again.

Maggie looked up. "Her name was Cynthia, and she called herself a Raven."

The air in the room grew heavy. I lectured my muscles to unclench. "Oh, she did, did she?"

Maggie's head snapped in my direction. "She heard about the Newcastle clutch that had been drinking werewolves, and that my blood wasn't just life-giving, it was intoxicating. That must have been years after they captured me, and that's when the real torture started."

The truth hit me like a ton of cinder blocks. "You were the source."

That brought everyone's attention to me.

Geri leaned forward. "What are you talking about? The source of what?"

Hesitation plagued me, but what the hell? Inga was dead. Tepeş was out in the open. The slayers he'd held, saved. WWL was under my control, or at least would be soon. No point in keeping a dead woman's secret when… what was the saying? The truth would set you free?

"Inga told me that Cynthia was in Chicago at Vlad's direction, trying to develop a serum that would undo werewolf mating bonds. But the active ingredient in the formula was something we were never able to trace, and one Cynthia and her conspirators were getting more and more stressed about as their supplies dwindled. That's why they were in Chicago working in Igor's lab. Inga feigned cooperation to keep an eye on their progress."

"But Igor told me his work was about restoring the slayer lines," Geri said.

I nodded. "*His* was, but he'd agreed to give Cynthia workspace at Inga's request. Keep your friends close and so on, you know? She hoped to find out who Asenaic Zero was, since every one of them Igor and Inga knew of was accounted for."

Tobias glared at his mother. "So they took da, only turned out he wasn't an asenaic. Then they came for Nick, but he wasn't an old, used-up alpha, weakened by his own loose mating bond to an exiled shewolf. Nick fought back, and they killed him. Still got what they needed, though. Enough blood to get a temp solution. But then they needed to test what they'd developed, so they took my mate."

Maggie's face screwed up, focusing on Geri. "The Dracule seized a hood?"

His throat bobbed as Tobias swallowed down his pain. "No, they took Kara."

Horace rejoined the table just in time to steeple his hands. "Are you trying to tell me you've had another mate besides this hood, boyo?"

Geri nodded permission to Tobias to answer. Like she would have been insulted or something.

"Yes, that's the truth of it."

The huey huffed into his hands. "I thought lupines only ever have one mate. Some of them with time may be able to have *relations* again, but a mate is forever."

The way Maggie hid her face at the term 'relations' told me Horace knew that from personal experience and that it hadn't exactly been something she was happy about. Whether that was contemporary to its happening or only in the rearview, I couldn't say. Tobias's mom may be a werewolf, but she was also a victim of kidnapping and torture, and if this asshat had taken advantage of that…

I didn't care if he was a huey or a supe; I'd flambé his ass.

"Not Tobias," Geri said. "He's claimed me as his mate. And I, him. We think it might be possible only because we're both asenaics."

"I see." Horace stood up, pulled down the hem of his sweater, and left the room once more. What in the hell was that guy up to?

Maggie was half out of her chair when Geri reached across the table and laid a hand over the shewolf's.

"Maggie, stop. I don't know what's going on here, but I can see enough to know he doesn't have your best interest in mind," she said. Good to know I wasn't the only one picking up on the passive aggressive vibe. "He's going to use your vulnerability right now to exploit you and make you stay here. You can't. Danger is coming."

"Think you understand what's going on, do you?" The shewolf reclaimed her acidic glower and snapped her hand free. "You have *no* idea."

No sooner had the words dropped than a wave of nausea rolled through me. In a moment, I crossed the room, pushed a suddenly-standing Geri and Maggie behind me, and placed myself between them and the front of the house.

Tobias shot to his feet. "Helsing, what the f—"

"Vampire. Front door."

No doorbell, which meant either it was attempting to get in unnoticed, or he could sense a slayer's presence, and who knew what effect that had on his plans?

"Can you tell who?" Geri peeked around him, her little hands settling on my forearm.

"I don't get unique buzzes off different vamps, Geri. It's more of a universal 'check engine' warning."

Horace appeared in the hall before us the moment the doorbell *did* ring. Apparently, vamps were kind enough to observe proper social etiquette when they showed up to attack you. He gave Maggie a smug glare before marching forward.

I rolled my eyes, even as I left the others behind to trail him. "Two more steps, *jefe*, and I'll make you a Baked Alaska."

The old man thumbed his chin at me before turning for the door, but before he could even lay a hand on the handle, it flew open.

The huey lunged.

My solarium flew.

But that wasn't what killed Horace, or what made his head take a permanent departure from his body.

As the headless form dropped away, its departed capital asset rolling until it bumped into a potted fern, I saw the source of my preternatural heebie-jeebies.

A barrel-chested vamp held a bloody sword, the medieval instrument a sharp contrast to the finely tailored black suit the perp wore. Armani, if I wasn't mistaken. An SUV as sleek as his ebony hair stood in the driveway outside and was probably worth more than the house in which we stood.

The vamp lowered the sword and stepped over the body, his eyes falling to the second burning ball of solar death in my hand. Immediately, his weapon fell to the ground and he held up his hands.

"Peace, slayer, I'm not here for you."

"So it's just coincidence that you happened to show up the same time we did?" I asked. "Right."

"There is no such thing as coincidence." God, his Italian accent was thick. "But if any of you want to still be alive two minutes from now, you'll get into my car immediately. The Dracule are coming."

FIVE

Someday, eventually, I'd think how cut it was that Tobias and I both tried to protect each other as a dark-haired vampire decapitated a huey and stepped over the still-jerking corpse. For the moment, we looked like fools, bumping into each other to become the other's human(ish) shield.

Caleb took position as sentry, the power of the sun balanced on his hand. The vampire, a man who defined tall, dark, and handsome with broad shoulders, ebony locks, and intelligent gray eyes, dropped his sword and pressed flat palms to the air, as though the danger we felt was from any weapon he might hold.

"I will not harm you." Never before had an Italian accent more suited a person, and something about it was so... familiar. "We are both enemies of the Dracule and of the Ravens in particular."

"Just because we both are gunning for Vlad doesn't mean we're simpatico," Caleb said. "Name and explanations now or I toast you."

The vampire didn't move as his gaze swept over Tobias and me. "My name is Massimo Bruneli. Igor Karmarov asked me to assist you if I became aware that the Dracule were coming for you. Two days ago, I learned they were. This huey is... *was* a Dracule initiate here to spring a trap."

Tobias squared his shoulders. "Igor couldn't have asked you to do anything. He's dead."

Massimo prickled. "Obviously, the request was made before his recent demise. The Dracule who call my city home understand that I expect loyalty to Republic before bloodline. They oblige, and those who do not are *permanently* removed. But Tepeş now claims he has the blood of an illustrian at his disposal, meaning the protection they may have felt before knowing he could do nothing to destroy them is gone."

"But he doesn't have the blood of an illustrian. He—"

The vampire jerked his hand up, cutting me off. "Do not tell me anything more, Hood, or you'll burden me with unwanted knowledge."

"*Your* city?" Caleb asked. "You don't mean—"

Massimo's chin tilted perceptively. "I watch over the Republic of Venice for Dark Ones and assure that they behave in such a way as not to endanger our community as a whole."

Venice? Suddenly, my memory snapped. Then I did, literally, and pointed an accusing finger. "You're the one I saw in my vision after Mina was born! The one Vlad asked for sanctuary."

Beside me, my mate's gaze narrowed. "Was he? I... I can't remember much about that time. I was so drugged up, so beaten."

No need for further inquisition. Massimo volunteered the truth. "It was me, Mr. Somfield. I was in the very room where you were being held."

"And you let him just stay a prisoner?" Caleb cocked back his arm. "Well, that settles that. Goodbye, Massimo."

"No, wait!" The vamp fell to his knees, throwing up his hands. "Bloodlines are not the only thing dictating the court's actions. Politics plays a bigger role than sanguine considerations. To have allied Venice with the Ravens would have been to declare the other republics enemies. Vlad does not respect much but he does honor nobility, at least where vampires are concerned. Fortunately, he yielded when I said no."

A quick look at me, a chance to read his expression, and I knew there was more to it than that. He wasn't lying, necessarily, but he wasn't telling the whole truth.

"To have allied..." Caleb trailed off. "Wait, *you're* the Doge?"

"Since 1687," Massimo acknowledged. "And until such time as I meet the sun, *a Dio piacendo*. The Eight Vampire Courts of Italy remain intact, though some in nothing more than name."

"That was around the same time Gerwalta Faust and Andreas Baron died," I said, more reflectively than anything.

"So you know your kind's history, *signora*." Massimo tipped an invisible hat in my direction as he stood.

"You knew Gerwalta Faust?"

"I considered seducing her." His face broadened into a grin. "Until it became clear Herr Baron would personally chew my arms off if I tried. It is my weakness. I've always had a thing for redheads."

Maggie, who had stayed silent, suddenly injected herself into the conversation. "So you stood by while the Ravens kidnapped and tortured my son, and now, I'm supposed to trust you with my escape?"

"I have a plane standing by at a private airstrip not far away," Massimo said. "We should all leave England as soon as possible. I assume you're bound for Germany, back to Schloss Wolfsretter?"

I nodded. "It's the only place we think Vlad wouldn't dare to attack. It holds too many advantages for us. Maggie will be safe there."

"The hell I will!" the woman in question retorted. "How can a wolf be safe in the hall of the enemy?"

Tobias summoned his inner asshat. "Good news, Mother: the Grand Matron declared that all asenaics are now righteous hoods. You're now an official wolfsretter," Tobias said, using the old German term. "Mazel tov."

Maggie blanched and looked as though she may argue before Tobias cut her off.

"We go to Triberg, at least until we figure out what to do next."

"Then I will assure you return there without harm." Massimo looked at Maggie. "If you wish to depart to Germany with your son, *signora,* I will assist you. I also extend you an invitation to my court in Venice, as I have no doubt the Dracule will be eager to reclaim you and my city is now safe from their tyranny. I can protect you where I failed to protect your son. Honestly, however, I believe you will be safer under the protection of the Red Matron."

Maggie rounded us with slow, haunted steps, her eyes fixed on the body whose only legacy to this moment would be the stain of blood he'd leave on the floor.

"Mum?"

The delicacy with which Tobias looked at his mother when I turned was a complete reversal from the attitude he'd spouted since we arrived.

Maggie looked away, her tough act softening around the edges. "I hoped if I was enough of a bitch, I could drive you away before Horace called them. I didn't want it to happen to you, what happened to me."

"Mum?" He stepped forward. "Mum, have you been..."

"Every day and every moment for years." Her hands raked over her scarred neck. "I've lived in fear that you would find me, and then, they'd do it to you."

Silence clung to the air, and only Massimo reasserting himself into the conversation snapped us all back to attention.

"I won't force any of you to leave with me," he said, pointing out the door to his vehicle, "but I suggest you do if you still wish to be breathing come dawn."

Just at that moment, our slayer clung to one of the dining room chairs for support. "Whoa…"

"Caleb?" He'd gone so suddenly pale. "Caleb, what's wrong?"

"Vampires." His knuckles bleached as he fisted his hands. "I've never felt so much energy. It has to be… I don't know, fifty? Sixty? A lot more than Istanbul or Spain."

Massimo had the gall to look smug, bowing and once again motioning us towards the door. The three of us exchanged one more look before hauling ass.

Could we trust Massimo Bruneli? I didn't know, but I did know that it was a lot easier to kill one vampire than sixty.

A BLOCK AWAY, a dozen vamps stood between us and the path forward.

"They knew there was a good chance a slayer was going to be with them," Caleb said. In the front passenger seat, he rolled up his sleeves. He wasn't wearing his usual designer garb, given the limited options of what Schloss Wolfsretter could provide, but old habits died hard and he apparently didn't want his clothes singed if he conjured up bigger solaria. "That's why they weren't right by the house, ready to strike. Why they used a huey as a watchdog. They wanted to make sure the trap was sprung before closing in."

"They promised Horace they'd take him into the crèche if he pulled off the operation." Sitting in the third row, Maggie's flat voice matched her distant expression. "He's been licking their boots for a decade trying to win a maker's bite. Bastard got what he bloody deserved."

"We are not all such hostile creatures, Mrs. Somfield," Massimo said.

Tobias, seated next to me, turned. "Mum, I'm not blaming you for what happened. Not in the least, but you're a werewolf. If it was just him and you there, why didn't you attack? Why didn't you escape?"

"That simple, is it now?" Her sudden caustic smile chilled me. "Where would I have gone?"

Any response was cut off by the engine growling, Massimo posturing to the horde that stood silent, waiting for us to move. "I can plow through them, but they will pursue. The fastest will catch us."

"How many of them you think qualify as the fastest?" Caleb asked.

"Hard to say. Full throttle speeds like I'll be able to do this time of night? Maybe one in ten. Then again, these are the Dracule, the strongest bloodline of my kind."

"But you forget, Mario, I'm a Helsing, the strongest bloodline of *my* kind."

"My name is *Massimo.*"

"I'll care if I survive." Caleb opened the door and shifted out of the seat. "Tell Amy I'll get to Chicago as soon as I can."

"Caleb?" I managed to grab his shoulder. "What are you doing?"

"Making sure you guys get out of here safe." His eyes twinkled as he winked at me. "Don't worry about me, Geri. I got this. Massimo, if I find out anything happened to them that's your fault, I'll personally come to the Venetian Court and engineer a bloody coup."

Massimo coughed a laugh. "Definitely a Helsing."

And just like that, my hand was empty as the car door slammed.

"Caleb!" I lunged, jerked back, lunged again. "Tobias, what are you—Let me go, he can't be out there alone. He—"

"He's doing it so *we* can escape." Tobias's arms wrapped around my hips, pulling me back even as I writhed. "Don't make it worthless."

Massimo took no issue with the slayer's bounce. Barely had Caleb stepped out of the vehicle when the engine growled. One of the vamps, either too slow or distracted, hit the windshield and went flying off the back. I followed the body, turning to see it land in the street behind us, all as the Wimbledon of solarium-tossing lit the rearview. Boughs of light exploded, casting our shadows forward.

"Behind you."

Massimo's warning let me turn just in time to discover an olive-skinned vamp materializing in the seat next to Maggie. He must have smoked in when Caleb left. The shewolf's eyes went wide as she flattened herself against the window. It was a honking big SUV, but it was still a tight space. If I swung a silver sword, I was as likely to get Maggie or Tobias with it as the vamp.

I pulled an ounce or two of silver from my stores, rolling it down my arm and into my hand. "Massimo, if this is a rental, I hope you got insurance."

His gray eyes found me in the rearview mirror moments before I turned. "What do you...?"

My lunarium illuminated the car. A shadow fell against the back window for a flash, right before it blew out the backside. Cracked glass flew, as much blowing out as falling in. Tobias did his best to pull his mother into his protection with a seatback between them. The vamp had just enough time to turn its black eyes on me before my weapon robbed him of his skin.

Just like it did with the Ravens.

A shriek unlike any I'd ever heard flew from the stricken creature's lipless mouth. My hands flattened against my ears, even as the impression of a high school anatomy illustration watched cinders chase up his knuckles, his palm, his wrist. By the time the damage reached his elbows, most of his hand had fallen in a heap on the back of my seat.

One more time, the vamp's eyes met mine. Slowly, his mouth cracked open as he let out a dead man's sigh. And then, just like that, he was gone.

I turned to the Somfields, pulling them off the side of the car's interior where they'd sought protection. "Are you okay?"

Tobias nodded, chest heaving but his relief evident.

Maggie, however, wore a novel expression. Curious... and perhaps, even frightened. "You're not just a hood, girl. You're the devil's spawn."

"A good thing, too. It sometimes takes a devil to kill a dragon," Massimo said as he squealed around the curb. "Hold on. I'm going to do the only thing I know to get us out of this alive: drive like an Italian."

SIX

AMY

REMEMBER YOUR INSTRUCTIONS. FOLLOW THEM.
CALL ME WHEN EVERYONE IS SETTLED IN CHICAGO.
SINCERELY, YOUR BELOVED SOLARI

P.S. NO FUCKING SLAYERS, BARBIE. THEY NEED TO
BREED... WITH EACH OTHER.

Clearly, Caleb Helsing was the Shakespeare of texting. Chalk up another point for Mr. Asshat. Forget the fact that, according to something someone had said, the male slayers that had been rescued were infertile. Caleb was convinced that something WWL developed could fix that, and he thought practice would help his guys hit one out of the park when the big game came around.

And by the way: Ew, as if.

I mean, a few slayers *weren't* so bad, but even I had some humanity. I wasn't about to go mattress-hopping with a man who'd spent most his life imprisoned, and the last month of it chained up in a basement with water coming up to his shins whenever the sun was down. I huffed as I slid the phone into my bag and got ready for take-off.

"Did he sign it Solari again?"

To my right, tiny Teiko managed to hold a baby on her lap and look comfortable in a coach seat. Of course, to her—to all the slayers, actually—the extreme economy class section could be Buckingham Palace. It was the first time they'd all been on a commercial airliner, and only the second time they'd been on a plane at all. Seeing as their previous experience had been while fleeing for their lives from Count Dracula, Teiko probably felt like the bag of overly salty peanuts Mina held was as good as caviar.

"Yup." I squirreled my phone out of sight and into my pocket before a passing stewardess slipped me the evil eye again. "At least it wasn't 'Solari and God's Gift to All Women' like it was last time."

Teiko shrugged. "He's arrogant, but that doesn't mean he's not valiant at the same time."

Mina's eyes fixed on a rattle Teiko shook just out of her reach, seeing it not as a toy, but as a thing to be hunted. She'd be walking by the time she was six months and getting a fake ID in preschool.

"He can be arrogant. He *could* be valiant. But I don't think he's capable of doing both simultaneously." I pulled the belt on even as the one male steward aboard opened his mouth to say something. Some people always found a reason to bitch. "I really wish Yan hadn't told him about that title for a chief slayer. Caleb already thinks he's three stars better than anyone else. Now that he's got something to put on a business card? He's going to be impossible to live with."

Teiko shifted Mina in her arms. "Oh, so he told you then."

"Told me what?"

"That you two will be living together back in Chicago," she said, like it was so obvious.

I was pretty sure I looked like a patient told they had some horrible disease. "Shut the fuck up."

Eyes wide, cheeks reddened, the slayer diverted her mask of shame.

Okay, now *I* was the asshat. "Shit, I didn't mean… Teiko, I keep forgetting you guys were so isolated and uber-serious all the time. I wasn't trying to insult you. I just… Did he actually say that?"

She turned back hesitantly. "Caleb said since you're only a huey, he's worried the vampires won't respect you unless they see you as his claim. He says you two need to appear close."

That could be perfectly true. Very sexist and a knock on eons of women's lib, but every day I discovered the supernatural world didn't follow human rules.

"Plus," Teiko continued, "Mina will be staying with you if anything happens to Geri and Tobias. He'd want to be near her. Don't tell him I said so, but I think Caleb's smitten."

I pushed a finger into Mina's chin, pushing down and making her smile. "Hell, I hate babies and I think she's the most adorable thing ever."

Teiko grinned. "I wasn't talking about Mina."

Then who was she— Oh…. *Nope.* A thousand times nope.

I fixed this woman with the glare of the criminally insane. "Caleb and I are *not* a thing."

"Maybe not. Or maybe just *not yet.*"

"Or maybe just not ever," I said. "Teiko, there's no delicate way to say this so I'm just going to say it. Caleb is a dick, and understand I say that with the utmost respect for all his slayer awesomeness and respect as the leader of your people. But on a very personal level? Flaming asshole after spicy food. He sees huey women as bullet points, as in, the summary of their importance is to point his bullet at them."

"He's what you hueys call a player, then?" The slayer's eyebrows arched. "Funny, I learned that word from Tobias, but he was using it to talk about you."

Add one Tobias Somfield to my shit list.

"Maybe I used to be, but I haven't slept with anyone in over six months."

Yeezus, had it been so long? No wonder I'd turned into the world's biggest bitch.

"Besides," I continued, "Caleb needs to be with one of you and make little bouncy slayer babies if you all are going to survive." I pulled out my phone and woke up the screen, sharing the recent text message. "See, he wants to make sure you all start with the sexy times as soon as possible."

"Actually, he was telling *you* not to make with the sexy times," she said. "It's because he wants you for himself."

"As his glorified secretary, and that's all he's getting me for, so case closed."

Thankfully, Teiko let it drop then, but I didn't appreciate that coy little smile of hers one bit. Hell, even Mina was grinning.

I focused my glare at the baby just as the wheels of the plane left the ground. *Dream on, baby girl. It ain't going to happen.*

SEVEN

GERI

I felt like a betrayer as the tiny private jet left English soil, which, given my name, I supposed was appropriate. The moon was nearly full and the sky cooperative enough to illuminate an earth tone palate beneath us. Caleb was down there somewhere. Dead or alive, I didn't know. If he had been killed so we could escape, how would I live with myself? Beyond what it would mean to the slayers, I lingered on what it would mean to me. He'd proposed; I'd declined. In hindsight, all my difficulties with the physical part of our relationship made sense. My heart was already bonding to Tobias. That kind of dedication wasn't supposed to happen until the couple slept together, but who knew what it was like for asenaics? Who knew what it was like for *me*?

But that didn't mean Caleb didn't have a place in my heart. In the last few weeks, he'd shifted into the big brother I'd never had. I needed him, needed my family.

"Cold drink, miss?"

A woman's voice fetched me from my reverie, wherein I'd sunk so deep, I hadn't even realized the others were talking.

"Thank you."

The glass clinked from a superfluous amount of ice cubes as I took it. Who knew such a small plane had flight attendants? Then again, if said plane was owned by an Italian vampire prince, anything was possible.

"You're welcome, miss." She made similar offers to both men sitting with me, before moving to the back of the plane and disappearing from sight.

I sat up and shifted my thoughts and my eyes to Maggie Somfield. She sat in the backseat, just as focused on what lay below us as I'd been moments before. Across a dinette set (though to call it something so plebeian seemed to undersell it), Massimo answered whatever question my mate had asked.

"There were… complications when Vlad dragged you through Venice. Though, here and now, please allow me to offer you my most humble and unworthy apologies for my inaction," the vampire said. "I found myself in a situation where it was necessary to play politics and expedite the Ravens' exit from my city. Also, after we met and later that evening, he did try to kill me, so it occupied some time."

Tobias's drink paused at his lips. "Suppose that's a good excuse, and you did just save us now, so all's even and such."

I slid into the conversation, picking up the loose thread. "What complications?"

Massimo's eyes darted around the cabin before finally, his gaze fell upon a window. "I was attempting to woo a woman."

"Oh, well, if that's it then." Tobias threw up his hands as he slumped back in his seat.

The vampire shook his head. "You do not understand. I wasn't simply trying to get someone into bed. I can do that easily enough. If Vlad had discovered that I was so…"

His words cut off, but I could still see the story written in his eyes. "If he knew you loved her, he could use her as leverage and force you to do anything."

Massimo's desperate gaze caught mine. "Yes."

I knew the feeling, had experienced the reality of it being carried out. Except for Igor, however, Vlad didn't threaten vampires. He saw them as some sort of sanctified creature. Why would he…

"She's human."

The realization fell from my mouth at the same time it dropped into my brain. I looked to Massimo, who didn't mount a denial. Instead, his jaw and fist tightened, as though I'd reminded him of the obvious and he was gathering his resolve. His love for a huey could fuel his determination, but it was also an incredible weakness his enemies could exploit. But at least for a vampire, there was a simple enough solution.

"You could turn her."

"I am not a maker," the Italian said. "Besides, it would be cruel of me to do so: to have won her heart, only to leave her behind when I meet the sun sometime in the next century."

The math was quick enough to do. "That's when you'll be five hundred?"

He nodded.

And then I, for some reason, proceeded to suggest something amazingly stupid and against my own self-interest. Blame it on my history with and sympathy for otherwise doomed relationships. "But you know you could extend that, don't you? Drinking supernatural blood, you could keep going as long as she would, and then you wouldn't lose her, and she wouldn't lose you, and…"

The vampire put up a hand to stop my babbling. "I do not wish this. Besides—" he grinned. "—she loves watching the windswept fields of sunflowers dance in the twilight. Why would I take that away from her?"

"What did Igor do for you?"

Maggie's voice took us all off-guard, and we turned to see her eyes fixed on the window. Good. She might be in shock from her sudden freedom, but she was still engaging with reality. I had no idea where her head was, though. My inner hood chided me, "An injured wolf can be a very dangerous thing."

Massimo's response refocused me. "He assisted me in expelling the Ravens from Venice the first time, then with seizing control of the court from his daughter, Luciana. Or as I believe you know her, Inga Rosethorn."

"Who's dead now, too," I said. "How did Igor go up against the Ravens, exactly? It's not like he could threaten to kill them. How did you two pull off a bloodless coup?"

The vampire grinned. "By recruiting the aid of your ancestors, Gerwalta Faust and Andreas Baron." He shook his head as he swiped a drink from his glass. "A shame what happened to them. They were so fiercely in love. Oh, when I knew them, they were still working that out for themselves, but anyone could see it. Their eyes pledged it with every blink."

I couldn't help but look at Tobias then, wondering if I'd find that same look in his eyes, but my mate wasn't a man easily distracted.

Tobias scooted to the front of his seat. "You're lying."

The vampire's head snapped back. Obviously, the Doge wasn't challenged often. "I haven't said one untrue thing."

"Fine," Tobias huffed. "Then you're holding back. You didn't rescue us because you owed Igor anything, though it made a good excuse, I'll grant. You rescued us because you think we're the most likely way to kill off Vlad Tepeş. You said it yourself: politics plays a bigger role than sanguine considerations. Now, why would a politician like you suddenly throw his lot in with a bunch of half breeds like us? What's changed since the Ravens dragged me through your court, beaten and delirious?"

Suddenly, it snapped. Unwanted knowledge, indeed. He'd just wanted to earn our trust and get us somewhere that we couldn't run away from him.

"He already knows about Mina. That's what."

The vampire chuckled. "You named the illustrian after a character from Bram Stoker? And they say irony is dead…"

So Tobias had hit the nail on the head, but that was only the beginning of the hammering. "Now you listen to me and listen to me good, Massimo. I don't give a tick's left ball if you did just rescue us and sweep us away on your luxury jet. If you threaten my daughter in any way, I will personally slice off your head, dip it in wax, and stick it to a pike in the middle of your city."

"Sounds as though your time at the side of the Impaler was most educational."

Massimo raised his right hand and snapped his fingers. The woman who'd given me a drink emerged from whatever crevice of the plane she'd stashed herself, carrying a silver tray. *Silver.* I doubted that was a coincidence. This time, instead of refreshments, it bore a tiny leather checkbook. The vampire took it with one hand while drawing an ink pen from inside his jacket pocket with the other.

"State your price. I will meet it."

My own remaining silver laced over my hands, grafting on to the end of my fingernails and giving me claws. "You sick fuck. Do you think there's any amount of money that we'd sell our child for?"

"Your *child*?" His dimpled cheeks looked so eerie without the ability to blush. "No, I'm afraid you quite misunderstand. I don't want your child. All I want is a bit of her blood."

Tobias managed to push me back in my seat before I went all Catwoman. Imagine that: a werewolf out-disciplining a hood.

"The answer's the same," my mate said. "I'm sure whoever it is you want to kill with Mina's blood has given you cause. But the moment word gets out that an illustrian's blood will let a vamp kill any other, including one of his own bloodline, there'll be hordes trying to find her."

"Kill vampires?" The Doge threw back his head and belted a guttural laugh. "Is that what you think it does? No, my children, an illustrian's blood isn't deadly at all."

Tobias's head tilted. "Then what's your interest in it?"

More importantly, what was Vlad's?

The Italian's eyes turned to slits, like he was questioning our sincerity. *Could they really not know?* he said in every way but with his tongue. Finally, he leaned forward, hands pushing against his knees. "I suppose if you consider that an illustrian's blood cures vampirism, takes away any potential for immortality then, yes, you might say it kills them, but that's a matter of perspective."

Cure vampirism? To some, that might be a fate worse than death. But even if it was true, I wasn't ready to pull in my claws. "Hueys are a hell of a lot easier to kill than supes. It'd sure help anyone get rid of their enemies."

"I can't deny the potential for that," Massimo admitted. "But that's not *my* intention. No, dear little hood, I want the blood for my own use. I'm in love with a human, and the only thing I want now from this world is to grow old with her. Your daughter's blood can let me give my beloved Portia a partner in this world, and a beloved in the next."

The truth of it then punched me in the gut. "That's what Vlad wanted. If he could make Igor human, he could do away with him without killing himself in the process."

"Leaving him the senior member of his line, and giving him tremendous influence over Dracule everywhere." Massimo nodded. "Illustrian blood is the way a paterfamilias goes from being an honorary position to a deity. If he can kill his own, he commands them. And that's why they're all doing what he says now, because most vampires still fear death. Perhaps more than a huey. Now…" He took up the checkbook again. "This is drawn from a bank account I keep in New York, which should help prevent tracking. The EU, as you probably know, has abolished the use of paper checks in recent years."

"It's not for sale."

Massimo's gaze rolled up to meet mine, and for the first time, I saw challenge in his eyes. "I'm prepared to give well into the high six figures for just a vial. Contingent, of course, on the death of all remaining Ravens. I think for either of us to cede our positions prior to that carries too much risk. But just think of the comfort you could enjoy with so much money once that comes to pass."

"Her blood is *not for sale*," I repeated. Then, after a drawn-out pause, "But I'd be open to an exchange."

Tobias squeezed my wrist, pruning his words. "What are you doing?"

"What I have to." I covered his hand with mine before turning back to Massimo and discovering an arched eyebrow. Good, he was interested. Maybe this could all work out after all. "I will offer you a vial of Mina's blood," I said, "in exchange for your life."

"My…" The vampire choked on the words. "You don't have much experience negotiating, do you, Mrs. Somfield?"

"My name is *Kline,* and on the contrary, I'm actually quite good at it." I leaned forward, ignoring *Mr. Kline's* gnashing of teeth. "I'm not asking for your death, Your Grace. Just… I don't know…ten years, maybe? Not long to a vampire but significant to a human. And if you're telling us the truth, you'll be human, won't you?"

"I'm afraid I still don't understand."

"Neither the bloody hell do I," Tobias snapped, pivoting to me. "Geri, once this gets out, imagine the consequences."

"I would think that someone as aged and wise as the Doge of Venice, whom I sure has many enemies and even more friends, would have a plan to… *disappear* himself," I said to my mate. "And if Caleb's going to have any luck resurrecting the slayers in anything more than name, he'll need help. Guidance, training, a link to norms and traditions from someone who's been around long enough to have seen it with his own eyes." I looked to Massimo. "You're an old vampire in a position of power; you must have known a great number of slayers in your time."

He turned his palms up. "A necessity of my position."

"Then help them," I said. "Dedicate the first ten years of your reclaimed human life to serving the solari, and I will give you the blood you want."

A broad grin erupted across the vampire's face. A moment later, his elegant hand struck out. "My office will reach out to coordinate after the Ravens are terminated. I'll need some time to settle my affairs and assure a smooth transition in my court, as well. My bride also probably wouldn't object to a honeymoon before we report for duty." This time I swore that Massimo *was* blushing. "In the end, I suppose I am still a romantic."

Beside me, Tobias crossed his arms. "You say that now but wait to see if she takes your name or forces you to take hers."

EIGHT

BRÜNHILD

"And this one?" Becky held up a brown leather jacket, the elbow worn by use and age.

In a moment, the memory overtook me. A motorcycle ride across the Pampas in the moonlight, a field of golden grass swaying in the breeze, a blanket... The smell of new leather as Pietro slipped the jacket over my shoulders. My head turned up, my eyes wide, my lips parted. I'd wanted to kiss him for a week, and then I was. According to my mother, Pietro was an abomination, one of the few living descendants of *Die Verräterin* and the grandson of an Argentine wolf killed for the crime of loving a hood. But he was *kind*. Compassionate. And, yes, very, very sexy. My senses filled with his scent, musk and leather and the breeze of the grasslands. I knew in a moment there was no hope. He could have me, if he wanted. The decision was entirely his, because *his* consequences could very well be permanent.

But he *did* want me. Despite all my biases when we'd first met and all the particulars of my heritage, he vowed to always love me. Then, a month into our mating, I fessed up. With crossed bloodlines of my own, my mother had forbidden us to have children. I waited for him to show that his heartache was stronger than any mating bond he had. I'd expected him to leave me, to ask the Grand Matron for an annulment. Mother would have granted it before the words even got out of his mouth. But no, he stayed. He stayed and he loved me through my fears and doubts, filling in the cracks of my anxiety with the warmth of his devotion.

I wished he were still here to do it again, but Pietro was gone. I'd lost my husband. For a while, I'd lost my daughter. If I didn't bring my people back together soon, I'd lose any chance to keep the hoods united in a time fraught with division. We were heading into a future that demanded we change. I only hoped we could.

But to move forward, I had to leave behind the things that tied me to the past.

"The garbage box," I finally said. "It's far too worn to give to charity."

Becky nodded and shoved the jacket into a bag filled with Pietro's things destined for the dump. "I see now why you wanted to have this house away from the Schloss. Must have been hard for the two of you, keeping secret what you both really were, all while the eyes and ears of the entire community were on you."

"Pietro had a rougher go of it than I did. So few living hoods had even seen a slayer, that they wouldn't know what to look for in me. But Pietro... Sometimes during full moons, the wolf in him took over. Not physically, of course, but he still felt the *spirit* of it. It's the reason he was the one I always sent out on patrol on *feuernacht*. It was both a way to hide his secret when hardest, and to allow him room to lean into the nature unquestioned."

"Seems to me, you two were well-matched." Becky gathered up the garbage bag in her arms. "Well, this one's full. I'll run down and put this in the garage with the others. You want me to bring a cup of tea or something back up for you?"

"No thank you, Becky. I'm fine."

"A nip of something with a bit more poison, then?"

Despite my sorrow, I cracked a smile. "No, but partake of whatever you like."

It was several minutes later when Becky rushed into the room to the extent that someone near ninety could. "Matron, they just pulled into the garage."

I dropped the pair of folded socks into the charity bin and jumped to my feet. "How many are in the car?"

"Only three, madame."

Halfway to the door, my feet froze. "Three?" So Margaret had said no.

"Gerwalta and Tobias," Becky continued. "And another woman."

My heart took the liberty to beat again until guilt struck a chord within me. "The slayer didn't make it?"

"They didn't say, ma'am. They asked that you come down immediately."

I arrived in the first-floor hall just in time to meet Gerwalta's eyes. It only lasted a moment, that look: the residual disdain mixed with the longing to be my little girl. I'd done that to her. I'd driven her away only to spite her for not pulling back. If that was the price for her survival, however, I'd learn to live with her contempt.

Tobias Kline followed in her wake.

"The slayer?" I asked.

It was the werewolf who spoke as my daughter swallowed her emotions. "We were separated in the escape."

"Escape?" My mouth suddenly felt dry. "Escape from what?"

"Dracule," Geri said. "Dozens of them. Apparently, Vlad's recovered enough to claim his role as the bloodline's paterfamilias. Interesting tip, by the way… Did you know that that was a thing? Kinda like a Matron or a pack leader. When Igor died, Vlad became the eldest in the bloodline, and now they all obey him. So that's just… super."

"I'll contact the Green Matrons nearest London. They might mount a search." Even if they had withdrawn from the council, it was in all our interests for each and every slayer to prosper. "What about Margaret Somfield?"

No sooner had I said the name than the woman came into view, standing in the shadow of her son.

Haggard. It was the only word that captured it. Hair that may have once been blonde hung limply, brass falling over her knobby shoulder. Wolves usually aged with a great measure of grace, but Tobias's mother could stand in line with a huey ten years her senior. Her most distinguishing feature, however, was the tortured flesh that ran from under her ear to where her skin disappeared beneath the collar of her shirt.

The shewolf loped a modest distance from her pup the moment she was through the door, clinging on to the wall for support. It seemed the mother-son reunion wasn't one of the warmest. Noting the distance of my own child, I had a feeling that Tobias's mother and I had more in common than the secrets of our overlapping heritage.

I straightened out my sweater. No cloaks in Rot Haus; it was a rule Pietro and I made early on. "Mrs. Somfield, welcome to—"

"It's Maggie." She cut me off as she walked further into the house, surveying the kitchen at the end of the hall. We all followed in her wake. "Am I your prisoner?"

The query cut me short. "Not unless you're experiencing lunacy or count yourself among my daughter's enemies. The intention was to rescue you. I—"

"I don't give an ounce of cat piss about your daughter, one way or the other, and I'm not moonmad."

I blinked when she headed me off a second time. If she had been a hood, I'd have sent her to shackles for a day. Even though I'd declared the asenaics de facto hoods, I didn't think there would be much gained in the act.

A cough cleared my throat. "Let me restart. Mrs. Somfield, I am Grand Matron Brünhild Kline. Up the hill—" I motioned vaguely in the mountain's direction. "—is Schloss Wolfsretter, where I stand in dominion over all the wolf-watchers of the world. I understand that it is a place synonymous with prison for many lupines, but it is also one of the few places we believe Vlad Tepeş would be reluctant to strike. Insofar as we believe he may now be in pursuit of asenaic blood in order to recover from some recent injuries, we also believe it is one of the safest places for *you* to be."

"It's where I've been staying with Geri, mum." The son looked at the floor while talking. How very curious. "Ever since they freed me in Spain."

"If the hoods freed you, and you aren't a prisoner, then what are you still doing here?" Maggie's face screwed up until she rediscovered Gerwalta. "Ah, that's right, you've mated the enemy."

"Guess that bitch thing wasn't all an act to drive us away, then, was it?" Tobias huffed. "If you keep insulting my mate—"

"Enough!"

Three sets of wide eyes turned on me. Despite my softening of late, perhaps they had forgotten that, while I was a hood, I was the alpha bitch of *this* situation and of *every* situation.

"We don't have time for family drama," I said, stepping between the two wolves. "Maggie, there are no prisoners here. If you want to leave, no one will stop you. But this is no time to be alone. It's obvious the Dracule have organized, and rather solidly. I'm not an expert in vampiric history, but I don't recall stories of their type having mustering tendencies. Except, of course, the last time it happened, when Vlad tried to embed the Ottoman army with vampires to destroy the werewolves of Europe. For the moment, I'd make a hopeful wager that his energy and commitment are focused solely on obtaining asenaics and slayers. You're part of a small target up against a much larger missile."

The shewolf squared her jaw. "I'll stay. For now."

Nodding, I turned back to my daughter and her besotted mate. "I will call together the remaining members of the council for a meeting a half-hour before dawn. You two will brief them on your experiences in England, and together, we will decide the best course of action going forward. For the moment, get some rest. The battle is upon us now, and ere we close our eyes again after tonight, it may be eternally."

Typical of her history, my daughter rolled her eyes, not caring for what she used to call my "melodramatic speeches." But as I watched her disappear into the sitting room en route to the bedroom, I knew in my heart I wasn't being dramatic at all.

I turned on Maggie, who remained, resolute and yet uncertain which direction to go. "I'm sorry."

Her face curdled. "I can imagine fifteen things you'd say that for. You have to be more precise."

No use in sugarcoating or distancing myself from my truth. Whatever Maggie Somfield had been through, she was a mother. She'd hate me, but she'd also understand. "I'd heard rumors that the Dracule had an asenaic for one of its senior members in England a year ago, but the last thing I wanted to do was expose anyone whose secrets might lead to my daughter's own. Then, last week, one of the green hoods informed me that you were the one being held. Obviously, it was a setup."

"So you sent your own daughter into a trap." Maggie crossed her arms. "I don't know whether to be more surprised by your deception or your betrayal."

"Greens are arrogant. They probably thought my relinquished daughter, a gigolo slayer, and a lone wolf stood no chance to outmaneuver their conspirators. But they don't know my daughter, and they certainly don't know *your* son."

"Even still…" Maggie cut herself off as knowledge lifted her eyes. "I think I know *you*, Brunnie. You didn't send my son to rescue his mother. You sent a hood to extract an asenaic, make sure I wasn't passed on to Vlad for his use. It wasn't until I became a strategic weapon that you had any interest in me."

"I'll accept any blame you want to assign me, but I will not apologize." I swallowed my anxiety, reminding myself I had nothing to be ashamed of. "He cannot win, Maggie. I may die, my actions may lead to the martyrdom of many a fine hood and wolf alike, but he *cannot win.*"

Maggie expected no less, it seemed. "I don't blame you any more than I blame a mosquito for its bite. It's your nature. I'm free now, all the same."

"Yes, you are, to the extent that you may make your way, or stay on. But I will *not* allow you to become their prisoner again. So leave if you like, but know if you do, someone under my command will be your shadow with the order to kill you if you're ever taken again."

"So what you're offering me, really, is the *illusion* of freedom."

"On the contrary, I'm offering you the terms." I turned into the living room. "Feel free to claim any available room in the house, and to join us when we depart for Schloss Wolfsretter before dawn. If you require anything, ask Becky. She'll provide a sympathetic ear. She knows a thing or two about being held against your will."

Maggie chortled as I got the stairs. "Another asenaic you took pity on and freed from the blood pits?"

"No, she's a huey. And I didn't free her; my mother did." I paused and fixed my son-in-law's mother in my gaze. "From Auschwitz."

The depth of desertion did not hit me in full until I stared across a table half-empty. Gone were the Greens, the Whites, the Browns. Still with me, the Blacks, the Blues, the Yellows (though I wondered if that was out of respect to Pietro and not to me personally), and the Oranges. The edges of the room were filled with as many of the castle's remaining hoods as could fit.

Gerwalta stood at the back, safe in the arms of her beloved after debriefing those present on the events of England. I'd watched as the cloud covered the moon, leaving every face in the chamber pale. They all understood now; the Dracule were coming. Yes, for the moment, only for the asenaics, my daughter in particular, but soon, we'd all be on their list.

What they didn't understand was why. I only prayed that what I was about to tell them would explain, worrying that it may only confound them more.

"In 1684, Gerwalta Faust of the House of Red, known to us as the Betrayer, died in this very castle. At the time, she stood convicted of the highest crime our kind recognizes: coupling with a wolf. Later that evening, her body, along with that of her mated lupine and the child their union produced, were skewered by silver and burned in the bailey just outside these doors. This, every hood knows. However, it's not the entire truth. In fact, Gerwalta Faust was carrying twins, and while one burned in the fire with her, the other survived."

The cloud turned again, this time from silver to black, a storm of disbelief thundering off the walls in the form of whispers and gasps. I put my hand up as I stood, calling for silence.

"The surviving asenaic child was smuggled into Spain, where she was taken in by Casa de Amarillo, but not before vampires living nearby discovered her blood's unique quality. You see, vampires are not, in fact, immortal."

I looked to my nephew's lover as I said this, Yan. As our resident vampire, he may have wished to silence me giving away their most treasured secret, but the time had come for the end of secrets.

Yan did nothing as I continued. "The maker's bite freezes time for them, but only five centuries, after which, their lives come to a natural end. Supernatural blood, however, can delay this fate. Hood and wolf for a few weeks. Slayers for a few months. Asenaics... In truth, we do not know for certain. Years, perhaps, though there's evidence that the effect lessens over time, requiring more frequent feedings. It's this blood which Vlad Tepeş wants, blood he can find in the remaining descendants from that infamous union. And..." I found Maggie in the crowd. "...in those who are the product of more *recent* unions."

"Can you speed it up a little?" Gerwalta said suddenly, drawing all the eyes in the room. "Stop being all mysterious and retrospective. Get to the vital information so we can make a fucking plan already. I'm tired of breathing every second knowing the most lethal vampire in history is gunning for us."

I crossed my arms, even as I heard my mother's voice in my ears. If the child wants rope, give it to her, then let us see if she builds bridges or nooses.

"Please, Gerwalta, why not tell all of us what you feel is crucial, since you're clearly the only one with skin in this game, the only one who will suffer, the only one in danger."

The fight died in Gerwalta's eyes. Clearly, she had been expecting resistance. A tiny part of me took pride in the fact that she had the courage to stand up to authority. If only she could now stay on her feet.

But then, her mate stepped forward instead. "Vlad Tepeş doesn't just want Geri. She's just the short-term goal because her blood can heal him quickest after the ass beating the Grand Matron gave him in Spain. The Dracule see all supernatural creatures as cattle that they have open rights to feed on. He would rule over the vampires, use slayers for food and pleasure, and destroy lupine society merely out of some century-old sick form of fucked-up revenge."

"What's so special about Geri's blood?"

I looked to my left, to the Orange Matron of the Council, Rona. The First Peoples of the Americas had stuck with us, even when the much-closer Greens of the British Isles had not.

"You, too, are an asenaic, are you not, Mr. Kline?" she continued. "Why is Geri's blood more desirable to them than yours?"

My daughter's eyes went to mine, asking permission. It was my truth now that they'd circled, my moment to see who would still stand with me after. I crossed through the crowd as she explained.

"It's because there is one blend of blood that holds more power than an asenaic, and I have it," Gerwalta said. "I'm more than an asenaic. Yes, I'm a descendant of Gerwalta Faust, and my great grandfather, it seemed, was also wolf, but it's more than that."

"It's because she also has slayer blood running through her veins." I turned as I took a position at her side. "The blood of my biological father, a slayer."

Whatever soft chatter had buzzed about the room came to a succinct stop as the English words were rendered into a dozen other languages. I decided to take the opportunity to just lay out the truth as I knew it.

"In 1953, a few years into my mother's tenure as Grand Matron, a slayer by the name of Hugo Victorious visited Schloss Wolfsretter. He believed that the reason their population had dwindled was due, in part, to the fact the slayers and the vampires they policed had become too close. The need for vigilance seemed moot, and many lost interest in continuing tradition, training children for a threat they believed had waned. Victorious thought that by liberating the slayers' most infamous enemy, he could revive the community and bring those who'd lost interest back into the fold. He convinced my mother to help him, revealing the hiding place of the silver jars in which the Dracule's worst spawn, the Ravens, were imprisoned. The product of that partnership was twofold: Vlad Tepeş and his generals were re-released into the world, and I was conceived."

Gerwalta stumbled forward. "Wait. That would mean, you're like..." Her mouth moved for a moment without sound. "Seventy-five or something? How is that possible?"

The confusion was understandable. Hoods aged somewhat slower than hueys, but not so much to allow for the discrepancy. "Slayers live much longer than other creatures. All the sources I've consulted suggest almost twice as long. But this is not what concerns us now."

Nive Larsen, a Blue Hood in residence studying the genealogy archives, emerged from the crowd. "What then does concern us?" she said, accusation rife in her tone. "You have been the most outspoken of us all on the importance of maintaining the bloodlines, and the whole time, you hid the impurity of your own? You *dare* to stand before us and call yourself Grand Matron? How could you?"

"Jesus Christ, you two-bit hood, you're the very example of why she didn't."

I, and everyone else among us, did a double-take when Maggie Somfield spoke. The weight of so many stares landed on her with all the mass of a feather. The werewolf strode forward into the crowd of those she'd been raised to consider the enemy.

"Are you really that far up your own asses that you don't understand... She knew you'd react this way, that's why she didn't tell you, you bleeding tarts. Is it true that she's a raging hypocrite for pushing a policy she herself couldn't meet? Of course, but if she didn't, she was afraid you'd come after her daughter.

Because if she didn't, she thought suspicion might grow about her own mate. Because if she didn't, you'd come after *her*. She's had to keep her family safe all her life from your bigotry and hate. So she seized the opportunity to become Grand Matron… Big flipping deal. She had to, because it was the best way to protect the people she loved."

Nive proved unashamed. "And that's all she's doing now too," she said. "She's in a pickle, what with Tepeş coming, and she's confessing because she thinks she can manipulate our emotions."

"Seriously?" Tobias planted his balled fists on his hips as he glowered at the Blue Hood, taking to his mother's side. "Newsflash for you: you're all in fucking danger. Vlad Tepeş doesn't care what hood politics are or what lupine families it destroys. He nearly wiped out the slayers, and the few that were left, he kept in a harem or locked in a dungeon. He forced a slayer to rape a werewolf to conceive a child whose blood would be lethal to other vampires. Brünhild recognizes this is bigger than her secrets. It's bigger than your judgments and your biases. Why can't you? She's trying to help save you, to save *all of us*, but if you want to stand there and cry about your wounded pride, then just go right ahead. I intend to stand with her and fight, because it's the best way I know to protect my mate. It's the *only way* to protect my daughter."

Off to the side, Geri beamed as Maggie Somfield guffawed, saying "What daughter?"

But the son ignored the mother. "I'm going to avenge the deaths of my father, of my brother, and of my…"

His voice broke, and for a moment, I thought he was done. Then, Gerwalta walked to his side, wrapping an arm around his waist and whispered something into his ear. The werewolf nodded before his eyes shot back open.

"I'm doing it to avenge my first mate, who the Dracule kidnapped, experimented on, and tortured. So, yes, I will stand by Brünhild, and I don't care if she's half-hood and half-water buffalo. The question is, are all ye hoods as willing to give your lives to save your own like the lowly dogs you think we are?"

As I looked around a room gone silent, there was no need for words. They understood the sentiment that had won the day.

The hoods were going to war.

And the wolves would be right beside them.

NINE

GERI

To anyone not in the know, it only looked like a garden shed. The structure lay outside the medieval walls of the compound, but within the modern 1960s security fencing. Inside, instead of hoes or a lawnmower, one would only find the top of a spiral staircase leading down into what was once a massive bomb shelter. Nowadays, it served as the Schloss's gymnasium, and it's where I found myself, unable to sleep.

I continued my forms as the "shed" door above opened, a red light blinking on the far wall indicating someone was on their way down. I didn't have to wonder who. There were only two wolves on the property, and Tobias was back in our room asleep. I swear, that man could slumber through a hurricane. I grabbed a towel and pressed my face into the cooled linen as a breeze carrying the scent of shewolf brushed past me.

"Hello, Maggie." I turned, pointing to a row of folding chairs on the side of the mat. "I was wondering when you were going to corner me."

Maggie assumed a seat. "A daughter, eh?" she asked without pretense.

"She's not an asenaic," I said, anticipating the meaning behind her furrowed brow. "But she's not… whatever I am, either."

"I see," she said in a tone that made it clear she didn't.

I pressed on. "Vlad forced a slayer to bed a wolf. The product of that crossing is our Mina. We adopted her after her mother died. The father, we were led to believe, was dead long ago."

"It seems I'm a grandmother then." A smile flickered on to her face, one I wasn't sure was born of joy or pain. "Do you… love her?"

A bead of defensiveness drew down the lines in my forehead. "I don't give a damn that she's not blood. She's my daughter. Your son loves her too, by the way."

"I'm certain he does. His emotions run deep. Always have. Even as a child, he—" She cut herself off, pulling back in on herself both figuratively and literally. "I wanted to ask you something. Something I must know, but I can't risk—I don't want to upset Tobias."

"Shoot."

Her head cocked to the side.

"What's the question," I amended.

"He mentioned having a first mate. What… What happened to her?"

I half-wondered if she expected to hear me say that I'd killed Kara. "The Dracule experimented on her, found a way to undo her mating bond. Tobias and I tried so hard to save her, but Kara was killed in the crossfire."

"Undid her mating bond?"

It surprised me that that was what hit her. But then again, after what she'd endured for years, a wolf killed by vampires was probably a mundane event.

After a moment, Maggie nodded, as though she'd confirmed something. "So, it wasn't because there was something wrong with him. The vamps did something, and then he could fall for you, betray his nature."

The implication threatened to derail my compassion. Like loving me would be evidence that her son was somehow damaged? But this was a woman who had suffered so her child could stay pack. I had to respect the intentions. "Honestly, we don't know why Tobias can love me. He's easily ten generations out from Gerwalta Faust and Andreas Baron. It's hard to imagine the DNA that would let that be possible would be so dominant still, but—"

"He's got more hood blood than even he knows."

Maggie's interjection stilled my tongue. "What?"

"My family's dirty little secret: *fur fever*," she said, her eyes as distant as her voice. "My grandmother was Grand Matron, one of the few that didn't come from your bloody House of Red. Unlike my other ancestors who were slaughtered when they mated a wolf, Lizza Wood was in a position to hide the truth and protect the babe. Everyone in the family knew my father was a halfie. He had wolfish tendencies, but never could take his fur, never became one of them."

I thought of my own father, of the recent revelation that he, too, had a recent lupine ancestor. Only after the fact did his contrary habits make sense to me. Growing up, I'd always excused his fits of passion and contrary tendencies to his being a foreigner. For a child, simple solutions solve complex problems. I hadn't asked my mother if my father could take fur, but I bet, like Maggie's father, he couldn't. Was it a male-female thing? Did the fact that hoods were matriarchal push the wolf traits in female offspring to be more pronounced? My university classes were playing hopscotch in my thoughts.

"But I did," Maggie continued. "The first full moon after my fire night. Ran away after that, never looked back. I knew if I did, all I would see would be a dagger coming my way. The House of Green ain't the forgiving sort."

I regained my feet as instinct brought my hands up, reaching for her. "Maggie, I'm…"

And just like that, her venom resurged. She turned, pulled away, her face screwing up. "Did you think I told you because I wanted your *pity?* Aye, but you feel it, don't you? You *pity* me. Pity yourself, girl. If the lot of you fails to put down the Dracule, you'll be me in thirty years. The shell of a mate. Nothing but the shell."

I jerked my hands back. "You're more than a shell. You stood up to a whole room of hoods yesterday and called them on their shit."

"Not much consequence of it for me, was there?"

"I hope it has all the consequence in the world, for all of us." She didn't want me to pity her? Fine. "No offense, Maggie, but if I get to be your age, I don't want to be anything like you. I've tried being bitter and self-justified. All that's ever done is drive people away. And while you've earned yourself a lifetime of the-world-owes-me-something credits, that currency doesn't go far in this court. I'd like to help you overcome what you've suffered. I'd like to introduce you to your granddaughter. But if you dare and try to tell me that I don't belong with your son for any reason, then you and I have a problem."

I watched in amazement as the corner of her mouth ticked up. "Might be hope for you yet."

I grabbed my towel and turned toward the door. "It's almost sunset. Come on, let's get breakfast and see how much of my mother's grand council had balls enough to stick around after two werewolves pantsed them yesterday."

"Balls? I thought there were only women on the Council of Matrons."

"Oh, that's true, but believe me, some of them have *cajones* the size of..."

The room shook as a boom came from above.

Maggie and I exchanged a look before we both took the stairs two at a time. We emerged from the shed to see a sunset sky bleeding flame.

Only, as my eyes focused, I saw it wasn't the sky that was on fire.

It was the Schloss.

TEN

Smoke hung in the air, a thick blanket that obscured my view. Silhouettes of nearby buildings showed no damage, so what the hell was going on? Then, as I did a second sweep, it hit me: all the smoke that I saw moved without wind, and whirled toward the castle, not away from it.

"Vampires."

Behind me, Maggie declared what suddenly became obvious. I turned, hoping to find an ally in this chaos, but instead discovering a woman who'd become a ghost of her own experiences.

I pushed her back into the fake shed, toward the stairs that led down to the gym. If she couldn't help, hopefully she'd stay safe and out of the way. "On the right side of the landing at the bottom of the stairs, there's a big, yellow button. Press it once you're through the door; it will lock down the facility airtight. The vampires won't be able to get in."

"But the others..." Her voice trailed off as, over my shoulder, her eyes widely tracked the cataclysm. "Tobias."

Another *boom* shook the air, and this time, it came with flame. I spun to see licks of red past the castle gate. Stone didn't burn, of course, but everything inside the compound, from the medieval tapestry to the books, to the furniture, wasn't made of stone.

"Don't worry, Maggie. Tobias is safe."

He'd volunteered to drive to Freiberg and pick up some supplies, leaping at a chance to distance himself from too many hoods. I didn't expect him back for a few hours.

I pushed Maggie more insistently. "Please, hurry..."

A scream ripped across the night, cutting off my words. I turned toward it, my eyes skirting up the external façade of the Schloss. At the top of the tower, I saw her. Becky Krantz, our sole huey resident, our castellan, my friend... looked out from a window that faced the inner bailey.

"Maggie, I have to go."

"But what about..."

"All the Matrons have a code that will get them in, but I know it, too." Passing benefits being the Grand Matron's daughter. "If no one comes in a few hours, just press the button again and it will unseal the door."

Finally, she yielded, giving me a passing look that approached gratitude before spinning and stomping down the stairs. I waited a moment until I heard the gym door close, then the sound of the compressed air and machinery working, sealing the gym off from the outside world. Even if everything up top turned to ash, she'd survive.

But now was time to make sure the worst case scenario didn't happen.

It didn't take a supernatural Einstein to figure out who was attacking or why. The Dracule, pissed off that I'd slipped their trap in England, had finally gotten desperate enough to bring the fight to the last place we ever thought they would. It might be revenge, or just a tactical move to weaken the biggest threat standing against them, but I didn't doubt for a second that capturing me was part of the plan as well.

Chaos claimed the outer bailey. Flashes of blue, yellow, and red swirled and bobbed as each hood at court took to battle, squaring off with vampires dripping into existence out of formless clouds by the dozens. Immediately, I fell back on years of training, looking for our strengths so I could sure up our weaknesses. They outnumbered us easily, but this was *our* land. Familiarity with the ancient structure and its hidden recesses, curved stairs, and high walls served *us*, not them. They also hadn't counted on the fact that we trained to fight in formation against packs. Vampires engaged mostly in one-on-one conflicts to hunt prey.

A hood was *never* prey.

A Yellow gave up just enough ground, feigning retreat, to bring a red-haired female vamp forward, lining them up with another dueling pair, two males, one wearing a blue hood. The Yellow spun, her silver sword taking the male vampire's head. The next second, the Blue used the now-voided space to force his silver spear into the redhead's chest, driving the tip clear through so the wooden staff touched her undead heart.

As I looked for a place to enter the fray, I heard Markus shout.

"Hey, Miss Kline!"

I turned to find my cousin and Yan on the edge of the outer bailey, fighting in tandem. The latter could move just as fast as his attacker, and he fought with the benefit of our training forms. Unfortunately, four vamps stood on the other side of their line, and the blows were unrelenting.

"A little help here?"

I had to get to Becky, but I wasn't about to ignore Markus. I'd only taken enough silver on me to the gym to do a little dagger practice, but it would have to do. The lunarium burned its way across the air, catching the attacking vampires with a touch. Three immediately turned to dust, but a fourth, a meek-looking female, had just enough time to turn and look me in the eye as my weapon struck, piercing a hole into her gut, the injection of sunlight quickly webbing up her chest and into her neck. It must have been a young vamp to go so quickly. She threw her head back as if to scream, only to dissolve the next moment.

No time to celebrate small victories, I ran by Markus without stopping. "I have to get to the tower."

"Are you insane? The whole building is going up in flames. You'll be trapped!" Markus's arm swung, throwing a potential attacker off my path.

"Becky's trapped up there. I have to try."

As I sped through the outer bailey, then the inner bailey, I threw what lunarla I could, picking off vamps both left and right. No point in hiding now, was there? I didn't know if all my attacks were deadly, but they had to at least hurt. Right outside the entrance to the castle proper, on the tiny drawbridge that spanned the dry moat bed, my mother sliced off the hands, then the head, of a particularly snarly member of the undead. She caught my eye as I ran by.

"Tower!" I said to her unspoken question. "Becky…"

She nodded once. "I'll get her."

"No, you're the Grand Matron. Stay. Command."

She turned back just as another vamp crashed against her. I didn't know why they fought. They could turn to smoke, whip past us and head straight for the windows. They couldn't fly, per se. Yan had explained to us that while smoke, a vampire could not reach any ground he wouldn't have been able to in a solid form. The smoke still obeyed physics; pushed against objects and was pulled by gravity, but still, a vampire was pretty damned agile in the flesh too.

Past the door, inside the foyer of the schloss, hoods of all houses dashed in every direction. Some headed to the exits to join the battle; some crisscrossed the main hall toward the escape tunnels hidden at the back of the castle; some turned circles, not sure which way to go. I ignored them all, making for the stairs. It was at times like these I wished I could fly like my mother. If only *that* trait were genetic.

Each step up the tower felt like scaling a ten-foot wall. My feet had never moved so quickly. I reached the last step, my chest working, my thighs burning. No sooner had I gotten to the tower landing than the whole of the castle shook again. I turned just in time to see part of the roof fall, blocking the path back down.

As Tobias would say, fuck.

No time to waste. The outer walls of the castle may be next to fall, and that would take the only other way out with it. One step into my mother's study, and I could see why Becky hadn't tried to escape. She sat in a chair beside the fireplace, her right leg bent at an unnatural angle.

With a grimace, she palmed the limb. "Next time the Schloss is under attack, remind me not to break my leg."

I crossed the office to the large painting hung behind the desk. It hid a secret staircase that we could use to descend the tower. The problem remained, however, that I had no idea how I would carry Becky *and* manage a ledge merely eight-inches wide that had to be traversed to get to safe ground.

No time for niceties, I threw the painting across the room. "I can carry you, but it's going to hurt like hell. You might want to consider passing out."

She managed a smile. "I'll do my best."

I got Becky to her feet and pulled her arm over my shoulders, trying to ignore the groans she made. There was nothing I could do for her pain.

"Wait!"

I stopped on the spot. "We don't really have time for…"

But before I could finish my sentence, Becky held up her free hand and a folded-up piece of paper it clutched.

"You need this," she said, shoving it into my chest. "I'm supposed to burn it or eat it if the vampires make it up here. Your mother said so."

I pushed Becky's hand back. "So listen to my mother. Hold on to it. The vampires haven't reached the tower yet."

Yet.

Before I could take another step, the growl of an engine forcing its way up the mountain met my ears. I turned, dragging Becky back to the window she'd been waving out earlier. And that's when I looked just beyond the castle walls…

…and locked eyes with the loathsome creature behind this all.

Skinless, hairless, fearless, but still unmistakably Vlad Tepeş. Time had done nothing to heal his injuries. Later, I could wonder how that was possible; vampires supposedly healed with time and feedings. Obviously, the damage done by a lunarium packed a little more punch.

A thunderous rev surged again, but what I saw down in the valley amid a patchwork of brown and black landscape put my heart in my throat. The only road which wound out of town and up our small cliff looked like a string of blue and white Christmas lights, a chorus of *woo-wee, woo-wee, woo-wee* underlying the clash of supe-upon-supe in the baileys below. What would we do when the hueys got close enough to see a plethora of smoke-then-solid vampires fighting with colorfully robed men and women bearing silver swords and notched bows?

"Becky, do we have a contingency plan for the invasion of the castle by hueys?"

The old woman harrumphed. "As if they stood a chance."

"Well, not independently, but in conjunction with vampires…"

Another light whisking its way up the hill caught my eye then, this one close enough for me to see that its moon roof was open, filled by a man holding a five-foot tube with a mounted sight.

I looked back over my shoulder at the old woman grimacing in pain, then back to the approaching vehicle. If they weren't already in firing range, they would be soon enough. Was it enough time to get down the stairs carrying Becky? Even at my fastest, I wasn't sure.

Becky's expression flatlined. "That bad?"

"Looks like a rocket launcher." They couldn't destroy the whole compound with it, but they didn't need to. The building could be used to destroy itself.

If they hit the tower.

Becky managed to relieve herself of my support, balancing on her uninjured leg. She took one look at me with the most resolute and determined boldness in huey eyes I'd ever seen and shoved the folded-up paper at me again. "Take it."

"Becky…"

"Take it!"

As old and frail as she appeared, I knew from experience the devil could be in this woman. I took the paper and shoved it into my sports bra.

She nodded her approval. "Now, to the window."

I turned wide eyes to her.

"You heard what I said, Gerwalta Kline," Becky snapped. "You're fast, but not fast enough to carry an old woman down a castle tower racing a rocket."

She said it all without the slightest bit of doubt or dressing. What could I do but concede?

Hobbling, we refilled the window frame. Becky leaned forward a bit and looked down.

"I won't survive that. My bones are made of faith at this age."

I shook my head. "Maybe if I use silver to make us a rope, then I can—"

"No time, my little girl. No time."

Her hand squeezed my shoulder, then moved down my back, and then…

Then there was only air. Air on every side and less of it beneath me by the moment. The tower grew tall in my sight, even as I screamed Becky's name and reached up, as though I could still pull her to safety, like I was in any position to save anyone. Oh, I'd probably survive, but it was going to hurt like hell when I hit. Gravity or dumb chance flipped me, and I splayed my hands out before me, as if I could springboard off the ground instead of smash into it. Because, why the hell not suddenly discover I was a werecat as well?

It was coming, coming… Sixty feet, fifty, forty…

Thirty…

I closed my eyes, ready to accept the earth as my lord and smasher.

Until, all of a sudden, it felt like the fall had been thrown into reverse. My eyes flew open but sight brought no clarity. Instead of getting closer to the ground, it was falling farther away from the two of us.

Two?

It didn't make sense. How had my mother seen me fall? She shouldn't have a view from the last position where I saw her. Even if she did, how could she have flown up to catch me that quickly?

Only, as I looked over my shoulder, I wondered if it hadn't been better that I hit the ground.

It wasn't my mother who had saved me.

It was my mother-*in-law*.

ELEVEN

An indifferent sun rose on a world of ruin and ash.

Not even my mother knew how old the schloss had been. Given its ample supply of antique books, rugs, tapestries, and dried-out wooden furniture, that it so quickly caught ablaze was no surprise. Funny how I never would have thought it possible, though. I mean, it was built of stone, wasn't it? How could stone be damaged by flame? But in the end, even the hardest materials could fail under the pressure of fire and time. The roof was gone. The grand hall, caved in. A few buildings on the edge of the grounds still stood but had been so thoroughly smoked, they'd be useless. Everything within the outer bailey walls crumbled when the tower, torn to pieces, crashed down.

I glared at anyone—first-responder hueys, mostly—who suggested that we were lucky. Only six people had died. What kind of luck was that for those who'd perished?

For Becky?

My mother, dressed in tattered civilian clothes and still wearing soot across her brow, crossed to a pickup truck where I sat on the lowered tailgate, sipping water and shaking. Divergent emotions warred for control of her face. Concern and a mother's instinct to comfort? The longing played in her eyes. But no matter what else had happened, she was still Grand Matron. For now, anyways. After this, who knew? Whatever was left of the Council of Matrons would either rally behind her or demand her head on a pike.

I took to my feet. "The vampires?"

Her eyebrows knitted as she turned, making sure any hueys were too far away to hear. "They scattered as soon as the tower fell, right before any hueys could see them, thank god."

I shook my head and closed my eyes. She thought the vampires had had enough smarts to uphold our veil, the one that kept our supernatural lives cleaved from human knowledge. I knew better. They'd come to wreak hell or else the operation would have been far more covert. In my memory, I still saw Vlad's vascular frame, that long, skeletal arm pointed to the sky as I fell. Vampiric smoke chased Maggie and me as she whisked us through the forest, desperate to escape. At some point, she must have felt that she'd pulled the pursuing vampires far enough away to double back, no hood the wiser. By then, it was too late to help; the place was crawling with firemen and ambulances and even a few villagers who'd driven up to lend whatever hand they could.

"And the hueys?" I said as Brünhild sat beside me. "What are you telling them about... Well, everything?"

"We've *confessed* to having an undeclared and unlicensed school. The best we can hope for is to play up to the least damaging story their minds will accept. We've blamed the explosions on our chem lab or kitchen or something. I don't know. I've handed that off to Alissa Hummel. She's native to this region, knows better what to say or not say."

"An unlicensed school?" The laugh came despite my best efforts to quell it. "You honestly think they're going to buy that?"

"Of course, I don't, but we've just experienced something traumatic. They'll be willing to give us the benefit of the doubt for now. In the end, I only have to stall them until nightfall. Markus is offsite hacking into their computer systems to clean any reports. Yan is calling in some favors. Some of his bloodline live in Vienna and they'll be here after sunset to help clear the memories of the hueys who come to investigate. We can't undo what's happened, but we can make sure it doesn't undo us."

"Geri!"

I leapt to my feet, my heart dropping as my wolf came into view. The mysterious bond we had told me he'd been safe but seeing spoke what instinct only whispered. Tobias caught me up and spun me off the ground, even as I pressed my lips to his and clung to his neck like I'd fall off the face of the earth if I let go. Several moments passed like that, until he gently eased me to my feet.

Tobias pressed his forehead to mine. "The second I heard... Jesus, woman, I thought I was going to lose you." A smile blossomed on his face as his hand wove through my greasy hair. It didn't matter that I looked like I'd just went a week without sleep. I was alive and touching me proved that to him. "Are you okay?"

I smoothed my hand over his fuzzy cheek. "I am, but there were others who... Oh, Tobias, five hoods are dead."

"Shush now." He cut me off, pulling me into the circle of his embrace. "It's okay, love. It's okay."

My mother cleared her throat behind us, reminding us that we weren't alone.

Tobias drew back, hooking me under an arm, and turned to my mother. "Matron, my sympathies for your losses."

"Thank you, Tobias." Brünhild folded her hands over her stomach and nodded. "If you'll excuse me, I need to attend to the injured."

The moment she walked away, my big, bad wolf turned into a frightened little pup. Pressing my cheeks between two large hands, he turned my head and neck this way and that.

"You sure you're not hurt?"

"I am," I assured him, pulling his hands off into mine. "But Becky… They found her body about an hour ago under some of the debris."

Deep lines grew in his face. "I'm sorry, Geri. I know you had a great deal of affection for her." After a moment of silence, his queries turned to the obvious. "We thought this was the one place they'd never attack. Even I believed that."

"If we were united, maybe. Now, with so many of the houses deserting…" I shook my head, coming to terms with the arrogance… *my* arrogance that cost six people their lives. "We should have known we'd be susceptible after what happened in London. Obviously, there are hoods sympathetic to the Dracule's cause. And after all the slayer's left, Vlad knew we'd be an easy target." Vlad. In the fallout of all that had happened, I'd almost forgotten. "Tobias, he was here. I saw him. But there's something… weird. He's not regenerating."

My head bobbed. "He doesn't look that much different than right after he was hit by silver flame. The lunarium. Whatever. Point is, he's not healing." Which meant only one thing. "He's getting desperate, starting to panic. A panicked Dracula is a dangerous Dracula."

Tobias ran a hand through his hair, grabbing the ends. "This has to end." He exhaled through pursed lips. "I should check on my mum. Do you know where she is?"

You mean the werewolf who can fly?

I closed my eyes against the memory. I owed it to Maggie to keep her secret. "Down in the gymnasium. We're using it as a temporary infirmary."

"She wasn't hurt?"

"She has a few scratches on her legs, but she's okay."

The way every inch of his frame melted told me my mate wasn't as indifferent toward his mother as he might pretend, but "Good to hear, I guess" was all he said.

Fine, if he wanted to keep pretending. I'd let him.

For now.

"Thank god we sent Mina away with the slayers."

Tobias nodded. "Any news from them?"

"They got to Chicago okay, but no one's heard from Caleb. Mina's good though, and Amy said they're all somewhere safe until they know what to do next."

"What to do next?" Tobias pulled his hands over his grimy face as he turned back over his shoulder. "Yeah, a lot of that going around lately."

"I know exactly what I'm doing now."

"That's your I-have-a-plan voice." My mate grinned. Wolves did love action more than words. "Do tell, love."

"Vlad's after me, whether it's to capture me or kill me doesn't really matter," I said. "We don't have to wonder where he's going to turn up. It'll be wherever I am. We should use that."

"And…what?" Tobias held his arms out wide. "Go on television? Make it a pay-per-view event?"

My jaw ground. "I'm supposed to be the sarcastic one, remember?"

"Hell, woman, I'm hoping you are, because it sounds like you're planning on using yourself as bait."

"There's no better way to catch a mouse than with some cheese."

"Vlad isn't a mouse and you'll bleed a lot more than a piece of bloody cheddar! I mean… You know what I mean."

His anger did nothing to change my mind, and he huffed and he puffed when he realized it. Fists anchored on his hips, his jaw worked.

"Where?"

"Home."

Tobias's face screwed up. "You can't mean we're going back to Paradise."

"Yes, we are." My mother had managed to sneak back up on us from the side without either of us noticing. We both spun to catch her questioning glare beaming on us. "But how did you know?"

The werewolf threw his hands up in the air. "Of course, she'd think your crazy plan is a good idea."

Brünhild turned to me. "What plan?"

I crossed my arms and pushed my back into Tobias. He better not breathe a word. After a lifetime turning the world upside down, my mother wasn't about to let me willingly step into the line of fire. "Going home, of course. It's been too long."

"I agree. I'm only allowing those essential to the cleanup here to remain." My mother motioned behind us, to the destruction. "Everyone else, I'm ordering home as soon as they can travel. There's nothing more anyone can do here, and after this kind of event, I think they would feel more at ease being close to their families."

"Aye, and that's probably the fifteenth miscalculation you made today."

I jumped back as Tobias rounded to find his much-shorter mother hidden behind him.

"God damn it, will people stop sneaking up!" Tobias exclaimed.

Brünhild stepped in closer. "You wish to register a contrary opinion, Maggie?"

Were they on a first-name basis now?

Maggie Somfield nodded. "You think you have kittens here, Grand Matron? Delicate little flowers who wilted from a touch of heat and need to be put in the cooler? Don't make me laugh. These hoods are warriors, ones just dealt a mighty blow. They don't need to be sent home to nurse from their mother's teats. They need to be pushed headlong into the line of the enemy. They need a chance for *vengeance.*"

"My *warriors,*" my mother said, drawing the term out, "were trained to hunt wolves, not puffs of smoke. Our silver does nothing to vampires unless we can get close enough to take off a head."

"Then get close!" Maggie snapped. "They're coming for your daughter either way. Oh, be compassionate. Send the wee ones home; send back the ones down there in the underground with broken bones and charred skin. But for those who can still fight, give them a chance to fight."

My mother, resolute as a mountain, pondered some length before snapping her heels together. "You'll be on the Chicago-bound flight tonight out of Munich. You'll need to leave for the airport within the hour."

And with that, she marched away. Maggie, looking proud as a peacock, chose to do the same in the opposite direction.

Tobias pivoted, eyeballing the retreating forms in turn. "Wait, did my mum just tell your mum off and get away with it?"

I waved my hand. "You know what they say: like mother, like son."

TWELVE

Maggie Somfield spent the entire drive looking out the window like what she saw didn't make sense.

"I can't believe this is what America looks like."

The wheels hummed against the grating of the Mackinac Bridge as we drove onto the northbound span. Winter had kissed the Straights, a prelude of ice clinging to either shore and around the islands in the waters below. The cold was closing in. Here, only a light dusting of snow had managed to claim land; by the time we arrived at Paradise seventy miles north, everything would be white. Thus, the reason we'd only been able to fly as far north as Traverse City. Marquette had closed after a hell of an ice storm, apparently.

"Where are the palm trees?" she continued. "The skyscrapers? The swamp people and storage locker lots?"

Apparently, imprisonment by the Dracule didn't limit one's intake of decade-old reality TV.

"The West Coast, East Coast, and way down in the South," I said. "We're on the edge of civilization way up here in the UP. Not much in the way of skyscrapers north of Detroit. A couple of big lighthouses, though."

"There are some storage lockers in Paradise," Cody added.

The Paradise Pack alpha reached up to adjust his rearview mirror. If ever I needed proof of how awesome a guy my ex was, this was it. He'd driven three hours to meet us at the airport and bring us home, even as Lisa was home with a one-week-old baby. He hadn't even been asked. My mother had called while we were in the air to let him know what had happened, and we walked out of baggage claim on our way to rent a car to find the old Ryland Family van at the curb. A blush had burned in my cheeks; that car and I had history, particularly its backseats.

"Don't think they get too much business, though," the alpha continued. "Most of us have enough land to store as much shit as we need and a bunch of shit we don't. And speaking of having plenty of room, Maggie?"

The shewolf stirred. "Alpha?"

Tobias's jaw worked at the implied insult, but there was still an hour to drive, and that could feel like an eternity when spent fighting with your mother. I knew from experience.

"I'm supposed to drop these two crazy kids at Chez Kline when we get into town." Cody jerked his head back to the third-row seats where Tobias and I sat together on a bench covered in more duct tape than stained cloth. "It's not far from the packlands, but it's not exactly across the street. Plus, you know, it's got enough silver laying around to start their own national currency. Lisa and I were wondering if you might want to come stay with us?"

"Your mate would be okay with someone… like me?" Maggie straightened.

Cody laughed. "Hell, we've put up with Geri for years just fine. She spent so much time at our house in high school, my mother packed both of us a lunch some mornings."

Forget the fact that as supes, our socializing tended to be nocturnal. The implication was still there.

Beside me, a low growl rumbled in Tobias's chest.

"Easy, Big Ben," Cody warned. "Don't become your mating bond's bitch. Not when you have Geri for that."

I laced my arms over my chest. "If I could slap you with a silver glove right now, Cody Ryland, I'd do it."

"I bet you would, Little Red." In the rearview, Cody caught my eye and gave me a wink.

Maggie bent over the back of her seat to face me. "I don't understand, is he saying that…" Her confused gaze landed on Tobias. "Things have changed since I was pack. First, you cheat on your departed mate with one of them, and then I find out she's a serial betrayer?"

"I'm sitting right here, Maggie," I said. "You don't have to talk about me in the third person. And nobody cheated on anyone. Tobias and I had no romantic relationship until about six months ago."

Like that made a difference. Werewolves mated for life. Even if a few had been able to have sex years after their mates had died, there was no emotion there.

Cody spoke from the front seat again. "Geri and I were never mated," he said, stating the obvious. Because unlike me, Cody wasn't a lab experiment in genetics that left instincts a twisted mountain road. "We just dated before she left for Chicago and I mated Lisa."

"I mean, technically, we were still dating *when* you mated Lisa."

Tobias's head snapped my direction.

I stared at the floor. "But probably not a point that needs to be made right now. And I'm over it. He's over it. *Everyone* is over it."

Except, apparently, Maggie. "I know I left when you were still young, but I would have thought I raised you better than this."

"Sorry to disappoint, *mother.*" Tobias's hand curled around my thigh, sending a wave of heat up my body that threatened to melt the ice on the windows.

Maggie faced the front once more. "Yes, Cody, I would love to stay with you. I think like any good wolf, I'd be much more comfortable with my own kind."

His grip never loosened.

For the next hour, Tobias simmered. Either Maggie and Cody didn't pick up on it or didn't care. Consequently, when Cody's van pulled away from the gate of the Kline family compound, I was standing in front of a bursting pressure gauge.

I flattened my hand on Tobias's chest. "Cody likes to tease. You know that's all that was, right? He and I...that's all in the past."

My mate's head cocked to the side. "You think *that's* what I'm angry over?"

"Well, yeah. Until you said that, anyway."

Tobias shook his head, his hands fisted so tightly I wondered that his palms didn't bleed. "Who in the hell does she think she is?" the wolf huffed. "Walks out on her own two children, letting us think she's dead, then has the nerve to question *my* mating bond?"

"In all fairness, she didn't walk out on you; she was exiled, then held prisoner for years."

Not the response he wanted to hear. "If she loved us, she would have made my da see reason. She would have forced her way back into the pack."

I forced my own silence as I punched the code into the panel on the security gate pillar. *You promised Maggie you wouldn't tell anybody anything. You promised.* Three shrill beeps sounded as the mechanical arm began to swing. The driveway lay under a coat of virgin snow, and the mechanism groaned as the gates became de facto snowplows.

"And then, what she said about you!" Tobias continued to huff. "Fine, let her take her potshots at me, but you don't insult a wolf's mate. If she wasn't my mother, I'd... Well, it's a good thing she is."

"You don't have to worry about me, Tobias. I don't bruise easily."

"Seriously? She basically called you a betrayer to your own kind."

"No," I said. "She called me a betrayer to the hoods, but it doesn't matter. We know the truth."

Or at least *I* did. God, I wanted to tell him. It felt like a lie to keep it in.

I trudged forward, the house I'd not seen with my own eyes in three years coming into view as the driveway wove through trees and brush. "Still, it's a little weird she'd take offense on behalf of the hoods and not the wolves. It's almost like...

My whole body seized as the realization hit me. I couldn't *tell* Tobias, but I had a way to get him to realize the truth on his own.

Tobias walked on before realizing I was no longer beside him. "Geri?"

"What pack did your mother come from?" A good leading question. "Was it the Morpeth pack? Your pack?"

His eyebrows knitted. "I don't know. I was so little when she d—*went away*. My dad didn't like to talk about her, so Nick and me didn't."

Letting my bag fall to the ground, I pulled out the slip of paper Becky had given me. It hadn't seemed like anything but a list of wolves when I'd first looked. At the top of the page, in scrawling German, it read 'to watch and advise if necessary.' Tobias's name was third. His brother's beneath was crossed through. Next to both was written "Morpeth Pack." Two more names I didn't recognize included pack designations from Donegal, Ireland and Mongolia. The last on the list were that of Ann-Marie Krueger, and her mother, Zelda, from Zeihern Pack, only Zelda's name was scratched out.

I held up the much-abused line paper. "I thought this was a list of asenaics, but me and my dad aren't on here. It's in my mother's handwriting, so maybe she was hiding us? Only, the Muñozes from Spain aren't on here either."

He took the paper from me and began to peruse it. "These are all wolves." He looked back up to me, his brow furrowed. "Where did you get this?"

"Becky gave it to me right before she died."

Something dark crept into his expression. "You said she was in the tower when the rocket hit the Schloss, when you were down in the gym. When would Becky have had a chance to give you anything?"

Shit.

"*Geeeeriiii?*" He pulled out my name like he was stretching taffy.

"I... I didn't want to worry you."

"Geri?" This time tart and to the point like the look he gave, a binding-me-with-Wonder-Woman's-golden-lasso-of-truth glare.

The self-built wall of omission broke, releasing the truth dam. "I was at the top of the tower when the rocket hit. But... it's fine! You see, *I'm* fine. And for the record, I was there trying to save Becky. She had a broken leg and couldn't move. And I was *going* to try to carry her down the secret staircase behind that ugly painting, but Becky knew we'd never make it, so she pushed me out the window, and then..."

When I turned, it was to the feel of Tobias's hands on my cheeks and his passion on my lips. He kissed me with a reverence that felt like Easter Sunday, the piece of paper crushed between us. When he pulled back, I saw unfallen tears glistening in his eyes.

"You beautiful git." Another kiss pressed to my lips, a declarative statement followed by open-ended ellipses as he dotted his lips over my cheeks and forehead. "I've already lost once, Geri. I can't survive that again."

The words, heartbreaking and simultaneously sweet, stung at my heart. Which was why I felt like a total asshole for writing it off so quickly.

I'd been able to paraphrase the truth without mentioning the surprise twist of my survival, but I'd an epiphany first and I felt like mine still had precedent.

"I'm not going to leave you, you fuzzy furball." I ran a hand over his twenty-three-hour beard for emphasis. "But can we focus?" I thrust the paper up between our faces.

He dropped his hands. "Would it hurt you to swoon once in a while?"

"I don't know, I've never swooned." He brushed off the comment with a smile as I continued. "So, it's obvious that this is a list of asenaics."

Tobias took the paper and re-read it. "But my mum isn't on here. Is it because Brünhild thought her dead when she made the list?"

"I don't think so. I asked Markus to run a search of our database for me. Zelda Kreuger died twenty years ago." I pointed to the entry on the list. "Tobias, I think this is a list of the asenaics who were raised as wolves. I don't think it includes ones like me and my dad, raised as hoods."

For a moment, nothing. Then, as his eyes went wide, his face lit up. "You're saying my mum was raised a hood?"

And the truth shall set you free!

But Tobias didn't look like a man experiencing enlightenment. He looked like a man experiencing a profound migraine.

My mate pressed his palms to his forehead. "I don't have the energy to think about what that means right now. All I want is a hot shower and a cool bed. Please tell me you have both in there." He pointed to the house.

That was all I was going to get from him?

Fine. I couldn't force Tobias to care about his mother's secret, the essential step to getting him to figure out how I'd survived a fall from the tower without a scratch. A secret, I'd note, that I so didn't tell him. Because I had made a promise, damn it.

"Did the last time I was here, but there's a chance my mother turned my room into a sewing den or a place to hang her collection of medieval torture instruments or something."

"Your family is so weird."

Said the pot to the kettle.

Beyond the front door, my childhood home stood frozen in time, a sitcom living room imbued with Yooper spirit. Each wall held a different taxidermied trophy mounted against wood paneling. The heads of a deer, a moose, an elk, and of course, a wolf all stared down on us with shiny plastic eyes. In our defense, it was a natural wolf and not one of the were variety. Lower Peninsula trolls often cocked a head at such displays. Same state, different state of mind.

I discovered, however, that my English werewolf wasn't any different. He just stood there, a visitor on an alien planet, failing to grasp the view.

"Tobias?"

My voice brought him back to the here and now. He turned on me, apologies written in his face. "Sorry. It's just, it's so... so..."

"Unlike the Packs' houses."

"You could say that again."

I pulled his bag out of his hand and together with mine, threw it on the couch. It and the love seat sitting perpendicular both had a little more wear than three years ago, but it was still the same old scratchy brown polyester weave with two intermittently stained tan throw pillows each. A massive, rectangular block of wood served as a coffee table while brassy floor lamps played host to airily wafting cobwebs. One could argue that the ceiling was white, but it looked like it'd been a while since it'd been washed. As much foot traffic as this room got, serving as the de facto headquarters of the Red Hoods of North America and sometimes beyond, keeping things clean was a constant task. Often, *my* task.

"I guess mom didn't hire a maid after I left. Either that or some of my cousins got in here while she's been gone and threw a kegger."

My mate still stood dumbfounded just inside the threshold.

I pushed him along a bit while closing the heavy front door behind us and passed into the hall to turn up the thermostat. "We'll do the grand tour after we get some sleep. Unless you're hungry? We probably have some venison steaks or whitefish in the freezer I could defrost."

Tobias took tentative steps like he expected the joke to spring at any minute. "I was expecting something posher. I mean, your mother *is* the Grand Matron."

"Brünhild Kline is the Grand Matron when she's in Triberg. When she's in Paradise, she's a Yooper mom who used to yell at my dad for getting potato chips down in the couch cushions. So, food or bed?"

"What?" He followed me as I made my way into the kitchen. "If you're hungry, then..."

I opened the freezer and found two ice-crusted bags of questionable content. I placed them on the counter. "Nope, but I'll leave these here for later. You said something about a shower? I'll go turn the water heater up. We keep it just high enough so the pipes don't freeze while we're away. You can jump in now if you want, but the water's going to be cold as hell."

"Don't care. I have to get the smells off me. I'm an archive of every person on that plane." He leaned in, sniffing my neck. "You are too."

"I'm not taking a cold shower."

Tobias flinched. "Not so tough after all, are you?"

"Oh, I'm plenty tough. I'm just also really spoiled when it comes to modern plumbing."

He dusted a kiss across my lips. "Fine, I'll go first, then you'll go in luxury."

While Tobias grabbed his own personal version of the ice bucket challenge, I climbed the stairs to my old bedroom, hoping to find a pair of pajamas I'd left behind three years before I'd fled in a fit of rage. Everything looked exactly like I'd left it. My bed was even unmade from the last time I slept in it. Which, frankly, would be embarrassing if Tobias saw. I quickly tidied that up, then headed to my closet to unearth some of my own t-shirts in the back.

A red velvet sleeve crushed beneath my fingers. A moment of confusion became a spark of disbelief. My old *feuernacht* dress. I couldn't believe it was still here. The style was decidedly old school Black Forest, right down to the white linen bustier and puffed red velvet sleeves. It had been intended to be the dress I wore when I someday claimed my fire and shed my nascent state. Instead, I'd worn blue jeans and a Black Crows tee (ironically), and had my powers awakened on the broadside of a solarium.

I took out the dress and examined it from top to bottom. Now that I was righteous, my hood would match it nicely. I wondered if maybe, just maybe...

When Tobias finally emerged from the bathroom wearing nothing but a too-small towel around his waist, it was to find me examining myself in the full-length mirror, rubbing my hands over the cinched waist of the dress that *almost* still fit. I had gotten it when I was a teenager, after all. Some of my curves had filled in since then.

I turned, cheeks blazing. "I was just... curious. If it fits. I didn't... I mean, I'm still a hood, too, right? And this dress was custom-made and cost a hell of a—"

"Shhh."

His eyes went dark. His mouth lulled open. The wolf stepped forward, the hunter sizing up prey.

He circled, and the dynamic between us shifted. Without laying a finger on me, I felt his touch over every inch of my body. Scents of lemon soap and tea tree shampoo enveloped my senses. His eyes glistened when he faced me again, his gaze slowly inching down my body, indexing the cut of the fabric, the dye of the cloth. I'd probably never worn more clothes in front of Tobias ever, and somehow, I'd felt more exposed than I ever had in my whole life.

"This is a bonfire moon dress."

The English name for what my Germanic clan called *feuernacht*.

I swallowed. "Yes, it is."

"You were meant to wear this when you took your fire," he continued, his finger tracing a path down my chest, over the rise of my breast. "On the night you became one of the righteous, became a *woman* so to speak."

He needed to be touching me more. "Yes."

"That would mean this is a little girl's dress. But, Gerwalta, you're not a little girl."

Something about him saying my full name did things to my knees that logic couldn't explain.

Tobias stepped away. "Summon it."

"Summon what?"

"Your hood. Put it on."

"So you can take it off?"

"No, the hood stays on." He pushed a kiss atop my forehead, trailing his lips in tiny refrains down the bridge of my nose, bypassing my lips and jumping to my chin, then to my neck. His hands encircled me, each sliding over my curves, taking a handful of my backside. "But the dress? I'm going to rip it off, piece by piece. I'm going to *free* the shewolf beneath."

Holy shit, how did he expect me to do anything? I was melting on the spot. Drive me ten hours north and I'd destroy the polar ice caps.

Concentrating long enough to draw the hood into being was almost impossible, particularly as his mouth sucked beneath my ear and one of my legs found itself wrapped around him. Nonetheless, I did it, the weight of the newly materialized fabric settling over my back, the pull of the button secured over my sternum pulling at the hollow of my throat.

No sooner had I given into his request than I heard the first *whrrpp*.

Part of the skirt sagged from the waistline, exposing a patch of hip beneath. I gasped as Tobias took my weight from me, pulling the other leg up and wrapping me around him just long enough to make his way to the bed. It wasn't meant to be shared by two, especially not if one of them was werewolf-sized, but at this point, it was either a full-sized mattress or an unvacuumed floor.

The bed involved fewer carpet burns.

Tobias lowered my hips until they touched the mattress, then pulled back up. Chancing a look down, I saw that the towel had somehow been sacrificed in the maneuver, giving me a delicious preview of this show's coming attraction. He leaned in over me, one hand working at the linen band covering my breasts. With one quick jerk, the patch of fabric ripped off its hems, exposing my chest, framed by the outer bodice of the dress, almost like two apples put on the edge of a velvet shelf.

My mouth fell open and my head tilted back as the pleasure we both felt wrapped me in a hypnotic positive feedback loop. I moaned. Lord help me, I moaned like some unbroken lover.

His smile broke the suction. "Not too fast, love." His hand hooked the fabric taut under my breasts and yanked hard. The seams surrendered, opening my midriff to the still-chilled air. "Take your time."

Seriously?

"Take my time?" With a thrust of my hips and a push of my foot against the mattress, I rolled Tobias off me, placing his body between the wall and me. Without further pretense, I anchored my hands on his hips and pulled him to the middle of the bed while simultaneously throwing my leg over him.

The ache of that joining, the feel of my lover, my mate, completing me…. The look in his eyes as my red cloak pooled around us and as I began to work myself over him… The love that flowed between us: in the air, in our bodies, in our souls…

The fear that this may all be temporary, his ability to be with me just a side effect of the very treatments and tortures our enemy had subjected him to…

"I want forever with you."

His hands settled on my hips, his push and pull aiding the gentle rhythm. "You have me."

His hips, his motion, his body… the delicious tension he caused in me….

I never wanted it to end.

But Kara had wanted that too. He had mated her with the same intentions, crossed oceans in an attempt to save her.

And she still died.

I wasn't stupid. Hoods and wolves died all the time. From accidents, conflict, old age…

Egotistical ancient vampires.

But right now, Tobias was mine. Here, in my tiny little corner of Paradise, we were one.

And as I reached my zenith, his body hard beneath mine, that was enough.

THIRTEEN

BRÜNHILD

No official sign or landmark stood where the unclaimed forest ended and the packlands began. It was the feeling in the pit of my stomach that told me I had crossed the border, that preternatural lurch a hood had when in the proximity of wolves. For me, it hit about a thousand feet out from the colony of houses owned by the Paradise Pack. I stood, waiting, listening to gusty licks on barren maple branches and shaking conifer needles. Winter wind was silence made tangible. It both overwhelmed the senses and deadened all else.

A flashlight bobbed through the trees, the rhythm familiar, keyed to the gait of the pack beta. Rick Ryland had no winter coat, though the faded, stained jean jacket he wore was so omnipresent, I was pretty certain he slept in it. Only at the state park, where he had a uniform, or while in his fur, during which he wore nothing, did it leave his person.

I shivered, remembering a distant day decades ago, a hidden place in the forest, an exception, when not only the jacket, but most of my clothing along with it, had been left on the ground...

"Hilda." He dipped his head but lifted a smile when he came into view.

I nodded back. "Rick."

Then, silence. Our encounters were always like this. Unspoken words lingered on our tongues, but in forty-five years, neither of us had said anything. Besides, Rick was a mated lupine. It didn't matter that he was a widower. The moment he consummated with his mate, anything he had ever felt about me was forfeit.

Anything sustainable on my side was impossible the moment I'd been born my mother's daughter.

The brightness in his face faded. "Heard about Pietro. My condolences."

"I..." My arm strapped across my stomach as my heart sank. I'd always been able to keep a straight face, to stay the Matron. But losing my husband, my love, my heart, the only man with whom I could truly be myself, who knew all my faults and my secrets and loved me despite them... My earth became quicksand whenever that pain returned, weakening my knees and pulling me under.

Stay focused, I lectured myself. You need to be strong for what you're about to do. You need to be the Grand Matron.

I pulled out a skin-deep smile. "Thank you, Rick."

He reached out to massage my shoulder, an act he'd never do if any of the other wolves could see. "He was like family to me, you know. From the moment you brought him home to Paradise, he had my back, and I had his."

"He considered you a brother of sorts." This time the grin proved authentic. "A brother he could never acknowledge in public but whom he loved, secretly."

"We did our best with the rules of the world we were handed."

I bit my lip. "If only we'd done better with the rules of the one we created."

The wolf straightened, dropped his hands to his belt to pull up his jeans, and looked around. "So, you want to do this all formal-like, or has the world finally gone batshit crazy enough that you'll take that giant stick out your ass and just act like a normal person?"

Good, old Rick. "Distinguished Beta of the Paradise Pack…"

Rick grimaced. "Stick still in ass, got it."

I pressed on. "I come in friendship and without qualm to seek an audience with your Alpha and ask permission to enter your packlands bearing no arms and no ill will."

Rick bowed, his arm swinging back. "Matron of the House of Red, on behalf of our alpha and the Paradise Pack, you are hereby granted entry to our illustrious packlands and welcomed as a friend. No harm will come to you, and you are considered our guest." He regained his height. "Now that that's over, come on. Greta Jansen made her potato salad, and if that's all gone by the time we get to the community room, I'm holding you accountable."

"I thought no harm shall come to me?" I said as we began to stroll towards the center of packlands life.

"That's only for being around. Depraving a man of Greta's spud grub? Hanging offense, as far as I'm concerned."

I put my phone back in my pocket and looked back up at Lisa and Cody Ryland just as the latter passed Baby Mandy to the alpha.

"Gerwalta and Tobias are almost here. Apparently they, and I quote, 'woke up late.'"

Lisa and Cody exchanged a knowing look.

"Just like the newly mated, huh?" Cody said. "*Waking up late* all the time."

Lisa giggled. "I think we *woke up late* for about three months there at the start, didn't we?"

I sipped at my punch, the orange sherbet nearly melted into the lemon-lime pop, as Maggie Somfield entered the community room. I'd rarely seen a woman so split in two. Part of her craved to be around people; you could see it in her longing gaze as she surveyed the room, like the new girl at school looking for a table in the lunchroom. The other part of her calculated each lupine present, sizing them up as either threat or irrelevant. She looked at the pack like a hood would. I knew that conflict intimately, for I had observed it all my life. In my husband born with a wolf's passions and raised in hood ways. In my daughter, saturated by tradition but drawn to its contrast. In my own mirror, a creature who held both the power of moon and sun, who drowned in the very shadows she herself cast.

I knew Maggie Somfield before I'd met her.

"Excuse me," I said to the alpha and his mate. "I need a moment."

For her part, Maggie didn't bolt when she saw me crossing the room, though her wide eyes and rotating gaze led me to think she was looking for an escape route.

"Mrs. Somfield," I said. "I was delighted to hear when I arrived back to Michigan this morning that you were staying in the packlands with the Rylands."

"Yes, well, they've been very hospitable." Then, echoing my formality, she asked, "Are things in Triberg stabilized?"

I nodded. "As well as we can manage, thank you. Our resident vampire and some of his bloodline were able to warp enough minds to let go of the immediate huey interest in the story. Unfortunately, Schloss Wolfsretter is damaged beyond repair."

"And will you rebuild?"

"The council hasn't decided yet. If we do, it will only be after we deal with our current situation."

We both turned to my left as the sound of a car coming to a stop outside met our ears. Gerwalta and Tobias, I imagined. I hadn't stopped by the house since returning earlier in the day, and though I'd never admit it, I longed to see that my daughter was still safe. Maggie's eyes also held some kind of desire, though different from my own. Son and mother may have been reunited, but that didn't mean they were amended.

"It's funny, isn't it?"

Maggie's head turned my way. "What is?"

"Any number of things, really. That you and I would become in-laws, for one. That hoods and wolves would be coming together to defeat a common enemy. That more than three hundred years after the fact, two different branches of Gerwalta Faust's lineage would find each other and fall in love."

"So you believe my son loves your daughter?" Maggie said.

It was such an odd question, I wasn't sure what to say.

Luckily, Maggie spoke on. "I've wondered it myself. If it was love or a mating bond. But he had a mating bond with another, I've been told. They're not supposed to get more than one, wolves aren't. It's supposed to be singular, and last forever."

I raised an eyebrow. "They?"

"We, us, wolves," Maggie amended. She drew a deep breath as our two children came into the room only to be circled by the whole pack. Congratulations flew for their mating, Tobias the recipient of more than one jab to the arm or slap on the shoulder. The shewolves took turns pinching Gerwalta's cheeks, leaving them fiery.

"They've both suffered for what they were," I said, keeping my eyes on the couple. "Through no fault of their own, they were born with conflicting natures. Perhaps there is some justice in this world still, that the two were able to discover what they did, do what they do despite it. I am thankful for that, Mrs. Somfield, aren't you?"

"You can call me Maggie—" Her eyes glistened when she turned. "And yes, I am."

The shared moment of hope and pride disintegrated the very next when Maggie added, "But you're nutters if you think this working together is anything more than the result of a temporary necessity. Wolves and hoods cannot live in harmony. Two individuals might be able to find a way, but our societies have too much tradition, history, and warfare between us to ever move beyond."

"I used to think that too."

Maggie's head cocked to the side. "You, the Grand Matron, think there's a way for it to be different?"

"I think..." I crossed my arms. "...not in my time. But in theirs? Perhaps. One thing I've understood since the time Gerwalta was born, Maggie, and that I think it even truer now: the only thing that brings two sides together better than a common enemy, is a leader who both can claim. Particularly if the last thing that she wants is to *be* the leader."

"Mom?"

I followed the sound of Gerwalta's voice, then the turn of her gaze. The community room had a small dais, one built of cheap pieces of lumber begged from overstock back when I was in high school. There, Cody Ryland urgently waved me on.

"Think on that a while, Maggie. I hope you can find a way to believe it too."

A minute later, every eye in the pack scrutinized me. I couldn't remember in my lifetime hearing a Matron—or any hood for that matter—attempt something like I was about to do. Truth be told, if my daughter wasn't friends with most of the pack, I probably wouldn't stand a chance.

A microphone mounted on a stand heavily fortified by gray duct tape squealed as Cody flipped it on. Every single person in the room, supernatural by some measure, covered their ears and groaned. The alpha waved his apologies and turned down the volume on a mixer board off to the side.

"Sorry, everybody, sorry." With a cough, he gathered their attention back. "So, not all of you have met Hilda Kline personally, but everyone knows her by reputation. And I know how weird this is for us all, to have the Grand Matron of all the hoods in the world here as an honored guest. But she's asked me a question, one even as alpha, I didn't want to answer until I heard what everyone thought. So with that, Hilda Kline."

I swallowed down my nerves. The pack may have played nice when I was just one person mingling among them, but now that they knew I was here with an agenda, the kindness I'd seen in their eyes faded. Would they believe me? Would they sympathize? Would they tell me to go to hell? I wouldn't blame them if they did. I'd ruled over them for more than twenty years, fiercely enforcing the separation between their kind and mine, all in hopes of keeping my daughter safe, my husband safe, *my secrets* safe. But all that had done was put all of us in greater danger.

The silver fist did nothing but choke. It was time to extend a hand of peace.

In my silence, expectations grew among the pack. Impatience festered. Annoyance sprouted. I closed my eyes.

"Members of the Paradise Pack—"

I fell to my knees, prostrating myself before them all.

"—we desperately need your help."

FOURTEEN

To say I didn't know if it was day or night sounded cliché, but bitch, I didn't know, so there.

My eyes cracked open to find Ginger Spice (red-haired slayer—what was his name again?) drooling on my shoulder. With a speed a Kenyan runner would have admired, I pushed him off me and proceeded to oog out. *Gross, slayer spittle.*

We had to get out of this freaking motel, and not just because I was running out of money. The wad of cash the hoods had given us when we left Germany couldn't last forever. While Bob's Roadside Inn 'n' Grub was an upgrade from Dracula's water-logged basement tortureland, even the slayers were beginning to feel worn down by stagnation. We'd shared three rooms for a month. One for the women to sleep in, one for the men, and the third which had become our everything-else-you-do-while-awake place.

So why was Drippy Doug (Doug!) giving me a spit shower?

The answer soon became clear. Because the sun was up. Even in our community room, that tended to knock out a few if they lingered too long. I pushed myself off the couch and looked over to one of the two beds. Mina's little arms danced up in the sky, Teiko stretched out beside her, racking up the z's.

I crossed the room, picked up a few napkins left over from the previous night's takeout, and cleared off my shoulder in preparation for a new kind of dribble. But, hell, if it was Mina, I didn't care. I'd even gotten over her spitting up on me. Mostly.

"Come here, little puppy." My biceps screamed as I lifted her. I swore that she'd doubled in size since we'd landed in Chicago. Geri and Tobias had sent me an infant. I was going to send them back a preteen if they didn't claim her soon.

Teiko pulled a hand over her eyes, blocking a ray of morning light that pooled over the bed. "I can take her if you…"

I shook my head. "She just needs a feeding and then she'll be down for the day. You go ahead and sleep. I'll be up and around."

The slayer didn't argue. Twenty minutes later, Mina had a full belly, a clean diaper, and pride in a job well done for staining my last clean shirt. I laid her back into Teiko's arms and headed out to catch some air.

At least I'd been able to buy a good coat in the Munich airport. The Chicago winter was in full effect, the wind touching me in places no man had for months. I pulled a cigarette from my pocket and cupped my hands over the end as the lighter fought probability to do its job. The first drag lit up my senses, tickling my throat and burning my eyes. It was a nasty new habit, but it was one that gave me an excuse to get out of those rooms and have five minutes to myself.

I hitched my foot up on a low-rise brick wall, leaned back, and found my happy place when someone spoke beside me.

"Since when do you smoke?"

I came off the building like a preacher off the pulpit.

He had the beard of a lumberjack and the clothes of a homeless guy, but you couldn't mistake those baby blues.

Caleb closed the distance between us, grabbed the cigarette from my lips, and threw it down on the ground, stomping it out. "No smoking," he commanded, wagging his finger. "It's going to be hard enough keeping you alive in the supe world. At least help me out a bit and don't give yourself cancer."

"You're... You're alive."

"Of course, I'm alive." He clutched his stomach. "Even if I have thrown up more in the last three weeks from seasickness than everyone else in the history of the world, ever, put together and doubled. If you ever want to lose ten pounds in a hurry, I'd recommend being stuck on a rickety old freighter in the North Atlantic in December."

"Stuck on... Caleb?"

"What?"

My hand swung forward, and lord help me, the beard and the man would have separate assault claims on me because I hit him hard enough to do both damage.

"Amy!" His hand reached up to nurse the wound. "What the fuck?"

"What the fuck?" I shouted back, even as three different room doors behind me flew open. "You were on a boat for three weeks, and you couldn't send a single message to tell us that you were *fucking alive*? We've been..."

"Caleb!"

Teiko practically bowled me over, her arms out and her beautiful bouncy breasts billy-bucking to her Solari.

"Teiko." And he opened his arms wide, of course, because that's who he was.

And I stormed off inside as the last of the slayers handed me off Mina in the doorway, only to slam the door and leave them all out in the cold.

Because that's who I was.

After Caleb ate, showered, and shaved, he no longer looked like a poster boy for Army Surplus. Sure he was thinner and had a few bruises on his forearms and cuts on his hands, but he assumed the role of the bold, charismatic leader every cult needed.

"Tell us again!" Doug, the sad little slayer-teen, prostrated himself on the altar of his idle, i.e. sat on the floor by the kitchenette sink as Teiko gave our brave and illustrious leader a haircut and asked him to revel us with the heroic tale of his sacrifice, endurance, and escape from the clutches of the evil Dracule.

"There's not much to tell," Caleb said, but I could see the smug smile he tried to douse. "There we were, Geri, Tobias, his mother, and the Vampire Doge of Venice, surrounded by sniveling, snarling, hell-bent Dracule. *We're all going to die*, Geri said. *If only there was a way to fight all these vampires, but I'm only one wolf!* Tobias said. It was then that I knew what I had to do. So I grabbed Geri Kline by the elbows and kissed that girl silly. Tobias, you know, growled and all that. And I just turned to him and said, *I know she's your mate, but I'm about to go out there and fight for you both and probably die, so just give me this.* Yeah, he hated it, but he understood. And then I leaped from the car and my solaria lit the night. The others got the hell out of there, leaving me in a crowd of vamps. Five, ten, maybe twenty of them closed in on me. I waited, letting them get close until..." He stilled, his hands held up like he was getting ready to pass some invisible basketball. "Kaboom!" And he threw his arms out wide, everyone reverberating. "One solarium from these mighty hands and they burned down to ash."

Thea, a Grecian beauty because all the female slayers had been gifted by the Gods of DNA, leaned forward on the bed. "And what did you do after that? Why were you gone for so long?"

Caleb wound a tie around his neck and set to looping it. "I was a single man in one of the most swinging cities in the world. You got to give me a little leeway to live a little, you know?"

I rolled my eyes. "As if."

Teiko gave me the stink eye before she focused back on Caleb. "How exciting. How brave!"

"And how full of shit."

Every slayer in the room handed me a bucket of daggers with their glares.

"Ignore her," Doug said to no one in particular, taking to his feet. "She's just jealous because she's not one of us. She'll never be able to do what Caleb can do."

I moved Mina over from one knee to the other. "Oh, I can spin a yarn like I'm Betty-fucking-Ross. The question is, why would I want to?"

Teiko's resolve cracked the tiniest bit. She turned back to the Solari, her voice soft. "You're not lying to us, right, Caleb? All that really happened, *riiiggghht*?"

Caleb pushed a cuff link through the buttonholes on his dress shirt (he'd brought a whole suit with him because... why?) before reaching up to pinch Teiko's cheek. "Of course, it happened, kiddo. Doug's right. Barbie's just jealous."

Before I could draft another response, we were cut off by a knock. Like a bunch of frightened rabbits, the slayers hunched down on the floor. All except Caleb who headed for the door.

"It's okay, folks," he said, opening the way to a short, bald white man in a three-piece suit. "That's just our ride."

"Our ride?" Doug ran across the room, past the suit, before reappearing over his shoulder a moment later. "There's a bus out here. But, like, a really fancy bus."

"It's here to take everyone to our new digs," Caleb said. "Grab yourself a seat on the party bus, everyone. We're moving uptown. Teiko?"

The Asian slayer took time turning, making sure to work a curve in the process. "Yes, Solari?"

"You take Mina and her things, okay?" Caleb ran a finger over her chin, and I tried not to barf. "I need to talk to Amy for a minute alone."

Teiko passed me a grin, clearly under the impression that I was about to be chewed out harder than a three-hour steak. As if. If anyone was going to be masticated, it was the beefcake she was trying oh-so-hard to seduce. Like *that* was ever going to happen. I knew what guys looked like when they were playing for power or playing for pussy. Caleb was flirting for favor, not fucks.

Even as Teiko took Mina, rushing out with the others to the party bus, the decent human being that lived somewhere inside me chastised my own inner thoughts. Teiko was a good woman. Hell, even Doug, while a little *drooly*, was pretty cool. All the slayers were awesome. So why in the hell was I being such a bitch about this? My problems were with Mr. The-World-Revolves-Around-Me, not them.

Shit, I was going to have to apologize, wasn't I?

The moment the door closed, leaving Caleb and I alone, I owned my attitude. "Look, that was wrong of me, I know. I'm sorry. I won't be so... *me* around them again."

"You're right, you won't."

His somber eyes drilled down on me as he slid his suit jacket on, all the snide sarcasm gone. A chill crept down my spine, a realization so stark it actually made me step backward. Caleb wasn't just an annoying male version of me. He was a supe. The guy could kill a vampire. If he'd wanted to, toasting me would be a walk in the park for him.

A corner of his mouth ticked up, but I couldn't figure out if it was because my reaction entertained him or reinforced his superiority over me.

"Just... let's not fuck up our shot to save slayerkind by bickering in front of the kids, okay?"

I nodded once, turned, then forgot everything I'd felt in the last thirty seconds. "I know you're lying by the way. You might be able to throw balls of sunlight around but detecting the bullshit men say to impress women is *my* superpower. And you know what? I don't give a shit if you lie to me, but those slayers look up to you. They *trust* you, and if they find out that you're pulling one over on them, they're going to be crushed so just—"

"Shut up, Barbie, you're right."

He'd copped to it so easily, I cupped a hand over my ear, inviting him to test my ability to hear. "Sorry, what?"

"I said, you're right." All his bravado? It fell away, leaving a smaller man than stood there moments before. "It's not all a lie, by the way. I really did get out of the car to give the others a chance to get away. And I really *did kill* quite a few Dracule."

I refused to let down my guard too quickly. "And?"

"And..." Caleb stuck his hands in his pockets. "And there were just so many of them. They overpowered me. And then took me back to a house in Southwark where they beat the living shit out of me, taking breaks to drink from me at will."

But that didn't make any sense. "How could vampires overpower *you*? You can turn them to ash."

"The house where they were keeping Tobias's mother? It was on the Thames." He chuckled into his shoulder. "The whole fight, I thought I was the one in control, but the whole time they were moving me toward the shore. The second they got me into the water, I was at their mercy. A slayer's powers... They don't work when we're grounded in water, remember? But I lucked out. One of the Dracule meant to watch me, she... She didn't want to kill *anyone.* She just wanted to go home. So I told her if she sprung me out, I'd get her there. Eventually, she trusted me enough to do it."

"And did you..." I clutched at my throat. "Did you get her home?"

His somber eyes met mine. "No, Amy. I killed her. The second we were far enough away, I turned her to dust."

I felt like he was looking to me for forgiveness somehow. Or maybe just understanding. But who was I to forgive him?

"I'm sure you did what you had to do," was all I could bring myself to say.

"So I keep telling myself. Like she probably told herself when she ended up there, too." He sucked in his bottom lip as he nodded. "The slayers need to believe in me because right now, that's the only way they can believe in themselves. So, please, just go along with my stories, okay? At least in front of them. When we're in private, call me on all the shit you want. Just as long as the arrangement is reciprocal."

"What shit do you think you're going to call me on?"

"You said you don't care about me." Caleb straightened as he crossed to me and cupped my cheek with his hand. "*Liar.* Like, you're at least ten percent happy that I'm back."

"More like eight-point-five." I pulled his hand down. "If I hadn't found out that you're demanding I live with you, it *might* have been a ten."

FIFTEEN

GERI

Cody's pack joined us on the first day. By the second, most of the Reds of North America had shown up on our front door. The Yellows followed, flowing in from the south, and then Blues and the Oranges gathered from east and west respectively. When Whites and Browns funneled in on the fifth night, I nearly passed out. But it wasn't until wolves from every corner of the globe filled out our ranks that I truly understood: something much bigger than anything the supernatural world had ever seen was coming.

In the span of twelve days, we'd gone from just a few to a hundred hoods and two hundred wolves. Paradise, a tiny town whose numbers swelled only during the summer tourist months, took notice. The sheriff threatened to ticket us for holding "some kind of backwoods tent revival without a permit." Luckily, Yan had also arrived, a few other members of his bloodline with him. Together the vampires twisted the authority's perceptions, and Sheriff Jensen drove away from the gates to our property muttering, "really, it's not *that* many people, and the Klines are such nice folk."

I kinda wished sometimes that instead of part-slayer, I could be part-vampire, just for their awesome Jedi mind skills.

Unfortunately, while we dodged huey fines and permits, vampire voodoo couldn't do everything. Our tiny little grocery store in Paradise was no match for such an unplanned onslaught. Amy, learning that we were running low on supplies, decided to max out the shiny new credit cards her father had sent, sending several trucks of dry goods and bottled water from the closest warehouse store two counties over. Still, every new arrival brought both joy from the increased support, and anxiety from having another mouth to feed.

"Kinda gives you a new respect for the phrase, 'an army marches on its stomach,' doesn't it?"

Tobias paused from laying out the framework of another tent. "Is that a thing?"

I looked up from my clipboard. "You've never heard that?"

He shrugged. "History was never my thing."

"Yeah, what was?"

"Detention."

Meanwhile, the need to command drew my mother from the recesses of her grief. Squads were formed. Drills were run. Discipline was instilled. For the first time, I saw beauty in her bravado. What I'd always taken as ego revealed itself to be obligation. She owed those coming to die honor in their sacrifice. She owed it to me. I, in turn, vowed to return the favor.

My father would have been proud.

Mid-December brought a fresh wave of winter hell; a two-day whiteout that left a hip-high blanket of snow and drifts the height of a grown man. Supes had a higher level of endurance against the elementals than hueys, but I still felt some guilt looking out of my bedroom window to the yurts and tents where hundreds slept in the cold.

A few days before Christmas, following a meeting between Cody, who had become the de facto Big Wolf, and my mother, several wolves from the packland's own camp showed up in the training yard inside our compound.

"This isn't like the centuries before now." Cody took center point, both local lupines and those who'd come from afar, answering our calls for help, soaking in the information. "Wolves and hoods have come to blows through the years, sometimes justified, sometimes not, but never before has there been a reason for us to fight *together*. The Dracule *are* that reason. But don't think this is going to be easy, just because we've joined forces with the hoods. Vampires are dangerous foes. They're wicked fast and deadly strong."

I took over. "But we learned some things from their attack on Schloss Wolfsretter. First, while many assaulted us simultaneously, their attack was not coordinated. They didn't come in formations, nor did they seem to have any strategy other than to push forward. The assault wasn't so much a single military campaign as dozens of individual attacks. They don't fight in groups, but we do."

"A single wolf or hood against a vampire—any vampire—stands little chance," Tobias assumed from there. "The best he can hope for is a draw. But even two wolves—"

"Or hoods," I interjected.

My mate smirked. "Or even two *hoods*," he granted, "taking on a vampire opens a two-sided battle that seems to bugger them up."

A wolf from a New England pack, his accent so thick it sounded fake, walked in from the edges of the circle. "Just tell us how you actually kill one of them bastards. Stake to the heart? Is that really a thing, or did I watch all that late-night B movie shit for nothing?"

I nodded. "Wood to the heart or brain works, if you can get close enough. Personally, I say go for the head with silver blades. Or you wolves have the option of *biting* it off, I guess."

"But be careful," Yan said. "We can turn to smoke and zip through the air faster than you can swing. It does take us an undistracted moment, however, to make the change. That's why you keep a vampire engaged constantly. If one of us should smoke, however, it's possible for a talented hood to encase us in silver. But keep in mind, the silver you wrap around a vampire then goes out of play, so only do it if there's no other choice."

"What we'd like to do now," Cody resumed, "is for you all to form squads, three or four people each. We have some friendly vampires here who are going to let you experience their speed and maneuverability."

With that, Yan's dozen or so brothers and sisters smoked through the crowd, rematerializing in the center beside us. The ease with which they seemingly appeared from nowhere drove the message home. All around, anxious eyes looked on.

"These are vampires of my bloodline, the Varanasi, a very old line whose origins are predated only by one other," Yan continued. "We're smart, powerful, and battle-rich. Training-safe weapons only for now, but otherwise, don't hold your punches. We'll recover from any light injury you induce in a day or so."

"In other words," Tobias said, "don't kill anyone, for fuck's sake. There'll be plenty of time for slaying when the Dracule come."

Cody nodded in agreement. "Concentrate on figuring out what each other's strengths and weaknesses are. And please, hoods, be careful not to touch any wolf with silver. It burns like a bitch. Geri, care to give a little demo?"

I nodded and turned, but instead of square off against my ex, I faceplanted into Tobias's back. My big, brutish, and ridiculous wolf stepped between me and the Paradise alpha, blocking my path and radiating defensive vibes.

"Are you barmy?" he barked. "That's my sodding mate you're talking about."

I wasn't sure what sodding meant. Didn't sound pleasant.

Cody grinned as I peeked around the hulking form in front of me. "Look, Johnny English, Geri and I have been sparring partners since... well, forever. I set this exercise up with plans for us to serve as models. We already know each other's styles."

"You think I don't know how to fight with my own mate?" Tobias barked. "Go find yourself a different hood, Cody. This one's mine."

I barely escaped an attempted dragging-away before I managed to pull my hand back, giving Tobias nothing but air to hold.

"Actually, Tobias, Cody has a good point."

The *Et tu, Brute?* stare... If it was over something serious, it would have broken my heart.

"But..." Tobias whimpered.

Lifting on the balls of my feet, my hands full of his sweatshirt for support, I pressed a kiss to his lips. "I promise, afterwards, you can be as Me-Tarzan, You-Jane as you want."

Something about my tone, my suggestion, bore down into his most alpha recesses. Hunger awoke in his eyes, a burning desire that I should be embarrassed was on public display, but on some level, I coveted.

"Fine." His forehead leaned against mine. "But you'll only have yourself to blame tomorrow when you walk through camp funny."

If a bomb dropped or the continents suddenly shifted, killing every person in the UP, archaeologists would someday wonder why so much silver had been hoarded in a private compound, a hundred miles from the nearest mine.

I loaded up, pulling the metal in a stream from bars piled on the edge of the practice area, to the palms of my hands, and then weaving it over my inner elbow and up my forearm. Meanwhile, Cody stripped in preparation to shift while Tobias, now standing at the edge of the crowd, did his best not to notice.

Cody turned as he dropped his boxers on top of his other clothes. Wolves had no qualms about nudity, but I realized suddenly that it was also the first time I'd seen my ex naked since we'd broken up. My memories had been watercolors compared to the 4K vision before me. Yes, I was mated, but my eyes didn't care.

"You know I trust you, Little Red, but if you get one burn mark on me, Lisa's going to pull out your hair."

I smiled up at him as the last drips of silver tickled my wrist and slid out of sight. "You do remember we've experimented with silver before, don't you?"

"Yeah, but that time we had... um." Cody cleared his throat. "A different goal in mind."

"You'll be fine," I assured. "Now, fur up!"

By the time I'd turned, the deed had been done. Wolf Cody was just... *damn.* Beyond the eye candy sheen of his coat, he was a beast of a beast. Gleaming white teeth, brindle fur, and nails that could slash flesh like Ginsu knives. Lupines resembled their wild cousins in every way but by size and eye color.

His haunches equaled my hip in height, meaning I could look into his brown eyes without looking down.

I pivoted and threw a leg over his back, mounting him in a way I never had during our years of dating. Not that I had mounted him *that* way either. Werewolves and love bonds and everything… To think I used to mourn that fact. But if I had given in to my love-struck self, I wouldn't have Tobias. I couldn't imagine my life without him.

Yan took position before us with the smoothness of James Dean walking into a soda shop. Hands in pockets, mussed hair tousled and covering his eyes, he looked like he was waiting for a bus rather than a battle.

"I'll be a gentleman and allow you the first move," he said, a hint of his Portuguese accent sticking out.

Cody threw his head back and howled as I wove my fingers into the fur of his scruff to keep balance. My silver obeyed my will, a dull blade the length of my forearm solidifying into being. I felt like Xena, Boadicea, and Wonder Woman all rolled into one.

An illusion that quickly evaporated as Cody lunged for Yan and I fell off his back and flat on my ass.

Cody pinned the vamp, but the lightened load must have alerted him to trouble. Both paws on the vampire's shoulders, he careened his head back, looking for me. The distraction gave Yan time to smoke out from under him.

"Oh, no you don't!"

My blade became liquid as I heaved it forward, one thin tendril balanced on a fingertip for control. Calling on more silver, the thickness of the stream intensified, creating a caldera in the air, redirecting the vampire mist to condense and rebound my direction.

Which seemed great.

Until the mist became a body that was heading straight for me, hands outstretched, fangs bared.

I pulled back the silver in a split second and molded it into a short staff, but not before Yan got to me. He grinned, cocky in a way only a vampire could be, as my ass hit the ground for a second time. Yan only had a moment to gloat as he pinned my shoulders to the ground. The very next, brindle fur rushed past my eyes as Cody knocked Yan off.

I was on my feet in a second.

But so was Yan.

Cody and I became binary forces to the vamp. I jabbed. Yan dodged. Cody nipped. Yan cried out.

We pivoted.

Jab, nip, swing, punch, dodge, thrust.

The vampire was losing dominance.

And the ability to hide his fear.

"Methinks this tactic should have been tested out long before now, Geri." Yan, his hands before him, ready to attempt a deflection, teeter-tottered his balance as we spun counterclockwise to his turning degrees.

"Better late than never?"

Yan nodded. "But only if you win."

The fear had been a ruse. Moving so fast my vision seemed to blur, Yan lunged.

I growled. Cody yipped.

And suddenly, I was on fire.

SIXTEEN

AMY

You'd think it was a prisoner transfer the way it all unrolled.

The bus—one of those executive types with blackened windows, leather seats, and a minibar—pulled into an underground drive off the empty downtown street at 3 AM. I thought at first that we were going into some sort of shipping and receiving entrance. Instead, through a set of glass doors rimmed with polished brass, a spectacle spread out before us. The lobby looked like a mythical creature who threw up cut marble and Christmas trees had gone on a bender and everything around had suffered the consequences. It was so Miracle-on-34ᵗʰ-Street that I wondered for a moment if we'd come to the wrong place.

"Where are we?"

"WWL, of course."

Caleb's hand landed on the small of my back, and it was only then that I realized I'd stopped walking, dazed and stupefied.

I shook my head as my feet gave into his will. "I've been to WWL before with Geri to drop Tobias's lunch. It didn't look like this."

"That's because you came in the huey entrance. This is the executive entrance. The *real* executives, not the ones you see listed on the webpage."

The security staff wore suits almost as nice as Caleb's (but they didn't look as good. No fault of theirs. Not everyone could hit the genetics lottery). Each nodded at him as we passed, then Teiko and Mina behind us, the rest of the slayers bringing up the rear, as we headed for a pair of gilded-door elevators.

"And what are we doing here?"

"It's our new home, Barbie. Stop being so … blonde. You look like a beached fish. Pick up the chin, drop the doe eyes."

I spun on him as both elevators opened behind me. "One, on behalf of blondes everywhere, I resent the stereotype that you're implying. And two, what do you mean it's our new home? Isn't this place crawling with vampires?"

Caleb pointed to the left elevator, which in a side-by-side, I noticed was much larger than the one on the right. "Everyone on. Reception is waiting for you on the thirtieth floor. They'll show everyone to their new apartments. There's ten total, but each has two bedrooms, so you'll have to figure out who goes where. You're all adults, I trust you to make good decisions."

They shuffled with grins on their faces as Caleb gently pulled Teiko aside. "Not you, babe. If you're willing, I'd like to have you come stay with me up on the thirty-third floor. Mina's taken to you and we both know Amy can't be with her twenty-four seven."

A century of female lib riled up in me. If he thought Teiko was going to be okay with the come-play-nanny line, when she was a supernatural being with phenomenal magical powers, then he was…

"Sure, Caleb," the pixie slayer giggled. "I'd love to."

Caleb patted her cheek. "Atta girl. Skip along with the others now. Amy and I will be along shortly."

Teiko and Mina *skipped* to the left as I found myself driven into the elevator on the right.

"Barbie, what did I say about the chin?"

The door closed, and not knowing what else to do, I closed my mouth and stared forward.

Bing Crosby crooned from the speakers above, singing in Spanish? I didn't know he knew Spanish.

"It's not fair, you know, manipulating her crush on you just for convenient babysitting."

Caleb kept his eyes forward. "Mmm-hmmm."

The bastard. "She's going to think you're into her."

"Who said I'm not?"

"Me. I know the playbook, Caleb. I worked it for a long time."

"Oh, you flirted with men so they'd babysit a supernatural baby?" He passed me a snide grin, and I had to tuck my hands into my pockets to keep myself from hitting him.

"Teiko's an amazing woman," he went on. "Intelligent, positive attitude despite what she's been through, an obvious affinity for children… Really, Amy, I'm surprised at you, dismissing my ability to recognize a woman's worth just because she happens to be beautiful *and* finds me attractive."

"You *are* attractive."

He rolled up on his toes, grinning. "I knew you were attracted to me."

"I said you're attractive, *not* that I'm attracted to you." I rounded, placing myself between Caleb and the doors. "I'm looking out for her. That's my job, right? Serve the slayers? Protect them? I promise you, Buffy, if you dick around with Teiko, I will run your balls through a shredder."

"Oh, Barbie. So kinky," Caleb cooed through pursed lips. "Do you remember the text message I sent you as you were leaving Germany?"

"It's hard to forget when my boss, or anyone, really, tells me not to fuck someone."

"I mean the part where I said that *they* need to breed," he said. "You don't think I don't know that includes me? I have to choose a wife, and Teiko is a good candidate."

"A cross-cut shredder. The kind that makes rectangles, not just strips."

Sincerity etched into his features. "Listen, Barbie, I'm planning on being respectful and courting her properly, so will you just let my balls stay as they are for now? They might come in handy later."

"Fine, but I'll be watching you." My eyes whisked down his frame. "And them."

"Fair enough." He pulled a cell from his pocket as it buzzed. "Ah, perfect, everyone's in the boardroom. And this… is the slowest elevator in the world."

"That's because you haven't pushed a floor yet."

He grimaced as he fixed me with an acidic glare and pushed an unmarked button. before sliding his phone back into his pocket. "When we're with the board, do me a favor: don't talk unless I specifically ask you a question, okay? Ideally, I'd like to come out of this meeting without them eating me alive. And if you could survive as well, that would be just peachy."

Any boldness I'd gathered fell around my ankles. "Is this dangerous?"

He gave me a this would be something new? glare.

"I mean, more than usual!" Sighing, I cocked my hip. "I get that you need to regulate the flow of info until you know who you can trust and who you can't, but if you want me to be your *aide du camp*—"

His eyes went wide at my throwing out the fifty-franc phrase. Why was everyone so surprised when I knew stuff? I *did* speak French, after all.

"—then I need to know what's going on."

"Are you familiar with the law of unintended consequences?"

"Of course, like how doctors discovered Viagra gives men boners because they were trying to develop a drug for hair loss."

Caleb's face screwed up, but he managed to shove the stick up his ass the very next second. "Vampires aren't like wolves. There's no alpha's prerogative, but the Dracule are lining up behind their new paterfamilias like good little soldiers anyway. When Igor sacrificed himself to save Geri, he never intended that it would leave Vlad even more empowered, but that's the result."

"Wait a freaking second. You're saying Count Dracula is actually the head of his vampire family tree now?"

Caleb nodded. "And he's using his position to build an army. Look what happened in England, then Triberg. But that's not really the clear-and-immediate danger right now."

I felt a chill creep over me as all the blood rushed from my face. "The Board?"

"Dennis Hoffman, reborn to the House of Dracule in the 1970s."

Truth bloomed like nightshade. "You're goin to kill him."

"Not just kill him, Barbie." Caleb navigated around me as the golden doors opened. "I'm going to make him an example."

SEVENTEEN

GERI

I jumped as the guest bedroom door opened.

Markus frowned, closing the door behind him, shook his head with the collective shame of our ancestors (must have learned that one from my mother), and planted balled fists on his hips.

"What the hell, Geri?"

"I..." I tried to swallow but my mouth had gone dry. "It was an accident."

"An accident?" His hand pointed back at the door. "You nearly killed them both."

Suddenly, my thoughts came bursting out without any filter. "Look, I didn't even know I could do that. Who in the hell thinks they can just oxidize all the silver they have and burst into flame? You know I would never hurt anyone on purpose like that. Jesus Christ, Markus, I'm not that person. Please, let me go in and apologize."

I tried to navigate around him, but no sooner had I taken a step than his beefy arm lashed out, pushing me back. "Lisa's in there."

"Good, then I can apologize to her, too."

"She wouldn't let you get the first word out."

I fell back, defeated. "At least tell me they're going to be okay?"

Finally, my cousin, one of my oldest friends in the world, softened around the edges. "Yan, thank god, is recovering pretty quickly, but Cody's got second-degree burns all over his back and shoulders. Oh, he'll heal up eventually, but he's probably going to have scars for the rest of his life."

There had been a time, if brief, where I would've revealed in that. Love Tobias as I did, that alpha had left me with scars of my own. Now, it was like the universe was playing some kind of cosmic joke. *You want to be a dangerous beast? Fine, we'll show you how dangerous you really are to those you love and everyone around you.*

It wasn't because of who I was. It was because of *what* I was. I'd worked all my life not to become the very thing I was apparently meant to be: a betrayer. Yan and Cody and everyone in the camps had put their faith in me, and in so small a test, I'd shown that it wasn't the enemy they needed to fear, it was me.

I turned for the stairs.

"Where are you going?" Markus called after me.

I couldn't stop. Every instinct was telling me to run, to get away before I hurt anyone else. Jesus, what if it had been Tobias I'd been working with instead of Cody? I could have killed the man who'd given my life purpose again. I couldn't stay here. I couldn't be the cause of any more pain.

I was down the stairs and nearly out the door when I ran head-on into a wall of muscle.

Ha, ha, universe.

"You're running."

I couldn't look up at him. I couldn't stand to see the disappointment I'd seen in everyone else's eyes in Tobias's too. "Not far."

My mate picked up my chin to meet his eyes. "Not at all. No one blames you for this."

Then, to round out the comedy set, the universe deployed my mother-in-law.

"Is the water to blame for the flood, or the storm clouds that brought it?" Maggie asked, hobbling in behind her son. "But it's worse than that. She's made everyone scared of her. Wolves, vamps, and especially hoods. No one knows what she is and what she's capable of, not even her."

Every ounce of tenderness Tobias had given me soured as he rounded on his mother. "What are you doing here?"

"I'm here to undo what she did," Maggie spit out. "I have the strongest asenaic blood of anyone here. And since I hear the vampire she almost killed won't see her, I've come to offer my vein to help his healing."

"You, do something altruistic?" Tobias said. "That's new."

Maggie scowled. "No one has time for your victimhood, *Toby*. Especially not me. Now," she scooted past him, "you managed to overcome one mating bond, maybe you'll be lucky a second time when this one is killed off by her arrogance or by her kin."

I could take anyone laying into me for what I'd done; that was only fair. But there was no way I was going to let a single soul, not even his own mother, take nips at my mate.

My fists tight, my jaw clenched, I turned. "You mean like your kind abandoned you, Maggie?"

The shot hit, turning her face white. "I don't know what you're talking about."

"Oh, don't you?" I paced forward, Tobias in my wake. Was it to pull me or his mother back? "The Schloss's castellan managed to give me this before she died." Fishing my hand into my pocket, I pulled out the wrinkled piece of paper. "A list of asenaics. Only, you know what? *I'm* not on it."

Maggie blinked. "But you're not really an asenaic now, are you? Even in our little pocket of the supernatural world, you're a freak."

That was a stone too far for Tobias. He lurched forward but I pushed a hand to his chest, holding him back.

"True enough." The admission took some of the wind out of her sails. "And that might explain it. Only, as I looked closer and saw who *was* listed, I noticed something. My father wasn't there, nor were the asenaics from Casa de Amarillo. Even then, I thought there might be a good explanation because all those people *knew* what they were. Maybe it was just a list of people who hadn't been told. Only then, I noticed one more name, one that told me what I was really looking at. Anne-Maria, the asenaic from the Zeihern pack that I met in Austria. She was there, and that's when I realized that what I had wasn't just a list of known asenaics. It was a list of known asenaics who were raised as wolves."

Maggie stumbled back, her hand shooting out to brace herself against the wall. "I don't know what you're implying."

"Oh, I'm not *implying* anything," I said, cutting her off. "Only I think I realize now why Tobias had such a strong, visceral hate for hoods and why he hated the Greens so much in particular when we first met. He was raised with that hate, wasn't he? By a woman who had been raised, then cast out, by that very clan?"

My mate licked his lips, his eyes bobbing about as he looked through his memories. "Mum, is this true?"

"Son, you can't understand what it—"

"IS IT?" Animalistic anger boiled his voice.

Maggie spent one more moment resolved before every muscle in her face collapsed. "When I took my fire at fifteen, my abilities awoke like it does for any hood. But the next full moon, out of nowhere, I took fur in front of my whole clan. They didn't waste a moment casting me out."

"So it's true." Tobias kept his distance, even as his chest cycled and his hands trembled. "How did you… When did you…"

"Come to be with your father?" she said, anticipating his thoughts. "A few years later, I'd moved to Morpeth just trying my best to survive in a world without family or clan. I got a job at a little pub. Working nights was a natural for me, aye? I lived in a rented room on the edge of town. Every full moon, I'd tell my boss I was going camping and head far out in the forests. But then, one night, I was pulling a beer from the tap, and your father walked in."

Maggie smiled at the memory. "Poor bloke, I think he fell in love at first sight. I must have looked like a little lost pup to him. He thought I was just another rogue, and told me he could take me home, claim me in his clan, that he was looking for a mate and he thought I could do. I knew he would love me; he'd bond to me the moment we were together. And I'd been alone and lost from the only world I knew, so I agreed. And for a while, we were happy. I think he suspected there was something different about me, but he never said anything. And then… the Dracule took me, and I did the only thing I could: I told your father the truth, and I begged, *begged,* for him to exile me. I wanted to put as much distance between the vampires and my boys as I could. He tried to talk me out of it, but in the end, pack over mate."

"But back in London, you told me…" Tobias's voice tapered off, as did the last hope he had to reconcile his memories with our reality.

Maggie wore her mea culpa in her soft eyes. "I said what I needed to drive you away, even if it didn't work."

Tobias shook his head. "But then, how did I feel you die? We all did. The pack knew you were dead."

"Oh, son, I've died plenty of times, but the Dracule who held me always knew how to bring me around again." Maggie shrugged, even as the tears welled up in the corner of her eyes. "But I managed to keep my tongue still, until you had to tie your luck to this lot…" She motioned vaguely at me. "…and put yourself on the Ravens' radar. All my sacrifice, for what? I spent every day being the ideal prisoner. Never fought, never complained. I did whatever it took for them not to have a reason to find my weak spots. That's what they do, you know. Find your weaknesses and hit them, over and over. If they had found out I had two sons whose blood might…"

Then, like a switch had gone off, her sorrow turned to anger. Her eyes narrowed on me. "I suffered all because I thought it was saving my babies. But you, Gerwalta Kline, have taken my sacrifices and thrown them in the gutter. I made sure Tobias would be safe, have a pack, a mate, a *family*. And you've ruined it."

Tobias's frame went rigid. "Watch your words, Mum. Geri *is* my mate, and I will defend her honor, even from you."

"At least she can kill Vlad," Maggie pressed on as though her own child hadn't just threatened her. "She nearly took out two supes by accident, I imagine she'd be outright lethal when she means to."

The son turned away from his mother.

Maggie straightened. "Why did you do that? What did I say that made you do that?"

Jaw tight, fists clenched, Tobias looked to me.

"Because," I said, "when I was being held by the Ravens, Vlad gave me a maker's bite. It inoculates the vampire who delivers it against the full brunt of a slayer's powers. All the slayers he held prisoner… They could hurt him, but their power wouldn't kill him."

Maggie cackled. "So even there, you're useless?"

"Mother, I warned you…"

Maggie held up a hand. "Don't bother, Son," she said. "I put my faith in hoods foolishly for the last time. I won't stay to make that mistake again…. or to watch my son follow in my footsteps and die."

Tobias didn't make a single attempt to stop her as she crossed the room and headed out the door.

EIGHTEEN

AMY

"You're nervous."

Ladies and Gentlemen, Caleb Helsing: master of the obvious!

I flexed my stiff fingers but tamped down my voice. I wasn't sure how thick the boardroom doors were. "I'm about to walk into a conference room on the thirty-third floor with only one exit, occupied by ten vampires, where I know one of them is going to die by a massive burst of solar energy while I, the only human in the room, watch. Why would I be nervous?"

"You make it sound dangerous."

"Crossing Michigan Avenue in rush hour is dangerous. This is insane."

Caleb shrugged. "Ninety-eight percent of the vampires in the world are good guys. I mean, except the ones that are chicks, of course."

"If you're going to be the CEO of this company, we need to review basic sexual harassment policies, ASAP."

"Especially given how much ass you and I both get."

Caleb unbuttoned, re-buttoned, and unbuttoned his jacket again. I considered calling him out on having just as many butterflies as I did, but while I was going to be *in* the room when the Solari staked his claim, Caleb was the one about to flambé a traitor. He had total dibs on anxiety.

"Okay, let's do this." Finally, Caleb's hand rose to push open the door. "Stay behind me and stay quiet. I wouldn't ask you to do this except that I need a witness. If it's just one slayer versus ten vamps, it's bad optics."

"Yeah, because vampires love it when a fleshy human is all up in their business." *Deep breath, Exhale. Big girl panties.* "If I die in there, I swear to God that I'll kill you."

"You don't have to worry about God. Geri will handle it before He even gets his boots on."

Caleb threw open the doors.

The thing about vampires—about all supes really—was that they don't look any different from humans. And yet, there's something extremely *inhuman* about them. The eyes, maybe? I'd read somewhere that eyes are the windows to the soul. A supe's eyes were windows that had "this house protected by Kick Your Ass Security" stickers all over them. Like the moment they looked at you, they were deciding if you were food, friend, enemy, or too insignificant to be troubled over.

I wondered which one of the corporate stiffs (undead *stiffs*, ha!) was Hoffman. Three chairs in on the left of the rectangular table's long side, I spotted him. Dude made it easy; he was the only one looking at Caleb and not glaring at me, wondering what I tasted like with hollandaise sauce.

"Ladies and Gentlemen," Caleb began, slapping his hands together. "Sorry to interrupt your meeting, but I have a very important announcement. Inga Rosethorn is dead and I'm now in charge of this company."

Okay, *now* they were all wondering what *Caleb* tasted like, hollandaise sauce or no.

Half on their feet, half pushing out their chairs, all of them crowing and cackling. More than stay behind Caleb, I became his shadow, giving myself a slayer shield in case one of them sprang up to attack.

A woman on the opposite end of the table, a short, hot latina with her ebony hair pulled up in a Dominatrix bun, spoke, throwing a wave of silence over the room. "Why would Inga Rosethorn leave control of a vampire-created company to the likes of a self-important peon of a huey?"

I stepped out into the open. "Hey, I'm not a peon!"

"They're not talking about you," Caleb pushed me back. "Ms. Vega, surely a vampire as old as you can sense what I truly am."

Vega narrowed her eyes but said nothing. As did I. Was it kosher to throw a woman's age in her face if she was a vampire? Seemed rude, at best.

"I know Inga told you the sensation you got whenever you were in certain parts of the building was because of genetic materials being kept in some of our labs. That's not entirely untrue, but can't you sense it here, right now?"

Vega grew even *squintier* before she threw the gesture in reverse and glared, wide-eyed. "Impossible. All the slayers are dead."

"Rumors of our demise have been… at least *slightly* exaggerated. You see…" Caleb held up a hand, sparking a solarium on his palm.

Starry-eyed children. Every single vampire in the room had become a starry-eyed child, marveling at the shiny fairy wand of the pixieland character before them.

Except one. Hoffman, who looked as smug as a three-balled gigolo. *Obs furshur* the Dracule had known about the slayers, and given how genuinely WTF the others were, he hadn't shared the info.

Closing his hand and extinguishing his weapon, Caleb took their attention back to his face. "Now that we have that settled, let me tell you how this is going to go."

Cue evil minion leaping to his feet. "Kill him!" Hoffman shouted, flinging out a *J'accuse!* arm. "The slayers are a plague, one we must eradicate from the Earth! How many of us did they kill through the centuries? If they return, how many more of us will die?"

I can think of one, I thought, grinning.

Vega folded her arms over her chest and huffed. "Typical Dracule."

"Better than a pacified, idealistic Xochi," Hoffman spat back. "It is *because* I am a Dracule that I know the truth. Yes, Inga is dead… because the Grand Matron of the wolfsretter killed her. The Grand Matron, whose daughter this man is dating!"

Vega turned to face Caleb. "Is this true?"

Caleb putzed. "I mean, we *were*. We broke up. Totally my idea, though."

"As if!"

Caleb looked back at me over his shoulder. "Didn't I tell you not to talk?"

I crossed my arms and tried to strangle him with my Jedi mind magic.

"I'm not referring to the part about your love life," Vega continued. "I mean is it true that the Grand Matron killed Inga?"

"Oh, that." Caleb redirected his gaze. "Yeah, totally true. As I'm sure Hoffman could tell you, Inga went to the dark side. Again. Come on, you guys know she does that every decade or two. She came after an innocent, and the Grand Matron, who happened to be onsite, killed Inga. *Ipso facto*, posthaste, and to wit, WWL's mine now because Inga didn't have a chance to change her will in between the time she was my protector and the time she decided all slayers needed to die, starting with one of mine."

The man sitting next to Vega, a pasty-skinned, partially bald vamp with the fashion sense of an accountant and the figure of a jellyroll (goodbye, all my teenage fantasies that every vamp was a sex god) cranked an eyebrow. "What do you mean, one of yours?"

"You know what, Partridge, I'm glad you brought that up." Caleb nodded at me—the signal he told me to look for while we were on the bus. I reached down in the bag hanging at my side and pulled out the stack of papers he'd had ready for me. Caleb threw them down on the table. "WWL's public face will remain the same, but our covert operations are shifting a bit. From this point forward, we will be a haven to those slayers who, as of ten minutes ago, are now residents of this building, and to find any slayers out in the greater world who may be hiding—or in bondage—and give them an opportunity to join us."

He stepped aside, bringing me into the line of vision. Never had I felt more like a piece of meat, and for me, that was saying something.

"I'd like to introduce Amy Popowitz," he continued. "I know she's only a huey, but since she's consigned her life to serving the slayers and me as the Solari, you are to treat her as you would me in my stead. She's my right-hand man." He shrugged and frowned. "A right-hand man with scrumptious breasts, but the point remains."

Yup, moving that harassment seminar to the top of my to-do's.

To my surprise, no one raised a single objection to this: to my place in the organization or the fact that I had delicious mammary glands.

Except for good, old Hoffman.

"Us, kowtow to food?" he spat, rising to his feet. "I will not stand for this." *Ironic.* "*We* will not stand for this."

"I'm not surprised to hear you say that, Dennis, since one, you are a Dracule and by default, given to be a rat-ass bastard, and two, I know that Vlad has ordered all Dracule to be on the lookout for slayers. I don't hold it against you personally, but I hope you understand that I can't accept fracturing in our ranks right now."

"Well, that's easily enough assured," Dennis spat back. "Surrender yourself and all the slayers to me and give me this huey bitch as a goodwill gesture, and I'll fall into line."

I was back behind Caleb again, but if he pushed me there or if I dove on my own, I couldn't remember.

Caleb leaned forward, his hands flattening on the table. "Anyone else want to second Dennis's motion?" He swept across each of the other nine vampires in turn. They either shook their heads or avoided his gaze. "Sorry, Dennis, your motion failed to carry. I'll accept your resignation and credentials on my desk by dawn."

The Dracule pulled down the lapels of his jacket. "Over my dead body."

Caleb pulled back his hand. "Terms accepted."

A wave of heat radiated from the man beside me as a solarium flew. It couldn't have been big—the size of a baseball—but, damn, it blazed. Instinct made me cover my eyes one moment, and curiosity the very next made me peek through my fingers. Vampires could move fast, but the way the slayers explained it to me, direct sunlight made many of the vamps' superhuman qualities go flying out the window.

Dennis didn't stand a chance. He had barely started to lunge to the side when the ball of light shot into his chest. I half-expected to see it come blazing out the other side and go shooting through the chair behind him. Instead, the ball nested, a wave of sunlight creeping up his chest, up the veins of his neck, and then, shot out of his eyes. For a moment, the vampire stiffened, a gray pallor overcoming him. Then, starting at the top of his head and cascading down, what had been a person crumbled into ash, falling in a pile all over the table and chair.

Caleb cleared his throat and straightened his tie. "Vega, as chairlady, would you like to survey the remaining members of the board to see if there are any more objections?"

The vampire turned her stunned expression from the ash heap. "No, sir, I don't think that's necessary. I will assure you that the board passes a resolution of loyalty and secrecy."

"Great." Caleb turned on his heel and headed for the door. "Miss Popowitz, if you please?"

After watching my new boss turn a dangerous creature of the night into a human-size pile of carcinogens, I did please very much.

NINETEEN

GERI

Rick Ryland's borrowed behemoth, outfitted with a plow, emergency lights, and doors emblazoned with the seal of the Department of Natural Resources, let us make slow time, even as the polar vortex pushed in from the lake.

"That was Amy. Seems Caleb turned up in Chicago last night."

"What?" Tobias's head lashed back and forth between me and the road. "How?"

"No details, just a quick FYI. Amy was busy with, and I quote—" I hooked the air with bunny fingers. "—'cleaning.' She said he just turned up at the motel out of nowhere and an hour later, Caleb charged in on the WWL Board of Directors and declared himself CEO."

"Son of a bitch, that cheeky bastard." It was a term werewolves didn't use often. They found the implication crass. Tobias may have meant it as a compliment, frankly. "About bloody time we got some good news."

"Well, there's a little more, if you can stand it. *Mina* has her first tooth. Isn't that crazy? She's barely two months old, and..." I cut off as Tobias's face fell. "Tobias?"

His voice dripped longing. "I miss her, Geri. I miss her so much. It's already been a month she's been away from me. Away from *us.*"

I laid a hand on his arm. "She'll be with us soon, I promise. One way or another, we'll make it happen."

Just then, my phone dinged. I picked it up to read the incoming messages.

"It's Markus." I scrolled through the text. "He says your Mom's phone is still reading the same location as it was fifteen minutes ago, near the corner of Front and Spring."

Thank goodness Maggie hadn't fought us on a hood-issued cell, maybe only one of the things she'd accepted from us without a snide comment.

Tobias shook his head. "I still don't understand how she managed to go clear to Marquette in two hours when it's taken us five to get this far in Rick's buffalo-killer."

My insides clenched. I knew exactly how. *Not yet*, I managed to tell myself before Maggie's secret came blurting out. Even among hoods, the ability to fly was extremely rare. My mother was the only one known in the last half-century with the talent. It had actually helped her become Grand Matron. Even in an age when we'd lost most of our overly zealous superstitions, flight still held divine right status among most hoods.

What would happen if the others found out that, not only was there another *uchan,* as they were called, but that she'd lived her life as a wolf?

Changing gears, I tried to picture the map of the UP's biggest city in my head. "If I had to bet money, I'd say she's at that café that claims to have the world's biggest variety of pasties. Nothing much else right there but a gas station or the hardware shop."

Tobias's jaw worked. "She knows the Dracule are desperately looking for powerful supe blood. She wouldn't sit out in the open like that without a reason."

Another ding. "Markus says my mom wants a report if there's any developments." *Ding.* "Also, Markus wants me to know he's still pissed at me and he's suggested I might want to just jump in Lake Superior."

Tobias moved his hand from my lap up to my head, pulling me into his shoulder. "Give him time, love. Everyone's still smarting right now over what happened."

"I know, but I didn't ask the fire to come. It just came."

"I'm not saying it's fair, but it just… is." He dragged the steering wheel left, navigating around a car pulled to the side of the road, stuck in the snow. Then another.

Then another.

And another.

"This seem odd to you?" Tobias said, now driving solidly in the middle of the street, even as the snow he pushed rolled to the right. "I thought you said this was just some quiet little college town?"

"It is."

And it should have been even quieter than usual, given that Northern Michigan University had already let out for winter break.

A flash of red and blue died down at the same time as a direct, white beam darted between us. Tobias pulled to a stop as we both covered our eyes, trying to keep from going flash blind. Outside my door, a lone figure bundled up in a winter coat and donning an Elmer Fudd-styled navy hat lowered his flashlight.

He knocked at the window. "Ma'am?"

Even without speaking, I could sense Tobias's hesitance. Apparently, his apprehension of authority figures extended to those of the huey kind. But to disobey would draw suspicion, and interference was the last thing we needed.

I rolled down the window, the old crank groaning in protest. "Officer?"

"Evening, ma'am, sir." The clean-shaven state trooper couldn't be more than a few years older than me. "I'm sorry. I know you're in an official vehicle, but we don't have any authorization to let DNR staff pass this way. It's dogs and mushers only on this road. Everyone else needs to come into town from the northside and park in the outer lots. You can pick up a shuttle from there for free."

"Dogs and mushers?" Tobias repeated. "That's just... so insulting."

Crap. We had to show up in Marquette at the same time as the annual dog sled race was kicking off, didn't we?

I did the mental math. In this snow, going around town, getting parking, and taking a shuttle in would take us another half hour at least. Already she might have sensed our proximity and gone. If Maggie left and got away from the crowds to take flight, she could be over Canada before we even got to the café. We couldn't afford that kind of delay.

"Just because she's your baby doesn't mean everyone sees *Toto* that way." I batted Tobias's arm even as his face screwed up in confusion, before turning back to the officer. "So sorry, Officer..." I focused in the dark on his badge, "Nyack. We're not technically mushers, but this is where they told us to come in. We got our search and rescue wolf here with us in the back. Maybe you heard of him, Tahquamenon Toto?"

Officer Nyack squinted. "A rescue wolf?"

I let my fake smile drop. "Oh, no, you *haven't* heard of him. Well, we don't take him out much, but we got a special invite to bring Toto by the opening ceremonies this year as sort of a public outreach thing. I guess they figured we should just park down this side of town with all the mushers, but if you want us to go around to the northside of town and take him in on the shuttle, no problem. I mean, he's massively huge of course, but most people...."

"No." Officer Nyack held up a hand. "Sorry, ma'am, I guess the message just never got to me." He cupped his chin. "A wolf, huh? I know some of the people up this way raise them, but I hear they can be real nasty too."

Tobias muttered from behind, "You got no fucking clue."

Luckily, Nyack seemed not to hear. He swung his flashlight to a plowed, extra-long spot about twenty yards up the road. "Go ahead and take that spot over there. Better hurry. The opening ceremony starts in about twenty minutes."

Tobias waited until the car was parked before turning to me, lips pursed. He stared, expectant, waiting.

Finally, I cracked. "What? We don't have time to drive around to the other side of town."

"Oh, no, Geri, I understand *why* you did what you did." He turned in place, looking into the exceedingly empty covered cab of the truck bed. "What I don't understand is how we conjure up a rescue wolf named Toto. Officer Nyack is still close enough to catch us in our fib if we wander away from the truck without one."

"I know. But you know what we do have?"

Tobias shook his head.

Waited.

Looked at me through bugged-out eyes.

Went red.

"No bleeding way. You are not parading me through town like some common mutt."

I caught Officer Nyack's silhouette in the rearview mirror. "He's still looking over here, and there's no other headlights heading this way. If I don't walk out of this car with a wolf in tow and soon, he's going to think I was lying."

"But you *were* lying."

"Do you want to get to your mom in time or not?" I asked, opening the door. "Rick always keeps some rope in the back. That should work as a leash. When I come back up in here in thirty seconds, it had better be to a cab full of fur."

<hr>

I'd never wondered in my life if werewolves were capable of glaring. After tonight, I could write a senior thesis on just how intently.

Another wave of anger rolled over me. I let it subside before yanking on the rope leash, pulling Tobias to a halt.

"Stop!" I bit at him. "Just because I can't understand what you're saying doesn't mean I'm not still feeling what you feel. Given our time limitations, there was no other way."

I'd also found one of Rick's ranger jackets and official hats in the back of the truck. I'd put on the coat, and Tobias was currently wearing the hat. I was hoping novelty and my sense of authority would distract people from asking what kind of wolf weighed in at two-twenty. (Or as Tobias was a fan of saying, eleven stone).

Two little girls, eyes wide and smiles nuclear, ran over as we rounded the corner a block from the café. They managed to run the distance between us before their parents promptly panicked and dove after them.

"But mommy, it's a *wool*," the younger said.

The mom looked up at me. "Is it tame?"

"So tame we sleep in the same bed." Tobias huffed, but I circled his scruff with my arm and rubbed his fluff. "Be a good boy now. These girls are just curious."

Frustration. Annoyance.

The second little girl reached up and took both his ears in her hands, despite the fact that she had to tiptoe to reach. Tobias's emotional profile shifted, and even I wasn't ready for where it landed. *Heartache. Longing. Hope.*

Mina.

A month had passed since we'd seen our baby. We'd hardly had that much longer with her at the onset. It didn't matter. The heart anchored in deep waters, no matter how wide the stream. But no time for that now. We had to focus. I stood and made our excuses, pulling Tobias's leash toward the café.

"Sorry, girls, but we have to be somewhere."

The café was more of a diner it turned out, an old-school greasy spoon complete with a jukebox in the corner and a checkered floor. Maggie sat at a table near the back in plain sight, like she wasn't even trying to hide. The building was small—the entirety of its interior could be viewed from the sidewalk out front, but it didn't seem a wise location to sit if you needed to make a quick escape. (Early Hood training had made this a constant consideration when on a hunt.) Only then, I noticed the rear exit door just a stone's throw from Maggie's booth. Even if danger came in the front, someone sitting there would have time to flee before the accoster could reach her.

Tobias whined.

I looked at my mate. "I see her."

He yipped.

"No," I said, guessing at his words. "No dogs allowed, not even during sled week."

The wolf's head cocked to the side.

"She's not really doing much of anything," I said. "Just sitting in a back booth, staring straight ahead, her hands wrapped around a mug of something. No, wait. She's doing something. She's…"

Maggie's big green eyes caught me.

Immediately, I dropped, but I knew it was too late. The only question now: had I scared her away, or was she still sitting there?

Tobias turned in place, pulling on the rope.

I shook my head. "No! You can't shift back here. Even in a college town, a giant wolf turning into a naked man isn't normal. Just… wait here."

I tied Tobias's leash to a light pole for show, pulled down my jacket, and went in, a wolf's whining accompanying my march.

Maggie didn't even look at me as I plopped down on the bench opposite her and ordered a cup of coffee, black, from the readily available waitress. At the same time, she didn't look like she was about to bolt, so I took advantage and just started to talk.

"Honestly, I get why you hate me, but you can't be out in the open like this. It's only a matter of time before the Dracule show up around here." I looked around and pulled my jacket tighter. "They may be here already, frankly. Please, come home."

Her eyes dashed to me quickly before again jutting away. "I can't be that close to him or anywhere near *you.*"

I slid back on the bench. "After so many years without a family, why are you doing your damnedest to not be a part of ours? And don't tell me it's because you think you'll draw danger to Tobias and me, because, hello," I motioned to myself with both index fingers pointed, "Dracula's filet mignon right here. No one's going to put your son more in danger than I am."

The shewolf's expression soured. "You're making a poor argument for why I should forgive you for seducing my boy."

"One," I counted out on my finger, "I didn't *seduce* anyone. We fell in love. Slowly, over a span of two years, for most of which I was trying really hard to land someone else. And two, I'm not trying to make the argument that I'm not putting Tobias's life in danger. I'm trying to make the argument that, if you stick around, you could help protect him. And, while you're doing that, he can help protect you, like a *family does."*

Maggie pulled her white ceramic mug to her mouth and drew a slow, languid pull of whatever dark elixir lay within. "You don't understand what I'm going through. I lost my family once. I can't do it again."

I reached across the table and wove my hands around hers, feeling the warmth of the mug through her fingers. "Then don't. Come back to Paradise with us."

"With us?" For the first time, a genuine sense of concern hatched across her face. "Please tell me you don't mean that Tobias is here."

"Of course, he's here," I smiled as a gust of cold air hit from behind, someone going through the rear side door I'd noticed before. "You don't think Tobias would let me come all the way to Marquette by myself in this kind of snowstorm and with Dracule running around, do you? I'm not you, Maggie. I couldn't just fly away if someone pissed me off."

"Why, Maggie Somfield, you told her your deepest, darkest secret. How *adorbs.*"

The voice. THAT VOICE. I hadn't heard it in so long, and yet, it scraped at my memory like the wounds it had cut were still fresh. Ice shot down my back and all the hairs on my arm stood. It was a visceral reaction, but it wasn't a supernatural one. It was the same one anyone would have if suddenly realizing they were in the presence of the very person who had helped to keep them prisoner once upon a time.

I turned to see the impossible made painfully possible. "Kai Yu. But it's…"

"Hello, Geri," the Hawaiian vampire said, shoving hands into his jeans pocket. He'd walked out of my memories and straight into my life again, looking the same as he had two years before. "Long time, no see."

"Not long enough."

Back when I'd first moved to Chicago and started in Igor's lab at the university, Kai and Cynthia had been introduced to me as two vampires working on a project to resurrect slayers through cataloging their DNA. Only later did I find out Tobias's mate, Kara, was their prisoner, and that they were developing ways to break werewolf bonds. Tobias and I, with some help from Igor, had killed Cynthia in an attempt at freeing Kara, but she died anyway. Kai had disappeared, and I'd never heard from him again.

Until now.

And while that was shocking, it wasn't as shocking as realizing what Kai had just said.

I spun on Maggie. "He knows you?"

"Of course, I know her," Kai said, scooting into the booth next to Maggie on her side of the bench. "You really think Somfield's mother just happened to come out from the woodwork *now*? It was quite convenient for *us*, of course, that you somehow found a way to hook up with a wolf who had already had one mate, *and* whose mother was in a Dracule feeding pen."

I turned sympathetic eyes to the scars on Maggie's neck, scars that had looked so set and ancient when I'd first seen them a month ago and had been healing so slowly since that I didn't even notice the improvement. They weren't old at all. Maybe a few months?

"Maggie…" I swallowed. "Please tell me you didn't do this."

"Oh, I'm sorry, Geri. She *so* did," Kai pressed on. "I'm afraid Maggie's been working for us all along. After the setup in London failed, she was told to keep an eye on you. Keep you safe, all while looking for an opportunity to separate you for… easy extraction. Almost got you in Triberg, but I don't think Maggie realized just how fast she was flying."

I locked the woman across the table in my sight and said the only word I could get to form. "Why?"

"Why else?" Her voice… flat, emotionless, matter of fact. "Because they agreed to spare my son if I did."

"Well," Kai interrupted, "spare, as in, they will be allowed to share the same cell in the pen, but you get her drift. Oh, but don't worry, Maggie, we're going to give you a loyalty upgrade. Hot water, a firm mattress… Maybe we'll even let you have a run in the garden every so often." The vamp gave a one-shouldered shrug. "At the end of a chain, of course. Now, the sled race will be kicking off soon and we want to beat the traffic out of town. How about you just come along quietly before the storm gets worse?" He grabbed his scarf, pulling it tight. "And I thought Chicago was bad. Makes me miss Hawaii."

"Feel free to go back there if you want, and don't forget to lay out on a beach at high noon while you're there."

"Geri…" The vampire clicked his tongue, his head shaking. "I remember you being so nice, so friendly."

"That was before your bloodline started killing people I love and taking others prisoner."

"That's just business, Brah." Kai leaned in, his hand on the edge of the table. "And you have to take your share of blame, you know. All Lord Tepeş wants is you and your mongrel. Give yourselves up, and we'll all coast the wave to shore."

I was positive Kai's surf lingo was lost on Maggie, but what wasn't was how she'd been duped. There was no deal that would let her keep her son and, better yet, take him away from me, but how could she have thought the Dracule would ever make good on that promise? Or had she lived so many years dependent on them that she felt she had no choice but to take what they said at face value?

But Maggie had reached her tipping point. She wasn't their prisoner, and she wasn't alone. Hope rose anew as the emotions played across her face and broadcast into my subconscious: disappointment, anger, shame, and finally: rage.

We didn't need to exchange words to make the plan together. A slow smile spread across Maggie's face and she nodded almost imperceptibly. I closed my eyes and let my chin dip.

"You know something, Kai?" Power welled up inside me, a beacon that vibrated in waves in every direction. Tobias's energy flooded my awareness, and I yanked at the tether connecting us. "You really should have come in the front door, then you'd know what a terrible mistake you were about to make."

The vampire had one second to give me a "what the hell are you talking about" look before the window of the diner shattered and a deadly growl rent the air.

TWENTY

Hueys, all with eyes on the supersized wolf that had just crashed through the front window, scattered.

Tobias barely had time to regain his balance before the lights started to flicker. It made no sense; a broken window shouldn't have any effect on the electrical. But when the bulbs above strobed, they illuminated a pair of swirling, snaking smoke streams bouncing over booth tops.

More vamps. Of course, Kai wouldn't be here alone. Luckily for us, the trifecta of wild animal, broken glass, and a blackout drove away the last of the hueys spectators. That wouldn't last. The police would come soon enough. Luckily, downtown was closed to vehicles and the lineup of the dogsled race just a block away. Word would reach them, orders given, but they'd need to form ranks and close in through a crowd that got here through a snowstorm.

Because it was Michigan, and a blizzard didn't get in the way of sports.

I did the mental math as the two hazy amalgam stacks solidified into humanoid shapes: two minutes, three tops.

"Hey, babe," I said to Tobias as he stalked past me. "I think you still owe Kai a little... what's the English phrase? Comeuppance?"

Tobias huffed as he closed in, his eyes set on the last living vampire that helped to capture and kill his first mate.

I had just enough silver on me to give myself some brass knuckles. Uh, *silver* knuckles. Not ideal since against vampires, my only hope was to chop off their heads. Unless I could run outside to break a branch off a tree and ram it through their heads or their hearts, that was. Tempting in terms of aesthetics, but not practical with the whole having-to-go-into-the-street aspect. Kai turned his wicked grin on Tobias as I sized up the others: a dark-skinned female knee-high to an alfalfa sprout, and a pudgy white dude who seemed to lack much definition even when he'd become solid. Enough light flowed in from the street to give me a view, but they'd still have the advantage where sight was concerned. Limited light didn't mean I couldn't throw shade, however.

I prepared to strike as the vamps neared. "I'm going to call you," I pointed at the dude, "*Doughboy* and you," I pointed at the woman, "*Sean Bean.*"

They exchanged a confused look before the woman asked, "Why Sean Bean?"

"No reason." Totally reasons.

Sean presented fists. "Whatever, chick. I'll kick your ass either way."

She lunged, I dodged, but Doughboy caught me on the swing, pulling me from behind as he wrestled my arms behind my back.

Meanwhile, a hot mess of *canine insaneicus* rose in the background. I got one quick flash of the scene as Doughboy swung me. Kai had broken one of the tables and was using its top as a shield.

Maggie, eyes wide and fingers splayed, had plastered herself against the back wall.

"You're a fucking werewolf, Maggie!" I groaned as I shifted all my strength into pulling my arms forward, attempting to break Doughboy's hold. "Act like—!"

Sean belted me in the solar plexus. My body attempted to collapse in on itself, but the male vamp's grip kept me upright. With a squeeze on my wrists, my hands opened wide. Two pings rang in the air as the silver knuckles hit the floor.

"You know the bitter part of all this?" Sean's backhand swung across my face.

Blood filled my mouth. It would heal. I spit it out in a stream, catching her shoe. "Having to park on the northside of town and taking the shuttle in?"

"No, it's that we're not allowed to kill you," Sean continued. "Not much use to Vlad if you're dead. I'm just supposed to hit you in the head until you pass out. Not that I won't enjoy it."

Her right hand took a turn, capped in a fist, and caught me with an uppercut, lifting my feet from the ground.

Doing me a huge solid.

I landed offset, my left hip aligned to Doughboy's right. Vamps were hellishly strong and lethal, but their tactics were designed with human prey in mind. They didn't get much exposure to hand-to-hand fighting, and it showed.

She cocked back, but I stopped her with a, "First, let me tell you what you're doing wrong."

It was just cocky enough to stall her. "Oh, do, Little Red."

"You're so small," I said. "*Petite,* I mean. Both of you are, aren't you? Actually, you're kinda quite cute. Kudos. But still, small. As strong as you are, you're still not going to have enough weight when you sink that swing. You need to use something heavier. Something like, oh I don't know, another vampire."

I stepped back one leg, lunged, and bent forward. Doughboy went flying over me. He hit Sean with the most gorgeous *kerplump* I'd heard in a while. The two of them toppled to the floor as I squatted, searching for my silver knuckles, hoping it would be enough fuel to make silver flame and send the vamps running. We didn't have much time before the huey police showed up, and even as busy as I was kicking ass and having my ass kicked, I could hear the crowd growing outside. A quick sweep revealed that Tobias had Kai subdued. I could have told the vamp that shields were terrible in a fight with a werewolf. All they had to do was jump in the middle of it and your big protective disk became your undoing as the lupine stood atop it, pinning you down.

"God damn it, where did they go?"

Suddenly, the weapon was foisted in front of my eyes. Like, two inches from my eyes.

I stilled, then tilted my head up.

"Looking for these?" Maggie asked, grinning.

She was... holding them. And she wasn't in pain. No burning flesh, no singed hair. And then, as I got to my feet, I realized that not only had she gotten her hands on my silver; Maggie was wielding it.

The metal shifted shape, morphing and reforming, until all that remained in Maggie's palm was a single, long string. She threw it to me just in time for me to catch the recovered Doughboy's lunge.

I jumped, lacing the string around his throat, and yanked. His head went flying one direction while his body went another. I looked for Sean, but only caught the tail end of her vapor cloud as she whisked out the front door.

I clenched my fist. "Fine, *Sean,* but this is the only time!"

Kai let out one more gurgling gulp as Tobias's maw closed, severing his neck.

Which was effective, but... I had to kiss that mouth later, and just... *ew.*

"Maggie?" I spun, looking for an explanation. "You..."

My mother-in-law was all grins. "You said it yourself, right? Start acting like one?"

She could wield silver, she could fly. If not for the fact that her son was currently in werewolf form beside us, I was beginning to think there wasn't the slimmest chance that Maggie Somfield had a drop of wolf blood in her.

Tobias yelped as he looked up at me, then at the door.

"I know," I said, inherently understanding his meaning. "Sean Bean got away. No time to worry about her now, though. Quick, get the bodies together."

Maggie for once didn't hesitate, toting Doughboy's head over to Kai's corpse even as she asked, "What for?"

I groaned as I plopped the bulbous body atop the other vamp, the physical exertion it took confirming that I had, indeed, found the perfect name for him. "Slayers can ash a vamp with a solarium. I wonder if my weak version of it would do the same? If we can get rid of the bodies and the clothes then the police will think this was nothing more than an out-of-control, rabid dog."

Behind me, Tobias yipped.

"Oh, calm yourself," I said. "It wasn't about you."

I sparked a garish ball of grey sunlight into being and commanded it to burrow into Doughboy's chest, working it through both vessel and vein. In a moment, he turned into a horror-movie-inspired skinless monster, just like the Ravens who'd been hit with silver fire back in Spain. Just as I was about to ask for suggestions, however, the form under my hand lost its integrity, turning to ash and leaving a pile of dusty clothes.

Great, evil undead bodies in zones where hueys could find them: no longer an issue. If only I'd had this ability back in that alley in Chicago. For the moment, escaping from a Marquette diner without the event crowds taking notice was still on our to-do list. If Tobias took his huey form, that might help... except he'd also be abundantly naked. The two vamps' clothing wouldn't help; my man had muscles where the others only had dreams.

I gathered up the clothes and shoved them into a busboy's collection bin, all as I swept the area to assess our options. "Maybe we try the side exit?"

Maggie pulled alongside me. "No, the front is better. The crowd will shield our identities *if* we can join up with it without being noticed. We need a distraction."

I nodded. "But what?" I turned to my mate. "Any chance you can sneak... by... and..."

My voice died as the incredulity in his wolfie expression broadened. Fair enough.

"I had to ask, you know. Okay, then what else can we—"

Before I could say another word, Maggie turned on her heel and headed for a set of double doors behind the diner counter.

"Where are you going?"

She didn't slow, even as I followed her into the kitchen.

"I was here for two hours. They didn't carry any rubbish through the dining room," she said. "Must be another set of doors leading to the snicket."

"To the what?"

"The alleyway, you blithe Yank."

"Oh."

Sure enough, we found the door behind the dishwashing area. I reached over to turn off the hot water left running by a worker who'd fled in a hurry.

"Give me thirty seconds, then run when the sheep outside do."

By sheep, I assumed she meant people. Such a werewolf thing to say.

"Without you?" I asked as she headed out the doors. "Absolutely not, you're the whole reason we came here and we're not leaving without you."

"You're right, you're not." She began to peel off her clothes and throw them into a nearby dumpster. "One of them got away, Geri. We both know what that means."

I did. It meant that our eventuality where the Ravens were concerned was soon to become an inevitability.

"You have a car?"

I nodded. "A few blocks from here. Can you follow Tobias's scent to it?"

"Not once it crosses paths with so many other dogs, no."

I leaned against the greasy brick wall. "Then how will you find your way back to us?"

"I suspect by you luring me there, the way you did in England." She cracked a smile as she deposited her last piece of clothing in the dumpster. "Just the way I lured you here tonight."

"The way *you* lured me here?" I reached out, touching her arm. "Maggie?"

"Peace now, Geri," she said. "Like you said inside, it's time I remembered who I am... and just what the hell I'm capable of."

And with that, my husband's naked mother took her fur and bolted.

Tobias fixed me with a concerned cock of the head when I came back into the diner alone.

"Don't worry," I said in response to the curiousity and concern spinning off of me. "She'll find us after we—"

Suddenly, a light beamed through the dark, hitting me straight in the eyes and stilling my words.

"Ma'am, are you okay? You alone?"

Hueys, damn it.

I sucked on my bottom lip. As my eyes refocused, the outline of a state trooper's standard-issue garrison hat was silhouetted against the street light coming through the broken front windows. "Um, not exactly."

The beam shifted, and I panicked. What would the officer do when he saw the giant wolf who, no doubt witnesses had reported, had crashed the diner? But to my surprise, what the light revealed wasn't covered in fur. It was covered in a supple spread of chest hair and a scruffy beard though, thank god, all his male bits were concealed from view by an overturned table. From the perspective of the people at the front, it would only look like Tobias was shirtless.

"Sir?" The officer stepped closer. "Are you injured? Do you need medical assistance?"

Perfect, I thought. Let them think that's what's going on.

Tobias conjured a groan as he pressed a hand to his forehead. "Oh, the pain. I'm so... I'm so..."

And then, because even though I loved this man, he was still male, Tobias started to laugh.

"I'm sorry, Geri," he said, looking up through his mirthful smirk and dancing eyes. "I can't. I just can't."

"Stupid kids." The officer grimaced. "Look, you all need to get out of here. We had a report of a bear or something breaking through—"

No sooner had the words reached us than the barking did.

The crowd filled the street at one end of the alley. A mass of hueys, the women crying, the men cradling their babes to their chests or atop their shoulders. A small contingent turned up our way, forcing the officer to forget about us and pivot in the direction of manic mushers and even a few unleashed sled dogs.

"That's our cue," I whispered, pulling Tobias behind a dumpster. "You might want fur for this next part, darling."

"My mom?" he asked again.

"She's coming. Let's get out of here." I had already mentally reached through the crowded streets and found the only other werewolf around, pulling on her tether as we began to move up the alley towards its mouth on the opposite block. "There is an upside to this, you know. My mom won't need to be debriefed. We'll just put on the evening news and fill in the edges."

TWENTY-ONE

And that's how I ended up driving out of Marquette with two massive wolves in the back of the pickup and arriving at Paradise with two passengers—one naked—instead.

My mother tapped on the driver's side window the moment Rick's truck came to rest within the compound. "Are you all alright?"

"I texted you that we were."

"I'd have the words from your mouth, child."

Was she actually... genuinely worried for me? "All good and accounted for," I said, switching off the ignition and any further thoughts on that question. "Tobias and Maggie are in the bed in the back. Maggie's going to need some clothes."

A nearby member of Cody's pack stepped forward, volunteering to go fetch something for Maggie, even as the nude woman in question and her son (who had thankfully left his clothes behind in the truck) shimmied out of the back.

My mother kept her eyes locked on me. "What happened?"

"What is the huey news saying?"

"That something spooked the sled teams, possibly that a bear had crashed into the Front Street diner."

"Bear, wolf, close enough," Maggie said as she rounded the car, walking up to my mother without a single ounce of shame in the fact that she didn't have a lick of clothing on. "Doesn't matter. We have bigger problems now. They'll be here tomorrow at sunset, Matron. I swear by it."

My mother gave the smallest moment of visible concern before brushing away the comment as a routine report. "And we'll be ready."

"Will you now?" Maggie grinned. "You and what army?"

Even I bristled at that. Other than my own youthful outbursts and a few notable exceptions of the Matron's Council, I didn't remember anyone ever having the courage to challenge Brünhild Kline.

Apparently, Mother didn't either. Her eyes narrowed; her frame went taut. "Excuse me?"

"I said," Maggie closed the distance, fists on hips, standing chest to chest with the Grand Matron, "you and what army?"

Brünhild cleared her throat. "I know your abilities are not as strong as they once were, Mrs. Somfield, but surely your eyes work well enough to see the two hundred or so wolves and hoods currently making camp within these walls. More are ready over in the packlands, doubling our number."

"Aye, I do see them. But I've also been kept in a Dracule feeding cage for the last two decades. When they first take you, they try to get you to forget who you are, what you're capable of, so that they can do the same. You become food to 'em, nothing else. Livestock, kept alive and healthy only enough so they can drink from you. And once you're nothing more than a cow, then they forget that you still got a mind inside you. They talk, and if you're a wise enough piece of meat, you chew your cud and you listen."

Maggie turned to a slowly-forming crowd as the shewolf who'd run off earlier returned with a robe.

"As soon as this here's Grand Matron's mommy gave the order that no asenaic would be allowed to bear children and that all the slayers they had known of were in vampire hands, them Dracule you're about to take on got panicked about their food supply. It's no wonder they want to break down wolf societies. They'll tell you it's for revenge, that their Vlad wanted to get back for what he saw as the humiliation of his country and his family, and that's true. But it ain't the whole truth."

I remembered the question I'd asked Vlad himself once upon a time. *But without werewolves, what is the purpose of a hood?*

An interesting query, isn't it?

"He's going to breed his food," Maggie said. "And he's been growing his bloodline to do so. The Dracule clutches have spent the last decade expanding, driving recruitment. Creating farmers, if you will. Now, they'll come here. You think you're fighting some kind of battle to protect your daughter, but you better be wiser than that, Brunnie Kline. They're coming here to get *all* your daughters. And your sons. All you've done by stacking up your cabal here is give them a bigger school of fish to net."

I stepped forward. "I'll give myself up, then."

Tobias was at my back in a second. "Geri, no."

"Vlad won't kill me," I said over my shoulder. "Like Maggie says, he needs my blood. He wouldn't be coming down this hard if he wasn't desperate for it."

"Doesn't matter." Tobias's embrace tightened around me. "*I* need you here."

The words warmed my heart, but they didn't alter reality. "I'm not good here. I scare people. I've *hurt* people."

"You didn't mean to."

"Like that makes a difference." I swallowed my nerves. "Maggie's right. We're not an army. We're a bunch of scared supes, huddling together for protection. Even if Vlad's top priority is me, then giving him what he wants buys us time."

Tobias's hands threaded my hair. "That won't stop him and you know it."

Markus had joined the growing crowd at some point. "You didn't nearly toast my fiancé to death just to give up, did you?"

I spun on my cousin. "Fiancé?"

He held up his left hand and showed off a gold band on the third finger. "Luckily it wasn't on him when you turned into Johnny Storm."

I didn't know if Markus and I were on good enough terms yet that I could hug him, but it didn't mean I didn't want to.

Mother, however, could be counted on to regulate sentiment to the sidelines. "I understand what you are saying, Mrs. Somfield—"

Maggie rolled her eyes. "You pretentious git!"

Brünhild recoiled. "Excuse me?"

"My name is Maggie," Maggie said. "Not Mrs. Somfield. Not even Margaret. Maggie, plain and simple. If we're going to be family, Brunnie, you should relax a little."

"Fine." Brünhild flexed her hand, cracking every knuckle along the way. "What is it you propose we do? Not fight?"

"Oh, no, we need every hand on deck, and I mean every hand."

Maybe my mother wasn't understanding, but I was. "You want us to call in the slayers."

Maggie turned, grinning. "Ah, there we go. Turns out my daughter-in-law is one smart biscuit." Then, looking to Tobias, she added, "My son chose his mate well."

It could have been a backhanded compliment, but I didn't really care at the moment. I was too happy seeing the rebirth of a shewolf.

Or was it of a hood?

"Besides Caleb Helsing, the slayers have spent their entire lives in captivity," Brünhild said. "They're not ready to face down the most dangerous vampire bloodline in the history of our world. Besides, Helsing is currently MIA."

My hand shot up like I was in elementary school. "No, he's not. Amy called. Caleb has turned up in Chicago."

Hydrochloric acid burned less than my mother's glare. I guess Brünhild really didn't want to be shown up right now.

Maggie, meanwhile, grinned. "Everyone wakes in the morning just as capable of dying, Matron. The Dracule will be here tomorrow. If we don't make our best stand with everything and *everyone* we got, then the next night, they'll be everywhere else. Call the slayers. We're fighting for their future as well as ours. They should at least have a chance to decide if they'll throw in their lot with us."

I pulled my phone from my pocket, but my mother's hands over mine stilled my dialing.

"What are you doing?"

I looked up into her awestruck face. "Calling Amy of course. She's their… whatever their version of a castellan is. She'll get the message out to them."

My mother looked back to me, nodded once, and played with the hood's button at her throat. "Fine, then." And then, turned and walked away.

Maggie gave us one wide, sloppy grin before she too meandered off. Even as she did, I saw those she passed by stand a little straighter, almost like they were being called to attention.

A queer feeling struck me as I turned to my mate. "Something here feels very off."

Tobias smirked. "Funny, that's what I've been thinking since a few hours ago when I saw *my* mum wield silver. But I guess discovering your mother is half-hood can be disorienting."

"A quarter, actually."

We both turned to see that Maggie hadn't strayed too far away so as not to hear us.

She eyeballed her son. "Geri, tell my boy how long your family has held the Grand Matronship since the council formed in the early nineteenth century."

"Practically the whole time," I said meekly, uncertain where she was going. "Except for when there was a Green Hood in charge for a few years right after WWII, but she was…"

"Executed by *your* grandmother," Maggie completed for me. "But not before the baby was born. Not before my father was smuggled away back home to Northumberland. You see, kids, the truth is, your relationship isn't really all that unusual. It happens every generation or so. Aye, but the Council of Matrons has been pretty good at covering them up by *any* means necessary. What's exceptional about us, is that we survived, because we had the seat of power protecting us from the floor upon which it stood."

She looked up to the sky. "Let's hope our luck holds out. Now, Geri, you were going to make a phone call?"

TWENTY-TWO

She was bloodly perfect.

Legs that went on forever. Breasts the perfect size for cupping. Lips that swelled every time I'd kissed her.

We weren't supposed to have mated. Not until things were official, anyway. But what the hell? From the moment we met, we knew we'd each found our other half. We didn't need any bond to seal us; our love had already done that.

The tiny curls on her head tickled my palm as I threaded my fingers through her hair. "I fucking love you, woman."

Kara's hand pressed to my cheek. "After what we just did, you better or you owe me a huge explanation."

My laugh melted into her mouth as I pressed my lips to hers. Kara lifted her head off the mattress, deepening the kiss, before letting go and pulling me down to her.

She sighed in the way only a content woman could. "Did you think you were going to feel like this?"

"What, you mean someday?" I traced a finger over her red, red lips. "Yeah, I knew it the moment I first saw you."

"You don't have to woo me anymore, love. I'm being serious."

"What? So am I. I remember it. It was at the Morrisons on Boxing Day. You had on that white sundress with the yellow sunflowers, even though it couldn't have been more than ten degrees out. You were grabbing some crisps, and I was grabbing—"

"I meant the mating bond!" Kara suddenly laughed out. "I mean, that *rush*. That moment we were one… That was… well, forgive the pun, but it was fucking brilliant. It was the most magical thing I've ever felt. Better than taking my fur for the first time. Better than chocolate!"

"Better than sex?" I completed for her.

"Well, vehicle of our thrill, and all." Kara tilted her head. "What was it like for you?"

I sucked on my bottom lip, hesitant. "I imagine the same as you."

"Tobias Somfield, don't you dare play cheaters on me! Do your own work."

A tightness spread across my chest. What could I say? I was a wolf. Kara was my first. Kara would be my *only*. I loved making love to her, even if it was an odd combination of thrilling and scary, not knowing if I was doing it right. I was a man, of course I'd seen examples in film, but still. I'd watched Usain Bolt run a hundred meters in ten seconds, but that didn't mean I knew the first thing about training to be a sprinter.

To my surprise, once we'd actually gotten into bed and gave it a go, everything came along pretty naturally. It had been wonderful, and judging by the sounds Kara made, I did things just fine and then some. But something *magical*? Some supernatural rush where my endorphins shot off and I felt some wave of unity?

I either hadn't had that or didn't notice. But I wasn't a bleeding idiot, so I wasn't going to say that to my girl.

"Like you said, best moment of my life."

Kara grimaced. "Better than when you cheated on me?"

I furrowed my brow and jerked up off the mattress. "What? How could I cheat on you? We just slept together. We *mated*."

Kara scooted out from under me as she, too, propped herself up on her elbows. "And yet you did. And with one of *them*, a hood. So really, not just cheated on me. You cheated on all of us. Your pack, your family, your mate."

"But I hate hoods." I shook my head. "No, I would never do that. I love you."

"Liar. You shagged the next piece of carpet under your feet. Then again, what would I expect from a descendant of—" She took to her feet then, taking a position over the bed and staring down on me in every sense of the word. "—*Die Verräterin*!"

"KARA!"

I shot to my feet, pushing aside whatever lay atop me and fighting the shaking. A hot dagger of light pierced my eyes, the sun licking out my retinas and leaving behind a burn. I threw my hands up, blocking the rays of dawn, giving my eyes a chance to adjust. When they did, it was to find myself not laying in my beloved's bed where we'd first made love, but in a hood's home in some far-off land.

Geri lay sprawled out on the floor, blinking and confused. Jesus, we'd been sleeping in her tiny childhood bed together. The weight I felt atop me... it must have been her, trying to wake me up.

"Geri?" I pulled dirty hands over weary eyes, cupping my face in my hands. "I'm sorry. I didn't mean to... I was..."

"Having some kind of bad dream," she completed for me. She didn't get up. She didn't even look me in the face. "Yeah, I guessed that."

But it wasn't a bad dream. It had been a good dream. A *great* dream. I'd been with my mate, in her arms, making love, and…

"I called out *her* name." I fell to the floor beside her when I tasted Kara's name in the back of my throat. "It didn't mean anything. It was just a dream."

"You don't have to apologize to me for dreaming about Kara." Her sad eyes drifted. "You aren't cheating on me by remembering her. You aren't even cheating on me by still being in love with her."

My rational mind knew that, but fuck all if I didn't still feel guilty. "You know you're my mate, right?"

The smile that she gave me went as deep as a frost on the leaves. "Of course."

Sitting back against the bed, I opened my arms, inviting her in. She hesitated, and that moment of reluctance burned hotter than any silver ever had. Eventually, she gave in, tentatively scooting toward me and resting her head on my shoulder.

"You've got to talk to me, love," I said. "Wolves aren't psychic."

"There's nothing to talk about."

"You realize we might both be dead this time tomorrow, right?" I wouldn't ignore that fact because Geri wasn't either. We shared a taste for blatant realism. "We won't be able to work this out after that. Tell me what's going on in your hoody little brain."

A momentary flash of her anger rushed through me, catching my breath.

"I was trying to be coy, but I'm going to stop digging myself deeper now."

The tension passed as she cycled a breath. "It's just something your mom said."

"Her moods and opinions aren't the most stable," I reminded her. "Don't put stock in it."

"It would have been true no matter when she said it." Geri pushed herself up to sit beside me, taking her warmth with her. "It's crazy—probably stress being the demon of my thoughts—but what we have… It isn't supposed to be possible, and I'm scared it's not. I'm scared that one day you're going to wake up and not love me anymore."

So that was it? "Well, that's a load of shite."

Raven hair fanned the air as her head spun. "How can you say that? Even if it's what you hope for, how can you say for sure that your feelings won't change someday? We don't know how long the effects of that serum the Dracule were giving you would last."

"For the last time, it's *not* the serum," I said. Her furrowed brow forced me to continue. "Lamb, let me tell you something I've never said, because I worried what kind of wolf you'd take me for. Back in Chicago, when we first met, I found you attractive."

Geri's eyes had grown as I talked, and now popped back to regular size. "A startling and upsetting admission," she deadpanned.

"Don't be a bitch about this, I'm serious. I was mated then. A mated wolf can think a woman beautiful, maybe even have the ability to understand why another man would fancy her. But I was *attracted* to you. And even if things didn't happen the way they did, that would be a sign that I was different. It shouldn't have been possible. I blamed it on the moon madness that was creeping up on me, but I guess now we know the truth."

Lithe, little fingers played with my chest hair. "You're supposed to be reassuring me, you ass."

"I thought I was."

"No, what you just told me is that I have to worry about you cheating on me because you were attracted to me when Kara was still alive."

"You just told me you don't blame me for still loving Kara."

"And I don't!" she assured me. "Only… I mean, you did just hear what you said, right?"

"Geri, I'm not going to placate you with lies. Not even hopeful assumptions." I reached up to stroke her cheek. "You want me to be a wolf here and tell you that I'm bonded to you, that my feelings can't change. I can't do that because it's not true. I still love Kara. I love her, and she's gone. But you're right here with me. Why would you think my love for you would fade any more than it has for her?"

My mate chewed that over for a moment. "In a weird way, that's kinda comforting."

I pulled her head back into my chest. "That's my girl."

We stayed like that for a few moments, enjoying the silence of day that the rise of night would shatter.

"Tobias?"

"Geri?"

"When I spoke to Amy earlier, she mentioned something."

"Still not psychic, love."

I felt her laugh against my side. Things were on an uptick. Good.

"She said Caleb got a report from WWL's Director of Internal Operations yesterday," she continued. "It included an inventory of what's sitting in their warehouses. One of the things on the list was extract of wolfsbane."

My muscles tensed, but I managed to keep my voice even. "They do have a large pharmaceutical division."

"Yeah, I know. But wolfsbane isn't a chemical. It's a herb. Caleb, I guess, was suspicious, so he asked to speak to the head of the division that was making it."

A hard lump went down my throat. "And?"

"And… that person… that *vampire* is no longer with the company. Caleb destroyed him when he arrived in Chicago, a research scientist who was also on the Board of Directors. A Dracule."

And… there it was. "They were stockpiling the serum."

Geri nodded. "Inga might have been working with the Ravens the whole time."

"Or she might have been pretending to work with them to keep in the loop of what they were actually up to and controlling their access to a very dangerous weapon. She definitely was aware of Kai and Cynthia's work at the university. She funded it. It could have been one of those 'keeping your enemies closer' things."

"Since she's dead, we'll probably never know. Either way, it doesn't change the facts." This time, the lump went down *her* throat. "If anyone wanted to have access to the serum…"

"Why would any wolf in his proper mind *want* to? Our situation aside, the bond between mates is what holds lupine society and packs together. It's so strong, that even when one dies—"

The words caught in my throat as the realization of what she was driving at hit me in the heart.

"I don't know if you have a bond to me or not," Geri said. "I don't know if because of both of our open buffets of genetics if that's possible. But if something happens to me tonight, or if another wolf should fall when the Dracule come, that serum could be a godsend. And if you want to take it, because… well, it was different when it was just the two of us. It would hurt like hell to lose you, but we're a pack now. I need my pack. *Mina* needs her pack."

Numero dos in the one-two punch of my mate's anxieties. "You want me to take the serum because you're convinced that our relationship is a side effect of that shite?"

Geri threw her legs over me, straddling my lap. Trembling hands covered my cheeks as she let her forehead fall against mine. "I don't want you to do anything, and the last thing I want is for your love to be a side effect. I want it to be the infection. But if comes down to it, then—"

"Shut the fuck up." I pressed a kiss to her lips as my hands circled around her back. "Okay? Shut. The. Fuck. Up. I love you. Not the serum. Not the alpha. Fuck, not even another hood. *I*, Tobias Somfield, love you. But you're not an infection, okay? You're my cure. You're my serum. You're my fucking salvation, woman."

She crashed into me, and I let her. I took every wave her oceans threw and rejoiced in the surf. And when we'd come down from our highs, I held her and swore to God, one way or another, this was ending tonight.

TWENTY-THREE

BRÜNHILD

Sunlight filtered throgh pines dusted with snow. The storm that had born down from the skies the day before had passed. The one that would rise from the lakeshore gathered on the horizon.

For the first few days, the influx of wolves and hoods alike had distracted me. Now, two weeks after arriving home, the emptiness of my bed in the daylight hours consumed me. I'd come to the woods to be alone, pushing out the voices and memories that tore at my heart. I missed my husband. My mate, my partner, my heart. I was never meant to fall in love with Pietro; I'd been sent to Argentina solely to deliver a decree from the Grand Matron. From *my mother*. And then things just… happened.

I tried to resist him. He persisted.

I tried to run away. He pursued.

I tried to threaten. He called me on my bluff.

I tried to mourn him. He refused to be forgotten.

"Oh, Pietro." I spoke to the trees, to the snow, to the ground. "Why did I let them take you? Why didn't I order you to remain behind? Why didn't I die too?"

A twig snapped behind me and I spun.

Maggie Somfield sat on a branch jutting out from a cedar about ten feet off the ground. How had she arrived without my hearing her? How had she arrived without my *sensing* her?

"Maggie." I dipped my head.

"Brunnie."

My eyes pressed closed. "I'm not a fan of the name."

"You don't expect me to go around calling you Matron, do you?"

"No, of course not. We are family."

With a graceful maneuver even I had to admire, Maggie dropped from the tree, landing with the lightest thud. "That must be odd for you, having a wolf in your family."

"You'd be surprised."

Turning towards home, I invited her to walk beside me. It had taken me a few minutes to fly out this far; walking back might take a half-hour. Still, as I now had company, it would seem rude to leave her behind.

The little voice within me that sounded remarkably like my mother chided, No, fine, take your time getting back when you know the enemy is nigh. At least they'll say you were polite when you die.

Long moments passed in which the only sound was the wind through the needles and the crunch of the snow beneath our feet. Nearer the lake, some of the drifts had been five feet high from the passing storms. Would that the woods were the same; it might slow the coming assault.

"How long did you know?"

I shook myself from my reverie. "Know what?"

"That the Dracule had me. That I, your son-in-law's mother, was still alive?"

"Not long. Rumors came first. The slayers were extensively interviewed when they came to Schloss Wolfsretter. One of them had overheard the Dracule in Vlad's company mention having an asenaic near London. I asked one of the few hoods in the House of Green I trust to investigate."

"And when did you *know* it was me?"

I owed her the truth, even if it showed how I'd been duped. "Two days before the raid, a vampire who owed me a favor got a tip that you were the one in that house on the Thames. I understand now that it was a trap, that someone used Massimo to pass along the information, hoping I'd send your son—and by extension, my daughter—to save you."

"And you played right into their plans." Maggie came to a sudden stop, causing me to do the same. "You're no silver-eyed nascent. Why did you get pulled into something so obvious?"

"Because you are my son-in-law's mother, and I thought he deserved a chance to rescue his only surviving blood relative."

"Because you allowed your emotions to be the dictator of your actions," Maggie corrected. "I don't fault your feelings. I figure even a hood must have them. But you were a fool, Matron. You put your child and mine on a silver platter."

Heat flared in my face. "I am not accustomed to insults from my guests, Maggie."

"I reckon you're not accustomed to insults from anyone." Maggie pulled her knit scarf tighter around her throat and kicked a patch of needles that had managed to stay above the snow. "Why aren't there more wolves here? More hoods? Why no slayers?"

My coldness rivaled Mother Nature's display about us. "Perhaps Tobias and Gerwalta should have left you to the Dracule in Marquette. Speaking of which... you are aware that as a reclaimed hood, your little maneuver of colluding with them could legitimize my leveling treason charges on you, don't you?"

"You won't do something like that right now." Maggie shrugged.

"It's within my rights."

"I know it is. I wouldn't argue against it. But you won't do it because you'd do the same thing. If you could give up my son to save your daughter, you'd do it."

If she expected to shame me, her plan had wildly backfired. "I would."

But to my surprise, Maggie just smiled and nodded. "Ah, Brunnie... We both really fucked up our kids and we did it with the best of intentions, dinna we?"

I didn't know where my smile came from. "Yes, we did."

"And that's why we both know what we're willing to do tonight if it comes down to it, don't we?"

"I suppose we do."

TWENTY-FOUR

GERI

I bit my bottom lip. "I don't know, Rick. It seems really... Are you sure?"

It wasn't the kind of war room you saw in movies. Our family kitchen didn't have banks of monitors or elite commanders with earpieces engaged, coordinating teams around the world. It did have a coffee pot which had done industrial work the last few weeks. Brünhild, Rick, Yan, Tobias and I stood shoulder-to-shoulder, marking out plans on a map of the State Park Rick had grabbed from his office. Maggie lurked nearby, glancing over our shoulders.

The Paradise Pack's beta blew his frustration with me out through a hefty sigh. "You grew up here, Geri, but you never had to plan a tactical battle here. According to our friend Yan—" He pointed at the vampire. "—vampires aren't trained in squad attack enough to form ranks. They want easy access, well-trodden paths to move large groups. The huey entry to the park is the only easy access, well-trodden way into that area, and that's relevent given the amount of snowfall we've had this week. Trust me, since we're choosing the battlefield, this is the best option."

"Never ran a tactical battle here…" My voice tapered off, but before I could follow up with the logical question, my mother interrupted.

"And you're certain there are no hueys in the park tonight?" she asked.

Rick nodded. "I ordered it closed for safety given the extreme snows two days ago. My rangers did a sweep of all the camping areas yesterday and chased out the last van-lifers. There are still some houses out on the main road that leads to the park entrance, but most of them are owned by snow birders and boarded up this time of year. The few that have residents are too far away or too old to give a damn."

Maggie Somfield's finger pinned a dot on the map. "And this? Is this not a house?"

"That?" Rick leaned in a bit. "That's the old lighthouse. It hasn't operated for years, since the old mill shut down. No big boats coming in to haul out lumber any more. But if the battle gets that close to the lake, we've done something wrong. The huey highway runs right by there. Not much traffic at night, but we can't be certain of it. The hoods will be standing ready in the open space around the gift shop, where the parking lot is empty. The wolves will be in the woods and will close in on the rear flanks of the enemy."

Yan moved to the table as he nodded his agreement. While his hair hadn't grown back, most of his burns had healed over thanks to a feeding from Maggie.

"The vampires Vlad are bringing are young, most under a century and of European heritage. There are a few who fought in the last great huey war, but the majority were made after the Ravens were released in the early 1950s. They were taught how to take down a single animal as prey, not how to coordinate on a battlefield."

So, that was that. The plans were made. The turf, selected. All that remained was for us to take position inside the State Park parking lots and wait for nightfall.

I crossed the room to where a block of silver sat and started to pull some of it onto my body.

Brünhild stepped away from the table. "What are you doing, Gerwalta?"

Seriously? "I'm gassing up. I could use a wooden staff, though. Since our main tactic here is going to be beheading the vamps, I'm thinking of going with a scythe."

My mother passed a loaded look to Tobias, who dug himself out from the woodwork to put his hands on my shoulders. "Love, you're not going to the front."

The stream of silver seized in an instant. "What do you mean, I'm not going?"

"Only a fool would let you be a hair's breadth from Vlad," Maggie said. "If he gets his hands on you and drinks, he'll be restored, maybe even unkillable if he takes in enough of you. We can't take the risk."

"But that's the whole reason I *have to be* out there. I'll lure him in," I argued. "We don't know for certain how many of the Dracule will continue to fight if Vlad dies. If we kill him off, then we only keep fighting the ones that insist on not giving up."

"Is that how it works for vampires? Like it does for wolves? Leaderless then listless?" My mother turned to Yan.

The vampire shook his head. "We aren't like wolves with alpha's prerogative. The ones that are coming are either following Vlad because they believe in his cause, or because he's holding something over their heads."

"We already know what, though," Tobias said. "They think he has an illustrian. He's told them he can kill them without risk to himself."

Yan balanced his chin on his balled-up fist. "I agree that's likely it. Of course, he assumes he'll win, and he assumes he'll get his hands on Mina once he has Geri. But, still…"

The vampire tapered off, but my mother persisted, asking Yan to speak openly.

"My bloodline has recorded all the details of the major events in supernatural history for thousands of years. An illustrian is so rare as to be thought rumor, but there's nothing in our records that indicates the deadly effect they have on vampires is any less subject to the same-bloodline risk. What does Vlad know that the Varanasi do not?"

"Probably nothing," Tobias grumbled. "He needed an army; he came up with a lie—or at least, a convenient twist on the truth—to get one. Given all the legends around him, why would they hesitate to accept one more he throws out at them?"

I couldn't believe they were ignoring the critical issue. "What do you mean I'm not going to the front?"

All their heads turned back to me. My mother, however, was the one who stepped forward. "You're just not, and that's an order."

"Oh, I see," I said. "I get special treatment because I'm the Grand Matron's daughter, is that it?"

"On the contrary, Gerwalta, if not for the obvious reasons Maggie already outlined, you would be ordered into battle *because* you are my daughter. I have never softened your obligations because you were mine. Why would you think I would start now?"

Well, she had me there. She'd always pushed me *harder* than the others who fell under her domain. "And where will I be, exactly?"

"You'll be staying here, guarding me."

I spun and tried to catch the pieces of my heart as they crashed to the ground.

One side of Cody's face looked perfectly normal, his boyish grin letting that dimple in his cheek peek out. The other side, however, was a canvas of glossy reds and canyons of blackened flesh. That Cody could smile at all was a miracle. That he could do it at me, a bitter tragedy.

He limped into the room, his right side still broken from the brunt of my blast a few days earlier. He came to a stop before me, carrying the tensions of all observing.

"Cody." I swallowed my nerves, not sure if I should apologize, or if the attempt alone would be an insult. "I—"

He held up a hand. "Don't. I know it looks bad, and hell, it doesn't feel great. But I already look three times as good as I did right after it happened, and Rick thinks I might be healed completely by the full moon. Not that I'm completely letting you off the hook for this, and not that Lisa ever will, but we have bigger things to worry about right now."

I tried to wet my palate, but my mouth had gone dry. "But you have to understand how important it is that every capable hand be in the battle and—"

He leaned forward. "You owe me this."

I recoiled. Not from the sight of him, but from his demanding tone. His *alpha* tone. "What?"

"You *owe* me this," Cody repeated, this time softer. "You did this to me and the way you're going to pay me back is to sit this battle out."

I surveyed the others in the room: Yan, Rick, silent Markus sitting on a stack of old newspapers, Maggie, even my mother and Tobias... Not a one appeared ready to lend me an argument.

Finally, Brünhild stepped forward. "If you die in this, even if you are only captured by them, then all this will have been in vain. We will stop the Dracule tonight, Geri, but the only way we can do that is if *you* are not part of the equation. Then no matter what, they cannot win. From the moment I gave birth to you, that decision was made."

My bottom lip stiffened. "I could disobey orders. I've done it before."

"You've done it professionally," Brünhild said. So, my mother *was* capable of sarcasm. "But you won't this time, because you know I'm right. I trained you to be a master of observation and strategy, and you can see the truth in this."

I hated to admit it, but she was right.

His teeth pulled on my bottom lip, his hands held on for dear life in the strands of my black hair.

"I'll be home by morning, love." Tobias's forehead fell against mine. "I promise."

"Make sure you do."

Markus cleared his throat behind us. I turned to find my annoyed cousin with a laptop in his hands. He opened it up and turned the screen in my direction as my mate and I unraveled ourselves.

"This will give you a rough view of what's going on but remember that these cameras aren't designed to be high def or work well at night," he said. "Your view won't be great, but you'll have some eyes on the field. I put a shortcut on the desktop called *wolfvision*. If you lose the page or the browser crashes or something, just double click on that and it will pull up. And don't click on this little icon here." He pointed to the feed on the screen and to the corner where something that looked like an eyeball appeared. "There are a few other cameras mounted around the park, places like the observation tower near the waterfalls and on the gift shop register and stuff. I've turned them off for now but if you click this, they'll turn back on and I can't stop them from broadcasting publicly. Those ones are managed by the big boys down in Lansing and my only option is to turn them on or off."

I took the computer and set it on the kitchen table. "I didn't even know there were security cameras anywhere in the park." Nervously, I began to scroll through *encounters* I'd had with Cody back in our dating days. "There's none up on the hiking trails, right? Or in the shack where the canoes are stored in the winter?"

My cousin passed me a quizzical look.

Cheeks red, I pressed on. "Thanks, Markus. You know, I've never asked. Where did you learn to do all this techy stuff anyway? I don't remember any part of my hood training that included how to hack into a state park security system."

"I went to college."

"What? When? Where? There isn't any college anywhere near your house."

Markus mussed my hair. "It's the twenty-first century, Geri. I did it online. You know, instead of throwing a hissy fit and running away to the big city in the middle of the night."

With a click, the screen brightened. The lights over the parking lot began to flicker on. Night was coming, and with it, battle. On the edges of the parking lot, near the tree line, hoods ordered in advance of the sunset were busily readying medic tents, pulling supplies from snowmobiles and sleds pushed into last-minute service. A small cart of silver bars had been deposited amid the area meant to form ranks, a resource for the hoods.

Markus gave Tobias a once-over. "The wolves are leaving from the packlands in about ten minutes. You better strip down and fur out if you're going with them."

Cody shuffled into the kitchen. "Tell Lisa and the other shewolves staying behind with the pups to close up all the homes and have wooden stakes within arm's reach at all times."

Tobias looked over my shoulder. "You must have laid down a heavy alpha's prerogative. I'd have thought the shewolves would be champing at the bit to take down some vamps. The only thing more dangerous than a male lupine is a female when you threaten her pups' safety."

"Lord, ain't that the truth?" Cody grinned. "They hate me right now for keeping them back, but at least they'll still be alive for it. Still, the Paradise Pack is sending in eighteen wolves, including a few cousins who came by dogsled this morning all the way from Newberry just for the occasion."

My face scrunched up. "When did you have a chance to issue an alpha's order? Did you go back to the packlands since... You know."

Cody shook his head. "Doesn't matter if they hear me say it or not. My pack adheres to my commands no matter where they are, as long as they're not *too* far away. Not sure about the limitations; we've never really had a reason to test it."

Tobias pulled his sweater over his head before handing it to me. "Any word from the slayers?"

"Caleb refused to let them come." Possibly because I had told him I'd never forgive him if he had, but that would stay our little secret. "Only the women have had their powers awakened, and they're too precious to risk if their race is going to survive. Besides, they have no combat training. They'd be more a liability than any help."

My mate grimaced. "There's probably a spot of truth in that. Still, you'd think after all his vows of revenge on the Ravens, Helsing would gird his bollocks and drag himself out here. But not to be done, I guess." Tobias's hand went to his belt as his mischievous eyes found mine. "Better look away now, love, or you might want to keep me home."

I faked up a smile, even though on the inside I felt like liquid death, and squeezed my eyes shut.

"Turn around just for good measure," he said.

I laughed but complied. "You just had to make me smile before you left, didn't you?"

But no answer came. Instead, when the lingering silence forced me to turn, it was to see he'd already taken his fur. Tobias gave one last, lingering look before turning toward the open door and running out.

Cody hobbled my way, putting his arm on my shoulder. "Kinda makes you thankful now, doesn't it?"

"What does?"

"That when I asked you, you didn't say yes fast enough."

My hand covered his. "And that I didn't dare say no when Tobias did."

TWENTY-FIVE

To have lived through the destruction of Schloss Wolfsretter…

To have survived Spain and rescued Maggie…

To have freed the slayers and infiltrated Vlad Tepeş's own home and harem…

To have lost Kara, Igor, Inga, Becky, and even my own father…

To have escaped the shadow of my name…

To have done all *that* and have it all come to this moment: me in my Yooperland home, sitting on the couch in my family room next to my convalescing ex, watching a grainy video feed of the battle five centuries in the making on a second-hand laptop.

I closed my eyes and tried to play out the way I hoped the battle would go. The vampires would file in through the main road, where our forces would already be stationed and waiting, the woods and rivers to their back. Normally a force wouldn't want such a formidable river so close, but my mother claimed it actually was a tactical advantage.

"The current and temperature of that river would drown or kill a huey, but Supes can endure long enough to cross it," she had said. "There's no bridge across until it spills into the lake a few miles away, and vampires cannot smoke over water. If we need to retreat, that buys us time."

I wasn't sure I agreed. True, the Falls didn't churn quite as much in the winter, being that some of the river water got trapped as ice up and downstream, but I had worked in that park long enough to respect Tahquamenon's power.

"Well, no, not yet," Cody said to his mate over the phone.

Three miles away, Lisa oversaw the shewolves barricading in the community center. There, they kept what pups couldn't be left at home by the lupines who'd come to Paradise to help. That included Cody's own, the younger only a few weeks old.

He should have been there with them. The alpha should be in the heart of his packlands, vigorously and heroically defending both friend and family. But he wasn't. He wasn't because I had torched him with my "awesome powers" and left him too weak and injured to take his fur.

"I mean, the sun *just* set a few minutes ago, so it's not like anyone would have had time to… No, actually, I don't remember that coming up. Hold on, I'll ask Geri. Say, Geri?"

"Mm?" I chewed on the pad of my thumbs, curled over, watching every micromovement on the video feed.

"How will the vampires know where the battle's taking place?"

A queer pang in my stomach made me sit up. "They know where we live, or at least, they'd be able to find out easily enough. It's not like we spent the last few decades buying up property through shadowy shell corporations like vamps do. We didn't know we needed to hide from them in that way."

It was a long way of saying, *Well, shit, I guess we forgot about that part.*

"So you're telling me the vamps will come to Paradise, and the one place they know to find hoods is this house?" Cody pushed the cell to his ear. "Honey, I'll call you back."

No sooner had our illusions of safety been shattered than we heard it: a slow, eerie creak as the back door of the house opened and a blast of bitter wind swirled through the kitchen and into the living room.

I was on my feet before Cody had managed to push the button to end the call, silver flame licking my fingers as I lashed my hand out to the side and sped into the kitchen. "You have two seconds to identify yourself or I make a tostada out of you."

Broad-shouldered and wearing a black winter coat, the figure managed to stay just out of sight, rendering himself a silhouette of terror just beyond the reach of the light spilling out of the living room. At least six feet tall, a Panama-styled hat added to his height. When he spoke, the voice, accented with a taste of the near east, was raspy.

"It was a wise decision for them to leave you here. So much needless bloodshed prevented when I capture you now."

Behind me, Cody growled a low lupine rumble in a human chest.

"Don't!" I shouted. "You're still too injured. It's too risky for you to shift."

"You kept a werewolf behind as protector, and yet, he cannot take his fur? You always surprise, Miss Kline. The Sultan was certain you'd have a phalanx of protectors." The figure's head tilted to the side as a long, veiny hand reached to pull off his cap and lower it into his chest. "My sympathies on your injuries, my lupine friend. Those who wield silver fire often do not realize its injuries cause more damage and death would be a better fate."

With two steps, he was in the house.

Behind me, Cody gasped, but I'd seen him before. A human frame absent skin and hair other than a few patches of scalded flesh over high cheekbones. The visceral structures of life, bones, tissue, and pulsing vessels twisted in a grotesque impersonation of a human face dotted with a set of vibrant green eyes.

"Miss Kline," the creature said, bowing his chin. "Such a pleasure to see you again."

"Geri, is he…"

I gave a step for each the vampire took, keeping Cody at my back. "No, that's not Vlad, but it is one of the Ravens."

"One of the only three you've left alive." I couldn't tell from the tone if it was respect or disdain that stained that truth.

Cody swallowed so hard, I heard it. "What happened to him?"

"I did."

"Same thing that happened to me?"

I nodded. "Except my mom hit him too, and her silver fire is even stronger than mine."

"Jesus, I didn't get off too bad, did I?"

Mr. Anatomy followed our conversation with a grim, bloody smile. "Come now, Miss Kline, you know I do not wish to injure you. Give me your neck so I can drink and be healed. If you do, I'll call Vlad and tell him to order back our line. No one will need to die today just to save—"

The flame in my hand coalesced, a tiny miniature moon punching forward to wallop the vamp in his chest. His smug smile burned into a growl as the bottoms of his feet came into my view. He flew backward, out the door, over the summer porch, and landed on his back where a well-trodden path led in from the training center.

We lingered in the doorway, my hand still cocked at my side, ready to conjure another lunarium at a second's notice.

"So that whole 'they can't come into your house unless you invite them' thing is a hoax," Cody said, peeking over my shoulder. "Is he dead?"

"I don't know." I stepped out on to the porch. "How do you tell if something without a regular pulse that doesn't need to breathe is dead?"

"We could poke it with a stick."

I turned dubious eyes on the alpha.

"What?" Cody said, glaring back. "I mean, it would probably piss off a vampire if it was still alive, right?"

"It would, but do you really want me to get close enough to a deadly creature to be within arm's reach and antagonize it to see if it fights back? Fess up: you became alpha because nobody else wanted the job, right?"

"You don't need to insult me. I haven't had as many chances as you to face off with the undead, and I..."

I turned back to the pathway, only to discover that I wasn't any wiser. I'd seen enough horror movies and dark comedies to know you should never take your eye off the bad guy when he's down, because the next minute...

"He's gone!" Cody peeped out.

"Yeah, no shit." I inched forward, surveying the landscape. No fresh footprints in the snow from where he'd landed, but so many people had walked through the area, that wasn't concrete evidence of anything. "He probably smoked away. He's not too injured if he managed that one. Come on, we need to get back inside, and—Cody, duck!"

My words were too slow; slower still was the injured werewolf.

A corpulent arm hooked Cody by the throat and dragged him back as a grotesque grin stretched long across a gruesome face. "Nice try, Little Red, but any damage your weak slayer powers could do to me, you've already done."

"Maybe I just need to be closer." The silver burned up my arm and ignited on my palm. "I know how your brood loves experimenting. Let my friend go and we'll see."

To my surprise, he did. The vampire sent the werewolf flying. Cody landed fifty feet away, face down in a knee-high drift, with a harrumph. In my peripheral view, I saw him plant his palms out and push himself up. He wasn't hurt if he could move like that, and I'd learned my lesson about distraction.

The vampire threw his arms out wide. "Go ahead. Like I said, your tiny little moonlight can't—"

The lunarium flew.

And then, I was on my ass.

Adrenaline pushed me to sit up, but even before I managed to look, I knew two things: something had caused the snow around me to turn instantly into a pool of toasty water, steam still clinging to the air, and that every stitch of clothing I had been wearing was gone, leaving only a thin coating of liquid silver glistening over my skin.

A thin coat that was being indexed currently by the eyes of one Caleb Helsing from the very porch I'd stood on just moments before.

"You ever read comic books?"

The non-sequitur made me blink like a meth-addicted rabbit. "What?"

"I'm just saying…" Caleb stepped off the back porch, marching over a blackened patch of sidewalk that ten seconds before had been a vampire and offered me a hand. "…you totally look like a female Silver Surfer."

"Geri!" Cody crunched his way over the intact drifts and into the three-foot radius of mud, in which I sat in the middle.

Caleb pivoted, firing up another solarium, forcing the werewolf to freeze on the spot.

"Caleb, don't. It's Cody. You met in Triberg a few months ago, remember?"

"*That's* Cody?" Caleb shielded his eyes, against what I hadn't the foggiest, and squinted. "Why does one side of his face look like Deadpool?"

"One, oh my god, how did I date you for so long and not know you were such a geek? And two, can you *please* help me up already? Cody, are you hurt?"

The werewolf looked himself over. "No. You?"

"I'm fine. Naked, but otherwise…" I shook my head as Caleb wrapped a hand around mine and pulled me to my feet. "What are you doing here? I thought you said you couldn't risk the slayers, that they were too inexperienced."

"I said *they* were too inexperienced, but I'm the motherfucking Solari."

Cody drew to a halt as I spun. "Whoa."

"What?" I followed his eyes down, seeing my silver skin wasn't *quite* as concealing as I hoped. And, frankly, I didn't hope for much. I lashed my arms across my chest. "Jesus, you've both seen me naked before. It can't be that big of a deal. Besides, what did you expect? It's cold out here."

"Then can I suggest we go back inside?" Caleb said, leading us toward the front door. "Good thing I decided to do the rude thing and just show up unannounced. When I sensed the vamp, I didn't bother ringing the doorbell."

"We don't have a doorbell." I shuffled myself inside, taking one of my dad's old coats off a hook by the door and letting it engulf me. "Was that the only one? Do you sense more?"

Caleb stilled as his eyelids closed. He shook his head. "Which only means not within a half kilometer or so. This guy either knew he'd find you here or just got lucky."

"It was the luck thing. I myself didn't know I was being written out of the battle until a few hours ago, and I doubt that information went outside of the command chain." But that got me to thinking. "Wait, how did you know to find me here? I know you knew we lived in Paradise, but no one gave you the address."

"Your mother did. She phoned me a few hours ago and I left Chicago right away."

Cody surrendered his body gingerly to a kitchen chair. "You drove here that fast?"

Caleb sneered. "As if. I'm a rich bastard now. I have my own jet. Anyways, Brünhild told me to come to the house. I assumed it was because she wanted me in the battle, but I doubt the Dracule forces total one veiny Raven. Which begs the question, why did she want *me* off the front lines?"

"Probably because you're the 'motherfucking Solari' and your bodily fluids are too precious to lose in battle."

"Finally, someone understands the value of my seed."

I let the passive-aggressive comment slide.

For now.

"So, then," Caleb continued, "just where *is* the battlefield?"

I pointed vaguely east. "State Park, a few miles from here."

"Great." He clapped his hands together. "Let's go. Or maybe you'd like to put some clothes on first? Though, you know, I'm cool if you don't."

Behind us, a growl rumbled in Cody's chest.

"Easy, Big Bad." Caleb put up his hands in a sign of surrender. "Just joking. Anyway, yeah, let's go."

I shook my head. "No. As much as I hate to say it, my mother's right. It's too risky for me to be there. And she was right to send you here for the same reason."

"And we're safe here?" One of Caleb's arms shot out toward the patch of muddy, singed ground outside. "Because that doesn't look like safety to me."

"I mean, we have a huge security wall surrounding the whole compound that's sealed shut and we didn't think the vampires would show up here when the battle is…"

The idea that had just popped into my head froze me in place and stilled my tongue. "Cody?"

Behind me, Cody spun.

"Call Lisa."

The alpha's face went white behind the burns. "Why?"

"They sent someone here to see if I was still at the house," I said, rummaging through Cody's pockets for his cell when he still hadn't moved. "They might have sent someone to the packlands too. They might have…"

The cell buzzed in my hand as I pulled it into view, Lisa's blonde tresses and blue eyes filling the screen.

Cody yanked back the phone from my hands, hit the screen, and pressed it to his ear. "Baby?"

I couldn't help it, I leaned in so I could hear.

"Hate to tell you this, dear," Lisa said, "but we just killed something over here. Something… disgusting."

TWENTY-SIX

Cody was in no condition to drive but try telling him that. Within ten seconds of hearing Lisa's words, he was in my house, digging through the basket by the door where we kept our car keys and using every ounce of his concentration otherwise *not* to take his fur. Though, honestly, fangs at that point would have been nothing more than a formality. His inner wolf was in charge, and the alpha was speeding towards his mate, all else be damned.

The shocking part was that he waited for me to get some clothes on and for Caleb and I to get into the car.

"If anything happened to any of my pack or those pups…" Cody hung an aggressive left, the back wheels of my dad's old Subaru wagon fishtailing.

His words tapered off, but the sentiment was palpable.

My hands shot out to the dash as the force of the turn threatened to knock me over. "Lisa said the vampire was dead, and given her description of what it looked like… What did she say? Like a horror movie villain? It was a Raven."

"Yeah, I get that, but what if he had backup coming? What if we show up there and there's fifty of them, and…" The engine protested as Cody punched the gas. "Come on, you stupid hood car, go faster!"

Caleb leaned forward, his hands white-knuckled over the back of my seat. "*If* we get there," he said. "Between the way you're driving and a Donner Party worth of snow, we're going to end up wrapped around a tree. We're supernatural, not immortal."

"Shut up, Helsing. This isn't your fight anyway."

Jovial Caleb took a metaphorical backseat, while the Slayer Solari, the super badass version of him I rarely saw, assumed the space. "The hell it isn't," Caleb snapped. "The Ravens killed my parents right in front of me. Vlad Tepeş took me prisoner, stuck me in his harem, and forced me to..." His eyes went distant before narrowing. "Don't tell me this isn't my fight. My whole life has been about getting revenge and seeing them all dead."

"Well, be that as it may..." Cody's tensions eased the teeniest bit. "If they've done anything to anyone in my pack or in *my* packlands, I have first dibs."

Caleb coughed a laugh. "I don't care who kills them, as long as every one of their asses dust at dawn. If it turns out one of your packlings killed a Raven, I'll buy them a new car as thanks. If they take down Vlad, I'll buy them a house." The slayer sat back. "That bastard dies tonight. Blood for blood. Oh, and that reminds me. Geri? Here."

One hand sank back behind the seat before it reappeared a moment later bearing a tiny glass vial filled with a crimson liquid.

"I practically had to arm wrestle Amy for that, so don't think she'll be willing to let you get any more of Mina's blood unless the world is coming to an end," Caleb said, falling back in his seat. "I just hope it isn't."

From the driver's side, Cody passed a quick side glance as I pocketed the item. "Why would you want a vial of Mina's blood?"

"I owe it to someone. Assuming we survive."

<hr>

THE CAR WAS STILL MOVING when Cody jumped from it, forcing me to dive to the floor and stomp down the brake with my hand before we crashed. Caleb, thank god, came to the rescue from the backseat, shifting the car into park and turning off the engine.

"That crazy lupine son of a bitch." Caleb pushed himself back into the backseat as I, instead, chose to worm myself out forward, dragging my body over the driver's seat and out on all fours from the car, bitter snow stinging my fingers. "Well, come on, Little Red, let's go see if there's an agreeable corpse waiting for us."

"We might also see if all the wolves are okay."

"Sure, if you insist."

The door of the community center cracked open, a set of blue eyes hovering above the business end of a shotgun. Just because a lupine could take any deer down with the equipment God gave them didn't mean they didn't also enjoy getting their Yooper on. The moment Cody got close enough to be in her line of view, the door flew open and Lisa was flying forward. The mates met in the middle, Cody picking Lisa up off the ground and Lisa throwing her arms around him, despite his compromised body.

"When you called, I thought—"

"He got inside and we don't know how and—"

"—I might have lost you—"

Their words became a waterfall of thoughts crashing over the edge of their emotions. I hung back, gathering the laptop under my wing as other members of the pack and wolves I didn't recognize crowded the doorway, many of them holding small children in their arms.

Caleb peeled off to the side, to where a pile of clothes oozed with thick, burgundy-colored blood. A kick to the corpse got no response. "Where's his noggin?"

Lisa looked up from Cody's embrace. "We threw it into the woods." She pointed out to a patch of trees. "Out there."

Cody ran a hand over Lisa's hair, which I suddenly noticed was darker than usual.

Blood. She was covered in vampire blood.

"You killed him."

Lisa's bottom jaw tightened. "You got a problem with that, Geri?"

"No, it's just..."

Just what? Inappropriate? Hardly. Lisa was a mom with an infant and a toddler. It was her duty to protect them. Surprising? Not in the least. A werewolf was a mighty creature, and Cody's mate was the alpha shewolf. Threatening? Maybe once upon a time, when I'd still been jealous of her, when she'd stolen the man I thought I'd spend the rest of my life with. So, what was it then? What was it that had me feeling all squishy and tingly on the inside?

I looked to the beaming eyes lingering in the doorway, to the frightened eyes of the children old enough to know there had been danger, to my high school sweetheart, flooded with relief that his mate was safe, and I knew. This was pride. It was gratitude. I was flooded by a sense of appreciation for a woman I once loathed.

I smiled. "I think it's awesome. Thank you, Lisa. For everything. For every, single thing."

Any grace I'd mustered bounced off the remembrance of recent events and died a quick death on the snowy ground. And that was okay, because she didn't owe me a thing.

Lisa's face screwed up. I knew that look. *Whatever, bitch.* I'd accept it. After all, I was still the woman who'd almost blown up her husband.

Cody's arms wrapped around his mate. "Helsing, any more of them nearby?"

Caleb looked up from the corpse. "No, but the crazy thing about vampires: they actually have this weird ability like bees. One dies, it sends out a smell that attracts others. I need to burn the corpse ASAP. Geri, can you go look for the head while I take care of this part of him?"

Eager to get out of the reach of Lisa's glare-of-death ray, I reached inside the community center long enough to deposit the laptop before skipping off in the direction the alpha shewolf had indicated. My shadow fell before me, Caleb's conjured solarium casting a warm glow behind me. A few steps away from the community center, drips of red on the snow served as breadcrumbs to lead the way. I must have been thirty feet away when I caught sight of two onyx eyes set in a wrinkled head still attached to half a neck staring up at the stars, a mask of profound suffering frozen in time. I recognized him from Spain, one of the vampires who held my dad while Igor, driven crazy by hunger, killed him. The vamp had suffered horrific pain when Lisa had severed his head from his body. I was glad. I was only sorry he'd been given the mercy of a quick death.

"Geri?"

Caleb's voice rescued me from the descent of my thoughts. I looked over my shoulder to see him doing his thing, manipulating the solarium with such ease, eating away at the tissues of the body. No puddles around his work; the nearby snow kept perfectly frozen. Damn, I needed to master that level of control.

"Yeah, I found it."

"Great, bring it here," he said, never looking up once. Hopeless gigolo he may be, but the man clearly didn't take his supe duties lightly. "If you can detach yourself from that pretty little blonde of yours, Cody, I wouldn't mind if someone fired up that laptop and checked if all hell has broken loose yet. As soon as I'm done with this, I'm heading to the front, no matter how sacred Brünhild Kline thinks my sac and swimmers are."

As Cody headed for the community center, reassuring shewolves and pups as he passed, I laced my hands through the vamp's hair, wishing I'd had my gloves. He might have been a Raven, but his *coiffure* needed an upgrade. A moment later, instead of the slippery sensation I'd expected from such a shiny 'doo, ice burned against my hand.

I looked down, forcing my assumptions through the strainer of reality, and landed in a mire of confusion. The vamp didn't have greasy hair at all. It had been wet, and it was frozen solid. But that didn't make any sense. Why would a vampire wash his hair as he was heading into battle? Why would he...

"Today, Geri!" Caleb demanded.

But I was lost to thought, the factoid bursting from the recesses of my memory. *Slayers' powers don't work in water.* That was why Vlad had kept his male prisoners in a dungeon flooded knee-deep. Why Igor and Inga took their day rest, not in coffins or even underground, but *underwater*.

"He wasn't looking for the battlefield."

"Say something, Geri?"

Caleb's solarium died away as he looked up from a steaming pile of ash. *Steaming*, not because of the snow underneath, but because the Raven's clothing had been saturated, then frozen. It was too cold outside for him to be so thoroughly soaked from falling snow, given a vamp's lack of substantial body heat. And since him having intentionally taken a never-nude shower, then showing up to the battle, held no tactical advantage, I was left with only one conclusion.

His clothes had gotten wet while he was outside and frozen *on the way to the battlefield*.

Urgency sped me, and I all but threw the severed head on the ground where the body had been only a few moments before.

"They looked for me on the field, but they didn't find me," I said, crossing to the hood of the car where Cody had set the laptop and was staring at it. "*Vlad* is here for *me*. When they didn't see me on the field, he sent out his trusted generals, vamps that had already been damaged by silver flame and couldn't be anymore if you remember what the one at my house said, to confirm I was safe. Hell, even to *keep* me safe, otherwise only sending one vamp after me doesn't make sense."

Caleb's hand dropped to his side; he took a few stumbling steps forward. "Geri, what are you—"

"He doesn't want me there," I said, cutting off the slayer. "This isn't just a battle to capture me. Even if I gave myself up willingly, he wouldn't trade my surrender for everyone's safety. I've pulled that one on him before and he's not falling for it again. He wants everyone but me dead, and he's brought a big enough army to do it."

Cody's brow furrowed. "That can't be true. You can see the field from all these cameras," he said, vaguely waving his hand at the laptop screen. "See, no vamps, not unless they can suddenly turn themselves invisible."

"Oh, they're there, hiding just beneath the surface." My finger landed on a wide-paneled shot in which the Tahquamenon River flowed in the background. "And if we don't get there to warn our side, they're going to be slaughtered from behind."

Caleb stepped up beside me as the screen filled with the security feed. All looked as it was before: neatly arranged rows and columns of hoods, each wearing their capes and bearing silver weapons in whatever form they thought best. Teams of werewolves patrolling the perimeter of the ranks, ready to aid or to rally. All of them facing the mouth of the parking lot, because that's where the vampires would be coming from, we'd assumed. It was the only way into the park if you were moving on foot with a large contingent. Hoods and wolves could move through trees like walking a path, but vamps needed clear open spaces.

We were so stupid.

I navigated the mouse to the little icon Markus had warned me not to click or I'd open the view to anyone who might be watching. Hesitation could be deadly, but so could alerting hueys to what I suspected was about to happen. To click or not to click? My imagination could be running away with me; it wouldn't be the first time, but there was even more risk if I *was* right.

And if I *was* right, then everyone I loved in that parking lot was about to get massacred by a surprise attack.

I said a prayer and clicked...

...And watched in horror as hundreds of figures streamed from beneath emerging from the waterfall, making their way through the river, and forming ranks behind our lines.

TWENTY-SEVEN

Cody clicked on the icon again, shifting back to the camera overlooking the parking lot. Some of the younger hoods were looking bored now. They'd been standing in formation for two hours, and the epic battle they'd been drilling for, beside wolves no less, had failed to materialize. The lupines, too, had begun to grow lax, one pair in the far background curled up in balls, sleeping. No one on the screen knew, as we did, that the danger lay at their backs.

"I have to warn them." I closed the laptop and threw it in the car through the still-opened driver's door. "I need a weapon in case I run in to trouble on the way over , but I don't have any silver left. Cody, do you know where Rick keeps his hunting rifles?"

Caleb's hand crooked over my shoulder, holding me back as I tried to dash forward. "Whoa there, Geri. You're not going anywhere."

"The hell I'm not. Or do you just want me to save myself and let all my people and hundreds of others get slaughtered?"

"It's not an either-or." Caleb pulled his phone from his pocket. "Technology, remember? We can let our fingers do the talking."

I shook my head. "My mother ordered all phones left behind. She didn't want distractions or someone's *La Cucaracha* ringtone going off."

Nearby, Cody nodded. "But won't your mom sense the vampires? I mean, since she's half-slayer, she should be able to do that like Helsing does, right?"

"Brünhild has some powerful solaria for a halfling, but she has to feed it silver to pull it off. She told me she didn't get any other slayer upgrades in the genetics lottery. Luckily, I'm one hundred percent, Grade A Helsing." He looked off into the distance. "You said this battlefield is only a few miles away? I can run that in a few minutes, if I really push myself."

I blinked my surprise. "Caleb, I've seen you move so fast you blurred."

He cocked a grin. "If we had ever actually made the beast with two backs, you'd discover my secret. Slayers weren't designed for endurance. Short bursts, maybe a mile? No problem. Running three while weaving through trees and hip-high snow drifts? I might dust a Kenyan but I'm not going to be able to keep that kind of pace for that long." Caleb swung his gaze to the car. "How long would it take us to drive there?"

"It's not far," Cody said, "but the packlands are at the end of a long, dead-end street. You'll have to go a few miles back up to the main road, a few miles up that, then turn again up the way that leads to the state park entrance. Then it's another mile from there into the park itself. In this kind of snow that's probably even longer than you running. Not to mention, the hoods won't know it's you. They see a car coming their way across a parking lot in a place that's supposed to be closed, they're going to shoot first and ask questions later."

"Then I run." Caleb sunk low, like a sprinter settling into the starting blocks. "Which way is it?"

Cody and I exchanged a look.

The slayer straightened. "Seriously? You guys can't hold out on this. One of us has to get there and this is the best option."

"They're not holding out on you." Lisa's voice made all three of us turn. The stately blood-splattered blonde stood a few feet away, arms crossed over her chest. "It's that you don't know these woods. They could point you in the right direction, but as soon as you get into those thick trees, you're going to get lost. It might only be a few short miles as the crow flies, but it's a few days away as the monkey wanders."

"As the monkey wanders?" The slayer turned to scan the woods. "I didn't know there were monkeys in the UP."

I grimaced, wondering how fast Caleb would be able to run while carrying me. "No, but we have the crows. But since we can't... No. No, wait a minute. We could. We *actually* could."

"Okay, counter-question. How did I date *you* for so long and not realize how many one-way conversations you have with yourself?"

Caleb's query fell on deaf ears because my brain and my heart were busy having an argument with each other.

Maggie Somfield had saved my life, and all she'd asked in return was for my silence about her ability to fly. It wasn't because she was ashamed of it, though for all I knew she may very well be. It was because if the hoods knew she could fly *and* she was half-wolf, then what did that mean for our history, our traditions, our social structure? Even though I'd long ago let go the idea that we were somehow inherently superior, even before I knew I was part-wolf, they hadn't. I had no problem destroying ignorance and fighting back prejudice, I just didn't know if it was a smart thing to do when the enemy was literally creeping up from behind. And it certainly wasn't a burden I should force on someone without their permission.

Then again, if I didn't use my abilities to summon Maggie, how many of those same hoods would survive the day?

"Is she having a stroke?" Caleb leaned in, snapping his fingers inches from my face. "I'm pretty sure she's having a stroke."

I grabbed his hand before he managed to press it to my forehead. "It's not a stroke. I'm having a moral quandary."

"Over?"

I shook my head. "How much shit I'm willing to eat for years to come to get there on time. Cody, go inside and warn the shewolves. This is going to hurt, but it's the best option we have."

Without a word more I closed my eyes, focused all my energy, and sent my summons racing over the landscape.

TWENTY-EIGHT

BRÜNHILD

Not a word of objection had been raised, but so many thought it and so loud, it crushed my eardrums. They weren't coming. We had practiced and planned and staged and feared, but the Dracule weren't coming.

For an hour, we'd kept formation, our fastest at the front, our strongest in the middle, our least experienced at the back as a last line of defense, wolves mingling about to support each in turn. The wolves, who had defied centuries of tradition and oppression by my ancestors—by me, to fight beside us. And now here we all stood, twiddling our thumbs, looking like fools.

Rick Ryland shed his fur and took his skin beside me. "Brunnie, I hate to say this, but the lupines are starting to…"

My raised hand cut off his words. "The hoods are as well. And frankly, so am I."

If the lupine could whine in his human form, he would be. "You don't think they went somewhere else, do you?"

My eyes shifted to Maggie Somfield, who thus far had trod the lines but refused to shift.

The shewolf shook her head. "I spoke to Dracule I'd been in contact with and *leaked* that Geri was hiding here in the park after what happened the other night. Either they no longer trust that I'm as self-serving as I once was, or they're simply somewhere that we can't see them."

I knew enough of the Dracule, both from Markus's research and my own experience, to suspect the latter, but I couldn't imagine just where they could be. My scouts had swept the forests on both sides of the river and the trail. All had reported back, and none had found any evidence of vampires. One of the reasons we'd chosen the hefty parking lot in the state park was due to its layout. The wide open space would allow us to see our enemy approach, give us the metaphorical higher ground with the wooded spaces behind us to retreat or regroup, and, according to Yan, was the kind of easily-accessible-by-huey-roads, developed space urban-centric vampires preferred.

So where were they, then?

"Mr. Ryland, perhaps another sweep of the forests in the direction of the Bayshore and the lighthouse? Perhaps they are *driving* in, like some of them did in Triberg. Any sizable number of cars on the highway would imply as much."

Rick bobbed his head. "Will do." And with that, he resumed his fur, barked and yelped at a half-dozen wolves nearby, and led a detachment away.

Maggie took up a position next to me, close enough to speak with confidence that not many would hear her. "This don't feel right, Brunnie. Something we're not seeing here."

"I concur."

"Possibly they smelled a trap? Or saw how much of a force we have gathered and changed their mind?"

"Doubtful. First, this is not a trap. Second, they don't credit us with much skill as to be daunted by us."

The shewolf's chin bobbed. "But how much longer do you intend for us to—"

The words cut off midsentence as Maggie doubled over. I spun, catching her just before the ground did. "Maggie!"

The son, of course, did not hesitate, shifting immediately back to his fur. "Mum, what is it? What happened? Is there—"

No sooner had the words tumbled from Tobias's mouth than he, too, bent over. Then, it was as though a wave crashed over the forces. Starting at the front and moving swiftly back and over to encompass the hundred or so lupines stationed at the front, the howling came. Not a camaraderie, but a sharp, biting yippy howl, high pitched and woeful, as though someone had a dog whistle and was blowing it.

A dog whistle? I wondered for a moment. Could the Dracule have defeated our wolf defenses by so plebian a measure? But with their sensitive hearing, surely, they'd have their eardrums pierced by such a sound as well. No, it was something supernatural, then, acting upon our wolves. Only, what had the power to affect so many and do so silently?

And with a sideways glance at Maggie, I knew.

I pulled Maggie to her feet. "Gerwalta?"

She nodded. "Yeah, it's her, the bloody, little—"

I bit my lip as Maggie cut herself off, either because of her pain, or to save me from mine. Gerwalta would only go through such desperate measures if she were in trouble. Or perhaps, something had happened to Cody? They were at the house together, hidden away. What could have happened? For the first time, I regretted not allowing a single cell phone to be brought along.

I shifted Maggie into Tobias's hold. "Take care of her. I must go."

"No." Maggie ground her teeth so hard, even I could hear it. "She wants me. She doesn't know how to direct it, but she's calling for *me*."

It was not time for my sensitivities to be pricked, but righteous indignation rose up all the same. "Why would she want *you*?"

The poisonous words were out of my mouth before I could recall them, and even I wouldn't blame Maggie for biting back. Only, that wasn't what she did at all. Oh, she glared, but she said *nothing*. Instead, it was what she *did* next that packed the punch. Maggie took two steps forward, out of Tobias's hold, looked skyward, and shot off into the air.

TWENTY-NINE

GERI

Maggie Somfield meant for me to die. That was the summation of my thoughts as she swooped down from the sky and pulled me from the ground, the Wicked Witch to my Dorothy.

"You *promised*!"

"I know." The pines below became broccoli on a flour-board landscape, bouncing off the light of the quarter moon above. "But I didn't know what else to do."

"They know now!" she bellowed back. "Do you know what this will do to my life? You're the Grand Matron's daughter. Your blood protects you. Mine will condemn me. They'll come for the wolf who can fly as sure as they'd come for an anathema alpha."

"Please, listen!" As cold as it was below, the wind this high up blew not air but ice, sending my teeth chattering. "We saw on the video feed," I said, my hands wrapping around hers, fearing she'd let go. "The Dracule are coming from the river. You need to tell them. They need to reverse the line before it's too late!"

Her scowl washed away. "Come again?"

"They don't need to breathe, and the Tahquamenon moves too fast to freeze. They've been hiding under the water, hidden near the waterfalls. They're going to attack from the back, where the weakest are. You have to flip. Move the front to face the forest."

"How many are there?"

I shook my head. "I don't know. We could only see what the camera could see, and it—"

"*How many?*" the shewolf growled.

I searched my thoughts for the only answer I could give with confidence. "How ever many Vlad was able to convince or coerce into coming."

"Geri!" Caleb's voice struggled to find me from far below. The solarium he sent up, however, came way too close.

"The slayers?" Maggie's eyes brightened, reflecting the blazing ball as it passed. "They came?"

"Only Caleb. The Ravens killed his parents and enslaved what remains of his people. He wants his vengeance. As do I. Please, Maggie, take me and Caleb to the battlefield with you."

My mate's mother bit her bottom lip, her eyes flashing between the ground and my face. Finally, she pulled me into her chest and dropped us at such a high velocity, it knocked the wind from my chest. I wasn't sure how she moved with such speed. Sure, my mother could fly too, but she couldn't compete with a jet the way Maggie could.

Caleb rushed to me, nursing me into his hold as I gasped and sputtered, trying to breathe. "If I didn't need your help, I'd burn your haunches for that, wolf."

"Hundreds of vampires are coming and you, one slayer?" Her disapproving glare cataloged Caleb from head to toe. "What good do you think your drop will be in this ocean? Save your fire for them, boyo. You'll need it."

Assured that I was going to live, Caleb pulled back. Trees about us lit up with an eerie glow as he pulled his weapon into being. "I'm not a drop, I'm a tsunami. You give me a clear shot and I can take out a dozen or more with a single blast."

"Do that twenty times, and it might help. All we need to be able to do is make sure no one gets in your way."

My forehead scrunched. "I can't tell if you're being serious or sarcastic."

Maggie fixed an iron gaze on me. "Can't you, now?"

She turned, walking away, even as Caleb doused his light and I, scrambling behind, followed.

"You two are children," she said. "Fired up, ready to die, not even knowing what it is you'd be sacrificing because you don't know the value of your life yet. These are Dracule we're going up against. Bloodline of the dragons. Fiercely strong, focused, and hell-bent on ruling us all in whatever form that takes. Stay here, stay free a little longer."

"Hey!" She was moments from taking off again when I grabbed her by the arm, forcing her to face me. "I get that you've suffered. I get that we're young and you think we don't know what we're risking, but I do. I have a daughter and a man, your son. I'm more than willing to die to protect them; I'm willing to *kill*."

I wanted to scare her. I wanted to shock her. I wanted to *convince her*. But the only thing I managed to do with my outburst was amuse her.

Her smile sickened me, but not as much as the words she was about to say. "The only one we need to kill tonight to assure that this ends is Vlad Tepeş, and you can't *kill him*, can you? Too weak physically, and your little sputter of moonlight power has done all it could possibly to him, I'm willing to bet."

All my righteous indignation withered. She knew. *She knew.* "No. He gave me the maker's bite. My powers won't kill him. Neither will Caleb's."

Beside me, Caleb huffed. "What are you talking about?"

"The maker's bite," I said, wondering if he wasn't aware. "You know, the one that makes them immune from a slayer's power? Don't tell me they let you linger in their harem that long without it."

"Of course, they drank from me, but it doesn't matter." The actual slayer before me grimaced. "That trick only works on chick slayers."

Even if that was such an obviously bad analogy, the overlaying premise began to worm into my thoughts and untie my understandings. Vague memories came back, of Alexa telling me something along those lines, but something still didn't add up. "But Vlad never bit my mother. Why did her attack only flay them, not slay them?"

"Because her powers aren't concentrated enough, duh."

"Interesting." I turned back on Maggie. "But that's not the problem you see, is it?"

She glared at me, daring me with that intense scrutiny to figure it out on my own. God, she could be so much like Brünhild when she wanted to be.

"I won't be able to kill him because I care too much," I said. "Because he'll convince me that if I go along with him, he'll spare the others, just like he's done before."

Maggie grinned. "The Dracule is like that. Told me if I stayed quiet and content in my little cage, they'd let my family be. When I go back to England, I'll take those words to the graves of my son and my mate and see if it resurrects their bones." She turned back again, and this time, I didn't stop her. "Stay here, Geri. Your head could win this battle, but your heart will cost us it. Mine won't. Your mother's won't. Your mate's won't. My Toby loves you and will kill anything that threatens a single hair on your head." Her shoulders cycled as she looked off into the distance. "But if the slayer wishes to fight..."

Caleb looked at the ground, nodded once, then turned his eyes up to me. "Sorry, Geri."

"Sorry about wh—"

He moved so fast, I spun in the wake. Even supernatural eyes couldn't track how quickly Caleb crossed to Maggie to be clutched in her hold and lifted from the ground.

"No, wait!"

Running after them was useless, but that didn't mean I didn't try. I'd barely gotten three steps when they'd disappeared from sight.

And with nowhere else to direct my frustration, I spun on the forest at large and began to yell at... no one.

"God damned wolves! Freaking slayers! What am I supposed to do here, knit socks?"

"Doubtful. I taught you many things, Gerwalta Kline…"

Clutching my chest, I turned to find the last person I'd expect to see away from the front with attack imminent.

"…but knitting was not one." Brünhild pushed herself off the tree she'd been leaning against. "Besides, she's wrong. I, for one, know the lengths a mother will go to to protect her daughter against overwhelming odds."

"Mother?" I looked through the trees, like I expected some kind of explanation to be on a neon sign just past the maples. "What are you doing here?"

Her eyebrow arched. "I thought you wanted a way to the battlefield?"

"What? I mean, I do. I did. I…" I felt like I was being set up. Even in the middle of a battle, I wouldn't put it past Brunhild Kline to leave the field just to show me up. "I thought yuo siad my beine there was too much of a risk. That I should stay out of the way."

"I did say that, but i doesn't mean I meant it."

Confusion froze my expression. "But… you… made me stay behind at the house."

"I never expected you to listen, though." She crossed her arms, her silver-lined black eyes twinkling. "Don't tell me you've finally decided to start obeying me now."

I hedged forward. "So, I can come to the front?"

"What better way to draw out Tepeş than wave you in front of his nose?"

Crestfallen, I crumbled. "So, it's just a tactic to you, then."

"I'd be lying if I said it wasn't. But at the same time, don't you feel like we both owe him an ass-kicking?"

Cursing? Having my English wolf around these last few months had clearly had an impact on my mother's sensibilities.

"Come on, let's go," Brünhild said without further ado, taking a few steps in the direction Maggie had flown just a few moments before. "If you face Vlad, you'll do what must be done, like the red hood, like the mother that you are. I did everything in my power to protect you as long as I could, and now you'll do the same for Mina."

THIRTY

The lighthouse near the shore, downstream from where the river met Superior, grew on the horizon as my mother started our descent. My hands woven behind Brünhild's neck, I held on for dear life as she cradled me in her arms, Superman to my Lois Lane. As we crested the slope, came out of the woods, and approached the state park, it was to see that news of the vampire's approach had reached the lines. It was the biggest game of Red Rover I'd ever seen, the front and rear flanks reversing position, those in the middle trying their best to stay out of their way. Maggie was nowhere to be seen, but near the tree line, my eyes landed on a brilliant glow. At first, I wondered who had brought a spotlight to the field and how they were powering it without a generator. Only after my eyes adjusted did I realize the truth: it wasn't a light at all. It was Caleb, his power crawling over not just his hands, but the entirety of his being. If what I did was silver flame, then this was a solar flare, a brilliant burst of sunlight that would toast any vamp that dared touch him.

Later, I'd have to ask him how he managed it without burning off his clothes.

My mother skirted the hoods shifting below as alpha and beta wolves yipped and barked, repositioning their own ranks. I tried to find my mate among them, but the moving mass of fur and legs made it impossible.

Brünhild slowed, approaching one of the small piles of silver bar reserves positioned for hood use. "Get ready."

I nodded, calling on the silver as my feet fell beneath me. I landed with a grunt, the dual swords already formed, hilts hot in my hand. I let my concentration lean just long enough to summon my cloak, and then, I stood.

A furry, wet nose brushed against my wrist. I looked down, and there he was: my mate, my life, my heart. My wolf. I spared a moment to pat his maw. "Couldn't sit this one out, sweetheart. Hope you understand."

He smiled, both fear and joy radiating from him in waves.

"You're afraid?" My chin ticked up, as did my anger. "Don't be. Be pissed off, like I am. I mean, aren't you tired of this asshat, arrogant vamp coming after us and the people we love? We're ending this tonight. And whatever Dracule survive, they do so on as tight a leash as the hoods can make for them."

It was about time we turned our considerable skills on the true enemy.

"Vampires afoot!"

I didn't recognize the lone voice that shouted out, but it didn't stay solitary for long. The commanders of each line barked out orders in a dozen languages.

Spanish, Persian, Russian… I looked to my left to catch the swirl of my mother's hood as she lifted above the crowds, trying to gauge the enemy. It wasn't necessary. Where moments ago there had been only snow and forest, forms twisted and writhed. Shadows solidified, a hundred haunted faces framed by dripping hair quickly turning to ice from the bitter wind.

Every color and every creed formed their ranks. Light-skinned, dark-skinned, tall, short, but all of them, fierce. Their eyes lit up when they spotted the Human Torch at the front of our ranks. I reminded myself that most of these vamps were young, few of them being turned before the Second World War. They'd been reborn to a world where slayers were either presumed extinct or secretly kept as cattle by elite members of the Dracule. To see one here, fronting the battle line, ready to fight, threw them. A legendary creature in turn saw one of its own legends made flesh. In that kind of state, anything—including defeat—may seem possible.

The enemy's confusion was a powerful ally.

My mother touched down beside Caleb, putting a hand on his arm, encouraging restraint. It didn't escape my notice that his powers had no visible effect on her, and suddenly I understood how I'd survived a direct solarium blast back in Istanbul. A full-blooded hood might not have been so lucky.

"I demand parley with your commander," Brunhild said, regal as she was righteous. "Let he or she be known."

A few vamps at the front exchanged amused looks, before a slender, bearded one belly-laughed. "Who are you to assume you have any right to—"

But before skinny vamp could finish, the sea of fangs behind him parted.

As terrifying as he was in my memory, he was five times worse in person. Whatever damage the other Ravens had suffered, Vlad's was worse. A sickly, oily slick covered exposed veins and bones, some of them still blackened by the silver flame. One eye looked like it was about to pop right out of its socket as his onyx peepers rolled to survey my mother, darted to me, then back to my mother. In his hand, a long wooden staff embellished with silver plating at the top, scrollwork whose beauty distracted from the sharpened tip. It wasn't merely utilitarian, though he did lean in as he walked. In a battle that included werewolves, what better weapon to have than the one they'd find the deadliest?

Vlad came to a stop and steadied himself on his staff. "Grand Matron."

"Sultan." My mother bowed her head. "So, it's finally come to this."

"You always knew it would." Tepeş's face inked into a repulsive smile, his back teeth showing through an absence of cheek. "You only have yourself to blame, though perhaps I can understand a mother's tender mercies. But if you'd let Inga kill the Inceptor all those years ago like she suggested, I'd have never learned of Gerwalta's existence. How many more of your clan and my clutches would still walk this earth today?"

"If you're trying to weaken my resolve through shame, then you should know this: it didn't work when *my* mother did it, and it won't work for you either." Brunhild whipped out a hand and splayed her fingers. On her palm, a tiny spark of silver caught a glint of moonlight and then, consumed it. White-hot energy coalesced into an orb, coronas of silver and gold striking out to connect with her fingertips. "And as for your clutches: they'll be fewer of them come sunrise."

"Such a thirst for bloodshed. A shame that we cannot claim your kind. You'd have made an exquisite vampire." Vlad cocked his head to the side. "But it needn't come to fighting. I have no desire to strike down these..." His hand rolled through the air. "Lesser dark ones. All I desire is the key to everlasting life..." Then motioning to the gathering as a whole, Vlad grinned. "...and the lock to deny it. I assume she's nearby, of course, Alexandra's child."

Brünhild bristled. "I told you in Spain, the illustrian died."

"Yes, you did tell me that," Vlad agreed. "But, why then, do I smell its blood here, on this battlefield?"

Instinctively, my hand went for my jeans pocket, pressing against the fabric, looking for signs that the vial had broken. The tiny cylinder's shape seemed intact, but when I looked back up, Vlad's eyes glowed with delight.

Shit.

"Yes, there you are." Vlad licked his lips, a sore-laden black tongue over thin, crimson flesh. "As I said, the illustrian lives, and Gerwalta has brought proof. Command her to come with me now, Matron, and I will protect her from harm while my troops destroy your kin."

Lashing her free hand to the side, silver streams ran down Brünhild's arm, curling themselves into solidity in her hand. At first, I thought it might be a club, but as the object took on definition, I was shocked to see it wasn't a weapon at all. It was a lantern.

"As the hueys are so keen of saying," my mother said, "over my dead body."

It all happened so fast. Brünhild raised the lantern high, crossing a hand over to place her lunarium in its chambers and sending beams of her power shooting into the eyes of the mesmerized vampire forces, blinding them. They wailed, cursed, covered their eyes, but their flesh remained intact, their clothing, undamaged. Caleb must have been right; my mother's power wasn't nearly as strong as his, especially when spread across such a large area.

Caleb marched forward. "Time to die, Vlad." The flames rippling over his body gathered, tendrils of fire and light pulling from his limbs and combining into a solar missile. The slayer threw his power forward, taking down three vamps who'd been standing near by. The unfortunate trio had a split second of terror before, in a snap, they were dust swirling away on the breeze. Through the cloud of the departed, I saw it: a pillar of black smoke I knew must be Vlad, zipping away to shelter.

My feet moved of their own volition, chasing through the mass of shrieking undead. Footfalls behind me pelted a four-two rhythm. Tobias flanked my right as Caleb overtook me on the left, his solarium no longer an aura, but a stream of concentrated sunlight, clearing a path before us. My lungs worked, forcing a miasma of ash and carbon to coat my throat and invade my tongue. The taste would haunt me, but I'd swallow the wine of death if it meant I could catch him.

Our pace made Caleb's aim poor, and the vaporous vampire we pursued managed to outmaneuver it. The river came into view, and still, vampires crawled from its depths, primordial creatures who raced forward toward the battle. My mother's strategy had been brilliant, but it was only a first strike.

"He's heading for the water!" I shouted as I sent a lunarium flying, disabling a dripping vamp moments before he intercepted Caleb.

Caleb sent a blast going to the right, clearing a path. "I step in there, I'm dead. I'll be powerless if my feet submerge."

"Just keep the vampires from coming in on us from behind. Tobias, jump him the moment he's flesh. I'll wrap him in silver as best I can with what I have left and Caleb can—"

Beside me, Tobias came to a screeching halt, losing his fur and throwing his arms around me. "Geri, wait!"

For a sliver of a second, I turned disbelieving eyes on my mate, working myself out of his hold. Tobias grimaced and picked me up off my feet, turning me at just the right angle to see Vlad reform on the edge of the river.

Maggie's head peeked above the surface just long enough for me to see her eyes. Bindings around her mouth kept her from screaming as two vamps held her in place. Vampires couldn't smoke across water, but they were just as strong in it as out.

How had he gotten her? Maggie could outfly vampires; I'd seen her do it. Now that her secret was out of the closet, there would be no reason for her to stay on the ground. Unless...

Unless he hadn't gotten to her at all. Maggie must have been trying to get to him.

Vlad cackled. "Every time we meet, Miss Kline, someone new for me to hold over you wiggles their way out of the woodwork. If you were wise, you'd stop making new allies, particularly ones so ready to throw themselves up in exchange for the lives of others."

Caleb ground to a halt beside us. "Let her go, Vlad!"

"You could take her place, Mr. Helsing," the vampire countered. "It's an exchange I'd make. Once I have the *Solari*, the other slayers will have no one to protect them, will they?"

"Alrighty, then." The slayer's hand glowed with a golden hue. "I'll just kill you now and get it over with."

A clap made by meaty hands produced an upsetting squish, like someone hitting two raw steaks together. The result, however, was far more disturbing. The vampires who had been crawling from the river, only attacking in passing, turned on their heel, each of them focused on where the three of us drew together, back-to-back-to-back.

"Go ahead and try," Vlad invited. "The moment I'm dead, my lineage will rend you limb from limb."

"Take me in my mother's place then." Tobias stepped forward, even as I attempted to claw him back. "We're old friends, Vlad, now. My blood did you lot well enough while you had me. Made your cheeks blush and your dicks hard. Take me again, let my mum go."

In the water, Maggie thrashed, giving the vamps on either side a fair fight. That was, until she lost her footing and disappeared beneath the surface. Only the working muscles of the vampires' arms testified that she hadn't been carried away by the currents. Her panic washed over me like the water washing over her, and neither of us could stand either for long.

Vlad clicked his tongue, even as Maggie resurfaced, coughing out the Tahquamenon. "Oh, come now, Mr. Somfield, how does that help your side? You'd only give me more leverage over Miss Kline. You haven't been around for as long as I have, and perhaps you've never served in battle at all until now, but one should never negotiate their only advantage. Nonetheless, I'm afraid I must decline. You see, in this... emaciated state..." He opened his arms out wide, inviting us to examine the tissue and sinew that clung to each bone. "... the only thing that can heal me is *her* blood."

"And you think she won't come easier if I'm part of the package?" Tobias crossed his arms, shaking with silent laughter. "Who's negotiating like a git now? Come on, Gramps. What is an old, used-up asenaic to you? Remember that pitch you made Geri back in Spain, when she kicked your ass the last time? Me and her and baby makes three, all under your loving embrace?"

Anger emboldened my step as I pushed Tobias back. "Hey, asshole. You do this, and there won't ever be a three, because I will cut your thing off."

Tobias caught my arms, swinging me, putting Vlad at my back. He leaned in, smirking. "Calm down, love. We don't want another blowup, do we? Remember what happened to Ryland last time you got carried away."

The glimmer in his eye wasn't a wink—Vlad would have seen that—and maybe it was because his emotional grid was suddenly so bouncy and bright, but the message got through to me.

"Besides," Tobias continued, moving me to the side. "You won't have to wait long, Old Drac. Geri's pregnant."

My whole world turned on its head, and the fact that my immortal mortal enemy was a few steps away, soaking up my mate's lies like dry bread in hot soup, didn't seem as important.

"What?" I said, spinning him around. "What are you talking about?"

"You're preggers, sweet. Only seems fair to bring it up, since our pups would be part of the deal."

"You got to be shitting me, Somfield," Helsing cursed. "You're seriously going to offer up your wife and your child to this blood-sucking pus sac?" The slayer shifted his hands, pointing his cocked palms at Tobias. "I knew she was too good for you, so I tell you what I'm going to do. I'm going to kill this asshole," His shoulder nudged in Vlad's direction, "and then I'm going to kill you, and then I'm going to take your mate as my wife, like I should have done back in Istanbul."

Okay, now I was confused. Was Caleb really going to pick this moment to try and make a "it should have been me" speech?

A cocky grin lifted one corner of Tobias's mouth. "Maybe you're right, Helsing. Maybe you should be with her."

"Yeah?"

"Yeah!"

"And maybe I should—"

No sooner had Vlad caught on that something was going on and lunged forward than Tobias hit the ground and Caleb leaped over him, hitting the two vamps in the river through their heads with twin solaria, all as I summoned all the silver on my body and let it rage into flame before directing it all at the last surviving Raven. The impact took him from his feet, sending Vlad racing back, his figure disappearing across the expanse of the river and landing him on the wooded islet beyond.

"Tobias, hurry! Get your mom." I focused my fire back to the vampires closing in on us from all sides, even as my mate dove into the river, paddling toward his mother. "Caleb?"

"Coming."

The slayer retook a position at my back, sending solaria flying in every direction, withering the unlucky victims to ash. I didn't hesitate to send silver flames in the gaps opened by vacating bodies. Even if it couldn't kill them, vampires, accustomed to enduring youth and vitality, were hesitant to give it up. Suddenly, it was as though a line had been drawn in the frozen banks of the river, the enemy hesitant to advance lest they fall victim to death or desiccation. Caleb's hands glowed with imminent power, while mine stayed up in a defensive posture. We couldn't afford to fund ignorance. They would advance. Even now, a dozen heads turned left and right, looking for a vantage of attack.

A splash of water made me look back over my shoulder for the slimmest of moments. Maggie spluttered as Tobias braced her arms, pulling her towards shore.

True to her nature, she pushed on despite her condition. "How…" *Cough.* "…are you going to…" *Cough.* "…get out of this?"

A good question. An excellent question. She could simply fly away. Maybe she could carry one of us, but not all three, and with Tobias present there'd be no doubt about who she'd choose.

Tobias picked up Vlad's staff, cautiously avoiding its silver embellishment. "Geri?"

"I'm thinking!" My mother's voice played in my ears, years of training dancing on the head of a needle.

What are your assets? Use them.

A slayer, two asenaics who tended wolf, and whatever the hell I was. If Tobias and Maggie took their fur, we'd have their maws. Solaria and lunaria would be enough to keep up our defensive perimeter, and the vamps would be foolish to come around behind us and push us away from the river. If they managed to get Caleb and I to step in, our slayer abilities would be neutralized.

Can you exploit the weaknesses of your opponent?

Doubtful, not unless I could make the sun suddenly rise hours before it was due or get the vampires to calmly and collectively queue while Caleb knocked them off in an orderly fashion.

If only I had a dozen Calebs, or even one really, really big one.

And then it hit me. My mom's lantern was a version of something Caleb had showed me back in Istanbul. Only, where my mother's powers had been too weak, a Helsing's wouldn't be.

I spun on Caleb. "Remember Hagia Sophia!"

He grimaced, even as he kept his eyes trained and his hands up. "Jesus, Geri, how many times do I have to say I'm sorry for that? I was aiming my solarium at the vampires who were coming to kidnap us. You just got stuck in between."

"No, not that. Remember what you told me about why the dome used to be plated in gold tiles?"

His arms slackened, but his glowing hands kept the vamps orbiting. "Yeah, but what good is that here? Is there a Byzantine cathedral nearby I didn't see in the travel guides?"

"This whole forest is our cathedral, and our dome is just up the river."

The lighthouse.

Caleb's eyes met mine, a singular moment in which we both knew what the other needed to do.

"Maggie, take Caleb and fly north as fast as you can. It's only a quarter mile away, you'll see it as soon as you're above the tree line."

Maggie marched to face me, toe-to-toe. "I'm not some jet you get to scramble, hood. And I'm not going to leave my son behind to die."

"And I won't leave without my mate," Tobias said, his chest pushing between the two of us, forcing his mother back. "So do what Geri says and don't kill us all by arguing it."

It was clear to me, as it seemed to be to Maggie, that where stubbornness was concerned, her son had taken after his mother.

All the fight left the shewolf in an exhale. Maggie's jaw tightened as she leaned over, focusing on Caleb. "Can you send out more of them big blasts like you did on the battlefield, boyo? Give them a little head time as I carry you away?"

Caleb's eyes moved, even as his posture remained attack-ready. "Of course, I can. I'm a Helsing."

With one nod, Maggie crossed to Caleb, hooking her arms around the slayer. "Then in 3...2..."

"Wait!" Caleb squealed so suddenly, even a few of the hovering vamps jolted. "What about Geri and Tobias?"

I turned toward the river, wading in as fast as I could and Tobias following in my wake. Even with a head start, we were going to have to book it. "We're going after Vlad."

THIRTY-ONE

CALEB

Comic books way oversold this shit. There was nothing beautiful or relaxing about being carried by a person who could fly. The feeling of being one sweaty palm away from the mother of all emergency exits failed to make the experience less thrilling. At least Maggie didn't hold me in front of her like I was a Stepford wife. At the get-go, she'd told me we'd be handling this piggyback-style.

"If your legs keep squeezing me that hard, boyo, I'm going to turn around so I can at least get something out of it."

"If you don't want me to be so panicky, stop panicking me, i.e. and e.g., *slow the fuck down*."

I looked over her shoulder, tears streaming from the corner of my eyes and freezing on the cleft of my ear, to find her smirking. This was *fun* for her. What a sick old woman.

I mean, not *that* old, but out of my window of targets.

The lighthouse grew larger with every passing second, a brick cylinder painted like a goddamn candy cane in stripes of red and white, little square windows buttoning up its front. Even twenty yards out I could see the windows surrounding its... whatever the hell the top part of a lighthouse was called, were caked in frost and dirt. The frost wasn't a concern; my solarium would vaporize that stuff on contact. The dirt? Not so much.

I pointed to an exterior catwalk platform that surrounded what I decided we were going to call the cupola. "Land there. We need to bust out the windows."

"Destroy public property? You really know how to show a girl a good time."

"You have no idea."

No sooner had my feet gotten a solid surface beneath them again (or frozen-over, iron-grate surface, as it was) than I lashed off my coat and wrapped it around my elbow. Luckily the hatch door on the copula wasn't locked. I guessed the designers of the lighthouse figured if you got this far from the outside, you deserved to get in.

Maggie landed and trailed me inside. "What are we doing up here anyway?"

"A bit of history: once upon a time, slayers figured out that the domes covered in reflective tiles could be used to take out a group of vamps if the need ever arose." The glass panes broke easy enough, each one bursting out and landing in shards on the catwalk outside. "And although a lighthouse lens isn't quite the same, it should let me... broadcast my solarium down there."

Maggie's head gave a preemptive nod. "You're going to be like a twat kid taking out ants with a magnifying glass."

I grinned as another window, then another, fell away, opening the entire side facing the state park. "Actually, *you* will."

The asenaic turned wide eyes on me. "What?"

"It'll be easy. Just point and shoot."

The blank stare rolled on forever.

I cocked a hip. "So, you didn't have any access to digital cameras while you were the Dracule's prisoner."

"I was more concerned about access to food and a working loo."

"Fair enough." I clapped my hand. "Yes, so, your analogy then. This," I tapped the edge of the cylindrical lens. "—is the magnifying glass. You are the little kid, and the ants, AKA vampires, are on the ground below. Only, instead of angling the magnifying glass, you're going to be angling the sun."

She turned, looking toward the inky eastern horizon. "Won't be coming up for a few hours though."

"No, Mags, I'm the sun. This is a lighthouse, not a searchlight. We can't angle the lens down, but we can change the projection of the light source. What I need *you* to do is to tell me which direction to point, because I'm going to be inside this thing pumping and I won't know where the hell things are going."

"I recall that's a problem for most men."

"You're a woman after my own heart, Maggie Somfield." Images of *The Graduate* played in my mind for the briefest of moments. "Another thing. It's going to be very important that I don't blast out the pillars holding the roof up over us or, you know, we'll be pancakes."

"If you do, I can fly away easy enough."

"Yeah, but I can't."

Her deadpan expression told me that didn't really matter a damn to her.

THIRTY-TWO

GERI

The Tahquamenon River has two sets of waterfalls—the upper falls tall, the lower falls, wide. The river forks at the second, creating a mini delta system in which several branches twist around a handful of islands. Vlad had landed on the biggest one, a piece of land that could take someone more than an hour to thoroughly explore.

"We don't have much time," I sputtered as I crawled on to the shore. "Even if that blast did knock him down, he's got to be back up by now. We need to find him and kill him."

Tobias stumbled out of the icy water, the unfortunate side effects evident thanks to his nudity. "Brought this," he said, holding up Vlad's staff as he bent over, recovering his breath. "Big, pointy stick, but it only will matter if Helsing manages to—"

No sooner had my mate started to utter the words than a beam ignited from the lighthouse at the mouth of the river. A ray of sunlight pierced the night, hitting the woods, setting off a cacophony of agony. Shrieks and screams carried on the wind as vampires fried up the river. I closed my eyes and said a prayer that the hoods and wolves were able to regroup in the wake of the dispersed solarium to turn the battle to their advantage. Even from a distance, however, suffering reached me. I knew that it wouldn't be a war without casualties on our side, but God willing, those lost would be few and not perish in vain.

"What if Vlad smokes again?" Tobias asked. "He can't get back across the water like that, but he can zip around this island and sneak past us easily."

I shook my head. "He won't. He doesn't have fangs when he's not solid, and he's going to want to bite me first and ask questions later. I bet he can hear his side getting toasted over there. Even for Vlad, that's got to be making him nervous." I reached out a hand. "Here, give me the staff. We need a lupine nose right now more than your bulging biceps. You go south, I'll go north. Sweep him into the middle, coming at him from both sides."

Tobias arched an eyebrow. "You sure splitting up is the best idea?"

"It's the last thing I want to do, but it's the tactically wise thing."

Tobias lowered the stick into my palm, but he didn't let go. Instead, he used it as leverage, pulling me to him, locking his lips to mine, sucking on my bottom lip as he pulled away.

"For Mina."

Mina. I'd been away from her longer now than I'd been with her, but the anchor held. There were many reasons I wanted Vlad Tepeş dead, the least of which was for my own sake. I owed it to my father. To Igor. To Kara. But I owed it most to our little Mina, who Vlad would never stop hunting just because her blood could...

My eyes went wide as I froze in place.

Tobias pulled back. "What happened?"

My tongue froze. How did you tell the person you loved that you figured out how to win, and all it would take was letting your enemy get exactly what they wanted?

I shook the surprise from my face and conjured up my most convincing lie. "I just realized that if we manage to pull this off, then we get to see Mina again."

My mate ate the poison and grinned from its sweetness. "We pull this off, and twenty-four hours from now, we could also be making our next daughter." His chin nested into his chest. "You do know that bit about you being preggers was a lie, right?"

"Of course, I do. I'd know if I was pregnant. And please, never use the word *preggers* again."

"Why Geri Somfield, I do believe I have placed a bee in your bonnet." Tobias smirked. "Now I do want to get you up the duff, just so I can annoy the hell out of you."

"I'm going to assume that means pregnant, *Tobias Kline*. But maybe first we should, I don't know, kill our mortal enemy?"

"If that's your idea of foreplay, lamb, I'm happy to oblige."

The form beside me vanished as my mate took his fur. Tobias's bushy, grey and black tail brushed tree trunks as he rounded the shore and slipped from sight. Alone, I counted to five, giving Tobias a head start, allowing his distance. If he caught on to what I was about to do before Vlad did, then we both were doomed.

I pulled the tiny vial of Mina's blood from my pocket and tucked it between my jaw and my cheek. The width of a cigarette but only half the length, I hoped it would be enough to cover the scent. If Vlad could smell it from several feet away on a crowded battlefield, then he might be able to trace it here as well. The staff would be too big to carry, but I still needed something. The wood, worn with age, might be smooth on the surface, but I was willing to bet it had a weak point. Holding it perpendicular to the earth, I gave all my effort into landing a side kick about a quarter way up its length. I didn't need something as high as my shoulder to slay a vampire. I just needed something I could wrap my hands around. It broke just as I'd hoped it might, with a jagged, splintery edge and short enough that I could tuck it up my jacket sleeve to carry it.

Wolves traveled on the ground; hoods maneuvered the trees. I had a theory that one of the reasons lupines were afraid of heights was because that's where a hood would attack from. With a leap, I hooked my free hands around a meaty branch of a young maple, tall enough to be a platform to the oak beside it. From there, I bobbed and wove, jumping from branch to branch, making my way to the center of the island. With each tree, Tobias's presence grew more distant, but it wasn't long before I felt the presence of another. Whether it was because he'd partaken of my blood before or because my inner slayer had awoken and sensed its natural foe, I didn't know. All I knew was that Vlad awaited me in the clearing ahead.

He grinned from ear to cartilage-spindled ear as I landed on the ground before him. "I would have heard you all the way from Istanbul. If you were trying to be stealthy, I'm afraid your mother hasn't trained you as well as she thinks she has."

"I'm not the best at making her proud." I hoped what I was about to do, however, would go against that trend. "I wasn't trying to run away from you, Vlad. I was trying to run *to* you."

"You really think you can defeat me in a one-to-one battle? Don't let my lack of flesh fool you, young one. I have centuries of experience and superior strength."

"I know you do, which is why…" I shook my head, holding my empty hands out. "I'm here to surrender."

He blinked rapidly, shifting his weight from one side to the other. "Sorry?"

"I sur-ren-der," I said again, mindful to separate each syllable. "Now call off your forces. I'll ask my mother to draw up a truce and a contract recognizing your claim over me, Tobias, and Mina."

The tiny tuft of remaining hair that served as his eyebrow quirked.

"You know, Mina, the…" What had they called her? "Illustrian."

"Ah, so she *does* live."

"Of course, she lives," I admitted. "And I'd like to keep it that way. If it means becoming your blood slave—"

"*Haseki,*" he amended, using the same word for me that he had for the female slayers he'd kept in his harem.

"Yeah, that," I said. "Then you uphold your end of the bargain. You let us live, and you let the hoods go in peace."

Shivers raced down my spine as he stepped toward me, his corpulent hand lifting to stroke my cheek. "If only you had agreed earlier, little lamb, then so many would not have died trying in vain to change the unchangeable."

"Ask my mother, I'm difficult that way."

When he laughed under his breath, his eyes lit up, then softened. "Accepted."

Then, moving his hand to the back of my neck, he coaxed me closer, even as I crossed my arms over my chest and hugged myself. We stood in a clearing, virgin snow beneath our feet and bare branches clacking in a breeze above. My body shook. Not with fear, though I couldn't deny I was afraid, but from the fact that I was freezing my ass off. I'd taken an ice bath and come out the other side into the cold night. Supernatural though I was, I was also still mortal.

"You tremble, though I cannot tell if it is from fear or from exposure. Do not fret, my pet. The sooner I drink you, the sooner I'll be restored." His breath tickled the hairs on my neck as he leaned in, scenting my skin. "Once I'm whole again, I will warm you." His cracked lips caressed a patch of flesh beneath my ear. "Yes, warm you and make you whole. I take good care of those things which I value."

I laughed beneath my breath, the shrieks of the battlefield carrying to us on the breeze. "Like how you led all your bloodline here to be toasted by a slayer?"

Vlad laughed into my neck. "I can always make more vampires, but recreating you... Now, that's a harder task."

The death mask grinned as Vlad pulled back to look at me. Not with loathing. Not even arrogance. No, he was looking at me with... adoration. With longing. Not for my blood, but for my understanding, for my reverence. Vlad was a vampire who wanted power, but not for power's sake. He wanted revenge. Revenge for what the werewolves had done to his country and his family. Revenge for what hoods had done to his freedom. Revenge for being denied by an immortal father and daughter.

He wanted to be understood, lauded, idolized, not because of who he was but because of what he could do. He'd kept a whole harem, indulging the women whose blood kept him alive with luxury, attention, comfort. He'd treated Alex as a queen!

He wanted to be loved, but more than that, he wanted to *love something.*

And suddenly, my plan changed.

"Yeah, yeah, yeah, so you say," I snapped. "So *everyone* says: I'm different. Different in a way that Inga Rosethorn told my mother to kill me as a kid. Different in a way that you're willing to throw your whole bloodline on the sword just to get me. How about we stop this stupid, on-going 'just what is she' suspense and freaking tell me the truth, huh? Because, obviously, you know."

Someone that wanted to be loved wanted to prove themselves worthy. How better to do that than sharing a dangerous truth about them that only you knew? And if I accepted whatever bullshit he was about to say, then Vlad might drop his defenses a bit. All I needed was a few moments of trust and weakness...

Corpulent lips pulled back over gleaming fangs. He liked it, both being taunted, and having his ego stroked. Vlad ran a finger over my cheek. "What you are is a thing nearly unheard of. The trinity of slayer, wolf, and hood? Even if circumstance allows such creatures to bond and mate, to conceive a child of such divergent lineage requires the strongest of pedigrees. In you, that has been realized. Red, Helsing, and Asena blood runs in your veins; no other amalgamation would have made you possible. You are the Chalice of Immortality, an inceptor."

I meant to feign surprise, no matter what he said. Turned out, I didn't need to pretend. Did he just say I was descended from a Helsing? Did that make Caleb my...

I shook off the thought and held to the moment. "An inceptor? But what in the hell does that mean?"

His smile turned to snarl. Vlad grabbed my wrist, pulled it between us, and sliced into my forearm. Blood, hot and free, flowed from the wound, steaming the air around us. *"This!"* he said, running a free finger in a smear past my elbow. "More valuable than a thousand Dracule, ten thousand slayers, and a million hoods combined. Your blood renews us. Yes, that you know. But more than that, feed it to a layman? To a *huey*? And it *makes* makers. New vampire bloodlines can be made with your blood, and that's exactly what I intend to do. Together, you and I will birth a thousand new fathers and mothers, all loyal to the Sultan." He dropped my wrist, both his hands pressed my cheeks. "And we'll—"

My chance had come, and three things happened all at once.

First, I pressed my lips to Vlad's, kissing him into silence.

Second, I bit down on the vial, breaking it and letting Mina's blood fill my mouth.

Third, I plunged the end of the broken staff through his frozen shirt and into his side.

The trees blurred around me as Vlad grabbed me by the shoulders and sent me flying. Panic seized me, and I couldn't contain the shock wave that went rippling across the island. A howl rang out even before I'd landed, luckily on a snowbank that absorbed the brunt of the fall.

I looked up, not knowing what to expect. Wide, white eyes stood out against a background of crimson and bone. Vlad's chest worked, his hands went to his throat, clutching like he could stop the poison from trickling down. And if I had just kissed him, he might have stood a chance. But by burying the shard in his side, I'd forced him to gasp, to pull back, to close his mouth, all at once.

I'd forced him to drink Mina's blood.

"What have you done?" His voice was a howl, a screech, a cacophony of anguish. "Damn you, hood, what have you done?"

His hands wrapped around my improvised weapon even as blood began to trickle from the wound. The vampire's jaw clenched, his eyes flew up, then down, then up again. Animalistic, guttural hefts rumbled in his chest before clawing up his throat. Pain, torment, torture…

Betrayal.

But no sooner had I started to believe that my plan had worked than Vlad's lips turned up and the infamous Dracula laughed.

"Oh, Miss Kline…"

He straightened, all torment washing away, taking my hopes with it. Vlad only winced when he pulled the wood from his side before holding it up for me to see, like a magician showing you your card pulled miraculously from the deck.

And then, Vlad the Impaler, proceeded to tsk-tsk me. "Come now, my dear. Certainly you know that wood is only lethal to a vampire if it touches the heart or brain," he said, shaking his head. "And again, the moment I let down my walls with you, you turn on me. No matter. I drank your blood just now, or did you think I didn't taste it on your tongue?"

"I knew you would," I said. "But that ain't all you just drank."

Suddenly, his smile withered, his laughing ceased. And Dracula… faltered.

Vlad held one hand out at length, then another, gawking at fingers firming and wrists growing supple. He spun, taking all the parts of his body in in turn. When he rounded again, it was no longer the face of a monster, of *my nightmares,* that met me. His chin, his forehead, his cheeks, his neck… Everywhere not covered by the folds of his clothes knitted together, a blossom of flesh and fat and structure.

"I don't understand. I—" His panicked eyes flashed up to me. "I drank your blood. You are an inceptor. Your blood should… make me anew."

"Yeah, funny thing about that." I beamed with a victory won after years of battle. "It wasn't *my* blood you drank."

"Geri!" Tobias broke through the trees, at my side as soon as he spotted me, pulling me to my feet.

"It's okay, Tobias. I'm okay." My mate caught me as one of my legs gave out under me. Broken ankle? Maybe even a cracked tibia. Such a small price to pay. "Help me. Take me to him."

Tobias's eyes went wide. "But he's renewing. He'll…"

"He'll do nothing," I said, cutting off my mate. "Now, please."

The werewolf dropped the argument. One of my arms stretched over Tobias's massive shoulders as he leaned down, becoming my foundation. We hobbled then, me on one foot, Tobias off kilter with my weight on him. Vlad fell to his knees, his throat closed by convulsion, his eyes fighting to stay trained on us.

"You know, I worried the smell would give it away," I said to him. "But the taste of your own hubris must have masked it. You wanted my blood. You expected it. You tasted blood in my kiss and assumed it, like me, was yours to consume. Only it wasn't my blood at all, Vlad."

"In your kiss?" Tobias said. "What in the—"

I sent a wave of submission out, and thank god, the tactic worked. Tobias's words stilled in a moment. That could come in handy in the future.

Vlad's eyes begged for answers when his mouth could only gape. I reached into my mouth, pulling the tiny shards of glass from my cheeks. Did it hurt? It should have, but there wasn't any pain. The euphoria of victory made me both feel electrified and numb at the same time.

"But I…" Vlad's chest pumped as luxurious black hair sprouted from his remade scalp. A full black beard popped like mushrooms growing in moss after a storm. But when his hand crossed over his muscular chest and flattened against the place where once his humanity had resided, I knew he understood what had actually just happened.

As did Tobias, it seemed.

"His heart…" The werewolf jolted as the sound echoed about us, turning wide eyes on me. "His heart is beating."

"Of course, it is," I said, grunting as I leaned over to swoop up the bloody shard. "He drank Mina's blood, and that means… he's human."

Vlad reached out to me. To attack me? To ask me for help? To offer his surrender? Who cared? He lifted hands to *take* something from me. Whether it was my life, my pity, or my forgiveness, it didn't matter. I would give him nothing.

I'd learn to forget the sound of the shard piercing his skull, but I'd never let go of the look in his eyes when he died, or how quickly it faded when I took his life and claimed back my own.

THIRTY-THREE

To expect that Caleb would have been able to destroy all the Dracule and let none escape wasn't practical. I wasn't worried. We'd killed hundreds, and those that were left would carry on the story for centuries. Slayers were no longer extinct, and vampires' immortality and love of gossip would work in our favor to protect our mortality.

It also would have been ridiculous to think we'd lose no one on our side.

Sixteen hoods, two of them my distant cousins. Seventeen wolves, including one from the Paradise Pack.

I still had no idea how Kim's mate would ever recover from her loss.

And all that remained was their memories. We bore our dead in our retreat. The bodies of the vampires had turned to ash under Caleb's assault or were claimed by the fire it triggered. Even in a winter wonderland, trees could burn. By the time the huey authorities showed up to battle the blaze, only the mundane remained to be covered by the footfalls and tire treads of their advance.

Luckily the fire also wiped out the cameras that might have shown the world the truth. Working technical muscles I hadn't known he had, Markus went all CSI on the park's surveillance system. There was only one user who happened upon the livestream of the battlefield during the few minutes it was public. If they understood what they were seeing, they hadn't tried to tell anyone about it yet. Not as far as we could tell, anyway. I prayed they never would.

A news story in the local press the following day suggested the blaze might have been connected to some local kids breaking into the old Northshore Lighthouse and managing to fire her up for a few minutes. Six ships radioed into base to report seeing the light. Luckily, the supposed shenanigans of some teenage Yoopers wasn't interesting enough to gather attention beyond Marquette, and the fire, quickly contained and extinguished, was written off as a freak occurrence.

It didn't hurt that some of Yan's family stayed around long enough to make sure everyone was in agreement on that point.

Unfortunately, vampire enthrallment and its ability to manipulate were powerless to quell my mother's anger. As, it seemed, was I.

"You *drank* an illustrian's blood?"

She sat in our living room, her jaw hanging, while Markus, Yan, Rick, and Caleb did everything they could to look away.

"Gerwalta, what a foolish thing. You had no idea what that would do to you."

I shrugged, hoping an air of dismissiveness would be inspirational to the Matron. "I already had werewolf and slayer blood in me, so what could have happened? Besides, I didn't drink it. I broke the vial in my mouth and forced it into Vlad's when I pretended to kiss him. Well, *actually* kissed him. Good thing for us that Dracula was still a man at the end of the day. He was either too stupid or too arrogant to question why a woman who hated him would want to kiss him. He just accepted it as obvious."

Take that, anyone who thought I'd never learned anything from living with Amy Popowitz for two years.

"I'm still not happy about that," Tobias mumbled from the kitchen as he grabbed a beer from the refrigerator. "I can understand why you didn't want me there. I don't agree with it, but I understand."

Coming back into the living room, he carried several unhatched bottles in his massive hands. Tobias began to disperse them like an orderly handing out medicine. I was surprised when my mother accepted one without hesitation. When did she start drinking?

Tobias collapsed onto the couch beside me, handing me his last spare. "I still think there was another solution to this that didn't involve snogging the enemy."

I took the bottle and readied it at my lips. "Sorry, but I didn't exactly have a syringe and needle on me at the time to covertly inject him with our daughter's blood." It only took one long draw for me to remember that I hated beer. "I... I... improvised."

Tobias's eyes drilled into me as he tipped his own bottle back. Oh, he'd stop huffing and puffing soon. A wolf couldn't stay mad at his mate for long, but the next time we were in danger, I wasn't sure he'd be as trusting with the whole you-go-that-way-and-I'll-go-this-way routine.

"You know…" Yan paused stitching a gash over Markus's eye. "It does make sense. In fact, some Varanasi scholars speculated that the whole reason slayers, wolves, and hoods came to be was because vampires were looking for a way to cure themselves. That is, not each kind of supe individually, but each an ingredient that would return one to a human state."

Tobias and I exchanged a look, and I knew we were thinking the same thing.

My mother, it seemed, was as well. She set the bottle aside and leaned forward, taking turns glaring at each of us. "The fact that Mina's blood reverses vampirism is a fact that must never leave this room. Now, even as Matron, I don't have the power to demand that of most of you. But as a grandmother, I swear to you that if I find out this has fallen into enemy hands and one of you is to blame, I will hunt you to the end of this life and well into the next, is that understood?"

Caleb removed the cold compress from his forehead and sat up in the threadbare armchair at the far end of the room. "One problem with that: Vlad used the rumor of Mina's existence to get all his children to line up behind him. I'm afraid the Dracule are going to continue to be a problem as long as that rumor's out there."

But Brunhild Kline was not a woman easily intimidated. "I guess it's a good thing, then, that they think she's in Chicago under the protection of the slayers. And after the way a single slayer was able to decimate their ranks, they won't be quick to make any attempt upon her, will they?"

It wasn't a question for which she expected an answer, and for once, Caleb was smart enough to keep his lips clipped.

"You needn't worry, Brunnie." Maggie came walking into the room carrying a bowl of hot water and a cloth. "I think after what happened last night, no one's going to ask you two ways on nothing. If they do, just use that glare of yours. That'll kill 'em dead."

"Speaking of what happened last night…" My mother leaned forward. "Maggie?"

My mate's mother, dabbing the cloth in the bowl, froze. "Deny it."

"Deny it?" Brunhild cackled. "There were a thousand witnesses. They might have looked the other way because of the threat of imminent death, but they still saw you."

Rick Ryland hissed as Maggie took to tending wounds won defending my mother, of all people. If someone had told me five years ago that the beta of the Paradise Pack would risk his life to save the Red Matron, I'd have called them crazy. "Come on, Hilda, you can cover up the existence of a cure for vampirism, but you can't pull the curtain over a hood who can fly?"

"A hood? Yes." She leaned back into the cushions, looking at her beer bottle with captive interest. "But Maggie has lived most her life as a wolf, and a wolf who can fly is something beyond my abilities to suppress. I can cast shadows, but I cannot deflect light. Maggie, there will be ramifications. There must be."

I sank down into the cushions and under the weight of my own guilt. "Shit, Maggie, I'm so sorry. That's my fault."

"No need, Geri." She looked at me over Rick's massive form. "You did what you had to do to protect your family. I understand that. I'm thankful for it even." She exchanged a quick look with Tobias, and a flash of motherly love shot through the air. "Nothing to be done for it now. I spent most of the last two decades imprisoned by vampires. It won't change my lot much to be hunted now by hoods."

"Hunted by hoods?" Brünhild took to her feet. "Do you think I'm looking to punish you? That I would accept the radicals among my kind who would want to harm you because of what you are?"

"You're the Grand Matron. What else would I expect?"

"You're right. What else *would* you expect?" My mother planted her hands on her hips. "But that's not how it has to be. You may be without clan and pack, but you aren't without options."

Maggie let the crimson-flocked rag fall into the dish and glared across the room. "What in the hell are you talking about, Kline?"

"I'm talking about..." My mother's hands kneaded an invisible ball of dough in the air. "Look, I know Northern Michigan is remote and difficult and not where you ever thought you'd end up. In the winter, it's colder than a witch's teat and in the summer, you'll find out why we say the mosquito is our unofficial state bird. But damn it, it could be home."

"Home?" Maggie scoffed the word like a curse. "Those Houses that denied your call, who walked out on your Council of Matrons... They'll be gunning for you as it is. Take in something like me? They'll not only question your leadership, Brunnie. They'll question your sanity."

Brunhild's jaw tightened. Her eyes narrowed. She turned back to grab her beer, more to fill space than to take a drink (though she managed to do both). Finally, she put it down, and pushed her index finger into the air. "You know what? Fuck them."

Of all the things that had happened in the last twenty-four hours, my mother's f-bomb was the most unbelievable and shocking of all, but she wasn't done yet.

"All my life I tried to force myself, force my daughter, to be the perfect hood, and it almost cost me everything. It almost cost you everything," she said, pointing at Maggie. "We're not hoods. We're not wolves. We're not slayers. We're… unique. We find our places, but we're never really part of any group. And now, my daughter and your son are going to attempt to raise a child who is just going to be not only out of place, but might be the target of some delusional vampires who think she's the solution to their problem. And you know what, Maggie, I think Gerwalta and Tobias need us to get through this. Us, if for no other reason than to be a living reminder that you shouldn't ever try to be anything else than you are, or you'll make yourself and the people who love you suffer. Now, what do you say to that?"

I pulled myself to the edge of my seat. "Who are you and what did you do with my mother?"

But she didn't cower or even laugh. Instead, my mother's chin went up in the air, as she OWNED IT ALL. "I am the woman who is going to try to be a better grandmother than she was a mother, and hope it's enough to make up for some small measure of all the terrible things that she did to you."

All eyes fell to Maggie as she put the bowl of water on the table and sat back on her heels on the floor, mulling. Seconds felt like hours, and only in the weight of her deliberation did I realize how much I wanted her to stay. If not for my sake or even for Mina's, then for Tobias's. I was finally going to get a chance to know the woman my mother actually was, and I wanted the same thing for him.

Finally, Maggie's expression cracked, a tiny tick of a smile daring to show itself. She looked up, and she couldn't hide the shine of her eyes. "Then I guess, for now, I'll stay."

And so would we. After all we'd been through, after all we'd lost, we'd finally won something back. We were pack. We were a clan. Soon, our daughter would be with us, and at last, all of us would be a family.

EPILOGUE

There was nothing special about the reunion. Certainly, the baby was adorable and the young couple who rushed forward to snatch her from the arms of a leggy blonde, attractive, but not exceptionally so. Of course, the hueys who witnessed the event couldn't know the black-haired man was a werewolf and his olive-skinned wife, a descendant of the real Little Red Riding Hood. Tell them the baby's blood had the power to cure the undead, and they'd probably call you crazy.

But as for the man in the finest suit any shop in Marquette could possibly offer who followed in the leggy blonde's wake... There was something about him that just caught the eye, turned the head, and yes, made the women flush. Hollywood good looks didn't begin to describe it. Anyone with the right genetics could pull that off. Maybe it was his swagger, how he walked with a little tilt in his step, how he flashed all the pretty girls a half-cocked grin. Maybe it was the Black Amex he'd flashed at the ticket counter to book a first-class seat to Chicago, or how his fingertips danced down the back of the leggy blonde, drawing circles on the small of her back. Maybe it was the fact that the air around him looked just a little bit brighter than it did anywhere else in the terminal, almost like he glowed.

Or maybe that was just everyone's imagination.

The four of them, plus the baby, took some seats at the coffee shop just outside the exit gate, laughing and pointing, regaling each other with stories. The blonde's mouth dropped open more than once. Soon enough, they just became another part of the scenery. That was, until you saw how the couple holding the baby looked at each other. Newlyweds, obviously. Probably couldn't keep their hands off each other when they were alone. The way that man looked at that woman was the way every woman wanted to be looked at. With reverence, with appreciation. God, he loved her. You wouldn't have to ask him to know it; he *adored* her. It was clear by the way she beamed at him that she felt just the same.

The leggy blonde and the suit? At ease with each other, for sure, though *she* made sure *he* got a number of admonishing glares. The hint would be taken, an apology would come in the form of a nod or a smirk, and the four would go on chatting. Only the keenest observer saw it happen. The suited man pulled a cup of coffee to his lips and the happy couple across the table laughed and looked into each other's eyes like no one else in the world existed. He'd sigh, and for a moment, for the *slightest* moment, the suited man's eyes turned to the blonde's face, she, in turn, looking at the baby and totally oblivious to the pedestal on to which she'd been raised. The longing, the desire that burned in that look. The disappointment that crumbled away whatever hope had sparked on his side alone. The baby squealed, everyone laughed, and just like that...

The moment was gone.

But that didn't mean it hadn't happened.

THE END

A NOTE FROM THE AUTHOR

BEFORE WE END WITH THE BEGINNING

Why is the prequel at the end?

It's a good question, and one asked of me often, of why the book that comes chronologically first comes last. The answer is there's a bit of an anachronism involved.

Reluctant was released June 2017. At that time, it was my first title under my current pen name. (Yes, my name is not actually Kendrai, because in real life, I'm not really that cool.) Prior to that (and recently again at the time of this writing), I wrote romances under the name Killian McRae. (No, my name isn't actually Killian either, for the same reason noted above.) When an author chooses a new pen name, it's like starting a new business. Part of that effort involves encouraging readers to sign up for my mail list, the only way I have to directly contact them without the purview of storefronts, public forums, and/ or social media observation. Not that there's anything wrong with those things, but I don't control them and thus, would have no other means to communicate if something should happen on any of them. A mail list is an author's driveway, our personal property.

Authors encourage readers to subscribe to a mail list by offering a "cookie," i.e. something they can only get by pulling into our driveway and trick-or-treating at our front door. *Requited* was the cookie when I first launched Kendrai Meeks. It was written both to be a prequel, but with the assumption that the recipient had already read *Reluctant*. Thus, while one could certainly follow the events of the novella, it gains fullness in the reader's orientated eyes. This is why it's included here, but at the end. It's definitely part of the series, but it's a special part that doesn't necessarily serve as an introduction.

In any event, I hope you've enjoyed Geri and Tobias's story. I've really enjoyed spending a few years with them. If you'd lie more of this world, I'm happy to share with you that there are three other series set in it.

Red Origins is a three-part novella series that tells the story of the original Betrayer, Gerwalta Faust, and her werewolf lover, Andreas Baron. Set in Central Europe during the seventeenth century, it functions as a romantic tragedy, a historical fantasy, and a supernatural suspense. You know the basic outline of the story from **Chronicles,** but parts of the history have been lost in Geri Kline's time. **Origins** was born of my own need to fully understand the truth of what really happened in the Black Forest three centuries before in order to properly balance it in the modern day. As I was sketching out the details, I decided to simply write the books. This series is complete.

Slayers, Inc. follows the continuing story of Caleb Helsing and Amy Popowitz as they try to negotiate being two outsiders living among vampires and with each other.

And finally, **Vampire Sovereigns** (launched 2020) is a new series "co-authored" by Kendrai Meeks and Killian McRae. Yes, these are both me, but I decided to approach it this way because they are both urban fantasy and paranormal romance. The first book, *Venice Dusk*, features a character that appears in both **Chronicles** and **Origins** (and who will also feature in **Slayers, Inc.)**, Massimo Brunelli, Vampiric Doge of Venice. Be advised: these books get steamy.

That's it from me. Thank you for your patronage, and please enjoy *Requited*.

*Yes, that is my actual initial.

REQUITED

1

Tonight, the harvest moon would rise to tempt those who walked the night into its light.

IN ANOTHER THREE DAMNED HOURS. I still had nine minutes of my shift left, minutes which felt like sandbags. On the other side of the hour lay freedom, dancing, fires, and clan chanting. So much chanting. Too much. I looked at the Reagan-era clock that hung over my desk inside the ranger booth and grabbed the walkie from its charger on the window ledge.

"What do you want, Geri?"

"No one else is coming in. You and I both know this."

The speaker registered a few clicks before the main office hailed back. "The second we say okay to you closing early is the second Joe Detroit and his two-point-five kids roll in and want a campsite for the night."

I pressed the send button and my luck. "It's after Labor Day, Rick. The two-point-five kids are back in school and Joe Detroit is working a double at the stamping plant. Besides, it's freezing out. No one is going to want to get out of their cars and stare at a waterfall when it's this cold."

"It's Michigan, kid. You know how the camp crowd is. Neither rain nor sleet nor common fucking sense…"

The silent buffer filled the space between us.

Finally, I heard a click over the radio when my boss hit the send button. "Look, Red, if you want to leave early, just say 'I want to leave early, Rick.'"

"I want to leave early, Rick. You know you do too."

He groaned over the air, and I could practically picture his scruffy face crunching from the annoying reminder of how the moon pulled us both: me to my clan, and he to his pack.

"I guess you could…"

I didn't hear the rest. With speed that would have shocked a hummingbird, I had the shade down, the RANGER STAND CLOSED sign out, and my backpack slung over my shoulder. By the time I crossed the parking lot and entered the gift shop through the employee's entrance, Rick had shut down the main office too. Guess Joe Detroit was S.O.L. if he decided to show.

I quirked an eyebrow. By-the-regulations Rick wasn't the type to close-up shop early. A moment later, a scent on the breeze gave away the reason, but I played along. "Have I been that much of a bad influence on you?"

"Your mother was worried it was going to be the other way around, if I recall." He jerked his head towards the breakroom door. "I know you said you didn't want us to do anything, but you knew we weren't going to listen, right? It's not every day we send one of our kids off to the big city to go to school."

My hands flew up. "Shhhh!" Sneaking past him, I snuck a look around the edge of the door and tried to figure out based on sound and smell who was in the breakroom. My senses might pale in comparison to Rick's, but I knew this landscape well. If someone uncommon was on the premises, I'd pick it up.

Three bodies, all human. All other workers at the state park. None of them my mother's informants.

Rick wore a know-it-all smile when I shrank back into view. "Still haven't told her yet, huh?"

"You know what my mom is like, and how pissed off she's going to be. I already get enough flack for me and Cody being friends."

"Friends? Is that what you kids are calling it these days?" Unconsciously, he crossed an arm over his chest and rubbed his opposite upper arm. "Don't take this the wrong way, kiddo, but I don't think I've ever met another woman more befitting of the name Brünhild."

"Amen to that."

When I was hired the summer after my senior year in high school, I thought the whole reason I got the job at the State Park was because everyone in town was scared shitless of my mom. I'm scared shitless of my mom. Rick, who was no doubt, scared shitless of my mom but hides it extremely well, proved that suspicion false on the third day of my employment, when she barreled into the gift shop, headed straight for his office, and told him in no uncertain terms that I would not be working there.

Rick just planted his fists on his hips, looked to the cash register where I stood trembling, and said to me, "Geri, if you were a minor, your mom would have every right to tell me you can't work here. At eighteen, though, the law considers you an adult. It's your call. You can quit like your mom here would like, or you stay on and learn how to do something other than terrorizing the local wildlife."

Eyes narrowed, finger pointed, and teeth grinding, Brünhild Kline had contemplated the man's murder, but knew where her domain ended and local labor laws began. "You've always had your nose wrapped up in other people's business, Rick Ryland."

Rick's nose had wrinkled as he bared his teeth at my mother. "Well, ain't that the pot calling the kettle black, Matron."

Running my hands under ice-cold water in the utility sink served two purposes: it washed away the grime that had built up from handling cash park patrons used for daily fees, and it distracted my brain from the buzz of hyperawareness brought on by the approach of night. Normally, I'd never have worked on the day of a full moonrise, but desperate times called for desperate measures. The University of West Chicago didn't exactly accept pieces of silver for tuition. The inheritance sitting in the bank that I'd received from my paternal grandmother would pay for my classes, but I still had rent and living expenses to manage. Unless I wanted to live in Bessie, which frankly, wasn't out of the question. I'd practicing laying down in the bed of my truck many times, albeit not to sleep, and it wasn't half bad.

Be a hell of a lot colder without a werewolf to curl up next to, though.

Rick put his arm around me and pulled me along toward the breakroom. "Gale made her German Chocolate cake. Try to ignore how lopsided it is, okay? She worked really hard on it."

"I would never insult her cooking, Rick. You know that. Everyone here is like family."

"I know, kiddo. And we're going to miss you so much. Offer stands: you ever want to come back and work at the park over the summers, all you got to do is call."

"You sure this job is going to stay open?"

"As long as that river keeps flowing and the falls keep falling, the park will always be here."

II

Each curve pulled heavy on the steering wheel, though I knew it was just my imagination. My rust-kissed but solid bull of a Chevy pick-up had never let me down. Considering what the average Michigan wintertime in the Upper Peninsula entailed, that wasn't a trivial thing. No, the reason I felt like I was slowly wading into a vat of molasses was because of the angle of the sun puckering up to kiss the horizon in my rearview.

I should have been home by now. That my mother wasn't blowing up my phone meant that either her battery was dead or she was. I shouldn't have stopped at my storage unit on the edge of town, but there was no way I was taking a chance with hauling home the final supplies I'd picked up for Chicago.

Paradise was more of a zip code than a town; a halfway point between Tahquamenon State Park with its legendary waterfalls and Whitefish Pointe on the tip of the U.P., most famous for its Shipwreck Museum and its exhibit on the Edmund Fitzgerald. During the summer, many a tourist crossed through this Yooper oasis, but stopped just long enough to hit up the one bar in town and cut their name into its much-tagged countertop. As far as small towns went, it lived up to all the clichés. Legacies grew as thick as the oaks and willows that carpeted the gently rolling hills that rose out of Lake Superior. It was a canopy of expectation that had blocked out my view of the sun my entire life.

At the last intersection on the way home, I paused, studying my options. I could turn left or right; both paths would take me out of town, away from home, and prevent the showdown with my mother. In both directions, the tall trees just beginning to blush with fall color and hit by the goldenrod rays of a fast-setting sun framed the roadway, like a mythic avenue of dreams. Ahead, the forest wove itself so tightly together that all I could see was shadow.

Running would imply that I was ashamed of what I was about to do. Though I feared my mother's reaction, I was not descended from fearful women. I would face her and stand my ground, taking whatever wrath she bore.

Besides, it was the last full moon at home, and the harvest moon at that. My skin crawled with anticipation for the fires. At the full moon's rise, my soul longed for the flame. How many lunar cycles in Chicago before the instincts deadened and I didn't feel this pull to clan and tradition?

My foot on the gas, I went boldly forward.

And that was when a flash of fur hit the hood of my car before rolling away to the side of the road.

III

I'd hit an animal; that much was apparent. But what kind? Out here, the possibilities could fill a zoo. Elk, moose, deer, bear? All possible, but given the hue of fur and the size of what had flashed before me, my suspicions were all but conclusive. Then, as I relaxed and connected with my senses, there was no doubt.

I pulled to the side of the road, cut the engine, and went for the utility box in the bed of the truck. Two gleaming silver blades met my eyes when I raised the lid, and next to them, my precious. A bow and arrow may have seemed a passé weapon-of-choice with all the firearms on the market today, but they had their upside. Light, portable, easy to shoot without riling up half the forest with the echo of the discharge. Plus, I just looked badass with one.

A bloodless trail relieved my immediate guilt that I'd severely injured something, but the consistently straight path concerned me. An animal just hit by a car should have been either limping from side to side, or instinctively weaving to avoid being pursued. As I got far enough into the forest that the light of day struggled to find ground, I realized either this animal didn't have the common-sense god gave a fruit fly, or I didn't. I looked back over my shoulder, but couldn't spot my truck through the growth. The thought of turning back crossed my mind only moments before the air from my lungs whooshed out as something slammed into me.

Face down on the forest floor, kissing dirt, an immense weight bore down and hot breath licked the back of my neck. The werewolf had me pinned.

Instinct ingrained by years of training and generations of breeding seized me. In moments, I took inventory of my situation. The ground provided a solid surface I could use to vault myself up. The bow was useless; my attacker would need to be in front of me. My best option would be to roll and hope the momentary shift of my body threw the wolf off balance. A few seconds would be all I'd need to access my weapons.

Overriding instinct however, I knew that my best option lay in ridicule.

My body went limp. "Most boyfriends just call when they want to talk, not throw themselves in front of their girlfriend's truck and give them a heart attack."

The balance of weight on my back shifted; brutish paws on my shoulder blades grew long and familiar. The wolf's hindquarters stretched, taking on their primate form. Soon, his long, muscular legs covered my own. His hipbones jutted into my lower back, followed by something definitively human, male, and solid.

"That's what huey boyfriends are like." Cody's voice, rough and airy and right against my ear, sent chills through my body. "But I'm not human, am I?"

He leaned forward, suckling my neck just below my ear. His touch stirred urges within, inspiring recollections what that mouth could do to other places on my body. We'd been rehearsing this dance for the better part of two years, a tenuous tango of desire and restraint. The full moon already hung low in the daytime sky and the primal instincts it triggered played havoc with willpower. Even as he shifted, Cody's hips rolled, making me suck in a breath and bite my bottom lip to quell my desires. One of us had to draw a line.

As usual, that would be me.

"You're moon mad, and I'm going to be late," I said. "If I don't get home, my mother will be combing these woods with a silver dagger etched with your name."

Unbothered, his teeth took to nibbling the bottom of my ear. "You want me. I can smell it."

Damn werewolves and their super senses. With a grunt and all my determination, I rolled. Cody could keep me down if he wanted; until I came into my full powers, any werewolf over the age of twelve could best me in a fair fight.

"Fine, let's do it," I said, teasing. "But you better make it one for the ages, because my mom will castrate you."

I barely paid any heed to the fact that he was naked as I stood up and leaned against a tree. I'd been around naked werewolves all my life – their human skin no less a layer of clothing over their true natures than a t-shirt or pants. Still, even I would admit that dynamic changed a little when the handsome, built, aroused male before you was your boyfriend.

"Really, castration? I've always pictured the Red Matron as more of the disemboweling type."

Cody sat back on his heels, rubbing his forelegs and calming his hefty breathing. I tried not to notice how ripped he was, or think about how fun it would be to explore all those ridges and dips with my hands. It was too risky right now. Under the pull of a rising full moon, us being around each other was way too dangerous.

"I wouldn't put it past her." Eyes above the belly button, Geri! "What are you doing out here, anyway? Doesn't your little werewolf handbook say you should stay close to the pack just before a full moon rise?"

He shrugged as he rose to his feet. "My uncle called me after you left work. Rick says you're planning on telling your mom tonight. I wanted to say good luck."

I ground my teeth. Wouldn't Rick have guessed that if I wanted my boyfriend to worry, I would have told him myself?

"I figured the rush of feuernacht would have her so giddy, she'd be a little less likely to skewer me."

Cody raised an eyebrow. "I don't think Brünhild Kline does giddy."

You should see her when she draws wolf blood, I thought. Instead of voicing my concern, however, I decided to distract my boyfriend by being all girlfriendish. Crossing to where he stood, suddenly looking sheepish, I rolled up on my toes and made doe eyes. "Thank you, Cody. That was really sweet."

He let my kiss land gently on his lips before his arms snaked around me and pulled me near. Like a racecar driver, I could count on his inner wolf to seize control of his libido this close to moonrise. Within moments, he'd deepened the kiss, his hands on my ass before drifting down and hitching under my legs, pulling me up.

"Too close… to full moon. Can't… Don't want to… resist you."

With every pause in his words, his hips undulated, tempting me with the promise of release even through the layers of my clothing between us.

"You have to. If you don't…"

Cody froze, pulling back to look me in the face, his gaze dripping with sincerity. "What if I don't?"

"Then you'll be bonded to me forever. You'll never be able to love another."

A quick peck of my lips, and he eyed me again. "I'm not sure I'm capable of that now."

With my hands on his shoulders, I pushed myself away, reclaiming my own feet. "Cute, Cody, but the full moon can make a wolf say…"

Anger pulled his brow taut. All the passion that a moment before had been focused on seduction erupted. "It's not the full moon, Geri. Damn it, can't you see that…"

I flinched, shocked by the spike of anger, my hand instinctively wrapping around the hilt of the two-inch silver dagger braided into my hair. Cody's eyes focused on my defensive reaction with regret in his eyes. In a moment, he softened; both his tone, and his rigid muscles straining beneath his skin. He ran a hand through his messy brown locks in a wasted effort to tame them.

"It's not just because of the full moon. I've been thinking about this for a while. I'm… You know I love you, Geri, and you love me too."

I didn't deny it. I'd told him the first time a year ago and I'd never taken it back since.

Reaching for my hand, Cody pulled it to his mouth and planted a kiss. "Mate me."

My hand snapped back out of his, and I had to suppress myself from slapping him. "What in the hell are you talking about?"

"I'm talking about you and me, man and wife. I want you, Geri. I want you forever."

This amount of crazy should require a license. "Cody, I… I do love you. But I can't do that to you. I can't be the reason you lose your free will."

"That's the way we wolves work. It's just how we are," he argued, stalking me. I stepped back with each footfall of his forward. "At least with you, I'd know you're with me because you love me, not because some genetic mating imperative was forcing you to."

"You think it's that simple?" My back flattened against a tree. "You're a werewolf, I'm a hood. My kind balances your kind, with violence and death if it comes to that. Besides, I'm leaving for Chicago in three days."

He had a simple enough answer for that, one that to Cody seemed so ingenious and self-obvious, it had him grinning like an idiot. "Don't go then. Stay. Mate me. Marry me, or whatever it is you hoods do to seal the deal."

Cotton in my mouth and electricity passing through my tongue, a vision cracked across the edge of my imagination: me, naked underneath the confines of my red hood, straddling Cody while the wedding drums played and fires burned outside our tent. I could practically smell the ash and taste his kiss on my tongue as we consecrated our union, simultaneously both by my traditions and his.

He wore a knowing grin when my eyes opened, adjusting to the fast dying light of the forest at twilight. "Tell me yes, Geri. I'll make you the happiest shewolf in history. Plus, you know it would totally piss off your mom."

A bonus if ever there was one. And I couldn't deny that in the gentle moments of daydreaming when good sense and reality drifted away, I had pictured what it would be like to be Cody's wife. Those fantasies dissolved in the rays of day, when I looked in the mirror and could imagine myself cloaked in red and wielding silver, readying myself for the hunt.

"But I've planned for going to Chicago for so long." My last-ditch attempt at a justification to say no came out as more of a whine than a retort. "I worked so hard, Cody. Pulled straight A's at Community, saved up enough from work to make the trip, applied for entrance and got it, all without my mom finding out. To have done all that for nothing?"

"Fine, then we'll go to Chicago together." He tilted his forehead against mine. "As long as I come home for a few days around full moon, I'll be fine." His hands braced either side of my face. "Marry me."

All my kick-ass skills and abilities washed away in flood of girly glee. "I owe my mom the truth about Chicago first. Let me just get that out of the way, and then I can make a decision. Just give me a couple days, after the full moon and after the fires. Okay? I'm not leaving until the weekend."

"I waited this long for you, I can handle a few days more." He placed another kiss on my lips, this one the perfect balance of sweet and spicy. "She brought it on herself, you know. Your mother, I mean. Naming you after Little Red herself? She was practically tempting fate that you'd end up with a wolf."

That she was. That she was.

IV

Smoke rose from the trees, creating a plume that I could see a quarter-mile from the entrance to our property. Fall bonfires were commonplace here, the easiest and most efficient way to get rid of the carpets of leaves. Even though it was still early for such practices in mid-September, I doubted anyone would even notice. Hoods were backwoods folk, a necessity when charged with the policing, and when necessary, destruction of werewolves. We lived where they lived – away from civilization as much as civilization would allow.

In Chicago, I'd be alone. No hoods. No wolves.

Maybe an occasional vampire.

No slayers. They were all dead.

The twelve-foot gate that surrounded our compound would raise eyebrows in the lower peninsula, but in the U.P., privacy was respected. Did the locals know that behind those gates, in addition to a house, a barn, and garage, was a state-of-the-art training facility for the House of Red? Unlikely. Cousins, aunts, and uncles had their own homes and mini-compounds dotted across our territory, stretching from the Great Lakes to the Dakotas above the forty-fifth parallel, but the head of the operation and the command of the region lay with the Matron of our bloodline, my mother.

The gates clanged shut behind me, and I felt the weight of the cameras pivoting as Old Bessie started her way up the half-mile drive to the house. The smoke here was thicker, and the taste of it tickled my tongue and scratched at the back of my throat. Tonight's bonfire must have been bigger than usual. I needn't wonder why. As I got close enough to the house, a sea of trucks, SUVs, and smaller all-terrain vehicles formed a veritable parking lot. It wasn't unusual for a few family members to drive out for feuernacht and spend a few days reporting to my mother, but tonight it looked as though everyone had shown up.

Great, my mother would be distracted and wouldn't have the vaguest clue that...

"And just where have you been, Gerwalta?"

My mother's voice could crack lake ice in January. I dropped my car keys in the basket by the door and found myself trapped in the entryway. Leaning against a wall, Brünhild Kline met descriptions of both terrifying and beautiful. Her long black hair streaked with gray sat atop her head in a severe bun. Her ivory skin still held a touch of youth, though the lines on her forehead and at the corners of her eyes grew deeper by the year. Solid biceps flexed as she crossed her arms and glared at me, waiting for an answer, a scowl contorting a face

837

that rarely knew smiles save when born of exacting pain on wolves or in the precious moments when my father could woo the little softness left within her.

"Like I said this morning, I had to work today."

"Yes, and you told me you were getting off at 5:30. It's nearly night now. Where have you been in the intervening two hours?"

The best way to lie to my mother was not to, to tell her only a partial truth and hope she didn't consider it worth her time to ask for more. "I ran in to Cody."

I bit my tongue before saying, literally.

"I know that much. I can smell the beast's stench all over you." She straightened her back and arched an eyebrow. "And exactly what were you doing with the alpha's son?"

The same thing we always do, mother. Making out and dry humping and wishing we could sleep together without so many consequences.

And also, he proposed.

"Just talking."

"Just talking!" My words rebounded, coated in a layer of acid. "Can I remind you, daughter, that someday when you are the Matron of our bloodline, he will be your adversary. That you talk with him is concern enough. That you two are friends is something that must end."

I stared at the carpet, feeling as tall in my mother's eyes as the faded shag beneath my feet. "Maybe I don't want to be matron."

Without pretense, she delivered a response so well worn, the edges had lost all color.

"If not you, then who? All this — all of it, I have built for you. You are my sole heir, my legacy. You are the path by which the House of Red shall retain its rightful place in our world. You must be a worthy leader. A pack will never respect you if they know you once pined away for their alpha, and a pack that does not recognize our authority grows dangerous."

"An authority that does not respect its own limits and fails those it protects breeds revolution," I spat back through anger held down with leather straps.

"Spoken like a modern woman." My mother stepped closer, gaining strength in proximity and brewing fear with reserve. "Yours is not the world of modernity, Gerwalta. Yours is an old world of myth and chaos and death for those who forget their natures. What kind of hood would think something like that?"

"I'm not a hood," I reminded her. "Not yet."

She met my retort with a slow bob of her head. "No, you haven't taken your rites yet. I may have granted your father's request to wait until you finished with your college thing, but that's done now, isn't it?"

I'd finished my associate's degree at the local community college in June. That this hadn't come up before astounded me, but I chalked it up to a suspicion that my father wasn't quick to inform my mother. He'd been my passive ally since high school. Maybe it was only the change in the seasons and the lack of a new tuition bill that tipped her off. Maybe she didn't know at all and was only bluffing.

I resorted to partial truths. "Yes, I finished all my classes at community."

A cat-that-got-the-cream grin pulled taut the corners of my mother's mouth; she wore a smile born of my pain. "Then you're lucky that most of the clan just happens to be here for your cousin Robert's fire. He's proven to be not as difficult as you."

The fact that Robert was three years my junior, and my mother's passive aggressive insult meant to point out that truth, didn't allude me. The moment I visualized the building of the fire behind our house, of the clan chanting the sacred words and my cousin's form stepping into the heart of the blaze, of his body consumed by flame, burning away the traces of his humanity and leaving only that part of him which was beyond human, stirred primordial longing in me. I couldn't deny that I'd felt the pull of the consumption, even dreamed of my own fire. Inside, my nature called on me to take rites and claim my hood. But deeper, I wanted change, freedom, to know that I chose something out of will and not breeding.

Cody's words reverberated in my memory, reminding me why I'd really resisted my birthright.

At least with you, I'd know you'd fallen in love with me before we'd been together, not because some genetic mating imperative was forcing you to.

Going through rites would only enhance my genetic hardwiring. I wasn't sure I could think of him the same way on the other side of the fire. If I were to have any hope of marrying him...

"Then we should wait for next month," I said, desperate to find any way to get myself out of this corner. "A fire burns for only one hood. Tonight, that should be Robert. I can't usurp his moon."

"Agreed." My mother crossed her arms. "But I want you to remember how much this means to you, even as you attempt to deny it. Go to your room, you will not join us tonight."

Like the wolves communally taking their animal forms on the full moon, the hood was called to clan and fire. Just like a juvenile wolf, I had the ability to forgo the gathering if needed. But it would hurt. My insides would twist, my heart would race, and I'd feel a thirst for appeasement. It was the worst punishment my mother could bestow for daring to argue with her, but even more so because it would be the last time I was with my clan for months or even years to come.

In the blink of an eye, I reverted to my five-year-old self. "But that's not fair!"

"Is that your best defense?" she asked, cool as the moon in the autumnal sky, and just as distant. "Since when has fair had anything to do with my decisions? I am just, whether or not you believe I am fair. When you feel like your body is pulling itself in two tonight, remember that you brought this on yourself. Now go."

I remembered suddenly what I'd come home hoping to do before I'd been distracted. Before I could chicken out, I put my hand on her wrist and held her back.

"Wait! I want to talk to you about something. Not about feuernacht or my rites. It can wait, but maybe tomorrow?"

A slow drip of consideration in her eyes proceeded her response. "Very well."

With a nod, she was gone, leaving me to climb step by lonely step to my bedroom. Hopefully I could open my window and at least smell the fire. With any luck, I'd take part of its heat within me and be able to stand up my end of the conversation better with my mother in the morning.

Through the night, the revelry rang out. As the sounds of howls and hoots, laughs and claps, swish and swirl floated up to me through my cracked bedroom window, the draw of my clan tormented me. Damn my mother, and damn those born with the blessing of not being her daughter.

The upside of my punishment, however, was that come next morning, I was fully rested while they were not. Right after the rise of the sun, I crept downstairs, determined to sneak out before anyone was the wiser. I knew I'd be telling my mother about Chicago later on in the day but I needed to get out to nature to clear my head first.

I was just about out of the kitchen door, my truck keys in hand, when a voice dripping with Latin flavor spoke up.

"And where are you going so early in the morning?"

As central as my mother was wherever she happened to be due to her brawn and bluster, my father was her equal in cunning and stealth. I'd heard stories of how he snuck up on a lone wolf driven mad with lunacy and slit his throat. I wasn't exactly suffering lunacy, but I was definitely about to have my head handed to me on a silver platter.

"She didn't say I was grounded. She only sent me to my room."

My father pulled a languid draw of coffee, not saying anything, a tactic he knew worked with me. If left in silence, I'd out myself through babbling for every transgression.

"Nothing happened," I insisted. No need to say anything more than that. My mother would have informed him.

"You mean, nothing has happened yet."

"Just because Cody and I are friends..."

His hand jutted up, blocking my retort. What my mother did with glares, my father did with gestures. "Please, boñita, do not insult my intelligence. I've understood for some time that you and Cody and more than friends. I have tolerated it because I know you are wise, and I do not need to tell you how dangerous that game is."

I closed my eyes. I couldn't see the look on my father's face when I told him the truth. "I love him, Papa. I've loved him for a really long time."

When I dared look again, it was only to discover my bomb had failed to detonate. Instead, my farther fixed indifferent eyes on me. "So what? Does that change anything?"

"Of course it does. I mean, if the Matron of the House of Red and an alpha were in love with each other, don't you think that would ultimately be a good thing for wolf-hood relations? Think of how many conflicts we could resolve through dialog instead of violence."

"And think how many more conflicts such a union alone could inspire. An alpha is, first and foremost, answerable to his pack. Even before his own mate, the needs of the pack have priority. The first time one of them disagreed with his dictate, they'd blame it on you. He'd need to appease them, or they would challenge his leadership. Either way, he might die, and you would then likely do the same."

I didn't know what drove such boldness. "He's asked me to marry him."

For once, my cool and collected father bristled. "Dios mio, porque no!"

"Why is it so crazy? I'm not lying, Papa. We've never slept together. If Cody loves me, it's because he loves me."

"I forgive you for your daydreams. Ignorance and youth blind us, but a wolf and a hood can never be together. Remember what became of Die Verräterin."

Die Verräterin, the Betrayer.

My father couldn't have chosen a more impactful way to drive his argument home. I winced as the images filled my mind, a child's imagination sketching out the rougher details. Gerwalta Faust, after whom my mother named me, paid dearly for the greatest transgression a hood can commit: she married a wolf and bore him a child. While the fairytale painted her as a heroine trapped by naiveite, the real Gerwalta wasn't as fortunate as the Grimm Brother's Little Red Riding Hood. She, her wolf mate, and their child were skewered on silver spits and roasted alive while her matron – her own mother - chanted ancient incantations, relinquishing her powers so she could not defend herself.

"You don't need to tell me to remember," I said in softer tones. "I'm reminded each time I sign my name."

Stroking his beard, my father's head dipped. "She named you after The Betrayer so you could make the name one of pride again, not follow in her footsteps."

I had had enough of bearing the expectations of the three hundred years of hood that stood between me and my namesake. "Sorry, Dad. I guess that was a bad decision."

Walden went to the woods to live deliberately; I went to the State Park where I had worked until only yesterday to live thoughtlessly.

In the measure of whom I loved more – my father or Cody – they were practically tied. Had it not been for my father's encouragement and willingness to have my back when my mother wanted to lash it, I'd probably have left home a long time ago. Not to run off to college and turn my back on all I'd known, necessarily, but at least to live with one of my cousins in Wisconsin, Ontario, or Montana.

As I followed the path toward the Upper Falls, I looked out on the rushing river, feeling the echo of my own struggle. For so many years, I had flowed along without conflict, letting the path I'd been born on move me. Then, as I became aware of my mother's sadism, and my father's tangential disavowal of her ruthlessness (to me in private, as he'd never openly question our clan's matron to anyone else), I began to rebel. I sped, I changed course, I rushed to jump over the edge.

I fell in love with a werewolf.

I stared at the falls before me, a series of aquatic plateaus cascading in seven different directions, and wondered which way to fall, and how much churning there'd be when I did. It took a few moments before I realized someone was talking to me.

I turned to see a woman, her head covered in dark cloth, biting her bottom lip.

I shook myself back to the moment. "I'm sorry, what?"

Her outstretched hand twitched again, offering her phone to me. "I said, would you mind taking a picture of us?"

Blinking away my inner thoughts, I smiled and took the device. When she backed to the railing and laced her fingers through the hand of a man wearing a yarmulke, I tried not to show the awkwardness I felt. I held up the Muslim woman's phone to square them in the frame with the mists of the waterfall rising behind them. Afterwards, the man moved on a few steps to get a better view as I handed the phone back to the woman.

Curiosity seized my tongue before I can stop it. "I'm sorry if I was gawking."

"Were you?" Her smile flickered. "No worries. We're used to getting looks. People don't expect to see a Muslima and a conservative Jew married to each other. We've learned to live beyond expectations, though."

An image of my father's anger-flecked eyes popped up in my mind. *A wolf and a hood can never be together.*

Because culture and history demanded it? Assumed it? Expected it?

Forbade it?

"I think that's..." I shoved my hands in my pockets. "...beautiful."

VII

It was time. Time to come to terms with everything I felt for Cody, and time to set out to do all I had decided to do with my life. Time to tell my mother about my relationship, about college, and that I'd decided to become the future alpha's bride.

I didn't need to take my fire to fuel the flames. I could make my own fire.

I'd accept what I wanted, stop feeling like it was something I had to hide or apologize for, and be a freaking adult. My mother's reaction wasn't my responsibility. If she wanted to summon her silver, skewer me, and roast me over the fires meant for my hooding, what could I really do to stop her?

All I had to do was find her and have done with it. In the training complex, I found one of the few cousins I considered a friend practicing his battle skills.

"Markus!"

The youngest of six siblings, Markus was the baby of his family, but "baby" was the last word anyone would ever use to describe him. Standing six foot three, he towered over me. When he wrapped me in his arms and spun me off the ground in his overly dramatic way, at least eight inches between my feet and the floor remained. He was a strong hood, one who took on his mantle at fourteen, the youngest of my generation. Once, my mother hoped I'd see him as a candidate for husband. Little did she know that Markus had been hoping to make a husband of our cousin Robert.

"There you are, Gerwalta. Why weren't you at the fire last night?"

He set me down like a feather on water, leaving me to straighten out my clothes. "Please don't call me that—it's Geri. And you know why. I was being punished."

"Your mother is mad at you again? Must be a day of the week that ends in y, then."

His light-hearted jab brought a much-needed smile to my face. "Speaking of the wicked witch, do you know where she is?"

"She was through here a little while ago, helping Robert adjust to all his new awesomeness and stuff. You should see his biceps ripple. I could watch that hood for hours." For a moment, Markus's face clouded over in a dreamy mask, and I tried not to picture what he must be thinking. Finally, he snapped back to attention. "Nope, she's not here. I thought I heard her say she had to go out for a summons."

My nose wrinkled. "A summons? I didn't know the wolves were having some sort of dispute that needed settled."

Markus grinned. "Just because you're tossing off the alpha's son doesn't mean you're the werewolf whisperer or anything. They're a large pack, Geri. Crowds create conflict. I'm sure it's nothing to worry about."

"I hope you're right. And just because I told you my secret doesn't me you can say anything about Cody and me around here. All the older hoods with their turbo hearing and stuff... Could get ugly if anyone finds out."

My cousin's eyes rolled. "You honestly think there's a single hood, wolf, or human in a ten-mile radius who doesn't know you two sneak off to the woods to polish bark all the time?"

I didn't want to ask what that term meant. "My mom doesn't."

"Right. You keep telling yourself that, and maybe sooner or later, it will be true."

VIII

I hovered in the kitchen until moonrise, only to be told by my father to go to my room and wait for my mother's return there. Early the next morning, after a sleepless twenty-four hours spent compiling mental lists, replaying the conversation by the falls, and listening to the sounds of my aunts, uncles, and cousins playing wargames inside the compound, I found myself and Old Bessie outside Cody's house. I didn't remember the drive, or even deciding to go. Something just... drew me there.

Cody's parents both worked in town during the day. I knew he would be home alone, if not only for the reason than we had taken advantage of that fact on several occasions. The spare key met my eyes when I opened the utility box panel on the side of the alpha's three-bedroom ranch house, its metal chilled from overnight temperatures that danced circles around the freezing point. I made my way for the back door, frosted leaves crunching beneath my feet.

"Screen door" was a symbolic name; I couldn't remember the last time it actually had a screen in it. Just beyond, I maneuvered the key to the keyhole and began to push it in the slot when I heard the sound of weather-stripping scraping wood. My eyes adjusted quickly to the dim light inside when I found the door unlocked and open.

"Cody?"

My voice deadened in a house strewn about with homemade afghans and carved wood knickknacks from local artisans. Carpet the colors of rocky road ice cream dampened the sound of my footfalls as I glided around furnishings and a stack of magazines piled up in the hall. Even though I was a nascent, a hood still not in command of all her strengths, I still had the innate abilities with which all my kind were born: stealth, agility, speed, superhuman senses. A little superhuman, anyway. Any righteous hood who'd gone through their rites would shoot past me on that one.

I moved through the interior of the house like mist over water. My hand on the open door, I paused, coaching myself for what I would do the moment I opened it and Cody set eyes on me.

I thought it over and you're right. We can make this work. Let's get married.

But I'm still going to college in two days, so we can get married in Chicago. For the moment, what do you say we just fuck and bond as a mated pair?

Okay, I might not use the term fuck, but damn it, there was no way either one of us was leaving this house a virgin.

I opened the door...

…and discovered one of us already wasn't.

The man who a moment before I had been ready to spend my life with, lay sleeping.

In the arms of another woman.

A naked woman.

I gave myself until the count of three, and proceeded to lose my shit.

"WHAT THE FUCK, CODY!"

Werewolves were gifted with speed that could make Olympic sprinters look like a child running through molasses in winter. One never could have guessed it from the way Cody's eyes languidly flickered open. Slower still was his ability to understand what was going on, or that he was currently using a brunette with half-inch blond roots as a blanket.

"Geri?" His hand slicked over his oily face. "What are you doing here?"

Just then, the shewolf began to show signs of life. Good, she was awake. That made it so much easier to kill her without guilt. Run, bitch, run. Give me an excuse to chase you.

"What am I doing here?" I vaguely motioned to the refuse on his bed. "What is she doing here?"

"Cody, sweetie, who is that?"

She had a voice, and judging by the amount of gravel in it, she'd been a smoker since she was in utero.

"Who am I? Who am I?"

Despite years of training to keep my emotions in check, my innate abilities were roaring to life through a vision of red. The shewolf's unkempt roots became my handle as I hoofed upon the mattress and dug my hand into her scalp, pulling her up to face me.

"I'm his girlfriend. Who in the hell are you? You're not one of the Paradise Pack, that's for hell sure. I know all of them."

Cody finally managed to sit up, pulling a fistful of twisted sheets and blankets over his lupine assets. He went from groggy to panicked in two seconds flat. "What the…? No, Geri, stop. Stop before you do something you're going to regret. Lisa is my…"

"Your what?" I demanded, waiting for the standard litany of male excuses to come pouring from his mouth. "Your sister? Your cousin? Your just-a-friend-and-it's-not-what-it-looks-like?"

"No, this is exactly what it looks like." My boyfriend's voice grew stern. The wolf shown through his eyes, sending a chill down my spine and loosening my grip. "Lisa is my…"

"I'm his mate!" The shewolf twisted away, crouching down in a position that would let her pounce and rip out my throat if she shifted forms. "I'm his wife, you crazy bitch."

My world.

Stopped.

"She's your…"

Tears, hot and as burning as the silent screams at the back of my throat, manifested at the corner of my eyes. A bare-backed Lisa began to rummage around the floor, picking up bits of clothing. Suddenly, the scene of what must have happened played itself out. Their touching. Their kissing.

Their mating.

Cody – my Cody – was gone.

"You're mated."

Whatever pity he could package together, Cody set it out in his features. "Yesterday we were joined, and this morning, we consummated. I've… We… Lisa, baby, can you give Geri and I just a few minutes?"

"Of course, sweetie." She had six pounds of sugar in a five-pound bag's worth of saccharine goodness in her grin as she leaned over the mattress to press a kiss against Cody's mouth, her ass pointed my direction. "I'll just go jump in the shower."

Lisa didn't worry that I'd negotiate my heart. She didn't worry that I'd try to make Cody see why this was all wrong. She didn't have to worry that my tears and my suffering would tug his heartstrings and bring him back to me.

She didn't have to worry about anything. They were mated, sealed in an eternal mystical bond, one that would last until death.

One that was supposed to have been ours.

"You're mated." I repeated the words as though comfort could be found in the stark truth, but it wasn't. I'd decided to turn my back on my family, my traditions, my birthright if needed, all to be Cody's wife. For nothing. "How? Why? When?"

"My father…" Cody shrugged. "Alpha's prerogative."

"Oh."

I didn't need any more explanation than that. Cody was a werewolf, and his father, not only the man he held above all others as a role model, but his pack's alpha. If his father were to decree that Cody would take a particular mate, he wouldn't have a choice. When the alpha gave a firm command, the packling had only two choices: obey or leave the pack. One kept you alive, the other could trigger a chain of events that ended in insanity and execution by hood.

"But why would he... Your dad has been... He liked us."

He liked me.

It didn't make sense. Cody's father hated the concept of alpha's prerogative. He boasted about how rarely he exercised the option. Their pack was made of wolves descended from Swedes and Finns. Like their human countrymen, they'd come to the new world with beliefs in hard work and community rule. When Michael Ryland put his paw down, it was only because he had no other choice.

Scooting to the end of the bed, Cody secured the sheets around his waist. Never mind that I didn't need a live model to recreate every inch of his body in my mind's eye.

"I know this is tough for you, Geri. Hell, it's tough for me. I fought my dad on it when he tried to get me to accept it of my own free will. When he ordered me, I did what he wanted, but inside, I was screaming for you. But the moment Lisa and I..." He had the nerve to blush, tucking his chin into his shoulder. "Then I knew she's the one I'm supposed to be with. She's the only one I could ever be with. I love her. I love her more than..."

A sickly suspicion began to leak in to the cracks of my horror. My hand shot up, killing his momentum. "Did he say why?"

Confusion marred his tragically beautiful brow. "What?"

"When you told your dad that you didn't want to mate Lisa. Did you tell him it was because you'd just proposed to me earlier in the day?"

His hand scratched the scruff at the back of his neck. "I told him I loved you. I told him that I only wanted to be with you."

"But another shewolf from another pack just happened to roll into town." The same time my extended family had come in from all corners to witness Robert's fire, leaving behind their own packs. Thunder rumbled in my chest as I leapt off the cliffs of my conclusion. "Did you mention you were planning on running away to Chicago with me and you'd only be home for full moons?"

Slack-jawed, Cody shook his head. "I didn't get that far. He told me in terms that left no room for discussion that you and me were through. He forbade me to talk about you until Lisa and I were joined."

The last twig of my patience snapped. "I have to go."

The shower in the bathroom came on just as I turned on my heel and started to march out of the room. I'd put down four steps when Cody's hand on my shoulder stopped me. I couldn't turn around, even though I knew inherently he wanted me to. No matter how this happened, and despite the fact that he was a werewolf, Cody Ryland was a good man. He wouldn't let me walk away thinking I'd done something wrong.

"You're a beautiful, intelligent, kickass woman, Gerwalta Kline, and any man—wolf, hood, or huey—would be lucky to have you. If there's ever anything I can do, anything at all…"

His voice trailed off, dragging the shreds of my hopes and dreams of our life together with it.

"Cody, I…" I couldn't get it out. No matter how much I longed for reciprocity, I wasn't there yet. I may never be there. To tell him that I wished he and his new mate well would be a lie. Deep down, I wanted to see them suffer. I wanted my heart to be avenged. I wanted to feed Lisa's blood to my silver blade and hear Cody's keening howl, knowing I took his mate from him.

I wanted to take my rites, let the fires consume the old me, and come out a righteous hood on the other side so I could have justice.

I wanted to become everything my mother wanted me to become.

I wanted to become my mother.

My chest fell as I exhaled my frustration, knowing there was only one place to turn, one person responsible for what had happened.

"No, Cody. There's nothing you can do. Good bye. Good bye forever."

IX

I flew into the house. A gaggle of cousins and two of my aunts in the living room barely registered as they called out, trying to get my attention. I had no interest in playing junior hostess. I needed to see my mother and I needed to see her now.

Brünhild looked like she'd been expecting me when I entered her formal office at the back of the house. Her hand wrapped around the handle of her favorite stein, one that depicted a pack slaughter in the Black Forest. One knee-high boot crossed over the other as she sat in her carved wooden chair, her gaze fixed on me at a distance. I stood at the door, my chest heaving, my thoughts racing, blood boiling.

"Out with it now, Gerwalta. We both know why you think you're here."

"Why I think I'm here?" Pain barely registered as my nails pressed so hard into the heels of my hands, I swore that blood must be running. "How could you, Mother? How could you?"

"How could I?" She repeated my question in a tone dripping with scorn. "What did you expect me to do? Allow you to go off and become some wolf's bitch? I didn't name you Gerwalta so you could repeat the same mistakes."

She rose slowly, like a queen staring down one of her unruly subjects, before stalking toward me. "Someday, you will command of our bloodline, and if you prove worthy, Grand Matron. A righteous hood of the House of Red cannot rule while opening her legs every night to the enemy."

I took two steps forward, meeting her glare with every ounce of fury I could muster. The thwack my flying hand made when it met her stoic face echoed off crimson papered walls, off the wood and stone hearth where a fire danced with an intensity that matched my own. My mother was my superior in every way; she could have stopped my assault midair had she wanted. Though I was curious why she didn't, I pressed forward, not knowing how much longer my luck would hold.

"This goes far beyond what you've done to me. What gives you the right to interfere in pack dynamics that way? What in the hell did you threaten Michael Ryland with to get him to command Cody to mate someone he didn't have any feelings for?"

"I didn't command any one. I only advised Michael that if his son ever attempted to bed a member of my bloodline, I'd have his pelt for my bedclothes. I suggested that Cody might consider taking a mate with a great deal of urgency. Luckily, my sister had already brought Lisa Kepler from the Ely Pack, who was hoping to find a match here in Paradise. How the alpha interpreted and acted on those suggestions was his own concern."

"That's what flies for diplomacy in your eyes? Threatening wolves you're charged with overseeing with death if they don't obey, and calling it their free choice when they kowtow?"

Her hands folded before her, she nodded. "If I cannot control an alpha wolf, I cannot control any wolf. And if we cannot control the wolves, they will grow wild and feral. Remember that we don't exist simply to make their lives difficult. Once upon a time, werewolves and vampires openly hunted defenseless humans, killing and consuming without limit. Slayers and hoods came into the world to make certain every species which shares it had protection from the others. When you're matron, you'll be wise to remember this."

"When I'm..." The words died in my throat. "I will never be matron, I'll never be a hood of your clan."

"We are what we are. Becoming a hood isn't a choice. It's an imperative. Becoming the matron isn't a birthright, it's the very reason you breathe and live. Enough!"

In a swish of arms, my mother beckoned her full power. The air sizzled with old magic, filling the room with the scent of pine needles and damp oak. Dressed in her common black hunting boots, black jeans, and ruby red button-down, her amber eyes flooded silver. Tendrils of power slicked back over her hair, down her shoulders, and blanketed her back, solidifying into a red cloak, the cloth that had given our kind our names.

"I grow tired of your insolence. It is time for you to pass through the fire and become one of the righteous."

Panic punched me in the gut. "That's why the family is all here, isn't it? It wasn't just for feuernacht. It wasn't just for Robert's hooding; they could have done that at any of the family compounds. It wasn't even as a cover to bring in a shewolf that you could force on Cody. You want them here as a sort of coronation."

"It's far more than that, child. I wanted them here in case there was need to hold an inquest," my mother said, standing tall. "If Cody could not bed the shewolf, I would have known that you'd blackened your name and lain with him. With the witness of the family, I would have ordered you to carry out the sentence and cut his throat."

The image of that fate made me see red. "I would *never* hurt Cody."

"Oh, really?" My mother's eyebrow arched. "Don't tell me that when you found him in the arms of another, you did not want to see his blood flow from his veins."

She caught the guilty flash in my eyes before I was able to turn away.

My mother preened her cloak. "As I said, we are what we are. A hood's nature is to destroy a wolf, not seduce one. Ask yourself, why hadn't you slept with him? It's because, in your soul, you are repulsed by the idea. Stop trying to reclaim the shame of your forefathers. Take your fire, and your rightful place at my side as the Grand Matron-in-training."

If I breathed deeply enough, I could taste how the magic scented the air, how it called to me to accept it in to my body. My mother was right about that much: this is what I was by birth. The power, the magic, the ability to run in time with werewolves, command silver to do my bidding, even fly if I was one of the lucky few gifted with the ability, was there for me to claim. All it would take would be my submission, and the elders of my clan calling on the ancient power that would grant me my own hood and imbue my body with the strength of my ancestors. In time, my ability, the respect and fear among both hood and wolves would equal that of my mother, maybe even surpass it.

I could think of no more horrid a fate.

"No."

"No?" Brünhild faltered. "What do you mean, no?"

I backed toward the door. "I would have refused to kill a man whose only supposed crime was loving me. I refuse to twist the hearts and minds of good wolves to further my political standing. I refuse to be like you. I am nothing like you."

"Oh, aren't you?" With her power, she beckoned a silver plate sitting on the fireplace. It sailed through the air, simultaneously morphing, reforming itself through my mother's unspoken command. When it hit her hand, what had been a simple round disc took on the form of a short sword. My mother held it up, the tip angled at my chest. "Which of us carries the greater shame from what you've done? You accuse me of being horrendous for simply getting your wolf to follow through on his instincts, while you spent two years drawing him away from his nature to get away from yours. Ask yourself, did you ever really love him, or did you just love the idea of doing something to piss me off?"

Even I couldn't deny that had been part of Cody's appeal in the beginning, but it had quickly grown into so much more than that.

"I was ready to be his wife."

"You were ready to be his doom. A hood and a wolf can never be together. Never. Our instincts to destroy each other are too great. Marrying Cody would only have set one or both of you up for an early death."

"At whose hands, mother? Mine, or yours?"

"They are the same hands." She raised her sword between us, the blade tip just inches from my heart. "Now, listen to me and listen well, daughter. I have tolerated your childishness and hesitance long enough. We are going downstairs now, and your aunts and I will summon the fire so that I can bestow your rites on you. You will pass through the flames. If you do not, I will gather our clan and destroy not only your precious Cody, but the entire Paradise clan."

The knob turned in my hand as my head lowered, eyes cast to the floor. "Yes, Matron. I will prepare for the ritual immediately."

I knew an empty threat when I heard one. Part of the reason that my mother held such a lofty position in our society was that her actions were firmly rooted in reason. Reasoned actions delivered with a silver-plated fist, perhaps, but she knew how hard she could press her position and when to pull back.

The ultimatum had not been given by Brünhild the Grand Matron. It was by Brünhild, the mother who felt she had no other options.

She might be right when it came to Cody; the community would probably back her slaying him if we actually had been together. But the whole pack? I knew there was no reason even she could conjure that would demand such retaliation, especially given that Cody was now mated to one of his own kind.

The werewolf threat had been neutralized. The threat from within — me, the rebellious hood — remained. I wasn't safe here anymore.

An old duffle bag became my impromptu suitcase. I wouldn't need much from here; I'd spent the last three months serendipitously gathering what I would need when I moved to Chicago and putting it in a storage locker Rick owned. Earlier in the week, I'd even drained my bank account – a bank account my mother didn't know existed – in preparation for leaving. The plan had been to skip town three days past full moon, after feuernacht, when the pull of my instincts would be on the downslide. And coincidently, two days before fall classes at the University of Southwest Chicago started.

Waiting wasn't an option anymore. I had to go, and go now, before the aunts came to escort me to the ceremony.

I had just zipped up the duffle when a knock turned me into ice. I stuffed the bag under my blankets, hiding the bulge with my body just as the door opened and my father walked in.

"Your mother said that you've finally agreed to the ritual. I came to see if–"

The pride in my father's eyes, shining as bright, died when he saw me. I saw then that he'd donned his own yellow hood, giving him away as a hood from the Casa de Amarillo. I'd always found it curious that for all my mother's arrogance about the House of Red, she'd married a man from a different clan. Shame wrinkled the edges of my resolve. In the closet, my formal feuernacht gown hung untouched. He took one more look at me, then at it, then me again.

He took the dress down, carried it over to me before gently attempting to hand the garment over. "Quickly. Your aunts are already building the fire."

I may have summoned the guts to lie to my mother, but I didn't hold enough animosity for my father to repeat the deception.

"I'm leaving."

"Leaving?" His brow wrinkled. "I don't understand. What's going on? What happened?"

"Did you know?" I couldn't bring myself to look at him, afraid what I might see. "About what she was going to do to Cody?"

My father's brow wrinkled. True concern shown in his features. "What happened to Cody?"

"Ask your wife, it's an engaging story." I peeled back the blankets, grabbed my bag, and flung it over my shoulder. "I'll be in Chicago; I'm not sure where. I'll call when I figure things out, but don't expect me to come here again."

"Chicago? *Cariño*, you can't be serious. You're a hood. How will you survive in such a big city, and with nothing but your innate abilities?"

"I guess the way everyone else does. Like a human."

POSTLUDE

Pietro Kline observed his wife's hooded silhouette against the massive, riving bonfire. He'd known a number of bloodline matrons in his life, first in his own clan in his native Argentina, then others as he migrated north when circumstances forced him from his homeland. When he'd caught a red hood's eye, one in line to lead her clan, it had been a shock, not only to himself, but to his mother and father as well. Yellow hoods had a reputation of being gentler with the wolves under their command, of preferring negotiation and diplomacy to solve problems and only resorting to the hunt when all other routes had been exhausted. The reds...

No other bloodline's cloak better matched their nature.

Their daughter had always embraced the extremes of their contradictory natures. He'd anticipated high expectations for any offspring wrought of their union... But how high sometimes took him aback. Pietro walked a fine line, between being his child's champion, being his wife's partner, and being the matron's second.

Brünhild glanced back momentarily over her shoulder, before returning her eyes and her concentration to the fire. "When will she be down?"

He side-eyed the nearby members of the clan gathered to observe the sacred rites, and stepped closer, leaning in over his wife's shoulder from behind. "Never."

Each of Brünhild's knuckles popped in sequence, but her voice remained a smooth plateau of emotion. "She's running."

"What did you think would happen if you backed her into a corner? You know who—and what—she is." Pietro heard the chastisement creep into his voice and aimed to soften it. "Our daughter hasn't changed. She's as unwavering and as unmovable as you. You won't hear from her again, Brünhild. Not until she decides it's time."

Brünhild clicked her tongue. "She can run from us, but she cannot run from her nature. It's welling up inside her, Pietro. I feel it. She feels it. Her destiny is calling to her, and its voice is getting louder. She will come to the fire soon enough. And if she does not, the fire will come for her."

MEEKSOLOGY

Red Chronicles*

Requited** - Book 0
Reluctant**- Book 1
Relinquished** - Book 2
Ravening** - Book 3
Rebellious** - Book 4
Righteous**- Book 5

Red Origins*

Beauty & the Betrayer** - Book 1
The Wolf & the Watcher **- Book 2
Red & the Restorer** - Book 3

Enter the Kingdom*

Court of Discontent** - Book .5
City of Cinders - Book 1
Freebird (A side story novella)
Isle of After - Book 2

Vampire Sovereigns

Venice Dusk

*Completed Series
**Also available in audio